W9-ABS-692

THE ROOT
OF HEAVEN
AND EARTH

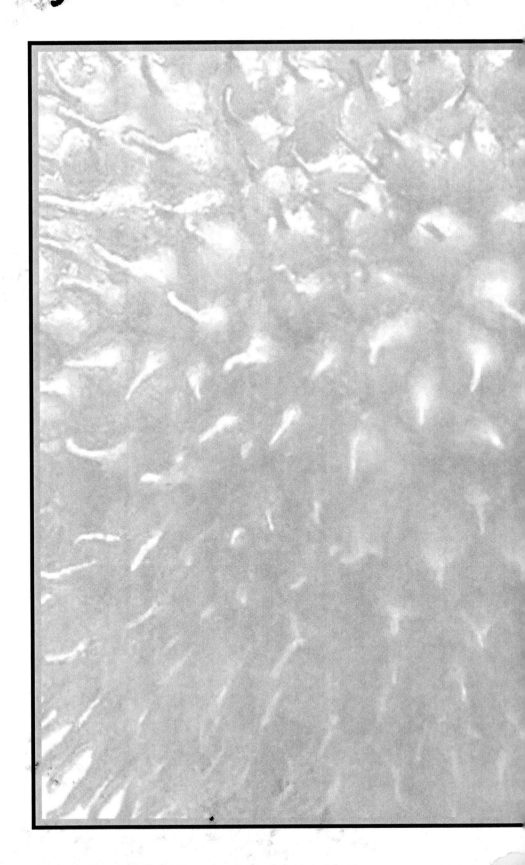

THE ROOT
OF HEAVEN
& EARTH

E. A. GRACE

ETHOSPHERE PRESS · NEW YORK

The Root of Heaven and Earth is the first book
by E. A. Grace. She lives in the United States.

The characters in this book and their names are fictitious.
They, the events in which the characters are involved, and the
locations at which those events take place, are products of the
author's imagination or are used fictitiously. Any resemblance
between them and actual incidents or persons, living or dead,
is entirely coincidental.

Ethosphere Press
1562 First Ave., #205-2005
New York, NY 10028-4004
www.ethosphere-press.com

Copyright © 2013 by E. A. Grace
All rights reserved, including the right to reproduce this book
or portions thereof in any form. First edition published 2013
Printed in the United States of America
20 19 18 17 16 15 14 13   1 2 3 4 5 6 7 8

Acknowledgements and citations for quoted passages may be
found in the appendixes at the back of this book.

Publisher's Cataloging-in-Publication Data

Grace, E. A.
     The root of heaven and earth / E. A. Grace.
         p.   cm.
     Includes bibliographical references.
     ISBN 978-1-938960-68-0 (pbk.)
         1. Social change—Fiction. 2. Nature—Effect of human
beings on—Fiction. 3. Self-consciousness (Awareness)—Fiction.
4. Culture—Origin—Fiction. 5. Future, The—Fiction. I. Title.

PS3557 .R1172 R66 2013
813/.54—dc23   2012923450

A tree is planted for each copy of this book printed.
Printed on archival paper

To Joan and Ned,
who made this book possible.

This passageway is known
as the root of heaven and earth.
Though barely perceptible,
its flow is eternal.
It serves many uses,
yet it never runs dry.

—Lao Tsu

PART I

EARTH

1

Paul knelt by his mother's bed, his face pressed against the sheet, his body shaking with deep sobs. His hand grasped her hand, which was already cool to the touch.

Outside the dimly lit room, a storm bellowed and raged, saturating the air with its magnetic charge. Paul heard the window behind him bang as it was pulled open by a sudden updraft. He turned toward it, and his attention was drawn outside—where, a moment later, he found himself standing on a bluff overlooking the ocean, with the storm still pounding around him.

Lightning broke the sky, revealing the water below, as surf crashed up against a sheer wall of land rising out of the sea. Then the light was gone—and everything around Paul seemed to be water, pouring in gusts and surges from the cloud-sodden sky and thundering in waves below him.

The wind grabbed at Paul's breath as it wound around him, yanking at his hair and trousers. Lightning struck again, branching in cascades above the water. In its light, Paul could see the ocean's surface below, frosted with little spurts kicked up by the falling rain. Every drop made its mark on the water.

Paul took a step toward the cliff's edge, hoping to see more clearly the broad spectacle of ocean and sky. As he did, lightning flashed once more, and a great gust of wind caught at him. In a breathtaking instant, he was pulled over the cliff's edge.

He plummeted toward the water, held in a long moment, illuminated by a single brilliant vein of lightning that lit and framed the sky...

Paul opened his eyes suddenly and took in the cold, gray wall of the apartment. His heart was pounding. Another bad dream! It had been like this for months—one disturbing dream after another—as though something was being stirred up inside of him, something which he felt would have been better left untouched.

This dream, like the others, seemed so vivid, so real! They brushed up too close to life, left him uneasy—as though they could somehow, in their vividness, break through the barrier between the dreaming and waking worlds.

Paul took another deep breath and glanced around Sheila's apartment, refocusing his attention on the real world. The bed he lay in was right next to the narrow cooking area and just a few feet from the bathroom. He recalled hearing that these had been spacious apartments when they'd been built a century before, but with the population always expanding, the apartments in this building, and in others like it, had been cut in half and cut in half until they seemed hardly big enough to turn around in.

Well, Paul thought, at least that was one thing about the dream that was definitely unreal; there was no place like that in the world anymore—so remote, so wild, with no evidence of human activity. But the part about his mother... He *had* found his mother like that, after she had passed away in the great *Muerte Azul* epidemic—one of the many epidemics that had swept the planet since the climactic disruptions began.

But Paul had been eleven years old then, not full grown like he was in the dream. So that part of the dream was unreal, too—though the dream on the whole had felt so lucid, visceral, with each sensation clearly formed. He had felt so vividly the rain soaking through his clothes, the electrical charge in the air—even, for a moment at the beginning, that piercing sense of loss over the death of his mother.

Paul tried to shake it off. He rolled over, so his sight fell on Sheila where she lay sleeping beside him, and propped himself up on one elbow, so he could see her better.

How beautiful she looked to him! It had always seemed remarkable to him that she thought herself no more than mildly pretty, when to him, she could not have been more beautiful. But it wasn't just her physical appearance, there was something about her, something he'd seen in her from the start—and still saw whenever he looked at her—that made him want to be with her, and to be there for her, always, and to never let her down.

Sheila moved in the bed next to Paul, as though by staring at her, he had summoned her from sleep. As he stared down at her, impressions of their love-making the night before played through his mind—its heat and passion.

Sheila squirmed, pulled the covers a little tighter, then opened her eyes. Paul was still up on one elbow, beaming his boyish smile at her. Sheila looked back, and for a moment she was there with him, her eyes clear, her attention focused his way—and in that moment, he saw in her what he had seen in her from the beginning, rising up from her depths, a strong, nurturing presence, which somehow, almost magically, made him feel right with himself.

He bent over and kissed her. She kissed him back with brief intensity, smiled a small smile, then stretched, reached for the media remote on the bedside table, and turned up the input volume of her implant to her usual daytime level. She seemed instantly absorbed in that feed and climbed out of bed without another glance at Paul. She walked around the bed to the little kitchen area and began heating a prepared food packet for breakfast.

As Paul watched her, he felt the desire he always felt—to please her, to do what was best for her, to be there for her.

He swung his legs over the side of the bed and turned his attention to his own day. This was not one of Sheila's shower days, Paul recalled, but it was one of his. He'd had some of his water allotments transferred over to her apartment, so he could shower here as well as at home. It would be easier to keep track of where his allotments were sent when their request for a shared apartment came through, he told himself. Then home would be home for both of them.

As Paul stepped into the bathroom and closed the door behind him, he caught sight of himself in the mirror, naked. He was a small man, about one and three-quarters meters in height, and well proportioned, with pale skin and short dark hair. At twenty nine, he looked fit and youthful. He pulled his arms up, bent at the elbows, and made muscles for the mirror, puffing himself up—then smiled a little. He had never taken much interest in his appearance until he had met Sheila, but he knew it was one of the things she liked about him, and so he had learned to appreciate it in himself.

Paul got out the bottle of dentoblast solution used for rebuilding tooth enamel, swooshed some around in his mouth, spit it out. He thought about Sheila and their love-making the night before. She had kept her implant running the whole time, tuned into sensory feeds to enhance the experience.

He had mixed feelings about that, though it was, he knew, a very common practice. He appreciated the pleasure it gave her, but it also drew her attention away from him and what they might share. And yet, everybody had those implants, even he did, and the world they made in one's mind was so seductive—in many ways much richer and more pleasurable than the real one.

Paul put the dentoblast solution back into its holder and reflected on how much more advanced today's implants were than the original ones. Both were set in under the skin at the temple, but the old ones had been hooked up to the visual and auditory centers of the brain, alone. The modern ones were far more complex, hooked up to replicate every kind of sensation—touch, taste, smell—everything. They could imitate an entire world; even the emotion centers could be skillfully stimulated. And one could run any kind of programming—Corprogov broadcast thousands of programs each day through the atmosphere using nanowave technology—and that was just for starters. An endless variety of alternate programming could be purchased cheaply on the black market. No matter how exotic one's tastes, something to please them could be found there.

Paul sat down on the toilet, thinking back to the time in his life just before he had met Sheila. How frustrated he had been in his work, how disenchanted he had become with his life! He had felt so alone in those days, and had begun to fear that he was throwing his life away in pursuit of a futile dream. Then he had met Sheila, with her *joie de vivre* and an approving light in her eyes. She had so buoyed his spirits then—it had felt as though a heavy weight had been lifted from his heart. She still did that for him, every time she smiled at him, whenever she would hold his hand, whenever they made love—even if she did do it with her implant running.

Paul realized he'd been daydreaming and got off the toilet. It flushed automatically. He said "start shower," and the bathroom computer checked his voice imprint, then started the shower with his preset temperature settings for his three-minute allotment. He got in and quickly went through an efficient system of bathing he'd been practicing since early childhood.

Paul was done with a few seconds to spare. He toweled off and asked the bathroom computer for the time. Quarter to ten. Damn, late for work again. He'd have to work late tonight. He had some catching up to do, anyway.

Paul dressed quickly and heated a food packet to eat on the way to work. He and Sheila shared a brief, sensual kiss, before Paul dashed out the door, his briefcase in one hand, the food packet in the other.

As he left the building, Paul took his media remote from his pocket and initiated a request for a float ship. The message was sent out through his implant, which automatically registered his location with the Central Command Center, where the nearest floater was automatically identified and dispatched to pick him up. Each floater could hold one or two people and transport them to a specified location. All movements of floaters were correlated though a central computer, so accidents were rare even though speeds sometimes broke two hundred kph. These small units hovered just millimeters above the roadbed, repulsed by magnetic polarities. Light, aerodynamic, and nearly friction-free, floaters kept the city in motion, while keeping energy use to a minimum.

Once on board, Paul used his remote to access his private area of the Stream, where he kept his personal files. The images appeared in his mind's eye as he checked today's schedule—May 14, 2136. He had a big meeting at 4 PM with a representative from the Corporate Government. Paul had to try to convince them that he and his team deserved better funding—more energy credits specifically—for their Depopulation Project. Without more energy credits, the work would stall.

Corprogov was sending someone named "Dr. Nakagawa" to today's meeting, Paul noted, as he tried to imagine how he should argue his case. It seemed to him that the project stood on its own merits, but maybe Dr. Nakagawa wouldn't see it that way. Paul thought about telling him how many members of his staff had had their education sanctioned and paid for by Corprogov. You've got to follow through on an investment, he would say—sometimes these things take decades to unfold. No use in dropping the ball now.

Paul sighed. Maybe he would mention that. You could hardly do anything in this world without Corprogov's approval—not choose a career, nor bankroll a project. It was essential that he got Dr. Nakagawa's support. Paul returned his attention to the Stream feed and reviewed the energy figures he intended to present to Dr. Nakagawa. Paul hoped the Corprogov scientist wouldn't look too closely at his numbers; if they caught on that he'd been buying energy coupons on the black market, he could land in jail for the rest of his career. Corprogov kept a very tight lid on things. But Paul was determined to see his project through, even if he had to take risks like these. At least, he thought, he'd kept books carefully enough that if he did get caught, he didn't have to bring the rest of his team down with him.

Paul turned off the feed and sat staring out the floater window as he whizzed across the city. When he passed the large boulder in the New Town Square (built during Strandford's big expansion about sixty years before), he knew he would be at his office soon. Paul liked that boulder; it seemed strangely comforting to see it there each morning, a rare acquiescence to the forces of nature in a time when everyone seemed so bent on denying or defeating those forces. It hinted at what the land had been like long before the town had been built up. For how long had that boulder been sitting in that exact spot? Paul wondered. Hundreds of years? Several thousand? Or perhaps many times more than that.

The floater pulled up in front of Paul's office building, and he got out. The town was abuzz with miniaturized, computerized transport units like the one he'd just gotten out of—they zipped and whizzed down the streets in great numbers. The people on the sidewalks seemed almost to be in slow motion when compared to the way the floaters dashed about. Paul looked into the faces of the other pedestrians as he passed them. He could see how their attention was turned inward—media junk spewing through their brains.

Why? Paul wondered. He kept his implant off most of the time—why did others so rarely turn off theirs? Were they that afraid of being alone? Paul looked around him—in a world that seemed so perfectly choreographed, so precise and in control, why did he sense so much panic? It was as though they were all afraid of just letting life move the way life moved. They couldn't choose a career without it being sanctioned and funded by the Corporate Government, couldn't have a thought without media programming overriding it. And when people did step out on their own in some fresh direction, there were harsh regulations designed to rein them back in. (Paul remembered hearing a friend say once, in hushed tones—"The criminal justice system? Did you ever really think about the term? The way justice is administered is *itself* a crime.")

Paul turned his course so he'd walk by the cherry tree in blossom outside his office. Why do people put up with so much regulation, he pondered? It was as though they believed there was something bad beneath the surface that would come through, that would break through, if things weren't always under such strict control.

Paul reached up and stroked the petals on one dangling cherry-tree branch. The scent was heavy and sweet in the air. How lovely, he thought. How very lovely. He looked up and saw the pink and white blossoms framed by an overcast sky. They seemed radiant, somehow, against that dull gray. Paul looked around for someone to share this with, a stranger perhaps, whom he could make eye-contact with. Surely there would be others who would pause to notice this great beauty in their midst? But they all passed him by with that same glassy stare.

◻ ◻ ◻

Paul drummed his fingers against his desk. Dr. Nakagawa would be here in about twenty minutes. Was he ready for the interview? If it didn't go well, they'd be without energy credits for the next year. The work was way past the theoretical stage—what would they do without the energy to proceed? The work would come to a standstill.

The window in the lab was open, and Paul could smell the scent of gathering rain. He glanced out the narrow window at a small patch of sky visible between the rows of tall buildings. Dark gray—another storm tonight. Paul sighed. He knew this was part of the reason he longed to get off this world, to go someplace new and vital, untouched and pristine—a place where the whole ecological system, including the weather, hadn't been thrown so severely out of balance as it had been here.

Paul ran his fingers through his hair, felt a hangnail catch on some of the strands. He absentmindedly took some small scissors from this desk drawer and clipped the offending hangnail. He'd have to make sure the equipment was all in good working order before Dr. Nakagawa arrived.

Paul stepped over to a small hydroponics system in one corner of the lab and pulled a carrot from the water. It was fresh and alive, its green top still attached. At one end of the lab was a raised circular platform, about one and a half meters in diameter, surrounded by poles going up to a metal awning about three meters above. The poles were surrounded by metal bands that stabilized the structure. In one section the bands had been left off, leaving a doorway onto the platform.

Paul took a bite of the carrot, while carefully keying in coordinates on the panel attached to the side of the structure. He rechecked his work and nestled a pair of goggles over his eyes. Then, holding the carrot by its green top, he stuck about two-thirds of the orange root section into the enclosure framed up by the poles and bands, and said, "Initiate preset procedure."

A brilliant flash of light radiated out from inside the enclosure. Paul lowered his goggles and removed the carrot from between the poles and bands—or at least, so it seemed at first glance—for in fact, the lower two-thirds of the carrot, the part that had been inside the area above the transport pad, had entirely disappeared.

Paul walked casually across the lab and picked up the rest of his carrot from a small raised platform at the far side of the room, where it had been transferred to. He took a bite of the piece of carrot that he had just picked up from the second platform, chewed it carefully, then took a bite from the portion of the carrot with the green top and chewed it.

"The same," he said, with a shrug.

He went back to the transport pad and, carefully referring to a star map set up next to it, keyed in some coordinates. He rechecked his work three times this time.

The door to the lab swung open and Paul's assistant, Jamie, poked his head through.

"Dr. Nakagawa's here to see you," he announced cheerfully. Paul glanced over at him—though Jamie was only three years his junior, Paul often felt the gap was wider than that, perhaps because Jamie, though capable and hard working, seemed unburdened by the sorts of responsibilities Paul carried.

"Okay, show him in," Paul answered.

Jamie disappeared for a moment, then returned with a small man dressed in drab business clothes.

"Dr. Nakagawa, this is Dr. Paul Rockwell. Dr. Rockwell, this is Dr. Masato Nakagawa," Jamie said.

The two scientists exchanged greetings and a hand shake. Paul tried quickly to assess the older man, in whose hands lay the purse strings for the whole project. Paul saw before him a man in his mid-fifties, shorter than he had expected, very serious looking—and somehow shy.

Dr. Nakagawa cleared his throat softly. "Well, shall we begin?"

"Yes, certainly," Paul answered. "Ah, I believe you are familiar with our basic program. The goal of this project is to try to humanely reduce the population of the world by half. The world's population, as you know, continues to soar," Paul said, as he casually directed his assistant and Dr. Nakagawa over to a display screen on the lab's wall. Paul hoped Dr. Nakagawa wouldn't be annoyed at being reminded of things he already knew, but Paul didn't want to leave anything out that might help build a case for the importance of his project.

"The population passed twelve billion within the past decade," Paul continued, "and is thought to be nearing thirteen billion now. We see all sorts of problems associated with these soaring population figures. The overcrowding in cities is especially apparent to us urban dwellers, as is the short supply of necessary resources—ah, such as energy—and food, potable water, basic materials for necessary goods such as clothing, equipment, housing. That is, even as we are all a part of the population problem, we all experience a reduced quality of life because of it."

Paul felt nervous as he spoke, but was pleased to hear his voice was steady. "Our farm lands are depleted, and our food, already short in quantity, is increasingly poor in quality, as well. Tensions between nations soar as various groups attempt to reclaim ancestral lands and the resources contained on them. Wars break out in areas in which we long ago thought peace was firmly rooted. You know all this, I realize, but it's important to remember the scope of the problem. It's not just overcrowding.

"As a result of having burned through nearly all the world's reserve of fossil fuel, we have dramatically altered the world's atmosphere. The cataclysmic destabilization of the world's climate that has resulted has also greatly reduced the world's food-growing potential. While we support a larger population than ever before, most now live a marginal existence.

"And the impact, of course, isn't just on people," Paul continued. "With the climate so altered and so little undeveloped land remaining, eighty-nine percent of the larger mammal species that existed a century ago are now extinct or survive only in zoos or other such preserves. The rate of extinction of other fauna and flora is also shockingly high. People have simply claimed most bio-sustainable land for farming, or housing, or other kinds of construction or use.

"With fewer people, these pressures could be greatly reduced. Some recovery might still be possible—perhaps, in time, even a revised kind of ecological balance. Surely not the same as it might have been a few centuries ago, and with far fewer species involved, but certainly an improvement is possible if these pressures could be relieved.

"Likewise, with a reduced population, the quality of life of those human beings remaining on the planet would be greatly improved. Not only would so many more resources become available to them, but the tensions over those resources would be greatly diminished.

"In short, we need fewer people, or we need more land. And we think we've found a way to provide both. At least we've made strides toward it."

"Yes, that's the project I'm here to review," Dr. Nakagawa said.

"That's right," Paul said. "As you know, for many years we've wished we could find another habitable world and send people to it. Even locating such a world is challenging enough, and the amount of time it would take to transport people such vast distances by conventional means—a rocket, for example—would be enormous. Some sort of stasis would be needed, for the trip itself would likely take much longer than a single lifetime.

"The solution we're pursuing, in contrast, would be instantaneous. Rather than traveling through space and time as we normally would think of doing, we've found a way to circumvent space-time all together; in effect, we simply step out of it at one location and then back into it at another."

"Yes, that's what you said in your funding proposal. How are your experiments coming along?" Dr. Nakagawa said. His tone was practical, businesslike, with what Paul hoped was a note of genuine interest.

Paul moved his hand in front of a screen on the wall of the lab. It lit up, displaying an image of a broad field of stars. "Map section QDR-231, maximum resolution," he said, and the display zoomed in, showing a few large, bright stars with four smaller dots scattered around one of them. Paul gestured toward one of the dots on the map. "You see here, this is G3-97, a planet circling a star about forty-seven light-years from here. Using our most powerful non-terrestrial telescopes, we estimate that it's a good candidate for habitation—the frequency of the light reflecting off it suggests it may have large bodies of water as well as land. It's a blue-green planet, like our own. It's a nearly ideal distance from its sun, with a regular orbit—not too elliptical. Temperature variations should be acceptable over much of its surface. Also, the planet's size and density are much like earth's. Its gravity should be comfortably in the range of 0.8 to 1.2 G's."

Dr. Nakagawa leaned over to take a look at the map, "What's the possibility of sending somebody there to scout it out?"

Paul took a deep breath, then let it out slowly. "We still have two major obstacles before we can proceed to that stage. The first is that we can only send electromagnetically unified sets," Paul said, as he put on some gloves and stepped over to a cage on a table a couple of meters from the display screen. Jamie lifted the lid of the cage, and Paul picked up a mouse from inside it.

"Ah, for example, we could send this little guy," Paul said, "as we already have some of his cousins—and he would go just fine because, as a biological organism, he *is* an electromagnetically unified set. But his hair and the unattached outer part of his nails—the part that extends beyond the nail bed—aren't tied into that system strongly enough. They would be left behind."

"Yep, and then we have a little pile of hair and nails to clean up afterward," Jamie chimed in.

"And people?" Dr. Nakagawa asked, glancing at Paul's assistant.

"Oh, it's the same," Jamie answered. He seemed to enjoy having something to contribute.

"Also clothes, equipment would remain behind," Paul added.

Dr. Nakagawa raised an eyebrow, shifted uneasily. "That sounds like a significant problem," he stated.

Paul nodded. "Yes, we'd like our first voyagers to go equipped for any contingency—even armed. Right now, we couldn't do that." Paul tried to sound factual, unconcerned.

"Ahm. Yes. And the other problem? You said there were two?" Dr. Nakagawa asked.

"Ah, yes," Paul answered. "We don't know how to retrieve them yet. Now, if you'd just come over here, we've set up a little demonstration for you. It's actually quite impressive what we're able to do so far." Paul strode across the room to the transport pad, trying to exude confidence. He was relieved that Dr. Nakagawa had allowed him to so quickly dismiss the second problem—hardly a small one. And of course, the problem was even bigger than Paul had suggested; not only were they talking about sending people forty-seven light-years away with no plan yet established for their return—but how could they even know if the equipment was aimed properly? What if it was off by even the smallest fraction? Projected over such a great distance, they could miss the planet altogether—or even its entire solar system.

"So this is the launch pad?" Dr. Nakagawa asked.

"Yes. We call it the 'transport pad.' And we now have our little voyager." Paul put the mouse down on the pad. "We've put these mice on an antibiotic, antiviral, antifungal regime—and sterilized them sexually. We don't want to accidentally transport any pathogens or pests into a pristine environment."

Paul handed out goggles and lowered his own into place, then signaled to his assistant, who rechecked the coordinates.

A moment later, Jamie nodded to Paul, and Paul said, "Initiate preset procedure." Again, there was a brief burst of white light—and the mouse was gone.

Paul looked at the transport pad and felt a small pang of guilt, sending the mouse off he knew not where.

"See, just the hair and nails," Jamie said, as he swept up the little pile and deposited it in the waste can.

"And the mouse?" Dr. Nakagawa asked.

"Has just been transported to the planet I pointed out to you on the chart," Paul answered. He hated to waste the energy on such an unnecessary display, but if it could help fund further research...

Dr. Nakagawa nodded his head slowly up and down. He looked thoughtful. Impressed—good, Paul thought.

"Okay, so let's say you solve the two problems you've just mentioned—how mass producible would this be?" Dr. Nakagawa asked.

"Well, we hope we would eventually be ready to take volunteers and send perhaps half the population of earth to an unpopulated planet. This process could be repeated as needed as Earth's population continued to increase," Paul answered.

"Very interesting. Very good," Dr. Nakagawa answered. He took a remote from a jacket pocket and reset his implant for credit-transfer protocol. "So what exactly is it you're in short supply of?"

"Well, as you can see, a functional prototype of the equipment has already been built. We just need the means to keep running it while we refine our experiments," Paul answered.

"Yes? Energy? Is this what you're referring to?" Dr. Nakagawa asked.

"Yes," Paul said. He hesitated to say the numbers he had in mind. He just about had his would-be benefactor hooked; he didn't want to lose him now.

"Well? What do you request?" Dr. Nakagawa prompted.

"Well, just sending a mouse like this requires roughly 185 kilojoules. We will need to continue with experiments at that level for some time," Paul said.

"One hundred and eighty-five kilojoules!?" Dr. Nakagawa exclaimed, incredulous.

"To transport twenty grams forty-seven light-years instantly? Yes," Paul answered.

"If it's that much for a mouse, how much for a human being?"

"We've estimated that would require approximately 750 megajoules," Paul answered.

Dr. Nakagawa looked stunned. He shook his head slowly. "And you think you're going to transport half the world's population with an energy demand like that?" he said, his voice rising at the end.

"No." Paul tried to sound very assured. "We would have to refine it, or find a better energy source. The work is young, Dr. Nakagawa—but vital."

"Dr. Rockwell, as I'm sure *you* know, having essentially run out of oil and coal, we've had to convert to archaic nuclear technology just to meet our current energy demands—and *that* presumes heavy rationing all around. Do you realize how long a single nuclear plant would have to run to produce enough energy to transport just one person to this G3-96 planet?"

"Yes—it would be roughly one half hour per person sent."

Dr. Nakagawa did some quick calculations using the mathematics functions of his implant. "Yes—and that plant would have to run roughly 350,000 years to send half the population of the world!"

"I know it seems daunting if you think of it that way," Paul said, trying to sound steady, "and that energy figure seems hopelessly large, I know. But a single person could be transported using an amount of energy equivalent to that released in just one lightning strike—and lightning strikes several million times a day globally. Of course, we've not yet figured out how to harness that energy, but all I'm saying is, there may be better energy resources in the future, and wouldn't it be good if this technology was ready when that time comes? After all, we've all invested so much in this research already. Sometimes these things take time to mature. We need to see this through."

Dr. Nakagawa looked thoughtful, glanced around the lab, sighed. "So what's the total you're requesting?"

Paul knew how these things were done. He carefully picked an inflated figure. "Twelve gigajoules."

Dr. Nakagawa sighed, then nodded. "I'll give you half—perhaps you'll find a way to reduce your energy demands." He spoke briefly into his remote, arranging the transfer.

"Thank you, Dr. Nakagawa. You're most generous," Paul responded.

"I hope that will be sufficient," Dr. Nakagawa added. "It *is* interesting work you're doing." He looked over toward Jamie and nodded.

"I'm sure we'll manage," Paul answered. Then he thanked Dr. Nakagawa, and they said their farewells, as Jamie opened the door and pleasantly ushered the visitor out of the lab.

◙   ◙   ◙

A heavy electrical cable rose up from a nearby power substation like a snake, curved over the top of a small hill, and dropped down to the fifth-floor rooftop of the building Paul's lab was in. Paul had his head out the lab's narrow first-floor window and was having a look at the new installation. He turned his face up and squinted his eyes against the wind and blowing rain. His usually boyish smile looked more like a grimace as he eyed the cable coming over the hill and down the side of his building, where it was bolted with bands of metal across it to hold it in place.

Paul pulled his head back inside the building and closed the window. He glanced around the lab at the cable running from the wall, through a rectifying unit, and into the transport pad's capacitor. Everything was hooked up and ready for the big current he'd just gotten energy credits for that afternoon.

Paul felt a little thrill at how things were coming together—the project was really under way. He'd worried that it was premature to commit to the expense of rewiring before the energy credits were assured, but he'd gone ahead and ordered the installation a week earlier. It had seemed an important gesture, and after all, what use would that money have been to the project without the energy to proceed? Now he was glad about the decision he had made.

Paul picked up a lab coat from the back of a chair and dried his face and hair with it. He reflected on the fact that these rains were in what once had been the winter rain pattern, but were now common this late in the spring (while the "normal" winter rains had arrived only twice in the previous decade). Paul returned the lab coat to the back of his chair, carefully setting the shoulders over the corners of the chair back. He was working late tonight—probably the only one in the building.

A soft buzzer sounded, and Paul took his food packet—a late supper—from the warming unit, then looked down at the silvery bag in his hand. Yet another meal of primary-grown nutrients from genetically altered yeasts—"Saccomite," as most people knew it. It didn't sound very attractive, he thought, but its widespread use was one of the few reasons his region hadn't been overrun by periodic famine, as so many other parts of the world had been. Paul wondered casually what the world's population would be now without such episodic starvation keeping the numbers down.

Paul sat down on the window sill and began to eat, turned sideways so he could look outside at the gusts of wind and rain. While he'd been working, he'd had his implant turned on low, with the Corprogov news feed running in the background. Now he turned it up and began to pay it some attention. He always found the way the news was announced annoying. The newscasters tried so hard to give a positive spin to even the most disturbing stories, their voices sing-song, artificially cheery. Still, this was the way the news was disseminated. If he wanted to know about things, he had to get it with all that syrup.

The news itself was much as usual. Impressions drifted though Paul's mind of the drought and famine in Western Europe, where frail children stood under a punishing sun. Next came images of camps populated by the so-called "permanent refugees" of the Great Amazon Fire, which had consumed the vast South American rainforest nearly half a century before, leaving in its place an arid savannah and a whole sub-class of people in constant need of outside aid. This was followed by a story about new rainfall records and flooding in the American Midwest, and then by another story about the persistence of "supremacy" or "identity" cults (which seemed endlessly to reassert themselves no matter how hard the larger culture struggled to overcome such bigoted views).

When that story ended, an old picture of New York City was projected into Paul's mind. This faded and was replaced by an image of narrow waterways above which the upper floors of skyscrapers projected like canyon walls. In the background, the announcer discussed the continued increase in global temperatures and the endless rise of ocean levels, fed by melting polar ice. Paul shook his head—he'd heard that had been a great city. Like so many others that had been lost or largely submerged—London and Tokyo, Miami and Shanghai, Alexandria and Mumbai...—their once-reliable steel structures now badly rusted beneath the waterline, their populations dispersed. The world was filled with underwater "ghost towns" that had once been great cities—and other, inland cities that had used up their water resources and "gone dry," prompting their populations to desert them, and crowd into a shrinking number of still-functional cities.

Paul sighed and turned off the Corprogov feed. No really new stories today. Paul used his remote to activate a file he'd bought from a local vendor. Immediately the sound of frogs singing played through his head. He smiled— a nice change from the news. This particular file wasn't something he could access through Corprogov's broadcasts. Corprogov considered the sounds of extinct animals too dreary a topic for general consumption. They believed that ready access to such sounds might encourage disquiet in a population now happily pacified with pleasing virtual experiences fed to them through their implants. Why it was thought that people might be distressed by the songs of frogs and not by the daily news feed, baffled Paul—except that perhaps the news could be seen as just "normal life," while the songs of extinct animals might inspire a realization of just how much of the exuberant tapestry of life had been irretrievably lost.

Paul leaned against the window frame and took another bite from his food packet. He turned up his implant volume a little more and the singing of frogs drowned out the sounds of the storm and all the ambient noises around him. Listening to the frogs, Paul remembered a conversation he'd had with his grandfather when he was a boy. The two of them had been hiking along a trail crowded with hoverboarders in the Santa Ynez Mountains, northwest of Los Angeles, and had stopped to look out over the Pacific Ocean below. His grandfather's eyes had glazed over sadly as he'd looked out toward the water. Paul, who'd been perhaps thirteen at the time, had looked up to ask a question and had seen the sad look in his grandfather's eyes.

Paul had long felt a special sympathy with his grandfather. Each of them had lost the one person in the world who mattered most to him, and for each of them it had been the same person: Paul's mother.

Paul had seen that sad look in his grandfather's eyes that day as he'd looked off toward the coast, and Paul had thought of his mother—though he was old enough to realize that there were many reasons his grandfather might feel sad. Still, whenever Paul saw sadness in his grandfather's eyes, he always felt a pang of sadness of his own—and of guilt.

Paul had looked up at his grandfather that day, and commented on how sad he looked.

His grandfather's expression was thoughtful, as he replied, "Down there, do you see those little islands just off shore?" His grandfather gestured, and Paul followed the line of his sight. "Those are the Santa Barbara Islands. There used to be a vibrant town in the lowlands below those hills—those hills, which are now islands."

"That was before the oceans rose, Granddad?" Paul asked.

"Yes," his grandfather said. "The hand of man has changed so much."

Paul was silent, as his grandfather stared out into the distance.

"When European explorers first came to America," his grandfather continued, "they sometimes wrote descriptions of what they had seen. What they saw was wonderful, and would seem strange to us now. One described the waters off the coast of Newfoundland as so teeming with fish that one could harvest them by lowering a basket into the water. They told of water at times so dense with cod that ships had trouble making passage through it. Inland, one could see to the bottom of lakes filled with water as clear as rain. It was said that sycamore trees in the forests of the Midwest grew so large that more than twenty people could take refuge in a single hollowed trunk."

As his grandfather continued to speak, images came up bright and alive in Paul's young mind: a vast prairie covered endlessly with bison so densely packed that the land appeared alive with their movements; passenger pigeons in flight, filling the sky from horizon to horizon for a day at a time, as their migratory flocks passed overhead; salmon climbing up rivers in summertime in such numbers that from a distance the water shone red, illuminated by their shining wet bodies pressing and pulsing together.

"People weren't alone on the planet then, as we very nearly are now," he told Paul. "The world was alive in a way we have forgotten to even think possible."

His grandfather was silent then, as Paul turned his own gaze out toward the water, trying to image how it might have been then. He wished he could have been alive to see such wonders! He stood there in the fading light of early evening and tried to imagine the old coastline with the water lapping up on a beach—which was, now, much too deep beneath the water for anyone to hold their breath and dive down to touch it.

Paul felt sad as he took another bite from his food packet and refocused his attention on the frog sounds. He found their voices, carried to him from more than a century before, soothing to hear. Listening to these sounds also made him feel more determined in his work—the idea that developed lands could somehow be re-opened, depopulated, and made wild again, excited him. While it was true that extinct animals could never actually be brought back, so much could be improved.

Paul so deeply wanted the project to succeed. He had had, since his early teen years, a passion for finding some way to make things right in the natural world again. Within a few years, he had begun to contemplate new ideas about extra-space-time travel—ideas that he had continued to explore and develop through college, graduate school, and then post-doctoral work at Caltech—all of which he'd completed in record time. Finally, he'd been able to establish the Depopulation Project, which he had been hard at work at for the last five years.

Certainly his ideas had not been widely accepted. He'd had to face a lot of obstacles and criticisms, and there had been times he'd felt discouraged—but maybe soon he'd be able to show what his work could really be. People would have to take notice. Paul wanted that validation, not just for the momentum and funding it would provide for his work, but also for the personal recognition it could offer. Somehow, deep down, he felt that if he could make things right in the natural world, they would be right in his own life, as well. Paul imagined the acclaim that would follow: the awards Corprogov would give, the public recognition—and the way Sheila would wrap her arms around him and love him as she had never done before. All of this would happen, he was sure, if he could just make the process work!

Paul saw a flash of lightning and distantly heard the rumble of thunder over the sound of his implant. He sighed. He'd finished his meal packet. No more daydreaming. He was a couple of days overdue on doing routine maintenance on the transport unit. He gathered up some tools and set them on the pad, then rechecked the basic programming on the external input panel he'd used earlier, still set for planet G3-97, where the mouse had been sent.

Paul climbed up onto the transport pad and crouched down to open an interior floor panel, where he could monitor and test the circuits.

Outside, the rain was coming down in sheets, blown and folded by the wind. A brilliant flash of lightning cracked open the air with a resonant boom, as it arced between a cable rising above a near-by hill and a clouded sky torn by storm. The heavy current from the flash cut though the insulation around the wires and traveled along that line, down the hill, to the bend where the cable met the building. The hot lightning energy sped along those wires, pulsing beneath the steely brackets that wed the cable to the side of the building, down one, two, now three floors of the building, running invisibly, wrapped in insulation, sizzling, racing downward.

Inside the chamber surrounding the transport pad, Paul had just opened the inner panel to take his measurements. He saw the lightning flash and heard the boom of thunder in the same instant. He looked around. He couldn't feel the electricity moving down through the cable from the hill, down along the outer wall of the building—but somehow he sensed it, like a wave rising up to overtake him. In an instant the energy had moved into the room with him, into the transport chamber. A brilliant flash of white light filled the room.

And Paul was gone.

Only his clothes, some tools, and a few small piles of hair and nails remained.

PART II

◉

ARRIVAL

◌ 2 ◌

When Paul woke it was dark. He lay face down in a sloping meadow covered with a tall, grass-like plant. The plant's stems pressed into his bare skin. He rolled over. Where am I? he thought. Wasn't I just in the lab?

His head hurt. He pressed his hand up against it to soothe the ache. His hair—where was it? Bald? Oh my god, he thought—I *was* just in the lab, working on the transport pad. He remembered opening the floor panel, the flash of lightning.

It can't be! Paul raised up on one elbow, shivering a little in the chill atmosphere, and looked around him. A large reddish moon hung low in the sky beyond some nearby hills.

No! He sat up, and a wave of dizziness and nausea moved through his body. No, no! He checked his nails. Short. He checked his hair. Gone, too.

He had been transported. But where to? He remembered carefully checking and rechecking the settings for G3-97.

"It can't be," he thought and began to tremble.

He tried to stand up, but as he did another wave of nausea and dizziness swept over him. He blacked out before he could get to his feet.

◌   ◌   ◌

Paul awoke again at dawn. The moon was gone, but now a clear, bright sun hovered just above the horizon. Paul remembered waking the night before. He sat up and looked around. He was torn between his excitement at having actually been transported to another world and the dread he felt at understanding that there was no likely means for his return. He took a deep breath into his lungs. The air was clear, breathable, unpolluted—perhaps better, even, than the air at home. He stood up, still a bit wobbly with the nausea and dizziness that had gripped him the night before, and looked around.

They'd done a good job selecting this place. Yes—it was quite earth-like.

He found himself in the midst of rolling hills covered with the same grass-like plant he'd felt pressing against his skin the night before. It grew in clumps that reached almost to his knee. Amid them were other plants that grew up higher still. Some of these put up long, slender shoots, which reached even above Paul's head and from the ends of which dangled small, flower-like purple growths. The land was scattered with plants like these, and with other, smaller, plants, many of which were covered with their own colorful growths.

Other vegetation sprouted up in the midst of these relatively low-growing plants. Large, tree-like plants grew out of the soil in fractal-like patterns, starting with thick trunks, then splitting and branching until the tips of the growths were narrow and twig-like. From them grew what appeared to be moderately sized "leaves," ready to catch the sun.

Paul looked around with admiration at the planet they had selected, then turned his gaze up from the "leaves" to the sun in the sky beyond, and was pleased to note that this sun shone with essentially the same spectrum of light as Earth's sun. That had been one of the requirements for the project; the size of the sun, the spectrum of its light, its distance from the planet, were all carefully selected so the ecosystem would be most earth-like and appropriate for human habitation. They'd done a good job.

Paul's heart pulsed with a shattered mix of emotion. He understood, perhaps better than anyone else could, just how truly desperate his predicament was. He had no clothes, no food, no water, no way of returning home—no way even of communicating with anyone there—and yet this, this world! A swell of pride rose in his chest amid waves of thrilled excitement and barely controlled panic. What he and his team had accomplished! He had been transported to another world, forty-seven light years from home—and not just any other world, *this* world, selected from countless others, carefully, in a process that had taken years. They had found this one, this one world, like a needle in a vast, galactic hay-stack—and here he stood now, breathing clear air, on a world so very much like his own! The fact that all their efforts had culminated in his accidental transport made little difference in this: it was a stunning achievement.

Paul steadied himself. He would have to stay focused, he told himself. This was no time for celebration, nor could he allow himself to fall prey to his fears. His eyes swept along the surrounding hills. He noted, again, the fractal-like growth pattern of the "trees." An especially striking specimen stood at the top of the hill Paul found himself on the side of. Its thick trunk rose up, then bent parallel to the ground for the better part of a meter before rising skyward again. Paul considered how the fractal pattern of its growth was typical of Earth's vegetation—in fact, it characterized patterns and designs of nature throughout Earth's ecosystems—and here he had found the same patterns on a world so far from home. It reminded him that Earth was not isolated from the rest of the universe, that the natural laws that had shaped his world had shaped the rest of the universe as well.

Paul turned and took in the scene around him. The hill with the especially magnificent fractal-tree at its top swept down toward a small valley with a long tree-studded meadow running the length of its center. On the far side of the valley rose more rolling hills, which were covered with the same "grasses" that surrounded him and with other low-growing plants, and which were dotted with the branching fractal-trees. Above was a sky, blue as any seen on Earth, spotted with small, white, puffy clouds. The air was soft and slightly cool, the sun warm, and though a gentle breeze blew across Paul's bare skin, he was neither too hot nor too cool.

Paul wanted so much to contact his coworkers in the lab back home. This place was magnificent! How useful this could be—a whole new land, sweet and raw and fresh, ready for new settlement.

Paul stood, his mouth agape, struggling between his fear of being stranded here and his overwhelming pride and awe at what they had accomplished, and accomplished so beautifully. If only he could contact his team and tell them—but there was no way. Even if they had agreed to some sort of light-based signal (a kind of laser-driven Morse code had been considered) the light itself would take decades to reach earth, and there would be nobody there waiting for it, watching for its arrival—even if Paul had had some way of building, powering, and properly aiming such a device. No—there was no way of communicating with his team, no way of telling them the transport had been aimed correctly, that he had survived, no way of coaxing them to send—what? Water? They had yet to figure out a way to make it sufficiently electromagnetically unified to transport—and even if they achieved that, how could they send the container? What then? Seeds? Yes, seeds, maybe, but the energy required... when they didn't even know if he was alive... And even if they could somehow be certain he had survived, with the energy budget they had there was no way they could send him enough to live on until he could plant and harvest a crop of his own. Even to try would likely bankrupt the program and mean its end.

No, there would be, could be, no help from home.

Paul's mind spiraled around the thought, and for a moment he perceived himself as though from a distance, alone and naked on a vast landscape, the only human in a new world. The image made his heart thunder, and he tried to rein in his thoughts. It was no good, it was no good at all, looking at it that way. He would manage somehow. He must attend to his own survival, here and now. He took a few deep breaths, and his heart slowed to something like its normal pace.

As calmly as he could, Paul assessed his situation. It's morning on a clear, bright day, he told himself. It may be hot later on. His first priority should be water, then some kind of shade or shelter. He hoped that water could be found. He looked again at the topography of the land. If rain did fall in this world it should run down these hills and gather at the lowest point, he reasoned. And wherever it had gathered, he would expect to find plants gathered there, too, drawing on that water.

Paul started down the hill in front of him, thinking that perhaps he would find adequately potable water lower down amid the trees at the bottom of the hill. The jarring of his footfalls brought his headache, nearly indiscernible since he'd woken, back to the surface. He tried to take gentle steps, both for his head and his feet, as he was unaccustomed to walking barefoot. After a few steps, he decided the best way to walk on this tall, stiff-stalked grass was to push the stalks down in front of each foot, bending the long, smooth fibers so they made a sort of "mat" he could step on. Walking like this was reasonably comfortable for his feet, a fact Paul found reassuring—he could walk a long way like this, he decided, even without shoes.

As Paul strolled along, naked under the bright, clear sun, he tried to reason out why the transport process had made him so ill. None of the mice they had transported within the lab had shown any sign of illness afterwards—although they had had a tendency to shiver at room temperature until their fur grew back. Paul suspected the ill effects he'd suffered had something to do with the great distance he'd traveled. Forty-seven light years, instantaneously! he thought. Incredible.

After a few minutes, Paul reached the bottom of the small valley. Up ahead was a cluster of the fractal-trees. Paul hurried on, strolling between widely spaced trees until he reached the cluster.

He stepped into its dark, quiet shade, then stood still for several minutes looking around and listening to the rustle of the breeze through the grass and trees. It was a beautiful spot, with the trees forming a kind of canopy, and the bright, clear day outside. Paul squatted down and pulled back the leaf-litter in search of a moist puddle, but found no water.

It's just the first stop, he reassured himself. No reason to expect it to be that easy to find water.

Paul continued along the valley floor and soon had left behind the cover of the trees. Out in the open, now, he spotted a large boulder and detoured just a bit so he could climb up on it and survey the land. Before him, the little valley he was in grew gradually deeper and wider. Another cluster of fractal-trees were gathered only another couple hundred meters ahead. In the area between where he stood and that cluster, the land opened up, forming an unbroken grassland with very few trees.

Paul climbed down from the boulder and proceeded along the gradually down-sloping ground in the direction of the next tree-cluster. After a while, he noticed what seemed to be a very small path at his feet, weaving serpentine through the grass.

A path! What sort of creature could have made it? Paul wondered.

He bent down, and as he did, his head began to throb again and a wave of nausea moved up from his stomach. Paul deliberately pushed aside these sensations and, kneeling, examined the path. He immediately saw the marks left by current—by current, yes, not a path. A miniature gully. Some sort of liquid, perhaps water, had flowed through here. He stood and looked ahead, squinting his eyes beneath the hot sun. The next cluster of trees was denser than the one he'd just left. His hopes rose that he would find water there.

He continued on and within a few minutes had reached the cluster and entered its shade. He paused and looked around. It was cool here and perhaps a bit damp. As his eyes adjusted to the shadows, he saw what looked like water standing at the base of some fractal-trees only a few meters ahead.

Since he'd started down the hill, he'd been able to push his fears to one side and stay focused on the task at hand. Now, suddenly, the importance of this moment shook through him. Here he was, an incomprehensible distance from home, naked, with no resources... If this was not water... He pushed the thoughts aside. It *had* to be water. It was unlikely there were strange elements, or even strange compounds, on other worlds, at least not world's like this one, with gravity so nearly the same as earth's.

The whole universe is of a kind, he reassured himself. It's all created by the same forces. A liquid, at this temperature—it had to be water. What else could it be? An oil?

Paul stepped up to the little pond. It looked like water—but was it? Even if it was, would it be safe to drink? Paul hadn't realized how thirsty he was until that moment. He knelt down next to the small pond (really no more than a large puddle) and sniffed. The smell was earthy—moist, rotting leaves, soil— that was all. He put his fingertips into the liquid, sniffed at his fingertips, put them to his lips. He tasted.

Water, he thought. Just water. He frowned a bit. He had no idea what micro-organism might be growing in it. If he drank, it could make him sick; without it, eventually he would die. He saw little choice but to go ahead and try it. He cupped his hands and lowered them gradually into the liquid, letting it run in slowly over his fingers, in at the base of his palms, trying to keep out as much debris as possible. Then he raised his hands to his lips and swallowed the liquid down.

Water. Yes. The taste was right. It had to be. But even so, he drank just that much. It was this to drink or nothing, he told himself, but still he wanted to be careful, to see first if it made him sick, before he drank his fill.

Resting back on his heels, Paul looked around the little grove that sur-rounded him. If this water turned out to be good and he didn't get sick from it, he decided, he'd make this shady area his base camp. He sat down by a tree and leaned against it, thinking about what would come next. Before long, he would have to do something about food—if he was even up to eating. He still felt queasy and a bit dizzy. He should rest before he did more, he decided.

Paul closed his eyes and leaned his head back against the trunk of the fractal tree, but he was too anxious to relax. Instead, he got up and stood under one of the trees at the outer edge of the cluster, just inside its shade, and again surveyed the surrounding land. He looked back up the valley in the direction from which he'd just come. The especially elegant fractal-tree with the bend in its "trunk" could just be made out at the top of a now-distant ridge. With his eye, Paul traced the path he had made down the hill and along the center of the small valley. As his sight swept along the curve his path had taken, it came to rest on the boulder from which he had earlier surveyed the area.

The boulder.

Hm.

The boulder looked awfully familiar.

Then suddenly it became clear to him—the lay of the land here, the size of the boulder—its exact undulations, its grooves and ridges...

He stared at it with stunned comprehension. But it couldn't be.

It made no sense—and yet, there it was, as plain to him as if he'd recognized another person's face.

It was the boulder the Strandford expansion had been built around. It was the same boulder he passed on his way to work every morning and again every night on his way home!

Paul felt dizzy, and the nausea he'd felt only fleetingly since the night before swept over him with force. He lowered himself to the ground at the base of the tree.

What was going on? Paul trembled. His thoughts blurred. It couldn't be!

Paul sat staring for several minutes, long minutes in which he felt perhaps more alone than he had ever felt before in his life.

After a time, the trembling subsided and his thoughts cleared a bit. He was a scientist. He would figure this out piece by piece. In his mind, Paul went over the theory of extra-space-time travel, the conceptual basis of his work. There had been naysayers all along who had suggested that cutting in and out of the space-time continuum in that manner could disrupt it, alter it in fundamental ways. Paul had had strong theoretical reasons to disagree, but now he didn't know what to think. Had he done something terribly wrong? Had he disrupted the space-time continuum in some way, changed the historic flow of events? Had he wiped out all the people? Had he destroyed them and all their creations, as it now seemed?

Paul sat on his heels with his knees and shins pressed into the grass, facing the boulder, the sky big and broad before him, the sun bright. His sun. The sun he'd always known.

This just couldn't be.

Paul sat very still for several more moments, then the trembling came over him again, and he bent over, wrapped his arms around his knees, and sobbed out his fears and confusion.

3

Hours later Paul woke, disoriented. Night had fallen, and as he roused himself from sleep in the darkness, for a moment he tried to place himself in his apartment. *Why so cold...bed hard...uncomfortable?* Then it came back to him: the transport, another world—no—*his* world...altered. Somehow. But how?

The afternoon before, Paul had lain on the rough grass, crying for a long time, but finally had allowed himself the comfort of escaping into an exhausted sleep. Now awake, he sat up and hugged his knees to his chest, shivering against a damp, cool breeze. The land beyond his little grove of trees was bathed in moonlight. Above, the moon hung, a brilliant white disk dappled with gray. Earth's moon, Paul thought. It was oddly comforting to see it there, so familiar, so exactly as it should be.

But why did it look so different last night, he asked himself? He recalled how it had appeared then: full and red, hovering just above the horizon. Just above the horizon... Yes, he'd seen it look large and reddish there before—a well-known optical illusion—yet he'd been fooled by it.

Paul rubbed his face with cold fingers. It was the Earth's moon he'd seen last night, he told himself. That was all. It was true—he'd never left Earth.

Paul again took in the view. It was earth's moon, all right—but this was not his earth. He again considered the idea that extra-space-time travel might disrupt the space-time continuum, corrupt the flow of events, but he still couldn't make it add up. Yet here he was, on an earth that had somehow been disrupted, altered.

A gust in the breeze made him shiver. He glanced around at the swaying boughs, listened as the leaves and branches rustled against one another, and as the wind moved through the grass. He cast his gaze around, and his eyes settled again on the boulder, in an open space between trees, framed in moonlight. So familiar! Another shiver caught him, but this time not from the chill. Home, but no home he belonged in.

Paul rested his chin against his knees and stared out at the grasslands, the boulder, the hill he had walked down the day before. He was aware of a gnawing feeling in the pit of his stomach, of his thirst, of the breeze and the sounds it made—and of other sounds, too, woven into the lift and sway of the wind. Other sounds. Soft, rhythmic. What is it? he wondered. Crickets? Yes, crickets—but something more. Paul tried to pick out the other sound he heard.

Frogs!

Frogs? But they're extinct! Paul's head swam with confusion.

"What have I done?" he whispered to himself. "Wiped out people, destroyed their creations—and brought back what people had destroyed?"

So surgical an effect. It didn't make sense.

Paul felt sick and weak, his tongue thick in his mouth, and he realized he was really thirsty. Only a sip of water since yesterday in the lab, he thought. No—it'd been more like a day and a half. Paul got to his feet and walked feebly over to the puddle he had drunk from the afternoon before. The air above the little pond was filled with the musty odor of rotting leaves. Paul hesitated before he drank. What other choice do I have? he asked himself, then submerged his cupped hands and let the dark, cold water flow in. He lifted his hands to his mouth, noticed the taste of the water—a thin, bitter tea—then drank until his thirst was gone.

Satiated and shivering, Paul found a spot, protected a little from the breeze, next to a nearby tree. He leaned back against the trunk and looked up into its branches.

Trees, he thought, shaking his head. Just earth trees.

If he hadn't felt so weak and frightened, he would have laughed at himself for having made so much of their "earth-like, fractal design." Yes, quite earth-like, indeed.

Paul closed his eyes, and images of the trees he'd seen the day before floated through his mind. Something about them jogged a memory from when Paul was maybe nine or ten. He'd been with his grandfather at his grandfather's apartment, sitting on the sofa, looking at a photo album. One of the pictures—it looked—yes, it looked like this land. Rolling hills covered with golden grasses and scattered trees. Trees like these with fractal-branches and deep-green leaves. And his grandfather was saying there had been many of these trees—live—live what? Live oaks. All over southern California. And they had died off because of some sort of disease.

Paul opened his eyes. The frogs, the trees, both missing from Paul's world, and yet here they were on this altered Earth. Paul thought for a few minutes about the stories his grandfather had told him, stories from his grandfather's youth, and stories from long before that, which his grandfather had read about in books written by the early European explorers and settlers. Those people would have seen these trees, Paul thought, and heard these frogs. Paul found himself wondering how much this altered Earth was like the way his world, his Earth, had been long ago, before Strandford had been built, before the settlers had even arrived.

"The past," Paul whispered.

The wind seemed to take his words and spread them across the hills, painting the hills in a new light. Paul lifted his head from his knees.

"The past," he whispered again, as though saying those words would somehow straighten out time, and he would wake and understand that he had just been experiencing an especially vivid program.

Could it be, that this is before the frogs went extinct? Before the trees disappeared? Paul thought. He looked out at the land around him. Even revealed only by moonlight, it looked so much like the picture his grandfather had shown him.

Could this be the past? Paul asked himself. As strange as that explanation seemed, it made more sense to him than the theory of space-time interference ever could. Besides, it was too strange to think that his effect would have been so surgical—that he could have somehow removed people and their creations, while reinstating what people had destroyed. No, it made no sense to think that the world itself had changed.

Paul shook his head, stunned as the thought became clear in his mind. Of course—he had been traveling in *space-time*. It was possible that, in stepping out of the space-time continuum, he had failed in his goal of stepping back into it at another location in space, but had instead reentered at another location in time—in the past, *before this land had been altered by human activity!*

Paul stared out at the moon-soaked landscape, trying to absorb this realization. The photograph his grandfather had shown him—it *was* a match, wasn't it? He wasn't just making this up? Yes, everything matched up right—the open space, the hills and trees. Everything. Everything—almost. Not the grass—not it or the other small plants that grew amidst it. The grass Paul had walked on grew in circular bunches, with gaps between those bunches where other small plants filled in. The photograph, as Paul remembered it, had instead shown one endless field of golden grain, tall and even.

Paul felt weary. His head still hurt some, and whenever he felt upset, the nausea he had felt so strongly the night before rose again in waves. He turned his head and lay his cheek against his knees, hugging his legs in tight against his chest to shield himself from the cold and wind. Did it even matter where he was, or why? He would still have to find some way to survive here.

Paul closed his eyes and let his thoughts drift for a few minutes. The grass in his grandfather's photograph came alive in his weary mind. The wind moved through it in waves, kicking up spray—no—kicking up seeds, which tumbled forward on the wind like spray on surf. The seeds were spread by the wind, by the waves, tumbling ever forward until it covered all the land—a great ocean of grass—like the ocean the settlers had crossed to come here, to come to this new land.

Paul raised his head and looked around. Of course. His grandfather had pointed at the photograph and had told him that the trees had been here and were now gone. And the grass—tall, golden oat grass—had been here since the settlers had come and spread their oat seeds a few centuries before—displacing the native plants and grasses, which had covered these rolling hills from the earliest times.

The earliest times. Paul stared out at the great, open, rolling hills. Untouched. Untampered with, unaltered since the earliest times.

Since before the settlers had come.

The past. Earth's past. It had to be.

The thought was at once exhilarating and terrifying.

But when? Paul thought. How far back had he traveled?

Paul looked back up toward the boulder lit in moonlight. How long had that boulder been there? A thousand years? he wondered. A million? Are there even people in the world now—or just ape-like creatures on some distant savanna, half a world away?

Paul's head hurt, and he pressed his forehead against his cold knees, staring into the darkness cradled between his arms. How could his calculations have been so wrong? He couldn't bear to think about it. He closed his eyes and wished that he had a warm bed to sleep in, wished that he would wake and find himself at home, at his apartment, with Sheila, warm and lovely, waking beside him—and not be in this place, not be in this place, anymore.

◘   ◘   ◘

Paul woke the next day, curled up like a ball at the base of the tree. He'd lain awake for hours the night before, cold and frightened, trying to think only pleasant thoughts, but finally he had drifted off and slept the sleep one has when the body demands attention. He woke feeling better than he would have expected—cold, stiff, and hungry—but better. He remembered having drunk a lot of water from the little pond the night before and was pleased that there were no noticeable ill effects.

The sun was up, and already the air had begun to warm. He had to admit it was a beautiful day. He stood and stretched, and it was like a conversation he was having with his body—each muscle, each joint announcing its complaint about his posture curled up against the cold the night before. His stomach and every other fiber soon joined in, the whole chorus demanding food.

Paul thought perhaps water would quiet his hunger until he could find some way of feeding himself. He stepped over to the small pond with the upbeat thought that, since he was in the distant past, the water was certainly water, and not some alien compound, and that the odds were good that it was free of anything that could cause him any serious gastronomic distress.

He squatted over the damp soil at the edge of the puddle. The sun was on the opposite side of the little cluster of trees than it had been the afternoon before, and reflected in the puddle's glass-like surface was the heavenly blue of the sky, bespeckled with the same sort of white, fluffy clouds that had drifted in it the day before.

As Paul leaned forward to take his drink, he was startled to find his own image reflected back. He was entirely bald, which he had already figured out, but it was strange to see himself without even eyebrows or eyelashes. His face, pink from too much sun, wore a tired, worried expression. At his temple was a large bruise—purple, mostly, and rimmed with a yellowish green. Paul brought his hand up and touched it softly. Sore. Apparently, his implant hadn't made the trip with him. Just as well, he thought. He would have no use for it where he was now.

Paul scooped up water and drank until the hollow feeling in his stomach was gone. He even splashed some water over himself in place of a bath—a move he quickly regretted, for it brought a sudden chill in the dry air. He squatted back on his heels, shivering, and it occurred to him that perhaps he should be more careful with his supply of water and not drink it when really he was hungry or splash it around. After all, what if he couldn't find more? This one puddle might have to last a long time.

Paul got up and took his morning pee out in the open, away from his little pond and the precious water it contained. Aside from having paused once to relieve himself on his journey through the trees the day before, Paul had no experience with doing so out in the open, and the action seemed daring and rule-breaking to him, even though there was no one around to see.

As he stood there in the open sun, he considered what he should do next. Food would have to be his next priority. He already could feel himself growing weak and didn't want to wait to try to find or catch something until he was too exhausted to make a successful effort of it.

He shook himself dry and looked up at the hill in front of him. It was taller than the hill he had come down the day before and might give him a better view of the land than the one he had had yesterday. Maybe if he looked from there, he could find a stream somewhere nearby, with clearer water than the puddle he'd been drinking from. He set off in that direction, and as he went, he continued to consider the question of how to get something to eat. The trees were all live oaks. They should have acorns in the fall, Paul reasoned, which might be edible, but now it was spring, and the trees would offer him nothing in the way of nourishment. Probably his best bet, Paul thought, was to catch an animal and eat it, but that answer only brought new questions in its wake. How would he catch it? How could he make a fire in which to cook it once it was caught?

The whole idea was foreign to Paul. He had only eaten meat a few times, on special occasions, and had never really gotten a taste for it. On his world it was a gourmet food, a delicacy, something for the very rich. In fact, many in his world objected to the whole idea of meat-eating, not because they thought it wrong to kill and eat an animal, but because they thought the food required to raise an animal to the stage where it could be slaughtered could better be used feeding some of the world's starving billions of human beings.

Paul reached the base of the hill and started up its side. He tried to focus his attention on the first of his questions: how to catch an animal? He remembered looking through one of the books in his grandfather's library when he was young. It was a book on historic Native-American culture. In it were pictures of tipis and hogans, of buckskin clothes and hand-woven blankets. On one page, Paul recalled, was a drawing of a large flat rock propped up with a stick. A short piece of string was tied to the bottom of the stick. Tied to the other end of the string was a lump of something, next to which the word "bait" was printed. In the shade of the rock, crouching and sniffing at the bait was a rabbit. The drawing had no action—it wasn't like the moving pictures the Stream provided—but action was implied. Paul had found that action-without-action quality interesting as a child. The rabbit would pull on the bait, and down would come the stick and with it the heavy rock, which would land on top of the rabbit, crushing it instantly.

It seemed like a simple enough plan, Paul considered, as he continued up the hill, but as before, one answer seemed only to raise more questions. The stick he could get easily enough, but where would he find a rock of the right size and weight? Or a string? Not to mention, he wasn't at all sure what he could use as bait. And how would he find the right location to set it up, where a rabbit or other small animal might just happen by?

The hill was steep, and Paul's feet were sore from all the time he'd spent walking barefoot the day before. He was concerned that even if he could answer these questions, he wouldn't be able to walk the distances necessary to accomplish all he would need to do. Also, he was aware that the skin all over his body was a sunburned pink from all the time he'd spent out in the open the day before. There wasn't much he could do about that, at least not right away, but it was discouraging and added to his anxiety, for it only called to mind more firmly how really ill-prepared he was for the circumstances he was in.

Paul paused near the top of the hill and looked back toward his small grove of trees with its puddle of water. Whatever he did, he mustn't lose track of how to get back to it.

Paul felt tired and squatted so he could rest for a minute, though he was now not far from the top of the hill. He stared back in the direction from which he'd come, out at the long valley between hills, and was again struck by how familiar the topography was. It made him think of Strandford, and of Sheila, and of how much he longed to be with her—and of how she would look at him, sometimes, when her attention was really on him, with such warmth and approval in her eyes; and of how, when she did, it made him feel like everything in the world was all right. He would give anything to have her beside him now, looking at him like that.

For several minutes, Paul stared out over the valley, lost in thoughts of Sheila—recalling a trip they had taken together to an exclusive high-rise hotel in the heart of Los Angeles about two and a half years before, in the early months of their relationship. Sheila had so wanted to go, and Paul had scrimped and saved so he could take her. What a good time they both had had! Paul remembered standing with her on the balcony there, looking out over the rooftops of the city, and talking together about the dreams they each had. He recalled Sheila turning and looking up at him, then, with such a deep, welcoming look in her eyes—as though there were nothing more she might wish for than to be there with him. They had made love that night, so beautifully, and Paul had felt he was the luckiest man in the world.

Sheila. Where was she now? he wondered. What was she doing?

Now. What was "now"?

Two days had passed since he'd disappeared. It had been—yes—Monday, May 14th, when he'd left. So that would make today Wednesday, the 16th, in the year 2136.

But that was her "today"—not his. How many centuries away from him was she now?

Paul shook his head, and in his mind he made a gesture, like draping a cloth over the question. It was painful even to think of it, and in any case, he might never have the answer.

Instead, Paul tried to imagine the scene at his lab when his team began to arrive on Tuesday morning. They would have come in fresh, with that air of early morning, and put on their clean lab coats, before entering the room with the transport pad. How would they have reacted when they saw what was left there, and realized he was missing? Paul wondered. Some with shock or even panic, he concluded, others with a cool detective's analysis of what had happened there. It would not have taken them long to arrive at the obvious conclusion.

And Sheila? How would she have responded?

Paul glanced down at his hands. A soft breeze blew over his sunburned skin, but he hardly noticed. He could see it very clearly. When he didn't come home Monday night, Sheila would have assumed that he was working late again. She would probably have intended to complain to him about not messaging her, and would have gone to bed without thinking anything more about it, until she woke and he wasn't there on Tuesday morning.

She probably would have gone to her job, Paul told himself, and tried to contact him after she arrived. Contact him at the lab—where Jamie would have answered and told her that Paul was missing there, too.

Would Jamie have told her about the evidence—the pile of clothes, nails, and hair on the transport pad? Paul wondered. Or would he have waited, till they could be more certain, till they could think things through? No, he would have just told her. Jamie could never keep his thoughts to himself. He would have told her, too, that the transport was set for G3-97, forty-seven light years away—and with no means of return.

She would have said, "Can't you send a rescue party?"

And he would have told her, "We would have no way of bringing them home, either."

Paul squinted into the sun, staring up along the little valley toward the hill where he had appeared two days before.

"'On G3-97, forty-seven light years away'—that's what Jamie would have told her," Paul whispered to himself.

"But that's not even where I am," he said softly. "No, Sheila, I'm not more than three or four kilometers from the lab right now." Three or four kilometers, he thought—and how many years? How many millennia?

Paul sighed, then dragged his eyes from the hill where one day his lab would stand. For a moment, he cradled his head in his hands, then rose, and as he did, his head spun for a moment. He steadied himself, and the spinning stopped.

Not well yet, he thought, and continued up the hill, carefully pushing and folding the grass down with each footfall.

Was Sheila distraught, he wondered—missing him? How could he let her down like this? He had meant to always be there for her, and now even this accident left him feeling guilty. Paul consciously returned his thoughts to his present circumstances. Where would he find rocks and clearer water? How could he make a cooking fire or clothes to shade his body from the sun? Why had he had to be on the transport pad when the lightning struck?

So many thoughts jumbled together and pushed for Paul's attention—but as he neared the top of the hill, not one was posing the question of what might await him when he reached the other side.

4

When he reached the top of the hill, Paul's eyes were on the ground, planning out each step so it would be easy on his bare feet. He almost crested the hill and started down the other side before he noticed that he had reached his goal. He looked up and scanned the horizon, starting in the north, then sweeping around so that the morning sun was on his back. Just more hills like the ones that lay behind him, was his initial impression—but as he scanned to the south, something caught his attention: a dark angular shape. It appeared to be part of something larger that was obscured behind a low-lying hill.

Paul's heart raced. He had to see what that was! He jogged along the ridge of the hill, moving southward, trying to improve his angle of view so he could see over the smaller, low-lying hill before him.

Suddenly his view opened up. The dark, angular thing was a building! A ranch house, Paul thought, of an old style, but bright and new-looking.

What year would that make this? What year did the settlers start to come?

People! Paul felt like jumping up and down but tried to keep his thoughts clear.

When would this be? The mid-1700s, maybe? Paul started down the hill. Yes, definitely a ranch house. He could see clothes hanging on a clothes line behind it. Just like in old photographs, Paul thought. What year would this be, before the grasslands went to oat grass? Could be mid-1800s. No telling, really. Paul had to admit he couldn't remember enough history to make a good guess.

In his rush to get down the hill, Paul put his foot down hard on a rock. He limped forward carefully, looking down to be sure of where he put his feet, and was suddenly aware, again, that he was entirely naked and stopped short.

Naked. That just wouldn't do. And didn't the Spanish colonize this area first? How early was that? Maybe he wouldn't even be able to speak English with the people in that ranch house.

Paul stopped his progress down the hill and, turning, walked back in the direction he'd come from, parallel to the ridge top, until the low-lying hill was again between him and the ranch house. Then he crept slowly down the hill he was on and up the low-lying one. When he was near the top of the small hill, he lowered himself to the ground and peered over its crest.

Paul squinted as the bright morning sun slanted across the land before him. It was a beautiful sight—the ranch house sitting there in the morning light. It was two stories tall, with what looked like a little extra space for an attic. It had a narrow porch, which ran along the west side of the house.

Paul couldn't tell what was happening inside the house, but the yard seemed quiet enough, except for a sort of rhythmic hum or buzz, which seemed to be coming from the far side of the house. Paul listened closely but couldn't identify the sound.

After a minute, he turned his attention to the clothes line. Clothes. He needed clothes. He thought about sneaking some from the line. There seemed to be no activity outside the house, except for whatever was making noise on the far side of it. He could probably take some of the clothes, if he was careful enough. He held his breath, thinking about it. What if he put on some of these people's clothes and then went to meet them? Wouldn't they recognize the clothes he was wearing?

Paul looked down at the line. Many of the clothes looked quite similar to others hanging there. A lot of the colors were muted earth tones.

Natural dyes, Paul thought. He noticed a lot of the clothes were the same shade of beige. Perhaps unbleached cotton.

As Paul lay at the hill's crest, looking down at the house and yard, he could feel his skin baking in the sun. Yes, a lot of the clothes *were* similar, he thought. He saw three pairs of blue pants and five beige shirts. Two of the beige shirts were of essentially the same design. If those colors and designs were common, Paul considered, then maybe it wouldn't seem strange if he wore them, too. Besides, what other option did he have? He couldn't just stay here in the sun to bake and starve. He could feel his body tense as he thought about what he'd have to do next. He just hoped no one would notice the clothes were missing—or at least not notice too soon.

Paul rose to a crouching position, then scampered down the other side of the hill as fast as his feet would tolerate. Soon, he was in among the clothes on the clothes line, looking for something that might be a decent fit. He pulled down one pair of blue pants and stepped behind a sheet to put them on. A little long in the leg and big in the waist, but they would do. He took one of the beige shirts off the line and put it on. A little big, too. He rolled up the sleeves to make up for their extra length, then buttoned up the shirt and tucked it in. Suddenly, he felt almost presentable. Grinning, he lifted his hand to run his fingers through his hair as a make-shift comb. Hair. No hair. That's right—no eyebrows, no eyelashes, either. Paul remembered his image in the pond.

And a bruise on my head, he thought. His heart was thudding in his ears, and he could feel himself trembling slightly all over. He was aware that he had no choice now but to present himself to strangers, to the very people whose clothes he had stolen—people to whom he would surely look strange, and with whom he might not even share a language—and he would have to ask them for their help. And he had to do it soon—the last thing he needed was to be caught standing among their clothes, wearing the clothes he had just taken.

Paul took a few deep breaths and looked toward the house, planning his route. A few high windows stretched across the back of the house facing toward the clothes line. If he was lucky, he could cross the yard and duck under those without being seen. He would then have to go around to the east or west. Not the west—someone might go out on that narrow porch and see him coming from the clothes line. So the east it would have to be.

Well, here goes nothing, Paul told himself. He dashed across the yard, then made his way quietly along the back of the house—or as quietly as he could, for he feared his thudding heart might give him away. As he turned the corner toward the east side, the rhythmic buzzing and humming seemed to grow louder. Paul ducked under another window, then paused to try to catch his breath and steady himself. He couldn't let his fear get the best of him, or he really would make a terrible first impression. He'd heard somewhere that in the old days, when the world wasn't so crowded, people were often quite helpful toward strangers. There was no way these people could suspect the truth, he told himself. They would see him as a stranger in need. It would be all right.

Paul took another deep breath and felt his nerves growing steady. He ducked under another window then crept the last couple of meters to the front of the house. He looked out across a broad front porch with a wooden railing, and into an open, dusty yard. Beyond that was a narrow lane, leading out through more hills toward the south.

Paul stepped out into the yard and saw then where the noise had been coming from. A woman, whose right side was turned toward Paul, stood between a couple of narrow, low tables toward the west side of the front yard perhaps twenty meters away. She wore a beige shirt, untucked, and loose brown pants. She was pushing a panel of sheet metal up and down in the middle of a plank of wood. Every time she pushed down came the buzzing sound, and every time she pulled up came the hum. It was hard for Paul to see from where he stood, but it appeared that with each stroke the metal panel moved a little further through the plank of wood.

Sawing? Paul thought. He vaguely recalled that there had been tools like the one she was using, long before the laser cutting tools.

From where Paul stood, he was facing the woman's side, watching the smooth, clean strokes she made with the saw. She had long auburn hair and tan skin. From where Paul stood, he could see enough of her face to guess she was in her late twenties or early thirties. She hadn't looked up since Paul had come around the corner. He felt certain she hadn't noticed him standing there. He thought again, briefly, about how he looked, then gathered himself to approach her.

Paul took a big breath, then strode as casually as possible into the yard, trying to make it look as if he'd come down from the hills to the east, rather than the north, as he had done—though he wasn't sure why the east should be any better. When Paul was about ten meters away he called out to her.

"Good morning!"

The woman stopped sawing and looked around. "Oh," she answered. "Good morning."

Paul stopped about three meters away from her. Good, she spoke English, he thought—and from his point of view, she seemed not even to have much accent.

"May I help you?" she asked.

"Yes," Paul answered. It felt strange to use his voice after not having spoken in two days. He cleared his throat, then added, "Ah, I'm lost—and I'm hungry. I was hoping you could maybe tell me where I could get some food."

The woman looked Paul in the eye. There was something about her look—penetrating, gentle.

In a moment she nodded slightly, then smiled. "Yeah, sure," she said, tipping her head in the direction of the house. "Marco's fixing breakfast right now." She pointed toward a door on the west side of the house, where the wide front porch wrapped around the house and became narrow. "Why don't you go on in there and see if he can give you something to eat."

"Thank you," Paul said. "That's kind of you." He took a step away backwards, then turned and walked toward the wide steps of the front porch. He had the feeling that she had assessed him and accepted him, as quickly as that.

"Watch out for the bottom step," she called after him. "It's kind of rickety. I'm getting ready to replace it now."

Paul stepped over the bottom step and climbed up onto the deep, south-facing porch, then walked around to the narrow porch on the west side of the house and knocked quietly on the door the woman had pointed at.

"Go on in," the woman called after him.

Paul, a little uneasily, opened the door and stepped inside. He found himself in a warm, brightly lit kitchen. The air smelled good, filled with the scents of cooking food.

A man standing at the range with his back to the door turned as Paul entered. He was a little taller than Paul, with straight black hair cut to the shoulder and warm-brown skin.

"Hello," he said, as he turned and saw Paul.

"Ah, hi. Are you Marco?"

"Yeah."

"The woman in the yard said just to come on in. She said you might be able to give me something to eat. I'm lost. I've been out all night."

Marco grinned a big friendly smile. "Oh, Anna? Sure, I can set you up with some breakfast." Marco started to turn back to the range, then cocked his head and looked at Paul again. "Are you doing okay?" He brought his hand up and touched the side of his own head in sympathy with Paul's bruise.

Mirroring him, Paul brought his own hand up and lightly touched the bruise. "Ah, I think it's okay. I must have hit it." Paul looked past Marco to the two pans with food cooking in them on the range. He wasn't sure what they contained, but it all smelled so good.

Marco nodded, looking Paul over with that same thoughtful expression Anna had had. "I'll get you something right now, if you'd like. Scrambled eggs with hash browns okay?"

"Yes, thanks," Paul answered, though he wasn't sure what "hash browns" were, or what made eggs "scrambled."

"Why don't you have a seat," Marco said. "I guess you already know I'm Marco—and you're?"

"Paul."

Marco smiled. "Do you want some coffee?"

"Uhm, yeah, thanks," Paul said. That, at least, he had heard of. It had been a common and well-liked beverage, as he recalled.

Marco poured Paul a cup of steaming brown liquid and set it down in front of him. He gestured toward two ceramic containers, which were already set on the table.

"I don't know what you like in your coffee, but there's the cream and sugar," Marco said, then turned back to the range.

Paul was glad Marco was so friendly, and he felt relieved, too, that nobody seemed too taken aback by his odd appearance. He looked into the ceramic containers and added a little from each to his coffee, guessing at what would be a normal amount, then looked up and around at the warm, homey kitchen. Paul figured if he was in a time period when ranch houses like this already existed, then there should at least be a small town in the area. It would be helpful to get a better idea of what the area was like now.

Paul took a sip from the coffee. It was hot and flavorful—sweet and a little bitter. Paul looked over at Marco, who was still facing the range.

"The coffee's good," he said.

Marco glanced over his shoulder. "Glad you like it."

"Ah, like I told you," Paul went on, "I'm lost. Could you point me in the direction of the nearest town?"

"Sure," Marco said as he turned the eggs in the skillet. "Just past those hills. It's not far," he said, pointing toward the southeast.

"And that would be...?" Paul began.

"Strandford," Marco said. That made sense to Paul. That's where the original town had started—long before it had expanded to the northwest.

Marco put a couple of knives and forks on the table, then got two plates out of one of the cabinets and began to serve up the meal.

"Hey, now I know why I made so much," Marco said.

"Yeah? Why's that?" Paul asked.

"You're here to eat it, aren't you?" Marco said, grinning, then set a plate down in front of Paul. Paul picked up a fork, but decided he should wait for Marco. The food made his mouth water.

"Go ahead and start," Marco said, as he scraped some of the eggs and hash browns onto another plate. "Anna's already eaten, and I'll be right there."

Paul took a bite. The food was heavenly. He didn't remember anything ever tasting this good, but then he'd never been this hungry before. Marco sat down with his own plate of food at the end of the table and began to eat.

Paul remembered again how odd his appearance was and tried not to eat his food too quickly, for fear doing so would only add to the impression of strangeness. Still, each bite was like ambrosia, and he had to deliberately pace himself as he ate. Between bites, he tried to focus on other questions he could ask Marco and on how to ask them. He wanted to try to figure out what year this was. Whatever the year, they sure had good food here.

"Is your head okay?" Marco asked. "It looks sore."

"Yeah, I think it looks worse than it is," Paul said, then realized he had no excuse for having seen what it looked like. He looked over at Marco, but Marco's face reflected nothing but concern. Paul took another bite of food and as he did, it occurred to him that he might be able to get some mileage from the bruise.

"Yeah," Paul went on. "I think I must have passed out. When I came to, I was disoriented, lost."

"That must have been frightening," Marco said.

Paul looked at Marco. "It was," he said simply. Paul was relieved he could tell him that much honestly, without worrying that he would reveal too much.

Marco nodded, his face sympathetic.

"It may seem strange that I would need to ask, but—can you tell me what day this is?" Paul asked.

"It's Wednesday, May 16th," Marco answered.

Paul's eyes grew wide. May 16th. It would be May 16th where he came from, too.

Paul held the fork poised midway to his mouth. "I, ah, I think I must have hit it pretty hard. Can you tell me what the year is?" Paul took the bite of food from his fork, trying to seem casual.

Marco gave him an odd look, but answered, "It's 2136, my friend."

Paul inhaled sharply, choking on the food.

Marco reached over and patted Paul firmly on the back.

"Are you okay?" he asked.

"Yeah," Paul answered, coughing, while trying to stop his head from spinning. Finally, he caught his breath and tried to answer the question he thought Marco must be thinking.

"For some reason, I was just having trouble remembering that this morning," Paul said. "Ah, was it 2135, or 2136? You know—it just wouldn't come to me."

"You must have hit your head pretty hard. Do you think you should see a doctor?"

"No, thanks—I think I'm okay now." But Paul didn't feel well at all. He felt another wave of nausea and dizziness coming on. He had left his world, yet he had not left it.

It's the present. The present. But not my present, he thought.

"I just think I need to rest for a while," Paul said, trying not to look stunned.

Marco looked at him, his eye steady, then he rose from his chair and squatted beside Paul. Marco took Paul's head gently between his hands and turned it first toward the window, then away. He did this two or three times, then sat back down in his chair.

"Your pupils seem to respond normally," Marco said. "If you like, after you finish eating, I'll take you upstairs. We have an extra room. You can rest there for a while."

"Yes, thanks, I'd like that," Paul answered. He wanted to lie down, but he also wanted a place where he could be alone to think.

Marco gave Paul a quiet, penetrating look, the same kind of look that Anna had given him in the yard, and Paul was afraid he would somehow see through him, see through everything, and know all. But if he knew all, what would he know...?

After a moment, Marco seemed satisfied and smiled.

Paul looked around the room, wanting to shift the focus.

"You know," he said, "from your house, I'd almost think I was in another era."

Marco looked around at the kitchen and smiled.

"Anna would like hearing that. We inherited this place two years ago. Actually, Anna inherited it." Marco's glance seemed to take in the room. "There aren't many of these old houses still around. Anna wanted to restore it to its original condition, from the 1870s, but we've definitely had to make some compromises." He gestured toward the stove. "We've got a biogas range, not wood. And the ice box is all veneer; it's a modern refrigerator on the inside."

Paul's gaze followed Marco's around the room. *It's 2136,* he kept thinking. *2136.*

The meal continued, mostly in silence. Marco asked Paul how he'd gotten lost, and Paul explained that he'd gone for a walk and fallen. When he'd gotten up, he'd continued on, but soon realized he was disoriented. Paul hoped Marco wouldn't ask too many questions. Almost as though responding to Paul's wish, Marco kept his curiosity to himself.

With every bite, Paul's mind hammered away at the date. He just wanted to be alone to sort this thing out.

When Paul finished the food on his plate, Marco offered him more, but Paul found, as hungry as he had been, he didn't have the stomach for it.

"No—but thank you. I really appreciate it," Paul answered, gesturing toward his plate. It was something, showing up at the home of strangers and being treated so kindly.

"Would you like to lie down now? I could show you that room," Marco said.

"Yeah. Thank you," Paul answered and stood up from the table. He felt wobbly and his head had started to hurt again, a little bit.

Marco got up and set their plates in the sink.

As they left the room, it occurred to Paul that it wasn't just that he was trusting these people out of desperate need, but that they had chosen to trust him as well. It was hard for him to imagine anyone being so open toward a stranger in his world, especially one who showed up as mysteriously as he had.

Paul followed Marco up two flights of stairs and into a small loft under the eaves on the third level. The loft had a small bed against one wall, and against another, a bureau and mirror. Adjoining it was a narrow bathroom, with a toilet, a pedestal sink, and a shower. The window in the bedroom faced east, and morning light filled the room.

"Another compromise," Marco said, gesturing around the space. "When the house was first built, this was just attic space. This room is hardly a part of the 1870s design. Anyway, there's the bed." Marco gestured toward it. "Make yourself at home. Let me know if there's anything else you need."

Marco stood by the door with his hand on the knob, waiting for Paul's response, but Paul was staring out the window at the rolling grasslands, at their familiar folds and curves. In his world, all this was so built up—dense, urban. Here—wherever, exactly, he was—it was wide open, natural. What must the population be here? Paul was thinking. The same year, but so much open space.

He turned to Marco, trying quickly to find a way to pose his question. It couldn't simply be asked straight-out.

"Yeah, thanks," Paul said. "Ah, you know, it's funny. I told you I had trouble remembering what day it was. It seems like there are other things that are a little fuzzy, also. Like, I was just thinking, I had this bet going with a friend of mine, and I can't remember how it came out." Paul shook his head.

"What was the bet?" Marco asked, and Paul could see he wasn't exactly interested, but wanted to be polite.

"We had a difference of opinion about what the world's population was. This was just a few days ago, so you'd think I'd be able to remember. We bet on it, and then we looked it up, but now I can't remember what the answer was— even which one of us was right." Paul put his hand to his bruise and sat on the edge of the bed. He felt terrible lying to this guy who had been so kind to him, but what was he going to do—tell him the truth?

"I'm not sure myself," Marco said. "Paul, if it helps, I think it's a little over three billion." Marco had a slightly quizzical expression on his face, as though he sensed, perhaps, that Paul was play-acting, but wasn't sure it even mattered.

"A little more than three billion. Is that right? I guess that sort of rings a bell," Paul said.

Marco nodded. "Let me know if you need anything," he said again.

"I will, and thanks for everything," Paul said, he hoped with enough sincerity to make up for the lie.

"Not a problem," Marco answered, then stepped out of the room and closed the door quietly behind him. Paul heard the latch catch as the door shut. He sighed and lay down on the bed. What comfort—a bed! He tried to quiet his thoughts a little, to regain his equilibrium, but thoughts kept rushing this way and that through his mind. *2136!* How could this be? At least now he could be pretty sure he wouldn't starve, nor spend the rest of his life without human contact.

Paul rubbed his eyes with the palms of his hands, and what Marco had just told him came back to him: *a little over three billion people! Three billion!* Paul couldn't get over it—just a quarter of the population of his world! No wonder it seemed so spacious and untrampled here.

Paul opened his eyes and stared up at the ceiling. His disorientation at discovering the date was resolving into a sense of curiosity. So this world was spacious, but what world was it? It was clear now that he wasn't in the past at all. As far as he could tell, he was on earth and in the present—it just wasn't the earth he knew.

Paul thought about quantum theory, and how one interpretation of the evidence suggested that at a quantum level many different probabilities can coexist. Paul recalled how he had explained this "many-worlds interpretation" to a classmate of his, when he had been studying physics in college.

"Imagine you close your eyes and throw a pair of dice," Paul had told his friend. "There are, what, a couple dozen combinations of numbers that might come up? If what is true of subatomic particles were true for the world at large, then every one of those combinations is there before you, in a kind of half-real way, until you open your eyes."

"But if I opened my eyes, I'd just see one combination," his classmate had responded.

"Yeah, right—you'd only *see* one—but at the moment you open your eyes and see which way the throw has landed, reality splits, and each probable way the dice might have landed *actually happens in some alternate universe.* You experience only one such universe—but the other universes are just as real and valid as our own."

Paul's classmate had looked skeptical. "Is that for real?" he'd said.

Paul had shrugged. "Who knows? Like I said, if the quantum evidence holds true for the world at large, sure. But nobody has any way of telling. We don't have any way to observe any alternate universes—to prove that they exist or that they don't. So it's all theoretical."

Theoretical, Paul thought, as he lay on the bed. He'd had several theories about where he was since he'd reached this world. What made this one any better than the others? Paul asked himself.

More information. I've got more information now, he thought. Paul stared up at the smooth, white ceiling, and absent mindedly ran his hand over the stubble on his head.

Evidence, he thought. What evidence do I have now? He thought through it all. The boulder was the same boulder. The land, the hills, were all laid out the same way. The trees were the same kind of trees that had once grown near Strandford in his world. He was near a town called "Strandford," now. And the date, the date was May 16, 2136.

Paul sighed and stopped rubbing his head. He thought again of the explanation he had given his classmate. It seemed a simple thing—so, the dice rolls this way, or that. But what if you've got a lot resting on that roll of the dice? In one alternate world you lose your shirt, in another you might hit the jackpot. Everything would be different after that—where you live, who you meet, who you marry, which children you have. And all these things turning out one way or another would depend on that single roll of the dice.

"If the quantum evidence is true for the world at large," he had said. Paul closed his eyes, trying to keep his thoughts clear. If it was true for the world at large, then every single time a choice is made, when chance would have it that events might work out in more than one way—then reality splits, it branches and goes forward, creating an ever-growing and infinite number of worlds—so that everything that *might* happen *does* happen in one or another of those worlds.

Paul pictured it like a tree with many branches, each sharing a common history, a common trunk. The further it grows, the more it branches. Each roll of the dice brings a new branching point, with each branch reaching out in its own direction.

And as it grows in each of those directions, Paul thought, it continues to split and diverge, leafing out into an infinity of alternate worlds—spreading so broadly over time that reality itself develops in fractal-like ways.

Paul rolled over on the bed. From each turning point, from each branching point—large or small—whole new worlds erupted. A branching point could be as small as a roll of the dice, or as large as an accident that might mean the difference between life or death. It could be a moment on the brink of creative insight, when the insight might, or might not, actually happen. It could be almost anything that would then set one world apart from another.

Paul thought about it for a minute. According to that theory, somewhere, in some actual world, Abraham Lincoln was never shot at Ford's Theater; somewhere, Adolph Hitler succeeded as a painter and never rose to power; perhaps somewhere, in the mid-21st century, an alternate energy source was found, and the Great Oil Wars never took place.

The list could be endless, Paul thought. Somewhere, someplace, each of these things could be real. Each of them *is* real—if the theory is correct.

And if it is right, then the best explanation Paul had for how he came to be in this world was that he had stepped out of the space-time continuum and into another world, a world that shared some of its history with his own, but where, at some point, there was some throw of the dice, some choice made or not made, and this world had split from his own and become this—this sparsely populated world with living frogs and rolling grasslands filled with native grasses among which live-oak trees still grew.

Paul found the thought exhilarating and strange. Was it true? Was this what had happened to him? It all seemed to make sense and fit with all the evidence he had. But if it was true, then what did it mean about his future? How would he live here? What were his prospects of ever getting home?

For a brief moment, Paul considered what it would be like if he just couldn't return. It *was* a beautiful world, from what he had seen of it. Would it be so bad if he just had to stay here? But then he thought of all the years he had put into the Depopulation Project. He couldn't just leave it that way, stalled, stuck—his world in ruins. *No.* And then Paul thought about Sheila, and for a moment he felt a pang of loneliness that seemed to cut all the way through him, followed by a wave of guilt at deserting her. He wanted to be with her, to feel the comfort of her lying beside him—and to be for her the steady and reliable presence he had always longed to be.

Paul rolled over on his side, hugging a pillow to his chest. From somewhere below, he could hear the sound of hammering.

Probably Anna was putting the new step in, Paul told himself. He realized he'd spent all the time since he'd come upstairs thinking and worrying, but not resting at all.

That was one thing he'd been truthful with Marco about; he did need to rest. Paul tried to help himself relax by focusing on the sound of hammering, finding the rhythms within it: a few steady strikes, then a pause, then the strikes again, sharp and regular.

As he listened, Paul could feel his fatigue sweep over him. After a couple of minutes, the hammering stopped, but Paul hardly noticed, wrapped as he was in the gathering dusk of sleep.

5

When Paul woke, he was surprised at how quiet the room was and how still the air. The room seemed dim compared to earlier, when the morning sun had come streaming in. Paul felt better for having slept. His head seemed clear and his stomach entirely settled.

Somehow, in sleeping, Paul had adjusted to the idea that he had arrived on another probable earth. It had gone from seeming a tenuous theory to being the only practical conclusion to draw.

Lying awake in the quiet room, Paul considered what he knew of this alternate earth. It was lightly populated and in good environmental condition. The air was the same air, but clearer, and as far as he could tell, the same languages were spoken here as on his world.

Paul smiled and stretched. Really, if they had planned it, things couldn't have worked out better. This world wouldn't take much adjusting to for the people who relocated here. In many ways it was clearly better than an entirely untouched world. People sent here from Paul's world would find at least some kind of light industry already in place. It would be possible for them to make themselves comfortable here quite quickly, and even though some space was already taken up by the current population, their numbers were so low as to leave room for several billion more to come from Paul's world, greatly reducing the population problem at home.

Paul thought about the dream that had propelled him now for nearly fifteen years. Ever since his early teens he had felt driven to somehow find a way to make right what had gone so wrong in his world. Now, it seemed the time was nearly at hand. He had never dreamed that he could come so far, so quickly.

Really—what could be better? Paul thought. He could hardly think of anything, except maybe to have someone with him. Like Sheila, Paul thought, smiling—although he knew anybody from the lab would be more useful in solving the technical problems.

Still, thinking of Sheila, Paul suddenly found himself missing her very much. He had always found her presence in his life so comforting. He wished he could have that comfort now.

No matter, Paul told himself. He would get back to her soon, and when he did, he would have a hero's welcome. The whole world would soon know what had come of his life's work!

First things first, Paul told himself, and began to wonder what sort of technology was available here that he could use in building a transport system to get back home. Yes, that would have to be the first step.

It troubled Paul somewhat that he hadn't seen very technically advanced equipment since he'd arrived, as he'd have to draw on such materials in building a new transport. He'd also have to somehow find a sufficient energy source. Those were all serious concerns, but perhaps the most serious of all was that, as the transport system was currently designed, it clearly had an aiming problem. Paul wasn't sure whether that was a result of some sort of flaw in the machinery itself, or in the theory behind its design—or even something in the nature of the lightning strike that (he was pretty sure) had triggered the device to send him here. In any case, that would have to be worked out before he could go back, much less arrange to return to this world with billions of others.

Across the room, a fly was battering itself against the window. Restless, Paul got up and walked over to the window, turning this problem over in his mind. He stared at the fly fluttering against the glass, trying to fly off into the open spaces beyond.

"You know it's there, but you don't know how to get to it," Paul said to the fly. He opened the window, and the fly zoomed off, quickly disappearing into a cloudless sky. For a moment, the distance between this world and his own seemed not so great to Paul, as though he too could fly off and find his home just beyond the field of his view, in the contours of those hills.

Something in that sense of nearness between worlds brought back a memory for Paul. He recalled a theory he'd read about in graduate school, when he was probing into the possibility of extra-space-time travel. The theory dealt with the idea that there may be some bond or link between certain probable worlds, created by a kind of interdimensional gravity. Paul had worried then that such a link might warp any extra-space-time transmission. The theory seemed to suggest that when transporting from one of two worlds linked in this way, it might be very difficult to end up any place else than on the other.

Paul had thought the theory intriguing, but in the end he'd discarded the idea as too theoretical and probably of no practical importance. Now that earlier conclusion seemed rash. Theoretical or not, it could quite possibly explain why he had ended up here, and not on G3-97.

It occurred to Paul that if Interdimensional-Linking Theory, as it was known, proved to be correct, it might well solve the aiming problem—at least so long as transporting between Paul's world and the one he now found himself on was all that was necessary.

Paul thought back through the basic arguments in Interdimensional-Linking Theory. He'd have to give it more careful thought, but he had a strong hunch it would prove to be correct. Its mathematical grounding, as he remembered, was solid. Paul shook his head, remembering the mad rush he'd been in for results in those years. He couldn't be bothered with unprovable theories that threatened to throw a monkey wrench into his plans.

Paul leaned against the wall as he stood staring out the window, and began methodically working through the steps he'd need to take if he had any hope of getting home.

First, he'd need to review the foundations of ILT. He hoped he could remember its details well enough. If it looked solid, then the next step would be to get to work on building a new transport. He'd need materials, and to get them, he reasoned, he'd need some source of money. And then there would be the energy problem—but then, his energy problems had always seemed insurmountable, and he had managed to get this far. He'd deal with it somehow.

Thinking through the details of his circumstances, Paul began to feel lucky about the whole thing. Really, things could hardly have gone better. If he was right about Interdimensional-Linking Theory, then the aiming problem might be no problem at all—and though it might be difficult for him to find the resources here that he'd need to build and activate a new transport system, it would surely be easier to find them here than on a completely uninhabited world. Even the fact that he was the one who had been accidentally transported struck him as a lucky coincidence, since he was the only one on the team with a sufficient overview of both the technology and the theory behind extra-space-time travel to be able to rebuild the transport system alone and from scratch.

The truth was, if the Depopulation Project was going to work, then somebody, sometime, would have to be sent ahead to some world. It seemed reasonable to conclude that this was about as good a world as could be hoped for, and that he was the right person to send. And why not now? It had to be sometime.

Paul felt excited, and the pleasure of the thought made him feel nearly well. He pictured himself returning home and the great excitement that would pass through his world when he announced what he had accomplished. If he could only tell his team back at the lab how well things had actually gone! Everything had added up so well, in fact, that Paul felt almost as though fate were on his side.

Paul stepped away from the window and, grinning, swung his arms around in the sunny, unpolluted air inside the room.

What great good fortune! he thought.

◙   ◙   ◙

Paul opened the door and went back downstairs. He found Marco and Anna in the kitchen, cleaning up.

"How are you doing?" Marco asked.

"Better," Paul said. "That was a good nap."

Anna pulled a plate from the draining rack and began to dry it with a hand towel.

"You slept for a while. We've already had lunch, but I saved some pozole for you," Marco said. "Are you hungry?"

"I sure am," Paul answered. He hated to take more food from these kind people, but he really was hungry.

"Well, sit right down here," Marco said, and as Paul sat down at the table, Marco took a bowl of food from the back of the range, then set it, and a spoon, down in front of Paul. The food smelled delicious.

"Thank you," Paul said.

Marco poured a glass of water and gave it to him, then Paul ate in silence for several minutes, while the others continued cleaning up.

When Paul was near the bottom of the bowl, Marco asked Paul what his plans were.

Paul looked up, hesitated for a moment, then answered slowly.

"Well, you know, actually, it looks like I'm going to be needing to find some work. I don't suppose you might be interested in hiring someone to work around the place for a few days?"

Marco glanced at Anna, and Anna looked at Paul. Anna's expression was once again as it had been in the yard—somehow all at once thoughtful, hard headed, and empathetic. Paul again felt that she was assessing him, and he realized how strange it must seem for him to have shown up lost, injured, and hungry, and then end up asking for work. He knew how strange he appeared, as well. And yet, Anna seemed to be looking into him, and not just at him.

After a moment, Anna nodded and said, "Well, we could give you maybe a few days work. We've been thinking about programming an ecobot to biomap the far southwest field. We'd like to see some perennials go in there, but the project would take more time than either of us would like to give it right now. I mean, ecobots are easy, but the programming takes time—and in any case, the planting is best done by hand." She glanced over at Marco, who seemed to be in agreement.

"If you want," Anna continued, "you could do the mapping with a hand-guided system, and we could pay you for that and the planting." She glanced again at Marco, then said to Paul, "maybe two hundred IC for the field?"

Paul nodded. "That sounds good," he said, though he had no idea what amount that actually was, or what the work would really entail. He was glad for whatever the money was—and anyway, he had a feeling that Anna was taking pity on him in offering him any work at all. In any case, Paul was relieved to hear they had what sounded like some sort of programmable robot technology on this world. If their technology was sufficiently advanced for that, then perhaps they would have what he needed to build a new transport system.

But still, it didn't quite add up—why, if they had such technology, were they still cutting wood and washing dishes by hand?

"Okay, then," Anna said thoughtfully, "you can stay in the room you were just using while you're here." She gestured toward the room he'd just napped in. "And you can join us for meals."

"Thank you," Paul said. He felt grateful and wished he could explain how important their generosity was to him.

"Are you up to working today?" Anna asked. She was looking at the bruise on his head.

"Yeah, I think I'm fine now," Paul said, lightly touching his temple. "Thanks for asking. Actually, I'd like to start as soon as possible."

Anna looked at the clock. "Well, I could get you started now, if that's not too soon."

"Sure, now is fine," Paul said.

"Have you had enough to eat?" Marco asked.

"Oh, sure. That was great," Paul answered. In truth, he felt he could go on eating for half the day, but he felt they'd been generous enough, and in any case, he really did want to get to work and move on with his plans.

Marco looked at Anna, then over at Paul. "You're going to need some shoes, my friend," Marco said. "Do you have any with you?"

"No," Paul answered. Marco cocked his head a little and looked down at Paul's feet, then stepped over to where Paul was sitting and put his right foot down next to Paul's left foot. Marco's foot was a little wider and longer than Paul's.

Marco rubbed his chin with one hand. "Well, let me see. I think I may have some old shoes that would fit you, or at least come close enough." Marco left the room. Anna put the plate she'd just finished drying on the shelf and picked up another one.

Paul asked if he could help with the dishes, but Anna told him no, not to worry, she was almost done. So Paul just sat there, uncomfortably waiting for Marco. He felt awkward intruding on these people's lives as he had, asking them for favors. At least if he was working, they would get something of value from him, as well, he thought.

Marco reappeared after a few minutes with a pair of old brown shoes and a couple of thick socks in one hand and something made of green fabric rolled up in the other.

"First, I think you'll need this," he said. He unrolled a soft, lightweight hat with a narrow brim. "It'll keep the sun off your head." Marco set the hat on top of Paul's bald head.

"And here are some shoes. They'll be big, I think, but the socks should make up for that. I haven't worn them in a long time, so if they fit you okay, you can keep them."

Paul pulled a sock onto his right foot and then pulled a shoe on over it. The shoe was a little long, but with all the adjustments done up right, it fit nicely. Paul went ahead and put on the other sock and shoe, then glanced up and saw that Anna and Marco were standing face to face by the sink, their arms around one another. They smiled at one another, then kissed briefly. Paul looked away. He cleared his throat, then stamped his foot against the floor, as though he were testing the fit.

"How are those feeling?" Marco asked, looking over.

"They feel good," Paul answered. "Thank you. That was kind."

"So, are you set?" Anna asked.

"Yep," Paul answered.

Anna looked him over. "Okay," she said. "Oh, you'll want some water, and maybe something to snack on, in case you get hungry. It's a few hours still until dusk."

Anna stepped over to the refrigerator and took out a bottle of water and a small blue sack, set them on the table, then stepped out of the room. A minute later, she came back with a large green bag swung over one shoulder and a small bottle in one hand.

Anna handed the bottle to Paul. "I thought you could use some Sun Stop, too—it's sunny out there."

Paul looked down at the bottle. It was half-full of small tablets. On the front it said: "Stop sunburn before it stops you!" Paul turned it over. "Dosage: one. Repeat weekly or as needed," it read.

"Thanks," Paul said. He glanced around the room. Anna was putting the food and water in the green bag. Marco had gone back to washing dishes. Paul looked at his sunburned arms, then opened the bottle and put one of the tablets in his mouth. It had a pleasant, fruity flavor. He chewed and swallowed.

Anna threw the green bag over her shoulder. "All set?" she asked.

"Sure," Paul said.

"Bye, honey," Anna added, looking over at Marco with an expression of such deep warmth that Paul, uncomfortable, glanced away. Anna turned to Paul with still a small look of affection registering on her face.

"Let's go," she said, with an upbeat lilt in her voice, as she opened the kitchen door so Paul could pass through ahead of her.

◻   ◻   ◻

They stepped out into another beautiful afternoon and set off to the south down a path along a fold between nearby hills. As Paul walked along, something to his right caught his eye. He turned his head and saw a tall, narrow, arch-topped doorway cut into the south side of the hill. Anna ignored it and walked on past. With effort, Paul avoided staring dumbly at it. Apparently, this was something one should take for granted on this world. As they continued on, Paul noticed more such doorways, and windows also, cut into the south-facing sides of the hills. Framing each window were narrow panels, which looked to Paul as though they might contain sets of some sort of high-density solar cell.

Paul hadn't noticed anything unusual about those hills when he'd gazed toward them, looking out beyond the old ranch house early that morning, but he'd been looking from the north, and these doors and windows all faced south. Paul presumed there were rooms, and perhaps whole houses, behind those doors and windows, but didn't want to ask. He had no desire to make it clear to either Marco or Anna how little he understood about them and their ways by asking questions any child of this world would know the answers to. He thought it couldn't help matters at all for them to see how much of an outsider he really was.

After a while, Paul saw someone come out of one of the doorways up ahead. Anna stopped him, and Paul overheard her ask the man if he'd seen the herd lately.

"No, not in some time," the man answered.

Anna shook her head, seemed vaguely concerned, distracted. There was something about her manner that got Paul's attention—she seemed confident, in-charge, not like the women he'd known, who took great interest in how they dressed and seemed always to defer to the nearest man. Paul watched as Anna casually brushed the hair back from her face. He found her intriguing.

"Well okay, thanks," she said. She started down the path again then turned and called after the man she had just spoken to. "Hey, tell Mei-Ling I said 'hi!'"

The man called after her, "Will do! Same to Marco!"

It was a broad, bright day, and Paul was glad for the hat on his head and the shoes on his feet. They strolled past rolling hills and sweeping fields before reaching what Anna called "the far southwest field." There, Anna set down the bag she'd been carrying and pulled some kind of compact machinery from it.

"Have you done this sort of work before?" she asked Paul.

"No," he answered.

"First, we need to evaluate the ecological health of this particular area of land. This machine is designed to take the needed measurements." She began to unfold the machine she'd taken from the bag.

"How's the information used?" Paul asked.

"It helps us to determine what sort of plantings would be most appropriate and what sort of support would be required for this particular piece of land. You know—enhanced ecology."

"Enhanced, ah, what?" Paul prompted her. She looked at him quizzically, surprised he didn't seem to know.

"You know the concept—when the whole ecosystem is most vital, each thing that's a part of it is most vital—including us, right? So we try to support the vitality and diversity of ecosystems." Anna looked at him as though that should have been enough to remind him. Paul looked back at her blankly.

"But sometimes we need more from a given ecosystem," Anna went on, as though to jog his memory, "than we could get from it in its natural state—so we create an enhanced ecology, supportive of the plants and animals we need, but still a complex, self-sustaining, balanced system."

Paul nodded.

"You know what I'm talking about?"

"No."

Anna shook her head and continued setting up the machine. "Well, that's half of it," she said. "The other part is to try to always give more than we take from the point-of-view of the thing we're taking from, while taking more than we give from our point-of-view."

Paul had the feeling that she was talking to him as she would to a little kid who needed the basics explained—but even with that, he felt confused.

"So," Anna went on, "we contribute a little bit of work to the ecosystem, adding enhancements, which add to its vitality and diversity, and in return we get food or other raw materials, which are worth more to us than the work we've put in. From our point of view, we get more than we give. We come out ahead. But from the point-of-view of the plants and animals that live within that healthy, enhanced ecosystem, they get to live in an ecosystem that has been helped along by us, while only giving up a portion of that to us as food or other raw materials—so it's better for them, too. When every member of a system comes out ahead from their own point-of-view, that's a healthy system. Enhanced ecology—you know."

Anna looked at Paul, and Paul could tell she was focusing on the bruise on the side of his head.

"Huh. Nice," Paul said, nodding like he understood while he tried to absorb what Anna had just told him. Healthy system. Everything comes out ahead. Right.

Anna made a couple more adjustments in the machine, then set it on the ground in front of Paul.

"I'd like it if you'd cross this field east to west." Anna pointed out the directions for him. "Keep your lines parallel to one another, if possible. You'll have to work around the trees, of course, but you'll plant around them, too, so that's fine. I'd just like to keep the data as orderly as possible."

Anna demonstrated rolling the machine across the ground. It plunged minispikes into the soil with each turn of the wheels. The spikes, Anna explained, were taking readings of nutrients, bacterial content, soil composition.

"Got it? It's very easy," she said.

"Yeah," Paul answered.

Anna pointed out landmarks that defined the area he was supposed to cover, which was necessary since there was no fence around the field, then called his attention to a warning light on the control panel, which would come on if he was going too fast for the machine to make its readings. She pressed some buttons on a small device she wore on her wrist and waited a moment while a little light flashed. Then she pulled a small panel out from one side of the wrist device. On that small screen the information she'd already collected with the soil analyzing machine was graphically displayed.

"It looks good so far," she said, looking over the output. "When you're done with this stage, I'll collect the readings, then we'll pull the right seedlings from hydroponics to go in the areas best suited for them here." She gestured around the field. "You'll be planting advanced perennials of various sorts. They have good, deep roots that hold the soil and offer some of the best-tasting produce on the planet, if you ask me."

Paul nodded, then ventured to ask, "With so many different kinds of plants growing in the same area, how do you harvest?"

Anna still seemed preoccupied by the data she'd just collected. "Ecobots. We program them to know what to look for." Then she turned toward Paul with a frown that seemed to say, "How can you not know that?" She glanced back down at her wrist device, pushed a couple more buttons, then closed the side panel.

"What's the energy source for the ecobots?" Paul asked. He was afraid he seemed both too eager and too ignorant with his questions, but he also wanted to know what sorts of resources might be available for him to use for his work.

"They're solar. Pretty sturdy little gals, too," Anna answered, looking up as she let her arms drop to her sides. "Once we get them programmed, they can stay out for years at a time, with a different function for each season. They're definitely hardy—can take pretty much anything Mother Nature dishes out. They'll even return home if something goes wrong, so we really don't have to keep track of them at all. They're always busy, and I can tell you, they make my job a whole lot easier.

"Well, I think you're set now. When you're done, I'll use the biomap you've made to program an ecobot to help you with the planting," Anna said, and took a step away. "If you come in around dusk, we'll have dinner for you." She started to turn away, then stopped and added, "Oh, I almost forgot—I'll leave the water bottle and snackpack for you under that tree."

"Okay. Thank you," Paul said.

Anna took the bottle and snackpack out of her bag, then said goodbye and strolled off in the direction of the ranch house, pausing only momentarily to set down the food and water for Paul.

While Paul liked Anna's company well enough, he felt relieved to be alone. It had been useful talking to her—he'd learned a lot—but he was uncomfortable making conversation. He felt constantly concerned that he would reveal too much about himself and come across not merely as ignorant, but perhaps as a lunatic, as well. The insane were often dealt with harshly on his world, and who knew how they were dealt with here. And besides all that, he still wasn't feeling well enough to really enjoy conversation with anyone.

With the mapping machine in front of him, Paul began slowly crisscrossing the field, watching for the speed indicator light to go off. As he did, he began thinking about where in this world he'd find the parts he needed for a new transport system and a suitable energy source for it, as well. Solar wasn't likely to offer the huge burst of energy he'd need. He came to the edge of the field and turned. Well, now at least he'd have some money.

Paul worked several rows of the broad field, trying to feel optimistic about his prospects. He told himself again how lucky he was, how much this world was like his—same air, same plants, same language. Ideal, right? But somewhere near his center he could feel a gathering tension—there was so much now he would have to attend to, to somehow make work. And he was, still, so very far from home.

◘   ◘   ◘

After dinner, Anna told Paul that she had left a towel for him in the bathroom adjacent to the room he was using, in case he wanted to take a shower. Paul thanked her, then started upstairs. Though he had last showered at Sheila's only two days before, in some ways it felt like a lifetime had passed since then.

Once Paul was upstairs, he went into the bathroom and stripped off the clothes he was wearing, but the arrangement in the bathroom was strange to him. He spent several minutes looking for the timing device, but finally decided there wasn't any. Then he fiddled with the knobs in the shower enclosure itself. They seemed to control both the flow and the temperature of the water. As soon as he got the water flowing the way he liked, he jumped in, careful not to waste a minute!

But it was seductive, to shower with no timer. It was the first time Paul could remember ever having done so. He felt giddy, like a little kid breaking the rules. He decided to relax and shower leisurely; by the time he'd gotten out, surely eight or nine minutes had passed!

As Paul toweled off, he was surprised to notice that his sunburn had begun to fade—even after another full day in the sun. It seemed to him that the Sun Stop tablets were as effective as the best creams of his world—and he was pleased that Anna had thought to offer him one.

Paul took a minute to rinse out the shirt he'd been wearing in the sink and to hang it to dry by the open window, then climbed into bed, exhausted from the stresses of the past few days. He lay in the darkened room with his eyes open, his naked body between clean sheets, trying to sort out where he was and what he would need to do next.

Paul thought about the wrist computer he'd seen Anna use and wondered if there was some sort of media access he could make use of to get information about technologies available in this world. He was once again stuck not wanting to ask questions that others would expect him to already have the answers to. He'd done enough of that today already. Maybe he could just wait. He'd go into town in a couple of days. Things might be very different there.

Paul heard an owl hoot outside his window. He recognized the sound from his recordings of extinct animals. He slipped out of bed and stepped to the window, where he peered out into a landscape flooded with light from the moon, which hung low in the eastern sky. Several trees stood in the moonlight on the hill facing the window, but Paul couldn't tell if the owl was in one of them. In any case, he was too tired to just stand there looking.

He climbed back into bed, where he lay awake, waiting. Soon, the owl called again. How exciting!—a sound that he would never, could never, hear on his earth.

Paul was struck again by the startling similarities and dissimilarities between this world and his own. In his mind, he again pictured the image of probable worlds developing like tree branches: how they share a common trunk, or history, until they separate at some "branching point"—a turning point of some kind or another after which each world splinters off, traveling down its own branch or path.

What had been the turning point that defined the difference between this world and his own? Paul wondered. He reviewed the differences he'd seen so far: the ideas about ecology, which Anna had espoused earlier, the low population, the frogs and owl—even the moments of intimacy he'd witnessed between Anna and Marco had a tenderness that was not commonly seen on his world. He wished he knew what may have caused these two worlds to split in just this way, but had to admit he didn't really have a clue.

Paul rolled over onto his side, with the pillow beneath his head. Thinking about how strange this new world was made him feel suddenly homesick and alone. For comfort, he tried to remind himself again of all the advantages this world held and how much it could mean for his Depopulation Project, but it made little difference to him in the mood he was in now—he felt tired, and alone, and longed for the familiarity of home.

Paul pulled the pillow in tighter beneath his head. With the lights out, it seemed like he could have been anywhere. He closed his eyes and pretended he was at Sheila's apartment, with her just a few inches away, lying next to him. He imagined putting his arms around her and pulling her close. The way her body fit so neatly next to his... He imagined that in a few hours his implant alarm would wake him and that he would get up and go to work, be surrounded by colleagues and assistants, focused together on a shared goal.

The idea morphed in his head, until he imagined himself actually being there with them, telling them about what he had discovered here. How excited they would all be—and how proud! He pictured Sheila there with him, too, in the lab, where she would never be. How proud she would be of him, too!

But how would he ever tell them? Suddenly the enormity of the task of building a new transport, alone, on this strange world, swept over him. In his world, he'd had others helping him. He'd had resources.

Here, he was so alone. So alone.

Paul pressed his face into the pillow, felt his skin slide along the cool pillow case. It was damp, and Paul realized that the pillow was wet with his tears.

He curled up in a ball and, squeezing his eyes tightly shut, refused to think any more about it, refused to think of anything at all. He lay very still, listening carefully to small night sounds. The tree outside his window rustled softly, caressed by a dark breeze. Somewhere, in another part of the house, a cricket sang its muted staccato.

Moments passed, and more moments flooded in to take their place, and through all of them Paul held himself gently braced and cradled between worlds. Finally, rescued by exhaustion, he drifted off to sleep.

◙   ◙   ◙

Over the next two days, Paul spent most of the daylight hours in the far southwest field, mapping and then planting, as Anna had instructed. Eager to move forward with his plans, he rose early each morning when the light was soft, and returned each evening as dusk set across the land. His days were hard and long, but his strength was gradually returning to him, and he soon had the biomapping done and had begun to plant.

Each evening, Paul intended to spend a few more hours developing his plans to build a new transport to return him to his world, and to deliver much of the population of his world to this, but each night, after dinner and a shower, he felt so exhausted (from the work and probably, still, from the lingering effects of the transport) that he found he could only retrace the steps of his plans in his mind before drifting off into a sound sleep.

On the morning of what would be his fourth day under Anna and Marco's roof, Paul again rose early and sat with them as they ate their breakfasts, listening as they talked about their crops and a few repairs they were planning to do around the old ranch house. As Paul listened to them discussing the details of their lives, he wondered what it would mean to them for him to bring countless others from his world to theirs, as he was planning to do. Surely it would change their world, and probably not in ways they would like. The thought troubled him, and he pushed it from his mind.

When breakfast was over, Paul helped clean up, and then headed out to complete the job of planting perennials in the far southwest field. He'd gotten nearly half of them planted the day before, and he wanted to be sure he finished up that day.

As he worked, Paul followed after the ecobot that Anna had programmed with the biomap of the field that Paul had generated. Every meter or two, he stopped to plant whatever type of seedling the ecobot spoke the name of, in holes the little robot had just dug. Though Paul was following the ecobot, the ecobot was following the information Paul had gathered while biomapping the field.

It was tiring work, and Paul felt glad to be getting through it—and to have a chance to observe the ecobot in action. In its basic mechanics, it did not seem so different from the robotic technology of his world, but it seemed responsive to signals from Paul in a way that surprised him. In many ways, it seemed more like a small animal than a machine, while its appearance seemed at once sleeker and more whimsical than the sorts of devices Paul was familiar with. In particular, Paul took note of the placement of its solar cells—they were small and overlapping, like the scales of fish, but they "fluffed" like the feathers of birds as they turned to catch the sun.

In the late morning, as Paul followed after the ecobot, gently lowering one seedling after another into the ground, he looked up and saw that people had gathered on some of the nearby hills, where they were picnicking and playing with their kids.

Paul stopped and stretched and looked around. He figured these people were probably the ones who lived in what he presumed were underground dwellings. This made sense to him—it would be Saturday, by now, after all. Why wouldn't they be out with their families, enjoying the sunny day?

Sometime later that afternoon, as Paul continued planting along the far side of the field, he heard a soft whirring sound and looked up to see a small, sleek, aerodynamically shaped vehicle coming up along the narrow road that bordered the field on that side. A little past where Paul was working, it stopped, and a young woman stepped out of it. Paul could see that the vehicle came barely to her waist. She looked around, then shouted to some people who were sunning themselves on a nearby hillside.

"Hey!" she called up.

One of the men on the hill sat up and turned toward her.

"Hello! What's up?" he called down.

"The herd," she answered. "It's coming in!"

A young woman stood up behind the man.

"Which kind?" she called out.

"*Too lee,*" the woman on the road called back.

"How far?" the man shouted.

"Not far—maybe six or seven kilometers."

Paul paused to watch the exchange. Most of the people within earshot seemed interested, and a few came down the hills and gathered around the woman who had brought the news. Paul realized he'd seen no fences and wondered what herd she was talking about. He considered going over and listening in, but he didn't see what difference it might make to him. Besides, the day was going fast, and he wanted to be done by nightfall.

◻   ◻   ◻

By the time Paul got in that day, it was deep dusk outside. He was tired, and the day had been a long one, but at least he was finished with all the biomapping and planting he'd agreed to do.

Marco had saved a plate of food, which he warmed up for Paul upon his arrival. A single light bulb hung over the kitchen table, casting shadows as Paul ate his dinner. Marco got a glass of water from the tap, drank most of it, then leaned back against the range and watched Paul eat for a moment before he spoke.

"How's the work going?" Marco said softly.

"Good," Paul answered, then swallowed. "I got it done."

"Well good, I'm glad. Anna said you've been doing a good job—made a good, clear biomap, and the plants have gone in looking healthy. It's hard work, I know—especially the planting."

"Yeah, well thanks," Paul said.

"No, thank you—the plants you've planted will be there for decades. Grains, beans, vegetables—we'll enjoy eating from them for a long time."

Paul smiled and nodded.

"Well, look," Marco continued, "I've got a couple of things I need to do, but I wanted to let you know—we're going to have a gathering tonight. People should start arriving in an hour or so. I thought you might like to have a change of clothes to wear. I've left a shirt and a pair of trousers on your bed. They're mine, but a little too small for me—I think they might fit you about right." Marco paused, measuring Paul with his eyes. "Use them or not, as you like. I just noticed you didn't have a change of clothes with you."

"Thanks," Paul said. He looked at Marco in the light's simple glare. "That's kind of you."

"There's nothing to it." Marco finished his water. "Enjoy your dinner," he said and left the room.

Paul finished up his food, then went upstairs to shower and change. The allure of an un-timed shower hadn't faded, and the "new" clothes—a soft brown button-up shirt and a pair of khaki trousers—were a pleasure, too. They were a bit smaller, and fit better, than the clothes he'd taken off the line.

Paul looked in the mirror and was pleased to see how close they came to fitting—and also to realize that his hair had come back in a little. Even the bruise was fading. He'd hardly noticed any such details in his fatigue over the last few days, but now he took some comfort in discovering that he looked a bit less strange than he'd imagined.

Paul carefully washed and rung out the clothes he'd been wearing, then hung them to dry by the open window—where he stood, for a while, staring out at the gathering night. He watched as the stars came out and recognized them as the same stars that shone in the night skies of home.

◘　◘　◘

By the time Paul joined the party, people were already gathered in the living room of the old ranch house. Paul was struck immediately by what an eclectic mix they were—many ages, also many ethnicities. Soft music played in the background while people sat in little clusters, talking.

Paul sat down in an arm chair tucked back into a corner. He felt uncomfortable at the idea of having to make conversation—after all, what would he be willing to tell of himself? As he settled into the chair, Paul looked around the room. He spotted Anna—she was sitting with a tall, lanky man on the long chair against the opposite wall. The man's appearance suggested a mix of Asian and African ancestry. No, Paul thought, looking at him—something more than that. Maybe European, too, or Indian? He couldn't tell, but as he looked around the room he realized that that was nothing unusual. Most of the people there seemed to have a heritage that reached back to more than one part of the world.

Paul's attention returned to Anna and the lanky man, and he noticed that they were holding hands, leaning toward one another, and talking very intimately. Marco came over to them and squatted down before them. He put his hand on the man's knee, and the man reached down and squeezed Marco's hand. There was nothing solicitous in the gesture, nor in the way he and Anna held hands. They all seemed relaxed, friendly. The man and Marco spoke, and the man nodded his agreement.

Marco got up and pressed on the paneling on the living room wall. A small doorway slid to one side, revealing a dark oval inside the wall. Marco moved his hand in front of it. Inside, a small display lit up. Marco touched the display, and the music, which had been playing in the background, faded out.

The lanky man kissed Anna on the cheek, then leaned forward and opened a satchel near his feet. He pulled out a small stringed instrument, a bit like a mandolin. Marco walked over to a little crowd on the opposite side of the room. He gestured back toward the lanky man, and the others began to pull instruments out of bags or from behind doorways, where Paul presumed they had been stowed when the musicians first arrived.

The musicians gathered at one end of the room and began to play, an upbeat melody in a style Paul was unfamiliar with. Some of the children got up to dance. A minute later adults began to join them.

Paul watched the kids dancing to the music. It struck him how few children there were for so many adults. It made sense, though—the population was lower here—they probably had fewer kids per couple. Paul noticed one small boy in particular, who was drifting from lap to lap during the music, but couldn't decide whose child he was. All the adults seemed to know him and relate to him caringly.

At one point, the musicians paused between songs, and a young woman came up and spoke to the man who had been sitting with Anna. She gestured toward the instrument the man was holding. He nodded pleasantly and handed it to her. The band started up again, this time with the young woman playing. The children, and a few of the adults, started dancing again. Paul noticed that Anna was now sitting with a woman. They were holding hands, whispering back and forth below the music. Paul glanced around the room and noted that a lot of people were holding hands as they talked. Even those who didn't touch were leaning toward one another with an air of intimacy.

Being alone in a room full of people who clearly knew one another well and felt close to one another just made Paul feel all the more isolated. He was glad to be tucked back into a dark corner of the room, where others could easily overlook him.

Sitting there, Paul began to think about Sheila. He imagined her missing him, worrying about him—and again he felt a wave of guilt at letting her down like this.

Paul rubbed his face, tried to console himself. How would she cope with this, really? She would turn up the feed on her media implant, he knew. She would set the emotional parameters unusually high, so they would sweep away whatever other sensations she was having.

Paul was glad to think of her not having to bear the weight of her worrying about him. She would take care of herself, he told himself, she would be all right.

Paul sighed and turned his thoughts to his team—surely they were wishing they could search for him, if there were only some way. Thinking this, for a moment Paul felt a piercing sort of loyalty to them and to his world. He longed to return home, to help solve the problems of his world—to make it a better world for all of them, but especially for Sheila. That was what he had set out to do, after all—to help repair the world he knew. He could not allow himself to be deterred now, at this time, when he had come so close to accomplishing that.

He thought again about the members of his team wishing there were some way they could send help.

That's just the way it is, he told himself. He was here all alone, without resources, without help. Even if they knew he was alive, even if they knew what he needed, Paul reminded himself, what could they actually send that would be of any use?

Paul sighed. "No," he told himself. "I can't think that way. I am going to get back—even if there is nothing they can do to help me." Paul imagined his return and the news spreading about what he had accomplished. Somewhere, Sheila would be tuned into the feed and would pick up this news. Then she would come to him, beaming with pride, and would put her arms around him. Sheila with the deep eyes into which he always wanted to throw himself. Sheila, in whom he saw a special beauty, unlike any other he had known.

Paul sighed again and looked around the room. What was he doing, wasting his time sitting in the corner at some party? He had finished the field. He would get paid and leave for town tomorrow. He'd seen the device behind the wall panel and the one Anna wore on her wrist—as well as the surveying tool he'd been using and the ecobot he'd worked with. It was completely clear that they had advanced technology on this world. Somehow, he would get what he needed to build another transport system. This world was probably connected to his through the principle of interdimensional linkage. If so, aiming would be no problem. He would build another transport and get back home. With the right materials and opportunities, it might just be weeks until he arrived—or more likely a few months, he told himself—and when he arrived, they would welcome him like a hero, a hero who could offer many of them—billions of them—a new life in a world prime for colonization. His team would be thrilled—and Sheila would turn to him with her eyes alight with love and pull him to her with such tenderness and passion!

Paul was aware of his heart pounding, as he looked around at the people gathered in intimate groups around the room. For a moment or two he wondered what it would mean for these people to have such an influx of strangers from another world as he had planned for them. Would it change their culture, their government, the way they lived their lives? Maybe, Paul thought, but it struck him that the needs of his world were far more urgent than theirs.

Paul turned these thoughts aside and considered instead what materials he'd need for the new transport unit. The first step would be to find out what materials and technologies were available on this world, he thought. Yes. He would go into town tomorrow, and maybe there he would find the information he needed.

Paul decided he'd had enough of the party and got up to go outside. He stepped out the front door then paused on the wide porch, taking in the nighttime scene as his eyes adjusted to the dark.

Marco and the lanky man Anna had been talking to stood shoulder to shoulder by the porch railing, in conversation. In their nearness and in the soft tones of their voices was the same intimacy Paul had seen between the people inside. Not romantic, Paul thought. They just seemed, well—attuned.

Marco and the man looked around and said "hi" to Paul, as Paul moved toward the steps.

"Hi," Paul said back, then turned to face Marco. "By the way, since I've finished with the field, I just wanted to let you know, I'll be leaving in the morning."

Marco nodded briefly. "Okay," he said. "Did you tell Anna?"

"Not yet," Paul answered. He wanted to tell Marco that he appreciated all the help, but somehow it just didn't come out.

"That's okay. I'll let her know," Marco said.

"Okay. Thanks," Paul replied, as he turned and stepped away. Behind him, he could hear a soft murmur as Marco and his friend resumed their conversation. Woven between the notes of their speech were the muted rhythms of the dance music, which flowed through hidden cracks and from around closed windows out into the night air.

Paul moved through and away from these sounds and out into the moon-drenched yard, which was littered with sleek, light-bodied, low-slung vehicles like the one the woman had been riding in that afternoon. Their windows glistened, but the rest of their bodies were like dark water in the moonlight. Paul stopped to look at one. It was covered with what seemed to be some sort of light-absorbing photocells.

Sun powered, Paul thought. He looked in the window. On the dashboard were an odd assortment of hand controls. On the floor in front of both the driver's and the passenger's seats were bands of metal that looked a lot like cyclist's pedals.

Paul stood up straight. What an odd mixture of advanced and basic technologies, he thought—then left behind the glistening, low-slung vehicles and strolled out of the yard. He climbed up a nearby hill (into the south sides of which, Paul presumed, windows and doors had been cut) and stood atop it, overlooking one of the enhanced-ecology fields to the south. The moon was brilliant, up high and nearly whole in a seemingly endless sky. The field below seemed almost to glow in its cool light.

Paul stood there thinking about the people back home, missing them. He hungered for Sheila's body next to his, for what he saw when he looked into her eyes—for what he saw in her, so deep and special, that could give him such unspeakable comfort. He could sure use some of that now.

Paul stared out from his hilltop, taking in the rolling hills beyond, drenched in moonlight. He wasn't sure why, but something about coming to this party tonight had made him feel suddenly eager to move on. He felt a desire to speed ahead, to get into town and seek out some kind of media link, to do his research on available technologies, energy sources, to begin to build his transport home.

Paul looked down at the ground in front of him, kicked at it a bit with his foot. He wondered what it was that was eating at him tonight. Probably it's just all this waiting around, he thought. Here he'd wasted almost four days biomapping and planting some field, when all he wanted was to start the research he'd need to do to complete his work.

Well, in any case he was set to go now. He'd get paid in the morning and would move on.

Paul put his arms around himself, as though for comfort, and raised his head. Just then some movement in the field below him caught his eye. An elk stood grazing in the field, as a couple more wandered out into the open from behind a hill.

Elk? Paul thought. Yes, they *were* elk. *Wild* elk? Paul's jaw slacked. He'd only ever seen them in a zoo! Very few still existed in the wild in his world.

Paul watched as gradually more and more elk appeared, until a herd of over a hundred had drifted from beyond the far hill and into the field below. More, still, could be seen in the distance.

Paul looked down at them in amazement. So many! He had to share this with someone!

Paul turned around and called out to Marco and the man on the porch.

"Elk!" he yelled. Marco turned toward him, then looked out in the direction of the field Paul was pointing at.

"How many?" Marco called back.

Paul glanced toward the elk, now spreading out and grazing on the ecologically enhanced field. "I don't know—a hundred? Two hundred?" Paul called back, but the truth was, there were more than he could count.

The man Marco was with pulled open the porch door. "Hey—the herd is in!" he shouted into the house.

Paul turned back to face the field. He felt a shiver run down his spine. They just kept streaming into the low area between hills, like a sea of living animals, spreading out before Paul and beyond the surrounding hillsides.

Paul heard someone coming up the hill behind him. He turned and saw it was Marco, followed by some others from the party. Marco stopped beside Paul, and together they watched as more elk drifted out from behind the far hills.

"It makes me feel good every time I see this herd come in," Marco commented. "At one time, there were only a handful of these elk left. Now, look," Marco said, and spread out his hands before him, a look of deep satisfaction on his face.

Paul followed the line of his sight. "What kind are they?" Paul asked.

"These are tule elk," Marco said, matter-of-factly.

Paul's head swam. *Tule elk.* Paul knew they had been long extinct in his world, but he remembered his grandfather telling him that they had once roamed in herds of thousands.

Paul stared dumbly for a minute or two, then began to think about what it meant to have so many animals on a field that was tended as carefully as the one he had biomapped and planted.

"Aren't you afraid they'll trample the field?" he asked.

"No," Marco answered, shaking his head. "The habitat was designed for them, too." After a moment, he added, "Besides, this land is as much theirs as ours."

Paul glanced over at Marco, who was staring down at the herd, and was struck again by the radiant warmth in his expression.

Paul remembered that morning, when the woman had shouted out, "What kind?" and the other woman had answered, *"Too lee."* Of course—"tule," was what she meant.

Nearby, someone pointed, and Paul turned his attention back to the field. He had been trying to tell himself all along how similar this world was to his own—English spoken here, same kinds of flora and fauna, same—no, better—air. But watching this herd of elk move casually through the field, Paul was overcome by an awareness of just how different this world was from his own. He shivered again—the elk, the clear air, all these people talking and sharing, no media Stream—it was just what he had dreamed of, wasn't it?

Still, what he longed for most in that moment was to get back home and tell the people of his own world what he had found here—a clean and open world, sparsely inhabited and full of life. Ideal for a new population.

Paul's thoughts swam with a vision of how it would be—how the attention of his world would turn to him, validating him, as word of his discovery went out across the Stream—and of how Sheila would embrace him and hold him, then, with an intensity and tenderness beyond any she had shown before.

$$\square \; \mathbf{6} \; \square$$

After breakfast the next morning, Paul stood in the kitchen with Marco and Anna. He was dressed in the clothes Marco had lent him for the party, because he felt more comfortable in them than the ones he had stolen. He had on, as well, the shoes and hat that Marco had offered him before he began his work in the field.

Anna was counting out money.

"There it is—two hundred IC," she said. She handed Paul the bills.

"Thanks. You've both been just great, really," Paul said. "Well, I guess I should get going but, well, I need to go change back into my other clothes, first."

"You like those? If you like them, keep them. Those don't fit me," Marco said, gesturing to the shirt and pants. "The shoes are old, I don't really wear them anymore—and that hat...," Marco said, shaking his head.

"It doesn't look good on him," Anna said.

"Look, keep it all if you like. They're all old things I don't need anymore. Besides, you did an extra-good job on the field."

"You sure?" Paul said. "I could pay you for them."

"No, no, no," Marco said. "They're yours."

Paul nodded. "Thank you both," he said. He stepped over to the kitchen door.

"You're welcome," Anna said.

"Don't worry about it," Marco said.

Paul put his hand on the doorknob and turned it, then turned back toward Marco and Anna once again.

"Thanks for all the help. It's meant a lot to me. Really. More than I can tell you," Paul said, then opened the door and passed quickly through it.

Outside, he paused on the porch, taking in the scene before him: rolling hills, green and welcoming, and above them, thin wispy clouds in a brilliant blue sky. Paul stepped off the porch and set off to the southeast, heading for town.

As he walked away, Paul glanced down at the money he had in his hand: ten twenty-IC bills. Across the bottom of the top bill it read: "International

Currency." So that was what the "IC" stood for. Good enough. Paul folded the bills and pushed the hand with the money deep into a front pocket of his pants and released the bills—the only thing in that empty space, the only thing he was carrying. He had money in his pocket, shoes on his feet. He was clothed and fed. He was so much better off than he had been four days before when he'd first arrived at the ranch. He felt grateful to the people who had helped him, but also proud that he was somehow making his way in this strange new world.

Marco had told Paul earlier which road to take to Strandford, and Paul set his steps along that byway. As he strolled along, Paul looked around at the rolling hills. How familiar the lay of the land was here, even without the businesses and buzzing floaters that would have enlivened this landscape in his world. Where he was now would have been part of the Strandford expansion on his world. He was heading in the direction of the old downtown—though on this world, from what Marco had told him, it was the only downtown Strandford had.

As Paul walked along, he tried to imagine in just which spots along the hillsides the shops and business from his world would have been located. It felt odd to try to superimpose those images of a bustling, dense, urban environment on top of this quiet scenic countryside. Paul heard a bird singing somewhere close by. He looked around, and his sight was filled with green hills and trees, a blue sky—a bright, enticing day. Alongside the roadway, the ground showed the marks of the large herd that had appeared the night before, but already they had wandered on, out of sight from where Paul was now.

Still, the world surrounding Paul seemed vibrant and alive. Once, he scared up a rabbit from some underbrush, then smiled as he watched it dash away, relieved that he didn't have to figure out how catch it for his dinner. Three times he was passed by one of the low-slung, solar- and pedal-powered vehicles. Each time the driver waved and smiled as he or she went past. At one point, the road Paul was on rose to the top of a hill, and Paul thought he could just make out the brown body of the elk herd far off to the west.

Amid these events, the walk into town gave Paul a period of quiet and solitude in which to contemplate what lay ahead. His first priority, he knew, was to resolve the aiming problem that had sent him here and not to G3-97. Interdimensional-Linking Theory was one possible explanation, but it was far from certain—and so long as the mystery of the aiming malfunction went unsolved, it would be pointless to devote the work and the expense of building a new transport unit to take him home. The unit would simply be too dangerous to use.

Paul thought through the possibility that the aiming mechanism would have worked just perfectly if not for an oversupply of power from the lightning strike, but that hypothesis just didn't add up. A power overload would have burned out the capacitor and shut the system down before the current even reached the aiming system, which was not only isolated from the rest of the unit, but had been built with what most of his team had considered entirely excessive surge protection. A lightning strike shouldn't have caused even the slightest fluctuation in its function.

That left the possibility that Paul's original calculations had been off. This also struck Paul as highly unlikely. Not only had he gone over those figures exhaustively himself, but his equations had been probed and reviewed in the most respected physics journals, and no one had punched a hole in them.

Which left Paul thinking, again, that Interdimensional-Linking Theory offered the best explanation of why he had come to this world and not been sent, as he would have expected, to G3-97. As Paul remembered it, he had considered ILT unflawed and yet unprovable when he had explored it in his graduate school days. Why had he finally decided to discount it then, he asked himself? Because he'd been unconvinced that alternate worlds actually existed—and of course, if they didn't actually exist, why should he complicate his work by worrying that Earth was linked to one? So he had worked out his aiming protocols without so much as a nod to ILT.

Paul shook his head and looked around. And now, here he was on what had to be an alternate Earth. Surely, he thought, Interdimensional-Linking Theory had to explain his arrival here, for what other explanation could there be?

Paul's thoughts turned to the transport unit he would need to build, and the parts it would require. He was excited about getting into town, where, he hoped, there would be some way of researching which technologies were available on this world. He didn't expect to be able to find exactly the same parts he'd used to build the transport system on his world, but he figured there ought to be similar ones available here, developed for use in other, related, technologies. If he was lucky, he would be able to find much of what he needed already built—parts designed to perform the same functions, but for other kinds of machinery. After all, Paul thought, a capacitor is still a capacitor, no matter what it's used for, just as quantum fusion parts had other applications.

Paul thought over the design of the transport system and began making a mental list of what parts he would need to have to build a new unit. For each part he thought of, he considered also what alternate uses it could be put to. For example, a part that he could use to transfer information from one component of his transport unit to another might have been built on this world for use in some kind of communications technology, or for, say, guidance feedback in robotics. Paul figured such a list of parts and their potential uses would help him have some idea of where to begin his search for the materials he needed.

When Paul had come up with what he thought was a fairly comprehensive list, he began to let his thoughts drift a little. They turned to a time when he and his team had nearly completed the prototype transport unit but were tangled in a lot of red tape from Corprogov, which was refusing to provide the necessary funds for a few essential, but very expensive, parts.

It was just about that time that Paul had started spending time with Sheila. They'd gone out to dinner and he'd told her all about the Depopulation Project and the transport system he was developing. Sheila had asked him then how the transport unit worked, but she didn't have the technical background necessary for him to explain it very fully. He'd thought for a moment, trying to decide how to tell her about it. He wanted to give her the facts—but he also, truthfully, hoped she would be impressed with the work he did.

"Well, it's a bit like the way a candle gives light," Paul had told her, formulating the thought carefully. "As the candle burns down, the wax and wick seem to disappear, but really they've been transformed into heat and light, a little smoke. The theory behind extra-space-time transport is a little like that," Paul had said, as he'd wondered privately if he would ever make it work. "We should be able to move matter from a material form to a probabilistic form that's energy only, then transfer it back to its original condition, all by shifting the frequencies of its subatomic components. Doing that would make it disappear and reappear. In order to make it reappear in a new location, we redefined it—well, this part's a little tricky, but basically, we redefine it as existing at new points in the space-time fabric. When it reappears, well, that's where it is."

Paul remembered how thoughtfully Sheila had listened—and how pleased he had been that she had appeared not just interested, but impressed, as he described the project that had so consumed his interests.

"So consumed my interests," Paul echoed to himself. It was true. Building such a unit had been his primary focus since he had first conceived of the possibility shortly before his twentieth birthday. The transport system had been his dream, his vision. He had devoted so much to it, and it had brought him here.

Paul took a breath of clear air and looked around at the open land—here, to a world better than he might even have dreamed of.

How impressed would Sheila be, now? he wondered.

Paul imagined himself building a new unit and returning home. Word would spread quickly after his arrival, he was sure. He imagined his picture being broadcast on the Stream: the hero who had found a new, inhabitable world—and who had gone there and come back alive! The image would skip from mind to mind, spreading like a kind of instant fire. It would remain active on the Stream for days, or weeks, or even months. Everyone would want to see his image. Everyone would tune in.

Even Sheila would tune in. She would wake up beside him and turn up her implant—and her mind would be instantly filled with Paul's face and with the amazing and wonderful thing he had done for their world! Paul could just imagine how it would be then—all her pride and approval as she turned toward him, with a look on her face that would fill him with such joy...

☒   ☒   ☒

It only took about half an hour for Paul to walk into town, and when he arrived he found the streets of Strandford were busy with the same sort of solar- and pedal-powered vehicles he'd seen cluttering the yard at the ranch house the night before. He walked around for a bit, taking in the town. Most of the street names were the same, but otherwise this place was very different from the Strandford he knew. This was just a sweet, rural town, not the highly developed urban area he was familiar with. Paul stopped a woman on the street and asked her where he could find an inexpensive motel.

"Inexpensive?" she said, her face open and friendly. "If that's what you want, there's the Wayfarer's Inn. I hear it's pretty bare-bones, but decent enough." She told him the intersection, and Paul thanked her and started to step away.

"You're a sojourner?" she asked. "The sojourners usually stay there."

"Ah," Paul said, spreading his hands halfheartedly, "yeah." He had no idea what she was talking about. He nodded, then turned and headed toward the intersection she'd named.

Paul was there within five minutes. He checked in and paid for two days in advance, then asked the clerk where he could buy groceries and was directed to a small store only a couple of blocks away. Paul stopped by the store and bought bread, cheese, and fruit to keep in his room, before settling in.

The room itself was small and sparsely furnished—but pleasant, in an understated way. With white walls and simple furniture, it had a clean and uncluttered look. Whatever "sojourners" were, it seemed clear to Paul that they had simple needs. Against one wall was a bed and basic straight-backed chair. Opposite that, a ledge-like table ran the length of the wall. Paul sat on the edge of the bed and looked around. Where was he going to find some sort of media access in this town? He remembered the panel he'd seen Marco open on the living room wall the night before and looked around his room for something similar.

On the wall above the long table opposite the bed hung a large plaque. Paul got up and looked at it more closely. It had two lines written on it—the name of the hotel and under that the words, "Intralink portal." Paul pressed on the plaque with his finger tips, emulating the gesture he'd seen Marco make, and an oval panel, about fifty centimeters across and thirty high, opened in the wall. Paul waved his hand in front of the opening, and a screen lit up inside. It glowed a pale sea-foam green, but nothing more happened.

"Oh great," Paul said aloud. "What is it and how do I make it work?"

"Please specify 'it,'" Paul heard a voice say. He glanced around. Nobody was there.

"What?" Paul said.

"Please restate your question."

"What is the device I've just turned on, and how do I use it?" Paul said. The voice, soft and neither feminine nor masculine, was coming from the panel.

"Intralink access system. Ask a question," it responded.

"Can you provide me with technological information?" Paul asked.

"Yes. Please specify desired information."

Paul opened the bag of bread and tore off a piece. It had been baked recently, and its aroma filled the air. Paul grabbed the chair next to the bed and set it before the screen, then sat down on it. He thought back over the list of parts he'd come up with on his walk, then picked one part and, speaking aloud, described its function and the sorts of technologies it might be applicable to.

"Please list parts of a similar design and function," Paul said.

The screen flashed, then displayed images of several small pieces of machinery. Paul touched one on the screen. It looked about right.

"Please further describe this one."

The display zoomed in on that portion of the screen, then rotated the image while animating it to show the way it was constructed. Meanwhile, the Intralink-portal voice described its various features and functions.

"I'd like to keep track of that one. Can you do that for me?"

"That item has been marked for future reference."

"Good," Paul said. He proceeded down through the mental list of parts he'd put together on his way into town, asking the computer to offer him matches for the characteristics he described. In each case he was offered a set of likely choices, from which he selected one or two.

As Paul went along, he noticed some differences in the kinds of technologies that were coming up, as compared to the sorts of machinery that existed in his world. For one thing, the machinery he was learning about produced only usable, nontoxic waste, like that which would occur in natural systems (for example, the solar technology of this world produced oxygen as a by-product, just as plants did). Also, much of the technology he was learning about was governed by a kind of synthetic intelligence, like the ecobots he'd learned about while working at Anna and Marco's place. (In fact, from what Paul was finding out as he used the portal, ecobots could receive very complex programming and not only assist in planting a field, but harvest it, tend to it, and respond to the needs of the plants and insects and other animals that were part of that ecosystem, as well. They could even do things as complex as evaluating and adjusting soil chemistry, and identifying and removing non-native species. The only thing they couldn't do really well, it seemed, was handle extremely fragile objects, like the seedlings Paul had planted—but apparently, what ecobots lacked in manual dexterity, they more than made up for in their ability to respond to a complex environment.)

Paul presumed that the computer he was using now was based on this same sort of complex synthetic intelligence. It seemed remarkably able to respond to his requests and to provide him with just the sort of information he was searching for. It was certainly better at sorting and compiling information than the media feed back home. Paul found it a pleasure to work with, and within several hours he had reasonable options for many of the parts he would need.

Paul stretched and stood up. He could tell by the shifting light in the room that the daylight outside was failing. He stepped over to the window, parted the curtains, and looked out at the setting sun. He felt good about what he'd gotten done that day. It wasn't everything—he still had more parts to find, and of course, that was just the first task. He'd still need to find funds with which to buy those parts, and he would have to build the transport—not to mention finding an energy source. But still, he felt encouraged. If it all went this easily, he would soon be on his way.

Paul let the curtain fall closed, then stretched again. He realized how tired he was. He'd been feeling stronger each day since his arrival, but he still tired more quickly than he was used to. He went over to the bed and lay down to rest. What a full day. Images of saying goodbye at the ranch that morning and of his walk into town played through his mind.

What an amazing world this was, with frogs, owls, elk, and that rabbit he'd seen along the lane. It seemed to Paul that he'd seen and heard more wildlife in the past few days than he had witnessed in his whole life before that. And here there were only a little over three billion people, Marco had said.

Yes, that was what he had said. Paul thought about it. But had he been right?

Paul got up and crossed the room to the Intralink portal. He sat down again in front of its view screen. The room had grown quite dark since he'd stopped to take a break, and the view screen seemed to glow more brightly now, with its sea-foam-green light.

"Question," he said to the portal. "What is the current population of this world?"

"For which species?" the portal asked, in response.

"Human," Paul answered.

"The human population is approximately 3.21 billion."

Paul shook his head. So Marco had been right.

He thought about it. That was roughly a quarter of the population of his world. He was impressed. How had they managed to keep the population so low?

Paul again was struck with the sensation that this world wasn't nearly as much like his world as he was inclined to assume.

He leaned back in his chair and recalled the media feed images he'd received on the Stream shortly before he'd been transported. It had been the news feed, he remembered, and had included images of New York City.

Was that different, too? he wondered—how much the ocean levels had risen in this world?

Paul wanted to ask the portal, but he knew he'd need some arbitrary standard of measure to make a comparison. Instead, he simply asked to see a current picture of New York City.

The screen flickered, and a moving image of city streets above which tall sky scrapers towered appeared on the screen. Down the streets rolled the same sorts of vehicles Paul had seen since coming to this world. The remarkable thing was—they were on solid ground.

In this world, New York was still above sea level!

My God, Paul thought. The ocean levels never rose on this world!

Amazing, he thought. Somehow on this world things had gone right where on his they had gone very wrong. Paul tried to make it all add up: low population, animals that had never gone extinct, lower sea levels. What had they done differently on this world, that things had turned out this way?

Paul rubbed both hands against the stubble on his head. Impressive, yes, he thought—it was impressive—but maybe it wasn't a sign of success. Couldn't all of these things be a by-product of some sort of natural disaster? A killer disease perhaps? Or a runaway war? Any of these things could have caused a big die-off of people, and so kept the population low.

Paul took a bite of bread, chewed it thoughtfully. And of course, with fewer people there would have been fewer greenhouse gases released by their activities, and thus there would have been less global-warming, less melting of the polar ice caps, and thus lower ocean levels. Ecosystems would have remained more stable, and there wouldn't have been as many people running around killing animals and destroying their habitats, and so there would have been fewer extinctions, as well.

Sure, there was no reason to feel impressed. All this may not be their success at all, but simply a positive by-product of some terrible event.

"That's probably all it is," Paul told himself—but still, he wanted more than assumption.

He leaned toward the portal. "Show a record of wide-spread epidemics for the past five hundred years." A graphic came up on the screen. Nope. There didn't seem to be anything particularly remarkable about the timeline he saw displayed. Yes, it showed the rampant deaths from tuberculosis and small pox among non-Europeans in the Americas from roughly 1500 to 1900, the influenza pandemic of 1918, the global impact of AIDS from its onset in the late twentieth century, and so on; but instead of seeing the incidence of epidemics increase during the past hundred years as they had on Paul's world, on this world epidemics had declined during that time.

Paul could find no evidence that an epidemic was the cause of this world's low population. He scratched his head. Perhaps the population had been decimated more than five hundred years ago, and it had only now had a chance to grow back up to these numbers. Paul picked some dates for which he was confident he knew the population of his world, so he could make a comparison between the two.

"State world human population for the year 1960," Paul said.

"Approximately 3.04 billion," came the answer.

"Now state world human population for the year 2000," Paul said.

"Approximately 6.08 billion."

Paul shook his head. That was correct for his world, too. He knew because he had memorized those numbers and dates in school as part of a lesson on the early days of the population boom. It had been taught that it had taken all of humanity's history to reach 3 billion—and then only another forty years to double that.

Paul got up and paced around the room. Whatever had happened to decrease the population of this world, it had happened since the year 2000—and it hadn't been the result of an epidemic.

Paul stopped before the view screen and leaned forward with his hands flat against the table.

Okay, if it wasn't an epidemic, then it had to be something else that caused such a steep decline in population, Paul thought.

"Portal, show timeline for outbreaks of famine since the year 2000," he said. On Paul's world drought-driven famine was a constant problem. It regularly killed off localized groups of people, only to have them replaced by land-hungry people from the surrounding regions, who swept in and claimed the land as soon as the drought that propelled the famine came to an end.

Surely, famine would account for some of the population decline here, Paul thought.

A new graphic appeared on the screen, but what it showed astonished Paul— there had been no major famine on this world since 2025.

"Show timeline record of droughts since 2000," Paul requested. Another image came up on the screen. Yes, there had been periodic regional droughts, though they were not as severe as they were on Paul's world, where rainfall patterns had been made unpredictable as a result of climate change.

"Didn't the droughts since 2025 result in famine?"

"No."

"Why not?" Paul asked.

"International cooperation to supply food prevented starvation."

Paul sat down in the chair in front of the viewscreen and rubbed his face with his hands. All of this was strange and a bit frustrating.

Not an epidemic. Not famine. Must be war.

Paul looked at the screen. "Show timeline for all wars since the year 2000," he said. A new timeline appeared, showing conflict in much the same places and patterns that Paul recalled from the history of his world—but only up until about the late 2010s. After that, the incidence of war began to decline on this world, and had dropped off entirely by 2050.

That certainly hadn't happened in Paul's world.

"When did the last war end?" Paul asked

"In the year 2048," the portal answered

Paul frowned. This made no sense at all. In his world, conflict had grown steadily as the shifting climate and dwindling resources had created new tensions between nations or had rekindled old ones. But not here, Paul thought, looking at the graph. Here, wars had simply stopped.

"Is that correct?" Paul asked. "No war has been fought anywhere in this world since 2048?"

"Correct. The last war was in 2048—a small conflict along the border of Kazakhstan and Uzbekistan," the portal answered.

"The last war was in 2048," Paul echoed softly, shaking his head. Eighty-eight years without a single war. Incredible. And what was stranger still was that he still had no explanation for the drop in population.

Paul ate the last of his bread and cheese while lost in thought, then got up and paced around the room.

After a few minutes, he returned to the Intralink portal. He asked to see death tolls for all the conflicts listed. He was sure he would find some one war that had been so terrible that it had decimated the population and left people too afraid of war to start another one.

The figures came up on the screen, and Paul examined them carefully. The numbers were unremarkable, and in any case not sufficient to account for the general decline in the world's population.

Paul shook his head. It was all very strange, and he was very tired. He'd had a long day. He ate what was left of his groceries, took off his clothes, and climbed into bed—then he lay awake wondering all over again what it was that made this world so different from his own.

Paul realized he'd been trying to think about this from a more-or-less social-science perspective. Now he thought of it again as a physicist.

Where was the branching point? he wondered. Where was the turning point, after which his world went one way, and this world went the other? What could it have been? What single event, what single roll of the dice, could have set this world on such a different course from his own?

Paul closed his eyes and again thought of a tree, where all the branches shared a common trunk—but in his mind it seemed that some branches arched so gracefully, while others became mangled by strong winds or gnarled from a lack of light.

What was it that had made this world and his so unalike?

The thought spiraled in Paul's mind, but his fatigue was deep, and sleep soon overtook him.

For the first part of the night, Paul dreams were plagued by machine parts, epidemics, and droughts—and by a single world that seemed to teeter back and forth between famine and incessant wars, and a stable, wholesome peace. Then, in the middle of the night, he roused himself from this troubled sleep just long enough to refocus his mind on Sheila. Sheila, whom he would somehow make his way back to again. Sheila, who would welcome him home—along with a whole world of admirers. Sheila, who could comfort him like no other.

7

Paul stood under the broiling sun on the same flat, Spanish-style roof, rimmed with a low wall, where he had gone to play when he was a boy. A cool breeze blew across the rooftop. Carried on it, Paul could hear the voice of his mother, calling to him.

He looked around, but she was nowhere in sight. He opened the door to go downstairs. He thought perhaps he could hear her voice rising up from within the darkness there.

Paul descended the stairs, surrounded by musty odors and the sounds of rats scuffling, then opened the door into the kitchen—where there had never been a door before. Across the room, curtains billowed near an open window.

Some part of Paul knew this was the way the room had looked the day she had died.

As he stood there, he could still hear her voice calling.

With gathering anxiety, Paul went from room to room, looking for his mother. Each time he entered, he caught a glimpse of her as she slipped away ahead of him.

"Mom!" he called. "Mom!"

He could hear her voice still calling him. He went from room to room, but he could never reach her...

Paul woke suddenly, out of breath. He felt like someone cast adrift in a sea of anxiety, but anxiety from a far different time than the one he found himself in.

Why this dream, and why now? he asked himself.

Another in the series, he thought. When had they begun? About two or three months ago, he decided. Just when things had started to get really good for him.

Paul rolled over and hugged the spare pillow to his belly. Things had been going well at work then, with the project coming along—and Sheila had finally agreed to share an apartment with him. They'd put in a request with Corprogov at the beginning of March.

Paul smiled as he thought about them getting a place together. Such a move was tantamount to marriage in a world where housing was so hard to get and so hard to change.

Paul had so looked forward to waking every day beside her, from then on, without fail, and having her there with him always.

He thought about the dream again. Why, when he seemed poised to gain something so good, had he had to start revisiting such a painful loss from his past?

Paul forced these thoughts from his mind, crowding them out by mentally reviewing the list he'd come up with the day before. He found himself wondering whether he could really make all these alien parts fit together. He was concerned that he was being too casual in how he evaluated how useful the new parts might be.

Paul rolled over, again pushing away the tattered remnants of the dream, which seemed still to press in around him.

What if the parts didn't fit? he asked himself. He was reasonably confident of the matches he'd made for parts that served only basic functions—but what about the really specialized sub-units? He thought carefully through the process of constructing the transport he'd already built. Some of those parts they'd had to have specially machined and constructed. Was it reasonable to assume that the new parts he'd found to match those would really do what he needed?

Paul sat up in bed, filled with a sense of anxiety. Everything was riding on him getting this right. It was daylight out, and he felt thirsty. He got up, drank some water, took a pee, then went to the Intralink portal and got right back to work.

He carefully reviewed every part he had added to the list the day before, spending most of his time on two or three that he considered most specialized in nature.

After spending a couple of hours at this, Paul finally concluded that he had come up with adequate matches for all but one of those parts, and even that one he was able to match after another half hour or so of work.

Paul asked the portal to keep a record of his revised list, then pushed back his chair.

"Food," he said aloud. He hadn't even had breakfast, and here it was already midmorning. He looked at the grocery bag on the table and remembered that he had finished all his food the day before. He'd have to go out.

Paul got up and showered, then put on the same clothes he'd worn for the past day and a half. He looked in the mirror. The bruise had faded considerably, and in any case, a lot of it was partially covered by the hair on his scalp, where it had started to grow back in. Paul's eyebrows and beard had started to fill in, too.

Paul rubbed his hand along the thick stubble on his jaw, trying to adjust to this new image of himself. Not bad, he thought. He'd actually seen images of people with a similar look once, when he'd wandered into a high-fashion corner of the Stream. It sure was an improvement over what he'd seen when he'd looked into that puddle a week before. Paul stood back and took in the whole effect: close-cut hair, brown shirt, khaki pants. Paul was pleased to think he actually looked pretty respectable.

Paul strapped on his shoes, checked the money and room pass in his pant's pocket, then headed out to pick up his breakfast. He was really hungry but didn't want to spend too much. He decided the best place to go would be the same grocer's he'd stopped at the day before—cheaper than a restaurant and only a short distance from the Inn.

As he walked over, Paul found himself missing the food packets from his world—whatever else could be said of them, at least they were convenient and filling.

When he got to the grocer's, Paul picked out two apples, four day-old muffins, and a quart of orange juice. He considered fresh fruit and juice a real treat. Though both were available on his world, only a few could afford them.

That's another difference between this world and mine, Paul thought, as he paid and left the shop. The differences between his world and this one just kept stacking up, and Paul found himself wondering all over again how this world had come to be as it was.

He started up the sidewalk thinking about that question and trying to recall all the differences he had discovered so far between his world and this, starting with when he had first arrived.

The land seems whole and well—back to its original condition, Paul reflected. People were friendlier, more open and connected. No implants. The technology was an odd mixture of basic and advanced. Lots of animals that were extinct on his world were not extinct here.

That seemed to pretty much cover what he'd found out before he got to Strandford.

Paul turned his attention to the information he'd gained through the Intralink portal.

The technology on the whole seems to involve more synthetic intelligence, and to be more flexible, Paul told himself—and this world's history is very different. No wars. No real problem with famine or epidemics. Low population numbers. Ocean at pre-global-warming levels.

It was an impressive list, and Paul couldn't help wondering again what the branching point could be.

He strolled along, lost in thought. What single difference—what one thing done, or not done—might have sent this world down such a different path than the one his world had taken? he wondered.

For years, Paul had focused on trying to solve, or at least lessen, the problems of his world through his Depopulation Project. It had always seemed to him the best hope for his world. With fewer people, there would be less stress on the environment and a healthier ecosystem. With fewer people, there would also be fewer demands on resources and therefore fewer wars, because there'd be no reason to fight over those resources. And of course, with less overcrowding, disease couldn't spread so easily.

Maybe, Paul thought, what he had struggled to achieve through technology on his world had somehow happened naturally on this one. Perhaps somehow, naturally, the population had been reduced here.

Whatever had lowered the population had to be key, Paul told himself. He felt sure of it.

Paul took a couple more steps and then laughed—yeah, he was sure of this, just like he'd been sure he was on G3-97, or in the past.

But still, it seemed a pretty good hypothesis, and Paul began to think of things that might have caused the population to be reduced on this world. His work on the Intralink the day before made it pretty clear that the people of this world hadn't developed their own transport technology, so it couldn't be that, and he knew from yesterday's searches that the population hadn't dropped because of war, or famine, or even disease. What else could have caused it? A virus that left most people infertile? Maybe, but that would have shown up in the record of epidemics he'd viewed the day before.

Paul crossed the street with his bag of groceries, then thought back over the various strategies that had been tried through the years to bring down the population of his own world. He remembered that in the late-twentieth century, China had established a policy of only allowing one child per couple and had used coercive methods to enforce it. It had worked, for a while, until the Second Cultural Revolution, when democracy had been established. After that, the one-child-per-couple policy, and other unpopular programs, had been brought to a close.

Maybe it was something like that on this world, Paul thought, but it would have to be more global in its effects. He thought about the money he had just handed the cashier. The bills were in "IC" units—International Currency.

That would make sense, then, he thought—a single autocratic government that keeps down the population numbers by restricting procreation.

Yes, that would fit, Paul told himself, as he approached the Inn. Such a government might enforce very strict environmental regulations, as well.

Paul thought about it for a moment more. It would also explain the lack of war. A single, entirely dominating world government—who would there be for it to go to war against?

When Paul got back to his room, he set the bag of groceries on the table next to the view screen and sat down. He had intended to eat while continuing with his research on parts, but now he was too excited with his new theory to go back to that just yet.

Paul touched the portal, which opened; then he waved his hand before the screen. As the screen lit up, Paul began asking questions.

It didn't take long for him to discover that this world did, in fact, have a single, unifying government. But the government, as it turned out, was not at all autocratic. It was a global union of peaceful, cooperating nations. All one hundred and seventy-eight nations of the world had joined together in this democracy. There were no laws regulating how many children a couple could have, though low numbers were encouraged and in some ways rewarded. Environmental regulations did exist, but they were put in place by elected agreement and were quite enthusiastically endorsed by the citizenry.

Paul leaned back in his chair. He took a bite of muffin, shook his head. The mystery just seemed to deepen.

Paul thought about it for several more minutes, as he finished the muffin, but he couldn't seem to get a fresh angle on the puzzle. Okay, he told himself, as he dug an apple out of the bag and called up his parts list on the viewscreen—he couldn't spend all day trying to figure out how and why this world was like it was. He had work he needed to do, and he hadn't gotten where he was in life at such a young age by ignoring his work.

Paul turned his attention back to researching parts for the transport system. But even as he continued to use the Intralink portal to explore various indigenous technologies, other thoughts kept turning at the back of his mind. By the time he'd eaten two apples and another muffin, his thoughts had drifted entirely away from the parts question again.

"The branching point," Paul whispered to himself, staring at the viewscreen. Maybe if he could identify just *when* this world became different from his, he could look more deeply into that period of history and discover the turning point. And discovering what the turning point was might just tell him *why* this world was as it was.

Paul hesitated for a minute, resisting an impulse to do something that would distract him from the work he knew he needed to do—but finally he admitted to himself that he would be distracted by the question until he had found an answer to it, and so he decided it would be okay if he spent a few minutes pursuing it.

Paul thought for a minute about how he could get the information he wanted. What he'd need to do was compare the history of this world to the history of his own and find the earliest point where they differed. That would be the branching point between this world and his own.

Paul thought back over the histories of epidemics, of famines, and of wars that the Intralink portal had displayed for him the day before. They seemed essentially identical—no, actually identical—to the history of his world up until sometime closing in on the middle of the 21st Century. After that, there were lots of differences.

No, it was earlier, Paul thought. More like 2025—wasn't that when the last major famine had been? After that, it seemed, the histories of the two worlds had begun to diverge rapidly.

Paul told the computer to clear the screen and ordered up a timeline of prominent events of the twenty-first century. "Run three parallel lines, one for the rise and fall of national leaders, one for the outbreak of wars, and one for environmental turning points, such as prominent extinctions, rate of natural habitat destruction, etc. Establish timeline from 2000 through 2050," he said.

Paul looked at the timeline of world leaders. Yes, yes, Paul said to himself as he looked down the list. Yes, they all matched Paul's recollections of history up until, ah, yeah, the 2016 American presidential election. The name of the person elected then—he was certain it wasn't the one who had been elected in his world. In Paul's world, the 2016 American election had marked a new upheaval, as the forces of corporate dominance had helped their candidate to achieve victory. It had been one of several turning points in the early development of Corprogov—though few people had had the foresight to recognize its full significance at the time.

Of course, Paul didn't have the names of all the past leaders of his world memorized, but he knew too well the ones who had been early proponents of the corporate-government movement—those who believed that government should be used to serve the corporations and the rich, while ignoring the needy. Over time, that philosophy had led to a kind of meshing of corporate and governmental institutions that had ultimately led to the establishment of the supranational Corprogov of his world.

Paul scanned the timeline. Clearly, after that, much was different. While several of the names of world leaders after that were familiar to Paul, those who had come to power with the rising tide of corporate control of government were absent. Apparently, that movement had never really taken hold on this world.

So, whatever had changed this world, Paul thought, had taken root enough by then—by 2016—to change the outcome of that election.

Paul looked next at the timeline for war, mentally comparing what had happened in this world to events in his own world's history. As he had noted earlier, the pattern of conflicts looked familiar up until the late 2010s—but after that, the frequency and duration of wars on this world declined much more rapidly than they had on his. In fact, the last war had come to an end almost ninety years earlier—in 2048.

Paul sat back and stared at the screen. As he finished his third muffin and started on an apple, he marveled that this world could be as it was.

He sat, staring at the screen as he ate the apple, trying to imagine what it would be like to live in a world where there could be such lasting peace—real peace—without autocratic rule. Then Paul raised his eyebrows and shook his head, tossed the core of the apple aside, and pressed on, eager to discover what the next timeline would reveal.

Paul leaned toward the screen as he scanned the timeline that displayed environmental problems. It was clear that wild-habitat destruction had been rampant on this world in the early part of the twenty-first century, just as it had been on Paul's, but on this world the rate of that destruction had begun to diminish by about 2020—while on Paul's world rapid deforestation and species extinctions had continued unabated until a dramatic decline in worldwide oxygen levels brought these problems to the world's attention, during the 2050s.

All sorts of moratoriums on cutting and building on new land were put into place on Paul's world then, but it had been too little, too late. By then, climate change had become a run-away phenomenon and had brought such severe warming to South America that within four decades most of the Amazon Rainforest had dried to a tinder and gone up in flames. Other rainforests around the world were little better off. An incredible numbers of species were lost for all time, as one habitat after another was transformed beyond recognition.

Paul sighed as he thought about it, then turned his attention back to the three timelines he had up on the Intralink screen. Among the possessions Paul had left behind on his world was a black-market file with information on species that had become extinct. He remembered it saying that the last tiger had disappeared from the wild in 2028, and that the last wild elephant had died sometime in the mid-2030s—Paul wasn't sure exactly when. However, he did know the date polar bears had been declared extinct in the wild—2025.

Paul looked at the timeline to see what prominent extinctions had occurred in this world in that time frame.

None were listed.

Could that be right? Paul wondered what the Intralink counted as "prominent."

"Portal, indicate date of death of the last wild polar bear, last wild tiger and last wild elephant on timeline," Paul said.

"Polar bears, tigers, and elephants are still alive in the wild," was the response.

Paul leaned back in his chair, his mouth a little bit open, trying to imagine a world with enough Arctic ice to still support polar bears. And just to think of it! Wild tigers and elephants still roamed free somewhere on this world! He shivered a bit. What a thought!

Paul stared blankly at the screen for a few minutes, imagining. He had always been enchanted by the idea of wild lands, where the forces of nature erupted without the constraints of human tampering. Polar bears, tigers, and elephants! In the wild! Images of a vast, icy coastline, of dripping rainforests, and of wind-swept savannas sprouted in Paul's mind. What would his grandfather think if he could only tell him?

For a moment, Paul tried to imagine it. How would he even express what he saw revealed in these simple timelines? That where the world they had shared together had been broken and diminished, this world was well and whole? For Paul, it was as though, his whole life, he had been cradling some precious elixir cupped in his hands and, powerless, had been watching it gradually drip away—while here, now, he found all that was precious gathered together again, still vital and alive and whole.

How could he tell his grandfather that? If his grandfather were still alive and here with him, how could Paul even shape the words? And yet, his grandfather would understand, would have understood perfectly, Paul knew, with hardly any words being spoken.

Paul stared at the screen, at the three timelines all stacked together. What did they add up to? What did they tell?

Paul could see no differences between this world and his before the 2016 American Presidential election. It seemed likely that up until that point—or a short while preceding it—the two worlds had been the same. But after 2016, Paul could see, the differences progressed rapidly. Within a few years after that point, the two worlds were obviously on drastically different paths.

Paul stared for a long time at the screen. Something had changed this world—reduced the population, prevented wars, protected the environment. Something had happened, something that could have gone one way, or gone the other—something that *had* gone one way in his world, and had gone the other way here.

Paul rubbed the short hair on top of his head. What could it have been? He thought again of the image of worlds diverging like branches growing off a single trunk. Somewhere, in the years proceeding 2016, the common trunk that these two worlds had shared had split, with one branch leading to Paul's world and another to this.

Paul leaned back in his chair and stared hard at the screen, then shook his head and stretched, popping the knuckles on both hands.

Oh well. There was really no telling, he admitted to himself. The roll of the dice, one way, or the other. Sometime before 2016, there had been a turning point. Something big, or something small—he might never know—but it had clearly made all the difference for the world he was now in.

Paul pushed the empty grocery bag aside, determined to get back to work on his parts list. He had taken much too long just trying to satisfy his curiosity. He didn't have enough money to casually squander time on nonessential activities. He still had parts to research if he was to make any progress at all.

He told the portal to clear the screen. "Display parts marked for future reference," he said. As the list of parts filled the screen, Paul realized he'd bought food for breakfast but hadn't even thought about lunch. That was just as well, he told himself. He wasn't really that hungry, and until he could be sure where his next paycheck was coming from, he should be careful about what he spent. He would just keep working until it was time for dinner and have a big meal then. It seemed to Paul that if he could just stay focused, he should have a complete list of parts by the time he stopped for dinner.

▢   ▢   ▢

Paul worked on for another few hours and did manage, finally, to come up with what looked like an adequate parts list. He asked the Intralink portal for a copy of the list that he could take with him, and it dispensed a small sphere, about a centimeter in diameter, from an opening just above the table top. The sphere appeared to be made out of some sort of iridescent blue crystal.

Paul picked up the small crystal from the table top. "The information is recorded in the crystal you just gave me?" Paul asked.

"Yes, it's on the data sphere," the Intralink device answered.

Paul stood and dropped the crystal into his pocket, then he dug it back out and turned it over in his hand. "Is it likely the sphere would lose data rattling around in my pocket?" Paul asked.

"No. The data can survive whatever humans can survive, once spherically encoded: pressure, electric shock, heat, cold, friction..."

"Okay, that's enough information," Paul said, cutting it off. He dropped the sphere back in his pocket, then glanced over at the window. The day was fading into evening. Paul felt tired and hungry.

He told the portal he was done, then closed the panel as the screen went dark. He wanted a big meal, but was concerned about what it would cost. At the rate he was spending, he would only be able to afford a few days at the Inn—and even if he had correctly identified the parts he would need, acquiring them would take money, surely very much more than what he now had, or could easily earn. This, finding an energy source, and being certain he had solved the aiming problem, were the problems he now faced.

And of course, Paul reasoned, there would be no point in buying parts from which he might build a transport, even if he did have money, if he hadn't solved the energy and the aiming problems. In any case, he concluded, he might as well spend money on food now.

Paul pushed in the chair, pulled the money from his pocket and counted it, then set out to look for a restaurant. As he left the Inn, images of the parts he'd been searching through cascaded through his tired mind. It struck him how sophisticated the technology on this world was, but also how little it was used compared to the high-tech, gadgety environment he'd come from. Paul stepped off of the hotel grounds and started down the street. Sure, Anna had had a micro computer on her wrist—but when she was installing the new step, she'd used a hand saw. And these solar-powered vehicles he saw buzzing by him seemed technical enough, but why bother to include pedals? It didn't add up. As fast as he was getting answers about this place, he was gathering up more questions.

Paul found a little restaurant about half a kilometer up the street and ordered a big meal. Though he was pretty satisfied with the solutions he'd come up with for parts, and though he thought it likely that Interdimensional-Linking Theory would prove to solve the aiming problem, the energy question still haunted him. Where in this world would he get the big burst of energy he needed to make his transport system work? The machines he'd seen people using, and those he'd explored through the Intralink portal, all appeared to have been designed to use as little power as possible. It was impressive how far they could stretch a joule—but his plans would require an intense burst of power, and there was no way around that. He'd seen no evidence of anything here that could provide that kind of power.

Paul's food was served quickly, and he ate hungrily. It didn't take long for him to finish his meal. He paid for his dinner and started back toward the Inn, but he was tired of spending so much time alone in that room. The days that had passed since his arrival in this world had been the most stressful of his life, and he couldn't help thinking how much better he would feel if he could go by one of the virtual sex shops that lined Encinal Road in his Strandford, and run one of his favorite programs. Those shops had all the stuff that was too steamy to be legally posted to the Stream and isolation booths to experience it all in, where there would be no problem of outside stimuli intruding and ruining the "reality" of the event. Paul had gone there often when he was younger, at times when he'd found himself feeling especially alone. He'd always liked the wholesome-looking women with the steady gaze. Deep down, he knew it wasn't the way they looked, so much as what their appearance meant to him, that made them so attractive. There was something about the way they seemed so tender-hearted, the rich illusion of their emotional embrace, that made him feel somehow recognized, valued, and less alone in his life. He could sure use that now.

Paul was only a few blocks from the part of town where those shops would have been located in his world. He decided to take a stroll in that direction after dinner and see what he would find. Sure, he knew no one in this world had the types of implants that would make the full experience possible, but he thought this world, with its subtle but sophisticated technologies, might have come up with an interesting alternative. He hoped they had, and that maybe he could find a little comfort that way.

Paul turned the corner onto Encinal Road, which would have been lit up with all sorts of flashing holographic signs in his world, but all he found was an ordinary street lit and populated no differently than the other streets in this small rural hamlet.

Paul felt depressed. He just stood there for a few minutes, looking around. Finally, he stopped another young man who was passing by and asked him as casually as he could if there were any sex shops in the area. The other guy tilted his head a little, looked surprised.

"That's a funny idea. Are you serious? Like paying someone for sex?"

Paul shrugged a little, then nodded a tentative "yes." He was going to suggest that it was *virtual* sex he had in mind, but he realized that would probably sound even stranger to this fellow.

"No, friend, there's nothing like that around here," the guy said, shaking his head. "Wouldn't be a lot of call for it, I would think—I mean, *using* someone like that."

He looked at Paul briefly, taking him in—and for a moment, Paul felt transparent, as though his mood were written on him as plainly as if he had been wearing a badge.

The other man took a step away, then he turned back and, with a sympathetic look, added, "When I feel lonesome—and, you know, if I don't have someone special like that—I find a friend who will put their arms around me and hold me close. Truth is, it comforts me better than any stranger could."

He shrugged a little, then added, "I mean, there's always someone who will at least put their arms around you, right?"

The man smiled a small, friendly smile, then turned and sauntered off, leaving Paul standing there, alone, knowing that there was no one in his life he could count on to hold him like that—not even Sheila, after sex, with her implant still running.

No, no one—not on this world, or any other.

As Paul watched the man disappear up the street, he felt his spirits dip. He should have known, anyhow, he told himself, as he continued on along the sidewalk. More and more he was aware of how different this world was from his own.

Paul was feeling sorry for himself and didn't want to go back to his room at the Inn. He was tired of being alone there, and tired of trying to find a way to cobble together a sophisticated piece of machinery from scavenged parts. In any case, he had gotten enough work done for one day, he told himself. He deserved a little time off.

As Paul walked along, the outer veneer of his mood continued to crumble. He thought about the work he'd been so focused on the last couple of days. So what? he told himself. Now I have a list of substitute parts—but no money to buy them with and no energy source even if I can scrape together the currency.

It all seemed futile. He was alone on a strange world—low on funds, trying to build some impossible machine. He didn't have enough money to build a new transport, even if he had the right technologies available. And in truth, he had nothing better than guesses as to whether the parts he'd picked out would prove useful—even if he actually could get his hands on them.

Everything Paul thought seemed to poke holes in his confidence. If he went back to the Inn, he felt sure his mood would just continue on its downward spiral. He remembered passing a little pub on a side street after he'd left the restaurant. He'd go there and treat himself to a drink, he told himself. And why not? What little money he had wasn't nearly enough to buy what he needed, anyway.

⊙   ⊙   ⊙

Paul stood at the bar, looking at a list of drinks posted on the wall behind the bartender. If he could keep his spending down, he'd have enough money for perhaps four more nights at the spartan Wayfarer's Inn, with just enough left over for food. It would be gone too soon, Paul knew, but still, he needed a chance to unwind. He asked the bartender how much for a half liter of stout on draft. The bartender answered, and Paul thought for a moment, then went ahead and ordered. Stout was a special treat. In fact, all traditional brewed beverages, whether beer, wine, or liquor, were hard to come by in his world because of the large amount of land required for growing the grains or grapes that went into them.

The bartender handed Paul his drink, and Paul handed the bartender a few bills, then looked around the pub for a place to sit. On the far side of the room, a small fire burned in a corner fireplace, with three chairs set before it. Paul went over and sat down in an upholstered arm chair near the fire. It was a quiet pub, and Paul could hear the fire crackling. He took a long draw of his stout, trying to sip the liquid beneath a thick layer of creamy foam.

Two middle-aged women were sitting in the other chairs facing the fire, talking softly to one another. Their manner revealed the same sort of quiet, amiable intimacy Paul had seen among the people at Marco and Anna's gathering two nights before.

Paul looked down at his stout, which he held cupped in two hands. It looked delicious and inviting. He took another draw, then rested his head against the tall back of his soft chair and closed his eyes. Waves of feeling rose up and fell within him, like the hills and valleys of ocean swells. He felt lonely, frustrated—he'd been thrust into this situation against his will, and now he had to somehow rise to the occasion. He felt sorry for himself, for the labors in front of him, for his running short of money, for his isolation in a world in which nobody else seemed to feel isolated. The more he found out about this world, the more tempted he was to fall in love with it, to embrace a world in which wars didn't exist, in which animals he had considered long extinct roamed wild and free. And yet, this wasn't his world. He felt keenly that he didn't belong in it, didn't know how to navigate within it. At this hour, even more than he craved the beauty and vitality of this world, he longed for the familiarity of his own, and for the secure place he had held within it.

Paul opened his eyes and took several swallows of his stout. He felt all at once torn between these two points, these two worlds, like a boat cast adrift on a sea, with all familiar moorings lost.

The alcohol settling in his stomach seemed to warm his blood. He relaxed, and his mind drifted. An image of the herd of elk he'd seen two nights before passed through his thoughts. How wonderful that had been! A sight he'd never dreamed he might see.

Paul tried to revive the image, animate it, bring it fully to life in his mind. He saw the first elk appear, then more entered the field, coming out from behind the hillside. And now the people coming out to watch, standing beside him, gathering beside him to watch the elk gathering below. Paul turned around to look, and the people were pouring in around him, pouring in from the house, from the surrounding hills. Millions of them. Billions of them. The people of his world streaming in and trampling out this world.

Paul opened his eyes and straightened himself in his chair. He didn't want to think about that. He didn't like those thoughts. He tried to think of something else that would keep his attention braced and away from that kind of thinking. Sheila. What would Sheila be doing right now? Would she be home from work? Would she be worrying about him? It had been, ah, let's see, could it really be seven days since he'd disappeared? Yes, a whole week—though it seemed like much more than that. Paul imagined Sheila sitting in one of the chairs in the small kitchen area of her apartment, worrying about him.

Paul looked down into his stout. He hoped she wasn't too upset. How was she feeling, right now? he wondered. Did she feel alone, as he did?

Paul sighed, then turned his gaze to the fire. The conversation of the two women next to him seemed rhythmic and soothing. He liked the soft sounds of their voices. He caught little bits of their conversation—"university," "attention to research," "it's nice to have the semester over." The words drifted in and out of his awareness as he stared into the fire and sipped his drink. Then a phrase caught his attention: "that's why I chose to focus on the twenty-first century," and Paul caught his breath. He leaned in toward them just a bit and began to listen more closely.

"The research is basically done," one was saying. Paul glanced over at her; she had graying, densely curly hair and brown skin, with a slight Asian cast to her eyes. "It's mostly a matter of writing up my findings now."

"I understand you've got a distribution contract already arranged," the other—paler, a few years younger—said.

"Yes, that part is..." Background noise drowned out her words.

"I remember you said you were...twenty-first century history, Professor...but I don't remember...precise focus," the younger one said.

"Twenty-first century ideologies."

"That must have been very interesting...major shifts during..."

Paul turned his head as though looking around for the server. With his face turned toward the two women, he picked up every word.

"Yes, and with the communications network in place, unlike previous centuries, there were such broad international patterns," the older one said.

"I'd certainly like to listen to a copy when it's done. It sounds fascinating."

"Well, thank you. I hope I can get it finished during the summer break," the older one answered. "Now, Mirika, I keep meaning to ask you, you said Jacob was having trouble with his ankle since that bad sprain..."

Paul turned his face back toward the fire and let out a breath. A historian, focused on twenty-first century ideologies. What luck!

A server, who apparently had seen Paul looking around, came by and asked if he would like another drink. Paul looked down at the glass in his hand— nearly empty. He swallowed the last bit and ordered another. He'd enjoyed the first, and besides, maybe if he sat here long enough he'd have a chance to speak to the professor.

Paul continued to listen to the conversation, but the bits he picked up seemed incidental, not on the subject that interested him. The server brought his second drink, thick and dark, with a nice head like the first, and Paul consoled himself with it as he waited for a chance to break into the conversation going on nearby.

After a time, the younger woman stood up. "I'm sorry to have to leave so early," she said. "I'm afraid I'm a bit over scheduled these days."

The older one stood and hugged the younger one goodbye, then sat back down as the younger woman departed. She sat looking at the fire for a moment, while Paul tried to gather up the courage to speak, then she pulled open a wrist display like the one Anna had used for field analysis, and began looking over the readout.

"Excuse me," Paul said. She looked over at him. "I couldn't help but overhear—you're a historian?"

"Yes."

"That was a fascinating period, the twenty-first century," Paul said. "I've been thinking lately about some of the changes that took place then, and I have a hypothetical question I'd like to ask you."

She smiled in the same open, relaxed way Paul had seen so many people smile since he'd come to this world.

"All right," she said.

"Suppose," Paul said, as he got up and shifted to the seat next to the professor. He was surprised to find himself a bit unsteady as he moved over. "Suppose that you had to pick out the single most important cause of all the changes that took place in that period—early in the twenty-first century, when so much began to change so fast—some one turning point that might have propelled all the other changes that came in the years after. What would you pick to name as that primary trigger?" Paul finished his question and took a swallow of his drink with what he hoped was a casual air.

The professor looked at him for a moment. He felt that she was sizing him up, then she smiled kindly and said, "Well, while there were many social and political movements that rose and fell during that time, the answer to that question is unequivocal. The one most important and enduring influence that arose during that era was the work of Dr. Indira Kumar. Most specifically, her memoirs, *Memories and Reflections*."

Paul nodded, still trying to seem very casual and not overly interested. "What year did that come out, exactly?" he said, sipping his drink.

"At the beginning of 2014. It was first published in the United States, then overseas. It quickly became an international favorite."

Twenty-fourteen, Paul thought. That would fit perfectly with the timeline information he'd collected. It was just two years before the American presidential election of 2016, and Paul was certain he'd never heard of either the author or the book before. If the book had been published in his world with anything like the same response, Paul felt certain, he would have at least heard of it. This counted as the earliest difference between the two worlds he had found.

"A-huh," Paul said. "What made her memoirs—what did you say they were called?"

"*Memories and Reflections*," the professor answered.

"What would you say made *Memories and Reflections* so influential?" Paul asked.

"Funny that you should be familiar enough with that period to ask what brought about its changes, and not be more familiar with her work." The professor squinted her eyes and tilted her head a little bit, then went ahead and answered Paul's question. "She had ideas about what defined and shaped us as human beings. Her ideas changed the way people thought about themselves and their relationship to others. It was a subtle effect at first, I suppose, but ultimately it had deep importance."

The professor looked thoughtful for a moment, then added, "I don't know where we would be without her influence."

"Like—how so?" Paul asked.

"Oh, in so many ways. We are a much more peaceful world than we would have been, I am certain. And bigotry—we've seen almost an entire end to bigotry..."

"And you credit her with that?" Paul cut in.

"Oh, not single handedly. But she catalyzed a change. Yes, catalyzed," the professor nodded thoughtfully. "That's the word for it."

Paul sat back in his chair, nodding. The word resonated with him. *Catalyst.* A roll of the dice, a branching of a tree, a single chemical—added in just a small amount—that completely transforms another chemical. Was she the element that had transformed this world?

"I'd like to find out more about her work, if I could. Where would you suggest looking?" Paul asked.

"Her works are available through Intralink, or for use on a personal player." The professor seemed to warm to the topic, as any natural teacher would when confronted with someone genuinely interested in her subject. "She was an impressive woman. Some would say that it was her training as an anthropologist that allowed her to see the underlying themes of human development and civilization with such telling clarity, but I give little credit to her traditional training, her perceptions cut at such odd angles to the conventions held in that context."

"She sounds fascinating," Paul said, and though he was trying to make conversation, he did mean it. "I presume part of your work is focused on her contributions?"

"Well, of course—one could hardly write about the twenty-first century without her."

Paul nodded. He was thinking about the crystalline data sphere the Intralink portal had provided as a record of his search. He wondered if it could be accessed on one of these "personal players," too. He'd like to be able to retrieve that data without depending on finding another portal like the one at the Inn.

"You said her work could be accessed through a personal player. Where do you suppose would be a good place to buy one of those around here?" Paul asked.

The professor thought for a moment, then suggested a store up the street about four or five blocks.

"And they'd have Dr. Kumar's memoirs available there, as well?"

"Oh, surely they would," she answered. "It's quite widely available."

Paul leaned back in his chair next to the professor and swallowed down the last of his stout. He stared into the blue light of the fire, now burning low, then felt suddenly uncomfortable at having intruded into this woman's solitude. Paul set his glass on the side table next to his chair, then thanked the professor for her help and excused himself quietly.

◻   ◻   ◻

Paul walked out of the pub and into the cool night air. Once outside, he set off in the direction of the shop the professor had recommended. The air was damp, and Paul turned his collar up against the cold.

"Dr. Indira Kumar," he repeated to himself, determined not to forget the name. He was certain he had never heard it before, and yet she, or her book at least, had apparently been dramatically influential in the world he was now in. And the year was right, too, he told himself: 2014. That was before the earliest difference he'd been able to identify between this world and his own—the American presidential election of 2016.

Paul had a strong hunch he had identified the branching point between this world and his: in this world, Dr. Kumar's book had been published and become famous. In his world, it had not. He wanted to find out what was in that book.

It wasn't long before Paul found the little tech shop right where the professor had told him it was. He stepped in out of the nighttime chill and found himself in a small, warmly lit room. A man, who had a little girl with him, was interacting with a woman who stood on the other side of a counter that ran across the front of the shop.

"We specialize in wearable technology," the woman was telling the man. "We have one of the broadest selections in town, and this is our best selling item for youngsters."

The man looked over an object he had in his hand, and then down at the girl. "What do you think, honey? Is this the one you want?"

"Is it the purple one?" the little girl asked.

"Yes, it's the purple one, honey," he said.

The little girl grinned up at him and nodded her enthusiastic approval.

"We'll take it," the man said.

"That will be 16.71 IC," the woman said, and gestured to a small indented area in the glass counter top. The man pressed his right thumb into the shallow indentation, then looked up and nodded at the salesperson.

"That takes care of it," she said.

Must be some kind of electronic transfer of funds, Paul thought, that uses his thumb print to identify his account. Paul stepped up to the counter.

"I'm in the market for a personal player," Paul said.

"Okay, which model are you interested in?"

"I'm not really sure," Paul said. "What sort of selection do you have?"

The woman spun a screen around so that it would face him and said "Carmile, please give graphic display of personal players in stock." The screen lit up with a chart listing nearly sixty models, along with indications as to which characteristics they each had. Paul reached into his pocket and pulled out the crystal with which the Intralink portal in his room had provided him.

"How many of them play these?" Paul asked.

"Limit display to those that play data spheres," the sales person said, and the listing on the display was cut roughly in half.

"I'm interested in getting a lower-priced model that I can also use to access Indira Kumar's book *Memories and Reflections*," Paul said. "What would you recommend?"

The sales person spun the screen halfway back around so she could see it, too, and tapped on the screen. "This model—it's a very good buy and it comes with any title of your choice pre-installed."

Paul looked at the price on the screen; it was one of the lower ones. He knew he should hesitate to spend the money, but with a little alcohol in his system he was feeling impulsive. Besides, he needed a way to retrieve the data he'd collected.

"Okay, I'll take one of those," he said.

The sales person turned and walked back into the aisles behind the counter. Paul looked around. The man was squatting in front of the little girl and was attaching a device, which looked a bit like a purple flower, to the front of her coat. Paul figured the little girl was about five or six years old.

"Do you know how to use it, honey? All you have to do is speak to it and it will respond, just like a person would. If you want to, you can name it and it will respond to the name you give it."

"Uh-huh," the little girl said.

"It works a lot like our Intralink portal at home. It can read you any story you want, and even talk to you about it and answer questions," the man explained, as the little girl nodded.

"And look," he went on, "it even has a screen, so you can see the pictures."

Paul watched as the man gently pushed a yellow button at the center of the device and a small screen unfurled to one side.

"I know," the child said, still nodding. "Sammy has one."

The man glanced over at Paul, shrugged. "They pick up everything so fast."

Paul smiled. Maybe the child didn't need the help, but Paul was glad at least he had the man there to explain it to him. The sales person appeared again from the back of the store and set a small blue-black device on the counter in front of Paul. It was slim and cylindrical—about six centimeters long and only a little over a centimeter across. The clerk demonstrated the scroll-out screen on one side of the device. The screen, when open, was as wide as it was tall.

"That's 23.54 IC," the clerk said, as she snapped the screen shut. She gestured to one of the indentations in the glass counter top.

"Is it okay if I pay cash?" Paul asked.

"Yeah, we can take cash."

Paul pulled the bills from his pocket and handed a few over to the clerk, who again stepped into the back, presumably to get change. Paul glanced over at the man, who reached down for the hand of the little girl and walked with her from the store.

"I think I'm going to name it 'Toby,'" Paul heard the little girl saying as the door swung shut.

The sales person returned with Paul's change. Paul reached for the player, but the sales person put her hand on it.

"Hold on, I have to install your text. Kumar's memoirs, right?"

"Memories and Reflections," Paul said.

The sales person picked up the player and said "Install Indira Kumar's *Memories and Reflections, SE.*" As she held the device a small blue light on one end pulsed slowly.

"What does 'SE' stand for," Paul asked.

"Special Edition. This version includes Dr. Kumar's "Preface to the Second Edition," all the appendixes, and a comprehensive collection of articles, reviews, and analyses related to the text. It's the most complete edition available." The light stopped pulsing, and the clerk unsnapped a metallic panel from the front of the player.

"I think it's the best version," she added, then reached up and attached the device to the pocket of Paul's shirt, with the curved front panel outside the pocket and the rest of the player inside. The two pieces snapped into place, apparently drawn together by a magnetic force. The outside piece was made of the same dark material Paul had seen on the sleek vehicles of this world— clearly, another solar-powered device.

"Some people think the preface is a little too technical and dry," the clerk continued, "but she is speaking to a university audience, after all. Anyway, don't let yourself get bogged down there. The rest reads like a novel."

Paul tugged gently at the personal player where it hung, just inside his pocket, and found it securely attached.

"You going to the retreat?" the sales person asked, rattling on without waiting for a reply. "A lot of the people who come here for players and who want her memoirs installed are on their way there. I went there a couple of years ago myself, spent a couple of weeks. It's a nice place."

"I don't know about the retreat," Paul said.

"You don't? You know all the sojourners who pass through town here? That's where they're headed. The Kumaric Retreat. It's up in the mountains east of town."

Paul remembered the woman asking him if he was a sojourner when he first got into town.

"What is a 'sojourner,' exactly?"

"Just anybody who makes the walk to the Retreat."

"Is it expensive to go there?" Paul asked. He still didn't know what he would do when he left the Inn in Strandford.

"Oh, it's free," the sales person said. "I mean, you've got to contribute some kind of work during your stay there—spend a little time in the gardens or the kitchen or something of that sort—but otherwise, they provide food and give you a little room to stay in. And it's a great education in Dr. Kumar's work, if you're interested in it."

"Sounds good," Paul said. "What do you have to do to get in?"

"Oh, anybody can go there. Like I said, it's free. You just show up. But they do have a couple of requirements: they ask people to already be familiar with Dr. Kumar's memoirs before they arrive—that's why I thought maybe you were going there—and they also encourage people to approach on foot. Though that's not strictly required, most of the people coming from Strandford do. It gives people kind of a meditative transition—helps people leave behind the whole 'hustle and bustle,' you know, and gear down a little bit before they get there, so they feel more reflective."

Paul nodded, intrigued. "Do they have access to Intralink there?" he asked.

The clerk smiled a little. "Well, they may want people to leave their daily concerns behind before they get there, but it's not like some kind of drastic isolation. Sure, they have portals there. I think there's one in every room."

Paul nodded thoughtfully. "So, how long a walk is it? How do you get there?"

"Depends on where you start the trail. Most start it up on Figueroa. There's a beautiful view coming down off the peak. It takes about three or four days from there. Others start the trail here in town—well, along the edge of town, really—out along Alamo Pintado Creek. If you're going to start here in town, that'll add a couple days to your trip," the sales person said.

"Alamo Pintado," Paul repeated. It didn't ring a bell. There were no creeks through the sprawling Strandford he knew from his world. "How would I get there?"

"Just head west from anywhere in town," she answered, pointing toward the back of the store. "Once you hit the creek, there's the trail. You can't miss it. It'll take you north, then curve around east toward the mountains."

Paul looked thoughtful, took a step toward the door.

"If you think you might be interested," the store clerk added, "you can get cheap camp gear for the walk to the Retreat at the store 'Wilderness Journey,' about three doors down, across the street," she indicated which direction with a jerk of her head. "They sell a lot of used equipment to sojourners, who then come back through town and sell it back to them. That's how they keep their prices so low."

Paul thanked her and stepped out of the store. He stood on the sidewalk, still a little buzzed from the alcohol. He was excited to hear about this Kumaric Retreat. He thought about going. If he went, maybe he would learn more about Dr. Kumar's work and more about the branching point between his world and this one. He'd have food and a place to sleep, and he'd even have access to an Intralink portal to do research on energy sources. Paul took a few lighthearted steps down the street. The more he thought about it, the more he liked the idea.

Paul crossed the street and stepped into the camping goods store with an air of impulsive enthusiasm. He greeted the sales clerk and told him that he was a sojourner and needed camping supplies for his walk to the Retreat. He knew he was still a little buzzed from the stout, but Paul didn't think that was the only reason he felt so good about this decision. The clerk set Paul up with a used torso pack, a simple sleep bivy, a small fire-starter kit, a compact flashlight, a canteen, a collapsible toothbrush, and a week's supply of travel food, as well as a map of the area—then threw in a small "sojourner's aid pack," which was a part of a giveaway special they had going on.

Paul asked the clerk how much water he'd need to bring along and was told there was water available along the way—either from creeks, or during dry periods, from cisterns left out for travelers. Paul was concerned about drinking the water from the creeks, but was told the water in the creeks was potable—that the biological organisms present had been rebalanced during the Environmental Reclamation Projects of the 2050s.

Paul asked the clerk to give him a subtotal of what he'd already set aside to buy, then added a used all-weather jacket, a spare shirt and trousers (both secondhand, as well—but in good shape), new underwear and socks, and a simple, lightweight solar razor to the pile of stuff he was about to buy.

Paul made his purchase and left the store. He stood out in front counting what little was left of his money. He'd already paid for two nights at the Inn, so that much was settled. Now he looked down at what he had in his hand. It wasn't even enough to cover a single night at the Inn.

He sighed happily. Well, I've done it, he thought. There's no turning back.

Paul walked back to the Wayfarer's Inn, feeling more lighthearted than he had in days. When he got back, he detached the new personal player from his shirt, then set it and his other new purchases on the table along the wall opposite the bed, and got undressed. He washed out the clothes he'd been wearing and hung them to dry in the bathroom near the open window. (He'd start out with his new clothes in the morning, he told himself, and would strap whatever was still damp to the outside of his pack to finish drying.)

Paul showered and shaved then—and afterward, as the steam cleared from the mirror, he stood back and appraised his reflection. His eyebrows, eyelashes, and hair had filled back in some. With that and the clean shave, Paul felt he actually looked pretty good. He might not be from this world, he thought, but at least he was beginning to look like he could be.

PART III

⊡

PILGRIMAGE

8

Paul woke early the next morning, not really hung over, but a little dehydrated from the alcohol he'd drunk at the pub. His mood, however, was bright, and he felt excited about the discoveries and the decisions he'd made the night before. The Kumaric Retreat was just what he needed: a free place to stay with free food and an Intralink portal for him to use—and all he would have to do in exchange was a little work while he was there.

Paul showered and put on clean clothes. The shirt he'd washed out the night before was nearly dry, and he decided to wear it and save the new one until he had reached the Retreat, but the new pants he put on. Though the fit wasn't perfect, it was good enough.

Paul loaded up the torso pack with all his food, clothes, and gear, with his drying trousers strapped on across the top, and the still-damp socks in a mesh pocket on the outside of the pack. Then he went to the office of the Wayfarer's Inn and told them he was leaving.

Much as he missed the certainty he'd felt about his life in his own world, it felt good to feel so untethered, Paul thought, as he left the Inn's grounds on that crisp spring morning. He stopped off at the grocer's and spent some more of what remained of his money on bread, cheese, and fruit—which he ate in a park under a live-oak tree, before setting off westward toward Alamo Pintado Creek and the trail that ran alongside it.

It was a short walk to the creek, which ran along the edge of town, and Paul had no trouble finding the trail. He set off on it, heading north, with the San Rafael Mountains ahead and to his right. As he walked along, he made plans for how he might connect the parts that he had picked out with the help of the Intralink portal at the Inn. Though each part had been designed for something different than the use he intended to put it to, he figured with a little ingenuity and some luck, he ought to be able to make things fit.

When Paul had walked a little way from town, he found himself in the same sort of terrain he'd transported into just a week before, and he began to marvel again at how untampered with this world seemed, even with over three billion people in it. It was beautiful. How had they done it?

How indeed? That was what he'd bought a copy of Dr. Kumar's memoirs for, wasn't it—to find that out? And hadn't the sales person at the tech shop told him he'd be expected to be familiar with it when he arrived at the Retreat?

He might as well get to it, he thought. It was no use having there be just one more thing he was ignorant about that everyone else around him understood.

Besides, he added, looking out at the pristine, tree-studded grasslands around him—he really did want to know what roll of the dice landed this world here, when his world was so different.

Paul stopped by the side of the trail, took his personal player out of his new torso pack, and clipped it onto his clean, dry shirt, as he'd seen the sales clerk do the night before.

Now, how do I make it work? he wondered. The darn thing didn't come with any instructions. Maybe it was like the other devices he'd come across—the music panel he'd seen Marco use and the Intralink in his room at the Inn.

Paul touched the front panel of his personal player, waved his fingers in front of it.

Nothing.

He pressed a button on top of the device, and a small screen unfurled from it at a right angle to the front panel, conveniently placed so that he could simply glance down and see it. Paul pressed the button again, and the screen was pulled back inside—but still, no lights or sounds came from the device.

"Darn, how do you make this thing turn on?" Paul said aloud.

"Several means are possible," the personal player answered, in a neutral, though not unpleasant, voice. "You may continuously touch the front panel for three seconds or more, or enter a voice-activated code. I can also respond to light signals. If I am named, you may address me..."

"That's good, that's enough, thanks," Paul cut in. "I'd just like to keep this simple, for now."

"Understood," the player answered. "May I suggest, then, that you choose a name to call me, and I will activate when addressed by that name. Simple set up also involves choosing vocal parameters."

"What do you mean, "vocal parameters?"" Paul asked.

"The sound of my voice," the player responded.

"Okay," Paul said, not sure what to ask next.

"Please describe a voice you would like to hear."

"Oh, okay. I'm not sure," Paul said. This didn't seem simple.

"Would you like me to play vocal samples?"

"Yes," Paul answered, and the player proceeded to engage Paul in chit chat about the weather, switching periodically from one voice to another.

"That one," Paul said, in response to some statement about how lovely the clouds were. He had selected a woman's voice, young, slightly high-pitched, but not at all childlike, with a certain warmth or kindness in its tone.

"Okay," the player answered, using that voice. "Would you like to select a name?"

Paul thought about it for a minute, and what came to his mind was the name of a friend he'd known in childhood.

"Yes," Paul said. "Kiki."

"Do you wish this voice to be used for all recitation," Kiki asked, using the voice Paul had just selected, "or do you wish the use of character-specific voices where appropriate in narration?"

"Character-specific voices," Paul repeated. "You mean a different voice for each character?"

"Yes," Kiki answered.

"I guess so. How do you decide how each voice should sound?"

"For fictional characters an attempt is made to match the voice to the author's description. For nonfiction—histories, etc.—wherever possible, voices are synthesized composites based on past recordings. Where such recordings are unavailable, voices of historical persons are based on descriptions made by their contemporaries. Every effort is made to achieve an accurate result," Kiki answered.

"Do you have voice recordings of Indira Kumar to base such a synthesis on?" Paul asked.

"The synthetic voice of Dr. Indira Kumar, who is best known as the author of *Memories and Reflections*, is a composite based on 1,168 individual recordings," Kiki answered.

"So it should really sound like her," Paul said to himself.

"Estimate of accuracy in tone is 98.9015%. Estimate of accuracy in inflection is slightly lower: 93.6845%," Kiki said.

"Okay, okay, good enough," Paul said. "Use character-specific voices."

"Done," Kiki responded, in her confident, female voice. "Basic set up is now complete."

"Good," Paul said. "I'd like to hear the book *Memories and Reflections*, can you do that?"

"Yes," Kiki answered. "Recitation is one of my primary functions."

Paul readjusted his torso pack and started up the trail. He felt excited. Something in this early twenty-first century text would unravel the mystery and reveal what had set this world on such a different course from his own.

"Please begin," Paul said, as he continued up the trail.

MEMORIES AND REFLECTIONS
THE MEMOIRS OF INDIRA KUMAR

PREFACE TO THE SECOND EDITION

To-day there is a wide measure of agreement, which on the physical side of science approaches almost to unanimity, that the stream of knowledge is heading towards a non-mechanical reality; the universe begins to look more like a great thought than like a great machine.

—SIR JAMES JEANS

Kiki began loudly and clearly, in a voice different from the one Paul had selected for her—still female, but softer, a little deeper, colored by accents of other lands.

Almost immediately, the voice shifted down an octave and a half as Kiki continued recitation. The new voice was male, educated, middle-aged:

Editor's note: In April of 2015, a little over a year after her memoirs, *Memories and Reflections*, were first published, Dr. Indira Kumar gave a talk to faculty and students at the University of Colorado (the school from which she had, only a few years earlier, retired). Margarite Jamison, who was a journalism student there at the time, wrote about the talk in an article that appeared the next day in the student newspaper, *The Campus Press*.

During her talk, Dr. Kumar made reference to quite a lot of factual information. Afterward, she made the sources for that information, along with a complete text of her talk, available through her University website. Those sources may be found in Appendix 1 ("Citations for the Preface to the Second Edition") which appears on pages A1-A3 at the back of this book.

What follows are descriptions excerpted from Ms. Jamison's newspaper article, coupled with the text of Dr. Kumar's talk, as it was posted online. (The note numbers which appear below refer to the sources cited in Appendix 1.)

Again Kiki's voice shifted as she read on, now youthful, female, clearly American:

On Thursday night perhaps two hundred people gathered in Old Main Auditorium to hear Dr. Indira Kumar, professor emeritus, well-known anthropologist, and author of *Memories and Reflections*, give a talk.

Just after 8 PM the lights were dimmed and the din of conversation fell to a low murmur. A few moments later, Dr. Kumar strode onto the stage. Some in the audience, being familiar with the great stature of her work, had expected someone of a similar physical stature, but Dr. Kumar is a small woman, no more than a couple of inches past five feet in height. She wore loose-fitting apparel with a scarf at the neck. Her short black hair was elegantly streaked with gray.

When she reached the podium, she greeted the crowd.

"Good evening," she said into the microphone. Her lightly accented voice, soft, yet direct, filled the room.

"What a crowd! How nice that so many of you have come." She glanced through the papers she had brought with her, then began her speech:

"Since my book came out, my memoirs, I've had an interesting range of responses...."

Kiki spoke, but again the voice was not hers—nor was it the voice of the young American student she had been using, nor the middle-aged editor, which had come before that. She had returned to the first voice, which was soft and accented. But it was more than that. It was gentle, thoughtful, poised.

Paul focused his attention as Kiki read on:

Some, apparently, read it just as a story of one person's life. Others read it with more of a focus on the ideas it contains. Of those, some have approved of the ideas, while others have taken issue with them. I suppose it's that way when anyone expresses their thoughts—some will agree, while others will disagree.

As most of you already know, I was not always an American citizen. I was born in India, in a small village not far from Varanasi. I didn't come to the United States until I was in my twenties. Having lived in more than one cultural context, it's clear to me from personal experience how much the basic assumptions that people share within a culture vary from one culture to the next.

I was surprised, when I first came in contact with Western culture, at some of the fundamental assumptions that underlie it. Having, over the past year, repeatedly had discussions with Westerners who take issue with some of the ideas expressed in my book, I've become interested in how Western views differ from those I've expressed in my memoirs. I've not just wondered how they differ, but have become curious to learn and to understand what the roots are, historically, of the attitudes I keep encountering—attitudes that have a great influence on what we perceive to be true today.

I'd like to take this opportunity tonight to share some of the conclusions I've come to as I've explored such questions.

My story begins in the distant past, during Europe's medieval period, an era that spanned a thousand years. During this time, the Catholic Church held sway over both religious and secular life in Europe. The overwhelming majority of people who lived there during this time adhered to the Church's teachings. The earliest European scientists—or "natural philosophers," as they were then called—were on the whole as deeply religious as their non-scientific contemporaries.[1] It was their hope that studying nature would help them better understand both scripture and the works of God.

The relationship between science and religion at that time was not at all what it is today. Rather, naturalistic study was expected to play the role of servant to religious study, augmenting and supporting religiously revealed truths, but never contesting them.[2] In the 1100s, for example, natural philosophers were intrigued with the Biblical account of creation, and became involved in trying to explain, in mechanistic terms, how the world was created in six days.[3]

The idea that what we would think of as scientific studies should serve religious ends went largely unquestioned in Europe from the inception of such studies at roughly the time of the fall of the Roman Empire, until the beginning of the modern era—that is, from roughly the year 500 to approximately 1550.[4]

After that, the climate of thought in Europe began to change.

It's hard to say just what brought about this change. Some would say that a new freedom of thought developed when the rise of the nation state in Europe, coupled with the Protestant Revolt, reduced both the political power of the Catholic Church and its influence on European thought. Others would focus on the seminal work of people like Nicolaus Copernicus and Issac Newton, or on the work of such influential thinkers as Francis Bacon and René Descartes—all of whom helped lay the foundations of modern science.[5]

Whatever the reasons, as the medieval era came to an end, natural philosophers began what would be a long, slow process of learning to trust the conclusions that direct observation and rational analysis led them to—even when those conclusions conflicted with the beliefs of their own religious faith. In 1543, Copernicus' idea that the earth circled the sun was first published—an idea that conflicted with the Church's stand that the earth was at the center of the universe.[6] Similar revelations followed. From the mid-1600s to the mid-1700s, natural philosophers cataloging the diversity of life on earth gradually came to recognize that a pair of each of so many different kinds of animals could not possibly have fit on a single ark.[7] By the early 1800s, scientists studying fossils and geological layers were concluding that the earth was vastly older than the years given it in the Bible.[8] But perhaps most shocking of all were the results of the research of Charles Darwin, whose *Origin of Species*, published in

1859, demonstrated that none of us, human and animal alike, had been created by God in our present forms, but rather had developed through a slow process of evolution.9

In short, just as Protestants had split off from the Catholic Church, thus freeing themselves to pursue truth in their own terms, Western science gradually took a path away from its own religious beginnings. By 1900, the course was clear; no longer would science be the servant of religious study, and no longer would its honest practitioners allow their results to be colored by their religious faith.

While many modern-day scientists continue to be religious in their private lives, virtually all reject the idea that religion, *or any information gathered through non-physical means,* has any fitting place in the practice of science.

Many take this even further, so rejecting the assumptions of faith as to conclude unequivocally that *all that is real is physical in nature,* and observably so.

Of course, today, such attitudes are not held exclusively by scientists, but have spread, and become accepted by many who are culturally Western, no matter their walk of life.

Now, it may be in part because I come from another culture, and therefore do not share in the heritage I've just described, but it seems clear to me that awareness attained through apparently non-physical means—such as intuition—*can*, in fact, be a useful resource in our quest to understand the world. Indeed, it is not uncommon for people to have experiences which demonstrate both the authenticity, and the value, of such perceptions.

I'd like to share with you, now, a couple of small stories, which I think will clarify my point. The first concerns events that took place about ten or fifteen years ago. A group of people I know decided to rent some cabins and spend a weekend together in the Rocky Mountains, a couple hours drive from here—but two of us, my friend Martha and I, couldn't get away on Friday night when the others drove up, so we decided to go together on Saturday morning and meet the others up there.

We arrived about ten-thirty that morning, and found a note saying the others had left for a hike at about a quarter to ten. With the note was a map of their route. After getting our things put away, and a quick bite to eat, Martha and I set off to join them. Since their hike had them returning by the same path they set out on, we expected to run into them on their return trip.

About ten minutes after we started up the path, Martha stopped and looked sort of puzzled, then said we had to go back to get something. I looked at my watch—it was a few minutes after eleven. I was concerned that if we didn't keep going, the others would be back before we even got started. I asked Martha why we needed to go back, and she said, "Someone's cold. I need to get a sweater."

It didn't seem likely. It was a beautiful summer day, both warm and sunny, but back we went, nonetheless. Martha took one of her husband's sweaters, which he had brought up the night before, and we set out again.

Now, I won't bore you with every detail of the story, but we ran into the others about forty-five minutes later, on their way back down the trail. One of them, Chris, had fallen into the water where the path had crossed a creek, and had gotten soaked.

In that clear, dry air, with just a little breeze blowing, he was freezing.

He was also complaining that the water had ruined his watch, which had stopped just before eleven o'clock—just minutes before Martha decided we had to go back for a sweater.

Another, somewhat similar story involves a friend of mine who gave birth to her first child, a daughter, several years ago. One night, when the baby was about three months old, my friend was awakened by a frightening dream. She had dreamed that the baby had gotten tangled up in its blanket and suffocated.

She woke horrified and rushed to the crib side, where she found her baby was, indeed, tangled up in her blanket, with part of the blanket caught around the baby's head.

Thankfully, the baby had not suffocated—though who knows what the outcome would have been, if not for that dream.

Such stories incline their participants to conclude that there is more to reality than what is physically observable to us. Indeed, few would argue against the idea that there is more to reality than what meets the eye, for what meets the eye does not include such known phenomenon as radio waves and infrared light. For these, we need machines to do the observing for us. And yet, experiences of the sort I have just described suggest that there is still more to reality, more than even what our best machines are capable of detecting.

The question I would like to raise is this: can science learn to accept the validity of intuitive perception, and to allow the fact of such perception to enter into our calculations about what is real?

My conclusion is not only that it can, but that it must, if it is to continue on its path of honest inquiry.

But what sort of truths would be revealed if it did?

Some scientific research already begins to suggest what new understanding such work might bring, and what sort of world it might describe.

Several years ago I saw an article in a weekly news magazine describing the research of a group of scientists trying to find a way to help ALS sufferers communicate. ALS (which is sometimes known as "Lou Gehrig's Disease") in its most severe form causes complete physical paralysis, while leaving the patient's senses active and their minds clear. People in this condition cannot so much as blink their eyes to communicate. They are completely "locked in."

When we think, our brains create electromagnetic energy. Most of us are familiar with this fact, and with the machines, called EEGs, that are used to measure brain waves. So long as we are alive, whether awake or asleep, our brains generate this energy. Only when we die is that energy no longer produced.

Most of us are also aware that, through biofeedback, people can learn to control the frequency of the energy their brains create.

The scientists working to help ALS patients knew about this, too, and wondered if it might become a useful tool. They found that by placing electrodes on the heads of these patients and hooking those electrodes up to a computer with special software, the patients could learn to modulate their brain wave frequencies in such a way as to control a computer cursor and spell out words.

This was great news for ALS patients, and the first notes written by the people in this study showed just how pleased and thankful they were. But something else about the article caught my eye. It concluded by saying, "But the scientists have dreams beyond the ABCs.... Even more visionary is the possibility of going wireless. If the electronics are sensitive enough, they might be able to grab brain waves out of the air."[10]

If a machine might be made that could be sensitive enough to pick up the energy of our thoughts from a distance, why should it seem so unreasonable to suppose that one person might be able to sense the mood, or even the thoughts, of another? A cheap radio can decode a tremendous amount of information encoded into radio waves. Why should we suppose that the human brain is incapable of decoding the information embedded into another person's thought waves?

We think of ourselves as being contained within our skin, and yet the energy of our thoughts radiates out into the air, as surely as the energy (in the form of light) given off by an electric light bulb radiates into the space around it.

Where, then, does the basic self begin and where does it end?

I wonder about this, also, when I read about the experiences of people who have clinically died and then come back to life. An article in the prestigious medical journal *The Lancet* surveyed 344 patients whose hearts had stopped and then been restarted. It found that 12% of these people had had at least a moderately deep near-death experience. The authors concluded that if such experiences were purely the result of physiological changes—such as an insufficient supply of oxygen to the brain—that it would be expected that most patients who had been clinically dead would report having had such an experience. Yet this is not the case.

Not only are such events inexplicable in physiologic terms; such stories challenge fundamental Western assumptions about the very nature of physical experience. One story related in the *Lancet* article, for example, was of a man who had been brought into a hospital in a coma, at death's door. CPR was performed on him for more than an hour and a half, including electric shocks to his chest, in an effort to reestablish a normal heartbeat. The man wore dentures, which had to be removed before a breathing tube could be put in. One of the nurses removed his dentures, then put them in a drawer in a crash cart. When the man was sufficiently stable, they sent him on to intensive care, still in a coma.

A week later, the nurse who had removed the man's dentures saw him in the hospital. The man had since woken from his coma. When he saw the nurse, he recognized her immediately. He said of her, "Oh, that nurse knows where my dentures are." He then addressed her directly, saying, "Yes, you were there when I was brought into [the] hospital and you took my dentures out of my mouth and put them onto that [cart], it had all these bottles on it and there was this sliding drawer underneath and there you put my teeth." He was able, also, to correctly describe, in detail, the small room where CPR had been preformed on him, and the others who had participated in his resuscitation, even though he had been unconscious at the time. He described, as well, how he had floated above the scene and watched as the doctors and nurses had worked on his body—hoping all the while that they would succeed in saving his life.[11]

More remarkable still is the story of a woman known by the pseudonym, "Pam Reynolds." During brain surgery, she felt herself drifting up out of her body. Hovering above, looking down on her body below, she observed the surgical team at work, saw in detail the unusual tools being used, even overheard a statement made during the surgery, concerning the small size of her veins and arteries. Her observations were later corroborated as consistent with events during the first stage of her surgery.

All this would be remarkable enough, but this particular surgery required drastic measures. In order to get at an aneurysm deep in her brain, in the second stage of her surgery her body was chilled to 60° Fahrenheit, her heart was stopped, and the blood was drained out of her head. An EEG hooked up to measure cortical brain activity at that time showed no activity—no brain waves. Her heart was not beating. She wasn't breathing. She was technically brain dead. By every conventional measure, she was made to die for the purpose of the surgery, then brought back to life when it was over.

In short, she experienced death on that operating table, but she did not experience a void, nor an "end of self." Instead, as she later reported, she found herself moving through a tunnel toward a brilliant light, where she was reunited with family members who had passed away before. When it was time, late in the surgery, she traveled back through the tunnel and reentered her body.[12]

Stories similar to these date back thousands of years, but have become much more common since modern medicine developed the means to resuscitate those who have passed beyond some definable point of "death."[13] Such cases suggest that not only can the energy of our thoughts extend beyond our bodies, but that our ability to think and to know ourselves is retained even when our physical bodies die. In short, we might infer that we are not our bodies—that what we are, at the most essential level, *is not even physical at all.*

The painstaking research of Dr. Ian Stevenson (longtime director of the Division of Perceptual Studies at the University of Virginia) serves only to reinforce this impression. Over approximately half a century of work, Dr. Stevenson recorded the stories of thousands of people, most of them children, who recounted memories of what appear to have been past lives.

Generally speaking, the stories Dr. Stevenson investigated were of children who described lives just preceding their current one. The children were often able to provide enough details about the earlier life (such as names, places, dates, and events) that it was possible to locate the living relatives of the deceased person whom the child claimed to have been.

In many of these cases, the child would possess remarkable knowledge about the deceased person's life—often recognizing and naming the deceased person's relatives (sometimes by pet names), describing events that took place in that life, and demonstrating personality traits characteristic of the previous personality.[14]

About 35% of the children Dr. Stevenson studied had birth marks or birth defects that they claimed were a result of wounds they had received in their former life. In 49 cases, Dr. Stevenson was able to attain a medical document—usually a postmortem report—describing wounds on the deceased. In 88% of these cases, the wound on the deceased was closely matched (that is, was within a matching 10 square centimeter area) to the location of the birth mark or birth defect on the child—and in many of these cases, the match was much closer than this would seem to suggest. Dr. Stevenson estimated the probability of such close correspondence happening by chance at 1 out of 25,600.[15]

All of these things—the idea that thoughts could be communicated through the air, that people may exist beyond their bodies at the point of death, and that children may remember previous lives and retain markings which resemble those left by injuries in a prior experience—suggest that the individual self is more than just the material body, and that the physical body may in some ways be shaped by the mind.

All of these things challenge the common Western scientific assumption that all reality is so rooted in the physical, as never to extend beyond it.

Now, I don't want to overwhelm all of you with too much information, but I'd like to expand this discussion into one other area before I conclude.

I'd like to suggest that not only is it possible that consciousness is not limited to a physical context, but that it may be the case that physical reality itself is not as it appears.

Early in the last century, the study of quantum physics began to reveal strange attributes of the subatomic world. The actions of subatomic particles, it was discovered, are *influenced by the act of observing them.* In addition, it was found that such particles, under some circumstances, interrelated in a way that suggested an essential, non-physical link between them—seemingly, *a kind of communication.*

In short, in the eyes of many quantum physicists, the new research seemed to suggest that even the smallest subatomic particle may be imbued with a kind of awareness, or consciousness. As the physicist Evan H. Walker described these findings—and I quote:

> Consciousness may be associated with all quantum mechanical processes...[and] since everything that occurs is ultimately the result of one or more quantum mechanical events, [one may conclude that] the universe is "inhabited" by an almost unlimited number of rather discrete conscious, usually nonthinking entities that are responsible for the detailed working of the universe.[16]

Another physicist, E. E. Witmer, reflecting on the same subject, said:

> These ideas only seem strange when we apply them to micro-objects because, by habit and by virtue of our cultural environment, we think of micro-objects as inanimate. It is no doubt true that to assert that micro-objects have volition is too strong a statement, but...they have attributes that are the vague beginnings of volition and activity.[17]

In other words, the actions of subatomic particles suggest that they may possess a sort of watered-down variety of consciousness. And of course, it is these particles which are the fundamental building blocks of the physical world.

Where some scientists suggest that matter is imbued with a kind of consciousness, others conclude that physical matter is not even physical at all. As Bernhard Haisch, Alfonso Rueda, and H. E. Puthoff wrote:

> Indeed, if that view is correct, there is no such thing as mass—only electric charge and energy, which together create the illusion of mass. The physical universe is made up of massless electric charges immersed in a vast, energetic, all-pervasive electromagnetic field. It is the interaction of those charges and the electromagnetic field that creates the appearance of mass. In other words, the magazine you now hold in your hands is massless.... Its apparent weight and solidity arise from the interactions of charges and field.[18]

The apparent nonphysical nature of the universe has also been described by quantum physicist Henry Stapp, who wrote:

> If the attitude of quantum mechanics is correct...then there is no substantive physical world, in the usual sense of this term. The conclusion here is not the weak conclusion that there *may*

not be a substantive physical world but rather that there definitely is not a substantive physical world.19

If we accept the conclusions of these scientists, we are left with an understanding that the universe is a field of energy out of which the illusion of matter arises, and that this energy, even in its smallest measure, is inherently imbued with an essential, rudimentary consciousness. If we are willing to extend this a little farther, we might suppose that all the apparently material universe, including life itself, has arisen from this basic energy matrix.

I love what Western culture has achieved, what science has achieved. I have chosen this culture to live in over the one in which I was born and raised—though that culture has its many beauties, as well. I mean no criticism of Western views, nor of science itself. I merely wish to suggest that it is time for scientists to widen our view, and to understand that the essential nature of reality may include far more than what we have credited it with.

If it is the case that the true nature of reality extends beyond the phenomenon of the physical, then surely we must be prepared to probe with tools that extend beyond the boundaries of that phenomenon as well, if we hope to gain a better understanding of what resides there. Without this, our comprehension of reality will always come up short. With it, who knows what mysteries may unfold.

Dr. Kumar gathered her papers as a few scattered hand claps of applause could be heard, then she leaned toward the microphone once more and added:

"If anyone's interested in my sources for the information I've given here tonight, I'll be posting those references along with the text of this talk at my webpage here at the University. Just look me up through the Anthropology Department site.*

"Thank you all for coming. It's been a pleasure speaking to you here tonight."

Dr. Kumar stepped away from the podium and the sound of applause erupted throughout the room. Several audience members, perhaps fans of her book or old friends from the University, rose to speak with her as she exited the stage.

❀   ❀   ❀

Kiki paused in her recitation.

"Is that the end of the preface?" Paul asked.

"Yes," Kiki answered. "End of preface."

"Then could you skip ahead to the citations in Appendix 1, and read me the sources listed there?" Paul said.

---

* As already noted, the sources for the information presented in Dr. Kumar's talk are provided in Appendix 1, on pages A3-A5, at the back of this book. —ed.

"Yes," Kiki responded, and she began again to read. Paul only half listened as Kiki read down the list. When she was done, Paul asked her to stop recitation for a while. He wanted a chance to consider all he had just heard.

As a physicist, Paul was well aware of the physical principles Dr. Kumar had referred to, but on his world the fact that the "material" universe was actually constructed of what amounted to non-material parts was not seen as having any particular larger significance. Recognizing that fact was useful in the application of certain technologies, such as the floaters he often used to get across town. The transport unit he had designed to reach distant worlds depended on such knowledge as well. Even the "communication" between quantum particles that Dr. Kumar had referred to had application in everyday technologies. The interface between brain and machine achieved by implants depended heavily on this fact. These were all practical matters to Paul. Never had it seemed to him to be worth the bother to contemplate their philosophical significance.

Paul reached a hilltop and looked back toward Strandford. He could recognize a few landmark buildings in the oldest part of town, but beyond that, it seemed strange to him to see the sprawling city he was so familiar with limited to so small an area.

As Paul continued up the trail, he thought again about the preface he'd just listened to. For a moment, he considered the fact that—as far as he could tell—up until the time *Memories and Reflections* had been published, his world and this world had been one. So the world Dr. Kumar was describing in her preface was really his world, as well. The thought gave him a little shiver, though the morning was warm and clear.

"Kiki," Paul said.

"Yes," Kiki answered in the voice Paul had selected for her.

"Please resume recitation where you left off," Paul said, and Kiki began again, with the intonations and accent of Indira Kumar.

◘   ◘   ◘

Chapter I

Open every living particle.

—Rumi

I remember, in early childhood, waking as the morning light came through the unglazed window of the room I shared with the female members of my family. On many such days, my mother or an aunt would already be up and be busy tending the *chula* fire in the inner courtyard or shaping *chapatis* by hand to bake for our breakfast. Sometimes, when the sun was just so, I would lie awake for a little while, watching the motes of dust sparkling in the sunlight streaming in through the open window. I still remember the scent of that room, in which I woke on nearly every morning of my childhood—a mixture of smoke from the cooking fire and the earthy scent of our mud-walled home, all mixed together in air thick with moisture from the Gomati River, which ran past our village.

When I was small, I would usually sleep on the same cot as my mother—or with one of my sisters or cousins. The women were up early each day, grinding grain for our breakfast or getting an early start on one or another of the many duties of the day. The water buffalo had to be milked, vegetables brought in from the fields, food cooked, cotton ginned and spun, and dung from the buffalo and oxen had to be collected and laid out to dry into the patties we used to fuel the fire on which we cooked our meals. I am quite certain my whole life would have been spent engaged in such activities, if not for some unexpected turns that lay in the path ahead of me.

My father's family had lived for many generations in the same small village in northeastern India, in the state of Uttar Pradesh, about twenty or thirty kilometers northwest of the ancient city of Varanasi. My mother's family was from a village nearby. As was the tradition, my mother came to live with my father and his family at the time of their marriage, when my mother was thirteen and my father sixteen. That was in 1944. I was born eight years later, in 1952, the third of their seven children.

Most members of my family lived their entire lives without ever having traveled farther away than Varanasi, where they, and many others, came to bathe in the holy waters of the Ganges River. Hardly anyone in my family had ever been educated past the eighth grade, for there was no high school in our village, nor in any of the villages nearby. Girls were offered even less education than boys, since most people considered it unnecessary to educate a girl, as the duties of womanhood did not require that sort of knowledge.

The life of my father's younger brother, Anbu, was, in many ways, an exception to the sort of life we saw around us. Those who knew him as a young man described him as charming and handsome, with an unusual thirst for knowledge. When he was young, and had completed all the schooling available in our village, he begged my grandparents to allow his education to continue. When finally they agreed, it was arranged for him to go to live with some distant relatives in Varanasi and to continue his education through high school there. Knowing the time and place in which I grew up, and the attitudes of my family, I have no doubt that if he had not made that step then, the life I would have lived would have been entirely different.

After moving to Varanasi, my uncle—who was at the time only fourteen years old—was told that he was expected to help out with the household expenses, and so he looked for work in his new neighborhood. He found employment at a store that sold fine fabrics. It was run by an Englishman who also ran an import/export business, sending Varanasi textiles to England and importing such English goods as were hard to come by locally.

The Englishman (a tall man with arthritic joints, who smoked an old wooden pipe) soon came to see that my uncle had a lot to offer, as he quickly learned the workings of the business and had a winning way with customers. For these reasons, the Englishman kept my uncle on after high school and trained him for a position of responsibility.

Under normal circumstances, my uncle would have married by the time he was old enough to finish high school, but my paternal grandmother was in poor health during those years and for a couple years afterward, and it was her responsibility to arrange a marriage for my uncle. Apparently, no one wanted to admit how ill she really was, so the process of arranging a marriage for my uncle was simply put off, with the thought that soon my grandmother would be well enough and would take care of it herself.

During this time, my uncle's esteem in the eyes of the English businessman rose steadily. My uncle's employer, who had grown homesick and begun to dream of a retirement in England, made my uncle an offer. He would, he told my uncle, provide funding for him to continue his education for a year or two in England, if my uncle would agree to study business management and various aspects of import/export law, and then return to Varanasi and take over the local shop and the Indian end of the import/export business. The Englishman would then return to England and oversee the sales of Varanasi textiles there, during his semi-retirement.

My uncle eagerly agreed and was soon off to England, where he spent a couple of years getting the required training. When he returned, at the age of twenty-one, he brought with him an English wife. I was about five years old at the time, but I still remember shocked murmurs within my family about the recklessness of embarking into a "love marriage." There was, however, nothing to be done about it, since the marriage had already taken place. After a while, though, my family forgot their objections and accepted my uncle's wife—my dear Aunt Mary—as one of their own.

Sometimes, when I was little, my Uncle Anbu and Aunt Mary would come to visit us from Varanasi. My aunt would bring me trinkets from their shop and invite me to sit on her lap while I played with her gifts. I fancied myself something of a favorite of hers. I spoke no English, and she no more than a few words of Hindi, but we had an understanding between us that was stronger than words. Perhaps it was that she didn't yet have children of her own, or that she found herself so far from her native home and family, but she allowed me to become special to her, and I welcomed the attention. It was through her early visits that I learned my first words of English and began to dream of a wider world beyond the boundaries of the small rural village that was my home.

Just as Aunt Mary's presence encouraged me to imagine a world beyond the dusty lanes and mud walls of my village, school coaxed from me an understanding that there were ideas and places beyond those thoughts and localities known to the average villager. For the most part, my early schooling was focused on the basics—learning to read, write, and do simple math. But starting in the fourth grade, our teacher began to spend part of each school day on history and geography, and my imagination caught fire. I remember walking home from school trying to imagine what the people in other times and places were like. Did they behave like we did—did they do the same work, eat the same food—or were they like my Aunt Mary, somehow always cloaked in the suggestion of worlds beyond?

My parents allowed me to stay in school until I had learned the most basic skills, but then began to think better of it—for of what value could school be for a girl, really? After all, wasn't it clear that I would follow in my mother's footsteps, as my mother had followed in hers? And she in her mother's before her? It seemed plain to them that there was little point in educating a girl, whose duties would not require schooling.

In any case, by the time I was ten, I was old enough to be of real help to my mother at home, and my parents began to believe it would be better to keep me there, where I could assist my mother and continue to learn the skills that I would really need in the life that so plainly lay before me. And so, during the break between fourth and fifth grades, it was decided by my parents that I would no longer attend school.

I was so excited by what I was learning in school, and by the promise it seemed to hold of a world beyond my simple village life, that I pleaded with my parents to let me go for one more year. After much discussion and several days during which they watched me sluggishly going about my chores, they agreed. In fact, in each of the following three years, they made the same decision to withhold me from school, and in each of these years I pleaded, and they relented, perhaps a bit more easily each time, as my determination wore them down. By the end of this time they were, surely, resigned to the fact that I was determined to have an education, but I knew, as the end of the eighth grade grew near, that that would be the end of it—for what high school could I hope to attend? There were none in my village, nor in any of the villages nearby.

I remember one day, late in the summer after I had finished the eighth grade, when my Aunt Mary and Uncle Anbu came from Varanasi for a visit. Late that afternoon, we were all gathered in the inner courtyard of my family home, finishing a dinner of curried vegetables, lentils, and yogurt. The sun was slanting low, its rays carrying the last cutting edge of the summer's sharp heat. As usual, the water buffalo and oxen were tethered nearby. A cake of their dung, which had helped fuel the fire that had cooked our dinner, lay smoldering in the *chula*, its smoke drifting into the air in thin wisps.

My mother and the other women of the family were squatting in a circle together, as they ate their meals. One of them mentioned the local school—which would soon begin a new academic year—and my mother commented, with some pride, that I had finished upper primary school. At least, she said laughingly, I wouldn't beg them again for another year of schooling! She said this lightly, sweetly, innocent of what education might mean to me, as she was herself uneducated. My Aunt Mary was amongst the women eating in that circle. I'm not sure what she under-stood of my mother's comment, but she asked Uncle Anbu, who was standing nearby, to translate. I remember how her forehead came together in concern. She looked over at my mother, then looked up at my uncle again. My aunt and uncle exchanged a few sentences in English. I knew very little English then, but I had the impression that he was explaining to her that there was no high school for me to attend in our village. My aunt and uncle continued speaking to one another in English as the talk around them began again in Hindi and moved on to other subjects. But my eyes stayed on my aunt and uncle—they were speaking about me, I knew, about my life, my future.

After a while, my aunt rose, and she and my uncle stepped over to the corner of the courtyard where my father sat discussing the day's events with some of my uncles. As Aunt Mary and Uncle Anbu squatted down to join the discussion, I eased myself over to a closer position and, as casually as possible, stood nearby so I could hear what they were saying.

"…invite her to come live with us…good high schools in Varanasi," I heard my Uncle Anbu saying to my father in Hindi. My father shook his head, gestured towards my mother, "…needs her here," I heard in his reply.

I casually squatted down near some of the younger children and looked around to see what was happening. My Aunt Mary had her hand on my uncle's arm. He was turned towards her as she spoke to him in English. Uncle Anbu listened, nodded.

"She would make some man a better wife, with an education," Uncle Anbu continued in Hindi, speaking to my father. "It's very helpful to me to have an educated wife." I watched my father's face as he and my uncles continued to talk, but he looked unmoved and unconcerned.

Finally, Uncle Anbu looked over at my Aunt Mary and shrugged. Then Aunt Mary slowly got up and rejoined the women in the middle of the courtyard.

The next day, Aunt Mary and Uncle Anbu left to return to Varanasi without another word being said on the subject. I remember going out into the fields that afternoon to bring in fresh vegetables for our dinner and dreaming wistfully of what a school in Varanasi would be like. I imagined a large classroom with paper and pencils for all the students to use—not the black-painted boards we used as writing slates in my village. And the ideas this school would offer! I thought, trying to imagine the unimaginable. I squatted down with the empty basket in my arms and began to poke around the leaves for whatever was ripe and ready to be picked. But surely such dreams could never come to pass, I thought, for it was certain, had always been certain, that my future would be like my mother's, and her mother's, had been.

One afternoon, several days later, my mother called me over to her as she was grinding wheat in the courtyard. She told me she had been speaking with my father. She paused for a moment, still grinding, then she looked up at me and said I should begin to think about getting ready—that I would be going to school in Varanasi at summer's end.

She told me this casually, almost as she might have told me to take the laundry down to wash on the rocks at the river, or as she might have said to help her with the spinning or the cooking. But when I called out for joy and a smile spread on my face, I looked into her eyes and saw her sorrow, and her happiness. She was preparing to send me away—because she loved me.

❀　　❀　　❀

And so I went to live with my Aunt Mary and Uncle Anbu in Varanasi and began high school there. Together, we lived in a small apartment above the shop they ran as a couple. I remember going to that shop for the first time, and how the scent of sandalwood incense drifted past the front door from the temple down the street. Inside, stacks of colorful saris lined the main aisle of the store, while off in one corner were the goods they had brought from England—woolen cloth, fine pens, stationary, pipes, tobacco, and the like. I was fascinated with these things, which had all come from such a distant land—a place where people looked like my Aunt Mary, wore strange clothes, sat in chairs, and spoke in English all day long.

The school I attended was just down the road. It was in a large two-story building with broad windows that overlooked the street below. In many ways, the school was challenging for me, for my education was not up to that of other students my age who had been educated in the city. Yet things were not as difficult as they might have been. I found I had an uncommon ability to remember things I'd seen or read, and this helped me to catch up with the other students, as did the extra tutoring I received from my Aunt Mary.

The subjects we studied were much like the ones at my school back home, except now I studied English and had a natural-sciences class as well. The science class was my first real introduction to Western ways of looking at the world. In it we learned that the world is made up of small parts called "atoms," that plants turn light into food, and that we all evolved from earlier forms and were a product of natural selection. It was surely a less magical view of the world than I had received through my Hindu upbringing; there was no Brahma to create the world, no Vishnu to sustain it, no Shiva to destroy. Nonetheless, there was something gracious in the clean logical lines of this Western reasoning which did appeal to me.

Of course, I was not always at school. In the afternoons, after homework was done, I would work in my aunt and uncle's shop or explore Varanasi with some of my friends from school. When the longer breaks from classes came around, I would return to my village and stay with my family, help my mother with the chores, and look after my younger brother and sisters. Sometimes, interesting things would happen during those visits home.

"Pause," Paul said aloud. He had long since left the relatively flat land of Strandford, where the live-oak trees grew thick along the creek, and had begun a long, uphill climb. The water in the creek now ran thinner and faster, and the trees along its banks were fewer and more spread out.

Paul had been walking in the open sun for about the last half hour, but had arrived at a low area where the trees gathered at the creek's banks.

"I'm going to stop here for lunch," Paul said, as though he owed Kiki some explanation for interrupting her recitation.

Paul took off his pack and sat down on a large flat rock at the creek's edge. It felt good to take the load off his shoulders (though in truth the pack was not all that heavy) and to take a load off his feet, too, since his shoes had begun to rub a little.

Paul felt hot and tired. He realized his energy level was not yet quite back to normal since the transport. He was close, though, he thought, and should be his old self again before long. Still, he found himself wondering again why he had gotten sick when he transported, when his lab animals had not.

Paul looked through the travel meals he had brought for his walk to the Retreat. He didn't feel much like hot food at the moment, but still was curious about the heating mechanism on the travel meals. Each came with a self-heating baton, which the instructions said to compress and insert into a narrow pocket on one side of the package that contained the meal. Paul tried it, and the baton began to heat immediately.

A chemical reaction, Paul thought—and it certainly produced a lot of heat for the small volume of the baton. He would have to remember to consider chemical reactions when considering his options for an energy source for his transport. He should ignore no possibilities until he had a workable solution, he told himself.

Soon his food was ready, and Paul found the quality quite good—better than the food packets from his world. He was sitting in the shade eating and considering possible energy sources, when he heard footsteps approaching. He looked around and saw a tall, lanky man approaching from up the trail.

"Hello, friend," the man said, as he stepped under the branches of Paul's tree. "You've found a good piece of shade. It's warm today," the man said, taking off his hat and sitting down a few feet from Paul.

Paul was accustomed to viewing strangers with some wariness, but it was hard to feel that way about this man and the relaxed, casual air he carried with him.

"Hope you don't mind if I make myself at home," the man added, nodding at Paul before looking into his pack, which he had slipped from his back as he sat down.

"Not at all," Paul said.

The man used a cup to scoop up some water from the creek and took a long drink, then looked back into his pack and pulled out a travel meal of some sort. It was not one of the self-heating kind; he pealed back its wrapper without further bother.

He seemed to enjoy the flavor. "These things get better every year," he said, then looked over at Paul. "On your way to the Retreat?" he asked.

"Yes," Paul answered.

"Just coming back myself," the man nodded. "Ever been before?"

"No, this is my first time," Paul said.

The man gestured to Paul's chest, where he had Kiki attached.

"I see you've got your personal player," he said. "Listening to *Memories and Reflections*, I'll bet."

"Yeah," Paul said. The man was asking a lot of questions, but none of them seemed very personal.

"Good. They'll want you to have done that. How far have you gotten?"

"I started listening this morning," Paul answered. "Just the preface, and a little bit more."

"The preface," the man said. "Yeah. Gets going better as a story after that. You ever listen to it before?"

"No—first time," Paul said.

The man looked a little amused, as though he had expected a different answer. "Well, we've all got to start at some point," he said. "I think you'll enjoy it."

There was a small lull in the conversation then, and Paul took the opportunity to look the man over. His pack and shoes looked practically brand new, and Paul took them to be of high quality—but his shorts and shirt looked

well-worn (in fact, the shorts had patches on the seat) and his hat looked like
it had been crushed and worn and reshaped a hundred times.

Paul puzzled over this—how the man seemed at once wealthy and poor—
and then recalled how people had been dressed at the party at Anna and
Marco's house just a few days before. Many had had on layers of clothes to
stay warm in the cool evening—often with the outer layer so worn that the
colors of the inner layer showed through holes in the outer one. It had given
them all an artful, casual look, and somehow had made Paul feel even more
a misfit—although the clothes Marco had given him to wear had some small
worn areas, too.

"I don't know where you're thinking of sleeping tonight, but there's a place
up ahead that offers food and lodging to sojourners. It's a good place to stay—
good food and soft beds—and I can tell you, you won't find a soft place to lie
down between there and the Retreat. Nice enough people who run the place—
not as talkative as some, but nice enough, anyhow. And I can tell you, it's good
to have a good night's rest going into that second day's climb. It's not too bad
after that—up and down, you know—but that second day's a doozy."

Paul thought about this for a moment and considered that perhaps the man
had a point. "How's the pricing?" Paul asked.

"Well, I don't remember exactly, but I stayed there on the way in, and I
remember thinking I'd paid about half what I had in town."

"Where'd you stay in town—the Wayfarer's Inn?" Paul asked.

"That's the spot," the man answered.

"Is it far?"

"The lodgings? Naw. I'd say you'll be there by late afternoon if you go steady
from here. It's where the path runs up next to the road. You don't want to get
in too late, because it's a popular spot, and they only have, I think, four beds.
Just their extra rooms, you know."

The man rubbed his chin. "Come to think of it, you shouldn't have much
trouble, not with all the hoopla around the conference in Cuyama."

"What conference is that?" Paul asked.

"The 89th Annual Conference of Kumaric Studies in Cuyama. They've
been at it a long time, and this time they managed to get Alizah Zahorjan,
Michael Keller, and Charita Royden to come. Quite a big deal—all the foremost Kumaric Scholars. It just ended a few days ago. Pretty much anybody
who'd be going to the Retreat now will have wanted to go to the conference
first and rub elbows, you know, and then would probably approach the Retreat
from there, along the north road. Or go to the conference instead of the Retreat.
I know a lot of people who said they were going to do that. I would have done it
myself—almost did—but I do a lot of talking on my job, and I thought, better
to take a break from all that and go for the quiet of the Retreat."

The man took the last bite of his meal, then scooped up more water from
the creek and drank. As he did, Paul wished that he had known there was
another—perhaps easier—route to the Retreat, but quickly decided that he
probably couldn't have afforded to pay for the transportation, in any case—
and approaching as he was doing, he told himself, would give him time to
listen to Dr. Kumar's memoirs and to think through what he needed to do

to build a new transport. In any case, he was glad there wouldn't be a lot of other sojourners on his route.

The man stood up and stretched.

"It's been nice visiting with you, friend," the man said, as he slipped on his hat and pack. "I've got a business meeting in the morning and still a long way to go before I'm home tonight, so I'm going to leave you here to enjoy the shade and the breeze. I hope you enjoy your sojourn."

"Thanks," Paul said. "I hope you have a good trip home."

The man nodded and smiled, then headed down the path toward town.

Paul stuffed his empty travel-meal package into a side pocket of his pack. Then he got himself a drink of water, stretched, and lay down in the shade. The ground underneath him was full of small sticks and rocks, and Paul thought longingly of the soft beds that lay ahead.

"Kiki, do you have a clock? Can you tell me when thirty minutes is up?" Paul asked.

"Yes I do. Yes I can," she answered.

"Good. Please tell me when thirty minutes is up—and keep telling me until I've answered, in case I've fallen asleep."

"Understood," Kiki said.

Paul lay quietly, listening to the sound of the breeze through the trees and to the trickle of water along the creek. It was odd for him to want to rest during the day. Still affected by the transport, Paul thought. But why? Why him and not the lab animals? Had he missed something? Had they been ill?

No, Paul felt certain—they had been energetic and had eaten well.

So why me and not them? Paul pondered. What was different?

Paul's best guess was that it had something to do with the fact that they had simply been removed from space-time and then reentered it at a different location, while he had been sent from one probably universe to another. Who knew what sort of stress that could impose on a person's body?

Paul shuddered a little and felt lucky he had at least shown up in one piece. He was glad, too, that he had learned it was possible, without first having to worry over the ethics of sending a human subject to who-knew-where. Again, Paul assured himself that he was lucky and that the work was actually going forward exceptionally well—but he was still nervous about what might go wrong on his return trip.

Paul had barely drifted off when he hear Kiki saying, "Thirty minutes has expired. Thirty minutes has expired. It's time to wake up. Thirty minutes..."

"Okay, okay," Paul said. "I'm awake." He lay still for a minute, staring up at the sun-lit leaves turning in the breeze above him, then rose to his feet feeling surprisingly rested for his short sleep.

Paul stretched and picked up his pack.

"Come on Kiki. Let's get going," he said, as he strapped on his pack and continued on up the trail. "Please resume recitation where you left off before."

◻ ◻ ◻

Late in the summer following my first year of high school, when I was back in my village with my family, I heard talk that there were four Americans—three men and a woman—camped out in their vehicle up the road a ways, by the river. I remember being interested when I first heard they were there, but I thought little more about them.

A few days later, a young cousin of mine left the door to our courtyard open, and our water buffalo got out. A bunch of us kids went out and hunted around for it, but it wasn't found until dusk, when two American men and an American woman came into town with it, asking if anybody knew whose it was. Somebody led them to our house, and my brother took the buffalo back in.

The next day, my mother cooked up a big bowl of *dal tarka*—lentils with fried onions, garlic, and ginger—to offer the Americans as a kind of "thank you" for bringing our buffalo home. Since I was the only one in the family there who spoke a usable amount of English, my mother asked me to be the one to carry the bowl of *dal tarka* and a pile of freshly cooked flat bread up the road and try to find the place where the Americans were camped. She told me specifically not to be foolish and leave the bowl behind, but to wait until they had finished the *dal* or moved it to their own jar or bowl. I took the food my mother gave me and set off, with the bowl held tightly to my chest as I walked along. The sun beat down, making the road dusty beneath my bare feet.

After I had gone a little over a kilometer past the edge of my village, I saw a strange vehicle, like a bus but half as long, pulled off along the side of the road. There was some sort of awning extending out from it on the side nearest the river. I stepped off the road and approached the microbus.

"Hello?" I called out. Nobody answered. I went around to the side facing the river and called again, this time louder.

"HELLO!" I said, and a pale young man in a blue shirt came out from beneath the awning.

"Hello! What can I do you for?" he said.

I cocked my head at this funny expression but remembered what I'd come for. I extended the bowl and *chapatis* towards him.

"Thank you for returning our water buffalo," I said to him. Actually, that's what I intended to say, but my English was still quite rough. I believe what I actually said was, "Thank you for to return our animal."

He smiled graciously, a little amused. He called out toward the bus, "Hey, guys, we've got some really good-smelling food here." He glanced at me and tilted his head towards the awning on the bus, as though inviting me to come with him, then stepped lightly back the way he'd come and disappeared beneath the striped cloth.

I came around to the opening under the canopy that extended out from the side of the bus and saw that the side doors were opened wide. Inside was a flat platform with some sort of mattress on top. A man and woman lay there, dozing in each other's arms. Another man sat on the platform's edge, his legs dangling out of the open doors of the bus. The man I'd given the bowl and *chapatis* to set them down on a small folding table that was set up under the awning.

"Hey Dan, hand me out some bowls and spoons, would ya?" he said, and the seated man turned and knelt on the mattress. He then reached up and opened a small overhead cabinet and took down some bowls and spoons. His movements disturbed the sleeping people. The man who had been lying down rose up on an elbow, rubbed his eyes.

"Hey, whatchya doin', man?" he said.

"Getting some bowls—that girl has brought us some food," he gestured to me, then handed the bowls and spoons to the man outside.

The woman opened her eyes and looked around at me. "How come?" she said.

"For bringing back their buffalo."

"How nice," she murmured as she sat up. She smiled at me.

The man outside was putting the *dal* into the bowls. I felt awkward and turned my gaze to the ground. Then I notice his hand was extended towards me. He was offering me a bowl with some of the *dal tarka*. I shook my head "no," looked up into his face—pale, and framed with dark hair, a short beard—and strangely, his eyes were blue! I had never seen blue eyes before. I was transfixed by the sight, amazed that anybody would have eyes such a color! I watched him as he handed the bowls and flat bread to the people in the bus (who now sat cross-legged on the sleeping platform) then sat down at the folding table and began to eat the *dal* and bread himself. Even though he was quite thin, there was something soft about him, perhaps in the way he moved—something gentle.

As people began to eat, they murmured about how good the food was. One or two glanced up at me and shook their heads "yes." I felt awkward standing there, not knowing what to say.

After a short while, I heard the strike of a match and smelled a sweet, smoky scent coming from inside the bus. The man who had been lying down had set down his bowl and was taking a long drag from a small brass pipe. His chest swelled as he inhaled—then, still holding his breath, he passed the pipe to the man next to him, who set down his bowl and bread and went through the same process, passing the pipe on to the blue-eyed man outside. That man glanced up at me from where he sat in a folding chair under the awning. His eyes looked like water. "Hashish," he said quietly. The wind rustled through the grasses at the river's edge as he, too, took a long draw from the pipe, then offered it to me. I looked down at the pipe. "*Caras,*" he said, using the Hindi word.

I had heard of this drug when I was in Varanasi, but I'd never known anyone who smoked it. I hesitated, with the man's hand extended out to me, his eyes, blue like the sky, looking up at me. What was it like? I wondered. Then I reached out and took the pipe from his hand, put it to my lips, inhaled, and immediately coughed out the smoke. Someone inside the bus suppressed a laugh, but the man outside gave me a steady look, brought a hand up to chest height and, with palm turned towards the ground, he made a small patting gesture.

"Slowly, then keep it down," he said in an airless, thin voice, and as he spoke, a thin band of smoke passed between his lips. I tried, again, watching his face as I did it, with my eyes on his eyes. I slowly sucked air through the pipe, and the smoke seemed less harsh this time. I tasted it, sweet and musty, as it went over my tongue, felt it enter my lungs— hot, sharp. I handed the pipe back to the man with the blue eyes, and he handed it to the woman in the bus. I coughed, then laughed nervously, and somehow this made the other people laugh and blow their smoke out into the air.

"What's your name?" the blue-eyed man asked.

"Indira."

I thought he was about to ask me if I lived in the village, but then realized that he knew that I did. Instead, he picked up my mother's bowl and put some more food in the smaller bowl he had balanced on his lap. Inside, the pipe was going around again. When it got to the blue-eyed man, he inhaled the smoke, then handed the pipe to me, making the same patting gesture in the air. I took the pipe, and this time the smoke went smoothly down, stayed there as I held my breath like the others. After a few moments, the blue-eyed man tilted his head back and, still looking at me, shot a plume of smoke upwards under the canopy. I turned my head and smoke came from my mouth as well. Then I stood there self-consciously. My eyes fell to my mother's bowl. What was I doing, accepting this strange smoke? I should be leaving, but my mother's bowl was still not empty.

The man saw me looking at the bowl and offered again to serve me some of the *dal tarka*. I shook my head. From inside the bus, I heard the woman speak.

"Hey, guys, finish up what's in the bowl. I think she's waiting for us to empty it so she can leave." The blue-eyed man handed the bowl into the bus. They passed it around, scraped the *dal* into their smaller bowls, then handed it out. The blue-eyed man took my mother's bowl and handed it to me, smiling. I smiled back at him.

"Thank you," the woman inside the bus said.

"Thank you," the men said.

"You're welcome." I nodded back at them. "Thank you for our animal to come home." Then I turned and started towards the road, feeling the eyes of the blue-eyed man following me.

As I walked back along the road, I wondered if it had been smart to accept the *caras*—the hashish—from these strangers, but since it seemed to be having no effect at all, I decided not to worry about it.

I didn't feel like going home right away, so a short way down the road, I stopped to sit beneath a chinar tree that grew on the bank of the Gomati River. I had often come to sit or play beneath this tree while I was growing up, and had always found the cool ground beneath its spreading branches a calming and happy place to be.

On this particular afternoon, the view from beneath the chinar tree was especially lovely. Its leaves turned and sparkled in the breeze, which blew in from the water, while the river itself reflected the tall clouds that stood gathering along the far horizon.

Suddenly, I remembered the bowl I was supposed to bring home with me. Had I left it behind? I glanced around me hurriedly—oh! what a relief. It was right there on the ground beside me.

I realized that my thoughts were getting confused and remembered the smoke I had pulled into my lungs. Perhaps it had done something, after all. I leaned back against the trunk of the tree, felt giddy. My thoughts seemed fragmented, disoriented. I closed my eyes and let myself drift amongst them.

Where the hashish had at first seemed to have no impact at all, now its effects came up like a wave overtaking me. I felt like I was floating, or falling, while immersed in a roar of lights and sound. It was as though all the pieces of my thoughts and senses had become fragmented and spun around.

I opened my eyes, tried to orient myself to the world around me. I felt my back where it was pressed against the tree, felt the hardness and curve of the tree trunk. I focused my attention on that—solid, real. I took a deep breath, focused on the air coming into my lungs, warm and moist. I looked out at the light sparkling on the water, at the water lapping up on the bank. Up and down, slowly lapping. Up. And down.

I became aware of some feeling moving within me like that. What was I feeling? Odd sensations. What sensation? Oh, the hashish! Why did I take it? I remembered the man with the strange blue eyes. He had offered it to me, gently, and with a sweet smile, and I had trusted him and said "yes." He was attractive. Yes, he was. Was that what I was feeling? I looked out at the water. Yes, I could feel that yearning lapping up inside of me, rising and falling with my breath, like the water on the river's bank.

I focused in on that feeling, let it become the center of my world. It seemed to swim up around me, to hold me. I was floating in it. Floating in it. What was it I was floating in? Oh yes, it was the feeling I was having. It was—*desire.*

I closed my eyes and fell into the roaring and rushing place again. Sound and light. For a moment that was all there was—sound, light, and a sense of motion. Then I remembered myself, remembered I'd been thinking—what was it? Not thinking, feeling. Feeling what? Feeling... *Oh!* Feeling *desire.*

What was *desire?* I asked.

I could feel that desire within me. But not as one thing. I felt it as many things, like the sparkles on the water. I felt it as the points of light reflecting off the leaves of the tree above me.

I was filled with little points of light, sparkling, *each with its own desire.* They came together—an interweaving—to make up my desire for the young man with the pale blue eyes. To make *all my desires.* To make *me.*

I laughed. Yes! And with the laugh, the impulse for laughter came like a little bubble to the surface and broke into being, and as it did, I felt a thrill at being alive. I looked out at the water, sparkling with many points of light, then I looked down at my body covered with soft cloth, and I, too, seemed to sparkle.

I leaned my head back against the trunk of the tree. I felt myself float-ing, or falling—falling into myself. And suddenly I knew, though I can't quite say how, that just as I was filled with all these particles of yearning within me—these potentials, these minute possibilities yearning to come into life—that I was in the same way a part of some even larger matrix of life that felt my yearning, my hope, and my desire like one of these points of light within itself.

It all seemed so wondrous that I laughed again, and my laughter was like bird song erupting from my lips, like the hush following a rain, like the way fish jump from the water and return splashing to it, or the glide of a bird as it comes home to roost—it was all life happening, a moment of yearning, then impulse, then expression—the full rich joy of life unfolding into the world. I was filled with these little bits of yearn-ing all threaded together—impulse wanting to become action, wanting to come into life.

Thoughts swirled around me in a big whirl. One would rush through my mind, and then another. No one thought held.

What had I been thinking? I couldn't hold it in my head...but...I could feel it—yes—*desire*—all the little desires within me. And when each comes into life I feel its burst of energy, of joy, like a bubble breaking at the surface of life, releasing happiness.

It all came back to me, and in the next instant, I again felt myself nestled into something larger and felt again that I was to it like one of these little bubbles of life I felt within me—desiring, striving to rise, to break surface into life, to turn yearning into action, into life.

Impressions drifted through my mind. I thought about school in Varanasi, the fragrances in the streets, incense through many doors and windows, the people gathering at the *ghats* on the river preparing for funerals, my aunt helping me with my homework in the evenings, the look on my younger brother and sisters' faces as they came running up to me when I got off the bus to come home. Home. Where the buf-falo had wandered off—where I was taking the bowl of *dal* to the young Americans.

I looked around me and realized how long the shadow from the chinar tree had grown. Had I been sitting here thinking all this time? What about? Varanasi—but before that? It had been something special.

The whirlpool which my thoughts had become after taking the smoke had slowed some. I tried to pace myself with it so I could grab hold at the right point, like running alongside a moving cart before jumping on. What was I thinking, before Varanasi—earlier? It had been interesting, I knew, and I longed to get it back.

Oh, yes—*desire*. I was thinking about desire, about yearning, about little parts of me, each of which feel their own promise, their own yearn-ing towards action, towards life. Yes, I'd been thinking about that, and the feeling, the feeling when that yearning is enacted, when it becomes life—that burst of joy.

Yes, that's what I had been thinking—that when a little part of me is given expression, I feel joy. And when I feel that burst of joy, the big thing I am a part of feels joy, too...and the thing it is a part of feels it...and on and on...spreading out like circles on a pond, radiating outward.

That's what I had been thinking. That's what it was.

I looked out at the view from beneath the tree. It all looked so beautiful. The sky, blue with tall clouds, had become tinged with gold as the sun crept towards the horizon. Beneath it, the river looked broad and strong, darkening in the slanting afternoon light.

I sat staring out at this scene for a long time, as thoughts and impressions continued to spin through my mind, crisscrossing at strange angles, rising and falling like my breath.

After a time, my eyes settled on the ground around me, on which were scattered a few bright green seed pods, like those which hung in great numbers from the spreading branches of the chinar tree above me.

I reached out and picked up one of the pods, turned it over in the palm of my hand. I'd seen these pods every year of my life, watched them develop from flower to fruit—then later fall as seeds. I looked at the one in my hand—spherical, with many little cones or peaks projecting out from it, its skin bright and waxy green. I turned it over slowly, letting the light play across its surface.

I was like one of those peaks, I thought. We all were. I held the pod up to the light, saw how all these smaller parts were joined together at their base. Each of us was a peak projecting off of the pod, each was rooted into the whole—something larger, which felt our life as part of it.

I stretched and let the seedpod fall to the ground, looked around me. The late afternoon sun cut in streaks through the hazy air. I'd been sitting there a long time, I realized. I should be getting home. I glanced around for my mother's bowl, at first not remembering where I'd set it, then spotted it, picked it up, and headed for home.

❀   ❀   ❀

I went to bed early that night, and the next morning woke with my head full of haze. I felt like being alone, so I climbed up to the wide, flat roof above my sleeping quarters, where I could see far off into the distance, as far as where the river took a long, slow turn, like a great snake.

I sat there under an early-morning sky for a long time, waiting for the clouds that filled my head to clear. After a time, I turned my gaze from the river in the distance down to the lane beyond our courtyard wall, where children were playing. Some of the younger children were turning somersaults, while two or three of the older kids were playing a game that involved kicking a ball of clay back and forth across the road. I watched, thinking how lighthearted and happy they all seemed.

Watching them brought to mind the ideas I'd entertained the afternoon before. I could almost see the sparks of yearning rising up in each of them as they played, almost see how each of those sparks turned fluidly into action, and how that action burst into the world—how each particle of

yearning was fulfilled in a moment of delight. I imagined each spark breaking into actuality, into action, into air—igniting in a moment of joy.

I sat, letting my thoughts drift, and found myself thinking about something I'd learned in school the winter before. We'd been studying English
prefixes and suffixes in my science class. Our teacher thought learning
about them would help us to more easily understand the scientific terms
we were studying. Some of the prefixes, especially, had lit my imagination.
I'd liked the way a whole new meaning could be created just by taking a
base word and attaching a prefix to it. I'd liked what the prefix "extra" did
to the word "galactic," for example. "Extragalactic," it became—existing
beyond our galaxy. Such an idea! I'd also liked the English prefix "intra"—
meaning "within" or "on the inside of." When combined with "cellular" it
took my attention *inside* an individual, living cell. But my favorite prefix
had probably been "proto," as in "prototype" or "protoplanet."

I pictured it as it had been written in the list of prefixes in my English
book. "Proto:" it had read, "the first, the original, the thing out of which
other things arise."

I heard a child's delighted squeal, and my attention was drawn to the
lane below. My youngest sister, Ananda, had been practicing somersaults,
and now she jumped up and down, happily calling out to the others to
watch. As they turned their attention towards her, she did another one,
almost perfectly. It made me smile, and I remembered how it was when I
was little and had just learned to do that, too. I had tried for what seemed
a long time before getting it right. I had been so happy, just as my little
sister was, when I'd learned to roll as well as the bigger kids did.

I felt happy for Ananda, rolling in the dusty road below, and thought
again about the sparks I imagined seeing in all the playing children.

Sparks of yearning, I had thought of them as—but perhaps more precisely they were sparks of possibility—the possibility of a well-turned
somersault, or a well-aimed ball of clay—and the yearning to make
them real.

Yes, that, but more than that, too, I thought. The thing that inspired that
yearning was broader, greater, than just the possibilities of the moment.
It was, it seemed to me, a sense each person feels of what they might be,
of what they might become.

I imagined how, with each small step taken towards those grander
prospects, a wave of joy rises to greet us—even if each of those steps is
itself no more than a well-turned roll on a dusty road.

I rested my chin on my arm, looking down at the children playing,
and imagined their whole lives spreading out in this way, each drawing upon their private well of possibilities, pulling those possibilities to
the surface and spreading them forward, a path winding through their
lives to come. And in each moment when a particle of that possibility
becomes actualized, I thought, they'll feel a burst of joy—just as we all
do, at such times.

I liked the thought and sat for a while, just letting it soak in, as I watched
the children playing below. The thought felt like a river, moving within

me. Near it, to one side, I could feel another thought growing, rolling, like a river in me, too.

I leaned back against the wall. The sun was climbing higher, the roof warmer, the sky brighter.

As I sat beneath that brightening sky, a new channel opened, and the two waters within me spilled together—and with that meeting, words I had thought only minutes before again came to mind.

The first, the original, the thing out of which other things arise, I thought.

"Yes," I whispered, as the waters tumbled and glided more smoothly into a common channel.

Yes, I thought. Just the right word for it: *Protolife.*

A smile came to my face. *Protolife,* I thought again, and tried to define it for myself: *A sense of possibility we long to give life to.*

I closed my eyes and tried once more: *A possibility we long to give life to—which feels real within us, but isn't yet real around us.*

My smile grew a little wider. Could it be as simple as what I was thinking, I wondered—that all life, all action, is inspired by a sense of possibility, of promise—of *protolife?* And that protolife, when fulfilled, brings us joy?

Was this *what joy was?* I wondered.

I opened my eyes and stared up at a blue sky across which scattered clouds drifted, glowing and bright.

I could not, in that moment, have been any happier, enjoying this fresh insight, newly arrived in my world.

All around me, the day seemed open. The sky seemed open. The world seemed so open to me.

❀　　❀　　❀

Perhaps there is something about being young which allows us to not only wish for a comprehensive understanding of things, but to believe that such an understanding is possible. If so, I was certainly no exception. In the weeks to come I became quite enchanted with the idea that I had arrived at an understanding of what joy was and of how it came into being. I felt about these ideas much as I had always felt about education. Each offered a window onto something larger than myself.

After that summer at home with my family, I returned again to Varanasi. A couple of weeks into the school term, I was aware that a close friend of mine, Komali, had missed several days of school. I went by to visit her in her home and was told that her father's mother, who lived with her family, had just a few days earlier passed away.

When I came to visit, Komali and I sat together in her sleeping quarters, and she wept as she told me about her grandmother's passing. Komali described her grandmother as being not just a grandmother to her, but a friend and confidant. She told me that each morning since her grandmother's passing she had woken somehow forgetful of her death, and rolled over expecting to find her grandmother still lying on her cot nearby.

Komali's eyes appeared swollen and red as she told me this. She finished her story, saying to me, "Oh, Indira, why does it have to hurt so much that she is gone?" Then her eyes settled for several moments on the corner of the room.

I had no idea what to do besides hold my friend's hand and listen, and be patient when she seemed unable to say more. I stayed with her for an hour or more, but she seemed so tired and sad, and it was clear that there was no way I could actually relieve her of her troubles.

I thought about her as I walked back to the home I shared with my aunt and uncle. I knew her question had been a rhetorical one, but still I wondered what the answer was. Nothing seemed very clear after talking to Komali, but one thing I felt certain of was that if Komali had never had a grandmother to love, she would feel no pain at her absence.

One day a few weeks later, I was sent on an errand by my aunt to another part of Varanasi. She wished me to deliver a package of goods special-ordered from England. I had just dropped off the package and was returning along a dusty, crowded lane when I saw a little girl, probably no more than six or seven years old, begging by the roadside.

It was certainly not uncommon to see someone begging in Varanasi, but this little girl got my attention. This was in part because she reminded me so of my own small sister, Ananda, but it was also because her physical difficulty was so obvious. One of her legs was withered, most likely from polio. It was bent in at her ankle and calloused along the outer part of her foot, where she was forced to put her weight when she walked.

I had seen many sights since moving to Varanasi, but had never become immune to images such as this. I felt terrible seeing this little girl, especially since she was so young and had a condition that was so severe. Of course, I wanted to help. I had already dropped off the package and all the money I had with me was for the bus to take me back home. On impulse, I put that small handful of change in her basket. She looked up at me, then, her eyes dark and expressionless. Our eyes met only for a moment, then I tore my gaze from her and started up the lane towards my home.

I felt so sad for her! When I was her age, I had run and jumped and played with the other children, but none of that was possible for her.

I walked up the narrow, cobbled street, threading in and out of the crowd, past the vendors set up in the muggy air with their aromatic pans of boiling milk or roasting peanuts, past a snarl in traffic where a wandering cow and her calf had blocked the movement of several rickshaw cabs—and through it all my mind remained full of thoughts of that little girl. What would it be like to have lost the use of a leg? I kept wondering. Surely she must long to run and jump and play as other children did.

These thoughts ran together with thoughts I had been having about Komali. I thought again of Komali saying how she would still wake in the room she shared with the other women and girls of her household, and for a moment upon waking still expect her grandmother to be there, to smile at her and hold her hand, and how, morning after morning, after the brief forgetfulness of waking, she was forced to discover again, with great sadness, that her grandmother was gone forever.

For both of them, I thought—my friend and that little girl—there was something longed for within them that could never, ever, be made real.

Each of them, I thought, held protolife that could never be brought to life.

The thought seemed terribly sad to me, and I wondered then whether, if it was true that protolife brought to life makes joy, then did it follow that protolife blocked from coming into the world would result in sorrow and pain?

Was that *what suffering was?* I asked myself.

I continued on towards home, winding endlessly through Varanasi's hot, narrow lanes, surrounded by ancient buildings, trying to get the image of that little girl's crippled leg from my mind.

Was she in physical pain? I wondered.

Was physical pain like other suffering? My mind swirled around the idea, imagining her body suffering—her cells.

Did her cells feel their own potential, their own protolife? I wondered. When injury or illness blocked the unfolding of our lives at a cellular level, did our cells call out in pain, speaking along our nerve's pathways, telling us there was something wrong?

A late monsoon rain began to fall, and all the ideas in my mind seemed to bleed together like laundry of so many colors. I looked into the faces of the people I passed on the road and found in their expressions so many emotions—sorrow, tenderness, fear, pleasure, humor, fatigue.

The rain kept falling, and the whole world around me became slick and wet. All the strangers were wet, and I was wet too. My young mind felt what I could not then have found the words to express—that we were all joined by these things, joy and suffering, and that the roots of these thing we share are intermingled in the mystery and the purpose from which all life comes.

I straggled home, wet and soggy, hours after I had been expected back. My aunt helped dry me as I tried to explain the reason for my lateness and, impossibly, in my fractured English, all the thoughts which still roared within my head.

The next year passed fairly uneventfully. I enjoyed the hours I spent in school and at my homework, for I was, as always, eager for my horizons to be stretched. I enjoyed, too, working at my aunt and uncle's shop, helping to display all the beautifully colored saris or packaging rich Varanasi textiles for shipment to Great Britain. But my favorite duty was waiting on the foreign customers who came to find familiar items in our import section and to peruse the beautiful, locally made fabrics. These people carried with them an air of far-away places, other customs and other lands, and I always found myself longing to know more about them and the places they had come from. I dreamed that one day I would travel and see those places for myself, that I would one day learn about how other peoples lived and how they understood the world. I was glad I had learned so much English from school and from living with my Aunt Mary, because it allowed me to talk to these people and ask them about their worlds.

The next summer, between my second and third years of high school, I went again to stay with my family in my village. There I once again milked the water buffalo, washed clothes with the other women at the river, spun cotton, ground corn, and brought in ripe vegetables from the field outside our home. In other words, it was life as usual, and if anyone had asked, I would have said that nothing new would happen anytime soon. But a few weeks after I had returned to school in Varanasi at the start of the next term, I was unexpectedly called home again.

Late on a Saturday morning, my Uncle Anbu took me to meet the bus, which ran once a day each way between Varanasi and my village, and gave me enough money to make the trip home. Neither of us had any idea why I was being called home. I climbed onto the bus and stared out the window as it bumped and jolted along.

I had been told by the messenger my parents had sent word with that I should prepare to stay overnight, and I had packed a light satchel, but I had not thought to change from the sari I wore in town. It seemed a bit too fine to wear in my village, made of brightly colored silk with a gold thread here and there showing through the weave. My aunt and uncle had given it to me for my sixteenth birthday, and I had felt proud, but now, looking around me on this rickety rural bus, it made me feel out of place.

I should not have been surprised then, when my mother, meeting me at the bus that Saturday afternoon, told me not to wear my sari in the city way, but to take the end of cloth from my shoulder and cover my head. We walked home together, and there was something in my mother's mood I had trouble recognizing. She seemed both excited and self-contained.

When we got to our house, my mother sat with me out in the courtyard and told me that the barber who came through our village every couple of weeks had told my father about a family looking for a wife for their son in the village north of ours. My father had sent a picture of me—one my Aunt Mary had taken the year before—for the boy's family to see, and they had approved. A dowry had been set, and so everything was arranged. My mother told me that the marriage would take place in just a couple of months.

At first I was excited by the possibility, like a door opening onto something breathtaking and new. And the event itself was exciting, too—a grand feast, and a ceremony which would as much mark my maturity as the beginning of my new life as a wife.

But then I had a thought.

"What about school, *Mati*?" I asked my mother.

She told me I would be pulled from school at that time, return to the village to marry, and soon after would be sent to live with my new husband's family.

I would not be able to continue in school!

I remember, it was like a cloud settled around my shoulders. I had been spending my time in Varanasi dreaming about my future, dreaming about the places I might go, the sort of life I might live, but I had forgotten to think of the very real, practical future right there before me—that I would be expected to marry without finishing school, without roaming the world, without learning other languages, or finding out about other peoples and other customs, as I had so longed to do.

I cast my eyes to the floor, knowing that my father had given his word about this arrangement. Though I felt saddened, I told my mother "yes," as a good daughter must do. My mother hugged and kissed me, her eyes aglow with her excitement at the thought that her oldest daughter would soon be wed. I kissed her lightly on the cheek in return. Then I told her I would like to go for a walk along the river again before returning to Varanasi on the bus the next morning.

I set off towards the chinar tree that grew on the river's bank. While growing up, I had often gone to sit there when I wished to clear my thoughts. My feet kicked up dust as I walked along the dirt road that ran beside the river. The afternoon air was thick with water and heat, the sky dense with knotted gray clouds. I felt numb—in a familiar place, but lost within myself.

When I got to the tree, I collapsed on the ground beneath it. A breeze blowing in from the river made the water ripple. Drying leaves rustled overhead. Oh! I had dreamed so much that now would not be! I pulled my legs up to my chest and wrapped my arms around them, then let my head fall against my knees. I could feel my tears soak through the thin fabric I wore wrapped around me. I imagined my tears like a river, running into this larger river I sat on the bank of, running with the river into the sea.

The breeze kicked up, and a few leathery seedpods fell from the chinar tree, dropping to the ground nearby. I picked one up, turned it over in my hand as I had a fresher, greener one a little over a year before. What had it meant to me then? It had been something special. Yes, it had made me feel special—my little peak coming off of the whole, propelling that part of the whole into the world, into life. Making happiness, making joy, just by being me.

I remembered that feeling in me, *of me*, delicate and proud. Who I was, the whole wondrous possibility of me living. It would not be fed by this wedding. It was the wrong way, the wrong way for me.

I squinted as a gust of wind came in off the water. When I was a child, I remembered, I had thought of the wind as being like a breath, blown out by the world. I looked down at the pod in my hand. All was quiet for a moment. A few drops of water hit the drying leaves above me. Then the rains came on, sudden and heavy—the clean warm rain of the monsoons. I stood up and stepped out from beneath the tree's protective reach, to be drenched by the downpour.

Wash over me, water—I told it—*carry me to the river. Carry me to the sea.*

Aimlessly, I turned and started back towards my village, smelling in the first rush of downpour the scent of dust the raindrops kicked up from the dirt road. I wore my sari wrapped over my head in village fashion, but even with it between me and the sky, in moments I was soaked through. My bare feet slipped and gripped at the suddenly muddy road, causing silty water to ooze up between my toes. I cried as I walked along, drenched in my own tears, the world wet all around me from the rain coming down. It seemed all one water, from my tears, from the sky, running down me, running off the sides of the road, running.

There is something cathartic about such a rain, and as I walked along my mood lifted a bit. My burden seemed washed away, and it occurred to me that maybe it didn't have to be like this, maybe the marriage could be postponed long enough so I could at least finish high school.

By the time I had arrived back home, I had gathered my courage to make this request of my parents. But I had raised my hopes too high. I had forgotten to think of how this arranged marriage would look through their eyes.

As I made my request of them, I could feel my hope slip away. We argued, and I realized then, perhaps fully for the first time, how strange they thought me for so wanting an education in the first place. I saw, too, how ungrateful they found my current behavior, asking them to go back on their promise to this young man's parents, when they had done such a good job finding me a husband from a good family, and now, while I was still young enough that my prospects would still be good. Seeing how my resistance looked through their eyes made me feel guilty and selfish. I was still quite young and not prepared to resist them both at once. So I again agreed to the marriage as any good, devoted daughter would be expected to do.

Afterwards, I went into the sleeping quarters, wrapped myself in a dry sari from my satchel, and collapsed onto a cot along the outer wall of the room. I lay awake in the shadow of dusk, my head filled with the din of confusion. A dividing line had been drawn. I felt what I could barely think—I was a part of something larger than myself, and my promise was a part of that, too. Didn't I have some responsibility to give life to what was in me? Yet my parents told me only that I was responsible to what others expected of me. It didn't occur to me to think that their choice might be best for me. My head swam, and my heart felt heavy. I pressed my cheek up against the mud wall of the sleeping quarters. It felt cool in the warm, heavy air of late summer. I cried quietly, trying to let my confusion run out of me, escape from me, or me from it. My tears soaked into the wall I lay beside, as the rain penetrated it from outside. In the middle, somewhere, I imagined them coming together. I drifted off to sleep with this image in my mind—a thin line of water running through the wall, connecting me to the rest of the world.

The next morning I woke very early. I could hear the oxen chewing and stamping in the courtyard. Light streamed in through the window over my cot. I felt something bristly and sharp in my hand. It was the seedpod

I'd picked up the day before as I sat beneath the chinar tree, still gripped in my hand. The individual points projecting out from the center of the pod had left impressions in the palm of my hand. I rose up on my cot and looked out at the new day. A state of calm had come over me while I'd slept. I looked outside at the peaceful morning, looked up at a sky cleared of rain, and I knew what I must do.

I would return to Varanasi quietly, as my mother directed, but from there I would write a letter home, explaining that the marriage must be called off, telling my parents clearly how determined I was to finish high school and apologizing for the shame I was bringing on my family. I believed my Aunt Mary would support me and that Uncle Anbu would support her. I sighed quietly, with relief—yes, I thought, I would finish high school. I looked outside at the bright sky and the sunny new day.

Yes, I thought—I would even go to college!

9.

"Chapter two," Kiki said.

"No, wait," Paul responded. "I don't want to start another chapter yet." While Kiki had been reciting, Paul had been listening closely, but now he wanted a chance to reflect and absorb—and to pay a little more attention to the surrounding landscape.

As he walked along, Paul thought about what qualities a person would have to have to so change a world and compared that to what Indira Kumar had been like when she was young. The desire to get an education seemed consistent, he mused—as, he supposed, did her inclination to see things her own way—but surely much more was needed to inspire so much change.

Paul looked up ahead. The path he was on followed the creek up between rolling hills to the east and a ridge to the west. Scattered sparsely across the landscape were trees of the same variety he'd seen when he'd first arrived in this world. Everywhere around him, the land seemed so vital, so full of life. Several times that day, Paul had spotted a kind of bird he wasn't familiar with. They often flocked together, he'd observed. They were good-sized, mostly black with white markings—and with a distinctive yellow beak. He wondered, now, what they were called. He had the idea his grandfather would have known.

Paul had also seen a number of ground squirrels and lizards, and two or three rabbits, since starting out that morning. Circling above, once, he'd seen a hawk—and in the distance, he was pretty sure, he had spotted a coyote. Paul had, on rare occasions, seen animals out in the open on his world, but never had he seen so many truly wild animals in anything like so short a time!

What a remarkable world this was!—so different from his own, Paul thought. He bet even the mighty Ganges River, which Dr. Kumar had mentioned in her first chapter, still flowed steadily year round here.

Paul thought about the history of that river on his earth. Most of its summer flow had come from runoff from the glaciers of the Himalayas. Indeed, the Ganges had been a river as great as the Himalayas were tall. Throughout history, Paul recalled, countless millions had depended on its waters just to live.

Paul remembered learning in school about the flooding that had resulted when the glaciers had started to melt rapidly—and about the waves of starvation that had followed once the glaciers were gone and the river had begun to fail. For thousands of years, crops grown along the river had been fed by its waters, but as its flow diminished, crops that otherwise would have flourished, instead withered and died in the broiling sun.

Paul sighed and thought again about the stories his grandfather used to tell him. So much of his world was not as it once had been—not as it should have been. But wasn't that just human nature, Paul asked himself—to be so careless, to be so selfish, to destroy whatever we touched? Certainly it seemed that way to him, coming from the world he knew so well. And yet, somehow, this world—so new to him—seemed to prove a different hypothesis.

Paul scanned the land around him, so much more vital than the same land on his earth, and dreamed of what he would like to do for his own world. If only the population could be brought down, he thought, perhaps the natural environment could, in some small way, begin to heal. Perhaps, in time, it could become a world filled with all sorts of plants and animals again—like it was in the stories his grandfather used to tell.

Paul glanced around at the surrounding hills. This world had such grand, open spaces—untouched and ready for habitation. He could do so much good in his world if he could just get the transport working and bring at least a third of the people here. Paul imagined how much less human suffering there would be, if only the resources of his earth were not stretched so thin.

Somewhere at the back of Paul's mind, he pushed aside the image of these unfettered, natural spaces being filled and trampled by the people of his world. It seemed to him that if this earth was really so special as it appeared to be, then it would somehow handle the influx—and if not, well, you have a right to grab for any life raft when you're drowning, don't you? And Paul's world, surely, was as desperate as that.

Paul thought again about the reception he would be offered as the news spread through his world that he had discovered another world ready to receive so much of the population!

People would celebrate in the streets, Paul told himself. They would lift him on their shoulders and carry him forward—and in the process, his world, which needed so much care that had been lacking, could finally begin to heal.

Paul strolled on under a wide blue sky, soaking up the sun, the clear air, and the sight of many wildflowers, as the afternoon stretched into the long shadows of evening. At one point he stopped to look back across the Santa Ynez Valley, from which he had just come, and at Strandford in its midst. It was so strange to see the contours of the same hills he knew, with so little the same built up among them. Paul imagined Sheila somewhere within those hills, in his Strandford, and wished that she was, in actuality, so near as the town he saw before him. He felt terrible to have, in essence, deserted her by coming here—though he knew quite well that he'd had no choice. He hoped she was managing okay in his absence and comforted himself with thoughts of her fully engrossed in the feed from her implant, and so insulated from feelings of worry and loss.

Paul continued on up the trail, swept up in thoughts of the steps he would have to take to return to his world. A new transport would have to be designed and built, an energy source found, the questions about ILT resolved, and on and on. Everything, he thought wearily, would take money, and time.

It wasn't long before he came to a place where the path ran along near the road up Figueroa Mountain. Paul climbed a low hill, and after cresting it, came across a woman sitting in a chair under a live-oak tree, with a small table set in front of her. She was doing some sort of work on a small machine which, Paul could see as he came nearer, was an ecobot. It appeared that she was repairing it.

"Hello," Paul said. The woman looked up. "Someone told me there would be lodging available where the path neared the road. Could you tell me how much further it is?"

"You're here," the woman said, gesturing to the hills behind her, and only then did Paul realize that the hills just off the road had doors and windows cut into them.

"Oh," Paul said. He looked at the device the woman was repairing. "What's wrong with it?" he asked.

"Got some grit in the principle joint on its claw. Was jamming up. Came home for some help. Not too much trouble to fix it."

Paul looked around, and it struck him as odd that she was sitting out in the open repairing an ecobot.

"Is this your land?" he asked. The woman glanced up from the table and gave Paul a funny look.

"Own it," she said, shaking her head. "I'd more nearly say it owns me. I can hardly imagine loving a place more than I love this spread. My husband and I run the lodging, if that's what you're getting at.

"Own the land," she repeated, shaking her head some more. She seemed amused. "You'll find my husband over there," she said, pointing. "He'll set you up."

Paul looked where she was pointing and saw a door nearby with a welcome sign on it.

Paul thanked the woman, then stepped over to the door and knocked.

"Come on in," someone shouted. Paul pushed the door open.

"I've come about lodging," Paul said to the man behind the counter.

"Then you've come to the right spot. Single or double?" the man asked. He appeared to be about the same age as the woman outside—late thirties or early forties. He had medium-length, dark hair, which was beginning to thin, and warm eyes. He struck Paul as fit for his age—but then so did most of the people Paul had seen in this world.

"It's just me," Paul said.

Behind the man was a long, narrow kitchen, in which two boys were standing next to a pot, taking peas out of their pods.

"Okay, single," the man said.

"If the price is right," Paul added.

The man named the price. It was as low as Paul had been told to expect.

"That includes dinner and breakfast," the man added.

The older boy in the kitchen flicked a pea at what Paul took to be his younger brother.

"Swamp it," the younger boy exclaimed.

"That will be fine," Paul said.

The older boy chuckled and flicked another pea at his brother.

"I said *swamp it*," the younger boy shouted.

"If you'll excuse me a minute," the man said to Paul. Paul nodded, and the man went into the kitchen.

"Tom, I told you—quit teasing your younger brother," he said.

"It's not hurting him. He can hardly feel it," the older brother said.

"That doesn't matter. He doesn't want you to do it," the man said, and it seemed clear to Paul that he was the boys' father.

"I'm going to pick them up. I'll rinse them off. They'll go in the pot," the older boy said. Paul guessed he was about twelve years old, the younger boy perhaps eight.

"Tom, think about how it is from Zaid's point of view."

"It doesn't hurt him," Tom said again.

"Remember last summer, at the Fourth of July picnic—Sika kept poking you in the ribs with her finger and laughing when you got annoyed?"

"Yeah."

"Did it hurt you?"

"No—but Zaid threw the first one," Tom answered.

"It slipped out of my hand!" Zaid exclaimed.

"I don't care where it started, Tom—you're responsible for your own behavior."

"A-l-l right," Tom sighed.

"You're coming along with those peas," the father said, glancing in the pot. "Good work."

The man emerged from the kitchen.

"Kids," he said to Paul.

"Yeah."

The man cleared the area on the counter for Paul to place his thumb.

"Could I pay in cash?" Paul asked.

"Sure," the man said. Paul dug into his pocket for his money.

"On your way to or from?" the man said, with the casual tone people have when making conversation.

"What?" Paul said.

"The Kumaric Retreat. Pack and all—you're a sojourner?"

"Right," Paul answered. "On my way to."

"People say it's a nice hike in," the man said, as Paul handed him almost all of the bills he was holding.

"Maybe so," Paul responded, "but I'm not looking forward to tomorrow's climb."

The man counted out Paul's change and told him how he could get to his room.

"Well," the man added thoughtfully, "if you don't mind a late start, I could give you a ride as far as Figueroa. I'm going to see an old friend in Lazaro Canyon—but not till dinner time."

"How far is Figueroa?" Paul asked.

"It will get you past that bad climb."

"Thanks," Paul said. "Just name the time."

"About five-thirty, I guess. I'll need you out of the room by three, though, but you're welcome to hang around."

"Great," Paul said. "Thanks."

"It's okay," the man said. "You want your dinner in your room or here with us?"

"Room," Paul said. "Thank you."

"We'll have it to you within the hour."

◘   ◘   ◘

The sun had dropped behind the nearby ridge, and the day was lost in shadows by the time Paul opened his door in a nearby hill and walked inside. The room he found inside was small but not cramped. It was lit by a large, oval panel in the ceiling, which was set to a bare glow. On the wall next to the door was a switch of some kind. Paul rotated it as far as it could be turned; the ceiling panel glowed a little brighter.

Not many windows, Paul thought. Must be dark living underground. It struck him as a sad way to live, when there was so much open space just outside and such broad, brilliant sunlight so much of the day.

As Paul got himself settled in, he thought about what he'd just seen in the kitchen. Diplomacy in action, even to settle the squabbles of children! It was never like that between Paul and his younger brother. They'd sometimes drawn blood.

But we turned out okay, Paul told himself. Still, he wondered if there was some relationship between what he'd just seen and the fact that there had been no war in this world for so many years.

Paul sat down on the edge of the bed and turned on a small reading light that was attached to the wall next to him. Then he took off his shoes and rubbed his sore feet—still puzzling over the differences between this world and his.

When dinner came, it smelled better than Paul thought food had a right to—and tasted as good as it smelled. Actual, whole foods—no yeast derivatives, like Paul had been accustomed to most of his life. He relished every bite.

Afterward, Paul spent the evening within his domed room, working and reworking the mathematics—as well as he could remember it—behind Interdimensional-Linking Theory.

Every way he could cut it, the figures seemed to hold, and yet Paul kept worrying that there was something he was forgetting or overlooking. He didn't know whether to take his safe arrival in this world as confirmation that this world and his were firmly linked, and that travel between them was, therefore, not just possible, but safe—or to see his arrival here as a kind of random occurrence—and to conclude that he was very lucky that something far worse hadn't happened, instead. After all, there could be quantum fluctuations involved that went beyond the current theories of subatomic stasis.

It seemed unlikely, but how could he be sure? No matter how carefully he worked through these equations, the fact was he would be gambling when he tried to return.

The more Paul thought about it, the more he fretted—but he couldn't get past his original conclusion that all the figures seemed sound. Finally, he decided that he really must put the whole thing aside and go to bed. But even so, he lay awake for a long time, unable to let go of his worries, before finally burying them in the soft darkness of sleep.

◘   ◘   ◘

Paul was back in his lab, only the lab wasn't the same as it had been before. The usual machinery was there, but it had all been redesigned.

Paul stepped over to the window to check the placement of the new power cable. He looked out at the open spaces beyond his building and saw elk in the distance and birds soaring through the air. It was only then that he realized that he was not on his world at all, but was, instead, preparing to return to it.

Everything was set to go. He had found an energy source, and had checked and rechecked the figures for his new aiming device. He had done everything he could to get ready, in every way he knew how.

Paul stepped onto the transport pad and looked around. He was restless and eager to go. He leaned forward and pushed the button that engaged the device. An instant later, a brilliant flash of light flooded the room.

Paul found himself tumbling down a long tunnel filled with light and noise. As he was held there, at that cusp between worlds, a sudden realization overtook him. What if there had been a flaw in his calculations? What if he wasn't returning to his earth at all, but to some other, unthinkably different, probable earth?

As Paul was propelled through the void between worlds, all sorts of possibilities roared through his mind. How different could different probable worlds be? he wondered.

How utterly different were the most extreme?

Paul felt himself falling—and then arrived, naked and vulnerable, in a blinding flare of light. With his first breath the air burned his lungs. He tried to open his eyes, but they were seared by the caustic atmosphere. Paul collapsed. A great, endless, howling wind battered his flesh.

Paul woke, trembling and clinging to the sheets in his quiet room beneath the hill.

Home, Paul thought. Home was where he wanted to be, with Sheila by his side—but how would he ever find his way there?

□ 10 □

Paul woke early under a ceiling panel that glowed as brightly as the light of day. He got up and fumbled with the wall switch to turn it down, then lay down again and tried to sleep a little longer. It was no use, though—he was awake now.

After a while Paul got up, got dressed, and went outside. He knocked on the door where he had asked for a room the day before, and was quickly invited in to join the family for breakfast. Only one other guest—a young woman, who looked rather sleepy—was up that early and had joined the others for breakfast.

Paul told the man he'd spoken to the night before that there was something wrong with the ceiling light in his room; he'd had to turn it up all the way to get a reasonable amount of light from it the night before, but this morning it had come on very brightly, all on its own.

The man just laughed and said to Paul, "You're not used to ground dwelling, are you?" Then he explained that the light was gathered in parabolic dishes outside, then transferred along optical fibers to the light panels indoors. There wasn't much of it at night, and there was a lot of it during the day—same as with windows. There were settings to keep it steady—by dimming the outside light or adding light from other sources—but they must have been switched off.

"I guess it takes some getting used to," the man added, "but ground dwelling has its advantages. Warm in winter, cool in summer, and leaves the surface land almost untouched." He took a deep breath. "And it feels good to know you haven't crushed too much under your footprint."

Paul nodded. "Yeah, I guess so," he said. "Thanks." Then he looked down at his breakfast and wondered how much more of what lay ahead would surprise him.

After breakfast, Paul returned to his room. After so much hard thinking the night before, he felt he deserved a break, and in any case, he had a book to listen to before he arrived at the Retreat.

Paul glanced over at where Kiki lay on the small table next to the bed.

"Kiki," he said, "please resume recitation at the beginning of chapter two," and in a moment, Dr. Kumar's accented voice filled the air, and Paul was carried along with it.

◘ ◘ ◘

CHAPTER II

Mind is the main thing, the forerunner of every act.

—BUDDHA

I looked out the window of the jetliner as it rolled down the runway. England. In a few hours this heavy bird would land in England, with me in it. I stared out the window as the broad fields and buildings flickered by, listened to the rush of engines, their whine and roar. The plane seemed sluggish, struggling, and I doubted what they'd said was true—how could it come aloft? Too big and ponderous. But as we rushed over the tarmac, I felt the seat come up beneath me, and in a few seconds I saw the shadow of the plane on the runway below us, the afternoon sun pressing it into the pavement, and moments after that we were turning in the air, looking down at the building in which I could picture my Aunt Mary, standing alone, waving her goodbye to this big jet plane, now like a speck in the air above.

I felt uncertain, imagined briefly that the floor might drop out from beneath me, then looked around at the calm of the other passengers. The engines continued their roar, loud and steady. I leaned back in my seat. I felt a bit numb; in a few hours I would step off this flight, and my life would be entirely changed. But now there was no more for me to do than sit here and pass the hours before my new world arrived.

In the past few weeks my Aunt Mary had spoken excitedly of home—summertimes spent boating in the canals of her childhood home of Birmingham; dense forests of dark-green trees, their leaves turning gold in autumn; the hard lines of tall, stately buildings, softened under blankets of winter snow; reading a book while curled up near the crackling warmth of a hearth fire. I had tried to feel her excitement along with her, but they were her memories, not mine. Still, it was comforting to have images of where I was going, of what to expect, no matter how exotic those descriptions may have seemed to me.

Now I was on my way, and in my hands was the farewell gift Aunt Mary had given me at the airport—a cloth-bound book with blank pages—a diary. I flipped through its clean pages, imagining what thoughts *I* might have which might seem worth putting there.

Aunt Mary had told me that I should write to her whenever I felt lonely, and that she would write back as soon as my letter arrived. She said she wished she could give me someone closer at hand to share my thoughts with. Then she gave me addresses for her family and friends around England and told me I should get in touch with them. Then she hugged me and gave me the gift, so I would always have a place to share my thoughts and feelings, she said. She wiped tears from her eyes, and I knew she wished she could come with me to England to smooth the transition.

I had said goodbye to most of my family in my village a few days before and to my Uncle Anbu as my Aunt Mary and I had boarded the overnight train to Delhi the evening before. We had reserved seats in sleeper class, and there shared a compartment with four other travelers. That evening, we ate our supper in the pantry car, and later were lulled to sleep by the rocking of the train as it passed through the deep night between cities.

I looked back out the window; the plane had continued climbing, and now below us were only clouds. They looked soft and near at hand—and they seemed a comfort, for I thought even if this plane might not hold me, it looked as though those clouds just might catch me if I fell, like a carpet of pale gray beneath us.

My farewell from my family had been a good one, and I was grateful that, though their traditions were different than the life I had chosen, they had come to accept me, as they had each year of my childhood, when I had begged to be permitted to return to grade school for one more term. They had finally accepted my schooling in Varanasi, my refusal to marry—even this, now—college in England. And when I had said goodbye to them a few days before, my mother had given me a gift for my journey: a shawl she had spun and woven herself to keep me warm that cold autumn in Oxford.

The stewardess came by and asked us all what drinks we might like to have. I asked for a cola, and she poured it for me, reached across the other passengers to fold down a tray from the seat back in front of me, and set the drink there on a napkin of its own. I picked up the cup and held it cradled in my hands. The ice had little bubbles of gas trapped in it. Little bubbles of gas floated up through the cola. I thought back to the time, two years earlier, when I had chosen to refuse the marriage my parents had arranged for me. How distant that moment in time seemed now, and yet how linked it was to this one. If my thoughts had turned a different way, if I had accepted the life my parents had laid before me, I would be in my husband's village now, spinning thread, maybe, or gathering vegetables for the evening meal. Not here, on a plane, to England. How slim a line between that world and this!

I set the cup down, looked back out at the clouds. And what had made that difference, really? I had come so close to accepting what they had planned for me. I remembered lying in my cot, crying as the rain came down outside. I remembered concluding that there was promise in me, and that it longed for something other than what my parents wished for me to be. I had believed in that, rather than believing in the traditions of my people, and that belief was carrying me away from them now.

One belief, one life, I thought, another belief, another life. Like the helm of a great ship, I told myself, our beliefs are what we steer by. They are the seeds out of which the lives we know and live grow.

It made me frightened, then, to think this—that I had taken so much into my own hands. I picked up my purse and slipped my new diary into it, then took out a pen and began doodling on my napkin to distract myself. I felt suddenly very alone and scared. I was going off by myself to a whole new world. Why? Couldn't I have been happy with the marriage my parents had planned for me? A quiet village life? It seemed at this moment as though that simple life would be a great comfort.

The man sitting next to me lit up a cigarette, blew its scent into the air from his lungs. I was remembering sitting in the airport that morning with my aunt, overhearing a conversation a man was having with his young son about Mahatma Gandhi. They were standing in front of a picture of the Mahatma at a display telling about India and her history.

"He was a great man," the stranger was saying to his child. "He dreamed of a free India, where we were not under the thumb of foreign rulers in our own land. Though the British fought him, arrested him, put him in prison, he would not give up this dream for India to rule herself, nor would he be turned from the path of nonviolence in making this dream come true. He was indeed a great soul."

I looked out the window, thought about how long the afternoon was lasting, with us chasing the westward-moving sun across the sky. I thought, too, about how sunny it was where I was, and how overcast the day would seem to the people on the ground below the carpet of clouds we floated above. I glanced around inside the cabin, and then, bored, went back to my sketching, and to thinking about what the man had said in the airport. The Mahatma had taken a path of his own design, which I felt I was also doing. But how, I wondered, had he known it was the right one? Many people resisted what he had done, but he was sure and stayed with it. How did he know what was right? I wondered. He must have felt it in some special place within him, like I had been sure I'd wanted to go to school, I thought. He must have listened to it, let it grow there—then brought it out where others could see it, led a whole movement based on what he believed.

What he believed. Hmm. What he believed. His beliefs had come up within him and shaped his deeds, then spread to others and shaped theirs, and collectively they had shaped the fate of my country, peacefully driven the British from power, and once again made our land our own. And his work had spread on, I knew from school, giving form and strength to Dr. Martin Luther King's work in America. It was from the Mahatma that the world had learned the way of nonviolent social protest.

I stopped doodling for a moment, leaned back in my seat, stared absently out the window. It was coming to me slowly—belief didn't just shape my life, it created the currents that shaped the world.

Oh, I thought, as I watched the clouds drift by beneath the plane. What if I made a wrong turn, and accepted the wrong beliefs? My beliefs had led me here—traveling on a plane to England. Gandhi's beliefs had shaped a nation. There were others... Hitler... and people had followed *his* ideas, too, and with such unimaginably terrible effect.

Uncomfortable, I turned my attention back to the tray in front of me and continued with the doodling. My life was destined to be shaped by my beliefs, I was realizing, and I was unavoidably going to believe something. It was an exciting, and frightening, thought.

I darkened the marks I'd made on the napkin, adding shading and detail. I thought of how I was going to this new land to study and to learn, and I found myself suddenly determined not to learn indiscriminately, not to just memorize the ideas others offered me, but to consider what sort of life, no, no, what sort of *world* might be made from those beliefs, and to try to form and embrace only those ideas which would lead down a worthy path.

I looked down at the doodle I'd been making on the cola napkin. I had been absentmindedly sketching out the shape of a chinar seedpod, with all the little spikes reaching out from a sphere-shaped center. Why had I drawn that? Like the seed my life was growing out of? I thought. But what life would grow from it? Would I be alone? Had I forsaken my one possibility of love in giving up the arranged marriage? Would I make good choices?

I could only guess. I had, in that moment, not even the first glimmer of what was to come, nor of how deeply I would soon delve into the layer of experience represented by the center of that pod. Nor could I have guessed, then, in what a surprising form love would one day find me.

After I landed in London, I gathered up my luggage (which included my Aunt Mary's old leather suitcase, a large satchel my Uncle Anbu had carried with him when he had traveled to England, and a smaller bag I had used for school) and took the bus from the airport to Paddington Station, following the directions Aunt Mary had given me. There, I bought my ticket and waited under the station's great arched roof for my train to arrive.

The air was cold compared to home, and I felt lonely and uneasy in this new place. I dug out the shawl my mother had made for me and wrapped it around myself, which helped me feel warm and not quite so far from home. Finally, the train pulled in, passengers got off, and I stepped into the sleek compartment. I stowed my luggage in the designated area, then walked down the isle and took a seat by a window at the far end of the car.

As soon as I was settled, I heard a voice asking if the seat next to mine was taken. I looked up and saw a young English woman with long, wavy red hair looking down at me questioningly.

"Oh, no, it's not," I answered.

She sat down and stowed her bag beneath her seat, then leaned back and glanced around briefly. She looked over at me.

"Where are you headed?" she asked.

"Oxford."

"Oh, yeah? Me, too. Is this your first year?"

"Yes."

"Mine too." She paused for a moment, then proceeded. "What will you be reading?" she asked. I knew from the materials I'd been sent by my college that this was how people referred to their course of study.

"I'm reading Human Sciences," I answered.

"Oh, how fine. Which college?"

"St. Hugh's."

"That sounds like a good choice. I thought about going there. I'm reading Theology at Lady Margaret Hall. My name's Laura, by the way. Laura Atherton."

"Hello, I'm Indira Kumar. Glad to meet you." We shook hands, and I was struck by how gentle she seemed, and how open and friendly. I realized I'd been worrying about how things were going to go since I'd left my aunt that morning, but with Laura there, suddenly it seemed that everything would be all right.

"Where are you coming from? Here in London?" Laura asked.

"No, India. I just flew in."

"India? That must have been a long trip."

"Almost ten hours—plus the trip by train from Varanasi to Delhi." I glanced down at my hands, not sure what to say next. "Where are you from?"

"Chelsea."

"Where's that?" I asked.

"In London—West End," she answered. We were both silent for a moment. I tried to think of something else to say.

"What does your family do there?" I asked her.

"Well, my parents are labor activists. They also run a small print shop—books, pamphlets for the movement, that sort of thing." She told me a little bit more about her family. She had three sisters, all older than she. Then she asked me how I felt, coming so far from home. I tried to tell her that I was frightened and excited all at once. I asked her if she was scared, and she said she had been, but that she'd decided not to waste time worrying about it. She figured lots of others had gone before her and that they'd managed all right, so she would, too. She'd said it brightly, and it seemed a contagious attitude, for I felt better hearing her say it.

The train started up then, and as it rolled along, we chatted about our families, the towns and cities we'd lived in—small details of the lives we were leaving behind. The time went by quickly, and before I knew it, they announced that the next stop was Oxford. Laura bent over and rummaged through a small travel bag at her feet.

"I was going to finish this on the way out, but I'm just about done, anyhow." She held up a small, hard-bound book with a gilded design imprinted on the front cover. "Have you read him, Rumi?" she asked.

I told her I had not.

"Really? He's delicious, and he's practically from the same part of the world you're from."

"India?" I asked.

"No, Turkey, really, but he spent his childhood in Afghanistan—that's near India, isn't it?"

"It shares a border with Pakistan," I told her.

"Sure, that's practically India." She smiled winningly. "So you should have it, I think. I'm practically finished with it anyhow."

"Oh, no—you should keep it, finish reading it," I told her. The train came to a stop then, and Laura stood up and picked up her bag, leaving the book on the seat she had been in.

"It's not that sort of book—you don't have to finish reading it. Just think of it as a 'welcome to England' present," she said lightly. She gave me a broad smile, and I was distracted for a moment by how clear her eyes were, how bright her skin, how red her hair. Then she turned, and in an instant disappeared into the crowd departing the train. I stood up, and for a moment thought I would go after her, then paused and picked up the slim, leather-bound volume. It felt solid and fine in my hands. "Welcome to England," I thought, and smiled.

Adjusting to life in England was, in some ways at least, more difficult than I had anticipated. Stories my aunt had told me had helped me learn what to expect socially—she had taught me about the currency, and how to get around on the trains and busses, for example—but nothing had prepared me for how different the place itself would seem. I found myself, that autumn, often lonely in what seemed a cold, strange land. The rich foliage my Aunt Mary had missed so much seemed overwhelming and dark to me. The sky seemed heavy and dark, as well, and all the more so as the school term wore on and the seasons turned. The reds and golds of the autumn season were bright and cheerful, but once the leaves had dropped, the trees seemed stark and spent. I found myself writing in my diary quite often and was glad my aunt had sent it along with me. I felt lonely quite a lot during my first term in Oxford and tried, as much as I could, to get out where I could meet other people.

Of course, it was not all bleak. I was enjoying my courses, especially my reading in "Society, Culture and Environment," a course which was well aligned with an interest I was developing in how people's viewpoints wove together to form a society. In addition, I would occasionally meet boys at parties or in tutorials and go out on dates, although it was harder for me than for the other girls, I think, for most of the young English boys didn't know what to make of a girl from India. Some were game enough to have a go, and I went out a time or two with two or three boys that autumn, but nothing much came of it with any of them. I liked the Rumi book given to me by the young woman on the train, and I would read from it and imagine the young man of my dreams as being so passionate and ardent as Rumi was in his love poems.

The few boys I did date were quite proper, main-stream lads, but I really had my eye on the young men who were known as "hippies." There was something brash and impulsive about them, from their psychedelic clothing and long hair, to their free manner and forthright opinions. I hadn't had a chance to spend time around any of them, really—though perhaps I was just too shy—and in any case, I presumed they'd think me too un-hip to take an interest in me. I'd also heard they used drugs, and in truth, I think this was part of their allure for me. After all, my one experience with a drug had stretched my way of seeing things and changed the course my life was on. I imagined all these young hippie men were somehow powerful and free, and enlightened beyond my comprehension. And I wanted one to like me, and to show me his world.

Most of my time, during my first term in Oxford, I spent pouring over my books, trying to make up for the shortcomings in my education, trying to catch up with the students from independent schools and privileged backgrounds, and hiding from my loneliness by being entirely preoccupied with my studies. Having an unusually strong memory for things I had seen helped me move forward quickly with my school work. It allowed me not only to be able, generally, to remember whatever I had read, but quite often to be able to read passages back to myself from memory, simply by visualizing a page as I had read it the first time.

But even as this unusual capacity for recall helped me shorten the gap between myself and many of the other students academically, it did nothing to diminish my loneliness, and day after day I struggled to find my way in a social world that was new to me.

Busy as I was with my schoolwork, I was still the same young woman, unsure of myself, trying to understand better, and more deeply, who I was. I felt as though the truth of myself was writ only faintly, where I could only barely glimpse it when the light was just right. I felt as though I were some fragile fabric with the patterns of myself just barely visible on it, a faint dye imprint I needed to observe, trace over, darken, make legible. But there I was, all the time bent over books, soaking up their ink, picking up their patterns of thought, their points of view, and in the process casting the fabric of my thoughts, my perspective, too dark with the ink of these endless printed words, obliterating my view of the fragile patterns which lay within.

It was the same when I looked out at the social world around me. I found there nothing to reinforce the self I once had known at home in India, nothing to reflect me back to myself. I felt like a sponge, soaking up the world around me, and in the process—though learning what I was hungry to know—I felt I was in many ways becoming less and less myself.

I had made a practice of reading little bits from my book of Rumi's poetry each night before bed. It was unlike anything else I was reading in those months—it was soulful and passionate, not dry and academic, and in it I thought I heard an echo of myself. I thought that if I could write like that, I'd find myself in the words which came forth. My diary became the means and medium of my early experiments with poetry, and by the time Hilary Term came around that winter, and I'd heard that Angela Murphy (an American writer who was then a visiting professor of poetry) was planning to hold an informal workshop-style writing class, I hurried to make arrangements to join it.

❋   ❋   ❋

The class, modeled after the American method for teaching writing, was held once a week, on Wednesday afternoons, at our instructor's home in a moderately affluent neighborhood near the campus. On the first day of class, in January of 1971, I left my dorm room a little before 3 PM and walked to Angela Murphy's home under a sky filled with heavy gray clouds. I managed to find the flat with time to spare, and dawdled outside for a few minutes, hoping I was not the first to arrive.

I could see other students approaching from up the lane and, checking my watch to make sure I would not be too early, rang the bell and waited only a few moments before I was buzzed into the building.

Inside was a small entrance hall with a door to my left and a stairway rising up beyond it. After a few seconds, the door was opened by a small woman, 30-ish, with long brown hair that fell in a single braid down her back. I could see past her into the flat, where others were already gathered. Ms. Murphy introduced herself as she ushered me inside, where I joined the others, who were milling around awkwardly as the last of the students trickled in. It was a different crowd than I was accustomed to on campus—all Oxford students, but a different collection than I saw in my lectures and tutorials. These were a bit older, overall, and of the eight or nine of us gathered there, perhaps four or five were hippies.

Ms. Murphy invited us through a second doorway, within which hung many strands of beads, which together formed a curtain we had to part before entering. The beads jingled against one another like chimes as we swept them aside with the backs of our hands. Incense was burning in the sitting room as we entered and unceremoniously settled into whatever spot was available to be seated in. Some sat on the sofa, a couple more took their places in stuffed chairs, while the rest of us settled on pillows strewn about the floor around the coffee table opposite the sofa.

Seated on a pillow near me was a tall, slender young man with pale skin and shoulder-length black hair. He sat very upright, as though practicing meditation, and I noticed at once the beads around his neck and his patched bell-bottom jeans, and I felt a little thrill that this attractive fellow was seated near-by.

Our instructor got the people on the sofa to scoot over and make room for her. She said we should all call her "Angela." Then she asked us to go around the room and each say something about ourselves. We started with the person to her left, and one by one people gave their names, told what they were reading, what year they were in, and at what school, and some of them then would add their reasons for wanting to take a poetry class. I uncomfortably took my turn, saying as little as possible, then turned to the handsome fellow next to me. He said his name was Jake Carlyle and that he was a second year student reading PPP at St. John's College. Angela stopped him and asked him to explain what "PPP" was.

"Psychology, Philosophy, and Physiology," he answered. He added that he was interested in studying poetry because he thought he might like to be in a band, and he wanted to be able to write good lyrics like Mick Jagger and Bob Dylan. Angela nodded, and we finished up with the rest of the people in the room.

Class didn't last long that day, for we hadn't yet written anything to be critiqued. We were given a list of a half-dozen words, seemingly chosen at random, and told to write a poem that included them, to type it up on ditto paper, underline the six required words, and to have the poem in her box on campus by Monday afternoon. She said she would have them run off and ready for us to read in class by the following Wednesday afternoon. She included only one further instruction for the assignment—no rhyming in the poems.

That was all—we were done in half an hour. The class scattered quietly into a winter afternoon covered in fresh-falling snow, and I watched as Jake walked off alone, a dark figure in a world turned white, his long legs swinging in strong, even strides.

❀   ❀   ❀

I had copied the six words into my notebook, and now, back in my dorm, I wrote them neatly across the top of a clean sheet of paper:

Disperse, Orange, Hollow, Ocean, Pluck, Birth

From these words I would have to create a poem. I looked at them on the page before me, tried to see some relationship between them that I could make a poem out of. Did oranges disperse? Could an ocean be hollow? I supposed an infant could be "plucked" from its mother in being born. You could disperse something into a hollow, I reasoned. An orange could fill a hollow. Something could be dispersed into an ocean.

I sighed, set my pen down, stretched. This was going to be hard. I sat still for a few moments, then looked over the words again. You could pluck an orange from a tree. A birth could leave a hollow behind, I supposed.

I began writing, combining the words in ways that made sense to me. It took a little over half an hour to get the words in an order I liked, start to finish. The poem was done; I would need to get some ditto paper, type it up, and drop it off at Angela's box within a few days.

❀   ❀   ❀

When the class next met, we all sat around the same coffee table in Angela's sitting room, and Angela passed out the copies of the poems written for the class. Each of us had a copy of everyone else's piece. One-by-one we read our poems, pausing between to critique them—to say what lines we liked, and what parts didn't work for us. When my turn came I read the poem I'd written a few nights before:

> You give birth and afterwards
> say you are sad at the hollow left behind.
> The next morning, I pluck an orange from a tree
> for your breakfast, wake you. You say
> you dreamed your sadness was
> dispersed in the ocean. I am glad for you,
> and bring you your baby, who rests quietly
> in your arms.

I had liked it pretty well when I had written it, but it now seemed very small and uninteresting as I read it to the class. When a poem was read, those who listened were expected to say something about it, and someone said they liked the idea of sadness dispersing in the ocean, from mine. I liked hearing that, but the truth was, several of the others had also written about plucking an orange, and two of the other women had mentioned a hollow feeling after birth. All in all, my poem seemed a bit stiff and unoriginal, and I felt awkward reading it, especially in the company of others who seemed "cool" in ways I felt I was not, who dressed and spoke in that loose, knowing manner that was part of the hip youth culture at the time.

The reading and critiquing took most of the time allotted for class, but when we were done, and all the students had read, there was still a little time left over. Angela pulled out a slim stack of papers—dittoed copies. She told us she had played with the assignment herself and had been unsure about whether she would share her poem, but since there was a little time left over, she would go ahead. She passed copies around the room, then read the poem to us:

> Thua Thien Province,
> Vietnam
>
> I disperse into a small-town breeze raised
> by the setting sun, fly across oceans
> and continents with the fading light
>
> to be with you in your blood-soaked jungle,
> under fire, night after night. I offer you
>
> milk from my breast. I reach up and pluck
> a ripe slice from the succulent orange moon

> to sweeten the hollow between your bitter lips.
> I summon down rain through air torn by shells,
>
> to wash away your machine-gun tremors,
> your vision of a friend shot through chest and eye,
> your dream where you wake with a knife
> at your throat, everyone dead around you,
>
> and so return your childhood to you—
> young warrior, unwitting mercenary,
> drafted innocent, forced to kill and die
> for a nation that has forgotten
>
> the wisdom of its birth. Even now,
> thousands of miles
> from you, my heart
>
> beats with yours.

I caught my breath as she read the last line, and her voice, fading out at the end, seemed to settle over the silent room like a powder. Everyone was holding their breaths. The poem was wonderful. It was so much more than any of us had done.

I was relieved when she didn't ask us to critique it. Instead, she simply told us to write a poem for the next session and have it in, on ditto paper, by Monday afternoon same as before. She said there was no specific assignment this time, just to write some poetry, but not to rhyme. Then we gathered up our belongings, and she released the class into the early darkness of a winter night.

When I got home that night, I dropped my papers on my bed and, dropping myself beside them, I looked again at the poem Angela had written. How had she done it? Where my poem seemed somehow obvious, too reasoned, hers was dream-like, magical. It came to life in a way mine did not. I looked over both poems again, trying to find the secret of their differing origins. Angela had used "orange" and "pluck" in the same image, as I had. In her poem, that image read:

> I reach up and pluck
> a ripe slice from the succulent orange moon
> to sweeten the hollow between your bitter lips.

while mine had said simply:

> The next morning, I pluck an orange from a tree
> for your breakfast, wake you.

Angela's image was dream-like; mine was very much a product of an awake, reasoning mind. I knew I had dreams as rich and strange as her poem—it was in me, but, I wondered, how could I get it out on the page?

I felt frustrated, and decided to leave this question alone for a while and to spend some time on my biology homework. I pulled out the heavy text book and stretched out on my bed to read it. I disliked this book—dry and dull, duller than it had to be to get the information across. I lay on my side, settled my head against my arm, and held the book so that the page I was reading stuck up in the air, then began to read about cell division.

It wasn't long before the words began to swim before my eyes, and as I edged towards sleep, I imagined the little cells preparing to divide. They were all sorts of colors—blues and greens, pinks and purples—and in preparing to divide they were doing a little dance together, jiggling from side to side in unison. They seemed very cheerful, and I smiled, and then realized I had been nearly dreaming. I rolled over and stared up at the ceiling.

Dreaming. Dreaming, but I was also still awake. I wondered if that was how Angela had written her poem. I sat up and thought for a minute, and realized what I could do. I reached for my alarm and reset it so it would next go off at 3 AM.

I woke in a wave of confusion as the alarm sounded in the deepest part of the night. I fumbled to shut it off, then remembered why I had set it. Half-asleep, I switched on the light, picked up the pad of paper and the pen I had left by my bed, then collapsed back on the bed and drifted nearly back to sleep.

I had been dreaming when the alarm went off, and wisps of the dream circled round me now. As images rose from the back of my mind, I let them join with words, and scrawled the words out on the paper, eyes closed, nearly dreaming. At first, I was back in my village, a pan of curried vegetables cooking for the afternoon meal, the goat butting one of my cousin's children. Other impressions spiraled in—my trip to England; the way I'd had to stretch to bridge the two places; my seeking of myself, even in that moment, in the words I put on the page. These impressions, these emotions, rose and fell in me like my breath, and I let them all come through, spilling from my pen onto the paper.

And then it was like a dream that is completed, and I knew there would be no more. I sat up and looked at the scrawled words on the page, barely legible. I copied them over while I could still make out what they said, then began shifting phrases around, replacing a word here or there, changing the break of lines.

When I liked pretty well what the poem had become, I looked at the clock once more—it was almost 4:30. I set down the pad and pen, turned off the light, and settled back into my bed to sleep some more before my morning lectures.

When I finished with my last tutorial the following afternoon, I went back to my dorm and read through the poem I had written in the night. It filled most of one page of my notepad, and it read:

> The eastern sun has risen above the roof line.
> Sunshine splashes across the courtyard:
> yellow light under empty blue sky.
> Our milking goat butts little Jafar, who laughs
> and chases, while a pan simmers above the fire.
> The aroma of curry and root vegetables
> wafts up with the steam, circling skyward.
> In bright light, my mother rebuilds the mud walls
> worn down by last night's rain, now blown far
>
> away, where I am going, to England,
> where snow drifts around my boots, circling,
> and the buildings last for centuries:
> hard stone and brick, which does not melt in the rain.
>
> Some days I am in both places, both houses, both selves.
> I wear my sari and carry my rucksack full of books.
> I remember who I am then, and who I will be,
> as though I am named by a word of many syllables
> which must be spoken with many breaths, arcing
> from past through present and future
> before it can be said completely.
> Only then will I truly know myself:
> when all the words I am
> have been spoken.

I hugged the pad to my chest and laughed. Ah! So that is how one writes in a dreamy way—one must first be dreaming!

The next time the class gathered, I read the poem I'd written when nearly dreaming and got a very favorable response from the teacher and other students. I remember in particular that Jake said he thought the poem was "very cool" and that he especially liked the part about saying "all the words I am." I remember, too, that one of the young women in the class asked if I really wore my sari and my rucksack at the same time, and I had to tell her "no, that was figurative."

When we were a little more than halfway through the three-hour session, Angela said that she thought the class had felt a little over-long the last time, without a break, and that we should all take five minutes to relax. Jake got up, put on his coat, and stepped out the door into the hallway beyond. I was glad for the attention he'd given my poem and hoped he would talk to me if I followed him out.

Pulling on my own coat, I passed through the small hallway and out onto the front step. There, I found Jake standing next to the stone face of the building, his hands cupped around the match he was using to light his cigarette. The sky above was the blue-black of evening, and as Jake took a draw of his cigarette, the tip glowed bright red in the snow-covered twilight. I stopped a few feet away from him and stood, pulling my coat tighter around me, and feeling unsure about what to say or do.

Jake blew out his smoke, and as he did, it mingled with the steam from his breath and filled the air. He turned towards me and let the hand with the cigarette in it dangle loosely by his side.

"That was a pretty cool poem you wrote," he ventured, stamping his feet to keep warm.

"Oh, thank you," I said.

"I like the way it sort of twists around, slides between different times and places." He glanced down, flicked the ash from his cigarette. "I assume you were on drugs when you wrote it?"

This surprised me. "Oh no, no I wasn't."

"Really. Well, I don't know how you did it, then." He drew on the cigarette. "So, you're from India, eh? That's pretty exotic."

I nodded, and he smiled down at me. "How long have you been in England?" he asked.

I told him when I'd arrived, and then we went on talking a couple minutes longer, until the door to the hall swung open and someone told us class was starting. Jake casually dropped his cigarette onto the pavement and put it out with his foot, then we both stepped back inside.

I felt excited during the rest of the class and had trouble paying attention. I kept glancing over at Jake, wondering if he might like me. He had seemed friendly, interested, impressed even. I was excited to think that perhaps by being and expressing myself, I had gotten his attention.

After class, Jake asked me which way I was going, then he walked with me back to my dorm, chatting about the poems we'd read in class that night, the bands he was into, who he thought the best guitarists were, and the like. He said there was a local band, which played in one of the pubs in Oxford, which he thought was good. He said he'd like me to hear them and invited me to come with him to see them play that weekend. We made plans to get together then.

So it was that Jake and I began spending time together. We'd go out to hear bands he liked or spend time hanging out with his friends. They were a good group, a little rowdier than I was accustomed to, but bright and eager for the experiences that life could afford them. Tommy had been an Oxford student the year before, but had dropped out and was playing guitar with one of the bands in town. Cynthia, who was Tommy's girlfriend, waited tables in a local coffee shop, wore frilly clothes and lots of makeup, called everybody "love," and knew how to find the fun in anything. Peter, usually called "Pete" or "Petie," seemed younger than the rest, although I don't think he actually was. He was small, and sweet, and had a way of letting you know he cared without actually having to say or do anything special. And then there was Hollie, who hung around, though she didn't seem to be particularly linked with any of the fellows. She was quiet, like Pete, and had a sweet, shy quality. Pretty quickly I came to be known as Jake's girlfriend, and that gave me standing in the group just because I was with him.

Cynthia especially was welcoming. We spent time together sometimes, and she helped me fashion a more stylish mode of dress, looking through the English clothes Aunt Mary had sent along with me (many of which were her hand-me-downs), telling me what was hip and what was not. I was surprised to find out that the few home-spun clothes I had with me, clothes made by my mother, were actually some of the hippest clothes I had. Cynthia even passed on some of her own clothing to me, when she thought something would suit me especially well. I was glad to have her as a friend.

I got in the habit of coming over to Jake's flat and studying with him there. We'd been seeing each other for more than a month then, and these evenings usually went about the same way—we'd study together for two or three hours and then make out for a little while. Then I'd disentangle myself from him, insisting that I'd have to get home and sleep, and then would leave.

But this particular occasion was different. It was evening, and we'd been studying for a little while on the sofa in the common room of Jake's two-bedroom flat. His roommate was gone for the night. A late winter rain was falling outside, while inside we could hear its steady hush. A cold, damp draft seeped in around an ill-fitting window, and Jake snuggled up to me, warming us both. We began to kiss, and he pushed our books aside and leaned towards me. Together we lay back onto the sofa, with him above me. He began to tell me how beautiful I looked and how much he wanted me, how much he wanted us to make love. He stroked my face with his hand, and as he did, his arm brushed against my breast.

"Oh, Jake, we mustn't," I told him.

"It will be fine," he cooed in my ear. "I'll use a rubber. You won't get pregnant." He pressed his body up against mine, and I could feel his heat and desire.

In truth, I wanted him, too, wanted his free and open world in my world, wanted to pull him towards me, up into me, to open the boundaries between us, but everything I had been taught told me, "no, one mustn't before marriage." He kissed me, now, and a slow fire ran through me— his lips on my lips, on my neck.

"Let me make you feel good," he whispered. I pressed my body against his. I should be stopping this, I knew. But why? For months I had been struggling with the question of what *I* believed, and why. I felt soaked in beliefs from my upbringing, soaked in beliefs from this new culture—but what were *my* beliefs? What should I believe, and why? Here, in England, amongst the hipper students, and amongst Jake's friends, it was normal for a girl to sleep with her boyfriend. Why did I believe I should not?

While kissing my neck, Jake brought his hand up underneath my blouse. Beliefs... Why?... I wanted to... He wanted to...

I was breathing heavily. I arched my body against his... I wanted to... He wanted to... There would be no baby...

"Yes," I whispered hoarsely in his ear, and with that change of mind I felt freed, and I plunged my hand down into his pants, down into the hot, frantic darkness within. He moaned and accepted my touch, and I desired him, then, in that instant as never before.

"Oh, Jake!" I thought, and the words spilled from my lips. I kissed him and pulled him to me. He reached up and unbuttoned my blouse, then put his lips around my nipple and kissed me there until I had nearly fainted. All the while I had my hand in his pants, caressing him, calling out to him wordlessly in my moans and whispers, calling him nearer. He undid his pants and offered himself to me, and all over again I was saying "yes" to him, "yes." We pulled down our pants. He quickly covered himself with a rubber, then entered me slowly, pressing and stretching till my young body made room for him there. All the months of loneliness I had been feeling since coming to England came pouring down over me, over me and away. He was there with me, and I with him. Together, now, yes... together... we... were... yes... together. Feeling him, his skin, pressed against mine, him within me, around me. Him, in me and around me, emotionally, physically. The feelings I felt from him, of him, wove together with the feelings of myself. The nearness. The nearness of him—his mind, his body, his mood. Yes, the closeness of it. Yes... I was... with... him.

We cried out and spent ourselves together and then clung together like the very young, our bodies hot with sex and chilled by the cold, damp air drifting in around the window.

"Oh, Jake," I said to him.

"Oh, baby," he whispered back.

❀   ❀   ❀

A few weeks later, the gang was out one Saturday night to hear Tommy's band play at a local club. The band wasn't very good, but Tommy's guitar playing soared. I was, as I usually was when I heard him play, genuinely impressed. When the band took their break, Tommy came over and joined us at our table. When he sat down, I leaned over and told him how good I thought his playing was.

"I know you're lying, love, but it's nice of you to say it," he answered.

Tommy was a handsome fellow, with a rugged build and a warm face. The look in his eyes always struck me as childlike, eager and open, and yet I always felt there was some piece of him held back where others couldn't see. He was a very good guitarist, and I always thought at some level he must have known it, but he would always deny it when complimented, and often launch into a list of the mistakes he had just made.

After Tommy sat down, Jake said something about America's war in Vietnam, and everyone started talking about all the problems in the world. Pete said something about how buggered up the world was, what with pollution, racism, the troubles in Ireland and Vietnam and all that, and Cynthia responded with a comment I'd often heard others make since coming to England.

"What we really need is a change of consciousness," she said.

"Yeah, but how bloody well likely is that?" Jake said a bit caustically, in an off-handed way, taking a swallow of his ale. A thin line of smoke drifted upward from the cigarette between his fingers.

"I think it is happening," Cynthia answered. "I see a certain number of flower children around here, if you might notice."

Tommy, sensing the tension, made some joke about "flower children" and putting the ones who were "into pot into pots." Petie laughed, and Hollie glanced at Petie and giggled.

I looked over at Cynthia, considered what she had said. I'd thought about this some since my plane flight to London several months earlier. It seemed to me that the main difference between the culture I'd left behind and the new one I'd found in England was the beliefs that people shared. Cultures were built up out of beliefs, I'd been realizing. When people hung together in cultural groups, what linked them, more than ethnicity or history, more than anything else, was the common agreement of their beliefs. They shared a uniform picture of the world—what it was about, what was important, necessary, how things worked. It seemed to me that if you changed the system of beliefs a group shared, the culture that grew up out of those beliefs would itself be changed—even transformed—by that change in their underlying belief system.

"I don't think it's so much a matter of when, but how a change of consciousness could take place," I said. "If people change what they believe, then they also change the actions that are based on those beliefs. A whole culture could change that way—just by reshaping its beliefs."

"Listen to her," Jake said, cocking his head towards me. "She thinks she's got all the bloody answers."

Cynthia hit him on the shoulder with the back of her hand. "Maybe she has something, if you'd just listen."

Jake, who was slunk down in his seat, glowered at her. "What, now you think she's going to change the world, clean up the rivers, create world peace? Bloody well likely." He seemed a little drunk. He frowned and took a drag on his cigarette.

Some of the band members were climbing back on stage. Tommy got up to join them.

"Well, you never know!" Cynthia answered Jake, unwilling to back down to his stubbornness. The band began to play, and the conversation came to an end. I looked over at Jake, who sat staring straight ahead, his drink and cigarette both held in the same hand, with the drink balanced against one knee in that casual, stylish manner of his. My feelings were hurt. I knew he was feeling moody, and that he was drinking, but I still couldn't imagine him cutting off the thoughts of one of his mates so abruptly as he had just cut off mine.

When the band finished their last set, we all filtered out into a crisp, clear night. Jake draped his arm around my neck, pulled me towards him, kissed me.

"Come home with me?" he asked.

"Not tonight," I told him. "I have to be up early," I lied. He'd had too much to drink, and I was angry at him, anyhow. Instead, I asked Cynthia if she'd like me to walk with her, as her flat was on the way to my dorm, and we set off together. Our footfalls clattered against the pavement as we left the others behind.

"I appreciate you sticking up for me with Jake," I told her, when we were a block or so away. "It hurt my feelings, what he said."

"Well, you shouldn't listen to him, love."

We walked along in silence for a minute, and I considered why it was that hurt feelings hurt.

"Did you ever think about it?" I asked. "Why it is things like that hurt your feelings?"

"No, what do you mean?" Cynthia said.

"Well, I think it's like, there are these little pieces in you that you want to let out, like little bits of life you want to bring forward, but when someone behaves like that, it pushes them back down inside you, and they don't come out. They get jammed up, and that hurts. But when someone says nice things, you feel encouraged, and you let what's in you come through. And you feel good when that happens, 'cause the life in you is moving."

Cynthia looked at me sympathetically. "Well, love, don't you think about it anymore. Men are just a bunch of sexist louts, and you shouldn't let their insensitivity hurt you."

We took a few steps in silence. "I don't know that word, 'sexist,'" I said. "What does it mean?"

"I learned it from a book I've been reading," Cynthia answered. "It says we birds should stick up for ourselves, that it's time to stop letting the blokes run everything. It says we think we have to play our sex roles, like a role in a play, but that we should break out of that and be complete people."

"Like a role in a play?" I asked.

"Yes, there are certain things we think we're supposed to say and do, just because we're women," she told me. "Like it's scripted. And the men have their own roles in that script, too."

We walked along talking about it for a while. I was relieved to be out of the club and into the quiet, open night. I was glad I hadn't let Jake coax me into going home with him.

"Here's my flat," Cynthia said, as we came to a stop in front of an old, gray stone building. "Well, love, don't you let him get you down," she said as she pulled her keys from her purse. "I liked what you said, whatever your boyfriend had to say about it." She smiled brightly at me as she started up the steps to her flat. She was giving me just the sort of support

I wished I could have gotten from Jake. At that moment, I could have kissed her, she'd made me feel so much better. I asked her if she would lend me the book, and she told me she would as soon as she finished it, and then we said "ta-ta" for the night, and I was off.

As I walked towards home, I thought about what Cynthia had told me. I thought about these "sex roles," and I realized that I knew exactly what she'd meant. In fact, I could see Jake was very attached to his. He wanted very much to be strong and masculine, knowledgeable and in-charge. Truth was, I thought, it made him feel insecure to hear me having my say.

I wondered for a moment why that would be, and then it came to me. I was the one his strength, his knowledge, his in-charge-ness was supposed to be measured against. If I seemed knowledgeable, he had to seem more so, especially out in public like tonight. And if he couldn't seem more knowledgeable, then he had to make my ideas look foolish, so he could still look and feel smarter. Sex roles really were like roles in a play, I thought, and for the play to go on, for him to be in his role, I had to be actively playing mine. If I stepped out of this role, my role—which helped him define his—he'd try to push me back into it: demure, following, less bright than he.

I felt angry, and I wondered—why were people playing these roles, anyhow? It struck me as strange that though Cynthia was complaining about role playing, she seemed very attached to her feminine role. I just couldn't understand it. It seemed that people were trying to live out a model of themselves handed them by their culture, instead of trying to discover and give life to what was really in them. What a waste of their real possibilities, I thought.

I got to my dormitory room and let myself in. Whatever was going on, I knew I needed a little space from Jake. Maybe if I could spend less time with him when he was with his mates, I thought. He didn't behave so poorly when we were alone.

❋   ❋   ❋

Our class gathered at Angela's at the end of Hilary Term in mid-March. We were all getting a lot from the class and didn't want it to end so soon. Angela, who was accustomed to the American semester system—and who thought eight weeks too short a time for a class, anyhow—encouraged us all to sign up for her new class, which would continue on during the spring Trinity Term, scheduled to begin in a little more than a month. Almost all the class expressed an interest in doing so, both Jake and myself included.

I had been seeing a little less of Jake after that night at the club, but we still got together once a week or so. During the break after Hilary Term, I focused most of my energies on preparing for the start of Trinity Term.

One night, a couple of weeks into the break, Jake came over, and we studied together for a few hours, with him seated in the desk chair, and me with my work spread out on the bed in front of me. When I'd done enough of the work I'd set out to do that night, I looked over at Jake where he sat, reading by the desk light. I noticed he was looking at a stack of the dittoed poems people had handed in for the poetry class that had ended a couple of weeks before. He noticed I was watching him and held up the poem he was reading. It was one of mine.

"I came across these papers mixed in with some other papers," he said. "You know, you've been writing some good poetry, Indira."

"Oh, thanks," I answered.

"I don't know how you do it. Your poems *breathe*. Mine don't breathe."

I looked at him. I liked it when he let his guard down a bit and was genuine with me in this way. "I have a trick, if you'd like to know it," I told him.

"Yes, I would. What's your trick?"

"Well, I've started thinking of it as 'free movement,' because it's a way of loosening up so your mind moves freely, so you feel the impulses rising, and you can recognize them and act on them." I went on to tell him how I'd learned to tap into the dreaming parts of my mind by waking myself in the middle of the night and writing then, half-asleep. It was getting, I told him, so I didn't have to do that at all anymore. I'd gotten familiar with that place in my mind and could get there when I was awake.

He sat quietly and nodded, thinking about it. Finally he said, "Free movement, dreaming, huh? Sounds like a good trick."

"It seems to work well. I've thought about it some, *how* it works to help write a poem—if you'd like to know about it."

"Tell me?" he asked. He was leaned back in the desk chair, his bare feet stretched out on the floor in front of him, the papers loosely grasped in one hand.

"I had a natural-sciences class in high school, in Varanasi. In the chemistry part we studied super-saturated solutions—you know, when you can get a liquid to hold more of some solid than could normally be dissolved into it?"

"Yeah," he nodded. "It's like when you heat water and you can get a whole lot of salt to dissolve in it, more than you could if the water were room-temperature, right?"

"Yes, and when it cools to room temperature, it really has more salt dissolved in it than it can easily hold. It's ready for the salt to precipitate out as a crystal. But it needs some starting point, some sort of trigger."

"Right. I've done that, in a class once—we put a string in the salty water and the crystals formed around that. They were pretty. Salt crystals."

"Yeah—you just need to get it started, and the crystal forms. And I think it's that way with our minds, too," I told him. "Our minds are full, over-full, with all the things we've felt and seen and picked up along the way. All you need to do is to drop something in there, into your mind, into that salty inner ocean, and you make associations around it, make connections to it, you dream something in association with it."

"So, you're saying the poem is the associations..." Jake began.

"...that come up around whatever you're focused on when you go into that dreamy inner place, that salty inner ocean, if you will, when you get ready to write. Whatever you're focused on, that's what you make associations around. So you create something that reflects that starting point, that bit of string or whatever it is the associations crystallize around. Like if you're depressed when you sit down to write, you'll associate together depressing images, and that's what you'll get when you write."

Jake shook his head, amused. "Yeah, like that one Sam Mallory turned in for our last week. Hold on, I just saw it," he said as he sat upright and shuffled through some papers on the desk, then picked out one sheet and read:

> Always I am following you,
> but never can get close.
> With every footfall,
> I can hear the ice cracking beneath my feet.

"Yeah," I said, and cocked my head to one side. For a moment I imagined what Jake had just read was a description of Sam's life, grown out of his somber attitudes, just as his poem had crystallized out of those same beliefs.

"Right, good example," I said, then went on with what I'd been saying, "but if you're only drawing from what you can hold consciously in your head at one time, well, that's not much, and it's only a small percentage of what you know. And the poem you make from there is going to reflect those limited resources. It's like your head's too small to hold all you know. You've got to think outside your head."

Jake nodded but looked a little confused.

"Like when you dream," I continued, "that's the sort of thing I mean when I say 'outside your head.' When you dream, you have access to all sorts of stuff—you loosen up and make associations drawing on currents in a much larger pond.

"You feel that awareness rising within you as impulses, as impressions. You have access to stuff from your childhood, things you thought you'd long forgotten. I think that's why dreams are so strange and magical. And if you write from a place where you're partly dreaming, you have all that vast resource, all that magical stuff to draw associations from, and to crystallize together to form your poem."

Jake looked very thoughtful, nodding his head slowly.

"So that's how you've been writing all that fine, trippy poetry," he said finally. Then he set the papers down on the desk and turned off the desk lamp. He leaned back in the chair, looked at me.

"Thanks for sharing that with me," he said. "I want to try it sometime." He had a soft, quizzical look in his eyes, as though he was considering me in a new way. He smiled sweetly, leaned forward, pulling his legs in and resting his elbows on his knees.

"Is there room in that bed for me?" he asked.

I set my work off on the floor and pulled back the cover. Jake, already barefoot, got up from the chair and took off his trousers, then slid in next to me as I reached up and turned off the light.

❀ ❀ ❀

Things were up and down between Jake and me in the weeks that followed. Sometimes he'd be aloof and condescending, sometimes he'd show up and be all there. I sort of felt like there was more than one Jake. I think he thought of me as more than one person, too. One he saw as soft and feminine, and he sort of idolized her, I think. On the other hand, he felt superior, and saw me as less than himself. In part, perhaps, he saw me as a dark-skinned person towards whom his upbringing had taught him to feel superior, and as an exotic woman who he could show off to his friends. Perhaps he was more than one person to himself, as well.

Though I had at first been attracted to the drug-using culture Jake was a part of, as I became more aware of what his drug habits really were, I wanted more and more to stay away from them and the part of him that chose that world.

Sometime that spring, perhaps as early as mid-April, I came by to see Jake at his flat one afternoon when he didn't expect me. I let myself in with the key he had given me and found him in his bedroom, hanging out with Tommy and Pete.

"Hello," I said, as I pushed open the bedroom door. The room was dark. The curtains were pulled closed. A candle was burning on the table by the bed.

Jake looked up from where he was sitting in the armchair under the window. He looked pretty out of it.

"Hello, love," he answered softly. I glanced around the room. Tommy and Pete were both sitting at the head of the bed, leaning back against the wall. Tommy, next to the night table, sat in the candle's glow, his belt draped over his shoulder. Jake got up and stepped over to the little table by the bed. He quickly moved whatever had been left out on the tabletop into the drawer. Then he blew out the candle and dropped back down into the armchair under the window.

"Hi, Indira," Petie said. He was looking towards me, but I had the feeling he might have been looking through me, or past me.

"Hi, Petie," I said.

"Have a seat," Jake said, scratching his neck.

I sat down on the bed near Tommy. He'd looked up when I'd come in, but now his eyes were closed, his head leaned back against the wall. His hands lay limply on the bed, but his fingers were moving slightly, twitching, as though he were imagining playing some guitar rift he heard in his head.

"Hello, Tommy!" I said. He opened his eyes halfway, gave a groggy smile.

"Hey," he said languidly. "How's it goin'?"

"Fine," I said. I wondered what they were all on.

I turned back to Jake, told him I'd just finished some schoolwork, thought I'd drop by and say "hi." We exchanged a few words, but the conversation was fractured; Jake kept drifting in and out. Before long, his head lolled forward, and he seemed to go to sleep. I looked over at the other guys. Tommy was still "playing guitar," and Petie was just staring into space, his eyelids half-shut, a wisp of a smile on his lips. I didn't see much point in sticking around. I got up and let myself out.

When I saw Jake a few days later, he assured me it was okay, told me how it made them feel so good to use it, like soaking up the warmth of a fire after coming in from hours in the ice and snow, but better, and that they wouldn't do it very often, anyway. But I had a bad feeling about it. I wasn't sure what it was that bothered me so much. Maybe it was the little line of blood I'd seen trickling down Tommy's arm, which no one else seemed to notice. Maybe it was how cordoned off they'd all seemed, away somewhere alone inside themselves.

In any case, I think it was about that time that they started using heroin.

❀   ❀   ❀

"Pause," Paul said to Kiki.

He'd grown tired of lying in bed listening to Indira Kumar's soft voice describe her Oxford days. He was beginning to feel restless. He sat up and slipped on his shoes, pulled a travel meal and his canteen from his pack, then attached Kiki to his shirt. Then he stepped out the door of his room under the hill and took in the rolling hills around him. Beyond them, a ridge rose up in the distance.

Paul climbed to the crest of the nearest hill and looked around. Above the ridge to the west hung a quarter moon, preparing to set, while the sun shown brightly, high overhead. Below him, to the south, he could make out Strandford—not his Strandford, of course, but a smaller one, better suited to a well world.

How had they done it, exactly? he wondered.

Somehow, he realized, Dr. Kumar's book had changed this world. But how? Somewhere, buried within this text, was the answer.

Paul thought about what he had listened to so far that morning—details about a young woman's social life, problems with her boyfriend, how she had learned to write poetry...

Was there anything there? he thought—some clue about what had made the difference? To Paul, the possibility seemed slim that a book such as this could possibly make such a difference—and yet, what had the historian in the pub told him?—that this book had been the most influential event, the single most important catalyst for change during the time period in which this world had begun to branch off from his own. It couldn't be a coincidence. There must be something here, Paul told himself.

Well, he'd have to give it time—after all, he was only a couple of chapters in. Maybe somewhere along the line, there would be some statement, some single important idea, that would clearly be the key to all of this. But more likely, Paul reflected, the thing that mattered so much in this book would turn out to be multifaceted—like a fabric woven of many fibers—not just one conspicuously placed idea, but a weave pulled together from many strands.

Paul looked down at the quiet community of Strandford where, he knew, elk grazed, and owls called, and people held one another in their arms—a Strandford so different from his own, in a world so different from the one he knew.

He had to be patient, he told himself. In time, he would unlock the mystery.

"Kiki, resume recitation," he said, as he made himself comfortable beneath a live-oak tree at the top of the hill.

◧   ◧   ◧

I was pleased when Trinity Term began, near the end of April, because it meant the continuation of my poetry class. I remember studying alone in my room one night, trying to get though some reading on the topic of sociology and demography. I was excited by my school work as a general matter, but I considered the poetry something special, time I could spend with myself and reflect, and on this particular evening I was trying to get my regular school work done so I would have time to come up with a poem for Angela's class.

When I had gotten enough of my reading done, I set my books aside and prepared to write. The young woman who lived across the hall from me had lent me her portable turntable for the night, and I had put on a stack of albums I'd borrowed from Jake a couple of weeks earlier. Side two of The Beatles' white album fell into place as I lit a couple of candles by my bed. The needle on the arm of the record player traced its way to the beginning of the first song, and Paul McCartney began to sing. I turned off the lights and lay down on my bed, trying to settle into a dreamy state of mind.

As I began to relax, I could feel impressions beginning to surface, but instead of them developing as poetry, I found myself thinking about protolife, feeling how it rose in me, like a swell coming up from some deep inner ocean.

I scribbled a few impressions on my pad of paper, hoping I could make a poem of them. As I did, I held the images in my mind's eye—an ocean, salty, and full of life of every kind; a deep place our roots drew life from, like the life-giving milk a baby pulled from its mother's breast. I imagined a chinar seedpod, its little peaks like mountain ridges rising from an ocean-filled world below, the roots of those peaks reaching down, down deep, drawing life and sustenance.

I became aware that I was making associations with my ideas about protolife—imagining an ocean, the chinar seed—just as I had described making associations when talking with Jake a few weeks earlier. But there was something more here; I was juxtaposing those associations. I was using them to make a mental picture, a mental model, which better represented the ideas and feelings I was focusing on than just associations alone could do.

Okay, I thought, waking up some from that drifty state of mind—so moving protolife to life wasn't two steps, as I'd originally supposed years before—it wasn't just inspiration and action. It wasn't even inspiration, association, and action, as I'd described the process to Jake the month before. I was beginning to understand that it also involved the making of a mental model.

I tried to get the process clear in my mind. I imagined an artist—a painter—feeling inspired to paint, then focusing on that feeling of inspiration, making associations with it, and then coalescing those associated impressions into a mental image of what she wanted to paint.

Perhaps she was feeling sad, then focused on that feeling of sadness, recalled images she'd seen of people looking sad, and then let those images coalesce into a single striking image that best expressed the sadness that she felt.

Then, I imagined, she held that mental image in mind, and used it as a model for the painting she would do.

The album side came to an end with John Lennon singing "Julia." The next LP dropped into place, and Blind Faith began to play "Sea of Joy." I sat up, set the pad of paper I'd been using aside, and picked up my diary from the floor. I opened the diary and wrote:

- *Focus on something we feel inspired by*
- *Make associations with that inspiration*
- *Form model from associated impressions*
- *Then take action to reproduce model in physical world*

The candlelight flickered through the room as Steve Winwood sang. I looked at what I'd just written, considered it. I imagined the painter visualizing the painting-to-be in her mind, moving the brush across the canvas, trying to reproduce that model, that image, imagining each brush stroke before she made it, modeling each brush stroke.

I thought about this, and a realization began to gather in my mind. As it did, I imagined the words I would use to express it. I wrote those words on the page:

For every action we take, there must first be a mental model. Without a model, we have no picture of how to act, no image to shape our actions around. Even with such simple actions as brushing one's teeth or tying one's shoe, one must first have a mental model of what to do. Every action requires a model.

I set down my diary and lay back down on my bed. It was exciting to be thinking this. But just what about it had me excited? I wondered.

The wavering candlelight made the shadows in the room shift and sway. The whole room seemed alive with that movement. I lay quietly on my bed, watching the light flickering around the room, and listening as Eric Clapton's soulful guitar cried out from the record player's single speaker. It was exciting to realize these things, I answered myself, because they seemed to hold in them not just a key to how people did art work, but how the very process of living shaped itself.

I lay there thinking about this as the candles burned and the record played. Focusing on what I'd been realizing, a clearer model of the process gelled in my mind. I sketched it out in my journal that night in early May of 1971. It looked something like this:

Focus on inspiration (protolife) — which is a kind of abstract model:

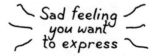

Make associations around that inspiration — drawing on a small resource (conscious mind), or on a larger (dreamy) resource (subconscious mind):

From associations gathered around the original inspiration, we generate a specific mental model, such as an image to be painted:

We then gather in more associations, which together help us recreate that model in life — drawing on a small resource (conscious mind), or on a larger (dreamy) resource (subconscious mind):

Lots of minor models rise up and take the form of impressions and impulses. These impressions and impulses may say, for example: "make this brush stroke," or "write this word." Using

free movement, we give these subtle impressions and impulses
life through our actions:

Such impressions and impulses, when acted on collectively,
bring to life a representation of the original source of
inspiration, refined and made more specific as it takes form
in the world. Thus protolife is expressed into the world. That
which was inside, takes form outside:

As I wrote, the Blind Faith album came to an end. The needle went "scritch, scritch," round and round till the arm picked it up, and another album dropped into place.

I smiled as I looked at what I had sketched and written, then glanced at the clock. It was getting late, and my poem was due in Angela's box the next day. I looked over what I had scrawled on the page when I'd first laid down to write. It didn't seem very poem-like—more like a descriptive outline of my thoughts.

I should try again, I decided, and as I once again settled down to write, I thought about my classmates, many of whom had continued from the previous term. I felt excited that the class would be meeting again and wondered how many of my classmates were scribbling out poems at the last minute, as I was.

A couple of days later, I found myself in Angela's sitting room, reading the poem I'd written that night. I had dashed it off quickly, and it wasn't one of my better efforts, but it turned out to be of some interest. It read, in part:

> The sun crested the horizon
> like the yolk of an egg, its light
> breaking across the broad plains below.

One might think there was nothing special in these few lines, but something interesting was going on in class that night, for of the seven or eight students present, three or four of us had overlapping images in our poetry. One student had written:

> They drove on till daybreak,
> stopped at a diner for steak and eggs.

Another had picked up the theme with these words:

> You hold an egg up to the light,
> see through its translucent shell
> to the new life stirring within.
> Pecking and straining, it breaks
> the egg's porcelain walls.

Several of us remarked on the surprising similarities, and on the odds of such redundancy in so small a class. A few students made jokes about it, one or two dismissed it as "coincidence," but I was fascinated. Had we all been writing our poems at the same time a couple of nights earlier, trying to get them done before they were due the next day? Had our thoughts somehow interwoven, and together drawn on the same creative resources? I had to wonder.

❀　　❀　　❀

Sometime a couple of weeks later Jake stopped by my room and asked me if I'd go out with him that weekend. We hadn't been seeing much of each other for a while. I thought he looked a little thinner than usual. He said he was low on cash, so we'd have to do something inexpensive. We settled on a film being shown on campus that Saturday night.

The film turned out to be pretty good, and we had a nice evening together. Jake was pleasant and seemed relaxed, and I came over to his flat with him afterwards. Things had been tense between us off and on, and it was good to be together on positive terms. I remember standing with him by an open window. It must have been mid-May. We were kissing, and he stopped and asked me sweetly if I would stay the night. We made love with Aretha Franklin singing in the background. Afterwards, we lay together, and I felt near to him in the way I had when we had first been together.

As I lay there, I could feel things shifting and rearranging themselves inside me. I had the desire to write, to let the words form, to let those feelings out where I could see them and discover what it was I felt brewing up inside.

Jake got up to use the toilet, and while he was gone I found a scrap of paper and a pencil on the floor next to the bed. I lay back down, let the feelings crest, the impressions form, the words come tumbling out.

When I looked down at the paper to see what I'd just written, I felt surprised, for it seemed unrelated to anything I'd been feeling or focused on. Jake returned from the loo and climbed back into bed. I showed him what I'd just written:

> The red boat is rocked by heavy seas,
> a great storm rising. A man in a dark rain
> slicker pulls in the sails, sets
> his teeth against the coming storm,
> with no land in sight.

Jake read through it, then frowned and asked, "Where did you get this?" He cocked his head so he could see my face from where he lay beside me.

"I don't know, it just came to me while you were gone."

"Are you sure?" he asked.

"Yes, sure. What's up?"

"This piece describes part of a story I've been meaning to write. I mean, I've been thinking about this very thing. I was thinking about it just now, after we made love. You see, I can't decide if I should have the boatman drown, or make it back to his wife on shore." He tapped the paper with the back of his hand. "I don't know if there's no land in sight. That's one way it might go. I've been trying to decide."

I took the paper back from his hand and looked at it. Jake scratched his head. "Pretty trippy," he muttered, then got up and left the room.

I slid down in bed and thought about it. It wasn't so different from what had happened in class a couple of weeks before, but I was closer to Jake, and this was more detailed, and it seemed clear that it had started in his head and not mine. I was aware of Jake rummaging around in the next room. I had this image of radio waves moving from Jake to me. The feeling of him. Yes, I could always feel him when we were close—his mood, his state of mind. It seemed perhaps there was more embedded in that awareness than I'd realized. I thought again about the radio waves. I'd learned in my science classes that radio waves were electromagnetic radiation, that they were energy waves within a certain frequency range. Our thoughts create electromagnetic radiation, too, I knew. That was what was read by an EEG machine.

Maybe, I thought, if we were tuned in right, tuned in to the right frequency, and if we were listening closely to the background sounds within us, as I did when I wrote—maybe we could tune into one another as a radio tunes into the radio signals moving through the air.

Jake came back into the room, still naked after our love-making. It was true—I could feel his presence. It was part of what I'd longed for when we were first getting together, part of what I was ambivalent about now—the way it linked me to him, to his world, to his viewpoints.

He sat down on the edge of the bed with an open book in his hands. "Do you know this fellow?" he asked, turning the binding so I could see the words printed there. "The Basic Writings of Carl Jung," it read.

"I've heard his name, but I don't really know what he was about," I said.

"Well, listen to this," Jake said, and then he read aloud from the book:

This deeper layer I call the *collective unconscious*. I have chosen the term "collective" because this part of the unconscious is not individual but universal; in contrast to the personal psyche, it has contents and modes of behavior that are more or less the same everywhere and in all individuals. It is, in other words, identical in all men and thus constitutes a common psychic substrate of a suprapersonal nature which is present in every one of us.

"I've been thinking about this since that class a couple of weeks ago," Jake went on, "where so many people wrote about the sun and eggs and all. I think maybe they were tapping into the collective unconscious. Jung says there's stuff already set up in that collective unconscious, archetypes, ah—like the fundamental patterns of living, which we all draw on when we live out our individual lives. Maybe when people create the same thing, they're drawing on the same archetypes."

"But Jake, *you* were writing that story."

"Well, maybe I wasn't. Maybe I was just drawing on some archetype, or something, and you drew on it, too." I could see this made him feel kind of small, like his creativity added up to nothing.

I picked up the book, glanced over what it said about archetypes. It looked pretty similar to my idea about inner models we draw on in generating action in the world, but in Jung's view, these were static models. It wasn't clear to me where they were supposed to have come from—they just were, and they didn't change.

"Jake, I know you were creating that story. I like this idea Jung has about a collective unconscious. Maybe Emma and Charlie and I were somehow in touch through it when we were writing our egg poems. But this archetype thing, I think Jung's got that wrong. I think we create the models we draw on in living our lives. And maybe sometimes we create them together...."

"That's not what archetypes *are*," Jake said sharply, cutting me off. "Oh, it's just like you—I tell you what a great thinker has to say, and you don't listen—you change his ideas to suit yourself! What makes you so bloody smart? You come here from some poor, barefooted nation and think you know so bleeding much!!" He picked up the book and threw it across the room.

I just looked at him, shocked. I felt hurt, angry, and what surprised me—I suddenly saw him as pathetic and small. He had these heroes, rock stars, Carl Jung, but he couldn't believe in himself.

I stared at him, and he must have felt how I saw him in that instant, because he got up and left the room.

I rolled over in bed, my back to the part of the bed Jake normally slept in. I thought about getting dressed and going home, but it was late and I was tired, and I decided to lie there for a few minutes. I didn't want to think about Jake or Jung. Instead I comforted myself with my own ideas.

I closed my eyes and imagined myself on a world shaped like a chinar seedpod, and I was walking down one of the peaks, going down deeper and deeper into myself. When I got to its base, I dropped my robe to the ground and dove into the salty waters that lay beneath. Brightly colored fish dashed and turned around me in the light filtering down from overhead. I swam through these warm waters, the source of all life, through forests of seaweed, and saw around me the roots of all the other peaks reaching down into these waters as well—down, down deep, where we were each a part of everything, and everything was a part of us.

✵   ✵   ✵

A lot of students went away for the summer, but I arranged to stay in my dorm and kept on studying. Jake was still in town, but I didn't see him often. With Jake not around much, and the regular term ended, I had a bit more time on my hands. I began to wish I could find a part-time job for the summer, to augment the scholarship money I was receiving and to fill in some of my free hours. I thought it would be nice if the job could give me a change of pace from all the studying I was doing. I was spending so much time reading and thinking alone. I wished I could be around people more and could be doing something I didn't have to think hard about.

Since beginning my poetry-writing class the winter before, I had become not only more aware of the impulses that gave rise to words and images, but of other impulses, as well, which rose up quietly as I went about my life. I gradually realized that there were impressions and impulses rising up in the background of my thoughts all the time, impressions and impulses that I would previously have ignored, having preferred instead to focus my thoughts, and make my decisions, quite consciously and deliberately. I was aware of how much my poetry had improved once I had learned to be aware of, and to follow, my impulses when writing, and I began to wonder how it would affect my life in general if I followed my impulses in other situations, as well.

One afternoon in late June, around the time I had started seriously thinking about getting a job, I had the impulse to go for a stroll and wander around town some. Instead of shoving the impulse aside, as I would customarily have done (and then staying home and focusing on my school work), on this day, I set my books aside and went out for a walk.

It was summer, finally, so I put on the sandals I'd usually worn when walking around Varanasi, and stepped out into a clear day beneath a sky speckled with clouds. I had begun thinking that I might like to take my walk through University Parks, southeast of Hugh's College, but by the time I got to the turn I'd intended to take onto Norham Gardens, I knew that wasn't where my impulse was leading me. Since the goal was to discover what would happen if I followed free movement in living as I had done in writing, I gave up the idea of strolling in the park and let the impressions which were drifting through my mind, and the impulses rising up from within, lead me.

I continued south along St. Giles, then, towards the center of town. It was pleasant to stroll along, looking at the grand, old stone buildings, or into the windows of the businesses that lined the road. It was one of those days when it's warm in the sun and cool in the shade, and I was enjoying being out in it.

I walked for a good little while, turning here and there as the inclination struck me. As I walked along one especially quiet side street, I glanced into the window of a little neighborhood food market and saw a "help wanted" sign had been posted there.

I stopped and looked around. It was a nice part of town, and it looked like a pleasant little store. I stepped inside and browsed the aisles for a few minutes to get a feel for the place. The front door had been propped open, and it smelled as much of sunshine and summer indoors as out. The place had a nice feel. I glanced around and caught the eye of a middle-aged man who stood behind the counter.

"Can I help you?" he asked, and I had the impression he actually wanted to.

"I noticed the help wanted sign in the window," I told him.

"Yes," he said. "I just put that out this morning. I need someone to work from one in the afternoon until close, three days a week. I have a girl who usually does it, but she's a student at the university, and she's gone away for the summer. It would only be for the summer, until the end of September, when she'll be back."

"I'm only looking for summer work, part time," I told him. There would be people around, I thought, and it would be a good break from my studies. It sounded like just what I was hoping for.

He smiled, and his look was relaxed and genuine. I liked him. He told me a little bit more about the job. I'd mostly be expected to work the till, but also restock the shelves when there was no one around. I'd also have to close up shop (tidy up, cash up the till, etc.) before leaving each evening. I nodded and told him I had done those sorts of things at my aunt and uncle's store in Varanasi.

We talked a little longer, then he offered me the job, and I happily accepted. We agreed I'd return in a couple of days for my first shift. I said goodbye and stepped back out into the sunny summer day.

It was just like when I wrote a poem, I found myself thinking, as I walked back towards my dorm—like when I wrote a poem, and in so doing, made in words a replica of the model I held in my mind. Only now it seemed, I had created *in the world*—not just on paper, but in my life—a replica of what I had held in my mind. The job I had modeled in my mind had taken form around me.

I wondered how it had happened, and it occurred to me that perhaps, in gathering associations, I was drawing not just on my own private conscious and subconscious resources, but on deeper resources that connected us all.

I pondered this as I walked back towards campus, past the heavy stone buildings at the center of town. Perhaps in that deeper, collective mind, I thought, an association had been made between the shopkeeper's desire for a new part-time summer employee, and my desire for a part-time summer job. The possibility had taken root, and I'd allowed free movement to carry me to it.

If I was right, then none of this could have happened if I hadn't first learned to listen to the dreamy impressions rising up from inside me. I felt lucky, as I walked home that day, and I wondered if that was what good luck was about—making a mental model of what we desire, and allowing free movement to carry us to it.

❋   ❋   ❋

My new job was easy to adjust to, as it was not unlike the work I had done at my aunt and uncle's shop in Varanasi. I liked helping the customers and getting to meet more of the townsfolk of Oxford, and not so much just the people connected with the University.

One day, on my way to work, I chanced upon Cynthia walking along. We stopped to visit, as I hadn't seen her in some time. I asked her how she was doing.

"Just fine, love—and you?" she said.

"Good. I've got a job at the grocer's down the lane," I told her, gesturing ahead of me. "I'm on my way there now. My shift starts in about ten minutes."

"Well, good for you. Don't let me hold you up," she said, smiling.

"It's okay, I'm early," I told her.

Cynthia paused before speaking. "Have you seen much of Jake lately?" she asked.

"Not really." I shook my head. "We don't seem to be getting on too well anymore. How's Tommy? I keep expecting to hear that he's run off to London to join a real rock and roll band. He's that good, you know."

Cynthia glanced off to the side, looked pensive for a moment. "Yes, but he wouldn't do that, you know." She looked down at her shoes. "He doesn't know how well he plays. Good as he is, he thinks he's not any good."

I found this strange. "You mean he *really* thinks he isn't any good?" I asked her. "I always thought, well, I don't know what I thought—it just didn't seem possible that he wouldn't know how talented he is, no matter how much he turns aside a compliment."

Cynthia looked at me. "No, love, he means it when he says that stuff. He *really* thinks he's no good," she said. "But you're right. He's the best guitarist in Oxford. He'd beat out most of them that's in London, I'd warrant. I think he sounds like Pete Townshend. You know, of The Who? But he won't believe me."

I shook my head. "How's he doing, anyhow?" I asked. "I haven't seen him in a while."

Cynthia paused again before answering, looking off to the side as she had before. When she spoke, her voice sounded shaky. "You heard anything about the three of them—Jake, Petie, and my Tommy—using heroin?" she asked. She looked me in the eye, then, and I could see she felt worried.

"Yeah," I told her. "I came over once when they were doing it."

Cynthia frowned, nodded, looked down. "It's wicked stuff. I don't think Jake and Petie are using so much, but Tommy..." Her voice trailed off, and her eyes seemed very far away.

"I'm sure he'll be fine," I said, trying to reassure her. I'd heard people talk about heroin. I knew it was illegal, and I had a general idea of its dangers, but it didn't seem very real to me that someone I knew would really get in trouble with it.

Cynthia looked at the ground. I felt like giving her a hug, she seemed so sad. I looked at my watch. I would be late for work if I didn't hurry up.

"It'll be okay," I told her. "It's probably just for a while, then he'll pull out of it." I put my hand on her shoulder. She smiled at me, though her eyes looked like she might cry.

"Yes, you're probably right, love." She nodded in the direction I'd been walking. "Now, you should get going, or you'll be late for work." We said goodbye, and I rushed off, leaving her there under her own cloud on a bright summer day.

❀　❀　❀

As I settled into work that day, I kept thinking about Cynthia, about Tommy using heroin, and about what Cynthia had said about Tommy really not believing in his own talent. It was a slow day, and my boss had restocked the shelves before leaving. There were no customers in the store just then, so I sat on a stool behind the register and thought for a while. How could Tommy not see how talented he was when it seemed so obvious to the rest of us? I wondered. He always noticed if he missed a chord change, or plucked the wrong string. He believed in his mistakes, so he could see those, I surmised—but he didn't believe in his successes, and so was blind to them.

I remembered what I had written in my journal: "Every action requires a model." Perhaps, I thought, every perception required one, too.

I considered this for several minutes, as I kept an eye on a fly that was busy buzzing at the storefront window. It seemed to me that if we didn't have a model for something, we couldn't see it, or at least couldn't really get it and interpret it right. I thought about the first time I'd heard English. It was when Uncle Anbu came over with Aunt Mary for the first time, when I was about five years old. I remembered they made all these funny sounds, but I hadn't the knowledge needed to give those sounds meaning. I had no models of what those words were, or what they meant. I heard the sounds, but not the significance of them.

Likewise, Tommy could hear himself play, but he couldn't understand that those sounds meant he was good at what he did. He had no model that said he was good—only models pointing up the mistakes he made.

I picked up a newspaper from behind the counter, stepped over to the plate-glass window where the fly was buzzing around, and began trying to shoo the fly towards the open door. I was thinking that if we had no model for something, then we might experience the sensations connected to it—hear the sounds, or see the sights—like Tommy did his music, but we wouldn't really grasp what it was we were hearing and seeing until we had a model ready.

The fly flew up high on the window where I couldn't reach it, and I decided it would have to find its own way out. I sat back down behind the register and thought some more about how Tommy didn't hear what the rest of us heard when he played, because he lacked a model that the rest of us had.

Then I got it—the model *was* the perception. Tommy couldn't perceive what he didn't have a model for—he couldn't perceive his own talent—because *the model was the perception.* The model was the pattern around which our sensations and experiences register and come to life in our minds.

Without mental models to make sense of what our senses tell us, I thought, those sensations would seem to be made up of nothing more than random and meaningless fragments. The models we create allow such uninterpreted sensations to coalesce and take form in our minds as perceptions.

Conception give rise to perception, I thought. And if that was the case, then it wasn't surprising at all that Tommy didn't go off to London and become a success. He couldn't even picture, or believe in, that possibility, since he believed so firmly that he wasn't talented. He couldn't conceive of it, and so he couldn't perceive it, either.

I felt suddenly relieved that when I had desired an education, I had managed somehow to believe in that possibility for myself. I had held that image in my mind and believed in it, though no other girls from my village had gone to high school before me—and certainly not to college!

A customer came in and bought a loaf of bread and a small tin of preserved meat, then left. I watched the fly for a couple more minutes, then decided I should check more carefully to be sure the shelves were stocked. I found we were low on a few cans of green beans, and I got a box from the back of the store. I was remembering sitting on the plane as I flew to England the year before. I had come to the conclusion then that our beliefs shape our lives. Now I was concluding that our mental models did.

I tore open the box of canned green beans and set the older cans out of the way so I could put the new cans at the back of the shelf. I put one of the new cans on the shelf, then picked up another. What was the connection? I was wondering. Beliefs and models. I set the second can next to the first. Of course—beliefs *are* mental models—they're models of what's real, or rather, of what we think is real.

Tommy doesn't believe in his talent, I thought. He has no model that it's real.

I sat back on my heels. I remembered Jake telling me how the heroin made him feel good, like it feels to become warm after being cold a long time, but better, and that that was why he wanted to use it.

Tommy must feel pretty wretched most of the time, I thought—he feels his talent, his potential, his protolife, but he believes it can never come to life—because to him it isn't real. In his mind, he's trapped in a life where he feels promise, but can never give it life.

I put a couple more cans on the shelf. No wonder it felt worth the risk to him to get high, I thought. I remembered how worried Cynthia had seemed. I hadn't let myself focus on it until that moment, but suddenly I felt a twinge of fear for Tommy, and for the other fellows, as well. I was glad, at least, that Cynthia hadn't seemed worried about Jake and Pete. I hoped she was wrong about Tommy.

I moved the older cans back in front of the new, and closed up the box of canned green beans. I returned it to the back of the store, and as I did, I heard a customer come in. As I came back out front, I did my best to push my concerns from my mind.

I think I must have been more worried about Tommy in the days that followed than I wanted to admit, because I had a strange dream about him a couple of nights after that. In the dream I picked Tommy up, like you'd pick up a sleeping child, and I carried him, cradled in my arms, and set him down inside a box, turned on its side, big and pale orange, with doors that spread wide like the wings of a bird. Then I got inside the box with him, and the doors closed behind us.

❋   ❋   ❋

A week or so after I had that dream, I gave Jake a call, and we got together for what would turn out to be our last date. He seemed much himself, on the whole, though perhaps more irritable and impatient than usual. I told him about running into Cynthia and how worried she seemed about Tommy, and Jake told me emphatically how ridiculous that was. He was in one of his moods that evening, criticizing everything I said. We saw a movie at the local cinema, and I went home alone afterwards, telling myself that I should resist the impulse to contact him. More and more it was becoming clear to me that he wasn't good for me, but I was young and alone in a country that was not my own, and it was hard for me to let go of the attention he paid me, however inconsistent its tone.

One thing that was gradually becoming clear was that he didn't see me as I wished to see myself. Whenever I spent time around him, I felt I was swimming upstream, trying to remember to see myself in positive terms and not fall into seeing myself through the uneven view of his eyes. All that I'd been learning was teaching me that the view I had of myself, my own positive mental model of me, was important—and that I mustn't let Jake undermine that.

Late one muggy afternoon near the end of July, during the last hour or two of my shift at the food shop, I found myself thinking about going over to Jake's flat. I told myself what a bad idea that would be—I didn't want to see Jake—and I pushed the thought from my mind. But as I went about my duties, it kept coming up. As time passed, I found myself feeling some urgency about it, and that annoyed me, because I didn't like the idea of feeling dependent on Jake or, at this point in our relationship, of even actively wanting to see him. So I kept pushing the thought of going over to his flat aside. And it kept coming back up.

I actually felt pretty anxious to get there, but couldn't see why I should. I didn't really want to see Jake, did I? I hurried closing up the shop at the end of my shift, and then stepped out onto the pavement. The traffic streamed by, and the gathering dim of evening made the world seem open and broad. I turned my feet towards home—away from Jake's place— but as I walked along, something was gnawing at me. After a couple of blocks, I stopped. The impulse was still there, and just as insistent: *go to Jake's*. I sighed, stood still on the pavement, considering, then decided to let the impulse determine my course, and turned my steps back in the direction of Jake's flat.

As I neared his flat, I was aware of how anxious I felt to get there. The night air was cool, but I noticed myself sweating as I hurried along.

When I got to Jake's flat, I knocked. The windows were open in the flat above Jake's, and loud rock and roll music poured out of them, filling the nighttime air.

I waited for someone to answer the door, but no one did. A dim light leaked out around the curtains of Jake's flat. I stood for a minute thinking, then got out the key Jake had given me months earlier and let in.

"Hullo?" I called out as I entered the flat. No one was around. The door to Jake's room was ajar. Light spilled out from that room into the otherwise dark flat. I pushed the door open the rest of the way. Tommy and Pete were slumped down, sitting on the bed. Jake was in the arm chair under the window.

"Hello!" I said again, as I came in. Petie looked up and smiled a sort of wan half smile.

"Hi, Indira," he said vacantly. A candle had been left burning on the table next to the bed, even though the light was on in the room. Next to the candle I could see a blackened spoon, a syringe, and a small bag of white powder.

I stepped over to Jake, called his name as I pushed his shoulder. He seemed to be sleeping. A breeze blew the curtain back from the open window, and I could hear Janis Joplin's ragged voice singing, defiantly challenging someone to break another piece of her heart.

Jake opened his eyes slowly and looked up. "Hey, love. What're you here for?"

"Believe me, I don't know," I said, shaking my head. I looked around the room. Petie's head was beginning to nod forward. Tommy's chin was resting on his chest, where he sat slumped down next to the night table at the head of the bed. Something about the way he was bent over didn't look right.

"Tommy," I said. But he didn't look up. I stepped over to him, put my hand on his shoulder, shook him gently. Nothing.

"Tommy!" I said louder, shook him harder. All the talk I'd heard about heroin came flooding back over me.

"Hey, Jake, I can't wake up Tommy," I said. Jake made a little snorting laugh. Petie looked up at me blankly, then with gathering realization.

"Do you think something's wrong?" he asked finally, as I continued to shake Tommy and shout his name.

"How much stuff did you use?" I asked, looking at Pete.

"Not as much as the others. I'm smaller."

"And them?" I asked.

"More," Petie said. "Tommy said he wanted a good trip."

I bent over and shouted in Tommy's ear, "Tommy, wake up!" Still, nothing. I put my hand on his neck. I could barely feel a pulse.

"I'm ringing an ambulance," I told Petie, and stepped over to the phone on the little stand outside Jake's bedroom door.

Jake spoke up. "Naw, naw—don't do it. He'll be fine. He's just in a little deep."

"Yeah—just a *little*," I said, picking up the receiver. I dialed the operator and asked for the ambulance service. Jake became suddenly animate, stepped over and tried to take the receiver out of my hand. I held tight.

"Don't," he hissed, his voice low so it couldn't be heard over the phone. "They'll bring the fuzz. We'll all wind up in jail."

"*Your friend is dying,*" I said to him slowly. I was starting to tremble.

Jake looked shocked as the idea registered. He let go of the phone. I heard the ambulance service answer on the other end. I put the receiver back to my ear.

"A friend of mine's overdosed," I told her. "I can't wake him." She asked a question. "Heroin," I answered. Jake blew out the candle on the bedside table, scooped up the drug works and dropped them into a bag, then swept past me and out of the flat without giving me another look. I gave the woman on the phone the address.

Petie had gotten out of bed and was hovering over Tommy, trying to wake him. I hung up the phone and came over to Tommy, and Pete got out of my way. "Tommy," I said again. I slapped his face hard enough to sting. I hoped it would bring him round.

"What can I do?" Pete asked from behind me.

"There's nothing you can do. Get out of here. Jake's right, the police might come."

Pete grabbed up his jacket on his way out of the flat. The door closed loudly behind him. The place seemed suddenly very still. I wondered what to do, and stood staring at Tommy for several seconds as Janis Joplin's voice continued to filter down from the flat above. Then I got ice from the freezer and touched it to Tommy's neck. Surely, that would bring him around.

I was sitting on the bed next to Tommy with ice melting in my hand, with Tommy still passed out in front of me, when the ambulance arrived, its yawling voice falling to silence as it came to a stop outside the building.

I got up and let them in—two men in uniforms, carrying a stretcher. They checked Tommy's pulse and blood pressure, asked questions about him, but not about the others. They put him on the stretcher, put a blanket over him, then carried him to the ambulance, loaded him in. One man went up front to drive and the other got in the back with Tommy.

"Should I come along?" I asked.

"Yes," the man in the back answered. "Come on, get in." I climbed in after him, sat down, and turned back towards the doors, spread wide like wings. The man reached out and grabbed the handles, then pulled the doors closed behind us. The ambulance pulled out into traffic, its siren wailing. I was in a box with Tommy, and the doors had closed behind us.

❀   ❀   ❀

Tommy passed away later that night. There was only so much they could do for him.

The services were held in Tommy's home town of Gloucester. Cynthia got time off from work to go, but when I came by to see her a week or so later, her roommate told me she hadn't come back—that she had gone to stay at her mother's house for a while, in Bicester. As it worked out, I wouldn't see her again for months.

In truth, I was sort of relieved that Cynthia wasn't around, much as I cared for her and wished I could give her comfort while she dealt with Tommy's death. Maybe I felt guilty that I hadn't somehow reached Tommy in time. Maybe I just so wanted to leave behind the whole world Jake had introduced me to, and Cynthia was a part of that.

I worried for a long time after that, wondered if perhaps I had left work when I'd first begun to feel like I should go to Jake's, if somehow things would have been different. But how could I have known? I told myself. And yet, at some deeper layer of myself, I *had* known. I just hadn't been quite conscious of it.

❀   ❀   ❀

I remember one evening, late that September, closing up at the grocer's. I knew the job wouldn't last much longer, and I was looking forward to the start of the autumn term. I cashed up the till, and began sweeping up inside the shop, as the light outside took on the deep blue of evening. I had the radio on, and the station I had tuned in was playing the latest album by the Rolling Stones.

As I swept, I was thinking about how things had gone between me and Jake. After Tommy's death, I just hadn't wanted to be around him anymore, not after seeing how selfish he had been when Tommy had OD'd. I had ended it officially, then, although things were pretty well done between us before that. I'd been aware in the weeks that had passed since then, how little interest I had felt in the hippie fellows who came into the grocer's when I was at work. They reminded me of Jake, and I had the feeling I wanted to stay away from them, too, where a year earlier they had all seemed so attractive to me.

Now, with Jake gone from my life, I was realizing, I felt freed from the job of alternately accepting and resisting his attitudes towards me, and I had gradually become determined all over again to listen to the promise I felt in myself, to believe in it, and to try to make the way open for it to come through into my life. I was relieved to feel that sense of promise once again actively pulling me forward in my life.

I stepped outside to sweep off the pavement in front of the shop, and as I did, I thought some more about how much my image of hippie men had changed. I had thought of them as free and modern. I had thought their drug use meant they were enlightened. But now, after Jake, I saw them as lost and troubled. *My model of them had changed.*

I looked up from my sweeping and down the lane just as a dark figure dashed across the street in front of traffic. At first I thought it was a man, and he seemed foolish, aggressive to thrust his unarmored body out in front of the oncoming cars. But then I realized it was a young woman about my age, and the impression which registered in my mind abruptly changed. Suddenly she seemed daring, bold, unbounded by convention. She seemed—attractive.

I almost turned my attention away, but then I stopped and made myself notice. Why had I found this fleeting figure—which now had disappeared down a side street—so appealing? And why especially so when I thought it was female, and not male?

The Rolling Stones album ended with "Moonlight Mile." The radio announcer spoke for a moment, then Jimi Hendrix's sinewy guitar introduced "The Wind Cried Mary." I paused and leaned against the broom, staring down the empty pavement to the corner where the figure had disappeared, and replayed the image of her dashing across the street in my mind.

Two different models of who that person might be, what that gesture might mean, based on one difference: the sex that person was. From a man, I assumed that gesture was part of the macho ethic of the age— an unreasoning toughness, aggressive and artificially immune. From a woman I saw the gesture as meaning something else—a counterpoint to her presumed gentleness, a rounding out of qualities; a freeing gesture outside the convention of demure femininity; a gesture driven by passion; a breaking free.

I continued sweeping slowly, pondering. A man dashing across the street might have had exactly the same emotions I had imagined the woman as having, and yet I had imagined those feelings as being hers, and not part of the model I'd invented when I had seen the figure as a man. Male or female, my impressions were likely complete conjecture in any case. I wondered how much of the world, as we perceive it around us, was simply this: invention projected onto the world, built up out of prior experience, and prior assumptions.

It wasn't so different, I realized, than how my feelings about the whole hippie-image thing had changed since I had arrived in Oxford. I'd seen hippies as romantic, free. I had been convinced by this myth, and attracted to Jake, thinking he had all this to give to me, and that he would broaden my world. But he and his friends were not free. Rather, they seemed burdened by unenlightened views. I was glad to be done with the world they made together, and with Jake's attitudes towards me. As a result, the way I saw others in that subculture had changed, too, whether rightly or wrongly.

I finished sweeping off the stoop, put the broom away, and locked up for the night. As I started for home, I thought about the school term ahead. A cool breeze blew through town that evening, and I knew the seasons were soon to change. I had a feeling about the changes coming in my life as well. Whatever they were, I felt ready, prepared in my heart and mind. I felt as though the world lay before me, as though an opening would soon appear, and I would pass through it.

I turned a corner and stepped out into a fresh breeze, laced with the scents of the coming autumn. That wind was blowing something new towards me, I felt, and happily I hurried into it, ready to embrace whatever it was.

❋   ❋   ❋

"Pause," Paul said.

"Pausing. End of chapter," Kiki responded.

Some of what Paul had just heard had gotten him thinking. Now he wanted a chance to stop and reflect on it.

He looked out from beneath the tree at the top of the hill, where he'd been sitting, and took in the rolling hills around him and the view of Strandford in the valley below. As a physicist, the part of what he'd just listened to that most attracted his attention was the idea that Indira Kumar had somehow foreseen the future in anticipating her friend's death. Under normal circumstances, Paul would have disregarded such claims, but having heard the story in detail, he now pondered over whether there might, on a theoretical basis, be something to the idea that such perceptions were possible.

As a physicist—especially one involved in the exploration of extra-space-time travel—Paul was well aware of the concept of "block time," and of the often-repeated quotation of the great twentieth-century physicist, Albert Einstein. "The distinction between past, present and future" Einstein had written, "is only an illusion." Paul recalled that it was Einstein's Special Theory of Relativity that had first introduced this idea to physics—that all of time existed simultaneously, even if we only perceive it one moment at a time.

Paul leaned back against the rough bark of the live oak he sat beneath and recalled how he had, in his own college days, struggled to understand just what this quotation of Einstein's had meant. He remembered how he had turned the idea over and over in his mind, until finally he felt he was able to grasp it.

The way we experience time, he had told himself then, was like walking along a wall while blindfolded—a great, long, endless wall, as long as time itself.

Sitting in his dorm room, Paul had pictured himself walking along such a wall. As he walked beside it, he touched it with only one finger—trailing that finger along the side of the wall. He couldn't see the wall because of the blindfold he was wearing, but he could feel the wall's surface.

Or—more accurately—he could feel only one small part of it at a time—the part his finger was touching.

Just as with time in general, Paul had noted, the part of the wall he had already touched faded from his perceptions as soon as he was past it. Though he could remember it, he could no longer sense it. And yet, that part of the wall still existed, just as surely as it had when his finger was pressed against it.

In just the same way, the part of the wall he had not yet reached was already real—though he had not yet touched, or sensed, or experienced it. It was like the future—real somewhere out ahead of him, but not yet real in his experience.

After studying the concept of "block time" and coming up with this image of the way time worked, Paul had worried some about whether this all implied that the future was already set—solid and immovable, like the wall he had imagined.

But Paul was a busy student and time passed as he continued with his studies. Soon, he learned about Quantum Mechanics, and the many modern discoveries that had developed since its inception. Through these studies, Paul gradually came to understand that time was not so much like a wall, as like a waterfall—a great, wide waterfall, as wide as the wall he had imagined was long—but different from the wall, since the waterfall was constantly in motion.

Paul had imagined himself strolling along a walkway built in front of such a waterfall, holding his hand in the water as he went. The waterfall behind him continued to exist after he had passed his hand though it, just as the part up ahead was real before he reached it. But even so, the entire waterfall was constantly in motion, constantly changing—a vibrant, fluctuating, vital thing.

The waterfall was real, and changing, before he touched it. It was real, and changing, after he touched it. It was always real and changing—just like time itself.

Paul looked out across the countryside, which was bathed in afternoon sun. He wasn't accustomed to thinking that someone could perceive anything outside of the moment they were in, but Dr. Kumar's experiences made him curious. Perhaps she *had* been able to glimpse what lay ahead, he supposed—but if so, how?

What a curious thing, Paul mused to himself.

He considered this for a moment. After all, he thought, how big *is* the moment we are in?

"What do you think about this, Kiki?" he said aloud. "Might it be possible to perceive a little bit of what we normally think of as the future, if the moment we normally think of as the present is somehow stretched out, or expanded? I mean, how long *is* the present moment? A nanosecond? A second?

"If stretched out, somehow, couldn't it maybe become an hour, a day—a year? Could maybe our perception of the moment expand to include a bigger chunk of time—or at least expand in such a way as to get *impressions* of a bigger chunk of time?"

Paul imagined spreading his arms, as he faced the waterfall, and leaning into it—touching an area far broader than one hand alone could reach.

"I have no data on that subject," Kiki answered.

Paul laughed. "No, I suppose not."

It *was* a bit off their topic—memoir recitation—which was the only set of files Paul had purchased for Kiki to run.

But still, Paul enjoyed such theoretical musings. He would never have been able to develop his ideas about the possibility of extra-space-time travel had he not been willing to take the time for reflections such as these.

"Never mind, Kiki," Paul said, then got up and stretched. He was content to be done with the subject now, anyway. As much fun as it was to play with such ideas, Paul was often uncertain what to do with them afterward. They all became like toys left lying around—all of them, that is, except his extra-space-time travel theory. That one he had done everything he could to nurse along.

After that, Paul let his thoughts return to the process of building a new transport and making preparations for his return. The math he had worked out the night before seemed to support Interdimensional-Linking Theory, and he tried to assure himself that things would work out all right, if he chose to depend on it to get him home safely.

After a little while, Paul was aware of the sound of approaching footsteps and turned to look down the hill toward the lodge. It was Zaid, the little boy Paul had first seen in the kitchen the night before, when he'd been shelling peas with his older brother.

Zaid reached the top of the hill. "My father said to come tell you you were supposed to be out of the room by three o'clock and that it's almost four," he said.

Paul took a close look at the boy for the first time; he stood about one and a quarter meters high, had dark straight hair and dark eyes. His skin was the color of the bare earth.

"All right," Paul said. "Thanks for letting me know. I'll come get my stuff."

Paul stood up and started down the hill, slowing his pace to make it easy for Zaid to keep up.

"Did you walk all the way here?" Zaid asked.

"Yes."

"Where from?"

"Strandford."

Zaid scurried along beside him. "Are you going to sleep outside?"

"Yeah, that's the plan, after this."

They continued on down the hill, with Zaid peppering Paul with questions: "Do you like to walk?" "How far is it?" "What's your name?" and so forth. Paul got to his room, still answering Zaid's questions patiently, and packed up the few things he'd taken from his pack.

"Why don't you go tell your father that I'm out of the room," he said to Zaid. He hoisted his pack over one shoulder, then quietly closed the door to his room behind them. Zaid took off running, which made Paul smile. Children!

Paul went and sat under a tree several meters away and went back to thinking about the new transport he would build and what it would take to get him safely home.

In a few minutes, Zaid returned and stood near Paul.

"My father says he may want to leave a little early and to ask you where he will find you."

"I'll be here," Paul said.

Zaid ran off again, then returned a few minutes later and stood nearby. Paul looked over at him. It occurred to Paul that there weren't a lot of other kids nearby for Zaid to play with.

"Do you like sleeping outside?" Zaid asked. Paul wondered how many more questions he could possibly have.

"Sometimes yes, sometimes no," Paul answered, thinking that he'd been pretty full of questions, himself, lately, but had had no one to ask them of— many of them about odd little things that any adult would have considered common knowledge. Maybe, he thought, he could ask Zaid some questions of his own.

"Do you like living underground?" Paul asked.

The boy shrugged. "I guess."

"Do most people live underground, now?"

"I don't know. Some. Some, they don't."

Paul nodded. "I've seen a lot of people wearing patches on their clothes," Paul said, thinking of the people at Anna and Marco's house and about the man he met on the trail the day before. "Why do people wear patched cloths—is there a depression?"

"A depression?" Zaid said. "Are they depressed?"

"No," Paul said. "I'm talking about an economic depression."

"Oh," the boy said.

Paul sighed. He hadn't spent much time around kids since he was one himself. "I mean, are they poor? Don't they have enough money for new clothes?"

Zaid frowned. "Why would they want new clothes if they have enough clothes?"

"Rather than having old, patched-up clothes? If you have holes in your clothes, wouldn't you want new ones without holes?" Paul asked.

Zaid shrugged. "Everything we take means life to something else," the boy answered, singing out the words as though they formed a much-repeated phrase.

Paul felt exasperated. It was a simple enough question, wasn't it? "What do you mean, Zaid?"

The boy stared at Paul with a look that suggested he thought Paul, perhaps, was strangely simpleminded. "Don't you know where clothes come from?" he said to Paul.

For a moment, Paul didn't answer. How do you reply, when someone else is making no sense at all?

The boy looked at his fingers and began counting off something he clearly had had to recite before. "Cotton and hemp comes from plants. Wool comes from sheep. Syn-thet-ics," he said, drawing the word out, "comes from plants, too, and from minerals and other things—and *everything* comes from the Earth, where all the plants and animals live, too. When we use the land or re-sour-ces, or the sunlight they need, then they can't live because we took it first."

The boy stopped there and stared at Paul as though he thought this answered Paul's question.

Beside the fact that this seemed to be something the boy had studied—probably in school, Paul thought—Paul was having trouble making sense of his reply.

"And so you patch your clothes instead of buying new ones...," Paul prompted.

"Because other things need to live, too. It's wrong to take what you don't need, because other people and other creatures need things, too. *Everything we take means life to something else,*" the boy said emphatically, much as another child might if Paul had suggested depriving a pet of food or water—after all, some things are just wrong.

"Okay, okay. Good answer," Paul said, placating the boy. "You're right, every living thing needs resources to live. It's wrong to take the resources they need if you don't really need them yourself."

And that was another difference between his world and this, Paul observed, to himself. Certainly no other child Paul had ever known would have made the sort of explanation this child had learned to give.

It seemed to Paul this was an exceptional opportunity to safely ask questions that he might not feel comfortable asking another adult. After all, what did it matter if this child thought he was odd? (In fact, Paul noted, what did it really matter if anybody thought so? It wasn't like people were going to figure out he was from another world—and even if they did, do what, then? Send him home?)

Paul remembered the response he'd gotten the day before, when he'd asked the woman—whom he'd taken to be Zaid's mother—if this land was hers. It was clear it seemed strange to her that he would even ask.

Paul pointed toward the hill with the door over which hung the welcome sign for the lodge. "Is that your family's home?" he asked the boy.

Zaid looked where Paul was pointing. "Yeah," he answered.

"Does your family own all this land around here?" Paul asked.

The boy gave Paul a funny look. "No. Nobody owns the land," he said.

"Nobody owns it?" Paul said.

The boy looked at him kind of strangely. "Nobody can own another living thing," he said.

"The land's not alive," Paul said.

Zaid frowned. "Some parts aren't—but other parts are. And the parts that are can't live without the parts that aren't—so, Mom says, they're not really separate."

"Huh," Paul said. "So nobody owns anything that's living?"

"Nothing that's living can own anything else that's living, 'cuz everything that's living owns itself," the boy said definitively.

Paul thought about it a moment. "So, if I said to your family 'I want to live here now, so you have to move,' would you have to go—if you don't own this land?" he asked, as gently as possible so as not to distress Zaid.

"No!" the boy said, surprised at the question. He squinted his face and cocked his head. "You don't have a re-la-tion-ship with it. We live here. We belong here." His tone had a sort of "don't you know this?" quality.

Paul rubbed his jaw with one hand.

Zaid took a deep breath and said, "People used to believe in right of do-min-ion. Now they don't. They use right of re-la-tion-ship. Living things don't own living things anymore."

"Why is that?" Paul asked. He wondered how much he could get this little boy to tell him about this world and the attitudes in it.

Zaid seemed frustrated. He picked up a small pebble and threw it, then collected himself. Paul thought that Zaid must consider him a especially thick-headed adult.

"My teacher said people used to believe in right of do-min-ion. They would buy land and never even go there, and then they would *cut down all the trees* and *kill everything on it*, just to make *money*. People who live on land, who have a re-la-tion-ship with it," Zaid said carefully, "would *never* do that."

"Why not?" Paul pressed.

"Just like, just like—you would never kill your family, would you?—or your cat or dog, because you have a re-la-tion-ship with them. And you can't take kids away from their families, but their families don't *own* them." Zaid seemed interested in trying to convey this to Paul, but also puzzled at his lack of understanding.

"Oh, I think I see," Paul said. "You have a right of relationship not to be separated from your family—or your land?"

Zaid frowned a little and nodded.

"But you don't have dominion over them," Paul added, somewhat to himself. "You don't *own* them.

"You learned this in school?" Paul said to Zaid.

Zaid nodded.

"Interesting," Paul said. He thought about the herd of elk he'd seen when staying with Marco and Anna. What was it Marco had said about them, when Paul had asked if he was afraid they would trample the field? Something about the field being designed for them, too—and that the land was "as much theirs as ours."

Paul wondered how far that herd roamed, and if everywhere people responded to it—and other herds—the same way.

It occurred to Paul that this wouldn't be possible on his world for any number of reasons—including that everything would be fenced off, and the herd wouldn't be able to go anywhere. But Paul didn't remember see-ing a single fence since he'd come to this world. He recalled something his grandfather had told him, years before—that fences were one of the many reasons so many animals had gone extinct, because they couldn't get where they needed to go to find the food that they needed, or to move with the seasons.

"Do you know what a fence is?" Paul asked the boy. He figured if he hadn't seen any here, maybe the boy wouldn't have ever seen any, either.

Zaid looked thoughtful. "That's when you put something really long in the way to stop you from going where you want to go?"

Well, at least he had the concept, Paul thought. "Have you ever seen one?"

Zaid shook his head. "They took them down."

"Why?"

Zaid shrugged and tilted his head a little.

Paul nodded. "How long ago? Where? Everywhere?"

"I don't know. I think maybe because of the buffalo?" Zaid said.

"The buffalo? You mean bison? How come did they take the fences down?"

"There got to be more and more of them, and they needed to eat, and other things needed to eat. Yeah, I think that's when they took the fences down. And now there are big, big, big, big bunches of them again," Zaid smiled, and spread his arms wide. "They go everywhere."

Bison! Paul thought. Was it true that there were huge herds of bison in this world, roaming free?!

"Hey, are you ready?" Paul heard a voice beside him say. He looked up and saw Zaid's father standing near him with a friendly look on his face.

"Yeah, I'm all set," Paul said. He stood up. "Thanks for the visit, Zaid," Paul said to the boy.

"The SPV's just over here," Zaid's dad said. Paul followed as they started in that direction. Zaid followed after them.

The "SPV," it turned out, was one of the kind of vehicle Paul had seen parked outside of Anna and Marco's place the night of the party. It was sleek and narrow, with room enough for two passengers, one behind the other. The outside was coated in what Paul took to be some kind of solar-absorbent material—and so Paul assumed the vehicle ran on some kind of solar power—but there were also pedals inside that the occupants could use.

Zaid's dad picked him up and gave him a big hug. "I'll probably be home in time to tell you good night, tonight. You be good and do what your mom tells you, okay?" He gave the boy a kiss on the cheek, set him down, then turned and opened the side panel of the SPV, which lifted at a hinge in the roof and gave access to the interior.

Paul threw his pack into the rear then got into the passenger seat. "What do you do if you have to go somewhere with the whole family?" Paul asked, as Zaid's father got in ahead of him.

"Bye, Zaid," the father said.

"Bye, Dad," Zaid answered.

"Bye," Paul added.

"We have a bigger model, too, which seats four," the man said, as he closed the side door. Paul could hear it as he started some sort of motor, which hummed quietly, and in a moment they were out on the open road, rolling quickly along. Ahead of him, Paul could see the man was turning the pedals at his feet with what appeared to be casual ease. Paul put his feet on his pedals, as well, and began turning them. It certainly didn't take much effort, considering the speed the vehicle was getting as they climbed the hill.

"This, ah, SPV—it runs on solar power, right?" Paul asked, emboldened in asking what might be silly questions by his success with Zaid.

"Yeah," the man answered.

"So what are the pedals for? Is the solar power not sufficient?" Paul asked, aware that they were not contributing much of the energy being used by the SPV right then, as they speedily climbed the hill.

"In most cases, it's enough, but sometimes, on an overcast day or a long trip, it runs a little low. It's a good idea to do a bit of the work and help keep the battery charged," the man answered.

Paul considered this for a moment. If this world depended mostly on solar power and kept their power use low with efficient machines, and pedal-power, and such—it worried Paul that he might never find the high-voltage power he would need to run the transport.

But then, just because some systems were efficient in this way, it didn't mean that they didn't have other, more energy-intensive industries, as well, Paul told himself, trying to calm his worries.

"And of course," the man went on, "people can't just hand all of their work over to machines, can we, or we'd get sick and die young, just like they used to do in the old days." He had the tone people have when making idle conversation. "Machines to *save* effort, machines to *make* effort—or to make exercise, that is. And I remember my grandmother telling me, often they would go unused, anyway—the machines designed to make effort—because work for work's sake isn't much fun. I learned a lot from her. Better to put your effort into what matters, something you can get some satisfaction out of doing—like getting you someplace you want to go—and not have so many machines."

"I guess all those machines were pretty hard on the planet," Paul said, thinking about how things still were in his world.

"Yeah—they just end up taking resources that could mean life to something else—and for what, really?"

Both of them fell silent for several moments then, as they pedaled along. Paul found the amount of effort he was expending satisfying but not strenuous. Not a bad way to live, he thought. He'd been wondering from the start why it was that the solar vehicles he'd seen at Anna and Marco's house had had pedals inside—and why Anna had used a hand saw when she obviously had access to more complex technology. Paul wondered if she had the same philosophy as Zaid's father. Perhaps it was common here.

"Yeah, over all, I guess we're a lot better off being focused on connection, rather than consumption. Seems like life must have been kind of sad, in the old days," Zaid's father added. "So many people alone with their machines."

Indeed, Paul thought, as he watched the land roll by—people alone with their machines, or their implants, or their isolated, virtual worlds.

After about half an hour spent riding up a long, steep hill, they crested the top and found themselves on level ground, with a breathtaking view of the countryside spread out to the south. Not long after that, Zaid's father pulled over to the side of the road.

"There's your trail," he said to Paul, as he pushed open the side panel of the SPV.

"Thanks for the ride," Paul said, grabbing his pack and climbing out.

"Glad to get you up that hard climb," the man answered.

"I hope you enjoy your dinner with your friends," Paul said as he stepped away. "And thanks again."

"Glad to do it. Hope you enjoy your sojourn," the man said, then closed the door and pulled out onto the road again—leaving Paul suddenly alone in a world nearing twilight.

As Paul stepped away from the main road and started up the wide, clearly marked trail, he took in the scene around him. They had gained enough altitude on the ride up to rise above the habitat of the live-oak trees Paul had found himself amid since his arrival in this world. In their place was a strange, tall, straight-trunked tree with slender green leaves the shape of needles.

Paul stepped off the trail and reached up to examine the leaves on one of the smaller trees. A remarkable scent—sharp and pleasing—filled the air around him. Paul remembered his grandfather telling him about such needle-leafed trees. They had carpeted much of the higher altitudes of North America before the time of climate change. As the weather had warmed, the climates of those areas had dried, Paul's grandfather had said, and the trees had dried also. As they became stressed for water, they became more susceptible to insect attack—much as people are more likely to get sick when their physical needs are not met.

That was when an epidemic infestation of bark beetles began. The beetles ate and burrowed their way into the trees' inner bark, carrying a fungus that blocked the flow of sap and killed the tree—thus creating the habitat the beetles needed for reproduction.

In addition to drying the forests, climate change had brought warmer winters. As a result, instead of being killed off by the cold each winter, the bark beetles just kept on eating. Soon the mountain sides, once carpeted with the beautiful green pines, were spotted with more and more dead and dying trees. Year after year, the infestation continued—having been provided the perfect opportunity through climate change. It took only a few decades for those once-great forests to be lost. Paul had never so much as seen one of those needle-leafed trees—until now.

Paul picked up a bundle of the narrow, green leaves, which had dropped to the ground. He cradled them in his hand, then pressed his nose against them and took in the aroma. He felt deeply touched, like someone else might feel when discovering a family heirloom, or a great work of art that they thought had been lost forever.

If only Granddad could see this! Paul thought.

He turned and looked around him. Everywhere he looked, there were pine trees!

Paul stood amid the pines for several minutes, taking in the fact of them, then told himself he didn't have time to spend being enchanted with the successes of this new world. Another world awaited his return, even if its inhabitants didn't yet realize it themselves.

Paul took a deep breath of the cool, pine-scented air and looked around once more, then reminded himself again that he now had an unprecedented opportunity to make a real difference in his world—just as he had been promising himself he would do since he was in his teens. He had worked hard in pursuit of this goal ever since. He couldn't, he told himself, begin wasting time now. He needed what the Kumaric Retreat could offer—and to take advantage of that, he had to be familiar with Dr. Kumar's memoirs before he arrived. After all, he hadn't gotten so far in life by permitting himself to become distracted—even if those distractions were as wonderful as discovering a living pine forest!

Paul dropped the pine needles he still held cupped in his hand and adjusted his pack. Then he stepped back on the path and continued along it toward the Retreat.

"Kiki, please resume recitation," he said. As her voice lifted up into the clear, scented air, Paul strode forward through the long, slanting shadows of living trees.

◙   ◙   ◙

CHAPTER III

When my thought absorbs yours, a world begins.

—ADRIENNE RICH

Michaelmas Term, in the autumn of 1971, began very quietly for me. As I had moved beyond the introductory course work of my first year of college, I began to find my studies of more interest, and I was, that autumn, more focused on my work than I had been the year before.

In particular, I was enjoying my readings in Sociological Theory and Social Anthropology. I remember handing in a paper for my tutorial on "Social Anthropology of the South Pacific," which compared and contrasted island cultures of Melanesia with those of Polynesia. In the paper, I explored the interplay between culturally held beliefs about identity, and how the people in these cultures experienced and defined their own selfhoods.

When it came time to discuss my essay with my tutor, she so closely questioned the details of my argument that at first I thought her quite displeased with it. But as the discussion went on, it occurred to me that her tone was not so much critical as interested. So I relaxed and enjoyed the conversation and the chance to share my ideas with another interested party. After this experience, I began to think about what an exciting field social anthropology would be to do research in, and how good it would be to share that work with colleagues who had interests like my own.

It was satisfying for me, also, to see how readily my fledgling ideas concerning the central role of beliefs in human culture could be illustrated by a discussion of the beliefs and culture of a specific region. I had been aware when choosing to do my reading in Human Sciences that the requirements for that degree included many courses that sounded interesting to me, but I now began to realize that my strongest interests lay within the area of social anthropology, and that I might like to make a career in that field.

Writing that paper that autumn held another significance for me, as well. Because of it, I began to think again about the importance of beliefs, and how they not only shaped the smaller elements of our cultural practices, but influenced, as well, the sort of world we collectively made, overall. It seemed to me that beliefs were extremely important, and yet we absorbed them from one another without paying much attention to how they were passed along, or actively considering whether we accepted or rejected any given belief.

It was clear to me, from the readings I'd done for my courses in social anthropology, that beliefs were passed along within a culture in many ways. Sometimes they were shared as concepts that parents explain to their children: for example, religious beliefs, or beliefs about what is proper or inappropriate behavior. But there were also more subtle ways beliefs were shared or spread within a culture. A nod of approval might indicate that a specific behavior was accepted or encouraged—believed to be good—without anything ever being said outright. Likewise, a person might offer an explanation for how some specific event came to pass, and that explanation might have embedded within its folds basic beliefs about the nature of the world. And these ideas would then be picked up by others and passed along, as well.

I remember sitting in my room in the Main Building, my chair turned so I could look down from my window and see the trees, which had just begun to show their autumn colors, in the gardens below. I was trying to decide if the process of accepting new beliefs had worked in my life as it had been described in my readings.

Specifically, I thought about contexts in which I had been exposed to the beliefs other people held. I had certainly become aware of beliefs held in common amongst Jake's friends, for example, pretty quickly after making their acquaintance. I remembered Cynthia explaining to me which clothes were hip and which were not, for example, and the look of approval on the others' faces when I had shown up dressed in the clothes Cynthia had recommended. It seemed that I had become aware of and accepted new beliefs through exactly the same social pathways my school books had described. But as I thought about it, it seemed to me that something more was involved in that exchange, something subtler. It seemed to me I had *felt* how Jake had seen me and had *sensed* attitudes of his—attitudes which had colored my world, though we had never directly communicated about them. Perhaps I had sensed something like that from Cynthia, Tommy, Pete, and Hollie, as well.

Only a few weeks earlier, I had heard the word "zeitgeist" used for the first time. I'd been told it was a German word and that it meant "spirit of the age." The person who had used it, an acquaintance of mine from my Human Ecology class, used it in reference to the youth movement which had begun in much of Western culture in the 1960s, and which was, then, just beginning to wane. He'd said how there was "something in the air," and how everyone could feel it. As I sat staring out my dorm window, I thought about that and wondered if it was true.

The window was open just a bit, and I could hear a soft rustling as the breeze passed through the trees outside. As I listened to the sound, my thoughts began to drift. I found myself thinking about the night I'd been at Jake's flat, when he had gotten mad and thrown a book. I was confident I had picked up impressions from him then, concerning the story he'd been thinking of writing, and I remembered thinking at the time about how that might work. I had imagined us all being like radio transceivers, broadcasting electromagnetic waves, while at the same time picking up electromagnetic signals that others sent out.

I wondered what it would feel like if many people were simultaneously focused on similar ideas or beliefs. I imagined such thoughts being "broadcast" by many people all at once, being picked up by others and rebroadcast, and being amplified, in a sense, through that process. What would it feel like to be in the midst of that? I wondered. If this effect was widespread enough, might someone have the impression that he or she was sensing "the spirit" of their age?

I leaned forward in my chair. My room was on the second floor of my dorm and, looking down, I could see students crossing through the gardens below. They were dressed so differently from how people their age would be dressed in India, yet so right for England. I dressed like them now. I thought about Jake, again. I remembered him throwing his book that night. What had gotten him so upset? I tried to recall. Oh yes, I'd said something about archetypes. I'd said that maybe we collectively create them out of a shared focus.

I smiled at the idea. It fit rather nicely with the thoughts I'd just been having about how the spirit of an age might be developed and spread. I wondered absently if perhaps, apart from Jake's distress, I had been right about archetypes.

Out my window, I noticed a young woman strolling across the garden. She was dressed in brown bell-bottom jeans and a bright yellow and orange shirt. So colorful—she reminded me of one of the trees! I rested my head against the window pane. I was still thinking about Jake, remembering how forcefully he'd thrown that book, the loud "thwack" it had made as it had hit the wall. What had Jake said? Oh yes, something about how backward I was, and how little I understood about Jung's ideas.

I leaned back in my chair, shook my head. I still felt annoyed, remembering it. But I had to admit he was right about one thing—I certainly didn't know much about Jung's ideas.

A week or so later, I was crossing campus when I noticed a flier someone had posted. It announced a talk by a visiting lecturer discussing Carl Jung—specifically, his ideas on archetypes and the collective unconscious. I made a note of the time and location and decided I would go.

When the date came around, I had to admit that I was disappointed in the lecture. Most of the time was spent discussing specific archetypes, and nothing at all was said about the source the archetypes were supposed to be derived from. I felt my understanding of the "collective unconscious" had been enhanced very little, as well.

But what made up for all of this was seeing a familiar face in the crowd—it was the woman I had met on the train when I had first arrived at Oxford the year before. I knew that if it had not been for her and her kind gift of the Rumi book, I would probably never have taken the poetry class the winter before, and my life would have been very different in many ways.

I was a few rows behind her, but I had seen her when she'd come in and sat down just before the lecture's start. As the lecturer had droned on about the "mother" archetype, and the "wise old man" archetype, and the various forms they might take, I thought about the book she'd given me and the importance that simple, kind gesture had had in my life—how welcoming it had been, and what interesting developments it had led to.

When the lecture was done, there was a brief question and answer period, and then we all got up to leave. I slipped between the chairs in the rows ahead of me and lightly touched her on the shoulder. As she turned around, she had that same warm and open look on her face that had made such an impression on me the year before.

I smiled and said, "Hello. I don't know if you'll remember me, but we met on the train, a little over a year ago. You gave me a book, and I want..."

Before I could even finish getting this out, she was saying that she did remember me. I thanked her for the book and told her how much I'd enjoyed it. She seemed quite pleased. We introduced ourselves again. Her name was "Laura." I think I'd almost remembered that. The room was emptying out around us, and we moved with the throng till we stood on the steps outside, where Laura asked me which way I was heading. I told her to my dorm, at St Hugh's.

"Well, good," she said. "It's LMH for me—what do you say we walk together?"

I was happy to agree. We stepped out under a soggy sky on that brisk, autumn night, and as we set off towards my dorm, Laura asked me what I thought of the lecture we'd just heard. I told her what questions I'd been hoping to have answered, and that I'd been disappointed.

"Yeah, I guess if that's what you'd been hoping for, you'd have to feel let down," she answered.

"What did you think?" I asked, as we walked along.

"It was a good change of pace. I'm reading Theology, you see. I'd really like to learn about lots of different religions, but the program here is mostly focused on the Western tradition, the Judeo-Christian tradition, that sort of thing. It's a bit narrow."

"Oh," I said. "What will you do? Will you continue to read Theology?"

"Oh, yes, I think I'll stick it out. I see it as sort of a first step. I've been thinking I'd like to go on to graduate school after this and study comparative religions."

I told her I had begun to think about future studies, as well, and we talked about that and many other subjects as we strolled along, listening to one another's voices and to the wind through the trees.

It seemed no time at all before we had arrived at my dorm, and Laura was asking me which one was my room. I told her and then asked where she lived, before saying good night. I thought it was nice that she had walked the whole way with me, and as I started up the steps to my room, I thought how smart and kind she seemed and how much I hoped we would become fast friends.

Laura and I began studying together pretty regularly after that. It was a casual thing; one of us would just show up at the other's room, and we'd talk for a while and then get to work. I remember coming by Laura's room one afternoon to study with her, but her roommate told me she had taken her books and gone to study in University Parks just south of Lady Margaret Hall, near the little pond that lay along the bank of the River Cherwell.

It was an unusually bright autumn day, I remember, with a clear blue sky. I crossed LMH's sunny green and entered the shade of the trees that bordered the north side of the park, trying to guess just where Laura might be found. It was that rare moment in autumn when the world seems filled with vibrant color. The ground was littered with gold and yellow leaves, while the trees still seemed filled with them.

I paused under a particularly tall and sweeping elm and looked at the wide green of the park. Laura wouldn't likely be out there, I reasoned— the trees were just too sparse. I looked back at the trees I'd just passed beneath and then over towards the pond. I couldn't see Laura anywhere, and wondered if she might, perhaps, have come and then left already. Just then I heard a rustling from above, as though branches were being shaken, and looked up just in time to find a shower of golden leaves tumbling down around me, followed by a delighted laugh from above. As the falling leaves cleared, I looked up amongst the interwoven branches and caught a glimpse of Laura's red hair and green jersey.

"Hey!" I called out, and before I knew it, Laura had jumped to the ground beside me.

I looked around in surprise. "What were you doing up there?" I asked.

"Studying," she said.

"Studying," I echoed, looking up into the tangle of branches.

"Sure. Sometimes when I just can't stand to read another word, it helps to find a new place to work." She reached up and grabbed a branch. "It's nice up there, and it's a warm day. Won't you join me?"

I watched as she pulled herself up, then stood for a moment, glancing around the meadow.

"Come on up," she called down to me. I hesitated, then wondered why I hesitated. Then I climbed up after her.

Spending time with Laura was like that. There were always surprises. She had a fresh way of looking at things, and she pretty much always did what made sense to her. Usually the things she did made sense to me, too, if I thought about them a little. I liked the way the world felt with her in it—bigger, with more possibilities.

I was happy a lot that autumn, with Laura around. She was generous with her possessions and with her ideas, and much as she had her own way of looking at things, she always seemed interested, and listened closely, when I talked about my thoughts. In truth, there was something in the quality of her presence that pleased me and made me feel better aligned with my own world. I continued to find her presence comforting then, as I had on the train the year before. It's hard to say just what it was, but I can say that there was something about her confidence that gave me confidence, and that somehow, the broadness of her world broadened mine. I liked very much having her around.

Near the end of Michaelmas Term, Laura suggested we take a break and spend a couple of days in London. We could stay with her parents, she said, and she could show me the town. Laura had an eye for the surprising and new, and when she couldn't find anything that was surprising and new to her, she delighted in introducing new things to me. So we made plans to go the first weekend in December, as soon as the term came to an end.

A few days before we were due to leave, I went into the city center to pick up a thing or two I wanted for the trip. As I was coming out of a shop, I saw Cynthia walking up the street under a brightly colored umbrella, beneath a dense gray sky, in the falling rain.

I watched her for a moment, before waving my arm and calling out to get her attention. We hadn't seen each other in some time, not since before Tommy's death.

"Cynthia!" I yelled. She turned my way, then smiled when she saw me.

"Indira!" she answered happily, and dashed into the doorway of the shop I was just leaving. We embraced.

"I haven't seen you in such a long time," I said. "I've been wondering how you were."

"Me too, love," she answered, closing her umbrella. "How have you been?"

I looked at her. She seemed a bit wearier than perhaps she once had, but good all in all. "I'm fine," I told her, and cocked my head, hoping she would answer my question.

"I'm in a bit of a rush right now, love, but why don't we meet for lunch soon and get all caught up?" she said. She suggested we meet in one of

the pubs in North Oxford, the Rose and Crown, and I told her sure, that
would be fine.

"All right then. I'm working this weekend, but maybe Monday, around
noon? You don't have any tutorials then?" she asked.

"No, the term just ended. But I'm going to London this weekend. I think
I should be back by then, but I'm just not sure. Maybe I could call you
when I get back?"

"Oh, what fun, London," she said brightly. "Well, okay—so, why don't
you ring me up when you get in, and we'll see how that'll work?"

"Okay. Are you at the same number?" I asked.

"No, let me give you my new one. But don't call too early—my new bloke
works the night shift."

"You've got a new fellow, eh?" I said, curious.

"Yes," she answered. She hung her umbrella on her arm and dug out
a scrap of paper and a pen from her handbag. "I met him when I was
back in Bicester. I wanted to come back to Oxford, and he came with me."
Cynthia wrote out her number and handed me the piece of paper. "His
name is Henry."

"So, you're sharing a place?" I asked, glancing at the number, then slipping the piece of paper into my bag.

Cynthia smiled that little girl smile of hers. "Oh, please don't be shocked.
It's really quite natural. The birds and the bees do it," she giggled. I was
glad to see she was her old self, after Tommy's death and all.

"Oh, I'm not shocked," I said, and smiled. I was glad to see her. "I'll give
you a call when I get back from London, then?"

"Sure, love. We'll have lunch, eh? Maybe Monday? It's so good to see you,
Indira. I've missed you." She gave me a quick kiss on the cheek, opened
her umbrella, and was off, her bright red boots sloshing through the water
that had showered down from the clouds above.

Laura's parents lived in a grand old house in Chelsea, the same house
Laura and her sisters had grown up in. Laura told me on the train on the
way to London that her parent's had bought the house together as a young
couple after the end of World War II. It had been a good price, and they
had, themselves, repaired some damage to the roof that had come as a
result of the blitz. In those days, Laura told me, the area had had a quiet
bohemian character, but the district had evolved since then, and was now
quite the fashionable place to live. Laura seemed to think this amusing,
as apparently she didn't consider her parents to be the sort to care much
for fashion. In fact, she said, her parents were somewhat radical, and had
often shocked or surprised her friends with things they'd said while she
was growing up. She said she hoped I wouldn't be bothered, then added,
"They're really quite harmless, you know."

The train ride to London passed quickly, and it was still morning when
we arrived that Saturday at Laura's childhood home. Nonetheless, I had
had time to worry on the way in about what this weekend would be like,

staying with Laura's parents and being unsure how they would behave. But I needn't have been concerned. Laura's mother seemed gentle and sweet, had a marvelous collection of books of every sort, and would occasionally make off-handed comments about how mistaken the government was in one or another of its social policies. Her father also seemed a gentle soul. He grew his hair longer than most men of his age, liked to cook, and welcomed me into the household like one of his own.

We had a wonderful time that first day, beginning with a family picnic at Kensington Gardens, for which two of Laura's sisters joined us, and ending with a quiet, home-cooked meal. Laura's parents did their best to cook a traditional Indian dinner, which I felt sure was mostly for me. I had the impression that Laura had told them I was homesick for the foods I'd grown up with, but had no way to cook them myself inside my dorm room.

The dinner, while not quite the same as home, was delicious, and I was delighted to have met these kind people. Laura, who'd clearly been a little concerned about how I would mesh with her family, seemed both pleased and a little amazed as she watched me talking like old friends with her parents about this thing and that, from my life back home in India, to the travels her parents had taken in their youths.

Later that night, Laura and I went for a walk along the Thames. I remember standing with her, looking over the railing into the water below the embankment. The reflection of the lights above our heads danced in the small waves kicked up by passing boats. It was cold out, but I was wrapped up warm, and I felt more content than I had in a long time.

Laura and I slept, that night, in the room she had shared with one of her sisters while growing up. We were on twin beds, separated only by a small bedside table, and after we turned off the lamp and settled into bed, with just a little light coming in through the window from the street lamp outside, Laura reached over and squeezed my hand, and told me how delighted she was to have me there with her, and to be able to share that part of her life with me. I squeezed her hand back, and we didn't let go until I had nearly drifted off to sleep. Then I felt her slip her hand from mine and heard her settle in amongst the covers of the bed on which she lay. I fell asleep thinking how lucky I was to have a friend like Laura.

The next morning Laura was full of plans for what she would like to show me around London. We had a quick breakfast of porridge and cream, then packed a lunch for later in the day. We left early and wandered down towards the river, with Laura pointing out sights along the way—the homes of her childhood friends, a house Karl Marx had lived in briefly, and the stylish businesses which were still springing up along King's Road.

When we got down to the river, we stopped off at a houseboat to see some old friends of Laura's parents, who were like an aunt and uncle to Laura. As it turned out, only the woman was home, but she let us in and was clearly delighted to see Laura. We sat in the cozy cabin of the houseboat and drank tea, listening to the frigid waters of the Thames lapping up against the boat outside. The woman, Kate, and her husband were soon to embark on their annual journey south. This year they would probably winter-over in Italy, but in the past they had sometimes gone much further, and had once spent the winter in Bombay. Indeed, some of the throw pillows, which added to the cabin's cozy feel, were covered in Indian cloth. It was strange for me to see these signs of home displaced, in a houseboat floating on the cold waters of an English river. But I was beginning to get used to this feeling, when I spent time with Laura, that the usual boundaries for my world did not apply, and that more was always possible.

After saying goodbye to Kate, we boarded a bright-red double-decker bus, and wound though the busy streets, past the grand old buildings of London, and began a day of sight-seeing. First off we went to Westminster Abby, against the grandeur and beauty of which I felt dwarfed, but within the hollow interior of which every whisper and footfall was made large. From there we strolled past the Houses of Parliament, and Laura told me about how, only a few decades before, when women were still trying to get the vote in England, suffragettes had chained themselves to the wrought-iron grille of the Ladies Gallery in the House of Commons and called down to the members, trying to convince them that women should be awarded the right to vote. They were ordered to be removed, Laura said, but as the women had locked themselves to the grille, nothing could be done until the grille itself could be wrenched from the surrounding stone!

"And so those women insured their voices would be heard," she told me. "But not without a cost. They were all carried off to prison afterwards." We paused, and I looked up at the building, trying to imagine the scene, and the passion those women must have felt for their cause.

We spent perhaps the next hour wandering through the city, past historic, regal buildings, all the while with Laura telling me stories about the places and the people who had inhabited them. Gradually, we made our way to Trafalgar Square, where we stopped and ate our lunch by the edge of a fountain, not far from a huge sculpture of a lion. Laura told me she'd sometimes come to the square as a child, with her parents, to attend political rallies.

"It's quite a feeling," she said, "to be part of a crowd of people who feel so united by a common purpose, even if you are just a child and barely know what's going on." She threw a corner of her bread to the pigeons, several of which descended on it at once. "I remember sitting on my father's shoulders looking out over this huge living, breathing sea of people," she said, spreading her arms, "who would occasionally break into shouts and cheers at something the speaker had said. I had no idea," she looked at me, "what the talk was about, or what ideas they were cheering for, but I could feel their restless energy, their passion, their excitement. It was a place to be." She took another bite of her sandwich.

"It seems you've had such a lot of interesting experiences," I said admiringly. She looked surprised.

"Does it seem so? Really? It's just my little life." She shook her head. "But you," she looked over at me, "you've lived in distant parts of the world, been exposed to different cultures." She tore another piece from her bread and tossed it to the birds, then looked back down at her half-eaten sandwich. "And you have a way of looking at things, Indira, in depth, that makes any situation you're in be more than it would be without you."

I smiled. I wasn't sure what to say. I felt sort of adoringly towards her in that moment. I wanted to reach out and take her hand, but felt too shy. Perhaps it was then that I first began to realize that the way I felt about Laura went beyond the feelings of simple friendship.

"We should hurry up and eat," Laura said, smoothing over the silence. "There's so much I want to show you."

And indeed there was. We went from there to the National Gallery, watched for a while as a man made detailed drawings with chalk on the pavement outside—then went in and toured the gallery, viewing art in the European tradition from many nations, and many eras, all housed together—work by artists ranging from Botticelli to Rembrandt to Vincent van Gogh. It was quite a thrill. I had had no idea such works even existed!

By the time we got back to Laura's parent's house that evening, there was barely time for a quick meal before we caught our train back to Oxford. It had only been two days, but I felt a whole lifetime had passed. With happy exhaustion, I fell asleep with my head on Laura's shoulder as we rode the train home.

❀   ❀   ❀

It was hard to say goodbye to Laura after being inseparable for two days. We walked from the train station together as far as her dorm, and then I went on home to mine alone. After I got in, I gave Cynthia a call to let her know I was back from London and would love to see her the next day. She sounded tired when she answered the phone, but brightened up when she heard it was me. We made plans to meet at one o'clock the next day at the pub she had suggested, and then said good night.

When I arrived at the pub the next day, Cynthia was already seated at a small table in a front corner of the room, near a big window looking out on the road. It was raining outside—a steady, wintry drizzle.

I closed my umbrella and stepped over to where she sat. As I neared the table, she saw me and got up to give me a hug hello. I thought she looked tired and asked her how she was.

"Oh, all right, love," she said, as we both took our seats. "Just a little sleepy, but I got myself a cup of tea, which should help a bit. Why don't you go ahead and order. I'll wait here."

I left Cynthia at the little wooden table and stepped up to the bar, where I ordered a ploughman's lunch and a half of bitter. Only two other customers were in the small room, visiting quietly in a back corner. I paid for my food and drink and waited a moment while the landlady drew my ale, then carried my drink over to the little table Cynthia had picked out.

As I approached, I was struck again by how tired Cynthia looked, as she sat staring out the window.

"Didn't you sleep much last night?" I asked Cynthia, as I sat down. Cynthia looked over at me and smiled sweetly.

"Oh, no, I think that's the problem—I slept quite a lot, nearly twelve hours. I'm having trouble getting my feet under me for the day."

"Twelve hours?" I echoed.

"Well, I didn't have much sleep the night before that, you see. Guess I was doing a little catching up."

"A big Saturday night, huh?" I asked her, imagining that she'd had a night out on the town.

"Big, I suppose you could say, but not the way you would mean." She looked down at her cup of tea, which she was playing with, turning it on its saucer. I waited for her to say more. She looked up at me.

"It's my new bloke I told you about, Henry. He got into a bit of trouble last Saturday night. I had to go up to Bicester and bail him out."

"Oh, no. What happened, Cynthia?" I asked. She was still toying with the tea cup, swiveling it so the handle faced first one hand and then the other. I took a sip of my ale.

"It's not such a big thing," she went on. "He'd been out to a pub in North Oxfordshire with some of his friends. They had a good time, I guess, and Henry was driving back and some farmer hadn't closed his gate properly, and his sheep were out on the road. It was a dark night," she said, looking up, "and Henry didn't see them until the last minute. He tied to brake, but the road was wet, and he slid right into them. An ewe was killed, and three or four others the farmer said he might have to put down. A constable came and took Henry into jail. Said it had happened because he'd been drinking, but I say that farmer should have closed his bleeding gate. Henry called me at two o'clock in the morning, and I had to drive up and bail him out. Imagine that, though, blaming him when that farmer couldn't keep his own gate closed!

"Anyway," she concluded, "the next day I had to be waiting tables at 6 AM. I guess I made up for it last night, but sometimes that's worse." She took a long swallow of her tea and, as she set the cup down, she got a funny look on her face. I picked up my ale and took a sip.

"I just remembered a dream I had last night," Cynthia said. She was looking out the window with her mouth a little open. Outside, people hurried by in the rain.

"Oh yeah? What did you dream?" I asked.

"I was asleep in our flat—I mean, in the dream I was—and in the dream I heard a noise from somewhere, and it woke me up. So I got up to see what the noise was, and it was Henry. He'd come in late. He'd been drinking. He lay down on the sofa, only, it wasn't the sofa where we live now. It was the one from the flat I grew up in. So he lay down there, and I pulled off his shoes and put a blanket over him.

"That was it, that was the dream. I just remembered it." Cynthia shook her head. "The funny thing is, I used to do that with me dad," she said, frowning a little, "just like that—put a blanket over him when he'd come home from drinking. Me mum would get awful mad if he woke her up, so if he came in late, he'd lie down on the sofa. I'd hear him come in and get up. I'd pull off his shoes and put a blanket over him. He needed me, I guess—or at least, I always felt like he did."

Cynthia stared past me for a minute, then shook her head. "Funny, dreaming of Henry like that. I've never done that with him—put him to bed like that, on the sofa, I mean." Cynthia's expression was blank, a little perplexed. She looked down and started playing with her tea cup again.

"I don't think I've ever heard you mention your father before," I said.

"Yeah, I guess I don't talk about him much," she answered. She was still looking at her almost-empty tea cup, but I had the feeling she was seeing something else. "He could really bend the elbow, me dad," she said quietly. "He'd stay out a couple of days at a time, sometimes, then come home full of ale. I used to make up stories for him, when the men from the factory came around to find out why he hadn't gone to work, or when the bill collectors called."

"Is that where you were staying, when you left last summer, with him and your mother?" I asked.

Cynthia looked up. "Oh no, love, he's been gone for years. He drank himself to pieces. Might as well have drowned in the stuff, I guess. Doctor said his liver was all eaten away. He was only forty-five. Left me and me mum to fend for ourselves."

I felt sad, thinking about it. "How old were you, then, Cynthia?"

"Just turned thirteen, when he passed away."

I shook my head.

"It was after that me and me mum moved out to Bicester to be with some of her people there." Cynthia looked off towards the bar. I followed her gaze and saw the landlady cut a good-sized slice of cheese from a larger block.

I looked back over at Cynthia. She was still staring, lost in thought.

"I'm sorry about your father, Cynthia," I said. "I didn't know."

Cynthia looked back over towards me. "Aw, it's ancient history," she said, shaking her head a little. She picked up the little tea pot her tea had been served in and carefully poured herself some more.

"You seen anything of Petie, Indira?" Cynthia said. She set the teapot down and looked over at me. "I hear he checked himself into a hospital and got cleaned up."

"Yeah, I heard that too," I said. "I guess he's really off the dope now."

"Word is, he's been clean for more than six months. I saw him. He looks well, seems happy," Cynthia said.

"I'm glad," I said.

"I don't think Jake checked himself in," she went on, looking up, "but Pete says he's not using, either."

"That's what I heard," I said. "I hope he can keep it that way." I didn't really want to talk about Jake. I looked around the room, then back at Cynthia. She looked very small and sweet sitting there—small and sweet like Petie was. "You know, I always thought you and Pete would make a pair. You're both such gentle souls," I said.

Cynthia made a face. "Oh, thanks, Indira—but, me and Petie? I could never think of him that way," she said. "He's a sweet one, all right, but, I don't know, it'd be like being with my own brother. I'm just not attracted to him." She shook her head. "Besides," she said with a little laugh, "I think Hollie would object. They've been going together, you know. I think they're both quite smitten."

I laughed. "I imagine Henry wouldn't be too thrilled with it, either."

"No, not my Henry," she laughed.

"Are you happy with him, Cynthia?" I asked.

"Oh, sure I am. He's awful good to me. You should meet him, Indira. He's such a real bloke, and it makes me feel like a real lady just to be around him. I like that." Her eyes sort of glowed as she said it. Then her face turned solemn. "Still, he's not what my Tommy was to me—but maybe in time he will be. Tommy was a good one. He was my prince, he was." Her eyes teared up, and she sniffed, then began playing with her tea cup again. "It does worry me some that he drinks, though." She seemed to catch her breath. "After Tommy and me dad, it makes me feel kind of scared.

"I don't know why I keep picking out these troubled men, Indira," she added.

I didn't know what to say. We were both quiet for a minute, then she looked up. The landlady had shown up with our food—bangers and mash for Cynthia and a simple ploughman's lunch of bread, cheese, and salad for me.

We both thanked the landlady before she stepped away, then Cynthia picked up her fork and took a bite of her mashed potatoes.

"Cynthia—you were saying something," I said. "I think you got interrupted."

Cynthia let her hands rest on the table, then leaned back in her chair and sighed. She looked back out the window, then said, "I guess they make me feel like I'm good for something, you know, blokes like that. Because they need me," she turned her gaze back towards me. "It means I have something to give to someone, Indira. Kind of makes everything feel more worthwhile."

I held her gaze, nodded.

"It feels like it completes something in me, I guess," she added.

"Yeah, I guess we all need to get that feeling from somewhere," I said. "I've thought about that, too."

"What have you thought, love?" Cynthia asked. She took a big bite of one of her sausages, and I could see the edges of her mouth curl up as she relished the flavor.

"Mostly just that we all feel our own promise," I answered, "and look for ways to give life to it," I took a sip of my ale and tore off a piece of bread, "and that one part of how we do that is through closeness with other people. We all give each other opportunities—for things we can learn, or ways we can be when we're around one another," I went on, putting butter on my bread, "like, well, like you're a really nurturing person, Cynthia, and Henry needs that from you, right? And that gives you a chance to give life to that part of yourself."

"Yeah, right," Cynthia said, "'cause I do like that, looking out for him, like you said."

She looked thoughtful for a minute. "It makes me feel whole somehow, when I have someone to give that to," she added. I had the feeling she was thinking about Tommy.

"Even if it does make me crazy sometimes," she added.

I looked off to the side, thought about Jake. "I guess we take our best guess at what sort of person might help us get that feeling." I looked back at Cynthia. "I have this idea that we make a picture of that in our minds, of what we think that person might look like, might *be* like. I did that before I met Jake. I had dreamed of someone who looked and seemed a lot like he did. Can you imagine? I really thought those hippie blokes had it." I shook my head.

"You really had a thing for them, eh? Yeah, me too, at one time."

"Yeah," I went on. "I thought they were hip and deep, wise and free— and Jake was *one of them*. The truth is, he hardly had to do more than look right, for me to want to open my heart to him."

Cynthia took a big bite of food, nodded to let me know she was listening. I thought about it for a minute, took a bite of bread with a piece of cheese. I felt sort of sad.

"You know it wasn't really there, what I'd imagined I could find," I said. I tore off another piece of bread, held it in my hand.

"Does it ever worry you," I went on, "that maybe what you're looking for, what you'd really be happy with, could be right beneath your nose, but you'd look right past it, 'cause it's not what you'd expected?"

Cynthia sort of cocked her head to one side. "No, love," she answered, "I guess I never really thought of it like that. You mean, like, maybe you'd meet up with some bloke in a business suit, and you'd be thinking: Well, *he* couldn't be very interesting. But maybe he could really be the heart of your heart?"

"Yeah, like that," I said. "Or maybe even something more surprising."

I took another bite of bread. Cynthia sat there, looking very thoughtful and sort of picking at her food.

"It's like that dream I had, like you say, how we picture what we're looking for," she said, and frowned a little. "I see something of my father in Henry. I know that. I've known that for a while. And now, with him needing my help, like that, after he'd been out drinking..." Cynthia absentmindedly used her fork to smooth out the mashed potatoes on her plate. "I wonder if that's part of the reason I want to be with him," she added, "that little bit of me dad I see in him."

"Were you very close to your father?" I asked her.

Cynthia smiled a sweet little smile. "Me and me dad were pals." She took a deep breath, leaned back in the chair. "You know, I don't think he really liked life so very much. That's why he drank. But with me, I think, well..." Her voice trailed off. "He used to call me his little gem. I think

I was one of the few things that made life sort of okay for him. He used to tuck me in before going round to the pubs. I really adored him when I was small."

We sat in silence for a few minutes. Cynthia picked up her tea cup, but instead of drinking, she stared out the window.

"Yeah, I guess sometimes the way we picture love," I said, "it looks like the love we've already had."

Cynthia seemed distracted by her own thoughts. "What's that you say?" she asked.

"Jake looked like my picture of love, so I picked him out," I said, somewhat absently. "Maybe, a bit, you picture love to look like your dad, because he loved you, and you'd like to have that love back."

Cynthia stared at me for a moment. I remember thinking, again, how really tired she looked. Then something in her seemed to catch. She set her tea cup down on its saucer, and I could see her eyes well up with tears. She looked away and blinked, and together we looked though the window at the rain falling along the lane.

One evening, later that week, Laura came by to study with me. We sat on my bed, our books and papers spread out around us. I liked having her there, and I remember thinking how different it felt to spend time with Laura than it had to spend time with Jake.

Laura looked up from her reading and saw me staring into space. She commented on how thoughtful I looked.

"I was just thinking about Jake," I told her. But it seemed more complicated than that, and I tried to gather my thoughts.

"When I was talking with Cynthia at lunch the other day," I said, "she was telling me about her new boyfriend, Henry, and she said how he was such 'a real bloke,' and how that made her feel like 'a real lady.' She liked that, feeling that way." I thought for a moment. "But when I was with Jake—well, this is sort of hard to explain. I knew he wanted to see himself as such a, well, as such 'a real bloke,' like Cynthia said, and," I tried to get the thought straight, so I could say it clearly, "and, well, for him to feel that way, it was like it was a role in a play, and he needed me to play the complimentary part. He wanted me to be weak and compliant, I guess, so he could feel strong and in charge."

"That must have been hard to live with," Laura said.

"Yeah, it's one of the reasons the relationship ended," I said.

"I thought you said it was because he was using heroin," Laura said.

I laughed. "That, and other reasons. A lot of layers, you know."

"Right," Laura answered, and there was something gentle and knowing in the way she said it.

"Anyway," I went on, "I was just thinking about how it felt to be around him. Sometimes it felt really nice, but sometimes, too, I felt like I had to struggle to hold onto myself, to not lose track of who I was. In some ways, at least, he really wanted me to be someone different than myself."

"I've had that feeling with some people," Laura said, "and like I said, it's hard to live with. Kind of makes you feel all jammed up inside—like you can't express yourself."

I could see she understood and was thinking about what I'd said, and somewhere in the back of my mind the thought gathered that this was part of what I liked so much about being with her—I felt understood and recognized, supported. I didn't have to struggle to be myself with her, as I had sometimes had to do with Jake. And here there was no sex role that I was expected to play. I felt free to be myself.

"Anyway," I went on, "I guess there's something in that role that Cynthia likes." It was sort of a strange thought for me, after struggling as I had to resist role playing with Jake. It occurred to me that there must be something in that role that fulfilled her, gave her life. Perhaps she saw it as an opportunity, for what was within it, while I saw it as an obstacle, for what was left out.

"We all have our own taste," Laura said.

"Yeah," I said. Then I told her a little bit about my idea of protolife, and said something about how maybe for some people a particular role fits, and that maybe it helps them give life to what's in them, but for others the same role would be a bad fit, and would just get in the way of what they were trying to give life to in themselves.

Laura seemed to think that was a pretty interesting idea, and we talked about it for a few minutes, then she got up from the bed and stretched. "Would you like a cup of tea? I was thinking of making some."

"That would be nice," I said. Laura stepped across the room. She picked up the tea kettle and turned on the tap. I looked back down at my text book. I could hear the water echoing around inside the kettle as it was filled, then heard Laura set the kettle down on the hot plate. She came back over to the bed and sat down near me.

"You know my sister, Maggie?" she said. "She was with us at Kensington Gardens, with her little boy, Nigel?"

"Yes, Maggie," I answered. "The one with the sense of humor."

Laura looked a little amused at my characterization. "Well, yes, all right. She is pretty funny, I guess. She's also quite the feminist, and she has some interesting things to say about sex roles." Laura pulled her knees up to her chest, and looked straight ahead as she gathered her thoughts. "Maggie says that sex roles are basically exterior and interior." Laura turned her gaze up to the ceiling. "Men's roles are exterior. Men are supposed to go out into the world and take action there. Women are supposed to deal with interior things, emotions, nurturance, and the like." Laura looked over at me. "But the reverse is true, too—men aren't supposed to be too interested in interior things. Women are supposed to leave the world of physical action to men. That's what those roles are about. That's what Maggie says. But the funny thing is, people keep playing these roles, century after century, all over the world. But why should they want to, right? I mean—why should anyone want to have half their world cut away?"

That seemed sort of poignant, and I nodded, thinking about it.

"I have a story about Maggie, if you'd like to hear it," Laura went on.

"Certainly," I said. I liked the stories Laura told about her family.

"Okay, then." Laura looked forward again. I had the feeling she was mentally lining up the pieces of her story. Then she looked back at me. "Well, when Maggie first got married, she and her husband agreed they were going to have a progressive marriage, no sex roles, none of that stuff. Right?"

"Ahuh," I answered.

Laura settled back against the wall at the head of the bed next to me, and I felt suddenly aware of how close we were to one another and of an impulse I felt to move closer. I wondered how she would feel if I did, but I sat still and kept listening to her story.

"It worked out pretty well for them the first couple of years, but then little Nigel was born. Before then, Maggie and her husband, Silas, they had both held jobs. Maggie had a job arranging flowers at a florist's, and Silas was doing repairs on some buildings in Soho." Laura gave a little laugh. "I remember Maggie commenting on how sexist their jobs were, you know, with her messing with flowers, and Silas doing construction, but she told me those were the only jobs they could get.

"Anyway," Laura went on, "when Maggie was about seven-months pregnant, she had some complications, and the doctor told her to stop work. She did, and after the baby came, she had to be at home to nurse him. So Silas became the breadwinner, and Maggie stayed home with the baby and just did the work around the house, there. She said that's how it all started—they began to play sex roles in their marriage. She got used to being the one to do something for Nigel when he was hungry, and when he was older and he was hungry it seemed like her job to something about it, so she'd get up and fix him a sandwich, or whatever—because she was used to feeding him, 'cause she started off nursing him."

"How did she feel about that?" I asked.

"I think it was pretty frustrating for her, in a way, to fall into these roles when they didn't want them, but she's an easygoing person, and I think she also thought it a bit funny, like she and Silas were playing these silly roles that didn't really fit them. But I thought it was pretty interesting when she told me that."

"Yeah, that is interesting," I said. I thought about it for a minute. "So," I said, "people just keep reinventing these roles because our biology predisposes us to certain habits?"

"That's about it," Laura answered.

I frowned a little, then said, "But what I don't get is why people get so attached to those roles. Like with Jake, he'd get sort of freaked out if I didn't help him play his."

"I know," Laura said. "With some people I get the feeling that they think they *are* their sex role. It's like they think if you take that away, they'll lose their whole identity."

I considered that as the tea kettle began to whistle. Laura got up to make our tea, and as she did, I watched her step across the room and thought about how much I liked it that she thought about such things, and that we could have such an exchange of ideas.

When Laura came back, she bent down and set the tea pot, steaming with the hot tea brewing inside, onto one of her school books on the floor, then she rose and put a couple of empty cups and a tea strainer on the bedside table. She sat down on the bed beside me, facing me this time, then looked at me and smiled. I remember noticing how graceful her movements were, and how beautiful her face looked in the light from the bedside lamp.

"I like talking to you, Indira," she said.

"Yeah, me too," I answered. Then Laura reached out and put her hand on top of mine. I smiled, and became aware that my heart was beating faster. I put my other hand on top of hers, and felt suddenly very close to her, and very happy. We looked at each other for a long moment, and then my attention was drawn to something I felt in the touch of her hand.

I looked down at her hand, then back at Laura. "What happened to your hand, Laura?" I said. "It feels sore."

Laura looked surprised. "How did you know?" She looked down at her hand. "I hurt it playing cricket. It doesn't look bruised." She looked back up at me. "I don't see how you could tell."

"I don't know," I said. "I could just feel it."

"That's very odd," Laura said. She picked up my hand and held it in hers, and I remembered what had happened with Jake when I had sensed part of the story he was planning to write.

"How *did* you know?" Laura cocked her head.

I shrugged. "I think it has to do with learning to listen to the impressions that skate by at the back of your mind," I said, trying to think of how to describe that sensation. "I was practicing it last year when I had that poetry class. Seems there's a lot there, if you just notice it." Then I told her a little bit about my idea that we could pick up thoughts and feelings from one another if we were tuned in the right way. I said something vague about radio waves, and how they're decoded, and that all living things put out energy waves just by being alive.

Laura looked sort of quizzical.

"You know," I went on, trying not to be too distracted by the fact that we were still holding hands. "It's like, maybe when you touch someone, a circuit is completed, and you can really feel for them, then, actually feel what they feel."

Laura looked down at our hands, the quizzical expression still on her face.

"You know, whatever you feel, inside your body," I added, "you feel because there's energy racing along your nerves—right?—up to your brain, where your brain decodes the information that's in that energy. Maybe when people touch, it's like two wires being put together. The energy goes from your hand to my hand—to my brain, then, too. Maybe that's why people like to touch. A connection gets made."

Laura looked up at me. There was something very sweet in her expression. "I love it that you think about such things," she told me. "You have the most interesting mind, Indira."

I smiled at her. I liked it that she was holding my hand. I liked it very much. I felt close to her, felt her presence now more keenly than ever, now that we were touching. I wanted more closeness, more…

Laura smiled back at me, a look of sweet tenderness in her eyes, and perhaps she, too, could feel what I was feeling, because she leaned in towards me and kissed me then. For a moment, I was surprised. Then a wave rose in me, and I felt weak all over—breathless and excited—and I leaned towards her, offering up my kiss to her.

Laura put her hand softly on my waist and pulled me gently nearer. She felt so close, and I wanted her closer. She put her arms around me, and I put mine around her. Together, we leaned back against the wall at the head of the bed.

We were tangled together awkwardly. I laughed, and she laughed, and we separated enough to each smile at the other and to gaze into one another's eyes.

I stroked Laura's face, then leaned forward and whispered in her ear, "I like you."

"Oh, I like you, too, Indira," she said to me, and then we kissed again, and slid down into the bed together, where we kissed and embraced for what seemed the sweetest eternity.

Finally, I looked up at the clock, which read quarter-past eleven. It was late. I looked back at Laura and whispered to her, "Will you stay the night?"

She looked at me, and I saw the green mixed in with the brown of her eyes, and a look of wonder on her face.

"Yes," she whispered back.

We looked at one another for a long moment, and then I raised myself on one arm and turned off the bedside lamp. We had just the pale glow of the full moon as it shone through the second-floor window, with the curtains spread wide. In the near darkness, I could see the white sheets and Laura's porcelain skin.

I touched her neck, followed its line down the "V" of her chest, to the top button of her blouse. I unbuttoned the first button. She reached up and guided my hand to the second. My heart was racing, and I felt dizzy with my desire for her. For her. Oh Laura! I bent over and kissed her neck while I undid the rest of her blouse, and as she undid mine.

I had felt her presence earlier, as she'd held my hand in hers, and I had felt myself afloat in her love as we had kissed and wrapped our bodies together on my narrow dormitory bed. But now, oh, as we drew off our clothing and touched one another in ways I had never before dreamed I might touch another woman, as we folded ourselves together, I felt myself diving into her waters, sensing her through her touch, now, more deeply than ever. I felt I was offering her everything I was, and it was being reflected back to me, made whole, realigned with her loving vision of me. And I was loving her in this way, too, cherishing each piece she opened to me, offering her all my joy and my comfort.

I slept little that night, for every time I felt Laura shift in my arms, or felt her hand drift from my waist to my thigh, or felt her breath on my neck, a fire erupted in me. I could not cool down enough to be drawn deeply into sleep. And each time the heat of this flame carried me up out of my restless dreaming, I surfaced with her name on my lips, soaking in her presence, and wanting to soak her up more.

I woke early the next day. The curtains were still parted, and bright morning light filled my white-walled room. I rose up on one elbow and looked down at Laura, still asleep beside me. Her pale, warm-hued skin seemed to glow in that sweet early light, and her flaming red hair spread around her face like a halo. I wanted to stroke her cheek, but feared I would wake her. As I stared down at her, I thought about how little I had been prepared to see in her the possibility of such a love when I had first met her on the train a year before, but my models had shifted, come more into line with what I was really looking for, and I was glad I had become ready for this now.

"Laura," my lips shaped her name. "How much life you give me," I barely whispered. Then I lay back on the bed and, staring up at the ceiling, wondered how I could live, now, with this happiness erupting inside me.

In the days that followed, Laura and I divided our time between schoolwork and one another's company, with schoolwork often getting the short end of that. We woke together and studied together; we dined and slept together. Every day we unearthed new treasures in one another's company.

Our world was filled with the discoveries of love and so, it appeared to me, was the world around us. Everywhere we went, it seemed, I saw other young couples in love, and wondered if they felt as inspired as we did. What caused any two people to choose one another, I wondered, from amongst all the people that they knew?

I remember one winter day in particular, when I was considering such questions. I was walking along Banbury Road, on my way to the Radcliffe Camera to meet up with Laura and study. A morning fog lay across the land—a low, tattered cloud. I was thinking about Laura, and about how it felt to have her in my life—about the happiness that always bubbled over in me whenever she was near, and the sense I had, whenever I was with her, that of all the places in the world where I might be, the one place I wanted most to be was right there with her.

As I continued on along St. Giles under winter trees shrouded in mist, I found myself thinking about how I had felt about Jake. In the beginning, I had believed so much in the model that had drawn me to him that I had been practically swept off my feet at the start. But in time I had come to see him in a clearer light, and that passion had slowly faded—just as this morning fog, which now clouded my view, would soon burn away in the clear light of day.

With Laura, it seemed to me, it was entirely different. It was only after I had gotten to know her that my love had grown, taking root in the ground of who she actually was. She was what I needed—what I had, deep down, been looking for all along. The model that had led me to Jake had been easily rewritten when I had seen who he really was—but nothing would ever convince me that the model that had allowed me to see, in Laura, the prospect of love, was a mistaken one, for it was plain to me already that this one was true and real.

I loved so much about Laura, I found myself thinking. So many things drew me to her—her open laughter...her sharp mind...her unerring gentleness...her willingness to engage in any adventure...

In so many ways, I thought, she helped me give life to what was in me—to what I most longed to give, and to share, and to become. No wonder I felt so much joy when I was with her.

I crossed St. Giles, and continued on along Magdalen Street, feeling astonished at my good fortune at having Laura in my life.

As I strolled along, my thoughts drifted like the fog around me, and soon I found myself thinking about the conversation I'd had with Cynthia at the Rose and Crown just a couple of weeks before, when she had told me about her new love.

I remembered her talking, that day, about how close she had been to her father, and about wanting to recapture the love and closeness she had felt with him. She had expressed, too, a desire to give nurturance—even if that meant looking after Henry when he was drunk. I remembered how Cynthia had held her cup of tea as she had spoken, and recalled her saying what she had said about liking it that Henry was a "real bloke" who made her feel like a "real lady."

I looked down at the swirl of fog kicked up with each step I took, and considered how uniquely her own Cynthia's desires were. Surely, no one else missed *her* father as she did, I thought—and perhaps no one else wanted exactly the same thing as she did from the sort of complex roles she played with Henry—being a "lady" to his "real bloke," but also his caretaker, and nurturer—all wrapped together in a private dance known only to them. It seemed to me that all the elements of Cynthia's desires combined and interwove together to create a composite exactly like no other in the world. And yet, I thought, as people saw these things, she would simply be defined as "straight."

I shook my head a little, as I stepped to one side to pass another pedestrian. It seemed so clumsy, I told myself, so diminishing, to reduce all the depth and meaning imbedded in Cynthia's desires into this simple term.

It was the same as Hollie would be defined, I thought. I considered this as I turned the corner at Broad Street and crossed to the far side, where painted storefronts lined the lively roadway.

That the same word would be used to describe both Cynthia's and Hollie's sexual orientation seemed strange to me. I knew they weren't both attracted to Pete. Hollie was "quite smitten" with him—wasn't that what Cynthia had said?—while Cynthia had screwed up her face at the thought of being paired with Pete, saying it would be like being with her own brother!

That they each felt so differently about Petie showed that their sexual orientations were not the same, I concluded, glancing down at the paving stones on the footpath. In fact, it seemed to me possible that—in all the world—they might not be attracted to any of the same people. And yet, somehow, meaninglessly, the same word would still be used to describe both.

Lost in thought, I strolled past buildings and past pedestrians heading the other way, only half aware of their presence and of the surrounding sounds of traffic, muffled by fog. Clearly there were many more factors involved in any one person's sexual orientation than just which sex or sexes the people they were attracted to were. I could easily count a score of reasons I was attracted to Laura—so why pick just one characteristic, out of so many, I wondered, and treat it, alone, as all important?

I rounded the corner by Exeter College and continued along the narrow side street. Up ahead, a young couple emerged from the fragile mist, walking with their arms around one another. The man, with short hair and a thick mustache, wore a pea coat and jeans. The woman wore a clear-plastic raincoat over a colorful dress. She carried a red purse and wore shoes to match. The woman whispered something in the man's ear, and they both laughed. Then they paused, turned to one another, and kissed a brief, passionate kiss, before continuing on. As I passed them, I wondered if they were newly in love, as Laura and I were.

So masculine and feminine—their styles of appearance—I thought. What part did the sexes they were, and the roles they engaged in together, play in the way they felt about one another? I wondered.

As I strolled along, my thoughts turned to the night I had walked Cynthia home, after we had all gone out to hear Tommy play with his band. I remembered Cynthia had told me about sex roles, then. "Like roles in a play," she had said.

I liked the analogy—as though the whole society was one vast theatrical production, with people cast most specifically, and deliberately, in the role of one sex, or the other.

I turned a corner onto the narrow lane between the massive buildings of Exeter and Lincoln College. As I turned, the sounds of traffic disappeared behind me. In their place I could hear the clatter of my footfalls as they echoed between stone walls.

It seemed to me that in a world where people invested so much in those roles, and believed so strongly in them, many people would naturally model their pictures of love in terms of what they expected from the two sexes— while other people (precisely because they did play the roles in which they had been cast) would then, in large part, live up to those expectations.

It would become a kind of self-fulfilling prophecy, I thought, going round and round—with belief creating experience, and experience reinforcing belief.

We would model love, then, with a specifically male or a specifically female face, confident that others would then play their part according to the particulars of the role prescribed for them.

And yet, where did the whole person, and the special promise within each of us, reside in all of this? I wondered.

Probably struggling to find a niche that worked for them in the midst of such confining expectations, I thought. Sometimes, with ambivalence, they would embrace the role offered to them, as Cynthia had apparently done. And sometimes, I imagined, they longed to find some situation, some circumstance, where they could escape those roles entirely—and might even be lucky enough to do so, just as I had been lucky, for so many reasons and in so many ways, in discovering Laura.

The narrow lane I'd been strolling on opened onto Radcliffe Square, where I could see the rotund figure of the Camera rising up above its grassy green.

As I started up the walk to the library, I thought again about the many facets of Cynthia's relationship with Henry, and what had drawn them together. It wasn't just Cynthia's sexual orientation that was complex, and multifaceted, and uniquely her own, I was realizing—it was that way for every one of us. No two people shared the same model for love, just as no two of us felt the same inspiration for it.

I reached the Radcliffe Camera and pulled open the library door. As I entered, I was picturing in my mind an image of people all over the world—on every continent, in every country—each of them inspired by the protolife borne uniquely within them, and each of them finding their own unique path for giving life to it.

I paused inside the door and looked towards the middle of the room, from which alcoves spread like pedals around the center of a blossom. Laura would be in the ground-floor reading room, she had told me, in the theology section. I started off to my right, looking in each of the alcoves as I passed, and as I did, I let my attention return to my thoughts.

I imagined all the complexities in each person's model of love, and the rare distinctiveness of each and every relationship. In a certain sense, I told myself, each person's life was an art of their own creation—inspired from within—then spilling out into the world around them.

As I glanced inside each alcove, I imagined all of that art arising and interweaving—and thus creating a larger work, with its own fluxes and meanings—a collective work, which became ever more complete as each of us became truer to the special promise within ourselves.

I paused again and looked around. I had gotten past the theology section, somehow, without finding Laura. Too lost in thought, I told myself. I looked back across the room, scanning each alcove of the elegant old library more carefully, then spotted Laura at the back of one, sitting at a wooden table in the soft light from the high, arched window above.

As I stepped across the room, I remembered how she had looked, that morning, when I had parted from her on my way to an early morning tutorial. Her face had been softly lit in morning light, her hair still tousled from sleep.

I slipped into the chair beside Laura's, and as I did she looked up from her books.

"I found you," I whispered, smiling.

"Indira!" Laura said, with delight. She looked at me for a long moment, her face seemingly lit from within. Then she leaned in towards me and said, in a whisper, "I am so glad you did."

❋   ❋   ❋

When Christmas came around that winter, Laura invited me to join her at her parent's house in London, and I was glad to go with her....

"Stop," Paul said. Kiki broke off recitation. The day was fading fast. The sun had long-since dipped beneath the ridge to the west of Paul, and even the soft glow in the sky beyond that ridge was nearly gone—and still Paul had not yet come to any sort of identifiable campsite.

Paul had been dropped off near the crest of a small mountain and had, in the short time he'd been walking, crossed over that crest to the north and started down the other side. Already the forest he had been so glad to discover had begun to thin and be replaced with smaller trees and shrubs as the path dropped to a lower altitude.

Paul decided, with the light so nearly gone, he had better just pick a spot to make his camp, and chose some high ground off to the side of the path, as it seemed to offer a sufficient area of flat, fairly uncluttered ground. Paul dug his flashlight from the side pocket of his pack and made his way up the hill in the darkness.

The view from the hilltop was stupendous. Spread out to the southwest were the lights of the Santa Ynez Valley, from which Paul had recently come. To the west of there was another glow. Paul paused to consider what town that might be. Santa Maria—yes, that must be it—the town he had grown up in.

Though it was only about fifty kilometers from his small apartment in the Strandford of his own world, Paul hadn't visited Santa Maria in years. Now, on another Earth, so far from his own, the soft lights of that familiar city seemed to beckon.

Paul recalled that he had left as soon as he had finished high school, but it had been a hard place for him to be for years before that—since, well, since his mother had passed away.

As Paul stood there looking at the lights of the closest thing this world had to his home town, a deep, stinging sadness came over him—a sadness that seemed almost to bridge into remorse.

Paul turned his back on the scene and searched through his pack for what he would need for the night. It was awkward holding the flashlight, and trying to hold the pack open with one hand, while probing within it with the other. This was certainly the last time he would let the sun go down before he made camp! he promised himself, doing the best he could to clear an area on which to lay out his sleep bivy. Paul was hungry and tired, and suddenly sad and frustrated—and yet, he reminded himself, it had been an amazing day!

Just the walk through the forest alone had been like nothing he'd ever known before. Within the shelter of these towering pines, he'd seen squirrels and what he thought were chipmunks (based on pictures he remembered viewing through the Stream); some sort of brownish-colored bird about a quarter of a meter in length, which walked in groups upon the ground; and large, black birds, which flew through the forest calling to one another with a throaty *caw.*

In the late afternoon, he had looked down a long slope and seen deer moving in and out among the trees, as well as grazing in the lowlands below. He had tried to count them, then, and was sure there were at least thirty, and perhaps as many as forty or fifty gathered there below! It was all too marvelous to imagine.

Even in the evening shadows, the world around him had seemed magnificent. Just then, as the sun had begun to fade, he had seen small bats darting and swooping through the air between the pines, catching insects for their evening meal.

For Paul, this wonderland had been like a dream come true. It had filled him with a kind of rare joy, as someone might have if they discovered that someone they loved, whom they thought had been lost in some disaster, had in fact survived. Paul knew that most of the animals he'd seen still existed in his world—but in nothing like these numbers. In truth, it made him wish he could somehow stay, and live in the midst of this splendor—but he wished even more that he could return to the world he knew and do what could be done to make right what had gone so badly wrong there. And in any case, he would never desert Sheila. He felt he had no choice but to return and complete his work.

Paul pulled his jacket from his pack and put it on, then went through the pack looking for the fire-starter kit, which he knew was somewhere within its cavernous body. At first it seemed lost in the dark shadows there, but eventually he managed to locate it. Then he gathered together a little dry wood from the area near his camp, cleared a space on which to burn it, and started a little fire using the kit.

Paul prepared one of the self-heating travel meals and sat eating it in the warm glow of his small fire. Soon, he found himself thinking about the book he had been listening to. Even if the love Dr. Kumar had expressed feeling for another woman had surprised Paul, its main effect on him was to make him lonely for love, and homesick for his own world, and for Sheila's presence within it.

How much was there, really, to do before he could get home? Paul asked himself. Funding would be a problem, he knew, but he would have to somehow get together appropriate parts for a new transport and get it built. At least this time he was certain the basic design could work. The first time, it was all theory. And he'd have to find a power source. Then there was the question of aiming and linkage, but Paul felt he had explored ILT as thoroughly as he could. It looked solid, he told himself. He assured himself that once the transport was built and powered, returning home should be an essentially simple and instantaneous process.

Paul finished his travel meal and climbed into his sleep bivy. Already, his small, makeshift fire was burning down.

Paul considered the power problem more closely. He had been assuming, he realized, that power that could be created on site—like solar or wind power—would be all he would find available on this world, but he realized he had no reason to assume this. Big energy industries had existed in the past of this world, just as they had on his—and still did on his. So why not expect some comparable high-voltage power to be available here, as well? he reasoned.

Perhaps this world could provide not only enough energy to fuel his transport home, Paul mused, but might provide it from an energy source as-yet unknown on his world. Perhaps then, he thought, he would not only have the means to get home, but might bring with him knowledge of how to fuel the transport of half the population of his world to this one.

Paul looked up at the star-filled sky. How many times, on his world, had he looked toward the sky and tried to imagine where their target world would be found there? After they had selected G3-97, he had even brought Sheila to the telescope at Sedgwick Reserve, to show her the region it had been found in—though its light was far too faint to be detected through any terrestrial telescope.

Now Paul looked skyward, as though he might find his own world spinning up above—though in truth it not only could not be found there, but was not actually there at all. (Instead, Paul reminded himself, it was exactly where this earth was, though his was in a parallel universe.)

Yet this small fact did no more to stop Paul from looking, now, than it had done before. He peered skyward, and pictured the people of his world spinning together on some far-away dot—on a little light lost somewhere in some night sky—a small ball of water and dust, with people packed on it.

He would unpack them, he told himself, picturing all the lonely, crowded, hungry people he would rescue and bring here. People from lands torn by war, from lands desiccated by a relentless sun, lands poisoned through generations of industrial toxin and pesticide use. Lands full of people living under the constraints imposed on them through puppet governments propped up by global corporations—for all of these people, Paul told himself, he would loosen their bindings. He would free them to come here, to this open, happy, well world, where the rain still fell when it should, where the oceans hadn't risen, and where the lands were not alternately baked and parched or drenched by flooding rains. They would come here, and even the people left behind would be unburdened, as there would be so much more left of everything to go around.

What a happier world his world would be, Paul thought, and how great a gift he would be giving to those who left it, and to those who stayed behind.

For a moment, another thought crowded in around the edges of this happy fantasy. For a brief moment, Paul thought of the people of this world and what an invasion of outsiders, unschooled in the ways of this world, would mean to the people here. Their population numbers would soar suddenly, swelled by people who were used to taking from the natural world whatever resources they chose to, without concern for the larger effect. Suddenly the population would explode with people accustomed to living under repressive laws and regulations that threatened horrible punishments. How would they behave when suddenly those restrictions were lifted?

These thoughts made Paul uneasy, and he pushed them aside. His duty was not to the people of this world. His allegiance belonged with the people of his own world, and with doing what was right for them. His whole adult life, and more, had been focused on this goal. So close as he was now, he would certainly not turn from it.

Paul rolled toward the dimming fire and stared into its gentle flames. His thoughts turned back to the people he hoped to rescue. He imagined returning to his world, triumphant. He would announce his achievement, and the news would spread quickly through the Stream. His face, his achievement, would be in everybody's thoughts. People would recognize him on sight. He imagined them turning toward him, with looks of adoration on their faces, as he passed them on the streets.

Paul smiled a little at himself, at how rich he had allowed this fantasy to become. Perhaps it would be like that, and perhaps not, he told himself—but in any case, he would have to remain practical, if he wanted to get there.

He returned his thoughts to the energy supply and to the possibility of having ample energy to transport the people of his world to this one. He wished it would be possible to transport them in large groups. He and his team had thought about this, early in the project—the possibility of building huge transport pads from which they could send whole groups at once. This way, it was thought, there would be no risk of the people becoming separated in the process and possibly landing kilometers apart, as the two world's spun through space and the alignment shifted gradually between them, while one person after another was transmitted. All in all, it was hoped that group transmission would be more efficient and would ensure that whole groups of people—such as families—arrived at exactly the same spot together—and were not spread out across the land.

So Paul and his team had worked on this idea of group transport and had, a few times, transported two mice together across the lab. The results each time were nothing less than gruesome. With the first attempt, the mice had arrived together on the landing pad—but not as two distinct mice. Instead, their bodies became entangled during transport, as though the transport unit had tried, insanely, to interpret their dual signals as one creature, with legs and teeth and eyes jutting and protruding out in every wrong direction. The monstrous creature had breathed a few breaths, before whimpering to a pathetic death.

Paul and his team had worked hard to understand the nature of the problem, finally coming to the conclusion that the reception nodes had become misaligned. They had realigned them, carefully, precisely, then tried again.

The results were no better—except that the second dual creature had, mercifully, been dead on arrival.

Months later, after adjusting some programming, they had tried once more. The bizarre, mangled, hairless thing that arrived across the room had lived a full five minutes and had, the whole time, lain panting and making a noise midway between a moan and a whimper.

After that, any plans for dual or multiple transports had been shelved.

Paul stared up at the stars. If he was lucky enough to wind up with an energy source of sufficient power and availability to return to this world with a third or more of the population of his, it would require building a great many transport pads. A whole industry would have to be erected on his world for building them. Others, sent ahead to this world, could be situated to receive the newcomers, provide them with clothing, and help them reconnect with loved ones. With any luck, it could be arranged that those who wished to arrive together would at least arrive nearby.

Paul lay awake for some time, imagining his return and trying to decide who in Corprogov he would contact for the boost in funding he would need to proceed with these plans, and who he could hire to help get started on building the new units.

Before drifting off, though, he decided that in the end, word of his accomplishment would be so widespread that others would surely come to him, offering funding, assistance, and support. What a fine day that would be, Paul thought—how well, and how smoothly, everything would go, once he got home.

◻ ◻ ◻

When Paul woke in the morning, he found the landscape had changed more than he had realized as he'd walked through it in the gathering darkness the night before. Before him now, stretching down the mountainside, was a terrain of grasses and shrubs and flowering plants of every variety—along with an assortment of smaller trees scattered about. The net effect was of a broad vista full of colorful plants and open sky.

Next to the cleared ground on which Paul had slept was an especially attractive blooming plant—a stemmy bush that stood about chest height and was covered in a boisterous display of lavender blossoms.

Paul pulled on his shoes and relieved himself behind the flowering bush, then rolled up his sleep bivy and stuffed it into his pack. He dug out a self-heating travel meal and got it started heating while he kicked apart the remnants of his fire from the night before, making sure there were no embers, and threw on his pack.

Soon he had started down the trail, striding along while he ate his breakfast. Ahead of him, the path sloped down a hill that stretched from the mountaintop behind him to the lowlands below. Beyond that, in the distance, another mountain rose up—forming the far side of a wide valley. It was a breathtaking view, full of mountains and sky in the distance, shrubs and flowering plants in the foreground—with all of it bathed in the soft light and shadows of the morning sun.

What had the sales clerk at the tech shop in Strandford said?—that most people pick up the trail on Figueroa, and something about the view coming down off the peak. That's where he was now, and if he remembered right, the clerk had said it would take about three or four days from here to reach the Retreat.

Paul considered this. It had taken him two days to get here from Strandford—two days of listening to *Memories and Reflections*, with three or four days left to go before he got where he was going.

In that case, Paul told himself, it seemed that he'd come more than a third of the way to the Retreat. He wondered if he was pacing things so he would finish Dr. Kumar's book by the time he reached the Kumaric Retreat.

"Kiki, what percentage of the text have you recited?" he asked.

"23.849376…"

"Okay, okay, you don't need to be that precise," Paul interrupted. "So, less than a quarter of the book recited with more than a third of the hike completed. At this rate, I won't have the book done by the time I get to the Retreat," he added, under his breath. He wasn't eager to arrive at the Retreat ignorant of what everyone else there knew—he had enough of that problem just being new to this world.

"Kiki, is it possible for us to skim ahead somehow, to hurry up this process?"

"I am programmed for text summary as well as recitation."

Paul thought about this. "I'm mostly interested in what Dr. Kumar may have written that would have influenced this world. I suppose the answer to that question is to be found somewhere in the ideas from her book. Is it possible to specifically identify those sections that deal most directly with her philosophy?" Paul asked.

"I am capable of identifying relative densities of story, description, and conceptual content in the text."

"What's the average conceptual content in the rest of this chapter?"

"It is relatively low, about 17.6092%. The margin of error for such estimates is ±3%."

"Okay. Can you summarize that material?"

"Yes."

"Please continue in summary mode until you come to a section with high conceptual content, then return to normal recitation mode at the beginning of that section."

"Please give 'high conceptual content' a numeric value," Kiki said.

Paul thought about this for a moment. "What numeric value would you give to the average conceptual content of the book on the whole?" he asked.

"The average for the book is estimated at 31.5413%," Kiki answered.

Paul gave it a little more thought. "Okay. Let's say 25% and above." He waited. Nothing happened.

"Are you ready?" he asked.

"Yes."

"Well, begin," he said—and as he resumed his trek down the trail, Kiki's melodious voice, delivered with her own pitch and intonation, filled the air around him.

◘   ◘   ◘

"The new year came, and Laura and Indira continued to spend time together," Kiki said. "Their relationship deepened, and their lives became more and more intertwined. Together, they dreamed of plans for their future together. With the next school year, their third and last as undergraduates, they decided to 'live out,' that is, off campus, and together they rented a flat in a quiet part of town. Both intended to continue their schooling by attending graduate school, but during Michaelmas Term in the autumn of 1972, Laura had a tutor with whom she did not get along, whose values and perspective were different from her own, and who was often critical of the approach she took to her studies. Laura became discouraged about her academic aspirations and almost didn't apply to graduate schools when Indira was doing so. Indira gave Laura encouragement. She told Laura how important it was that all people pursue the fulfillment of the promise that lay within them. She said that that was how people brought their gifts into the world. After this, Laura remembered how long she had felt interested in studying religion, and how important it was to her. Together, she and Indira both applied to graduate schools at the same time—and to the same schools."

"Did they get in?" Paul asked.

"Yes, they both began at Columbia University, in New York City, in the autumn of 1973, after returning from a three week summer excursion to Indira's home in India where Indira reunited with her family, heard details of their lives from the years they'd been apart, and told them stories of her life in Oxford and of her admission to graduate school. Laura went with her and was pleased to have an opportunity to meet the cast of characters Indira had been telling her about since they'd first met. They did not tell Indira's family that they were in love with one another, only that they were dear friends. Indira's family enjoyed meeting Laura and were pleased to see that Indira had such a caring and loyal friend as she, who would continue to be her friend and companion in America. They thought it was good that she would have a friend already with her in that strange and distant land.

When Indira and Laura arrived in New York, Laura began graduate work in the Sociology of Religion, where her interests turned to the patterns of belief that appear repeatedly in various religions around the world. Meanwhile, Indira began working on her Ph.D. in Sociocultural Anthropology, focusing especially on the relationship between value-based beliefs and cultural practice. They both worked hard and had to be thrifty because they had such limited funds, but they found their school work satisfying, and enjoyed living together in New York and being exposed to the diversity of cultures the city had to offer."

Paul was pleased to be racing forward through the text at this rate. He worried a little about what he might be missing, but felt he could trust Kiki to slow down when the time came.

"Laura completed her doctorate in May of 1978, and finding no work in her field available to her in the New York area, she took a temporary administrative position while waiting for Indira to finish her degree. Indira was awarded her doctorate in December of 1978 and was quickly offered, and accepted, a post-doctoral position assisting a professor of hers at Columbia. Meanwhile,

Laura was becoming increasingly concerned that if she did not find some sort of professional work soon, she would not be taken seriously when she went to apply again. Finally, in desperation, she applied for a post-doctoral position at the University of Colorado, even though it would take her far from Indira. She was awarded that job, assisting a professor whose research dealt with the ways local and world religions blend to create unique amalgams. Specifically, Laura was hired to assist in conducting interviews and making records of the forms of religious beliefs such syncretism had led to among the Northern Cheyenne.

"Laura left New York for the Northern Cheyenne Reservation in southwestern Montana in late August of 1979. It was the first time she and Indira had lived apart in seven years. It was very hard on both of them, but they could find no other way to sustain the careers they had both worked so hard to prepare for. They both hoped they would find a way to be together again, soon."

Kiki paused for a couple of seconds, then continued: "End of chapter three," she said.

She paused again, and when she spoke next, her voice took on a formal tone as she presented the new chapter.

CHAPTER IV

Perhaps all who are terrible, in their deepest essence,
are the helpless, who want help from us.

—RAINER MARIA RILKE

"Summary resumes:" Kiki went on, in her normal voice. "The professor Indira was assisting was as much a friend as a supervisor. He knew about her relationship with Laura and was sad to see them apart. When Thanksgiving break came around that fall, Indira made plans to fly out to Montana to see Laura, but was frustrated that she would spend so much money and still only get to see Laura for three or four days. The professor whose work she was assisting in encouraged her to take off a full week following Thanksgiving and to make it up by working longer hours when she returned.

As things went, Indira couldn't get a flight out in time for Thanksgiving but got a ticket for the next morning—Friday, November twenty-third. She would be with Laura for a little more than a week, until her flight back on the morning of Sunday, the second of December. Unfortunately, Laura was offered no equivalent time off, and so would have to continue with her work while Indira was there."

Kiki paused. "Normal text recitation resumes here, approximately 5.2751% of the way into chapter four."

Paul hadn't realized she'd been speaking more quickly than usual until he heard Kiki's voice slow as it took on the pace and intonation she used to simulate Dr. Kumar's voice, as she began reading from *Memories and Reflections* once again:

> I woke early that morning, filled with excitement at the thought that in just a few hours I would be on a flight west to see Laura. I got out of bed, and as I did a dream I'd had in the night came back to me. I'd been with Laura, and we'd been scaling a mountainside. We'd been hiking through rocky terrain above the tree line, and sometimes the going was

rough. The light was half-bright, like twilight. We moved up the steep slope with care, picking our way between boulders.

When we neared the top, I looked up. The sky was filled with the most beautiful golden light. Birds swooped and turned over our heads, and the air seemed fresh and clear. Together, Laura and I made the summit. Below us, I could see a broad landscape open up. We were looking down and out across a great forest. We could see only the tops of the trees, dark green and rolling on for endless mile after mile. Any open space between the dense branches was filled with mist, so the ground was invisible far below us.

From within those mist-wrapped trees, voices rose in song—a rich, rhythmic music unlike any I'd ever heard—so musical, and so filled with joy. The sun finished rising, and the air was filled with light and music, and I was there with Laura on the mountain top.

I lay back down on the bed and thought about the dream for a minute. So beautiful, and so out of step with the way my days had darkened since Laura had been gone. It wasn't the first time I had dreamed that dream, either, I remembered with a strange sense of irony. I had dreamed a dream that was the same, or at least very similar to the one I had dreamed the night before, when Laura had first been offered the research assistant-ship at the University of Colorado—the same job that had since taken her to the Northern Cheyenne Reservation in Montana. That job had seemed such a good foot-in-the-door position; not only would it mean she had found work in her profession, but they had told her that an assistant professorship was expected to open up the following year and hinted that she would be well situated to fill that position if she took the job. We had both been so worried about being apart—and how long that separation might last—and had been hesitating to accept the job offer, when I had dreamed this dream of the mountain top.

I remembered it so clearly, the way, I think, we often recall turning points in our lives. I had woken up happy that morning, after two days of worried indecision, and told Laura about the dream I'd had, and expressed to her what a good sign I felt it was. It would be all right, I had told her. We would manage the distance somehow. Not only had the dream lifted my mood, but I had felt there was something telling in its details. We might have a rough hike up ahead, I told Laura, then, but I thought it was the right choice for both of us in the long run. I felt that it would help us to eventually arrive someplace good.

I had told Laura that, and she had listened to me. She had taken the job and gone someplace far away. And here we had been apart now, missing one another, for more than three difficult months—though it seemed much longer than that.

I got up from the bed and stumbled groggily into the kitchen. I took the coffee pot off the shelf and filled it with water, then plugged it in and measured out a small scoop of coffee.

"Good omen," I thought cynically, as I recalled the difficulties of those three months. I put a couple of slices of whole-grain bread in the toaster and sat down at the little kitchen table to wait.

Laura had arrived in Montana knowing no one, doing research that many in the town saw as an imposition. It took time to make social connections and gain the trust of people in the area. It had been hard for her the first month or so she had been there, and continued to be a challenge even now.

And while Laura had been there trying to make things work for her, I had found myself in a New York that seemed suddenly unfamiliar. Always it had seemed bright with Laura living there with me. Perhaps, I thought, it had felt that way because all paths I had taken then led, ultimately, back to her. The city had always been full of strangers, but they had been strangers with whom I had always felt a sort of communal fraternity. Now, when I walked through those crowded streets, I felt thoroughly alone, and the end of my path was a dark, empty apartment which was most defined by the simple fact that Laura was not in it. On how many mornings had I woken and reached for her, only to find, again, that she was gone?

The toaster popped. I got up from the table, took the jar of peanut butter from the refrigerator, and spread a generous amount on each piece of toast. Laura had always told me this was no proper breakfast, but it seemed sensible to me, and I enjoyed it. It made me smile, thinking of the way Laura would tilt her head when she commented on it.

"Oh my!" I thought with a shiver of delight. "I'm going to see her later today!"

❀   ❀   ❀

My flight arrived in Billings, Montana, about two-thirty that afternoon. After picking up my...

"Stop," Paul said. All this talk about Indira and Laura's relationship and their longing for one another's company was affecting Paul's mood, and he wanted a break from it. He walked along in silence, thinking about Sheila and how hard it was to be forced to be apart from her. He had, from the start, felt such a desire to be there for her, completely and unfailingly, and to have it be, now, that they had been forcibly separated (without him even having the opportunity to tell her where he was, or that he was fine, or that he was doing everything within his power to return to her) weighed on him heavily. All he could really do was try to be practical at each step and to keep pushing forward.

Sheila—oh Sheila—I'm doing all I can to get home to you! Paul thought, and for a moment he felt regret—no, something closer to remorse—that he was failing, however unwillingly, to be present when she might need him.

How sad was she now? Paul wondered. Did she think he had been lost forever? Did she blame him, as he blamed himself, for letting her down?

Somewhere in Paul's mind, he knew how hard he was being on himself, how unreasonable—and yet the feeling was still there. He had set a standard for himself, to never desert or fail her, and yet he had done just that.

Should he not have continued with such dangerous work, once he had become committed to her? he wondered. And yet, who would have known it could be this dangerous? A lightning strike—who could ever have predicted that?

For a moment, Paul mused at the irony of imagining that perhaps he should have given up his work for her—when part of what had drawn him to her in the first place had been how inspired she made him feel, in general—and how much she inspired him in his work, especially.

Paul remembered the first time they had met, at a party at a friend's house. He had seen her across the room and had felt something for her at first sight—not passion, exactly, but something tender and strong, nonetheless.

He could picture in his mind now, so clearly, how she had looked in that first moment—tall and slender, in the sort of synthsilk jumpsuit that was considered the peak of fashion at that time, standing under a light at one end of the room. Her face had been softly lit and had seemed to Paul to almost glow beneath that light. It wasn't an extraordinary face, Paul knew—not extremely pretty, or fine—but a good face, one in which he saw something reflected, something special that took his breath away.

Paul had stood for a long time watching her, glancing up from his drink to peer past the shoulder of another woman who was attempting to engage him in conversation. He had kept on looking until Sheila had glanced in his direction and seen him watching her.

Paul stopped along the trail to adjust his shoes. This long downhill trek was throwing his feet forward inside them, and they were beginning to rub. Paul was glad the shoes Marco had given him were as adjustable as they were, but the truth was they weren't quite the right size, and he would have to be careful how he wore them if he didn't want to raise blisters.

Paul stood back up and made some adjustments in the fit of his pack, as well, before continuing down the long incline, zigging and zagging across the landscape with one switchback after another.

Soon, Paul's thoughts had returned to the night of the party. The party had been held at his friend Tyler's house—with drinks and dinner—and when it came time to be seated, Paul discovered that the tall, slender woman who had observed him watching her from across the room had made arrangements to be seated next to him.

Paul felt so smitten, at first, that he could hardly make conversation, but Sheila leaned toward him and plied him with questions about himself and his work. At one point, a friend of Paul's who was sitting across the table chimed in, telling Sheila that Paul had recently earned a prestigious award for his scientific work.

"Oh, real-ly," she said. "A famous scientist—is that so?"

"No, no, actually—I'm not famous, and it's not a particularly prestigious award," Paul answered. "It's just that the organization that gave it wants to promote its population-related work."

"Don't listen to him," Paul's friend responded. "You have to be doing quality work to get such an award, no matter what motives they have for taking an interest in your project."

It was clear from the impressed look on Sheila's face that she was unshaken in her conclusion that Paul was somehow famous and had received a high-status award. Her eyes seemed lit as she looked at him—her expression so full of warmth and approval that Paul found himself suddenly taken with her all over again.

They continued talking throughout the meal. Sheila seemed impressed with Paul, and Paul felt something stirring in him in response to Sheila—something remarkable and pure, as though he wanted to be a valiant knight for her, to meet every need, and answer every plea. It was as quick as that, the way he felt about her. It was like that from the start.

Paul looked down the trail and saw some other hikers approaching—two women and a man. When they were near, the man called out "hello!"

"Hello," Paul answered back.

"Sojourning?" one of the women asked, as they grew nearer. She had the most pleasant smile.

"Yes," Paul told her.

The three stopped to speak to Paul.

"It's good hiking weather," the man said.

"The creeks are high, but not too," the woman who had already spoken said. "You won't have any trouble with most of the crossings—you just go from rock to rock—but one you'll have to wade across."

"It's not bad, though," the other woman added.

"Thanks," Paul said.

"We were going to go to the conference," the first woman said, "but now I'm glad we decided to do this instead. Weather's perfect for it. It's just been beautiful."

Paul guessed they were all a little younger than he. All had the happy look of having spent time out in the fresh air and sunlight.

"Well, we're heading up to Figueroa—gonna go sprawl out in the shade," the man said cheerfully.

"Thanks for the news about the creeks," Paul said.

"Enjoy your sojourn!" one of the women called back, as they continued their way up the trail.

"Yeah, thanks!" Paul said, then headed on down the hill. As he went, his thoughts turned again to Sheila.

She had seemed so impressed with Paul on that first meeting, he recalled, so prepared to think him brilliant, or famous, or anything good. And the truth was, Paul had been so in need of some encouragement then that he had opened to the flattery like a blossom to the sun.

He had been having a hard time for months, as his work had been slowed almost to a stop by a lack of funding. With the work still in the theoretical stages then, just three years before, even the most open-minded of those in the Corprogov structure were unwilling to stick their necks out enough to give the extraordinary boost in funding needed to begin the building and testing of his transport machine. Paul hoped the award he had recently been given would help turn the tide, but it was still too soon to tell what effect it would have, and Paul had begun to lose faith in himself and his work—not because he doubted the basic theory behind it, but because it seemed the it was too much to hope for that he could somehow find the practical means to complete the work, and so transform his world.

And so here he was at this dinner party, at a particularly low point in his life, talking to a woman in whom he saw, mysteriously, something very deep and special, who, for some reason quite beyond him, insisted on believing that he was someone special, too.

Even then, that first evening while talking to Sheila, Paul had found himself thinking that he *would* push forward—that he would somehow clear the way so that he could build his transport to another world. He would use it as he had planned to all along: to lower the population of his world and so renew and revive the world—and he would do it for *her*, for this enchanting woman who leaned toward him and caressed his arm as they spoke.

And that's just what I should be focused on accomplishing, even now, Paul told himself, as he made his way down the hillside.

And to do that, he thought, he would need the haven the Retreat could provide—and to be accepted there, it would be necessary for him to be familiar with Dr. Kumar's book. He was only wasting time daydreaming about Sheila now.

Paul took a couple more steps down the trail as he convinced himself to shift his focus to the necessary task ahead, then spoke aloud.

"Kiki," he said, "please resume recitation at the beginning of the current section."

And with that, Kiki's voice again filled the air with the tones and cadence of Indira Kumar's voice.

◘   ◘   ◘

My flight arrived in Billings, Montana, about two-thirty that afternoon. After picking up my luggage, I took a cab to the Greyhound bus station, and from there caught the 3:45 bus to Crow Agency, a small town just outside the Northern Cheyenne Reservation. Laura had no car, but she planned to meet me there with a friend, in his car, and together we would return to Lame Deer, where Laura was living.

As I boarded the bus, I was struck by the smells of cleaning fluid and stale cigarettes. I got a seat with no one next to me, and with a good view out the broad, clean window beside it. As we rolled out of Billings and out onto the highway, I thought about where I was headed. Lame Deer was the center for the tribal government, and though under two thousand in population, it was the largest community on the reservation. Laura was living there in a small, one-bedroom house rented for her by the University of Colorado. I had often tried to picture her there, imagining it just as she had described it to me in her letters.

The house was very small, as houses go, painted blue on the outside, with just one bedroom, a bathroom, and a small sitting area off the kitchen—which Laura had referred to as "the lounge" when she first got there, but which eventually became her home office. She used the office to do interviews in when she didn't go out to people's homes, and to type up the tape recordings of those interviews in the evenings. The house was located near the edge of town, Laura had written. Out one window she could see pine trees on a hillside, and out a window on the other side of the house she could see an old car rusting in the yard.

I stared out the window of the bus at the great open grasslands rolling by along the highway, and tried to picture her house in a similar landscape. She had written to me that the place she was living was very quiet—so unlike the city. She didn't miss all the noises we could hear in our apartment in New York, she had written to me—just the sound of my voice within it.

The bus stopped at every small hamlet along the way. A trip I had been told could be driven in a little over an hour would take almost two hours by bus. The vast grasslands rolling by my window seemed just as drawn out.

The great American West—was it all like this, stretching on, mile after mile? I had been hoping for weeks that Laura and I might be able to rent a car for a few days to look around the region, as we had done one October weekend, after coming to America, to see the autumn foliage in the New England states. That had been a lovely vacation for both of us, and I hoped this trip might become a vacation of a similar sort. Even if Laura would have to work while I was there, I hoped she would be able to spare a couple of days for such an excursion.

It was dark by the time I arrived in Crow Agency. I got off the bus and, with the driver's help, collected my luggage from its cargo compartment. Then the driver boarded again, closing the bus door with a slight "hiss." The bus pulled away, and I waited alone outside a building which had already closed for the night. A steady breeze blew, rustling through the leaves of a cottonwood tree that grew near the parking lot. From somewhere, not too far off, I heard a horse whinny. The soft, chill air was filled with the scent of wood smoke, and still a hint of diesel from the departing bus.

Before long Laura arrived, riding in the passenger seat of an old green sedan. As she got out of the car, her face was filled with joy. I think I will always remember how she looked in that moment. Laura and I embraced. After three long months apart, holding her was like the sweetest kiss of heaven.

❀   ❀   ❀

I woke the next morning, as first light filtered through the bedroom curtains, and looked at my watch, which was still on my wrist from the night before. It read just after nine o'clock. But that would be New York time. In Lame Deer, it was two hours earlier, and Laura still lay peacefully asleep in my arms. I pulled my arm out from beneath her pillow, and rose up on that elbow to look down on her. She looked beautiful, resting there, but also tired. I knew she'd been working very hard, stretched thin by all the work required of her, and I hoped somehow our time together might offer her some relief.

I lay back down and drew her near me between the warm sheets, then lay drifting in and out of sleep for another half hour or so, in the quiet of that small rural town, until Laura's alarm went off.

We lingered in bed for two hours or more, talking and making love. When finally we got up, we were famished and fixed a large omelet in which we inventively included a bit of most things Laura had in her refrigerator. The joy I felt being with her was so in contrast to my somber mood of the last few months that I felt like someone who had been lost in a dark forest, and now, found, had suddenly rediscovered sunlight.

Laura was as delighted as I, and as we dawdled over brunch, we filled one another in on all the details of our lives. Even with so many letters having been sent back and forth, we never could fill them with all we wished to share.

The conversation soon branched off to a discussion of Laura's work there in Lame Deer. The house she was living in had been rented for her by the professor from the University of Colorado whom she was assisting. He had ties to tribal government and so had been able to arrange it, although normally people who weren't tribal members were not allowed to live on the reservation.

But even with his pull, the transition had been difficult for Laura. When she first arrived, she knew no one in Lame Deer. For the first month or more that she was in there, Laura spent most of her time looking for ways to make herself known to the community and to help people understand the nature of the work she was doing there. As friendly and generous as she found the people in Lame Deer and the surrounding area to be, no one seemed too eager to participate in a study that at first glance appeared to promise little other than an outside intrusion into their private lives and traditions.

It was only after Laura got to know Joseph Young Bear that things began to improve. Joseph took the time to learn about the research Laura was doing. He understood that she wasn't probing for the most personal details people could provide, only for an understanding of how outside religions had been integrated into Cheyenne traditions. He understood, too, that the overview her research could provide might be of some value to the tribe.

I had met Joseph just the night before—a tall man with broad shoulders, clear eyes, and a warm handshake. It was he who had been kind enough to drive Laura all the way to Crow Agency to pick me up and take us both back to Lame Deer. He and I hadn't spoken much that night, as Laura and I had been so busy catching up, but I knew already from Laura's letters that he was a leader in the tribal government, and that he had helped put Laura in touch with people she could interview for her study.

Sitting across the table from me as we ate brunch, Laura filled me in on details which might not have found their way into her letters.

"I showed him the research process," she was saying, "exactly how the information would be gathered, analyzed, and used to create an overall picture of how elements of outside religions had been interwoven into the religious beliefs and practices of the Northern Cheyenne. He was hesitant at first, but eventually decided that the project had value. Now when he talks to people about being interviewed, he tells them that what I'm doing helps to make a record of their beliefs—of who they are now, in the twentieth century. He tells them he's glad for the records there are of their ancestors, and that records made now will be of value to those who come later.

"Most of the people involved in the study are people Joseph sends my way. He's been such a huge help, Indira," Laura told me, "and good company, too. We've gotten to be good friends. I think you'd like him. He's thoughtful about things the way you are, and very smart. I really hope you'll have a chance to get to know him while you're here. I think you both would like each other."

We were sitting at the little table in the area next to the kitchen, which Laura used as her office and lounge. It was relaxing just to sit there, listening to Laura talk. It was such a delight just to hear her voice and to be able to watch her gestures and facial expressions again.

The table was next to a small window, and as absorbed as I was in the conversation and in watching Laura smiling and talking and gesturing with her toast, it had been dark when I'd arrived the night before, and I was curious to discover just where this little house I had woken up in was situated, so I kept shifting my gaze between Laura and the view out the window.

Outside, I could see other small homes scattered about. Beyond them was the pine-studded hillside Laura had mentioned in her letters, somehow larger and more rugged than I had pictured it. The ground between the houses was covered with grass, which must have been green and lush in the summertime, but now had turned brittle and brown. In shady spots I could see patches of icy snow left over from the last snow fall. The sky was bright and surprisingly blue, with power lines passing between the houses and along the main road.

I looked back over at Laura. "Didn't you write to me that Joseph was in Vietnam?"

"Yeah, he was there," Laura answered. She looked thoughtful. "He said it was pretty weird—in all the ways you've heard about Vietnam, and more. He said when he first got there he heard some of the other men in his platoon refer to Viet Cong territory as 'Indian Country.' Like they were the cowboys or settlers and the Viet Cong were the Indians."

Laura's voice had turned serious. "Joseph told me it felt really strange to him," she went on, "and made him think about the conflict and what the U.S. was really doing there. It made him wonder who these people were who he'd been hired to fight.

"In Saigon, on the way in, he saw some graffiti left by a U.S. soldier. It said, 'The only good gook is a dead gook.' Like white people used to say about Indians." Laura winced a little as she said it.

"Anyway, he said it all felt really strange. He said after he got there, it seemed different than he expected, and he had a lot of trouble getting his head around what he was really doing there." Laura picked up her tea cup and looked at it absently before taking a sip.

After a moment of silence, I asked, "How'd he end up there? Did he enlist—or was he drafted?"

Laura set her cup down carefully on its saucer. "He joined up," she answered. "I think he said in '66. He said it's work that's respected in Cheyenne culture, and there really weren't many opportunities available here on the reservation. He was young. I think it just sort of happened that way. I don't think he'd really set a course for himself yet."

Laura paused, as though weighing what she would say next, then added, "He'd been there for barely five months when he got shot—hit in the leg and hip. He said where he got shot in the leg the bullet went clear through and nicked an artery. He said there was blood everywhere. The hip wound fractured his hip, but the bleeding wasn't so bad there. He was walking point, I think he called it, at the front of his group. They were ambushed, and he went down in heavy fire. When he saw all the blood, he thought he would die for sure. He was only nineteen years old, and he thought his life was over."

Laura leaned back in her chair and looked out the window, then back over at me.

"Like I said, he was up at the front and under heavy fire, but a friend of his, his platoon's medic, made his way to Joseph's position and tied a tourniquet around Joseph's leg above the wound. The medic was rushing, trying to get to the others who had been hit after Joseph went down. He told Joseph to apply pressure to the hip and to loosen the tourniquet every few minutes and then re-tighten it. He was kneeling over Joseph, who was on the ground—helping him, like I said, under heavy fire—and just then a bullet hit the medic in the cheek and blew out the back of his head. He died instantly."

Laura was silent for a few seconds. "Sorry, I didn't think about how heavy that would sound."

"It's okay," I answered.

"Anyway, I think it says something about Joseph. Not the event itself, but the way he responded to it. He felt his life had to count for something after that—not just because he had come so close to losing it, but because someone else, a friend, had given his life saving Joseph's. Because of that, Joseph felt his life didn't just have to count, but had to count double.

"After he came back—he was discharged after he was wounded—after he got back he was determined not to just drift through life letting whatever opportunities came his way shape the sort of life he was going to live. He wanted to do something that mattered, and he knew if he was going to, he would need to create better opportunities than the ones he saw around him," Laura paused and bit her lower lip, looking thoughtful, like she was trying to decide what parts of Joseph's story she could tell, and what would seem too personal to him.

"He'd, ah, he'd finished high school with pretty good grades," she went on, "but there was nothing remarkable about his time as a student, so after he was discharged he got a job to pay the bills and spent his nights and weekends studying. After a year he took his SATs and ACTs and got excellent scores on both. He applied at a lot of Ivy-League schools. He got into Harvard on a scholarship."

"That's pretty impressive," I said.

"Yeah," Laura answered, "and not only impressive that he set a goal and got himself into Harvard, but that he was somehow confident enough of his own identity to do it."

"How do you mean?" I asked.

"Well, for example, Joseph told me that he has a cousin who feels strongly about maintaining Cheyenne traditions. When Joseph was getting ready to leave for Harvard, his cousin more or less accused him of being a collaborator—serving the purposes of whites who want to undermine Indian culture," Laura said. "Both Joseph and his cousin had gone to the BIA school, the government school, in Busby, where they did everything they could to wipe out anything culturally Cheyenne in the children—punished them for speaking their own language, that sort of thing. So his cousin saw school in that light and wasn't pleased to see Joseph going off to one."

"So how did Joseph respond to that?" I asked.

"He told his cousin it wasn't that way. That first of all, Harvard wasn't that way, and then he told him, 'Think of it like this—I'm sneaking into the white camp to gather up supplies we need here, and bringing them back with me.'"

I nodded, trying to imagine how that would have seemed to his cousin.

"And that's basically what he's done," Laura went on. "After he got his BA..."

"Wait," I interrupted. "What did his cousin think about that?"

"I don't know, exactly. I think he thought that sounded okay. They get along now—they're close—that's all I know."

"Okay, go ahead," I said.

"Anyway, after Joseph got his BA," Laura continued, "he went on for his Master's in, I think he said Public Policy. Then he brought those resources home and began to use them to create better opportunities for the kids coming up here today. He's done a lot of good for the people around here. Worked with other veterans in the area—either helping them or getting them involved in helping others. He's working to bring in grants for small businesses. They're trying to establish more Indian-run businesses, so when people spend their money on the reservation, the money will stay in the community and continue to build here." Laura absentmindedly straightened her fork where she had set it on the table next to her empty plate. Her expression was serious as she went on.

"I have the impression from what people say that he's really done a lot of good around here. He's a good man. I have a lot of respect for him," Laura concluded.

"It sounds like he deserves it," I said.

Laura nodded, looked up at me. "He does," she said, her look still thoughtful.

Laura reached across the table, picked up my hand, leaned forward and kissed it, then quietly set my hand back down and rose to begin clearing the plates from our meal. I smiled up at her, filled with delight that I could be there with her.

I stood up and picked up the empty skillet and both of our glasses. I was thinking about what an interesting world Laura had found herself in when she'd come west. It was one of the things we'd both shared from the beginning—a desire to expand our horizons and learn more about what the world holds.

"You know something I'd like to do while I'm here," I said, as we walked into the kitchen. "I'd like it if we could go sight-seeing together, see what the area is like."

I set down the skillet and glasses by the sink. "I know you'll have to work while I'm here, but I thought maybe if you could take off one weekday, next Friday," I continued. "Maybe we could rent a car and look around some. Go to Yellowstone, maybe? We could be back Saturday night."

"Take off Friday," Laura echoed, looking thoughtful. "I could take it off if I can make up the time elsewhere. Friday—oh, Indira, that seems so soon—and you fly out Sunday morning!"

Laura set down our plates next to the sink, then turned and leaned against the counter, facing me.

"Suddenly the week seems so short!" she said, shaking her head. I leaned against the counter next to her. She put her arm around me and rested her head on my shoulder.

"To think I'm going to be without you again so soon," she said, then looked over at me. "But I've got you now," she added. "Let's do it. The sight-seeing would be fun. But I'll have to make up the time, I guess today or tomorrow, while it's still the weekend, if I'm going to take off a whole day this coming week." Laura sighed and cast her gaze down.

"I'm sorry about that, Indira. It's just that I'm so behind already." Laura's voice sounded sad and more than a little overwhelmed.

"It's okay, love," I answered. "It'll be wonderful just to be here with you." I gently turned her face toward me and kissed her briefly on the lips. "Why don't I clean up the dishes and let you do what you need to do to get some of that work cleared away?"

Laura accepted, and apologetically suggested that she would have to work both weekend afternoons, if she was going to take off the whole day, the following Friday. As I got started on the dishes, I thought about the letters she had sent to me in which she had written about the circumstances surrounding her job there in Lame Deer.

As hard as Laura had been working since she had arrived, she had found herself constantly behind in her labors. She had been asked to aim at completing and typing up two interviews each week day. Not only had she gotten off to a slow start in her first weeks there, as she had tried to meet people and encourage them to take part in the study, but it was hard even now, with all Joseph's help, to line up as many as two interviews in a day.

From the start, Laura had felt it was important to spend some time with each participant before beginning an interview, to give them a chance to feel more at home with her before launching into asking them questions about their religious beliefs and practices—a subject most people, the world over, will consider to be personal. She not only thought this approach was kinder to the people she was interviewing, but better for the project, as people will generally tell more when they feel more at home with the person they are talking to—and will be more likely to encourage others to agree to be interviewed if they found the experience pleasant, themselves. But because Laura was careful to deal with each person in a positive way socially, and never approached any of the interviews with an impersonal or clinical tone, it often took her three or four hours interacting with someone in the process of completing an interview that was intended to take only two.

The professor who had planned this project had imagined that it should be possible to complete and type up two interviews a day—though this had little to do with the actual reality Laura found herself dealing with. All things considered, Laura felt lucky if she could complete the requisite two interviews a day—quite apart from the time it took to type them up. A single interview would generally take three or four hours to type, as Laura's typing couldn't keep up with the actual pace of conversation, and she would have to keep stopping to rewind the tape. Just to complete her expected day's work could easily take twelve to sixteen hours—and that allowed no time for meeting people and lining up interviews in the first place.

Still, as impossibly demanding as her assignment turned out to be, Laura felt she had to do her best to live up to it if she hoped to be offered the assistant professorship she had been told would soon become available. While she enjoyed meeting the people she interviewed and felt the work was genuinely interesting and valuable, she felt constantly stressed by the demands of expectations she couldn't possibly hope to meet.

When I finished with the dishes, I reminded myself that even though Laura had to work, I was on vacation. I spent a little while reading and then napped through the better part of the afternoon.

When I woke, Laura was still hard at work at the little table we'd eaten brunch at—typing away at her electric typewriter, transcribing the tape she was listening to on headphones plugged into a reel-to-reel tape recorder. I felt hungry, but since we'd finished brunch so late, and it was so close to dinner time, it didn't make sense to start a meal just then. Instead, I made us a simple version of afternoon tea, with just one sandwich for Laura and me to share, and a pot of tea for the two of us.

I brought our food to the little table Laura was typing at. When I set the tray with our tea and two half sandwiches on the table, Laura stopped typing and took off the headphones.

"How's it going?" I asked.

"Pretty well," she answered. She seemed tired, but cheerful.

"Finding lots of examples of syncretism?" I said, turning towards her. Laura smiled.

"Maybe. Some interesting things, anyhow," she answered. "The man whose interview I'm transcribing now told me he prayed to Jesus before leaving for his fast at Bear Butte. He had a vision there, but the vision contained no Christian symbols. I asked him why had he prayed to Jesus, and he just said, 'I thought it might help.'"

I sat down on the edge of the table, listening. Laura had already told me in one of her letters that much of Cheyenne religious philosophy had to do with the way *exhastoz* gets moved around. *Exhastoz* translates roughly as "cosmic energy" or "blessings." Some Christian practices were seen as additional ways one might receive such energy or blessings—but they don't replace traditional ways, just add to them.

"He told me a little bit about the vision he had," Laura went on. "He left out some details, he said, because he didn't want to waste their power talking about them. The part he did tell me was beautiful, though."

"Do you think it would be okay to tell me about it?" I asked.

"Yeah, I think so—at least the amount he told me. He did agree it could be part of the study—but really it's not, I mean, there's really no syncretism in it.

"He's one of Joseph's veteran friends. He'd been having trouble with nightmares," Laura went on. "In his dreams, he'd be back in Vietnam—maybe separated from his unit, alone in the jungle with the enemy all around, and him out of ammunition, unable to protect himself. Stuff like that. Really terrifying stuff.

"He went to Bear Butte—a very sacred place—to fast, and had a vision there. In the vision, he was back in the jungle. He could hear sounds all around him. He was surrounded by the North Vietnamese, but his unit was far away. He was trembling, really terrified, and just then he looked up. A hawk was flying up above, and the trees were strangely open, not like the jungle, so he could see where it flew to. It called to him to follow, and he did.

"The hawk led him out of the jungle and into open grasslands, prairie, where he could see for miles and miles around. He could see that there was no one there, so he knew that he was safe.

"He said it was the first time he'd really felt safe since he left for Vietnam." Laura paused, and then added, "It's beautiful, I think—his vision. His dreams have been much better since he had it."

"Yeah, it is beautiful," I said.

Laura looked thoughtful for a minute, and then added, "It pleases me to hear stories like that, where Cheyenne traditions can be so powerful for people still. So much has been taken from these people. Their land. Their way of life. Many no longer speak their language. I've thought about it since I've been here. I've thought if you were here you'd point out how much pain comes from people being cut off from their dreams, from their—what did you used to call it? from their protolife. How bad it would be to be cut off from the possibility of making life from it.

"Anyway, it's hard for people here." Laura turned her gaze out the window. "Most Cheyenne live in poverty today, struggling with an outside world that doesn't recognize them. I think it says a lot about their strength as a people that they've managed as well as they have, but its a hard path they've had to walk." Laura turned her eyes back towards me.

I nodded, thinking about what she'd just said, then let my gaze fall to the floor. After a moment, I said, "Sometimes I think life is just a hard path for everyone, one way or another."

I looked at Laura and saw her looking up at me, surprise written on her face. "Indira, that's so unlike you! You were always my cheerful optimist!"

I looked back down, frowned a little, bit my lip. "I guess I've just been feeling that way lately," I answered.

Laura reached for me and pulled me to her. I slipped from the table and stood beside her where she sat. She held onto one of my hands and wrapped her arm around my waist.

"I'm going to have to cheer you up while you're here, I can see that," she said.

I looked down at her and smiled, stroked her hair. "You do that," I told her. "It'd probably be good for me. But first, you have work, and I promised not to interrupt you if we're going sight-seeing at the end of the week." After working and studying in one another's company for so many years, we had each learned to be careful not to interrupt one another's labors.

I kissed her on top of her head, then turned and set her half of our avocado and cheese sandwich and her cup of tea (darjeeling, with milk, just as she liked it) off the tray where she could reach them while she worked.

When I turned back towards her, Laura was looking up at me with such light in her eyes.

"My beautiful Indira," she said. She tenderly kissed the back of my hand, then slid her chair back in close to the typewriter. She reached down and picked up her headphones and put them on, then took a bite from the sandwich.

"Oh, good!" she said, her words a bit muffled by the mouthful of food. She took a sip of tea and swallowed, then added, "Thanks so much, Indira. I hadn't even realized I was hungry."

I smiled at her, then picked up the tray and carried it across the room to the easy chair and side table by the opposite window. From behind me, I heard the whir of the tape player and the clatter of keys as Laura began to type.

I sat, staring out the window, taking bites of my half of the sandwich between sips of tea. Out the window I could see the old car Laura had written to me about. A group of children of various ages clamored through, on, and around it. I found myself considering how cynical I'd sounded when talking to Laura just then. She was right, I knew—I would somehow have to lose this cynicism which was seeping into me. It was becoming part of the model through which I saw the world, and so was becoming a part of the world I created around me. I would have to pay more attention to what I was telling myself, I thought, and to the picture I was making when I looked out at the world.

I stared out at the kids playing on the car. One appeared to be pretend-ing to drive it, while two more alternately sat in the back seat or ran around outside. Two more kept climbing up on the roof and jumping down from there. Those two looked to be about eleven or twelve years old, close to the same age as a boy who lived in the building in which Laura and I had shared an apartment in Manhattan—and where I was still living alone.

That boy's name was Emil. His story, I felt, was a part of this somber mood I had been feeling, was one of the building blocks of this new cyni-cism that was gathering within me.

The first time I remembered seeing Emil was shortly after Laura and I had moved into our apartment, when we'd first come to New York about half-a-dozen years before. We were both on the staircase landing our apartment and his family's apartment opened out on to. I'd lost control of a paper bag full of groceries while taking out my keys to unlock the door, and some oranges had dropped out of the bag and rolled over to where Emil was standing outside his apartment door. He'd reached down and picked up two of them and held them up towards me with both arms extended.

"Come along, Emil," his mother had said, beaming down at him proudly. Emil had handed me the oranges, then turned and disappeared into the apartment. I'd say he was about five years old at the time.

Sitting in Laura's Lame Deer home, I recalled how warm it had been in New York that autumn, and how I had often sat with the window open, working at a small desk in front of it. I would sometimes hear Emil and a couple of the other children from the neighborhood playing on the sidewalk in front of the building. I was very happy with our new home. Even though the city seemed dense and difficult in some ways, I felt I had found a good home there with Laura, in a place where children played and sweetened the air with their laughter.

There's something about sharing a building with people. When walk-ing down the street, the strangers change with each passing day, but the strangers in your building are always the same strangers. Even if you don't stop and speak to them, you come eventually to feel as though you know them.

Emil's parent's were recent émigrés. They had moved to America as a young couple from Yugoslavia, before they'd had any children. I only knew that much about them because Mrs. Koffel, the building's gossip, had insisted on telling me a little bit about everyone in the building when Laura and I had first arrived—although I think mostly what she wanted was to find out something about us.

Emil was his parent's oldest child. He had a sister who was two or three years younger and a brother younger than she, who had been just a baby when Laura and I had first moved in. I would see Emil in the hallway, sometimes, with his parents. I would nod at his parents, who never seemed especially friendly, and then glance down at Emil, who would look up at me with the most lovely, open expression, full of child-like delight and curiosity.

As he got older, the eye contact continued. We wouldn't talk, but somehow, he would always look me right in the eye, as he had when he was little, at least for a moment, at least a momentary glance where we connected. And I felt related to him somehow, linked to him in a way that's hard to define or explain. I was always interested to know more about his life.

Sometimes I would run into Mrs. Koffel, while coming or going, or picking up the mail. She would start to tell me about the building's other residents. It's hard to know how she knew what she knew, or if it was even true. I felt guilty listening to her stories about the other tenants—and wondered what stories she told about Laura and me. Mostly I avoided these conversations, but when she had news of Emil, I would listen—a bit guiltily, but listen.

When Emil was about eight or nine, he was caught shoplifting. He had to go to juvenile court and was put on probation. I saw him with his parents in the stairwell about that time. They didn't look my way as they unlocked the door to their apartment. They seemed subdued, burdened. I wondered if they were embarrassed by their son's behavior, ashamed somehow to be seen with him.

I remember on that occasion they had hurried him inside as I passed, but Emil looked back over his shoulder at me, that same innocent, open look behind his big brown eyes, perhaps now clouded a bit with sadness, and then the door had closed behind them with a click that echoed in the empty hallway, bouncing between the linoleum floor and the hand-plastered walls and ceiling. I walked past their door and over to my own on the other side of the landing and, fumbling with my keys in the dim light, let myself in.

Most of the time, in those days, I was busy with my studies, or grading papers for one of the classes I was helping teach, or savoring the few hours Laura and I could salvage from our other activities to spend in one another's company. I didn't think much about Emil for a time. I would sometimes pass him with other members of his family on the stairs, or hear his family's voices through the walls.

It gradually dawned on me, as the months passed, that it had been a long time since I'd seen either of his parents look at him with that expression of parental adoration and pride I'd seen in his mother and father's eyes so often in the first couple of years I'd lived there with Laura, and the tones of family turmoil I'd heard through the walls on occasion—a raised voice, a scolding word, a child crying—seemed to be coming more frequently now.

I wondered what was happening—was the father out of work? Was his diminished income creating stress in the family? Had Emil's shoplifting episode been an outlet for some sort of stress building up at home? Or had that act, somehow random and childish—an attempt to fit in with the rough and tumble kids of the neighborhood, perhaps—had it been the starting point for this increased discord? Had his parents decided he was a difficult child from whom they would withhold their approval and affection?

In time I saw Emil with his family less and less, and more and more
I would see him outside of the building, on the street, hanging out with
the other neighborhood kids, tough kids, a little older than him.

I remember one rainy night passing him with two or three other boys,
standing in a doorway, smoking, their collars turned up against the cold.
Still, he looked at me, as I passed, with that same sweet and guileless
expression, that same openness in his eyes. I wondered what had pushed
him from the arms of his family into the company of these tough neighborhood kids—if perhaps they offered him a degree of acceptance his
family would no longer provide.

But no matter what company he kept, nor how tough he became on
the outside, Emil always looked me in the eye when we passed, a habit
so deep, so ingrained, it could not be let go of—a sideways glance, quick
but somehow steady, in the hallway; or a quick look up at me as we'd pass,
him climbing the stairs, and me descending; or on the street with him
situated in his new world—there would still be that look, and still his eyes
were dark wells of innocence, something spacious and tender living there,
no matter the years that passed, nor how tough his clothing.

So perhaps it shouldn't have surprised me when Mrs. Koffel told me, a
few weeks after Laura had left town, that Emil had been arrested again,
for theft. She said he'd grabbed cash from the drawer at a convenience
store while his friends, a couple of the kids he hung with in the neighborhood, had created a disturbance. The store was run by a couple, an old
man and woman. The man had been out, but had returned just in time
to catch Emil in the act. Mrs. Koffel surmised that it probably wasn't the
first time they'd done this—just the first time he'd gotten caught.

"Kids like that!" she'd exclaimed, shaking her head.

"Where is he now?" I asked her, imagining him back in the juvenile
detention center.

"The police have him. His parents won't pay bail this time—they want
him to learn a lesson. I say, that's the right thing to do. Kids like that—
making trouble! And they caught him, dead to rights. He'll probably stay
away for a while this time."

I nodded, and started up the stairs. The news depressed me. I kept
thinking about Emil when he was small, him playing games with the
other kids on the sidewalk, his laughter floating up in the warm evening
air of summer as I sat studying by the open window above. I thought of
his clear eyes meeting mine every time we passed in the hall. His parents
would leave him in jail to rot. What lesson was there for him in that? Just
more of the hardness that had sucked him in in this difficult city, the only
home he'd known, the only world he understood.

I looked back out the window and suddenly an awareness of time passing caught up with me. Only a couple of the kids were still playing around
the rusted car. The sky above them had turned blue-black with the last
shreds of evening.

I sighed. Emil. Yes. I was sure his story was part of the sourness that
was now clouding my view, but only one part of it. Without Laura, the
city seemed a harder place in other ways as well. All of the bumps and

bruises of life, which her loving arms would have comforted me through, now stayed with me a little longer, and I took more notice of them.

Emil, I thought again, and wondered if I had been right—that his parents had lost faith in him after the shop-lifting incident, had seen him no longer as their jewel, but as a bad kid whom they had to press into line. And the more they'd pressed, and restrained, and scolded, the more they had driven him from them, into the waiting arms of the streets below. Where they had repressed, he had broken free. Where they had disapproved, he had incorporated their vision of him into his own—and then seeing himself as worthy of disapproval, he had acted accordingly.

For a moment, sitting there, I wished he could have been my child, to raise with approval and encouragement. I looked over at Laura at the desk, still at work. She was concentrating on what she was doing, but even within her concentration, I could see her gentleness. It felt good just to be in the same room with her. It had always felt that way.

I rested my head back, staring over at Laura, and it occurred to me that I had never told her about Emil.

Laura looked up and saw me looking at her. She stopped the tape player and took off her headphones.

"I've glanced over at you now and then, but each time you've been deep in thought," she said.

"I've been thinking about Emil," I told her.

Laura looked puzzled for a moment.

"Oh, the boy in our building," she answered, nodding. "What's up with him?"

I told her, then, about what had become of Emil. Somehow, just telling her about it made it seem less bad. Laura listened closely, then commented on how sad that was, but that he seemed a very bright boy, and might still find a better course. Then she looked out the window next to the table, staring out into the blue-black twilight.

After a minute or two, she took a deep breath, then looked down at her watch.

"Quarter of five," she said, with a note of surprise. "I don't know about you, but I'm getting hungry. How about I finish up a few things here, and then get started fixing us dinner?" Laura said.

"How about I cook dinner while you work?" I offered.

"Oh, no—I have something special planned. I want to cook for you."

I smiled. "Well, at least let me fix us another cup of tea in the meanwhile."

Laura smiled and agreed to that. I started towards the kitchen, then turned back towards Laura.

"Oh! But I finished the milk when I made tea this afternoon," I said.

Laura made a little gasp. "Oh, that's right! I'm sorry—I knew I was low. I meant to get more before you arrived, but I ran out of time."

"Don't worry about it," I said, and offered to go get more while Laura worked. Laura hesitated, but then agreed and drew me a little map so I wouldn't get lost along the way. Soon I had slipped out the door and was

on my way by foot to the only convenience store in town—just a little
closer, Laura had told me, than "the big store."

I set off for the store, down the quiet road through Laura's neighborhood, listening to the sound of my shoes striking the pavement, watching
the light from the flashlight Laura had handed me as I'd left, dancing on
the road ahead. The air was fresh and crisply cold, laced with the scent of
pine smoke. Above me hung a crescent moon in a star-splattered sky.

I was thinking again about how I had begun to pick up the cynicism
Laura had noticed earlier. Partly it had been that I had felt sad to have
her gone, but more importantly, I realized, her absence had caused me to
focus more of my attention on the world outside the life Laura and I had
shared together—a life that had always been so purposeful and fulfilling,
always so loving and warm. With Laura gone, I had taken more notice of
the people my life crossed paths with, and what the lives they lived were
like—and those were not always happy stories.

I had begun to wonder, with Laura gone, if my old perceptions hadn't
been a little too positive—this simple equation that life was driven by a
longing to fulfill protolife, and that when protolife was fulfilled, we felt
joy. Likewise, I had for a long time considered suffering to be simply a
block in this process, but now, after Laura's long absence, suffering had
begun to seem a very dark and complex thing, and I no longer felt I had a
handle on its causes or nature. Not that I had thought about it and decided
that my earlier conclusions had been wrong. After all, the ache I felt was,
simply put, a longing for Laura's presence, unfulfilled. Nonetheless, in
the months I'd spent without Laura, I'd been seeing such a hard side of
life, and I'd begun to feel overwhelmed by those perceptions.

I reached my first turn where the road split in a "Y" and looked down
at the little map Laura had handed me as I'd left for the store. Her handwriting, as usual, was smooth and elegant. The note indicated I should
turn here at the "Y" and then again at a "T" up ahead. I smiled. It was
sweet that she had drawn it for me.

As I put the note back in my pocket and headed off down the left branch
of the "Y," I started trying to remember what other events had happened
that may have colored my view. Certainly, Emil's recent incarceration
had been disheartening news, but my change in attitudes had begun
much before that.

The evening breeze seemed stronger after turning at the branch in the
road, and I slipped off one glove to button the top button of my coat. It was
a cold night, with the temperature close to freezing, and I was glad I had
listened when Laura had advised I bring my warmest coat with me from
New York. All buttoned up, the coat felt snug and warm. As I slipped my
glove back on, I let my thoughts drift, trying to recall what other events
may have influenced me.

An impression came to me of stopping at the fruit and vegetable stand
a couple of blocks from my apartment one sunny autumn day, perhaps

two or three weeks after Laura had left town. As I recalled, it had been rainy and chilly earlier that week, but that day was sunny and clear. I was shopping for vegetables for a salad when an old woman came and started picking out tomatoes next to me. I glanced over and realized she was someone I recognized from the neighborhood—a small woman with gray hair, perhaps in her mid-sixties. I remembered encountering her at the same produce stand once, months earlier, when I had come just to pick up one item Laura had forgotten to buy for dinner. The woman had been just ahead of me in line that time, and had insisted, in a somehow grandmotherly way, that I take her place in line, as she had two baskets full of what she was buying, and I had just the one item. It had seemed a kind gesture, and I had remembered her for that reason.

I glanced over at her that sunny autumn day, sure she did not remember me. Just then, she reached in front of me for a red, ripe tomato. The sleeve of her sweater had been pushed up, probably because the day had turned so warm, and there on her forearm, I could see—a line of numbers had been tattooed.

A moment later she had her tomato and stepped away to look through the onions. I only saw it for a moment—yet sometimes a perception as fleeting as that can color other, more lasting, perceptions.

After that, I found myself looking at people whom I previously might have assumed lived lives of harmony and happiness, and instead began to wonder what terrible heartaches they may have endured.

It occurred to me then, walking through Lame Deer on my way to the convenience store, that it wasn't just that my perception had changed, but that I had become more receptive to hearing about the suffering of others as a result of that change in perception. I began to expect their life stories to include suffering, and so they found in me a listener who expected, and in a certain sense invited, them to tell such tales.

But it was more than that, even, I thought as I walked along. Being alone, without Laura, had made people feel more comfortable telling me private stories of all sorts—stories they could tell to one person, but never to a group, not even to a group of two.

I reached the street I was supposed to turn at and took a right-hand turn. Having examined it once, now, the little map Laura had drawn was firmly anchored in my mind. I glanced over it mentally. This right, and then another left at the next "T" just ahead, and I would be about halfway there, I thought. Then I let my mind turn again to the events of that autumn, and another memory came to me.

I was working late on campus one evening. I'd done that a lot since Laura had left town, as it put off my inevitable return to an empty apartment. On this particular evening, a professor I barely knew, named Matthew Drake, stopped by my office. He asked if Will Mosley, the professor whose research I'd been working on, was around, and I told him no, he'd already left for home. Matthew and I were what I would think of as "good acquaintances." We'd been introduced a time or two, and always said a brief "hello" when we passed in a hallway, though I wouldn't say we crossed paths more than once or twice a month, at best. On this particular evening he stood in my doorway and chatted with me for a while. He mentioned that he had a son who was in school at Dartmouth College, and that his daughter had just begun that fall at Sarah Lawrence. He seemed restless and not eager to leave. He said that he'd thought he might find Will working late and had hoped that Will would join him for a beer. Matthew told me, also, that his wife was away at a psychology conference in Ontario—and that he just hated to go home to an empty apartment.

I realized that all he was telling me amounted to a kind of invitation, and paused to consider if I might like to go with him. I didn't know him very well, but he seemed like a nice enough fellow, and I knew that Will thought well of him.

As I considered this, I recalled seeing Matthew with his wife, who was also on the Columbia faculty, in the hallway one day. She was talking with someone, and he was waiting for her. I had just glanced over at him, as I'd walked by, and his eyes had been on her. His look had been so gentle, so adoring, that I'd smiled, noticing it. I was sure it was as he was saying—he just wasn't eager to go home to an empty apartment. The truth was, I wasn't, either.

I told him I'd share a beer with him, if he'd like the company. He cheerfully agreed, as though my suggesting this removed any awkwardness from him having stood at my office door talking about his circumstances.

I took a few minutes to tie up a few loose ends in the work I was doing, and soon we were on our way to a quiet bar down the street.

We took seats right at the bar, rather than at a table, I suppose because it felt like the thing that "pals" do, and that acting like pals removed whatever edge of awkward intimacy there was in the two of us going out for drinks together.

Matthew was middle aged, tall and graying, with a little too much weight on what must once have been an athletic frame. His voice was soft, and his manner of communication attentive and nuanced.

For the first half hour or so we were there, we talked about the research I was working on with Will Mosley. Matthew had heard about it from Will, and said it was interesting to hear another take on it. But after a time, I'd had enough of talking about my work, and encouraged Matthew to tell me about his.

I'd been a little sketchy about what field he was in. I knew he was friends with Will, and that his wife was on Columbia's Psychology faculty, with an office in the main part of a building my office was in an extension on. But it turned out that Matthew wasn't at Columbia at all—he was a professor in the Anthropology Department at NYU, and knew Will Mosley from graduate school, years earlier. Matthew's area of research was child-rearing practices around the world. I asked him some questions about his research, then asked him how he got interested in studying child rearing to begin with.

Matthew looked at me for a moment, his face thoughtful, as though he were measuring his response, and then answered in the same quiet voice he'd used all evening. "The truth is my own upbringing was less than ideal. My father was a violent man. He believed in 'spare the rod, spoil the child.' He regularly beat me and my brothers while we were growing up," he told me.

"What in the world for?" I said.

"Anytime we were 'bad,'" Matthew said, shrugging and holding up his fingers to make the quote marks around the word "bad."

"Nothing remarkable," he went on, "the usual kid's stuff, I guess. But he thought he had to keep us under control, not let our 'bad' impulses get loose. It was the way he was raised. Also, he had a lot of anger, and he drank. That's a bad combination. He was raising us the way he thought was right. 'Putting the fear of God' in us, and all that. But it also gave him the opportunity to take his anger out on somebody. Which must have been a sort of relief for him, I suppose.

"He never would admit he'd been wrong in raising us the way he did, but I think he began to have his doubts when he saw me raising my kids without ever touching them in anger. They're good kids. He could see that. You don't need violence to make someone be good."

I looked over at him, listening closely. Matthew slowly turned his beer on the counter in front of him, then looked back over at me.

"But for me, growing up," he went on, "I just thought that was the way it was. When I got pretty nearly grown, and I realized other people didn't raise their kids like that—that it was an aberration, not the norm—I became interested in finding out what normal was, and all the different ways that normal could be expressed around the world."

"You seem like such a gentle man, Matthew," I said. "I would think it would be hard not to be burned up with bitterness, growing up like that."

"Well, I'll admit, I was a pretty confused young man. I hated him for a long time, and would sometimes get lost in thoughts of how I would get back at him. Those thoughts could be pretty violent, I'll admit," he said with a kind of quiet sadness. "I used to want to give him a piece of the same thing he'd given to me and my brothers."

Lit the way the bar was, Matthew's beer seemed to glow with its own amber light. It shone as he turned it slowly on the counter in front of him, its sides wet and glistening.

"It kind of haunted me," he continued, "for years, even when I was grown and living apart from him. It was something I knew I needed to work out, but it was hard to think clearly about it. I had the worst fantasies, for a while, when I was a young man, thinking about what I'd like to do to him. I wanted to make him see what he'd done to us, by somehow making him hurt like I had hurt, and like my brothers had.

"But then one day I realized what I was doing—I wanted to make him understand, you see," he looked over at me, his expression pleasant, calm. "I wanted to cause him the pain he had caused me and my brothers because, somehow, deep down, I thought it would change him. I wanted to make him see, make him understand. I thought if he really understood, personally and vividly, the pain he caused in us, that he couldn't have done it. I wanted him to become a *different sort of person* who would be safe for me to deal with."

I nodded, wanting to understand what he was telling me.

"That was what I really wanted," Matthew said, "to disarm him, make him safe for me and my brothers. I wanted to give him the pain, so he would understand it."

"Because if he understood the harm he'd been doing, he wouldn't do it?" I said, echoing what he had just told me.

"Not if he understood in a way where it reverberated through him. Not if he really *felt* it. Not if he *really understood*," Matthew told me. Then he added, "Not just for me, but for my brothers, also."

"You're the oldest?" I asked.

"Yeah. In a way, I think it was harder to watch him do that to them, than even to have it happen to me." Matthew looked over at me, his face at once intense and surprisingly serene.

"I'm sorry you had to go through all that," I said.

"Thanks," Matthew said, his voice quiet. He looked me in the eye, then down at his beer.

"Do you still think of him like that?" I asked.

"The violent fantasies—no, not in years," Matthew answered. "Like I started to say, once I realized I thought like that because I wanted to be safe from him, things started to change. Seeing that helped me take the next step—which was realizing I *already was* safe. He couldn't reach me, nor my brothers, anymore. We were men—big and strong—and we'd all moved far away. We were free of him—and I didn't have to make him understand, didn't have to make him see how terrible his actions were, in order to be safe from him."

Matthew took a sip of his beer. "I could even see him on occasional holidays and feel safe, after that," he added.

Matthew smiled a little, looked relaxed. "It helped meeting Mira, too," he said, referring to his wife. "She taught me what gentleness is. She's a lovely woman."

I smiled a little, too, then took another swallow of my beer. Matthew cradled his glass on the counter in front of him. It was his second pint, still half full.

"Well, I had no idea I'd tell you all this," he said, after a minute's silence. "Get me a little lonely, and give me a beer and a patient listener, eh? I'm sorry, I hope I haven't talked your ear off."

I assured him that wasn't at all the case—I'd found what he'd had to say interesting and appreciated his candor.

We visited a while longer, on less intimate subjects. When we'd both finished our beers—my first, his second—Matthew pointed out the hour, and we both decided it was time to go.

As I rode home in a cab from the bar that night, I thought about what Matthew must have been like when he was a boy. He was such a big man now. His father must have been a big man, too, I thought, as I watched the city lights stream by outside the cab window.

I reached the street Laura had marked as "4th Street" on the map and turned onto it. It should be only a couple more long blocks now, according to the map, I thought, and I would be at "the little store," as Laura had referred to it. I was glad to be getting near. Even dressed warmly as I was, the cold was beginning to seep through. My hands felt like ice. Each breath took form in the air like a cloud in front of me.

Just then a car slowed on the road alongside me, heading in the same direction I was going in. I looked over and recognized it as the same car Laura had come to pick me up in the night before. I bent down enough to see inside. Joseph Young Bear was driving. He pulled over near me, and I opened the passenger door.

"Want a ride?" he said.

"I'm just getting milk at the little store. I'm almost there."

"That's okay. It's cold. I'll drive you."

I could feel the warm air coming up from inside the car and realized I was letting out all his heat. I hurried up and got in.

"You looked pretty deep in thought," he said to me. "I hope I didn't startle you."

"Oh, no problem," I answered. Joseph pulled away from the side of the road. I had an impulse to tell him what I'd been thinking about, but it seemed an awfully intense conversation starter. Then I remembered what Laura had told me earlier that day: "He's thoughtful about things the way you are... I think you'd both like each other..." and decided I might as well go ahead. "I was just thinking about a conversation I had with somebody in New York, a while back," I added.

"Yeah?" Joseph said.

I nodded. "Yeah. Interesting man. He had the idea that the impulse people feel for revenge is basically the impulse to give the other person the same experience they've caused you—and that people have that impulse because deep down they feel that if the other person really understood the pain they caused, they wouldn't do it again. Not that an act of vengeance would actually be likely to wake anybody up to anything, but still, he thought that was where the impulse comes from—a really raw impulse towards communication."

We pulled into the parking lot of the convenience store and stopped by its big glass window, in the glare of its lights. I looked over at Joseph. He seemed thoughtful.

"Yeah," he nodded. "It's like anger."

"How so?" I asked. Joseph still had that thoughtful look. He left the engine running, with the heater on. The cold night air seemed to press in around us, but the engine chugged, and warm air blew out from the dash.

"Well, what do people do when they're angry?" he said.

I shook my head. "What?"

"They raise their voices, maybe shout. It's like they're saying 'listen to me,' you know, 'my needs aren't being met. Listen to my needs.' Like that. I think the voice of anger tries to get attention for some need that's not being met. It wants communication."

I looked at him, nodding. "Yeah, I think that's right," I said, surprised. I wasn't really accustomed to meeting people who thought about things like that.

I gave it another moment's thought, then added, "but sometimes when people get angry, they also get violent. Is that the same thing?" I said.

Joseph shook his head a little from side to side. "I think violence comes when people give up believing that communication can help solve their problem." He paused a moment, and the car was silent except for the chug of the engine.

Then Joseph went on.

"Like, at first you're not angry and you say, 'Please don't do that.' Then, if they don't listen, you get angry and you shout 'Don't do that!' If they still won't listen, maybe you feel like shoving or hitting to get their attention. But when people believe there is no way communication can work, and the problem is a bad one, then they may try to kill or destroy the source of the problem," Joseph said, "even if it's a person."

He seemed very serious and looked thoughtful for another moment. "That's why there are wars," he added, "because people reach a point where they believe no one will listen."

I thought about it for a long moment, with the engine chugging in the background. "I think that's true," I said quietly. Out the car window I could see just a patch of sky, but the lights from the convenience store seemed to have wiped all the stars from it.

"Why don't you go ahead and get the milk," Joseph said. "I'll wait here and give you a ride back."

"Yeah?" I said. I didn't want to put him to any trouble, but it seemed nicer to ride back with him and talk a little more, than to walk home alone in the cold. "That would be nice," I answered. "Thanks. I'll only be a minute."

I pushed open the car door and stepped out into the cold. I was thinking about Laura and how she always seemed to know who I would like.

It only took a couple minutes to get the milk. Joseph and I talked more on the way home, mostly about how important communication was in solving problems. When we got back, I invited Joseph in to join us for dinner, but he said he already had other plans and needed to get where he was going when he'd first stopped to pick me up. I thanked him, said goodbye, and brought the milk in to Laura.

Already the small house was filled with the scents of the chicken, mushroom, and penne dish she was cooking—a favorite of mine, which I hadn't eaten in months.

The next morning Laura and I went for a walk into the hills near her house. The land rolled out, spacious and unencumbered, so unlike the clogged cities I had been living in for nearly a decade. It made me think of my home in India, when I would walk out beyond the edge of town, where the land and river seemed together to reach and stretch endlessly.

It was Sunday, but still Laura had to work most of the afternoon. I spent part of that time reading, and then walked to the big store, where I bought what I would need for dinner. I had brought spices and a few other items I thought might be hard to find in Lame Deer with me from an East Indian market I liked in Manhattan, so I could fix Laura some of the foods she'd been missing since we'd been apart. That evening we had *aloo gobhi tahri*, *kevati*, and *matar paratha* for dinner (or seasoned potatoes, cauliflower, and rice; curried beans; and spicy green peas), and finished with *rose phirin* (sweetened rice with nuts, raisins, and rose water) for dessert. We had a lovely evening, dining by candlelight at the little table in Laura's "lounge," then went to bed early—though I can't say we went to sleep early at all.

No matter how late our night, though, Laura had to be up early. She showered, dressed, and ate a quick breakfast before leaving for an interview she had arranged to conduct in someone else's home. I slept in, curled up in the warm spot that Laura had left behind, had a late breakfast, then spent the next hour or so catching up with my journal entries.

After Laura returned, we walked together to the post office to pick up her mail. The day was clear and crisp, and felt surprisingly warm, since the sun was out and shining brightly.

Laura's mail included a letter from Carl Sandler, the professor she was working with at CU in Boulder. He had decided he would like to come up and see for himself how the study was progressing. The letter said that he planned to leave Boulder after his last class let out on Thursday and drive up alone, arriving in Lame Deer sometime Friday, probably late in the morning.

Laura read the letter aloud standing outside of the Post Office, her voice hollow as she shaped the words.

"I can never be ready in time," she said, a look of shock on her face. She handed me the letter, then started walking towards home. I fell in beside her.

For a few minutes she said nothing, then launched into explaining how she was certain he was checking up on her, and that he must have considered her earlier progress reports insufficient.

"You don't know that, do you?" I asked her.

"You haven't seen the letters he's written back to me," she answered. She was walking quickly, with her eyes on the ground ahead of her.

"Well can't you explain that the work takes more time than he expected?" I asked.

Laura shook her head. "He would think it's my fault," she answered. "I'll just have to get it done." She said it with a lack of inflection, like someone talking about a death they had just been told about but couldn't yet accept.

"But how can you?" I asked.

"I can't," she answered plainly.

"Maybe I could help," I said. Laura looked over at me for the first time since we'd left the Post Office grounds. She looked scared, tender, grateful, and angry, all at once.

"No, love—it's so nice of you to think of that. We don't have the equipment. We might be able to scare up another typewriter—but the reel-to-reel—if it were on cassette, maybe—but everything's on reel-to-reel tape. I don't know where we'd get another deck. No, I'll just have to work..."

As her voice trailed off, her eyes turned forward again. We went on for several strides without another word spoken, then Laura looked back over at me, her eyes wide.

"Oh, Indira—our trip on Friday! All the time I was going to spend with you. It's all shot." Laura stopped and I stopped, too. She looked me in the eye. She looked weary. Her eyes brimmed with tears.

"I'm so sorry," she told me.

"Not to worry," I said. We were on a side street, about a quarter mile from home. I put my arms around her and hugged her for a minute, then we continued on towards home more slowly, with my arm around her shoulder, all the time Laura discussing what parts of the study she could pull together most quickly, and what she could do to show general results from the amount she had accomplished so far, so it would seem that all she had left to do was fill in the gaps. If she could help him see that the work was of high quality, and that it had been necessary to spend time really talking to people to gain their trust and cooperation, and not to be just one more person who comes and tramples on what they cherish... She turned the thoughts over, without quite setting them down. If only she could help him see what she was accomplishing, and not how she was coming up short.

When we got to the house, I fixed us tea, then spent another twenty minutes with Laura discussing strategy—which part of the work to put her energy into finishing, and how best to present it to Sandler when he arrived—and then left her alone so she could get to work on it.

It was true that the news was very disappointing. Not only was it necessary to cancel our sightseeing adventure, but it was clear now that we would have little quality time to spend together during the rest of my stay. It was as though I had shown up to visit with Laura just before the start of exam week. And yet, disappointing as this was, my main sentiment was that my heart went out to Laura. She had been stressed all semester and really needed a break, and now rather than getting one she was having the screws tightened even more.

As much as I wanted to help her, all I could really do was stay out of her way and let her focus on her work. Just the fact that I was there made things in some ways worse, because in addition to the burden of her work, she also had to deal with her guilt at having to ignore me.

That evening Joseph dropped by with information about more contacts for Laura's study. I understood how much Laura appreciated his help and wanted him to know that she did. She and I hadn't had dinner yet, and she invited Joseph to stay and join us. This time, Joseph accepted.

Laura began getting out the leftovers from our meal of the night before and heating them on the gas range. She seemed hurried and a bit distracted. Joseph offered to help, and I suggested he rinse and tear up lettuce for a salad, while I got the other vegetables ready. I wasn't sure our leftovers would be enough for three people, but with a salad added, I thought there would be plenty.

I was rinsing vegetables at the sink and listening to Laura tell Joseph about Sandler coming to visit, when I heard Laura let out a short yell followed by the sound of a pan coming down hard against one of the burners.

"Oh, Laura!" I exclaimed. I dropped the vegetables I'd been working on and came to her side. She was holding her right hand cupped in her left.

"What happened?" I said.

"I had the flame up too high. It heated the metal part of the handle," she said, shaking her head. "Stupid. Stupid of me."

I got a chunk of ice from the freezer, wrapped it in a dish towel, and handed it to Laura. She put the ice on her hand, and I put my arms around her and held her for a minute.

A moment later I stood back and looked at her hand. "Is it bad?" I said.

Laura bit her bottom lip a little, looked at her right hand. "No, I don't think so. It will probably be okay if I leave the ice on it a while."

"You're having a hard day," I said sympathetically.

Laura looked at me, accepting the sympathy. "Yeah," she said.

"When will Sandler get here?" Joseph asked.

"Friday," Laura told him, "and I'm going to be at a dead run until then."

Laura left the food to heat slowly and sat down near Joseph. He asked to see her hand, and agreed it didn't look too bad. Then they went on talking about the people Joseph had found for her to interview.

It wasn't long before the meal was ready, and we sat down to eat. Joseph had only eaten East Indian food a couple times before, but said he liked it a lot. The conversation turned to a trip Joseph and some others were planning to leave for the next morning. They were going to drive down to Colorado to a place called "Sand Creek," where a massacre of Cheyenne and Arapahoe people had taken place in 1864. They planned to be there when the sun came up on Wednesday morning. The massacre had been a dawn attack, and they would be there one hundred and fifteen years later to remember the people who had been killed there that day. Joseph looked very serious talking about it. He said they would make blessings and offerings. He said it wasn't just important for people to remember the event and those who had died there, but he hoped that for the people who went, remembering how much had been lost would help them also remember the value and importance of the lives they were living now.

"We are all flowing in the same stream," he said, "then and now. You can't say one part of it is valuable without realizing that it's the same for the whole flow."

Joseph continued to look solemn and thoughtful, and then said to Laura, "You have been wanting to learn about Cheyenne culture and traditions, and I've liked the sort of questions you've asked and the way you've asked them. I know this doesn't have anything to do with the syncretism you're studying, but I had planned when I came tonight to invite you and Indira to join us, if you would like. But I guess now you won't have the time."

Then Joseph turned to me, and I was surprised by what came next. "But you're both invited—together, and individually—if either of you wants to come. We'll be gathering at Sara Spotted Elk's house about eight o'clock tomorrow morning."

I looked at Joseph, and he looked at me. I was really quite surprised that he would extend the invitation to me, even if I would have to come without Laura. He and I had only been around each other a couple of times and had only really had the one conversation, the night before. But there was something in his look that assured me that he felt comfortable making the invitation.

I looked around and saw that Laura was looking at Joseph. He looked over at her.

"I'm really honored that you would choose to invite us, Joseph. It means a lot to me," Laura said, then sighed. "I wish I could come. Any other time, and I would have said 'yes.'" She shook her head sadly. "I can't speak for Indira, but you're right, I won't be able to make it."

Joseph looked back over at me. "Won't the others mind?" I said. "They don't know me. I'm afraid my presence would be an intrusion." I didn't say so, but I was feeling a little disoriented by the invitation. The event seemed so solemn, and yet it opened doors to a much wider world than I had expected to see. And then there was Laura. Could I be of any use to her if I stayed?

"I'm the one who suggested the trip. There are just a few coming, and they've all been told that you would both be invited. It's all right. Everybody is in agreement."

I looked at Laura. "You should go if you want to," she said. "I'll have to work in any case."

I sat for a moment, thinking about it.

"You don't have to decide tonight," Joseph said. "Like I said, we're gathering at Sara's house about eight tomorrow morning. If you want to come, be there."

I looked at Laura. "I know where that is," she told me.

"How long will you be gone?" I asked Joseph.

"We'll drive down to Denver tomorrow, stay over with Deborah Highwalking and her family for a few hours to sleep, then drive down the rest of the way to Sand Creek before dawn. We'll have to come straight back here afterwards. Russell Hollowbreast is working the night shift at the little store Wednesday night, so we'll have to get back in time for that."

We talked a while longer about it, but I was still uncertain about going when Joseph left that night. I was concerned that Laura would need me while I was gone, and we stayed up and talked about it some that night.

I told her I could fix her food and maybe help make things easier on her that way, but in the end she convinced me that she would really rather see me go and have this experience, and see some of the West as I had hoped for. She said if I stayed, she would only feel bad about ignoring me while keeping me from other things.

In the end, I decided to go, and packed a small bag that night. It felt strange to be leaving Laura, even for just a thirty-six hour trip, after having waited and wished for so long to come and see her.

❊ ❊ ❊

"Pause," Paul said. He stood on the bank of the creek the trail now ran along, trying to figure out how to get across. It was the third crossing he had come to that morning. With each of the others, he'd simply allowed Kiki to continue talking as he had made his way across, stepping (or occasionally jumping) from one rock to the next—but this crossing was different. As he stood on the stream's bank looking at the placement of the rocks protruding from the water, he could see no way to get across while remaining dry. At some point, he would have to take off his shoes and start wading, he reasoned—and it might as well be now, when he could comfortably sit on a log, and not crouch on a rock midstream, all at once trying to balance there and to remove his shoes.

Paul sat down on the trunk of a tree that had fallen along the creek's bank and took off his shoes. Then he rolled up his trousers and walked out into the creek. With each step, he could feel the smooth rocks beneath his feet and the cold water flowing around his calves. Carefully, he made his way through the water, which was dappled with the bright sun and the shade of the oak and sycamore trees that grew along its banks. As Paul was nearing the far side of the creek, he stepped near one of the larger rocks in the water and saw a fish shoot out from under it. It was brownish green and covered in dark spots, and was at least half a meter in length.

When Paul reached the far bank, he looked back out at the rock-strewn stream and wondered how many of the other rocks had such fish lurking in their shadows. Curious, he waded back out a couple of meters to another rock and scared a good-sized fish from its shade. This fish, too, had the same olive tone and spotted markings. He tried a few other rocks, then, and found that most of them had fish lurking in their shadows. They varied in size, with some almost as big as the first one.

The creek must be full of them! Paul thought, and wondered how many more he would have seen had he been looking for them in the early morning or in the cool of evening, when the fish would not have had reason to seek out protection from the glaring day. Surely, there had been many concealed near the rocks he had stepped on during his creek crossings earlier that day.

Paul stood at the stream's edge, with its cool waters caressing his tired feet. He was remembering his grandfather telling him about a kind of fish that used to be abundant in the waters around the area where Paul grew up. They started their lives in the fresh-water streams, then migrated to the ocean. Paul remembered his Grandfather telling him that the younger, freshwater fish started out with spots—like the ones Paul had just seen—but when they migrated to the ocean they would begin to change, taking on a steely silver color and growing even larger. By the time they returned to the freshwater to spawn, they could well be a meter long!

When the settlers had first come, Paul's grandfather had told him, these fish were so plentiful in the rivers and streams during spawning time that in the early days the ranchers would hunt them with pitchforks and could easily catch a great many this way.

Paul could just imagine these fish, these "steelhead trout"—pulsing their way up the rivers to spawn, crowding the waters with their muscular bodies as their scales glinted silver in the sun.

Paul's grandfather had told him that in time the people had started damming the rivers and diverting the water so it could be used elsewhere. In doing so, they choked off the water the steelhead depended on to live and caused the rivers to run dry for part of each year. One year, as the parched Santa Ynez River lay baking and drying in the sun, people had gathered up the steelhead trout between its banks and estimated their number, then, in that one desiccated river alone, at over half a million—and this at a time when the steelhead had already been cut off from much of their ancient spawning grounds for many years! How great must those numbers have been when the rivers ran truly wild and free, and the fish could travel unfettered in their clean and ample waters? Paul wondered.

Now, on Paul's world, none of these native steelhead trout remained—but here, apparently, on this earth that Paul had discovered, things were different. Paul was pretty sure all the spotted fish he'd just scared up from the shadows were steelhead trout, still too young to make their journey to the ocean. Here, they seemed to be lurking under nearly every rock and within almost every shadow. How many more would there be when it came time to spawn, here, in the very place where Paul now stood? Would they fill these waters, with their bright, undulating bodies flashing in the shining sun, as they made their way upstream to spawn?

Paul started at the shining creek, full of wonder at the thought.

After a minute or two, he climbed out of the water, then dropped his pack to the ground and pulled off his shirt. He sat on a large rock on the creek's bank and used his shirt to dry his feet, smiling all the while.

Soon, he was done, and returned his shirt to his back and his shoes to his feet. He paused to take a no-heat travel meal from his pack, before he put it back on and continued up the trail.

As Paul walked along, he felt glad about the day. He had been a little concerned that the repeated creek crossings would cause problems, but they were going fine—better than fine—wonderfully, really. Beyond that, he had passed a couple of designated camp sites along the way—all with cleared ground, a hearth, and a small latrine. He knew he shouldn't have too much trouble finding one for the night, if he was just sensible enough to stop while he still had light to find one by.

For Paul, the whole day seemed to sparkle. Now that he was down that long hill, the path Paul was on wound along near the creek, and was, most of the time, in the shade of the oaks and sycamores growing along its bank. The branches above him were filled with small twittering birds, whose songs made a pleasing background chorus behind the voice Kiki was simulating for Dr. Kumar.

Paul could hardly imagine his good fortune, to be someplace such as this, where there were so many creatures visible around him! Indeed, the day itself seemed perfect; the sky was clear, the air warm, the breeze soft and cool. What better day could there be than this? Paul wondered, as he again asked Kiki to resume recitation.

◙   ◙   ◙

We set Laura's alarm for an hour early, but I still woke before it went off and lay awake for a little while, thinking about the coming day, and the journey ahead. As I lay there, I swallowed, and realized my throat felt sore, but after swallowing a couple more times it felt better. I slipped out of bed and put the coffee on, so it would be ready by the time Laura got up, and then got a quick shower.

Laura and I ate breakfast together in the dusky morning light, and then visited for a little while before I left for Sara Spotted Elk's house. Laura had wanted to walk me over, but we both knew she didn't have the time, so instead she drew me a map to help me find my way, and I set out on my own.

By the time I got there, it was after eight, but I wasn't the last to arrive. Joseph introduced me to everyone who was there and to each of the others as they arrived. We all stood around for a while finding things to talk about, but when finally everyone was present, it was clear that some people had brought along a friend. Instead of the five or six people expected, the group had swollen to eight—too many to ride in Joseph's sedan.

It took the better part of an hour to come up with an alternative. We ended up with an old Ford station wagon Russell Hollowbreast borrowed from his cousin. It was wood-sided and perhaps twenty years old or more, but it had the distinctive quality that part of the cargo area could be folded up to create another full-sized bench seat running the width of the back and facing forward. After setting up that back seat, Russell pointed out that it was a little tight for people with long legs. Since I was shorter than most in the crowd, I got in back there.

It was almost half-past nine by the time we set off, rolling west along the road out of Lame Deer, heading for the highway that would take us south towards Wyoming and then Colorado. I looked back towards town through the wide side widow of the station wagon. A great, wide sky swept out above us, streaked with thin, high clouds. It curved down as it spread till it touched the vast, tree-studded prairie below. Russell turned on the car's AM radio, which sputtered out a song by Led Zeppelin. Between the bits of static, I could make out the words, as Robert Plant sang about a woman who had sworn she would never leave him—and I thought about Laura working alone in her little house, a spot of blue in the world falling away behind us.

✿   ✿   ✿

The land in the American West is breathtaking. Even standing in one place, one feels a sense of grandeur in the openness of the land. But on a highway, rolling through it, one gets a sense of its real immensity. On and on the land spreads out and keeps on spreading. In the distance, mountains may rise—great peaks covered with snow, made small only by the grand scale of the land they are placed within.

Along the road into Wyoming, I saw a herd of antelope dashing across the open prairie, saw it out the wide side window by my seat at the back of the station wagon, looking out into all that openness. If not for the roadway cut and gouged and plowed out of those grasslands, if not for the thin wire fence, which paced the highway everywhere, and which seemed to rush by constantly in a stuttered blur, it would all have seemed perfect—endless, breathtaking, and free. I felt a sense of wonder looking out at it. I only wished Laura could have been there to share it with me.

As we traveled south, the car was filled with the warm buzz of the wheels against the pavement, with music from the radio, and with the quiet murmur of conversation as people visited with whomever they were seated nearest.

I felt a little cold, sitting in the far back, as the blower, which picked up the heat put out by the engine and forced it into the body of the car, was half broken and would only cough out air in a soft whisper that spilled half-heartedly into the front seat. I was glad I had on my warmest coat, so the chill leaking in from outside didn't bother me too much.

We stopped for lunch at a little diner in Casper, Wyoming, a little past mid-day. After the meal, we bought gas, then continued south toward Colorado. Most of us took the same seats we'd been in earlier, with Joseph in the seat just in front of mine. Outside of Casper, the road turned east for a while, and we passed through an area which had more trees than the area where we had been traveling. Joseph turned back towards me, then, and told me that the road here ran alongside the North Platte River. The North Platte, he said, marked the northern boundary of Cheyenne and Arapahoe lands as stated in the Treaty of Fort Laramie, from 1851.

"According to that treaty, we are on Cheyenne land now, and will be for the rest of the trip, all the way to Sand Creek—and we still have another four or five hundred miles to go."

The people who were sitting nearest heard what he'd said to me. A few of them nodded, and a conversation ensued as to which land was promised in which treaties. I listened to them, watching out the window as the land rolled by, trying to imagine what life had been like for the ancestors of my companions hundreds of years earlier, before roads and fences and all the other changes Europeans had brought with them.

My throat, which had hurt a little when I'd first woken up that morning, had begun to bother me again, and my eyes stung a little. I closed my eyes and rested my head against the window, which felt as cool as ice. I could feel every bump in the road, which the old shock absorbers of the station wagon let pass through without resistance. As we rushed down the highway, the rumble of the road, the sound of the radio, and the conversation around me all wove together like a soft blanket of sound, and I drifted off to sleep.

I don't think I could have been asleep more than a few minutes when I was woken by a loud hiss and sputter and the sudden swerving of the car. We must have cut off someone in the right-hand lane, because a pickup went roaring by us on the left with its horn blaring, as Russell brought our car under control and pulled off onto the shoulder on the right-hand side of the road. I heard someone say "close call" and another "blew a tire," as I looked around. We were near the top of a low rise in the land. Though the car had stopped on a level shoulder, I could feel the station wagon slope down towards the corner of the car where I was sitting. Everybody started getting out of the car, and Russell came around to the left rear wheel. I glanced out the window next to me and saw him looking down.

"Shit," he said.

"I hope we've got a spare," Dorothy said, as she came up next to him.

"Better check," Russell said.

I followed the others out of the car, as Russell opened the tailgate and lifted the lid to a compartment beneath the cargo area. He lifted up the full-size wheel that was in there.

"Shit," he said again.

"Flat," Hank said.

By then everyone else had gathered around.

"What, the spare's flat?" Sara said.

"Yeah," Russell said. "Shit."

"Is it really flat, or just low?" Joseph asked.

"Flat," Hank said, then added, "And it's got a nail in it, see?"

Everyone was silent for a minute, and then Sara said, "Someone will have to hitch into town to get it fixed."

"I'll do it," Russell said, sounding not too happy. "I can get it plugged in Douglas."

"How far back do you think that is—fifteen...," Joseph said.

"More like twenty miles," Russell cut in. "Shit." He was shaking his head.

"I'll come with you," Joseph said.

"Naw, it'll be easier to get a ride if I'm alone," Russell said. "But thanks."

Russell set down the wheel and went around to the front of the car to get his coat. The others discussed how much the repair would cost, and everyone pitched in something. Russell came back with his coat on, and Sara handed him a small pile of cash.

"Thanks," he said. "Well, might as well get going." He picked up the wheel and carried it to the side of the road. He waited for a few seconds as a three or four cars roared past, then crossed the south-bound lanes, walked across the big, grassy median, and crossed to the far side of the north-bound traffic. There, with the wheel leaning against his leg, he stood with his thumb out, waiting for someone to pull over and offer him a ride.

The rest of us stood around for a few minutes, talking about how long it would be before Russell returned. Everyone agreed that Russell would be doing well if he got back in time to get the tire on with any daylight left. Some of the group went back into the station wagon to take colorful blankets from the bags they'd brought with them. They wrapped themselves in the blankets and went and sat in a group in the open grass several meters from the edge of the highway. Those of us who hadn't brought blankets, or who didn't want to get them out, wandered over to join them.

The place they were sitting was at the top of the rise we'd been climbing when the tire blew. The sun was shining, but there was a chill in the air and a small breeze blowing. It was possible to see for miles in every direction—no development, just endless grasslands.

I sat down near Joseph and looked back across the highway, where Russell still stood with his thumb out. One car after another drove past him. Some of the people near me were still discussing something having to do with treaties, and then someone commented on how little some of the younger Cheyenne knew about their own history.

"They sure won't learn it going to school in Busby," a woman named Rose said.

"They sure won't," William echoed.

"I hope at least everyone here knows the history of Sand Creek," Sara said.

I looked back towards the group, and Joseph looked over at me and smiled a little, then said to the group, "I think everyone does, except maybe Indira. She's not from around here."

"What tribe are you from?" Rose asked me, and I thought of the similarity in my appearance and theirs—we all had straight black hair and brown skin. It was only because of this similarity that they were called "Indians," I knew, since the early European sailors had thought they had landed in India when they first got to America.

"She's not Indian," Joseph answered. "Well, she is, but she's from India."

"Oh," Rose said, nodding her head. I smiled.

"Do you know about what happened at Sand Creek?" Joseph asked me.

"Only what you said last night," I answered.

Hank suggested that Joseph tell the story. "I've heard the way you tell it," Hank said to him, "you make the picture whole." Then Hank added that it would be good for everyone to hear it again, while taking this journey. Everyone in the group looked over and nodded, encouraging Joseph to talk about Sand Creek.

Joseph agreed, and we sat in silence for a minute, while Joseph gathered his thoughts. I looked back over at Russell again, but realized he had gone. His absence suddenly made all the land seem empty—a great endless emptiness around us, through which a thin, chill breeze blew.

I buttoned my coat at the collar, then turned my attention back to Joseph.

❋   ❋   ❋

Joseph's silence lasted for perhaps a minute. When he started, he spoke slowly, feeling his way through the story he wanted to tell. He gestured to the prairie rolling out from the rise we were sitting on.

"In the days before white people came into this country, all of this was Cheyenne land. The buffalo roamed across this land in herds so large that if you stood on a rise such as this one and looked out at such a herd, you would not be able to see the end of it. You could ride on horseback through this land for days and days and never lose sight of them. When they ran, they made the earth tremble like thunder.

"The buffalo ranged from the Rocky Mountains to the Mississippi, north into Canada, and south as far as the grass grows. Sometimes they would wander west of the Rockies, when there was rain enough. I have read that there were buffalo east of the Mississippi River, too— and there they ranged almost to the Atlantic ocean, from the Gulf of Mexico to almost as far north as Canada. These eastern buffalo looked different from the ones in the West. They were bigger, with no hump and shorter hair."

Joseph turned towards me. "In New York state, for example, there were buffalo at one time," he said. Then he focused his attention back towards the group. "By sometime in the early 1800s, all the eastern buffalo were gone—not even one of them was left.

"Wolves in the East had hunted the eastern buffalo, but with all the buffalo gone, the wolves were hungry. They hunted deer and other wild creatures, but they also hunted the cattle and sheep the Europeans had brought with them.

"The philosophy the Europeans had brought with them from Europe, and which remained the philosophy of the American settlers, was that wild creatures like wolves were savage, vicious, and bloodthirsty. To them, it was part of what it meant to be 'wild'—and they saw wolves in particular as something dangerous that had to be controlled or destroyed.

"To them, wolves were the wildest of the wild, and they did all they could to wipe them out. They didn't just hunt the wolves that hunted their cattle and sheep. They hunted and trapped and tried to kill all wolves, and when they could, would follow a wolf back to its den, then kill that wolf and all of its pups, too. To these people, the wolf was not civilized, but they thought of themselves as civilized. But a wolf would not even attack a person, unless rabid or maybe cornered, while they, so 'civilized,' tried to kill off all wolves.

"The early Americans settlers never learned enough about wolves to know they were wrong about them. They never sat on a hillside and watched the adults playing with the pups, nor saw how far an adult would travel in a day to find food to bring back to the young. Once, wolves ranged over most of North America. Now, with the exception of Canada and Alaska, nearly all of them are gone.

Joseph paused for a moment, then went on. "At the beginning of the 1800s, very few white people were in the West. The few who were here were mostly trappers and traders. For the most part they got along with the people they met along the way. In the early 1840s, settlers began

coming west along a trail they called the "Oregon Trail," which came
through Cheyenne land. Along the way they killed buffalo, and then
left them to rot on the ground. Their oxen, mules, and horses spread
out and ate the grass that the buffalo fed on, while all the activity in
general drove the buffalo from the land. Soon, fewer and fewer buffalo could be found. In 1848, someone found gold in the area that is
now California, and white people began to flood into the West in search
of gold. Through most of this time, there was no fighting between
Cheyenne and white people—except that in, I think it was 1856 or '57,
there were three or four fights between Cheyenne and soldiers. Mostly
those fights were over misunderstandings, and most of the time, the
soldiers were firing on people who did not want to fight. So there were
some skirmishes, but not a lot, and the Cheyenne tried hard to avoid
a fight.

"The next year, in 1858, gold was found in the area where Denver now
stands. More white people flooded into the West, but this time they were
coming specifically onto Cheyenne and Arapahoe land—and not just to
pass through. We had no interest in the gold. You couldn't eat it, nor wear
it, nor hunt with it. We told them, 'Go ahead, take the gold. I'm glad for
you because it makes you so happy—but once you have found it, then
please leave this land.'

"But the people didn't leave. They built Denver and settled on Cheyenne
and Arapahoe land.

"The Cheyenne still hoped to have peace with the settlers, but the settlers saw us as they saw wolves. They thought of us as wild and uncivilized,
and therefore assumed we were savage, vicious, and blood-thirsty. They
didn't know us any better than they knew the wolves. They thought it
would be just a matter of time before we would be fighting with them.
Some thought they should try to change us—to make us 'civilized' like
they were, but many thought they would be better off without us, just as
they thought they would be better off without wolves.

"By this time, the white people were fighting between themselves in
the East—it was at the time of the Civil War. The soldiers in Colorado
Territory had been called east to help in the fighting, and new soldiers
had been raised from amongst the settlers, so they could defend themselves, if need be, against us. Their leader was a man named Colonel
John Chivington."

Joseph looked around the group, and I could see some of the others stir
at the mention of this name.

"Chivington had been a fire-and-brimstone-style preacher," he went
on. "I guess he wanted to rid the world of everything he thought of as
evil things, like wolves and Indians. He had preached to Indians when
he was younger, but apparently he had never learned to see through his
own prejudices. The world was black and white to him, good and bad, and
Indians to him were part of a ruthless, lawless wildness that threatened
everything good. He saw us like so many of his countrymen saw wolves.
He thought we should all be exterminated, and at least once made public
statements to that effect.

"In the spring of 1864, the white settlers were pretty nervous. There had been violence between some of the settlers and some people of other tribes, but the Cheyenne had not been fighting."

Joseph paused and looked thoughtful, then turned towards me. "In most cases," he said, "the other tribes had wanted to keep peace, also." He looked back towards the others. "A joint committee of Congress formed after Sand Creek to investigate the treatment of Indians concluded that this was the case. They said the 'large majority' of wars on the plains were started by white men acting outside the law.

"Amongst the Cheyenne, our chiefs—Black Kettle and Lean Bear and others, like White Antelope—wanted to keep us at peace.

"That spring, some Cheyenne men were traveling north and found some mules wandering loose. They gathered them up and brought them along with them. That night a white man came into their camp and claimed the mules were his. The Cheyenne who found them said, 'sure, you can have the mules, if you give us a present in exchange for the trouble we went to rounding them up.' The white man left and sent the soldiers to attack them. The Cheyenne fought back, and people were hurt or killed on both sides. After that, the soldiers kept hunting for the Cheyenne and trying to kill them. When the soldiers would attack, the Cheyenne would fight back. When the Cheyenne saw the soldiers marching towards our villages, we would run from them—and when the soldiers found our villages empty, they would burn them to the ground. Our people couldn't understand why the soldiers were doing these things.

"Once, after about a month of this, the soldiers came to Lean Bear's village. Lean Bear was a great chief who tried hard to keep the peace. He had been to Washington and met with President Lincoln. When the soldiers arrived, Lean Bear rode forward to talk to the soldiers, but they wouldn't talk. Instead, they shot him from his horse and then rode up to him and shot him again where he lay on the ground. This made everyone very angry and very sad.

After this happened, the other chiefs could no longer keep the young men from fighting against the soldiers. And so this is how the war between the white people and the Cheyenne began.

"That spring and summer there was a lot of fighting, but Black Kettle and White Antelope and many others still hoped for peace. They were afraid to go to where the soldiers were to ask for peace, because they were afraid the soldiers would refuse to talk and would kill them when they approached, as they had done with Lean Bear.

"The soldiers had orders to do this—Chivington had told his men to kill any Indians they came across and not to take prisoners. At a public speech in Denver late that summer, he had said that it was his policy to kill all Indians, both little and big. He had said, 'nits make lice,' meaning that if you don't kill the baby lice when you kill the big ones, the little ones will get big, and you will still have lice. He was talking about killing Indian babies.

"He was hardly the only one to have such opinions. Major Jacob Downing, who had fought against the Cheyenne who found the mules, has been quoted as saying that he believed Indians were an obstacle to civiliza-tion and should be exterminated. The *Rocky Mountain News*, Denver's newspaper at the time, ran many editorials calling for the extermination of Indians. In the Denver Opera house about a year after the massacre, someone asked the crowd if they thought Indians should be 'civilized' or should be 'exterminated.' The crowd began loudly shouting, 'Exterminate them! Exterminate them!'

"It was a popular idea amongst those who had other plans for what this continent would become. They considered us to be a threat and in the way. At the time Columbus first came to this continent, there were probably more than five million people living on what would eventually become the contiguous part of the United States, and all of that land was ours. By the end of the last century, our numbers had dropped to about four or five percent of what they were in 1492—and today we possess only about three percent of that land. They did not exterminate us, but you can see how close they came, through war, and massacres, and the diseases they brought.

"Sand Creek is only one part of a very long and terrible story—but it's the part our journey is about now.

"So," Joseph said, looking thoughtful. "Even though the soldiers had started the fight with the Cheyenne, and there had been a lot of blood lost on both sides, Chief Black Kettle and Chief White Antelope and others still hoped for peace. One Eye and his wife and Min-im-mie decided to put their lives on the line and travel alone, just the three of them, to Fort Lyon, in the hope that they could convince the soldiers to talk to them and not just kill them on sight. They wanted to tell the soldiers that the Cheyenne wanted peace. It was worth risking their lives to them to deliver this message.

"Luckily, Major Wynkoop was in command at Fort Lyon, and he ignored the orders Chivington had given him to kill all Indians in the vicinity. He agreed to talk to One Eye, and later he agreed to meet with Black Kettle and the other chiefs.

"Major Wynkoop tried to help our people make peace. He traveled with some of the chiefs to Denver to meet with Chivington and the governor to talk about peace. But Chivington and the governor didn't really want peace, although they wouldn't come out and say so. Chivington told our leaders that he controlled all the troops in the area, and that he would stop fighting with anyone who laid down their arms and submitted to military authority. Our leaders left the meeting with the understanding that the white leaders would let them know the answer to their request for peace in time, and that in the meanwhile they should go with Major Wynkoop and gather their people near Fort Lyon under Wynkoop's protection.

"So the Cheyenne, along with some Arapahoe, gathered not far from Fort Lyon at a place called "Sand Creek." Also, many Arapahoe went right in and camped by the fort.

"But soon after, Wynkoop was removed from his command and replaced with Major Anthony, who felt about Indians much the way Chiving-ton did.

"Those who had gathered near the fort left good hunting grounds to go there. Near the fort, food was scarce. Wynkoop had been handing out rations from the fort's supply, but when Anthony arrived, he didn't much like that idea. He commented once that starving all the people gathered there would be an easy way to dispose of them—but that was the sort of man he was. He told the Indians staying nearest the fort, who were mostly Arapahoe, if they were going to stay there they were going to have to hand in their weapons, and the people did this. Anthony had red eyes from scurvy. Some called him the "Red-Eyed Soldier Chief." Many wondered if they could trust him. He did eventually pass out rations, and he continued to promise protection until an answer came to the request for peace.

"After a while, Anthony stopped passing out rations and told everyone they should go hunt for themselves. He returned the Arapahoe's weapons for them to hunt with, and when the chiefs came to talk to him, he told them they should go camp with their people at Sand Creek and await word of peace. Anthony promised that they and their people would be perfectly safe there. Little did our leaders know that he just wanted to keep us nearby, so when he had enough soldiers gathered, he could attack. This was the same intention Chivington had."

Joseph stopped talking for a minute and looked out at the land around where we sat. The sun had dropped low in the sky, and the air was growing cooler in the evening light. I had been so engrossed in what Joseph had been saying, I'd hardly noticed how cold I was getting, nor that my head had begun to hurt. I swallowed, and my throat felt raw.

Joseph was looking over his shoulder, back towards the highway. "I wonder how Russell's doing," he said.

For a moment, no one answered, then Dorothy responded, speaking quietly. "I'll bet he's got the tire fixed by now," she said.

Joseph nodded, then looked down at the ground in front of him. Everyone was very quiet. After several moments, Joseph looked up and continued speaking.

"So, both Chivington and Anthony had met with the Indians—both Cheyenne and Arapahoe—camped at Sand Creek. Both Chivington and Anthony knew that the people at Sand Creek had come seeking peace. Both knew that those requested to do so had peacefully surrendered their weapons and that some—mostly young men—were away hunting game. But in the dark hours before dawn on November 29th, 1864, in the Month of the Freezing Moon, they rode together with seven hundred soldiers (mostly short-term volunteers who had signed on just to fight Indians) towards the village at Sand Creek.

In the first light of dawn, the soldiers could make out nearly one hundred white Cheyenne teepees, and just a little apart from them, another ten Arapahoe lodges. There before them, about five hundred Cheyenne and Arapaho lay peacefully sleeping, confident that they were resting under the protection of the soldiers.

"At dawn, the soldiers attacked. Quickly, Black Kettle raised a large American flag and a white flag, to show the soldiers that the people there were at peace with them, but this did no good. The soldiers kept coming, firing into the village.

"The soldiers encircled the camp, killing everyone in sight—old people, women, and children, that's who mostly was there. Having few weapons, the people had no choice but to try to run away. People scattered, most running north along the creek. The creek bed was mostly dry, just pools of water here and there, some ice. Where they could, they dug pits into the tall sandy banks along the creek, and tried to defend themselves there, but there were too few weapons. Most of the young men had taken their weapons and were off hunting buffalo. The soldiers shot into the pits from a distance, killing anyone who seemed ready to fight, and then came into the pits and killed all the others—old people, women, children. Women begged for their lives and the lives of their children, and then were killed, and their children killed. The soldiers killed everyone, young and old, little and big. The ground was red with their blood. Not even the infants were spared.

"After the adults were all killed or escaped, some of the soldiers tested their skills by taking turns shooting at a little boy whose parents must have already been killed in the slaughter. He was small, maybe three years old, and was wandering naked amongst the dead bodies. He was nearly out of range of the soldiers. They wanted to see who could hit him, and took turns shooting at him. Finally, on the third try, one of them killed the little boy.

"At the height of the killing, when it was clear what was happening to his people, and that he could do nothing to stop it, White Antelope walked out into the middle of Sand Creek and sang his death song. He was shot and killed. After the killing was over, the soldiers came and cut parts off his body to save as souvenirs. Many of the bodies were cut up in that way, including many of their private parts being taken.

"All of the while, Chivington watched and did nothing to stop any of this. He had given orders to take no prisoners. At least one of the officers from Fort Lyon who had known the Indians staying there and sworn to protect them refused to fight, and refused to order the men under him to do so. Others had voiced objection before the fighting, but they were few, and that did nothing to stop the slaughter."

Joseph was silent again for several moments, looking down at his feet. Then he looked up again and went on speaking. "I had family there that day. Some in my mother's family, some in my father's. One, my great-great-grandmother, woke when she heard the sound of many animals running in the distance. My great-great-grandfather was away hunting buffalo, but she was there with her parents and with her son, my great-grandfather. She thought maybe it would be buffalo making that sound and went outside to look. Then the soldiers came into view. Many people just stood there, at first, believing the soldiers would not hurt them. Black Kettle called out to everyone not to be afraid, but my great-great-grandmother was afraid. She called to her parents to wake up, then grabbed a rope and picked up her baby son. Together she and her parents ran for the horses on the other side of Sand Creek, but she was younger and faster than her parents, and even carrying a baby, she got to the horses before they did.

"The horses were agitated, but she managed to catch one and climb on with her baby son still in her arms. She turned back to look for her parents, but all she saw were people running everywhere, and many of them falling. By then bullets were screaming through the air around her. The soldiers were trying to gather the horses, but instead mostly they were scattering them. The horses began to run, and hers ran with them—off across the plains, leaving the fighting behind her.

"She spent a cold night alone, with just her son, far from the village, worrying about her parents and everyone else. The next day she found some of the others who had escaped. They had to wait another day, maybe two, until the soldiers had all left, and then together they went back to look for survivors."

Joseph paused again, and then added, "When they returned, they found more than one hundred and fifty dead, with almost four times as many women and children dead as men. Many of them had parts cut off their bodies. Her mother and father's bodies were found there, in the same condition as the rest."

Everyone was silent for a minute or two, then Joseph looked over at me and said quietly, "Most everybody here has ancestors who were at Sand Creek." I looked around the group. Everyone looked very solemn, and I wondered what stories each of them were remembering.

I looked away, not wanting to intrude, and turned my eyes up, beyond the group, to the west where the sun was setting along a vast line of open prairie, the sky crimson and gold, casting my companions in silhouette, each with their head downcast.

I hadn't realized when I'd left that morning that the trip I was on wasn't just a journey to some historical site, a remnant of a nearly forgotten past. I hadn't realized how deeply felt and personal that history was, a part of the lives of the people I was traveling with, a hole in each of their hearts, a wound carried down through generations.

Finally, Joseph stood up, and the others rose around him—and I along with them.

Joseph stamped his feet. "It's cold," he said. Hank came over and spoke to him quietly, I think thanking him for talking to the group. People milled around, talking softly.

After a few minutes, Dorothy came over and spoke to Joseph. I heard her say something about getting the car jacked and the wheel off while there was still light, then she, Joseph, and Hank went over to the car and started looking for the jack and lug wrench.

I looked back towards the setting sun, feeling very sad. I stood with my arms wrapped around my body against the cold, watching as the sun touched the horizon. Sara came and stood next to me, her eyes turned toward the brilliant sunset, her blanket wrapped around her shoulders. After the most vibrant colors in the sky were lost, Sara asked me if I would like to walk along the highway with her a little ways, to try to warm up. It was kind of her, I thought, as I really didn't know anyone there, except Joseph a little, and he was busy with the car.

I knew we wouldn't go far, as Russell could show up at any moment, but I was cold, almost to the point of trembling, and my throat had begun to feel as fiery as the fading sun.

Together, Sara and I paced along the highway, striding through dry grasses, trying to warm ourselves in the gathering dusk, she draped in her blanket, and both of us draped in sad thoughts which chilled our hearts as much as the cold November air.

❊   ❊   ❊

It wasn't long before Russell had returned and the repaired spare tire was in place. By the time we got underway, there was only the slightest deep-blue glow of light in the western sky. In the east, stars were appearing, while dense clouds gathered along the southern horizon. I was still cold when I took my seat again in the back of the car. With the night's cold, the car's heater was of even less use than before.

I wasn't feeling well, and Joseph's story had pitched me into a very somber mood. My feet felt cold, and trying to wiggle my toes inside my shoes to warm them was like trying to warm up inside a block of ice. Different parts of Joseph's story kept running through my mind—vast herds of buffalo slaughtered; Joseph's great-great-grandmother looking back to find her parents, never to see them alive again; soldiers taking turns aiming at a little boy.

I didn't want to think about any of that. The way I felt, I didn't want to think about anything. I put my left arm over the hump above the rear wheel, and bending awkwardly, rested my head against it.

I must have dozed like that, for the next thing I recall it was as dark as pitch out, and a light snow was falling. It must have gotten quite cold, because the snow was like powder on the road ahead. When I turned my head and looked forward along the side of the car, I could just make out in the backward glow of the headlights how the snow twisted in eddies where the front wheels spun along the road.

I closed my eyes again and shivered. So cold. It hurt to swallow, and I wondered if I had a fever. Not only was I feeling chilled, I noticed, but my thoughts swam uncomfortably, the way they did when I was sick. My thoughts kept shifting between what Joseph had talked about earlier, and thoughts about Laura working alone, when I wished so much she could be with me. Mostly, I just tried to stay quiet and rest. It was clear I was getting sick, and this wasn't a good time for it.

I don't know if I dozed again, but the next thing I remember the car was pulling off the highway. I sat up and looked around. Stopping for gas, that's all. Outside the world was dusted in white.

I got out and used the restroom, then went with some of the others to the convenience store next door. We'd all planned to fix dinner when we got to Denver, but it was late and everyone was getting hungry. I bought a coffee, a cinnamon roll, and a package of aspirin.

I stopped outside the shop to take the aspirin. Joseph paused to talk to me when he came out of the convenience store. He saw the aspirin and asked if I had a headache.

"No, sore throat," I told him, and I was surprised at how much I could hear it in my voice.

Joseph put his hand on my forehead. "You're like fire," he said.

"Yeah? I'm freezing," I said and stamped my feet.

"It's too cold in the back," Joseph said sympathetically.

"Do we have a lot further to go?" I asked.

"A couple hours more to Denver," he answered. "We should have time to fix dinner and sleep for a while before driving to Sand Creek." Joseph threw a wrapper in the trash can.

"You should sit up front. It's warmer," he said. I said there were already people there, but Joseph said it wasn't a problem. He walked me back to the car and helped me get settled in up front, in the middle spot on the wide bench seat. He explained to the others who'd been sitting there that I was getting sick and needed to be warm. This started a ball rolling, and by the time we left, Rose, who'd been in the far back with me, and who was also cold, was sitting next to me.

As we pulled away, Rose took her blanket and spread it over both of us. Russell switched on the radio, and Sting's voice spilled out around us, singing about countless castaways, searching for a home. I tried to turn sideways a little, so I could rest my cheek against the seat back, but there was no way to do it without crowding the others.

In minutes we were back on the open highway, and the town lights had receded behind us. Ahead of us, the headlights seemed to grab the road and pull it towards us out of the darkness. I stared out the windshield at the snow falling through the headlights. It seemed to be rushing towards us. I felt ill at ease with myself—sick and sad. I had been feeling for some time that the understanding I had of the world was out of step, lacking, but that night, feverish and saddened by the terrible story Joseph had told, that sense of inadequacy had suddenly deepened.

I kept thinking about the ideas I'd had about protolife years before, and how they had seemed to explain so much about life, about the joy we sought, and about how we gave the promise in us actuality. I'd seen so much beauty in those ideas, and in the world as I'd understood it through them. Human nature—all of nature—seemed so beautiful to me in that light. But what struck me now, as we rolled along through the vast snowy plains of Northern Colorado, was that I had paid very little attention to what goes wrong in human nature, to the harm and hurt that is done, and to the reasons behind it.

Was there anything in those ideas I'd had years before that could adequately explain the sorts of deeds Joseph had talked about? I wondered.

I recalled the ideas I'd had about suffering, about how all suffering, even physical suffering, resulted from a block in the process of life expressing itself.

Yes, that much I had considered. But that only explained why such terrible deeds caused pain. What seemed incomprehensible to me was how people could perpetrate such crimes in the first place.

I felt as though I was looking into a well, too dark, too deep to see into. I stared into the falling snow as we drove along. Fine and powdery, it swirled in eddies on the way down, caught up in the turbulence around our vehicle. Most of the road had turned white, but there were two black lines where the tires of the cars ahead of us had compressed and melted the snow. We were driving into a powdery darkness, following two dark stripes on the road. I knew there was a whole world around us, but I could only see this much.

I swallowed, and my throat hurt. I didn't want to think too hard right now. I rode along for a long time just staring, letting my thoughts swirl like the snow drifting outside. The heater was blowing steadily. Near it, and with Rose's blanket over me, I began to feel warm.

My eyelids grew heavy, and I let them close, but each time I drifted off to sleep, my head would nod forward and wake me. Rose must have noticed. She touched my arm, then gestured that I could rest my head on her shoulder.

"Thank you," I whispered, trying not to let the words rub against my sore throat. I put my head against her shoulder, glad for her warmth and kindness, and slept like that the rest of the way to Denver.

❋   ❋   ❋

Rose woke me when we got to Deborah Highwalking's house. We climbed out of the car, and Joseph told me that some of the others were going for groceries and would fix a quick dinner, and then everyone would sleep for a while before leaving again in a few hours for Sand Creek. He asked how I felt. I told him I was sick.

Joseph felt my forehead. "Come on, let's get you to bed," he said.

Joseph showed me into the house and introduced me to Deborah. Still groggy and feeling lousy, I murmured a "hello." Joseph spoke to her quietly for a minute, and then they led me into a small bedroom off the kitchen, in which two small children slept on a large mattress on the floor. Deborah picked up first one child and then the other, and moved them to one side of the bed. I wouldn't find out until later that these were the most comfortable accommodations available in the house, and they were being offered to me. I gladly accepted. I set down my pack, slipped off my shoes, and lay down. Deborah stepped out of the room for a minute and came back with two warm blankets. Joseph laid them over me. I shivered.

"You should sleep," Joseph said. "I'll bring you food when it's ready."

"Thanks," I croaked. Joseph nodded, then he and Deborah quietly stepped from the room, leaving the door open just enough for a narrow band of light to slide in. A single bulb in the nightlight near the bureau created a general glow. I could just make out the clock on top of the bureau: a little past nine, it read.

I closed my eyes. For a few moments, I seemed to still feel the rocking of the car—but only for moments, for soon I was fast asleep.

I dreamed that I was with others in a car driving to a place called "Sand Creek"—except that in the dream, it was not the massacre site we were going to, but rather a place where I was going to go to search for Emil.

We drove on through darkness, through a swirling mist of snow and fog. When the mist finally cleared, I was standing alone in front of my apartment in New York. The others were no longer with me.

As I started up the steps towards the front door, I could hear my feet on the cement. The scent on the air seemed just right—smog plus a hint of ocean air—but still, somehow, everything else seemed off.

Off-scale, that was it—everything was the wrong size. But even so, it all felt very vivid—real and sharp—as though I'd been spinning a dial, and now everything had come suddenly into focus.

I heard somebody call my name, and I turned around to answer. Then I realized—"Emil," that's what they had called me. *Emil.*

"Hey Rudy," I answered, as I saw a teenage boy approaching. Rudy was one of the kids in the neighborhood. I went back down the steps at a trot to greet him.

"Hey man, what's happening?" I said. I saw that another boy, Clark, was with him. It was spring, with still a little chill in the air. My body felt young, energetic. I looked up to these guys, Rudy and Clark, admired how they were—older, smarter, faster.

"We need your help on something, Emil," Rudy said. They were short on cash, he explained, and needed me to help them get some. They explained to me what I'd have to do, spelled it out—and as they did, each detail seemed to be painted in the air before me. While they made a disturbance at the back of the corner store, I was to jump over the counter, push the lower right key on the cash register, grab the twenties, close the drawer, jump over the counter, and book it out of there as fast as I could. They'd follow me out, and we'd split up the money.

I followed them towards the store. I'd never done anything like that. Rudy walked ahead of me. He had a way of moving—very smooth and strong. Self-confident. I wanted to be like him.

Rudy turned back towards me, put a hand on my shoulder. "I only need a minute of your time, my man," he said. He smelled like tobacco and a hot day in the sun. I wasn't sure what to tell him, but I followed along as they walked.

When we got to the sidewalk in front of the store, I still wasn't sure what I would tell them. Rudy turned to me and said, "Okay, now just do what I told you," then he and Clark went on inside. Soon, I could hear a ruckus coming from the back of the store. I watched from the sidewalk as Mrs. Meyers left the cash register. Now or never. The ruckus continued. Now or never.

Rudy, so smooth and confident, had asked for *my* help.

I dashed through the open doorway, scrambled over the counter, pushed the lower right button on the register, not even sure I would take anything.

The drawer slid open with a "*ding.*" In it were neat stacks of bills. Rudy had said just grab the twenties, close the drawer, and get out of there. I grabbed the twenties, not even thinking, pushed the drawer closed, and jumped over the counter. My feet hit the ground in unison on the other side, and I was off running, out of the store and down the street. My heart was racing so fast it sounded like the way it had sounded once when I'd gone to a foot race. I'd stood right by as the whole pack of runners came past, and I could hear all of their feet pounding at once.

Every muscle in my body worked as I raced up the sidewalk. I had done it! I had done it! I pulled up half a block away, and looked back as I watched first Clark, then Rudy, exit the store, then join together and come towards me at a fast walk. Rudy was smiling. He put his fist in the air like, "right on, man," for me. Rudy was making that gesture for me.

I looked down at the money in my fist. There must have been five, maybe ten, twenties. Mrs. Meyers' money. I could feel a kind of sadness start to well up inside me, but then I looked back up at Rudy. A bubble of doubt had started to rise, but my heart was still racing, the thunder of footsteps still going past, and I looked up at Rudy now, almost with me, smiling. It was like I could hear the crowds cheering, too, drowning out any other small voices.

Mrs. Meyers would be okay.

Rudy and Clark got to me and patted me on the back. They towered over me.

"Good going, Emil," Rudy said. "I knew you could do it." He took the money from my hand and looked over at Clark. I looked up at them, as they both grinned.

"I'll tell you, Emil, you're my main man," Rudy said, and I was glad. I had done it! I had done it! I had had the courage to do it, and I could see I'd made Rudy proud.

I was pulled from the dream by a light tapping on the door, then by Joseph's voice.

"Indira?" he said. I opened my eyes. Joseph was squatting near the mattress, a bowl of something hot and steamy in his hands. The dream still swirled through my thoughts. Emil. I'd been dreaming about Emil.

"I brought you some chicken soup," Joseph said.

"You guys made chicken soup?" I asked, looking up at him.

"No, hamburgers, but Deborah thought this would be easier on your throat. It's from a can. Chicken noodle."

"Oh, thanks," I said, then added, "Thank Deborah, too, please." It was uncomfortable to speak. My throat felt swollen. I sat up and picked up the bowl of soup.

"Is there anything else I can do for you?" Joseph asked.

"No. This is perfect," I said, my voice ragged. I felt touched by the kindness of these people, whom I barely knew.

"Okay, then I'm going to go have my dinner," Joseph answered. "Hopefully, there'll be enough time for us all to get some sleep before leaving for Sand Creek."

Joseph stood up. "Do you want me to wake you when we get up, and see if you feel up to going?" he whispered.

"Yeah, sure," I said. "Maybe I'll feel better."

"Okay. Give a holler if there's anything else you need." Joseph stepped through the door, carefully leaving it open enough for the light from the kitchen to light my meal.

From where I sat cross-legged on the edge of the mattress, I could see through the doorway into the kitchen. The room was lit by one light in the middle of the ceiling. The floor showed a seamless pattern of pale blue and cream-colored linoleum. I could see the backs of some of the people I'd come with at a table at the far side of the room. Joseph carried a plate to that table and joined them.

I took a spoonful of my soup. It tasted good—hot and salty. Steam rose from it, drifting upwards in the light from the doorway. I ate the whole bowl, then lay down again.

Huddled beneath the covers, I began to drift between fragments of dreams.

In one, I was packing to go see Laura, but I couldn't find the shoes I wanted to wear.

In another, I was in a cab on my way to the airport, but the tunnel was closed, and there was no way out of the city—no way to be with her.

As I looked out the window of the cab, the city seemed dark and troubling. I looked up and down the street, then I found myself walking along the sidewalk. I was still in a city, but it wasn't clear which one. The streetlights flickered as I walked past.

I was walking towards home, with my belly full of the warm numb of liquor. I could feel my body, as I walked: massive, muscular—masculine.

I arrived at my doorstep and fumbled with the stubborn lock, cursing under my breath as my frustration grew. Everything about the world seemed against me.

My boss had yelled at me again that day. What an idiot, I thought. I'd like to see if he could do any better himself! But all I had said to him was, "I won't let it happen again."

The key turned, and the next thing I knew, I was in the kitchen, expecting my dinner would be ready—but the table had been cleared.

"Martha!" I bellowed, "I work all day to pay for your room and board, and all I expect of you is one thing—*my dinner!*"

My wife appeared, whining about how late I'd come in, her voice thin and pleading.

I grabbed a beer and shoved past her—almost tripping over a pair of shoes left in the middle of the floor. Matthew! I fumed. Twelve years old—he should know better! And in my own home!

For a fleeting moment, I struggled to contain my rage, but the frustrations of a day—of a life—gone wrong welled up in me. I picked up his shoes and started towards his room. There are rules, and he has to follow them, like anybody else! I would straighten him out.

I turned down the hall, then found myself in Matthew's room. He was sitting on the edge of his bed, listening to music. I threw the shoes at him. He stood up—got up like maybe he thought he would stand up to me, so I smacked him upside the head, and then again just 'cause I didn't like the look on his face. That'll teach him where to leave his stuff!

I could see in his eyes he wasn't showing me enough respect, and I took my belt off.

"Please, no—don't," he cried. I walloped him a couple of times. He wilted under the belt. I looked down at him. He seemed much smaller than when I'd come in.

Give a kid an inch to start going wrong, and it'll be like a growth that takes over all of him, like a cancer. I was doing him a favor to set him straight, now, while he was still young and could be bent to it, like my old man did for me.

I put my belt back on...and then I was sitting by the TV, with a beer in my hand.

"Martha!" I yelled. And she brought me my dinner.

It's not my fault the world is against me. What they take away from me out there, I take back here. A man has to rule his own castle.

I swallowed, and the pain of it brought me back to where I lay, on a mattress in the children's room in Deborah Highwalking's house. I rolled over. What an awful dream, I thought. What a really awful dream.

I felt sleepy and nearly drifted back to sleep, but held myself back out of it for a little longer, until I was certain the dream had passed, and I wouldn't fall back into it.

After a while, I stopped resisting, and I slipped back into sleep. And this time the sleep was dark and smooth, with no dream in it.

❋   ❋   ❋

After a time, I was awakened again by Joseph's soft voice. I opened my eyes a little. The clock on the bureau read a little past two.

"We're going to be ready to leave in a little while," Joseph whispered. "Are you up to coming?"

"Coming?" I whispered. I was barely awake. "Oh." I swallowed. My throat felt raw, my mouth parched. "Water?" I said.

"I brought you tea," Joseph told me. "*Mohkta wise-eyo*—purple coneflower tea. It's good for a sore throat." Joseph was squatting on the floor near the mattress. He held a mason jar full of dark liquid between two hands. I sat up a little, and Joseph handed the jar to me. The tea was hot. I tasted it—woody, pleasant.

"Sorry, I couldn't find a mug big enough. But the jar will do," Joseph added. "You think you'll be up to coming with us?"

I set the jar down on the floor, lay back down. I shook my head a little.

"No," I said. "Thanks for the tea."

"You're welcome. Don't worry," Joseph told me, "Deborah says you're welcome to stay here while we're gone. We're planning to come by here again on the way up—maybe get a little more sleep before heading back to the Res."

His words seemed to come to me from a distance.

"Good," I said. "Thanks."

I swallowed again, and tried to gather my thoughts. "Joseph," I said, staring up at the dark ceiling.

"Yes."

"The story you told earlier," I said, turning my gaze towards him.

I frowned a little, then finished my question. "How can people be that way?"

I looked at him, and my eyes stung with fever. Joseph looked very thoughtful for several long moments, nodding his head a little.

"Yes," he said softly, as though agreeing with me, then reached over and pulled the top blanket up closer to my head. "You're sick. You should rest now."

Watching him, I could see him thinking. "You have ideas about this?" I said, with difficulty. Joseph looked me in the eye.

"Tell me, I'm not too sick to listen," I said, and the words sounded like dry leaves blown along a sidewalk.

"I've wondered it, too," Joseph answered. He rubbed his jaw for a minute. He had been squatting but now sat down on the floor. "I guess it has a lot to do with how they saw things," he said. "It's like what I said on the way down, many of the settlers and soldiers thought that Indians were all 'wild savages'—that we were all dangerous—and not just dangerous, but bad in a wild, uncontrollable way that could never really be fixed. They believed we were bad in our very essence. It made sense to them that destroying something that was so basically bad was a good thing to do."

I tried to take in what Joseph was telling me. *Believed we were... bad in... essence.* His words went through my head. *Destroying... bad was... good.*

This was how Joseph explained such violence. Could this really explain it? I wondered.

Joseph sat quietly, still looking thoughtful.

I glanced over at the children. "We're not being too loud for the kids, are we?" I whispered. "I don't want to wake them."

"No," Joseph said softly, glancing up from his thoughts. "It won't bother them, not if we keep it kind of low."

Joseph paused again, then went on. "When I was in 'Nam, after we arrived, as part of our training, they made a point of teaching us to see the people we were fighting as the enemy, and not as human beings. They told us over and over that we shouldn't think of the North Vietnamese as human." Joseph shook his head. "I guess the idea was, you've kind of got to believe the people you're fighting are subhuman, or just plain bad, or worthless, otherwise it's too hard to pull the trigger. They told us when we were out on patrol to think of it just like we were going hunting back home. I think a lot of the soldiers saw it that way. It was a kind of craziness that made the craziness of what we were doing seem less insane, if you know what I mean."

Joseph was silent for a few moments, and I thought how comforting it was just to have him in the room with me. His presence seemed to pull me further from the troubling dreams I'd had earlier.

"Anyway," he said, his voice soft and steady, "like I was saying, the way I figure it, both Colonel Chivington and Major Anthony really believed in the whole 'Indians are uncivilized, savage, bad' thing, and so it seemed to them it was good to kill Indians. I don't think they could see the humanity of people who were right in the same room with them, not if those people were Indians. Chivington and Anthony were so convinced that Indians were savage and dangerous that it was easy for them to believe all our efforts at peace were insincere. Anthony believed we were just trying to postpone the fighting until spring, when it would be easier for us. Chivington believed we were asking for peace so we could avoid the 'punishment' he thought we had coming to us. That's how he saw things. They believed these things, and so fighting us, then, even when we had surrendered and asked for peace, seemed to make sense to them."

"How do you know so much about this?" I whispered, my voice rough against my throat.

"I grew up hearing about it," he said, his voice still soft. "And I read a lot. Did a long paper in college. I dug it out a couple of days ago, when I was thinking about driving down here."

Joseph picked up a small rubber ball from the floor in front of him, turned it over in his hands absentmindedly. "Anyway, not all the soldiers were as blind as Chivington," he went on, "Major Wynkoop and some of the lieutenants under him—Cramer and Soule, especially—all tried to help make peace. Wynkoop believed the 'savage Indian' stereotype at first but, unlike Chivington and Anthony, when he met real people he could see who they were, so his blindness didn't go that deep."

Joseph looked thoughtful. "I'm trying to remember what Wynkoop wrote about his first meeting with One Eye and Min-im-mie, when they, and One Eye's wife, risked their lives to come seeking peace. If I remember right, it was something like, 'I was confused at seeing such patriotism on the part of two savages,'" Joseph said, looking up towards the ceiling. "He said something about how he felt he was, ah, 'in the presence of Superior beings,' something like that."

Joseph rubbed his jaw thoughtfully, and then added to the quote, "'and this when I had always considered Indians to be, without exception, cruel, treacherous, and blood-thirsty, incapable of feelings of affection for friend or family.'

"I may have changed the words some, but that's about what he said," Joseph concluded. "When Wynkoop finally met with One-Eye and the others, he could see the real people in front of him. He could see that what he had been taught about Indians was wrong. I'd say Wynkoop was a good man, even if he had been taught wrong to begin with," Joseph added.

I tried to imagine that meeting, what it would have been like for him to have believed he was fighting a vicious, subhuman enemy, and then to have finally met with some of them, only to realize that they were honorable people prepared to risk their lives in the hope of peace.

I looked over at Joseph, who looked at me. "So some could listen and learn—while others could not," he said. "Cramer and Soule and some others were there before the massacre, and tried to stop Chivington and Anthony from attacking. But Chivington and Anthony wouldn't any more listen to Cramer and Soule than they had been willing to listen to Black Kettle and the other chiefs who asked for peace. They had their own views, and nothing could shake them from them."

Joseph took a deep breath, set the little ball on the floor near him, then leaned back with his hands behind him for support. "There's also evidence that Chivington had private reasons for wanting to get into a big fight with Indians," he said. "Chivington had just failed in a run for Congress, and may have thought if he could gain a reputation as an Indian fighter it would help him get elected. So from his point of view, it was a good thing to kill Indians in general, and also he likely believed it would help him politically. It didn't matter to him if it was in a sneak attack after we had surrendered and asked for peace. In fact, I imagine he thought that was better, because we'd be easier to find and he'd be less likely to be killed himself."

Joseph was silent for a few moments as I tried to make sense of all he'd just told me. It reminded me of something I'd read while helping to teach a class at Columbia.

"Two, maybe three, years ago," I said, and realized immediately how much it was going to hurt to talk, but I wanted to finish what I'd started to say, "I helped teach an introductory class in Social Anthropology." I swallowed painfully, and then went on slowly. "The text book had an introduction that, well, I guess the author was trying to get the students to have an open mind about other people's cultures. It said, the text book said, that it's reasonable to define 'good' as what we see as being 'desirable,' and 'bad' as what we think of as 'undesirable.' It said," I closed my eyes, trying to remember it, and after a moment was able to picture what had been written in the book in my mind's eye.

I took a deep breath and swallowed again before speaking. "It said, 'We come to our own personal definitions of 'good' and 'bad' by evaluating what we think of as 'desirable' and 'undesirable.' We desire happiness, so we conclude that it's 'good.' We feel pain is undesirable, so we conclude that it's 'bad.'"

I opened my eyes. "Good and bad—desirable and undesirable. It's pretty obvious, I guess," I croaked out, "but it was what they said next that I wanted to tell you. They said why would anybody actively pursue doing something that they themselves thought of as being an undesirable thing to do? There would be no reason. The author suggested that it's in our nature to attempt to do good, or the desirable, as we understand it from our own points of view."

My voice was a hoarse whisper as I added, "They went on to talk about how it was important to remember that when viewing other cultures—that people naturally do what seems desirable, or 'good,' to them. But I thought it was interesting; we're all trying to do what we see as 'desirable;' we're all trying to do what we see as being 'good.'"

I swallowed again, and rested my head against the pillow. Joseph was half lit by the glow of the nightlight. He looked very thoughtful. I closed my eyes for a moment, distracted by the pain in my throat.

"Yeah. I guess that's right," Joseph said, after several moments. "We all work out what we think is right from our own perspectives. From what I've read, even Chivington thought of himself as doing good."

I opened my eyes. "Yeah, it's amazing," I said. I could feel each word as it formed like a sharp thing in my throat. "I've even read that Hitler thought he was doing good—thought he would be remembered as a kind of savior throughout the 'thousand year *Reich*' for ridding the world of Jews—and not just Jews, but gays, Gypsies, Afro-Europeans—anybody he thought of as detracting from his so-called 'Aryan ideal.' It's amazing how narrow a person's perceptions can be—that they can do incredible harm and never truly grasp how bad the thing they're doing is." I swallowed painfully and hoped I wouldn't think of too much more to say.

Joseph nodded thoughtfully. "It's like the only people's eyes they can see through are the ones who see the world just like they do," he said. "Everyone else's world is invisible to them."

I was thinking about what Joseph had just said when the noise coming from the next room got my attention. It sounded like people were gathering in the front room. I imagined it was my companions getting ready to leave.

A moment later, someone tapped on the bedroom door. "Come," Joseph said in a loud whisper. Russell stuck his head into the room.

"Ready?" Russell asked. He pushed the door the rest of the way open and stood silhouetted in the doorway. "You coming, Indira?"

"No, too sick," I answered hoarsely.

"Oh," Russell said sadly, and I could see he felt bad for me. "I hope you feel better soon," he said.

Joseph got up. "Is there anything else I can get for you before I go?" he asked. They both seemed so sweet, standing there looking down at me.

"No," I answered. "Thanks for the tea, and the talk. Mostly I think I just need to sleep."

Joseph and Russell both nodded. "Okay," Joseph said. "I'm sure Deborah would tell you to help yourself to anything you need."

"Okay. Thanks. I hope it's a good trip," I said.

Joseph nodded. "I hope you feel better soon," he said quietly. He looked down at me for a moment in silence, perhaps wondering if there was anything more he could do, then he and Russell both turned and slipped silently through the door, pulling it shut behind them.

A few minutes later I heard the front door open, followed by the shuf-fling of feet, and imagined all of my companions leaving the house and climbing into the station wagon. The sheer curtains on the window next to the bed were pulled just a little open. Through the gap I could see out into the dark night, where a light snow was still falling. Moments later, I heard the car start and then pull away into the darkness.

I drank some of the tea, then lay thinking about the conversation Joseph and I had just had. I thought, too, about the stories Joseph had told and the dreams I'd had. I thought about how the settlers believed it was good to push Indians off their land in order to spread "civilization," and how the soldiers had thought it was good to kill Indians because they believed Indians were just plain bad. Doing good. Doing good. They all thought they were doing good. How strange it was.

Impressions from my dream about Matthew's father came to mind. He was returning from the bar, angry, frustrated. Had he thought he was doing good, too? Had it felt good to him, I wondered, had it seemed *good* to him to take out his frustrations and sadness on his sons? Had it made him feel powerful to take out his rage, like that, on his powerless children, in a world that had made him feel so powerless? I thought of the man in my dream, his rage all bottled up inside him, like a pressure building. Might it have felt good just to have let it out? Yes, maybe—good and powerful, an active force finally, in his own life—if only for that moment.

Another part of the dream came back to me, then, about Matthew's father "straightening out" his son before Matthew could grow in the wrong way—like some sort of misshapen growth was inevitable if it wasn't controlled. His own father had done a "favor" for him, he had thought in my dream, and he would do this "favor" for his own son.

A good act, it might have seemed to him, I thought—and not just for the moment when his rage was released.

My thoughts turned to Emil. Dear, young, sweet Emil. Had he felt there was goodness in his actions? Sure, as I'd dreamed it, at least, he'd lived up to the expectations of the other boys in the neighborhood—older boys he had admired—and he had gained their respect. How thrilling—how thrilling and satisfying. What a desirable thing that might have seemed from his perspective. How good that might have felt.

Emil. I felt sad thinking about it. Was this how he had lost his way?

I rolled onto my side and pulled my knees up close. I felt lousy, physi-cally and emotionally. I closed my eyes and tried to stop thinking, tried not to feel, even, the soreness of my throat or the aching in my body. Before long, my thoughts began to swim together, and I found myself drift-ing off to sleep. Fragmentary impressions coursed through my mind—images from the dream about Matthew and his father; Joseph talking about Chivington wanting to "punish" the Indians; a bloody raid at dawn; a peace flag flying; children crying as soldiers took aim...

For a moment, I struggled back towards waking, trying to clear my mind of these impressions—but even as the fever unsettled my thoughts, the sickness drew my body towards much-needed sleep, and I could feel myself being pulled back down into that dark hole. The impressions swirled around me like falling snow, as I descended into a landscape that seemed already made before I arrived.

I was riding on horseback through a smooth darkness, broken only by patches of snow glowing in starlight.

Up ahead, I could catch glimpses of someone—someone we were following. I knew he was not our leader, but a guide. Two dark figures rode along beside him—the two officers I had put there to guard him and make sure he led the way.

He had tried once already to mislead us, and I thought he might try again. It was only through threats that he'd come this far. He had family at Sand Creek, and had some idea of what was to come there...

I rolled over in bed, still dreaming, like someone held deep beneath the water, longing to get back to the air and light. But the dream continued to swirl around me, and I was pulled deeper—a swimmer unable to let go of a massive weight that kept pulling her down and under.

I could hear the other riders and horses around me. Fighting back chills, I shivered against the cold night. My thoughts had been drifting, as I rode through this dark, unchanging landscape, and now they settled on the past—on my days as a preacher, before I'd become a colonel, before this long night's ride.

I had tried to do what I could to save all of those with Christian souls from the fires of eternal damnation, I told myself—but it was hard, especially here in the West, with so much gambling and drinking going on. Satan's hand could grip anyone's heart, and it was well to remember that!

I pulled my coat tighter around my neck with one hand, while holding the reins loosely with the other. My thoughts continued to drift through my past.

"Our Lord is a vengeful Lord, and He will smite down the wicked and the sinful," I had told them. In the world there is so much depravity. It is the work of Satan, a stream running beneath the surface of the human heart, a stream which all must struggle to keep suppressed, or the hand of Satan will take hold in their lives!

I turned back in the saddle and looked at the soldiers following behind me. These were good, brave men, and I felt honored to be leading them. Some were a bit wayward, it was true, but they were good Christian men, and it is good Christians Our Lord loves, as it is His will that this good Christian nation sweep across this land like the light of a rising dawn. It is His will, as well, that all the heathen savages who stand in His way be smited down.

On this very night, on this cold, dark night, we are traveling into darkness to do God's will. Soon there will be light, and it will be the Light which clears away Darkness.

We are the Righteous Ones.

These savages are sly. They are backwards, and they are simple minded, except for their infernal trickery. But I would not be taken in by any trick in which they pretend to seek peace while hoping only to avoid the righteous wrath they have earned! Unlike those Indian-lovers, Cramer and Soule and the others. Damn any man in sympathy with an Indian!

Such Indian lovers as Soule and Cramer are half heathens themselves! I'd have liked to have shot them! Have they no love of our good, Christian women and children—the purest amongst us—no desire to make this land safe for them?

A shiver of passion ran along my spine. Can't they see that it is God's will that these untamed savages be cleared away to make room for His Light to spread? For His Light to spread and to bring with it His Civilization and His Cultivation to this fallow, unused, wasted land?

I could see myself on a grandstand speaking to a great crowd, telling them about our mission and about the blood—oh, yes, the blood!—and how it ran deep and purified the land, making it safe for our mothers and sisters, our wives and children.

And the crowd, hearing that, would rise up with me, for me, and honor me with their cheers, with their well-wishes—and with their votes!

The thought made me smile. I could see myself striding up the steps of the U.S. Congress. Oh, the power which would be in my hands! The thought felt vitalizing and good, like the way it feels good when you're young and have strength in your body and know you can run a long way.

I shifted in the saddle and looked up ahead. Beyond the endless miles of snow, the faintest deep-blue glow had begun to gather in the eastern sky. I stared into it and could feel—the time was growing near. What was I doing, I told myself, thinking about the future far ahead when I should be preparing for that which was right at hand?

I would have to rally the troops before sending them into battle. My blood stirred at the thought of it. Oh, the gore—yes, soon I will be wading in it! The gore and the glory—I will be covered in both! We will all be! I thought, with satisfaction.

My heart quickened, and I knew just then how to prepare the troops. I will point out to them that I am not telling them to kill all ages and sexes, for they have heard before my orders to kill all and take no prisoners. No need to repeat them now. I will just remind them of all those dead at Indian hands, and they will know just what to do...

I twisted awake, sweating heavily, even in the cold night. No, oh no. Chivington. I had dreamed up Colonel Chivington's thoughts as he approached the massacre.

Such strange and dreadful dreams I was having tonight!

Half trembling, I sat up and drank some tea, trying to shake off the sickening feeling of the dream. I was glad for the nightlight that illuminated the room, as it helped me find my way back to the here and now.

I set the jar down and rubbed my face. Just as Joseph had described him, I had dreamed him, I thought—with all that certainty that the Indians were bad and that he was right.

I lay back down and pulled the covers over me. I still felt shaken by the dream, and my thoughts felt uncomfortably scattered by the fever.

Impressions of violences large and small kept swimming through my mind—soldiers taking aim at a child; a crowd shouting "exterminate them;" the satisfaction, even, that I'd dreamed Emil had felt after he'd stolen the money.

Words Matthew had said to me in the bar went through my head: "Not if he understood in a way where it reverberated through him. Not if he really *felt* it. Not if he *really understood*," Matthew had said, talking about what it would have taken to make his father wake up to his own cruel deeds.

Matthew had been suggesting that if his father had seen through his sons' eyes, if he had really known their pain, he would have become incapable of any longer willfully inflicting such pain on them.

Was Matthew right? I wondered, pulling myself up out of my feverish thoughts a bit. Maybe so. Maybe so, I thought.

I closed my eyes and an impression of how I'd felt when I'd seen Laura burn herself the night before came to my mind. I'd seen her jerk her hand back and heard her call out. I'd felt for her like a spasm going through me.

Poor Laura! I couldn't bear to see her hurt. I never could.

Her pain had reverberated through me the way Matthew had hoped his own pain would resonate in his father.

Had Matthew been right that his father had never really felt the pain he'd inflicted on his sons?

I thought about that for a minute and again recalled the moment Laura had gotten burned. I had heard her call out and had thought, immediately and vividly, about how it must have felt for her—*as though her experience were my experience.*

Yes, I thought—I had imagined her pain. In truth, I had imagined her pain as clearly as if it had been my own.

I rolled over and thought about that for a moment. Put differently—*I had included her perspective within my own.*

Surely, this was a way Matthew's father had never perceived his sons.

I thought about the dream I'd had about Chivington. Nowhere in the impressions I had dreamed up for him had he shown any concern for what his violence would mean to the people he was preparing to attack. Their perspective was invisible to him. Like Joseph had said: "It's like the only people's eyes they can see through are the ones who see the world just like they do. Everyone else's world is invisible to them."

I thought back through everything Joseph had told me about Chivington. It was true, nothing had suggested that Chivington had thought, even the smallest bit, about how what he planned to do would actually affect his victims.

Perhaps such a lack of awareness was part of this pathology, I told myself. Perhaps, like Matthew's father, Chivington had no real comprehension of what others experienced at his hands. How could he have borne it, I thought, if he had somehow imagined, truly, and with full comprehension, the torment he inflicted? How could anyone?

I thought back through the dreams and impressions that had been passing through my mind. It was like both Chivington and Matthew's father had lived on islands of their own, too far from the lands other people inhabited to imagine what those people really experienced. To them, the experiences of people dissimilar to them were invisible.

Even the good-natured Emil had shown this flaw to a degree. He had been out of touch with what his actions would mean to the shopkeeper.

I rolled over, raised myself on one elbow, and pulled my journal out of my pack. I set it on the floor next to the mattress I lay on, opened it to the first blank page, and wrote:

1. *Insular perspective:*
Failing to see through other's eyes.

Under the dim light from the nightlight, I could just make out what I had written. I underlined it, then beneath it, in smaller letters, I wrote, "one piece of the pathology." Then I rolled onto my back, wondering what other pieces there were.

I thought through what Joseph had said about Chivington's views, and how he'd believed that Indians were all bad—and I wondered if that, too, was part of the problem.

Then I remembered what Joseph had told me about the training he and the other U.S. troops had received when they'd first arrived in Vietnam. They'd been taught, quite deliberately, to see the enemy as less than human, Joseph had said. How had he put it? "You've kind of got to believe the people you're fighting are subhuman, or just plain bad, or worthless, otherwise it's too hard to pull the trigger."

Yes, I was certain that was part of the reason that Chivington and the soldiers he'd led at Sand Creek had been capable of the terrible things they'd done. They'd been out to destroy something—something they misperceived as being essentially bad. And even Matthew's father, as I had dreamed of him, had been trying to fight—or at least to suppress—a tendency toward "badness" he thought he saw in his sons.

I rolled onto my side again, picked up my pen from the floor next to my journal, and wrote:

2. *Belief in a bad or worthless nature.*

I underlined it, set my pen down, then lay back down, weary from the effort.

Tired as I was, I was also excited by the ideas gelling in my mind. Both of these items I had listed, it seemed to me, predisposed people to destructive acts—like a broken brake line or a gas leak in a car could turn an otherwise safe machine into something very dangerous.

I thought about it for a minute. In what other ways did the "machinery" break down in cases like the ones I'd been thinking and dreaming about? I wondered. I thought about Chivington and Anthony and about how they both had known they were attacking people who had surrendered and who were seeking peace. But they hadn't listened to the truth—they had both assumed it was some sort of ploy.

Clearly this was part of the reason things had gone so wrong. I thought again about what Joseph had said—that Chivington and Anthony had both failed to listen and to change their views when the chiefs had come seeking peace. But Wynkoop had listened—there had been no block in communication—he had listened and adjusted his opinion.

I ran that around in my head for a little while, then thought again about Matthew. He had wanted to communicate with his father, show his father the pain he was causing, but Matthew had found no way to get through to his dad. In my dream I had imagined Matthew calling out, "Please, no—don't." The communication, the words, had reached between them, but had failed inside his father—just as the chiefs had said the right words, but Chivington and Anthony hadn't listened.

The block was in the perpetrators, I thought. They were unprepared to hear.

I rolled over on one side, picked up my pen, and wrote:

3. *Failure to Communicate — with oneself, and with others.*

Then I set the pen back down on the floor. I repeated the three items to myself under my breath: *Insular perspective. Belief in a bad or worthless nature. Failure to communicate with oneself and with others.*

I raised up on one elbow and sipped some of the tea Joseph had brought to me. It was a little woody and bitter, but I still liked the flavor.

I lay back down and repeated the items on my list to myself again: *insular perspective (or failing to see through other's eyes)—belief in a bad or worthless nature—failure to communicate with oneself and with others.*

What was this a list of exactly, I asked myself?

How things can go wrong in the machinery within us. Yes, that was it.

I pulled the blanket closer around me. From the position I was lying in, I was looking through the jar of tea Joseph had brought me and towards the nightlight behind it. The tea was a soft brown with just a hint of green in it. It looked lovely with the light from the nightlight shining through it.

It was so kind of Joseph to have brought it to me, I thought. He had been kind to me, also, when we'd stopped for gas and snacks and he'd helped me get a warm seat in the front of the car.

I rose up on one elbow, picked up the jar, and took a sip—then lay back down and considered Joseph's kind acts. He must have been thinking about how I was feeling to have offered me the help he had—the warm seat, the soup, the hot tea. What a kind man, I thought. *His perspective was hardly an insular one,* I told myself. He'd really empathized with what I was experiencing.

He must have really been listening, too, when we'd stopped at the convenience store, and I'd told him how bad my throat felt. He'd gone to the trouble then of finding me a warm spot in the car.

Good communication, I thought. Yes, he'd really listened when I'd told him about my sore throat.

I still felt feverish, but somehow the interest I was feeling in these ideas pulled me up out of the aches and pains of my body. It was exciting to see a pattern developing.

I rolled onto my back and stared up at the ceiling. And *bad?* Did he see me as having a bad or worthless nature?

No, clearly not. Every gesture had revealed that he thought I was *good*— that I was *worthy* of his care and attention.

Clearly, I told myself, Joseph's actions reflected the *reverse* of all three items on my list!

I smiled and thought about Laura. I thought about how considerate she always was of whatever I was going through, and how willing she was to see a situation from my point of view. I thought about how easy she was to talk to, and about how much she believed in me.

I translated that for myself silently:

• Considerate of my feelings and willing to see my perspective = *perspective not insular.*

• Easy to talk to = *good communication.*

• Believed in me = *saw me as good and worthy.*

Again, all three items in reverse, I thought.

My smile grew a little bigger. It seemed to me that it was common for people to get all three of these items right. So often, people *do* pause to imagine how their actions would seem from someone else's point of view. So often they *do* communicate. So often they *do* value one another.

I thought about the people who had tried to help the Indians at Sand Creek—who had worked for peace early on, or who had tried to keep the massacre from happening. Joseph had mentioned Wynkoop and a couple more soldiers named Cramer and Soule. I thought about them and their actions in relationship to these three items:

• *Insular perspective*: No, their perspectives were not insular. They had seemed to understand the views and the needs of the people they were dealing with.

• *Belief in a bad nature*: No, they saw the Indians as valuable enough to try to stop the violence against them.

• *Failure to communicate*: No, they had communicated well. They had listened and understood when the Cheyenne and Arapahoe chiefs had asked for peace.

It all seemed to crystallize for me then. Where we do harm, the machinery within us is failing in one or more of these three ways. And when we do good, none of these—none of these *impediments*—were in the way.

I felt a quiet joy gathering in me. I felt like I had uncovered something important, something fundamental and yet simple: *the three impediments to the full expression of the native goodness within each of us.*

Yes, the three impediments, I thought—the presence of which causes the machinery within ourselves to malfunction and so create distorted and dangerous effects—the absence of which allows the fundamental goodness and beauty of our natures to reveal itself, unimpeded.

The room was gradually filling with the first light of dawn. We *are* truly, elementally beautiful, I thought. I needn't have doubted it. When the mechanisms of our selves are functioning smoothly, our native longing to do good, to fulfill ourselves, and to find joy is expressed directly into the world as good-doing, as fulfillment, and as joy. That's how the machinery runs when there are no impediments in its way.

We desire to do good, and without these three impediments, that's just what we do. But like the car I'd ridden in on the way to Denver, if an essential mechanism fails—whether that failure has to do with *perspective, communication,* or a recognition of the *goodness and worth* in everyone; or whether the failure is a blown tire, or a broken brake line—*if an essential mechanism fails,* that machine becomes a danger to those around it, no matter how sleek and beautiful it may be when running smoothly.

I thought about our car swerving when the tire had blown, and how lucky we had been not to collide with the truck in the next lane. Our car was not evil. No car is. But when the machinery failed, the danger was no less real.

I picked up my journal and put it on the mattress, then rolled over on my stomach and began to write:

> We are good. We are beautiful. But sometimes obstacles form which get in the way of us expressing the natural goodness and beauty within us.
>
> That can happen:
>
> - when we fail to see through another's eyes — and so become insensitive to their experience,
>
> - when we see others as being bad or lacking in essential worth — because then we feel justified in treating them cruelly,
>
> - when we fail to communicate — because this makes it hard to see the real situation we are dealing with and so may lead us to take actions inappropriate to it.
>   Also, when we don't communicate, emotions may go unexpressed — and so pile up, like water behind a dam, and eventually break loose with too much energy behind them.
>
> But if we can keep clear of these three impediments:
>
> > Insular perspective
> > Belief in a bad nature
> > Failure to communicate
>
> then our natural beauty shines through.

"Our natural beauty," I read back to myself, smiling.

I underlined the last phrase twice, then lay back down. I felt lighter, relieved of some sort of burden I'd been carrying. It was as though the storm clouds I'd felt gathering around me for months had suddenly cleared. Funny, I thought, that it would take such a storm in myself to blow them away.

"That was it," I thought, feeling almost giddy.

I sat up and drank the rest of the tea Joseph had so kindly made for me, then lay back down and gathered the blankets around me, smiling. The sun must have just crested the horizon, for a thin beam of light broke through the opening in the curtains and, spreading, washed across the ceiling at the far side of the room.

I looked out the window at the gathering dawn, which had turned the sky a deep shade of rose, and found myself thinking about my new friends, who would just then be gathered at Sand Creek, and suddenly the reality of this journey, of their journey, came back to me.

I imagined the sun washing across the open grasslands with that same reddish glow, across a place of such pain and sorrow that the seeds of heartache cast there one hundred and fifteen years before could still be felt now, passed down like a virus in the blood through five generations.

Learning how a machine can be converted into a bomb, I thought, makes its blast no less deadly. And yet, somehow, the insights I'd had while lying there did give me hope. You can't defuse a bomb until you can see how it was made and set, I thought.

I pulled my knees up to my chest and for some time sat staring out the gap in the curtains at the brightening sky. I didn't know what sort of blessings my friends had planned to make that dawn, but I made my own while sitting there.

After a time, I leaned forward and pushed the curtain back enough to see a bigger piece of sky. The land was draped in a blanket of fresh snow, but the sky was bright and filled with a multitude of small white clouds.

I imagined others waking beneath such a sky one hundred and fifteen years earlier. I wished that somehow my blessings could be sent back to them, draped over them like that clean, white snow, offering them protection as they woke that day from their peaceful slumber to the thunderous approach of seven hundred mounted soldiers.

❀   ❀   ❀

As I lay in thought watching the brightening sky, I heard the door to the bedroom I was in quietly creak open. It was Deborah, whom I had met the night before. She smiled at me when she saw I was awake, then stepped softly over to the bed to wake the children.

There were two of them, a girl of about eight and her sister, perhaps two years younger. I wondered how they would feel about waking to find a stranger in their bed, but they seemed unfazed. The older one seemed sleepy but otherwise unconcerned. The younger, I thought, seemed pleased to have a new person appear. As soon as she was up, she wanted to show me some special rocks she'd found, but her mother hurried both kids on to get them ready for school.

I lay there for a while, listening to them moving around the house, then got up to use the bathroom. The house was small and simple, but had the atmosphere of a real family home, and I felt glad to be there, though a little concerned about imposing. Deborah insisted on fixing me breakfast (eggs and toast), and mixed me up some orange juice before she and the kids dashed off to work and school, respectively.

The sun was well up by then, and I went back into the bedroom and lay in the broad splash of sunlight spilling in on the bed. I spent half an hour or so writing in my journal about the journey and the realizations I'd had the night before, then lay back down, relaxing and soaking up the sun. My throat still felt raw, but I was certain my fever had broken.

I closed my eyes and enjoyed the warm glow of light that soaked through my eyelids. The house was very quiet, the room warm, and soon I had again drifted off to sleep, but this time my dreams were not the sharp and rugged creatures of the night before. This time I dreamed that Laura and I were sailing across a sea as wide and open as the prairie had been the day before, below a sky as broad and blue. We were being carried by the wind and the way was open before us.

The sun was high in the sky by the time Joseph and the others returned from Sand Creek. Joseph woke me gently, as before, and was pleased to see how much better I felt.

It wasn't long before we were all on our way north again, hurrying to get Russell home in time for his late shift. Joseph again secured me a warm spot at the front of the car, and we rode home together under that endless Western sky, which was rapidly clearing of clouds.

It would be years before I fully understood the importance of the ideas that had unfolded for me in Deborah Highwalking's house that night, years before I fitted them into the puzzle that would eventually allow me to stand, as it were, on a mountain top and look out towards a brightening future. But I wasn't thinking about that that morning as we rolled north in an old, wood-sided station wagon. I was thinking instead of Laura, and how soon I would find myself, again, and for a few days longer, in her warm and tender arms.

❀   ❀   ❀

"Pause," Paul said.

"Pausing. End of chapter," Kiki said.

Paul had been looking for a good place to pause the text and take a break from listening. Now, he stopped at the side of the path and dug a travel meal from his pack, then strolled along eating his lunch in the shade of the over-hanging trees. He wanted to leave Kiki silent for a little while, to give himself space for his own thoughts. Listening to Dr. Kumar describe her feelings at being separated from Laura earlier in the day, and now listening to her express her eagerness to reunite with Laura, had sharpened Paul's distress at being taken from Sheila. He found himself again feeling guilty about abandoning her (however much he knew, rationally, that it wasn't his fault) and worrying about what needed to be done to return to her.

Paul had done all he could to review the mathematics behind Interdimensional-Linking Theory during his stay at the lodge two nights before, but he still didn't feel as confident of it as he would like to feel of something he would entrust his life to—and the dream he'd had later that night had left him even more uneasy—but what other choice did he have? ILT was the only explanation he had for why his would-be transport to another planet in his universe had brought him here, to a parallel earth. All he could really do was trust that whatever natural laws had warped the transportation process during his journey here would be constant enough to do the same on his journey home.

He'd done what he could to work this out, Paul told himself, and he wasn't going to let it worry him now. Instead, he let his thoughts drift, and soon he found himself thinking again about the night he and Sheila had first met.

That night, as the dinner party was coming to an end, Sheila had leaned in close to Paul and, in a hushed tone meant for only him to hear, asked him if she could download his avatar. Then she sat back and, with an expression both playful and seductive, awaited his reply.

Paul was well aware that people often made these "avatars"—these virtual replicas of themselves—to share with others. Within a certain fast-living set, it was often the case that the first intimacy between a couple would take place in a virtual setting, where each alone might plug the other person's avatar into a program to run privately through their implant. If both were pleased with that virtual experience, they might then encounter one another in the actual world.

Paul looked at Sheila for a moment, then, taking in her expression. He'd always thought the practice of avatar swapping superficial, and in truth, off-putting—but this woman—my God, what an effect she was having on him! He thought perhaps he would follow her anywhere.

"I have no avatar," Paul told her simply. "I've never constructed one for myself."

"Intriguing," was Sheila's reply. "A purist." She tilted her head a little, and her smile expressed a new curiosity.

After a moment's thought, Sheila leaned toward Paul again and asked him if he would join her for a gallery opening the next weekend. She said, with a tone of near reverence, that the work of Vespucci Andreoni would be displayed.

When Paul hesitated, not sure whether to tell her he had no idea who that was, or just to answer regardless, Sheila seemed somehow to recognize that he was not in the know, and added that Vespucci Andreoni was a very famous and very influential experiential artist who had been commissioned by Corprogov to design virtual art experiences for the Stream.

Paul had little interest in what he considered to be unnecessary distractions such as experiential virtual art, but he was, at the moment, feeling so smitten with Sheila that it would hardly have mattered what she had invited him to. With hardly a thought, Paul found himself agreeing to go.

Sheila smiled and commented lightly that she'd had to pull strings to get the tickets—and that she would be delighted to have a famous scientist accompanying her.

Paul protested again that he could hardly be called "famous," but somehow he didn't feel like protesting too much or trying too hard to correct the way she saw him. The truth was, he was enjoying her affirming view of him.

Paul smiled at Sheila, in whose face he saw some deep mystery, some special beauty calling to him. Who was this woman, he thought, who seemed so willing to give him the benefit of the doubt, and to offer him such generous approval?

Paul leaned in toward her, then, and told her how pleased he would be to be there with her, as well.

While he'd been thinking about Sheila, the path Paul was on had wandered a little away from the creek, and it now put him in the open sun. He stopped to get out the hat Marco had given him, then continued on.

Sheila had left the dinner party a little before him that night, Paul recalled. As Paul had watched Sheila across the room, saying goodbye to a last friend or two before slipping out the door, Tyler had stepped up to Paul and clapped him on the back.

"She's sizzlin'," Tyler said.

Already, Paul didn't like someone describing her that way.

"She was asking about you earlier," Tyler went on, "—who you were, what you did." Tyler looked at Paul with a knowing smile and patted Paul on the back again, then moved on to say goodbye to one of his guests.

It would be three years since the night they'd met, come August, Paul thought, as he strolled along the trail. And how many times had he asked her to marry him in that time?

Paul knew that Sheila thought the idea old fashioned, but he hoped that one day she would agree. In the meanwhile, they planned to get an apartment together—which practically amounted to marriage, Paul told himself, half-seriously. After all, with the apartment shortage, and Corprogov's sluggish response to requests for reassignment, people could hardly separate if they wanted to once they had moved in together.

Paul and Sheila had just started their wait for a shared apartment a little more than two months before his accidental transport. Paul had been eager to get them moved in and settled into their new place—whenever one might be assigned to them—but Sheila had held out hope that with Paul's Corprogov connections, he might be able to pull strings and get them a place larger than the combined space of their two single apartments. Paul thought that would be nice, but knew too well that he lacked that sort of influence, no matter how much Sheila wanted to believe he had some special importance within the Corprogov structure.

Well, maybe now I will, Paul thought—or at least, maybe I will once I get back with news of what I've accomplished.

Again, Paul found his attention pouring back into his dream of a happy return. This time he pictured himself walking down the street outside his office, with everybody he passed recognizing him, and all faces turning toward him with expressions of complete praise and approval.

He imagined walking into his lab to meet with a Corprogov official, who offered him not just unlimited material resources and energy credits for his work, but also a spacious hillside apartment in the best district in town.

Soon the path returned to the creek, and not long after that Paul came to another campground. This one had been established in an area where two small waterfalls, which fell around a massive boulder in the water's path, had widened and deepened the creek, making a pool large enough for swimming. Oaks of various sorts hung over the water and the adjoining campsite, creating a carpet of shade.

It was late afternoon, Paul was tired, and his feet were sore. He pulled off his pack and dropped it to the ground on the creek's bank, then pulled off the shoes Marco had given him and put his sore and weary feet into the cool water. This place would be his home for the night, he decided. Though it was late in the afternoon, it seemed too early to eat dinner or even to do the little involved in setting up camp for the night, so instead Paul sat quietly on the creek's bank and went over, in his mind, the parts he'd picked out when using the Intralink portal at the Wayfarer's Inn in Strandford, and tried to reason out what exactly would be required to fit one part to another.

As he imagined adapting one part to fit another, he wondered if each part would have to be changed in ways that, in turn, might make each more difficult to fit into the next. As Paul imagined it, the process became like a giant three-dimensional jigsaw puzzle, where each part was in flux, having to be adapted, and then adapted again, to fit into the series of parts around it.

Finally, Paul sat up and rubbed his head. The truth was, he told himself, that he wouldn't really know which adaptations were possible or necessary until he actually had the parts in his hands and could examine them more closely. One way or another, he assured himself, he would make the process work.

Paul sighed and stood up. He already had his shoes off, but now began to strip off the rest of his clothes, preparing to take a swim in the creek. As Paul unbuttoned his shirt, he reflected on how things now stood for him. Though it was plain to him that any number of obstacles still lay in his path, he was eager to tackle and overcome them. He wanted so to push forward, but there was frustratingly little he could do from here.

He could, at least, listen to more of Dr. Kumar's book, he told himself, as he unfastened his pants—but even there, he felt the progress was too slow.

What was it he had figured out that morning? That he'd come more than a third of the way on his trek, while listening to less than a quarter of the book. Perhaps he could find a way to speed things up further.

Paul stepped out of his pants and pulled off his shirt. Ideally, he might find a way to skim ahead in such a way that he would still learn enough about the material he was skimming to seem adequately informed at the Retreat. If he could accomplished this, then it stood to reason that he would also more quickly find out just how it was that this book had so influenced this world.

Paul lay his clothes on some rocks above the water, making sure that Kiki remained high and dry there, then jumped into the creek where the water was wide and deep beneath the falls.

The water was fresh and clear. Cold, but not terribly cold—invigorating. Paul splashed around in it, washing himself as best he could, then took a deep breath and swam down to the bottom of the pool. As he turned to swim back up, he looked up through the crystal-clear water to the light playing along its surface.

My God! Paul thought. What an incredible world he had found himself in!

Paul rose quickly to the surface and filled his lungs with air. Looking around, the whole day seemed somehow brighter, clearer, now, from within this bright, clear water.

Paul knew he had work to do, but didn't want to leave the water quite yet.

"Kiki," he called out from the middle of the pool, "is there some way you can determine which sections of this book had the largest social impact?"

"Yes," Kiki answered from the stream's bank. "General patterns can be assessed." Paul could hear her clearly enough above the burbling of the small waterfalls.

"How would you do that?" Paul asked.

"By surveying reviews and analyses in search of references to social influence."

"Do you have such articles on file?" Paul asked, treading water.

"Yes."

"What—they came with the book?"

"Yes," Kiki said.

"Okay. Well, then would you please identify the next section with high conceptual content and/or extensive social influence, and jump ahead to it?" Paul said.

"Shall I use the same parameters for defining 'extensive social influence' as you set for defining 'high conceptual content?'" Kiki asked.

"Yes," Paul answered, as he began to swim back to the bank. As refreshing as it was, the water was too cold for him to want to linger long.

"Identified," Kiki said.

"Good. Please begin recitation at that point," Paul said, then climbed out of the sparkling water as Kiki began to recite.

The next morning over breakfast, I mentioned to Irene that I had started the article on animal intuition that I'd found in a magazine in the sitting room, and that it looked like it would be quite interesting. She said she was done with that magazine and that I could take it with me if I liked.

We had finished packing and brought down our bags first thing, but I remembered to run upstairs and get the magazine before our taxi arrived. And arrive it soon did. We all said our quick and excited farewells, and Laura and I set off on a bright, cold January morning, whisked away in a black London cab, on our way to Africa.

"Wait—Africa?" Paul said, as he pulled on his trousers and looked for a sunny spot to warm up in. "Why are they going to Africa?"

"To do research on the Mbuti Pygmies."

Paul picked up his hat and his shirt, with Kiki still on it, and sat on a large rock in the sun. He positioned himself so he could lean on another rock and stretch out a little.

"Okay, look," Paul said to Kiki, "is this the beginning of a chapter?"

"No. We have skipped approximately 79.7835% of chapter six," Kiki answered.

Paul sighed. "Chapter six? And what did we finish last—chapter four?"

"Yes."

"Okay, Kiki, if you can, would you please summarize chapter five? And then would you please begin recitation again at the *beginning* of chapter six?" Paul smiled to himself as he noticed how politely he was speaking to his little, wearable computer.

"Yes," Kiki answered, and then promptly began her summary, as Paul stretched out in the sun.

"At the end of the week she'd spent with Laura in Lame Deer, Indira returned to New York City and continued with her post-doctoral work there. Laura stayed in Montana for another six months, then moved to Boulder, Colorado, where she continued to assist Professor Sandler in typifying and quantifying the data she'd collected.

"In 1980, Indira applied for and was offered an assistant professorship at the University of New Mexico at Albuquerque. She gladly accepted, for this would move her much closer to Laura, who was still in central Colorado. They began taking turns visiting one another on weekends and so, at least, no longer felt quite so far apart.

"In 1981, Laura's post-doctoral work came to an end. She had applied for jobs at various universities around the country, including a tenure-track position that had opened up in the Religious Studies Department at the University of Colorado at Boulder, where she had been working. Laura was delighted to be offered this position and accepted it.

"Meanwhile, Indira had been working very hard. During her first year at the University of New Mexico she saw the publication of her doctoral dissertation, which presented some new perspectives and caused a small stir in her field, and had completed two more papers, one of which had already been accepted for publication.

"When a tenure-track position in Cultural Anthropology opened up at the University of Colorado at Boulder, Indira applied for it and was hired to that position to begin in the fall of 1982."

"So they were both at the same school, then?" Paul broke in.

"That is correct." Kiki answered.

"Both tenure-track positions?" Paul asked.

"Yes," Kiki answered.

"They were lucky to manage that," Paul said.

"Indira thought so, too," Kiki answered. "She wrote:

It had been three years since we had lived in the same city, and although we knew we were fortunate to be able to arrange work at the same school so quickly, it felt as though it had been altogether too long a time that we had been apart. We settled into our new home in the shadow of the Colorado Rockies with a sense of joy that I could hardly find the words to express....

Kiki paused and then asked, "Shall I proceed with the summary?"

"Yeah—so what happened then?" Paul asked.

"Indira and Laura spent their time teaching and doing research, occasionally taking hikes on the weekends or having dinner with friends. They took in a stray cat, which they named 'Bubbles' for his enthusiasm for chasing soap bubbles, a fact they discovered one day while doing laundry. In the autumn of 1984, both Indira and Laura took and passed an exam that granted them United States citizenship. They celebrated this by taking a two-week vacation in Mexico during the winter break between semesters, during which time they visited Mayan archaeological sites and went scuba diving off the Yucatan coast.

"For the most part, though, Indira and Laura stayed close to home. Both of them enjoyed their jobs and the splendid scenery that surrounded them in Boulder, but over time they both came to feel some frustration at how specialized their intellectual explorations had become. Indira especially had always had a yearning to grasp the 'big picture,' as it were, and felt frustrated at what a small corner of knowledge she was polishing as she probed the relationship between beliefs and culture. Still, her work was stimulating, and regardless of this frustration, she couldn't think of any other work she would rather have engaged in.

"Indira published frequently in her first years at the University of Colorado, and her work continued to get noticed. When the University of Wisconsin at Madison showed an interest in recruiting her in 1985, her department rushed to entice her to stay by offering her tenure. Indira was pleased to accept tenure at CU in Boulder, for it did not appear that Laura would also be offered a position at the University of Wisconsin, and Indira had no intention of leaving her behind.

"They had both come to love Boulder and to appreciate the environments they found within the University there, and so hoped very much that Laura would also be offered tenure there. They were, therefore, both relieved and delighted when Laura was granted tenure at the beginning of 1987.

"We have reached the end of chapter five," Kiki said. "Shall I resume recitation at the beginning of chapter six?"

"Yes. Proceed," Paul said.

◌   ◌   ◌

Chapter VI

If Truth were an ocean and I a scuba diver,
I would be diving into her blue-green belly.
And in her midst, in all her many endless acres,
I would see only a few of her fish, a little
of her seaweed, and a single silvery crab,
whose pincers work like water.

—Angela Murphy

What is now proved was once, only imagin'd.

—William Blake

In the spring of 1987, Laura flew off to Chicago for a conference titled "Local Religions in a World Context," which focused on religious beliefs in traditional societies and how these beliefs are influenced by outside forces. There, she attended a talk by Andrew Poulin on the Mbuti Pygmies of the Ituri Forest in Eastern Zaire. His research focused on how the Mbuti maintained two, mostly separate, systems of religious belief—one that they practiced privately in their forest home, and one that they had largely adopted from their neighbors the Bira, which they practiced only while they were in the Bira's territory.

Laura had become increasingly interested in the degree to which various religions reflected and encouraged a perspective of belonging (or by contrast, one of isolation) and was then working on a paper on this aspect of various religions around the world. When listening to Poulin's talk, she was particularly taken with his description of one of the Mbuti beliefs. Within the aspect of their religion that they practiced when they were in the forest, away from the Bira farmers, was the idea that the forest they lived within had a spirit (the "forest spirit") that watched over

them and influenced what happened in their lives. They knew this forest
spirit wished them well, so when they found themselves in hard times,
Poulin said, the Mbuti assumed it had to be because the forest spirit had
not been noticing their problems—and so they would sing to it to get its
attention.

Laura saw this belief as reflecting a sense of belonging with what they
saw as the conscious, caring forest in which they lived, and she was
curious to learn more about these people and their religions. Laura told
me later that after Poulin's presentation she spent some time talking
with him, asking him for details about the religion the Mbuti practiced
in the forest.

After talking for a while, and finding that he could answer some but not
all of Laura's questions, Poulin recommended some books and journal
articles in which she might find more comprehensive answers. He had
then looked thoughtful for a minute, Laura later told me, then suggested
that she could join them, if she liked, at the on-going research site he and
some of his colleagues had set up in the Ituri Forest. That way she could
ask whatever questions she liked, directly of the Mbuti themselves.

The idea really caught hold in Laura's imagination. After she got back
to Colorado, she began reading about the Mbuti and their forest home
and would, every once in a while, repeat to me some Mbuti story she had
just read in one of a pile of books on the Mbuti that she had checked out
from Norlin Library, or read a passage from one of these books describing the Ituri Forest.

The Ituri was part of a larger forest that covered an area almost half the
size of the contiguous United States, she told me. Not only did the forest
itself cover a vast area, but the trees within it were large, as well—as tall
as fifteen-story buildings.

"Can you imagine the scale of it, Indira?" she had said. "It would be
like walking down a city street in the shadow of tall buildings—only they
wouldn't be buildings, they'd be trees, each trying to outreach the other
to find the sun above."

Laura was truly enchanted with this possibility of traveling to the heart
of Africa, and of doing research with people who lived as hunter-gatherers
in a verdant, ancient rainforest. She realized there would be difficulty in
coming up with a research project and in arranging the funding—but
the one real obstacle, which made this possibility more fantasy than reality, was that she didn't want to plan a research project that would, once
again, take us so far apart.

Still, Laura pursued this new interest and kept a pile of books on the
subject by her side of the bed, from which she would read at bedtime,
like a kid enthralled with an adventure story. Whenever she'd find a particularly interesting passage, she would read it aloud to me, and after a
time I found myself reading those same books as well, for the Mbuti were
remarkable and intriguing in any number of regards.

One of their more remarkable qualities was their unusually small stature; they typically have light, compact builds, and average less than four
and a half feet in height. Another is the fact that they have been living

in the same rainforest in central Africa for at least 4,500 years, and in a manner that seems to have changed little over that time.

As Colin M. Turnbull wrote in his book about the Mbuti Pygmies, *The Forest People*:

> The earliest recorded reference to them is...a record of an expedition sent from Egypt in the Fourth Dynasty, some twenty-five hundred years before the Christian era, to discover the source of the Nile. In the tomb of the Pharaoh Nefrikare is preserved the report of his commander, Herkouf, who entered a great forest to the west of the Mountains of the Moon and discovered there a people of the trees, a tiny people who sing and dance to their god, a dance such as had never been seen before.... The Pygmies...were evidently living, all those thousands of years back, just where they are living today, and leading much the same kind of life, characterized, as it still is, by dancing and singing to their god.*

As others told it, this was just the tip of the iceberg. Some believed the Pygmies first settled in this region of Africa tens of thousands of years ago and were still living a lifestyle essentially unchanged in all that time, hunting and gathering for food as all people once did, before agriculture first appeared in the world some 10,000 years ago. By this argument, it was believed that the Mbuti may, more than any other living population, be able to reveal something meaningful to us about what the earliest people were like—how they viewed the world, and how they lived within it.

This idea of how the earliest people may have lived within and viewed the world really caught fire in my imagination—what *had* life been like then, during the dawn of both human belief systems and human culture? Whatever the answer, it was a history shared by all people alive today. What could it tell us about who we had become, and why?

I found myself wondering not simply how we had made fire or found food, but how we had *seen* the world. If it was true, as I had long believed, that the world we make around us collectively is an outgrowth of the world we model in our minds—then, I wondered, how had the views we'd held *then* led to the world we lived in *now*?

It seemed a delicious topic to ponder.

I remember one day, in the fall of 1987, sitting out on the back step of our house in Boulder with a cup of tea, grading papers. Bubbles, our old tom cat, lay in the sun nearby in his usual state of complete contentment.

After getting through about half the papers I had to grade, I took a moment to stretch and look around. I remember noticing that the maple tree in our back yard had started to show its autumn colors, and how I then looked up at the Rocky Mountains, which formed the western border of the town—craggy and elegant in the afternoon light—and found

---

* 1961, New York: Simon and Schuster; 15.

myself remembering a time when Laura and I had been young together in Oxford, and we'd gone rowing out along the River Isis.

Laura had rowed powerfully that day, and we'd gone skimming along, floating on brilliant water, which held reflections of blue and white from the sky and clouds above. After a time, Laura had pulled the oars in and, letting the boat drift, had slipped backwards off her seat and leaned back with her head and shoulders against the gunwale behind her, with her legs resting on the seat she had been sitting on. I looked at her as we drifted along, noting how brilliantly her red hair shone in the daylight, how sweet her face looked, turned up to the sun, with her eyes closed. After a time, I leaned back, too, and stretched my legs out. The sun was warm, and I remember watching the trees drift past and noticing how quiet it was—just a little breeze through the leaves above, and hardly any other sound.

It seemed very serene, and after a time Laura opened her eyes and began to tell me about how, when she was growing up, she'd dreamed that one day she would climb tall mountains, or perhaps be shipwrecked on some desert island and have to fend for herself, or would maybe, one day, build her own boat and sail around the world. She lifted her head a little, so she could look at me, and said that she knew that she would probably never do those exact things, but, she said, looking back up at the drifting clouds above, she hoped, more than anything, that at least she would never become one of those people whose life was comprised mostly of habit.

I picked up my tea and took a sip of it. It was one of those days when the air is cool but the sun is warm, and I took off the sweater I'd put on for sitting outside. I felt bad that Laura was hesitating to go to Zaire because of me. It wasn't just that she didn't want to be away from me, I knew, but that she didn't want me to be left alone for months without her. I wondered if there were some way she could still do this research without us having to be apart.

Well, I thought, maybe if I were to go with her. But what would I do there? It wouldn't really make sense for me to go, unless I were to be doing research on the Mbuti, myself.

I took another drink of my tea and pondered this. I had been thinking about the fact that the Mbuti saw the forest as being alive, as having a spirit of its own. I had also been thinking about the fact that they lived in a way that was environmentally sound. They didn't throw the ecosystem out of balance, but rather lived within it and were a part of it. It would be interesting to know to what extent their beliefs about the environment shaped the way they behaved towards it.

I set down my tea cup and thought a minute. Maybe Laura and I could *both* plan research projects involving the Mbuti and could take that trip together!

I smiled—now wouldn't Laura be excited by *that* idea? I knew just when we could do it, too—my sabbatical leave was due to start in less than two years, while Laura's was due in a little less than one. If Laura could arrange for her leave to be postponed by a year, we could take our leaves together, and go to Zaire.

❋   ❋   ❋

Laura was, of course, thrilled with the idea, and while we had already considered ourselves hopelessly busy with our work, we now became even busier, continuing with the research we had already started, teaching, learning more about the Mbuti, writing up research proposals for the work we intended to do in Zaire, and keeping track of all the daily tasks that filled our lives from morning till night.

During this time, I continued to read about human prehistory and became increasingly fascinated with the question of what people had been like in the earliest days of human culture. Although the subject was too far from my area of expertise for me to become involved in it as a part of my professional work, it still fascinated me. It seemed to me that learning about human prehistory was like finding out what a friend had been like as a child—what circumstances he or she had grown up in—and through those discoveries having a chance to have some real insight into who that person had become as an adult, and why. And so, in what little free time I could arrange, I found myself reading all I could find on what was known about the earliest expressions of human culture.

The further I delved into it, the more mysterious it seemed. Various questions arose, which no one seemed able to answer. For example, in creating the earliest art, people of that time had shown remarkable skill in rendering images of animals—but in depicting people, their art was typically vague and ill-formed. Why, I wondered, did they not apply the same skills in depicting people?

Other questions arose, as well. For 100,000 years or more, anatomically modern humans had lived exclusively as hunter/gatherers—but then, within a period of just a few thousand years, agriculture was developed independently in at least seven distinct locations around the globe. Why had it suddenly appeared, like that—and in so many places—so nearly at once?

Another mystery archaeologists had been unable to resolve had to do with the fact that agriculture had been chosen over the earlier lifestyle of hunting and gathering, even though, at each of the originating sites, its advent had meant less nourishment, more disease, and shorter lives. Why had these people made such a choice?

Mysterious as well was the fact that art, like agriculture, had begun to be produced in many separate locations within a relatively short window of time. Why was this, and how had it happened?

The more I read, the more inexplicable these mysteries seemed. I thought about it in my spare moments, and in pondering these questions, I found myself wondering who we had been then, and how the events of that early era had set the stage for who we had become. It all fascinated me and made me hungry to read and learn more.

As the year wore on, I continued to delve into the mysteries of prehistory, even though I was terrifically busy with all sorts of other obligations. Laura was caught up in an assortment of projects, as well, and so our days were full, and time passed quickly. It was sometime that fall that Laura was informed that her sabbatical leave postponement would be allowed.

The next year—1988—went quickly as well. In preparing for my sabbatical leave, I worked up several grant proposals and was eventually awarded a small sum for the work I planned to do in Zaire. Laura also managed to arrange funding, and as the months went by, we found ourselves growing steadily closer to the actual event.

Sometime during the winter of '88/'89, Laura and I attended a party held by a friend of ours, Roger Rivlin, who was in the Physics Department. Several other friends from other departments attended, as well, and after spending some time discussing various research projects we were each involved in, some of us began to express the frustration we felt that we could not more fully allow our work to follow our interests as they developed—because the subject matters we found ourselves interested in exploring were too far outside our areas of expertise; or because the ideas that had caught our interest were too far beyond the accepted paradigm; or simply because the ideas themselves, while having interest at a theoretical level, could not be empirically verified. While we were certainly free to write on such subjects if we wished to do so, we feared that doing so would hurt us professionally.

"I think its important to apply clear standards to the information we accept as factual," I remember Roger saying, "but just because I can't actually *prove* a given idea, that doesn't mean it's not worth exploring or having a dialogue about."

Yasmina Youssef, another friend and a psychologist, nodded. "Yeah. I'm not interested in displacing, or even challenging, the usual system for publication, either, but I'd like to have some context for exchange that is more about the process of discovery than the product—a place to have a dialogue about ideas that don't fit in the usual channels."

"Yes. And not just within one's own area," Laura added. "I just read an article in, what was it?—some popular magazine—about discoveries in physics and what they seem to say about the most basic workings of reality. I was thinking how interesting it would to explore the parallels between the world view that's suggested by quantum physics and the world view shared by various religions. It would be fascinating to write an article on the subject, but I know too little about physics to write it and be taken seriously—only what I read in that article—so I wouldn't try to actually publish something of this sort. But I'd still like, somehow, to engage in an exchange of ideas on the subject."

Roger took a sip of his beer. "That could be an interesting subject," he said.

I remember Yasmina started to say something about creating a forum, but I was distracted for a few minutes when another friend stepped over to say "hello." When I returned my attention to the conversation, they were all discussing the possibility of starting a small newsletter, which we would circulate only amongst a few trusted colleagues, and in which we could broach whatever subjects interested us, and so invite a more open exchange of ideas. Laura and Roger immediately began to discuss coauthoring a paper on physics and religion, and someone cut in to suggest that we choose a name for the newsletter.

Our group got quiet for a minute, and the noise from the rest of the party seemed suddenly loud. I remember watching Billy Doyle, a friend of ours in engineering, who had been listening attentively but not saying much, as he slowly swirled the ice around at the bottom of his glass, as though gathering his thoughts there. He kept looking down into his glass, as people tossed out various names, then he looked up and waited quietly for a pause in the conversation.

When one came, he said softly, "We could name it the Huginn/Muninn Newsletter."

The words didn't sound familiar, and I wondered if I'd misheard him. "The what?" I asked.

"The Huginn/Muninn Newsletter," he answered. "From Norse Mythology—Huginn and Muninn were the ravens who sat on the shoulders of the Norse god, Odin."

Laura tilted her head a little to one side, as she considered this. Roger and Yasmina were also paying attention.

"Their names mean 'the thoughtful' and 'the mindful,'" Billy told us. "They would fly all over the world for Odin, everywhere—even to the edges of time, even into people's dreams—to discover the thoughts and memories of the people. Then they would return to Odin and deliver these thoughts and memories to him, one on each shoulder, whispering into his ears. They supplied him with the fodder for his wisdom." Billy shrugged. "I thought it might make a good name."

"Yeah, I remember that story," Laura said, nodding. She thought about it a moment. "I like the idea." She glanced around at our little group. "What does everybody else think?"

"I like it," Yasmina said, and Roger and I joined in, voicing our approval. And so the *Huginn/Muninn Newsletter* got its start.

❋   ❋   ❋

As the time grew nearer for our trip, it grew shorter for everything else as well. Laura and I spent the spring and summer of 1989 teaching classes and tying up various research projects we had underway, as well as refining our plans in connection with the other researchers at the Ituri Forest site. Andrew Poulin was no longer doing field-research there, but he put us in touch with a colleague of his, Lisa Xiang, who had kept the site going, and who was just as welcoming as Poulin had been. We made arrangements for when we would arrive, and began to complete a list of what we would need to take with us when we went there.

That summer, we also made arrangements for our house to be leased by visiting faculty—a couple who both normally taught at the University of Edinburgh, and who were coming to the University of Colorado for their sabbatical leaves, along with their three-year-old son. They agreed, also, to look after Bubbles while they were staying in our home, and Laura and I were pleased to have all that settled.

That fall, I finished writing a paper I had been working on for some time and submitted it for publication. Laura was informed that her paper, "From Belonging to Isolation: A Multi-Cultural Analysis," which she had been working on when she had first met Andrew Poulin a couple of years earlier, would be published in the March issue of *The International Journal of Religions*. But for the most part, we spent the fall refining and finalizing our plans for the trip. We were due to arrive at the research site in the Ituri Forest in mid-January of 1990. We would have to get an international flight into Kinshasa, the capital of Zaire, and then find other transportation to the research site from there. Laura wanted to fly to London and spend Christmas with her family there, and then go on to Kinshasa. That seemed an attractive plan, and certainly her family was eager to see her, for she hadn't made it back to London, then, for over four years. So we agreed to begin our trip with a stopover in London—and to conclude our journey with a brief stay in and around Varanasi, to see my family there.

Amongst the items we planned to bring with us on our trip was a new type of computer, a "laptop" made by Cambridge called the "Z88." We were unable to locate one for sale in America, but Laura's parents agreed to order one for us that autumn and have it waiting for us when we stopped over in London at the end of the year. We were quite excited by the prospect of this new device. It weighed only two pounds and was able to run 20 hours on four penlight batteries. Its screen would display only a few lines of text, but we nonetheless thought it would make an excellent tool for organizing and processing the data we would be collecting. In Boulder, we bought rechargeable batteries and a solar charger to be used with it. We were assured the charger would work, if only slowly, even in the dim of the rainforest.

While deciding on a stopover in London had been easy, deciding what to do once we were inside Zaire turned out to be a little more complicated. The flight from London would land in Kinshasa. The simplest way to go from there would have been to catch another flight from Kinshasa to Kisangani, and then somehow arrange ground transportation to get to the research site inside the Ituri forest. But Laura had been reading about Zaire—and about the barges, left over from colonial days, that still carried passengers up and down the Congo River between Kinshasa and Kisangani—and the idea of taking such a trip had sparked the same sense of adventure in her that had been brought to life when she had first started dreaming of going to Zaire in the first place.

At first, I didn't share Laura's enthusiasm for the barge trip. From what I had read, the quarters on the barges were cramped, and while a flight from Kinshasa to Kisangani would take no more than two hours, the barge could take any amount of time, from ten days to two weeks. But while going by barge seemed largely an inconvenience to me, for Laura it would be a dream come true. I had grown up near a great river, and I had lived in more varied circumstances than Laura had, and it seemed somehow unfair to deny her this just because I had already had the satisfaction of adventures of this sort. Laura suggested that we could travel first class on the barge, and so make that part of the trip a bit more pleasant—and she pointed out that if we brought work along, the time we were on the river wouldn't seem quite so frivolously spent.

This was enough to relieve my reservations, and I agreed, and even began to look forward to this part of the trip myself. I had already been planning to bring various resources along for my work with the Mbuti, but now I began to plan out what I would bring along to work on on the barge, as well.

Laura and Roger had by then written a paper for the *Huginn/Muninn Newsletter* dealing with parallels between the model of the world proposed by quantum physics and one suggested by many religions. I had thought that it had come out quite well, and that they had presented the subject in an enlightening and satisfying way.

For example, their paper included an explanation of how two particles that are bound together may be split apart, and how the two parts then go zooming off from one another at the speed of light. If some action is then taken that has an effect on one of these particles, then, remarkably, the other (now physically distant), instantly displays the effect of that action, as well.

In other words, their article explained, the particles start out joined, but once separated, continue to share a certain interconnectedness.

Roger had written that part of the paper. Then, in the next section, Laura had described the belief, present in many religions, that we all come from some single, unified source, and how, though now separated—made individual—we still share a basic interrelatedness, much as the two particles (once joined together but now split apart) still participate in a kind of "wholeness."

The paper had ranged widely through such subjects as this, and I had enjoyed reading it. In fact, as I'd seen what sorts of articles people were submitting for the *Huginn/Muninn Newsletter* in general, I had become much more excited about the whole concept of having such a newsletter and had begun to think about writing an article for it myself.

Nineteen eighty-nine was an interesting year in the arena of world events. The Exxon Valdez ran aground in Alaska's Prince William Sound that spring and spread eleven million gallons of crude oil along the pristine Alaskan coastline, killing countless sea birds and sea otters, and blackening the shore for a thousand miles. Laura and I, tucked away in our home in the scenic foothills of the Rocky Mountains, watched this environmental horror as it unfolded on television, and then in newspapers and magazines.

Less than two months later, we watched as another shocking event developed half a world away—in China—where the government responded to a peaceful student protest in Tiananmen Square with tanks and guns, and hundreds of college students were shot to death or run over by tanks in the streets of Beijing, for nothing more than gathering together in a call for democracy.

In the weeks that followed, I found myself reflecting on these events, wondering why the world was as it was, and what we all might do to make it a better place.

One afternoon, while biking home from the market with food for our dinner, I found myself recalling a time, during my first year at Oxford, when I had thought a lot about how we modeled the world in our minds, and how we then acted to give expression to those models—and in so doing, how we then created in the world around us representations of the very things we had mentally modeled. Through that process, I had concluded, that which is inside takes form outside.

I got home and put the groceries away, then sat out on the porch while I waited for Laura to get home, pondering how this principle might relate to events in the world at large.

Over the past few years, a feeling had been growing in me, as I had been so whole-heartedly engaged in pursuing my career. This feeling would surface sometimes, and then it would get brushed aside as I dealt with the demands of my daily work. I was a successful professor of anthropology— but I worried that I was not doing enough to help solve the problems of the world around me. It seemed to me that the world I lived in was at a critical juncture, faced with mass extinctions, skyrocketing population numbers, warfare fed by ever-newer technologies, and the perennial issues of prejudice and oppression, hunger and poverty. It always seemed to me, when I stopped to reflect on my life and work—on the anthropology classes I taught, and the papers I wrote on culture and beliefs—that the work I was involved in did too little to help solve any of the pressing issues of my age.

So I sat on our porch swing on that warm autumn afternoon, rocking gently back and forth, and musing about these things. I very much wished there was some way I could help address such larger questions, and thus help bring us even a small step closer to solving the world's problems. It seemed so important, and I doubted the work I was doing could qualify as that.

As I have mentioned, around this time, I had been thinking quite a bit about who we had been in prehistory and how the beliefs we held in our ancient past may have set us on a course towards the present. As I had read more and more on the subject, I had had some insights that I hoped might at least begin to unravel some of the great mysteries remaining from that ancient past.

So, as I sat on the porch that day, my thoughts drifted through all of these topics:

I thought of the idea I'd had in college that we make the world as we model it.

I thought about my desire to do something of worth in the world.

And I thought about the insights I'd had about how the earliest people may have seen themselves and the world around them, and—yes—about how they had *modeled* their world.

These thoughts pulled together and mixed in my mind. They seemed threaded together by a single feeling. They seemed almost to breathe together. As I mulled this over, time took on that slowness it has when one first wakes in the morning. A car went by. A small breeze rustled the leaves of the maple tree in our front yard. Somewhere, a mockingbird sang.

Then, across the street, a car door slammed. The moment was broken. I sighed, and looked around. Somehow, those ideas were related.

I thought about it some more. Somehow, what had happened in the past helped set us on a course to the present that we now knew, and, in turn, to the future that would develop from here. How we saw the world then...how we see the world now...what the world is today and what it would become—these things were all interrelated.

Could some good come of this line of thought? I asked myself—but I couldn't, at that moment, as I sat on the porch, see how these insights might help change what happened in the world I lived in. Still, I was intrigued with the possibility that some light might be shed on current events by this probing of the ancient past, and that some good might come of it.

It occurred to me then that I would like to write an article about the foundational beliefs and perspectives out of which modern human culture had grown—and in the process of writing it, draw together the insights I felt gathering along the horizons of my mind. What new comprehension, what new discoveries, might unfurl as I went about the process of writing such an article?

It was an exciting thing just to think about, and I felt suddenly energized by the thought. But I was also aware that the fledgling ideas I had on this topic were still very fresh and unformed, and quite theoretical—and I knew I would not consider trying to prepare this material for any sort of traditional publication—but it struck me, then, that this *was* quite an appropriate topic for the *Huginn/Muninn Newsletter*.

I began to get excited and wished Laura would get home, so I could tell her about these ideas, and this new, exciting, plan. As I sat there, waiting, I imagined working on this article in a cabin on a barge, cruising up the mighty Congo River with Laura by my side—along each bank a tall and ancient rain forest rising up—and in that quiet and solitude, away from the demands of my life in Boulder, I would pour myself into these thoughts and untie the knots imbedded within them!

I can't describe what a jolt of energy it gave me to think about this. The trip suddenly seemed romantic in every dimension. I swung more quickly on the porch swing, smiling and anticipating how things would be. Laura would be home soon, and I would tell her all about it.

Laura and I spent a good deal of time that summer and into the fall, engaged in language study. Different groups of Pygmies in the Ituri Forest speak different languages, but we only troubled ourselves to learn one language, Bira, the language spoken by the group of Mbuti we would be staying with and learning from. Lisa Xiang helped us out by sending us audio tapes for studying Bira. We spent hours listening to those tapes—playing them while showering, or while eating breakfast, or on headsets as we biked to work. But once we had decided on the barge trip, our language problems doubled.

More than two hundred languages were spoken in Zaire. French was the official language, left over from colonial times, when the Belgians ran the country. When we had thought we would cross most of Zaire's vast width, from Kinshasa in the west to Kisangani in the east, by plane, we had assumed the French that Laura already spoke would be enough to get us by. But now we planned to follow the Congo River as it snaked through the heart of Zaire, and there we would also have need for the language of commerce—the same language that was used by the military, and that was spoken most commonly along the great reaches of the mighty Congo River: Lingala.

So, as the year neared its end, we prepared for Christmas in London and months in the tropics. We wrote letters to friends telling them we would be out of touch for the next half a year. We got shots to protect against tropical diseases, bought rain gear and mosquito netting and quinine. We struggled to put our old research projects into some kind of order before embarking on our new ones, and we spent countless hours repeating back words in Bira and Lingala as we listened to our language tapes. We gathered together the materials we would need for our research with the Mbuti and for the work we would each do while on the barge. When mid-December finally came around, and we were about to embark for England, we were both so exhausted that we wished for nothing so much as a fortnight spent daydreaming on a sunny beach somewhere. But wish this as we might, when the morning of the twenty-third of December rolled around, we checked all the luggage and gear we would need for a six-month trip and boarded our plane for London.

"Pause," Paul said. The sun was getting close to the horizon, and Paul thought it a good time to stop and attend to domestic matters. He picked a clear spot not far from the creek, but still under the protective dome of the overhanging oak trees, to lay out his sleep bivy—then gathered dry wood from the area to build a fire with. He'd caught sight of fish in the pool beneath the falls a couple of times since Kiki had started reciting chapter six, and he'd begun to think that fish would be nice for dinner—but he wasn't sure how he would catch one.

Paul stopped to consider the problem, then recalled that he'd been given some sort of bonus "sojourner's aid pack" at the shop where he'd bought the camp gear in Strandford. He dug it out and discovered that it contained an assortment of handy tools and materials, including a small first-aid kit, a rudimentary fire-starter kit (probably not good for more than one or two starts), a phosphorescent emergency light, a small utility knife—and a fishing line, hook, and fishing fly.

That would do just fine, Paul thought—or at least he hoped it would, as he'd never had the experience of actually fishing (though he'd once tried it as a virtual experience on the Stream.)

Paul used the utility knife to cut a green bough from one of the trees, tied the line securely to one end, then set about fishing, dropping the lure near big rocks like the ones he'd discovered the fish hiding under earlier that day.

Before long, he had caught a fish almost too large to make a meal of—and had spotted several more lurking in the shadows. Soon he had his dinner cleaned and cooking on a spit above his fire.

That night, Paul went to bed much happier than he had the night before. He was tired but well fed, and the bit of earth he had spread his sleep bivy on was smooth and comfortable. All along the stream, frogs sang in a boisterous chorus.

Paul lay awake thinking about that—countless living frogs in a world where they had never gone extinct!—and about all the other animals he had encountered in just that one day: rabbits scared up from the tall grasses along the path; a nearly endless number of lizards sunning themselves on rocks and trees; both fish and an occasional turtle swimming in the stream; and many times along the creek's bank he'd seen the hoof prints of some sort of animal—deer, perhaps, or maybe more of the elk, though they seemed a little small for either. Whatever the prints were from, they were so plentiful!

What an amazing world! Paul thought. What a priceless treasure!

How was it that this world had remained so vital, while his had grown so wretched? Every day he observed evidence that the natural environment on this earth was whole and well in a way it had long since ceased to be on his— but he knew, from what he had discovered through the Intralink, that the wellness of this world went far beyond the health of its plants and animals.

How had this world put an end to war and famine? he wondered. How had they created a system where, apparently, everybody had what they needed? How had they managed this, while on Paul's earth the problems had just piled up, endlessly compounding one another?

On Paul's earth, wars had never ceased, but rather had grown more virulent and frequent as the population soared, and people fought over diminishing resources. As climate change baked the earth—speeding evaporation in one place, then dropping that water in deluging rain or snow somewhere else—it brought both droughts and floods. It heated ocean waters, which in turn fueled terrible storms—storms that lashed those coastal cities that had, somehow, survived the rising ocean waters; storms that spun off powerful tornadoes inland. Over and over, storms ravaged the land. Over and over, crops were lost to drought or floods, and people were left starving. Economies failed in response to these onslaughts—then struggled back to their feet, and failed again. Epidemics swept through the human population, which was often stressed by war and shortages of food and other necessities—while one species after another, unable to keep up with the changing planet, disappeared forever from the face of the earth.

This was the world Paul knew, the world he had always known. It was the world all the other people of earth—his earth—knew as well. The people of his earth had so little to hope for, so little to dream of. All they had that was real was a stricken world, and all they had in answer to all that hardship and despair was the solace their implants provided, through endless downloads from the Stream—countless enticing yet superficial offerings put in place by Corprogov to placate the restless billions.

Paul felt suddenly very sad, and found himself missing Sheila intensely. He knew this was why she lived so much within the world her implant provided. It was not she who was unusual in her way of living, but Paul who stood out from all the rest. It had never troubled Paul that Sheila left her implant running through so much of the day—it was at night when they were together that he had so often wished she would turn it off.

Paul lay awake, thinking about how frequently Sheila left her implant on when they made love and how it made him feel. Paul knew the sensations fed to her through her implant could seem almost as real as reality itself—or, as some would claim, even more so. It had made him jealous, at first—and sometimes keenly so—that Sheila was experiencing another man's touch, another man's body next to hers, even as she and Paul made love together.

As Paul lay awake, he remembered telling her how he felt on one of those occasions, and how she had answered him then.

"But Paul," she had said, "you're such an attentive, responsive lover. No piece of virtual programming I could get would give me that. They just run and do what they do. You *respond* to me. Really, the feed is just an enhancement—like listening to music. *You're* the one I'm with."

Paul rolled onto his back, and his sleep bivy rolled with him. He had finally come to terms with it, he recalled, by focusing on the fact that he was her only flesh-and-blood lover—but even so, it had troubled him that she was unwilling to give up something as trivial as a simple "enhancement," in order to keep from causing him heartache.

Still, Paul thought philosophically, the world they lived in was such a sad and troubled place; everybody needed some sort of escape from it. For Paul, his escape was through his work, and through his dream of changing his world for the better—but for most people, the only answer was the virtual experiences they downloaded from the Stream. For what was there around them but a dissipated world, growing always more ruined and depleted?

Paul stared up at the starry sky where it shown through the limbs above him and thought about holding Sheila close to him. As always, he felt such a desire to be there for her and to give her what she needed. If only he could use this vital world he had found to help return vitality to his world—to her world, to make her world well again. If only he could bring her this as a gift, like a jewel he might lay at her feet—what sort of vitality and renewal might it bring to Sheila herself?

Paul thought of her response as she discovered this gift he had brought to her—as news of his success spread through the Stream. What warmth and pride she would shine upon him! he thought. She would offer him her acceptance, then, and shower it over him, as she had never done before. She would be made more whole, somehow, more well, Paul imagined; somehow, in some way beyond words, she would be revived and replenished.

Paul sighed and stared starward, and as he did, he sensed that he, too, might then be made well, made whole, in a way he hardly knew how to describe.

⊡ 11 ⊡

The next morning, Paul woke stiff and sore from days of unaccustomed activity. Not only were his shoulders sore from carrying the torso pack, and his legs sore from walking, but his feet were covered with reddish areas where his shoes had been rubbing. His feet complained as he pressed them back into the shoes for another day—then Paul took a minute to heat a travel meal, before throwing on his pack and started out along the path.

Paul had made an early start of it—the light was still soft, and a thick fog hung in the low-lying areas along the creek. He strolled along, listening to the burbling creek and the sound of the breeze through the trees, too groggy still to want to resume recitation. It was, in any case, too beautiful a morning to want to distract himself from it. Small birds twittered in the branches above him, hopping from twig to twig. At one point he startled a small herd of deer, drinking at the creek's edge, and watched them disappear quickly among the trees and shrubs. Once, when crossing a meadow, he scared up a rabbit from the bushes near the path. He stood completely still, and watched it retreat through the meadow sloping away from the trail. When it had reached the middle of the meadow, Paul saw what he thought was a bobcat bound out of the tall grass and pounce on it. He felt so amazed by all the life happening around him that he could almost forget his aching muscles and sore feet.

Around each turn in the path, it seemed to Paul that new wonders appeared. It wasn't long before he came across a herd of pronghorn antelope—perhaps three or four dozen in number—which scattered as he approached, disappearing into the tall grass and bushes in great bounding leaps. As they lifted off from the ground with each bound, it seemed to Paul almost as though they were taking flight!

As he stood, spellbound, watching them disappear, Paul recalled something his Grandfather had told him about these antelope. His grandfather had said that when Europeans first came west, they found pronghorn antelope *in herds numbering into the thousands* in the open plains of the Central Valley of what would later become California. Pronghorn had gathered in their greatest numbers in those open grasslands, but, as Paul remembered his grandfather explaining, had never been so plentiful in the coastal mountains—the sort of terrain Paul was in now.

So, Paul thought, if a herd as big as the one he had just seen existed *here*, where he was now—then how was it now in the Central Valley on this earth? How large might the herds of pronghorn be there?

Paul tried to imagine it—two or three thousand antelope gathered together, jumping and floating through the hot dry air, moving in unison in the shimmering heat.

What a place this was, Paul thought, that such a thing might even be conceivable here!

Paul took a deep breath and began again down the trail. Soon, he crossed the creek another time and began making his way up a steep climb, following the switchbacks on the trail. As he went, he began to feel hot and uncomfortable and decided to distract himself from his discomfort with more of Dr. Kumar's book. He was about to ask Kiki to pick up where he had left off, when he realized he was having trouble recalling what had been happening when he had stopped with recitation the day before.

"Kiki," he said, "would you please recite the last two sentences you recited before stopping yesterday, and then go on from there?"

"Yes," Kiki answered, and soon the cosmopolitan voice of Dr. Kumar filled the air along the Sojourner's Path:

When mid-December finally came around, and we were about to embark for England, we were both so exhausted that we wished for nothing so much as a fortnight spent daydreaming on a sunny beach somewhere. But wish this as we might, when the morning of the twenty-third of December rolled around, we checked all the luggage and gear we would need for a six-month trip and boarded our plane for London.

❀ ❀ ❀

Laura's family was given to large family gatherings, and this Christmas, with Laura and me in town, was even more festive than usual. On Christmas morning, Laura's sisters and their families arrived with gifts in hand and pots and pans of every shape and size filled with food for the potluck dinner. Laura's parents, Irene and Drew, had given up having a Christmas tree for environmental reasons, and instead had gathered all the house plants together on a table in one corner of the sitting room and decorated them lavishly with every sort of ornament. As the family arrived, gifts were placed in and around the plants and cascaded down off the table and out into the room. The kids raced around, excited and impatient to start opening gifts, but first we all shared a quick breakfast in the room off the kitchen with the big window looking out over the street below. All in all, it was a beautiful day, and I enjoyed being in the midst of a big family again, after the cozy home life Laura and I shared in Boulder.

Our days in London were filled with social activities. Laura looked up old childhood friends, and we had more than a couple dinners out at various friends' homes around London. We saw Sarah Wilkinson, who had been a friend of Laura's since secondary school, and who was now involved with a charity group providing prenatal care for single mothers—and Jimmy Lyons, who Laura had known since they were both five, and who was a talented painter (who preferred to work in the neo-abstract expressionist style, but who actually made his living doing art for greeting cards).

We spent an evening, as well, with Edmund Canby and his family. Edmund had grown up just a few doors down from Laura, and they had oftentimes played cricket in the park, along with some of the other neighborhood kids, when they were both small, and in their teens they had rallied around various liberal causes together. Now Edmund was edging up on middle age. He had grown quite stout and increasingly conservative in his politics, and everything about his home had a reserved, don't-draw-outside-the-lines sort of quality. It all reminded me of how the perspectives we hold become the mold in which our lives are cast and recast, over and over again as the years go by—always changing, and always reflecting the mental views we hold at any given time.

Visiting friends and Laura's old haunts around the city, we thought, too, of Kate and her husband, whose houseboat Laura and I had visited on my first stay in the city years before, and we wondered if they were off to some tropical location for the winter. Laura's parents said sadly that Kate's husband, William, had died a few years before, and that she had sold the houseboat and moved into a flat a few blocks from her beloved Thames. We stopped by to see her one chilly December afternoon, just in time for tea. She seemed much older than on our last visit, but still cheerful and full of life. She had started dating a man she had met at the community garden and seemed still pleased with life and its possibilities.

London, full of its ancient stone edifices, seemed at once so solid and unchanging, and in other ways so altered even in the few years since Laura and I had last gone together for a visit. Everyone was older, and the styles along King's Road, always in flux, had changed once again. The streets were full of late-1980s chic—a lot of black leather, with multiple piercings and tattoos, and a really extensive variety of hair styles. I wondered how Laura felt returning to her home streets every few years, and each time finding them so transformed.

Still, for all the changes, the city itself carried with it a weighty, Old World feeling of constancy. The landmark buildings were as they had been for centuries, and Kensington Gardens, where I had joined Laura and her family on a picnic during my first stay in London eighteen years earlier, seemed the very picture of its old self.

Laura and I went for a walk there one day in the last days of December and wound up hiring a couple of horses for a ride in Hyde Park. It was a chilly overcast day; we hired the horses for an hour, but not fifteen minutes into our ride snow began to fall in heavy, thick flakes from the leadened sky, and the world was, in surprisingly short order, seemingly remade. I remember looking over at Laura, seated on a large gray-dappled gelding, trotting over white earth, through white air, her red hair bouncing as the horse took sharp, quick steps. As we trotted along in this whitening world, Laura pointed out spots she'd visited as a child, or where she'd hung out with friends in her teens, and I stared around me, transfixed with the wonder of it all. I never dreamed in that moment how far away that scene would seem to me even one week later, as we boated up the muscular brown Congo, bordered by lush green tropical forest on both sides, under an achingly endless blue sky.

Even while we filled our London days and nights with many various and interesting activities, I was always aware that this was but a brief interlude in anticipation of something else. I remembered reading somewhere about one of the American plains Indian tribes whose members, when taking a long journey, would stop every few days along the way to allow their spirits to catch up with them.

I thought about this repeatedly during the last days we were in London, but for me the sensation was not that I had left my spirit behind in Boulder, and was waiting for it to somehow make the trans-Atlantic journey and catch up with me in London, but rather that it had gone off ahead of me—and there she was, Indira on the Congo, Indira venturing into Africa—and here I was, body bereft of soul, hungering to catch up with her. Having anticipated this journey for not months, but years, it was hard to involve myself fully in this transitory interlude in London. My thoughts were always racing up ahead.

On the last full day we were in town, Laura and I spent the afternoon going through our belongings, making sure that everything was gathered and organized for the trip ahead. We unpacked the winter clothes we'd brought for our stay in London and left them in the dresser in Laura's old bedroom—we would retrieve them when we stopped by again on our way back to the states in six months, having been, by then, to both Africa and India.

Laura's parents had fulfilled their promise to have our new laptop computer waiting for us when we arrived, and we packed it away carefully in Laura's briefcase, then slipped her briefcase into one of the bright-yellow watertight bags Laura had bought from a shop specializing in river-rafting gear in Boulder. I put my briefcase, with all my important papers in it, into another such bag, hoping that we had planned far enough ahead and were adequately prepared for our trip into the rainforest.

With our packing all taken care of, we went downstairs for a final diner with Laura's parents, then turned in early, hoping to get a good night's rest before our morning flight.

I climbed into bed, and Laura turned off the light at the switch by the door, then got into bed with me. We snuggled under the cold blankets and whispered with one another about our excitement at our imminent departure, now just hours away. Then we grew quiet in the still darkness, and soon I could feel Laura's breath slowing as she settled into sleep.

Laura, whose excitement had inspired this adventure, was fast asleep beside me, while I, who had started out so complacent about our journey, lay brightly awake, staring with eyes open into the darkness around me. I was in gear, ready to travel. No part of me was ready for sleep.

I made myself close my eyes and tried to rest, but in my mind I kept going over all we had packed and where we had put each item, and comparing that list in my mind to all the activities and environments I expected us to encounter in the next six months.

After doing this for what seemed only a short time, I looked at the clock lit up on the night stand next to the bed and saw that I had been lying awake for more than two hours. Slowly, so as not to wake Laura, I lifted myself out of bed, as quietly as possible located my slippers and bathrobe in the darkness, then crept downstairs to the kitchen where I warmed some milk in a pan on the stove.

While the milk was heating, I looked through the cabinets for a suitable mug, then stood leaning against the counter for a couple of minutes while the milk got hot. I poured it up, then went into the sitting room, turned on the Christmas lights covering the amassed house plants, and looked around the room for something light and distracting I could read. I found a likely looking magazine, turned on a small table lamp, and settled into the old easy chair next to the house plants. Yawning, I thumbed through the magazine and settled on an article, the title of which was something like: "Intuition and the Animal Mind."

The article began with a story of a dog who would begin waiting by the door for his owner's return some twenty or thirty minutes before the owner would get home from her day's work. The woman worked as an electrician, and her hours were irregular, so even her husband didn't know when she would come home each day—except that the dog would begin waiting, and so her husband would expect her.

The husband had become interested enough in this phenomenon that he started to take note of the time the dog began its wait each day, and to ask his wife where she was at that time once she got home. It became clear to them, the article had said, that the dog began its daily vigil at the time the woman first *decided* to head for home. Once or twice it had begun its wait early, given up, then resumed it at a later hour. On those occasions, it turned out the woman had decided to go home and then changed her mind and taken care of some other business before return-ing. It seemed, the article stated, that it was the woman's intention to return that the dog was responding to, even though they were miles apart, and the dog could not have been aware of her, through any sensory means, from that distance.

I set the magazine down in my lap, picked up my mug from the little table next to the chair, and drank some of the warm milk, which had cooled to an acceptable temperature. I leaned my head back and closed my eyes, wishing I would feel sleepy. The story about the dog had reminded me of an old woman who had lived in my home village in India when I was a child, and I began thinking about her. People said that she always knew when her oldest son would visit from Varanasi, even though she had no phone service by which he could contact her. She would just have the feeling he was coming and would prepare his favorite meal of curried vegetables with rice and dal and have it waiting when he arrived. I had taken this as a normal part of life when I was young—so different from the Western view I would later be introduced to. Now, snuggled into an easy chair in the glow of house plants lit by Christmas lights, I wondered if she had somehow sensed his intention to come home—and if so, what sense had she used?

I realized I was still cradling the warm mug in my hands where they rested in my lap. I drank the rest of the milk and set the mug down. I stretched. Was I sleepy yet? I asked myself. I picked up the article as though I would go on reading, but instead found myself thinking about my time in college and how I had paid such careful attention to what I could sense intuitively, then. Like tuning into a radio signal, I had thought of it then—a signal that could not be perceived through sight or sound, or smell or touch or taste. And yet it was real....

I felt my head lull forward, then jerked awake. I opened my eyes groggily—must have just drifted off, I told myself. Slowly, I got up and turned off the lights in the sitting room. I left the mug off in the kitchen, and then, with magazine in hand, climbed the stairs to rejoin Laura in our room above. At the time, I had no idea the valuable role this article would play in my thinking in the weeks to come. Like a key turning a lock, it would help open before me a new understanding of who we had once been—and who we might yet become. But for now, it was just an interesting article, which I carried with me as I went back to bed.

The next morning over breakfast, I mentioned to Irene that I had started an article on animal intuition, which I'd found in a magazine in the sitting room, and that it looked like it would be quite interesting. She said she was done with that magazine and that I could take it with me if I liked. We had finished packing and brought down our bags first thing, but I remembered to run upstairs and get the magazine before our taxi arrived. And arrive it soon did. We all said our quick and excited farewells, and Laura and I set off on a bright, cold January morning, whisked away in a black London cab, on our way to Africa.

Our flight took off from Heathrow a half an hour late, but otherwise our departure was unremarkable. I stared out the window as we took off, saw the land grow small below us, watched the city shrink to tiny roads and "model cars," saw the countryside become a patchwork shaped by roads and farms—then the English Channel and its great expanse of blue—and then I leaned back in my seat and got out the magazine Laura's mother had given me and began to read again.

The article continued with a discussion of how the stories it contained had been collected and verified. It seemed the person who had gathered the information had been quite careful on this point. The article continued, then, with three stories that involved animals seemingly knowing the location of other animals or people to whom they felt attached, without the benefit of any apparent physical source of information.

The first of these stories involved the work of the American naturalist William J. Long. In the late nineteenth and early twentieth centuries, Long spent part of each year in the woods of New England and Canada. There, he spent time tracking wolves, and so became quite familiar with their habits. Though wolves live in packs, they range widely, often traveling far from the other members of their group. Through close observation, Long came to believe that the individual pack members always knew where the other members of their pack were, even though an individual wolf might wander countless miles while separated from the group. As an illustration of the sort of circumstances that had led him to this conclusion, Long wrote about a wolf he had tracked who had an injured leg, and who had temporarily left the pack to heal up in a sheltered area.

After following the injured wolf to its den, Long left it there and later picked up the tracks of the pack in the snow. He was not far off when the pack killed a deer, and so he knew that they made the kill and fed in silence, many miles through thickly wooded hills and valleys from the wounded wolf.

Long followed the pack for a while after they finished feeding. Later, when he returned to the kill site to observe the attack patterns in the snow, he found the fresh tracks of a solitary wolf with an injured leg, coming in at right angles to those of the pack. He followed these tracks back to their place of origin and discovered that it was the trail of the wounded wolf he had been observing, which had come in a straight line from its isolated den, many miles away. It had somehow known, Long proposed, that the others had made a kill and had come directly to that spot, though the wind was wrong for it to have known of the kill by scent, the distance too great and the land too rugged for it to have known by sight, and the other wolves too silent for it to have known by sound.

I looked over at Laura, who had gotten out some of the materials she had intended to work on on the barge and was looking through them. I glanced around the plane. All the seats I could see from mine were taken, and I casually wondered if the plane was full. Some of the people I could see from where I sat were talking, but I couldn't hear any of their conversations—the noise of the engines seemed to muffle all other sounds. As there seemed to be nothing of interest going on around me, I looked back down at my magazine and continued reading.

The next story was about a boy who had come across a stray homing pigeon in his back yard. The boy had fed it, and the pigeon had become his pet. The pigeon's leg was banded with the number "167." Sometime later, the boy was taken to a hospital for an operation. The hospital was about a hundred miles from his home by road, seventy by air. On a dark, snowy night, about a week after leaving home, while the boy lay in his hospital bed, he heard a fluttering sound at his window. He asked the nurse if she would open the window, which she did, and in came a homing pigeon with a band on its leg. The boy recognized the pigeon as his pet, and asked the nurse if she would check the number on its leg. It was 167. Somehow the pigeon had found him, all those miles away, on a dark, snowy night, and had even selected the right window to look for him behind.

The third of the three stories about animals locating their friends or loved-ones concerned a cow and her calf. They had been taken to market and sold separately, and had then been sent to two different farms, several miles apart. Sometime during the night following the auction, the mother cow broke out of the farmyard to which she'd been taken and walked to the farm to which her calf had been sent, though she had never been there before. In the morning, she was found there, nursing her calf. The two were positively identified as mother and calf by the auction labels still stuck to their rumps.

I stopped reading again as the flight attendant came around to offer us drinks. I nearly asked for coffee, but I hoped I might have a chance to sleep a little on the plane, and so got fruit juice instead. Laura asked me to get her pen for her from the bag at my feet, and I rummaged around for it for a few minutes till I found it in the bottom of the bag, then finished my juice and went back to reading the article. It continued with various stories of dogs and cats who became distressed or agitated at the same time that their owners fell ill or were injured or even died at some location distant from where the pet was then staying. Some of these stories were quite remarkable, but for the sake of brevity, I will not try to recall them here.

I will say, though, that the author of the article offered an interesting theory as to how all this worked. He suggested that this sort of awareness-at-a-distance of such things as the location or welfare of others was associated with circumstances where creatures felt especially emotionally interconnected, as one might with others within a family, tribe, or pack. Not only were these circumstances correlated, the author argued, but such awareness-at-a-distance was dependent on quite practical, literal links, which were by-products of this sense of "emotional identification" or "communal belonging." That is, the author suggested, people and animals don't just *feel* connected when they are emotionally bonded—but are, actually and literally, connected in this way.

Such awareness, he argued, was not limited to the present moment. Rather, it was possible for this awareness to spread out from the current moment in time and permit an intuition of—or *foreknowledge of*—events that had not yet come to pass, especially of those future events that could affect the welfare of the animal itself or of others within its communal grouping.

Although I had been quite open-minded about such ideas when in college, I had in the years after allowed myself, to some extent, to be steered away from entertaining such thoughts, as they were viewed as ridiculous by so many people around me. Still, while not as explorative of such ideas as I had once been, I had not so much rejected them, as set them aside. In any case, though somewhat skeptical, I was intrigued and went on reading.

As I recall, several stories that addressed this question of precognition in animals followed. Many of these carefully documented stories concerned animals reacting to impending air raids during World War II. In at least some of these cases, the animal's warning behavior would begin long before the air-raid sirens went off, at a time when the planes themselves were still hundreds of miles away. Apparently, many of these animals (dogs, cats, and birds) did quite an impressive job of alerting the people around them about an approaching attack, but unfortunately, the crisp details of these air-raid stories have not stayed with me over time.

One story dealing with foreknowledge in animals I do recall quite clearly, however. In it, a woman and her dog, a border collie, lived together somewhere in the Bitterroot Mountains of Idaho. She was an avid bicyclist, and would, on most days after work, go on a twelve-mile ride with her dog loping along at her side, following a dirt road which cut and looped through the steep mountains near her home. At one point on this ride the road sloped down steeply for a half mile or so, and then made a hair-pin turn. As other traffic on this isolated road was rare, the woman and her dog would race down this hill together and take the turn at the bottom at great speeds.

On one bright afternoon in spring, after several days of rain had kept them from their usual activities, the woman prepared to take the dog and go for a bike ride. The dog appeared sullen, clinging near the woman's side, and seemed only to get in her way as she took the bike down from its rack in the garage. They started off together. The dog took up its usual loping gait at her side, and the ride progressed as it had a thousand times before, with the two of them racing along through the bright mountain air—until late in the ride, when they reached the crest of that hill. As they started down, the dog barked, then sped up and cut in ahead of her, getting in her way so she had to brake to keep from hitting it. She cut around the dog, and it raced ahead of her, turning and barking again.

They continued like this down the long hill, with her braking and swerving, and the dog racing and barking and getting in her way. She scolded the dog and continued as best she could down the hill, but her usual rapid descent was slowed to a snail's pace. By the time she reached the turn at the bottom of the grade, she was barely creeping forward. She rounded the turn—and squeezed down hard on her hand brakes. Where once the road had been, now a cliff dropped for a hundred feet. A landslide had taken out the road.

"I don't know how she knew," the woman said later. "It was like she was trying to herd me back up that hill. I wouldn't be here today if it weren't for her."

I don't remember much more about the article, but I do remember wondering if these animals were somehow sensing this sort of information through some physical, though invisible, means—and if so, if such abilities were somehow built into their bodies physically, as the sense of sight or smell would be. I remember staring out the window, then, and pondering briefly if such capacities were built into the human animal, as well, and if so, how things might have been for us in the days long ago, when we lived more by impulse, or instinct, than by deliberate reasoning.

I put the magazine down and leaned my head against Laura's shoulder. She turned her face towards mine and, with her voice soft and gentle, asked me how I was doing.

"Fine," I answered. "Just going to nap a little, now."

She reached over and stroked my hair once, then went back to the work she was doing, and soon I had drifted off to sleep.*

---

* See Appendix 2 (pages A6-A7) for more on the article on animal intuition.—I. K.

Chapter VII

In morning light, after a night of rain, it appears that everything gathers at the river: tributaries from the surrounding land; animals of every stripe and feather; even time itself seems to stretch out along the river's endless, misty, muddy banks.

The blue clouded sky, which woke with us at dawn, may now be found in the river—and we, peering into the water's reflective depths, find ourselves there, too, wide-eyed and full of wonder, as though discovering ourselves for the very first time.

—HUME SOMERLEY

It was well after dark by the time we bounced to a halt at Njili airport in Kinshasa. We disembarked onto the tarmac and immediately noticed a pungent, smoky odor in the thick tropical air. We waited by the side of the plane as our gear was unloaded, and then were directed by one of the flight crew towards a one-story building nearby, through whose windows light shone brightly into the dark night. We had heard stories about the difficulties involved in getting through customs when flying into Kinshasa, and were prepared with the requisite bribe when our turn came around, and so got through without too much trouble.

With a bit of huffing and puffing, we managed to lug our gear (a fully loaded backpack, a daypack, and an over-stuffed briefcase bagged in yellow plastic, each) out to the curb, where we got in a waiting cab.

"*L'Inter?*" the cab driver asked in French.

"*Comment?*" Laura responded, asking what he had said.

"*À l'Hôtel Intercontinental?*" he explained.

"*Ah, non, à l'Hôtel Estoril,*" she answered, directing him to the hotel we'd picked out from one of our guidebooks.

We pulled out into traffic, and soon we were zipping along the avenues of Kinshasa. The cab, a decrepit old sedan without even the semblance of shocks, seemed to amplify every bump in the road, bringing home with full sensory emphasis the fact that we had arrived—we were *here*—and the journey had gone from dream to reality.

We pulled up in front of the *Estoril's* white-washed front, paid the fare (which involved not a little haggling on Laura's part—we should have agreed on a price up front), then collected our luggage and carried it inside. We signed in and were given a comfortable, carpeted room on the second floor, with a balcony overlooking the street. Before we settled in that night, I spent a little time describing the day's events in my journal—something I hoped to do without fail throughout our stay in Zaire.

We had reserved a space on the barge that was scheduled to leave the following afternoon, but when we walked over to the ONATRA office the next morning (it was only three or four blocks away) we were told that while the barge had arrived on time (a rare event, someone later told us) it was in need of repairs, and would not be ready to leave until the next day. That was all well enough, Laura and I decided, for now we would have time to get our money changed to *zaires* and to buy several gallons of purified water for use on the barge. (We had been told that none would be provided; most of the local people would drink the water from the river and take the risks that involved.) We also needed to buy kerosene for the little cook stove we'd brought along, as bringing it on the plane was not permitted, and we expected to have need of it later in our trip, not just to cook our food, but to boil water to sterilize it when our initial supply of purified water ran out.

We stopped back at the *Estoril* and asked the desk clerk where we should go to buy these things and where to go to exchange our dollars. The clerk, answering Laura in French, recommended a store for the goods and named a couple of banks nearby where we could get our money changed. She then added that we would get a better exchange rate on the black market and said we could find people who would make such an exchange in the café across the street from the U.S. Embassy.

Laura translated this for me, and we discussed it a little. Then Laura asked the clerk if she knew what the current exchange rate was. We knew that inflation was a big problem in Zaire but were still surprised when she told us the exchange rate had grown to more than six hundred *zaires* to the dollar.

The clerk agreed to exchange a small amount for us there, so we could do our shopping first, if we wished to. We exchanged twenty dollars, and Laura thanked her. Then we turned away, trying, between the two of us, to put away a pile of bills amounting to nearly 13,000 *zaires*.

We hadn't gone more than ten paces when Laura said to me, "My gosh, Indira, if we're going to exchange a few hundred dollars for our trip, we're going to need a whole extra suitcase to carry it in!"

Of course, she was right, and we realized then why everyone we'd seen since our arrival, men and women alike, were carrying some sort of bag or purse—they needed a whole bag just to carry enough money for a day's use! So we went shopping that morning not just for kerosene and water, but for an extra piece of soft-sided luggage as well, just to carry our money in.

We set out on foot on a clear morning, under a brilliant and burning tropical sun. The heat and humidity were in strange contrast to the cold of London and Boulder from which we had so recently come, and it felt good to soak up some of this new land's moist heat, so like the summertime weather of my homeland. Laura, I will say, was a bit uncomfortable, but she was never one to complain when there were new things to be explored.

Kinshasa was a remarkable city, full of life and varied textures. Beautiful trees with broad leaves lined the streets and provided a comforting shade. Tall buildings dominated the business district, and the streets were busy with traffic. All of these things suggested a vibrant, moneyed city, but along those same streets people begged, and we were told that if one wandered into the poorer parts of town, the picture was one of stunning poverty. The government in place at the time, under Mobutu Sese Seko, was referred to by some as a "theftocracy," as its members were known for their practice of skimming the best of what the country had to offer for their own private use, while leaving the rest of the citizens to struggle, unaided, through hungry, impoverished lives.

I remember after we returned to the hotel that afternoon, sitting and staring at our new bag, filled with the local currency. I kept going back and forth in my mind between thinking we must be amazingly rich, with this incredible quantity of cash, and having another feeling—that we were now about to go off on our journey with nothing but a big bag of play money to pay our way with. It had been just as odd to see people in the streets with bags of money, while knowing the poverty that underlay that scene.

That evening, Laura and I took a cab across town to the Restaurant Mama Kane, where we had our first genuinely African meal. We stepped outside afterward and waited for the cab we had called for the return trip. All along the street small fires were burning, with little groups of people huddled around them. The night air was warm and filled with the smoke of these fires. I watched as someone nearby gathered together a little pile of the rubbish that littered the street and lit it on fire, then began using it to cook something in an old metal can. I realized, then—the streets were full of fires being used to cook people's evening meals. The odor of burning trash scented the air.

I put my hand on Laura's back. "That's what the smell is," I told her, gesturing. She nodded solemnly. It was a beautiful and depressing sight—the street lit up like a festival, and the poverty that made it so.

We spent a second whole day in Kinshasa, waiting for the repairs to be completed on the engine boat that would push our string of barges upriver. We spent a little time sightseeing that day, went to a museum full of elaborate hand-carved masks and figurines, then took a walk along the bank of the Congo, which reminded me, in its power and size, of my beloved Ganges back home. While out walking, we got caught in a downpour—steamy rain falling in wind-blown sheets, the air full of big, wet drops—and then, after drying off back at our hotel, had a leisurely dinner of Portuguese food (of all things!) on the patio of the *Hôtel Estoril*.

When finally, on the morning of our third day in Kinshasa, Laura and I again made the walk to the ONATRA office—and were told this time that our barge was ready. We were also ready to leave Kinshasa and begin our journey upriver.

❀   ❀   ❀

It wasn't past mid-morning when we arrived by taxi with all of our gear, but the dock was already pulsing with life—a great sea of people carrying metal trunks and cardboard suitcases, bundles and blankets and bolts of cloth, foam mattresses and straw sleeping mats, pots and pans and iron contraptions I later learned were charcoal grills, all pouring down the rickety metal staircase and across the floating dock onto the barges chained together below. Along with them came an assortment of animals: chickens, goats, and an occasional pig.

When we'd gotten out of the taxi we'd been approached by a tall and muscular man who seemed eager to carry our luggage on board for us. With all our original gear, plus the four five-gallon containers of water (enough to last two people two weeks in the tropical heat) and an additional five gallons of kerosene, Laura and I knew we could use an extra hand, and she negotiated a price with him. That done, he picked up the gallons of kerosene, which we had tied together with a rope, and slung them around his neck like jewelry, then he tucked one five-gallon container of water under each arm, picked up the other two in his fists, and began pushing his way through the crowd towards the barge. Laura and I hurriedly grabbed up what was left and set out after him. (We later estimated that he'd been carrying close to two hundred pounds, but he moved forward with as little visible effort as if the containers had been empty.)

As we came to the top of the staircase and the crowd parted in front of us, I could see a line of barges tied up to the dock below, already alive with the crowds that had been boarding since dawn. Where painted, the barges were white, and where unpainted, they had rusted to a brilliant orange-red. To our left was the engine boat, facing upriver. It was three-stories tall, and at once beat up and old after decades of use, and still grand in her neglected glory. On a plaque beneath the wheel house the name of the boat was displayed: *Colonel Tshatshi*. To our right, in front of the *Tshatshi*, was a two-story barge, and beyond that, tied to this two-story barge's port side, I could just make out the outline of a second two-story barge. In front of all three was one more barge, this one flat and already covered with the people who would be camped out there during the journey upriver.

We found our cabin on the third deck of the engine boat. Laura had promised she would arrange the best accommodations offered, and this was it, the *"cabine de luxe,"* as the metal plate above the door announced. We paid the man who had brought our water and kerosene, and Laura went to look for someone who would let us into our cabin.

Our cabin was at the rear of the *Tshatshi*, and from where I stood outside our cabin door, I looked out at the river stretching out behind us. It wasn't long before Laura returned with the steward, a small, barefooted man in a starched white uniform, who unlocked the padlock on our cabin door and, after dawdling briefly with a few friendly remarks, left us with the lock and key.

Inside our cabin the air was stagnant and stiflingly hot. We pulled back the curtains and opened the windows on the starboard side of the room, then dragged in our gear, but left the door open and the screen door shut, hoping a little breeze might blow through. The room included two rickety metal cots, a small table with two beat-up chairs, an armoire, and an air conditioner built into the wall. The floor was tarred timber, and the walls were made of metal.

I imagined that the room might have seemed quite nice—a half-century before, when it was new! We took a look at the bathroom and found everything in working order, although there was no plumbing for hot water, the porcelain was deeply stained, and no toilet seat was provided.

Laura had already been casting me looks of concern, but when we pushed the two cots together, so we could share them as one bed, and cockroaches scattered to find new hiding places, she sighed and said sadly, "I'm sorry, Indira."

But it was really all right. Through the doorway, we had a beautiful view of the water reaching out behind the boat, and although the air conditioner didn't really work, it did blow the air around enough to make it *seem* a bit cooler.

We spent the rest of the morning settling in, cleaning up the place a little, putting our clothes away in the armoire, and doing what we could to chase out the gargantuan cockroaches which came with the room, no extra charge.

We were just trying to decide where to leave the water and kerosene where they would be most out of the way, when we heard someone banging on something not far away and stepped outside to see what was up. It turned out it was a boy banging on a large metal pan with a spoon. Laura asked him what he was up to, and he told her it was his job to call us to lunch in this manner. We had both been feeling hungry, anyway, so we locked up our cabin and found our way to the first-class dining room, where meals would be provided as part of our passage.

The dining room was a nice-sized room with windows looking out over the water. It had six large tables, all covered in aging, but clean, white table cloths—and it was quickly filling up with passengers ready for lunch. I had hoped we might be offered a menu, but instead we were each brought a plate of the going fare: four meatballs, a baked potato, and cooked carrots.

Laura again winced with concern. While not keeping strictly with the Hindu religion of my upbringing, I had nonetheless never adopted the practice of eating beef or pork, and Laura had come more and more to eat as I did, although she didn't mind a meaty meal, on occasion.

Laura called the waiter back over and spoke to him for a minute in French.

"He said they serve beans and rice to the passengers traveling second and third class," she told me. "You can get a fresh plate with beans and rice in place of the meatballs, if you want."

"That would be great," I said to Laura. *"Merci,"* I said to the young man. Laura said something else to him. He answered, then scooped up my plate and disappeared with it.

Laura put her hand on my hand. "I promised him a good tip for each meal, if he makes sure you get rice and beans instead, whenever meat is served." Then she leaned in a little towards me, and added, "I think he thinks we're both a bit crazy, sending back meat," she said, and laughed.

❄   ❄   ❄

After lunch we spent some time exploring the four boats on which we expected to make our home for the next couple of weeks. Our *cabine de luxe* and the first-class dining room were both on the top deck of the three-story riverboat that would push the other barges up the Congo. After strolling around the outer walkway of the *Tshatshi's* top deck, we went down and looked around the next two decks. These decks held the other first-class accommodations—narrower rooms with bunk beds and no air conditioning. Some of the people whose rooms these were had set up stools on the railed walkway that ran around the perimeter of the boat. They seemed relaxed, visiting with one another and listening to loud Zairian dance music on their radios.

The *Tshatshi* was flat across the bow, and the two-story barge ahead of it was flat at the stern. They were lined up here and cabled together bow to stern, and we had to leap across the gap to get from one boat to another. This two-story barge, named the *Kasongo,* and the other two-story barge cabled to its port side, the *Myanza,* held the second-class accommodations, and jumping across the gap from the *Tshatshi* to the *Kasongo* was like jumping from one world to another, for we found ourselves suddenly in a rush of activity. People filled the walkway around the outer edge of the barge, overflowing the dark, steel-walled cubicles which were the second-class cabins, laying out merchandise for sale in every available space. Animals were tied up here and there, though the bleating of goats and the clucking of chickens could barely be heard above the vibrant strains of the Zairian soukous music coming from every radio. We made our way down the corridor, and people greeted us in Lingala.

"Mbote!" the merchants said, then gestured toward their goods.

"Mbote!" we answered back, and we could see the surprise on their faces as we said "hello" in their language.

We went past the *Myanza* without boarding her, and made a second leap onto the flat barge at the front of the line. It housed the third-class passengers, if you could call it "housing," for here they would have no rooms at all, just a piece of rusty, steel deck on which they would lay out their straw mats, their goods if they had some to sell, and perhaps set up a piece of canvas to keep off the sun and rain.

Everywhere people were setting up shop and house amidst a cacophony of sound and activity. Music blared, goats bleated, babies cried and were picked up and nursed by their mothers. Most of the men wore western-looking clothes, while most of the women wore brightly colored African shirts, with a length of fabric wrapped around their waists, like shortened *saris*. Some of the women were pounding manioc root into flour, holding carved mallets and thrusting downward over and over into cylinder-shaped wooden bowls. Others fried bananas or sweetened balls of manioc dough—a sort of doughnut—cooking on the charcoal grills we'd seen people carrying on board earlier.

The air was filled with the scents of these charcoal fires; of smoked fish and roasting meats; of the sweat of people who lived each day in the broiling sun; and of the fresh river breeze, which blew over the deck. Together, these smells hung in the air, along with the visible smoke and water haze, and blended into the singular scent of barge life.

As unaccustomed as I was to these sights and sounds and smells, the combined effect was a melding together of natural elements—but parked in the middle of the deck, incongruous amidst all the hubbub and clutter, was a gleaming, seemingly brand-new, white Land Rover. I vaguely recalled having seen it there as we were boarding earlier, and thought that must be right, for however it had gotten on board, it must have been done early, before these people had begun to stake out their claims to a couple of square meters of deck each.

I nudged Laura and pointed out the Land Rover, and we discussed whether they had driven it on by ramp, or perhaps lifted it on by crane. However they had gotten it on, it could not hold our attention long amidst all the activity. All around us, people swayed to the strains of soukous music as they went about their chores. Where people were setting up shop, a wide variety of items appeared, from malaria pills to Bic pens, from little bags of salt and sugar to bolts of colorful cloth, from needles and thread to plastic cups, matches, spiral notebooks, Ayu soap, and the Primus beer we'd seen everywhere since coming to Zaire. Everybody was busy, preparing for their trip upriver—and I wondered what this place would be like in a day or two, once everyone was settled in.

❀   ❀   ❀

After spending an hour or so exploring the barges, Laura and I headed back to our cabin. We were tired and wanted to get more settled in, but once back in our room, we decided to lie down for a little while first. The room was muggy and warm. When we turned the knob, the air conditioner coughed to life, sputtered and hummed, and moved a little bit of air around. We closed just the screen door, leaving the door and windows open, and so managed to coax a small breeze through our room.

We lay down on the two rickety cots we had pushed together earlier and knew nothing more of the world until we were startled awake by the sharp call of the *Tshatshi's* whistle. I opened my eyes and heard the diesel engines beneath us give up a great roar and throb to life. I sat up and looked around our little room, as the setting sun streamed in through the open doorway, filling the room with an orange haze. The sun was setting over the river behind us, and the water was magnetic with color.

Knowing we'd overslept anyhow, I nudged Laura and got her to sit up and take a look. She was sitting a little behind me and wrapped her arms around me, resting her chin on my shoulder. A moment of breathless thrill passed through me, as it often still did when Laura was near, even after so many years. I wrapped my arms around hers, and we sat like that as the barge slowly pulled out into the current, leaving frothy lines where the propellers stirred up the water in our wake. We stared out at the river as the sun continued to dip lower in the evening sky, and I could hear Laura's voice soft in my ear.

"Thank you, Indira," she whispered.

"What for?" I asked, turning a little towards her.

"We're here."

Where at lunch I had expected a menu to chose from, at dinner I had expected, at least, a change of fare from lunch, but there would be none for the duration of our journey. They had apparently stocked up for only one meal and kept repeating it with a sort of dull inevitability for the entire trip. Laura was again served meatballs, a potato, and cooked carrots, and I was provided with beans, rice, a potato, and cooked carrots. Around us, the other passengers ate without complaint. Apparently, such unvaried fare was to be expected.

With dinner over, Laura and I stepped out onto the promenade. It was night now, and the air, though still warm, was cooler than during the day. A steamy mist clung to the river, turning in wisps that barely revealed the steely-black water beneath. We strolled along the walkway, watching as search lights scanned the water ahead.

A crew member walked by. Laura stopped him and asked him something in French. He answered, gesturing out at the water, then walked quickly away.

"They're using the lights to look for islands and marker buoys, and also to keep a lookout for signs of sandbars. Apparently, the river is low this season, and there's some danger of running aground," Laura told me.

Out along the river we could see the faltering ignition of fireflies, like pulsing stars in a low-hanging sky. We seemed to be moving though a world of mist and darkness, lit only by the glow of insects, and the powerful beams of light probing the misty air and inky water.

As we started to our room, I was aware of the pulse of life on board this array of river barges, like a whole city put afloat. Rising out of that vaporous darkness came a clamorous montage of sounds, which reminded me of life in New York City: voices, laughter—somewhere, a baby crying. The mix was sweetened by the absence of traffic noise and the omnipresence of Zairian soukous—dance music permeating the mist, seemingly from all directions at once. All around us, it seemed, there was a party going on.

As we reached the corner at the blunt bow of the *Tshatshi* and turned down her starboard side toward the stern of this, the last boat in the chain, the sounds of nightlife faded. About mid-way back we paused by one of the pillars supporting the awning over the walkway, and looked off toward the shore. We were far from Kinshasa now, and the searchlights, when they strayed ashore, revealed only glimpses of marshy lowlands, with palm trees rising up along the banks.

As we stood there, I became aware of a muffled sound coming from the room behind us. I listened to the soft noise, trying to identify it. It was the sound of a man crying—deep, heart-rending sobs, which, from the sound of it, he was trying to contain, keep quiet. There were no voices, no comforting coo of a companion. He seemed to be alone. I looked at Laura and tilted my head toward the door, gesturing. She heard it too, and we stood for a minute in sympathetic silence, then tiptoed past, leaving whoever it was alone in his solitude, and his misery.

The rest of the evening was unremarkable. We returned to our room, where we did a little more settling in, then spent a few hours reading or going over the material we'd each brought along to work on. I spent a little bit of time, as well, sketching out our day in my journal.

It was past eleven when we finally locked our cabin door and turned in for the night. But though the hour was late, it seemed no one else on our chain of barges knew it. Drifting up from the lower decks of the *Tshatshi* and over from the other barges, through the misty night, came the murmur of voices and the constant rhythms of soukous. They blurred together with the unvaried pulsing of the *Tshatshi's* engines, and try as I could to fall quickly asleep, I found myself lying awake for hours, alert to the continuing activities in the world around me, as we chugged upriver, a dot of light and liveliness in a world of darkness spreading out for countless miles around.

The noise, which had lasted late into the night, rose again with the morning, and though I'd been awake quite late, I woke about eight to the sound of someone calling out a boisterous greeting on the deck below. I woke up thinking of the paper I would write for the *Huginn/Muninn Newsletter*. Now that we were on the barge and settled in, there was nothing holding me back. I don't think I'd realized until then how much I'd been looking forward to this—a time that was dedicated neither to my regular work, nor to the distractions of daily life, a time in which I could pursue this probing interest which had been growing in me over the past couple of years.

I got up, pulled back one of the curtains a little, and looked outside. The sky was thick with clouds, and a light breeze was blowing. It was a little less hot than the morning before, but the air seemed especially thick and heavy.

I left the curtain pulled back a bit, and opened the cabin door so that a little air might blow through. Laura was still asleep, so I tried to move quietly, and hoped the additional light wouldn't wake her.

I got out the notes I'd been keeping for the article I intended to write, sat down on my cot with my pillow propped up behind me, and began going through my notes, trying to put the details in order in my mind. My notes were filled with facts and dates I wanted to include in my paper. Looking over them, I was reminded of the arguments I had planned to make, and the conclusions I had meant to draw from them. To begin with, I wanted somehow to set the scene of how the culture of our ancient human ancestors had developed over time—specifically, how incredibly slow paced those developments had been over most of our prehistory. Next, I would need to call the reader's attention to the fact that by about 30,000 years ago *something* had changed, such that the rate of cultural evolution had begun to quickly increase.

I absentmindedly tapped the paper with my pen, and then stopped because I realized I was making noise. Laura slept so peacefully beside me; I didn't want to wake her. Then I remembered our new laptop computer. I quietly got it out, and set my pen and paper aside. One of its selling points, I remembered, had been its unusually quiet key action.

I sat down on my cot with the computer propped up on my lap. It was unlike modern laptops, with no lid to open—just a narrow screen at the top above the keypad. I was glad I'd reviewed the user's guide one evening in London. I started it up by pressing both shift keys.

As I stared down at the little flashing cursor, I tried to collect my thoughts.

Some 30,000 years ago, things had begun to change quickly. Yes, but it wasn't just how much the rate-of-change had acceleration that intrigued me—it was the baffling nature of the changes themselves.

What did I want to say about it, exactly?

I knew the people reading my article would be from any number of disciplines, and would know little about the subject I was discussing. That meant I would need to somehow supply them with the basic groundwork, as well as the sort of detailed evidence that they, as academicians, were accustomed to receiving.

I sighed, and ran my fingers through my hair. Okay, I said to myself. There were mysteries involved in these changes, and I would have to go step by step and show what was so mysterious, before I even got near the material I was most excited to tell about—that is, the material about how I thought those mysteries might be solved.

I went back to looking through the notes I had brought along, trying to apply to them the structure that was forming in my mind.

After a few minutes, I heard a tapping at the screen door and looked up. It was our barefooted steward, carrying a tray with our breakfast on it. I got up and opened the screen door, and he stepped in and set the tray on the little table next to our cots, then smiled and slipped from the room without a sound. The smell of fresh coffee and biscuits filled the cabin.

I looked over at Laura sleeping, and at the hot, fresh food, then sat down on the bed and put my hand on Laura's head, stroking it gently.

"Breakfast's here, Laura," I said to her softly. She rolled over and opened her eyes.

❀   ❀   ❀

"Pause," Paul said. He was sitting on a fallen tree near the path, trying to adjust his shoes. He was finding it frustrating, as it seemed that nothing he could do would give him a comfortable fit. All day his feet had been growing sorer, as he'd struggled along through the rugged terrain—climbing first up a long, steep hill, then down the switchbacks on its other side. Only recently had the terrain begun to level off, but too late for his sore feet.

Paul sighed as he gave up on the adjustments he was trying to make to his socks. He stripped them off, dug through his pack to find the spare pair he'd bought in Strandford, then put them on, hoping they would be softer and rub less.

It would help, too, he thought, if he had a day off from hiking for his feet to mend. He wasn't ready to promise himself that, but he could, at least, stop early for the night tonight, he told himself.

The red spots on his feet were noticeably worse than they had been that morning, and it was clear that blisters were rising beneath them. Paul sighed again. Yes, an early stop was in order. He had already passed one campsite since setting out that morning. When he came to the next one, he would stop.

It took another couple of minutes for Paul to get his shoes back on in a way he thought was as comfortable as they could be made to be. Then he sat still for a minute, drank some water from his canteen, and reflected on the part of Dr. Kumar's book he had spent the morning listening to. Certainly it was an engaging enough story, but he was beginning to feel a restless desire to hurry on to whatever it was in this book that had helped to make this earth so different from his own.

Paul put away his canteen, then said, "Kiki, does this section meet the criteria I set before for high conceptual content and/or extensive social influence?"

"Yes," Kiki replied.

Paul scratched his head. Sometimes he wished Kiki was more conversational. But then, it occurred to him, maybe the problem was that he wasn't being conversational enough with her.

"I've been wondering," Paul said. "I remember when Dr. Kumar was describing her time at Oxford, she wrote about visiting a pub with some friends of hers, where she said something to them about how the way we model the world in our minds influences the sort of world we create—and, well..."

Paul looked down at the ground and rubbed the back of his head with one hand. Oh, what *is* my question? he asked himself.

Paul looked out across a narrow creek, which the trail had joined after splitting from the first one early in the day. "I suppose that has something to do with it, somehow. Anyway, I keep trying to figure out how what she's saying in this book has anything to do with the way this world developed."

Kiki made no reply.

Paul waited, then realized he hadn't asked a question.

"Kiki, could you please tell me—does the material in the rest of this chapter have anything to do with the cultural changes that followed the publication of this book?"

Paul waited again; this time, the answer came quickly.

"It would appear so," Kiki replied. "Many analysts of *Memories and Reflections* suggest that the ideas in this chapter influenced the way humanity understood itself. Multiple allusions are made to correlated changes in society."

Paul took a moment to take this in. "Well, I guess that would qualify as high conceptual content and extensive social influence," he said, more to himself than to Kiki. He stood up and tested the way his feet felt in his shoes.

"Okay, go ahead and resume recitation," he said, then continued on up the trail.

◘   ◘   ◘

It was a lighter breakfast than either of us were accustomed to, but it was a treat to have it brought to us. Laura told me she'd slept well—that the throbbing of the engines had lulled her to sleep like a baby. I laughed, but was glad that at least one of us had gotten a good night's rest. We finished breakfast, and afterward, Laura slipped her camera into her fanny pack and went on a stroll around the outer deck, while I went back to gathering myself together to write my article for the Huginn/Muninn Newsletter.

As Laura and I had munched our breakfast and visited about the events of the day before, the notes I had reviewed earlier that morning had begun to find an order in my mind. Now, I wanted nothing more than to burrow into the work, and in ordering it, and revealing it, discover what was buried there.

I dressed quickly, and returned to my cot with our laptop and my pile of papers. I spent another ten minutes or so reviewing the notes I had brought with me, but there was no real need; I knew now how I would start. I stared out the window at the passing hills and the waving palms along the shore, as I let the words form in my mind, then placed my hands on the keypad and began to type:

> For most of the past 4,000,000 years, from the time the first hominid walked upright on the plains of Africa, we see extremely gradual changes in the cultural evolution of the ancestors of modern people. It wasn't until 2,500,000 years ago that our ancestors made the first tools out of stone. It took another 1,000,000 years for them to refine this technology and begin making finely crafted stone hand axes. The next major hallmark in our cultural evolution didn't come until another 1,000,000 years had passed. At this time, 500,000 years ago, our ancestors first learned to use and control fire.[1]

I typed a number where my first citation would go. It was frustrating, but I hadn't been able to bring my source materials with me. I certainly had enough to carry and keep track of without them. I would have to add my citations when I got back to the States. For now, all I could do towards that end was put in numbers where my citations belonged.*

I went on typing:

Only with the pace of cultural change having been so glacially slow, would we think to say that it picked up a bit in the following 400,000 years. About 200,000 years ago, our ancestors developed a technology for making tools from stone flakes.[2] The first beads had been made by 110,000 years ago.[3] Some 90,000 years ago, our ancestors began to make elegant tools out of bone.[4]

But then, beginning just over 30,000 years ago, the rate of cultural change really began to accelerate. At about this time, the practice of making art took hold at isolated locations in Europe, Australia, Asia, and Africa[5] (every continent then inhabited by people) and was well established the world over by 10,000 BP.†[6] The practice of making and using beads began to flourish around the world during roughly this same time frame.[7] Then, between 10,000 and 5,000 BP, people in at least seven separate locations on at least four different continents independently began, for the first time, to domesticate plants and animals.[8] Agriculture was born, and by 2,000 BP most people the world over had given up their traditional lifestyle of hunting and gathering and had either invented or adopted agriculture to take its place.[9] All in all, in a space of perhaps 30,000 years, the face of the human experience had been transformed.

Many mysteries surround these changes, and conventional explanations leave much in doubt. I propose here that a full comprehension of the motivations and inspirations that fueled this cultural transformation requires a new understanding of the essential foundations of human nature, and of how our modern sensibility developed—a sensibility that reflects developments in both our sense of time, and our sense of self.

I paused to think. It seemed the essay could turn in a couple of different ways at this point, and I wanted to pick the right one. Now I would have to fill in the basic details and, hopefully, make these mysteries come to life.

People passing by outside our cabin spoke to one another brightly in Lingala. For a moment, I was distracted by the sound—so musical—and I listened as their voices trailed off as they went down the walkway that ringed the *Tshatshi*. I sighed, and looked back at my papers. I would have to trust the facts to tell the story, I decided—and suddenly it seemed clear what to write next:

It is believed that the first anatomically modern human beings (*Homo sapien sapiens*) evolved in Africa between 200,000 and

---

* See Part I of Appendix 3 (pages A8-A15) for the citations that were eventually included with this article. —I. K.

† "BP" indicates the number of years "Before Present." —I. K.

100,000 years ago, and then gradually dispersed from there, populating Asia first, then Australia and Europe, and eventually the Americas.[10] These early people were essentially indistinguishable from us anatomically: their skulls were the same shape as ours, their brains were at least as large as ours are today. It may be presumed that if a child from this time period were to somehow be transported forward in time, and raised and educated as children are raised and educated today, we would find them no different from their friends and classmates—for they were modern people, in a physical sense, just as we are modern people, in a physical sense, today.[11]

But they lived very differently from how most of us live today....

I glanced up as Laura came in from her walk.

"How was the world?" I said.

"It's beautiful out there," Laura said, a little breathlessly. She sat down on the cot next to me. "I can't quite believe we're really here." Her eyes shone intensely.

I touched her cheek and smiled. "I'm glad we could come," I said, then glanced around. "It is exciting, isn't it?" I added.

"In all sorts of ways," Laura said, then looked down at the computer in my lap. "You're writing, aren't you? And I've just come breezing in. Don't let me interrupt you." She stood up, then paused beside the cot, looking down at me.

"How's the little machine?" she asked quietly.

"Good," I said, glancing up.

Laura smiled, gave me a quick kiss on top of my head, then picked up her briefcase and quietly cleared a place to work on the table beside me.

I reread what I'd just typed, scrolling through the little screen, hoping to pick up the thread I'd lost.

...were essentially indistinguishable from us...would find them no different...were modern people.... But they lived very differently from how most of us live today.

Once I found the thread, I went on:

They were hunter-gatherers, hunting wild animals and gathering wild plants for food. If we might extrapolate anything from the experiences of twentieth century hunter-gatherers living in the sort of tropical climate in which we originated, then we could presume that our ancient ancestors, like their twentieth-century counterparts, wandered freely, lived life largely from one moment to the next, took a leisurely and playful attitude towards their labors, and felt an almost religious sense of belonging with the natural world around them.[12]

For 100,000 years or more, anatomically modern people lived in this way. As we spread around the planet, new environments may have imposed new pressures. Those who reached the colder climates

of Europe around 40,000 BP, for example, would likely have lived
less in the moment as they learned to prepare for the cold winter
months ahead—but for the most part, though we spread widely, our
hunter-gatherer lifestyle remained unchanged.

Then, comparatively suddenly, between 10,000 and 5,000 years
ago, a new lifestyle was *independently developed* at several distinct
locations around the globe. During this time, people began to plant,
tend, and harvest crops, and to keep animals for food—gradually
domesticating local species.

What prompted this relatively sudden shift towards domesticating plants and animals, we might wonder? At first glance we might
assume that people made this change in order to increase their supply
of food—for surely we may assume that farming is a more efficient
way of acquiring food than hunting and gathering is.

But the truth is not so clear....

That was right, I thought, the truth wasn't so clear—but what exactly
did I want to say about it? I got up and poured myself some more coffee
from the pot on the tray that Laura had left resting across our backpacks
when she had cleared the table to work. I wanted to try to emphasize how
strange it was that people had chosen to give up hunting and gathering, and begun to domesticate plants and animals instead. It seemed so
natural to people today that of course we would be farmers, but it hadn't
always been that way.

I poured some coffee for Laura, as well, then returned to my spot on
the cot, where I sat staring out the open doorway of our cabin—out at
the big blue sky beyond, trying to figure out how to go on with my essay.
Finally, I decided once again to just let the facts carry my argument, and
I began again to type:

Certainly it is possible to get more food from a given piece of land by
farming it than by hunting and gathering on it—and yet the archaeological record shows that, at the locations where agriculture was first
developed, the food supply for the hunter-gatherers who preceded the
first farmers was especially good—both in terms of the quantity and
the variety of foods available. In other words, the initial transition to
agriculture *was not motivated by a need for additional food.* Agriculture
did not originate where there was a shortage of available food, but
rather *where there was a surplus.*

So much food was available and near at hand that the hunter-
gatherers who preceded the first farmers lived a very comfortable
and stable life—they did not need to wander far in search of food, as
we might imagine, but rather stayed in the same location for most
of each year.[13]

Nor did the transition to agriculture bring improvements in their
diet. The evidence shows that as a general rule, the first farmers were
less well nourished, experienced more disease, and lived shorter lives
than the hunter-gatherers who preceded them.[14]

In addition, knowing what we do about the nature of farm work, it can be assumed that the labor of the first farmers involved a good bit of repetition and drudgery, and lacked the excitement and variability which are inherent elements of the work of hunter-gatherers.

So why, we shake our heads and wonder, did people all over the world so unanimously choose agriculture as a way of life, when this transition implied such a reduction in the quality of the lives they lived?

As Anne Birgitte Gebauer and T. Douglas Price write in the introduction to their volume, *Transitions to Agriculture in Prehistory*:

I searched around for the scrap of paper I'd brought with me with that quote on it, though I thought I might be able to remember it on my own. I found it at the back of my pile of notes, and carefully typed it in:

Rather than the result of external forces and stress, the adoption of domesticates may well have been an internally motivated process. The consequences and conditions [associated with the advent of agriculture] in fact suggest that human populations were pulled into the adoption of farming rather than pushed. But what or who pulled, and how?

...This question of *why* humans adopted farming remains elusive and at the same time one of the more intriguing in prehistory.[15]

Intriguing, I thought—yes.

I scrolled back through what I had written that morning, and felt fairly pleased with it. I thought I had done a pretty good job showing how remarkable the series of cultural changes that had started about 30,000 years ago were. I felt, too, that I had made a good case for the idea that there had been no externally motivated need pressuring people to invent agriculture, and I especially liked the quote I had ended with. I read back through it: "may well have been an internally motivated process...." That was very much the point I had hoped to make.

I set aside the little computer, then took what was left of my coffee, which was now no better than lukewarm, and went outside. I leaned against the railing at the rear of the *Tshatshi* and watched the water spreading out in her wake, reaching out towards the two shores, each growing more distant as the river widened from the narrows near Kinshasa. The hills, which had looked mostly clear-cut near the city, with just a few tall trees standing along the ridgetops, had given way to low swampland, full of bushes and tall grass. The world had a feeling of vastness here, with the river wide, the land seemingly endless, and the sky arching bright and blue over it all.

After a few minutes, Laura joined me out on deck. She brought the map and guidebook.

"I thought I'd try to figure out where we are. It'd be nice to keep track as we go along." She opened the map and looked at it for a minute, then asked me if I would hold it while she looked in the guidebook. I set my coffee down on the deck near the railing, and took the map from her.

"I had an interesting experience while I was out this morning," she said, as she peered through the book.

"Yeah?" I said, trying to hold the map so the breeze didn't pull at it. "What happened?"

"I wandered about for a while, looking around and taking pictures. Not a lot of pictures. I took some from the bow of the *Tshatshi*," Laura said, gesturing casually toward the front of the boat, "looking off toward the other barges, then I wandered down to the lower decks and was taking pictures of the shore." She looked up from the book and caught my eye. "It was early. Not a lot of people were around. There was a woman down there, sitting out on a chair outside her cabin. She got my attention and told me I should stop taking pictures. She said the military police would think I was a spy and have me arrested. I didn't think she could be serious, but she said she'd seen it before. A few trips ago, she said there was a foreigner taking pictures. He was taken off the barge in Mbandaka, and he didn't get back on when the barge went on upriver. She didn't know what happened to him."

I was concerned. "Did you see any military people around when you were out this morning?" I asked.

"No," Laura said, "I told the woman there weren't any military police around to see me. She said it didn't matter—they had spies."

"Spies, huh?" I said.

"Seems the military are very concerned with spying, one way or another. I wonder if it's all true," Laura said, and looked back down at the guidebook.

"Did you think she was telling the truth?" I said. My thoughts turned to all I had read about the corrupt government of Zaire, which had come to power through a foreign-assisted coup d'état and assassination.

"She seemed quite serious," Laura answered, a bit distracted by the guide book. I would say she seemed oddly unconcerned, but it wasn't odd for Laura—she never let herself worry.

Laura read a little in the guidebook, then looked over at the map I was holding. "I think we're right about here," she said. "The distances and vegetation seem about right."

"Where's Mbandaka?" I asked.

"Ah," Laura looked over the map. "It's right here. About three days away, I'd say."

I looked at the spot on the map. "Please don't take any more pictures," I said.

"I'll be careful," she answered.

❂   ❂   ❂

At lunch, Laura and I took a seat where we could see out the windows on the *Tshatshi's* port side. The waiter came around and brought us our food—the same as yesterday's fare. I half-heartedly took a few bites.

While the food was not spectacular, the view was. From where we sat, we could see the stern section of the *Myanza*; the river; the far shore, full of shrubs and towering elephant grass; and above it all, the thickening sky, now knotting up with heavy gray clouds.

Most of the other passengers dining with us were Africans, so, when a man of European descent sat down near us, I found myself unintentionally glancing over at him. He took this as an opening for conversation.

"Looks like you've managed to find a little variety here," he said in English, gesturing towards my beans and rice.

"They don't seem to mind if you downgrade to what the second and third class passengers are eating—well, at least not if you offer a tip," I told him.

He laughed. "A tip, or a bribe?" he said. Although his remark might have sounded a little cynical, he said it in a good-humored way, and I smiled.

"My name's Raymond Maddock," he said, smiling warmly and offering me his hand. I gave it a firm shake and took a better look at him. There was something about him that seemed somehow boyish, even though he was, I supposed, only a few years younger than Laura and I—perhaps in his early to mid-thirties. He was moderately tall and looked quite fit. He spoke with an accent in a light, even tone.

"I'm Indira Kumar," I told him, then gestured to Laura, "and this is Laura Atherton." He and Laura shook hands.

"Where are you headed?" he asked.

"The Ituri Forest," I told him.

Raymond frowned a little. "Are there Hutus and Tutsis there? Is that right? I know there are across the border, in Rwanda."

"I don't think so," I said, and looked over at Laura.

"Only various Mbuti and Bantu groups that I know of, in the area we're going to," Laura said.

Raymond nodded. "So what takes you there? Sightseeing?" he asked, and again his accent caught my attention. The waiter came around and gave him a plate of the usual food. He broke apart one of the gravy-covered meatballs with his fork and took a bite.

"No," I answered. "Research."

"Really?" he said, and swallowed. "In the Ituri? What sort of research?" He seemed quite interested.

"Yes, in the Ituri, with the Mbuti Pygmies," I answered. "Laura is examining to what extent their religion fosters a sense of interconnectedness, and I'll be researching how their belief system affects their relationship with the forest ecosystem." I took a bite of beans and rice, while Raymond nodded thoughtfully.

"And you," I asked, swallowing. "What brings you to Zaire?" I looked out the window at the wide river, choppy and dark under the clouded sky. "It's a remarkable place to be."

"Yes it is," Raymond answered, following my gaze out the window. "Actually, I'm also here on research." He gestured towards the bow of the *Tshatshi* with his fork. "I'm heading for a research site near Bomenge—studying bonobos."

"Bono...? What?" Laura asked.

"Bonobos," Raymond said. "They're one of the great apes—you know: chimpanzees, gorillas, orangutans—and bonobos. Not many people have heard of them, though. They come from too isolated a region to get much attention, and they were misidentified as a variety of chimpanzee for a long time, anyway."

"Yeah?" Laura said. "What do they look like? Like chimps, I suppose?" I smiled a little—it was something I'd always liked about Laura, that her curiosity became engaged so easily.

"In some ways, yes, in some ways, no," Raymond answered. As I listened to him speak I tried to guess his accent and wondered if perhaps he was Australian.

"Bonobos have more slender, lighter builds than chimpanzees," Raymond went on. "For bonobos, their arms and legs are about the same length, whereas chimpanzee's arms are longer than their legs. So bonobos are more like us in their proportions. Ah, and their faces are different from chimps, too, but that's a little hard to describe. Also, Bonobos walk bipedally more of the time than chimpanzees do." Raymond took another bite of his meatballs.

"They walk how?" Laura asked.

"Bipedally," I answered for Raymond, as his mouth was full. "That means 'on two feet.'"

"So they walk like we do?" Laura asked, trying to get this straight.

Raymond swallowed. "Part of the time," he said. "It's quite remarkable to see them walking upright, which they do, say, when they have something they want to carry in their hands. They're more upright than chimps. It looks strangely human."

Laura looked off into the distance, and I could see her trying to picture this.

"How long have you been doing research at this site?" I asked Raymond.

"Just over two years now," he said, frowning. "I've been away for the past month." He drummed the table a little with his fingertips, then stopped. "I'm eager to get back to it. The bonobos are just beginning to get habituated, ah, that is, they're just beginning to get used to having people around, staring at them—well, they're getting used to it enough that at least part of the time we can get some real observing done. I feel like we may really be able to move forward, now. In the first months we were there, we felt lucky if we could get a few good glimpses of them in a day. Now it's not uncommon to get in an hour or two of more or less continuous observation in a single day.

"So, it'll be good to get back to that," he concluded, nodding.

"Could you get them to sit still and be looked at, maybe, if you fed them?" Laura asked. "I used to do that with squirrels, when I was a kid."

"I'm sure we could do better if we provisioned," Raymond answered. "That is, if we fed them, like you say. They do that at Wamba—that's another bonobo research site—but my research is focused on observing their foraging habits, so there would be no point in trying to get them used to us by offering them food. We'd just disrupt their natural patterns."

Outside, the clouds looked darker than when we'd come inside, and the wind was starting to blow.

"If you've been doing research here for that long, you must have spent a lot of time on these riverboats," I said.

"No, actually—I had been flying into Basankusu and then driving to the site. But the last time I took off from Basankusu one of the bloody engines went out right after we got in the air. The whole time we were aloft, we were wavering from side to side." He gestured with his hands, swaying. "We landed safely, but it sure spooked me," he raised his eyebrows and caught his breath. "Nothing's kept up in this country—it's too poor, and supplies aren't available. So," he concluded, shrugging, "I decided to take the barge this time."

"That must have really been frightening," Laura said.

"Enough to make the inconvenience of these barge trips look a bit more attractive." Raymond said, and the conversation fell into a lull, as we all took bites of our altogether too-familiar meals.

After a couple of minutes, I asked Raymond what institution he was affiliated with. He took a sip of his water, and answered.

"Australian National University, in Canberra. And both of you?"

"The University of Colorado, in Boulder—in the U.S.," Laura answered.

"That's funny, I wouldn't have pegged either of you as Americans," Raymond said.

"Well, neither of us started out that way," Laura answered.

An unexpected gust of wind swayed the *Tshatshi*, and I looked outside at the dark clouds congealing above the water. Laundry, hanging out on the railings of the *Myanza*, flapped in the wind. As I watched, lightning flashed, followed quickly by a loud clap of thunder. Rain began to fall as suddenly as turning on a shower. I could hear it hitting the roof of the dining room. Across the water, I could see the wind tugging at the tall grasses on the far shore, while the river itself, gray beneath a gray sky and pelted by rain, had the look of hammered pewter. I looked again at the *Myanza* and saw people on her deck dashing about, picking up merchandise they had set out on the walkway to sell, and pulling in laundry that had been left over the railing to dry.

One young man jogged the length of the barge, rushing to gather in goods (which he had apparently left in someone else's care) before they got blown away or soaked by the rain. Once he arrived, he offered a bright smile to the woman who had apparently been watching the shop, and together they moved their merchandise inside.

Something appealed to me about this scene. The people had rushed to protect their goods from the weather, but they had seemed somehow more lighthearted about it than I had come to expect from people in the West. Perhaps it was something of the third world, of poverty, of a life where one has only so much power over one's circumstances and must make the best of it. Perhaps there was something in their gestures that reminded me of my own upbringing in India. It was hard for me to pin down, but whatever it was I had glimpsed, it made me want to go out and meet the people who lived this riverboat life—blown by wind, and filled with music, and sky, and the great muscular Congo.

The cloudburst had caught Laura and Raymond's attention as well, and I glanced over at both of them. Laura's face seemed lit from within, her expression enthralled. She was having the adventure she'd dreamed of, and she couldn't have been happier. Raymond's expression had turned, too—not animate and engaged, as he had been in the conversation— instead, his face had clouded over, as though shaded by the heavy sky outside. He seemed someplace solemn and shadowy within himself.

After a few minutes, the gusting wind, which had announced the storm's arrival, abated. As the rain came steadily down, we all returned our attention to the conversation, and the moment of light and shadow passed. Laura wanted to know, if the bonobos were good at walking bipedally, like we did, did that mean they were more closely related to us than other apes were?

Raymond calmly answered that there was, actually, a good bit of debate on the subject. He said that both chimpanzees and bonobos shared about 98% of their DNA with us, which was more than either of them shared with their next-nearest relative, the gorilla. He said that both chimps and bonobos had a common ancestor that had broken off from the human family tree about five or six million years ago, and so from that point of view, they were both equally related to us.

Outside, the rain was falling in thick sheets. Occasionally lightning, now distant, brightened the sky. Thunder rolled softly over the water.

But it really wasn't that simple, Raymond continued. He described how it was thought that chimpanzees had evolved more quickly in those five or six million years than bonobos had, because they had moved to new environments. So from that point of view, he said, bonobos are most like the ancestor that chimpanzees, bonobos, and humans all have in common—and could be considered, therefore, to be more closely related to us than chimpanzees.

"By that reasoning," Raymond said, "we're more closely related to bonobos than we are to any other living creature."

"That's fascinating," Laura said, leaning forward, bright and cheerful. Raymond looked at her, and his expression was strangely intense. At first I thought his look tender, then melancholy.

Laura pushed her plate away. "It's good to have good conversation—it makes it easier to forget how unvaried the food is," she said brightly.

"Yes," Raymond said, nodding. He set his napkin on his empty plate.

I was nearly done with my meal. Around us, I had the feeling that other people were lingering over the last of theirs, waiting for the rain to slow before going outside. Raymond, Laura, and I stayed around, too, watching the rain splattering against the deck outside.

"Doesn't it sort of make you wonder what we could learn about us," I said, "by seeing what *they* are like—as they're so closely related to us?"

"Kind of like the paper you're working on," Laura commented.

"Yeah, a little," I said.

"What paper are you working on?" Raymond asked.

"It deals with human cultural evolution over the last 30,000 years or so," I told him.

"That sounds interesting," Raymond answered, looking at me, and again his expression seemed comfortable and relaxed.

"We both agreed we'd bring something to work on on the barge, so the trip wouldn't seem quite so frivolous," Laura said, smiling. I thought how much she seemed to be enjoying everything about this trip.

"So you're working on it here, on the barge?" Raymond asked. He sounded a little impressed.

"That's how I spent the morning," I answered.

"Well, I've got to credit you. I've got some work with me, but I've been finding it a little hard to concentrate. All the noise and commotion..." He waved his hand, indicating the surrounding scene. "It will be better when I'm back in the forest."

I glanced around at the packed dining room, then over at Laura. Her head was tilted a little to one side. She looked thoughtful. Raymond casually pushed his plate away from him.

"So," Laura said, "if bonobos are our nearest animal relatives, what are they like? I mean, well, how do they behave? Are they smart like chimps are, for example?"

"Yeah, they're as smart as chimps, I'd say." Raymond answered. "Their intelligence is focused a little differently, though. They're more socially oriented than chimps are. Actually, they're pretty remarkable animals. They're very smart, very peaceable, uncommonly empathetic—whereas groups of chimpanzees have sometimes been known to wage war on one another: chimps killing chimps. It's not uncommon for chimpanzees to kill monkeys for food, but bonobos have never been observed deliberately killing another animal, except insects, which they sometimes eat."

"Yeah, I can see what you mean by 'peaceable,'" Laura said.

"Yes, and that's not all. Some people have referred to them as the 'make love not war' apes. Whereas chimpanzees resolve social friction with gestures of aggression, bonobos most typically resolve conflict by having sex. It's like with human couples who make love to make up with one another after having a fight. But with bonobos, they make love whenever there's any social tension, and most of the time that's long before any real fight has happened. Sex serves much more than a reproductive function for them; it's the glue that binds them together socially. They use sex to smooth over conflict, and to make and reinforce all sorts of social bonds. And not just the males and females, but all members of the group. To put it simply, they're extremely bisexual animals, although I would say that the female-female bonds are the strongest combination amongst bonobos." Raymond paused, with a somewhat quizzical look on his face. I supposed he was wondering what we thought of these animals he was so devoted to studying.

"Anyway," he went on, directing his words to Laura, "this relates to another remarkable aspect of bonobo social life. The female-female bonds form the social backbone of any given group. Physically more powerful males can't dominate bonobo females, as the males do amongst chimpanzees, because the bonobo females stick together. It's always a mature female who leads in bonobo groups."

Raymond looked off to one side for a moment, casually drumming his fingers on the table. "Yeah. So, I'd say those are the bonobo's most remarkable behavioral characteristics," he concluded.

"They sound really fascinating," I told him. "I don't suppose we'll find any in the Ituri Forest?"

Raymond looked back over at us and shook his head. "No, they live only in a very localized area, south of the arc of the Congo River," he answered. Outside, the rain had slackened off, and the crowd in the dining room had begun to thin out.

I set my napkin on the table and pushed my chair back a little. "Well, I'd like to meet one someday," I told him.

"Yeah," Laura said. She had that far away look she got when she was thinking. Raymond smiled a little, then nodded.

"I feel lucky to be able to research such remarkable animals," he told us.

The dining room was just about empty. Laura turned sideways in her chair, with one arm resting on its back, the other on the table.

"So, where is this research site you're going to? Will you be on the barge all the way to Kisangani?" she asked him.

"No, just to Mbandaka." He looked around at the empty tables, then stood up. "I've really enjoyed our conversation," he said, and once again gave us a look I found hard to interpret. Was it just sadness, tenderheartedness—or some sort of longing?

"Maybe I'll see you both around the barge," he added. Laura and I told him, yes, and that we'd also enjoyed the conversation.

He was just about to leave, when it occurred to me I had something else I wanted to ask. I told him about Laura having gone out with her camera early that morning, and what the woman had told her about taking pictures being dangerous.

"It seems so unlikely," I said, "that someone could be arrested for spying just for taking some travel photos—do you suppose it could be true?"

Raymond listened thoughtfully, and nodded. "I'd be careful," he said, keeping his voice low, as though he didn't want others to overhear. "Things may seem normal enough on the surface, but this *is* a military dictatorship, and there's not much out there to rein in the military, if they want to set paranoid regulations and enforce them as they please. Most of the time, all they're looking for is a bribe—but I'd still do the best I could to steer clear of any potential problems. I keep a camera at the research site, but I don't travel with it for just this reason."

I took a moment to let the thought sink in. "Thanks," I told him, and looked over at Laura. I hoped she would listen. She had a tendency not to take danger very seriously.

"Too bad your bonobos aren't setting the regulations," Laura joked. "I'll bet they'd be more sensible."

"Probably," Raymond said, and laughed.

We finished saying our goodbyes, and Raymond left. Laura and I took a minute to leave a small pile of *zaires* on the table as a tip for the man who had brought me my beans and rice, and then we, too, left the dining room, and headed back to our cabin.

That afternoon I spent a couple of hours rereading and refining what I had written that morning, while Laura continued to review the ethnographic data on the Mbuti she'd collected before our trip. We'd left the door of our cabin open again, and at one point I looked up and saw where the sun had broken through clouds over the river behind our riverboat, streaking down to the water in broad shafts of light.

Each time I would look up, the scene would be different, the sky clearing, the day brightening, the sun reflecting on the water, which now was almost as wide as my beloved Ganges back home. I found myself feeling nostalgic for my childhood home, for the smoke rising from the funeral ghats along the banks of the Ganges River in Varanasi, with the sky endless and spreading wide above, and for the people I had known in my youth. Several times, when I would look up from my work, images from my childhood would pass though my mind. Interlaced with these images were impressions of the scene I had watched earlier, of people dashing along the deck of the *Myanza*, when the wind and rain had come. I kept trying to refocus on my work, but I was yearning to explore the life that surrounded me here—full of river, rain, and sky—and to discover the people who lived it.

Finally, I set my work aside and suggested to Laura that we go out and see what had become of the village we'd watched people erecting on the flat barge the day before. She was happy to agree, and we set off into a day that had grown bright, muggy, and hot.

The scene, which had just been taking form the day before, had really erupted into life while we had been tucked away on the *Tshatshi*. The tarpaulins, which had been tied by a corner here or there and had been flapping in the breeze the day before, were now sturdily erected to protect the people beneath from the sun and rain. The goods shopkeepers had just begun to display the day before, were now carefully laid out on straw mats, where they might catch the eye of any passerby.

At the bow of the barge, people pulled up buckets of river water and poured them over their heads as an impromptu shower. Before us, the river, blue and gray under a sky now bright with late-afternoon sun, stretched a mile from shore to shore. Behind us lay the vital barge life, a scene which was at once home, business, and party. The place had the sound of a festival, a great musical murmur full of voices and song.

The buckets of water hauled up from the barge's bow had also been used to wash laundry, which lay now in bold, decorative colors wherever it had been left to catch the sun and breeze. Most notably, it covered the white Land Rover we'd spotted the day before, giving it a surprising, colorful, tropical appearance.

Laura and I wandered back in amidst the stalls. The day was growing late, and the sun's shadows had begun to stretch long across the deck. Many of the charcoal grills were in use, and on them many women had begun to cook their family's evening meal. The air was filled with the scents of charcoal and cooking meat. The sun cut in and out of the smoky haze, making the air visible in slanting bands.

I was looking over at a couple of men who had scratched out a checkered pattern on the rusty deck, and who were playing checkers on that "board" with the caps of Primus beer bottles—caps turned up for reds, down for whites—when I felt a lunge beneath my feet, and felt the barge come to a sudden stop in the water. I was barely able to keep my footing. For a moment, everyone on deck went silent, and then the voices rose again.

"What was that?" I said to Laura. The deck felt strange beneath my feet, as though it slanted down a little from bow to stern.

Laura shook her head, then turned to a man standing near her and asked him the same question I had just asked her, this time in French. It seemed not to be the language he was used to, but he managed to answer Laura.

Laura translated for me, saying that we "must have hit a sandbar." I asked if this was a big problem. As she passed on my question, I could hear the engines on the *Tshatshi* roaring at full throttle.

The man shrugged and answered. "He says we are stuck," Laura said, then spoke to the man again. He shrugged, again, and answered. He had that relaxed, unworried manner I'd seen when watching the people on the *Myanza* earlier.

"He says it could be minutes or days—or maybe we'll never get off," Laura told me.

The man spoke again. Laura listened, and then added, "He says you can see them sometimes, the barges, the old ones, still stuck in the river."

A woman, sitting near my feet, frying bananas on a charcoal grill, spoke to the man, delivering her words quickly and forcefully. The man answered in the same manner, and then turned around and went back to haggling with a customer. The woman called up to me—said something to me in French, which I didn't understand, and I answered her in Lingala.

"*Nayoki te,*" I said—"I don't understand."

She looked surprised, then repeated what she had said, but this time in Lingala. I had trouble with some of the words, but managed to understand that she was telling me that sometimes the barges could be stuck badly, but usually they could get free in a short time.

"*Natondi yo,*" I said to her, thanking her.

Laura smiled, and I had the feeling she was pleased someone was speaking to us in Lingala. "*Mintela nsolo malamu,*" she said to the woman, stumbling through the words for "bananas smell good." Laura's smile broadened, and she gestured towards the food the woman was cooking.

I think Laura meant only to be making conversation, but the woman smiled and spooned some of the fried bananas into a bowl, then handed it up for Laura to try.

"*Eloko te,*" Laura said—"that's all right"—and she waved her hand a little, as though to say "you don't need to give that to me." But the woman extended her hand a little further, nodded her head towards Laura, and said something bright and cheerful in Lingala—which neither of us understood.

Laura took the bowl and ate a bite. *"Ezali malamu! Natondi yo!"* "It's good! Thank you!" Laura said. I tasted it, too, and echoed my agreement, *"Iyo! Ezali malamu—natondi yo!"*

We introduced ourselves (a somewhat belabored process, in the rough Lingala Laura and I spoke) and discovered the woman's name was Nsambi. While we spoke, the *Tshatshi's* engines continued to roar and grind in the background. Our new friend seemed unconcerned, but it worried me some. We'd set aside a certain amount of time for this trip. People would be expecting us. I listened to the engines struggling, but felt no movement in the barge and wondered just how firmly we were jammed up onto this sandbar.

Meanwhile, Nsambi was asking various questions—like where we were from, and why we were traveling—and we both did our best to answer.

We stood there visiting like this for perhaps ten or fifteen minutes, then something happened. I could hear the engines roar particularly fiercely, then something gave way, and we slid off the sandbar, moving in reverse. A happy murmur rose from the crowd as the barge slid free. The riverboat continued in reverse for perhaps a minute, then turned sharply astern and continued upriver around the sandbar.

"Ah," Nsambi said, looking around, *"likambo te"*—"there's no problem"—and smiled. Laura and I, both pleased to see the barge free, nodded and cheerfully agreed.

It seemed as good a time as any to end our conversation and move on, so Laura and I returned the bowl, thanked Nsambi again for the delicious food, then stepped back into the throngs of people covering the flat barge's deck, and went on our way.

"That was really nice," Laura said to me, but then expressed her concern about taking food from someone so poor as the people traveling on the flat barge must be.

We wandered around for another half hour or so, looking at the goods on display and chatting with people. After a while, we came across someone with some really big, delicious-looking, ripe pineapples for sale. Laura suggested we buy one. She had the idea we could take it to Nsambi, ask to use her knife, and then share it with her.

We picked out a really beautiful one, then wandered back the way we'd come, browsing in the stalls on the other side of the aisle as we went. When we got back, it appeared Nsambi had called her family around her for dinner—three children under seven, and a young husband with a smile as warm as hers. She looked up and welcomed us when we returned. We shared the pineapple with all of them, while Nsambi smiled the same radiant smile she had offered us earlier, then insisted on serving each of us up a bowl of the spicy stew she was cooking, full of Congo River catfish, tomatoes, and onions.

Laura tried to wave her off. *"Eloko te,"* she said, shaking her head, but Nsambi insisted, smiling. They went back and forth for a minute, but it was clear that Nsambi really wanted us to stay.

"Let's do," I said to Laura, and Laura smiled and nodded her agreement.

"Natondi yo," Laura said, thanking Nsambi. As Laura reached for the bowl Nsambi was holding out, a thoughtful look came across her face. Laura took the bowl, then asked in halting Lingala, *"Olingi masanga?"*— "Would you like beer?"

"Ah—Natondi yo," Nsambi answered back happily. Her husband grinned, and the woman in the next stall looked our way with a smile.

Laura smiled back at them. She handed me the bowl, told me she'd be back quickly, then disappeared into the crowd. She returned a few minutes later with an armload of Primus—plenty for all.

Nsambi gestured for us to sit down, which we did, and we began chatting with her and her husband.

The children's attitude seemed one of excited, happy caution as they peeked out from behind their parents, then disappeared in giggles when we smiled at them. Gradually, the oldest got up the nerve to come sit close to us, and eventually the younger ones followed. They seemed especially fascinated with Laura's white skin and red, just-past-shoulder -length hair. They pointed and whispered to one another, and after a while gathered up the courage to touch Laura's skin and hair—and my hair, too, for though it was dark like theirs, it had none of the curl they were used to.

The catfish stew was delicious, and I felt so glad to be eating out under an open sky with these friendly people. Strains of dance music could be heard pulsing and throbbing from every corner of the deck, carried aloft on the evening air. The sun, just dipping into the water in the river behind us, lit the sky in hues of orange and red, making a magnificent display. We felt happy and well, and were in good company as we settled down to the best food we ate on that river journey, and to more friendly questions about the countries we were from and what we were doing on the river. The stars came out above us in the warm, humid night, and we sat, surrounded by the sounds of music, the *Tshatshi's* engines, and the soft rising and falling of a thousand voices, as some of the people around us revved up for a night of festivities, and others sang their children to sleep.

When the meal was over and the evening finally wound down, Laura and I wandered back to our cabin, a little dazed with drink and with the general good cheer of the evening. On the way, we stopped at the bow of the *Tshatshi* and looked out from the upper deck. Search lights cut through the clear night air, playing along the equatorial waters, searching the surface for that faint sign, that distinctive warping of ripples, which would reveal the next sandbar beneath. I wondered if there would be another, and if the next would be so easily dealt with. I put my arm around Laura and pulled her near me, then we turned and went back to our cabin, and our two metal cots, for the night.

❋ ❋ ❋

We had been up late the night before, and I had been sleeping restlessly since the morning clamor had begun just after dawn, so when the steward tapped on our door at about eight o'clock, I got up to answer it in a fog of sleepiness. I took the breakfast tray from him and thanked him, then set it down on the table myself and crawled back into bed, wondering a little what he made of our having pushed the beds together. I think I might have decided to try to sleep a little bit longer, but Laura had heard the knock, too, and was soon up pouring us coffee, full of bright morning cheer.

I moaned, swung my feet over the side of the bed, and accepted the cup of coffee Laura was holding out for me.

"I really like the music around here," I said. "I'm just not sure why it has to go on so nearly twenty-four hours a day."

"Just think about how it would be if we were staying on one of the other barges," Laura said. "At least back here we're away from a lot of the commotion." I looked at her with half-open eyes, as she sat down on the cot beside me.

"Maybe so, but it's still plenty loud back here," I said. Laura looked concerned.

"Oh, don't worry about it," I added. "I'm sure I'll sleep again someday."

We dragged our little table and chairs through the cabin's doorway, so we could have our breakfast out on "our verandah"—as we had come to call the piece of the ship's walkway that was outside our cabin door—and there sit looking at the river stretching out behind us, and at the water churned up in the *Tshatshi's* wake.

We sat there for an hour or more, sipping coffee with cream and sugar, eating biscuits and jam, and reading whatever light reading material we could lay our hands on in place of a morning newspaper. After a time, Laura got out the map and guide book, and tried to estimate where we were along the river. She noted that the river had widened considerably, and guessed that we were probably near Bolobo, at about two degrees south latitude. The day had started warm and clear, but I assumed we would not get through it without at least another shower. So long as we were south of the equator, we would be in the rainy season. Once we passed to the north, I had read, it would be drier—but we would not cross the equator until we'd passed Mbandaka, which, Laura estimated, was still a couple of days away.

I found myself thinking, again, about the possibility of trouble in Mbandaka, but Laura seemed to have forgotten the matter entirely, and I even had to dissuade her from taking some additional shots of the Congo's shore, where the morning light cast playful shadows amidst the trees.

As I said, the day had broken bright and clear, but it was still relatively dim and cool in our cabin, so after breakfast Laura and I brought our furniture back inside, took turns showering, then opened up the door and window and got out the work we had brought with us.

I hoped to pick up writing my Huginn/Muninn article where I had left off the day before. I got out the laptop (which Laura seemed not to mind my having laid claim to) and sat down on my cot, ready to go—but found myself staring out through the screen door, instead, watching the water turned up by the boat's passage.

I was ready to write, but nothing was coming to me. After a few minutes, I realized what the problem was—I wasn't sure exactly what it was I had already written, or what it was I was supposed to be going on with.

I started up the computer and began skimming through the text I had typed in the day before, trying to pick up the key points. "For most of the past 4,000,000 years," I read, skipping ahead, "...we see extremely gradual changes in the cultural evolution of the ancestors of modern humans."

I scrolled further down the screen and continued to skim:

> Just over 30,000 years ago, the rate of cultural change...began to accelerate.... The practice of making art...was well established...by 10,000 BP. The practice of making and using beads began to flourish.... Then, between 10,000 and 5,000 BP, people in at least seven separate locations...began, for the first time, to domesticate plants and animals.
>
> Many mysteries surround these changes.... A full comprehension...requires a new understanding of the essential foundations of human nature...developments in both our sense of time, and our sense of self....
>
> The first anatomically modern human beings...evolved in Africa between 200,000 and 100,000 years ago.... They were modern people, in a physical sense, just as we are modern people, in a physical sense, today....
>
> They hunted wild animals and gathered wild plants for food...and felt an almost religious sense of belonging with the natural world around them....
>
> Then, between 10,000 and 5,000 years ago...people began to plant, tend, and harvest crops, and to keep animals for food....
>
> What prompted this...shift...we might wonder?...
>
> The evidence shows that as a general rule, the first farmers were less well nourished, experienced more disease, and lived shorter lives than the hunter-gatherers who preceded them....
>
> So why...did people all over the world...choose agriculture...when this transition implied such a reduction in the quality of the lives they lived?...
>
> "Rather than the result of external forces and stress, the adoption of domesticates may well have been an internally motivated process."

I smiled. That had done it; now I knew where I was, and where I wanted to take it. I picked up the laptop and continued typing:

Doubling the mystery of why agriculture was chosen as the preferred lifestyle of the great majority of the world's population, is the mystery of why it developed *when* it did—independently at multiple locations in such a relatively narrow window of time—though people had been, we might assume, intellectually capable of comprehending a process as complex as planting and harvesting for at least 100,000 years.

Perhaps a partial explanation can be found in the fact that the climate became more stable at the beginning of that time period and has remained unusually stable to this day. Surely this would have made it more possible for people to successfully plant and harvest crops.[16] But while a stable climate would have provided an increased opportunity for the successful production of crops, it offers us nothing in the way of an explanation as to why people would have wished to become farmers in the first place, when the cost of making that initial transition was apparently so high.

What had I said about that? I asked myself. I looked back at what I had written before, and found the phrase: "less well nourished, experienced more disease, and lived shorter lives." Good, I thought—then I had made it clear how high that cost had been. I went on writing:

What's remarkable is that this sort of broad-scale shift in human culture is not unique to the beginnings of agriculture. A surge in human rock-art production took place in a similarly short time period—appearing for the first time at widely separate locations throughout the then-populated world, from about 32,000 to 27,000 BP[17]—a development that cannot be correlated with any widespread change in the physical environment, such as a shift in climate would involve.

So if we are to understand what motivated these changes, we must look beyond evolution (for we had achieved modern status and dispersed long before these changes occurred), and we must look, also, beyond widespread environmental changes as an explanation for these developments, for no satisfactory answer is offered there. The answer, I propose, can only be found by looking deeper, into the very heart of human nature itself.

I sat back and thought about how to get at this idea. I had a feeling for the thing I wanted to say, and I wondered how I could convey that feeling, as well as the ideas that shaped it. I thought about this for several minutes, and gradually an idea took form.

"I remember visiting with a friend of mine, in her home, when her daughter was about four years old," I typed.

While my friend and I spoke, her daughter idly entertained herself by putting her hand, with fingers spread, against a blank piece of paper. She then drew around it with a crayon. When she was done, she held up the paper and shook it happily.

"Look, Mommy," she exclaimed. "It's my hand!"

I remember, as a young child, helping my mother repair the mud wall of our home after the heavy monsoon rains. While building up the old walls, I would often simply imitate my mother's motions, smoothing the mud out in front of me, but sometimes I would stop and lift my hand from the mud, thus leaving an impression of my hand there, an action from which I would take a certain delight, for it was *my* hand which had left that impression—like no other hand. No other hand would fit there. And so it was something I had made, which in a certain sense represented myself.

Such hand stencils and hand prints, done in paint on cave walls, are amongst the most common images in prehistoric art, and can be found all over the world: in Africa, Asia, Europe, Australia, and the Americas.[18] It seems it is a rather universal human impulse to make such a mark, and perhaps it has as universal a motivation behind it. It seems to be saying: "There before me is something *I* have made, which represents myself."

I looked around for some quotes I had brought along, which I thought would go well in the next paragraph. When I found them, I went on typing:

This experience of self-discovery through art is part of the great heritage of artistic expression, and is known to artists young and old. Art is inherently an act of expression, and through our own expression we encounter our selves. As the painter Joseph Glasco said: "You paint, then, not what you see, but what you are," an idea which is echoed in Jackson Pollock's statement: "Painting is self-discovery. Every good artist paints what he is."[19]

Perhaps the wave of interest in artistic expression, which began to gather in so much of the world at about 32,000 BP, and which continued to deepen and spread thereafter, represented a growing interest in just that—self-discovery.

I sat back and smiled. I thought that made the point quite well, but it was an important point, and I would need to reinforce it by discussing the details of how people expressed themselves during that era. I thought about this and decided I could best begin by talking about the beads that had been made during this time period.

I was excited to go on, but first I asked Laura if she would mind if I had half of the last biscuit, left over from our breakfast.

"Take the whole thing, if you want," she said, and handed it to me. I took it, had a bite, and began to type again:

A similar interpretation may be inferred from the bead-making activities of the people of that time. While evidence for bead-making dates the practice back to more than 100,000 BP, the making of beads did not become prevalent until after 36,000 BP, and had not fully taken root around the world until perhaps 9,000 BP.[20] So, roughly speaking, during the same time frame in which art was becoming a well-established practice globally, so was bead-making. How the beads were principally used—in trade, or for personal adornment—we can only guess, but it is not unreasonable to assume that at least part of this gathering interest in bead-making was fueled by an increasing interest in self-adornment.

As anyone who has dressed him or her self in special attire for a party can attest—how we clothe and decorate ourselves is part of how we represent ourselves, not just to others, but to ourselves. It is a form of self-expression, and as such, of self-discovery, as well.

What we see, then, beginning to take root by not later than 32,000 BP, is a gradually increasing interest in the self, as revealed by an increased engagement in behavior that involved self-expression, and the self-discovery that, at some level, invariably accompanies such expression. But how focused or active was this dawning interest in self, which these activities reveal?

I set down my laptop computer and got up to use the toilet. When I came back, Laura asked me if I would like to go to lunch. I lay down on the bed and pointed out to her that they hadn't banged on the pot to summon us yet.

"Indira, they did that about twenty minutes ago. You must have been really engrossed in what you were writing," she said.

"Wow. I guess *so*," I said. So we quickly pulled ourselves together and set off for another repeat of the same meal we had had every time we had eaten in the dining room so far. While we were dining, we heard the *Tshatshi's* engines throttle down, and then go silent. The barges coasted for several seconds longer, and then came to a smooth stop in the water. Laura asked one of the waiters what was going on, and he told her he didn't know—it was an unscheduled stop. From the windows which ringed the room, we could see perhaps half a dozen large dugout canoes rowing away from the flat, foremost barge, each holding between five and ten passengers, heading for shore.

Other than this unexpected promenade, it was an uneventful meal. Afterwards, we stood out on the deck outside the dining room doors and talked a little about what we wanted to do with the afternoon. My writing had been going so well, I kind of wanted to get back to it. Laura was agreeable to spending some more time on her work, as well, so we headed back to the cabin.

To make things a little nicer for ourselves, and because our cabin had gotten hot in the afternoon sun (a problem which no amount of running our debilitated air conditioner could cure), we decided to pull our little table and chairs back outside, again, and set them up so our chairs would be facing the water. We put the little table against the cabin wall between us.

It was surprisingly quiet with the engines halted, and I sat for a time staring absently at the shore—at the way the sunlight sparkled on the leaves of the trees as the breeze lifted them, at the water birds gliding overhead, and at the dark shadows at the river's edge where, I supposed, hippos lurked.

After a time, people appeared from out of the dark recesses of the rainforest, climbed into their canoes, and began rowing back towards us where we were, still, anchored to the muddy bottom of the Congo River.

I pulled my chair up close to the railing so I could prop my feet there, and with knees bent, put the computer on my lap and scrolled through what I had written before lunch. It was such a beautiful day, with a blue sky, and a handful of clouds strewn about, and I was still enjoying soaking up the tropical warmth after a winter begun in the foothills of the Colorado Rockies. With a full stomach and a quiet breeze, I had to read through what I had written earlier two or three times before it really came into focus for me.

I remember trying to simplify what it said in my mind. I picked up a scrap of paper I had written other notes on, and wrote out this summary of what I had written so far, just to get it clear in my own thinking:

Art developed over a wide area, in a comparatively short period of time, as did agriculture. Its development reflected a growing interest in self-expression and self-discovery.

Right, I thought, and reread the last line I had written before we had gone to lunch: "But how focused or active was this dawning interest in self, which these activities reveal?"

If I was going to carry this forward, it seemed to me that first I had to somehow describe what the art of this era was like—to show some of the patterns in the types of images rendered—after all, I thought, which images an artist chooses to create says a lot about who that person is and what's going on in his or her heart and mind.

As I picked up the laptop to write, I both heard and felt the *Tshatshi's* engines rumble to life beneath me. I glanced up—the canoes were gone from the water. "They must have arrived back on the barge," I thought, as I looked out at the empty water they had just crossed and at the dark trees hanging above. It seemed the barge had made an unscheduled stop to allow some people to make a trip ashore.

As we got underway again, I positioned the little computer more comfortably on my lap and began to type:

To answer this question, let's look in more detail at the art of this era—from roughly 32,000 to 10,000 BP.

I paused to think about this for another minute or two, trying to order in my mind what I would have to say, and in what sequence I would say it. I would start with art that portrayed animals, I concluded, and then discuss art that displayed images of people. I began again:

Animals are amongst the most common images in the art of this time. They are rendered in a variety of artistic styles in different traditions around the world. They are sometimes stylized, but are more often naturalistic in their representation.

The artists of this era often showed a remarkable skill in making beautiful and accurate images of the animals they depicted, with every facet of the animal's physical form carefully represented, from skillfully drawn heads and faces, to well-formed bodies, legs, and tails.

Human images are also a part of this early art, though they appear less frequently than do images of animals. What's of interest, though, is that while artists showed their skills for creating detailed representational art when depicting animals, they did not bother to apply these same skills when rendering images of human beings.

In European art of this era, for example, human bodies may be roughly sketched on cave walls, or more carefully crafted in stone, but human faces—if rendered at all—are most generally indicated with only a few casual lines. Indeed, as one looks around the world at the art of this time period, one finds that human faces are either barely indicated, or more commonly, are not represented by any marks at all.[21]

I paused, and then typed in a note, in brackets, to myself: "[uniformly true?]" it said. I would have to check on it when I got back to Boulder.* I reread the last few words I had written—"human faces are either barely indicated, or more commonly, are not represented by any marks at all"— and then went on typing:

The collective effect is that these are generic human images— *and not pictures of individuals*—for what, in visual terms, more defines the individuality of a given person than the features of that person's face?

Where the face is lacking, then, so is the sense that the image is of a specific individual. So, while we may see an early fascination with self-expression (and the self-discovery that accompanies it) revealed by the making of beads, and of hand prints and stencils, and by the creation of art in general, during the time period between 32,000 and 10,000 BP, we do not yet see a really focused fascination with individuality itself.

A true interest in, and preoccupation with, the qualities of the individual do not fully develop until the following era (from 10,000 BP to the present). During this time, it becomes more and more common for people to render human images with fully drawn faces, a development that suggests an increasing interest in the individuality of the people so depicted. Eventually, this interest would give birth to the

---

* For one notable exception to this pattern, see the note at 21a in Appendix 3 (pages A10-A12). —I. K.

art of portraiture, in which the individual is not simply depicted, but is artfully revealed through the process of visual representation.

I smiled to myself and stretched, then set the laptop, and a few notes I'd held on my lap, on the deck beside my chair. It seemed to me that the article was going reasonably well, but I'd had about enough for one day.

I got up and stood by the deck's railing, looking out at the forest, which was now incredibly tall and dense as compared to yesterday's view. The river had turned north, and we were, at that moment, much nearer its eastern shore than its western one. Here, the forest seemed to rise up like a great wall of green beside us. Not only had the forest seemed to have erupted out of nowhere since the day before, but I was now much more conscious of what Laura had pointed out that morning—the river had expanded to an impressive width. It was now perhaps half a dozen miles across and spotted endlessly with islands, around which the splintered currents ran.

Such a view! I thought, as I looked out across the water. Above and around me, the sky had again begun to fill with clouds, and the wind had picked up a little.

Laura came and stood beside me, and together we looked into the forest as we motored past, wondering what sort of wildlife we might have spotted if it had not been chased away by the loud pulsing of the *Tshatshi's* motors.

We both wished we could have gone ashore and wandered into that green world. It looked cool and inviting, mysterious and elementally alive. We both felt a little sad to think that it would be another couple of weeks before we reached the Ituri and could really immerse ourselves in a forest like the one we saw passing right now along the river's eastern shore, so tantalizingly close.

A gust of wind caught us off guard, and we dashed to pick up our papers and things before the wind could take them away. After that, we moved our belongings back inside and spent the rest of the afternoon there, with Laura continuing to read her book on the Mbuti, and me listening again to the Bira language tapes with which Lisa Xiang had provided us.

❀   ❀   ❀

"Pause," Paul said.

"Pausing. End of section," Kiki responded.

It seemed a good time to take a break from the story, Paul thought, as he took a bite of the no-heat travel meal he had fished out of one of the side pockets of his pack a couple of minutes earlier. It was a little late for lunch, and Paul would have liked nothing better than to take a load off his feet for a while, but even so, he had decided not to stop while he ate—in part because he hoped that if he kept going he might reach a comfortable campsite soon.

Where Paul was now, the trail had become separated from the creek, and he was hoping that by the time he reached the next campsite, the trail would have rejoined it. There, he hoped, he would ease his sore feet out of his shoes and soak them in the cool, running water—and not have to put his shoes back on again for the rest of the day.

Paul was beginning to wish that he had stopped at the first campsite he had passed, earlier that day—but his feet had seemed to be holding up then, however marginally, and he had thought it too early in the day to stop. Now, his progress was slowed by the blisters on his heels, and he had begun to feel that he would never reach the next campsite, though they had seemed well spaced the day before.

While the campsites gave the impression of being more spaced out, the trail now seemed busier than it had the day before. Paul had crossed paths with two sets of hikers—the first, made up of two young men, had passed Paul on their way in, but had not spoken (probably, Paul had thought, because they could hear Kiki reciting to him in Dr. Kumar's voice). Later, Paul had passed an older woman hiking alone on her way out. She had nodded and smiled at him warmly—but again, had not interrupted the recitation.

As Paul walked along now, he tried to distract himself from his sore feet— and his worries of not being able to go any further until they healed—by thinking again about the transport he would build, and how he might fit together the various parts he had identified during his stay at the Inn in Strandford.

Paul so wished he could actually get his hands on these parts now, so he could tinker with them and see how they might actually be combined together. He tried again, as he had the afternoon before, to turn each part around in his head and imagine how the various connections could be made to work, but again came to the same conclusion he had then—that there was no point in struggling to make such guesses. What he needed was to have the parts before him, along with all the tools that might be necessary to make adjustments.

Somehow, Paul thought, he would have to find a way to pay for the parts— and do so sooner rather than later.

As Paul limped along, he began to think about what he would be able to do to earn money in this world, and not just a little bit for mapping and planting a field, but substantial money, enough to buy all the specialized equipment he would need in order to construct a new transport.

What such work might be seemed impossible to guess at. For one thing, he had no idea what work might be available that would match his specialized skills—just as he had no idea what such work might pay or what the parts and equipment he needed would cost. No, all in all, he thought, there were too many variables to make any but the wildest guess.

Still, Paul found himself trying to make comparisons between this world and his, assuming similar relative values were placed on his labor in both worlds and on the parts needed to build a transport. He could certainly not have funded his own research on his salary in his world. He had had to depend quite heavily on Corprogov funding to pay not just for the parts, but for the costs associated with running a lab, the salaries of his assistants, and so forth.

But now would be different, Paul assured himself. He would make do without a lab, or assistants. Instead, he would work alone, perhaps in a small room he would rent and live in. And he would not waste time and resources on early models or prototypes—but rather just start out building the transport he would use. That would help save funds, too.

Even in his world, he might have made such an arrangement work, if he had already had experience with building a fully functional transport (as he did now) and—Paul thought with a smile—if he had not been so determined to set aside money from his salary to buy nice things for Sheila.

Sheila. She was certainly a more pleasing subject of thought than frustrations in building a new transport, and now Paul let his attention turn to her. It was, after all, nice to have some reason to smile, even when his feet hurt so much.

Twice since they had met, he had bought them transportation to the Santa Barbara Islands, and gone to the best hotels and restaurants there. Both of those trips had been wonderful vacations, and both he and Sheila had come back tanned and relaxed.

Once Paul had purchased transportation for the two of them to Lake Tahoe (which was farther away than most people ever got to go in a lifetime), but Paul had found that trip depressing, because he remembered too well the stories his grandfather had told him about how that lake had once been. The water, his grandfather had told him, had been so crystal clear as to give the impression of floating on air when looking down from a boat through twenty-five meters of it—and while floating on all that "air," one could look down at the bottom of the lake, and all in one view, see trout by the thousands swimming there in the sunshine.

At the center of the lake (where the water was so deep that a building one hundred and sixty stories tall could be hidden in it upright) the water had been cobalt blue, not merely reflecting the sky, but seemingly taking on its own true color. Around the lake had been virgin forests with tall stands of pine and fir, within which all sorts of animals had flourished.

The land and lake, Paul discovered when he went there, were far different from what they had once been. The water of the lake was foul-smelling and full of algae, which turned it a greenish brown. It harbored very little life. Worse still, the growing heat of climate change not only had changed the nature of the lake, but had dried the region and left the water level so low that a great, white "bathtub ring" lay on the rocks around its shore, where the drying water had left mineral deposits behind. The mountainsides surrounding the lake were nearly bare, having lost most of their trees to drought, bark beetles, and fire. Along with the trees, all the other plants and animals that depended on that forest ecosystem had died out, too.

Still, Paul had to admit that the trip itself was pleasant enough, if one's expectations were held low, and Paul had thought the vacation had pleased Sheila greatly—if only for the glamour of traveling so far and being able to tell her friends about it—and in the end, the fact that it had pleased Sheila had pleased Paul, and made the trip all right for him as well.

All in all, once a year since they had met, Paul had provided a vacation of some sort for the two of them. He remembered Sheila telling him with delight about how jealous it made her friends feel. Paul had smiled, pleased he could do something that gave Sheila such pleasure. It was much the same when he bought her clothes or expensive jewelry—or some of the hard-to-find food items that he knew she liked especially well.

On such occasions, Sheila would always squeal with delight and throw her arms around his neck. Often, later, Paul would see her showing these things off to her friends. It gave him such pleasure to know he could offer her these few, fine things, in a world in which any luxury had become so hard to come by. With shortages of various sorts and rationing in effect, many people with money had trouble acquiring anything that offered special comfort. Paul, however, had had to work out ways to get around such limitations. Because of his work and the importance of having the materials he needed, Paul had sometimes had to resort to buying goods on the black market. This could be dangerous, because it was illegal, and the punishments Corprogov imposed were harsh—but once Paul had established connections there, he was willing to use them, occasionally, to purchase something special for Sheila.

The truth was, he wished he could give her so much more, to protect her from any hardship, and to give her the fruits of the work he had strived so long to accomplish: a well world, and a secure and comfortable place for her within it. Perhaps in time, he could make all of that hers.

Paul came to the top of a small rise and started gingerly down the other side. He was aware, of course, that it might be nice to be valued in other ways by Sheila, though he was happy he could please her with the things he could provide. He knew that he loved her in a way that resonated deeply within him, and he suspected that she loved him like that also—though such things were never expressed directly between them. After all, why else would she have chosen him from among so many others? Paul reasoned. Surely, he felt, any man would see in her what he did, and any man would choose to be with her—and yet she had picked him out of all others.

It was mid-afternoon by the time Paul came to the next campsite on the trail. The path, by then, had rejoined the small creek it had trailed along earlier. The campsite was located along it, at a place where a pool formed. Scattered pine trees grew around it. Above the camp was a steep rocky ridge, with broad bands of some sort of white rock intermixed with bands of brown. It had quite a striking appearance.

Paul stopped at the camp with a sense of relief and dropped his heavy pack to the ground. Every step had become painful, due to the blisters on his heels, and his pack (which had seemed quite light when he'd set out four days before) had grown to seem burdensomely heavy as the day wore on.

Paul took off his shoes and carefully peeled the socks from his feet, before gratefully plunging his feet into the cool water of the pool.

For several minutes he sat quietly, then pulled his pack a little closer and dug out the pair of socks he had worn earlier that day. He washed both pair in the pool, rung them out carefully, then left them drying nearby on a sunny bit of rock.

It was a beautiful spot, Paul thought, as he looked around the campsite. Not a bad place to be stuck for the rest of the day. As Paul had eaten lunch along the trail earlier, there was little else to do now but recline at the pool's edge and let the cool water take the sting out of his blisters.

Paul lay down and closed his eyes against the dappled light filtering down through the trees above. A soft breeze played along his skin, while birds sang and twittered in the trees. Somewhere, a squirrel scolded.

Paul lay like that for a little while, thinking of nothing in particular, then realized he could be listening to Dr. Kumar's book and asked Kiki to resume recitation. Kiki's voice drifted up from where she was clipped on the front of Paul's shirt and filled the little grove around the water with the softly accented speech of Dr. Kumar.

◇   ◇   ◇

Laura and I went to dinner in a warm drizzly soup that passed for rain. The day was dimming, and somewhere, I imagined, the sun was setting over the water, and the forest stood, somewhere to the west of us, but amidst the foggy rain we traveled within, it was hard to say just where.

We entered the dining room and looked around for a place to sit. The room seemed surprisingly bright in contrast to the watery dusk outside. Everywhere around us were people wearing brightly colored fabrics of Africa. Floating on the warm, humid air was a melodious cacophony of voices, speaking in French and Lingala.

I saw two empty chairs at a table to our right and stepped towards them just as a couple of young men arrived at that table and seated themselves in the spots I'd thought to claim for Laura and myself. As I turned back towards Laura, I caught a glimpse of Raymond at a half-empty table in the far corner of the room. He had caught sight of Laura, and was looking towards her with an expression that seemed to me, in that fleeting moment, an amalgam of pain and longing, love and bitter tenderness.

A moment later, Laura turned in his direction, and Raymond's expression widened into an open smile. He waved at Laura to get her attention. She saw him and waved back, then turned towards me to make sure I had seen him also, and started across the room to Raymond's table.

We took our seats, facing out towards the misty night. The others at the table were with another group, and until our arrival, Raymond had been eating alone. It occurred to me then how different this river trip would be for a solitary traveler than it was for Laura and me, traveling together. I thought a little about the look I'd seen on Raymond's face, when he'd first seen Laura, before she'd turned his way, but he greeted us with such boisterous good cheer that any discomfort I may have felt was soon swept aside.

Dinner was, of course, a repeat of previous meals, and after we were served, we poked at our food and chatted about how strange the weather had gotten, and the peculiar fact that the barge had stopped for an hour or two in the middle of the afternoon.

"It was a funeral," Raymond told us. "Someone in the crew told me that a passenger on the flat barge, a child, had died of cholera, and they stopped the barge so that her body could be taken ashore and buried."

"That's so sad!" I said.

"Oh, her poor family!" Laura said, and then added, after a moment, "So—there's cholera on board?"

Raymond nodded. "There must be. I haven't heard of anybody else being sick, though."

From where we sat, we could see the searchlights cutting into the misty rain—white light swallowed up in a white fog, which was quickly turning to gray. Raymond stared out into this dimming world of mist and rain, and for a minute or two seemed lost in solemn thought, then he appeared to reel his feelings back in, and he turned to me with a sober, friendly look, and said, "So, you said you've been working on a paper—is that right?"

"Yes," I told him, and I realized I, too, had been lost in thought. There were more potential hazards on this journey than we had realized when we'd set out.

"How's that been going?" Raymond asked, then took a bite of cooked carrot.

"Pretty well," I answered. "I got a little more written today."

"I wish I could claim to have spent my time so productively," Raymond said, shaking his head. "I spent a good bit of the day browsing the stalls and eating *mandazis*."

"What are *mandazis*?" Laura asked.

"Those fried dough balls, really a sort of doughnut, you see them making around here," Raymond answered.

"Oh, I haven't tried them," Laura said. "Are they good?"

"Delicious," Raymond answered, with a little smile on his face. He unenthusiastically split a meatball with his fork, then glanced my way. It occurred to me that this must have been his fifth meal of meatballs since boarding the barge. "You said your paper was about, ah, human culture in prehistory? Do I have that right?" he asked.

"Pretty much," I said. "What I was working on today had to do with how our sense of self evolved over the last 30,000 years or so." I was vaguely aware of Raymond having navigated the conversation to more pleasant topics and away from the death on board.

"Interesting subject," Raymond said, raising his eyebrows. He took a drink of water. "That's something primatologists concern themselves with, you know—self awareness." He picked up half a meatball with his fork.

"No, I had no idea," I answered.

"Yeah. Not all animals are self aware, you know—but the great apes are." He put the piece of meatball in his mouth.

"How is it possible to know that?" Laura asked. It seemed an obvious enough question—how could someone tell what an animal's perceptions were? Raymond swallowed and answered.

"Well, a man named Gordon Gallup came up with an ingenious experiment about, ah, well, in the early '80s. He left a mirror in a cage that housed chimpanzees and watched how they responded. For the first couple of days, they reacted as though there were another chimpanzee in the mirror. They made social gestures of various sorts towards their "new companion," but by about day three they seemed to realize that it was their own reflection they were looking at, and they began to use the mirror to examine parts of their own bodies they hadn't been able to see before, like inside their mouths, say, and to make faces in the mirror, I suppose just to entertain themselves. It seemed pretty obvious they were consciously examining themselves in the mirror, but just to make sure, Gallup put red marks on their foreheads and ears without their knowing it, and then let them loose with the mirror again. The chimpanzees looked in the mirror and repeatedly touched their own foreheads and their own ears where the red marks were—they understood it was their own reflection they were looking at."

"That's fascinating," I said. "And so this represents self awareness because..."

"Because for them to be able to look in a mirror and say 'that's me' they must first have a concept of 'me' to begin with. You can't say 'I see myself' unless you can conceive of yourself," Raymond answered. "Anyway, the test has been done on all sorts of animals since then. All the great apes— orangutans, gorillas, chimpanzees, and bonobos—are capable of self awareness, although with gorillas it's a bit iffy, though certainly some gorillas are capable of recognizing themselves in a mirror."

"What about other animals?" Laura asked. I looked over at her—she was nearly half done with her dinner—and I thought with a smile that she was never one to be picky about what food she was served, nor how often she was served it.

"Lesser apes are not self aware, nor are monkeys. But monkeys and certain other animals, pigeons for example, can use information reflected in a mirror to learn more about the environment they're in—like, say, they can use a reflected image to locate an object that wouldn't be visible to them otherwise."

"Huh," I said. "So they could think, for example: 'hey, there's some food that the mirror is reflecting,' and go find the food, but when they see their own reflection, they think: 'hey, who's that monkey?'—or pigeon, or whatever."

"Yeah, that's about it. There's also been research done on dolphins," Raymond told us.

"Oh, yeah?" Laura said. "And how do they do?"

"They pass. Dolphins can conceive of themselves," Raymond said and took another bite of his potato.

"What fascinating research," I said, and thought for a moment. "I'm just trying to imagine if there's some way of relating this to the work I'm doing." I looked out the window at the deepening white night. The world seemed filled with the swirling, warm mist. Through my mind danced impressions of people painting on cave walls—murals filled with images of bison and deer, and next to them, faceless human figures. These impressions were followed by images of apes peering into mirrors, examining red spots on their ears and foreheads. Together, they made a dizzying blur.

"Well, we *are* related to the great apes," Laura offered.

"Yeah," I said, frowning. That was true, but I couldn't see how to use it.

"One of the ways this research has been used," Raymond offered, "is to try to guess at what point in the evolution of primates..."

"Wait—are we primates?" Laura asked.

"Yes," Raymond said. "We—the apes, monkeys, lemurs—and of course, the ancestors we all hold in common for perhaps the last sixty million years. So, I was saying, this research has been used to estimate at what point in our evolution we first became self aware."

"How does knowing about modern animals tell us anything about that?" I asked.

"Well," Raymond said. He looked thoughtful for a moment, then set down his fork and pulled a pen and a small pad of paper from his breast pocket. "It's like this," he said. He opened up the pad and sketched out something to show us. It took him a moment, and then he set the pad on the table. What he had drawn looked like this:

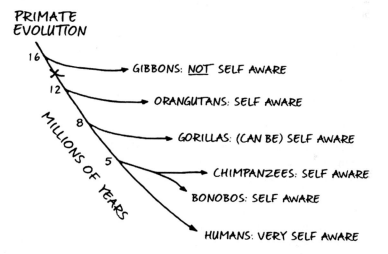

"This represents developments in primate evolution," Raymond said, pointing at the piece of paper with the tip of his pen. "We last shared a common ancestor with gibbons about sixteen million years ago, with orangutans about twelve million years ago, with gorillas eight, and with bonobos and chimpanzees about five or six million years ago. All the great apes—orangutans, gorillas, chimpanzees, and bonobos—are capable of self awareness. Gibbons are not. So, it's presumed that somewhere in here," he pointed to an "X" he had marked on the page, "between sixteen and twelve million years ago, the capacity for self awareness first appeared within the order of primates. And so it's present in all the great apes today—and in us."

I looked closely at the piece of paper and nodded my head. "May I keep this, Raymond?" I asked.

"Sure," he answered. He tore the piece of paper from the pad and handed it to me, then pocketed the pad and pen. "I don't know if that's of any use to you," he said. "It's certainly much before the time period you're talking about."

"That's true," I said. "But it's really interesting, and it kind of puts things in perspective." I slipped the piece of paper into my pocket.

The conversation moved on, then. We told Raymond about our afternoon and evening on the flat barge the day before, the people we had met, and the delicious food we had eaten. We discussed the journey upriver, the commotion and vitality of barge life, and the research we all planned to do when we reached our destinations.

When dinner was over, we said good night to Raymond and walked back towards our cabin. The rain had stopped, and the world was filled with a milky mist, which was white wherever light hit it, and which made a foggy wall of black everywhere else.

On our walk back, Laura and I stopped and peered over the railing for a while. The mist was thickening, and the search lights penetrated it haphazardly, revealing patches of dark water where the light cut through. I was thinking about what Raymond had said, about a chimpanzee having to live with a mirror for about three days before it could look into it and come up with the realization: "Oh, that's me!" I didn't think an adult human who had never before seen a mirror would take nearly that long.

"You know," I said to Laura. "I was thinking about what Raymond said about self awareness, and I think it's helped me pin down what I'm trying to say in my paper."

"Yeah?"

"Yeah. Well, it's clear we have been capable of self awareness for a long time, but in the time period I'm writing about, we quickly became much more *preoccupied* with that sort of awareness. We went from being capable of self conception, to becoming preoccupied, to some extent at least, with how we conceived of ourselves—with who we were. And it may be that it's that preoccupation, that active awareness of and focus on selfhood, that distinguishes us from other primates—and other animals in general."

Laura stared into the mist, looking thoughtful. After a few moments, she told me, "I'm not sure I could say why, exactly, but that rings true for me, Indira." We stood there for a while, watching as the fog swirled around us and the search lights danced through it. There was something sort of hypnotic about the swoop and sweep of the lights.

After a while, I said, "We were lucky to meet up with someone who's as good company as Raymond."

"Yeah, I guess that was lucky," Laura said. The two search lights swept through the scene ahead of us with an irregular cadence, which made me think, somehow, of moths fluttering in slow motion.

"What do you think of him personally?" Laura added.

"He seems like a nice enough fellow," I said. "Why? How does he strike you?"

"He seems nice enough, I guess," she said, but there was something hesitant in her tone.

"But...?" I prompted.

Laura shrugged and sort of squinted up one side of her face. "But...well, I have the feeling there's something else going on with him, that's all. I can't quite put my finger on it. It's like, there are things going on on the inside of him that aren't what he's showing us." She paused, then added, "It just makes me a little uneasy."

The fog above the river was thick in places, torn thin in others. Riding through it was like passing through veils.

"Yeah, I have a feeling like that about him, too," I answered, then told Laura about the look I'd seen on Raymond's face when we'd first gone to dinner that night. It was a look of longing, I told her, sweet, but also troubled. It had made me uneasy, as well.

Laura said she'd seen him looking at me like that, too, a couple of times. She hadn't known what to make of it.

I remember just standing there then, as waves of mist, which seemed to have been torn apart by the search lights, passed over the barge.

"Well, you know, it really doesn't matter," Laura added finally. "He said he was getting off in Mbandaka, didn't he?"

"Yeah, I think so."

"Well, that can't be more than a couple days away. After that, I doubt we'll ever see him again," Laura looked towards me, "and until then, it's like you said, we're lucky to have someone around who's such good company."

"Yeah," I agreed, nodding.

Laura stepped back from the railing. "Want to head back?" she said, cocking her head towards the cabin.

"Sure," I said. We put our arms around one another and strolled back to our room, and I wondered if I would ever find out what Raymond's story was.

When we got back to the room we both read for a while. I made another journal entry, then we decided to retire early for the night. I was glad to do so, as I hadn't slept well at night since we'd boarded the barge, and since I was exhausted, too, from days filed with new sights and sounds and much concentrated thinking. I went right to sleep, early as it was, but Laura told me in the morning that she'd laid awake for hours, imagining the forest to come, the Mbuti, and all she hoped she might discover from the research ahead. She said a short while after I'd gone to sleep, the barge's throbbing engines had fallen silent, and we had come to a stop in the water. She'd looked outside, and found that the fog had thickened and filled the dark night. We were blind in the water, and could not go forward until the fog cleared, presumably hours later.

In any case, I was glad to get a good night's rest, the only one I got while we were on the barge.

⊙ 12 ⊙

"Kiki, stop recitation," Paul said. He had begun to feel groggy and had moved to a more comfortable spot in the shade of one of the trees, where he had lain down to take a nap. His feet, he had decided, had soaked long enough—now sleep was what he wanted.

By the time Paul woke, it was late afternoon. He felt hungry and stiff and sore, but his feet hurt less than they had on the trail. For a little while, he lay quietly under the pines, taking in their scent and the soft rustling sound the breeze made through their needle-like leaves. A squirrel came part way down the trunk of one of the trees nearest Paul, stopped to look at him, then went the other way. A small group of birds with blue backs and white bellies hopped and skipped around the open ground, looking for insects.

Paul smiled, filled with delight at this remarkable scene—then he stretched, and sat up, and took a look at his feet. The blisters on both heels were open and rubbed raw. They stung when the breeze hit them, but otherwise produced only a dull ache. Paul was concerned about how they would feel when he had to put his shoes back on the next morning and decided to go through his pack and see if there was anything he might use as a bandage to keep the shoes from rubbing.

Paul had almost forgotten about the "sojourner's aid pack" he had been given at the store in Strandford. He opened it now, and looked through the small first-aid kit inside. It contained a small vial labeled "Immuno Enhancer." Other vials said "System Boost," "Venom Blaster," and "Sun Stop."

None of these seemed at all relevant. Paul dug a little deeper through the small silvery box and soon came across a slim, sealed envelope, which said "Dermo Mend" on its label.

Paul pealed back the envelope, which contained two of something he took to be some kind of self-adhesive bandage. He thought they might form an effective barrier between his shoes and his heels, so he put them on.

Each patch wrapped neatly around a heel. Paul noticed immediately that both the sting and ache were instantly gone.

Pretty good, he thought, then carefully slipped his feet back into his shoes. Still pain free!

Pretty darn good, Paul thought, then looked back through the vials he had pushed aside, searching for something that might be good for soreness. He settled on "System Boost" and, without much thought, went ahead and took it.

Certainly, there was no instantaneous effect like there had been for the patches. In fact, as Paul sat waiting, it seemed there was no effect at all.

Oh well, Paul thought—so long as it didn't hurt him, he didn't care. The blisters were the real problem, and that seemed to be solved.

Paul could see that he had a good bit of daylight left and decided to spend it setting up his sleep bivy and eating dinner. The travel meal he chose this time was spicier than the others, which was nice for a change. Paul sat at the pool's edge, eating it and listening to the slow movement of water.

When the meal was done, Paul's feet still felt fine. He was restless, and in any case, with the surrounding trees casting the long, slanting shadows of late afternoon, it was clearly far too early for bed. He decided, instead, to take a stroll up to the ridge, which overlooked the camp on its north side, and see if he could climb up the steep ridge face far enough to take in a view of the surrounding land.

Paul stood up and stretched, then pulled his jacket from his pack and set off for the ridge.

He didn't have far to go before the terrain turned steep, but he managed to make his way up the sharp incline by carefully choosing his footing and often using his hands to steady himself as he climbed the more vertical sections.

Soon he had reached a height where the view was impressive. Paul smiled as he took it in, then started looking around for a place to sit. A narrow, level area, almost like a path, ran along the face of the ridge. Paul followed it a little way, then spotted a wide ledge a few meters below him, cut out of the white rock.

Paul looked around carefully for a way to get down to it. The only route he could see—descending directly from his little "path" above—was covered in loose rock. Paul looked it over carefully, then concluded it was too dangerous to attempt the climb down. The terrain was very steep here—much of it like a cliff—and he was afraid he would slip and not be able to stop his descent. Instead, Paul climbed a couple of meters above his path, where an outcropping of rock protruded from the ridge.

As Paul took a seat there, he felt pleased with the spot. The view was extraordinary—well worth the climb—and remarkably, his feet hadn't bothered him at all during it.

As Paul settled his gaze upon the land to the south and the broad sky above it, he noticed four large birds circling in the evening air. They soared almost motionless in great arcing circles. They didn't seem to be coordinating their flight at all, as they were far from one another.

One of them was much nearer to Paul than the others, and it was only when it glided over the ridge on which Paul sat that he got an idea of how truly enormous it was. He had the impression, then, that if he had lain down beside just *one* of its wings, he'd have found that wing to be almost as long as he was tall!

Paul sat a long time, his mouth agape, watching the birds soaring effortlessly above him and trying to remember the stories his grandfather had told him about birds with a vast wingspan, which had once lived all along the West Coast of North America, from British Columbia in the north, to at least as far as Baja California in the south.

His grandfather had told him, Paul recalled, that these birds had been known, at times, to attain wingspans of more than *four meters*. Four meters! Paul thought—when he himself fell well short of two in height!

Paul remembered his grandfather telling him that these birds—these "condors," as they had been called—had been seen gathering by the *hundreds* to feast when carrion was plentiful, though typically they had been seen in far fewer numbers than that.

Still, Paul thought, as he stared skyward—it must have been an incredible sight to see such huge gatherings of birds which were so remarkably large that seeing one alone was a sight worth remembering!

Sadly, Paul thought, on his world, these "condors" had not survived the onslaught against them, and had eventually all been wiped out.

Paul watched in wonder as the four enormous birds smoothly glided through the sky, high above him, without even a wing beat—as though they had become part of the air itself, and so could float effortlessly within it.

Somehow—wonderfully, amazingly, Paul thought—*here, the condors had survived!*

Paul couldn't imagine his good fortune at seeing these amazing birds and wished that somehow his grandfather could have been there with him to take in the sight. He sat like this for a long time, watching the birds in the fading day, and remembering other stories his grandfather had told him about the one-time abundance of animals in the California wilds.

Paul's grandfather had told him of explorers and settlers who wrote of bears so numerous that they roamed in groups by the dozen; sea otters gathering and playing in countless colonies of several hundred each, spread out all along the coast; shellfish so plentiful that the Indians had made huge mounds of their empty shells; and of a broad lake described as being "as full of white geese as of water."

What a world it must have been! Paul thought, as he stared up at the soaring condors. What a world his earth *had been*—and what an amazing world this earth *still was!*

As evening gathered, one after another of the birds disappeared from the sky. Home to roost for the night, Paul thought. The western sky was rose-tinted, while the east had begun to gray. Paul had begun to wonder if it might be possible, once he had his transport working (and he had returned home to deliver the news of this new world), for him to come back to this world and collect animals from this earth to send home and repopulate extinct species there.

The thought, once it had occurred to him, seemed thrilling—but all sorts of problems came quickly to mind. First, aiming mechanisms would have to be made highly precise, as there would be no point in delivering hairless, nailless, featherless creatures to his world unless he could be certain he could contain them in some sort of enclosure once they arrived, protect them, and then deliver them to fitting habitats where, hopefully, they might reproduce and multiply.

And then, of course, there was the question of where that habitat would be. With climate change having so affected the weather and the seasons, simply placing an animal in the area where that species had once lived would not be sufficient. And, of course, with so many plants and animals having gone extinct, even if one could discover a place that had the right climate for a given species, the creatures that species had evolved to eat might not exist there at all—or perhaps not anywhere in Paul's world.

Clearly, even if the aiming and energy problems were solved, simply sending back animals would be of no use. Whole ecosystems would have to be rebuilt in unison. Preparation and planning would be essential to the success of any such program.

Paul glanced around and realized how quickly the light had begun to fade. If he didn't get back to camp soon, he would have trouble seeing well enough to make his way.

Hurriedly, Paul got up and began to climb back down from his perch above the narrow pathway—but when he was nearly to the path below, his feet slipped in the loose rocks and he began to slide. He tried to catch himself by reaching out for the larger rocks along the way, but this did nothing more than dislodge these rocks, as well.

Down Paul went, and he didn't stop until he had landed on the wide, white ledge he had spotted earlier, as he had looked down from the narrow path above.

Paul's heart was racing, and his hands and arms scraped a bit, but otherwise he seemed to be intact. Shakily, Paul rose to his feet and began to try to make his way back up the steep face of the ridge. In the west, the sun had dropped below the distant hills, and only its glow was left in the evening sky.

How foolish, Paul thought. I've lost the sun, and the moon hasn't yet risen.

He looked for a good place to put his feet and hands, so he could pull himself back up to the path above, but each attempt he made only resulted in a shower of small rocks and a quick return to the ledge that had broken Paul's fall. On perhaps the fourth or fifth attempt, Paul managed to make it a little higher—but this only resulted in an uncontrolled fall, which came uncomfortably close to throwing him over the edge.

Frightened and trembling, Paul sat down to try to assess the situation. He had too little light to really see what he was doing, and he knew that another mistake like the last one could easily result in his death.

He tried to steady himself and think about this rationally. It was clear to him now that there wasn't enough light from the sun left for him to safely climb out of there, and he wasn't sure when the moon would rise again.

He tried to remember how late it was when the moon had risen the night before, but couldn't remember seeing it at all.

No, all the light he could remember had come from his small campfire.

In fact, when *had* he seen the moon last? he wondered, as he took deep breaths to try to slow his beating heart. It must have been the morning before last, when he had climbed the hill outside the lodge to listen to Dr. Kumar's memoir.

Yes, that's right, he thought. He had seen a quarter moon above the ridge to the west—and that had been late morning, after he had spent hours listening to recitation in his room.

If it was up that late before it set, it must have risen late the night before, Paul thought. He sighed. He had really gotten himself stuck. He had no flashlight with him, and, he was realizing, it could well be hours before the moon rose. And it would be a crescent moon, in any case, when it did rise— not even full enough to cast much light.

Paul sat grumbling to himself for several minutes, as he came to terms with the choice of spending a cold night on the ledge or trying to climb out without enough light. He stood up and looked at the wall again. He could see no better way to approach climbing it than what he had tried before.

After several minutes spent pointlessly reexamining the situation, Paul sat back down—worrying, now, not about how he would climb out in the darkness, but about how he would climb out at all, even with all the light the next day would bring.

What if he couldn't make his way back up? Paul pondered. He was too far from the trail for anyone to notice him here, or perhaps even to hear him if he called out to them as they passed along the trail below. And he knew no one in this world. No one would miss him. No one would come looking for him.

Paul shook his head. Whatever the morning brought, he concluded, it was clear there was nothing left to do now but get settled for the night. He lay down on his side, testing the space to lie in. It was ample enough and, with his back against the rocky wall, he was pretty sure he would be far enough from the edge not to roll off it during the night.

The rocky face of the ridge protruded out beyond the west end of the ledge Paul lay on. That should help block the westerly breeze, Paul thought—and so, he hoped, it might help to keep him from getting quite so cold during the night. At least he had thought to put on the lightweight jacket he had bought in Strandford, before leaving camp. Still, cold or not, he would just have to make the best of it, he told himself. He had no doubt he would be uncomfortable—but he was just as sure he wouldn't freeze to death. For the time being, the best thing for him to do was to try to get as comfortable as he could, and to do his best to avoid worrying.

As he thought about how little he had with him with which to make himself comfortable, he remembered that he was still wearing Kiki on his shirt.

"Kiki," he said aloud.

"Yes," she answered.

Good, it's not damaged, Paul thought. He found it strangely reassuring just to hear her voice, as though it meant, somehow, that he was not so alone in his predicament. He looked around the rocky ledge in the fading light. So this would be his home for the night, he told himself—but at least he would have Kiki for company. He considered asking her to resume recitation, but decided to make himself as comfortable as he could, first.

Paul sat up and loosened the binding on his left shoe and was about to take it off, but decided to leave it on for warmth. As he opened the bindings on his right shoe, he reflected on how he'd been finding the story told in Dr. Kumar's memoirs quite diverting—and was finding the article she was writing for the *Huginn/Muninn Newsletter* interesting, as well—but as involving as he was finding these things, he wasn't listening to the memoir to be diverted or entertained. He wanted to know how this book had helped create a world so different from his own, so much better. The truth was, he still found himself feeling skeptical that material of this sort could actually, in fact, have had any meaningful influence on this world.

Paul thought about it some more, then shook his head.

"I just don't see how any of this book could have so changed this world," he heard himself muttering aloud. Though he had not directly addressed Kiki, he realized that he had hoped she would answer.

"I'd appreciate a response, Kiki," he said, with a bit of a sigh in his voice.

"My data suggests that this chapter meets both of your criteria: high conceptual content and extensive social influence," she said.

"Just what data do you have indicating extensive social influence?" Paul asked.

After the briefest pause, Kiki, responded, "Of 7,418 articles reviewed, 68.3511% make specific reference to this chapter. Of the 2,109 articles that specifically deal with the influential effects of *Memories and Reflections*, 97.5624% make reference to this chapter," Kiki answered.

Paul rubbed his head. He wished she would be a little less technical—especially now, when he felt he could use some comfort.

"Okay," Paul said. "Kiki, could you select a passage from one of those articles—one that refers to this part of the book—and recite it to me?"

"Yes," she answered. "Identified."

"Then begin," Paul said.

Kiki's voice—now male, mature, and educated—filled the darkness around them:

> As we follow Dr. Kumar on her journey, we find her probing deeply into ideas that seem to us, somehow, cool and distant, out-of-step with the fecund tropical landscape that surrounds her. We wonder why she is taking us here, and how these puzzle pieces might fit into the larger mosaic of this legendary book.
>
> And so we choose to ride along, motoring up the Congo and into the rainforest with her. And as we go, her cool descriptions of fact, like a snowball sent gently rolling downhill, gradually pick up other insights, gathering mass and speed as they move along, until, near the end of her journey, we arrive at a splendid crescendo, when the true weight of her discoveries settles upon us.

Paul shook his head. "Okay, Kiki, you've got me convinced," he said. "I'll keep on listening. Continue recitation of Dr. Kumar's book."

Paul lay back down along the rocky wall, glad of the warmth the sun had stored there, as Kiki's voice once again took on the timber and intonation of Indira Kumar's.

◻   ◻   ◻

I woke early to the sound of people laughing on the deck below. Laura, lying next to me, continued to slumber undisturbed. I pushed back the blinds a little and discovered the day had dawned bright and clear, in surprising contrast to the milky thickness of the air the night before.

I got up and showered. I was hungry, but our breakfast would not be delivered for another hour or so, so I got out some dried fruit we'd brought along and snacked on that. I wanted to get back to work on my Huginn/Muninn article, but it was still early, and I was afraid if I pulled back the blinds so I could see, the light would disturb Laura's sleep, so I quietly carried one of the chairs outside and set to work out there, wrapped in a soft breeze and in the early morning light.

First off, I reread what I had written the day before, about the remarkable increase in art production, and what it suggested about a developing interest in selfhood, then set to typing again:

> All in all, it seems reasonable to believe that this ancient trend towards increased art and bead production reflected a parallel trend towards an increased interest in self-expression and self-discovery.
>
> But does finding a satisfactory answer to this mystery help in any way to resolve other mysteries of that era? Specifically, does it help us to answer the question of what inspired people to make the transition from hunting and gathering, to agriculture?
>
> To try to get a clearer picture of what motivated people to start domesticating plants and animals, let's begin by looking at the circumstances in which agriculture was first developed.
>
> It can be said, most simply, that agriculture developed where it could be developed. It developed where the food supply was so rich that people did not need to wander far in search of food, but could stay in one place and tend crops during their first fledgling attempts at plant husbandry. Agriculture developed, then, where the food supply was especially abundant and varied, where the soil was rich and receptive to the growing of plants, where the water supply was good and steadily available, and where there were already plants present in the environment which could be easily, and successfully, adapted to domestication.[22]
>
> But all that this tells us is that agriculture developed where the circumstances supported it—not why people would choose to engage in it, even in circumstances that were so conducive to its development. In order to answer the question of *why* this choice may have been made, let's start by imagining a person living in that environment and try to guess how and why such a person might have come to plant the first crops.

I sat still for a while, staring out at the sunlight, which slanted low through the morning sky and reflected in dazzling sparkles from the water's surface. I was trying to refine the impressions I had in my mind of just how someone would have come to plant the first crops. What would they have had to know to become prepared to do this? What might their motivations have been? What aspects of this experience would have filled them with a sense of potential—of possibility or promise?

I had been thinking about these things, now, for over two years, and the ideas I had had about them had gradually come alive in my mind. I hoped I could convey some of that feeling of reality and vitality to the people who would read my article. I liked the idea of describing all of this in terms of the motivations and actions of a single person, because then, I thought, the intuitive sense of it, and that quality of reality, could be better conveyed to the reader.

I looked over the last part of what I had just written. "Let's start by imagining a person living in that environment," it said, "and try to guess how and why such a person might have come to plant the first crops." I put my hands on the keyboard and began to type:

We can presume that this person ate well, and that, with such an abundance of wild foods available, this person—let us say "she"— completed her daily work with time to spare, and so had a certain amount of leisure time available.[23] We'll imagine her living in a vital, fertile environment with rich soil and plenty of water. Somewhere nearby grain-producing wild plants grow. She has, all her life, gathered the seeds of these plants as food and has brought them home with her, where she grinds, and cooks, and eats them.

Some of the grains fall to the ground as she carries them home. At times, she has noticed where the grains she has dropped have lain on the fertile soil near her doorway. She has seen them, after it has rained, begin to sprout, and sometimes when this has happened, some of the seedlings have taken root and become plants. Sometimes these small plants have continued to grow to maturity, and have produced more seed. She understands this cycle. And she has seen that the germinating seeds need to stay moist, or they die before plants can grow from them.

On some occasion, in an idle moment, she tries pushing some of these seeds down into the moist soil so they won't dry out in the sun. These, she notes, come up sooner and stronger than the ones left lying about.

"Look at what *I* have done," she tells herself, and understands that somehow, by pushing those seeds down into the soil, she has made the plants that grew from them the tallest and strongest of the bunch.

The next time a growing season starts, she tries pushing more seeds down into the ground and carefully keeps the soil around them moist so it won't dry out. Later, she looks on with pride as these plants flourish, and, like an artist standing back from her creation, she looks at the impact of her actions in the world as a kind of art which reflects her self, and she feels a sense of pride and self-efficacy, just as people still feel to this day when they look at a garden they have planted and see the plants there—tall and green and draped in their brightly colored and ripening fruits—satisfying and in every way worth the effort of their cultivation.

I was pleased with how this was going, and took a moment to stretch. I could hear someone knocking on a door nearby, and when the door was opened, I could hear the steward's voice wishing the occupants *"bon jour."*

Ah, breakfast! That would be nice to have.

I decided to wait to start writing again until the steward had brought our breakfast tray. I poked my head inside to see how Laura was doing—she was still sound asleep in the darkened room. It would be good to let her sleep a while longer, I thought.

When the steward came, I tiptoed inside with the tray and set it on the table. I took coffee and a biscuit for myself, then went back outside and continued writing:

> With each of the following seasons, she plants more seeds and feels a special satisfaction when she harvests the seeds of the crops she has planted, for this is something *she* has made come to pass.

Yes, that was it, I thought—*her* creation. I would like to emphasize that a little more. I took a bite of my biscuit and thought for a moment before continuing:

> And if she makes a simple bread by grinding and cooking these grains, then this bread seems somehow better to her than other bread she has eaten, because this is bread that she has made from the ground up. Before, she felt supported by the environment around her. Now, she feels she is supporting herself, and so feels a new sense of independence. All of life becomes a kind of art through which she expresses her *self.* She is filled with a dawning sense of satisfaction and self-volition—and with an expanding and deepening sense of self-identity.
>
> Others have seen what she's been doing and join her in what is, as a practical matter, a new art form, for food is still amply available without anyone having to produce it in this way. They domesticate animals and create croplands—and everywhere they look they see the canvas of the world filling up with their creations, marked by their intent. It seems more and more that the world is a mirror, showing them something of who they are, and what they are capable of.

I paused and read back through what I had just written with some satisfaction, then went on typing.

> As viewed in this way, agriculture was, in its earliest form, a new artistic medium—and like any other new medium, it not only

expressed these artists in new ways, but required them to develop new skills and resources in order to work within the new artistic form.

Laura stuck her head out the door, looking sleepy.

"There's coffee and biscuits on the table," I told her.

"Smelled them," she said, then went back inside, letting the screen door fall shut behind her. I could hear her pour coffee, and then a few minutes later, I heard the shower start.

I looked back over the last few sentences I'd typed, and felt suddenly tired. Okay, so what comes next? I asked myself. Yes, right, so the adoption of agriculture involved a kind of self-expression; it was a new art form, which changed the land around us.

Right. But—I wanted to say something more—I wanted to say that the adoption of agriculture didn't just change the land—*it changed us, too*, in ways that had far-reaching effects and that powerfully influenced who we were to become—who we were today.

I sat staring out onto the green banks of an island in the river as a flock of egrets took rise from the shallow waters along its banks. Above, the sky stretched wide and blue, with tall clouds along the horizon. What a breathtaking day, I thought—all light and breeze, and the world so alive!

I turned my thoughts back to the paper I was writing. I would just have to go through it step by step, I told myself—first showing how things had been for us as hunter-gatherers, then describing how becoming agriculturalists had changed all that—how the new medium of art had required that we perfect new skills, which in turn had further changed our relationship with ourselves, and with the world around us.

I sighed and tried to order these ideas in my mind, then set my hands on the keypad and began to type:

Throughout most of our evolutionary past, our ancestors lived in warm climates with little seasonal variation. In such environments, it was not necessary to store food in one season for use in another. Ample food was available year round. An individual living in such an environment who spent the day hunting or gathering had little reason to plan for the future, or to consider much outside the moment he or she was in. *Should I wander this way, or that? Should I look for plants here, for game there?* Such were the sorts of questions we would have had to address on a daily basis.

During that time, as is common amongst hunter-gatherers who live in such climates today, the majority of our attention was focused on the moment we were in, for the world was alive, and it was necessary to be alert to it.[24] We spent our days looking for game, for fruit or nuts or tuberous plants, and when we found what we were looking for, we threw a spear at it, or picked it, or dug it up from the ground. Drifting off into thoughts about the past or future, for the most part, would only have interfered with the task at hand.

Eventually, though, we were pressed to change the way we related to time. For some, this pressure was a result of a move to a more challenging climate, where, for example, it may have been necessary to plan ahead for the winter months. For others, this transition was made as agriculture began to spread around the world.

Once we had turned our attention to farming and become dependent on it, living in the moment no longer served our purpose, for farming by its nature required considerable attention be paid to both the future and the past. Not only was it necessary to plant and tend crops months in advance of when they would be needed, but farmers must constantly look to the past for information about what is the best course of action to take in the present.

When I put this much water on my crops two years ago, did they do as well as when I put this other amount of water on them last year? Based on my past experiences, what amount of water should I use now to best insure the future results I desire?*

I heard Laura rustling around inside the cabin, and in a few minutes she came outside and joined me, bringing, one by one, the table, the breakfast tray, and another chair with her. She had the book on the Mbuti she'd been reading with her, and after giving me a quick good-morning kiss, she sat down near me and began to read. I went back to my work.

Engaging in agriculture not only pushed us to think about time frames other than the moment we were in, but it required us to somehow become adept at distinguishing between results we found desirable and results we found undesirable, so that we might, then, select between them. In other words, it became necessary to develop a conceptual framework for making evaluative judgments, and so we began to think in terms of certain results being "good" (that is, desirable) and others being "bad" (that is, undesirable).

We had stepped out of the impulsive actions of the moment, and had begun to build a world through conscious intention. We planned more actively than we ever had before, and we spent our time carrying out those plans. While agriculture may have attracted us as a means of self-expression and discovery, it soon became a medium that also shaped the very self that it expressed.

We went, then, in a period of a few thousand years, from being in many ways childlike (living in the moment, impulsive and

---

* As already stated, this shift in how we related to time may have begun first amongst hunter-gatherers who migrated to climates outside the tropics, where they would have had to plan ahead to preserve food, clothes, or shelter for the harshest season(s). In that context, a developing awareness of how present actions may affect outcomes in the distant future would not have been coupled in the same way with an emerging desire for self-expression and self-directedness—and would have begun much earlier than the inception of agriculture, perhaps by as much as 30,000 years.

See note 24 in Appendix 3 (pages A12-A14) for more on this subject.—I. K.

dependent—suckling, as it were, at the breast of Mother Earth), to being like teenagers: more deliberative in our process, and intrigued with the prospects of our own self-definition and self-determination.

The sense of self-discovery and independence we gained in growing plants and domesticating animals was rewarding enough to be worth the increased tedium of the labor involved—as well as the costs of transitioning to a diet that, while still plentiful, was less varied and nourishing than what we had eaten before. Like teenagers driven by a desire to explore our independent selfhoods, it seemed worthwhile to us to, in essence, accept tedious jobs and move out on our own, leaving behind the comforts or our parents' home and table.

I looked back over what I had just written, trying to assess if I had succeeded in saying what I'd wanted to say. Skimming back through the text, I picked up key phrases:

> They domesticate animals and create crop lands—and everywhere they look they see the canvas of the world filling up with their creations, marked by their intent.... Agriculture was...a new artistic medium...
>
> As...hunter-gatherers,...the majority of our attention was focused on the moment we were in.... Engaging in agriculture...pushed us to think about time frames other than the moment we were in... It required us to somehow become adept at distinguishing between results we found desirable and results we found undesirable....
>
> We had stepped out of the...moment, and had begun to build a world through conscious intention.... We...were...like teenagers...intrigued with the prospects of our own self-definition and self-determination....

So far, so good, I thought. I held my hands over the keypad, poised and ready to type more. I felt there was more I wanted to say, but for the moment, I couldn't seem to get clear on just what it was.

After a while, I set the laptop down under my chair, then stood up and leaned against the ship's railing. It was such a beautiful day, with the forest coasting by, cool-looking with its towering trees, its dense foliage and shade, and the sun bright and sparkling on the water. From the forest canopy along the near shore, a large bird took flight, its wings cutting through the air in big muscular strokes. In the water, mats of water hyacinths floated by, dotted with pale purple flowers which jutted up into the air above.

As I stood watching, I caught sight of a little cluster of thatch-roofed huts built along the water's edge. I wondered what life was like for the people who lived there, at the border of river and forest, surrounded by such wild beauty.

"Hey, Laura—look," I said, pointing at the huts. She looked up from her book and craned her neck to try to get a good view of what I was pointing at, then she closed the book she'd been reading and came and stood by me.

"The huts?" she asked.

"Yeah. Who do you suppose lives there?" I said.

"You know," she said, squinting and holding her hand above her eyes, "I think they're on stilts."

"Are they?" I said, and looked harder at the little huts we'd just chugged past. She was right. "I guess the water must get pretty high sometimes," I said.

"I wonder if we'll get a chance to meet any of the people who live in that forest," Laura said, as she looked out across the water.

We stood staring off the back of the boat together for a while, and then Laura said, "Hey, there's something I'd like to share with you, in the book I've been reading."

"Okay," I said. Laura went back and picked up her book from the little table she'd carried outside.

"It's very curious," she said, as she flipped through the pages.

I stood watching her as she looked for the right passage. Light reflecting up from the river danced across her face, so that her eager expression seemed to shine. I thought about all the times she had read to me from books like this one, and for a moment I felt nostalgic for our cozy bedroom back in Boulder, for our friends, and for the mountains that rose up so tall, nearby.

"There are these stories, traditional stories the Mbuti tell. Well, they're referred to mostly as 'Pygmies' here, rather than 'Mbuti'—and sometimes as 'Mbuti Pygmies.' But anyway," she turned some more pages, "these are stories the Mbuti tell about themselves and about animals, and about the relationship they have together. The stories have some recurring themes," she looked more closely at one page, and then turned to the next one. "One of which is how close that relationship is—but somehow," she said, looking up at me for a moment, "something always goes wrong."

She sat down in the chair she'd been using, turned a couple more pages, then stopped. She looked up at me again. "In these stories, the Mbuti and the animals are close, but at the same time, they can't really connect," she said, gesturing with one hand. Then she looked back down at the page and ran her finger along it, looking for the right place to begin.

"Okay," she said, "here's the story I was going to share with you. It's strangely enigmatic." She began to read, and as she did, her voice (which was, as always, pleasing—soft, and a little reedy) rose above the sound of the engines pulsing from two decks below.

"An elephant and a Pygmy were friends," she began. "The Pygmy was called Mbali. He went to visit his friend, the elephant."

I moved my chair closer to hers, then sat back down, settling comfortably into the chair, feet stretched out ahead of me, listening. A slight breeze stirred, and the sunlight reflecting up from the water cast patterns on the ceiling of the promenade. I closed my eyes as Laura's voice drifted over me.

When he arrived at the elephant's village, the elephant was delighted and said to his wife, "My friend, Mbali, has come; make us a nice dish of mashed plantains." So his wife pounded the plantains, added salt, and put the dish over the fire. When it was ready the elephant took some red-hot embers and held them to his feet, and the elephant fat ran into the food. When there was enough he turned to his friend, Mbali, and said, "Eat well." The two of them sat down and ate up all the food. The Pygmy said, "This is delicious." He went back to his camp.

The next day the elephant said to his wife, "Now I will go and visit my friend, Mbali." So he cleaned himself up and set off. When he arrived at Mbali's camp, Mbali saw him and called, "Welcome, friend! Come and sit down." He told his wife that his friend had come, and that she should prepare some mashed plantains for him. When it was cooked the Pygmy took some red-hot embers and started putting them...

The sentence seemed to linger in mid-air as Laura turned the page,

...to his foot. The elephant said, "Don't do that, it will kill you. My feet are big and heavy, let me do it." "Don't be silly," replied the Pygmy, and put the embers to his feet. He screamed with pain and almost died. The elephant took hold of him and brought him back to life, then said, "See, I told you it would kill you." The elephant then took the hot embers and put them to his feet so that the oil ran out into the plantains, and they all sat down and ate.

When the meal was finished the elephant returned to his home. His wife greeted him and asked if he had had a good time. He said: "It was terrible. My friend, Mbali, took red-hot embers and put them to his feet and almost killed himself. I shall never go back there again, never."*

Laura finished reading, and I opened my eyes as she looked over at me. "Isn't that curious?" she said. She looked back down at the page thoughtfully.

"What do you make of it?" I asked her.

"Well, I was thinking about this while you were writing," she said. "I've seen the principle Mbuti religion—the one they practice in the forest—as expressing a fundamental sense of connectedness with the natural world. I mean, that seems obvious enough if you look at it—they sing to the forest, which is alive and responsive to their needs. They have these stories in which they are friends with the animals. So there's this larger sense of belonging and connection, right?"

"Right," I said, nodding my agreement.

"But what I was thinking while you were typing is that there's this other element, this thing that's amiss." She gestured towards the book she'd

---

* For anyone interested, Laura was reading from this book: Colin M. Turnbull. *The Mbuti Pygmies: An ethnographic survey.* Anthropological papers of the AMNH; v. 50, pt. 3. New York: American Museum of Natural History, 1965. 265–266.—I. K.

just read from. "I mean, take this story about the Mbuti man and the elephant," she said, tapping the page, "they're so close, and yet, well, the pieces don't quite line up for them, do they?"

I nodded my head a little as I listened.

"And I gather from what this book says that it's like that with other Mbuti stories as well—there's a connection, but the pieces don't quite fit together. So I was thinking about it, and the more I thought about it, the more it seemed to me that in the Mbuti world that sense of belonging, or connectedness, is never quite perfected; it's never really complete."

She looked down at the page thoughtfully for another moment, and then over at me. "Even with their religion, which is so beautiful, and which suggests such a sense of interconnection, there's, well—they have to *sing to* the forest—don't they? It doesn't just *know*, and respond. Even then, in that beautiful belief about a benevolent world that responds to their needs, there's a hint of separation coloring the closeness."

"Yeah," I said, and once again nodded my agreement. "I think you've got a point there."

"It's going to make the research more interesting, I think," Laura said, "sorting out these threads of connection and separation."

We talked a little about how this new insight would affect the research she had planned, and then Laura went back to her reading.

After a while, I got up and stood by the railing, ruminating over the things we'd been talking about. I wondered what we would both discover once we actually got to meet the Mbuti, and how much we would each have to make adjustments in the research we had planned.

I was looking out at the great river, noticing how perfectly it caught and reflected the cloud-speckled sky, when a motion I glimpsed out of the corner of my eye caught my attention. I turned and saw three massive dugout canoes passing on the starboard side of the *Tshatshi*, heading downstream. Each of them held perhaps half a dozen people, most of whom were standing and rowing with long oars in great sweeping motions, bending their arms and backs with each stroke. Looking down into the canoes, I could see that they were filled with woven baskets of various shapes and sizes, which appeared to contain an assortment of goods.

I got Laura's attention and pointed to the passing canoes. We both watched as the powerful strokes of the rowers sent the canoes skimming across the water.

"Can you imagine the size of the trees they were cut from?" I said.

Laura murmured her agreement as she sat up straight and peered out between the railings. I estimated the longest canoe at about fifty feet in length.

"I wonder if they're heading for that little village you spotted earlier," Laura said. I wondered this too—after all, where else might they be headed, in all this wilderness?

Laura went back to her reading, but I stood and watched the canoes for several minutes, until they became little dots far down river. I found myself wondering not only where they were going, but where they had come from—as there was nothing around us at this point on the river, except the barge itself.

❋　　❋　　❋

Laura and I sat out on our veranda the rest of the morning, with Laura reading, and me either contemplating what I would write next or listening to our Bira language tapes. All in all, the morning went quickly, and it didn't seem long before the pan was banged to announce lunch.

As we walked over, I suggested to Laura that our waiter might know something about where the canoes had come from, and were going to. After we were settled at our table, and our waiter came to bring our food, Laura asked him about what we had seen. The two of them conversed back and forth in rapid French for a few minutes, with Laura asking questions, and the waiter answering them. A time or two, the waiter pointed upriver, or made a line in the air tracing the shoreline. Finally, Laura nodded and smiled, then thanked him, and he went back to his duties. Laura looked over at me, still smiling a little, then casually broke apart one of her meatballs with her fork.

"It didn't make much sense, did it," she said, "for all those people to be setting up their wares all over the barge, just to sell to one another?" She took a bite with a studied nonchalance. "I had been wondering about that," she added, nodding thoughtfully.

"Yeah—okay," I said, "so what did he say, Laura?" I was eager for her to get past her preamble and tell me. Laura swallowed and took a sip of water.

"He said many of the passengers are here just to sell their goods to the people who live along the river. That's what they do for a living." She let her smile break through a little, again, then leaned towards me. "You think this place came alive in the first twenty-four hours after we left Kinshasa? Apparently, it's really hopping now." I could see the excitement in her eyes as she pointed to the near bank.

"People from all along this side of the river row out in their canoes—they're called 'pirogues,' by the way—to sell and trade their goods and buy whatever provisions they need. They stay for a while and then drop off and return to their villages before the barge carries them too far upriver." I could see a gleam in Laura's eyes as she paused and set down her fork. "He said they know when we're going to arrive. Do you want to guess how, Indira?"

"No," I said. "How?"

"They talk to one another with drums! The villages send word upriver in some sort of drumbeat language. They put out word once someone sees the barge is on its way." She looked thoroughly delighted and leaned back in her chair, glancing around the room.

"I don't know, Indira." She shook her head. "For some reason, I always thought that talking with drums was some sort of myth made up by Hollywood." Our eyes met, and Laura's smile widened. "What do you say we go have another look around after lunch? I have the feeling we may have been missing a lot, tucked back here in our quiet quarters at the end of this flotilla."

"Sure," I said and smiled back. Her eagerness had touched off a certain excitement in me, as well—though it was hard to imagine the barges becoming any more lively than they had seemed when we had explored them last, a couple of days earlier.

❉   ❉   ❉

After lunch we stopped back in our cabin so Laura could put on sunscreen, and also pick up her fanny pack, as she wanted to have a little spending money with her.

The day could not have been brighter nor clearer, but this also meant the sun was really beating down. First we wandered through the decks and corridors of the *Kasongo* (where Laura bought a straw hat to keep the sun out of her eyes) and then out onto the deck of the flat barge, at the front of our array. And certainly Laura was right, for there the vital mix of party, home life, and business was even louder and more fervent than it had been when we had visited before.

I followed Laura as we made our way through the throng, past merchandise that was a mixture of the city offerings (fish hooks...condensed milk...bars of soap...) and goods brought in by the villagers. Six-foot-long catfish and fresh, ripe pineapples; riverine eels and smoked monkey carcasses; long manioc tubers and fragrant papayas; giant snails and wiggling, thumb-sized palm grubs were all amongst the offerings now being brought on board. Laura bought some roasted caterpillars from one vendor, who wrapped them up in a broad, green banana leaf before handing them to her.

"Are you actually going to eat those?" I asked, as Laura poked one in her mouth. She squinted up her eyes and bit into it—then smiled and said, "Actually, they're good." She offered me one, which I declined, then continued to munch them as we walked along. A little while later I bought a dollop of what I thought of as "manioc-root porridge," a thickish, cream-colored paste, also wrapped in a banana leaf, which I thought might make a good dessert—though it was, in truth, more starchy than sweet.

We gradually made our way up to the barge's bow, where we stood for quite a while looking out at the river, which was brilliant under the blue, cloud-specked sky, with verdant islands scattered about. We had just passed another cluster of huts built on stilts, like the one Laura and I had seen earlier, and we could hear the rumble of drums, calling out to the next village, letting them know we were on our way.

We stood quietly together, looking out across the placid water before us. It seemed so peaceful, somehow, even with the hubbub of the crowd behind us, and after a few minutes I realized I was relieved to be away from the incessant pulse of the *Tshatshi's* engines.

"We probably couldn't hear the drums before because of the engine noise," I said to Laura.

"Yes, you're probably right," she answered.

Though it was nice standing at the barge's bow, looking out at the water, the sun was punishingly hot. People were still using the area as a kind of impromptu shower, stripping to a minimum of clothing, then dragging up buckets of water and rinsing themselves off. It seemed almost private in this area at the edge of the barge, with the crowd behind us and the endless river ahead. I was tempted to join them, it looked so cool and pleasant.

We stood there for some time, looking out at the water and eating our snacks, and then Laura tapped my arm and pointed ahead of the barge. A couple hundred meters ahead, I could make out a cluster of slender lines afloat on the water. It took me a few moments, and then I realized—it was a group of canoes! People had rowed out in their pirogues from one of the villages and were waiting in the water as we approached. For several minutes they just floated there, poised, but as we drew near, they kicked into action, tearing at the river with their oars, pushing their crafts upstream, trying to come up to speed with the barge as it motored upriver.

Laura and I left our vantage point at the bow and moved towards the starboard side for a better view of the action. As the barge caught up with the cluster of canoes, the oarsmen—who stood as they rowed—struggled to match our pace, as they guided their pirogues alongside. The best of them smoothly docked with the moving barge. One overturned in the turbulent water. Another was not fast enough, and the oarsmen failed to catch hold before the barge had passed them by. All of it amounted to a little bit of drama which, I realized, as I looked down the side of the barge and saw the collection of pirogues docked there, had probably been going on, off and on, throughout the day.

Laura and I made our way down along the side of the barge, weaving in and out of the crowd. We were curious about what the canoeists had brought.

"Did you notice," I said to Laura, "that all the rowers were men?"

"Yeah, I noticed that."

"I've noticed, too, that all the people I've seen cooking are women," I added.

Laura glanced over at me and nodded, "me too."

"I've gotten so accustomed to our life in Boulder. It seems strange to see people divide things up that way," I added.

"Yeah," Laura said, making a quick nod with her head before she took a step ahead of me to fit through a narrow place in the crowd. As I stepped in behind her, I wondered how rigid people here were with these roles—how would they react if they saw a man pounding manioc, I wondered, or a woman rowing a pirogue?

We got near one of the canoes that had docked successfully and looked down into it. It was filled with the same sort of woven baskets filled with goods I'd seen in the canoes that had rowed past us that morning.

Up ahead there was some commotion, and we continued on towards it. We worked our way through the crowd along the starboard side of the barge. One of the pirogues that had just docked had, resting in the bottom of it, a large, live crocodile. A length of old rope was wrapped tightly around it snout. Another held all four of its legs pinned against its back. A man stood in the bottom of the canoe, his foot on the animal's head, taking bids for it. This went on for several minutes. Finally, a price was named, and the sum of money handed down. The buyer jumped into the canoe, and the two men began to try to hoist out the crocodile, which was longer than either of them was tall. As they did, the animal was using all the force pent up inside its muscular body to try to wrench itself from their control. Even with one man holding onto its tail and the other gripping its upper body, it nearly capsized the flat-bottomed canoe, which even so seemed remarkably stable in the water. Some of the men on deck reached down to give a hand, and the animal was heaved up on deck and unceremoniously dropped against it.

It was about this time I became aware of a familiar mechanical sound in my ear, but what happened next was too distracting for me to take much notice of it. As the crocodile crashed against the deck, the old rope binding its legs tore apart. The crocodile was still tangled up in the rope, but the rope had loosened enough for it to have some mobility. It started to turn toward the water. One of the men stepped forward to grab it, but the crocodile brought its tail around with stunning force and sent the man flying. By then, the man who'd bought the crocodile was up on deck, trying to keep it from making its way back to the water. Then a young man—or perhaps I should say "a boy," for he was still quite young—dove at the crocodile from its side, and, with the full weight of his body on the crocodile's back, he used his arms to pin the animal's head to the deck. The crowd gave up a happy cheer, and the boy looked around, grinning exuberantly as others stepped in to help tie the crocodile's legs again.

I noticed the little mechanical noise in my ear again, and looked towards Laura, who had been standing next to me, taking pictures of the whole event!

"Laura!" I exclaimed, in a hushed voice, as she took one last picture, then slipped the camera back into her fanny pack amidst the piles of Zairian currency.

She zipped the bag shut and looked over at me. "Nobody was looking at me, Indira," she said quietly, "they were all watching the crocodile."

"It's too big a risk," I said, in an emphatic whisper. We looked at one another for a long moment.

"Okay," she said.

"You promised you wouldn't take more pictures," I said.

"I promised I would be careful," she corrected.

We gave each other another long look. She could be so damn bull-headed! I was really upset—the idea that she would risk getting arrested by some unchecked, power-hungry military police—for some damn photographs!

I looked at her pleadingly. "Would you *please* not take any more pictures until we can be sure that it's safe?" I implored her. She looked at me, and then suddenly her expression softened, as it sank in, I guess, that I was genuinely afraid for her safety.

"Okay, Indira—I promise I won't take any more pictures till we can both be sure that it's safe," she told me.

I nodded and thanked her, then looked around. The crocodile had been carried off, I knew not where. The sun seemed unbearably hot. I wiped the sweat from my face.

"Do you want to go back to the cabin?" Laura asked, as though reading my thoughts.

"Do you mind?" I asked her.

"No. It all seems a bit much, all of a sudden."

❋   ❋   ❋

I think it had brought Laura down for me to get mad at her, and she was quiet as we walked back to our room. When we got back to the cabin, Laura got out the map and guidebook and stood out on the promenade outside our door, trying to estimate our location, but at the moment, I didn't want to be reminded of how close we were getting to Mbandaka. I couldn't see how she could be very accurate with so few landmarks along the shore, anyway, but I had to admit that we were a day closer than we had been the day before—and that Mbandaka couldn't be far away now.

I was hot from having spent too long in the sun, and I retreated to the darkness of our cabin, where I propped myself up on one of our cots, so I could stare out the window at the passing trees. We were hugging the shore at this point on the river, and the forest drifting past seemed tantalizingly close. How wonderful it would be, I thought, to step into its deep, shadowy recesses. The thought of another week in the blazing sun as we slowly crawled upriver depressed me—and the thought of our arrival in Mbandaka, and what might follow, filled me with a quiet dread. Why couldn't Laura have been more careful? I thought, but then sighed as I considered how ridiculous the regulation was that she had chosen to ignore. It all seemed so crazy.

After a while, I got up and turned on the air conditioner (which sputtered and blew hot air) and got out the laptop to look at what I had written earlier that day. Laura came in, sat down beside me on the bed, and we talked a little about the disagreement we'd had. Laura told me she hadn't planned to bring the camera with her that day—but she'd found it in her bag, and it had been too tempting not to use it once the crocodile got loose.

"Anyway, I'm sorry I upset you, Indira. You're probably right that it was a reckless thing to do. I'm not used to living in a military dictatorship, you know." She smiled a little, and I reached over and took her hand in mine. I gave her hand a squeeze.

Laura smiled some more, and her eyes had that light in them that I always adored.

"I want to get a shower," Laura said, tilting her head a little towards the bathroom. "I don't know when I've been so hot. Maybe it'll help me cool off." Then she leaned over and kissed me.

I held her hand for a moment longer, smiling at her. "I just want you to be safe, you know," I said.

Laura nodded. "I'll try to do that." She stood up. "This cabin is like a tin can in the sun," she said, and moved towards the bathroom.

I watched as she disappeared into the narrow room, and heard the shower start, then turned my attention back to the little screen on the computer I held on my lap.

I read and reread the first few lines on the screen, but as much as I tried to concentrate, I felt thickheaded and couldn't seem to focus my thoughts.

After a minute or two, I looked up and out the window, where I could still see the treetops gently coasting by on the river's near shore. How much cooler it would be beneath their branches, I thought.

I could hear the swoosh and sway of the shower as the cool water poured down over Laura.

"How much cooler," I thought, again. Then I got up and closed the door to the cabin, stripped off my clothes, and followed Laura into the shower.

❀　　❀　　❀

We made love that afternoon on the narrow cots in our steamy cabin, which seemed for the first time not so hot, after we'd been chilled by the cool water of the shower. We both drifted off to sleep afterwards, wrapped together in one another's arms.

I woke long after Laura did, in a room half-lit with evening light. I rolled over and looked out through the screen door at the fading day. The light was low, streaking long across the water, which appeared steely blue in the half light. Above, the last flames of the yellow, setting sun met the evening-blue of the sky with a band of green, like jade—or like a painter had nicked her brush in the tree-tops and smeared the color into the darkening sky.

Next to me, Laura sat reading by the bedside light. She was dressed, but apparently had made sure I was well-covered with a sheet before opening the cabin door to let in the evening breeze.

Laura told me they'd banged the dinner pan only a few minutes before. Groggily, I pulled my sheet around me and stepped into the bathroom to dress. Soon we were both ready to go. As we left, Laura paused to lock the door behind us, and I turned to look out over the water again, just as the last curve of the setting sun was dipping below the horizon.

I'd had the feeling we'd nearly slept through dinner, but in fact, we were some of the first to arrive. We were served promptly, and as we began to eat, Laura looked around at the room filling with people and commented idly, "I wonder where Raymond eats when he's not here."

I was still too groggy to say much in response. Laura was only a little bit more lively herself, and dinner progressed quietly, with little conversation, though it felt good just to be there with her.

Small sensations seem large when one has recently wakened. As I ate, my senses seemed filled with the taste and texture of my food, the thick warmth of the air, the clatter of silverware at the tables around us, and the steady murmur of voices, which fell like a shower throughout the room.

After dinner, Laura and I stopped at the bow of the *Tshatshi* and looked ahead as the searchlights swept the river. Insects, drawn to the lights, hovered in clouds in that glow, where bats, swooping in at odd angles, devoured them. Over the water, where the beams dispersed, the air was clear—no mist. The slick, dark water looked all the more impenetrable without that draping of white—yet the whole scene, as beautiful in its own way as on any other night, didn't hold our attention. It's an odd thing about traveling, how quickly the remarkable and the new dissolve into the common and the familiar. We didn't linger long, as we had on other nights, but turned the corner and started down the starboard side of the *Tshatshi.* We could hear the sounds of a party floating up from the deck below. Ahead of us, the barefoot steward was standing at someone's door, knocking and holding a tray of food. As we approached, I recalled that that was the door Laura and I had stood in front of on our first night on board, when we had looked out at the grasslands on the shore and heard the man crying.

When we were only a few strides away, the door was opened, and the warm glow of incandescent light flooded out along the walkway. A male figure stepped into the doorway—medium height, athletic build—accepted the tray from the steward, then disappeared back inside. He was only visible for a moment, and with the light from inside I could see him only in silhouette—but even then, I was pretty sure it was Raymond.

I looked over at Laura, who was glancing over the railing towards the sounds of music and festivities drifting up from the deck below. As her gaze swung back, she saw me looking at her, and smiled. I smiled back, and I wondered again if that had really been Raymond. It seemed that if it was, I had just discovered something very private about him.

In a few minutes we were back at our cabin, and as we paused at the door to unlock it, I told Laura about what I had just seen. She looked very serious for a moment, and I imagined she was remembering that night. Then she nodded slowly, acknowledging what I had said, and we went on inside.

I spent the rest of the evening recording the day's events in my journal and rereading what I'd written so far for the Huginn/Muninn article. I knew I wanted to comment on the near-synchronicity of certain events in prehistory—that is, on the fact that agriculture had developed separately in several places in such a relatively short period of time, and that the development of art had followed a similar pattern—but the details of what I wanted to say wouldn't come clear. I kept reading and rereading what I had already written, but couldn't seem to move on to what to write next. It was as though I were picking up blocks I wanted to give some sort of order to, but kept tripping over some unseen thing—everything would go flying, and I would have to start gathering and sorting all over again.

As it happened, the evening passed with no more accomplished than my having written a pile of jumbled notes.

The night wore on, and finally, tired and frustrated, I set my work aside and got ready for bed. Laura wasn't quite ready to stop working, so I lay awake on my cot in the stagnant air of our steel-walled room, listening to the throb of the engines, the cough of our overtaxed air conditioner, and the endless sounds of nightlife drifting through the open window.

After a while, Laura switched off the light and joined me, snuggling close despite the heat, and we lay together in the unquiet darkness, waiting for sleep to arrive. As I rested there, I again went over the progression of ideas from my paper in my mind. It seemed to me that I knew what I needed to say, but whenever I tried to turn my thoughts towards it, it kept slipping away.

Eventually, I felt myself drifting towards sleep, and as I did, an impression rose in my mind. I was kneeling beside a lake or pond of some sort. Its edges stretched out into an impenetrable darkness. Its surface was black and oily. I wanted to see something that was hidden beneath that water, but I wasn't sure what it was. No light seemed to penetrate beyond its slick skin. Bravely, I bent over and pushed my head into the water—but as I did, I shut my eyes against the water's sting. I felt the liquid flowing over my head, but with my eyes closed, I saw only darkness.

The image jarred me, and I opened my eyes as I lay on my cot. Through the window, I could see a three-quarters moon hanging over the rainforest beyond. Mist drifted through the treetops on the near bank. I thought again about Mbandaka, now less than a day away.

Oh, why did Laura have to take pictures of that crocodile? I thought. From the lower deck, I could hear the throb of the engines as they pushed us ever farther upriver. For a moment I felt cold, even in the stifling heat.

Shh, I told myself. Shh. I'll think about these things tomorrow. For now—sleep. Just sleep.

Laura woke before me. When breakfast came, and I didn't wake to the sound of the steward's knock or the smell of coffee in the air, she figured I must be tired and could use a little extra sleep and decided not to disturb me. As it worked out, I had not gone to sleep quickly the night before, but had lain awake, listening to the dance music floating up from the deck below, and fretting about what was to come.

I woke feeling more tired than when I had gone to bed. Laura was already busily at work, and we only spoke for a minute before I got up and stumbled into the bathroom for a quick shower.

Breakfast was cold coffee and biscuits—although in truth they were nowhere close to cold in the steamy tropical weather. While Laura continued to work, sitting on her cot with papers spread out all around, I brought the little table and a chair outside so I could eat breakfast and work in the open air.

Sipping coffee and munching biscuits, I looked back over the material I had written since first boarding the barge. I felt pretty satisfied with the case I'd made for people having shown a gradually increasing preoccupation with selfhood over the last 30,000 years, or so.

I dipped my biscuit in my coffee and considered again what needed to come next in my paper. I was aware that I had hit some sort of impasse in my writing the day before and that there was something I was uncomfortable with about the material that came next—but I really wanted to get somewhere with this paper, so I decided to do my best to push forward.

I wanted somehow to unravel the mysteries surrounding the appearance of both art and agriculture—to explain how such impressive developments could have appeared so nearly simultaneously in so many different places. In particular, I asked myself, how could such cultural revolutions have erupted in multiple locations without any physical means of communication between the people at the various sites?

The idea seemed to have a sort of slickness, which made it hard to grab hold of, or to break apart analytically. I sat staring dreamily out at the water. I could feel my thoughts splintering into fragments, like the way water flowed around the many islands that filled the river. It was morning, and I was tired. I let my thoughts drift. As I did, an image began to unfold in my mind, of a rain-soaked field under which the root system of a giant plant inched along here and there, sending up strong, healthy shoots into the open air and sunlight. Each shoot appeared as a separate plant, yet each was tied by its roots to the others.

I rubbed my eyes, shaking off sleep. I set the little computer on my lap to write, but as I did, I had to admit that I had no idea where to begin. I was addressing an academic audience, even if an especially open-minded one, and I would need facts, arguments, proofs, for anything I wanted to say.

I let my hands fall to my sides, and I found myself staring down at the water in the *Tshatshi's* wake. Dual ridges spread out where her two propellers spun beneath the river's surface. The v-shaped swells, which rose behind each propeller, crashed together where they met behind the middle of the barge, while their outer ridges spread in opposing arms toward the Congo's two shores.

As I sat, staring, I was reviewing in my mind what was known about the advent of art and of agriculture. The archaeological record of agriculture's development was plain:

- Agriculture had been independently invented at at least seven separate sites on at least four continents within a period of only 5,000 years.
- Agriculture's invention had been motivated, I believed, by developments in how people related to their own selfhoods. It was a form of self expression.

While it could not be proven that art was actually invented at each of the separate sites at which it first appeared (as it could be with agriculture, due to evidence of the gradual domestication of local plants), the pattern of art's advent was very similar to that of agriculture:

- Art appeared on all the continents then inhabited by human beings within a period of only a few thousand years.
- The invention of art, I believed, had been motivated by changes in how people related to their own selfhoods. It also was a form of self-expression.

How was it, then, I asked myself, that these developments had been synchronized?

I imagined the root system, again, inching through the earth, sending up shoots. Could it be as simple as that, I thought? Some circuit that tied us all together? Some shared medium through which waves of change could move, spread out, and then become expressed by individuals?

I again lifted my hands to type. The air held the scent of coffee and biscuits. I could hear people laughing in a cabin not far away. I would be telling this to the Huginn/Muninn crowd, I thought—people who would surely consider this argument impractical, unprovable. I would be risking my professional reputation, even with them, if I went down this road.

I set the laptop on the little table I had carried out on deck, then slowly finished the last of my coffee while staring down at the turbulent water in the *Tshatshi's* wake, feeling the currents of my own thoughts bending and twisting around obstacles in my mind.

After a time, I looked up. Clouds were piling higher in the sky, and the morning breeze was gusting a little as it came around the corner of the *Tshatshi's* upper deck. I sighed and set my mug down. I stretched, trying to release some of the frustration I was feeling. I took a last bite of my biscuit, gathered up my work, the little table, and the chair, and took them all inside. Then I told Laura I was going to take a break and go for a walk.

❀   ❀   ❀

I tried to set aside all my concerns as I walked up along the *Tshatshi's* port side. The river was wide and brilliantly lit by a sun that muscled its way between the gathering clouds. I wasn't heading any place in particular—I'd just wanted to get out and move around. I got to the bow and headed down the stairs to the second deck.

It's a funny thing about traveling, how much we may be steeped in the newness of a place, in its sights and sounds, it surprising foods and interesting people, but wherever we go, we arrive and stay and depart within the environment we make within ourselves. On that bright, sunny, tropical day, filled with the smell of cooking food and the sounds of laughter and festive music, I felt all jammed up on the inside and unsure of what to do about it.

I circled the second deck two or three times, then stopped and stood on its starboard side. Leaning on the railing, as I looked off towards the shore, I tried to keep myself from wondering how soon Mbandaka would come into view there. We were motoring up the middle of the river today, with the forest a trim line of green in the distance. Birds swooped and turned over the river, looking for a meal in the water below. From the lower deck, I could hear the voices of the women who had gathered there to wash out laundry where the water jetted through. As they worked, they sang and chattered brightly. I could just catch sight of them and the colorful fabrics they wore, if I leaned out a bit past the railing and looked down.

I had just righted myself from taking this view, when I felt a powerful jolt. For a moment the air was filled with the piercing whine of failing metal, as we came to an abrupt halt in the water. A brief moment of still silence passed, then a common voice of surprise rose from the deck below, with people speaking rapidly in Lingala. It felt a bit like when we'd hit the sandbar a couple of days earlier, but this was a harder jolt, and the barge listed distinctly to one side now, as though we had come firmly to rest on the uneven bottom.

I walked to the stern and looked over the railing. I could hear the engines struggling, but we stayed as motionless in the water as an island, and I remembered what the man had told us a couple of days earlier, about the fates of barges that had gotten badly stuck on the river's bottom.

I looked down and could occasionally see an arm pointing out from the first deck, gesturing out over the water. I had the impression of a crowd gathering, and decided to go down and see what I could find out about the situation.

I walked back to the bow and started down the stairs amidst the roar of engines and the clatter of voices, but as I reached the first deck, the engines fell silent.

A crowd had, in fact, begun to gather, and I made my way through it towards the stern of the boat, along the port side. I managed to make it as far back as the railing at the stern, but could not get past the corner where the stern met the port side. The tilt of the deck seemed even more noticeable to me now, where I stood.

I leaned out over the railing, so I could see past the crowd. I could see the captain standing at the rear of the boat, talking to some of the crew. As I watched, one of the crew members stripped to his waist and jumped into the shallow, green water—which barely came up to his chest.

He dove under the *Tshatshi*, and nearly a minute passed before he surfaced, gasped for breath, and plunged under the water again.

He did this three or four times before emerging a final time. As I watched from my perch, he stood there with the river flowing past him, looked up at his captain, and announced something in French.

The captain looked upset and shouted down to the young man, who answered and climbed back up on deck, guided by the helping hands of the other crew members. Then he stood and spoke to the captain for a couple of minutes more, intermittently pointing towards the water and gesturing with his hands.

I couldn't hear what they were saying, but a murmur moved through the crowd like a wave, starting where the captain and crew members stood, carrying a report of their conversation. Around me, people were passing along a phrase in Lingala. I had the impression they were explaining to one another what was going on. I tried to grasp what they were saying, but could only pick out a couple of words. "*Kipakapaka*," I heard them saying, and "*ebuki.*"

"*Kipakapaka ebuki*," I said to myself, trying to keep the sounds fresh in my mind. The diver put his shirt back on, and the captain and his men began to walk away.

"*Kipakapaka ebuki*," I repeated to myself, turned, and started towards our cabin, moving along the port-side walkway and up the stairs with deliberate quickness, repeating the two words to myself as I went, so I wouldn't forget them.

Finally, I came around the corner and stepped into our cabin. Laura was still sitting on the cot where I had left her, looking over papers.

"*Kipakapaka ebuki*," I said to her.

"What?" she answered, looking up.

"Where's the Lingala/English dictionary?" I asked. "*Kipakapaka ebuki*," I repeated under my breath. Laura picked up the dictionary from a little pile of books on the floor beside the cot and handed it to me.

"What do you suppose is going on with the barge," she said. "I felt a jolt, and we stopped. I think we're tilting"

"Yeah," I answered, nodding. "*Kipakapaka ebuki*," I said, again, and began flipping through the pages of the dictionary. "Yeah, I think we're on a sandbar. I heard what people were saying." I turned a couple more pages. "I'm pretty sure '*ebuki*' means 'broken.'"

I found the page. "*Ebuki*: Broken. Yes," I glanced up at Laura. "They were talking about what's going on with the barge. *Kipakapaka, kipakapaka*," I repeated to myself. "How do you suppose you spell '*kipakapaka*?'" I asked.

"*Ki-paka-paka*," Laura said slowly, listening to the sound of the word. "K-i—p-a-k-a—p-a-k-a," she guessed. I pictured it in my mind as she spelled it out.

"Oh!" I said, looking up at her. "I've seen that word." I could see it in mind's eye, plain as day, just as it had looked when I'd seen it sometime before, neatly printed out in our Lingala/English dictionary. Next to it on the page was printed its English equivalent. "Oh gosh," I said, as I returned my gaze to the dictionary and began again turning its pages. "I think it means 'propeller.'"

"Really?" Laura said, as she sat up straight on the cot. "If you think so, Indira, you're probably right—with that photographic memory of yours." She leaned towards me, waiting for me to find the word.

"*Kipakapaka*," I announced, and placed my finger under the word, where it appeared on the page. "Propeller," I said.

I stared at the book for a moment, then closed it and looked up at Laura.

"So the propeller's broken," she said with that blank tone people have when an idea has just begun to sink in.

"It sure sounds that way," I answered. "They were saying more—that's all I caught."

Laura collapsed back on the cot. "Oh god—if the propeller's broken, how long will we be stuck here?"

I sat down in the chair by the little table, and for several minutes Laura and I contemplated what this would mean for our journey. But before long we heard the ship's engine come to life and begin struggling again.

Laura cocked her head. "What's the use of running the engines if the propeller's broken?" she said.

Together we got up and went out on deck. As soon as I looked over the railing, I could see what the answer was.

"Look, Laura," I said, pointing. "Usually there are two places where the water is churned up—one here, and one over there. Now there's just one."

Laura nodded. "So there are two engines and two propellers. They're trying to back us off the sandbar with the one that's still left."

❀   ❀   ❀

For the rest of the morning the one good engine struggled and strained, but we didn't budge an inch. Two strong engines had run us onto that sandbar, and one alone was having a heck of a job getting us off.

Laura and I both tried to get some work done, but with the strain of the one usable engine constantly reminding us of our predicament, it was a little hard to concentrate. When the pan was banged to announce lunch, we were both glad to have an excuse to stop our useless struggles and do something a little more pleasant.

Lunch, of course, consisted of the usual fare, and Laura commented on what it might be like to be stuck on board for days or perhaps weeks longer, eating constantly the same meal, over and over again, but I pointed out that they would have to run out at some point, and that seemed to cheer her some.

After a while, Raymond showed up and conversation quickly turned to the stuck barge. Laura told him what I had overheard people saying, and how we thought the propeller for one engine was broken. Raymond listened thoughtfully.

"*Kipakapaka ebuki*, huh?" he said, nodding, repeating what we had told him. "Propeller's broken—it sounds like that's what they were saying." He took a bite of his cooked carrots, chewed for a moment, then added. "Well, that's pretty serious, if that's the case."

"There was more to what they were saying," I said, "but that's all that I could catch."

Raymond listened, then added, "What I don't understand is, well, there are two barges out in front of the engine barge—why didn't they run aground first and bring the whole chain of barges to a halt before the propeller even reached the sandbar?"

Laura nodded and took a sip of water. "I was thinking that, too—but the *Tshatshi's* a three-story boat. It's heavier, and it has the weight of the two engines on top of that. I imagine it rides deeper in the water, with the propellers deepest of all. I picture the front barges just skimming over the sandbar—then the *Tshatshi* and her propeller hit."

"Right," Raymond added, "and in that case, it would make sense for the propeller to be hardest hit."

"Yeah," Laura nodded. "I figure it went something like that."

"Laura and I have been trying to guess how long it will take to get us unstuck and underway again," I said. "Someone we talked to a couple of days ago said that barges sometimes stay stuck a very long time. If they're badly enough stuck, they just desert them."

"Yeah, I don't have a lot of experience with river travel," Raymond answered, "but I suppose that could happen. Parts can be hard to get. And if the river's low, like it is now, well, they might decide to wait till the water rises and try again, I guess." He stared off into space for several moments, contemplating this, then picked up some potato with his fork and held it hovering above his plate.

"Someone in the crew told me last night," he said, "that we were due into Mbandaka by late morning today—so we can't be far from it now. I was going to get off there, anyway." He took a bite of his potatoes.

"I'm trying to remember—is that where you said your research site is?" Laura asked.

"The Ikelemba River runs into the Congo just past Mbandaka. The research site is up the Ikelemba, actually on a tributary to it, near Bomenge." He glanced around the dining room, as though assessing the situation. "I suppose if we're not unstuck by tomorrow morning, I might as well hire a pirogue and leave from here." He returned his gaze to the table, then added, perhaps a little too eagerly, "You're both welcome to come with me. You could stay at the site for as long as you liked. You might get to see some bonobos. The site's not so far from Basankusu—when you're ready to go, Mvula or I could give you a ride there—they've got a good-sized airstrip where you could catch a flight to Kisangani.

"It's probably a more reliable way to go than barge travel," he added. "That is, if you don't mind air travel." I had the idea that he seemed relieved, somehow, at the idea of us coming. He looked at us both expectantly.

"I don't know," Laura said, glancing over at me, "it's awfully nice of you to invite us, but I think we'd like to see what the situation is here first."

"Oh, of course," Raymond said, "and I suppose that should be a good deal clearer by tomorrow morning."

"Do you think we'd see bonobos?" I asked.

"Well, as I've told you, they're very shy, and they're not fully habituated yet, and you would be new to them," he tilted his head a little bit, "but then, the *Dialium* trees should still be in fruit, and we could situate ourselves near one and probably get a good view of them eating in the upper canopy."

He leveled his head. "You might not get a very close look, is what I'm saying, but we should be able to arrange for you to see some, I would think. And of course, Mvula will have been keeping track of where they've been foraging and should be able to help us find them."

"Who's Mvula?" Laura asked.

"My field assistant," Raymond answered.

"Is it just the two of you at the site, then?" Laura asked.

"I have two graduate assistants, also—but they left a couple weeks after I did and won't be back for another week," he glanced up in the air, "yeah, week—a little more. So, I'd enjoy having you come, if you want a way off the barge." He looked at us and added, "Please consider it."

"We will," I told him. "It's very good of you to offer."

"Yes, it is," Laura said, smiling, then added, "That's an interesting name, 'Mvula.'"

"He's Mongo. It's a Mongo name. He really knows the forest, and he's smart," Raymond said, picking up another forkful of food. "I was really lucky that he came poking around when I first set up camp. He was interested in what I was doing there. I ended up hiring him, and it was the best decision I've made since coming to Africa. Like I said, he's very smart—in another time and place, I would be working for him—but as it is, he's glad to have the work, and I'm lucky to have him as an assistant.

"Makes me look good," he added, grinning.

All through the conversation, the sound of the struggling single engine had been rising and falling in the background. Now it caught my attention again, and I found myself contemplating how stuck we were and what our options might be. I didn't at all like the idea of landing in Mbandaka only hours after we got unstuck—nor did I like the idea of remaining stuck, and the thought of going with Raymond somehow made me uneasy, though I wasn't sure for just which reason.

"Well, I'm sure it would be an interesting experience to join you," Laura said, picking up half a meatball with her fork. "It's been interesting being on the barge, too," she added, gesturing around the room with one hand. "Yesterday, Indira and I were out on the flat barge. Someone had brought a live crocodile in one of those dugout canoes, and it came untied when they brought it up on deck—quite a lively scene! They hauled it off somewhere—I don't know where they took it." Laura put the half a meatball in her mouth.

"Yeah," Raymond nodded. "I was out on the forward barge this morning. Some people were hauling aboard chunks of forest elephant. They're endangered, but that doesn't stop people from hunting them." He looked down at his plate and pushed the food around absentmindedly with his fork.

"What I don't understand," Laura said, "is where all this meat is going. I don't see all that much of it being eaten."

"No," Raymond said, looking up at her. "I'm sure most of it's being put in cold storage for sale in the cities. There was someone I heard about, who took this barge trip a year or two ago. He was particularly concerned with the number of primates being killed for bushmeat..."

"Bushmeat?" I interrupted.

"The meat of animals from the bush. I think maybe they call it game meat in America—something like that?"

I nodded.

"Anyway," Raymond went on, "this fellow counted up more than three thousand primate carcasses in cold storage at the end of one riverboat journey. The impact is enormous. It's terribly popular in the cities now to eat bushmeat. It's created quite a demand—not just in Zaire; the meat is shipped out to countries all over the world."

"Can't they pass a law to protect the endangered animals?" Laura asked, then took her last bite of food.

"They have those laws—they're not enforced," Raymond said. "Logging has opened up roads into the interior. Before, the local people had traditions that kept them living in balance with the natural world around them. Some animals, like bonobos, weren't hunted at all. In some areas, bonobos were seen as relatives of a sort, 'our brothers of the forest,' that sort of thing. It was taboo to hunt or eat them. But with the logging roads, outsiders came in—did the hunting themselves, or paid others enough to get them to break their taboos.

"The whole effect is devastating. The logging destroys habitats, which hurts not just the animals, but the human population that depends on those habitats. It leaves behind roads, and, well—you can see how it spirals down," he said, shaking his head. "Primatologists keep trying to guess how long it will be before all the great apes—gorillas, chimps, bonobos, orangutans—will be extinct in the wild. But nobody really knows." Raymond took a deep breath and looked solemnly down at his plate. He seemed to be trying to steady himself. Finally, he looked up and met my gaze.*

"Anyway," he said, "it's a damn shame. I'm hoping that the research I'm doing will draw at least some attention to the bonobos and that maybe if the international community becomes interested, something can be done to protect them, before it's too late."

Raymond set down his fork. He hadn't finished his food, but I had the feeling he wasn't interested in it anymore.

"I'm sorry to hear about this," I said.

"Yes," he said simply. He looked off to the side for a minute, and when he looked back, his expression was considerably more cheerful.

"So," he said, "if we're still stuck in the morning, I should have some way of locating you, to see if you want to come with me." He looked at both of us. Laura asked to borrow his pad of paper and wrote down our

---

* The storm clouds Raymond saw on the horizon seem small compared to the storm which blew through that region only a few years later. It was not just the animals of the forest which fell victim to this violence, but the people of Zaire (later known as the "Democratic Republic of the Congo") themselves. Less than a decade after Laura and I visited this country, it became the focal point for a five-nation war, sometimes referred to as "Africa's World War," which is estimated to have caused the deaths of more than five million people.

Sadly, the bonobos fared no better than their human counterparts. For more on the current status of these animals, go to: bonobo.org

cabin number for him. Raymond slipped the pad back in his pocket, then stood up.

"Sorry to go on so, about such a distressing subject," he said, and looked thoughtfully off to the side. "I tracked down a poacher once, last year, a local fellow. He told me his three-year-old daughter was sick, and he needed the money for medicine. The logging roads spread disease, too. It's not a simple picture."

Raymond glanced down at the floor, then back at us. "So, anyway, sorry about going on."

"Don't apologize," Laura said. "No need."

Raymond nodded, and repeated that he would look us up in the morning, if we hadn't gotten underway—and then added a quick farewell, in case we did get moving, and he was left off in Mbandaka in, say, the middle of the night.

Laura and I said a goodbye as well, just in case—and as Raymond walked out through the dining-room doors, I tried to push aside an impression I had of Laura being dragged off the *Tshatshi*, at Mbandaka, in the middle of the night.

❋ ❋ ❋

After lunch, Laura and I went for a walk and discussed our plans. The future seemed a blur of uncertainty. We both had a desire to complete our original plan of taking the river route to Kisangani, if that could only be done without further trouble. On the other hand, it would be interesting to go to a bonobo research site and have a chance to see some bonobos, but we weren't sure how soon we would be able to catch a flight from Basankusu to Kisangani.

I was worried, too, about what might happen to Laura once we reached Mbandaka, if we stayed on the barge, but Laura was of the opinion that very few people had noticed her taking pictures, and that there was nothing to worry about. She *was* uneasy, however, about the two of us going off into the wilderness with Raymond, and reminded me of how he had looked at us both on various occasions, and the sense we'd both had that there was something not quite right with him.

We strolled around the outer decks of the *Tshatshi* for an hour or more, talking, but in the end we decided that if the barge was good and stuck, we would go ahead and leave with Raymond—for what better choice would we have? And if we pulled free, or if it looked like we would do so soon, we would try our luck with the barge, and stay put.

Having come to a decision, we headed back to our cabin with the intention of getting some work done, but the afternoon progressed like a slow-moving beast. The air around us was thick and stagnant, the barge unmoving. Huddled in the dark heat of our cabin, our world was filled with the intermittent roar of the one good engine and the sputtering hum of our fruitless air conditioner. I believe Laura managed to get some work done, but I lay on my cot, alternately attempting to distract myself with a light novel, and staring out the door at the water slowly drifting past the barge, replaying the events of the day in my mind, and anticipating those of tomorrow.

After dinner that evening, when the sun hung low over the river, I stood out on the deck and looked out at the river in the radiant twilight, as it flowed in ripples over the sandbar. Beyond it, the forest, tall and dark in the soft light, seemed impenetrable, ancient, indestructible—and yet, I realized, somewhere out of sight, like the sandbar beneath the water, this forest was being logged and dragged away tree by tree, gnawed away at by the fanatical determination of men and machines.

It struck me that there were always layers to the world like this, undercurrents, active but unseen, shaping the world. Even our thoughts were like this, I considered—not themselves visible, but forces which have great impact nonetheless.

I scanned the line of trees with my eyes. From this vantage point the forest seemed utterly wild, untouched—primordial. I felt soothed, looking out at it, and for a while I was able to set aside the worries that had occupied me throughout most of the day.

Standing there, I imagined the people I had been writing about, evolving in a forest much like the one before me. I imagined how they had lived, and tried to conceive how the world of the present had grown out of that world of the past. Somehow, I thought, the mental framework our ancestors had embraced had been like a seed from which the current world had grown.

I ran my fingers through my hair, took a deep breath, and leaned up against the railing. What a contrast there was between that world and this! Ours was a world in which people could write symphonies and circle the globe in airplanes, from which people had gone to the moon—a world of high-powered computers, in which the anatomy of an atom was understood, in which failing hearts could be repaired, from which people could look out through telescopes and see the other side of the galaxy, or with the push of a button on a television, observe events as they transpired on the other side of the globe—*this* world had somehow grown out of the world of the past that I had been exploring.

I looked down at the river flowing past. The choices our ancient ancestors had made, the directions they had picked, had somehow brought us here. Just as what we chose now would, in due course, take us on to the world of the future.

"By how we set our sail, we steer our course," I said softly to myself.

I looked again at the ripples in the water over the sandbar, saw how they caught the fading rays of twilight and threw them back towards the sky. Small bats swooped and swarmed in the dim evening light, chasing insects that had risen from the shadows, as the sun sank low towards the water.

Tomorrow, I thought, if all went smoothly, we would wake to find the propeller repaired, and would pull free of this spot. Perhaps we would head on to Mbandaka and be given no trouble concerning Laura and her picture-taking—and we would continue on east, to Kisangani, which lay waiting where the river made its turn towards the south.

But maybe not. Maybe not. Laura could be pulled off the barge and interrogated, held. Or we could leave with Raymond, whom we hardly knew, and head into that deep forest, into the land in which all human ancestors had evolved, and in which our nearest animal relatives still lived.

I rubbed my neck. Everything was so uncertain. The light played softly across the water. This world was so beautiful, and so difficult.

I looked up at the forest, and remembered what I'd been thinking about it before. Yes, every human success—from science to art, from literature to technology—had somehow evolved from the direction we had set for ourselves thousands of years ago—but so had our failures—all the rigidness of a society capable, sometimes, of arresting someone for no more than the taking of photographs; a world in which people were restricted by narrow sex roles; in which animals were hunted to extinction; in which whole ecosystems were torn to the ground; a world which had love and beauty, but also war and violence and bigotry; a world in which Laura and I must hesitate to show our love in public, for fear of the reactions we might get. All of these things, also, had somehow grown out of the beginnings I had been studying about.

It was awesome to think about. Just how, I wondered, had the events of the ancient past paved the way for the world we knew now?

I looked out across the water and watched, as the sun—a half disk, shimmering orange above the water—sank slowly into the river.

If we could understand how the world we lived in had grown out of the past, I wondered, could we then learn how to better choose the sort of world we made for the future?

I stood staring for a long time, pondering this.

When finally the sun was lost into the great river, when it had doused its light in the heavy folds of night, I sighed, and stretched, then turned towards the cabin Laura and I shared, and to her welcoming arms for the night.

✸   ✸   ✸

The next morning was filled with shadows and noise. I slept restlessly and dreamed intermittently—once about a mountain I was struggling to climb, but the ground around me was covered with a slippery shale—another time about swimming in deep water, down, deep down, where the light filtered through in thin blades.

I was pulled abruptly from sleep by someone knocking at the door. I opened my eyes, and the world was bright and coated with the sounds of metal on metal—a grinding and banging rising from the decks below.

Laura sat up on the cot beside me, rubbed her face with one hand. "They're making such a lot of noise," she said, swinging her legs over the side of the cot. "Maybe they're getting things fixed."

She got up and answered the cabin door. It was the steward with our breakfast tray. She took it from him, thanking him, then set it down on the little table and crawled back into bed beside me.

I was tired. I had the feeling that the pounding and grinding had been going on for hours. Since daylight I had been fluttering in and out of sleep.

I got up and poured myself some coffee, then sat down and drank about half of it, ate a biscuit. The noises seemed somehow louder now that I was up, but Laura appeared to have gone back to sleep. I got out some fresh clothes, stripped off my T-shirt and underwear, and turned on the shower in the bathroom. The sound of the water dimmed the noise from the decks below. I ducked under the warm spray and let it wash over me.

❋   ❋   ❋

I stepped out of the shower into near silence—no banging, no engine noise, just soft voices drifting through the cabin walls. I dried off and slipped into the main cabin to dress.

Laura was just waking. With her eyes half open, she looked over at me and smiled. She looked groggy but well rested. She rolled onto her back and stretched, then got up, stood on the cot's edge, and took a look out the window. She let the blinds fall shut and turned towards me.

"I sort of thought we might have moved," she said, yawning, then walked across the cots and took a seat in one of the chairs by the little table. She sat there loose-jointed in the damp tropical air.

"That's wishful thinking," I commented, as a great metallic grinding rose up again from the decks below.

"Is the coffee still warm?" she asked.

I chuckled. "Isn't everything?"

Laura smiled, stepped over to the little table to pour herself a cup of coffee, then glanced back out the window. "I wonder where we'll be this time tomorrow," she said absently, then she carried her cup into the bathroom and swung the door mostly shut.

I heard the shower start and looked around the cabin. It seemed somehow changed from the day before. Would it be hours or weeks longer we would stay here? I wondered. The thought made me feel directionless, and I spent a little time cleaning up. Laura came out of the shower, dressed, and sat down for breakfast, spreading a biscuit with jam. I opened the door and window, pulled back the blinds the rest of the way—letting the day in from outside.

"Good morning," I heard Laura announce. I looked around and saw Raymond standing at the screen door.

"Good morning," he answered. Laura invited him in.

Raymond stepped in and stood awkwardly at the foot of one of the cots.

"Have any idea what's up?" Laura asked. I gestured towards a chair, and Raymond sat down in it. "All kinds of banging and grinding going on this morning," Laura added. She sounded hopeful—maybe things were getting fixed?

"I talked to the captain a little while ago," Raymond answered, shaking his head. "He said it's not so much the propeller that's broken, as the propeller *shaft*. Seems a propeller blade hit a submerged log and stuck. The engine kept turning the shaft, but the blade wouldn't budge. The shaft twisted till it was torn in two," he held out his hand and turned his forearm until it wouldn't turn anymore.

I sat down on the edge of a cot. "So what's it going to take to fix it?" I asked.

Raymond shook his head again. "They've been trying to get it loose all morning. They've got one piece out now. Massive sucker. I had no idea. The engine that turns it must be huge. They're working on the other piece now. When they get it free, they'll take both pieces into Mbandaka by pirogue, get them welded, then bring the repaired shaft back and reinstall it."

Laura had leaned forward. She was looking at her hands, or the floor, I couldn't tell which. "So that should take about how long?" she asked, glancing up at Raymond.

"A few days, if they're lucky, I guess. Could be longer. It's hard to say. The problem is, once they get everything back and put back together, they'll still be stuck on this sandbar."

Laura sat up, nodded thoughtfully. "But we'll have two good propellers then. That ought to make a big difference—that is, in pulling the barge off."

"Sure," Raymond said, "but from what the captain said, they're not sure how badly we're stuck. The barge might slide right off—or it might not. The captain was talking about trying to lighten the load by unhooking the *Tshatshi* from the other barges so she can pull free, then rehooking and pulling the other barges off one by one. The thing is, it's anybody's guess how long it will take."

Raymond put his hands on his legs, and for a moment I thought he was about to stand up. "Whatever happens," he said, "I'll be long gone by then. I was just about to go to the forward barge to see if I could hire someone to take me on upriver to my research camp."

He looked at us both intently, and I thought for a moment I saw a flicker of that longing look he had cast at Laura in the dining room a couple of nights before. He seemed nervous, and also eager.

"So," he said, flexing his hands where they rested on his knees, and again I thought he was about to stand, "I'm on my way, and I wanted to know if the two of you would like to join me. It's likely you'd see some bonobos," he cocked his head, coaxing, "and you'd get out of this stifling sun and into the forest. And of course, you'd be off this barge, and who knows how long...well, it's hard to say, but you're welcome to come with me."

Once again, his expression was hard for me to interpret. It seemed a mask of many emotions. But one thing was clear—he wasn't just offering. He really hoped we would come.

Laura and I looked at one another. I was already uneasy at the thought of going with Raymond, and it didn't help to have him seem a little over-eager for our company. But it was like he had said—we could sit here in the glaring sun for who knew how many days as the repairs were made, and then again as they struggled to get the barge unstuck. Or we could go with him. Or, I supposed, we could wander off on our own—but then there was the bonobo site, and the ride we'd been offered to the airstrip at Basankusu. It seemed a lot to pass up on. And if we stayed on the barge, it seemed almost a certainty that we would arrive late for our rendezvous at Epulu.

"Really, I would be delighted to have you both come," Raymond went on. "Mvula would be there, of course. We could make you quite comfort-able there."

Laura and I were still looking at one another, and I felt her thoughts mirroring my own. But it was what we had agreed, wasn't it? That if we were really stuck, we'd go with Raymond? Hadn't we settled it the night before?

I saw Laura make a small nod, and I nodded back to her. I looked back around at Raymond.

"Sure," I said, then glanced over at Laura to reconfirm her wishes, but Laura had already turned her gaze to Raymond.

"Yes, thanks Raymond. We'd be delighted to come," she said, expanding on my brief reply.

As though at some signal, we all stood up.

"Right, then. That's great," Raymond said, his face still just as unclear to me. "Great. Well, I guess I should get on with making the plans." He paused for a moment. "I'll need to find someone with a good-sized pirogue who knows the river," he said, almost to himself.

He glanced around the room. "This is the stuff you'll be bringing?"

"Yes," Laura and I both answered.

Raymond nodded. "Right. Good. Well, I'll come back around when I've got things settled. I'd like to get off as soon as possible, so we can make some headway before it gets late. Do you think you could be ready in the next hour or two?"

Laura and I looked at one another again, nodded, and agreed.

"Good. Then, I'll come back when I have things settled," Raymond said, and slipped out the door as quietly as the breeze.

For moments, there seemed a vacuum, a pause in time. I had the impression the puzzle of life had just shifted, and suddenly made a new picture. We were here. And we would be leaving.

Yes.

And then it struck me with a forceful suddenness—we would not be stopping in Mbandaka at all. Laura would not be stopping there.

A bubble of joy rose up in me. I looked over at Laura, who seemed lost in thoughts of her own. I was smiling, and I turned my gaze out the window to the deep forest along the shore, and to the cool and beckoning shadows which hung like a mist below its canopy.

Yes, I thought—we will be leaving.

✵   ✵   ✵

After Raymond's departure, Laura and I set to work ordering our belongings for the trip and getting packed. We still had most of our purified water and all of our kerosene. For the most part, we figured our earlier preparations should serve us well for this unexpected leg of our journey, but we were both a little concerned about the canoe trip, and what might get wet. Of course, we had the two yellow river bags we'd bought to keep our papers and our laptop computer dry in the rainforest, and the backpacks were supposed to be mostly waterproof, but we still decided to repack, using plastic bags we'd brought for trash to seal up our clothes, food, money, and other items we wished to keep dry.

When we were mostly done, Laura left to go see the captain. She wanted to let him know our cabin would no longer be needed, and also to hire a porter who would help us carry our gear to the pirogue, once Raymond had arranged for one.

While Laura was gone, I finished with the packing, and before long the room looked much as it had when we'd arrived, with our two backpacks, two daypacks, a money bag, two briefcases covered in strong yellow plastic, all surrounded by a great jumble of water bottles and kerosene cans, all stacked together in the middle of the room between the two cots.

By mid-morning, Laura had returned, and everything was set. Raymond came by with his luggage in hand and told us he had hired a big, sturdy pirogue, which he thought should be ample for all of us and our gear, and a couple of men who would take us past Mbandaka, and part way up the Ikelemba River. After that, he said, we would have to make other arrangements—but not to worry, for it shouldn't be hard to find others who would be happy to earn a few thousand *Zaires* for taking us on the rest of the way to the research site.

Laura got the attention of our porter, who was waiting outside, and we loaded up our possessions and followed Raymond along the walkways of the *Tshatshi*, then the *Kasongo*, and finally out onto the deck of the flat barge. We told our porter we would pay him a little extra if he would see to it that our gear was safely stowed, to which he quickly agreed, and Laura and I took a few extra minutes to dash into the bazaar and buy food to eat on our trip. Laura bought deep-fried palm grubs, which were scooped up by a grinning, nearly toothless woman, who wrapped them up for Laura in a banana leaf. For me, it was eel and rice from a few stalls away, also wrapped the same way.

The sun had not yet reached its apex when we finally climbed into the pirogue and, after a few minutes spent arranging ourselves amidst our possessions, shoved off from the stalled barge. I was thinking about the trip ahead, and hoped Raymond was right that we would have no trouble finding a flight from Basankusu to Kisangani. And what would the forest hold? I wondered. Bonobos? Other animals? What people would we meet? Such an adventure!

A cool breeze drifted over us as we distanced ourselves from the barge. I looked back at Laura where she sat behind me, ready to share my excitement with her, but was surprised to see her staring back at the barge, a solemn look on her face. I followed her line of sight, and as the two oarsmen stroked rhythmically upriver, the array of barges gradually shrank into the distance—an island of vitality and sociability, which we had, I realized, all too abruptly left behind. I thought about Nsambi, then, and her family, and wondered how long they would be sitting on that same piece of river. (It would be some time before it even occurred to me to consider how casually Laura and I had accepted Raymond's word, when he had told us the barge was stuck too badly for us to stay.)

I turned forward and felt the breeze on my face, full of the scents of rainforest—a dusky smell I would soon come to recognize, full of dark shadows and green things growing. In front of me, I could see the strong, bare back of the oarsman where he stood rowing in steady strokes, and beyond him, stretching out into the hazy distance, was the vast shoreline which lay ahead.

. 13 .

When Kiki's voice fell momentarily silent, Paul asked her to stop.

"Stopping," she answered. "End of chapter."

Good, Paul thought. He had been listening a long time, and now was feeling groggy enough that he thought he would be able to sleep, even on this rocky ledge.

For several minutes, Paul lay on his back with his eyes open, staring up at a sky strewn with stars. Never on his world had he seen the night sky so distinctly without the aid of a telescope! Here the air was so clear, so free of pollution, and the light of distant cities so dim, that the sky truly sparkled. The Milky Way was so beautifully illuminated that Paul was reminded how the name had come to be—for there, above him, a broad band of milky white stretched across the sky, revealing the stars of earth's galaxy as they spun around its center—a center that the earth, itself, spun around, too.

Paul rolled onto his side and scrunched up against the wall behind him, trying to stay warm. Though the nighttime air had turned quite cool, Paul couldn't grumble too much about it, as it seemed fresh beyond anything he had known on his world. Here it carried scents, not of pollutants, but of living things.

Along the horizon, Paul could see the soft glow of Santa Maria's lights, and though he reminded himself that he was on a whole other earth now, they seemed to him to be the lights of his childhood home, rising up in the distance.

Paul stared a long time, letting his thoughts drift, then began to feel melancholy and decided it really was time for sleep. Paul reminded himself again not to roll toward the cliff's edge during the night—then, wrapping his arms around his body, he nestled up against the rocky wall for safety. Soon he had drifted off into the enfolding darkness of sleep.

◘   ◘   ◘

Paul was running as hard as his young legs could carry him, cutting across the lot beside the pharmacy where the reprocessed building had stood, up

Concepcion Avenue, then down the narrow alley between his building and the next. It was a hot day, and something was wrong with his legs, as though the air had grown thick around them and held him back as he ran.

He pushed open the door of his building, with the package still in his hand, and was suddenly inside the cool interior, pounding his way up the endless stairs, surrounded by the echo of his own footfalls. Floor by floor, he breathlessly ascended, but it seemed that, with each turn, another turn was added, and he could never reach the top.

Time went on forever—and then suddenly Paul was inside the apartment, looking from room to room. He had a package; he had to give it to her. Each time he would enter a room, he would see a bit of her—a leg, a shoulder, the back of her head—as she turned from him and disappeared.

"Mom," he called, as she slipped away ahead of him. He understood just how she felt. She was angry at him and wanted him to stay away.

Paul started to cry. Somewhere, his brother was crying, too.

Paul went to Casey's room, but he wasn't there. Paul went from room to room, looking for Casey. As he passed a window, he noticed how bright it was outside—while everywhere inside, it was deathly dim.

Finally, Paul found Casey beside their mother's bed. Her arm hung loosely over the side.

"Mom!" Paul called out—but she wouldn't listen to him, or even turn toward him.

"Mom!" Paul called out, louder, and woke as the sound of his voice was lost in the empty nighttime air. His face was wet with tears. He opened his eyes, but around him was only darkness. Even the stars had faded before a dim moon.

Paul's heart was pounding, and his skin was damp with sweat. He was filled with a terrible, almost unbearable, sadness—mixed with piercing regret.

Paul sat up, trembling. He almost stood—then remembered where he was, and why, and how near to the cliff's edge. Instead, he leaned back against the hard rock, and thought about his mother, and how she had died.

In the dream, he had caught many glimpses of her—but had never seen her face. How many years had it been since he'd been able to remember what she had looked like? he wondered—and he hadn't even a photograph to remind him.

Paul looked out at the bare glow of Santa Maria's lights and thought how strange it was that he would dream of her like this, would come so close to seeing her in a dream, now, when he was the farthest he had ever been from the home they had shared—on a whole other world, entirely!

Paul lay back down, still trembling, and soothed himself with thoughts of Sheila. Sheila, who looked at him with such warmth in her eyes. Sheila, who admired him far beyond what he deserved—and who spoke of him to others with such approval. Sheila, to whom he would soon return, and who would envelope him in her loving arms when she discovered him—well and whole—at her door, and hold him as she had never done before.

Sheila, Paul thought, as the tears rose up in his throat. He focused on her fiercely, trying to push aside the feeling the dream had left him with. He missed her now, in this moment, more intensely, more bitterly, than he had ever done before. Soon, the tears overtook him, and he cried against the unyielding rock, wishing so to be home, to be with her, and to receive the solace that she gave him.

◻   ◻   ◻

When the morning came, Paul had the sense that he was having to rise up from a great depth to meet it. Somewhere within him, he was struggling with something dark and unnamed, something that clung to him and wrapped itself around him, almost suffocating him.

Paul opened his eyes and immediately remembered his circumstances. On another day, he might have wanted to rise and quickly begin searching for a way down, but on this morning he woke already feeling overburdened.

Paul closed his eyes and struggled again with the feeling he had found himself entangled in as he awoke—then remembered the dream he had had the night before. As it came back to him, it unsettled him further, as though it bore into him at a level below eye sight, pouring through him in currents that wore away at something solid and secure within himself.

Paul rubbed his face and sat up. Maybe he was just feeling unsteady from having spent a night on a cliff's edge, he told himself—but as he, for the first time, took in the world around him in the bright light of day, he knew this wasn't so.

Why this dream, now? he asked himself.

He could make no sense of it. It had been eighteen years since his mother had died in the *Muerte Azul* epidemic, which had taken so many lives. Paul recalled how it had gradually crept up along the West Coast from Central America, and how it had eventually "ignited" and spread like fire through much of the Southwest, before the quarantines Corprogov had clamped down forced it to burn itself out.

But by then, many people were dead. In many of the affected cities, half the population had become sick with it, and as many as a third of those infected had died.

The truth was, Paul reflected, they had been lucky that it had only taken his mother, and not him and his brother, Casey, as well—and that his father had been one of the few to get inoculated (which Corprogov had permitted because of the importance of his food-distribution work) though the inoculant was in short supply.

Countless times, Paul had tried to tell himself that they had "gotten off light" compared to other families that he knew of—but he could never convince himself to feel that way. The truth was, he could still hardly bear to think about those times. Even now, he felt uncomfortable with even these few thoughts on the subject, as though each such thought was a burden too heavy to carry.

Paul stood up and looked around. The last thing he needed, he told himself, was to burden himself with these thoughts now.

Paul stepped to one side of his ledge and relieved himself over its edge. The sun was up, the air was clear, birds were singing in the bushes nearby. This was no time to wallow in the pains of the past, Paul told himself, as he looked along the length of the ledge for some way to get down.

He turned and looked back at the rock wall he had slid down in the twilight the evening before, examining it. It was quite steep and covered with loose, gravelly rock. Clearly, there was no good way to climb up along that route. From there, Paul traced his eye along the whole perimeter of the ledge on which he'd slept. The ledge was perhaps a meter deep and three meters long—or maybe a bit longer than that, Paul thought, as he noticed that one end of it disappeared around a curve in the rocky face of the ridge.

Paul stepped over and looked around that bit of rocky outcropping, and realized that the ledge actually continued on a good way after that, where it met up with some less-steep terrain. There, to Paul's delight, he saw an accessible way down.

Paul glanced around, as though he might notice something he would otherwise forget and leave behind, before recalling that he had nothing with him but what he wore. He bent down to tighten the bindings on his shoes, then started carefully along the ledge, following the various twists and turns, which led gradually downward. As he moved along, he realized that all of his sore and aching muscles had resolved themselves during the night, and that all his pain was washed away. Even his feet still felt good!

Paul stepped carefully through the uneven terrain, baffled as to how this could be, but then remembered that he'd drunk some sort of elixir he'd found in a vial in his free "sojourner's aid pack" the day before.

Paul steadied himself with his hands as he navigated a slope covered in loose rocks. It seemed the "System Boost" he had taken had worked wonders on his muscles—seemingly mending them overnight, just as the "Dermo Mend" patches had helped his sore feet.

Whatever this world had to offer in terms of technology, Paul thought, at least when it came to making people feel better, it seemed their technology worked quite well.

Paul came to the bottom of the ridge and zigzagged his way through the brush and grasses until he made it back to the path, and from there back to camp.

Once back in camp, Paul sat by the pool, breakfasting on two self-heating travel meals, and eyeing his sleep bivy enviously. It would have been much nicer to have slept in that, he thought—but then things had worked out all right. He had survived and was all in one piece.

Recalling the night brought back the dream he'd had in it, and Paul's mood, which had lifted once he'd found his route down, began to sour. Paul immediately pushed aside the impression of his dream, telling himself he had more important things to focus on.

Soon, he had his breakfast finished and all his gear stowed and had started off down the trail along the creek, in the shade of pines. As much as he tried to shake it, the mood the dream had brought with it continued to haunt him, threatening to pull him back into the hole he had arisen from when waking.

"Kiki," Paul said—and found himself almost startled by the sound of his own voice, the morning had been so quiet—"please give me something else to focus on. Resume recitation where we left off last night."

In a moment, the tones of Dr. Kumar's voice lifted into the air around him. Paul allowed his attention to follow it, carrying him into the world she lived in, and away from the thoughts and feelings that troubled him.

◙   ◙   ◙

CHAPTER VIII

*All who are in touch with the natural world can sense energies,
emotions, and intentions of people and animals. If we listen, we can
know—all we need to do is give up being in charge. Knowing inside
is not something unusual; it is how we are. All humans can have
that connection with All-That-Is. The connection is within us.*

—Robert Wolff

Whatever solemn mood had settled on Laura as we left the barge lifted by
midday. Though clouds gathered in the northeastern sky, the air was clear
above us, and the sun sparkled radiantly on the water as we skimmed
along. It felt good to be close to the river, not meters above it as we had
been on the barge. Every once in a while I would see a fish jump to catch
an insect hovering in the air above, or see a bird dive with its talons open,
ready to scoop up a fish from the water below. One oarsman stood at the
pirogue's bow, the other at its stern, and their posture, standing above the
low-riding craft, reminded me of when Laura and I used to go punting
on the River Cherwell during our Oxford days.

The punt was new to me when I first arrived in England. Like the
pirogue, it is a flat-bottomed boat, though a good deal shorter in length
than the pirogues of the Congo, and perhaps twice as wide. When punting, one person stands on a platform at the stern of the boat and pushes
off from the river's bottom with a long pole. Much as one might handle
an oar from a standing position, the pole is swung forward, plunged into
the water, pushed against, then lifted and swung forward again. As I sat
there in the sunshine, coasting along, I thought how much the oarsmen
looked like punters, and commented on this to Laura.

Before I knew it, Laura was making her way to the stern of the boat.
She made rowing gestures to the oarsman standing there, then pointed
towards herself and reached out for the oar. The man grinned at her, then

handed her the oar and stepped out of her way so she could take his place at the stern. The front oarsman, noticing the drag on the water as the other man and Laura traded places, glanced back to see what was happening, then stopped rowing to watch as Laura took up her oar. I made my way forward then, and took the spot of the front oarsman.

I'd say we made a pretty good showing, Laura and I, though it had been many years since either of us had held an oar, or a punting pole, while our guides had spent most of their lives navigating this river. We managed to get up a little speed, though I'm sure it was nothing compared to what our oarsmen might have done on a good day. Still, it felt good to stand at the bow of that pirogue, in the sun, on that muggy January afternoon, as we propelled ourselves up the Congo River. And I dare say it gave those two men something to talk about when they returned to their village the next day.

I'd say that Laura and I only stayed at these posts for fifteen minutes or so, and were glad then to return our oars to those whose muscles were more seasoned to the effort. I leaned back against a pile of packs and water bottles then, and tried to think about what to add to the article I'd been writing, but under that warm sun I got no further than to let my mind drift over what I had already written, interspersed with odd, dreamy images of bonobos examining themselves in mirrors and ancient humans decorating their bodies with paint.

Sometime around noon we passed a small city on the Congo's eastern bank. By this time, the clouds from the northeast had pushed in, sweeping over the domed sky like the closing of an eyelid, and a few drops of rain had begun to fall. The river had splintered around islands, and we were traveling along a northeastern course, in deep water, perhaps two to three hundred meters from shore. Raymond said the city was Mbandaka, and as we coasted by we could see its dilapidated structures, which seemed to have slipped quietly from the grasp of the forest and come to a stop at the river's edge. The forest, which must once have been cleared to make room for the city, seemed to have crept back in amongst these tired buildings, which together displayed themselves in an uneven patchwork of green and white and rust red. This broken medley of buildings and overgrowth sprung up with a disconcerting suddenness after so many miles of unbroken forest.

So this was Mbandaka, the city that had caused me such worry and fear, I thought. It seemed, from our vantage point, so innocuous and insignificant—a mere jumble of run-down buildings. And from theirs, I realized, we were hardly more than a speck on the water. We drifted past with barely a ripple.

By early afternoon, we were in a steady downpour. The clouds, which had piled up against the southwestern horizon, had begun to clear in the northeast, where a narrow ribbon of light lit the border between earth and sky. Our oarsmen continued to move us upriver, their inexhaustible muscles rippling beneath their bare, rain-soaked skin. By mid-afternoon, we had already come to the mouth of the Ikelemba and turned up it. It was a substantial river, and I might have thought it impressive if I had not had the Congo and Ganges to compare it to. It looked dull gray under the wet and clouded sky.

Before long we passed a village on stilts, closer than we had passed by other villages when traveling on the barge, and I got a better look at this one. Children were playing in the clearing around the huts. I saw a cluster of pale monkeys with dark faces, surely killed for their meat, hanging from a stake stuck in the ground. In a clearing back from the water, I caught glimpses of corn and manioc growing. The huts themselves stood on young, narrow trees cut from the forest—they were stripped of bark, and I could see the knots where branches had been removed.

Then we were past, and the river bank was once again a wall of green rising suddenly from the water's edge. A few minutes later I heard the rhythmic pounding of drums and wondered what the message was, and if it was possible they had noticed us passing and were announcing our journey up the river, just as other villages had announced the passage of the barge.

As we continued to wind our way upriver, the day around us began to fade. The clouds continued their journey across the sky, clearing first where they had gathered early that morning, and gradually disappearing over the opposite horizon. The rain had slackened off, first to a weak drizzle, and now, finally, it had stopped all together. The sun dropped low into the western sky, brightening the remaining clouds, above, and the water, below, with its crimson glow. We were hanging close to the shore, rowing upstream in the slower water near the river's edge.

The horizontal light cut though a low mist, which draped itself over the water like a moist breath the forest had exhaled. There, in that half light, in that misty dusk, we passed through a cloud of small lavender butterflies, which so filled the air around us that the world seemed showered with their tiny, fluttering shapes. They lifted and swirled in the air, afloat in the turbulence our passage made, like snowflakes swept by the breeze on a winter day.

For the longest time the sun seemed to hover above the river, as though hesitant to extinguish itself in the watery depths below. Though the tropical twilight had felt surprisingly brief on other occasions, this one seemed to stretch on, linking an afternoon draped in clouds and forest shadows with the clearing skies of night. When the rays of the evening sun shot through the remaining clouds in bands of color, the oarsman at the pirogue's bow lifted his oar out of the water, then turned to Raymond and spoke to him in Lingala.

His speech was too soft and quick for me to catch what was said, but I watched as the man gestured upriver, and Raymond nodded his agreement. Then the oarsman returned his oar to the water and began again his long, steady strokes. Raymond turned to Laura and me and told us that we would stay the night at a village where our guides had some relatives. There, they would find others to take their place, and then would leave for their home village the next morning.

We glided on in silence. The world darkened around us. The water took on even more the appearance of the sky, with stars reflected in its blackish surface and shreds of mist hanging above it like small clouds. I found myself uneasy, imagining the departure of our oarsmen with the morning light, and realized how much confidence I had placed in these two men, who knew the territory we were passing through. But they weren't really our companions on this trip, I reminded myself. It was just Laura and me—and Raymond.

We coasted on through darkness as the landscape around us became increasingly one of sound rather than sight. A chorus of insects, frogs, and other animals flooded out of the forest, which towered over us on one side, blocking even the starlight there. The demarcation between that black wall and the milky, star-lit sky above us seemed to be our only guide as we worked our way up the dusky river.

The world took on a timeless quality as we glided over the water in darkness, and I found my thoughts slipping from one subject to another, helter-skelter. What would the journey hold? I wondered. What would this village be like tonight? How could I revive my work on the article, which seemed to have closed itself off from me like a seed? Why that look of concern I had seen on Laura's face as we had left the barge this morning? This morning. Yes, that was just this morning. Raymond seems all right, doesn't he? Was that what Laura was worried about? The guides seem good—friendly, open—too bad they will be leaving us tomorrow.

All day I had been distracted by the newness of our adventure, but now, as we slipped through an invisible world, lulled by an invisible chorus, I looked at the fretful turnings of my mind, and realized how exhausted I was. Too many days spent concentrating on the article, too many nights kept just above sleep by the noise and activities of barge life. It should only be another day before we reached the research site, I told myself. Maybe it would be quiet there, and I would really sleep.

Up ahead, on the shore, firelight flashed and flickered between the trunks of giant trees. It seemed almost to pulse or sway, as though dancing, as we coasted along.

A few minutes later, we made landfall on the Ikelemba's southern bank, amidst a clutter of pirogues. We all stepped ashore, unsteady, as though dazed by the light from the handful of camp fires that burned there, surrounded by a clearing and half a dozen huts raised high on stilts.

❋   ❋   ❋

"Pause," Paul said. Kiki's voice seemed to hang in the air for a moment, then trailed away in the breeze. Paul had begun a series of switchbacks rising above the creek, up along the canyon wall.

"I'm not sure how soon I'm going to get to the Kumaric Retreat," Paul said, "but I don't think this recitation is going fast enough. Could we skip over some of this, try to move a little faster?"

"I could continue in summary mode," Kiki responded.

"Okay," Paul said, considering that option. "But I like feeling caught up in the story, so don't skip too much."

"You have set the parameters so that I should return to recitation mode for material of high conceptual content and/or extensive social influence. Do you wish these parameters expanded?"

Paul sighed. "Yes." He thought for a moment. "I like the descriptions. I like the way they give me a feeling for where they are, where they're going. Include that material, too. Do you have that?"

"Descriptive passages will be recited, not summarized," Kiki said.

"Good," Paul answered, looking back down into the ravine below him, and at the creek, barely visible now, at its base. He was glad he'd stopped to refill his canteen earlier, when he'd noticed that the trail branched away from the creek up ahead.

Paul turned and continued along the trail. "Please begin," he said to Kiki.

"They were met at the shore by people from the village," Kiki said, "including the sister and brother-in-law of their lead oarsman, and some of their children, who were themselves nearly adults. The travelers were led into the village and fed dinner, a vegetable stew of ground peanuts, corn, manioc leaves, and onions, seasoned with hot *pili pili* peppers. A bowl of live palm grubs was set out for them to eat, as well, though only the oarsmen and the villagers ate them.

"'The moon drifted up above the forest canopy like a slow-moving balloon,'" Kiki added, momentarily switching to a tone lightly colored by Indira's intonations as she added a brief descriptive passage to her summary, then continued in her own voice.

"Throughout the village people squatted near low-burning fires, laughing and chatting. Many gathered around the travelers and listened as the oarsman and his sister told each other stories about events that had passed since they'd seen one another last. The travelers 'held bowls from which steam rose into the nighttime air—air which was scented with wood smoke, the simmering stew, and the sweet and musty odor of the forest.' The children watched the strangers from their parent's sides.

"One little girl, naked and not more than five years old, squatted near Laura, 'playing with and snacking on the palm grubs in the bowl, and staring openly at Laura, whose red hair and fair skin she seemed to be fascinated with.' Every once in a while, Laura would glance over, and the two would exchange a smile. Soon all the children—even the little girl—lost interest and began a game in which first one and then another would hide in the shadows beneath the huts and be sought by the others.

"When the meal was over, their guides introduced them to a couple of 'strong-looking' young men, named Isinga and Dibaya. 'They had bright smiles and an easy, youthful enthusiasm.' Indira thought neither of them could have been more than eighteen years old. She had the impression that Isinga was their lead oarsman's nephew. Both were interested in the job of taking the three strangers on to the research site. Laura and Indira thought they seemed likable and were ready to hire the young men on the spot, but Raymond wanted to see their pirogue first. As Indira watched 'they strolled to the river's edge, and Raymond looked down into the canoe, combing it with his flashlight.' The pirogue was fine, and they soon settled on a price for the young men's services."

Kiki's voice took on the thoughtful, accented tones of Indira's voice as she switched briefly to full recitation mode:

That night we slept on straw mats high up above the ground in the hut built on stilts that our hosts lived in. The roof was low (or perhaps I should say the floor was high) and the whole place had a musty smell from the thatched roof and woven wall coverings. We slept without so much as a sheet to cover us, and none was needed, as the muggy tropical air blanketed us. The house was full of small noises—whispers of the teenage boys who lived there, the sounds the straw mats made as people turned, trying to find the most comfortable position from which to fall asleep. Beyond, the forest seemed to breath with life, its constant chirps and songs woven together into a single sonorous noise, which I might describe as "soothing," had it not been so loud. Finally, I fell asleep, and dreamed that I was a child, sleeping in the room I had shared with my sisters, and that there was a great tropical rainforest outside.

The light tones Paul had programmed as Kiki's voice returned:

"They were up early the next day and breakfasted on manioc porridge, which their hosts prepared. The day 'broke bright and clear.' After breakfast they went down to the river and moved their gear from the pirogue they had arrived in to Isinga's pirogue, which was shorter than the first, but 'of adequate size and solid build.'

"They paid the guides they'd traveled with the day before, thanked them, then said goodbye to them and to the people of the village, who had made them feel so welcome. Indira felt a certain sadness at parting, though the contact had been so brief.

"'We climbed into the pirogue and started up the Ikelemba,'" Kiki said, again adopting Indira's voice:

The sun was still low in the eastern sky as we set off. The water around us was slow-moving and brown in color. I told Laura that it looked like tea, and we discussed how this water had percolated down through the rainforest to get here. The river was in fact, we concluded, a kind of tea made of the whole rainforest, steeped under the hot tropical sun.

And hot it was—what clouds and mist lingered from the day before burned off with the morning light, so that the sun shone boldly down on us and our open craft. Where the water hyacinths weren't too thick, we stayed in the slow-moving water along the river's shore. There the tall trees rising along the river's bank caught and tangled the breeze so that little of it reached us, as we baked in the bare sun below.

Sometime around noon, Isinga and Dibaya said they would like to eat and to rest somewhere out of the sun for a little while. We agreed, so they gathered up their net and cast it over the water. We were just passing a stream that emptied out into the river, and the water of the river there was two-toned, with a clearer blue thinning the deep tea tones.

Soon Isinga and Dibaya had caught half a dozen bright, wiggling fish, which they hauled on board. We dragged the pirogue up onto the muddy red bank and retired to the forest's shade. The fish were quite an assortment, though all were fairly small (none as much as a foot in length). Some had scales tinted with aqua-blue and a fringe of red along the outer edge of their fins. A couple looked like some sort of catfish. Another had a long dorsal fin (which grew, non-stop, along the ridge of its back, almost into the tail fin) and was covered with a sort of leopard spotting, in gold and black.

When Isinga and Dibaya opened the net, all the fish flopped about except for the leopard-spotted one, which righted itself to its belly and began to try to make its way back to the water, pushing itself along with its fins, which stuck out to the side like little legs. Dibaya laughed when he saw me staring at it. He picked it up and said, as best I could understand him in his lilting Lingala, that this kind of fish does not need water to breath, and can live in the air, or even in the mud.

Kiki returned to summary mode. "Soon they had a fire going. Dibaya and Isinga prepared the fish over a little fire while Laura and Indira watched, then they all ate together. Dibaya and Isinga had brought along, as well, a package of live and wiggling palm grubs, wrapped up in a banana leaf. They set it out to share—though of the three foreigners, Laura was the only one brave enough to try one. After eating, everyone rested in the shade for an hour or so. Then they set off again, with the sun still high in the sky.

"Within an hour they had passed Boyenge on the northern shore. Much of it seemed 'veiled by the dense forest' but Indira had the impression that it was a much smaller city than Mbandaka. Not long after, Raymond said they would have to start looking for the red sash Mvula had left tied to one of the trees at the mouth of a tributary. They would need to turn up that waterway to get to the road to the bonobo research site, he told them. He said it was the same sort of marker they used to identify trees used by the bonobos. By mid-afternoon, they had caught sight of it—'a simple reddish band of plastic wound round the trunk'—and turned up the tributary.

Again Kiki adopted Indira's voice:

This river was narrower and, at places, the trees shooting up alongside of it arched over it, far above. I lay back against our gear and looked up into the branches, glad to find myself in that soft, dappled light. The air was filled with the high-pitched chatter of monkeys, and I could see several kinds leaping from branch to branch high above. I asked Raymond what they were. He looked up and named them casually as we rowed along—redtail, mangabey, he said. A little later on he pointed out some red colobus, and blue. The trees made an arched ceiling high above the narrow river we were traveling on—like the painted ceiling of a cathedral, I thought, as I looked up at the branches drifting past—but this bright mural was a living one! And indeed the analogy fit the scene, for I did have the feeling I was entering some sort of grand, living cathedral. The awe

I felt reminded me of the first time Laura and I had visited Westminster Abby together, years before.

"They continued up the tributary," Kiki said, "until they came to the place where it met the road to the research site. There they unloaded their gear, paid Dibaya and Isinga for getting them there, and said their farewells. The road was 'barely more than a rutted dirt track through the forest.' Raymond suggested that he hike up it to the research site, then come back with the jeep for them and all their gear. He set off alone, while Indira and Laura sat down under one of the trees to wait."

"Pause," Paul said. Kiki's voice fell silent.

The trail Paul was on had climbed. He stood, now, on a path cut into the canyon's wall, looking out over the open spaces beyond. He stopped and pulled his canteen from his pack, then turned his head up as he took a drink from it. In the sky above him, two—no, three—condors circled lazily.

Paul smiled, filled with a sense of wonder at the sight. He'd been keeping his eyes on the trail as he'd walked along, but now he scanned the scene around him. The sides of the canyon were covered in wild flowers of every variety. Below them, at the bottom of the canyon, was movement—like a carpet of brown, moving in and out among the trees and brush.

Paul wondered what was there, as he peered carefully downward.

Yes, he was sure—more of the same sort of elk he had seen at Anna and Marco's the week before.

Paul's smile grew bigger. It was wonderful to be, at once, reading about a world in which so much life existed, and to be in one!

Paul put his canteen away, took another look at the scene around him, then continued up the trail.

"Kiki, resume summary," he said, and again Kiki's voice filled the air around him.

"When they arrived in camp," Kiki continued, "they were introduced to Mvula, a middle-aged man in whose face Indira saw 'a quiet patience.' Mvula was a small man, but strongly built, his hair 'dusted with grey.' He had begun cooking dinner after Raymond had come to get the jeep. They all ate together, sitting around the open-air hearth outside the kitchen hut. They visited in a mixture of Lingala, English, and French. Mvula spoke English about as well as Laura and Indira spoke Lingala, and though he appeared to speak some French, as well, Indira could not converse in French, so little was said in that language.

"Mvula reported on the activities of the bonobos during the few weeks since Raymond had left and concluded by saying that the apes had just found an *elimilimi* tree that morning, which was in full fruit, and that they had nested near there for the night. Raymond asked Mvula if he would show him where it was in the morning, when the bonobos would be there feeding. He then invited Indira and Laura to join them. Mvula said the tree was about an hour's hike away, and Raymond told them they'd all have to be up by 4 AM if they

wanted to have time to eat breakfast and make their way to the fruiting tree
before the bonobos arrived, shortly after dawn.

"Tired as Indira was after so many nights of short sleep, she and Laura
both eagerly agreed to come along. After all, Indira had had a feeling since
arriving at the camp that they really were going to get to see some of the
shy, elusive bonobos, and she figured this would probably be her best
opportunity.

"After dinner, the four of them sat around visiting for some time, then
Raymond showed Laura and Indira to the hut normally used by his two graduate assistants," Kiki said, and then switched to recitation mode:

The hut was at one edge of the clearing, not far from the kitchen hut
outside of which we'd had our dinner. Raymond said this opening in the
forest had been cleared by local farmers for growing crops. He said they
would clear an area, grow crops there for a couple of years, but when the
land got tired, they would leave it and clear a new swatch of land. So the
huts sat in this open area, and behind them, only a few meters away, rose
the forest, dense and shadowy. The huts (there were four of them, counting the kitchen hut) were all squat, one-room structures built right on
the ground, with red clay walls and thatched roofs. There was no glass
in the windows, but there were screens and shutters.

Raymond opened the door to the hut we were to stay in, then strode
across the darkened room and lit a kerosene lamp that was resting on a
foot locker at one end of the room. As the light spread across the room,
warm and yellow, I saw that the two cots inside were each draped in mosquito netting, a thin whitish fabric which, in the dim lamp light, seemed
almost a kind of mist hovering between floor and ceiling.

Laura and I went to get our luggage from the jeep, and Raymond was
kind enough to come along and help. We left the water and kerosene in the
jeep, but gathered up everything else to haul back to the hut. I remember
Laura was full of questions about the bonobos. In particular, I remember
her asking Raymond about where the bonobos slept. Raymond described
to her the nests they built in trees by folding one branch over another,
thus making a kind of cradle to sleep in.

When we got back to the hut, I set down my backpack, daypack, and
yellow-clad briefcase in one corner of the room. Laura asked Raymond if
it might be possible for us to go to see where the bonobos slept after we
were done observing them in the morning.

As Laura said this, I turned around. Laura's back was to Raymond as
she set her backpack on one of the cots, and Raymond was watching her,
again, with that expression of tenderness, or longing—his eyes brooding,
intense, and dark.

"Sure," he answered softly, "we could do that."

I felt a little shiver. I had almost forgotten. It was like there were two of
him: the normal one we had been traveling with, and this one—strange,
intense, hard to decipher—who had shown up again now that we were
so nearly alone with him in this seemingly endless forest.

"Raymond said good night and left," Kiki said, continuing in summary mode. "It was almost 9 PM by the time Indira and Laura got into bed—early for them, but late considering they intended to be up long before dawn. They pushed the two cots together to share as one and snuggled close to one another, whispering in the darkness for half an hour or so, until finally Indira 'heard Laura's breath fall into the slow rhythms of sleep.' Then she 'tried to turn toward slumber' herself, but something held her back from sleep.

"Indira found herself lying awake, thinking about Raymond, about what the next day would bring, and about the article she'd been working on."

"Hold on a second," Paul said. "I want to know about the article. Could you please back up and recite that segment?"

"Yes," Kiki answered, and her voice once again modulated itself to express Dr. Kumar's pitch and intonation.

With Laura sleeping so quietly beside me, my thoughts began to drift. I found myself remembering the look I'd seen Raymond give Laura—that night, and also earlier, on the barge. Passionate—yes—there was some passion there. Longing—yes, that too. What did he feel for her? There was something raw, almost bruised in his expression.

Don't worry about it, I told myself. Don't think about it. It doesn't matter—we'll only be here a day or two—won't we?

I tried to sleep, but my thoughts kept moving, surfacing. The bonobos. Would we see some tomorrow? Mvula seemed to know where to look for them. I thought it would happen.

Sleep, I told myself again, but the current of my thoughts kept pulling me along. I thought about the paper I had been working on on the barge—about the changes that had occurred in human behavior during prehistoric times, and about how each of these changes had arisen at widely separate locations in such relatively short periods of time.

The window next to my cot was shuttered closed. I got out of bed and opened it, then stood looking out across the clearing and into the same tall and ancient forest that I had been yearning to explore since I'd first seen it growing along the sides of the Congo River, as we'd motored upstream on the barge. A full moon floated high above the trees. Its light entered the room like a flood.

Outside, insects and frogs, and perhaps other animals of the forest, were having a rumpus. Their voices filled the air. A thin mist wove itself through the tall stand of trees, glistening in the moonlight. The forest was so close, I thought, and still it seemed I had yet to really enter it.

I thought again about my article, and how I had gotten stuck trying to explain how and why the most remarkable cultural changes of our deep past had arisen together. There was something about that part, the place where I kept getting stuck—something about how I held it braced, framed up in a certain light, carefully packaging it and preparing it to show to my colleagues.

It came to me slowly, then, that that framing, that point of view, somehow didn't fit what I wanted, or needed, to say. The thing I *did* want to say, I could feel, like a dark space in my mind towards which I was having trouble turning a light, but within which I could nonetheless feel something brewing, like a familiar presence waiting there.

I told myself to let go of the way I had been looking at it, to forget it, and to let a new structure surface, to let myself come to wherever it was the material was really leading me, regardless of how it might look to people involved in the *Huginn/Muninn Newsletter.*

I sighed and closed the shutters, then climbed back into bed beside Laura, who now seemed lost in a blissful sleep.

Moonlight leaked in around the shutters and made a small glow at one end of the room. My thoughts were filled with the sensation of what it was I did want to say, but I couldn't quite get close enough to it to name it for myself.

I told myself to go to sleep, that I would have to be up early the next day, but there was something in the dark quiet of that room that seemed to encourage thought.

After a time, I glanced over at our little travel alarm, with its small hands glowing dimly on the bedside table, and saw that it was almost 11 PM. Oh no! I thought—I've got to get to sleep—up early—tomorrow—bonobos. But it must have been close to midnight before I finally drifted off.

Kiki paused. "End of segment," she said.

"Okay," Paul answered.

"The following section falls within the parameters you set for high conceptual content and/or extensive social influence," Kiki continued. "Shall I resume recitation mode?"

Paul paused on the trail and looked around. The morning was nearly gone, and the Retreat was coming ever nearer—and yet, as fast as time was passing, he had so much of the book yet to listen to. Still, he couldn't very well skip or skim through this section—not if he hoped to ever really have his questions about this world answered. But still, he did wish that things were going faster.

Finally, Paul sighed and said, "Yeah, okay. Resume normal recitation. Go ahead," and as soon as he had spoken, Kiki's voice rose again, and again Paul found himself listening to Dr. Kumar's soft, accented speech.

◘   ◘   ◘

Laura shut off the alarm, then rolled over with a deep sigh. The moon had set, and it was pitch black in our little hut. A few seconds passed, then I heard Laura get up and fumble around for a moment, swearing softly under her breath. I heard the scratch of a match and saw the sudden glow as she held the match and lit the kerosene lamp. As the light flooded the room, I looked over at Laura, who stood slumped in the middle of the small dirt-floored room.

She looked back at me. "Ready to start the day?" she said, her voice rough with sleep.

"No," I answered, then told her how late I'd been awake, and that I was going to beg off the bonobo-viewing trip, as I had slept too little for several days.

Laura sat down heavily on the side of her cot and sighed again. She pushed the hair back out of her face with one hand.

"Okay, that makes sense. Go on back to sleep," she said, her voice tired and sympathetic. She reached over and turned the lamp down to a bare glow.

I lay with my eyes closed while Laura dressed quietly and quickly, then turned the lamp down until it sputtered off.

"Sleep well, love," she whispered, as she slipped out the door.

"Goodbye, have fun," I mumbled, and was soon back to sleep.

It was about nine-thirty when I woke again. I got up and stretched. I was hungry. After a week of restless nights on the barge, I finally felt as though I had slept deeply. I wanted to get something to eat, but had the feeling that if I gave myself half a chance, I could sleep the rest of the day.

I pulled on some tan shorts and a green T-shirt, and put on some sturdy boots, then stepped out into the glare of the tropical sun. Pinned down by a rock on the ground outside our door was a note left for me by Laura:

Indira—
     Gone bonobo watching. Probably won't be back till mid-after-noon—Raymond wants to stay to observe (that is, if we do find the bonobos).
     Yummy manioc porridge for breakfast if you like—look on table in kitchen hut. Coffee, too.
     Love,
          Laura

I sighed. She'd gone off without me—just as I'd asked her to do. I looked over at the forest just beyond the little clearing. Somewhere in there was Laura.

It wasn't until that moment that it occurred to me that she'd gone off with Raymond. With *Raymond*—who'd given her such a strange look just the night before.

I thought about it, and for a moment felt distressed. But then I real-ized—they weren't alone. They were with Mvula. Mvula was all right. I'd had a good feeling about him. He had patient eyes, and that warm, grandfatherly smile.

"They'll be okay," I told myself.

I wandered over to the kitchen hut and got a bowl of the porridge and a cup of coffee, both cold, then took them outside to one of the camp stools by the fire site, where we'd supped the night before, and sat down. The porridge was good, with its starchy-but-not-quite-sweet quality, but I soon realized that there was too much sun for me there, at that naked spot in the clearing. I eyed the shade by our hut, then remembered a folding chair I'd seen just inside the door. That would do nicely, I thought, and soon had myself set up in the shadows cast by the forest, in front of our little hut, where I sat, eating and reading and sipping coffee.

I spent the next hour or two sitting in the shade, reading about the Mbuti. The sun continued to rise until it was high overhead and little shade was left in front of the hut. I picked up the folding chair and carried it around to the side of the hut. There the edge of the forest was only a few meters away, and the upper branches of the trees hung over the clearing, casting a dappled shade. I set my chair down beside the hut and sat down to read some more.

As I sat there a small cloud of golden butterflies gathered around me, hovering in the air. They were brighter and larger than the ones we'd seen on the river two nights before. It seemed they were attracted to the light reflecting off the pages of my book. I felt surrounded by shimmering bits of golden light, all quivering and alive. After a minute or two, I closed the book and watched as the cloud lifted and, seemingly lighter than air, fluttered off into the forest from which they had, presumably, only moments before come.

I stared at the spot where the butterflies had entered the forest. The day was hot, even in the thin shade beside the hut, and I felt relaxed and sleepy, like one might after a hot bath. I leaned back in the chair until its back rested against the outer wall of the hut, and closed my eyes.

My thoughts began to drift, and I found myself thinking about the bonobos and wishing that I hadn't been so tired, hours earlier, when the alarm had gone off—wishing that I could have seen them. I began to imagine what their voices might sound like as they called to one another, and to think of them moving through the forest as Raymond had described. They took life in my mind as shadowy forms, swinging through the trees and walking, sometimes upright, like people, on the ground.

After a time, I opened my eyes and went back to my reading about the Mbuti, but I had trouble concentrating. Something was tugging at my attention. I would look at the page, read a few lines, but then my thoughts would drift again.

What *is* it? I asked myself. I sighed and looked up from the book.

The forest—*yes*—the cool, dark forest, which I had been watching from the barge, which I had been longing to enter and explore. What was I doing sitting here in the clearing? *The forest is right there.* I stared into its cool, green depths. An odd feeling settled over me. "There," I thought. "I want to go *there.*"

I got up and stretched, looked at my watch. It was almost noon. I carried the folding chair and book back inside the hut and left a note for Laura telling her where I had gone. I paused to take a drink from my canteen, then I closed the door behind me, and walked back to the edge of the clearing and into the forest.

I pushed through the dense growth at the clearing's edge, then stood looking around me, waiting for my eyes to adjust to the dim light. The air was humid and still, and filled with the rich bouquet of rotting leaves and scented foliage. All around me trees shot skyward. Fifty meters above, their branches spread and interwove into a broad, green ceiling. Younger trees with slender trunks stretched almost to the height of the older, massive ones, all striving to stake out their bit of sun above. Thick vines wound around tree trunks and draped themselves through the air. The forest floor was surprisingly open, sparsely covered in low-growing, stemmy plants, which reached perhaps to my knees or a little higher.

The feeling that had coaxed me into the forest was still with me, and I felt that I knew just which way to go. I set off, paying close attention to the trees I passed, and every once in a while turning around to look back at where I had just come from, so I would have good visual reminders for finding my way home.

The place was like a wonderland. I don't think I had ever really grasped the scale of it, as Laura had shared story after story with me in our cozy bedroom in Boulder. This was not like any forest I had visited before. Though the trees varied a lot in size, the largest had trunks wider than the distance I could spread my arms, with sprawling, above-ground but-tress roots that extended on for meters, eventually snaking off into the underbrush—while above, their branches arched so high overhead that I again had that feeling of having entered a great cathedral. From amidst their branches I could hear the chatter of monkeys, the songs of birds, and a gentle swooshing sound as their leaves ruffled in the breeze above.

I wandered along, weaving between the trees and stepping over roots. Once, I paused to enjoy the delicate pattern on the bark of a tree, and realized there was a stream of small red ants interlaced with it, moving up and down the trunk industriously. Every inch of this green, sonorous world was alive, I realized. And it felt alive, like one great organism I had entered into and become a part of. I was sad that I couldn't be sharing this vibrant world with Laura, but reminded myself that we would be together in a place much like this one for months to come.

I kept walking, picking my way between the trees, and continued to have the sense that I knew just in which direction I wanted to go. It reminded me of my college days, when I had philosophized about "free movement" and wandered here and there on a whim, just to see where it would get me. I remembered how good it had felt to wander like that, and how helpful I had sometimes found it. It had even helped me get a job once, I recalled.

I mused about this as I walked along. Where did this strong feeling I was having come from—this feeling of knowing in just what direction I wanted to go? I had had such feelings of "knowing" when I used to wander during my college days, I recalled.

Gosh, I hadn't done this in a long time, I realized—just gone someplace because I felt some wordless impulse to do so. I felt sad thinking that I would have to be so far from my usual duties and routines—halfway around the world, in fact—before I would let myself move so freely again as I had when I was young.

I walked along, taking in the world around me. I saw a small bird with an iridescent-blue back and a tangerine chest and face, light delicately amongst the underbrush, then take flight again, weaving between the tall trees. A couple of times I saw brightly colored butterflies drifting through the forest, or sunbathing where strands of light rained down through the canopy and puddled on the forest floor. It was a world filled with green, from the canopy above, to the small plants below. Even the air seemed somehow scented with green.

After walking for half an hour or so, I began to feel as though I should be slowing my pace. I continued on a little bit farther, but then found myself standing still, looking up at the trees around me. The feeling that had called me into the forest had passed.

I stood, aimlessly looking around. Here I was, I realized, but where was that? I took a few tentative steps in one direction, but it just didn't feel like where I wanted to go. I took a couple of steps in another direction, but found myself stopped and staring around me again.

Well, this was interesting—I seemed to have arrived at wherever it was I was going to. I looked around for a place to sit and think about what to do next. I climbed up on a big root growing out from the base of a tree, and sat perched there, with my back against the trunk. At the bottom of the tree, in front of me, was a small opening in the forest, only a few meters across, just enough to let a little sunlight drift down.

I sat there, thinking about what I wanted to do next. I wasn't ready to go back to camp yet, and I didn't seem to feel like going anywhere else, either.

More butterflies appeared, flitting through the air in the little clearing. I sat and watched them as they dipped and hovered. I felt silly just sitting there, but it seemed to be where I wanted to be, and I decided to just trust the feeling I was having, like I would have done in my old college days. And so I just sat there, with my head resting back against the trunk, watching birds or butterflies, and every once in a while dusting insects from my arms or legs, if they mistook me for a bit of bark they might crawl upon.

I'm not sure how long I sat there like that—perhaps ten minutes, perhaps twenty—but after a time I heard a crashing sound in the underbrush, and a hoot, answered by three or four other hoots, not unlike the calls chimpanzees make, but somehow thinner and lighter.

I held very still, and waited. The crashing sound grew nearer. I felt my heart pounding. Was it possible? Were these bonobos I heard approaching? Seconds passed, during which time I held so still and tried to be so quiet that I found that I had forgotten to breathe.

I drew a quiet breath, and then, a few moments later, an animal that looked very much like a chimpanzee, but with a lighter build and longer hair around her face, casually knuckle-walked into the little clearing with an infant on her back. She sat down more or less opposite me, staring off to my right. After a moment, she swung the infant around to her front and began to nurse it.

A few minutes later, two young adult males entered the clearing, and then another mother, this one with two offspring—a young one which clung to her chest, and an older one which rode on her back. The second mother sat down by the first and began grooming her. The one being groomed glanced over and, looking the other one in the eye, gave her a brief kiss on the mouth. Then she looked back down at her nursing infant.

The older offspring of the second mother got off her back and began climbing a small sapling. The youngster would climb part way up, then ride the sapling down as it bent under her weight, then do it all over again. Meanwhile, the two young-adult males began a sort of sport, chasing one another playfully, scampering about between the trees, and all the while calling out with apparent delight.

After a few minutes, I heard some more rustling in the underbrush around me. A call came from perhaps twenty meters away and was answered by one of the bonobos near me. The second of the two mothers rose, gathered her young, then continued on in the direction they'd been moving when they first came into sight. The two young-adult males went with her. The first mother was still nursing her infant, and quietly watched them go. Then she looked around the clearing and seemed to notice me for the first time. Her eyes met mine for a moment. It was a calm, patient look, curious maybe, but not alarmed. It was a look of surprising intelligence. Then she rose, with her baby still nursing, and followed the others out of the clearing.

For the next few minutes I could hear others in the group passing through the underbrush near by. There has to be a bunch of them, I thought. I sat listening as the sounds passed by, then grew farther away.

Finally, I was aware only of the same sounds that had surrounded me since I'd entered the rainforest. I sat for a few more minutes, and gradually it occurred to me that I no longer needed to be where I was; it was over. The feeling which had led me to this particular spot, and which had convinced me to wait there, was gone. I got up and began to walk slowly back to camp. I was left only with a sense of wonder at having found myself in the midst of this intimate family group.

❀   ❀   ❀

I strolled back towards camp, feeling absolutely delighted—the bonobos! I had seen the bonobos! I couldn't wait to tell Laura about it—and hoped that she had had as good an experience wherever she had been in the forest, waiting for them to come and feed. I thought back over what Raymond had told us about these animals, and remembered in particular what he'd said about bonobos being arguably our nearest animal relatives, about how they were surprisingly unchanged from the common ancestor we had shared with them and with chimpanzees, some five or six million years ago. I thought about how affectionate and spontaneously playful the bonobos had seemed. Was this part of our lineage? Had our human ancestors, prior to the creation of art and agriculture, been so loving and impulsively playful, as well?

Whatever our shared past, I felt lucky that I had found the bonobos, lucky that somehow, just by following my impulses, I had come to a place where I could see them, watch them nurse and play, even be able to look one in the eye.

Lucky. What was the definition of luck I had come up with in college? It took me a moment to recall. I had thought then that someone who seemed "lucky" was someone who was able to use free movement well. Yes. Use free movement well. Hadn't I done that just now, in finding the bonobos? And certainly it made me feel lucky.

As I walked back through the forest, I found myself thinking about the article on animal intuition I'd read in the magazine Laura's mother had given me the morning we'd left London. I thought about how the animals discussed in the article had been able to locate loved ones or forecast danger. It seemed to me that people might describe those animals as "lucky"—but I thought it was more than luck, more than coincidence. Surely it wasn't mere coincidence that the cow had gone to the farm her calf had been taken to, though she'd never been there before—or that the wolf had traveled through dense forest straight to the kill left by its pack. No, surely what these animals had done was more than coincidence— more than what people usually meant by the word "luck."

I wondered if those animals had used free movement, too.

I tried to recall the article in more detail. I remembered that it had begun with a story about a dog who knew when its owner was coming home—a story that had reminded me of a woman who'd lived in my village when I was growing up, and who somehow knew when her oldest son was coming home from Varanasi. The article had included other stories, as well, about various other animals who also seemed aware of the location of their loved ones, even when they were far apart.

I tried to picture the magazine as I'd held it in my hands on the airplane. (At times like this I always felt grateful that I could so easily remember things I had seen—what Laura liked to call my "photographic memory.") I could clearly see the magazine before me. Yes—there'd been the dog, and then the story about the wolf and its pack, another about a pigeon and a boy, and next came the story about the cow finding her calf.

I turned a page of the magazine in my mind. What came next was a set of stories about dogs, cats, and birds who, during World War II, had given warnings to their owners before enemy air raids. That's right—and the article had said that their warnings had started far enough in advance that the enemy planes could not possibly have been heard—when they would, in fact, have still been hundreds of miles away.

I turned another page in my mind's eye. I could still remember the slick surface of the magazine pages, and the way the light from the airplane window had reflected off them. Next—and last—there'd been the story about the border collie who had slowed the progress of the bicyclist down the hill, and so stopped her from going over the cliff.

I turned my attention back to where I was, walking through the forest. It was important that I didn't forget to notice where I was, and where I was going—I didn't want to get lost. I looked around me. The area looked familiar. Good. I knew where I was.

My attention turned back to the article I had read. All the animals in it had seemed to have a kind of knowledge their physical senses could not possibly have provided them with.

So how had they known?

Had they somehow used free movement—and if so, how? I wondered.

I shook my head and stepped over a root. How does anybody use it? How had I used it just now?

I remembered that I had thought I'd understood how it worked back in my college days, but now I was having trouble recalling even a general sketch of what I'd come up with then.

I tried to pull my thoughts together. Somehow, however I had thought it had worked, it had involved people following their impulses—I was sure of that much—and in so doing, making real things that would otherwise have just been longed for, things that would just have been desires or a sense of possibility. It was a way of making possibilities into realities, I remembered, and I had thought it applied equally to how we create art, and how we create our lives.

I knew, too, that whatever it was I'd come up with years before, it had involved a series of steps. If I could just remember what those steps were, I wondered, would they apply to the way animals lived, as well?

I tried to recall the process, but it had been such a long time—nearly twenty years since I had considered such things in college. Still, I thought perhaps I could piece it back together.

I stepped past a real giant of a tree, with vines dangling everywhere, and for a moment I was conscious, again, of the scent of the forest, and of its great, green living mass. I recognized the tree with the vines as one of the ones I'd passed on my way into the forest and was pleased to be assured that I was heading in the right direction.

As I continued on, I kept trying to piece together how I'd thought free movement had worked. Let's see, I said to myself: step A. You feel some sense of possibility, some inspiration or desire, right?

Yes, that's how it starts. You feel a sense of possibility or promise.

In the treetops above me, monkeys called to one another. I could hear the recoil of limbs as the monkeys swung from one branch to another, releasing the first. I paused to look up at them.

This had something to do with protolife, I thought. *Protolife*—how had I defined it? It was something like, "life in its potential form," wasn't it?

Yes, that was it, I thought.

I turned my eyes from the monkeys and began to walk again, thinking about how I had used free movement that day.

So my longing to see the bonobos was a longing for a kind of potential—for a little piece of potential life—for protolife, I thought.

That was right. Okay, then: B. What would come next?

I had pictured myself seeing bonobos in the forest. I'd been anticipating it, picturing it—a kind of fantasy—and that fantasy had taken shape as a mental model. Right—had I created a mental model of how that protolife might be fulfilled.

That was it. And so that made "C" simple.

"Letter C," I said to myself: I had followed my impulses—that is, I had used free movement—and in doing so my impulses had led me to the bonobos.

Sure, that seemed right. That's how it had worked. Everything was adding up.

I paused for a moment to get my bearings. The last thing I wanted was to get lost on this walk, when nobody even knew what direction I'd set off in. The trees in front of me didn't look especially familiar. I turned around—this wasn't quite right.

At first I thought maybe I should backtrack, find the last place on my path where there were trees I recognized and start over there, but first I decided to just turn slowly in a circle and look carefully at the trees I could see from where I was. After a somewhat worrisome minute or two, I recognized a tree about ten meters away. I'd have to be more careful—I'd begun to wander off track.

I walked over to the tree and looked around until I felt that I'd gotten myself oriented again, then set off. I was still enchanted with being in the midst of the forest. It was funny—I was the only human being any-where around, and yet I felt not alone, but rather kept company by all the vibrant life around me.

It was beautiful here, and as I walked along, I enjoyed the sights and tried to keep track of familiar-looking trees as my guide to finding my way back—but after a time my thoughts returned to the question I had posed for myself: *How did free movement work?*

"Okay, that's three steps—A, B, and C," I said under my breath. What had they added up to? I tried to recount them in my mind:

A. *Focus on protolife.*
B. *Create a model of protolife fulfilled.*
C. *Follow free movement to give that model expression, make it real.*

I thought about it for a moment. That's what I had come up with, all right, but somehow it didn't seem quite right. I had the feeling that when I'd thought about these things in college, there'd been more steps.

I thought it through again. There had been links between them, I felt—yeah—how you get from A to B, and from B to C.

I began again to try to lay it all out in my mind—all the while stopping every few minutes to look around and make sure I didn't wander off my path again. I was glad I'd paid attention to the most remarkable trees I'd passed earlier—without them, I felt certain, I would have been lost.

Okay, I said to myself. So what were the extra steps I'd left out? I had the feeling they had involved, somehow, making associations.

That seemed right. I went through all the steps again in my mind, more carefully:

1. *I had focused on my longing to see the bonobos. That is, <u>I had focused on protolife.</u>*

2. *I had imaginatively allowed associations to gather around that sense of possibility or desire. That was it. Yes. I had made associations.*

3. *Those associations had taken shape as a fantasy of seeing bonobos. The fantasy of seeing bonobos in the forest became a mental model of what it would be like to see them. I nodded to myself. I had, through fantasy, generated a mental model.*

Good. So, what was next? I was aware that somewhere, deep within me, I must have somehow known where those bonobos were going to be, and when. Otherwise, how else would my impulses have led me to them?

I liked the feeling this gave me. It reminded me somehow of the feeling I'd had when I'd stumbled on just the sort of job I'd wanted in college. I liked the idea of having hidden within me a kind of veiled knowledge.

But if I had somehow known where the bonobos were going to be, if I had somehow known this in some deep and nearly invisible place within me—how had I gotten access to that knowledge and brought it to the surface? The question seemed a big one, and I walked for quite a while simply turning it over in my mind. I had the feeling that somehow I knew the answer to this question, that I had answered it for myself years before. I felt as though, somewhere, I had all the pieces to this puzzle, but didn't know where they were, or how to turn them to make them fit together.

As I walked along, I was still aware of hearing the monkeys I'd passed a few minutes before, still aware of trees towering above me, of the many scents and shadows around me. The forest itself seemed so alive.

I was becoming distracted by my surroundings, but as I did, something loosened and shifted inside me.

I smiled. That was it—I had made associations around the mental model, the fantasy, of seeing the bonobos, and in so doing, I had drawn on all layers of my awareness, even the layers veiled within me. I had drawn on awareness that was conscious, subconscious—and part of *the collective unconscious!*

Yes. Yes—that was it! That's what I had concluded!

4. *I had made associations with my mental model, but not just any associations—I had made associations that drew on collective awareness.*

I stopped for a moment and stood thinking about this. If I *had* somehow drawn on some sort of deep, shared awareness, then how had it surfaced, how had it become conscious enough to lead me to the bonobos?

I puzzled over it, and as I did, I was glad to see the pieces gradually becoming aligned. I smiled—it was like looking at a picture coming slowly into focus.

5. *That deep knowledge, or awareness, surfaced in the form of impulses and impressions.*

Yes, it did—of course—free movement had led me to them. That was it. Somewhere within that collective consciousness, my mental model of what I longed for, my model of seeing the bonobos, had been drawn together, through some sort of deep associative process, with other information related to it. *That information, drawn from a collective awareness, had surfaced as impulses and impressions of actions that were aligned with my model—that could complete or fulfill it.* And then, using free movement, I had followed those impulses and impressions—my impulses and impressions—and had found myself at that little clearing, where the bonobos were also heading.

It seemed almost simple. Only a few easy steps. Only usually, I realized, we weren't aware of the process of making the associations. That seemed right, I thought—and if I ignored the steps involving associations, considered them to be invisible, then the process really did seem simple:

1. *I had focused on protolife.*
2. *I had fantasized a model of it being fulfilled.*
3. *I had followed my impulses and impressions as they brought deeper awareness to the surface.*

That was it—and that was exactly how I had found the bonobos:

1. *I had focused on my desire to see them—had focused on the possibility of seeing them.*
2. *I had imagined seeing them.*
3. *I had followed impulses and impressions, which had led me to them.*

So simple!

I thought again about the animal stories in the magazine, delighted, now, to see the connections lining up. Was that how the cow had found her calf? Had she longed to be with it, fantasized about finding it, and trusted the impulses and impressions that arose from some deep associative process within her? and the pigeon who had found the boy behind just the right hospital window dozens of miles from home? and the injured wolf, hungry and unable to hunt for itself, who went straight for the kill left by other members of its pack? Had they all longed for something, fantasized about finding it, then drawn on deep awareness that surfaced through impulses and impressions?

It seemed suddenly not just that it was possible to think of this as simple, but that it really was, essentially, a simple process. I grinned, then paused absentmindedly and scratched my head.

Was that right? Was it that simple? What about the dog who had tried to chase the cyclist back up the hill and away from where the landslide had taken out the road? or the animals who had warned their owners of impending air raids during World War II, when the bombers were still hundreds of miles away?

Had they somehow been aware of events *before* they happened, and if so, how could *that* be part of the collective awareness?

It seemed a lot to try to sort out, and for a while I just strolled along, enjoying the forest, and letting my thoughts drift. I thought again about having seen the bonobos, and again felt eager to tell Laura all about it. I wished I could describe to her the look in that bonobo mother's eyes when she had looked right at me before leaving the clearing.

The clearing, which I had wandered into just in time to see the bonobos... I had had a feeling of just where to go. How I wished I could tell Laura about that, too!

How had that happened? They weren't there when I arrived. But I had waited—like I knew they were coming. Like I knew *where they were going to be.*

I would have thought this too incredible at that moment, I suppose, if I hadn't just been thinking about animals that seemed to have some knowledge of events before they happened. But at that moment in time, in a forest that itself seemed somehow magical—wondrous, strange, and vast—it didn't seem too strange to me to imagine that I had, at some level of myself, *known about what was soon to happen,* even though I, like the animals in the article, had no physical means for knowing that.

Still, the thought gave me goose bumps and delighted me. I thought back through the article in my mind. It had described intuitive abilities in dogs, cats, birds, cows, and wolves. I wondered if bonobos also had such abilities—and if they did, did they use them, maybe, for finding food, or locating one another in the forest? It seemed a practical sort of ability to have, useful for survival. Had our ancestors, I wondered, been able to do this?

I came to a fallen tree that lay in the direction I was headed. I was happy to remember passing it earlier, and in a moment of exuberant pleasure I climbed up on its broad trunk and continued my walk there, striding along its mossy back. I was happy with these entertaining thoughts, and delighted, too, just to be in the forest. It all would have been perfect if only Laura had been there with me.

So—I asked myself—had our ancestors really made use of such intuitive abilities?

Our ancestors. I had thought so much about what they might have been like on the barge, and in the months, even years, before our trip, but I had never considered this.

Had they been able to do this, to use their intuition like the animals in the article?

Well, why not? I thought, as I strolled along the center of a log as wide as a sidewalk. Why not?—apparently, lots of animals could do such things. Even I could, when I set aside my deliberate plans and intentions, and just followed my impulses and impressions instead.

It seemed the thought reminded me of something. What was it? *Set aside plans...just followed my impulses...*hm.

My thoughts spiraled back to the time I'd spent on the barge, and to the writing I'd done there. I'd written about how, in the long-distant past, before there was art or agriculture, our ancestors had lived life focused in the moment. We had followed our impulses from one moment to the next. After that, wanting to express our own intentions, our own *selves,* we had learned to plan—to consider both the past and the future—and our attention was drawn away from so crisp a focus on the present moment. We had become focused on our individual selves, then, and in the process, we had become focused on our own individual, conscious intentions.

The idea took a long moment for me to gather it in, and then it broke like a sudden rain shower, seeming to make every connection at once: We had begun to make plans and follow them—and so we no longer lived in the moment. Because of this, we stopped following free movement. *We stopped listening to and trusting the impulses and impressions that rose up from within us.*

The idea seemed to shake me as it took form in my mind—until we became so focused on our *individual selves,* people had lived more like other animals live. We drew our wisdom from the well of collective awareness—and would have, surely must have, had the sorts of abilities I'd read about in the magazine.

We had lived in the moment, trusting in, and responsive to, our impulses and impressions. *We had drawn on that inner wisdom, which had been like a root system—drawing deep water to the highest branches.*

The thought so stunned me, I stopped and sat down on the log I'd been walking on. My head was spinning. The thought seemed at one level so simple, but also to require an essential recalculation of how I saw the world. A paradigm shift. For several long moments, I could hardly take it in.

I looked up at the green canopy above me. I could see the leaves shimmer as they were turned by some distant breeze in the world above the forest. It reminded me of how once, on vacation, when Laura and I had gone snorkeling in the ocean off Isla Mujeres in Mexico, I'd looked up through the strands of blue-green light filtering down through the water from above and noticed how the sun and breeze made patterns there, where the water met the air.

Only now it was a canopy of leaves I was looking up at, and the forest was like the ocean, surrounding me.

I looked back down and glanced around me. It seemed so quiet and lovely sitting here. Everything was so green—green above me and below me, green moss everywhere—like being in a big, green, living organism. It was so beautiful, so vital. The place had a kind of presence, a sense of the combined life of everything living there: the trees and vines, the monkeys and ants, the birds and butterflies—and me.

Had life in the ancient past really been the way I had been imagining it? I wondered, as I stared into the forest.

Had our lives really been infused with love and play, as it was for the bonobos I'd watched?

Had we really experienced each moment in especially rich detail?

Had we really, I wondered, been able to find the food we desired and to locate our loved ones—even to avoid danger—simply by trusting ourselves to the spontaneity of the moment, and the impulses which rose up within it?

I ran my fingers through my hair, as though somehow that might untangle these wild thoughts.

Had we, I wondered, felt *lucky?*

✳ ✳ ✳

"Pause," Paul said.

"Pausing. End of chapter," Kiki replied.

The trail Paul was on was winding its way back down the canyon wall. Below him, Paul could see the creek and what appeared to be another campground on its far side. He had begun to feel hungry and was considering stopping for lunch.

"Kiki, what time is it?" he asked.

"11:14 AM," she answered.

No, too early for lunch, Paul told himself, but when he reached the creek, he could at least stop and refill his canteen.

As Paul made his way down the last bit of the winding path and out into a small meadow that lay between him and the creek, he thought again about how he had imagined the nature of time, when he was in school, as being like a wall or a waterfall; though we could only sense a little of it at once, the whole of it was constantly in existence. And though it was constantly existing, it was also constantly in flux, constantly changing—such that each probability that might exist, did exist, up ahead of us somewhere—until the future (in all of its potential variations) became the present, singular and solid around us.

How did this relate to the sort of serendipity that Dr. Kumar had experienced? Paul wondered. Had she somehow sensed a little of what lay ahead? Had she been drawn to a particular probability, or possibility, and somehow aligned herself with it?

Paul reached the creek and crossed it easily, stepping from one rock to another. He sat down on a rock near the water on the far side and refilled his canteen. In the trees all around him, birds sang. In the water, he could see the forms of fish lying low in the shadows—and in the shade of one of the rocks, he spotted a good-sized turtle.

It surprised Paul how easily he could adjust to this natural environment—so untouched, and so unlike any he had known before. How quickly he had come to feel as though he had been living in it all his life!

Paul put his canteen away and threw on his pack.

"Kiki, please resume recitation," he said.

As Kiki began again, Paul followed the path, which continued through the campground and away from the creek, weaving its way through a thick stand of sycamore and cottonwood trees, which went on for as far as Paul could see.

CHAPTER IX

Each of us, as Jung realized and as a quantum view of consciousness would explain, may find in his or her own depths the collective yearnings, the collective fantasies, and the collective potential of the whole human race.

—Danah Zohar

The mental and the material are two sides of one overall process.... one energy that is the basis of all reality.

—David Bohm

When I got to the edge of the clearing, I wasn't far from where I had entered it a couple of hours earlier.

Good job finding my way back, I told myself. I looked around the camp—everything was just as I had left it. Everything. Nobody was around. I didn't know why, but for some reason I had expected Laura to be back by then. I had imagined she would be there with Raymond and Mvula, perhaps sitting and talking at the fire site, or in a bit of shade alongside of the kitchen hut. But nobody was there.

I went to look in our hut. I found the note I had written for Laura just where I had left it. I had a heavy feeling as I sat down on one of our cots.

I realized I was starting to worry. No point in that. Laura had said she probably wouldn't be back till mid-afternoon, and it wasn't yet two o'clock, I pointed out to myself. And it wasn't like she was alone with Raymond. Mvula was with them. It was silly to worry. And I certainly shouldn't start worrying when she wasn't even late.

I started to take off my boots, but then realized I was hungry. There was still a little of the manioc porridge (*fufu,* I'd heard somebody call it

428

on the barge) left from breakfast, but I didn't want more of that. Besides, it would have been sitting out for hours. I decided to settle for some trail mix, and pulled a bag of it, which Laura and I had brought from Boulder, out of one of the packs, then picked up my water bottle, which I had left by the door. While I was at it, I got out my journal and a pen. I'd promised myself when we were planning this trip that I would keep a journal the whole time, and here I hadn't made a single entry since we'd left the barge. I had some catching up to do, and in any case, it was good to keep my mind occupied till Laura returned.

I kicked off my boots and stretched out on the cot with my trail mix, water, and journal. I spent some time describing the trip by pirogue, the weather, the oarsmen, the people of the stilt village, and so on. It was warm in the hut, warmer than it had been in the shade of the forest. By the time I'd gotten up to date on my journal entries, I was feeling sleepy. It seemed a good idea to try to get caught up some more on my rest.

I got up and closed the shutters to keep out the light, took a drink of water, then stretched out on the little cot. I wished Laura was there to lie beside me. Laura.

Where *is* she? I checked my watch. It was nearly three o'clock. I told myself again not to worry. It would be okay. It *felt* like things were okay, didn't it? Sure. She wasn't even late.

I let the sleepiness come over me and burrowed my head into the pillow. With the shutters closed, the air in the room was still and seemed warmer than it had before.

I draped myself limply across the cot and the ideas I had been having on my walk drifted past me: *at some level we're all aware of events taking place at a distance—even, somehow, at a distance in time.*

Groggily, I wondered how that might work. I could feel myself relaxing into the cot in the warm darkness of the hut. It was sort of as though one part of my mind was drifting, while others passed thoughts forward from some dreamy place out of sight.

I remembered that I used to think about people as being like radio transceivers, sending and receiving invisible signals. I had an impression of those days, of being with Jake at his apartment, of sensing how he felt. I remembered, too, the similar poems we'd all written for class.

Maybe it *was* like that, I thought, like we were sending and receiving radio waves—at least, when people were nearby—but that didn't seem enough to explain what I had been thinking about in the forest.

No—whatever it was that made this bridge of awareness, whatever it was that allowed one creature to know where another creature was when they were distant from one another, or to somehow sense what was soon to happen—well, it would take more than some sort of radio-wave-like signal to make that possible. Any radio-wave-like energy our brains might emit would be a weak signal, and surely would not be able to carry so far in space, nor jump over the gap of time.

I rolled over, searching for a soft spot on the hard cot, but had to settle for a cool bit of sheeting. Perhaps it was the daylight leaking in around the cracks in the shutters or my concerns about Laura, but tired as I was,

I found myself lingering a long time at the edge of sleep, where thoughts get slippery and come easily alive.

Everything within me seemed awash with impressions. I remembered sitting on the fallen tree on my way back that afternoon, and how alive the forest had seemed. I had felt a part of it. The sensation came back over me, like the way the sensation of waves rising and falling might return to someone after a day spent playing in surf or riding on a boat above ocean swells. Ideas and impressions bobbed and floated through my mind... *the long-distant past... before art... before agriculture.* I imagined people moving through the world, then, with the same sense of belonging, of being part of a larger web of life, as I had felt when I'd been in the forest that afternoon.

But not quite the same as I had felt, I realized. Amongst the earliest people, this sense of interconnection would have been even deeper, more complete, because those people were not yet focused on their own individuality—on the thing that set them apart.

Lying there on the cot, I was almost dreaming. I saw the people of our ancient past hunting for food, making stone tools, and interacting with their loved ones. They were keenly aware of the cool touch of rain, of the sounds of animals moving behind the screen of trees, of subtle scents carried on the breeze—and of the silky threads of intuition, which rose like gossamer from the deepest layers of their own consciousness.

For them, each moment was rich and vital—magically unfolding.

But there was something more.

I tried to let the idea surface. What was it? Some wordless longing, which rose, also, from within them: *a sense... of possibility... of some unnamed thing... a sense... of satisfaction... when...*

What? The thought seemed to gather slowly, like the way snow, when first falling, melts and disappears, then gradually amasses.

There was a sense of satisfaction... *when...*

Yes. What? *Oh—when "I" act... and the world reflects "me."* A well-made stone tool. A hand print in the mud. When I act *and create things that reflect me.*

Of course—we had felt a longing to know and express *ourselves.*

Our *selves.*

That was it.

Again my thoughts returned to that deeper sense of belonging, which rose like surf beneath me—the feeling that had enveloped me in the forest. An impression took shape in my mind: We had felt this longing to know *our own selves,* and that longing had been like a bubble, rising to the surface from deep waters.

❋   ❋   ❋

I stretched and turned on the narrow cot, and felt myself slowly spiraling up towards waking.

Where was this going, I thought?

I found myself lying with my eyes open, staring at the wall. The sun crept in around the shutters and entered the room in narrow bands of light. I was hot. I could hear a fly buzzing around the window at one end of the room.

I remembered looking up at the trees surrounding me in the forest, and at the light in the canopy above, and how it had reminded me of the light on the water above the kelp forest Laura and I had dived in off the coast of Mexico.

The image passed, and I rolled onto my back. I lay quietly in the hot stillness of the room. I wanted to sleep, but for some reason, instead, my thoughts drifted to the article Roger and Laura had written together for the *Huginn/Muninn Newsletter*—the one they'd written on physics and religion.

I remembered that somewhere in that article Roger had put together a particularly interesting chain of ideas. What were they? I felt they were somehow related to the sense I had had of being part of the life of the forest.

Let's see, I thought, focusing my attention. Roger had started off talking about a physicist named David Bohm.

That's right. He'd talked about how Bohm believed that the universe is a seamless whole.

I remembered sitting in the easy chair next to the lamp in our living room in Boulder holding the article in my hands, when I was helping Laura proofread it. I'd looked at it very closely then, and hoped now, even though a few months had passed since that close reading, that I would still be able to recall it clearly.

I tried to picture the first page of the article in my mind, to picture what I'd seen written there.

As I remembered looking down at the paper, I was pleased at how easily the words began to come into focus. It was helpful, I knew, that I had been lying so quietly, with my mind cleared of distracting thoughts. Now, bit by bit, in my mind's eye, I managed to scan down the first page of Laura and Roger's article and then began the second. About midway down on the second page, I found the passage I'd hoped to find. I turned my attention to it, like someone else might turn their attention to remembering the look on someone's face after a surprise party—remembering weeks or even years after the event how that person had looked at the moment the crowd had shouted "surprise!"

In that same way, I was able to bring that part of the page back into focus and read a passage from it back to myself:

Bohm believed that this perception—that the universe is made up of separate parts—is fundamentally misleading and incorrect.

Roger had written—and with that, the gist of what he had said in the article began to come back to me.

I continued to scan down the page in my mind's eye, picturing it the way it had looked then (a loose stack of white papers, each printed neatly in black ink) before it had been printed in the newsletter. I was skimming, looking for a particular passage.

Soon, I found what I was looking for. Again, I managed to bring the passage back into focus, and so read it to myself. Roger had written:

> John Stewart Bell's inequality theorem demonstrated how one could experimentally test whether the universe is in fact an indivisible whole, or is actually made up of separate parts.

Curious, I thought, and with that, the page dissolved back into a vague pattern of dark marks and white paper.

Curious, I thought, again. *An indivisible whole.* I remembered finding that idea fascinating at the time I had gone over the article with Laura—and to actually be able to *test* such a thing!

I rubbed my eyes. I could feel thoughts moving within me, gathering together a sense of the overall direction of what Roger had written in his section of the paper.

As I remembered it, Roger had described how scientists had applied Bell's theorem in experiments carried out on pairs of entangled particles—that is, the experiments were carried out on subatomic particles that had been bound together in a certain way.

The experiments had shown that if one splits apart a pair of entangled particles, and then takes some action that affects one of them, the other particle is also *instantly affected—no matter how far apart they might be when that action takes place.*

Roger had said this meant that, at the level of the smallest particles, *location has no meaning and nothing is really separate from anything else.* He'd called this property "nonlocality."

Yes, that was right, I remembered—*nonlocality.* It was called that because location has no meaning where the particles are concerned. *Even after the particles were split apart, they functioned as though they were still united, not separate, not at separate locations.*

Again, I skimmed down the page in my mind's eye. I was surprised at how easily the text was coming back into focus. It helped that I had slept in that morning, I thought—and that I was relaxed now.

I continued to mentally skim down the page. Soon, I found the passage I was trying to remember. It was a long one. I took a deep breath and let it out slowly, and as I did, the irregular black marks on the white page sharpened into focus. Roger had written:

> What this research demonstrates is that such particles remain connected outside the context of space and time, even when they are physically separated within it.
>
> As impressive as this may seem, what makes this result so remarkable is that, since the big bang, all matter in the universe has been bound together, or "entangled," just as the particles in the experiments had been. And thus, as "split apart" as everything may seem

to us to be, everything in the universe is, in fact, still bound together in a context outside of space and time.

In other words, David Bohm's conclusion is fundamentally correct: everything in the universe, including us, is part of a single, seamless whole. The appearance of separateness is, fundamentally, and for all of us, only an illusion.

I lay still for a moment, reabsorbing what I had read first just a few months earlier. I remembered that when I'd first read it, I'd thought the idea delightful, and wondered if it could really be so. Certainly it was consistent with many religious teachings—which, I recalled, was the thread Laura had picked up in her section of the paper. She'd said this concept of nonlocality, or wholeness, was similar to ideas held in many religions.

Again, I struggled to find the words I remembered having read, but soon they were there, too, leaping up out of the page in my mind's eye. Laura had written:

Such a belief in an essential oneness of all beings and all things is widespread in Eastern religions (Hinduism, Buddhism, Taoism, etc.) and is present in varying ways and degrees in the Abrahamic religions, as well (that is, most prominently, Judaism, Christianity, and Islam).

I lay quietly for a moment, imagining the page as it had looked in Laura's final edit, with a few marks here or there in Laura's elegant handwriting—and then it occurred to me that I wasn't sure why I was thinking about this at all. I recalled that I'd been daydreaming about the earliest people, and then, somehow, had switched over to this.

My attention was drawn back to the room by a second fly, which had begun buzzing outside the mosquito netting. I wondered why it had to make so much noise, and then laughed at myself, thinking that a fly could sound noisy after all the noise on the barge. I stretched and rubbed my face, and my hands came back damp with sweat. I considered opening the shutters to see if I could catch a breeze, but decided I liked the darkness of the room more than I disliked the heat.

Lying in the humid darkness of the hut, I was aware of the smell of the thatched roof baking in the sun. I rolled over, closed my eyes, and pressed my body against another relatively cool patch of sheet.

"Sleep," I told myself, and tried to let my thoughts relax and drift. For several moments I felt myself tumbling towards sleep, but as I did, I watched vaguely as my thoughts again drifted to the distant past.

We had been aware of impulses and impressions arising from deep within us—I found myself thinking.

Before we focused on our separateness, we had felt connected.

Impressions of the article Roger and Laura had written drifted through my mind, too, interweaving with these ideas about the past.

Separateness is . . . only an illusion. Everything in the universe is, in fact, still bound together . . . outside of space and time.

All of us are still bound together . . .

All of us . . . yes . . .

All of us . . . felt connected. . . . were connected, I thought, *in a context outside of space and time . . .*

All of us are connected.

Now—and in the past.

I tried to gather my thoughts. It seemed I was on the edge of something, of some way all this could come together. My thoughts felt fluid, dreamy. I tried to lay it out before me.

In the past . . .

In the past we had felt a seamless sense of belonging. We had lived in the moment, moving fluidly. Life had seemed rich, even magical. Lucky.

We had felt lucky . . .

But we had craved something more.

What had we craved?

Selfhood.

That's right, to explore our own selves, I thought, pulling the ideas together, struggling to concentrate without coming too much awake.

We had felt a desire to explore our own selves—and this desire was a kind of protolife—like a small hot coal burning in all our hearts.

This desire, this protolife, was latent within us, dormant there, waiting for the right time, the right spark, to set it alight.

Yes—just as striving for independence in adolescence is the blossom of a seed already planted, even in the newborn child. *This desire to explore and express ourselves had been latent in all of us;* it had been there in all of us, *burning in us all.*

In us all. All of us. I turned that over in my mind. And we were *all bound together . . .*

Was the wholeness Roger had talked about somehow related to Carl Jung's idea of a collective unconscious? I wondered, waking a little. Did it constitute a layer of awareness from which both people, and other animals, could gather subtle knowledge—an ocean, a deep well, from which we could all draw?

Were the wholeness of matter at a particle level, I wondered, and the wholeness of the collective unconscious, both part of some fundamental oneness—an entanglement in which we all are somehow *"bound together"* in some *"context outside of space and time?"*

I remembered wandering in the forest, wondering how the animals in the article had known what was happening at a distance, or what was soon to happen, wondering how I myself had seemingly known where, *and when,* to find the bonobos.

Bound together . . . outside of space and time.

Was it possible that at some level of our awareness, at some depth within us, space and time, *distance and time* were meaningless—and that if we sensed at this level, what we sensed might stretch beyond the limits of the here and now? Was that how the dog had known to warn the cyclist? Was that how the animals had warned of air raids? Was that how I had known where to go and wait for the bonobos?

Had we each drawn from a deep level of our own awareness—a level at which we were all entangled, all bound together outside the defining boundaries of space and time?!

The thought seemed stunning. For a moment, I recalled the trail of feelings I had followed to the little clearing in the woods where I had seen the bonobos—amazed, again, that somehow my impulses had led me there.

Lucky, yes—I had certainly felt that—as perhaps had we all, in a distant past, before we sensed or knew the full possibility of our own individuality.

❀   ❀   ❀

I lay still for a few moments, savoring the idea of our ancient ancestors feeling lucky, imagining them wandering across a wide land, trusting the flow of possibilities rising up from deep within them.

Our ancient ancestors—who had developed art, and agriculture...

Yes—amongst whom first art and then agriculture had arisen at so close to the same time, in so many parts of the world.

"An internally motivated process." The words I had quoted on the barge echoed in my mind.

Internally, I thought—yes—*from deep within them.*

Perhaps from the same place I had drawn from in finding the bonobos— from a place of essential oneness, beyond the bounds of space and time.

The thought seemed crazy at first, but as I thought it, I felt an odd sensation, like a fog was clearing from my mind—as though perhaps now I had all the pieces of the puzzle I'd been trying to put together.

I lay quietly assessing this feeling for a moment, then decided to go ahead and let my thoughts proceed along these lines, regardless of how odd they might seem to me.

I closed my eyes again, and imagined the people of the ancient past, spread out across the world, each silently longing for self-discovery and expression.

I pictured them in my mind, felt these feelings along with them.

They felt this longing deep within them—*in a place where they were not alone.* They longed quietly, collectively, *in a place where separateness has no meaning.*

Deep within them, I thought—in a shared place where space and time, where location, has no meaning—each contributed his or her own latent longing.

Gradually, collectively, they gathered associations around that protolife, around the longing for self-discovery they hoped to fulfill.

Excitedly, I let the chain of thoughts continue to unfold. These associations, I told myself, began to take shape deep within them—*deep within us.* These associations, gathering in a place of collective awareness, began to take form as new models. Yes—*as new models afloat in an ocean of consciousness, shared by all.*

As I lay in the warm darkness of the little hut, listening to the buzz of flies, the story continued to gather before me:

In the small actions of every day, these new models, these *shared models,* began to surface.

Their longings took form in these models, and the new models helped them express those longings.

Yes, I thought.

New impulses and impressions surfaced within them—and the people, still focused and alert in the moment, freely moved to enact them.

Following their impulses, they began to make hand prints in the soft soil.
Following their impressions, they began to decorate their bodies with paint.
Following what arose from within them, they began to make art.
Yes.

The story continued to unfold in my mind, and I imagined these impulses and impressions surfacing through the lives and acts of people in many parts of the globe, in all the places in which art or agriculture had appeared. I imagined these impulses and impressions gradually unfolding, drawn up into the individual mind from a webwork, a deep ocean of shared awareness—from the collective unconscious—from the whole of which we were all a part (and of which we are all still a part).

These collective impulses, these shared impressions, arose and were given expression *on every continent people then lived on—rising up within us all.*

I rubbed my eyes. What was I saying?

No, no, I told myself—this was too wild, too theoretical. How could I possibly prove it?

I wondered if these were the ideas I'd been feeling around the edges of since I'd been on the barge—feeling, but been unwilling to look at. Had I been afraid to say, to even *think* this, for fear it would damage my career?

Just exactly what *was* I thinking, I asked myself?

I had the feeling I could compress it, make it simple:

Out of a shared sense of protolife—specifically, the promise of self knowledge and expression—we had grown new models for fulfillment. But not just new models—new <u>collective</u> models. New <u>archetypes</u>.

"New *archetypes,*" I repeated to myself. Yes. A new archetype for *The Artist*—and then, later, a new archetype for *The Farmer.*

There was some other word I wanted. What was it?

It took me a moment to find it.

Zeitgeist—that was it—"the spirit of an age."

As I imagined it then, lying on the cot in the sweltering hut, listening to the drone of flies, these new archetypes had erupted as new zeitgeists, drawn to the surface of our awareness by impulses and impressions. I imagined waves of change arising from within us, arising and spreading across the face of the planet—like a sort of slow, dawning light, rolling forward, seeding cultural change.

Could it be, I wondered, that it had really been like that—that both art and agriculture had begun with a kind of collective longing?

I tried to let the steps of what that process might have been become clear in my mind:

> *First, from deep within us, we had felt desire—a sense of possibility, of protolife.*
> *Then we had dreamed of those desires fulfilled.*
> *Our collective dreams—our fantasies—had become new models —new archetypes.*
> *And finally, the new archetypes had surfaced in our actions . . . and we had remade the world.*

The ideas seemed to flutter through my mind like the butterflies of the forest.

The change began with a longing rising up from deep within us . . . and became a new way of being, which had spread across the world.

The idea seemed fantastic and lyrical, large and breathtaking. It settled over me softly, like a blanket. I felt myself hovering at the edge of sleep. Thoughts floated to the surface of my awareness, then drifted past.

Art and agriculture—we had brought them into being, I mumbled to myself, my thoughts drifting. Then words surfaced again in my mind:

It was "an internally motivated process."

"An internally motivated process." The phrase seemed to echo through my head.

Independently—yes—it had erupted in many places, *independently.*

But had it?

I pushed the idea back on itself. Well, independently, but not so independently, I thought. It was true that both art and agriculture had appeared spontaneously at a number of separate locations, but if what I was thinking now was correct, their genesis was not achieved independently. Their creation had not been independent, but rather *shared.* A shared process. *A collective change.*

I felt a certain excitement as the idea hardened, and came into focus in my mind. *That* was what I wanted to say in my article—we had *collectively* brought art and agriculture into the world.

I opened my eyes and it came to me what I had been thinking. Oh no! I thought. I could never say that to my colleagues. They would never accept it. Where was my proof?

I curled up on the hard, narrow cot. I thought for a few minutes about why we had started the *Huginn/Muninn Newsletter* in the first place. In large part, it had been to give us all a forum to express ideas that could neither be proven nor disproven, but that might, nonetheless, be valid, and valuable.

I sighed and rolled onto my stomach. Could I say this? I didn't know. I didn't want to decide now. Sleep—that's what I wanted. I pushed aside all complicated thoughts and felt myself sinking into my cot as my muscles untied themselves.

Where is Laura? I thought. Surely she'll be back soon, won't she? Yes, soon—and she'll come snuggle with me. I imagined her lying beside me as I felt myself drifting off, surrounded by soft light and the warm drone of flies.

✱   ✱   ✱

"Stop," Paul said, when there was a momentary lull in the sound of Kiki's voice.

"Stopping," she answered. "End of chapter."

Paul surveyed the land around him. After crossing the creek and then leaving it behind earlier that day, Paul's path had passed another campground, then crossed a broader creek. The path now wound westward along the course of that stream.

While he'd hiked, Paul had become hungrier and hungrier, until now, with the sun high above him, he decided it was time to stop.

He climbed on the back of a fallen cottonwood that lay beside the stream and began to poke through his pack for another of his travel meals. As he'd listened to Dr. Kumar's memoirs that morning, he'd quietly pondered her ideas about animals using "free movement" to find what they needed, about human ancestors being guided by such currents as well, and about broad cultural changes that arose out of a shared longing for individuation and a shared consciousness. He'd been unsure of what to make of her ideas, but it has been interesting to listen to. Meanwhile, his own mood had been uneven all morning, and now some of the shadows that had clung to him as he woke that morning began to gather around him again.

It troubled him that he would dream about his mother as he had done. Why had he dreamed that she was mad at him—why had she disappeared, avoided him?—and why, for that matter, had he not been able to remember her face for so long?

These were troubling thoughts. Part of him wanted to think through them, as though they were part of some long road he might reach the end of, be done with, and be able to put behind him. At another level, it seemed to Paul that these thoughts, and all the troubled feelings that accompanied them, rose up from some sort of deep pit within him, and that the more he dug down into the darkness from which they came, the more likely it was that he might get lost there among them.

As he sat, eating his travel meal and ruminating on these matters, Paul recalled an event that had taken place at school, a few months after his mother's death. He had gotten in a fight with one of the other boys. He'd been playing kickball with some of his classmates on the school court during break, and one of the boys had shoved Paul too hard.

Paul had thought the action deliberate. In response, he had spit on the ground, then looked the other boy in the eye and said, "roach eater."

It was the worst slur any of the kids knew, and as cutting as the words were in the culture of that schoolyard, thinking back on it, Paul supposed he had expected the other boy to just glare at him for a minute, then go back to the game, but instead the boy had held his ground, answering:

"You should know—since your *mother's* one."

That childish retort had inflamed something still aching in Paul's young heart, and in a flash he had lit into the other boy, fists flying.

Both boys had wound up bruised, and the fight had ended with teachers pulling them apart, with Paul still furious and openly crying in front of his schoolmates for the only time in his childhood.

Paul thought about it. He remembered how, for the rest of that day, impressions of his mother had bounded through his young mind, and he had felt an overwhelming sadness—perhaps the only true grief he had ever permitted himself to feel over his mother's death. It was never something he could really bear to think about.

Impressions of the dream dashed fleetingly across Paul's mind. For a moment, again, Paul saw his mother slipping from the room, avoiding him.

Paul rubbed his face. What was he doing, sitting here, thinking about this? He couldn't fritter away time if he hoped to succeed in his plans—to finish listening to Dr. Kumar's book, to get to the Retreat, to build a new transport and—yes—to return home to a hero's welcome!

Paul got up and threw on his pack, then continued up the Sojourner's Path, eating his travel meal and weaving a little as he adjusted the weight on his back.

"Kiki, resume recitation," Paul said, and in a moment Dr. Kumar's voice once again spread through the afternoon air.

◙   ◙   ◙

Chapter X

Nature is the incarnation of a thought, and turns to a thought again, as ice becomes water and gas. The world is mind precipitated.... Every moment instructs, and every object: for wisdom is infused into every form.

—Ralph Waldo Emerson

The soul of Jonathan was knit to the soul of David, and Jonathan loved him as his own soul.

—1 Samuel 18:1

I woke uncertain about where I was. The barge? No—there was no motion, no roar from the engines, no soukous music drifting up from the deck below or the cabin next door. The room was pitch black. With one hand, I felt the cot pushed up next to mine, expecting somehow to find Laura resting beside me, but there was no one there.

Where's Laura? I thought groggily, and then it all came into focus. We'd left the barge. We were in a little clearing in the forest, and Laura had left earlier in the day—with Raymond. And now it was after dark, and she had not yet returned.

"Laura?" I said aloud, hoping I would find her in the room's shadows, but there was no reply.

I sat up in the bed, my body heavy with fatigue, and felt for the flashlight I remembered leaving on the bedside stand.

Laura! Where was she?

Worried, I switched on the flashlight, then left it resting beside me on the bed while I tied on my boots. Where would I look for her? She could be anywhere in the forest. They'd gone to find the bonobos near some kind of tree. *"Elimilimi,"* Mvula had called it. Where in the world would that be?

I stood up wearily, still caught up in the shreds of sleep. I felt a sense of worry tinged with panic, but behind that, somewhere, at the edges of my awareness, was the sense of something having shifted inside of me. Something had opened and become clear.

What will I need? I asked myself. Going into the forest at night—I might need extra batteries for the flashlight, insect repellent to stave off mosquitoes... I dug through my pack until I found those items. I put the batteries in my pocket and started to apply the mosquito repellent.

I must have been out cold, I thought. Even worried as I was, I was having trouble waking. Every motion I made felt heavy and sluggish. My thoughts seemed a scattered fog.

I went back to the pack for a compass and snack bar, put them in my pockets, picked up the flashlight again and, hoping I had thought of everything, stepped out the door.

Outside the hut, the night was warm and filled with the song of insects. In the forest beyond the clearing the moon had begun to rise. It hung low in the sky, tangled in the tree's upper limbs. I stood still for a moment and looked around me, scanning the compound. I was immediately aware of the glow of lights coming from the direction of the kitchen hut.

How foolish, I thought—they're back, and here I am, ready to search the forest for Laura.

I wondered for a moment if I should go and look, to be certain that's who was there, then almost laughed at myself. Who else would it be, here, in this remote location?

I stepped back inside the hut, making excuses to myself for jumping to conclusions (half asleep, unfamiliar circumstances) and returned the compass and snack bar to my backpack. Then I stopped to straighten my hair and clothing, and used the flashlight to guide myself to the little latrine at the edge of the forest, before washing up and joining the others near the fire site outside the kitchen hut.

If not for being so sleepy and distracted, I might have paused to appreciate the rugged beauty of the scene before me. Laura and Raymond sat on camp stools near the cooking fire, empty bowls on the ground beside them. The fire before them was built on a platform raised for cooking. The platform rose nearly a meter from the ground and was made of the same red clay the huts were built from. The fire lit the little clearing with a golden glow, casting bands of light and shadow, which made the tall trees at the edge of the surrounding forest seem to dance and sway in its shifting light. A few meters away, a lantern hung from the eaves outside the kitchen hut. It cast its brilliant, white light across the top of a small wooden table set against the wall, showing its grain in bold bands of rust red and blackish brown. A battered aluminum cooking pot was set on top of it.

The bright glow in the area near the kitchen hut, and the flickering fire light swaying amidst the towering trees beyond, made the world seem at once very small and grandly large. I slipped into that pool of light and took a seat on the camp stool nearest Laura. Raymond, seated across from us, offered a brief greeting, and I nodded a reply. Mvula was nowhere in sight.

"Hey, you woke up," Laura said, looking over at me and flashing a warm smile. "I didn't want to disturb you, you looked so sound asleep. There's lots of stew left, and it's still warm, if you want some. We've been back about an hour—just finished eating." She paused, then added, "Did you sleep all day?"

I laughed a little, glad to see Laura. "No, not at all," I said.

Laura looked at me, still smiling. "Actually, when I saw that you were napping, I wondered if you'd been able to get back to sleep at all after I left this morning. I wasn't sure how much sleep you'd had, so I didn't want to wake you."

"I went back to sleep okay—and then I wanted a nap, too," I told her. She reached over casually and stroked the back of my head and neck. I smiled at her sleepily.

"Well, I'm glad at least you got some rest. I was sorry you had to miss the bonobo-watching trip. I hope at least you had a good day?" she said.

I looked into Laura's warm, tender eyes. "It was good," I said, then an impression of what I'd been thinking about as I'd fallen asleep a couple of hours earlier came back to me. "I've had some wild thoughts," I added.

"Really? Do you want to tell us about them?" Laura asked. I still held her gaze, squinting my eyes in the light from the camp fire and lantern. I was glad just to see her cheerful, lovely face.

"No, you look sleepy," Laura said, shaking her head as she answered her own question. "Why don't you wait until you've finished waking up, then you can tell us what you like. And I can fill you in on our day, too. We found the bonobos! Indira, it was so exciting. I really wished you could have been there."

I smiled at Laura sleepily. She looked so happy. I wanted her to tell me what she'd seen, but she was right to wait. I knew I couldn't give her my full attention until I'd finished waking up.

"Here, I'll get you a bowl of stew," Laura continued. "It's the same as last night, but still delicious." She rose and stepped over to the little table against the wall outside the kitchen hut.

"It's still good?" I asked. "It didn't sit out too long—since last night?"

"No, they have a little refrigerator they run off a car battery," Laura answered.

I nodded, then looked over at Raymond. "That works, huh? A car battery?"

Raymond had been watching Laura. He looked back over at me. "Yeah, it works fine, though the batteries run down faster than I would like.

We have a generator, too, which we crank up sometimes, but it makes a bloody racket, and I'm afraid it will chase away the apes. So we just use it to charge up all the batteries once a fortnight or so."

Laura handed me a bowl of the stew, then sat back down. I noticed she'd turned down the lantern a little, possibly because she'd seen me squinting in the light.

"Thanks," I said to Laura, then filled in the silence which followed by asking Raymond where Mvula was.

"He went home to his family for the night," Raymond said. "They live in a village a few kilometers up the road. It's people from that village who cleared this patch of land," Raymond gestured around him. "He'll be back in the morning with the jeep."

"That's nice—that his family is nearby," I said. I took a small bite of the stew. Laura was right—it tasted good—but I really wasn't ready to eat yet. I glanced around at Laura and Raymond.

"Well, anyway," Raymond said as he turned to Laura, "it's just amazing the amount of information that has been gathered through the years, and then entirely disregarded." He shook his head. I had the feeling he was just finishing a thought he had begun before I arrived.

Laura turned to me and said, "We were just talking about bonobo sexuality and animal sexuality in general—and about how common same-sex sexual relationships are in nature, but how severely underreported they've been in scholarly writings, at least until very recently."

"Well, actually, things are better, but I don't think we've really begun to get the old prejudices out of the way," Raymond interjected. "Ideas have a lot of inertia."

Raymond looked over at me. "We like to think of science as somehow pure," he said, "that people observe facts and then draw reasoned conclusions from them. But as I was just telling Laura, in animal research, especially on the question of animal sexuality, what researchers have *expected* to find has greatly colored what they allow themselves to perceive and report on.

"For so long," he continued, explaining to me rather than Laura, "it was assumed that for animals the only possible purpose for having sex was to produce offspring. So when scientists researching animal mating behavior would observe animals of the same sex mating with one another, instead of responsibly reporting what they had observed, they would assume right off that it was an aberration, and so disregard those observations in their findings. Hardly scientific! They wanted the actual world to match their view of the world, to conform to their own social and scientific prejudices, instead of factually observing the world as it was. So we had skewed results for decade after decade—actually, for century after century."

I nodded and took another bite of the stew, then looked over at Laura as she added, "And their findings only reinforced the social prejudices that had, in the first place, convinced them to ignore those kinds of observations."

"Right," Raymond responded, "and round and round it's gone, with prejudice encouraging further prejudice."

"It's amazing how an official view like that can become established," Laura said, "even if it's incorrect, and then just keep being passed on and on, reinforcing itself. Like all that stuff in the Bible that people think of as condemning same-sex relationships as immoral—if you go through it bit by bit and look closely at the earliest texts, it's clear that's not what was intended. That impression is based on mistranslations and other kinds of misunderstandings."

"Oh, really?" Raymond answered. "That's interesting. Like what, for example?"

"Like, well, for example, if you read a correct translation of the ancient texts and add to that an awareness of the times in which they were written, it's really quite clear that Sodom and Gomorrah were destroyed for the sin of inhospitality, not for any sexual misconduct," Laura said. "The idea that it had something to do with sex between men is based on a mistranslation of the Hebrew word that means 'to know.' It's actually extremely rare for this word to imply carnal knowledge—but even so, when the townspeople say they want 'to know' the strangers who have come into their town, it's commonly translated as meaning 'to have sex with them,' rather than meaning that they want 'to know who they are'—even if this second translation would seem much more obvious."

Laura shook her head a little. "Anyway, what most readers don't know is that the value of welcoming strangers into your home—or in this case, your town—was a very common and important one in Biblical times. Outside of urban centers, travelers had no inns to stay at. They depended on the hospitality of strangers for their welfare—for their survival, even, traveling through a desert region.

"The people of Sodom and Gomorrah were hostile towards the angels, who had come as strangers into their town. The town was destroyed, but Lot was spared, because Lot, unlike the rest of the town, showed the angels hospitality by feeding them and giving them a place to stay.

"It was the same with Jericho," Laura added. "When it was destroyed, the only ones spared were a prostitute and her family—because she, again, had offered hospitality (in her case, by giving lodging and protection). Hospitality was a *very important value.*"

Laura paused and rubbed her neck thoughtfully. "There's other information, too," she went on, "including a passage in the New Testament—something that Jesus said—that indicates that he also thought the sin of Sodom and Gomorrah was inhospitality. It all really adds up, if you know all the details."

"That's all very interesting," Raymond said. He looked thoughtful.

Laura picked up a stick from a pile of wood next to the fire and tapped the ground with it absentmindedly. The look on her face told me she was having trouble remembering some details she wanted to share with us.

Finally, Laura shook her head and went on. "Anyway, another example," she said, glancing at both of us, then thoughtfully poking at the fire, "there's a passage in Leviticus that gets translated as, I think: 'Thou shalt not lie with mankind as with womankind,' but a literal translation of the ancient text would actually be: 'Thou shall not sleep the sleep of a woman with a man'—which is pretty ambiguous, it seems to me." Laura again looked over at Raymond and me.

"Whatever, exactly, that means," she went on, "the line which follows it appears to condemn it. It's usually translated as: 'It is an abomination.'"

Laura frowned. "But that's a mistranslation," she said. "The word translated as 'abomination' is actually a Hebrew word, 'toevah', which means basically 'this is something that is unacceptable within a given cultural or religious framework.' For example, in Genesis, Moses refers to Jewish religious practices as being *toevah* from an Egyptian point of view. He's certainly not saying such practices are fundamentally immoral—just not accepted by Egyptians.

"So, what we're being told," Laura concluded, "is that sleeping 'the sleep of a woman with a man' was considered unacceptable for the Jews of that place and time. They were being told in that passage not to be assimilated into Canaanite culture. Apparently, the Canaanites had the reputation of sleeping that sort of sleep, and it wasn't considered a very Jewish thing to do. The larger point was: 'Don't disregard our social conventions. Don't put at risk the security and communal identity that conventional practices help provide.'"

Laura sighed and shook her head. "In any case," she said, "'*toevah*,' doesn't mean 'an abomination,' and it certainly doesn't mean 'immoral.' It just implies a practice that is considered foreign and not accepted. Like eating shellfish is *toevah*—which is another 'abomination,' as it's commonly translated."

"Eating shellfish is an abomination?" Raymond asked, a little astounded.

"Yeah, the way it's usually translated," Laura answered, smiling at Raymond's look of surprise. After a moment, she returned her gaze to the fire and used her stick to push a half-burned ember back towards the flames. "Anyway, it's possible to go through the whole Bible that way," she said, "bit by bit. The most informed interpretations and translations simply do not support the idea that the Bible condemns same-sex relationships as immoral. In fact, some Biblical passages are quite affirming—including applauding some same-sex relationships that may well have been passionate ones—but unfortunately, mistranslations and misinterpretations have left an unreasonably negative impression.

"And I'm sure a great deal of violence and bigotry has been inspired by those misunderstandings," Laura added, a note of sadness in her voice. She tapped her stick lightly against the ground, lost in thought.

"I have the impression that there's a lot in the Bible that doesn't exactly fit well with a modern sense of morality, anyway," Raymond said.

"Well, yeah, in many ways that's true," Laura answered. She looked over at Raymond and nodded a little, then added, "Like in Exodus, it says if you beat your slave so badly that you kill him or her, it's okay—so long as they don't die right away. In fact, there are any number of passages, throughout the Bible, that condone slavery—and that would definitely not be considered moral in the modern world."

"Yeah, that's the kind of thing I was thinking of," Raymond said. "I have the impression there's a good bit of stuff like that, though I can't think of it offhand."

I wondered, watching them have this exchange, what Raymond's religious background was, but like so much else with him, I was having trouble figuring out exactly how he saw things.

Laura looked thoughtful in response to Raymond's comment. She took a deep breath. "Yeah, let's see," she said, looking up towards the starry sky. "It does say, as I remember, that a man and a woman who have sex while the woman's on her period should both be sent into exile. I guess that's the sort of thing you had in mind?" Laura asked, looking back over at Raymond, who nodded his agreement.

"And somewhere, I think it's in Leviticus," Laura went on, again frowning slightly, "it says that kids who curse their parents should be put to death." She paused and shook her head. "I mean, you're right, it's true—it really is not a modern document. But hopefully we've learned a thing or two in the thousands of years since those things were written.

"And of course, there are other, very positive things in the Bible," Laura added, turning to face me. "What was it you told me, sometime, Indira—that Mahatma Gandhi was inspired, in part at least, by the idea of turning the other cheek, when he came up with the concept of nonviolence?"

I had just taken another bite of stew and hurried to swallow so I could answer her. "Yes, in part—also Hindu teachings, and *Civil Disobedience* by Henry David Thoreau. And his wife, in fact, he said taught him by example."

"Right—so it was a part of it, though. And it is an important concept," Laura said, looking back over at Raymond. "I like the Beatitudes, too. I think that's the only part of the Bible my mother ever had memorized," she said, smiling a little. "I used to hear parts of it, sometimes, growing up. You know, 'blessed are the merciful, for they shall obtain mercy... blessed are the peacemakers...'"

Raymond nodded at Laura thoughtfully, then turned his gaze into the fire, which popped and sizzled as its smoke rose toward the star-strewn sky. For several moments, nobody said anything.

I began thinking again about what Raymond had been talking about, about animal researchers discounting what they had seen with their own eyes. I had another bite of stew, swallowed, then said, "I'm curious, Raymond, about what you were saying—about the animal researchers. Was there more to that?"

Laura nodded. "Yeah, me too. I didn't mean to sidetrack the conversation."*

Raymond seemed a little distracted, as though we were dragging him back from some deep thoughts to another topic he'd already left behind.

---

* See Part I of Appendix 4 (pages A16-A17) for more on same-sex relationships and the Bible. —I.K.

"Ah, well," he said, then sat a moment longer, staring into the fire and rubbing his jaw with one hand.

"Well, you know," he began again, "one reason there has been so much resistance by researchers to recognizing the prevalence of same-sex mating in animals is that a competition-based model of evolutionary theory was, and really still is, so deeply ingrained."

"I'm not sure what you mean by 'competition-based model,'" Laura said.

Raymond smiled a little. "Oh, yeah, sorry," he said. "I mean, the way they see things, they think the more surviving offspring an organism has, the better off they are in an evolutionary sense. In other words, the more offspring they have, the more likely their genes are to be passed on, and keep getting passed on, and still be around multiple generations down the line. They see that as the code for evolutionary success.

"But the idea that whoever has the most offspring wins is really simplistic," he went on, "because of course, if you produce *too many* offspring, they will compete against one another for whatever food is available, possibly overrunning their environment so that the food supply gets used up, a whole bunch of them starve, and there's a huge crash in the population. We've seen that sort of thing in deer populations, for example, when people have killed off their natural predators. For a little while there are way too many deer, and then suddenly there are way too few, because so many of them have starved.

"So it's just not an effective evolutionary strategy to keep pressing the limits of what the environment will sustain, because a collapse of that sort, even once every several generations, can incur such great losses as to overwhelm any temporary gain. The best long-term evolutionary strategy is to match the production of offspring to the resources available to them. And to my way of thinking, this implies a more cooperation-based than a competition-based model."

Raymond seemed to think about this for a moment longer, then added, "It's sort of the same thing as if you, as a parent, were trying to decide how many kids to have. If you can only afford to send two kids to college, you don't then plan to have eight. It's just not a good strategy if you want a successful life for your kids. Instead, you only have the number you can really take care of and that the environment around you can reliably sustain."

"This is like what you were telling me before Indira joined us," Laura added in, "about how costly it is for some kinds of animals to reproduce?"

"Certainly," Raymond told her, smiling a little. I had the feeling he was enjoying her taking the sort of interest she was in what he'd been telling her, and I wondered again how it had been for the two of them when they'd been off in the woods together that afternoon. So far, at the fire since I'd joined them, I hadn't had that uncomfortable feeling about Raymond at all. Yet it had been like that with him since we'd first met him on the barge. It was almost like he was two people, one friendly, enjoyable even, the other colored by a disquieting hunger, a bruised longing of some sort, which made me uneasy just to be around him. I wondered if Laura had seen that part of him when she'd been with him in the forest earlier, then reminded myself that she had not actually been alone with him then. Mvula had been with them until just shortly before I had joined them for dinner at the fire.

Laura turned to me. "I never really thought about it," she said, and I realized I'd been lost in thought, "but the risk involved in reproduction is really different for different kinds of animals. Lots of kinds of animals may lay hundreds, thousands—or even *millions*—of eggs at a time, most of which get eaten, but by that time in most cases the adults are long gone. There's no changing diapers and midnight feedings, or all of that, you might say. They just lay the eggs and scram.

"But, as Raymond was just explaining," she continued, "for mammals and birds there's a lot of work involved in reproduction. Mammals are especially vulnerable to attack by a predator when giving birth, and of course, there's risk in the birthing process itself—and birds have to just sit there on their nests hour after hour, day after day. Mammals have to nurse their babies; birds have to feed their chicks. It's a lot of work for them—especially compared to animals that just lay their eggs and then disappear!"

"Exactly," Raymond said, still looking at Laura with a pleased expression. "It's not advantageous for them to get one offspring half-raised, allow it to die, and then have to begin again on another one. Quite apart from the emotional impact, it's not a good evolutionary strategy. Just getting an offspring born or hatched has involved a lot of risk, and big sacrifices, so for mammals and birds, the strategy is to have just a few offspring, and then to be sure that a very high percentage of them live to adulthood—at which point, they'll be able to pass on those genes again."

"And this is what's really interesting," Laura said, again turning to me. "Animal species in which same-sex mating has been most commonly observed are typically ones that have just a few young and put a high premium on seeing to it that they survive until adulthood," Laura glanced back over at Raymond, "and they also characteristically form groups of some sort, ah—flocks, herds, pods..."

"Right," Raymond said, now addressing himself more to me than to Laura. "Not that same-sex pairings are at all limited to animals in these two categories, but they do tend to be more commonly observed in the circumstances Laura just described. So that would include various sorts of birds—gulls, swans, flamingos, penguins, for example—also antelope, bison, giraffes, sheep, elephants," he rubbed his jaw as he thought of more, "as well as whales, dolphins, seals, gorillas, bonobos, ah...well, that would be some of them. It's really quite a long list.

"Anyway, the idea is," Raymond continued, "that sex doesn't just create new individuals, it creates bonds between group members," he held his hands out in front of him, with one hand gripping the other. "Those bonds increase group cohesion—and that added group cohesion improves the likelihood of survival for all group members."

"And of course the more intricately interwoven the bonds are in a group, the stronger that group cohesion is, and the greater its benefits. Species that have enough flexibility built into their sexual nature to allow such bonds to form between male–male couples and between female–female couples, as well as female–male pairs, generate a much more elaborate system of social bonds."

"Which means they're more likely to survive because they're more likely to share food when they find it, to alert one another to danger," Laura told me, counting the items off on her fingers, "or even to risk themselves to protect other members of the group from danger—ah, and to care for abandoned or orphaned young.

"Raymond was saying it's sort of like an insurance policy," Laura went on. "Everyone invests in the group, and the group uses its resources to insure the welfare of its members." I smiled, looking at Laura. She had that engaged, happy glow she got when she'd discovered an interesting new idea.

Raymond nodded, glancing at Laura, then back at me. "This is all highly related to the research I do. Bonobos are especially group-oriented animals and are extremely flexible in forming sexual bonds. They use sexual bonding in all sorts of social relationships, and the social and emotional bonds within the group are very strong. An adult bonobo will risk its life, for example, to save any of the infants in its group, no matter what their relationship is to it. Sadly, I know of an instance where someone was trying to poach a live bonobo infant for the pet trade, and a dozen bonobo adults gave their lives trying to protect it."

Laura and I were both silent for a moment.

"That's terribly sad," I said.

"Yes, it is," Raymond said. "But the point is, the bonds within a bonobo group are very, very strong.

"And they are in other regards, too," he added. "A bonobo mother may nurse her babies for four or five *years*, and as a rule, her sons can be expected to stay with her their whole lives."

"That is all really fascinating," I said, setting my empty bowl on the ground beside my chair. "And you say these kinds of sexual relationships, the sort of same-sex sexual bonds that bonobos share, are common in other animals, as well?" I asked.

"Oh, yes," Raymond said. "Same-sex mating occurs in all the species I just listed, and in a great many more. How common it is within a species varies quite a lot from one species to the next, however. In some it can be very common, in others less so. Nearly all bonobos are bisexual, for example—though the females on the whole are more focused on same-sex relationships than the males. Similarly, homosexual activity is very common amongst bottlenose dolphins of both sexes, but in that case, especially between males. In bottlenose communities, for example, one might expect to find as many as three-quarters of the males pair-bonded with another male at any given time."

"*Three-quarters!*" I said.

"Yes," Raymond answered, "and there's a great deal of sexual activity between females, as well." He paused for a moment and glanced up. "Ah, let's see," he went on. "I think it's black-headed gulls, in which so many of the males nest together. Yeah, that's right. More than a third of male black-headed gulls will at some time in their lives form a 'pair-bond' with another male. That means they engage in an elaborate courtship ritual together, then build a nest together. And many male couples nesting together have been observed to have sex, as well."

"And if they're bonded with another male, do they reproduce somehow—I mean, obviously not with each other, but...?" I asked.

"Amongst black-headed gulls? The males that bond only with other males?" Raymond asked.

"Yes," I said, nodding.

"Generally not," he said. "What I remember from the research I've seen is that about one out of five—roughly 20%—of the males bond exclusively with other males. That is, they never form a pair bond with a female gull. Sometimes a pair of males will take care of eggs abandoned by mix-sex couples, then raise the chicks, but the chicks aren't their own.

"Another 15% or so of males," he added, "will spend some seasons bonded with a male and other seasons with a female. But like I said, more than a third of male black-headed gulls overall spend at least one season pair-bonding and nesting with another male."

I thought about this for a minute. "But if the males that bond only with other males never reproduce," I said, "from an evolutionary point of view, how are the genes of those individuals passed on?"

"In other words," Raymond answered, "why wouldn't the genes that permit such same-sex bonding die out, if the birds with those genes don't have any offspring?"

"Exactly—right," I said, nodding.

"Yes," Laura chimed in, clearly curious, "and even the bisexual ones—I would expect they would have fewer offspring overall. Wouldn't that put them at a disadvantage, in an evolutionary sense?"

"Well, presumably," Raymond said, "the answer is that the genes don't die out because they are shared amongst all black-headed gulls, and that the genes don't *determine* sexual orientation, but rather allow for *flexibility* in sexual orientation—so they are part of the genetic makeup of even those birds that engage exclusively in mix-sex coupling.

"Let me put this in context," Raymond went on. "Think about wolves, for example. All wolves share the genes that define them as wolves, right? That is, any two wolves will have most of their genes—virtually all of their genes, in fact—in common, just because they're wolves.

"As a general rule, each year only two wolves in each pack reproduce— the alpha male and female. That is, whichever pair happen to be the alpha pair that year. The others don't do nothing, however. They help guard and care for the pups, and they hunt. Think of it as a reproductive strategy for the whole pack. The alpha female has a litter that includes, typically, about five pups, give or take. Meanwhile, she and all the other members of the pack engage in behavior that helps insure that those newborn pups live to adulthood.

"This gives good insurance that the genes held in common within the pack get passed on. If they all reproduced, scarce food resources would have to be allocated to all of the pups. And at the same time, there would be fewer hunting adults, because all the mothers would have to be on hand to nurse their pups. On the other hand, maybe they would all hunt, and the pups might be left unguarded and, for stretches of time, unfed. A much higher percentage of the pups would die. And even so, those that didn't die from these causes would still compete with one another for limited resources, and possibly precipitate a food crises in which much of the pack, if not the whole pack, could starve. So it's a practical matter for wolves to have a limited number of reproducing members, with the others helping out.

"So my point is," Raymond went on, "animals that aggregate in a group of some kind—a pack, pod, flock, herd, etc.—in a certain sense function as a single organism. One of the things I tell my classes when we discuss evolution is to think of a whole species as you would a single animal," Raymond said. "Think of the members of a wolf pack, say, as being like physically disconnected cells of the same organism—and with each 'cell' having almost exactly the same genes as every other 'cell.' The organism has to produce enough new cells with each generation to continue to exist—enough cells—not too many, not too few. If it overproduces, there's not enough food to go around, and starvation and die-offs result. If it underproduces, the population gradually dwindles away, right? Long-term survival of the genes shared in common within this organism is best guaranteed by having the *right number of members* to fit well within its environmental niche."

"Which is like what you were telling me before—a cooperation-based model of evolution," Laura said.

"Right," Raymond answered, "cooperation and balance mean success. You can even think of whole ecosystems this way, with each species being like an organ in a single body. Each species has to play its role in balance with the others if the system, overall, is going to be healthy."

Raymond looked thoughtful for a moment, then looked over at me. "Sorry to be so long-winded," he said, "but I want to go back to your question about the gulls. You wanted to know how their genes get passed on. Well, perhaps that number—that approximately 20% of the gulls that never have any offspring—is the percentage of members that have to abstain from reproducing in any given season in order to create the optimal number of new offspring for the flock to continue to be *of an appropriate size* to fit its niche—not to outgrow its food source, nor to under produce and gradually die off.

"And theoretically that number may not be set," he added, "it could become a higher percentage if the number of flock members begins to grow too large. It could become a smaller percentage when there's plenty of extra food and other resources for new members.

"So for this species of gulls, sharing a gene that permits males to have the flexibility to bond sexually with other males may provide a certain adaptive flexibility, allowing a more niche-appropriate rate of reproduction, and a greater likelihood that the flock on the whole will survive—

and therefore that the genes of black-headed gulls will continue to exist in the world.

"And theoretically," Raymond added, "that gene would be present within all black-headed gulls—and passed on by the ones that *do* reproduce—just like wolves all share the genetic basis of their social structure, in which only the alpha pair is likely to reproduce."

"That's really interesting," I said, then we all sat quietly for a moment, as Laura and I pondered what we'd just heard. I had never before thought of a whole flock, or a whole species, as being and functioning like a single, multi-celled organism, with all its cells each carrying essentially the same set of genes.

I got up and served myself what was left of the stew. As I sat back down, I noticed how thoughtful Raymond looked, sitting with his legs stretched out in front of him, as he stared into the fire. I took another bite of the stew. Then Raymond cleared his throat and added to what he'd been telling us.

"There's more to the story than that, even," Raymond said, and there was something about his tone, the carefulness of his speech, which suggested to me that he wanted to clarify some point. "The gulls could get the benefits of a more balanced rate of reproduction simply by evolving to have a certain percentage of their members abstain from sex in each season.

"Do you see what I'm saying?" Raymond asked. "From an evolutionary standpoint, all I've just explained is why it's advantageous for some members not to have the sort of sex that results in more offspring. So there won't be too many offspring, right? But then why, from an evolutionary stand point, do the male couples engage in sexual coupling at all? And the answer is, of course, as with bonobos, that with sex comes bonding. Bonding leads to more cooperative behavior within the group, which in turn also increases the likelihood of survival for all group members, including the likelihood that the eggs already laid, and that the chicks already hatched, will survive."

"Wait," I said. I knew Laura had said something about this earlier, but I wondered if I had been a little too groggy to take it in at the time. "Can you tell me again, exactly how does the fact that these birds have bonded with one another increase the likelihood that the young will survive?" I asked.

"Sure," Raymond answered, smiling a little, patiently. "Birds within a flock aid in one another's survival in a few different ways. First, they may aid one another in finding food. Second, they all act as sentries for one another. If one bird in a flock becomes aware of a predator approaching, for example, it will give a warning call and take flight. The others hear the call, and take to the air also. Thirdly, birds in a flock will dive at a predator that has already caught, but not killed, a flock member. The predator may be distracted by this and unintentionally release its prey. And fourth, bonded adults in a flock, including same-sex couples, may take care of orphaned and abandoned nests and chicks.

"In fact, co-parenting of young by same-sex couples has been observed in quite a variety of animal species. But of course, all of this depends on there being strong bonds between those individuals, and within the flock in general, and sexual bonds are particularly strong bonds," Raymond concluded.

"So it sounds like it's advantageous for there to be some members that don't reproduce, but who still do form sexual bonds," Laura said—"and that same-sex coupling allows that to happen."

"Right," Raymond said, looking over at her with a slightly surprised expression. "My point exactly. It helps keep the population from over-growing its niche, while contributing to an important network of social bonds. And it leaves some adult couples available to care for orphaned and abandoned young."

"That's fascinating," I said. "I've thought in the past about how important sexual bonding is for people—the way sex forms a kind of interpersonal bridge. But I never thought of that bonding as having evolutionary value."

"But it certainly does," Raymond said.

I took a bite of my stew, which was hardly warmer than the warm tropical air now, but still quite good. Laura and Raymond were both quiet for several moments.

The fire snapped and popped in front of us, then Laura turned to Raymond and said, "All of that makes sense if all the animals in a given flock, herd, pod, or whatever, had 100% of their genes in common, but how much do they, really? How much of their genes does a pack of wolves, or a flock of black-headed gulls, have in common, for example?"

Raymond looked thoughtful, then answered. "Well, I can't say specifically for wolves or gulls, since I don't offhand know of any research into it, but I can tell you that you share nearly 99% of your genes with—guess who—Indira? Me?"

Laura frowned a little. "Well, your ancestors were European, and so were mine, so I guess I should pick you."

Raymond smiled. "Actually, I was thinking of that young bonobo you saw in the tree right above you this afternoon," Raymond said, then laughed at the look on Laura's face.

"You're serious?" Laura said.

"Yes," Raymond answered. "Ignoring duplicate copies, we human beings have nearly 99% of our DNA in common with both bonobos and chimpanzees."

Raymond paused and then asked Laura, "So what percent of your genes do you suppose you and, say, Indira share?"

"Well, I'm not going to guess blind twice," Laura answered, looking a little chagrined, "so I would just say, well—a lot?"

Raymond smiled, clearly enjoying the game. "And you would be right!" he said emphatically. "In all likelihood, there's more genetic diversity in that group of bonobos you watched this morning than in all of humanity."

"All of *humanity*?" Laura responded, incredulously.

"You and Indira share at least 99.9% of your DNA. Any two human beings do," Raymond answered, nodding. "Getting awfully close to that 100%, isn't it?"

I thought about this for a moment. "So it makes sense biologically for human beings to take risks to help one another, like birds and bonobos do," I said.

"Right," Raymond answered. "Just as it makes sense for us, in other ways, to function like cells within a single organism—including that it may have an evolutionary value for a certain percentage of people to form same-sex sexual bonds, especially in circumstance where we may be overgrowing our environmental niche, or when there are children who need adopting."

Raymond paused, then added, "To come at all this a little differently, it would appear that it's natural for us to have the sort of flexibility in forming social bonds, and the kind of devotion to those we're bonded to, that we see in our nearest animal relative—the bonobo," he concluded.

"With whom we share nearly 99% of our DNA," Laura said, still looking a little amazed at the idea.*

❀   ❀   ❀

I was vaguely aware of the pleased expression on Raymond's face as he took in Laura's reaction, but my attention was turning to an impression forming at the edge of my mind, somewhere just out of reach. It was some feeling, hazy and indistinct—a piece of memory gathering and pressing forward. Gradually, it came back to me.

"I remember, sometime, some of the physical anthropologists in my department talking about something like that, how much we all have in common, genetically," I said. "One of them was saying that the concept of race as defining genetically distinct groups of people is bogus, an invention. I think it was Sue Ann," I added, turning to Laura. Laura nodded.

"Anyway, what I'm remembering her saying was that, of that small difference—of that 0.1% difference which exists between people—only about a *tenth* of that difference has to do with what we think of as racial characteristics, and even that doesn't sort out along racial lines.

"As I remember," I went on, "she was saying that what we think of as 'racial' traits, genetically, pertain to very superficial characteristics—that race is, in a very real sense, just skin deep." I thought about it for a couple more moments, trying to recall more about the conversation—and then it all seemed to come into focus.

"That's right," I said, glancing down at my hands, then back over at Laura. "It was at the winter solstice party at Dulcea's house a year or two ago. James Caldwick was there, too, and a student I didn't know, and they were explaining to the student that we all started out as Africans with dark skin, and then dispersed from there."

---

* See Part II of Appendix 4 (page A17) for more on same-sex coupling in animals. — I. K.

"Anyway," I said, refocusing on where I was, with Laura and Raymond at the fire. "As I remember, the idea was that sunlight makes our skin produce vitamin D, and having dark skin in a tropical region keeps you from being poisoned by overproducing vitamin D, because the darkness of your skin blocks out some of the sunlight. But as people migrated north and the sunlight dimmed, people needed to be better at producing vitamin D. Then the people with the palest skin were most likely to have surviving offspring—and over time, people in the north gradually got paler and paler. And more so the further north they went, because there was less light to produce vitamin D from.

"Another interesting detail I remember—it was James who told me this," I said, looking over at Laura. "You remember me mentioning him, don't you—James Caldwick?"

Laura looked a little unsure.

"Well, he's the one I told you about whose family had pushed him into becoming a lawyer when he was young," I told her, hoping Raymond wouldn't mind my little aside to Laura. "Don't you remember? He'd really hated it—being a lawyer. He was really miserable doing it. Then he got diagnosed with cancer. His doctor said, statistically, the odds were he wouldn't live more than another couple of years. Do you remember him? He decided then that if he wasn't going to live very long, he was at least going to spend his time doing something he loved, and he went back to school to study anthropology. That was at least twenty years ago."

"Oh—yeah, yeah, now I remember you talking about him," Laura said.

"Well, anyway," I went on, "he said that people who eat a great deal of fish and the fat of marine mammals get a lot of vitamin D from their diets, and that this is why people who live in the arctic—like the Inuit, for example—still have fairly dark skin, even though they've migrated so far from the tropics, because they have that sort of diet, and don't need their skin to be able to make a lot of vitamin D from the dim sunlight in the far north."

"Yeah, that makes sense, I mean, it matches the way people actually look, doesn't it? Almost everywhere where people have evolved, their skin color matches the amount of light," Laura said. "I remember coming to basically the same realization about race when I was, oh, a teenager, I guess. I saw a map to which little pictures of the people who lived in each region had been added. Little circles with the pictures of individuals—little smiling faces in each of them in spots all over the map, so you could see what the people looked like, all over the world.

"It really was impressive in its effect, because you could really see how gradual the changes in appearance were from one region to the next. Like from here, people get gradually lighter and lighter in skin color as you go north, until you get to Scandinavia, where they are really pale. The changes in appearance are gradual, just as the changes in climate are gradual. There's no line like, here, suddenly, there's another race. To a degree, I guess, maybe the change can seem less gradual where there are major physical obstacles, like the Sahara or the Himalayas, which have kept people apart, but mostly the map showed only slight differences between neighboring peoples. It really drove home for me how much the whole concept of race is, well, just like what you said—just a concept, not a reality. People can't really be divided into such distinct groups," Laura concluded, glancing first at me, then over at Raymond, then back at me again.

I nodded at her, then found myself looking into the fire. There was something tugging at my attention, and I let my thoughts follow in the direction in which they were being pulled. As I did, I was vaguely aware of Raymond adding a story of his own, about some similar realization he had come to when he was young.

When Raymond finished, I looked over at Laura. "You know, thinking of James reminded me of something. I remember when he first told me that story about how he had gotten over his cancer after deciding to do what he loved, I was thinking that, well, that was probably why. I mean, deciding to do what really fulfilled him, what really gave him joy, had probably given his immune system a boost," I said. "It had helped him get well." I didn't want to use the word "protolife," because I didn't want to stop to explain it to Raymond, but that was what I was thinking—that doing what brought his protolife to life had given him joy—and health.

"Yes, I've heard about things like that," Raymond said, "that a positive frame of mind aids the immune system. And I think there's medical research to support that."

"Yes, I've seen that, too," I told him. "Our immune systems are strengthened when we do things that make us genuinely happy. In fact, being in a positive state of mind has a lot of benefits. Ah, for example—people who are depressed are more accident-prone, just because they're kind of out of it. They're not alert—their reflexes are slowed, their reaction times are down."

I paused. Laura and Raymond were both nodding politely. "But I was just thinking—imagine what kind of effect that sort of thing could have over time."

I set my bowl down, trying to think of how to explain this. "Imagine you have two groups of people, one of which has some physical resource— a certain sharpness of mind or, say, manual dexterity—which permits them to do the things that they find fulfilling—the things that give them joy. Right?"

Again I looked at Laura and Raymond, and again they nodded politely. "And then picture, in contrast," I said, "a second group of people who don't have that resource, and who, as a result, go through their lives feeling unfulfilled, joyless. Who's more likely to survive?"

"Ah," Raymond said, nodding now with more interest. "The ones who are alert and have quick reaction times are less likely to, say, fall off a cliff or get eaten by a predator."

"Right, right," Laura said, "and those same ones—the ones who feel joyous and fulfilled—they're more likely to survive because their immune systems work better. They're less likely to die of disease."

Now I was nodding. "Right," I said, "and the ones who lack the physical traits they might find fulfilling to have—the ones who are unhappy, joyless—they're more accident prone, more likely to get eaten," I gestured toward Raymond, "and more likely to get sick and die of a disease." I glanced over at Laura.

"It's just a thought," I went on, "but doesn't it make sense to think that who we are now *physically* has been shaped, in part at least, by what we, as a species, have found inspiring and fulfilling in the past? That we have evolved towards having the capacity to fulfill ourselves because wherever a trait which enhanced that capability developed, it would have been selected for? Doesn't it make sense that that trait would have made us more able to survive, and therefore would have been passed on to the next generation, and the generation after that, and so on?"

"Fascinating," Laura said.

"Yeah, that's very interesting," Raymond said, looking first at me, then out past the fire, thoughtfully.

"It just seems to me," I went on, "that we have this idea of evolution as being fundamentally meaningless, a machine that builds itself for no good reason. But I'm just thinking, maybe there is meaning shaping the course our evolution takes. Maybe the evolution of all creatures is shaped by what fulfills them. Maybe ours is shaped, and has been shaped, by what fulfills us." I paused, and looked at Laura and Raymond, both of whom looked very thoughtful.

I turned my attention to my own thoughts, as well. Perhaps, I told myself, who we are physically had taken shape around our protolife—just as every other species may have been shaped by its protolife, as well.

A vision of the whole natural world took form in my mind—so vast and colorful and wonderfully alive—with all of it being subtly shaped, over millions of years, by the pursuit of meaningful fulfillment.

We were all silent for several long moments. The fire popped and sizzled. Then Laura turned to me and said, "Well, you seem entirely awake now. How about if I tell you about the bonobos we saw today?"

"Sure, that would be great," I answered.

"It was dark when we set out," Laura began, leaning in towards me. "We needed to use flashlights as we walked through the forest. The trees were amazing, Indira. They're huge, and they have roots and vines running everywhere. Being there with just the flashlights for light—well, it seemed a bit surreal.

"Anyway, we walked a long while, and Mvula led us to the *elimilimi* tree that the bonobos had nested near. I don't know how he did it. I think I would have been lost.

"We got there just as the sky was brightening and hid in the underbrush, trying to be as quiet as possible. We waited there till well past dawn, but the bonobos never showed up. Mvula was right—it was a big, gorgeous tree, and it was fruiting out all over the place. Huge tree, tiny fruit. And no bonobos anywhere.

"So Raymond suggested we keep looking. Mvula said he knew of another tree where the fruit was near ripening, so we set off for it. It was a bit of a hike, but not as long as it had taken us to get to the *elimilimi* tree." Laura glanced over at Raymond. "I still don't know how Mvula does it," she said, then looked back at me.

"The sun was well up by the time we found the other tree. It was a—what kind of tree?" Laura asked Raymond.

"*Ntende,*" Raymond answered.

"*Ntende,*" Laura said. "And sure enough, we found bonobos there. It was so exciting, Indira. I so wished you could have been there. There must have been a couple dozen of them."

"I counted twenty-eight," Raymond cut in.

"Twenty-eight," Laura said, accepting his count. "They were way up high eating the fruit, which grew in these big orange clusters, with each piece of fruit about the size of a fig. There was so much of it! I ate one of the fruits that had fallen to the ground. It was good—sort of sweet and sour all at once. Most of the bonobos were eating when we arrived, but later on some of them made nests by folding one tree limb on top of another. Then they would sit or lie down in the nests they had made. They're beautiful animals. Sometimes they would gather up fruit and then climb or swing through the branches to a place where they could sit and eat it more comfortably. It's amazing to see them move, way up in the air like that, like some high-wire act."

Laura glanced over at Raymond, then back at me, as though trying to remember what else she wanted to tell me.

"Oh yeah," she added, "the, ah, *ntende?*" She glanced over at Raymond for confirmation. "The fruit on the *ntende* tree was ripe, but it usually wouldn't be quite ripe yet this time of year, Raymond said. For some reason, it ripened a little early, which is why the bonobos weren't at the *elimilimi*—it's also called *Dialium*, right?" she asked Raymond. "They weren't at the *Dialium* tree because they like the *ntende* fruit better—probably because it's easier for them to eat. The *Dialium* fruit is so tiny."

Laura paused and took a deep breath. I always loved seeing her excited like this, and even though I was realizing that I'd probably had a more close up encounter than she'd had, I wished then that I could have joined her in the forest and shared in her excitement as the day had unfolded. It was, after all, our hope of giving Laura a chance at just this sort of adventure that had drawn us here from Boulder in the first place.

"That's marvelous," I told her. "Did you get to see any of them close up?"

"Sort of," she said. "One of the young ones, a young female, I guess got curious and came down a little closer than the rest. But still, she must have been at least ten meters above me. I did get a pretty good look at her face, though. They have such a presence, Indira. They remind me more of people than any other animal I've seen. I do wish you could have been there."

Laura finished up by describing how they had stayed at the *ntende* tree until about noon, when the bonobos had swung off through the treetops, then dropped to the forest floor and disappeared into the underbrush. Laura, Raymond, and Mvula had tried to follow as long as they could, but the trail had turned cold quickly, and so instead they had stopped in a little clearing and eaten the lunch Mvula had packed, and had then spent the rest of the afternoon marking trees where the fruit was ripe or soon to ripen, or where bonobos had recently built nests, and then making the long hike back to camp.

The conversation moved on, then, and I told Laura and Raymond about my own journey into the forest, and all that I had seen there. I didn't try to tell them about the thoughts I'd had then, just about where I had gone and what I had seen. Laura, I think, was a little bit jealous when I described how the bonobos had appeared so close at hand in the little clearing in front of me, but I pointed out to her that I'd only seen them for a few minutes, not nearly as long as she'd been with the ones she had seen at the *ntende* tree.

As I continued with my story, Raymond had a lot of questions for me about just where I'd been and what exactly the individual animals had looked like. I did my best to answer him, though I think my descriptions for the most part lacked the details he wanted.

Finally, I finished my story by describing how the two mothers had kissed, and how they had then all wandered off into the underbrush.

"Wow, I can't believe you saw two of them kissing close up like that," Laura told me. "They were doing all sorts of things up in the tree above us—eating, grooming, napping, probably having sex now and then from the calls they made—but they were so high up, and there were so many leaves and limbs in the way, I could only get a clear view part of the time. How lucky you were that they stopped right in front of you like that!" Laura shook her head. "That's really something, Indira. And then you made it home okay? You didn't get lost?"

"Yeah, I was fine. I had to pay attention, but I found my way back okay. And then I took a nap after I got here."

Laura looked thoughtful for a minute, then turned to Raymond. "You know, her mentioning the two bonobos kissing reminds me, I had another question for you about what you were telling us earlier," she said. "You were saying before that same-sex mating occurs in some species that do *not* fit the pattern you described—that is, they don't form groups and care for just a few young. I'm just curious—what would some of those animals be?" she asked.

"Well, orangutans are one," Raymond said. "They're very solitary creatures."

"But they don't have many young, right?" Laura asked.

"Only one at a time, generally, like us," Raymond answered. "Butterflies are another example. They may lay a lot of eggs, and they don't raise their young, but on the other hand they also may gather in groups. I'm not sure how common same-sex mating is amongst butterflies, however," he said. "I just know that it has been observed."

Laura nodded. "So what would you say the evolutionary strategy is there?" she asked.

"Well, I guess from one point of view you could say they're getting half the benefits of the pattern we discussed before," Raymond told her. "But the thing is, not everything fits into neat compartments. Bonobos fit in both categories, but it's unlikely their same-sex mating serves any function in population control. Since bisexuality is the norm for them, and they're *so* sexually active, they probably have just as many offspring as they would if all the sex were heterosexual. But for them it's clear that their sexual activity is very important in forming all sorts of group bonds—bonds that aid in their survival.

"This is different than the case with the dolphins I mentioned earlier, where males may be exclusively focused on same-sex relationships for many years of their lives, but may still mate heterosexually and reproduce at some point. They probably do have fewer offspring than they would if they didn't spend so many years in same-sex couples—which in turn may help the pod they are in fit better within its ecological niche. And of course, again, such bisexual bonding greatly enhances the network of bonds within the group. But the exact mix of these sorts of things is different for each kind of animal.

"So what I'm saying is, even within the groups I already described, there are all sorts of variations—and the range of variation just extends out from there.

"I mean, just look at how rich and various nature is," Raymond went on, gesturing around him. "So many different kinds of plants and animals. Such rich variety. It makes sense to assume that nature would provide as much variety in terms of sexual expression as it does in every other area of life. After all, within all that marvelous variety, we would expect to have just as great a range of evolutionary strategies present.

"The fact is," Raymond concluded, "I can't tell you what the evolutionary strategy is in every case. It's a fascinating topic, but I think we've only just scratched the surface when it comes to grasping the broad range of evolutionary strategies that come into play when creatures reproduce themselves."

While Raymond had been speaking, I had been holding in my mind an image of orangutans coupling. The big orange creatures had always seemed so human to me in their gestures and facial expressions. In my mind's eye, I pictured two of them making love, bonding together in a tender, loving, intimate embrace, with colorful butterflies fluttering in the air around them.

I noticed a pause in the conversation and looked up. "I was just thinking about the orangutans," I told them. "Maybe their coupling is of evolutionary value," I said, "because it *feels meaningful to them.* Maybe it makes them feel joyous and fulfilled to be together, just as intimacy has that effect on people."

I paused, searching for the words to give form to my thought. "Maybe when species have that sort of flexibility built into their natures," I continued, "life has more opportunities for meaningful fulfillment for them, and so as a group they are more likely to survive and pass their genes on."

"*Right,*" Laura said, drawing the word out thoughtfully. "Like the capacity to create art, or to sing, or, or," she paused, "to appreciate humor. What evolutionary value do *they* have?"

"Exactly," I answered. "That's right. Perhaps they exist *because they are fulfilling.*"

Laura and I smiled at each other for a moment, then I turned my gaze out into the forest. I again imagined the butterflies circling around the orangutans, and wondered if their love-making felt fulfilling for them, as well. Did they rejoice in those moments of intimacy with another of their kind?

Looking at life from that vantage point, all the natural world around me seemed so bright and rich—a great up-flux of life designing and refining itself, naturally opening the way to untold fulfillment and joy, multiplied endlessly by all the many and various creatures, and all their many and various lives.

I looked back over at Laura and found her watching me, the smile still on her face. "Well, you're full of surprises tonight, aren't you, love?" she said sweetly. It was the sort of moment where, if we had been alone, she might have added, "I've always loved that about you." But instead, there in the forest with Raymond, she said simply, "I guess that sleep did you good."

Then Laura paused, and added, "Hey, speaking of which—what was it you were going to tell us, Indira? You said you'd had some wild ideas today."

✺   ✺   ✺

"Pause," Paul said, as Kiki's voice—emulating Dr. Kumar's—fell silent.

"Pausing. End of chapter," she replied.

It seemed to Paul that he had been climbing either up or down all day. Now he was on another upward stretch. It was just this sort of terrain that had caused his feet to become sore in the first place—and he was impressed to find that, after having applied the Dermo Mend patches the night before, his feet were still not hurting. It seemed so impressive, in fact, that it had begun to worry him. Were the patches protecting his feet—or were they just making them numb to the damage the shoes were inflicting? He didn't like the idea of some invisible damage going on beneath a patch that obscured his vision.

Paul dropped his pack and sat down beside the trail, then slipped off his shoes and socks. Apart from the patches stuck to his heels, Paul's feet looked perfectly normal—no redness, no swelling.

Paul pressed against the patches with his fingertips. He could feel the pressure of his touch—but no pain along with it.

Very good, he thought—and again felt impressed at the quality of this technology.

As Paul was putting his socks and shoes back on, he heard a sound coming from ahead of him on the trail and looked up as another hiker approached. It was an older woman, with gray hair and a broad-rimmed hat to keep the sun off her face. It appeared she was hiking alone.

"Hello," she said cheerfully, when she caught Paul's eye.

"Hello," Paul answered. The woman looked at him, and something in her look made him suddenly conscious of his appearance. Paul dragged a hand over his scalp. Thick stubble there. Eyebrows must be the same. And he hadn't shaved since he'd set out on this walk.

"Sojourning?" the woman said, just as cheerfully.

"Yes," Paul answered.

"Well, I hope you enjoy your hike! You're most of the way there, by the way. You'll probably be there by this time tomorrow." The woman smiled as she passed Paul. As odd as Paul knew he must look, her manner was nothing but friendly.

"Thank you. You, too," Paul answered, then watched as the woman disappeared down the trail. How remarkable it was, he thought, for a stranger to be as friendly as that. It seemed there was nothing about this world that didn't surprise him.

Paul rubbed the stubble on his face. He'd have to remember to use his solar razor before he arrived at the retreat tomorrow, he told himself, then looked back down at his shoes. He adjusted the bindings carefully, then stood, lifted his pack to his shoulders, and continued on his way up the steep trail.

The temperature had risen as the day wore on. The path, too, had climbed a good bit since Paul had left camp that morning. As Paul came around a curve in it, he found it looking out over a small, sunny valley. In its curved basin, Paul could see animals grazing. He stopped and looked more carefully. Elk, he was sure they were. There were a lot of them. Tule elk, he thought—the same sort as he had seen at Anna and Marco's.

This herd was large, too, stretching out among the brush and grasses of the small valley, and into the ravines leading into it. Could this possibly be the same herd he had stood on a hill watching just a week before? Paul wondered. He knew they had wandered on, even before his own departure.

Paul stood watching for several minutes, listening to the distant lows and grunts of the animals below. For a moment he was tempted to climb down to where they were, to get a closer look, but then thought better of it, and instead turned and continued up the trail.

"Kiki, please resume recitation," he said, then listened as the voice of Indira Kumar rose around him, drowning out the soft din rising from below.

◙   ◙   ◙

Chapter XI

In the days when natural instincts prevailed, men moved quietly and gazed steadily. At that time, there were no roads over mountains, nor boats, nor bridges over water.... Birds and beasts multiplied; trees and shrubs grew up. The former might be led by the hand; you could climb up and peep into the raven's nest. For then man dwelt with the birds and beasts, and all creation was one.

—Chuang Tzu

I was still thinking about the idea of protolife shaping life, even at the most basic biological level, when Laura asked me about the ideas I'd had before my nap.

As I tried to collect my thoughts, Raymond swatted at a mosquito on his neck, then got up quietly and stepped over to a small pile of wood that had been left a short distance from the fire. He picked up a small log, then set it down and picked up another.

"Sorry. I don't mean to interrupt," he said, setting down the second log and picking up another of about the same size. He repeated this another time or two before apparently finding what he was looking for.

"This'll do," he said, then stepped back over and added the log he'd selected to the fire.

"The others weren't good enough?" Laura asked, smiling.

I smiled, too. In truth, all the logs had looked about the same to me.

"I was looking for a green one. Sometimes the smoke helps drive off the mosquitoes. I should have brought some goop out with me. I'm not used to staying this long after dinner."

"Yeah, I'm starting to get bitten, too," Laura said.

"You know," Raymond said, looking around, "I think I may have seen some repellent in the kitchen hut."

He got up and lifted the lantern off its hook under the eaves, then carried it with him into the hut. Laura and I were left sitting in the glow of the fire, with the forest rising up around us beyond the clearing. Stars shone overhead.

In a moment, Raymond was back, a bottle of insect repellent in his hand. He hung the lantern under the eaves again, then stepped over to Laura.

"Here," he said to her, as he sat back down, "you can take the first crack at it." He handed it to her.

"Thank you," Laura said, and squirted some into her palm. "You need any?" she said to me.

"No. I just put some on a little while ago."

She handed the bottle back to Raymond, who squirted some into his palm, then held the bottle between his knees while he applied the liquid.

"Sorry for the interruption," he said to me. "Have to be careful in the tropics. Seems everything's a vector for some disease."

"Not a problem," I said.

"So," Laura said, looking from Raymond to me. "Did you want to tell us..."

I nodded, and tried to turn my attention back to what I'd been thinking earlier that day. I remembered the impression I'd first had when I'd woken from my nap, like something had shifted inside me—like an obstacle had been removed, or a door opened.

I rubbed the back of my neck. "I guess relaxing and getting some rest helped move a log jam," I said tentatively.

I frowned, thinking for a moment, then went on. "The way it feels, well—things I've been working on on the barge the past few weeks have begun to shift, somehow."

I looked over at Laura and Raymond. "It's funny how things you've been looking at a long time can suddenly begin to look really different. It reminds me of the way an image shifts in a kaleidoscope—it's the same pieces, but something changes, and suddenly they just add up differently."

I frowned again. "Anyway, this all has to do with what I'd been thinking about on the barge," I said.

"Do you mean the paper you were writing?" Raymond asked. "What did you say it was about?—prehistory and individuation?"

"Yeah, that's it," I told him.

"So, how does it seem so different now?" Laura asked. I looked over at her. She was leaning forward a little, her eyes intent.

"Well, I feel like all that stuff I was working on on the barge has crystallized, somehow," I said. For a moment, I thought back over the ideas and impressions that had flowed through my mind as I'd lain in the heat of our hut, smelling the thatched roof baking in the sun and listening to the soft drone of flies.

"The frustrating part is," I said, turning my attention back to the scene around the fire, "I really feel like the material is right, like it's true—and, well, I've got a lot of good supporting material for most of it—but some of it, the part I've been thinking about today, in truth, I don't see how it could possibly be proven or disproven."

"So what makes you inclined to believe it?" Raymond asked. He had screwed the lid back on the bottle of insect repellent, and now set it down so that it leaned against the leg of his stool.

I stared at the bottle as I thought about my answer.

"Well, for one thing," I said, "it's consistent with the information I do have. And, well, it just seems to fit somehow. But the truth is," I added, looking back up at Raymond and Laura, "we don't have a lot of data about the ancient past—cave drawings, bones, tools—that's about it. It's like putting together a jigsaw puzzle without all the pieces."

Raymond laughed. "It's like me studying the bonobos," he said. "I watch them playing together or grooming one another. They make all sorts of facial expressions, some of which look very human, and I wonder just what they are thinking. I can sometimes make a pretty good guess, I think, based on one thing or another, but I could never prove any of it."

Laura smiled a little at Raymond, then said to me, "But you said it feels like things are crystallizing for you, huh?"

"Yeah. It's interesting," I said, nodding. "It's almost like a story, the way it's taking shape in my mind."

"Can you tell us about it?" Raymond asked, as he got up and stepped back over to the kitchen hut. He turned down the lantern to a low flame, then came back to where we were sitting and stirred the fire, which was burning brightly. The smoke from it drifted upwards, illuminated by the flames.

I thought for a moment. "Well, I could tell you about it, I guess—but it seems pretty complicated, especially if I were to try to give all the supporting data. That would be a mess."

"Well leave it out, then," Raymond said, as he laid the stick he'd stirred the fire with on the ground near the fire.

"Sure, just tell us a story," Laura added.

"I could," I said, thinking about it a moment more. "Yeah, I guess I could do that. Do you want me to?" I looked over at them.

Laura nodded. "Yes," she said.

"Sure," Raymond said, and gave an encouraging nod.

"Well, okay then," I said. I thought about it for a couple of moments, trying to decide how to best make a story of it—then I began.

"Imagine our early human ancestors, moving through a forest not unlike this one," I said...

❋   ❋   ❋

"Wait. Pause," Paul cut in.

"Pausing," Kiki said.

Paul looked down at his feet as he made his way up another hill, then shook his head a little.

"I don't know," he said, half to himself and half to Kiki. "This is all interesting enough, but I just don't see how all this stuff about what we were like in prehistory, or how we evolved, or whatever, can help answer the question of how this world became the way it is."

Paul looked up and took in the bold blue of the sky. "Kiki, what do you say to that?" he asked.

"The material appears to be relevant," Kiki answered, after a moment. "Its numeric value for social influence is 63.5781%.

"And as Dr. Kumar herself observed, earlier in her memoirs," Kiki added, then switched to Dr. Kumar's voice as she continued:

Somehow, what had happened in the past helped set us on a course to the present that we now knew, and, in turn, to the future that would develop from here. How we saw the world then...how we see the world now...what the world is today and what it would become—these things were all interrelated.

Paul thought about that for a moment. All interrelated—yes, he supposed they were. And in any case, if Dr. Kumar had seen these things as being related in this way, then it made sense that this material might lead to the answer he was seeking.

Paul glanced back toward the little valley he had stood gazing into just a few minutes before, full of tule elk grazing in the sun. Yes, he truly would like to know how this world had become as it was!

"Okay, let's keep going," he said. "Please resume recitation again, where you were just before I asked you to stop."

And with that, Kiki's voice rose again, speaking with the soft tones and accent of Dr. Kumar, weaving together a story about the past, as Paul continued up the trail.

◻︎　◻︎　◻︎

"Imagine our early human ancestors, moving through a forest not unlike this one," I said, gesturing toward the forest beyond our little circle of light. "We were self-aware in the way you described other animals as being self-aware, Raymond, like chimpanzees or bonobos are, but this was a long, long time ago, 30,000 years or more, perhaps much more, into our past. We were aware, conscious of our own selfhoods, but not *focused* there, not particularly interested in that awareness.

"We were, in a certain sense, like a child might be today—capable of a certain sort of independence, but much more naturally oriented to its parents, its family. We lived within the framework of nature, just as a child lives within the framework of its family, and we were just as oriented there, guided by instinct and intuition, just as a small child turns to its parents for guidance.

"And like a child, too, we lived focused in the present moment and thought very little about the past or the future.

"Time passes, and that child grows older, and something begins to gather within her, a certain sort of longing to know and be herself, a longing to probe more deeply into that self-awareness, which she had previously felt only tangentially, vaguely, along the borders of her awareness. She feels a desire to discover and define what she finds lying there.

"This same longing was there, arising within all of us. Beginning perhaps 30,000 years ago, we came to a kind of "teenage" stage of our development as a species, and like teenagers, we pushed away from the source from which our existence had arisen, and sought our independence. We wanted to know and be ourselves in a self-conscious and deliberate way. We longed to express and discover ourselves.

"And so we began to make beads to adorn our bodies, and to make paintings on cave walls—expressing ourselves into the world, and discovering ourselves there, reflected back.

"Then, starting some ten thousand years ago, we began to sow seeds and harvest plants, which *we* grew where *we* chose, turning the landscape of the world around us into a kind of giant canvas onto which we expressed our*selves*, and through which we, again, discovered ourselves reflected back.

"In other words, we began to make our mark on the world, and to discover ourselves through our creations."

I thought about this for a moment, then went on. "Agriculture required of us that we plan ahead, and that we draw on past experience as the basis for that planning. We turned our focus from the present moment then, and involved ourselves more and more with thoughts of the past and the future. We began making decisions for ourselves—consciously, deliberately—planning ahead in pursuit of the specific outcomes we preferred.

"We began to define those outcomes in our thinking as either "desirable" or "undesirable," sorting out which choice to make on that basis. And so we began to interpret our experiences as either 'good' or 'bad,' and to see the world in those terms.

"Gradually, in time, we began to make a different sort of world around us. We began to build the world we know today."

I stopped and thought for a moment, then said, "That's about how far I'd gotten while we were still on the barge."

I let a moment or two drift past as I tried to decide how to tell them about the ideas I'd had earlier that day. Those ideas felt fully formed in me, somewhere just beneath the surface, but consciously they still seemed raw and fresh and tangled together, and perhaps too brazen to tell about.

After another moment, I heard Raymond's voice.

"I have a question," he said. "Who exactly does this pertain to? I know you mentioned the transition to agriculture. Would this only be people who became agriculturalists, then? Not hunter-gathers?"

I turned my attention back to our little gathering around the fire.

"The way I picture it," I told him, "we all made this transition. That is, we all became interested in exploring our own selfhoods, and we all sought the means of self-expression, which could include self-adornment, art, agriculture. But agriculture, as remarkable as it is as a means of self-expression," I gestured around me, "—as much as it allows us to paint our will out onto the canvas of the world, to express ourselves onto the land and the fruits of the land—as remarkable as it is in those terms, it just wasn't for everyone. Not everyone was in an environment where agriculture made sense, or where it was even possible. For example, you don't grow plants if you live in the arctic.

"So I think this change happened for all of humanity, but it was expressed differently depending on climate, environment, the availability of plants and animals that could be effectively domesticated, that sort of thing."

"That makes me think of the Cheyenne," Laura said.

"Yeah?" I said.

"Well, there's reason to believe they grew crops, in addition to hunting and gathering, when they lived in the Great Lakes region. And in fact, at least some of them farmed pretty intensively for a while after they were pushed out onto the Great Plains. Eventually, though, they gave up agriculture entirely and lived the way we think of them as having lived—riding horses and followed the buffalo herds. I guess it didn't make any sense to try to keep growing crops once they started following the buffalo. But apparently they had grown crops when the circumstances were right for it."

"Is that so?" I said. "I didn't know that. Yeah, that fits perfectly." I thought about it for a moment, then went on, trying to finish answering Raymond's question about who participated in the change.

"Like I was saying before," I told him, "agriculture would have pushed us to relate to time differently than we had before. We had to learn to plan ahead. In the same way, hunter-gatherers living in a climate where they had to stockpile food, or make warmer clothes in preparation for the harsh winter ahead, would have had to learn to think about future and past times, as well, and to plan for the future, just as agriculturalists did.

"So both of those groups would have needed to think outside the moment, to plan ahead, and to make decisions based on the desirability of outcomes. They wouldn't have survived if they'd just lived impulsively, hand to mouth, moment by moment.

"But I think some groups that did not develop agriculture, and that lived in tropical areas, where food could be found year round—and where there was, therefore, no need to plan ahead for the winter—probably never had to learn to really step out of the moment, nor to deal with that kind of planning."

"Like the Mbuti," Laura said.

I looked over at her. "What about them?" I asked.

"I'm not sure where I read it," she said, "but their time sense is different than ours. They live very much in the present moment. I think it was in one of Colin Turnbull's books, actually. It said, essentially, that the future and past were pretty much insignificant to them—that it was the present that mattered."

"Oh yeah," I said, "I have the feeling I've read that, too, now that you mention it. And it certainly fits, doesn't it? Hunter-gatherers like the Mbuti, living in the tropics where there's hardly any seasonal variation, do hunt and gather the same way year round. They don't need to plan ahead, at least not for more than what they'll do that day."

I looked back over at Raymond. "So, to answer your question more clearly, it applies to everyone, except that the part about time and planning may not apply so much to at least some hunter-gatherers living in the tropics today," I said. "Also, hunter-gatherers who migrated into areas with wide seasonal variations, where it was necessary to plan ahead for the winter months, would have gotten a much earlier start on the time and planning aspect of this—by perhaps as much as 30,000 years. So the timing and ordering of changes may have been different in different contexts, but the whole set of changes is pretty much universal—and all of it happened very quickly if you measure it against the speed of change throughout most of human prehistory."

Laura looked thoughtful, then asked, "So you said that's how far you'd gotten on the barge—what were the ideas you had today?"

"Today? Well, I've been thinking about this change that took place in the human perspective—in human *consciousness*, I guess you could say— when we started focusing on our individual selfhoods. And today, for the first time, it occurred to me what it might have been like to have been *inside* that change."

I stopped and wondered how I could possibly tell them this strange and complex story. I looked first at Laura, whose face beamed with affection and interest, then over at Raymond, who looked calm and intrigued, invisible thoughts ticking past behind his eyes.

I thought for a moment longer about how to tell them about these ideas, and as I did, I began to find the thread that wove through them like a story.

The fire cast a reddish glow around us. The area near the campfire was very quiet. From beyond, in the darkness, I could hear the hoots and howls of monkeys and could make out the occasional crash of limbs, as the monkeys swung from one branch to another in the ancient forest encircling us.

"Set aside any question of proof and tell it like a story, you said?" I asked them.

"Yeah, sure, go ahead," they both told me.

❀　❀　❀

I stared out into the darkness, beyond the glow of firelight. The moon, which had been just cresting the trees when I'd left our hut earlier that evening, now hung high in the sky, full and brilliant, casting a shimmer of light through the tops of trees, like sun on water.

"Imagine," I began, "how life might have been for us in the far distant past, before we became focused on our individual selfhoods. Imagine a time before that change, when people lived instinctively, like animals do. Imagine a time when we were focused within the moment—moving freely, impulsively—trusting our intuitions to rise up and guide us.

"We felt a deep sense of belonging and interconnectedness with all the life around us then. We didn't merely live on the land, or in the forest, but rather were part of the life of the land, part of the life of the forest."

I thought for a moment, following a thread of thought like a rope pulled up from deep water.

"This was not the sense of independence that came later, but a feeling of belonging within a larger network of life, like a child feels a sense of belonging within his or her family.

"When a child is small it doesn't matter if his sense of self is barely formed, or if he is not yet ready to be self-determined, because his parents and his family form a context around him, and provide him with the guidance he needs.

"Like that child, our sense of self was young and undetermined. The natural world formed a context around us, cradling us. From deep within our own natures, impulses and impressions rose up—wordlessly, like water rising up through a root-system—providing us with the guidance we needed," I said carefully, still tracing that line within myself.

"We felt the promise intertwined with each moment, and followed it intuitively, surprised and delighted by where our impulses led us. Our minds were not yet focused on planning for the future, nor recalling the past. Our attention was in the present. We felt a certain joy at each moment unfolding, and were crisply aware of each sensation within it: the soft patter of rain on leaves, a scent carried on the breeze, the feeling of the wet earth beneath our feet.

"But buried within us, within all of us, was that budding desire to become more fully ourselves, and to discover and articulate that selfhood.

"We continued to follow our impulses until finally they arose collectively, out of that shared depth, and like a field of wildflowers blooming in unison, gave rise to one wave after another of individual expression around the world.

"The advent of personal adornment, the advent of art, the advent of agriculture—each wave was so closely aligned as to seem nearly synchronized when viewed spread out against the larger timetable of human development.

"And I guess what I'm saying is, what I realized today is, with that process something was born—but something was also lost. We traded in a kind of free-moving existence for our workaday worlds, full of deliberated plans and living up to expectations.

"In the deep past, I believe, we had a sense of unspoken—and unspeakable—belonging, of being a part of something much larger than ourselves, something whole and alive, something that we gave expression to *through even our smallest acts.*

"We were aware of those impulses traveling through us, like waves cresting from some deeper current.

"But we traded it in, even though doing so meant a reduction in the quality of our food and an increase in our labor, because *we hungered so* for the development of individual identity in ourselves, and for the discoveries it would hold.

"That hungering, which began as a collective act, which rose up from the deepest currents within us, turned us away from that sense of collective belonging.

"We became individual in a way we never had been before—but we became, also, alone as we never had been before.

"In making that change, we gained all the possibilities our individual lives grant us, but we left behind a certain sensation of—or awareness of—wholeness, and of belonging, I think," I told them. "And today, for the first time, I guess, I realized what sort of sacrifice we'd made, to pursue these changes which have since set us so apart from the rest of the natural world.

"Up until today, I had mostly thought of this process as a kind of advancement," I concluded. "After all, without this change we would never have developed art or agriculture. We would never have created religion or science. We would have none of the technologies we've developed since the stone age. But sadly, I'm realizing, on the path to all of those innovations, we lost something really valuable along the way."

I stared into the fire, and for a moment imagined our ancestors finding food or locating a loved one just by trusting their impulses. How magical the world may have seemed to them then, and how deeply rooted we may have felt within it, I thought.

For several long moments, nobody spoke. The fire popped and sizzled, dancing in flames of orange and blue. The words I had spoken had come from that place where ideas become interwoven during sleep, and I was still absorbing what I had said, even as the words themselves had vanished in the nighttime air.

"That was some story," Raymond said quietly.

"Yeah, it was some story," Laura said, nodding. "And a familiar one, as well."

"Familiar?" I said, surprised. How could this insight still settling within me seem already familiar to Laura?

"It sounds like creation stories from religions all over the world," she said, smiling with that little smile which says, "come on, Indira, think."

I looked at her blankly. "It does?" I said, squinting my eyes.

"The article I just got the proofs for before leaving town? You remember? The one that's coming out this March in *The International Journal of Religions*. 'From Belonging to Isolation: A Multi-Cultural Analysis,' I called it?"

"Right," I said, remembering the article she was talking about, but not at first recalling what it said.

Laura turned to Raymond and continued. "It's a comparison of traditional stories from many religions around the world, with all of them depicting a particular recurrent theme. All the stories I analyzed dealt in one way or another with an early time of often harmonious belonging, in which we felt a kind of oneness or nearness to 'the Source'—whether it was referred to as 'God,' 'the Great Medicine,' 'Nature,' 'the One who causes all things to be,' or whatever else within a given tradition. All of those stories described how we had begun with this sense of 'oneness,' and then passed through some sort of transition, where that original sense of closeness and harmony was lost."

Laura looked back over at me and laughed a little. "Really, Indira, the story you just told us fits so nicely, I can hardly believe you didn't make the connection yourself," she said, still smiling and shaking her head a little.

I shrugged. "I just had the idea today. I guess I hadn't had a chance to make the connection. I did think about your other article—the one you wrote with Roger," I said. "You just got there ahead of me, that's all."

Laura reached over and squeezed my hand. I felt sort of thickheaded, the connection seemed so clear now that I recalled the article.

"I guess," I added, "I just took such a different route to get there, I didn't see that I was arriving at so nearly the same place."

"Yeah, it is nearly the same place," Laura said, nodding thoughtfully.

"You know, one of the things I found so interesting in compiling those stories—and they really are widespread throughout the world," she said, looking over at Raymond again. "They appear in Asia—Hinduism, Taoism; in tribal religions in Africa, South America, North America, and the Arctic; and of course, the Abrahamic religions, which originated in the Middle East, but have spread all over the world: Judaism, Islam, Christianity—all of which share the Garden of Eden story."

Laura looked back over at me. "But what really struck me as I was compiling these stories is that within each tradition from which a given story originates, that story is not told as a 'myth.' Instead, each of these stories, within their original contexts, are considered *history*—the story of how we came to be as we are now—a history that is thematically very similar, even though the stories developed independently in so many different parts of the world."

Laura looked pensive for a moment, then added, "And they match so closely with the story you told us here tonight, too. I just think that's interesting."

We all sat in silence for several moments, reflecting on this, then Laura looked over at me again and said, "What part of the article I wrote with Roger were you relating this to?"

"The part about wholeness and, ah, non-locality," I answered. "I think before we became so focused on our individual selfhoods, we would have felt that sort of essential interconnection much more strongly."

"Oh, I thought you were going to relate it to the wave/particle stuff," Laura said, looking thoughtful.

"Really? The wave/particle stuff? That's interesting. How so?" I asked her.

Laura shrugged a little. "Well, you know," she began, and then looked over at Raymond. "Are you familiar with the idea that light can be both a wave and a particle?" she asked him.

"I might have heard something about that, but no, not really," Raymond answered.

"Oh," Laura said, then paused, apparently trying to decide how to explain it to him.

"Light functions as either a wave or a particle," she began again, "depending on the context it's in. When an individual photon (that is, the smallest measure of light) is being observed at a particular location, then it functions as a particle—in other words, it is a specific physical thing at a specific physical location.

"When a photon's not being directly observed, however, it displays wave dynamics. The way Roger explained it—he's the physicist I wrote the article with—when photons are displaying wave dynamics, *they don't actually exist at any specific location.*"

Laura paused, raising her eyebrows and cocking her head a little, as though to say: *Isn't that crazy?*

"Roger said," she went on, "that when photons function as waves, they are in fact in a state *on the verge of being.* They're located in a kind of *partial way everyplace they might be,* but are not *actually located at any one place.*

"Photons can go back and forth between those two states. When they are observed, they have a specific location. Instead of being in a wave state then, they're in a particle state. When they're not being observed, they sort of partway exist everywhere they might be, and they function like waves. Back and forth, wave and particle, particle and wave, depending on whether anybody's looking," Laura concluded.

"No kidding?" Raymond asked, frowning a little.

"No kidding," Laura answered. "That and other such strange things—according to Roger—is why particle physicists talk about 'quantum weirdness.'"

"Yeah, that's pretty weird all right," Raymond said.

"In the article we wrote together," Laura went on, "I relate that wave/particle duality to different states of consciousness.

"Analogously, when we're in a "wave-like" state, our consciousness, our sense of identity, is broadly spread out, and not so focused on our own individual perspective. We may feel an expansive sense of love for and empathy with other people and other life. We may feel a deep sense of belonging with all of nature, or with all of humanity, or we may have a particularly strong sensation of connection with God.

"Different people experience that state of mind in different ways," Laura added. "It's often felt as a religious experience. In fact, as I wrote in the article, certain religious practices are designed to help us achieve that state of consciousness—meditation, fasting, prayer, repetitive tasks like drumming or chanting—all of them may be used to still or occupy the, well," Laura glanced over at me, "the *locally focused* parts of someone's mind, and thereby free up the rest of their mind to reach this expanded state.

"In contrast, when we're focused on our own individual experiences, or our own self-interest, I described that as analogous to the particle state. Then, our consciousness is locally focused, not diffused into a larger sense of interconnection," Laura added, then looked over at me again.

"That's what I thought you were going to say you were remembering from the Huginn/Muninn article Roger and I wrote," she said to me. "I thought you were going to say you were thinking that we as a species had moved from being mostly in a 'wave-like' state of consciousness, to a more 'particle-like' state."

Laura stopped for a moment and looked thoughtful. "And maybe you would even have said that we use religious practice as a way of trying to get back what we have lost."

"Huh," I said, a little surprised. It was an interesting idea.

Laura looked back over at Raymond. "It's all just analogy. I have no idea how you'd begin to measure actual consciousness directly, or in any way determine if it's literally in a wave- or particle-like state."

※   ※   ※

I followed Laura's gaze over to Raymond and realized he was beginning to look a bit bleary-eyed.

"You look tired, Raymond," I said.

"I am," he said, nodding. "I'm not used to staying up this late, but you've both made the conversation so fascinating, I've kept thinking I'll just stick around a little bit longer."

"What time is it?" Laura asked.

"Quarter-past nine," Raymond said, looking at his watch. "And I got up at half-past three this morning. I wanted to prepare things for our trek.

"I've been feeling pretty weary lately, anyhow," he added, in a tone that seemed to speak more than his words, "so I think I should be heading off to bed. I don't mean to break up the party."

Raymond stood up. "So will I see you both—oh, that's right, I guess we should talk about what's happening in the morning."

"Yeah, I guess we should," Laura answered, then said to me, "Raymond said Mvula is overdue for a day off. He said sometimes when he has time off Mvula likes to take the jeep and drive into Basankusu and pick up some supplies for his family and neighbors. Raymond gets him to pick up supplies they need here, too, and still pays him for half a day. Anyway, Raymond told me Mvula might like to go soon, and he could drive us into the airport there when we're ready." Laura glanced up at Raymond and back at me. "I told him I thought you might like to stay another day or two, so you could get a chance to see the bonobos, too—but seeing as you've already seen them...," Laura paused.

"I don't mean to rush you out of here," Raymond said. "Mvula could wait another couple of days. I'd really love to have your company a while longer."

I looked up at Raymond. His eyes looked tired, but there was also something pleading there. Perhaps it was just the flickering firelight, but his expression struck me in that moment as somehow deeply sad—almost hauntingly so—and full of longing.

Laura nodded at Raymond, then addressed herself to me. "...and seeing as we may be late arriving in Epulu as it is...," she continued.

"No, you're right," I cut in, seeing where she was headed. Then I looked back up at Raymond. "I'm sorry, but I think we really should go."

As I heard myself speak those words, I thought how funny they sounded—*I'm sorry?* For not accepting the hospitality of a stranger any longer? And yet I was sorry. After all, his eyes looked so very sad.

Laura nodded and looked back up at Raymond, also. "Yeah, I think that's right. It's wonderful, all the hospitality you've offered us, though," she told him.

"Okay, when...," Raymond started.

"Probably in the morning," Laura answered, looking to me for confirmation.

I nodded. "Yeah."

"All right, then," Raymond said. "I'll make sure Mvula sticks around in the morning. And I'll say goodbye to you both then." He made a sort of funny half-smile and began to turn away.

"Oh, by the way, there's a bucket of ash under the table there." He pointed to the side of the kitchen hut. "You can use it to snuff out the fire, when you're done." Then he said one final good night and strode off in the direction of his hut.

Laura and I watched as Raymond strolled away. When he was clearly out of earshot, Laura leaned over towards me and said quietly, "He can be an odd fellow, sometimes. I had the feeling he *really* wants us to stay."

"Yeah," I said, feeling a moment of concern for him. "I thought he actually looked kind of choked up. He's likeable in a lot of ways, but... I mean, he hardly knows us. Why would he care so much whether we stay or go?"

"I know," Laura said. "It's hard to make him out.

"Well," she added, "we'll be on the road again soon." She moved her camp stool over close to mine, and we snuggled up together. Around us the trees loomed large. I felt so close to her there in that little spot together.

"What was it like to be in the forest with him today?" I asked her.

"He was fine," she told me. "He's good company—knows an awful lot about bonobos. Besides, Mvula was there." She paused, then added, "I like Mvula. He doesn't say an awful lot, but there's something very calm and patient about him."

I lifted Laura's hand and kissed the back of it. It felt surprisingly warm.

I turned towards her, then, and pressed my cheek to hers.

"You're a little hot," I said.

"It's hot weather," she said.

"Do you feel all right?" I asked her.

"Ah, I don't know. Kind of run down, actually. But I think I'm just tired out," she answered.

I looked at her with concern.

"Don't worry, I'll be fine," she said, and smiled. That was Laura—whatever it was, it was bound to be fine.

"Maybe," I said. "But I'd hate to see you get sick way out here." I thought perhaps she looked a little pale, though it was hard to tell in the dim light.

"Don't worry," she said, pausing to observe my look of concern.

"I'll tell you what," she added. "I am tired, though. Remember, *I* stayed up when that alarm went off this morning. Maybe it is time we hit the sack."

"You go on," I told her. "I slept half the day. I'd just lie awake if I went to bed now. I'll be along in a while."

Laura agreed and stood up, then paused to kiss me on top of my head before stepping off towards our hut.

"Hey, Laura," I said as she walked away. "Take the lantern with you, why don't you? Without it, you won't even be able to see well enough to find and light the other lantern when you get inside."

"What about you?" she asked.

"I have a flashlight," I answered.

Laura agreed, stepped over and lifted the lantern from its nail, then carried its light with her into the darkness.

I felt such love for her, watching her go. I hated even to think of anything bad happening to her, she meant so much to me.

❋   ❋   ❋

For a long time after Laura left, I just sat there quietly. It seemed to me that even with all the sleeping I'd done, it had been a long day, full of complicated thinking. I thought some about Laura, and then let my mind turn to Raymond. "Odd fellow," had been Laura's comment, and I had to admit it was true, even if it seemed a bit unkind to think it when he had been nothing but friendly, generous, and helpful to us in everything he had actually said or done.

I sat there musing over this for a while, and as I did I recalled what I had noticed on the barge, which I had almost let myself forget about entirely.

It was from Raymond's quarters I had heard the man sobbing that night.

As I sat there thinking, I remembered having noticed Raymond's eyes in the flickering firelight earlier that evening. What sadness had I seen lurking there?

Was it, perhaps, not the sadness of our departure I had glimpsed in him then? I wondered. I shook my head. How would I know? Still, there was something in him that I found perplexing—odd, yes, as Laura had named it—something not quite lined up right.

I didn't much enjoy thinking of Raymond this way, whatever it was that was going on with him, and instead turned my attention to the discussion we'd all had earlier that night.

I thought about what I had told Laura and Raymond, about what it had meant for us to have become so focused on our own individual selfhoods. I remembered how those ideas had come to the surface in me, somehow interwoven and made whole in my thinking in a way I hadn't expected them to be.

In a certain sense, it seemed to me, I had discovered those ideas along with Laura and Raymond, as I had told them about what I'd been thinking. How surprising that had been—like recounting a dream that comes back a little bit at a time, until finally, as you finish telling it, you discover it for the first time in its entirety before you.

Was what I had said really so much like the stories in Laura's article? I wondered. It would be interesting if it were. After all, as Laura had pointed out, the stories her article dealt with had all been viewed as history in their original contexts. Was it possible that the story I had told by the fire was really a true account of the human experience? Had events really unfolded in much that way? And if so, was some sort of corroboration to be found in the stories Laura had written about in her article—stories that were seen, within the cultures they originated in, as a record of factual events?

Factual events, I mused. Yes, of course I knew that the most fabulous or magical aspects of these stories didn't fit at all with my beliefs about how things actually work in the world—they couldn't be factual in that sense. In fact, in most ways, the stories had seemed more symbolic than factual. But I knew, as well, that each culture has its own way of keeping track of the most important events in its past, and symbolic storytelling can sometimes convey a truth with more meaning and potency than can be communicated through a simple retelling of the unadorned facts— especially when such stories are part of an oral tradition where the stories must be succinct and pithy enough to be effectively memorized and recalled by succeeding generations of people. In that case, factual events may be formularized, stylized, in a certain sense, and then remembered and recounted in symbolic rather than factual terms. At that point, out- siders see them as "myths," while those within the culture in which they originate view them as "fact." Perhaps the truth was that they were myths that held within them the symbolic representation of fact.

As I remembered it, Laura had told me that all the stories in her paper had originally been part of such an oral tradition—in all probability this was even the case with the Garden of Eden story, shared by the Abrahamic religions of the Middle East. The only stories she thought were at all likely to be exceptions to this pattern were two stories about an ancient "golden age," and another one written in ancient China—but even though they had been passed on in written form for thousands of years, she had told me, she had no idea what the history of those stories had been before they had been written down. They, also, may have been derived from an earlier oral tradition of story telling.

If that were the case, I wondered, might even the most symbolically stylized of the stories that Laura had written about hold a certain truth within it? Might they actually be, as they were viewed within their cultures, a kind of "history" passed down through countless generations—factual in terms of their broader significance, if not in their details?

If that were so, it might suggest quite a lot. After all, as I remembered, the stories Laura had written about had appeared all over the world—from Asia to Africa, from North to South America, from the Arctic to Europe to the Middle East. They were widespread, just as the dawning of art and agriculture had been widespread. If they, in some way, agreed with one another, what might we glean from them about the most ancient aspects of the human experience?

All of this intrigued me and made me want to remember more specifically what Laura's article had said. I turned my attention, then, to trying to recall the details of what Laura had written.

My memory agreed with Laura's about the proofs having come sometime in December, when we were getting ready for our trip to London and then on to Zaire. I'd helped Laura go over them then, checking to make sure that all of the corrections had been made, and that no new errors had been introduced.

Laura had read her original copy aloud, while I had followed along, checking what Laura read against the proof copy sent by the journal's editor—going through it word by word, comma by comma.

As I thought about this, the way the pages had looked began to come back into focus in my mind, with a line or two of text, here or there, becoming clear. I struggled to pull more of the page back into focus. It was late in the day, and though I had slept late that morning and napped that afternoon, I was tired now, and that made the task more challenging

As my eye scanned the page I imagined before me, I tried to find more lines that would come into focus, or to glimpse enough to jog my memory about what was written there.

"The first age was the golden age." Laura's words were printed in the left column, about midway down the first page. I mentally skimmed down through that column, picking out the words and phrases that I could most easily visualize. "Their lives were carefree," I read, "without work or misery." Further on the words "feasting" and "never ill" caught my eye, and then a whole sentence from Laura's text came clearly into view. "The earth provided them with abundant food, which they gathered in leisure contentment," Laura had written.

That last part could certainly describe a hunter-gatherer existence, I thought. I remembered having read that passage before, and recalled that Laura had written that the text she had based that description on had been written in ancient Greece—most likely late in the eighth century BC. Had it been based on an earlier oral tradition? I wondered.

The Greek story had stood out for me, I remembered, because it had reminded me of another story from my own Hindu heritage—another story about a "golden age," which Laura had written about, as well. The Hindu story about an ancient "golden age" also told of a carefree, happy time, one in which people wandered freely.

Wandered freely, I thought. Yes, that fit too—could this happy era of easy satisfaction refer to an early time when we wandered freely, as we hunted and gathered?

Laura had written that the Hindu golden age had come to an end when people no longer felt fulfilled merely by existing. "It was then that another form of fulfillment was begun," she had written.

I thought about this for a moment, trying to decide just what that meant. Did it mean that this era of joy and contentment came to an end when people had sought fulfillment in a new way? Might it have ended when we sought to fulfill ourselves by exploring our individual selfhoods?

I pondered this for a few moments, but soon felt eager to move on and find out what other parallels might be drawn between the thoughts I'd been having and the other stories Laura had described in her paper.

Again, in my mind's eye, I glanced down the page.

The next passage that caught my eye was also from Asia, this time from the Taoist tradition in China. It was by Chuang Tzu, who had lived more than two thousand years ago. I skimmed that section, picking up lines. Chuang Tzu had written about an earlier time, now past, "when natural instincts prevailed" and when "all creation was one."

"Natural instincts," I thought. What were "natural instincts?" Might they be expressed through impulses and impressions? I wondered.

When "all creation was one," I repeated. Yes, that also fit. It seemed to describe a time when we felt a sense of oneness and deep interconnection.

So Chuang Tzu's story was also similar to the story I had told, I mused, and wondered how long it might have been passed on orally before he wrote it down.

How fascinating—a Grecian story from Europe, and Indian and Chinese stories from Asia, had been covered so far—and so far they seemed to line up well with the story I had told to Laura and Raymond.

I continued to mentally scan down the page.

About two-thirds of the way down the right column of that first page was a subtitle that read: "Africa." I remembered that part. It was a discussion of a particular story—one that was told in versions that varied somewhat from place to place, but that was mostly the same across much of that continent.

Sitting there by the fire, staring into its hypnotic flames, I recalled having read that section. The story had had to do with an early time when God—or perhaps it was "the One who causes all things to be"—had lived on the earth with the people, or perhaps very, very near to the people, in the air just above them. The details varied, depending on the version told.

I tried to focus my attention on what I could recall of the various versions of this story, and some details gradually came back to me. As they did, the different versions of the story swam together, interweaving in my sleepy mind.

In that early time, there had been no sorrow or hunger, and though the people had very little, they had been content with what God had given them.

In those days, God sometimes lay on top of the earth, and sometimes he floated just above it, like a low-hanging cloud. He was very close to the people—too close, really. The smoke of their cooking fires kept getting in his eyes. People would sometimes bump him with the pestles they used for pounding manioc, or they would use him as a towel on which to wipe their dirty fingers. Also, their quarreling bothered him. And one old woman would cut chunks off of him to add to her soup.

I knew I was mixing the stories together, but I couldn't seem to straighten them out. But still, the pattern was clear—in an early, happy time, before hunger or sorrow, God had been very close to the people, but the people's behavior had annoyed God.

Then what? I tried to remember.

Then someone had gotten greedy and demanded more than what God had given them. This angered God, who went away, then, to his present location, high up in the sky.

Yes, that was one version. It seemed to me that another version had described how people had learned to control their environment. Yes—to control fire, and to hunt effectively. *Their behavior seemed cruel to God, and so that was why he went way up into the sky, out of reach, to get away from people.*

Another story said he had gone and hidden in the forest. *Nobody ever saw him again—so nobody today can really tell what he is like.*

Whichever of the African stories I thought of, I could see the repeating pattern—we had been very near to God, or "the One who causes all things to be," but because of our own actions, we had driven him from us.

I looked at the symbolism embedded in this story and tried to guess what the people who had first told it had meant to record there. What real-life experience did this story seem to represent?

I thought about it a moment. Might it represent an earlier time, a time of happiness and plenty, when we felt close to some essential creative source—and a time, later, when we lost that sense of closeness and instead felt a certain separation or isolation? Might it also suggest that we felt that this new sense of isolation as a result of something we had done, some choice we had made?

It seemed to me that Laura was right—this story, also, seemed related to the one I had told earlier.

I rubbed my face and tried to remember what had come next in Laura's paper. My arm began to itch where a mosquito had bitten it. Apparently, the repellent I'd put on earlier was beginning to wear off.

I recalled there having been something in Laura's paper about a story that was told in various versions through much of South and Central America—a story about a "tree of life."

I remembered what a vivid image I had formed in my mind when I had read descriptions of that tree. As I had pictured it, it was tall and broad, with overarching branches that cast a deep and cooling shade. From it grew all the many and various foods that people needed to survive. According to the story, it was the only such tree in the world, the single source of life-sustaining nourishment.

As the story went, people sought out the tree, and when they found it, they cut it down. In some versions of the story, water poured out from its severed trunk, flooding and changing the world.

In at least one version, the people who cut down the tree of life chopped it up into small pieces, so they could all plant their own gardens from it. According to this version of the story, the destruction of this tree marked the beginning of labor and of agriculture.

Yes, I thought; here was another story that described both an early time in which we were close to a unified source of some kind (in this case, a tree that made abundant food available for the finding)—and a later time, in which we became separated from that source, lost access to the abundance it offered, and thereafter had to labor to meet our needs.

Again, I thought, the story was symbolically consistent with the story I had told.

So the pattern continued—the stories Laura had selected from Europe, Asia, Africa, and South America as part of her research all seemed aligned with the story I had arrived at by a very different method.

I smiled a little. On so many occasions since I had known Laura, our interests had overlapped or interwoven in some way. It was nice when it happened, as it made it so much easier to share the things that were happening in our lives. Even this trip to do research with the Mbuti was like that.

As always, I was glad she was in my life, and I was glad, now, too, that I had helped her proofread her paper, since it seemed to me that having given it such careful attention then was making it easier for me to recall these details about it now.

Again, I tried to visualize the pages, catching bits and pieces that helped remind me of what was there. In my mind's eye, I was on the third page now.

Near the middle of the page, in the left column, I could make out a section subtitled "North America." In it, Laura had written about stories told within traditions ranging from the Hopi of the American Southwest, to the Cheyenne and White River Sioux of the American plains, to the Netsilik Inuit of the Canadian Arctic. These stories, I remembered, described an early time when people had lived very close to the earth and the animals, and had had so much in common with the animals that they could understand and talk to one another. In a couple of these stories, as I remembered, people could become animals, and animals could become people, so close was their connection.

I skimmed down the page and was able to pick out a few lines. "Many people...could talk to a bird, gossip with a butterfly," I read from a passage quoted in the section about the Sioux.

"Both people and animals.... spoke the same tongue," I could see in the part about the Inuit.

As I scanned the page, it seemed to me that Laura had given the most space and attention to the Cheyenne and Hopi stories, both of which she had provided substantial quotations from. In my mind, I could see the shape of that section on the page, with two indentations where the quotations were set in from the margins.

I tried to focus in on the quotation from the Cheyenne story first, and after a few minutes of trying, I could make out most of it. From what I could recall, it went like this:

In the beginning the Great Medicine created the Earth, and the waters upon the earth, and the sun, moon, and stars....

[The Great Medicine] created human beings to live with the other creatures. Every animal, big and small, every bird, big and small, every fish, and every insect could talk to the people and understand them. The people could understand each other, for they had a common language and lived in friendship. They went naked and fed on honey and wild fruits; they were never hungry. They wandered everywhere among the wild animals, and when night came and they were weary, they lay down on the cool grass and slept. During the days they talked with the other animals, for they were all friends.*

It was a beautiful quote, and I could see why Laura had wanted to include it in her text. I wondered where she had found it, and if she had, perhaps, first learned of it when she had been living on the Northern Cheyenne Reservation, years before.

Certainly, it seemed consistent with my ideas about an early time in which we felt a great sense of interconnection and belonging with the rest of life around us—a happy time in which food was found easily as we wandered freely in the world.

I let my mind's eye continue scanning across the page. It settled next on the quote from the Hopi story halfway down the next column. For several minutes I tried to bring back into focus what was written there. I sat quietly, staring into the fire and listening to the night sounds spilling out of the forest, but try as I could, the details of that quote would not come back to me, and after a while, in frustration, I gave up.

---

* The quotation as presented here is the correct version, without any errors that I may have made in recalling it then. See Laura's appendix (Appendix 5, pages A18-A21) for citations for quotations and other material from her article, "From Belonging to Isolation: A Multi-Cultural Analysis." —I. K.

One thing I was pretty sure I did remember right, without drawing on my visual memory at all, was that Laura had made some specific point concerning the Hopi story, something that set it apart from the others.

For a minute or two longer, I sat wondering about this as I stared into the fire's warm glow, then something began to take form in my mind.

That was it. All of the North American stories had talked about an early time when people and animals had been especially close and could talk to one another—and it was clear in all of them that the stories were about an earlier era that had long-since passed. But, as Laura had pointed out, there was no mention in the Cheyenne or Sioux or Inuit stories of how that era had come to an end. Only the Hopi story gave those details.

I rested my face in my hands, rubbing it gently. *Details. Come on Indira, details,* I said to myself. It was late in the day, and I was beginning to feel worn out, but still I thought I could do it. How did the Hopi story say the era ended?

I took a deep breath, then let it out slowly, and as I did, my memory became clear.

A few words came into focus on the page before me: "the First People...were happy.... they felt as one."

Yes, that was it! I thought—then the rest of the story came back to me.

As the Hopi story told it, after the time of happiness and closeness with other people and with the animals, the people lost respect for their Creator and came to believe in the differences that set them apart—differences that separated people from animals, and that separated one group of people from another. Then, believing in the differences between them, they grew suspicious of one another and began to fight.

I thought about this for a moment more, trying to relate it to the story I had told to Laura and Raymond just a little while before. All of the North American stories described a time of ease and closeness with all the natural world, but the Hopi story added to this, explaining that it had ended when people began to believe in their differences—in the things that separated one group from another.

In short, there had been a time of ease and deep interconnection that had ended with a new sense of separation. Was this, perhaps, the sort of separation we would feel as we began to see ourselves as individuals? I wondered. It seemed to me that this story, too, could represent the sort of transition I had been thinking about.

I took a moment to take this in, then skimmed on a little further, to the next page. I had begun to feel quite tired, and was having trouble concentrating, but I decided to press on a bit longer. I knew the end of the article was near. My eyes trailed down through my mental image of the fourth page, until I got to another subheading. That section dealt with a story shared by the three major religions coming out of the Middle East: Judaism, Islam, and Christianity.

It was the story of the Garden of Eden.

The passage about that story wasn't very long. Laura had discussed it only briefly before going on to the final section, subtitled "Conclusions."

At the bottom of that column in the Middle Eastern section, just before
the concluding section began, I could make out the shape and form of
a footnote.

I had the feeling there had been something of particular interest about
that last note, and turned my attention there, to the bottom of the page,
trying to bring the slightly smaller print of the note into focus.

I sat quietly, feeling tired, and tried once more to clear my mind, bringing my concentration to bear as I might once have done in school in the
middle of an exam, trying to recall the details I needed to answer the
questions in front of me.

Gradually, the note came into focus. It read:

> 21 According to one Gnostic Christian interpretation, the Garden of Eden
> story tells how we 'fell' from an awareness of our divine origins into
> ordinary human consciousness.

I sat there staring into the fire, vaguely aware of the sounds of frogs
and insects singing in unison from deep within the forest, scratching
my arm, and wondering just how well this Gnostic interpretation fit with
the story of the Garden of Eden.

It seemed to me it certainly fit well enough with the story I had told to
Laura and Raymond before they'd gone to bed—at least in as much as I
had been talking about the loss of a kind of deep awareness that was then
replaced with a more superficial one. But what about the Garden of Eden
story itself? Did this interpretation really fit there?

The story of the Garden of Eden was not part of my religious heritage,
and I wondered if I could even remember it well enough to consider this
question properly.

I was feeling very weary. I turned my wrist towards the fire and looked
at my watch. How had it gotten late so quickly? I wondered. It was already
after eleven. I would have to go to bed soon, I told myself. I was beginning to feel quite sleepy, but I wanted to finish with my thoughts before
I went to bed.

How did the story begin? I asked myself. I wanted to remember and,
as drifty as my thoughts had begun to be, I let myself follow where
they led.

There had been the garden, and a tree in it, I told myself. *A beautiful tree.*

I pictured the tree shimmering in the moonlight—*its leaves turning like
chimes in the nighttime breeze.*

I imagined Eve sitting in a clearing near the tree. *It was late. Something,
a dream perhaps, had interrupted her sleep.*

It had been like that for her, lately, I thought. *She would wake sometimes,
at night, prodded by a strange and new feeling at the back of her mind—like
something calling to her. A possibility. Some promise. An urging she couldn't
name and didn't yet know how to act on.*

Adam lay beside her, the soft moonlight playing along his naked body.

Eve looked down at him lovingly.

The images swirled around in my mind. Was this even the right story? I knew I was changing it.

In my mind, these were not the first people, only the first ready for the change.

Eve trailed her hand along Adam's shoulder, calling him up from sleep. He rolled over, took her hand, kissed it, then closed his eyes and drifted back to sleep.

Eve sat, waiting, listening to the thing that had been calling to her late at night—or during the daytime, sometimes, when she was quiet. A sweet longing, a kind of music she couldn't quite find the tune for.

She looked around her, saw the tree shimmering in the moonlight, heard the music of its leaves. Was this the music she had been hearing, the music that had been beckoning to her?

She rose and walked the short distance to the tree.

There, in the moonlight, it was more beautiful to her than it had ever been before.

Its fruit seemed bright, almost iridescent in the moonlight. She picked one. She could feel something in it, an unnamed thing. A possibility.

Eve held the fruit in her hand and felt wonder and fear. She knew if she ate this fruit, imbibed of this possibility, swallowed down this nectar, she would be forever changed. Like a drug transforming her, her view and vision of herself would be transformed, and she, and the world around her, would never be the same.

It was tantalizing. It felt wondrous, crazy.

Just then, she was aware of Adam standing beside her, and suddenly she knew that he had been awakened by the same dream, too.

He picked the fruit, too, and together, staring into one another's eyes, they ate of it, the sweet nectar running down their chins.

For the first time then, they knew themselves, and knew that they were naked.

They lay back down, then, and together they wept, out of joy and wonder and sorrow—for now, for the first time, they were alone together, and felt their aloneness. And so they held one another, and waited for the dawn, and all that would follow it.

For them, the world was forever changed. In their sight, now, some things were good, and some were bad, where before it had seemed that all of existence had been woven of a single shining thread. Where before they had eaten what had grown wild on the land, now they would plant and harvest, working day by day to live in a world of their own making.

My attention came back to the low-burning fire, glowing and warm in front of me. What an odd, dream-like story I had made for myself. I was certain it was different from the original, that I had left things out, changed things here and there.

I felt very sleepy and rubbed my face with both hands, then stared blankly for a while at the low flames of the fire and the red embers they drifted along the backs of. The moon was nearly overhead now, and as the fire's light had dimmed, the light of the moon had seemed to strengthen, so that all the world around me seemed to glow in its blue-white light.

I thought about Laura, already sound asleep now for perhaps two hours, and about the next leg of the journey we would embark on tomorrow, and as I thought about these things—the trivial details of living—a thought drifted forward in my mind, one I had called for and not received just a while earlier, but now it was being passed to me, as though dutiful workers had been busy locating it while I had thought about other things.

I had in my mind, crystal-clear, an image of the quotation Laura had used from the Hopi traditional story. I read it off to myself slowly, just as it was written, savoring the words and the fact that I could find the words now, so complete, just as I had wished for:

> So the First People kept multiplying and spreading over the face of the land and were happy.... They felt as one and understood one another without talking. It was the same with the birds and animals. They all suckled at the breast of their Mother Earth, who gave them her milk of grass, seeds, fruit, and corn, and they all felt as one, people and animals.

They all felt as one.
In the past, before they came to know separateness.

Yes, Laura was right; these stories—told around the world about the events of our prehistoric past—seemed not only to agree with one another in essential, symbolic terms, but to agree with where my thoughts and discoveries had led me, as well.

In the ancient past, we had all felt as one—but in time, we had come, instead, to know separateness.

This was what my prehistory research suggested to me. This was what these stories, told as history, had recorded.

I sat quietly before the dimming fire for a few minutes, then shivered in the warm nighttime air as I realized how well all these things lined up.

As the embers burned down, I stretched and snuffed out what remained of the fire with the ash, as Raymond had requested. Then, using only the moonlight to light my path, I headed home to the little hut I shared with Laura, and to the sweetness of sleep on a quiet night.

. 14 .

Kiki's voice fell quiet.

"Pause," Paul said.

"Pausing. End of chapter," Kiki responded.

Paul walked along in silence for several minutes. Ever since he was a kid, Paul had dreamed of living in a well world, vibrant and full of life. Now, as he hiked, he thought about this idea of a sense of oneness, as Dr. Kumar had described it. The more he thought about it, the more the idea resonated with him—as though, perhaps, this was an element of what he had longed for all along: to be part of a web of life that was vibrant and whole—to belong somewhere so deeply that he could never, ever, be torn from it, nor it from him.

Paul remembered the world of the past as his grandfather had described it to him, whole and well and teeming with life of every kind—a world that was alive and could support life—not the half-dead and dying world that Paul had grown up in. Paul had often wished he could live in a world like the one his grandfather described—a world like the one he was traveling through now.

Paul remembered that he had, at one time, imagined himself joining the off-world team, once the transport was ready and a means of return was established. He had hoped to be one of the people sent to explore a new world and its untouched wilderness. To explore it, but not to stay permanently—because he also had a desire to see his world's ecosystem repaired, to whatever extent it might be possible to do so, and that could only truly begin once the population there had been reduced.

Paul remembered how he had once hoped Sheila would join him in traveling to another world, and that they might stay there together, in that new world, for a few years. He remembered talking to Sheila about how he had dreamed of going to a new world and there having the chance to see nature whole and pristine.

He encouraged her to go with him then. He said the plan was to select most people to go by lottery, but others could volunteer. Paul made it clear to Sheila how important this was to him, and for a time Sheila seemed willing to at least consider it—though she disliked the idea of leaving "civilization" behind and facing all of the deprivations and discomforts that would surely follow.

Paul was thrilled with the idea that she might come with him, even if she lacked any real enthusiasm for the possibility. He imagined how they would set out together—two young lovers ready to engage a new world, to face its challenges side by side, and to seek refuge, when need be, in one another's arms—but the plan had fallen through once Sheila learned that she would arrive both naked and bald on a planet she envisioned as "barren," with neither clothes nor jewelry brought along. Then, Sheila's initial lack of enthusiasm resolved quickly into a stubborn determination to have no part of the project. She didn't want to leave her friends, she told Paul, or her things—and could, in any case, hardly imagine what he meant when he talked about experiencing nature "whole" and "untampered with."

Paul coaxed her, saying how empty the world she knew would seem with so many of the people gone.

"But they'll leave their stuff behind, won't they," Sheila responded, "if they'll go through naked and can't bring anything with them?"

A smile spread across her face, as the realization came fully to mind.

"Imagine how much more we could have here, Paul," she added. "Double-size apartments would be easy to find! We could probably get *two*, and knock the wall out between them! Think of the space we would have! And imagine the sorts of jewelry that would be available on the black market. Travel, lodgings—imagine how much less everything would cost! Imagine how we could *live*, Paul, with all those people gone!"

Paul sighed, remembering it, as he continued along the path. It had disappointed him, truly, that this was her response—in part because he so wished for this chance to go, and for her to come with him, but also because it saddened him that she would not make this compromise to help him fulfill a dream he had dreamed, and worked toward, for most of his life.

The fact was, though, that even then, in that first year of their relationship, he had loved her very deeply already, and with a kind of determined devotion. He would never let a difference of this sort come between them. If her home was in the world they shared, then it would remain his home, as well.

Some would think it a great sacrifice, Paul considered, as he walked in the shade of trees along the stream, which tumbled down the long grade beside him, but he had to balance it with all she gave him—all the approval and the encouragement—all the compliments she would pay him when they were alone, and especially when they were with others. Paul had never been with anyone else who made such public displays of approval, nor who accepted him so openly. And of course, there was the feeling he had whenever they were together, as though he had been swimming, his whole life, against a current, trying to reach somewhere—and that the place he had been trying to reach was, somehow, the very thing she held open to him.

As Paul wound his way up the steep path, impressions of the discussions he and Sheila had had about off-world travel swept through his mind. As he remembered, she had taken more interest in his work after they had talked about the people leaving and the goods that would be left behind. After that, she was always asking when the project would be completed—but remained determined not to join him on it.

Paul rounded a turn and spotted a campsite up ahead, in the shade of the cottonwood and sycamore trees that grew near the stream. As he neared the camp, he could see that it was vacant. Good, he told himself. He had passed several campsites already that day, and had begun to worry that he would pass too many, and would be stuck between them, again, when the sun went down.

Paul made short work of setting up his sleep bivy and getting a small fire going (though he had no use for one, other than the "company" it offered). Before long, he had heated a travel meal for his dinner. He sat eating it and staring into the dancing flames, as the dim of evening flowed in around him.

It seemed to Paul that at every break he had taken that day, an uncomfortable mood had gathered around him. Each time, he had pushed it away, and each time it had returned.

Now, as the mood settled around him once again, he decided not to push it away this time. Instead, he let it gather. It rose up now, within him, as though drawn from the deepening shadows of dusk.

It was the dream of his mother, Paul realized, that was haunting him still. It lingered with him, like an unpleasant aftertaste. Why that dream? Why now? Why had he dreamed of her as he had—angry and avoiding him?

Paul had been sitting with his knees pulled up to his chest. Now he rested his forehead against them as he tried to sort out the feelings he was having. Fragments of memories related to his mother's death rose within him. His father had been away, Paul recalled, doing work for Corprogov, when all of them had become sick—his mother first, then he and his brother.

As Paul thought about it, a feeling of great sadness enveloped him. Sadness—but something more than sadness. *Wrongness.* Yes—his mother's death had always seemed so *terribly wrong* to him.

Paul rubbed his face with his hands and looked into the fire again. How many other children had felt that way, Paul wondered, when the *Muerte Azul* epidemic had taken one of their parents? How self indulgent it made Paul feel now, to conceive of his own mother's death as being so especially tragic, so especially wrong, when so many others had been lost, as well.

Nonetheless, Paul reflected, why had the feeling lingered so? Why did he still feel so unremittingly terrible, whenever he remembered it?

Paul thought again about the circumstances surrounding her death. His father had been away, doing food-distribution work for Corprogov, but because of the quarantine, had not been able to get back when the outbreak had occurred, even though he had been inoculated—and so Paul's mother, and brother, and he had had to fend for themselves, even as the illness had swept through the household.

Paul remembered sleeping and waking, delirious with fever. He remembered his father showing up and nursing him and his brother until they were back on their feet. But not Paul's mother. She had passed away while Paul's father was still out of town.

Paul remembered standing by her bedside and touching her hand while it was still warm. Though he couldn't quite picture her face, he somehow could remember that it had been a pale blue—the "blue death" that the name described. *Muerte Azul.* Because in the end people's lungs filled with fluid, and they suffocated to death. Without oxygen in their blood, their blood—and their skin—were tinted blue.

Even then, as he stood above his mother's bed, his own fever had been gathering, Paul remembered. What a dark time that was! Paul told himself, as he pushed himself away from the subject.

It so pained Paul to remember that day that he had rarely ever let his thoughts probe this far. Now, he rubbed the thick stubble on his scalp and looked around the campsite. Enough of wasting time with such self-indulgent thinking, he told himself. If he wanted to blend in at the Retreat—to seem as though he were actually of this world—and if he wanted to understand, too, what had shaped this world to be so different from his own, then he had a book to listen to, and that's what he should be doing now.

Paul lay down on his sleep bivy and looked up, through the spreading branches of a cottonwood tree, at the brilliant stars above. From far off in the distance, he heard the sound of coyotes calling. He listened closely. It was a sound he had only ever heard before on recordings.

Something in the undulating calls of the coyotes reminded Paul of his own heartache. He was tempted to lie there, listening—but knew he must not. Here he was, lost on a strange world, with few resources—this was no time to become self indulgent.

"Kiki, resume recitation, please," he said softly.

Soon Kiki's voice filled the air around him, overshadowing the sorrowful voices rising out of the darkness, and the sorrow rising up in Paul, as well.

CHAPTER XII

For formerly the tribes of men on earth lived remote from ills,
without harsh toil and the grievous sicknesses that are deadly
to men. But [Pandora] unstopped the jar and let it all out, and
brought grim cares upon mankind.

—HESIOD

The next morning I woke to soft light and the quiet rustling of cloth.

I rolled over and found Laura standing beside the cot next to mine, folding, then rolling, a pair of shorts, which she then pushed into the lower compartment of her backpack.

"Morning," I said, my voice thick with sleep.

"Morning, love," Laura answered, smiling. Her voice was soft and cheerful. She had already dressed for the day.

"Have I overslept?" I asked.

"Not at all. I didn't want to wake you too early."

I stretched, still foggy with the last wisps of sleep. "What's happening with our trip?"

"Mvula has agreed to take us into Basankusu," Laura answered. "He's gone to his village to see what people want from the market there. He'll be back probably in an hour or so.

"There's *fufu* leftover from breakfast, if you like," she added. "I would have woken you when it was ready, but like I said, I didn't want to wake you too early.

"It's still warm. All nice and gooey," she added, smiling. "I've already eaten." She folded and rolled a T-shirt, then set it with a neatly stacked pile of rolled shirts on the cot. "It won't take long to get us packed up.

"Oh, and if you're quick about breakfast, and there's time," she went on, her voice still soft, "there's a *Dialium* tree not far from here. We passed it yesterday on our way back. Raymond said he would show it to you, if you'd like. I said you probably would. He said it's not likely there'll be any

493

bonobos feeding there now, but at least you could get a chance to see one of the sorts of trees they feed in—and in fruit, even!"

I stared at Laura, as she pushed the set of rolled shirts into the lower compartment of her pack, then set a bag of travel snacks—trail mix, pemmican bars—in on top of them.

"Wasn't it packed well enough?" I asked.

"Things had gotten shifted around. I thought it would be nice to know where they were," Laura answered.

I nodded. "Why don't you come with us?"

Laura looked at me blankly for a moment. "Oh," she shook her head, "I saw the tree yesterday. In fact, I spent a good deal of time under one like it yesterday morning." She pushed a plastic bag with her toothbrush and other items in it into a side pocket of her pack.

"Besides, I don't really feel like a walk. I thought I might lie down for a bit after I get this done."

"You don't feel well?" I asked.

Laura shrugged, then stopped what she was doing and looked at me. "Not great. My stomach's a bit churny," she said.

"I'm okay, though," she added, as she reached into the top of her pack and moved her sunglasses and sun screen to the side pocket opposite the one with her toothbrush.

"Do you think you have a fever? You felt a little warm last night," I asked.

"I don't know. The sun's barely up and already it's hot. It's like living in a sauna. I feel warm, but it could just be the weather."

I sat up and reached across her cot to feel her face.

"Well?" she said.

"You're warm," I said.

"Hum," she said, nodding like I'd said something obviously inconclusive.

"I don't know how quickly Mvula will be back. I'd like you to have a chance to see that tree," Laura said.

"Is it really that interesting?" I asked, as I got up and started to dress.

"I don't know. We came all this way, Indira. When else will you have such a chance?" Laura asked.

I looked over at her and smiled. That was Laura. We'd come all this way for her to have the sort of adventure she'd dreamed of all her life, and now she wanted to share it with me.

"Okay," I said, "I'll go grab some breakfast first. Where will I find Raymond?"

"He's around. If he's not still at the kitchen hut, check his hut. He's expecting you," she said.

I finished dressing, slipped on my boots, and opened the door to go. "I'll find him. But you rest," I told her. "That stuff doesn't have to be that well organized."

As I left the hut, I glanced back at Laura and noticed how pale and tired she looked.

The door swung shut as I turned to walk away. It was just the travel wearing her down, I told myself. Still, I couldn't shake an uneasy feeling.

I found Raymond at the table outside the kitchen hut, going over some papers, which I took to be the records of bonobo sightings and movements that Mvula had kept while Raymond was away. Raymond looked up just long enough to say "good morning," then returned to his work. He appeared to be concentrating, like he had something on his mind, and I didn't bother him with more talk.

We sat together in silence while I ate my breakfast—which was fine with me, as I never felt like chatting much first thing in the morning. When I finished, though, and got up to clear my bowl, Raymond looked up and said, if I was interested, he would be glad to show me a *Dialium* tree in fruit. I agreed, left my bowl with others to be washed, and we were soon on our way into the forest.

I again had that sensation of leaving the openness of the little clearing and entering the depths of a dense, breathing, living forest. Together we strode beneath towering trees and stepped over enormous buttress roots, which snaked here and there along the forest floor. Above us, monkeys of one sort or another called down from the treetops.

As I followed Raymond through the forest, every once in a while he would glance back at me—at first I thought just to make sure I was following—but after a time I began to feel there was something furtive about these glances. A time or two we made eye contact, then Raymond looked quickly away. His manner seemed strange, and again I remembered how oddly he had behaved at various times since we'd first met—all the peculiar, brooding looks he had given to Laura and me, first on the barge, and again after we had arrived at his camp. His expression on those occasions had seemed to me to be full of ache and longing—blending a note of tenderness with something dark and troubled beneath. I thought of the word Laura had used to describe him the night before. It was "odd"—an odd contrast to the face he showed us most of the time.

Now, walking through the forest with Raymond, I wondered which face he was preparing to show me now. I was alone with him, trusting him to lead me deeper into the isolation of the forest—and as good company as he was most of the time, I had to wonder what, exactly, lay ahead.

Soon, Raymond stood with his hands on his hips, looking up into the branches of a towering *Dialium* tree.

"As I expected," he said, "there are no bonobos here. I think they'll stick with the *ntende* tree as long as it's in fruit."

Raymond glanced back at me, then up at the tree. Now that we had arrived, he seemed his usual self, sharing information and talking about things of interest. It was as though a curtain had been pulled back briefly on the walk here, revealing something dark or troubled deep within him, and then allowed to fall shut again.

"The bonobos climb way up to get to the fruit, which is out on the smaller branches near the crown," he said, pointing upward. "They seem to have a natural sense of just how much bending a branch can take without breaking. They'll go way up where the branches are thin, holding at least two different branches with their hands and feet and shifting their weight as they need to to keep any from breaking. They'll gather up the fruit there, and then bring it to a more comfortable spot to eat it."

"What does the fruit taste like?" I asked.

"It's hard to tell you. They're sweeter than the *ntende* fruit. I'd say they're really quite delicious." Raymond looked around at the ground. "You can see there's a good bit of fallen fruit here," he said, picking up one tiny, rounded specimen. "But I wouldn't recommend eating these old ones—though the bonobos may eventually pick through them, once the season's past and that's all that's left. They'll even eat them when the outside gets moldy. You see, you just peel back the skin," he said, demonstrating, "which you wouldn't want to eat anyway, and there's the fruit inside."

Raymond dropped the small, dark fruit, then looked back up into the high branches of the *Dialium* tree.

I followed his gaze up toward the upper branches, then turned and looked around at the surrounding forest. It looked much like the part of the forest I had been in the day before, except for the prominent red marker ribbon tied around the base of the *Dialium* tree. I wondered if I might have passed right under another such tree the day before, without even noticing all the fruit it carried.

I looked back up into the leafy crown with its specks of light and shade, and I thought about being alone here with Raymond, and about the day ahead. I wasn't sure when Mvula would return and be ready to set off for Basankusu, but it seemed to me there was no use staying here any longer and possibly delaying our start. I had seen what I had come to see—and in any case, in truth, I would feel more comfortable once we were back at camp.

I was just about to suggest to Raymond that maybe it was time to head back, when I looked over at him and realized he was staring at me. How long he'd been staring, I didn't know. He looked uncomfortable when I caught his gaze. He turned his sight to the *Dialium* tree, then the ground, then back to me again.

A moment passed, then he took a step towards me and said, "Indira, there's something I've been wanting to say to you, and to Laura, almost since I first met you on the barge." His face had, again, that hurt, bruised look, marked by some tenderness, or longing, as though he was filled with unspeakable emotion, just as I had caught him appearing when he had looked at Laura or me on the barge, and later still after we'd arrived at his research camp.

I felt my body tense as Raymond went on, talking awkwardly, as though he were expressing something he himself might rather conceal.

"There's something about you both, something I really needed..." His speech faltered. "No, let me begin again. I should have thought about this more carefully. I'm sorry." Raymond glanced up into the branches above and took a deep breath.

"You may have wondered," he began again, "why I was in Australia. It wasn't for a holiday. It was for a funeral."

He paused again, and it seemed that all the color had left his face. "It was for my sister, Ida. My younger sister. She died suddenly in an auto wreck three weeks ago."

"Oh, I'm so sorry," I said, and suddenly my sense of ill-ease with him passed, and he seemed again, to me, to be the pleasant, personable man who had been such good company for both Laura and me since our journey started.

Raymond nodded. "Thank you," he said softly, then sat down heavily on a nearby log, and for a moment cradled his head in his hands.

"I haven't at all gotten used to it," he said. He paused again, taking in a deep breath. "What I wanted to tell you was, well..."

He steadied himself, looking directly at me. "What I'm trying to tell you is that the accident was her fault. She'd been drinking. She'd been drinking a lot in recent years." He looked at me, watching me listening, then went on. "She died instantly. But the driver of the other car did not. He was in a coma until a few days before I left to come back here. The doctors decided it was hopeless, then, and took him off the respirator. He didn't make it. He was a father of three. Kids, all of them, still." Raymond shook his head. "His oldest is twelve."

Raymond stood up, and then, standing, didn't seem to know what to do with himself, and sat heavily back down.

"I'm so sorry," I said, again.

Raymond nodded, his face solemn and appreciative. "She wasn't always like that—a drinker," Raymond continued, his voice thickening. "She was so bright and full of life, even just a few years ago—so interested in everything. So alive. The world was hers, I always thought."

He was in such pain telling me this. Surely, this must be the bruise I had so often seen in his eyes?

"She got married right out of college," he went on. "They had a little girl. 'Aria' was her name. Beautiful child. Almost angelic. My sister Ida had been a journalism student. She'd planned to be a reporter and travel the world, but when Aria was born, she put it off. She had really exacting standards for herself, all her life she did, and she figured if she was going to be a mother she wanted to do it 'right,' you know—like she wanted to do everything—so she planned to stay close to home for a while, while Aria was little.

"Anyway, Ida and her husband, Sam, had just moved to a new house in Sydney, where Sam had gotten a job. This was," Raymond took a breath and sighed slowly, closing his eyes for a moment, "um, four, four and a half years ago. Aria was just, ah, well, about two and a half then.

"I'm sorry if I'm making this story long, but I want to tell you—and I hope you'll understand. I've been wanting to tell you and Laura about this for a while, but I haven't been able to bring myself to do it. I've thought of it often enough, but it's just been too hard."

Raymond again took a deep breath, let it out slowly, then continued. "My sister had been eating lunch on the back porch right after they moved in. Sam was at work. Aria had already eaten her lunch and was playing with these, uhm, with these sort of blocks that connect up, out on the lawn where Ida could watch her. Beautiful day, Ida told me later. Perfect weather, she said."

Raymond stared past me into the forest, then returned his gaze to me. "I'm sorry." He shook his head. "It's just that..." He looked down at his hands.

"It's all right," I said softly.

Raymond nodded. "They hadn't even unpacked yet," he said, "not even the answering machine. Sam was expecting an important call, so when the phone rang, Ida dashed inside to get it."

Raymond looked around at the forest, as though what came next was too painful to say. I wondered why he must tell it. What was it he had felt so strongly that he wanted to tell us, as to be worth putting himself through this?

"It was a beautiful yard. Like a little garden, really," he said. "With a koi pond. When Ida came back outside, that's where Aria was. Floating in the water. Face down. Ida had only been inside for a few minutes. She'd just taken the call, rummaged around a bit for some paper to write the message on, then come back outside.

"She could never forgive herself. We did all we could to convince her that her mistake was small, even if the consequence was very large, but nobody could get through to her.

"That's when she started drinking. Her marriage fell apart after that, too. God, what a downward spiral! Since I got word of Ida's death, that was all I'd been able to think about. First Aria gone, then those years of drinking, then Ida gone, too—and she'd taken someone else with her.

"It's all so terrible," Raymond said, shaking his head. "She was my kid sister. I wasn't that much older, really—but she was always my kid sister." Raymond stared blankly, then turned his attention back to the story.

"But all I could think about since the funeral," he went on, "was how terribly everything had gone, how really terrible everything was. One tragedy after another. Until I met the two of you on the barge," Raymond said, looking up at me. He bit his lower lip for a moment, then added, "You're both so smart, so interested in the world, so ready for adventure. Like Ida was, before things went so wrong for her, and for everyone around her.

"You gave me that back," Raymond said, his eyes deep and soft. "You and Laura brought back to me *who she was* before all the terrible things started happening—before she lost Aria, and then lost her way. Such life in her, such possibility! It's still terribly sad—and I'm sure it always will be—but at least I have that much now. You've brought who she was back to me. I could never thank you enough, really. But I'll have that now. I'll keep that now, and I thank you."

Raymond stood up, then, with an air of having had his say.

"Do tell Laura for me, won't you? As you can see, I'm not very comfortable talking about it just yet. It would be kind if you would tell her for me."

"I'll be glad to do that, Raymond," I told him, then stepped forward and, spreading my arms, offered him a hug.

Raymond's face again clouded with emotion, but this time I understood why. He stepped forward and accepted my embrace, choking back a sob or two before straightening and stepping away.

I remembered again, then, that Laura and I had heard a man sobbing on the barge one of our first nights on board, and how I had realized later that the sound had come from Raymond's cabin.

How had I missed the possibility, I asked myself, that there had been some tragedy? Why had I not understood his intense gazes as suggesting something like that?

Raymond looked aside, wiping away tears with the back of one hand.

"We should really go," he said, his voice soft and ragged. "Mvula will be back soon. You'll want to get an early start if you and Laura hope to make it to Basankusu before nightfall."

Kiki paused, and when she spoke again, it was with her own voice.

"Returning to summary mode," she said.

"Together, Indira and Raymond..."

"Wait," Paul cut in. To him, the transition seemed jarring, intrusive—and all the more so since he was lying at his campsite in the dark, and the story he had been listening to had filled his awareness, vivid and real. Paul considered telling Kiki to continue with recitation, then reminded himself of the importance of finishing the book, if possible, before he reached the Kumaric Retreat.

"Okay," he told her, "but like I said before, include the descriptive passages, too, all right?"

"Understood," Kiki said. "Returning to summary mode using previously set parameters."

"Oh," Paul said. "Okay, right. Begin."

"Together, Indira and Raymond returned to camp," Kiki went on. "Mvula had returned shortly before they got back, and together he and Laura had made sure the jeep was loaded with all the gear Indira and Laura had brought with them, as well as a satchel Mvula was bringing along.

"To Indira, their parting from Raymond seemed rushed, after the intimacy of their exchange in the forest only a short while before. Indira and Raymond hugged goodbye, which brought a look of surprise to Laura's face. Laura, though, 'got in the spirit of things' then, and gave Raymond a hug goodbye, as well, before she, Indira, and Mvula climbed in the jeep and set off down the red clay road, waving goodbye to Raymond. Indira 'felt sad to see Raymond's lone form disappearing amidst the trees,' as they rounded a turn on the way out of camp. She felt dismayed thinking back to their exchange in the forest. All that time, she and Laura had regarded Raymond with distrust, while he had been 'nothing but good' to them. If only, she thought, 'we had understood more about him earlier on, we could have treated him with the kindness he needed and deserved.'

"As Indira watched the road 'unrolling behind the jeep,' she thought how sad Raymond must feel, being left alone in camp at a time when 'so much had already been taken from him.'

"Returning to recitation mode," Kiki said. When she began again her voice settled into the tones and rhythms she had synthesized for Dr. Kumar.

As we bumped along, I turned and focused on what lay ahead. The road itself was a simple dirt track through the forest. Though it was badly rutted in places, Mvula handled the road well, straddling the deepest ruts by running the tires on one side of the jeep along one edge of the road, while placing the other two tires on the ridge between the ruts. In other areas, though, the road was smooth enough for normal driving, and one way or another, Mvula managed to make good time.

The forest rose up quickly on either side of the narrow roadway. Tree limbs arched and intertwined above us, letting in a dappled light, which littered the dirt track ahead like so many radiant leaves. Even the stickiness of the steamy tropical air and the roar of the jeep's motor didn't dim for me the fairy-tale quality of passing through so deep a forest, so beautifully lit.

As we rode along, my thoughts kept returning to Raymond, and what he had told me about his sister. I looked at Laura, sitting in the passenger seat ahead of me, and wanted to share his story with her, as I had promised to do, but this didn't seem like the place to have that conversation—in an open air jeep, roaring and bouncing along. I didn't want to shout about it. Besides, I wasn't really sure how much English Mvula understood, and the subject was a private one. I would wait until Laura and I could be alone together, someplace quiet, I decided.

Still, my thoughts kept returning to Raymond's story. How sad about the death of his niece! How sad, too, that his sister had judged herself so harshly that that death had led to years of drinking and, ultimately, her own death and the death of the other driver.

If only someone could have gotten through to her, I thought. If only, as Raymond had suggested, someone could have helped her see that while the consequences of the actions on the day her daughter died were truly dire, that didn't mean there was something essentially wrong with *her*.

Maybe she might even have come to this realization on her own, I thought, if she hadn't been keeping herself so numb with alcohol—unable to communicate, then, even with herself.

I imagined how it must have been for her, after Aria's death. I imagined her in so much pain that she, like a burn victim, could not bear even the slightest "touch," not even the whisper of soft winds coming up against the part of her which bore that injury.

I imagined how she had covered that injury, cloaked it, suffocated it with alcohol, so that her perspective on those events—*that it was her failing that had caused the death of her child*—became isolated, insulated within her, separated from her other thoughts. She couldn't, as I imagined it, learn or grow or think her way out of it, because she held it so still, so perfectly still, where nothing could touch it.

And so she couldn't learn how to release the piece of hate she had turned against herself.

I stared ahead, as we rumbled down the road. The breeze the jeep's motion created was welcome on so warm a day.

There was something familiar about these thoughts I was having, it seemed to me, but what was it? Why did I feel like I had thought them, or something much like them, before?

Several moments slipped past during which I thought about nothing in particular, trying to let that sense of familiarity take clear form in my mind. It was like I was thirsty, and I was trying to let my thoughts gather, like rainwater, to quench that thirst.

Soon, I found myself thinking about another trip I'd taken by car, along a very different road, a decade earlier, from Montana down through Wyoming and into Colorado, the year Laura was working in Lame Deer.

Why that trip? Why think about it now? I asked myself.

And then the circle closed.

Insular perspective, I thought, then, remembering some of what I'd thought about on that trip.

Oh right, I thought. Raymond's sister had used alcohol to help *insulate* herself from the world—from the thoughts she had with which she accused and attacked herself, and from her feelings of loss.

The accident at the koi pond hadn't just taken her daughter's life— surely, it had taken something from Ida as well. She must have lost faith in herself, have come to see herself as capable of a monumental, irreversible, horrible mistake—of an unforgivable error.

Yes, I thought—she had come to believe in an essential and irreversible failing in herself.

She had come to *believe in the badness of her own nature.*

The idea resonated as I realized that that, too, was part of the ideas I'd thought about on that trip down from Lame Deer to Denver, years before.

My thoughts returned to Raymond's sister. And so the pain of loss had been overlayered with the pain of self-loathing, I thought. She felt two unbearable pains, laid one on top of the other, and so she had walled herself off from both of them, *insulated* herself from her own thoughts and feelings.

Others had tried to reach her, I remembered Raymond saying—family members, friends perhaps, too—but she wouldn't let them in.

And so she had *failed to communicate with herself—and with others.* (Another thought from that trip!)

And so Ida had drunk, and driven—and through those actions the pain she had felt had been expressed out into the world. It had radiated into the world, and engulfed others, as well.

I sat still for a moment, amazed at the pattern becoming clear in my mind. I remembered writing in my journal about these very same three ideas on that snowy night in Denver, all those years before. If my memory was right, I had written about exactly those three things: *insular perspective, belief in a bad nature, and a failure to communicate with oneself or others.*

I had had a name for them then, hadn't I? I asked myself—a name for those three things?

I thought about it, and then it came to me: Yes—they were *the three impediments.*

The three impediments to us revealing the true goodness of our natures.

I remembered how I had thought about it then: from those three impediments arose so much of the trouble in the world.

If we could somehow shed those impediments, I remembered concluding, then the true beauty of human nature would shine through.

We drove on through the morning. At times I would try to lean forward and talk to Laura or Mvula, but the road was too uneven for that to be a comfortable position in which to ride. At other times I would talk, nearly shouting, with me nestled in the back seat, and Laura turned part way in the front to answer, but the truth was it took too much effort to make ourselves heard, and so conversation only took place in fits and starts.

After a few hours we stopped for lunch. As it turned out, neither Laura nor I had planned for meals on this leg of our trip any more than to think we might make a lunch out of our travel snacks, or possibly cook up some of the freeze-dried dinners we'd brought with us from Boulder, but Mvula quickly got a little fire going and fixed us up a simple meal of *fufu* and manioc greens, cooked together with dried fish—all with the now familiar *pili pili* hot sauce.

As simple as the meal was, it was delicious. The three of us sat, making conversation over lunch, and I soon came to realize how well Mvula understood French. He had spoken relatively little of it when we had supped together two nights before, but I realized over lunch that he was trying to use only English or Lingala to converse with us, as they were the only languages all three of us shared. However, when Laura spoke to him in French, he understood her perfectly and answered her in French with no trouble at all.

It was pleasant sitting there together in the shade of the forest, visiting quietly in whatever language, but we all knew that the trip would grow no shorter so long as we lingered there, and so we soon finished up, did what little cleanup could be conveniently managed, and were on our way again.

As we set off down the road, I thought about Laura, and how little she had eaten at lunch. Though she had said she wasn't sick, it seemed to me that something was amiss. It would have concerned me no matter where we had been, to see her that way, but it troubled me especially to see her less than well in a tropical rainforest, in which so many different sorts of illnesses dwelled.

I told myself not to worry, though. Even if she were sick, worrying wouldn't make it better.

Perhaps in order to distract myself from worrying, as much as anything, I turned my mind again to the ideas I'd been having about "the

Change"—as I had begun to think of the transition that had taken place when people had begun to focus on their individual selfhoods.

So much had developed in my thinking since we'd left the barge, I hardly knew what to do with all the new material. It troubled me that what I had been thinking was so theoretical. I felt much more at home with material that could be proven or disproven, outright. And yet, the bits and pieces I had to work with just seemed so intriguing.

I stared into the forest rolling by in flashes of dark and light, letting my thoughts drift for several minutes. Up in the trees above the road ahead, I could catch glimpses of monkeys fleeing from the sound of the approaching engine. Since leaving the research site, we had now and then passed small villages along the sides of the road—clusters of huts, built right on the ground like the huts at the research site, but of simpler construction, with walls built of mats rather than clay.

We passed another of these villages. In a small clearing between the huts and the road were three women, together, pounding manioc root. Small children played nearby. The women looked up and waved as we drove past, as did some of the children. I remember noticing the strands of sunlight revealed by the drifting smoke from a cooking fire.

I smiled and waved back at them, surprised in that moment with the simple sense of human connection I felt from even such momentary contact with strangers.

Connection. That was something we would have felt less of after the Change, I told myself—as we shifted from an undifferentiated sense of belonging to a focus on our own individual identities.

I considered this as we continued on down the red-dirt road. Yes—we would have become isolated in our individual viewpoints, insular in our perspectives, and so lost that deep sense of belonging.

Insular in our perspectives. The phrase echoed in my mind.

Yes, that made sense, I told myself. As we became more focused on our own individual perspectives, our perspectives would have become more insular, insulated—more separated from everything else.

I could feel my heart beating hard at the thought. *Insular perspective.* That was one of the three impediments!

What was another one? I asked myself.

Failure to communicate with oneself or others.

Could that possibly have been an outgrowth of the Change, too?

I thought about it for a few minutes as we bumped and jostled down the road. Perhaps so, I concluded. After all, as I now saw it, we had become separated from the deepest layers of our own self-awareness in order to focus on the most individual aspects of ourselves. Wasn't it likely that that would have affected communication?

I thought of the image I had come up with years earlier, which I had thought of as symbolizing the essential structure of human consciousness. It was based on the shape of a chinar seedpod—a sphere with many little peaks rising off of it.

This symbolic sphere or globe, as I had imagined it, was filled with water—a vast ocean—and each of our individual consciousnesses were rooted in that "inner ocean," in which dwelled a kind of "collective unconscious"—while the most individual aspects of our selves were represented by the little peaks, each separate and distinct.

Was that how it was, really? After the Change, had we each become so focused on our own individual peak that we had lost touch with that place of collective awareness within us—that "inner ocean?"

I thought about the traditional stories I'd remembered the night before. It seemed to me that a story about people having climbed up out of an ocean of abundant life and collective belonging and onto little, isolating peaks might have fit well amongst them. Yes—it was that same theme, again: *from belonging to isolation.*

I imagined the people before the Change, then—imagined how we might have been before we became so focused on our own individuality. I wondered in what ways we had been able to share ourselves, then, and what sort of communication had been possible between us.

An image of two lovers in an intimate embrace came to mind, and I found myself considering how different it feels to be with someone who is ready to share the deepest parts of themselves, than to be with someone who is not. So much more is communicated, even when no words are spoken.

Was that how it would have been, in the early days, before the Change? I wondered. Would people, in living their daily lives, have felt that sort of deep, emotive communication within themselves, and between themselves and others?

And if that was how it was before the Change, how would it have been after people became so focused on their individual selfhoods? When we turned away from that "inner ocean" within ourselves, wouldn't that sense of mutual connection have been pushed aside, as well? Wouldn't that easy, emotive connection and communication—that simple empathy—have largely disappeared?

I imagined the people after the Change relating like two lovers who had become estranged from one another. Though their touch might have been as intimate, it would never feel as deep.

Was that really how it had been? I wondered. And if so, wouldn't that reduction in communication, that "failure" in communication, have brought new problems into the world?

I looked out at the world jostling by as we bumped our way down that uneven, rutted road. So that was two impediments, I thought. What about the third impediment—*a belief in a bad nature?* Might it also be, in some way or another, a by-product of the Change?

I remembered, on the barge, writing about how the development of agriculture had meant that we had to start to plan for the future, had to start to distinguish between "desirable" and "undesirable" outcomes, and so, in turn, had to begin to think about certain results as "good" or "bad." It seemed to me that even the possibility of conceiving of a "bad nature" had its genesis in the Change I'd been contemplating.

The three impediments, I thought, with a strange feeling of dread. Had we created them, or at least made them palpably worse, by choosing this path in which we had become so focused on our individual identities?

Had we, in doing this, opened a door through which all kinds of troubles had been ushered into the world?

I felt suddenly very tired thinking about it. Though it was still early in the day, the air was hot and muggy. The road rolled by in a mesmerizing pattern of shadow and light. Even in the open-air jeep, I felt surrounded by the constant drone of the engine.

I turned to the rear of the jeep and pulled my daypack from the open cargo area. I set it on the seat beside me, then leaned against it, using it like a pillow, and closed my eyes.

Soon I was aware of nothing more than the rumble and hum of the jeep along the road, and the flickering of light behind the red glow of my eyelids.

I'm not sure how much later it was, but I remember hearing Laura say something to Mvula in French, almost shouting at him above the roar of the engine, and then feeling the jeep pull abruptly over to the side of the road. I sat up in time to see Laura jump out of the jeep, carrying the daypack which she had stowed at her feet, and run off into the woods.

Laura came back several minutes later, looking paler than usual, and worried.

"What's wrong?" I asked.

"Would you get my canteen? It's there beside my seat," she said, then added, "I'd like to wash up."

I found the soap in her pack where she said to look for it, and helped her with the water and soap as she needed them.

"It's diarrhea," she said.

"Is it bad?" I asked.

"Like a faucet," she said. "I'm nauseous, too. Thought I would throw up, but didn't."

I touched her forehead. "No doubt now," I said.

"Fever?"

"Yeah."

"I felt that," she said, glancing around for something to dry her hands on, then drying them on the sides of her pants. "It'll pass," she said. "Probably something I ate."

She looked concerned. Her words seemed aimed to reassure me.

"You should drink plenty of water," I told her, handing her back her canteen.

Laura took it from me and drank, pausing a time or two to catch her breath, or perhaps to calm her nausea. Then she screwed the lid back on and put the canteen by her seat.

"You good to travel?" I asked her, feeling concerned.

"I'll manage," Laura said.

We drove on then, with Laura again in the passenger seat up front, and me in the rear, watching her and hoping she would not turn out to be very ill.

It wasn't more than twenty minutes before Laura again called for Mvula to pull over and, leaping from the jeep, disappeared into the forest. When

Laura returned, she reported that her diarrhea was "like water," and that she had thrown up this time. Already, she had begun to look worn. Whether it was from something she'd eaten or not, Laura was clearly quite ill.

I refilled her canteen from one of the five-gallon containers we'd brought with us on the barge.

"Please drink as much as you can," I said, as I handed her the bottle. "I don't want you getting dehydrated." Laura took the canteen from my hand and drank from it. The air was stiflingly hot in the half shade by the road.

"I'm afraid next time, Indira, I won't make it in time," she said. She handed the canteen back to me, then slipped into the front seat of the jeep.

Laura gestured wearily up the road with one hand while mumbling something to Mvula in French. Mvula started up the engine, and we all continued up the road to Basankusu.

Where before I had tried to deal with my concern about Laura by thinking about other things, now I turned my attention to the question of her illness, and what could be done about it.

Something she had said echoed in my mind: "Like water."

My thoughts returned to the time when the barge had stopped and several pirogues full of people had rowed ashore.

It had been cholera, I'd found out later. A child had died of cholera, and people had rowed ashore for the burial.

Cholera. I didn't know a lot about it, but I remembered reading somewhere that its main symptom was watery diarrhea.

We stopped three or four times in the next hour. I remember riding behind Laura between stops, noticing the way she sat, twisted in her seat with her head resting on the seatback, like a wilted flower. I wanted so much to do something for her, but had no idea what to do.

The next time we stopped the road was in deep shade. Mvula pulled over quickly, near a giant tree whose raised buttress roots extended beyond its trunk for several meters.

When Laura disappeared behind it, I did my best to ask Mvula how far it was still to Basankusu, and understood from his answer that we still had two or three hours of travel ahead of us. With Laura looking sicker and sicker with each stop, I wondered if we could make it there.

Just then Laura emerged from the forest. As I watched her walk towards me, I could see an unsteadiness in her gait which was unlike her. Her face looked pale and drawn. I helped her wash up, but instead of standing up straight after she was done, she remained bent over, her arms resting on the side of the jeep, and her head on her arms.

"I can't keep this up, Indira," she said. Her voice was soft, a little hoarse. "I really feel awful. I want to find someplace and lie down. I'm not going to make it to the forest next time. I'm afraid I'm going to make an awful mess." She kept her head down, her eyes closed.

"We need to get more water into you. That should help," I told her. I refilled her canteen again with the water we'd been traveling with since Kinshasa and handed it to her to drink. She swallowed down half the bottle, then handed it back to me.

"I don't know what good it does," she said, resting her head on her arms again. "I drink it and drink it, and it just runs right through me. Water in, water out. After all I've drunk, I'm still dying of thirst."

I looked at her and nodded. I hated to hear her choose those words. I knew that if it was cholera, there was a risk she could die of dehydration, no matter how much water she drank. Her body could lose it faster than it could be absorbed.

Laura just kept staring at the ground between her feet.

"I wish we had some sort of medicine to give you," I said, feeling helpless to properly care for her.

"We have some... oh, I don't remember what it's called," Laura said, then added, "It's supposed to sort of put your intestines to sleep. Stops you up."

"Want me to get it? Where is it?"

Laura shook her head. "I don't want to take it. People's bodies get diarrhea to get rid of the infection, clear it out. I need to throw it off."

"Laura, if it'll make it possible for you to get to Basankusu...?" I paused, then added, "You said you couldn't keep this up."

For several moments, Laura didn't move a muscle. She just stood there bent over with her head resting on her arms.

"Okay," she said finally.

"Okay," I said. "Where is it? With the first aid kit?"

"Yeah, I guess," she said, still not moving.

"Where's that?"

Laura told me where to look. I dug it out, then pressed a single white pill into the palm of her hand.

Laura stood up then, and looked down at the little pill, then extended her other hand towards me.

"I'll take it," she said. "Maybe it will make it easier to get to Basankusu."

I put her open canteen into her outreached hand. Laura swallowed the little pill, then drank a long time before handing me back her canteen.

"We should get going," I said to her softly. "You want to ride back here, so you can lie down?" I started to get up.

"No, you stay," Laura said. "I'll put my head on your lap."

We drove on...

"Pause," Paul said. Kiki's voice fell silent. It was growing late, Paul told himself, and he wanted to get a good night's sleep before his last day on the trail, so he really should stop listening for the night. What he wouldn't tell himself was that the descriptions of Laura's illness were stirring up recollections of his mother's sickness and its aftermath. It was making him feel more and more uncomfortable as Dr. Kumar's story moved along.

Paul rolled over on his side and tried to push away all the unpleasant impressions that had flowed in around him as he'd listened—but as he lay there trying to quiet his thinking, he felt like someone standing in a pool of water, struggling to push the water away. Everything he pushed aside just poured back in around him.

Soon, specific parts of those impressions began to surface, and Paul found himself recalling how much of the time his father had been away in the months following his mother's death. As an adult, Paul understood that his father had had little choice. He worked for Corprogov and so had to go where they needed him. After all, with all the food shortages, his job as food-distribution officer was considered quite important. But for Paul, as a child, it had been hard to understand.

Paul thought about his father, trying to comprehend how life had been for him. Paul knew his father had found his job depressing. He was supposed to help make sure resources wound up where they were needed (for example, that the grain and primary yeast reserves were routed to the famine areas most in need) but he had encountered so much graft, especially from those above him in the Corprogov hierarchy, that it was impossible for him to properly do his job. Often, he had to stand by and watch people suffering because of the greed of others.

He had felt burdened, as well, Paul understood, by the responsibility of looking after two young boys, alone, after his wife's death—but here, again, Paul had to struggle not to feel resentful toward him. Paul and his brother, Casey, had been left alone a lot after their mother's death—left to fend for themselves. It was hard on them. They had survived mostly on Saccomite and had quarreled a lot. With little comfort or adult guidance, their pain and sorrow had welled up like a blister between them.

Paul stared upward as thin clouds drifted between him and the starry sky. Was that when his grandfather—his mother's father—had come to live with them? Paul wondered. It was strange how sketchy his memory was on this subject. Surely, he'd been old enough to remember more.

Paul scanned his memory for other details. Yes, he was sure that was when his grandfather had moved in with them (in fact, Paul recalled talking to Casey about it, once, years later). Their father had made some excuse about not wanting their grandfather to be alone—but the truth was, they all needed him, and that was why he came to stay.

Certainly, Paul's father had been of little use, even when he was at home, Paul remembered. It wasn't like that before his mother died—but afterward, Paul's father was drunk on torich much of the time.

Torich—it really was a sort of plague of its own, Paul thought. Cheap and readily available on the black market, it made people feel as though all their troubles had blown gently away. Or it did, so long as they were on it—but in the meanwhile, the health costs rose, like a pool that the user eventually would drown in. Paul's father had lived long enough for Paul to tell him that he'd finished graduate school with a PhD in physics, but it had hardly seemed worth doing, as his father had been deep in the haze that torich wove around him.

As Paul lay there, it seemed to him that he had never really known his father. His father had been absent for one reason or another for most of Paul's life. It had been nearly six years now since his father's death—but much longer than that since Paul had felt his father's presence in his life in any meaningful way.

At one level, Paul felt that he couldn't really blame his father. Who knew what stresses he felt from his job (the corruption, the visits to the famine zones...) and Paul could only guess what his mother's death had meant to his father, who seemed so crippled by it.

But for all of this, a part of Paul still saw his father as he had when he was young. When his mother was dying, and Paul and his brother were in need, his father had failed to be there until it was too late, and their mother was gone. But he *should* have been there, Paul had felt. He should have been there when they needed him most.

Paul felt a shiver and turned his thoughts away from a dark area in his mind. He didn't like thinking so much about his mother's death, or any of the events surrounding it.

Paul got up and stirred his small fire, coaxing a little more life out of it, then sat back down and watched the sparks floating skyward. At least things were pretty good between him and his brother, he thought. They got along well when they saw one another—but those times seemed to be getting spread further and further apart, as they each grew older and more wrapped up in their own lives.

It would be nice to see his niece and meet his nephew, Paul thought. They must be pretty big now. When was it he had seen his brother and his family last—had it really been three or four years now?

Paul lay down on his side, facing the dwindling fire. Dawn would come soon enough, he thought. He should sleep while it was dark.

Paul closed his eyes, then, and turned himself toward the numbing embrace of sleep.

◻ ◻ ◻

Paul woke with the feeling that he had been dreaming, but he couldn't remember any dreams. He sat up and rubbed his eyes, then looked around in the soft light of early morning. There was a chill in the air, and Paul reached for his pack to pull out his jacket.

He got up, pulled on the jacket, then, barefooted, walked to the side of the camp that was farthest from the stream, where he relieved himself at the edge of a meadow. When he was done, he stood and stretched and let out a loud yawn.

A noise in the grasses near him caught his attention, and he turned toward it just in time to catch sight of a rabbit before it disappeared into the underbrush. Paul looked around. The grass glistened with morning dew. In the air was the sweet scent of things green and growing. The stream burbled and hummed as it flowed past his camp. Birds in the trees along the stream's banks were full of early morning song and chatter.

What an incredible world this was! Paul thought, as he stepped back toward his things. If only he could share what he had discovered here with his grandfather—but that would not be possible, not on this or any other world, since his grandfather had passed away several years before.

Not on this or any other world, Paul thought again, and as he did, he wondered if his grandfather had ever been born on *this* earth, and if so, if he might still be alive somewhere here.

Who knew? Paul thought, as he sat down on his bivy sack. With so very many things different on this world than on his own, it seemed to him there was no reason to expect that the same people would have met, and married, and had the same children they had had on his earth. In fact, with the population as low as it was here, it was clear to Paul that the people of this earth had had far fewer children than had been had on the earth his grandfather had been born on.

Surely, Paul thought, the odds were slight that this world would have produced another one of him—and even if it had, that man would know nothing of Paul or of the close bond they'd shared.

Paul pulled his pack over to him and began looking through it for his solar razor. As he did, he recalled the thoughts he'd had about his grandfather the night before. Funny, the way he had trouble recalling the details of events from around that time—like when it was that his grandfather had come to live with them. If it weren't for the conversation he had had with his brother, Casey, on their last visit, Paul reflected, it would all be even more of a jumble.

Paul thought back to that last visit. It had been difficult for Paul to gather together enough energy credits to make the trip, but Casey had married since Paul had seen him last, and he and his wife had had a child, and so Paul had thought it important that he go and meet them both. It had been good to be with Casey's family, Paul recalled, and he had had a particularly good visit with Casey—especially one night when the two of them had stayed up talking.

Paul found his razor and worried for a moment about whether it would still hold a charge after having been in his pack for a few days, but it turned on just fine. Paul went to the side of the stream and used the calm waters at its border as a mirror while he shaved.

His hair had filled in pretty well, Paul noted—more like an uncommonly short hair cut, now, than the baldness he'd seen before. Even his eyebrows had come to look fairly normal.

Good, Paul thought, as he finished shaving. He took off his shirt and used a few splashes of the cold water to clean up with, then used his shirt to dry off with. Then he put the shirt back on and, stepping away from the side of the creek, returned his razor to its place deep in his pack.

Paul dug around in the pack a little longer then, until he found just the variety of travel meal he was in the mood for. It was slightly sweeter than the others and gave off a fresh-baked scent when warmed. Paul compressed the heating baton that came with the meal to get it started heating, then slipped it into its slot in the meal packet.

Paul stretched again, as he waited for his breakfast to warm up. Not many of the comforts of home, he thought—but he had to admit that he'd been enjoying the way he'd been living and wasn't as eager as he would have thought he'd be to arrive at the Kumaric Retreat.

As Paul sat waiting for his breakfast to warm, his thoughts drifted back to his visit with his brother and how things had been between them in recent years. Yes, it *had* been a long time since they had seen one another, but with energy credits so hard to come by, and the demands of their jobs, it was bound to be that way.

Funny, Paul thought, how much people's lives steer them, and not the other way around. Casey's path was set for him as soon as he'd been old enough to get an official job. Their father had pulled a few strings and gotten Casey a job doing the same sort of work their father had done—food distribution for Corprogov—and Casey, knowing a great opportunity when he saw one, had taken the job. Then Corprogov had deployed him to Omaha, where he was trained for a position opening up there. Paul had only seen him three times since. It seemed just to get harder to get together as time went on.

Paul was glad he had been able to make that last visit, though—not just so he could meet Raya and Carmen, but because he and Casey had had such a good visit on that one night, in particular. They'd stayed up talking about subjects they had never before spoken of in such depth—about their father, their grandfather, and their mother's death.

Paul took a bite of his travel meal. "He was all right before she passed away—solid, stable," Paul recalled Casey saying.

"Dad?" Paul answered.

"Yeah. I mean, he worked a lot," Casey said. "I know he was away a lot of the time—but he seemed pretty happy when he was home with us. But after Mom died, he drank so much torich! When I try to picture him then, I always picture him with a bottle in his hand. He tried to be a good dad—and he helped me out a lot, getting me set up with Corprogov work. You know how many people would die to have the doors opened for them that he opened for me? But after Mom's death, well, he really got tripped flat."

"Yeah, I guess that's right. I really hadn't thought that much about what he was like before and after," Paul said.

"How could you not have? It's like the difference between day and night," Casey said.

Paul smiled. "Maybe. But you know, I was older. Maybe I just wasn't that focused on things with the family."

"Yeah, you were out of the house a lot, for a while—getting in trouble," Casey replied. "Until Granddad came and straightened you out."

"He didn't 'straighten' me out," Paul said.

Casey smiled a little. "Maybe, but you were in pretty thick soup before he came. That's why Dad got him to come."

"No—that's not why Granddad moved in with us. He was lonely after Grandmom passed away," Paul explained.

"*No*, Grandmom died when I was really little, Paul—like when I was two. Granddad moved in before I turned nine. I remember him being there—living there—on my ninth birthday, less than a year after Mom passed away. He hadn't been there that long. If he was lonely, why'd he take so long to get lonely? No, you were the reason Dad asked Granddad to come. Dad had to be away all the time, and he wanted another grown-up around, I guess. You shaped up pretty well after he got there. I think you liked having him there, and he liked you. It seemed to calm you down."

"Yeah, I liked having him around," Paul said. "He was always patient—the way Mom was. He explained things. He didn't shout."

"Yeah, well, like father like daughter, I guess," Casey said. "I just wish Dad hadn't burned all of Mom's pictures. I would have liked to have had more to remember her by."

"What do you mean," Paul asked, "burned her pictures?"

"Don't you remember? Dad, thick on torich one night, took all her stuff up to the roof and burned it."

"Oh—yeah," Paul said. "I'd forgotten all about that." Paul thought about it a minute.

"I'm going to get us something to eat," Casey said, "I've got some genuine, true-meat salami. A supply was going to the UC, and my boss let me hold one out. I'll make us a couple of sandwiches."

"True-meat salami?" Paul answered. "Pretty nice to be near enough to the fabled Corprogov Upper Crust to get a little of their leavings!"

"Just one of the perks of the job," Casey called back, as he left the room.

Before long, Casey was back with the sandwiches and a couple of drinks.

Paul took a bite of one of the sandwiches. "I should visit you more often," he said.

"You should," Casey replied.

"You know, I was thinking about what you said, about Dad burning the pictures. I remember him coming back from work one night and going into their bedroom, after Mom had died, and starting to box up all her things. I asked him what he was doing, and he said somebody he worked with had told him it would help. He didn't say much else. He just kept boxing."

"Yeah, I remember that, too," Casey said. "And then, one night—about, well, I don't know how long it was. Like weeks, maybe, or a couple of months—but one night, when you were out—this was before Granddad came to live with us—he took all that stuff up to the roof. I could smell the torich. He was really thick on it. He lit up a fire on the grill he kept up there and began burning it all. I was crying—eight years old, and he's burning everything that's left of my mother! I started to scream at him to stop, and he grabbed me up by the shoulders—picked me way up in the air like this," Casey gestured. "I thought he was going to throw me off the roof—but instead, he just dropped me. I shut up after that. Just sat in the corner and cried, and watched him burn it. He had tears streaming down his face the whole time—but he did it. I don't know where you were."

"Dad wasn't one for halfway measures," Paul said quietly, thinking that he would have felt the same as Casey, had he been there.

"No, he wasn't one for halfway measures," Casey said, shaking his head slowly. "When I got this job, everybody knew him already—when I got here, I mean. They said he'd gotten where he was because he'd always followed through. Give him a job, and he'd do it. Well, he sure followed through on that."

Paul sat, staring at the floor, then looked over at Casey. "It's funny, how much more you seem to remember—more details, I mean. After all, you're three years younger than me. I should be the one who remembers more."

"Well, you were pretty spun out for a while—even after Granddad got there. I don't think you really evened out until you started coming up with all those schemes to—I don't know what you were up to—to transform the planet, or something."

Casey laughed. "I remember one time, you told me you were going to extrapolate the DNA of extinct species by making comparisons between the DNA of their closest living relatives—then reconstruct their DNA from scratch and clone them."

"It may have been possible to come close—but then there wouldn't have been any right habitat, anymore...," Paul started.

"Oh, and what was the other thing you said? Oh, yeah—you were going to construct these giant, like, *wings* to float above the planet, and create enough shade to help cool it back down, so more things could live..."

"All right, all right," Paul cut in. "That would have worked, too—but can you imagine the cost? They'd have to be HUGE—and you'd have to place them really high up..."

"That's what I mean," Casey said, "you had these wild plans—but you quit getting into trouble."

"... besides, if you fixed things," Paul went on, "people would just ruin them again. That's why you have to make it so there are fewer people."

"Not that the plan you have now is crazy," Casey hastened to add. "You tell me it can work, and I believe you. I tell everybody I work with, my brother is a genius mad scientist."

Paul looked at his younger brother. "You give great compliments, you know that, Casey?" he said wryly.

"Hey, not everybody can have a genius in the family."

Paul finished the last bite of his travel meal, stuffed his bivy sack into his pack, then picked up his pack and slung it onto his back, still smiling a little, as he remembered. Casey—he'd have to go and see him when he got back, he told himself—if he could truly find the resources he needed to build a new transport, find an energy source, and aim it all properly.

Paul started up the trail, which led up a hill beyond the camp. As he went, he thought about the references Casey had made to him getting into trouble when he was young.

It was true, Paul thought. He must have seemed a real handful to his father after his mother's death. For a while, he had certainly had a knack for picking out the wrong sorts of friends to associate with.

Thinking back on it now, Paul realized that he'd been in pain and had found other troubled boys—who were, themselves, hurting, for one reason or another—to associate with. Paul remembered the feeling of it—like he was running away from something in himself, and they were running away from something in themselves, and together, somehow, they could all run faster.

Together, they had roamed the streets, daring one another and testing the bounds of their friendship. Looking back, Paul could see that he'd really had nobody at that time—except his younger brother, who was just a kid—and his father, who was around just enough to pretend that he was responsible.

So Paul had turned to the company of other boys his own age to give him the companionship he needed, and a sense of belonging.

Paul remembered how, one morning, one of those boys had gotten mad and sworn at one of the teachers at school, and the teacher had grabbed the boy by the collar and dragged him into the solitary detention area. The teacher had left the boy there through lunch, and hadn't let him out until the end of the day. Paul and his friends had all agreed this was unacceptable, and had retaliated by breaking into, and vandalizing, the teacher's office after he had left school that day.

The administration of the school knew Paul had been one of the quiet and studious students in the years before and that this was his first serious offense. They also knew about his mother's death, and that his father was in a position of some responsibility with Corprogov—and so they had agreed, in response to his father's pleas for leniency, to go easy on him. Paul had been given a month's detention, he remembered—though some of the other boys had received far harsher punishments.

Paul remembered coming home from the last day of detention and talking to his grandfather, as his grandfather got settled in his room.

So, Casey really was right, Paul thought. It *was* just after that that Paul's father had turned their small dining room into a bedroom, and Paul's grandfather had come to stay.

Paul looked at the trail up ahead and recalled what the woman who'd passed him the day before had told him. He would reach the Kumaric Retreat in just a matter of hours, now, and here he was daydreaming his time away with memories of his brother and childhood.

Paul sighed and shook his head, then tried for a moment to remember what had been happening in Dr. Kumar's story before he had stopped listening the day before.

Yes, that was it—they were traveling to an airport, and Laura was very sick. She had just taken some medicine Indira had offered her, then decided to ride in the back of the jeep with her head on Indira's lap.

Though Paul lacked enthusiasm for listening to a story about a loved one who was ill, he nonetheless asked Kiki to resume recitation.

With that, Kiki began again, her voice modulated in imitation of Dr. Kumar's.

◻   ◻   ◻

We drove on then. The medicine was helpful, but even so we stopped a number of times before we arrived in Basankusu. The land opened up some as we neared town, with the dense forest thinning and palm trees sprouting up in the open spaces.

Mvula had agreed to take us directly to the airport. It was too late for the market that day, in any case, and I had begun to feel worried that Laura and I might show up just minutes too late for the only available flight to Kisangani—the second largest city in Zaire, perhaps only an hour away from Basankusu by air, and a place where I thought a good doctor could be found for Laura.

It was after dark when we pulled up in front of the airport (which was little more than an airstrip, really) on the outskirts of Basankusu. My worst fears were not realized, but they might as well have been. There had been a flight to Kisangani the day before, and no more flights were scheduled for that destination for nearly a week.

As I didn't speak French, Laura had dragged herself to the reservation desk only to be told this disappointing news. By the time we made it back out to the jeep, where Mvula waited with all of our gear, Laura was trembling with weakness and fatigue. I could see from the way she moved that every gesture took effort.

I helped steady Laura as she climbed back into the jeep. Mvula had been quiet during most of our trip, but now in the dim light cast out in front of the terminal building, I could see his look of concern for Laura. We gave Mvula our news, and he told us, then, in a mixture of French, English, and Lingala, that he knew of a place nearby where a woman had a couple of huts she would rent to travelers—people who came to town for the market or the airstrip. With the same gentle tone I had learned to expect of him, he offered to take us there.

Laura had only one question before agreeing to go: Would there be a latrine?

Mvula assured us that this place was *"moderne,"* and had latrines dug and *bifelo* (walls) built around them.

Laura wished for only two things by then: a latrine and a place to lie down. And so we went.

The huts were built beside the Lulonga River, which bordered Basankusu to the north. They were built on a small rise above the water, which shone beautifully in the moonlight. Palm trees swayed on the near shore, their ample leaves fluttering and glistening in the same light that lit the river.

I waited with Laura in the jeep as Mvula went to make arrangements with the proprietor. How could the world be so beautiful and so filled with sorrow, all at once? I wondered. I looked down at Laura, with her head resting in my lap, and thought how very pale she looked in the moonlight. The hair around her face was damp with sweat, her eyes dark and hollow. In all the years I'd known her, I'd never seen her look so ill. I stroked her face, aware that her fever had grown.

Mvula returned and told us that one of the huts was occupied, but the second was available. He pointed out the latrine nearby, then led me to the hut while Laura stayed in the jeep, resting.

The hut was nothing more than a squat thatched building with an open doorway and a bare floor. In one corner, sleeping mats were loosely stacked. As basic as the accommodations were, the space was large enough for perhaps half a dozen sleepers and would provide us with shelter for the night.

I returned to the jeep and helped Laura to the latrine. "Just leave me here until you have a bed ready," she told me, her voice barely a whisper. "I'm tired of running back and forth."

I pulled enough of our gear from the jeep to set up for the night (including a ground cloth and foam pads, a flannel sheet we'd brought in place of sleeping bags for use on cooler tropical nights, and a piece of mosquito netting to drape over the open doorway of the hut), then returned to the latrine, where I helped Laura wash up with water from my canteen, and then steadied her as we walked the few meters to our hut.

Seeing how exhausted Laura had become, I worried that we had made the wrong decision in coming here. We should have gone straight away to look for a doctor once we'd made it to Basankusu. If it *was* cholera—and the thought that it even might be terrified me—then I knew it could kill quickly, sometimes within hours.

Laura lay on her camp pad, limp and pale, with the moonlight streaming in around her through the open doorway. I told her I thought I should get her to a doctor. She opened her eyes and shook her head.

"No. I'll be fine," she said. "No doctor. Let me rest."

"Laura, I'm not sure you will be fine. Have you thought about why you might be sick?"

Laura just looked at me, annoyed at being pestered when she felt so awful.

"No," she said finally.

"Do you remember when the barge stopped on the river, and all those people rowed ashore?"

Laura nodded a little. "Yes."

"It was for a funeral. A child died. Laura, do you remember—there was cholera on board."

Laura's eyes grew wider. "You think? It could be cholera?"

She looked worried now. I hadn't wanted to worry her.

"I think it could be. I think you need medical care."

Laura stared up at the ceiling. When she spoke, her voice sounded fragile, like wind through dry leaves. "Lisa Xiang told me, you have to be careful. She said, there are stories of needles being reused, especially in remote areas. There's a lot of AIDS in Zaire, Indira."

Laura looked into my eyes. Her face was drawn, the area around her eyes dark.

"They'd want to give me an IV, for all the fluid I've lost."

"I think you need it. Oh, Laura, why didn't we plan ahead, somehow, so I could take better care of you?" I wiped tears from my face with the back of one hand.

Laura reached over and squeezed my other hand. "It'll be all right," she told me.

I looked down at her, and she held my gaze for a moment. I thought how like her, to be trying to reassure me, in a situation like this, even when I should be reassuring her.

Laura turned her eyes towards the open doorway and frowned a little. "You know," she said, in a hoarse whisper, "I think I remember something."

She closed her eyes for so long then that I wondered if she'd gone to sleep.

When she opened them, she asked me to get a plastic bag from the bottom of the lower section of her pack. It had all the travel information Lisa Xiang had sent to her before our trip.

I brought it to her, and she said to look through it for a magazine clipping.

"Lisa sent you a clipping?" I asked.

"No. I clipped it and put it in there, so it would come with us. I think. Last fall. Forgot all about it."

I located the clipping, then held it in the moonlight so I could read it. It was a short piece, no more than a filler, really—just three or four inches long.

I skimmed through it: "ORS ... scourge of diarrheal illnesses ... simple as water, sugar, and salt ... saves more than a million lives each year."

I kissed Laura's hand, then stepped over to the doorway, where I pulled back the mosquito netting and read the full article in the moonlight.

I had never heard of them before, but apparently Oral Rehydration Salts were becoming well known around the world. According to the article, a person could force their body to absorb water faster than it was lost, even during illnesses as severe as cholera, simply by drinking an exact mixture of three common ingredients: a liter of water, eight teaspoons of sugar, and one teaspoon of salt.

Luckily, Laura and I had stockpiled ample supplies of all three of these ingredients, along with other necessities, in preparation for our time in the field. We agreed that Laura would try the solution, and that we would do our best to get her to a good doctor as soon as possible.

Before long, I had Laura's canteen filled with the formula, and had placed her daypack where she could lean against it while she took sips of a solution that, I hoped, if necessary, might save her life.

By the time Mvula came and told me dinner was ready (and I hadn't even realized he was fixing it), Laura had finished that canteen full of the solution and begun on another. She wasn't interested in eating any food, so I left her with what I had hopefully begun to think of as "the elixir of life" and went to join Mvula by the little cooking fire. Nearby, the Lulonga River continued to flow, slow and sinuous, and the palm trees to sway brightly in the moonlight, but all I could think of was Laura, and all the hope I was putting in that unnamed article and the simple solution of common ingredients it recommended.

I don't even remember what Mvula prepared that night, but I do remember eating it sitting, looking out across the river, while fireflies flashed their mating calls above. A low mist hung over the water, with the fireflies hovering above it like stars above clouds. Overhead, the sky had clouds, too, pushing in from the east, while the moon retreated in the western sky. All around, crickets sang their lonely calls.

Mvula and I said little during the meal. I was too tired and preoccupied to try to find the right words, in any language, to share with him, and perhaps he, sensing the seriousness of my mood, thought it best to allow the silence. When the meal was done, Mvula kindly encouraged me to return to Laura's side and leave the cleanup to him. I accepted, though I was concerned that he was ending up with an unfair portion of the work. On the way back into the hut I stopped to pick up the rest of our personal items from the jeep, as the sky had begun to look menacing—leaving behind only a five-gallon container of kerosene; three five-gallon water jugs, two of which were empty; and Mvula's personal items, which I expected he would bring in for the night.

I thought perhaps Laura seemed a little stronger when I again helped her to the latrine after dinner, but I was worried, still, and didn't want to get my hopes up too much. I helped her back to bed and convinced her to have some more of the rehydration solution before settling down to rest. Soon, she was fast asleep. It was long after dark by then, and I felt exhausted after a day of travel and worry. I lay down next to Laura, watching her in the small glow of our camp lantern. Its flickering light seemed only to accentuate the dark circles around her eyes.

From somewhere along the river, I could hear the rhythms of "talking" drums. It seemed strange to me that there was life going on elsewhere in the world, when my life and attention were turned so entirely to my concern for Laura.

After a little while, Mvula finished with the cleanup and slipped silently past our curtain of mosquito netting, carrying his travel satchel and a few stray kitchen items. He paused to ask how Laura was doing (I could tell him only that I didn't know) before he settled in by the far wall of our hut for the night. I didn't want the light of our lantern to disturb him, so I turned it off, then, and tried to sleep, myself.

I awoke to the sound of Laura stumbling to her feet and to the steady hush of falling rain. I picked up a flashlight and went with her as she made her way again to the latrine, steadying her over the muddy slope, which was now slippery with rain. Afterward, I helped her to wash up and to wipe the mud from her feet, before she lay back down. It was a process we would repeat many times that night. But I was heartened, on this occasion, that Laura seemed perhaps a little stronger than on the last.

I encouraged her to drink more of the solution before she drifted off to sleep again, then I went and sat in the doorway and looked out in the direction of the river, and the dense night between me and it. The moon had set, or the clouds which had brought this rain had covered it, for it was all darkness in the world around me now.

It seemed I had slept just enough to take the edge off my fatigue. Now, in mid night, I didn't feel I could sleep any more. Weary but not sleepy, I sat there wondering why Laura had gotten sick and not me. I knew illnesses with symptoms like Laura's often arrived through contaminated food or water, but all I could think was that we had eaten the same foods and drunk the same water when staying with Raymond—but not on the barge. We'd eaten different foods in both the dining room and on the flat barge, there. And so it seemed plain to me that Laura must have gotten this sickness on the barge.

Through my mind drifted images of pirogues rowing ashore, and of a child's small body wrapped in cloth, ready for burial. *No, Laura—not cholera, please! The world would be nothing for me without you to share it with.* I leaned my head back against the doorjamb then, and tears slid down my cheeks, like the rain falling around me. Not so far off, in the darkness, I imagined the strong Lulonga flowing, slowly gathering in all the waters falling around it, gathering strength—like a creature crawling through the darkness, quenching its thirst.

In the dark mood I was in, so worried about Laura as I was, the world seemed a troubled place, and all the troubles of the world seemed to get caught up in the net of my thoughts, like so many gasping, struggling fish.

I put my head down on my knees. My thoughts swam with impressions of all the sorts of violence and disharmony that existed in the world, like a news reel playing off images—of war (machine gun fire through darkness, bombs being dropped), of a married couple fighting (shouts, cries for help, a bloody fist), of bigotry (people beaten for being the wrong race, loving the wrong person), of a woman raped, of a forest toppled, of toxic rivers flowing into the sea…

How had we come to make this world, full of so many troubles, where we could do such harm without even comprehending the impact of our actions? I wondered.

How had we become so insulated from the damage we inflict that we might hardly know or sense it?

How could we strike out with such violence against others we considered "bad," without understanding that from their own, perhaps limited, perspectives, what they did seemed acceptable—even good?

How could we, over and over again, fail to bridge these gaps by simply communicating with one another?

But I knew how, or was beginning to understand it. It had all become clear to me earlier that day, as I'd ridden along in the jeep, thinking about the three impediments. *This* was the sort of world we had made—and we had ushered in all of these problems along with it.

I lifted my head and stared out, through the rain and black of night, in the direction of what must have been a gradually rising river, and let my thoughts flow, as that river flowed, slowly past in the darkness.

Everywhere around me the rain fell, forming threads of water, which reached towards the Lulonga. Though I was barely conscious of it as I sat there, my thoughts had begun to gather like this, too—with new bits and pieces appearing dimly amidst a larger landscape, gathering together, forming rivulets, braiding together into stronger bands, and moving towards a larger mass of ideas already gathered and flowing— slowly, gradually, coming together and interweaving with a story about our ancient past, which I had, already, begun to tell myself.

❈   ❈   ❈

Kiki's voice fell silent.

"Pause," Paul said.

"Pausing. End of chapter," Kiki responded.

Paul decided this would be a good time to stop for a rest. He was tired of the slow, uphill climb, and of the warming temperatures, which seemed to climb steadily as the morning wore on. As warm as the day was, that warmth was relieved, somewhat, by the soft breeze, and by the shade of the oaks and pines that grew along the river.

Paul dropped his pack to the ground and sat down on a log overlooking the stream. He was thinking about the troubles Dr. Kumar had described as existing in her world and how much they reminded him of the world he knew. Was it true, he wondered, as Dr. Kumar had suggested, that these problems were all outgrowths of the three impediments?

Certainly it was common in his world for people to be cut off from one another, Paul reflected; after all, it seemed to him that their attention was focused mostly on their own individual lives, and on the feed from their media implants. It seemed to Paul, as well, that most of the people he knew believed in some sort of fundamental error in human nature—a kind of basic "badness" that had to be suppressed and never let out. Surely, Paul thought, most of them saw no reason to try to foster communication with either themselves or others, when things went wrong—for how could that "badness" ever be made right? Instead, it made sense to them to just try to suppress things further.

In any case—Paul reflected, shaking his head—that was certainly the way Corprogov did things.

He looked down at his feet, which still felt fine, then knelt over the stream and splashed water on his face and neck. Even in the shade, the day was still warm, and after the exertion of his long, uphill hike, it just seemed warmer. Adding to Paul's discomfort was the fact that it was hard for him to listen to this story about Laura's sickness. It reminded him too much of what had happened in his own life.

Paul took a long drink of water, refilled his canteen, then threw his pack back on and continued up the trail, but decided to wait a little bit longer before beginning recitation again. Instead, he let his thoughts drift back to when his grandfather had first come to stay with him and his brother and father.

In the months before his grandfather moved in, Paul had had such a hard time dealing with his mother's death. During that time, whenever his thoughts neared the subject of her passing, he would feel overcome with a sense of how very *wrong* it all was—and of how wrong he was, somehow, in connection to it. Each time this happened, he wanted to shove the subject away, to run away from it, and to leave it behind him for good.

Paul's grandfather, on the other hand, spoke about her death unhesitatingly— as though it was a subject that belonged, naturally, in clear view. Whereas Paul preferred to keep her death cloaked in the shadows of his mind, his grandfather pulled the subject, piece by piece, out into the open. Gradually, based on what his grandfather said, Paul was able to make whatever sense of it he was eventually able to achieve.

It was good to have his grandfather there in many ways. After his grandfather moved in, Paul was required to come directly home after school. Once there, his grandfather was patient with him (much as Paul's mother had been) and spent time with both the boys, helping them with their schoolwork and, eventually, preparing foods grown in a small rooftop garden he designed and planted with the help of the two boys.

Having his grandfather around soothed Paul in a way that the boys he knew through school had never been able to do, and soon their grandfather/grandson relationship became one of friendship, as well.

Paul's grandfather spoke to Paul about a past when all of nature was whole and vibrant, when the climate was still in balance, and when wilderness and vitality pervaded the world. He spoke, too, about the various effects that human activity had had on the world, and why it had become as it was today. Through these conversations, it became clear to Paul that the epidemic that had taken his mother's life—and very nearly doomed him and his brother, as well—was not a random occurrence, or even a natural event.

According to his grandfather, the pathogen that caused *Muerte Azul* originated in the tropics of Central America. It had first been named and classified at a small clinic in El Salvador, perhaps a century before. Through the years that followed, occasional outbreaks occurred there and in neighboring countries—but it always stayed in the same region.

About thirty or forty years after it was first classified, people realized that the disease was spreading. It was slowly traveling north, through the Corprogov Provinces of Guatemala and Belize, and into Southern Mexico.

With each decade it went further. As clear as it was that the disease was migrating, for a long time nobody was quite sure why. The first real clue came when a particular breed of bat was identified as the reservoir animal. These bats carried the disease; though they might be made sick by it, it rarely killed them. Though the disease might die off entirely within the human population, it always survived within this particular species of bat. Periodically, people would be re-exposed through contact with the bats or their droppings, and a new outbreak would begin.

Identifying the reservoir animal was seen as a big step, Paul's grandfather explained to Paul—but the question of why the disease was spreading to the north remained a mystery.

The answer to this question, which scientists eventually arrived at, was that as the planet warmed, the bats that carried the disease were gradually migrating further and further north to keep pace with the changing climate; as they went, they carried the disease along with them.

By 2115, the bats had spread throughout much of the Southwest Quadrant—from El Paso to Denver, and all along the Pacific coast south of San Francisco. When the next major *Muerte Azul* outbreak occurred, it took place there and spread like wildfire throughout an overcrowded, and often undernourished, population.

After the *Muerte Azul* epidemic had burned through the area, many people, embittered over the loss of their loved ones, blamed the bats and made efforts to eradicate them. They attacked not only bats of the specific species that carried the disease, but any and all bats they could find, thus devastating the bat population.

It was as foolish as many other deeds that people had committed through-out the centuries when dealing with the natural world. What people little understood was that many of the species of bats they destroyed ate insects that people considered to be pests. With the disappearance of the bats, insect numbers climbed sky-high.

By that time—in the early twenty-second century—most insects had evolved a resistance to the insecticides that people had spread, so casually, over the previous two centuries. Now, with their numbers suddenly swelling and the bats' numbers in such decline, there was little people could do to combat the swarms of insects. So it came to be that endless acres of crops were consumed by countless numbers of hungry insects. For this reason, the *Muerte Azul* epidemic of 2118 was followed closely by the food shortage and famine of 2120.

The rooftop garden Paul's grandfather planted made this time less difficult for Paul's family than for most (as Paul's grandfather was able to effectively screen off his plants from the hungry insects) but the lesson for Paul was nonetheless clear; human beings had greatly wronged nature, and when we wronged it, it would inevitably wrong us—perhaps taking from us that which was most precious and dear.

This lesson helped define the way Paul understood the loss of his mother. It was as though the wrongness that had invaded his young life and had taken his mother from him, had begun as a swarm—a swarm that had swept up like a wave out of Central America and zeroed in on his family's home.

Though Paul felt, deep down, that the piece of that wrongness that he car-ried in himself could never truly be put right, the knowledge that his grand-father had shared with him gave him some hope of righting what was wrong in the world at large. As Paul understood it, the natural world had been forced out of balance by the actions of human beings, and great harm had come of it. Somehow, that balance had to be restored.

Soon, Paul had all sorts of schemes spinning through his young mind, each aimed at the prospect of putting things right. In addition to his early plans to reconstruct the lost DNA of extinct species, or to shade the world (and so to cool the fever inflicted on it by climate change), Paul also toyed with plans to genetically design plants to suck carbon dioxide from the air at a vastly enhanced rate and to then sequester it in their roots. He had plans, too, to rebalance the ocean's chemistry (ruined by an overload of carbon dioxide absorbed from the atmosphere) so that all the myriad creatures that had once lived there could survive there once again.

It wasn't until Paul was in his late teens and had read, in a magazine, about research into the possibility of extra-space-time travel, that he began to dream of a way to transport great numbers of people off the earth—and so make space for the world to heal itself, in whatever ways were still possible.

It was from these early, perhaps visionary, musings—and from many years of study and hard work—that the Depopulation Project was eventually born.

That thought brought Paul back to the present, where he found himself thinking about the current status of the Depopulation Project, and wondering if his team would go on working in his absence. He was just trying to decide which of his team members would be best able to take his place—even temporarily—when he followed a turn in the path and came face to face with a large black bear, which stood on the path about twenty meters ahead of him.

Both Paul and the bear stood and stared at one another for a full half minute, then the bear swung its massive weight around and lumbered off into the brush.

Paul stood perfectly still as it retreated, his heart pounding. He had never dreamed, in his life, that he would ever see such a sight!

"What a world!" Paul whispered under his breath, amazed again at how enormously different this earth was from his own.

Paul wondered if any of the hikers he had passed that morning while he was listening to *Memories and Reflections* had encountered that same bear.

He stood very still for another minute, until he was quite sure that the bear was gone, then set off up the trail again. As he went, Paul wondered briefly what the terrain would be like in the area around the Kumaric Retreat, and what sorts of plants and animals he might see there—then realized how very little time he had left for listening to Dr. Kumar's memoirs before he arrived.

"Kiki, resume recitation, please," Paul said, as he hit his stride going up the trail. In a moment, the tones of Dr. Kumar's voice again filled the air.

CHAPTER XIII

Currents drift;
liquid thoughts
settle out of mist.

—CARMEN RUIZ

———•·•———

Urged on by fog and falling rain,
the rising river carries us to new shores.

—HUME SOMERLEY

I woke much earlier than Laura and lay awake with the rain falling out-side in a steady drizzle, worrying over how to get Laura to a doctor we could depend on. I finally decided that we might be able to get a flight to Kisangani if we first flew to a neighboring city—perhaps Gemena or Bumba—and then caught a flight on to Kisangani from there. Once in Kisangani, we could look up a Catholic brother we knew of at the mission there (someone who Lisa Xiang had given us the name of) and ask him for assistance in finding a good doctor.

Having, just the evening before, looked through the papers that Lisa had sent to us in Boulder, had reminded me that she had recommended Brother Frank Bohdan as someone we could turn to if we needed assis-tance when in Kisangani—especially if we needed help finding transpor-tation from there to Epulu. It seemed to me, as I lay awake listening to the rain striking the thatched roof above, that if Brother Frank knew so much about the comings and goings between Kisangani and Epulu, he ought as well to know his own city and how to find good medical care there.

I thought about this for an hour or so after waking, going back and forth over the details in my mind, considering how best to get Laura to Kisangani, and how to get her to a good doctor, once there. At one point,

Laura stirred, and I thought she would waken, but instead her stirring seemed just a ripple in her sleep.

"Oh, Laura," I whispered—in a voice so soft it blended with the gentle rain and slipped through my lips as quietly as raindrops falling—"you are the love of my life."

I couldn't imagine she could hear me, though her face lay only inches from mine, even if she had been awake, but she rolled towards me then, and opened her eyes with a sleepy smile.

"And you have always been mine," she whispered back.

I smiled at her and stroked the damp hair back from her face. "How are you, my love? Any better this morning?" I asked, even though I knew this was for her the end of a long and difficult night.

Laura nodded a little. "Yes, I think—maybe not so weak." She paused, then added, "and the nausea is better, too."

We talked a little about how much good the ORS had done, and I told her about my plan to get her to a doctor in Kisangani, if she was up to traveling. She said she thought she probably would be, if she took some more of the medicine she had taken on the way to Basankusu the day before.

Soon, Mvula was up, too, and after a simple breakfast—prepared on our cook stove just inside the doorway of our hut—we loaded up the jeep and set off for the airstrip amidst the steadily falling rain. We had agreed that Mvula would leave us there to make inquiries while he went to the market to make the purchases he had planned to make for himself and others in his village. When he was done, he would return to the airstrip, and there we would consider what was possible, and what should be done.

The drive was a short one, as it had been the night before. Before leaving us at the airport's terminal building, Mvula helped us unload all of our gear (as it could not be safely left in the open-air jeep while he shopped at the market) and place it in a pile inside, near a row of seats that looked through a broad window and out onto the muddy runway beyond.

❋   ❋   ❋

After Mvula's departure, Laura and I asked questions of the reservations agent, who carefully laid out for us a complicated web of flights and possible connections.

As we left the reservations desk, we were approached by a man in a uniform, a soldier, who asked (or should I say "insisted"?) that we show our papers and explain our reasons for traveling in Zaire (it seemed that as foreigners our activities were inherently suspect) though he did not, for some reason, require of us the bribe that Raymond had warned us to expect. (I thought perhaps he was being more lax than usual because Laura looked so ill.)

When finally done with these matters, Laura and I went and sat by our gear and discussed our options. We had been told that a flight was available to Gemena that night, but that none would go on from Gemena to Kisangani for several more days. No flights from Basankusu to Bumba were available anytime soon, but we could fly from Gemena back to Mbandaka, and from Mbandaka to Kisangani. If we did this, we would arrive in Kisangani in four days. The reservations agent suggested that if we were eager to get to Kisangani, the shortest route (in time, at least) would be to return to Kinshasa by air (from which we had set out by barge more than a week before) and from there catch a direct flight to Kisangani. If we did this, we would leave Basankusu the following afternoon and arrive in Kisangani two days after that.

Laura, adventuresome to the last, was inclined to take the first route, though Gemena and Mbandaka, as it would allow us at least a passing glance at two more Zairian cities (she said our having floated past Mbandaka on the river didn't count)—while I preferred the second option, as it would get us to Kisangani one day sooner, and might even give us time to get Laura to a doctor in Kinshasa (although we had no one to recommend a good one there).

We discussed this for a while, and then decided to give the conversation a rest. Laura needed to make a trip to the restroom, again, anyhow (and was glad to finally be somewhere with running water).

When Laura returned, I said to her, "You know, I never told you about what happened when Raymond and I went for a walk yesterday morning."

"No—did something happen?" Laura asked, with a tone of concern. She slumped down in her chair and waited for me to continue.

I shook my head. "No, no—at least, not like you're thinking." It made me sad to think how badly we had both misunderstood him. "No, actually, Raymond told me a story, and he asked me if I would tell you, also."

I went on then to relate to her, as accurately as possible, what Raymond had told me. It was a sad story, and when it was done, Laura sat, looking weak and weary, starring down at the floor.

Finally, she said, "Well, I wish I'd known sooner. I'm glad at least we were able to offer him some sort of comfort. I'd like to try to find some way to write to him. I'd like to give him some sort of response."

"I know how you feel," I said. "Maybe when we're back in Boulder—by then, I think, he'll be back in Canberra. We could maybe write to him at the university there."

"Yeah, or maybe I could send a note back with Mvula today. But—no, I'd rather wait and write later, when I can give it more thought." Laura didn't look like she felt up to writing much of anything.

We both sat very quietly for several minutes.

"I was just thinking how he was at dinner," Laura said finally, "the night before last—before you came out from the hut. He was very, well, sweet. He did all of the work getting things together—warmed up and all—for dinner. I kept having the feeling he wanted to do something nice for me, but I couldn't figure out why."

Laura paused for a moment, then went on. "He said something interesting before you joined us. It was when he was talking about the sexual bonds bonobos form, and how they do that in so many different sorts of relationships. He said friendship, the way people experience it, may be like a watered-down form of romantic or sexual bonding, and that the tendency of people to form complex networks of friends is sort of like the intricate network of bonds that bonobos form. He said friendship offers many of the same advantages as the sort of bonding we discussed—just like for birds within a flock, or whales in a pod, or whatever.

"Anyway, he said we—humans—are very flexible in forming social bonds, just like the bonobos, but for most of us, most of the time, those bonds take the form of friendship."

I thought about this, and while I was thinking, Laura added, "I have the impression he thinks you and I are just very good friends."

Laura glanced over at me and smiled, a little amused.

I smiled back. "Of course that's not all wrong," I said. "We *are* very good friends." I picked up one of her hands and kissed her palm.

I looked at her then. She seemed so pale.

"You doing okay?" I asked.

"No," she said, shaking her head slightly. "I think I've been up too long." Then she pushed her daypack off the seat next to her and lay down, curling up onto two of the interlocking chairs, with her head on my lap.

I draped one of my arms across her shoulder, holding her hand, then rested my other hand on her hair. I was aware, being close to her, that as much as the ORS had revived her, and the medicine she had taken that morning had quieted some of her symptoms, her fever was still quite high. And still we were so far from Kisangani, and reliable medical care.

❋   ❋   ❋

I sat for a long time, staring out at the palm trees on the far side of the runway and at the rain falling into countless puddles on the unpaved ground. From somewhere far off in the distance, I could hear the low rumble of thunder.

Laura was sleeping and the day was ticking past, without us ever having decided what we would do, or where we would go. It seemed to me there was no rush in deciding—we would go somewhere, that night, or the next day. Laura could rest for now.

After a time, a man—tall, of light build and European decent—entered the terminal. He approached the window beyond which the runway lay, red and damp in the falling rain, then paced back and forth beside it, looking out in all directions. A time or two he stopped to glance at his watch. He turned and looked around the terminal, then noticed me watching him.

He crossed the small piece of floor between us, then spoke to me in French.

"I'm sorry," I replied in English, trying to keep my voice low enough not to wake Laura, "I don't speak French."

"*D'accord,*" he said, glancing down at Laura and lowering his voice to match mine. "Then I will speak to you in English. Please tell me, have you seen a plane land, *urh,*" he looked at has watch, "anytime in the last half an hour, and unload many boxes?"

"No," I told him, "I've been here much longer than that. No planes have landed in that time, and the ones before that only had people and luggage on them."

He looked relieved. "I wasn't sure if I was late or if I was early. You never know in this country. Nothing runs on time."

"Where are you from?" I asked him. I had the feeling he wasn't from Zaire.

"France," he told me, beginning to seem less rushed. "I am with an aid agency. We are expecting a shipment of vaccines. They have to be kept cold. I thought, perhaps, they came and were left lying someplace." He glanced back toward the large window behind him. "At least there is not too much sunlight today."

As quietly as we had been speaking, our conversation had woken Laura. She sat up beside me.

"Where are you traveling from?" the man asked me.

"The United States," I told him.

"Oh, well, I am pleased to meet you," he said, extending his hand. "My name is François Chevalier."

Laura and I introduced ourselves and shook hands. I noticed how caringly he took Laura's hand, as though he understood that she wasn't just resting, but was ill.

We told him we were trying to arrange a flight to Kisangani, but none was available for nearly a week. The fastest route we could find was to return to Kinshasa and fly to Kisangani from there. It was a mess.

He shook his head. "You should not have to go so far," he said. He paused and looked thoughtful. "The plane I am waiting for will go to Kisangani from here. I am certain they will have extra space on it. I will arrange for you to ride on it, if you like," he said.

Laura and I were both happy to accept his offer. François excused himself then, and walked across the room to the reservation desk.

Laura leaned her head against my shoulder, and I encouraged her to have some more of the ORS.

A few minutes later, François returned and told us that he had managed to get information about the flight he was there to meet, and had found out it had left almost two hours late.

"So," he said, "I will not wait here, but will return," he again glanced at his watch, "in an hour to wait the plane. You will be here?"

"Yes, certainly," I said.

"D'accord. And I will arrange a ride for you on it," he said. Laura and I expressed our appreciation, then watched as he crossed the terminal and left through the front door.

Laura looked over at me. "Who, exactly, was that?" she said.

"François Chevalier, who is here with a French aid agency providing vaccinations."

"I got most of that," Laura said, then shook her head. "That's amazing. We have a flight." She lay back down and put her head on my lap again.

"Now that's something you'd never expect to happen in the States," she said, "but I guess here, where services are in short supply..."

"...maybe people help each other out a little more," I finished for her, feeling amazed at our good fortune.

Sometime, early in the afternoon, Mvula returned, carrying a cluster of a dozen or so bananas. Laura and I told him we had managed to make arrangements for a flight to Kisangani. Then, with Laura's help translating, I told him how much I appreciated the help he gave when Laura was sickest.

Mvula shrugged, answering that he did very little—just a little food and driving. He then seemed to remember the bunch of bananas he was carrying, and offered them to us, saying they were for our lunch.

I took the bananas from his outstretched hand, while saying in English, "Thank you so much, Mvula! But please let us pay you back for this—and for all the meals, too."

While Laura translated, I picked up my daypack thinking I would give him one of the several bundles of *zaires* I had stashed there, then remembered we hadn't yet paid for our share of the hut, either.

I pulled out three of the bundles. "For the food, and for the hut," I said. Laura translated, while Mvula waved the money away, saying something in French.

"It's too much, he says," Laura told me. It was true, I knew—the thick bundles of cash probably amounted to nearly twice what we owed.

"Then get something at the market for your wife and children," I told him, again with assistance from Laura.

Mvula's eyes met mine. "You helped make it possible for me to take care of Laura," I told him. "Please let me do something nice for your family, as well."

Mvula's eyes had that calm, patient look they so often had, and as I listened to Laura translate my words, I could see his resolve soften. I think he understood that I wanted to make some gesture and that this was all I had to make it with.

A moment passed, then Mvula's face lit with a kind smile, and with that I pressed the bundles into his left hand, then reached across and took his right hand to shake it goodbye. Mvula thanked us as we thanked him, then we all said our farewells, and parted.

As Mvula walked away, I realized that our last connection to our trip on the barge—however vague that connection was, at this point—was leaving with him. Our carefully planned trip had transformed into a completely unscripted adventure.

When François Chevalier returned, Laura and I were sitting together, eating bananas and trail mix. We invited him to join us. He appeared less rushed than before and seemed glad to have something to eat. Outside, a break in the clouds had allowed a little sun to shine through.

François looked at Laura thoughtfully, then said to her, "I hope you will not be offended, but you do not look well."

Laura shook her head. "I'm not offended," she answered. "I'm sick."

François smiled a little, nodding. "I am a doctor. If you tell me *how* you are sick, maybe I can help."

Laura and I explained to him, then, what her symptoms had been, and how suddenly they had come on. We also told him about the ORS she had been taking, and about the presence of cholera on the barge.

François nodded, listening. "Well, you will be glad to know I do not think it is most likely you have cholera," he told Laura. "It is not usual for there to be a fever with adults. In children, yes—but usually, adults with cholera do not have a fever."

He asked a few more questions to try to narrow it down, then shrugged and said, "Without a lab test, I cannot know—possibly *shigella*, maybe *e. coli*... it is impossible to say. Whatever it is, you are doing the right thing for treating diarrhea. An oral rehydration solution is what we would give you," he squinted, and pushed his lips out a little, "only we would give you a little better mixture, with potassium and something to help balance pH. There will be some with this shipment. I will give you some when the plane arrives."

With my most pressing worries largely relieved, it seemed the day went quickly after that. Once the plane arrived, and the shipment was unloaded, François did give us several packets of his improved ORS mixture and told us to be sure to find a doctor if Laura's symptoms persisted, or if she took a turn for the worse.

By late afternoon we were underway—bouncing down the muddy, rain-soaked runway, and lifting into the air under a low ceiling of clouds. I was relieved at how smoothly everything had gone—we were even allowed to bring our five gallons of kerosene onboard. ("Not to worry," we were told, "we will put them where they will not slide around.")

Soon, Laura was asleep with her head resting on my shoulder, lulled by the drone of engines. I sat thinking back over the events of the day and what Dr. François Chevalier had told us about Laura's illness. Certainly his remarks about the unlikeliness of cholera were reassuring—but still, she had been so sick, and I knew so little about the other illnesses he had said she might have. I would be more comfortable once Laura could be thoroughly checked out and tested. I was so glad we would be in Kisangani soon.

I sat, staring out the window at the dense clouds below, thinking about the rain-drenched land which they concealed. I found myself thinking about the night before, when I sat in the doorway of our hut and stared out at a dark world covered in rain.

Soon, my thoughts rejoined the stream of ideas that had carried me along then. My thoughts drifted through the problems that had persisted in human culture throughout recorded history, gathering in stray ideas about the things that so often go wrong in the world.

They continued to drift down that stream of ideas, as I considered each problem—then turned as I rowed back upriver, looking for the headwaters where those problems could have originated. More and more it seemed likely to me that all these problems had, in fact, flowed out from a common source—that they were, indeed, all by-products of the Change.

I must have been deep in thought, because it seemed as though we had just gotten aloft when I felt us starting to drift downward. As I looked out the window, it seemed as though the clouds were rising to meet us.

Soon, we were in their midst, and then down below them, and landing in a dense evening rain at the Bangoka International Airport in Kisangani.

⁕　⁕　⁕

It was almost six o'clock before we disembarked onto the asphalt runway outside the terminal building, and another hour before we could gather our possessions and hail a taxi to take us into town.

We checked into a room on the second floor of the rather decrepit *Hôtel des Chutes*. Laura immediately crawled into bed, while I did my best to order us some dinner from the French-language room-service menu.

Laura ate only part of her meal. I fixed her up some of the ORS François had given us. She drank some, then soon drifted off to sleep. She had only had to relieve herself half a dozen times since taking the medicine that morning, but I wasn't sure whether to be pleased at this as an early sign of recovery, or to worry that we had prevented her body from defending itself in the only way it knew how.

I took a quick shower, then climbed into bed beside Laura. I lay awake for a long time, listening to the rain blowing around outside and splattering against the window—and following each little rivulet, each little stream of my thoughts. If it was true that the Change had set the three impediments in motion, then it would make sense, I told myself, that many of the problems of the world would have developed from that same source.

But was that really how it had happened?

Carefully, I laid out for myself a list of what those problems were, and began to wade through them, carefully, meticulously—and as precisely as I could—tracing each back to its source.

I lay like this for an hour or more, slogging dutifully from one problem to the next, until finally drifting into a fitful sleep.

I woke a few hours later, when Laura rose to use the bathroom. Now, with a well-lit bathroom and indoor plumbing, she no longer needed my assistance, but I got up with her, nonetheless, and made sure she had plenty of the ORS mixture prepared, then I went to the armchair by the window, pulled the curtain back, and sat staring out at the falling rain, softly lit by streetlight.

I had been dreaming when Laura's movement woke me, and now the dream came back to me. It had been raining in the dream (just as it was, now, raining in real life) but this had been a thick, dark, impenetrable rain, and though I couldn't see it, I could feel and hear it falling.

In fact, I could see very little in the dream, but I knew somehow, all those individual drops, all those little splashes of water, were being blocked and stopped somewhere—somewhere up in the hills above me, beyond me—in a place from which I had, in some distance past, come.

Somewhere in those hills the rain was piling up behind a dam of some sort. The dream ended when the dam broke, and all the land was ravaged and torn by a savage flood.

I woke wondering—*how could each of those fine little drops have amounted to this?*

Somewhere, far off, lightning struck, and for a moment the wide Congo River (which lay, a hundred meters away, at the end of the road my window looked out on) was finely etched in brilliant light. Thunder rolled past like a heavy fog.

I got up and dug out my journal from my daypack, then returned to the armchair. Outside, streetlamps burned along the old colonial roadway. Down the road rushed a torrent of water, gathering all the falling rain and pouring it in one deluging stream down the hill towards the river below.

I opened my journal and quickly jotted down a rough description of my dream, but even as I wrote, I knew there was some meaning in it beyond what I was then uncovering.

"Coming back to bed?" I heard Laura ask. I glanced over as she climbed back in, pulling a sheet over her.

"Soon," I answered, thinking how beautiful she looked in the thin light drifting in from outside.

As Laura settled back to sleep, I turned my sight, again, towards the window—and as I did, my thoughts wound round my dream again. I was more aware of the feeling of the dream, now, than of its particulars. It seemed somehow—in mood, or in timbre—to be part of the other thoughts I had been having as I'd laid awake after first going to bed. It felt to me, somehow, to be more about the problems that pervade our world, than to actually be about the events in the dream itself—but still, I couldn't name exactly how.

I leaned forward and opened the window just enough to let in a little of the rain-scented air. The air, which blew in thin puffs through the narrow opening, felt cool, almost cold, against my bare skin. After so many days of muggy heat, it was a relief to even think of coolness.

After a time, I became aware of the steady tones of Laura's breath in sleep. I was glad she was sleeping well—so much better than the night before. I thought again that I should go back to bed, but there was some restlessness in me, and so I sat, instead, watching the rain fall in billowing sheets beneath the light posts, watching the rain flooding toward the river, watching a world shrouded in rain.

Slowly, then, I picked through the thoughts I had begun at bedtime. Again, one by one I probed through each of the major—the widespread, the continuing—problems of the world. War and poverty, crime and violence, prejudice and oppression, environmental destruction, overpopulation; so many such problems troubled our world.

One by one, I took them apart, trying to understand what propelled them. Step by step, I put them back together. Bit by bit, piece by piece—like a machine dismantled and reconstructed—I tore them down and rebuilt them, seeking to understand, to my own satisfaction, how each was constructed, and why each ran as it did.

I'm not sure how much time passed as I thought these thoughts, but eventually Laura woke again—needing again to use the bathroom—and found me sitting there, just as I had been when she'd fallen asleep before.

As she crawled back into bed this time, she said, "Come. Come to sleep, Indira. It's almost three o'clock." She pulled back the sheet from my side of the bed, then lay very still, looking at me.

She was right, I knew—it was silly to pursue this line of thought until I was exhausted.

Wearily, I pulled myself up from the chair and lay down beside her. Laura pulled me close, then, wrapping her arms around me. I felt a thrill at having her near, as I had felt such a thrill at her nearness now for more than eighteen years.

I picked up one of her hands and kissed it tenderly. Her fever was down a little, I noticed. Good. Good for Laura.

As Laura's breathing stretched out into the even cadence of sleep, I tried to slow the spinning of my thoughts.

Gradually, I caught the corner of sleep, and pulled it in around me.

I woke before Laura and spent some time in the big chair beside the window, thinking about the dream I'd had the night before and writing in my journal about it.

Outside, the day was bright and clear. The street, which had been so deluged with water the night before, was drying in the sun, under a blue sky strewn with small, tattered clouds.

How the world transforms itself! I thought, as I looked out at the scene before me. It seemed to me remarkable, just then, all the ways nature makes and remakes itself, in ways both ordinary and extraordinary—most of which we take for granted. And not just such changes as turns in the weather, like this one, but the whole arc between winter and summer, or the growth of a small seed into a vast tree. The more I thought about it, the more it seemed to me that in nature, nothing holds steady—storms come and go, seasons change, creatures are born, live, and die. Transformation is the norm in nature. Nature never holds still.

I sat a long time by the window, thinking about one thing and another.

When Laura woke, about mid morning, I suggested to her that we both have breakfast, and that I then go alone to see Frank Bohdan and ask him for advice about finding a doctor—and also about how to make arrangements for transportation to Epulu.

Laura said she was feeling better and no longer needed a doctor. I told her that I very much wanted her to see one. After worrying about her for days, I wanted her to at least get checked out.

I looked over at her, hoping she would give me her agreement—she was still pale, and the circles around her eyes still dark—but Laura was adamant. She argued first that François had said that she didn't have cholera, to which I answered that he had said it was not "likely."

To this she replied that the cholera had been on the barge, but that she didn't think she had become sick from any of the food on the barge—where all she had eaten had been thoroughly cooked—but rather from the raw grub she had eaten on the way to the research site.

"I don't think grubs carry cholera," I told her.

"No, I don't think so either," she said. "I don't think I've had cholera. Don't you remember, the night at the village built on stilts, the people eating palm grubs?"

"Yeah."

"I remember one of the children, a little girl, who squatted near us and kept smiling at me."

"Yeah, " I said. "I think she liked your red hair."

"Maybe," Laura answered. "But she was handling the grubs a lot and sometimes dropping them back in the bowl. One or two, I think she may even have put in her mouth before dropping them back in. It wasn't very sanitary."

"But you didn't eat any grubs that night," I said, shaking my head.

"But where do you think Isinga and Dibaya got the grubs they had with them the next day, when we stopped by the river?" Laura replied.

"Oh," I said, considering this. "You think they brought grub leftovers?"

Laura nodded, smiling a little. "Yes—and we don't have any reason to think there was cholera in that village—but I think that's where the germs that made me sick came from, whatever it's been.

"I don't know what I have, Indira, but I'm *so* much better. I only was up twice last night, and I haven't thrown up since the night before that. I think my fever's gone, too."

I went and sat by her then, with a dawning sense of relief coming over me. I put my hand on Laura's cheek and then her forehead. Cool. She was cool, no fever.

To my surprise, I could feel my eyes brimming with tears. I had been so worried the last few days, so hesitant to let my hopes rise when Laura so clearly needed my care, and now she was, clearly, as she had put it, doing *so* much better.

I looked down at Laura and smiled. Dear Laura—she had seemed special to me since that day, nearly twenty years earlier, when she had given me the book of Rumi's poetry on the train—and I had loved her, I think, since the night she had walked me home after the talk on Carl Jung. And I had loved her every day since. But there was something about nursing her while she'd been so sick that had made me know—in a way I had never had to contemplate before—how unbearable it would have been to have lost her from my life. She was, indeed, the shining light that lit my world.

Laura had waked genuinely hungry for the first time in days, so I encouraged her to look over the menu, written in French, which had been left in the room, and to pick out something she'd like to eat for breakfast. I needed her help, also, in picking out something for me. Laura was even up to calling in the order for room service, she said—though in the end, neither one of us was able to get someone on the other end to pick up the line.

Finally, I decided just to go down to the dining room myself and order our food there. I asked Laura how to say "room" in French and then, armed with the menu and a scrap of paper on which I'd written our room number, I set out for the hotel dining room.

As I left our room, I found myself thinking about our night in the huts in Basankusu, and how worried I had been about Laura then—and how I had, almost bitterly, blamed the Change for all the problems of the world.

Funny, I thought, that I had forgotten the conclusion I'd come to on the barge—that the Change was, just as much, the source of our most remarkable achievements. It wasn't so much the source of something bad, as the source of everything that human life had become—both good and bad, both desirable and undesirable. Our greatest achievements, as well as our greatest failures.

I paused along the half wall that bordered the walkway outside our room and looked down into the *Hôtel des Chutes*' inner courtyard, full of papaya and banana trees. The day *was* beautiful—just warm enough, with the air clear and bright.

I thought again about the street outside our window, so warm and sun-drenched after a night of torrential rain, and about Laura waking feeling so much better.

Yes, it *is* true, I told myself—life does transform itself!

I continued on along the walkway and started down the stairs, thinking about the transformation I had named "the Change"—about the time when we had all become so focused on the nature of our individual selves—and all that had followed. As I thought about this, I could feel another thought pushing forward from somewhere deep in my mind. Even before it took shape in my mind, I could feel there was something soothing about it—soothing and delicious, like ice cream on a sunny day.

The thought rose to the surface. Was it possible, I wondered, if we found the right key, that *we could transform ourselves again?*

I paused on the landing, then, looking out at the dense foliage of the courtyard plants. I imagined humanity gathering together around a new longing—another step past the one that had so ignited our sense of possibility, of promise, so many millennia ago.

If it was true that all the most major and persistent problems of the world had one originating source—might not an answer to all of those problems stem from one source, as well?

We had remade the world once—could we now, willful and self-determined as we had become, remake it again?

I reached the lobby and looked out at the dry, sun-kissed streets of Kisangani, and again remembered how they had been, soaked by torrential rains just hours before. One process of nature had turned the streets to rivers, and another process of nature was drying them out.

Transformation is natural, I told myself. It is the way nature works, and we are part of nature.

I stood lost in thought for a minute, then remembered my mission and went on into the dining room. One of the people on the staff spoke to me in French, I believe offering to seat me.

"*Non, merci,*" I replied, then pointed to the menu items that Laura and I wanted. I finished by saying "*chambre*" while showing the piece of paper on which I'd written our room number, then pointing up towards our room. The woman nodded and said something agreeable sounding in French. I was fairly certain I had succeeded in placing our order, so I thanked her and started walking back to our room.

On the way back up the stairs, I found myself remembering how, when I was in college, just after the end of the 1960's, people had often said that what was needed was "a change in consciousness."

Yes, I thought, that was what we needed—what we still needed: a new zeitgeist—a new "spirit of the age." The Change had been that. It had brought a new way of being into the world.

Could we really do that again? Could we remake the world again, and this time not leave seeds that would grow into all kinds of problems?

The idea was so delicious, so exciting, I had an impulse to dash back to the room and tell Laura all about it—but told myself I should wait, at least, until I had thought it all out more clearly. As it was, it still seemed rash, grounded more in conjecture, at this point, than clear analysis.

Yet still…the idea was so tantalizing.

I paused again by the inner courtyard, beside the half wall along the walkway outside our room, and stared out at the jungle of tropical-fruit trees. I kept thinking: *what an exciting idea!* If one change of consciousness had truly gotten us all here, perhaps it was plausible that another change of consciousness, as natural to us as the first, might move us beyond all these problems—and into something entirely new.

As much better as Laura was feeling, she still wanted to rest when she was done with her breakfast. I was glad to see her willing to take care of herself, rather than pushing to continue her adventure. (I knew it must be tempting for her, being, as she was, in a brand-new city, where she had never before been.)

As Laura rested, I set out alone to see Brother Frank Bohdan. I found him just down the road from our hotel, in the Procure of the mission—a massive red-brick edifice left over from colonial days. Rising up above the Procure, at its far end, was a small version of a European-style cathedral. It appeared to have been made of, or covered in, concrete, to emulate the gray stones of Europe, but was somehow much more elegant than that would suggest.

Lisa's note to us had said that Brother Frank spoke English, and I had assumed that meant as a second language, but as it turned out he was a transplant from Idaho and spoke with an easy American drawl. He had various relics from home around his office, including a cowboy hat, which hung from a hook by the door. He was comfortable to talk to, and soon I felt right at home with him.

I told him about our research and our need to get to Epulu, and that it was Lisa Xiang who had recommended we contact him. He clearly knew her name and seemed eager to help. He said the mission in Mambasa was expecting a new Land Rover to be delivered soon. They hoped it would be on the next barge heading upriver, but word had come in that the barge had gotten stuck on a sandbar just below Mbandaka and broken a propeller. They had managed to transport the propeller to Mbandaka by pirogue to get it repaired, he had heard, but apparently there were difficulties reinstalling it with the barge still stuck.

It was hard to say when the barge would arrive in Kisangani, he told me, but more importantly, he couldn't even be certain the Land Rover had been put on it in the first place. But it had been ordered, he assured me, and when it did arrive, he would be sending a driver with it up to Mambasa—and Laura and I would be welcome to ride along.

I told him then that I knew something about that barge, as Laura and I had been on it until it had become stuck almost a week earlier. I described to him the Land Rover we'd seen parked on the flat barge. It was gleaming white, I told him. He asked if it had a winch. I thought about it for a minute, then told him I thought it did have something mounted on the front, then described for him what I remembered seeing.

"Well, that should be our Land Rover, then," Brother Frank said, his tone brightening. He nodded and looked thoughtful.

"And with all this rain," he continued, "perhaps the river will have swollen enough to float the barge free." He thought about it for a moment. "The propeller shouldn't take long to attach, if that's the case, I would think. Well, it's just possible the barge will be in by the end of the week. As I said, you'll be welcome to ride as far as Epulu."

I told Brother Frank how much I appreciated his help, then, and gave him the name of our hotel and our room number. He told me he would contact us once he was notified that the barge, and the Land Rover, had arrived. Before leaving, I asked him if he could recommend a good doctor there in town (mostly, I think, because I had been planning this for so long and had not completely let go of my worries) and he gave me the name of the one used by the people at the mission.

As I said goodbye and stepped out into the brilliant sunlight outside the Procure, I felt a gathering sense of excitement, for I could see now that the way was clear for the last leg of our journey—to Epulu and into the Ituri Forest, homeland of the Mbuti Pygmies.

During the days that followed, Laura spent most of her time dozing and reading, while I found myself swept up in thoughts of just how we, as a species, had arrived at our present circumstances—a condition so ripe with all of our successes, and all of our failures. I found myself contemplating, in more and more detail, just how each of the characteristics that we assumed to be essential qualities of human nature had come to be developed.

Where I saw problems, I found myself examining them, following in each a branching stream, which led, time and again, back to the "Original Change" (as I had now begun to think of it), then following these same branches of the stream as they flowed out into the future, where I would imagine how each of those problems might be transformed by a "New Change"—a sense of new possibility, which was, then, taking clearer and clearer form in my mind.

When Laura was well enough to be up and about, we spent a little time each day sightseeing. We went first to see the "Wagenia nets"—which were elaborate structures built across the Congo River along the rapids at Boyoma Falls, just outside of Kisangani. These "nets" were actually giant funnel-shaped fish-traps attached to a sort of scaffolding built by the Wagenia people.

We also spent some time exploring the old colonial city itself, full of its dingy whitewashed walls, red-tile roofs, and broad avenues. We were taken with the local market along the north edge of town, full of the noise and commotion of crowds and bartering, and of endless stalls in which an impressive array of goods could be bought.

In a city which could be, apparently, so difficult for people to arrive at, we were surprised at the diversity of restaurants in town. We were served fish and chips in one restaurant and Greek cuisine at another, as well as more local fare. For dessert one day we stopped at a patisserie where we were served Belgian-style pastries and sweetened yogurt.

But as much as we enjoyed these short excursions in and around Kisangani, we returned to our hotel after each of them with the hope that we would find waiting for us there the message that Brother Frank had told us to expect.

Finally, on the afternoon of our third day of sightseeing, we returned to our hotel, where we found a note waiting for us, telling us that Brother Frank had sent word that the barge was in and that the Land Rover would be ready to leave the next day. It had been nearly a week since I had gone to see Brother Frank at the mission. We set aside the rest of our plans for that day and stopped by the Procure to see him, so we could let him know we had received his message, and also to nail down some final details of the trip.

By the time our alarm rang early the next morning, all the streams of ideas running one way and another through my thoughts had knitted together into one strong, pulsing waterway. Collectively, it seemed, they revealed a clear map of where we had come from, and where we might go.

It seemed to me that our world, produced by one Change, could indeed be changed—yes, *transformed*—again.

In fact, it seemed to me that it was as natural for us, having first gone through the Original Change, to move on to another, newer change, as it was natural for a child, having first gone through adolescence, to move on to adulthood.

As I saw it, the New Change was, after all, simply the natural next step in a journey we had all set out on together a long time ago.

✴   ✴   ✴

"Pause," Paul said, as Kiki's voice fell silent.

"Pausing," Kiki answered. "End of chapter."

All morning, Paul's path had climbed slowly uphill, and many times along the way Paul had had to cross the stream that the path followed up the mountainside. As Paul had walked along, the landscape around him had gradually changed, with more oaks and pines, and less brushland.

Paul found a comfortable spot, now, on the stream's bank, where he could wash up a bit, then sit and soak his feet in the water. It felt good—though the relief of it was hardly needed. The combination of the Dermo Mend and the System Boost had kept his feet, and the rest of him, feeling well.

Paul dug through his pack for a travel meal—one of the spicy ones of the no-heat variety—and sat thinking about Dr. Kumar's memoir, as he ate it. Everything he had learned pointed to this book being the key to why this world was so different from his own, but Paul still had trouble imagining quite how it had brought these changes into being. Had introducing these ideas alone been enough to make the difference?

Oh well, Paul thought. He wasn't likely to figure this out without listening to more of the book—and failing that, he would probably be able to find out more when he reached the Retreat.

The Kumaric Retreat—how far away was it, now? Paul wondered. The woman he had met on the trail the day before had said he would probably get there by this afternoon.

Paul sighed. It hardly seemed likely that he could finish Dr. Kumar's memoirs by then. It certainly didn't seem like they were anywhere close to being over.

"Kiki, what percent of the book, *Memories and Reflections*, have you recited to me now?" he said aloud.

"Approximately 63.4418%," Kiki answered, after a brief pause.

Paul shook his head and felt, suddenly, a bit deflated. There was no way he could finish Dr. Kumar's book by the time he arrived.

He had failed to complete that goal—and how far had he really gotten in preparing to build a transport, for that matter? He had made a list of possible parts—which he hadn't been able to look at since he left the Inn in Strandford five days ago. He hadn't yet figured out how to afford those parts, which might, or might not, turn out to be usable. He had made no headway at all on finding an energy source. And even if all of those things could be made to work out, he was still dependent on Interdimensional-Linking Theory proving to be correct. If it turned out not to be, who knew where he could end up!

So many uncertainties, Paul thought. Couldn't he at least have completed Dr. Kumar's memoirs before he arrived at the Retreat? Paul felt as though he was not only climbing uphill on his trek toward the Retreat, but was climbing uphill in his life, as well.

Paul took another bite of his travel meal, then lay down in the shade. He closed his eyes and let his thoughts drift, listening to the hush of the stream beside the trail.

The dream he had had while stuck on the ledge two nights before had left a sort of residue, a mood that persisted just beneath the surface, and which came and went within the frame of his awareness. Now that mood, that feeling, came back over him again—a sort of scared, lonely feeling, tinged with—what? Sadness? Regret? Remorse?

Paul opened his eyes, uncertain of whether to run from this feeling or examine it. He had tried often enough in the last days to escape it, push it aside, but it kept coming back to him.

Why this feeling? Paul asked himself. Why had the dream made him feel like this—and why was the feeling lasting so long?

Impressions of the dream came back to him. He saw the apartment as he searched through it, saw his mother retreating ahead of him—angry, avoiding him, wanting to stay away.

Why? Paul asked himself, but as he opened his thoughts to search for an answer, instead an impression of Sheila unfolded into his awareness. As that impression came forward in his mind, Paul suddenly found himself missing her very intensely. Sheila, he thought—oh, Sheila—how I want to come home to you!

He felt terrible, in that moment, for abandoning her, for disappearing without a word. He had so meant to be there for her—absolutely and resolutely, without error. And instead he had disappeared without so much as a "goodbye." How could he have so let her down?

In thinking this, a new determination welled up in Paul—a determination to move forward and solve the problems involved in building and operating a new transport, and so to return to her—to bring home the news of what he had accomplished, and in so doing to help repair her world—to right the wrong that had been done to it, and restore its balance—for *her*, for Sheila, so that she could live in it without having any of that wrongness inflicted on her.

Paul fantasized about offering Sheila this gift of a world made well (more well than, in truth, it could ever again be). He pictured it like a blue-green gem he could hang around her neck.

Paul imagined Sheila putting her arms around him, then, and pulling him close to her with a tenderness she had, in fact, never previously shown.

If he could give her this gift, this repaired world, Paul felt, all would be made right and complete.

With his determination renewed, Paul sat up and stowed the wrapper from the travel meal in his pack. He drank his fill of water from the stream, put his socks and shoes back on his feet—then stood, lifted the weight of his pack onto his shoulders, and continued on up the Sojourner's Path.

"Kiki," he said, "the break's over. Please resume recitation."

With that, Kiki again modulated her voice to replicate Dr. Kumar's, and continued with recitation.

◙　◙　◙

CHAPTER XIV

*An acorn falls
in still water. Countless
ripple circles spread.*

—Mizuki Inoue

*It is today that we must create
the world of the future.*

—Eleanor Roosevelt

As Laura and I finished packing a few things and arranged a taxi to take us and our belongings the few blocks to the mission, I found myself thinking about our meeting with Brother Frank the day before. Things had not gone as expected. The driver Brother Frank had arranged had broken his leg in an accident the afternoon before, and so couldn't make the drive.

At first Brother Frank had asked us if we would wait a few days while the mission in Mambasa sent one of their drivers down to pick up the Land Rover, but Laura had pointed out that she could do the driving herself, at least as far as Epulu, where the driver from Mambasa could be sent to meet us. It would save time and effort for everyone, she'd said. It was the practical thing to do.

Brother Frank was polite about it, but clearly doubted she had sufficient experience to handle what he described as a deeply rutted, muddy, tropical road. He said there'd been road work going on for months, starting in Kisangani and working its way towards Epulu, but he wasn't sure how far it had gotten—at least as far as Bafwasende, he knew, but he wasn't sure how much past that.

Road work was a rare thing, Brother Frank told us, as the government seemed to see bad roads as a kind of insurance. "You can't overthrow a country's government if you can't get to its capital," he pointed out. But still, as the commerce along those routes provided funds that fed the government, from time to time some road maintenance did take place.

Brother Frank told us then that past whatever point the repair crew had gotten to in its work, the road would be hard driving. At its worst, there could be whole stretches with deep mud—thick stuff we could easily get stuck in. In other places, he said, heavy trucks used for transporting goods had displaced so much mud as to carve narrow canyons as deep as the trucks were tall, and just wide enough for the trucks to pass through. He said the mud was especially bad at the bottom of these narrow "canyons," as water tended to gather there. Even the most experienced drivers often got stuck.

As daunting as this all sounded to me (for I certainly had no wish to attempt the drive myself—I hadn't even learned to drive until after Laura and I had moved to Boulder, and even then did relatively little of it), to Laura it sounded like a grand challenge. She encouraged Brother Frank to reconsider. She told him that her aunt and uncle had a small farm near Winchester, in Hampshire, where she had spent a good deal of time while growing up. During the autumn rains, Laura told Brother Frank, the old roads through the property could become a real mess, but she knew how to make her way through them without getting stuck in the soggy mud.

Beyond that, Laura pointed out, if we got stuck on our way to Epulu, the driver from Mambasa (and whoever had come along to drop him off) would just have to continue on past Epulu until they found us. Then they could help pull us loose, and we could continue on. The odds were that we would still have saved everybody some time, Laura said.

Brother Frank finally shrugged and agreed. After all, it's hard to win an argument with Laura. She is always perfectly polite, and relentless, and though not always entirely right, she is never far wrong. In the end, Brother Frank sighed, said something to the effect of "at least there's been very little rain the last several days," and agreed to let us take the Land Rover as far as Epulu.

After I went to bed that night, I lay awake for some time, wondering what sort of difficulties we would be greeted with after leaving Kisangani the next day. Finally, I drifted off to sleep, imagining endless tracks of dark, thick mud; and tall, rutted canyons carved from the red clay road, with water passing through them.

The taxi ride from the *Hôtel des Chutes* to the mission was very short, and the Land Rover—gleaming white and brand new—was parked right out in front. We unloaded our gear next to the Land Rover, and I waited with it while Laura went to find Brother Frank.

Along the road outside the Procure, artists were setting out paintings to sell to the passersby. It was another beautiful day, and it occurred to me that I felt just a little sad to be leaving Kisangani, which I had only just begun to get to know.

Before long, Laura was back with Brother Frank. Brother Frank looked as though he had stepped right out of the American West, with his cowboy hat and loose, lanky walk. He took a little time to go over some information we would need to have (who we were to meet, and when, and where) as well as information about the vehicle's gearing, its four-wheel drive, how to use the winch in case we got stuck, and how many kilometers it was to Epulu. He also gave us the name of the man in charge at Epulu Station, and told us that if for some reason no one from Mambasa was there to meet us, we could leave the Land Rover in his care.

Brother Frank wished us good luck with our trip and other endeavors in the Ituri, asked us to tell Lisa Xiang he said "hello," then handed us the key to the Land Rover. We expressed our appreciation for all his help, and soon we were loaded up and on our way.

We had managed to get an early start, and the sun was still low in the sky as we drove eastward on our way out of Kisangani. Soon the buildings disappeared and were replaced by an open landscape from which the forest had been cleared. All along the road, crops had been planted. Fields of corn, manioc, and papaya alternated with the huts of the people who had planted them. The road itself, though narrow, was smooth and even, and I felt hopeful that it would turn out to be an easy trip, after all.

The speedometer on the Land Rover showed a steady fifty kph, which was pretty good time for us to be making on a dirt road. Brother Frank had said the drive itself should be a little over four hundred and fifty kilometers. At this rate, I thought, we might be there by evening. I could only hope the good road held, and we wouldn't encounter any of the horrendous "canyons" Brother Frank had described.

The Land Rover had a radio on which I was able to pick up a station out of Kisangani, and we rolled along in the bright sunlight, listening to Zairian dance music and saying little. My thoughts had returned to the stream of ideas I had been exploring for the previous week, and I cast those thoughts adrift in the air around me, where they wove together with the rhythmic strains of trumpet and electric guitar.

Now and then, we passed a truck on the road, carrying goods to Kisangani. I tried not to pay too close attention to their mud-caked tires, or to their tarp-covered loads, with dried mud streaked along their sides.

After a time, the radio station I had tuned in began to grow staticky, and the patches of horticultural land disappeared as the shadows of the mighty forest rose around us. Trees arched above us, making a great tunnel of dappled green and red, through which we perpetually drove. It was soothing to pass through it—aside from the rumble of the dirt road which, though recently repaired, still set the whole vehicle humming.

Outside of Bafwasende, we stopped and hurried through a simple lunch of bread we'd bought at the patisserie, peanut butter, and bananas, and soon were on our way again. Brother Frank had told us that if we were lucky, we could expect to spend at least one night on the road (and perhaps a good many more) but considering the sort of time we'd been making so far, I thought him oddly pessimistic.

The road continued on, like a tunnel passing through an ocean of green. Occasionally, we would pass people selling animals hunted from the forest. The cadavers of porcupines, monkeys, and duikers hung by their hind feet in the shadows along the side of the road.

Other areas, as well, showed the impact of human activities. Villages and planted fields came and went. Other areas showed the ravages of clear-cut logging. I felt a desire to get away from the road, to go deep into the forest, where the wilderness was still pristine.

Perhaps an hour after we'd stopped for lunch we passed some equipment broken down by the side of the road. To my dismay, I realized it was the road-repair crew with their bulldozer and leveler. The hood over the engine of the bulldozer was open. The leveler was parked nearby. The crew was scattered around, sitting casually in the shade.

I wondered what the problem was, and if they were awaiting parts they needed for a repair. Certainly the scene showed little activity, as they sat by their silent, hulking machines.

Soon we were past, and the road turned rugged and rutted. The bottom of the Land Rover began to drag against the ridge between the ruts. Laura backed the Land Rover up, then threw the engine into low gear and forced the vehicle up onto the ridge, so we were driving with the two right wheels along the side of the road and the two left wheels running along the center ridge.

"It's those darn trucks," Laura said. "They've cut the ruts too deep for us."

The Land Rover tilted slightly as we rolled along, but Laura seemed to be managing.

We made slower time after that, although Laura's ridge-driving kept us out of the muddy area at the bottom of the ruts, so at least we didn't get stuck. In places, the center ridge gave way under the weight of the Land Rover, and we skidded about some in the mud, but Laura proved true to her promise to be up to driving in the mud, and we continued on.

Even with all the evidence of past traffic on the road, we felt alone in the forest, as we went quite some time without seeing another vehicle.

By the middle of the afternoon, we discovered why the traffic on the road had been so light. As we came over a low rise we could see a line of ten or twelve trucks parked in the middle of the roadway, with about half heading in one direction and half in the other.

We ground to a halt behind a big tarp-covered vehicle.

We just sat there for a minute, then Laura put the Land Rover into park and turned off the engine.

"What do you suppose the problem is?" I asked.

"Don't know. Let's go have a look," she answered.

We both climbed out of the Land Rover and started forward along the right shoulder of the road.

As we walked along, I asked Laura if she'd noticed what the odometer said.

She shook her head. "Not for a little while," she answered, "but I think we've come about two-thirds of the way, maybe a little more."

We passed another truck, this one with a green body and a brown tarp over its load. Its crew of barefooted, muddy-looking men stood around talking and smoking cigarettes, while the driver, dressed all in white, sat in the cab.

One of the muddy-looking fellows approached us. He spoke to Laura in French, then showed us his foot. He had a long, shallow gash along the top of it, apparently left by a shovel. It looked a little infected.

Laura and I went back to the Land Rover and dug out our first-aid kit, then helped him by cleaning and bandaging the wound, with a good layer of antibiotic ointment included. I hoped it would help, but couldn't imagine how he would keep it clean with the sort of work he was expected to do along the road, getting down in the mud and digging out the heavy truck whenever it got stuck.

When we were done with the man's foot, we put the first-aid kit back, then started up the road again. Laura wanted to see if the shoulder was wide enough to drive along, and so allow us to bypass this traffic jam.

After passing several trucks sitting idle in the road, we made it up to where the problem was. Apparently, the roadway had been dug out by the passing of successive vehicles, leaving a long, narrow channel—the sort of "canyon" Brother Frank had spoken about. A truck had gotten stuck at the bottom of it—a depression so deep that the top of the vehicle barely protruded above its walls, even though the truck itself (stacked high with goods as it was) was at least three, possibly four, meters in height.

Laura and I peered down into the hole. It was dim down there compared to the glare of the hot sun, but in a moment our eyes adjusted. Workers were busy around the front of the truck, where the bumper had dug into the ridge between ruts. The front tires seemed to have sunk into the muddy ruts, lowering the whole vehicle too much to pass. The workers were digging around the front end—and in the process, making the hole even deeper.

Laura and I stepped back from the edge.

"That will take some time," Laura said.

I looked back at the long line of vehicles, then forward at more heading the other way. Trucks coming from both directions were waiting to pass through that single hole. I wondered how many of them would get stuck, also.

I could see that Laura had followed my gaze. "We'll never make it by on the shoulder. It's just too narrow," she said, squinting in the bright light. "Come on, let's get out of the sun."

Together, we went and sat in the shade alongside of the road. In the forest's shadow, insects hummed. One of the workers from the road crew for the stuck truck climbed out of the hole carrying a bucket of mud and dumped it on the ground.

After a while, I found myself thinking about the dream I'd had several nights earlier in Kisangani, in which the rain had fallen and gathered behind a dam of some sort, then rushed out of the surrounding hills through the darkness as a flood. It had been one of the those sorts of dreams that are as much about the feeling of the dream as the events, and that leave an emotional residue that stays with you long after.

Laura looked over at me. "You've been awfully quiet, lately," she said.

I told her I was just remembering a dream I'd had about a week before, in which a hard rain had fallen behind a dam high up in the surrounding hills, and how the dam had broken, and a flood had ravaged everything.

"The dream had a strong feeling," I said. "I've been thinking about that, off and on, trying to put things together, figure out what the feeling was about."

"Yeah? Have you figured it out?" Laura asked.

"Well, I think it has something to do with something I'd been thinking about before I had the dream. Do you remember what I told you about the last night we were at Raymond's camp? At the fire? About how, maybe, there was this point in our past when we'd become caught up in the whole idea of individuality, in discovering our individual selfhoods, and that it had brought a lot of changes?"

"Yeah," Laura answered. "It's what you were working on, on the barge."

"Yeah, but more about what I thought about after that—about the changes that resulted," I said. "Well, since then, I've been thinking more about some of those changes."

I thought about this for a moment, then went on, piecing the ideas together. "Years and years ago, I think it was during the time you were in Lame Deer," I told her, "I had this idea about what goes wrong in human nature, when people do terrible things—or even just when things go wrong on a more ordinary scale, because I think it's all the same thing. I called it the 'three impediments.' I doubt you'll remember."

"Well, maybe I do," Laura said, scrunching her face a little.

"Well, they all had to do with why things can sometimes go so wrong, when human nature is really basically very good. They had to do with how things go wrong when people believe there's something essentially bad or worthless about themselves or someone else; or how things go wrong when communication breaks down, either communication between people, or just inside of one person; or how problems develop when someone has a perspective where they don't take in someone else's point of view—when that happens, people will sometimes do cruel things without really realizing how cruel they are."

"Ah-huh," Laura said, nodding.

"Anyway, before I had the dream, I'd been remembering about that. I was thinking about how the three impediments—and other problems, too—grew out of our having become so focused on our own individual identities. I was thinking about how all that grew out of that original, early change—or out of 'the Change,' as I've been calling it.

"After all, it's easy to see how that shift to focusing so strongly on our own individual identities could have generated the three impediments." I pushed down on first one finger and then another, as I listed my examples. "It did make our perspectives really individual, really insular. It did made us start breaking up how we perceived the world into "good" and "bad" and made us start to define ourselves and one another in those terms. And it did separate us out, isolate us, and create a kind of distance, a kind of insularity that would have affected communication, as well." I took a breath. "But the dream, well..."

I thought about this for a minute, while Laura listened patiently. "The dream was, it was like there were all these impulses to give life to something. That was the feeling in the dream, and I think that's what all the drops were: little bits of protolife falling like rain. They fell, and they kept coming down, but there was something blocking them. It felt like—it felt like—well, like if you felt something strongly but you couldn't really act on it. So it welled up inside you.

"Like if you saw a puppy about to get run over by a car, and you wanted to rush out and help, but you couldn't act on that impulse, couldn't rescue it. Or if somebody was doing something mean and you just wanted to tell them to cut it out, but you couldn't, you couldn't tell them, and so they just kept doing it—and so you just begin to want to shout, or to knock them down or something. You know how feelings pile up? They can pile up. Like all those drops behind the dam. Sometimes if you just keep not saying something and not saying something—something you really want to say—it will all pile up and then come out all at once. Sometimes people will just snap. They'll yell when they could have spoken softly. Like that—the dam breaks, and it all comes flooding down, and wrecks everything."

"Yeah, I know that feeling, when stuff piles up," Laura answered.

I nodded. "Right, and even though things can get pretty wrecked when that dam breaks, it's not like there's anything wrong with water, itself, in its basic nature—*even when it floods.* Water is still just water. And it's not that there's anything wrong with the basic impulses which pile up inside us, either. We're as innocent as water. But when you let things pile up, they sometimes come crashing out."

Laura nodded, listening. Several meters away, in the bright sun, another man climbed out of the hole carrying a bucket and dumped the thick mud onto the ground.

"Anyway," I said, "I think that's what the dream was about—that kind of situation where everything piles up and then breaks loose—and I think I dreamed it because I'd been thinking so hard about what the Change had done, what changes it had brought. And I've been thinking about it since. Once we stopped being so impulsive, once we began to question every impulse and to make decisions more deliberatively, a lot more impulses would have been pushed aside, left to pile up. We would have started having a lot more of those outbreaks, it seems to me—and they might have been ugly—could have caused problems. They still do cause problems.

"And I've been thinking, well," I said, using a twig to poke at the red, clay-like soil near my feet, "we would have looked at that and said, 'now, that's a bad thing'—not a good thing. We'd have thought—'now, that's a thing to be avoided.' We'd see that these unpleasant floods would rush forth from somewhere inside, and crash all over everywhere. Maybe someone would yell, or hit someone, say—because they'd pushed aside impulses and then lost control when everything built up too much. So people would have begun to think, 'there's something bad inside us, something we really should suppress, really should keep in check.' Like that. And so they'd suppress things all the more, and so what they'd suppressed would break loose even worse the next time, with an even bigger flood, and so they'd just suppress things more, and believe more in the badness within them.

"And of course, the more people began to really suppress their impulses and their feelings, the more out of touch they became—and the less able they were to communicate with themselves or others about what was really going on with them.

"So there's another impediment cropping up. They were, by this point, believing in a bad nature, and communication was failing more.

"And I think the cycle just kept getting worse, because the more out of touch we became with what was going on inside ourselves and one another, the more insular our perspectives were—and the more mistakes we made as a result of having such insular perspectives, or of failing to communicate. And when we looked at those mistakes—and the people who got hurt as a result—we just believed all the more that there was something bad about us, something bad in our nature.

"In other words, once all these problems had developed, they just kept on compounding one another."

I finished, and looked over at Laura. On her face was a look of both mirth and seriousness.

"Wow," she said.

"Yeah?" I said.

"That's pretty amazing."

"Why are you smiling?" I asked.

"I'm not smiling," Laura said.

"You are, kind of," I said.

Laura cocked her head. "Well, you're just so amazing. I get such a kick out of you, Indira," she said. "So, is that it? Are we doomed? Does it just keep getting worse and worse?"

"No. No, not at all," I answered. "Actually, I think it's quite possible to reverse it all."

I looked up and across the little clearing that separated us from the road. One of the men from the green truck, whose foot we'd patched up earlier, was walking towards us with a couple of orange bottles in his hands.

When he reached us, he smiled a beautiful smile and extended the bottles towards us. Again, he spoke in French, and Laura answered him.

Laura turned to me. "You want an orange soda?" she asked.

I glanced at the bottles—each made of clear glass with a bright-orange liquid inside—then back at Laura.

"Yeah," I said, nodding.

Laura spoke to the man again, then he took a bottle opener from his pocket and pulled off the caps of the two bottles. He handed the bottles to Laura, who thanked him brightly in French.

I nodded and smiled, too, echoing her *"merci."* The man again smiled a broad smile, then turned and walked back to his truck.

"Apparently, this is what their truck is full of," Laura said, handing me one of the bottles. "He thought we might be thirsty."

"That was nice of him," I said.

"Yeah, it was," Laura answered. "We fixed his foot. I imagine he wanted to do something nice in return." Laura took a swallow of her soda, then set the bottle down in a puddle of light, so the sunlight cut through the orange liquid. Around us, insects continued their warm buzz.

"So," Laura said, with enthusiasm in her voice, "you were about to tell me how you reverse, ah—what did you call them? The three..."

"The three impediments," I said.

"Yeah," Laura said, staring intently across at the top of the truck sticking out of the mud hole.

"Well, it's not so much that you reverse them," I said, "as that, well—I think the Original Change was part of a larger process—just one step in a larger progression. There will be other..."

"I'm sorry. Excuse me," Laura interrupted. "I just had an idea. Do you want to come with me? I want to go have a look." She looked towards the road, then back at me.

Together we got up and, carrying our bottles of soda, walked back over to the road where the tarp-covered top of the truck stuck up out of the 'canyon' in the road, then stepped around in front of it, where the road leveled again.

When we got to the other side of the road, Laura stopped and looked around.

"I don't know why I assumed that if the shoulder was too narrow on the right side of the road, it would be just as narrow on the left," she said.

We walked the rest of the way forward along the line of parked vehicles, then all the way back to the Land Rover on the left side of the road. On balance, the left shoulder was just a bit wider than the right, though there were some snug spots here and there.

When we got back to the Land Rover, Laura said, "Well, you want to have a go of it?"

"Let's try," I said.

So Laura and I climbed in, and Laura started up the engine. We crept carefully out of line and along the left side of the road. As we passed, others whose trucks were parked on the road turned to watch our progress or stepped aside to make way for us.

We made it past the first six or seven vehicles without too much trouble, but were stopped where some thick vines grew across our path. There was no room to squeeze around them, and they looked too strong to just force our way through without risking damage to the front of the Land Rover.

Laura backed up a few feet, then we both got out to examine the situation. Together, we tried to pull the heavy vine aside to make room to pass, but it was rooted at one spot and anchored to a nearby tree at another. We couldn't move it out of our path.

A small group had gathered to watch our efforts, all the while murmuring comments. When we were done trying, a young man stepped out of the crowd with a machete and began hacking at the vine for us. It took him a couple of minutes to hack through it, but in the end he did a neat job of it.

I would say the small crowd took nearly as much pleasure in this as Laura and I did, for there was little else for entertainment as they waited in the hot sun.

Laura and I gave the man our enthusiastic thanks, then climbed back into the Land Rover and crept along the rest of the way until we reached the open road beyond the mid-forest traffic jam.

As we headed away from the "canyon," I realized we'd been in a particularly low-lying area, and that that probably had something to do with why the road had become so bad there, where the water gathered. Soon we were on a piece of road a little higher than the rest, where the mud and rutting weren't so bad.

"We should start looking for a place to sleep, I think," I told Laura. "It's taken us eight hours to go this far, and most of the road was in much better shape than this."

"It's only four o'clock. We could go a bit further, don't you think?"

"A bit. But we'll have no sun after six—earlier, really, because the trees will block the light before sunset," I answered.

"Okay, we'll drive on a bit further and keep an eye out for a nice spot," Laura said. Then, in a moment, she added. "You were going to tell me how to fix everything."

"Fix everything?" I said. "Oh, you mean the three impediments."

"Right."

"O-kay," I said. I tried to gather my thoughts. Laura glanced over at me a couple of times, but didn't say anything.

"Well, there are all these problems that just keep appearing and reappearing throughout human history," I began finally. "They may take different forms, but they're really the same problem. They come up in all sorts of different cultures, in all sorts of different time periods. They're things like war, violence in general, prejudice—sexism, racism, homophobia, whatever form—abuse of the environment. Lots of different sorts of problems that just reoccur.

"People have a tendency to sort of shrug and say 'well, that's human nature'—but I don't think it is just human nature. I don't think we have to have these sorts of problems."

"No?" Laura said, glancing over with part of a grin.

"No—it's more like it's human nature *at the stage we are at*. It's like, if you think about it, when you're a young child, you identify deeply with your parents, with your family of origin. You have a deep sense of belonging with that group, with that 'source,' which you came from. Like we were talking about at the fire at Raymond's research site, I think humanity started out with this feeling of oneness, and we start out our individual lives that way, too.

"So, then you get a little older—you reach your teen years—and you push away from that with which you have so deeply identified. You want to strike out on your own, to make your own decisions, to become your own person, form your own identity—to know and define yourself.

"Well, that's sort of the stage we're at, as a species. We've been very caught up in our self-identities and in striking out on our own. But there's another step that comes after—and if I'm right about this, then it's a natural, almost inevitable step."

"And that's...," Laura prompted.

"That's, well, it's like when you really grow up, and you can turn around and realize that it's okay to identify with your parents—you won't lose your own identity if you do. You won't lose your independence. It's okay to feel a sense of connection with them, and to appreciate what they know or have to offer—you won't lose everything that you've gained in going off on your own. You'll still be your own person.

"It's sort of an inevitable step," I added. "People do it with their parents, their families, when they become confident of themselves.

"I think we lost our sense of our own place within nature, of our own connection with nature and with the rest of life," I continued, "when we pushed that sense of interconnectedness aside in order to define our individual selves. I think we know ourselves as individuals well enough now that we can turn our attention back to that larger, deeper sense of interconnectedness without losing what we've gained in striking out on our own.

"We can have both now. That's what I've been thinking. We can reach our true adulthood."

Laura took her eyes off the uneven road long enough to glance over at me. "That's fascinating."

"In fact, I think we've already begun," I added.

"Hm," Laura said, her brow furrowed the way it did when she thought hard about something. "So how does this reverse the three impediments?" she asked finally. I could see she was enjoying having something to think about.

"Well, if you think of the Original Change—that's how I've started thinking of it—if you think of the Original Change as a time when we started focusing on a narrowed down, specific, individual sense of self, then the Next Change, or the New Change, is about expanding that sense of self to include more—not so it gets diluted, but expanded—more gets added to it. Like if you have a family, you identify with each of them—you have an expanded sense of identity, which includes more. Only now, that expansion has to go far beyond that.

"To really undo the three impediments, we would need to identify with all living things—with all life, with everything there is—to regain that deep sense of oneness I think we had before, but to keep our sense of individual identity in the process.

"If we did that, our insular perspective would be replaced with an expansive, inclusive perspective. So, that's one impediment reversed," I said.

"And of course, part of that move away from an insular perspective would involve a deeper willingness to relate to others and to ourselves. Right?" I said. "I mean, that just follows."

Laura looked thoughtful, nodded. "Right. Yeah," she said.

"Then in turn, that willingness to relate more deeply with ourselves and others would naturally inspire more and deeper communication," I went on. "Right? So, that's two impediments down."

"Okay," Laura said.

"And as we identified more and communicated more, we would see more clearly what we were really motivated by and what motivated others. We would see that we all try to achieve what seems 'desirable' or 'good' from our own perspectives.

"People would therefore stop seeing themselves or other people as having an essentially bad nature," I said. "Also, in identifying with, and communicating with, and understanding the motives of others, we would have a window onto who they were—and would naturally see their worth. So that's the last impediment—believing in a bad or worthless nature. That's all three impediments."

"Wow," Laura said. "Very interesting argument." She was nodding thoughtfully, her eyes on the road.

"Of course, people would still make mistakes," I added, "but with the three impediments out of the way, when there were problems, we would look into the mechanics of what went wrong—we would see from other people's points-of-view, communicate more clearly, value one another— and so, just in general, we would be able to solve problems much more quickly and effectively.

"To tell you the truth Laura, if what I've been thinking is correct, then all of those persistent, perennial problems I spoke about before—war, bigotry, and all that—they all grew out of the Original Change, and they would all be solved by the New Change."

"That's fascinating," Laura said, then was silent for several minutes as she considered what I'd told her.

After a few minutes, I spoke again.

"There's a poem by Rumi," I said, "that reminds me of that sense of broad identification, that sense of being connected to, being part of, everything—that state of mind I think of as part of the New Change," I glanced over at Laura and then back at the road. "I've been thinking about this, and I remembered that poem. I've been thinking about it, lately. It's the one that begins 'I am dust particles in sunlight.' Do you remember it?"

"I think, yeah—but I can't think of the words," Laura said.

"'I am the round sun....,'" I recited. I carefully visualized the poem as it was printed in one of my books of Rumi's poetry, back in Boulder, then went on:

> I am morning mist,
> and the breathing of evening.
>
> I am wind in the top of a grove,
> and surf on the cliff.
>
> Mast, rudder, helmsman, and keel,
> I am also the coral reef they founder on....

I paused, and Laura prompted me. "Both candle..."
"...and the moth crazy around it," I went on,

> Rose, and the nightingale
> lost in the fragrance.
>
> I am all orders of being, the circling galaxy,
> the evolutionary intelligence, the lift,
>
> and the falling away.

I paused again. "There's more, but that's the part that really resonates with me."

I looked over at Laura. Her face looked the same in profile as it had years before, and I thought of her as the young woman she had been when we had first met on the way to Oxford, and she had tried to make me feel welcome and at home.

"Thanks for giving me that first Rumi book all those years ago," I said to her softly.

She glanced over at me. "What? On the train?"

"Yeah."

Laura glanced over at me again, smiling. "You seemed so sweet, and you were so far from home. I wanted to do something nice for you."

I sat staring at her as she carefully watched the road ahead. It was only a little over a week since that night outside of Basankusu, when I had felt so afraid of the illness that had taken hold of her.

"I'm so glad you came into my life, Laura," I told her. "Even after almost twenty years, I'm still so thrilled that you are part of my life. Everyday."

Laura glanced over at me with a tender look, then reached for my hand. "I feel lucky every day you're with me, too, Indira," she said.

We held hands another hundred meters, then she let go to grasp the wheel as we hit another stretch of particularly rugged road.

The sun had dropped behind the forest's crown, and the world was cast in the long twilight of the forest, by the time we picked a spot to pull over and put up our tent for the night. It was an area that had apparently been used before, as the brush had been cleared back a short distance from the road.

We soon had our tent up and our camp stove working. Laura dug the cook pans out of her pack, and together we chose one of the freeze-dried dinners that I had stowed in mine. It was quick business to get it prepared.

When it was done, we sat together on a nearby log, surrounded by the scents of damp wood and green growth. I thought it strange, now that I was here, that I had ever expected the forest to be quiet. With the sun low behind the trees, and the evening dim gathering around us, the night music of the forest had begun to rise. Invisibly, in the shadows, all sorts of small creatures sang.

As we sat together over our dinner, Laura seemed lost in thought.

Finally, she said, "So, Indira—do you really think people can attain that sense of interconnection, of belonging, that's in that Rumi poem? Now, I mean. Not just that we had it in some far-distant past?" Her face looked wistful as she spoke.

"I kind of doubt people would put it in those terms—you know, not so poetically—but I think that potential is in us, in everyone of us. Anytime you want to help a stranger, protect an animal from coming to some harm—anytime you care in a way that is unselfish—it's part of that, I think," I said.

I reminded Laura of the image I'd first thought of years before—long before she and I had met—of a chinar seedpod, with all the little spikes rising out of it, and how each of those spikes represented our individualized consciousness. The way I thought of it, the deeper we delved into our own selfhoods, the more we entered into the sphere at the center of the pod—entered into that deep, ocean-like place that represented the collective unconscious—a common area, shared by all.

"Right," Laura answered, nodding. "It's sort of like a stand of aspen trees."

"Yeah? How is that?" I asked.

"You see a whole stand of aspen, and you think 'there are a whole bunch of individual trees,'" Laura said, looking first at me and then out at the forest beyond our campsite, "but that's not how it actually is. What you're really looking at is one gigantic organism, which has put up a whole lot of different shoots." She looked back at me, delighted at the idea. "Each tree is just one shoot growing up out of the larger whole. Aspen 'stands' can be huge things—covering a hundred acres or more—and they're all one organism.

"So, what I think you're saying," she went on, "is that we're all like shoots growing up out of the same stand of aspen; if we just go deep enough, we'll realize we all share the same roots."

"Right, exactly—that's great, that's a great image!" I said, smiling as I took it in. "And not just people. It's *everything*—*everything* works that way. We can all trace ourselves to the same set of roots." I looked out at the trees, at the forest, so like the forest I had walked through at the bonobo research site, and remembered the sense of life I had felt within it.

"I believe that the deepest roots of consciousness are shared," I added. "We just need to get back in touch with that—to rediscover it in ourselves."

"'Mast, rudder, helmsman, and keel—I am also the coral reef they founder on,'" Laura said.

"*Right,*" I answered, smiling. "'Both candle—and the moth crazy around it.'"

We both looked at one another for a long moment, smiling, then our attention turned to a rattling sound coming from down the road.

In less than a minute, a bicyclist came into view, heading up the road in the direction of Epulu. When he saw us, the cyclist stopped his bike and called out.

"*Jambo!*" he said.

Laura and I were unsure of what this meant.

"*Mbote!*" we answered, greeting him in Lingala. He cocked his head a little.

"*Bon soir,*" he offered.

"*Bon soir,*" Laura answered. The man then said something to Laura in French, and Laura got up and stepped over to him. They spoke together for several minutes, during which time the man pointed up the road in the direction in which he was heading, and then back down the road in the direction from which we'd all just come. He seemed excited about something.

When they were done talking, the man climbed back on his bike and continued on up the road. As Laura walked back over towards me, I watched the man depart. He appeared to be in a hurry, something that seemed out of step with what we'd experienced so far as we'd traveled through the relaxed culture of Zaire.

Laura squatted down beside me and stared up the road at the retreating cyclist.

"Well," I said. "What's up?"

"A man was attacked and killed by a leopard last night in a village just up the road from here. That fellow had gone to Nia Nia this morning to inform the authorities there, and is trying to get home now before it gets dark."

"Isn't that pretty unusual, for a leopard to attack a person?" I asked.

"Yeah, apparently. He said, when they log the forest, the animals go looking for food other places—places where they wouldn't normally be. He told me the leopard came into his village the night before last and ate some of the chickens. Then last night, it apparently came back for more and went into this man's house by mistake, and when the man woke the leopard must have felt cornered and attacked him. Killed him—and ate part of him before it was driven off."

"Is there any danger from it here, where we are?" I asked.

"Hard to say," Laura said, but she looked concerned. "They think it may attack again, now that it knows how easy it is to kill a person. This fellow on the bike didn't seem to think it would be safe to camp here. That's why he stopped—to warn us."

We discussed it a little bit and decided that, while the odds that the leopard would come this way and bother us in our little campsite were very small, we both would feel more comfortable if we put more distance between us and the last attack before settling down for the night.

We finished our meal in the gathering dusk, then broke camp, piling everything back into the Land Rover—and then set off again, with the night settling in around us.

❋   ❋   ❋

"Are you sure you don't mind doing the driving?" I asked. "You've been at it all day."

Laura glanced over at me. "I don't mind it, but you could do me a favor."

"What's that?" I asked.

"Just, well, talk to me. Tell me something interesting," Laura answered. "Driving—even on this road—can get a little monotonous."

"Okay, what do you want to talk about?" I asked.

"Well, you said before that you thought all sorts of perennial problems of the world grew out of the Original Change and could be made better by the New Change, right?" Laura said. "Well, why don't you tell me how that would work."

"Okay," I said thoughtfully. Ahead, the Land Rover's headlamps made dark craters of every hole. We bumped along, with Laura dodging the worst of them, and careening here and there to avoid the biggest-looking spots. I could see this night-driving was going to be difficult.

"Well, oddly enough, I guess the place to start is with the Original Change and how things were before it.

"I talked some about this at the fire that night. I think before the Original Change, we lived very much in the moment, without concern for the future or the past. The way I see it, when everything was okay in the moment we were in, then everything was, for us, okay—because the present moment filled our awareness. It was all there really was for us.

I thought about it for a moment longer, then went on. "So we didn't bother to plan ahead, or to plan out our actions, we just trusted our impulses as they came to us, and acted on them, naturally, living within the flow of the moment—and life was good. We felt safe and secure, for the most part, because in most moments we were safe and secure.

"I think in a lot of ways we were like the animals in that article your mother gave me—the one I took on the plane. You remember me telling you about it?"

Laura nodded. "Yeah, I think. Animal intuition?"

"That's right. I think before the Original Change we focused on what we longed for and acted according to our impulses. And we didn't let those impulses build up, either, like water behind a dam. We just let them flow forth, unquestioningly—like animals naturally do."

I paused and thought for a second. "Here, you know what," I said, "I think I wrote about this, in my journal, a few days ago. Maybe it would just be easier for me to read you what I wrote."

I unzipped my daypack, which was resting at my feet.

"It's not that I think I *know* this stuff," I said, as I pulled out my journal and penlight. "It's just that this is how it seems to me. This fits with the research I've done, but it's not something I could prove. It fits with my experiences, though, and I guess you could say it just makes sense to me."

I opened my journal and flashed the light on, then turned through the pages until I found the right passage.

"Here it is," I said, and began to read:

When we followed that flow, drawn impulsively forward towards the good things we longed for, life tended to go our way. Life may have seemed magical to us; we may have felt lucky, day by day, just living our lives out in the easy flow of one moment into the next.

In the time before the Original Change, when our attention was drawn to what we longed for, we allowed it to linger there. That focus on our longings became a kind of seed material around which the possibilities we sensed gathered. Sprouting, and informed by the possibilities we sensed, those longings then gave rise to impulses— impulses that we followed, and which, in turn, led to events that seemed by magic to fulfill our longings.

But in the time after the Original Change we became worried about what we began to think of as "bad results" and "bad people," and our worries more and more clouded our minds. More and more our impulses were either avoided and repressed (so that they would break loose abruptly, propelled by too much force, and so caused unnecessary havoc) or we would follow impulses formed around the seed material of our worries and our fears. When we focused on things that made us feel angry and upset, or on things we dreaded and wished to avoid, then our actions often reflected these models and replicated them in our lives.

Our lives lost their sense of magic and were no longer full of the joyous happenstance that had naturally occurred in the time when freely focusing on our longings, and following our impulses, had led us to fulfill the protolife rising up within us.

Indeed, our lives became tinged more and more by our worries and our fears. Impulses that might have led to joyous fulfillment got pushed aside, as we set about living our lives according to plans that were carefully and consciously constructed. While the process of planning opened new doors, some doors were closed, as well. That protolife which, by its nature, required planning could now be fulfilled, but the rewards of living within the wise innocence of the moment were left behind.

I finished reading and turned off my penlight, then mostly closed my journal, letting the penlight rest between the pages.

"So," I said, "the Original Change opened up the possibility of new forms of fulfillment—nobody ever could have become a concert pianist or listened to a symphony, for example, if we hadn't started down this path—but something was lost, too. We were no longer living in the moment, soaking up the pleasures of the moment, free of long-term worry."

"It sounds like you're saying we lost a certain sense of security, like animals have. I've sometimes felt sort of jealous of Bubbles," Laura said, referring to our cat in Boulder, "the way he is when he lies in the sun, completely relaxed. I've seen pictures of animals in the wild—like lions, for example—lying in the sun like that. And other animals, too—like when you see sheep out grazing in a field, or birds flying through the air. There's a pattern they seem to have, like you were saying—like if there's no problem in the moment they're in, then for them, there's no problem at all. And that's what you're saying it was like for us in the past, too. Is that right?"

"Right, exactly," I answered. "And it's not that problems never occurred—I'm sure they must have—we just didn't spend time worrying about them until we got there. So you could say it was like that, like an animal lying in the sun, soaking up life, with no worries about the future, no worries about who we were, or who we were going to become. But the Original Change changed all that. It opened up opportunities and introduced problems that had never existed before."

"Right, and you were going to tell me how those problems developed, and how they could all be solved."

"Well, that's what I'm working on," I said. "So, then," I gathered my thoughts, "we started out in this state of mind, living in the moment, where when we were fed and safe in that moment, we felt deeply contented—no worries at all. We may have felt intense fear in moments of high risk, but in most moments we were safe and felt safe. We trusted the flow of the moment and felt a sense of interconnection with the life around us.

"But after that, after the Original Change, people found themselves in this time when they began to struggle with new problems—when they had shifted their focus away from the moment and begun to actively worry about the future and the past—a time when they had lost a certain sense of belonging and connection and of creature security. That sense that 'all is well' when all is well in the present moment, had been a given before, an essential aspect of life. Once that was lost, people longed to regain it—to regain that simple, lost sense of security, that 'security of innocence.'

"But by now, it's after the Original Change, and that 'security of innocence' *is* lost. There is no turning back, now. We've eaten the fruit, so to speak. We now have plans. We now sort out what's desirable and undesirable, good and bad. We now worry about the future. We're out of Eden, you might say, and we want that security—that sense of safe belonging—back, but all we have to replace it with are our plans and deliberate actions, and whatever else we can grasp at that we hope can make us feel safe and secure and connected again.

"So once the Original Change had come to pass, people began to get pretty uptight," I went on. "They instituted systems and rules and ways of doing things that were supposed to insure that they were secure, and that they stayed secure. They instituted systems of laws and customs, which—if everyone followed them—were supposed to make sure everything came out all right."

"Yeah, I can see this," Laura interjected, "the growth of human civilization as we know it."

"Right," I said, "and it involves these basic motivations to create security and exert control. But once all these rules and laws and customs are set in place, if people went outside of them, other people would get pretty upset, because it was the certainty, the stability, the regularity of these laws and customs that gave people the sense that they lived in a known and adequately controlled world, in which they were secure.

"You might say, we had at one time entrusted ourselves to the natural system and fluidly lived within its boundaries, but after the Original Change, we separated ourselves from that naturalistic flow and put our faith, instead, into systems of our own construction."

"Interesting—yeah," Laura said, nodding her head as she carefully kept the Land Rover on track along the center ridge and the edge of the road. Ahead, we drove into a pool of light from which the narrow roadway and the trunks of enormous, vine-covered trees erupted.

"While you were still sick—or at least resting—at the hotel, I was thinking about this, and remembering a program we saw on public television a couple of years ago. Do you remember? It was on the American Civil Rights Movement. I think it was called '*Eyes on...*'"

"*Eyes on the Prize*—yes, I remember," Laura answered.

"There was a part of it where they showed a bunch of people—both African-Americans and European-Americans—riding a bus together into the South, integrating the bus at a time when, I guess, that just wasn't done."

"Yeah, they were called 'Freedom Riders,' I think," Laura said.

"That sounds right," I said. "And when they got where they were going— was it Birmingham? Or maybe more than one spot? Anyway, when they got off the bus, the crowd beat them really badly. The crowd was so angry, they were so terribly angry, that these people would dare to integrate this bus. Do you remember that?"

"Yes, I do," Laura said. "It's hard to comprehend."

"I thought so, too. I wondered why—how could they be so angry, so violent, about something so fundamentally harmless? And I thought about it."

"What did you decide?" Laura said, avoiding a dark patch of road that the headlights couldn't penetrate.

"I think it's something like this," I answered. "Imagine that your *sense of security*, your whole sense of who you are and how you're oriented to reality, *is dependent on external social structures*, that is, on the laws—both written laws and laws of custom—that define the external social structure of the world you know.

"Now imagine that somebody threatens that security," I went on, "threatens to tear down those laws and those customs, threatens to break down the thing that tells you who you are and where you fit in, and that gives regularity, predictability, and certainty to the world you know. Imagine, in addition, that your very sense of self, your sense of your own identity and of your place in the larger workings of things, are all dependent on the thing that is being torn down..."

"Then you're going to freak out," Laura said.

"Exactly. You'll be angry, upset, fearful—desperate, even. Because the world you know is only that deep," I said, holding my index finger and thumb a little bit apart. "For somebody like that, their sense of self is too shallow, I think. It's just them on the little tip of one peak rising off of the sphere. They don't know who they are in their essence. Their self identity is formed around only the most individualized, insular aspect of who they are. For them, their whole sense of identity, of security, may be extremely dependent on their cultural framework. For them, their role and identity within that framework *is* who they are. If you threaten their role, if you threaten their place within that framework, if you threaten to take that away from them, then you threaten them at the deepest level of their being—that is, at the deepest level that they, with their shallow sense of self, know."

"Wow," Laura exhaled, "and so you change the rules around them, and their role within that, and they feel like you're destroying who they essentially are."

"Because that's how they know themself. That's it; that's my best guess," I concluded. "And so you see where I'm going with that—how would somebody get to that place, where their identity was that small, that fragile?"

"Right. I see," Laura answered, nodding. "They're too focused on their individual self, and too focused on social structures to give them a sense of security, or identity—because that's part of the fallout of the Original Change."

"That's it," I said. "The Original Change opened a door to let in the mindset of bigotry—the mindset in which people grasp hold of narrow social structures and desperately hold onto them."

I could hear Laura take in a deep breath, then let it out slowly.

We drove on through the darkness in silence for a while.

"I have a question," Laura offered, after a time.

"Yeah," I said, drawing my attention back from thoughts of my own.

"What about the sort of groups people who are like that tend to form—like white-supremacy groups. If they're so caught up in individuality, what's the deal with those groups?" she asked.

"Yeah, I know, I got there already," I said. "But the idea, the way I see it, is that, if you deeply know who you are, you'll be able to identify with people who are unlike you without feeling any threat to your own identity—like, for example, you're not going to be washed away, you're not going to lose track of who you are, because you identify with someone who's distinctly different. But if you only know yourself in the most superficial way and define yourself in only the most superficial terms, then your sense of self can be washed away easily—like thin topsoil that a strong wind can blow away.

"If that's the case," I went on, "then you'll look for ways to shore up that identity. You may look for others who have a similar, superficially defined sense of self to stand with, to create a kind of solidarity with, in which each group member reinforces the others in the same, specific, superficial definition of self."

"Right. That makes sense," Laura said. "And a lot of times there's some message of superiority or specialness in those groups, too, I guess."

"Another kind of shoring up for people who are fundamentally not confident about themselves," I added.

Laura looked thoughtful, and for several minutes we were both silent. I felt tired and was content just to stare into the darkness.

"You know what it seems like," Laura said, after a time. "It's like the aspen trees. If you think that all you are is the upper branches, then you fear even the slightest breeze. But if you understand how deeply you are rooted, then you know that no wind will ever topple you."

Laura glanced over at me, and I smiled at her.

"That's it, exactly" I said. "And that's why the New Change would fix that sort of bigotry, because people would know themselves down to their roots."

❀   ❀   ❀

As we crept along through the darkness at a fraction of the speed we had set out at earlier that day, I wondered if we would see the village where the leopard attack had taken place, or if it would be lost under the canopy of forest shadows, and we would pass it by unnoticed.

Perhaps we already had, I thought. We had not seen the bicyclist again—but did that mean he had turned off long ago, or that he was still out there ahead of us on this rough and rutted road, traveling faster than a car could be driven?

Around us, the forest was so dense, and in the darkness it was so hard to get any sense of distances. For the first time since we had entered the forest, I found myself feeling uneasy as I thought of what might be lurking there—and worried, as well, when I thought of the missing cyclist and what might have become of him.

Laura glanced over at me and picked up the thread of our conversation.

"So, does that apply to other forms of bigotry, too, do you think?" She paused, then added, "What about homophobia? What about sexism?"

I didn't answer right away. I was still staring out the window at ghostly tree trunks caught in the glare of the headlights.

"Remember the deal—you're supposed to keep me going with lots of good talk," Laura added.

I smiled. I was glad Laura considered these ideas "good talk"—after all, they seemed so bold, so new to me still—and still so theoretical.

Regardless, I myself found these ideas exciting, full of mystery and possibility, however much they might be stitched together with theoretical suppositions, and I was pleased that Laura found them intriguing, as well.

"Homophobia and sexism," I echoed. "Well, you know, you've given me plenty of time to rummage around in my own thoughts, lately, and I've had some ideas about that, too," I told her, gearing up to do my best to hold up my end of the bargain.

"The basic answer is 'yes,'" I went on, "the Original Change set the stage for bigotry of all sorts, and so it applies to those, too. But it seemed to me, when I was thinking about this before, it occurred to me that there's a deeper question here: why *those* bigotries? We've talked before about why sex roles exist at all. After all, there are some biological tendencies, which sex roles take hold of and exaggerate, amplify," I said.

Laura glanced over at me.

"Like mothers nurse their babies—men can't—and so the role gets expanded to include the feeding of kids when they're past the nursing stage, and then expanded further to include feeding all family members. Or like hunting—someone had to hunt, but there were times when it might have been difficult for a woman to do so—like when she had to keep her nursing baby near at hand, or late in a pregnancy, or perhaps when menstruating, and the scent of blood might have been a problem.

"So that would have created a tendency for men to hunt more than women. But after the Original Change, that tendency would have become exaggerated. It would have been used to define set rules—or specifically, roles that people were expected to follow: *men hunt, women don't.*

"So sex roles grew out of a context where there was already some sort of pattern there, and then that pattern was amplified or exaggerated to create a rigid structure." I glanced over at Laura, hoping she was following what I was saying.

"Right?" I added.

Laura nodded in agreement. "Sure. Works for me."

"But that still leaves two questions," I went on. "One, *why* make those roles so rigid, so that, in a traditional context, one sex is *supposed* to play one role, and the other is *supposed* to follow a different one? Why impose any rigid roles at all? Why not have the attitude that people should do whatever suits them? Why did people *insist* on other people playing these roles? *Why did they become required?*

"And so that's one question. The other question is: *why has the women's role so frequently been one of lower status?*"

"Do you have answers to those?" Laura asked.

"I think so. You can tell me whether you agree that they make sense. The first one is easiest. Before the Original Change, there'd been a kind of natural innocence; we'd lived moment-by-moment, trusting our impulses, unconcerned for the future. We'd felt secure in the present moment, regardless of what the next moment held.

"Like I was saying before, though, the Original Change had washed that sense of security away. For the first time, we stepped out of the present moment and looked out across a future we knew we had little control over.

We knew full well the importance of all the choices we had to make, and knew, too, that we were responsible for the results of all those choices. We felt anxious then. We felt worried about the future. We'd lost the security we'd once felt, when we'd lived in the innocence of the moment."

"Right," Laura said. "That's like what you were saying before."

"Yeah, right—and I don't mean to repeat myself—but it was a big deal when we lost that. And because we'd lost that, after the Original Change, people had a desire to try to recreate that sense of security—and to do so by creating social structures that were predictable, knowable, and definable. The world at large was so unpredictable; it involved so many unknowns. People wanted the world of human activities, at least, to be something they could control, and define, and count on.

"The ability to control and predict returned to them a little of the feeling of security they had lost. They began to depend on the predictability of social norms as the source of their security. For this reason, once a social norm of some sort was established—like that women did the feeding, or men the hunting—then that comfortingly familiar pattern was quickly translated into a rule. The most predictable, usual thing quickly became the required thing."

"Oh, yeah, yeah—that makes sense," Laura said. "And if people stepped out of the bounds of that, didn't do the most predictable, required thing, people would feel insecure, feel threatened, even."

"Right. And because they felt insecure and threatened, they would get upset—like they did at the freedom riders," I added.

"Or like those blokes in Hampshire did when Jimmy grew his hair long," Laura said.

"Oh yeah! I hadn't thought about that in years," I said. Jimmy was one of Laura's cousins. Sometime, about 1969 or '70, a group of clean-cut young men had threatened to beat him up for wearing his hair long, but he'd taken off running and slipped into a shop up the road. I remembered, around that time, hearing other stories of long-haired young men who had met with similar threats and hadn't been as fortunate in the outcome.

"He broke the rules for male role-playing, so they went after him," Laura said.

I thought about that. It always amazed me how much so many people had had to go through just to claim back a little of the latitude that was native to us as human beings. How remarkable it was to me that human beings had, through the centuries, decided to give so much of that freedom away, just for a little added sense of security!

"So you were going to tell me why the prescribed sex role for women has traditionally been one of such low status," Laura prompted.

"Oh, yeah. Well, let's see," I said, turning my attention back to that question.

"First, let me say, if I'm right, then there's no reason to assume that women always had a low status," I said, then paused to think about it a moment longer.

"Imagine how it would have been, before the Original Change," I went on. "People lived in the present moment, with little concern for the future.

They had personal experiences, but very little consciousness of having an individual identity. They had no need for plans, or rules, or self definitions. They lived moment-by-moment, impulsively.

"That's the way I've been seeing it, and if that's right, there would have been no sort of deliberate sex roles imposed on people's lives—or roles of any other sort. We would have had no use for that sort of ordering of things. But even without sex roles, there would naturally still have been a conscious awareness of differences between the sexes. After all, people weren't stupid then—their attention was just focused differently."

"So when I was thinking about this sort of thing, when you were sick," I told Laura, "I asked myself—I wondered—how would the sexes have been viewed, then, if not through the prism of sex roles?"

"And what did you decide?" Laura asked.

"Well, think about it. In that context, which one of the characteristics that distinguish the sexes would have most stood out?

"It seems to me that the act of giving birth—the capacity to give birth— is the most dramatic," I went on, answering my own question. "Even today, as jaded as we are, and as removed from the process of nature as we are, most of us still respond to the act of giving birth as somehow magical. Even if we are told that it isn't magical, that it's just a process—still, some- how, we feel like it is. So imagine how much more magical it might have seemed at a time when we had no scientific explanations, before we ever sought to control nature or to put our mark on it through agriculture."

Laura nodded. "Yeah—even more so."

"And if we identified with nature then," I went on, "in a very deep, per- sonal way—felt a deep oneness with it—well, I'm just guessing, of course, but it seems to me that before we resisted that identification, that sense of belonging with the natural world, the act of birth must have seemed hallowed, in a certain sense—truly mystical and wondrous. And if that's true, it seems to me that women's status would likely have been higher because of it—but of course in a loose, unregimented kind of a way. After all, this would have been before the Original Change—before there were a lot of deliberate social structures."

"Okay, I'm with you so far," Laura said. "We felt a deep belonging with the natural world, and giving birth was nature at its most miraculous. So women—the birth-givers—would have been held in higher esteem."

"That's it, in a nutshell," I said. "In fact, there are a lot of figurines of women from European archaeological sites, dating from as far back as, oh, I think it's about 30,000 years ago—a significant portion of which may have represented women who were pregnant. In contrast, relatively few figurines of men have been found. So that does seem to suggest, perhaps, some sort of early preoccupation with women—however it might have been motivated."[*]

"That's interesting," Laura commented, as we bumped along the road. "Okay—so let's say your guess is right, that there was an early time when women enjoyed a higher status. Why didn't women keep that status?"

---

[*] See Part II of Appendix 3, Note 1 (page A15).—I.K.

"Well, think about it," I answered. "If women were originally given a high status because they were seen as the conduit through which the deeper forces of nature brought life into the world—if they were known for that and seen in those terms maybe long before anybody ever conceived of making an artistic representation of it—then how would women have been viewed after it became *en vogue* to try to dominate and control and act independently of the forces of nature?" I paused and waited for Laura to respond.

Laura glanced over at me, her eyes wide. "You'd have to dominate and control women, too—wouldn't you, if that's what women symbolized?" She shook her head. "Wow."

"If women represented the thing we were trying to be independent of, trying not to be influenced too much by...," I trailed off.

"Then you'd have to be sure women had very little influence, as well," Laura said, and again glanced over at me with a look of surprised discovery.

"That's the idea." I told her. "And in that context, men would symbolize the opposite. Like a big play in which everyone was cast in roles, and men took on the opposite role—the role of outward action, of independence from the rest of nature."

Laura shook her head. "That's such a trip. Do you really think that's how it was?"

"Well, you see that kind of thing in families, don't you? People take on roles relative to one another. Like in a family where the parents put the kids under a lot of pressure to succeed, all the kids will feel ambivalent about that, but they tend to sort it out into roles, where there'll be maybe one hyper-achieving kid, and another kid who rejects the pressure and decides to just relax and be a failure. There's a kind of drama in the family, and it turns into roles that people play.

"I think human beings were ambivalent about the Original Change, too—how could we not have been? We were going forward into something new and promising, while at the same time, we were leaving behind something that was, in some ways, better.

"As I see it, that ambivalence got dramatized, got displayed in the cultural roles we set up for ourselves—with men representing the generally admired forward thrust, and women representing the deeper ties we were trying to maintain control over. Women could still be admired, but mostly only if they remained neatly 'tamed' within their prescribed role—tamed like the rest of the natural world, which they had come to represent."

Laura shook her head again. "You're something, Indira." She looked thoughtful for a minute longer, then added. "So, you're saying, men somehow created this role, and kept women within it..."

"No, no—I'm not saying men did this to women. I'm saying we all—both sexes—did it to ourselves and to one another. And certainly it's been limiting for women, but it's also been limiting for men. We all signed up for this play, so to speak—we all wrote it together, and regardless of who has a higher or lower status within the play, we all signed up for it—and we all inducted our children into it, as well. Both women and men teach their kids to play sex roles. It's a cooperative venture.

"In short—all people helped create the Original Change—and we all contributed to the symbolism, roles, and rules that developed out of it."

❄   ❄   ❄

After a moment, Laura nodded and said, "Okay, I see that." She looked thoughtful for another moment or two, as I watched her in the glow of the dashboard lights, then added, "So I think my original question was, 'if the Original Change brought all these problems into the world, how did it create homophobia and sexism?' I think you've answered the sexism part, but..."

"But what about homophobia?" I said.

"Yeah," Laura replied.

It was nice to be able to share all these thoughts with Laura. I'd wanted to, often enough, when I'd been coming up with them—while she'd been sick and then recuperating—but I hadn't wanted to bother her then.

I thought about her question for a minute longer, before offering my reply.

"Okay. I would come at that like this," I said, then stopped and thought for few seconds longer. "Yeah, well, I guess the place to start is by talking about sexuality, in general. I'd say that it's in the nature of sex to build intimacy—to create a kind of bridge between people. You might say that through sex, we go deep together—and in the midst of that intimacy, we find that we share the same root."

Laura glanced over at me and smiled. "I like that idea," she said—then added, more quietly, "That's how it feels."

I looked at her tenderly for a moment, as she watched the road. I reached over and touched her arm, then went on with what I was saying.

"But part of the fallout of the Original Change was that we had started to distrust and push away from that sort of deep sense of interconnectedness. You might say we were afraid we would lose our sense of self back into it—our fledgling, new, young, not-completely-formed sense of self.

"So as attractive as sex was, it could also have seemed a bit frightening, a bit scary, too, because it opened up the boundaries between these new, hardly formed self-identities, and blurred the lines between them."

"Yeah, I can see that," Laura said.

"So, the way I think of it—the way I've been thinking of it," I said, remembering sitting in the hotel room in Kisangani and watching the rain falling outside our window as I'd considered this point the week before, "we would have wanted to place some sort of control over these sorts of experiences—sexual experiences—so that we didn't get too swept away with them, or if we did get swept away, we did it in some context we had some sort of control of."

"Kind of like sex roles?" Laura asked.

"Yeah, kind of like sex roles—we wanted an external structure we could impose on our lives to give them a definable structure we could depend on. So sex could still take place—it *had* to still take place, or the species would not have been able to survive—but it did so increasingly in a way that was regulated.

"In much of the world, sex is considered taboo outside of the framework of marriage, for example. And even within marriage, sexual acts that can serve no procreative purpose—like oral sex, for example—have often been considered unacceptable. I think there are even laws against such non-procreative sex within marriage still on the books in the U.S. You know, laws that tell married couples what they can and cannot do together sexually."

"That's true. I've read about them," Laura said.

"Yeah, I think it's Maryland's laws I've heard most about. It's a felony there, by the way—with prison time! But I think these laws are pretty common in the U.S.,* and other countries, too," I said, and tried to remember where else I'd heard of them. I had the impression that laws restricting sexual expression—even between consenting adults—were widespread, but I was having trouble recalling just what laws were in effect where.

"So, you were saying...," Laura said.

"Oh, right," I said, casting about for the thread of my thoughts. "Right, okay, so we put all these controls around sexuality," I continued. "Often the controls on sex have focused on controlling women's sexuality, specifically. After all, women are most strongly associated with that deeper sense of connection from which we were trying to distinguish ourselves—so you have everything from chastity belts in old Europe to female genital mutilation in Africa—things designed to control or destroy not just sexuality in general, but especially to suppress women's sexuality.

"So you're saying there was a general sense that sexuality had to be controlled, or managed, and women's sexuality especially so," Laura said.

"That's right," I answered, then paused, trying to collect my thoughts.

"Okay," I said, after a few moments. "So people created roles and rules around the expression of sexuality. We were depending more and more on a social system to give us security, and sexuality had to fit within that social system. Sexuality had to be regulated, because it threatened to blur the lines of individual distinctiveness and—as we would have felt at that point—throw us into chaos. And that regulation of sexuality had, at the very least, to permit heterosexual sexual expression, because people still needed to reproduce.

"And, like I was saying, while there is a lot of variation around the world, overall, in one way or another, we see some sort of regulatory norms placed around the expression of sexuality—and especially around the expression of female sexuality.

"So, sex became restricted and regulated, with the only universally accepted form being reproductive sex within the framework of marriage," I concluded.

---

* In 2003—thirteen years after Laura and I had this conversation—such laws were found to be unconstitutional in the United States and were removed from the law books.

"So only the most necessary form of sex, within the most regulated context," Laura said.

"Right," I said. "And mostly people went along with those regulations, whichever ones applied in their specific cultural context, just like mostly people went along with their sex roles—and pretty much those things fit together, because if you'd, say, set aside half the qualities natural to being human in embracing your sex role, you might find it very desirable to form a union with someone who had other, necessary qualities—the very qualities you'd rejected in yourself. In other words, the sex roles made a complimentary set, and that, especially, made them attractive to one another.

"That is," I went on, "they did for those who agreed to play sex roles. But for some people those sex roles just didn't fit—they went against their basic nature, their basic protolife—and for them the prospect of being in a relationship in which they would have to constantly play such a confining role didn't fit, either. These people might have found themselves wanting to push aside the whole system of rules and roles that the society was attempting to impose on their lives.

"A man in that situation might have met another man who felt the same way, for example, and they might have been drawn to each other—offering one another freedom from those constraints, and a sympathetic understanding of one another. Perhaps they would have fallen in love..."

"Oh, I see where you're going," Laura cut in. "But the act of them falling in love, the act of them being together, would have been seen as a rebellion, not just against what they personally found confining..."

"But against sex roles, restrictions on sexual expression—against the whole set of social structures that had created that confining environment in the first place," I said. "So anytime two men or two women were together romantically, or sexually,..."

"Right, right. I see it," Laura said.

"...just the act of them being together would have been seen as a symbolic threat to that whole system of roles, rules, and regulations upon which people depended for their sense of security. It was as though the couple were saying to everybody else: 'Hey, these structures you live by are just a house of cards. They're not absolute. They're not permanent. They can't be depended on. They're just made up, and they can be disregarded and discarded this easily,'" I finished.

"And if you think someone might be beaten up just for wearing their hair too long...," Laura began.

"Or for sitting in the wrong place on a bus—it's all the same thing. People get really upset if you show them that the structures that define their world—the structures that they rely on to define themselves—are ephemeral. If you do that..."

"They're likely to freak out," Laura finished for me.

"Exactly," I said. "If you do something that makes people think that the world upon which they depend—and according to which they define their very selfhoods—isn't dependable, or unshakable, they may try to destroy the one who makes their world look so uncertain. It's a desperate act—an act of desperation. And the hostility that is at the core of homophobia—or of any other prejudice—is part of that. They're responding to a perceived threat to their security and their selfhoods."

"When in truth, the thing they find so threatening is just two people loving each other," Laura added, shaking her head.

❊   ❊   ❊

We drove on through the darkness, each lost in her own thoughts. Before long we came to an especially bad stretch of road. Here, there were no matching set of ruts running in parallel lines down the center of the road, but instead, an irregular scramble of tracks going this way and that through deep mud.

One of the problems with night driving is that you can't see the road very far ahead, and we were well into the muck before we realized how really bad the road was there. Laura gunned the engine, and we went skidding along, trying to maintain enough speed so that we wouldn't sink in and get stuck. I'd say that particularly bad stretch covered perhaps fifty meters, and we were a good two-thirds of the way through it before we lost our momentum and found ourselves stuck, motionless except for the spinning of our wheels.

"Shit," Laura said under her breath.

She sat perfectly still for a second, then threw the vehicle into reverse and gunned the engine—but it was no use.

Laura reached behind her seat and dug her flashlight out of her pack, then we both got out to take a look at the situation.

The mud sucked at our boots as we circled the Land Rover, examining the conditions around each wheel. Laura looked dismayed.

"Even with four-wheel drive, I don't like it. That front left wheel looks like we might be able to get some traction, if we had some sand or something to throw in with it." Laura glanced around. It was as though the forest were an ocean of darkness surrounding the small island of light thrown off by the Land Rover's headlights.

"Do you want to just find a place to put up the tent and sleep here?" I asked. "We'll have better light in the morning."

Laura looked down at her shoes, which were covered in mud, then back up at me. She sighed.

"No," she said finally. "I don't know when people will start driving through in the morning. I don't want us to be trying to get unstuck while there's traffic piling up."

"That's a point," I said.

Laura shone her flashlight out into the forest, perhaps looking for something she could jam in around the tires to give traction.

"I guess we're going to have to dig out. If we can clear enough mud from in front of each tire so that we can roll forward, and get up a little momentum..." Her voice trailed off.

I knew Brother Frank had sent along a shovel. One shovel between us, and the amount of labor...—I thought, dismayed, as well. Then something occurred to me.

"What about the winch?"

Laura, who had looked unspeakably tired the moment before, now seemed to fill with new energy. She smiled.

"Yeah!" she said, and walked around to the front of the Land Rover to look at the electric winch, which was bolted on there.

It took us a good half an hour to decide on the right tree to lash the cable onto, to read through the instructions for use in the manual we found in the glove box, and to get set up—but soon we had the cable attached and were ready to give it a go.

We had hooked the winch cable to a tree ahead and to the left of us. It wouldn't be a straight pull, but it was the best we could do. Laura and I knocked what mud we could from our boots and climbed into the Land Rover. Laura started the engine, and as she put the Land Rover into gear, I started the winch using the remote-control cable. The winch whirred into life, and it was as if I could feel the whole vehicle straining beneath us. I could feel us slide a little in the direction of the tree, but as much as the wheels spun, and the winch strained, we couldn't escape the suction of the mud.

"It's no good," Laura said finally. "Anyhow, I'm afraid we'll burn out the winch."

Laura looked weary and sat staring ahead into the glow of the headlights. I got out and took another look at what was holding us there.

A moment later I was back. "Come have a look," I said to Laura.

She climbed out and followed me.

"See," I said, "the winch is pulling to the side, at about a thirty degree angle, while the wheels are pointed forward. We need to turn the wheels—drive towards the tree—then the winch and engine won't fight one another."

A slow smile spread over Laura's face, then she laughed.

"Gee," she said under her breath. "We weren't thinking, were we? Let's try it."

We got back in, but this time Laura turned the wheels before we revved up the engine and the winch. As we listened to the roar and whine of the motors, we felt ourselves creeping forward.

We stood in the glow of the headlights, in front of the Land Rover, which was parked on a relatively solid patch of clay along the left side of the road. The winch cable and accessories had all been stowed away, and Laura and I were busily scraping the mud off our boots with twigs we'd picked up along the edge of the forest.

"How much further do you think we have to go?" I said to Laura.

"I don't know. Maybe another fifty kilometers, maybe more."

"We could perhaps look for a place to pitch the tent—do you think? It's been a long drive. We'll get there in the morning," I said.

Laura stood erect and looked around. "We could," she said, "but the shoulder here is pretty narrow, and we sure don't want to pitch a tent in this mud."

I still had the flashlight from when I had gone to look at the wheels earlier. Now I pulled it from my pocket and cast its light at the looming trees along the road.

"It looks like it gets a little wider over there."

Laura, who had gone back to working on her boots, turned her face in the direction of the light, and as she did, from somewhere in the dark forest beyond the roadway, we heard a terrible scream.

Laura stood up straight and turned to face the sound. A cold shiver went down my spine.

It was the sound of a woman screaming. It repeated over and over— five or six times.

Then there was silence.

I shone my flashlight into the underbrush, but there was no motion, no sign of life, nothing to tell us where the sound had come from.

Both Laura and I stood perfectly still, scanning the forest with our eyes. I could feel the hair standing up on the back of my neck. I remembered the man on the road, on his rickety bicycle, riding out ahead of us into the darkness, and remembered his warning. We would have long-since passed him and his village.

I looked over at Laura. Her face looked strained and uncommonly pale in the harsh light of the headlights. Then she turned towards me, a slight frown on her face.

"You suppose—a hyrax?" she said, her voice caught between dread and curiosity.

It took me a moment to place the name, but then I remembered—the hyrax was an animal whose call was said to sound like a woman scream-ing. I had read about it when we were still in Boulder.

"Oh, I sure hope so," I answered, and suddenly realized I hadn't been breathing. I took a breath. "They repeat like that, don't they?"

"Yeah, I think so."

"But the leopard...," I said.

"I know. But it didn't sound quite human. Do you think?"

I listened to the sound still echoing through my mind. "No, no, you're right. Not quite human," I said. "The repeats were too much the same, I think. It was a call."

We both looked at each other, then off into the darkness in the direction from which we'd heard the screams. I remembered what I'd read about the hyrax—a small animal, about the size of a rabbit. It lived in trees and was a distant relative of the elephant.

"Right, so it was a hyrax," Laura said. After a moment, she added, "Let's drive on to Epulu. The last thing we want is to get woken up by that bloody thing in the middle of the night. What a night that would be!"

I conceded that she had a point, then bent and scraped the last big chunk of mud from my left boot.

"Are you sure you're up to it, Laura?" I asked. "I can drive, if you want. Remember how sick you were just a few days ago."

"I'm happy to drive if you'll just keep talking," Laura said. She pried a thick slab of the sticky mud from the bottom of her boot. "Anyhow, I'm hoping we'll get a good stretch of road up ahead. It can't all be like this."

I agreed to her offer, and as I did, I remembered what Brother Frank had told us about this road, and hoped Laura was right about what lay ahead. Certainly it hadn't all been this bad. We could keep our fingers crossed.

I finished with my boot, then climbed in through the driver's door, so I could avoid the mud on the other side. A moment later, Laura got in after me.

"Here we go," Laura said, then threw the Land Rover into gear, and we leapt forward, keeping as much as possible to the slightly higher, more-compact ground along the side of the road, but still sliding around a good bit until we cleared that particularly bad stretch of road.

Soon, we were driving along as we had most of the time since passing Bafwasende, with the Land Rover positioned so it straddled the right-most rut of a rutted but otherwise fairly stable road.

As we rolled along, we both had a laugh at the cold shivers that had run down our spines because a rabbit-sized animal, somewhat resembling an overgrown gerbil, had called out in the darkness.

Regardless of the reason, though, it felt good to be on our way again.

❀   ❀   ❀

"Pause," Paul said, and Kiki's voice fell silent. Even as he'd walked along, listening to the recitation from Dr. Kumar's book, Paul had been ruminating, at the back of his mind, about how these ideas had actually changed this world. He would have been entirely skeptical, in fact, if not for the fact that this world *had* been changed, and apparently by this book. But how? The question had run through his mind so often since he had set out on this hike, it seemed to have been a constant thread in the background of this thoughts. After all, Paul was a physicist, used to dealing with the world in precise mechanistic terms, and so had kept probing for the precise mechanism of change.

Paul looked around him as he continued along the trail. The path had climbed even higher since he'd stopped to soak his feet a couple of hours before. Now, he walked through deep pines, under a sky bluer than any he had ever seen. The air all around him was bright and clear and perfumed with the scent of pine. For Paul, it was like a wonderland—an impossibility on his earth, yet a fact on this one.

Perhaps he had been looking at it wrong, Paul thought, as he considered the question that had been echoing in his mind for as long as he'd been listening to *Memories and Reflections*. Maybe it wasn't these ideas, alone, that had changed this world. Maybe they were just the first step. After all, a large portion of the memoirs was still left to be read. Maybe, Paul thought, Dr. Kumar didn't just come up with the idea of the New Change, but somehow saw a way to more speedily propel it into being.

Paul considered this possibility, turned it over in his mind a couple of times—then set it down again. Of course, he had no way of telling if this was correct. There was really no more he could do than continue to listen to her book and wait to find out. And after all, he must be very close to the

Retreat by now. He wanted to get as much read as possible before he arrived.

"Kiki, please resume recitation," Paul said, as he once again looked around at the magnificent pines.

Kiki's voice again took on the distinctive qualities of Dr. Kumar's, and drifted out into the clear mountain air.

◻︎   ◻︎   ◻︎

We rolled along in silence for quite a while after that. I looked over at Laura, softly lit in the cool, green glow of the dashboard lights. She held the wheel steady, even as the Land Rover rumbled along beneath us, and again I felt glad that it was she, and not I, who was driving.

A moment after thinking this, I remembered my promise.

"So, would you like me to keep talking, Laura?" I asked.

Laura glanced over. "That's the deal. I drive, you talk. Is that still okay with you?"

I smiled. "Sure, even if I am getting the better end of it. What do you want me to talk about? Do you still want me to talk about the Change?"

Laura's face looked thoughtful in the dashboard light. She rubbed her chin with one hand.

"Ah, well—yeah—I would," she answered. "It seems like you were going to tell me how the New Change would solve the problems we were talking about. I'd like to hear that."

"Do you remember what we were talking about last?" I asked. "What was it—homophobia..."

"And sexism," Laura said.

I tried to collect my thoughts. Our time struggling to get the Land Rover unstuck, and the episode with the hyrax, had pushed everything else from my mind.

"You with me?" Laura said, glancing over.

"Yeah—I'm on it," I answered. "I think the answer for both of those problems—homophobia and sexism—is basically the same. If we embrace the New Change, our sense of self will deepen. And, well—I see this as having, basically, two steps—the two steps which would have to happen for the New Change to heal sexism and homophobia.

"First, if the New Change happened—that is, if we developed an expanded sense of self—then we'd know ourselves more deeply and feel more interconnected with others. I mean, that's basically what the New Change is. I guess you could say we'd travel down through the peak on a chinar seedpod, so to speak, widening and deepening our sense of self, and discovering how interconnected we are at our root.

"We would all know our own selves so deeply, then, that when we identi-fied with others—when we allowed ourselves to see the world from their point of view, to explore their perspective, their culture, their customs—we wouldn't feel any threat to our own identities, or our own viewpoints, in doing that."

"So you're saying, it's like we'd be too deeply rooted for any such wind to blow us over?" Laura suggested.

"Yeah, that's good—that's right. That's very poetic," I told her. "And, of course, once that happened, sexuality itself wouldn't seem so threatening—we wouldn't fear that we might lose our very selves within the intimacy it provided, as I imagine that we did after the Original Change. We wouldn't worry that we might get washed away by it, so to speak—and so people wouldn't feel the same need for the restrictions the society has placed around sexual expression."

"I think that's already going on, don't you?" Laura said, glancing over at me.

"Sure, I do. I think we've already started down this path. And when we really get there, when we've really arrived at the New Change, I think we'll find that so much more intimacy will be possible. Not just sexual intimacy, but intimacy, closeness, of all sorts. People wouldn't need to feel so alone, anymore."

I paused and thought about this for a moment, then went on. "So I said there were two parts to this. The second one is, with the New Change, we would be more in touch with our own intuitions, with our ability to be in the right place, at the right time. We would begin to trust ourselves to free movement, again, but in a more conscious, knowing way. We wouldn't want to try to control the world so much, or to make it all predictable, because we would have a sense of our own place within it, and the rightness of that.

"The way I've been thinking of it, once we reach that point of confidence, people will just be able to be themselves, to get in touch with their own protolife, and live lives that they find fulfilling—without a lot of roles or social regulations to restrict them," I said.

Laura dodged a rough patch of road, which looked as though it might be especially muddy, then steered the left wheels back up onto the center ridge.

"Okay, so let me see if I have this," Laura said. "You're saying, with the New Change, we would feel more secure in ourselves, and so wouldn't seek security by creating a rigid society, with artificial roles in it..."

"That's right," I said.

"...and people wouldn't need social conventions to make them feel secure, and so they would no longer feel threatened by unconventional relationships," Laura concluded.

"That's it, exactly," I said, pleased to hear her put it so succinctly. "And so there's the end to any sort of rigidly imposed sex roles—and to the sort of sexism that goes with them. And there's the end to homophobia, too—in a nutshell. There'd be no reason left for people to feel threatened, simply because two people loved each other."

I glanced over at Laura, softly lit by the light from the dashboard. She looked deep in thought.

"So you've thought about this," she said finally, "and it applies to *all sorts* of problems? Isn't that what you said?"

"Yeah, as clearly as I can think it through. It's theory, of course, but it all adds up for me."

"Good. Well tell me another example, would you? This is interesting, Indira. I'd like to hear it."

"Well, you pick something," I said. "Some persistent problem. Something that's been part of the human experience for a long time."

"Okay," Laura answered, watching the road. "Well, what have we been through so far? Rigid, repressive cultures; sex roles; sexism; homophobia; racial and ethnic bigotry—really, bigotry of all kinds—and all of them would be solved by the New Change." Laura glanced over at me and smiled.

"How about war and violence?" she added. "Do you have an answer for that one? Did war come from the Original Change? Would it be solved by the New Change, according to your theory?" Laura asked.

"Yeah. I do—it would—but you know, you left off loneliness. We just touched on it, but I wanted to add that I think people could have a lot more deep, rich, close relationships—and not just sexual ones," I said. "I think the Original Change created a kind of isolation, which we wouldn't need to have if we continue on to the New Change."

"Right," Laura said thoughtfully. "It's what you said—no more fear of losing yourself in intimacy."

"Yeah, right, because your identity is so strong, so you trust it and let it happen. And you know yourself better, and it's easier to share what you know." I thought for a moment, then added, "And because people would identify more deeply with one another, and there's an inherent intimacy in that, as well."

Laura nodded her head thoughtfully.

"And I think that ties into environmental problems, too," I said.

"Really?" Laura asked. She glanced over and flashed a smile. She seemed entertained. "Okay, let's do that one first. No—first could you get me something to snack on? I'm getting hungry."

"Sure. You drive, I get," I said. I reached back behind Laura's seat and pulled her daypack from the floor, then set it between my knees.

"I'm remembering right, aren't I? You've got the trail mix in here?"

"Yeah."

"Is that what you want? I think maybe there are some bananas on the back seat."

"No, they're kind of smushed. The trail mix will be fine—although I may regret it in a week when we run out," she said.

"You're right. We should have brought more."

"That's okay. I won't have that much now. It's in the bottom of the main compartment."

I pulled the bag out, opened it, and held it out for Laura to take some.

"So, loneliness and the environment," Laura prompted, speaking with her mouth full.

I stared out at the narrow track between the walls of forest which lay ahead. As we bumped along, the light of the headlamps jumped and jolted between trunks and branches. Every once in a while the light revealed a monkey swinging away from the approaching noise and light, or a bird disturbed from its roost, but for the most part the forest seemed sterile and motionless in the cool light.

"Loneliness and the environment," I echoed to myself, and then set about trying to explain to Laura what I had thought about days earlier in our hotel room, while she lay sleeping.

"The Original Change had all sorts of effects on our state of consciousness," I began. "We weren't just more focused on our individuality. That focus on our individual selfhoods created a sense of isolation, a sense of separateness—and therefore loneliness.

"As we looked off away from the present moment in time and began to prepare, in each day, for the future days that lay ahead, we became anxious, and sometimes fearful, about the future and what could go wrong in it.

"And even though the Original Change was, itself, in larger ways, fulfilling—in terms of the smaller, moment-by-moment acts of life, we had lost the rich infusion of fulfillment we had created by fluidly giving expression to our impulses.

"So there came a time," I went on, "when, as a result of the Original Change, we were living lives that were lonelier, more fearful, and less fulfilling than the lives we had lived before. This left us in an odd emotional state, in which we were carrying around a certain unhappiness with us all the time. In a certain sense, I guess you could say, we were carrying around a 'hollow' space within us—a kind of empty, aching sorrow—filled with loneliness, anxiety, and longing. It was a hollow we longed to have filled.

"To imagine how it was, think of someone feeling isolated, living within a context of rigid rules and roles where only certain sorts of intimacy would be permitted. Imagine that this person has the prospect of having children to love and bond deeply with. Anybody might long to have kids to love and hold, but now this person has this hollow aching within them, and the prospect of having children takes on a new dimension of importance. They now feel it with a kind of need that wouldn't be there otherwise.

"Now imagine somebody," I went on, "who's worried about the future, worried about how they'll survive in their old age, about having enough to eat, having someone to take care of them. These sorts of fears were not there when we lived in the moment, day by day—because, regardless of what the future held, we didn't worry about it until we got there. But after the Original Change, these sorts of worries took a new place in our lives—and for many people the answer, again, was to wish to have more kids than they might otherwise have wished for, so we could increase our security in the future and reduce our loneliness.

"Obviously, this wouldn't have affected the population much until we developed the ability to have some conscious control over how many children we had, but I think it's been an influence overall, as I think most people do feel that hollow. So, I think the problems we have with overpopulation today are in part, at least, an outgrowth of the Original Change," I said.

"Which in turn affects the degree of impact we have on the environment," Laura said.

"Exactly—because there are so many more of us to have that impact."

"And the New Change would fix this?" Laura prompted.

"Because we would develop deep bonds with a lot of people, and so wouldn't any longer feel so alone, and because those deeper, broader connections would create other kinds of security networks. So those extra motivations for having children would disappear, and the population would start to drop.

"And we would treat the environment better in other regards, too," I went on. "We would identify more deeply with other life, and so would feel for the harm we were doing it, and would really want to make whatever adjustments we had to to stop doing that harm. It would be worth going to the trouble to learn what we have to do, and to do it—just like people are willing to do whatever it takes to protect their kids, because their identity is broad enough to include their children. You know, 'heart of my heart,' and all that.

"So, what I'm saying is, if our identities expanded enough to take in all other life, we would be much more responsible in how we dealt with it."

I stared out the window as we passed by massive tree trunks—rising up in the glow of the headlights, then disappearing into the shadows above—and thought about the barren land we'd passed earlier that day, clear-cut from the forest.

Laura put out her hand, and when I didn't respond right away, she felt around on the stand between our seats.

"Where's the trail mix?" she said softly.

I picked up the bag and held it open for her. "Sorry, I got distracted," I said.

"It's okay. It's all very interesting, Indira. I'm glad one of us had some good ideas. When I was sick, I was just sick. That was my whole world."

"I'm sorry you had to go through that," I said.

"Well, I was the one who wanted to go on an adventure," Laura answered, as she slowed the Land Rover to examine an especially rough bit of road, then backed us up and came at it with enough speed to slide though it.

"Still, I'm glad to have the adventure, even if I did get sick," Laura commented.

"And I'm glad you're driving," I said.

"And I'm glad you're talking," Laura said. "Do you have more?"

"About the environment? Sure. Let me just think for a second."

A moment later, I began again. "So, after the Original Change, we had this hollow feeling—like I was saying—this combination of loneliness, anxiety about the future, and this feeling that while some aspects of ourselves were really being fulfilled, other parts of our selfhoods—the parts that somehow didn't fit within our neatly defined societies—those parts of ourselves were left suppressed, set aside, unfulfilled. And so, like I said, there was this sort of lonely, anxious, restless, hollow feeling that people began to carry with them."

"And people wanted to soothe that hollow feeling by having more kids than they would otherwise have," Laura offered.

"Right, that's one thing, but it had lots of other effects, as well. People began to want to compensate for feeling isolated or unloved by representing their value to others through the goods that they possessed. You know the kind of thing: 'Here I am, I have this sexy sports car, which you're going to love, and because I have it, you're going to love me.' You don't get real love that way, but if you're lonely enough, desperate enough to be loved, it can still seem pretty desirable to go that way.

"So people began to seek love by trying to impress others with what they owned or possessed—with their house, their clothes, the number of cattle they had, that sort of thing. It became just one more reason people began to possess more than they needed—to take more from the earth than they needed, with all the environmental effects that implies.

"In other ways, too, I think," I went on, "people were just trying—are still just trying—to fill the hollow. If you're feeling anxious or lonely, and you want to comfort yourself, you're likely to feel temporarily better if you buy yourself some new things—even if you don't really need them. Food is the same way—we fill ourselves with food to temporarily fill the hollow left over from the Original Change—and then later, we fill ourselves again.

"People will sometimes do the same thing with sex, by the way—seeking out physical intimacy when they feel very alone, but do it with someone they're not bonded with, and so they just feel alone afterwards, too.

"And, of course, none of this really helps. Temporarily, maybe, yes—but in the end people are just as lonely, as anxious, as unfulfilled after they have shopped, or eaten, or had casual sex, or whatever—because the basic problem hasn't been solved," I concluded.

"And the New Change would solve that?" Laura said.

"Sure—because as we came to know ourselves more deeply, and to relate more deeply in our connections with others, that loneliness would disappear. There would be security in that, too—in the social networks that those deeper connections would help form. That sense of security would be revived, too, as we regained our trust in our own intuitions.

"And as we trusted and followed the life rising up within us, as we more freely gave expression to the promise we felt there, more and more we would feel fulfilled, and more and more we would feel the joy that comes with that fulfillment. We would, in short, have filled the hollow."

Laura took another handful of the trail mix, chewed it thoughtfully.

"Hm," she said, after a few moments. "So we'd be less lonely, more secure, and more fulfilled." She nodded thoughtfully. "That's pretty impressive. Does it just keep going on? Does the theory come out that way in every situation—crime, poverty, drug addition—whatever the problem, does it work with anything you would pick?"

"I think so," I said. "Like drug addition, apart from its physiological basis, psychologically, socially, I think it's another example of trying to fill the hollow. Really, any sort of addictive behavior is.

"And poverty—well, obviously," I went on, "this theory doesn't have to do with producing more goods, but just the goods we have, just the food and other necessary goods we already grow and make, would be enough to go around if people weren't so busy trying to fill their personal hollows, trying to accumulate so much for themselves. And if we identified more deeply with others, we would want to be of more help when we saw others in trouble.

"So I think true poverty would be a thing of the past, too," I concluded, then thought for a minute about how I had felt, years before, when I'd first moved from India to England. There was so much wealth in England—so much, even, that went to waste—which could have done so much good where I had come from.

"And crime?" Laura asked.

I turned my attention back to the conversation, and paused for a moment to form my answer. "Well, I think I would tie that in with what you asked before about war and other violence."

"Yeah?" Laura said.

"Sure—think about it. There's a kind of violence in doing something that is harmful to another person, that is against their wishes or their well being—and that's basically what crime is, isn't it? I mean, maybe sometimes we use the word when maybe we shouldn't, for some things that technically aren't crimes...," I said.

"Like what?" Laura asked.

"Like that student I had last year who was arrested for smoking pot—or really, for possessing a small amount of it. I couldn't really see how he was hurting anyone," I answered.

"Right—the so-called 'victimless crimes,'" Laura said.

"Yeah—society decides to regulate some behavior just to have standard norms. But in situations where one person is hurting another, there's a kind of violence in that. There's violence in crimes, there's violence in wars. There's even violence in the punishment of crimes, where the society decides to hurt the perpetrator," I said.

"And would you say that all comes from the Original Change, as well?" Laura asked.

"I can't say all violence does. There's violence in nature. But I do think the Original Change shifted the balance so that it made more sense to us to use violence as a tool.

"Remember, the Original Change encouraged an insular mindset where we did not identify deeply with other life in general—and also didn't identify, specifically, with other people who were different from us. When you don't identify, you don't see things from another person's point of view; you don't empathize. If somebody has something you want, you just take it. You don't care about them; you don't feel for what it means to them to lose it. Criminal acts can seem to make sense to people who see benefits for themselves, and who don't feel for the cost to the victim.

"And of course," I went on, "the same sort of problems can exist on a larger scale. If you live in one tribe and you see another tribe living on a prime piece of land—and if you don't see how things are from their point of view, if you don't empathize with them, if you don't feel for how they feel—then what's to stop you from deciding that it would be most convenient for you just to kill them and take their land for your own people—that is, for the little band of people you do identify with?"

Laura nodded as I went on.

"The same mindset may have led to slavery, too," I added. "You want work done, but you don't want to do it yourself—so why not just force somebody else to do it for you? That insular mindset, which developed as a result of the Original Change, makes that sort of conclusion seem acceptable—even practical."

I glanced over at Laura. "We do the same thing with animals," I added. "People think they can own animals and do to them whatever they want. They think they can own land and clear cut it, destroying all the life on it—because an insular perspective permits such logic to seem sensible. If we identified with that other life, if we felt for it, we could never do such terrible things," I said.

"And wars are just the same thing, I guess," Laura said. "You want some resource, you want some piece of land..."

"So somebody invades," I said, "and then the nation that's been attacked feels they have no choice but to fight back. Pretty soon both sides are demonizing the other—seeing them as having a bad nature, and feeling justified in any actions they may take against the other. Communication falls to the wayside. All three impediments come into play—all outgrowths of the Original Change. Whatever the actual initial motivation for war, I think that picture is pretty much the same.

"You might be interested to know, by the way," I said, "that the earliest evidence of war from an archaeological site dates to about 12,000 years ago—when the Original Change was really coming into its own. There's no archaeological evidence of war ever having taken place before that time."*

I paused for a moment, then added, "All these problems would be vastly improved with the New Change. Each side in a conflict would want to understand, would be prepared to listen, and to identify, to feel for the needs of the other, and to see from their perspective. After that, it becomes more possible to work out reasonable solutions—whether it's in the context of international struggles, or interpersonal ones. Or even in dealing with nature—with other creatures—the New Change would prepare us to seek to understand the needs of all involved, and to try to meet all of those needs. The circumstances that we have known for thousands of years—that have led to so much conflict and destruction—could be so greatly improved upon."

For a long time, then, we bumped and rattled along in silence. Out my side window, near the tops of the trees towering above the road, I could see a half moon dangling. I found myself thinking that when we had set

---

* See Part II of Appendix 3, Note 2 (page A15).—I. K.

off on this journey, I had thought of it as an adventure for Laura. I had had no idea how much it would mean to me, nor how much I would be changed by it. The ideas I'd had already had profoundly changed my outlook on the world.

I looked over at Laura and watched her face in the green glow of the dashboard lights, and suddenly was overcome with a feeling of how very precious she was to me.

Perhaps she felt me looking at her, but regardless, she looked over at me then, and offered me a warm smile, before returning her eyes to the road.

"You know, Indira," she said, "what you've been talking about, about the mindset of the New Change, I was just thinking about that. In Buddhism, when they talk about enlightenment, they talk about it being like 'a dew-drop slipping into the shining sea.' But as some people—like Huston Smith, for example—will point out, it really makes more sense to think of the dewdrop opening, and the entire sea entering into the dewdrop."

"That's the sort of thing you're talking about happening, isn't it?—symbolically, I mean—that we expand our sense of self to take in more," Laura asked.

"Yes, it is," I said, thinking about the image of a dewdrop being filled with all that was in the ocean—vitalized, fulfilled, enriched.

Laura paused, then said, with a note of hope in her voice, "Do you really think it's likely that that's what lies ahead—the New Change, I mean?"

"I not only think it's likely," I told her, "I think it's sort of inevitable. What time frame we're talking about, I'm not sure, but if I'm right about the sort of development we've been through already, we could no more stop the New Change from happening than we could decide to keep someone a teenager forever and never let them become an adult. I think it really will happen—it's just a matter of *when*."

I rode along in the darkness, listening to the rumble of the tires against the road and the hum of the engine, and thought about this for a little while.

"You know, Laura—the truth is, we've already begun. We've already begun to learn to set aside our prejudices, to identify more freely and deeply; to care more about people with customs or backgrounds different from our own; to care more about the animals, even the plants, that fill our environments. Our social structures are less rigid, less repressive to individuals. We turn more and more to diplomacy—both interpersonal, and international—to solve our problems.

"We've already started into that long turn that will eventually line us up with the New Change, I think. It won't happen overnight, but I think we're really going to get there. I really think that this is right. I know I can't prove it, but it all makes sense to me. And it's consistent with the facts. I think about where we've come from and what's inspired us in the past, and I think it's inevitable that we'll keep going forward. How quickly or how slowly is up for grabs, but it would be almost impossible for us not to get there. This *is* what lies ahead: *the real adulthood of humanity*."

"The real adulthood of humanity," Laura echoed. "I like the idea a lot, Indira. I sure hope you're right."

We continued on along the narrow road, traveling through a tunnel of forest aglow with the light of the Land Rover's headlamps.

I asked Laura what the odometer said, and we estimated that it would be perhaps another hour to Epulu, barring another mishap—though in the end the way was clear, and we shaved a little off that time. Though I'd promised to keep Laura entertained with talk, I didn't find that I had so much to say after that, and together we rolled along mostly in silence with, I believe, both of us thinking about a world with no more wars or violent conflict; a world in which people felt a part of a larger community of life, and in which the natural world flourished in all its facets; a world without bigotry, in which each person identified openly with others, and thus perceived the person, and not the stereotype; a world in which people were not isolated, or restricted by narrow roles or rules, but rather truly knew and fulfilled themselves, and formed deep, tender bonds with others; a world in which so much possibility was set to unfold.

By the time we arrived in Epulu, it was nearly midnight. Laura and I were both weary, but thrilled to be there. We set up camp in an open, grassy area near the Epulu River. In the darkness, we could hear the rush of the water as it slid dimly by in the glimmering moonlight. From the forest all around us we could hear a chorus of frogs and insects and, from somewhere deep within the forest beyond, the sound of people singing.

Laura and I stood listening next to our half-erected tent. The voices rose and fell rhythmically, striking alternating pitches. It was a sound I recognized from recordings Laura and I had listened to back in our home in Boulder—a bright and joyful sound. It was the Mbuti Pygmies.

I nudged Laura. "We're here," I whispered softly, not wanting to invade the music with my voice.

We finished getting our tent set up, then crawled inside and lay in silence for a long time, listening to the voices from the forest.

In the morning, we would get in touch with the man who ran Epulu Station and make arrangements to store some of our supplies there, then ask him to use his shortwave radio to contact Lisa Xiang for us.

Was Lisa with the people who were singing now? I wondered. Were they gathered around a fire whose sparks floated upwards, like stars, towards the high forest canopy—which itself lay like an uneven carpet below the star-spattered sky?

I thought about the research we had come here to do and wondered what this song the Mbuti were singing was about. I knew that they believed that if they had problems, the forest spirit must not have noticed what was going on, or it would have helped them—so they sang to it, to get its attention.

Was that what they were doing now? It wasn't the only reason that they sang, I knew, but as I found myself listening to the rise and fall of voices, I wondered if they were calling to the spirit of the forest to bring them good fortune.

I imagined their small dome-shaped houses, covered with leaves as large as platters. I imagined them dancing around a fire that sent its sparks drifting up amidst the interwoven branches of a vast, living forest.

Here were a people, I thought, whose lives were so deeply intermeshed with the life of the forest around them—and yet they sang *to* the forest.

"Have you thought about that, Laura?" I asked.

"What?"

"The Mbuti, they sing *to* the forest."

"Yeah," she answered.

"If it were before the Original Change, they would feel no need to. They would simply be of the forest. There would be no 'I' to sing to 'you.' There wouldn't be even that much sense of separateness.

"I mean, here we are," I went on, "we've come so far to meet these people who belong so deeply with nature, here living in the cradle of humanity, but even they passed through the same Change."

Laura was silent for a moment, then answered. "It's like I was saying to you on the barge," she said. "They have all these stories where there's something keeping them apart from nature, from the animals—some gap, some misunderstanding."

"Like the elephant story," I said.

"Yes. They never quite, really belong," Laura answered.

I listened to the song rising up from somewhere within the forest, listened to it interweaving with the chorus of frogs and insects, and with the sounds of the river.

"They sound like they belong," I said.

"Yes. It sounds like that," Laura said softly, thoughtfully. "And they believe the spirit of their forest cares, and will listen when they sing to it—but like you said, they do have to sing to it to get its attention. They and the forest are not one."

I rolled over so I was facing Laura. I couldn't see her at all in the dark inside the tent, though she was only inches away.

"So it really was all of us, wasn't it?" I whispered. "*All* of us made the Change, even those who still live in the moment—who were never pushed to make plans by growing crops, or by living in a cold climate. We all know ourselves, and we all feel a certain separateness because of it."

"You sound sad about that," Laura said.

I wasn't sure how to answer. Maybe it did seem sad. But it shouldn't, really. Maybe we were just that much more ready for the New Change.

I could hear a rustling as Laura turned towards me. Suddenly, I was aware of her presence.

"We're alone together," I whispered.

Laura reached over and touched my shoulder, then trailed her hand down my arm and let it rest near my elbow.

"We've come all this way and finally arrived in Epulu," I said. "And we don't have separate cots," I added, "and you're not ill or recovering."

Laura gently pulled towards me, and I moved closer to her—and as I did, I remembered a dream I'd had, many years before, before Laura had left New York to go to Lame Deer.

In the dream, Laura and I had been climbing a tall mountain and had arrived at the top before a beautiful vista, with a great forest spread before us, and from below us, somewhere, had arisen the sound of people singing. The dream had seemed a good omen, somehow, and had cheered me enough at the time that I had encouraged Laura to go ahead and take the job in Lame Deer.

Now, remembering it, I felt that we had, indeed, arrived somewhere after a long climb—and here we were, in the presence of a vast forest and a beautiful song, while stretched out before us was a breathtaking view of the future.

I caressed Laura's cheek in the darkness.

"We have arrived," I whispered, then pressed my lips to hers.

CHAPTER XV

Rise up nimbly and go on your strange journey
to the ocean of meanings.

—RUMI

The months Laura and I spent with the Mbuti were a time full of happiness and discovery for both of us. In addition to the opportunity to do research in the field—something we both very much enjoyed—it was a time of personal satisfaction for me, as well, for the quiet of those months gave me a chance to reflect on the ideas I had developed on our journey there.

I found myself eager to find a way to take hold of the promise of the New Change, and actually engage in making it real around us.

It seemed to me that the deliberative consciousness that we had arrived at through the Original Change could be a tool we could use to speed up this process. There was no need to wait the thousands of years it had taken us to pass through the Original Change. We could apply our abilities to plan and to set our own course, to setting sail for this destination, and not have to simply wait as an inevitable tide caused us to drift slowly towards shore.

In the weeks and months that followed, as Laura and I spent our time with our new Mbuti friends, sharing in their daily lives and taking notes on their beliefs and activities, I found my thoughts returning often to this question of how to encourage the New Change. I understood that it depended, as the original one had, on it being dreamed of, longed for, and modeled in the minds of those who wished for it—but there was more we could do, as well.

It seemed plain to me that the first step of this new path must involve a deepening encounter with the individual self—for only when our sense of self grew large enough would our narrowed perceptions widen sufficiently to take in the experiences of other people and other life. Only when we understood the nature of our own impulses, could we see the inherent goodness in that unfettered flow, and therefore see the inherent goodness in one another, and in the very nature of things. Only when we improved the communication within ourselves would we know ourselves well enough, and empathize deeply enough with others, to really bear the fruit of what communication, at all levels, could be.

Clearly, I thought, if we were to leave behind our adolescent posture towards the world and grow into our true adulthood, the first steps would involve an adventure of self-discovery.

I found myself wishing to use my time with the Mbuti not just to discover what I could about the ways and beliefs of our often-ebullient hosts, but to use the solitude I found in that deep and ancient forest to delve deeper into myself, as well.

The Ituri Forest is perhaps the most enchanting of places within which one might engage in such an adventure. Its tall trees rocket to the sky, while below them narrow streams sparkle like strips of sunlight cast upon the ground. Wherever the Mbuti travel within the forest, they are at home, singing songs to lighten their labors or to add joy to celebrations. Each day, life begins anew, with astonishingly few worries carried over from one day to the next.

A few weeks after our arrival, I spent the day with Kamaikan, first helping her as she rebuilt a section of her leaf-covered hut where the rain had gotten in the night before, and then following her and the other women into the forest, where we foraged for mushrooms and nuts.

I had so many questions about how the Mbuti viewed the forest and the other creatures within it, and about how those views influenced their behavior....

❊   ❊   ❊

"Pause," Paul said, as he came to the crest of a rise.

"Pausing," Kiki responded.

Before and below Paul were a group of small buildings with roofs as shiny and dark as pools of deep water. They ringed a larger building, which was at the center of the meadow in which they were all cast about, like coins scattered in the sun. Around them, people strolled, or mingled with one another. Near the large building at the center of the green was a tall fir tree, in the shade of which people sat quietly, as though in study.

Paul trailed his sight along the path before him until it met up with the cluster of buildings below. Over the Sojourner's Path, just before the first building, was an arched sign, which read: "Welcome to the Kumaric Retreat."

Paul stood quietly for a minute, taking it all in and listening to the birds singing in the trees along the path. He had come all this way to reach this place, he thought—and for a moment it seemed that he had come, even, from another world, just to be here.

Paul rubbed his chin, and was glad to find it relatively free of stubble, then rubbed his head, and was glad to find it relatively full of hair. Even the bruise on his temple (which he recalled noticing in the stream when he'd stopped the day before) had faded enough to be hardly perceptible beneath his new tan.

Well, Paul thought, he couldn't be more ready than he was now—and he started down the short slope before him, toward the Retreat. As he went, he thought back over what he had listened to of Dr. Kumar's memoirs, and wondered if perhaps the biggest difference between his world and this was that in this world they had sought ways to encourage or speed up the New Change—while in his world, he was sure, the New Change was never so much as dreamed of.

Soon, Paul was off the slope and walking across a wide green meadow toward the nearest building. Before him, the sign proclaimed its welcome.

It was a fascinating question, Paul thought, as he strolled the final meters to the Kumaric Retreat: What, exactly, had they done in this world to make the New Change happen so quickly?

PART IV

◉

RETREAT

. 15 .

As Paul passed beneath the arched entrance to the Retreat, he noticed that the meadow surrounding him included quite a variety of plants. While some Paul recognized as native to the area, others were clearly cultivated plants grown for food.

Ahead of him, and just off the path, a young man was bent over, gathering vegetables from the meadow and putting them in a wheel barrow.

"Excuse me," Paul called out.

The young man stood up. In his hand was a large, purple-red tomato.

"This is my first time at the Retreat," Paul said. "Could you please tell me where I should go?"

The young man brushed the hair back from his eyes and smiled. "Sure, glad to," he said. "If you follow this path it'll take you to a large building at the center of the Retreat. There's a door there," he pointed, "just across from that tall tree. That's the director's office. She'll help you out."

Paul thanked him, then continued on toward the director's office. As he went, he passed people standing or sitting on the open meadow at the center of the Retreat, engaging in conversation.

In only a minute or two, Paul found himself at the door the young man had pointed out. It was made of some sort of solid, stone-like material. On it was etched an image of a sphere with many cone-shaped projections rising off of it. The cones were all narrow at their peaks, then sloped down, widening at their bases, where they connected with the body of the sphere. Paul was pretty sure this emblem was a stylized representation of a chinar seedpod, like Dr. Kumar had described in her memoirs.

Paul glanced around. On a stone plaque on the wall to the right of the door was engraved:

WASEME YABANN
DIRECTOR

Just below that, and a little smaller, a few more words were carved:

Flow down and down in always
widening rings of being.

—RUMI

Paul smiled. For a moment it seemed to him as though the world of the book he had been listening to had seeped out into the world around him—a door with a chinar seedpod on it and a quote from the poet who had meant so much to Indira Kumar!

Paul lifted his hand and knocked on the director's door. Immediately, he heard a voice call out, inviting him in.

As Paul stepped inside, he was struck with how light and bright it was inside the office—almost as bright as it was outdoors. The whole ceiling seemed to glow. Paul wondered briefly if the light was delivered through the same sort of fiber-optic technology he'd witnessed in the underground room he'd stayed in his first night on the trail. On shelves and corners all around the room, plants soaked up the sunlight.

"Hello," a woman said, as she rose from a chair on the far side of her desk. Paul took her in at a glance: a couple decades older than he was; her face, eyes, and hair a rich palette of browns; a manner as warm and bright as the room itself.

"Hi," Paul said, as the woman stepped around her desk to greet him. He reached out his hand to shake hers and was surprised when she took his hand in both of hers.

"Welcome to the Kumaric Retreat," she said. She turned her head slightly, then looked at Paul with a kindhearted, explorative expression. "I don't believe I've seen you here before."

"No, it's the first time I've been," Paul answered.

"To *our* Retreat, or to any of the Kumaric Retreats?" she asked.

Paul was surprised to learn there were others—but then thought that he shouldn't be. Clearly, Dr. Kumar's ideas were widespread.

"To any," Paul replied, hoping this answer wouldn't set him apart too much—but the director didn't miss a beat in replying.

"Well, then welcome all the more," she said, smiling. She introduced herself, then gestured toward a chair and encouraged Paul to set down his pack and have a seat, which Paul gladly did. It felt good to get off his feet after so long on the trail.

"You've been listening to *Memories and Reflections*?" the director said, gesturing toward her own shirt, while looking at Paul's. Paul glanced down and saw where Kiki was attached.

"Yes," he said.

"It's a long book—were you able to finish it?"

"No, actually, I just got as far as her starting her research in the Ituri Forest."

The director nodded. "We like people to have listened to it all, of course, but that will be okay. The concepts in the last third are what we emphasize here. You won't miss out," she said, as she sat back down in the chair behind her desk. Though the setting was somewhat formal—with them seated across a large desk from one another—the director seemed so relaxed that it put Paul at ease, as well.

"Since this is your first visit, let me tell you a little bit about the Retreat," Director Yabann went on. As warm and unhurried as her tone was, it was also authoritative. Each word was spoken clearly and with measured emphasis. "This particular retreat was completed in 2031," she said. "It was the seventh established in the United States, and the twenty-third worldwide. It was much smaller when it first opened its doors—we've added quite a number of buildings since then.

"It was, of course, after Dr. Kumar's book came out that people first began to dream of how we might collectively move forward toward the New Change, to speed up the process of creating an expanded sense of self. It was hoped that by having a place where people could gather and practice together, helping one another, that goal might be achieved more quickly.

"I'm sure you know most of this, but in case not, that's when some people got together and, with Dr. Kumar's blessing, in 2017, began construction on the first retreat. The purpose of Kumaric Retreats has been unaltered in all the years since—to provide a place were individuals may come to work on self expansion, and so add their influence to the creation of the collective change we all desire.

"That was the focus of the work they did in the first retreat, just as it's the focus of the work we do here, even to this day." The director paused, as though to give this point more weight, then went on, speaking in the same deliberative manner, her gaze resting gently on Paul.

"The process of developing an expanded sense of self is done in three stages," she said, waving her hand over a white square, about fifteen centimeters across, on the surface of her desk. Instantly, a semi-transparent three-dimensional image was displayed above the square. It appeared to Paul to be a holographic image of a chinar seedpod—but more naturalistic, and less stylized, than the one depicted on the director's door. (The one projected above her desk had far more cone-shaped projections rising off of it. Each differed from the next in subtle ways—in height, in thickness, in angle of ascent.)

"The first stage is designed to help people expand their awareness of themselves at the individual, or private, level," the director said. The hologram zoomed in, now, so it showed just one of the cones rising off of the sphere. The director picked up a pen and pointed to its tip. She paused, then she pointed a little lower, at the middle of the cone.

"The second stage is intended to help people explore the layer of themselves that they share in their relationships with others, and to help them expand their awareness of the personal experience of others. In other words, stage two has to do with interpersonal awareness."

The director moved her pointer down to the cone's base, with the pointer angled downward toward the body of the sphere.

"The third stage is intended to help people discover the deepest layers of themselves, and to help them develop a deepened sense of connection with all life. It is at this stage that people learn to sense the oneness of all life and to tap into the collective awareness that is at the root of all consciousness." The image zoomed out to show the whole seedpod, once again.

The director looked at Paul. Paul nodded. He had to admit to himself that there was something appealing about such clear and concise symbolism: the deeper we go in ourselves, the more we discover of ourselves and of our connection with others. How had Dr. Kumar described that deepest layer within us, Paul tried to recall—"*an ocean of consciousness, shared by all*"?

"With each stage," the director was saying, "information is offered to people to help them gain facility with the new awareness that they're developing. It's like when you get your first SPV. You know that it may take you far, and to many new places—but first you must learn how to drive it."

Paul had the feeling he had heard the term SPV used before. Oh yes, he thought—Zaid's father had used it. It meant Solar Powered Vehicle, if Paul's memory was right.

"So it is when we open up new territories within ourselves," the director went on. "Possibilities abound—but new skills must be learned for those possibilities to be fully actualized. To truly gain the freedom that lies dormant within us all, we must first learn to work the machinery of self. For this reason, with each stage of exploration, novice sojourners are offered new skills—new 'tools,' you might say—for navigating through each of these new layers of awareness.

"As Dr. Kumar once wrote, '*Life is an art, and we are the artists.*' We hope to help people learn what they would need to know in order to delve into the truth within themselves and bring their protolife to life—and in so doing, to make within the 'art' of their lives the experiences they would find most fulfilling.

"After all," the director concluded, "the more individuals succeed in creating around them the sort of world they, personally, would wish to live in, the more that is the sort of world we collectively create. The New Change grows out of the change in each of us. The Kumaric Retreat is here to help people create that change within themselves."

"So, those are the three stages, in a nutshell," the director told Paul. "Each novice sojourner is expected to find an experienced sojourner to work with as they go through the three stages. It's generally recommended that novice sojourners work with more than one experienced sojourner during their stay here, for the breadth of experience that provides. We ask experienced sojourners to wear a purple vest, so that those looking for such assistance will know who they can turn to. Feel free to approach these people to ask for help. If you have trouble finding someone you feel comfortable working with, you can come back to me, and I'll help you find someone.

"We want to make everyone feel welcome here, of course, but there's not space to let everybody come and stay forever. There's a two-week limit for novices, while experienced sojourners are permitted to stay longer—three, perhaps four, weeks if they are busy with their work assisting others. We are grateful for the time they spend with us. They are all volunteers.

"In addition to working individually with novice sojourners, many experienced sojourners also hold open classes, workshops, and discussion groups of various sorts, through which they share their expertise—all of which are available to those who wish to participate. You can find a listing of what's available through the portal in your room—or if you stumble on a gathering that looks interesting, feel free to join in.

"Everybody gets assigned a chore," the director added, as she again left her desk and stepped over to a wall panel near the door. "We try to split the chores up fairly. Let me see here." She waved her hand in front of the panel, where an Intralink portal opened up before her.

She called up a graphic of work assignments, then told Paul, "We had somebody here who was washing dishes for Monday, Wednesday, and Friday dinners, who left just this morning. If it would be all right with you, I'd like to ask you to pick up that duty."

"Sure," Paul answered. "Just that one thing?"

"That's right."

Paul smiled. "That'd be fine," he said. He had been told by the store clerk in Strandford that he would have to work while here, and was glad to discover that he would not be required to work every day, or for very much of any day. That would leave more time for him to prepare for building another transport. He felt quite fortunate to have found such a fine place to stay and continue his project.

"Good," the director said. "All right, then. Let's get you a room." She called up another schematic.

"This is a map of the Retreat," she said. "We have an unoccupied room here. It's west facing and has a very nice view, especially around sunset. I hope it will suit you."

Paul nodded his agreement, and at that, the director gave a command, and the portal delivered a small, sphere-shaped crystal. She gave the crystal to Paul.

"Keep this with you," she said. "Your room will sense it's with you and allow you to enter."

She turned back toward the screen. "You're here now," she said. "The dining room is here, and here's the kitchen just behind it. Halwerd will be in charge of the kitchen on the nights you're dishwashing. You won't need to work tonight, but tomorrow, check in with him before dinner is over, so he'll know you haven't forgotten."

The director turned toward Paul, her face still as warm as when he had first entered.

"Do you have any questions?" she asked.

"No."

"Then you're set. Feel free to come back, if you need my help for any reason. Also, there are portals all over the Retreat. If you need to see a map, a schedule of workshops, access to Kumaric texts, Intralink access—anything of that sort, you'll find what you need there.

"I hope you discover, during your stay here, all you have hoped to discover," she told Paul.

Paul thanked her. They shook hands again, and again she held Paul's one hand in the two of hers.

Then Paul picked up his pack and, with it pulled over one shoulder, stepped back out into the open day.

◘　　◘　　◘

Within minutes, Paul had arrived at his room. He closed the door behind him and dropped his pack heavily to the floor. It felt good to have arrived in a place he knew he would have entirely to himself for the next two weeks. Paul glanced around the room, taking in every detail. A long, narrow window ran across much of the wall opposite the door, revealing a panoramic view of the land and mountains west of the Retreat. To the right of the window, on the same wall, was one of the sort of panels Paul recognized as concealing an Intralink portal. Just below and in front of it was a small desk and a chair.

From the wall to Paul's right a long, narrow bed projected into the room. Just beyond the bed, on the same wall, was a doorway. Opposite it, on the far wall, was another door, and next to that door was a large engraving, which Paul could easily read from where he stood by the door. It read:

> *The superior person settles her mind as the universe settles*
> *the stars in the sky.*
> *By connecting her mind with the subtle origin, she calms it.*
> *Once calmed, it naturally expands, and ultimately her mind*
> *becomes as vast and immeasurable as the night sky.*
>
> — FROM THE HUA HU CHING

Paul finished reading it, then explored what lay beyond the two doors. The one nearest the bed, it turned out, led to a small bathroom with a shower, sink, and toilet. The other door led to the closet.

Paul stepped over and waved his hand in front of the wall panel, then watched as the portal opened up. He smiled. Everything was working out very nicely. A private room with a portal—and all he'd have to do for it was the three-stage thing the director mentioned, and wash some dishes, and for that he'd have room and board and a quiet place to work out what, exactly, he would need to do to build a new transport. He thought he could easily steer clear of all the voluntary workshops, classes, and discussion groups—and spend most of his time right here, focusing on his own work.

Paul sat down on the chair and slipped off his shoes. He'd been worried his whole way here about trying to get Dr. Kumar's memoirs finished before he arrived, and now was relieved to discover that the fact that he hadn't finished it didn't seem to matter. What had the Retreat director said? Those concepts would be emphasized here—and even without finishing it, he wouldn't miss out.

Good, Paul thought. He was glad to have one fewer thing to have to worry about.

Paul looked up at the portal in front of him and felt excited and energized as he took in the fact that he had arrived and could now focus on his work. For a moment, he was tempted to get started right away, refining the way he would connect up the necessary parts, looking for an adequate energy source, and trying to find some way to fund the purchases he would, eventually, have to make—but then he remembered how many days he had been without a bath, and decided it would be best to get a shower and a shave, and maybe even a short nap, before getting to work.

Paul woke to the sound of a chime coming from the Intralink portal near his bed. He opened his eyes and looked over at the portal. It was lit up and showed a map leading from his room to the dining area. A message below that read: "Dinner is ready."

It took a moment for Paul to adjust to his surroundings. So here he was, finally, at the Retreat. He wondered if he would discover here what he hoped to learn: how, exactly, they had made the transition to the New Change happen so quickly on this world, while on his world, it had not yet happened at all.

Paul stretched, then sat up and rubbed his face. He had only meant to sleep for twenty minutes, but instead two hours had gone by. It was six o'clock, now, and time for dinner.

Paul got up and dressed quickly in his cleanest clothes, then set out for the dining hall.

The room in which dinner was served was large enough to comfortably hold seventy or eighty people. It had a high arched ceiling and a broad fireplace along one wall. Above the fireplace was some sort of ornate machinery.

Paul stepped through the door and stood looking at that machinery. The line from the buffet reached almost to where he stood.

Someone near Paul followed the line of his sight, then said, "It's interesting, isn't it? Those contraptions were so large when they first started making them, back when this Retreat was built. I have one at home, but mine is so small, you hardly notice it."

"What is it?" Paul asked.

"A carbalizer," the man said.

Paul looked at him blankly.

"To recapture the carbon from the smoke and fumes. This one converts it all into a black powder—looks like soot. Last time I came here, I worked in the garden, burying that stuff. It's great in the soil, terrible in the air. In the ground, it holds the nutrients right where you want them. I think that's why they grow such great vegetables here."

Paul thanked the man for the information, then got in line for the buffet. If the carbalizer really did capture the "fumes"—the gasses—from the fire, Paul thought, it would take energy to convert it into something that looked like soot—but if so, what was the source of the energy used for that conversion?

As Paul considered this, the line for the buffet moved steadily forward. In only a few minutes, Paul was at its front. Moments later, he had a full plate in his hands and was glancing around the room for a place to sit.

The room was quite welcoming—the tables solid, the chairs padded and comfortable looking. Around each table sat groups of people, interacting with one another. Paul took a seat near the middle of the room and began to eat. The food he had selected from the buffet (fresh vegetables in a rich bean and barley stew) was marvelous—so different from the Saccomite of his world and the travel meals he had existed on for the last week.

Paul glanced at the woman next to him, who caught his eye.

"The food's really good," he said.

"Yes, it is. That's what you expect at a Kumaric Retreat. It's part of the Kumaric way," she said.

"Good food is?" Paul asked.

The man seated beyond her leaned forward. "Whole food is. If you want balance in your life, that has to include balance in your body. If you eat food that's been refined, stripped of its nutrients, you'll always feel hungry, and you'll never feel well. That's part of the pleasure of coming here—food just the way that nature made it, grown on site."

Paul looked around the room at the people visiting, and enjoying their meals. They all looked so well, so fit and healthy. But it was more than that; they seemed vibrant and warmly engaged in their interactions. They reminded Paul of the people who had gathered at Anna and Carlos's house, in their way of dress and in the intimacy of their gestures.

"Your first time here?" the woman asked Paul.

"Does it show?" Paul asked, as he turned back toward her.

"The way you were looking around when you came in, and just now," she said.

"Yeah, it's my first time."

"My name's Abigail," she said. She offered her hand. Paul reached for it to shake it, but instead, she took his hand in both of hers.

"I'm Paul," he said, as she smiled, then released his hand.

"Have you found an ES yet?" she asked casually, then took a bite of food.

"A what?"

"An experienced sojourner to work with?"

"No," Paul answered.

Abigail chewed and swallowed. "I know someone who likes to work with novices. He's good. If you'd like, I'll introduce you."

"That would be fine, thanks," Paul said. He was half pleased and half not. In the back of his mind he had almost hoped he could complete just the work requirement, but not actually have to waste his time on the three stages. On the other hand, he thought, if he risked it, he might not be permitted to stay—and then where would he go?

"Okay," Abigail said. She took another bite of food, then looked around the room. She glanced at Paul cheerfully, held up an index finger to him, then got up from the table and crossed the room.

A minute later, she returned with a man with graying hair, olive skin, and sparkling brown eyes. He was wearing a purple vest.

"This is Farsan," she said to Paul. "Farsan, this is Paul."

Farsan took a seat on the other side of Paul. For a few minutes, they spoke. Farsan asked Paul a few questions, though none were too probing. It seemed to Paul, instead, that he was probing with his eyes, as his face had much the same sort of attentive expression that Paul had seen in both Anna's and the Retreat director's faces. As they spoke, Paul was aware of something fatherly in Farsan's expression—well, not so much fatherly as grandfatherly, Paul thought. Something in Farsan's presence (the warmth in his eyes, his thoughtful manner, a certain gentleness, perhaps?) reminded Paul of his own grandfather, though this man was younger and somehow more physically vigorous than Paul remembered his own grandfather as having been.

After a few minutes, they both agreed to meet the next day at two o'clock. Farsan told Paul the room number, then stood and patted Paul on the shoulder before returning to his dinner at another table.

Paul glanced around the room. People were still streaming in through the same door through which Paul had entered only a little while ago. Some held hands—men and women, men and men, women and women—but it struck Paul, as it had at Anna's and Marco's, that most of these relationships were friendly, rather than romantic, in nature.

What a strange world, Paul told himself, as he took another bite of his dinner. Then he allowed his thoughts to drift, once more, to the welcoming he would receive when he returned to his world, triumphant, and told them of the treasure he had found for them! He imagined, too, how it would be to see Sheila, and what the look on her face would be after she had heard of his success through the Stream.

Yes, everything was going exceedingly well, he told himself. After dinner, he would spend a few hours on the Intralink portal in his room, going over what he still needed to learn about the parts he would need to build his transport. And when he was done, he would lie down and get a good night's sleep on a real bed for the first time in many nights.

◘   ◘   ◘

Paul was climbing stairs that went, somehow, from the building next door, into his building. He felt he had never come this way before, but now he had to try.

The climb was long. Something sticky on the stairs sucked at the bottoms of his shoes, which made the climb harder. The stairs seemed to go on forever. Paul's legs ached, but he kept climbing, running as fast as he could up the stairs.

Suddenly, Paul was inside the apartment and everything was silent. He looked down at his feet. He had taken off his shoes so he could move more easily. He stepped forward on his young, steady legs. He would find her now. He had to.

He had a package in his hand. He went from room to room, calling for her, but each room was empty. The curtains fluttered, and light leaked in around them. Everywhere, there was a sense of hollowness, a kind of emptiness.

Finally, Paul found her, lying alone in her dimly lit bedroom, with the curtains closed and a band of light coming in through the open door.

"Mom," he said, but she didn't answer. The room was hot and still.

"Mom," he said again. This time, she rolled over with a moan and turned her face toward him. Her eyes were cool and distant, closed off to him.

Her face! Paul realized—he could see her face! Even though he was dreaming, he understood that it had been a very long time since he had been able
to remember it—and yet there she was before him!

As Paul looked at his mother, her eyes bored into him: remote, hard—and
accusatory.

Paul looked away for a moment, unable to bear it, then slowly turned his
eyes toward her again. Only now the face of the woman before him was no
longer hers.

It was Sheila's.

"Mom!" Paul shouted, but this time his own voice stirred him, and he came
awake in his darkened room at the Retreat, with the impression of Sheila's
appearance still before his eyes. She looked like she had when they'd first met,
when she had sat beside him at dinner and said such encouraging things—
her expression open, pleased, coaxing.

In that moment, Paul remembered her and longed for her embrace, and for
all the comfort he had found there. He closed his eyes tightly and tried to escape
back into the dim nothingness of sleep—into the hollow between dreams.

◻   ◻   ◻

When Paul woke in the morning, the dream that had awakened him in the
night still lingered within him, like wisps of a fog the day would soon burn
away. It stayed with him long enough for him to remember the appearance
of his mother's face. How many years had it been since he had seen her, even
in his mind's eye? he wondered. Yet he still knew her when he saw her—even
like this, briefly, in a dream. It *was* her face, he knew.

But why was it, Paul wondered, that it had been so many years since he
could recall how his mother looked?

And why was it that, after so long, his first memory of her would be like
this, on her deathbed, with such a hard look in her eye—his mother, whom
he *knew* had been so kind and so gentle?

And why, he lay there wondering, when he could finally recall her, did her
face disappear before him again—only to be replaced with Sheila's?

Paul lay with his eyes wide open, staring at the ceiling. He had come so
very far, and through it all he had been so certain of himself, and of his
purpose—but something in this dream pulled at something within him—
something deep, that other things had been built on, like a tide tugging at
the posts beneath a pier.

It was as though Paul could hear the wood creaking and moaning beneath
his feet. He was afraid that if he wasn't careful, the pier might shatter, and
he would be dropped into the chilly water beneath.

Paul sat up and rubbed his face, hoping that he could finish waking, and
so scatter the lingering fragments of this discomforting dream—and the
strange, wordless ache it held within it.

16

Paul looked up and around the room. Something about the wall opposite his bed caught his eye. Something was different.

Paul stared for a moment before he realized what it was. Something about the engraving had changed. It seemed to him that there were fewer words now.

It took a moment for Paul to accept the fact, but what had been written on the wall the day before was no longer there. In its place, the engraving now read:

People only see what they are prepared to see.

—RALPH WALDO EMERSON

Paul stepped over to the wall to take a closer look. The lettering, which had appeared solid at a glance, was actually slightly transparent. Colored glass? Paul wondered. He reached out his hand to touch the material, but where he had expected to find a smooth surface, he found no surface at all. Instead, his fingers entered into the material without so much as a ripple.

Paul withdrew his hand quickly. It only took a moment for him to realize that the reason the material wasn't solid was because it was made of light. It was a hologram.

No wonder the words could be silently changed while he slept, Paul thought—then laughed a little at himself, for his initial confusion.

Using the sink in the bathroom, Paul took a few minutes to wash out some of the clothes he had worn on the trail, then pulled the remaining clothes from his pack and began to dress for the day. As he put on his shirt, the portal lit up and displayed an announcement that breakfast was ready. Good, Paul thought. He was hungry—and after the fine dinner he had had the night before, he was especially looking forward to breakfast.

He put on his shoes, made sure the pass to his room was still in his pocket, then set off for the dining hall.

Paul found his breakfast enjoyable and uneventful. He sat quietly by an open window, looking out over the Retreat. His only tablemate was another young man, who seemed as disinclined to engage in small talk as Paul was.

After he was done eating, Paul decided to take a few minutes and look around the Retreat. He had planned to return immediately to his room and use the Intralink portal there to help him refine his plans for building a new transport, but decided he could spare a little bit of time to discover more about the Retreat. After all, he told himself, he might even be able to figure out what the power supply was for the Retreat—in which case, the time he spent looking around would have been well spent.

Paul strolled around, examining the buildings for any sign of where they got their power. Perhaps some sort of solar-absorbent material was built into the walls and roofs, he considered—but if that was the case, then that material had clearly been designed to look no different from any other building material, for Paul could find no evidence of it.

Paul thought that perhaps he could trace the power supply back to its source by looking for wires going to or from the buildings, but when he looked, he could see no sign of external wiring at all, or any other means for power coming to or from any of the buildings.

Frustrated with what he could find outside, Paul decided to take a look inside one of the buildings. He chose a long, single-story building nearby and went inside.

The building had a hall running through the middle of it. On either side of the hallway were doors. As Paul started down the hall, he could hear voices coming from behind some of the doors. About midway down the hall, on Paul's left, one of the doors stood open. As Paul approached, he could hear laughter coming from that room.

Paul smiled and stopped near the open door, just out of sight of the people inside. On the wall next to the door, a few words were engraved. They read:

MODELING-REALITY CLASS

Odd, Paul thought—that the room would be so consistently used for one purpose that they would engrave the words there permanently—then realized the words were no more likely to be permanent here than they had been in his room, before.

Paul stepped closer to examine the lettering. As he did, the words shimmered and redrew themselves:

WE PERCEIVE WHAT WE MODEL

they said. Paul recognized a certain transparency and pressed his finger into the lettering just as the words shifted again. This time they read:

We see things not as they are, but as we are.

—IMMANUEL KANT

Paul stared, thinking about the technology required to produce this effect and whether he could make any use of it, or any of its elements, in his project.

As he reflected on this, the words reverted back to the original phrase—"Modeling-Reality Class."

Paul leaned over and peered through the doorway of the classroom. Inside, the lights had been dimmed. The classroom itself was ordinary enough, with the obvious exception that a holographic projection—of a star-filled sky above a distant mountain range—filled perhaps a third of the room, at the end furthest from the door.

"Can anybody point out the constellation 'Leo' for me—also known as 'the Nemean lion?'" the teacher asked. She stood facing the hologram, with her back to the door—young, slender, with dark, wavy hair that fell loosely around her shoulders. The students all shrugged or shook their heads.

"All right. I'll show it to you, then," the teacher said. She turned, now, so that she stood in the light from the doorway. Paul noticed that she had on a purple vest. He took in the sight of her: not quite as tall as he and no older, with an expression, somehow, at once serious and playful.

She's beautiful, he thought, and it struck him then that she looked unlike anyone he had ever known—such a mix of qualities from around the world—her features full and faintly African, her eyes with a slight Asian cast, her cheekbones high, her skin smooth and golden brown, and a flash of bronze in her dark eyes as she scanned the classroom.

She tilted her head forward and said something to her personal player, which was attached to her shirt just below her left shoulder. As she spoke, lines appeared between a set of stars in the holographic sky, revealing the constellation she'd asked the class to identify. The lion—with its thick head, neck, and torso—appeared to be striding through a field of stars on spindly legs, while trailing a wiry tail.

"There," the teacher said. She stepped over to the display and pointed out the brightest stars in the constellation, naming them. Then she spoke again to her personal player, and the lines demarcating the lion disappeared again.

"Okay," she said to the class, "can anybody point out the constellation of 'Leo' for me?" she asked again, smiling.

Nearly every hand in the class went up. The teacher called on one of the students, who stepped into the skyscape, pointed out the right stars, and described the image of the lion.

"You can see it, now," the teacher said to the class. "Now that you have a model for it in your minds, it's visible to you. Imagine how the stars look to people once they have learned to recognize a dozen, or two dozen, constellations! Why, it's more like a mural for them, than the way the night sky looks to most of us—and yet the stars are the same.

"For most of us," she continued, "the night sky is full of dots scattered aimlessly—but after we've formed mental models of constellations, we see patterns in the stars to match those constellations, just as though the constellations really existed outside ourselves. The stars exist outside of ourselves, but the constellations come from within," she said.

"I'd like to share another example with you," she said. Paul watched as she again spoke to her personal player, then lifted her head and casually brushed the hair from her face as a new holographic projection appeared before and around them—this one of a room in an art museum. At one end of the room, a large abstract painting was prominently featured.

Paul, who was taking as much interest in the teacher as the class, remembered what the director had told him about feeling free to join in. He quietly slipped through the doorway and took a seat at the back of the room.

"What do you see here?" the teacher asked the class.

"A painting, with a lot of blue, smudgy dots," a young woman with short dark hair, who was sitting to Paul's left, answered.

"Okay, good," the teacher replied. "Anybody else? Do you see anything more in this?—any patterns in the dots?"

"Not really," a rugged-looking man near the front said. "The dots are close together in some areas, far apart in others."

"There are bands with more blue. Other areas are almost all white—but no real pattern," an older woman near Paul added in.

"Okay," the teacher responded. "Anything more?"

Some of the students glanced around the room.

"It's just an abstract painting—and kind of a boring one," a young man in a red and green shirt said. Other students nodded.

"Okay, good. Then I'd like to show you another picture," the teacher said. She again gave a soft command through the personal player attached to her chest. The hologram shimmered, and a different room—apparently in the same museum—took form around them. The effect was very much as though the whole class had simply been transported to another room in the museum.

In the new museum room, the class was positioned before another large painting—this one comprised of a few bold, blue strokes against a white canvas.

"This," the teacher continued, "is a character in Chinese—in the earliest simplified style. It means 'joy' or 'joyous.' Take a close look. Okay? Now we'll go back to the first painting."

She gave another word to her personal player, and again the image around them shimmered. In a moment, they were all seemingly transported back to the first room in the museum.

As the first painting reappeared before them, Paul heard a couple of small exclamations from the class.

"It's the same thing," a young man with long brown hair said.

"Yes," someone else chimed in. "The blue parts match."

"It *is* the same," the teacher said, her tone full of encouragement. "The pattern was there all along. I counted on none of you having studied archaic Chinese writing, so no one—none of you—would have already formed a mental model for this Chinese character for "joy."

"So let me make this very clear: to begin with, you could see the dots that made up the painting, but you couldn't identify the pattern those dots formed—a pattern for the word "joy"— because you had no model for it. Perceiving patterns in the world around you is a mental construct. It is an interpretation of the world. It happens in your mind, not outside of you. Until you have the pattern—the model—in your mind, you will never see that pattern in the world around you.

"You might say, if you want to find joy, you have to form a mental model of it first. You have to believe in it, first—or you will never find it—for, after all, *a belief is nothing more than a mental model of what's real.*

"Okay, so—can anybody give me an example of how this might work in real life?" she asked the class, then said a word to her personal player, and the museum hologram disappeared. The classroom lights came up as the light from the hologram faded.

"What you're talking about—isn't that the same thing Dr. Kumar wrote about in *Memories and Reflections*," the young woman with the short dark hair answered, "when she talked about her friend Tommy, the guitar player? He had no mental model for being good at what he did, so he could hear the same notes everyone else heard, but the patterns he would pick out matched the mistakes he made, not his successes."

"Right, because he *did* have a mental model for himself as a mistake maker," the young man with the long brown hair said.

"That's right; that's a good example," the teacher told the class. Paul watched her. He continued to find her beautiful, but it was something more than just how she looked. There was something beautiful about *her*—about how warmly she turned toward the students in the class, how brightly she spoke to them, and with what enthusiasm. There was something open and fresh about her, Paul thought—like a beautiful lake, as clear as the sky above, into which one might wish to dive.

Paul smiled, and for a moment wondered if maybe someone like her could possibly take an interest in someone like him, and just as quickly discounted the idea. Still, it was nice to sit there and enjoy watching her teach.

"It's like that saying," a young woman near the front of the class said, "'*You can't perceive it till you conceive it'*—or conceive *of* it, I guess."

"Exactly. Very good," the teacher said. She looked around the class. "This reminds me of a quote, originally from one of Dr. Kumar's journals: 'We do not see as real, or existent, anything we do not have a model for.' Wait. You'll like this better as a projection."

She spoke briefly to her personal player, then stepped to one side of the room. The lights in the classroom dimmed as another projection came up. This one appeared to be of someone's study, dating from the early twenty-first, or perhaps late twentieth, century. It was a small room, with a large window looking out over a residential street, beyond which rugged mountains rose skyward. A woman—small, with straight gray and black hair, and dark eyes and skin—sat at a desk, writing in a journal. In a moment, a voice filled the classroom, and Paul realized it was intended to convey what the woman was writing. He recognized the voice immediately as that of Indira Kumar:

> We do not see as real, or existent, anything we do not have a model for. If a person does not believe that others will treat them kindly (that is, if their model tells them that this is not the way of the world) then people who commit kind acts will seem to them only to be behaving strangely. Rather than viewing such kindness as a natural part of life, those who disbelieve in kindness will, instead, be suspicious of those who are so 'odd' as to commit kind acts.

For them, such individual acts of kindness will exist in full view—like the stars visible in the night sky—but those kind acts, joined together, will not form interpretable constellations.

While these kind acts may seem nice enough on their own, they will seem, then, to make no sense in the larger picture. For those who see the world as unkind, the kindest among us will appear only as strangers, whose behavior is uninterpretable, and therefore deserving of suspicion.

The fact is that none of us are comfortable with people behaving oddly. We prefer, instead, the company of those whose actions seem understandable and interpretable to us. Those for whom kindness appears as an oddity may, therefore, choose the company of the unkind, for in such company they find a context that matches their model of reality—a context that is known and predictable and with which they feel prepared to cope. In that sense, it seems to them a safer context, as well.

Just as patterns of kindness remain invisible to those initiated only into the unkind, opportunities of all sorts, when left unmodeled, will remain invisible to us, as well.

If there is some sort of work someone would love to do, and they do not believe that it will be possible for them to attain it, then the path that might lead to that work, and the life that goes with it, will be as invisible to them as a constellation they have yet to imagine in the night sky. The cobblestones that mark that path will seem to them randomly scattered, or aligned in strange patterns that hold no meaning. They will not follow a path they do not see.

To discover in life what we wish to find there requires first that we model it in our minds. Only after these patterns are established in our minds, will we be able to perceive them when they occur around us.

"I've always liked that passage," the teacher said. She looked admiringly toward the figure of Indira Kumar as the image faded away.

"What Dr. Kumar is telling us here," she went on, "is that if you want to have an experience—to have career success, say, or a loving relationship with someone who treats you well—then you need to first form a mental model of those things happening, to believe in it, and to be prepared to see it in the world around you—or those opportunities will pass you by, as invisible to you as the Chinese symbol for joy was to you just now.

"All right. Now, time is getting short, and I want to get in one more projection before the class is done—so I'm sorry, but I'm going skip discussion on this so we can fit everything in. Here, again, Dr. Kumar speaks of constellations."

The teacher bent her head once more and spoke into her personal player. The scene in the study reappeared, and once again, Dr. Kumar's voice filled the room:

Reality is more complex than is our ability to perceive it. Unable to take it all in, we instead pick out and emphasize those aspects that seem most significant to us. Thus the world we perceive is never more than a minor subset of the actual world around us. We are like the ancient astronomer looking at the heavens, identifying constellations. We take note of only a few select stars out of the countless many.

Each of us tries, by connecting the dots of his or her reality, to tell ourselves true stories about it. In the process, we ignore many elements that we regard as insignificant—but which may, in fact, be points of light around which whole worlds orbit.

By picking out a handful of seemingly significant details and throwing away the rest, we provide ourselves with a necessary ordering of perception. In so doing, we choose to attend to the bus about to run us down, while disregarding the old leaflets in the gutter. It is essential that we prioritize and emphasize certain perceptions over others—yet that process has its hazards, as well.

We are predisposed to see, in the world around us, patterns that duplicate the patterns we hold in our own minds. Someone who believes the world is full of greedy people, for example, will attend to those elements of their experience that are consistent with that belief, while ignoring, as irrelevant, just as valid evidence to the contrary. So it is that what we model and believe will seem to us persistently proven and reproven, for there are always enough stars in the sky to give shape to whatever patterns we seek in them.

It is this way for those who believe in greed, or in generosity, or in anything else. We find evidence for what we model and believe in in the complex field of perceptions that surrounds us—even as we dismiss, as small and irrelevant, everything that does not fit our view.

For this reason, the world we actually know and experience begins within us. The story of our lives is told in the constellations that we draw.

As the projection faded once again, the teacher stepped to the front of the room.

"Okay, everyone—you've been a great class. I'm so glad you all could come. For those who would like to come back for more, I'll be here at 9 AM Mondays, Wednesdays, and Fridays from now through June 8th. Come again if you like. Each day will be something new on the topic of 'modeling reality.'"

"I wouldn't miss it, Jessica," Paul heard the rugged-looking man say, as he passed her on his way to the door.

"I won't be back until next Friday. I've already made plans for Wednesday with my ES," the young woman with the short dark hair said.

Paul thought about saying something to the teacher, too, but didn't know what it would be. Instead, he stepped from the classroom with the rest of the class, and soon found himself back in the same hallway, wondering if this was really the best way to spend the brief two weeks of room and board he had walked so long to acquire.

As Paul turned his thoughts to this question, he chastised himself for wasting time so impulsively. Quite apart from the time he'd spent in the classroom, what was he doing looking around the Retreat for its power source, anyway? What mattered was what was available on this world, not what just happened to be being used at any one location on it.

Besides, Paul noted as he stepped back out into the sunlight, any place as remote as this place was, was probably designed to run efficiently and on less energy than he would need to run his transport. Why should he hope to find the sort of power supply he would need here, anyway?

Paul felt frustrated with himself as he headed back to his room. The fate of a whole world depended on him. He would have to do better at keeping his mind on that in the future, he told himself.

17

It seemed to Paul that he had hardly had time to get anything done on his project before the portal screen flashed and displayed an announcement that lunch was ready. Frustrated, Paul decided to ignore it. Instead, he told himself, he would eat one of his remaining travel meals in his room.

He canceled the portal's announcement, then reviewed what he had been doing. After returning to his room, he had first spent some time with the portal asking questions about current patterns of world power use—what percent was derived from solar, from wind, from combustion, and so forth—but having found nothing promising that way, he had begun to ask, instead, about the power requirements of various machines and industries. It frustrated Paul, but it seemed the machinery of this world was very energy efficient. Nothing he could think to ask about depended on the sort of intense blast of energy his transport would require.

If he could only build a low-energy solar-powered transport, Paul told himself cynically, he would be all set.

After spending time looking for a power source, Paul turned his attention to exploring the list of potential parts he had stored on the crystal before leaving the Inn in Strandford, but quickly became frustrated at how little he could tell from the data he had saved about such things as relative sizes, elasticity and durability of materials, and what amounts of energy the parts would require to function properly. He asked questions about each of these variables as he went along, and the portal supplied him with details, but it was hard to get a clear overview from such scattered sets of numbers. He wished he could somehow examine these parts first hand.

Paul reviewed all this mentally as he sat staring at the flat portal display. How long had he been back in his room, now? he wondered. A couple of hours, perhaps? Yet it seemed all this reviewing of parts had gotten him no further along than where he had started.

Paul ran his fingers through his hair, then muttered to himself, "I wish I could at least see these things in 3D!"

At that, the lights in the room dimmed, and a glow rose in the part of the room beyond the foot of Paul's bed.

Paul turned toward the glow. It was the parts he had been examining, displayed holographically in three dimensions.

Paul stepped over to them with a look of pure pleasure on his face. Then he glanced back over at the portal and asked, "Are the sizes displayed their actual sizes?"

"Yes," the portal answered, in its soft, genderless voice.

Paul was surprised at the answer; the parts looked much smaller than he had expected. Then he remembered how much nanotechnology was built into these units—which was one area where this world had plainly advance faster technologically than his. This was a world of small and efficient devices.

Paul circled the projection, examining it from all sides, then reached for one of the parts instinctively, as though he might grasp it—but his hand passed right through the image. Paul chuckled at himself: the image was, after all, only light. Still, that impulse gave him an idea.

"Can I interact with these parts?" he asked. "Can I move or rotate them, for example, or add labels with more information?"

"Yes. You can do all of those things," the portal responded.

"Okay, if you can, move these two parts," he pointed, "next to each other—and display above them the amount of energy they require for optimal functioning."

Immediately, the results Paul had requested were displayed. He smiled.

"Good. Now," he said, "all the other data I've been asking about for the last couple of hours—display it next to the part or subpart it pertains to."

Paul felt something close to joy as all he had been trying to work out in his mind took form before him. He quickly set about reordering the positions of the parts. As he moved each, its data went with it.

Paul could feel how engrossed he was becoming in this work. "Portal—can you tell me when it's quarter till two? I have an appointment I can't miss," he said, then added, under his breath, "not if I want to be sure I don't get booted out of this place."

"Yes," the portal answered.

"Then do so," Paul said. He went to his pack and dug out one of his last few travel meals, then returned to the projection.

"Now, move this part here," he said, "and this part here."

Paul watched as the parts moved through the air. "No, rotate this one so this side of it is next to this side of this other part," Paul said, gesturing. "Good. Now, will these two parts connect in this way without an adapter of some kind between them?"

"No," the portal answered.

"Then highlight the area between them in red. I'll come back to it later.

"Now, rotate this one 180° within the same plane as the last," Paul continued, and smiled as he watched the piece rotate into position. For the first time, his odd assortment of parts was beginning to take shape for him as a single thing: the new transport he would build to return him to his own world, bringing with him word of an incredible accomplishment—that he had traveled not only between worlds, but between parallel worlds, and now had the key to rescuing his earth!

Paul took a bite from his travel meal, and pushed forward with his work.

◘   ◘   ◘

As Paul left for his meeting with Farsan, he hoped it could be kept short so that he could return quickly to the project he had started in his room. Paul felt he was making real progress now. His mood was lifted by this fact, but at the same time he felt some annoyance at being required to waste his time doing whatever, exactly, it was he was on his way to do.

Paul arrived a few minutes early and found Farsan already there waiting. The room they had agreed to meet in was constructed around the same floor plan as Paul's, but this one was equipped with a small sofa and a stuffed chair, instead of a bed. The room's window, which faced toward the center of the Retreat, was covered with curtains—for privacy only, apparently, since they were made of a sheer material that let in a great deal of light.

After greeting Farsan, Paul sat down on the sofa, which faced a wall with an inscription on it. The inscription read:

> *When we feel our relationship to other life, we naturally seek to protect it. When we see other life as something apart, then we may use and abuse it without a second thought.*
>
> —JALEH REGENBOGEN

Paul looked it over. "What's the idea with these quotes, anyway?" he asked.

Farsan followed the line of Paul's gaze. "Oh, on the walls? They're just a bunch of quotes. Each relates somehow to the Kumaric Tradition. I think at first they were just going to use quotes found in Dr. Kumar's writings—things she wrote, herself, or things she copied down—but they keep adding to them."

"Waseme calls them 'reflection points,'" he added, as if he thought the term a little self-important, and amusing in that way.

Farsan himself seemed not at all presumptuous. His appearance was fit and casual, his manner relaxed and friendly. Paul saw in him again the same congenial warmth that had reminded Paul of his grandfather the evening before.

Farsan sat down in the stuffed chair, which had been set at an angle before the sofa, so it faced Paul where he sat.

"So, how are you doing today?" Farsan asked.

"Oh, fine," Paul said. "Just eager to get to work." He figured the sooner they got started, the sooner he could get out of there and back to his project.

"I'm agreeable to that," Farsan said. He smiled a little and looked at Paul the same way the Retreat's director had the day before, the same way Anna had when Paul had first arrived in this world—a penetrating look, tinged with warmth and understanding. Paul wasn't quite sure how he felt about it. He didn't like the idea of being exposed, and yet there was something so friendly about it, too—as though Farsan was ready to give aid and support.

"Are you comfortable there? Do you need anything to eat or drink?" Farsan asked.

"No," Paul shook his head. "I'm fine."

"Good. Then let's get started," Farsan said. He sat leaning slightly forward. He glanced down at the floor between his feet before looking back up at Paul. "I imagine you are aware of the basic structure of the work people do here at the Retreat, but I like to go over the fundamentals, anyhow, when I work with a new sojourner."

Paul nodded as Farsan continued. "The process here is divided into three stages. In the first of these people explore their individual, or personal, selves. In the second stage, they move on to an exploration of the interpersonal self—that is, their relationships, and their awareness of others. In the third stage, they explore their awareness of the transpersonal self—or, you might say, their place in the larger web of life, and their connection to it. We'll be starting out with an exploration of the personal self here today."

Paul tried to look as though he was more interested than he actually was. While he still hoped to discover exactly how *Memories and Reflections* had made such a difference in this world, he didn't think the answer would be found in such uninspired details as these.

"As Dr. Kumar explained," Farsan went on, "our lives are a kind of art. If we wisely choose what we create in this art, we may experience lives full of meaning and fulfillment—and therefore full of joy. She taught that the art of our lives is like any other art. It begins with the mental models we form, which then become expressed and represented in the world around us. That is, in shaping the mental models we form, we also shape the circumstances and events they give rise to.

"It's important for us to become conscious of the models we form and to choose them carefully, because they will greatly influence the lives we do, in fact, live. Part of the work we do at the Retreat is to help people refine that 'art,' and in refining it, to more consciously choose what they create in their own lives—and in the world around them.

"Now, following free movement—following your impulses and impressions, that is—will lead you to express whatever's in you. It's important to remember that, because if you're carrying around rage and resentment, for example, then that's what free movement will lead you to express. Historically, many people have come to distrust their natural impulses and inclinations for just this reason—but the solution is not to learn to suppress what's in you, but rather to learn to shape what's in you, so that when you give it expression, naturally, through the everyday actions of your life, you will be pleased to discover what you have given form to in the world around you.

"Stage one—the personal stage—is intended to help people explore what they're carrying around within them, help them get to know themselves better at an individual level, and help them choose and shape their personal models—so that when they give expression to what's in them, and so create that on the outside of their lives, they'll be creating something they want to live with. That is, they'll be creating a life they want to live within, and not just, for example, a representation of some anger or resentment they may have been carrying around with them.

"Is that clear enough?" Farsan asked. His delivery had struck Paul as somehow patient and fatherly.

"Perfectly," Paul said, and it was true. After all, what Farsan had said seemed quite familiar to Paul. It reminded him of material from Dr. Kumar's memoirs—especially the part about her college days, when she was learning how to use free movement in her poetry and in her life. Then, she had written about just this sort of thing: how what we hold within us takes form around us.

"Good," Farsan said. He smiled. "Then we can move on. I'd like to talk a little about what's involved in observing and re-forming our mental models. Often, the ones that are the most important to rewrite are ones that resulted from an injury of some kind. As Dr. Kumar wrote—hold on, I'll need to call this up on the portal to get the quote just right. I know some people can remember these things, but I don't have a knack for it and have never used Synaplast."

Paul wasn't sure what he was talking about, but decided just to wait as Farsan got up and stepped over to a rectangular panel on the wall to Paul's right. Farsan waved his hand over the panel, which slid back to reveal the portal screen. It only took him a moment to find the right quote, which he read aloud to Paul:

> Emotional injury that lasts is injury that causes us to write negative stories, which we then tell ourselves about ourselves, or about our lives. When we reclaim those stories and rewrite them for ourselves in more positive form, we heal from those injuries. The possibility to heal is always with us, because we can always reclaim the power to make, and remake, our own stories—about ourselves, and our lives, and the world around us.

Farsan closed the panel with the wave of a hand, then sat back down.

"The idea is that," he continued, "as conscious beings, we are in some ways like self-programming machines. We have the capacity to chose what we believe—that is, to choose the mental models we form to represent reality. As Dr. Kumar suggested, we have the capacity to write, and rewrite what is, essentially, 'the code of our own programming.' It's an important idea."

Farsan leaned back in his chair and looked at Paul. "There's a story I sometimes like to tell people when I work with them on stage one. I think it makes it especially clear how much difference this sort of programming can make in a person's life—this sort of 'rewriting of stories.' I'd like to share it with you now, if I could?" He paused, and Paul realized he expected a response.

"Sure, that would be fine," Paul said. The truth was, he was finding it quite pleasant to sit there, listening to Farsan talk.

"Good," Farsan said, and again his face lit with an easy smile.

Paul smiled back. He found Farsan relaxed and personable, and was pleased at how little effort it was taking for him to meet this requirement for staying at the Retreat. If he was going to have to take a break from his work, this was quite an acceptable way to spend it.

"This is a story my grandmother told me the summer after I finished college. I think she had waited until I was grown and would be able to understand it, to tell it to me." He paused, as though gathering his thoughts.

"When my grandmother was young," Farsan began, his face quite serious, "a man came to stay with her family. He was a friend of her father's—of my great grandfather's, that is—who had been laid off from his job in another city and had come to the town where they lived because he had heard that jobs were available there.

"They were old friends, my great grandfather and this man—had been friends for years, from when they had all lived in the same city—and my great grandfather wanted to help his old friend out while he got back on his feet. And so my great grandfather invited his friend to come and stay and look for work in the area.

"My grandmother had just turned thirteen when this man arrived, but she looked old for her age, and the man took an interest in her. One day, after she had come home from school, and while her parents were both still at work, her father's friend came to her and pressed her to have sex with him. It seemed, at first, that he was trying to seduce her, but when she said 'no,' he wouldn't listen." Farsan paused, as though giving a moment for the thought to sink in.

"And so that's how it happened," he concluded. He glanced off to one side. "It changed a lot of things."

For a moment, Paul wasn't sure what to say. "What did it change?" he asked finally.

Farsan looked at Paul. "Well," he frowned a little, "she told me it changed the way she felt about herself. And it changed how she felt about men." He thought for a moment. "She told me—I remember she said it had felt so deeply invasive, as though a part of herself, and not just her body, had been touched—a part of her so deep that maybe *she* didn't even know how to reach it—had been reached by someone else, and changed, and in a way she didn't like. In a way she would never have wished for."

Farsan glanced to one side. "It was terrible for her to discover that another person could enter *her* like that, could enter into her *self* in that way, and change something there, within her. It was terribly invasive, she told me."

Farsan looked at Paul. "But that wasn't all, because while that was happening emotionally—and I remember her describing this. We were sitting in the kitchen of our family home, where I grew up." Farsan rubbed his jaw, took a deep breath, and continued with the story.

"She told me, then, that while all that was happening emotionally, her body was responding to the sex as sex. The physical sensations were sexual, and pleasurable in the way sex is. So while one layer of her was rejecting this invasive, disorienting, disturbing event—and I should really say 'these events,' because he came to her again and again—another part of her was responding to it, receptive to it. It cleaved something in her, she told me, as though she couldn't trust herself to be on her own side anymore."

Farsan paused, then added, "That's what she told me." He looked down at his hands as he finished the sentence. His face was clouded, his brow furrowed.

"It must have been terrible for her," Farsan said factually. Then he took another breath and looked back up at Paul.

"It was hard for her too, because she had been so alone since moving to that area. It was the town where her father had grown up. They'd gone back there just a year earlier, when he'd been offered a job, after being laid off from the same production team from which his friend was later laid off. She'd left good friends behind, but hadn't really met any others. Maybe she was too shy. Then there was this man in her house, giving her attention, when she was lonely—but it was so much the wrong sort of attention. And as I said, it was disorienting and destructive for her. I think when people *feel* bad, they have a tendency to conclude that they *are* bad, and her self-esteem plummeted. And so it became even harder for her to make friends.

"Eventually, her father's friend got a job lined up in another state and left her family's house. So he was no longer there to use her, as he had been doing, but this was the legacy he left—a very confused and disheartened teenager who had lost faith in herself, who felt different from and isolated from others, and who had been harshly awakened from the dreams of intimacy and romance, which are perhaps part of the formula of how we grow into adulthood. Instead, there was this nightmare of invasion and a feeling of disconnection from herself."

Farsan paused. He looked thoughtful and sad.

Paul's voice was soft. "Why did she tell you about it?" he asked.

Farsan drew a long breath, then rubbed his jaw with one hand. "I suppose she wanted to teach me something," he said. "Something about where I came from; something I would need to know to live a good life. I would say, she wanted to transfer to me a lesson she had learned, that maybe she had always wanted to teach me, but she had had to wait until I was old enough to really understand it.

"It was the summer after I finished college, like I said. I came home and one day, we were sitting in the kitchen talking, and she began to tell me this."

Farsan paused again, nodding thoughtfully. "And I agree with her. It was a good lesson. That's why I like to tell it sometimes, when I work with people here."

Farsan leaned forward. "Shall I go on?"

"Certainly," Paul said. He had become quite interested in the story.

"So, basically, the years went by, and she carried that with her," Farsan continued. "They were lonely years, she told me, during which she never seemed to fit in. So many of the things that teenagers go through and discover and share with one another, seemed different to her because of these experiences—when her friends were talking about their first date, or their first kiss, what was she to say? She felt that she never belonged with the people around her."

Farsan paused for just a moment—to reflect, or to collect his thoughts? Paul wasn't sure, but it interested him to hear a man speak with such concern about the experiences of a woman. The sensitivity, the thoughtfulness, the topic of discussion—all of these seemed remarkable to Paul, in contrast to the norms of the world he was from.

"As she grew older," Farsan went on, "she would sometimes spend time with young men she knew, in whom she took some romantic interest, but no matter what happened in these relationships physically, she would always keep her guard up emotionally, she told me, because she knew how destructive it could be to let someone else in—and now that she was older and more self-possessed, she could better control how receptive she became, even during sex."

Farsan looked toward Paul. "So she was constantly lonely, and one relationship after another fell to pieces." Farsan paused again, as though, perhaps, to allow a moment for the thought to sink in.

"Then one summer," he continued, "when she was about twenty-five, a friend got her interested in coming to a Kumaric Retreat. Not this one. One up in Oregon. There, she worked with an ES—a woman who was older than my grandmother was, someone who had had similar experiences when she was young. My grandmother's ES helped my grandmother remember the romantic dream which is, perhaps—like I said—something that we all have some inborn sense of."

"I'm not sure I know what you mean by that," Paul said.

Farsan looked thoughtful. "Well, we all dream of romance, at some time or another. Where does that dream, that hope, come from? The way my grandmother explained it to me, we don't have to be taught it, or learn it by observing. We just feel it. One day, when we are young, the longing for it wakes up in us, and we find ourselves longing for a girlfriend, or a boyfriend. We all know the feeling. It's in us because we're human. We don't have to be taught."

Paul nodded. "Okay," he said.

"Anyway," Farsan continued, "while working with this ES, my grandmother came to realize to what a great degree she had lost sight of that romantic dream—or really, had come to disbelieve in it. She realized she had become guarded against men in general—against intimacy in general. She realized she had come to feel that any man she let get close to her could potentially use whatever space she gave him to become, not tenderly close, but to invade her as soon as her guard was down. She realized she had become determined, without even noticing it, to never again take the risk of letting her guard down in that way. She had created a cycle in which she would meet men she was attracted to, but then never actually give them a chance to become emotionally close to her.

"My grandmother knew enough about Kumaric philosophy to realize that so long as she thought that romantic or sexual intimacy was dangerous, then to her it would seem so, and that all the people with whom she might share such intimacy would, then, always seem suspicious and dangerous to her. She understood that the only way she would ever meet—and recognize—the sort of person (the sort of man, really, since it was men she was attracted to) that she might wish for, was if she could first imagine and believe in him—that is, to model him, and the relationship they might share, in positive terms instead of negative."

Paul thought about this. "Because, in order to really see him, she'd first have to have a mental model that would allow her to recognize him? Like finding a constellation in the sky. You first have to imagine the pattern?"

"That's right. That's exactly right," Farsan said. "She realized she'd first have to form—and believe in—a model of a nice guy who could romance her and never be invasive. She would have to replace the negative story—like Dr. Kumar said in the quote I just read you—with a positive story, if she was ever going to heal the injury left by the experiences she had when she was young."

Paul frowned. "So how did she do that?"

Farsan seemed pleased at Paul's interest. "She had to imagine a man being good to her in that way. But to her, that seemed wrong-headed and dangerous, because clearly there *was* a danger there—a danger she had already experienced—which she had to be vigilant to protect herself against. Do you see?"

Paul nodded. "Yeah—that makes sense," he said.

Farsan smiled a little, then went on. "So, the woman my grandmother was working with pointed out to her that she didn't have to imagine *all* men as being the way she wished they could be, but only some—even, really, only *one.*

"So my grandmother set about trying to imagine how someone would have to be to fit into the dream of romance she still felt in her heart. She spent that whole summer at the Kumaric Retreat—and you could stay for whole summers then, in the early days—rewriting the code, you might say, rewriting the story she carried within her of how men might be, and how she might relate to them. She created a new model for it.

"Of the men who came through the Retreat that summer, she made a point of picking out the ones who seemed especially caring and considerate, especially aware of the feelings of others, to spend time with. By being around them, she told me, she began to form an image in her mind of a type of man who would never push past the limits she set—who, in whatever way she let him in, would always be gentle, and respectful, and kind.

"She told me it was an important lesson, and it took her time to refine it. She kept practicing after she left the Retreat. It was nearly two years after that when she met my grandfather. She told me she saw everything in him that she had come to dream of. She told me she was certain that if she had never rewritten the story she carried of what intimacy could bring—never revised that model—she was certain she would never have seen my grandfather for who he was, and she would have shut him out as well. For without the new model that she so carefully formed, she could never have recognized in him what was, truly, there.

"So I sat there at the kitchen table with my grandmother that day, and she told me, 'As you go through life, always notice what stories you tell yourself, Farsan. Notice what you believe to be true. *Make sure you have models that form a story you want to live in your life, because the story you tell yourself forms the framework for the life you will live.*'"

Farsan leaned back in his chair. For a moment, he rested his hand on his chin, looking off to one side, then he lowered his hand and continued. "Then she leaned toward me and put her hand on my knee, and said, 'This is a powerful thing to know. It reshaped my life; it changed your grandfather's life; and without it—your mother first, and then you, *truly*, would never have been born.'"

Farsan was silent for a moment. Paul imagined he was thinking about how powerful a tool his grandmother had wielded when she had set about rewriting that "story," that "bit of code." Then Farsan looked over at Paul.

Paul looked back at him silently, turning over in his mind the story Farsan had just told.

"What about all that other stuff you said your grandmother went through," Paul asked. "Like her self esteem, stuff like that? Was she okay, eventually?"

"Yes," Farsan said, nodding slowly. "Starting that summer at the Retreat, she found more people she could talk to. Of course, this was a long time ago, and in those days, the sort of experiences she had gone through when she was young were, sadly, all too common—as were other forms of sexual abuse and assault. She told me that at the turn of the last century—between the twentieth and the twenty-first, so not long before she was born—girls in the United States had a nearly thirty percent chance of experiencing some sort of sexual abuse before they reached adulthood. It was about half that chance for boys. Once she began to talk about her experiences—and was around others who would be open with her, as well—she found a great many other women, and quite a number of men, who had been through such things, themselves. She learned not only that her experiences were not uncommon, but that her responses to those experiences had been entirely normal.

"After that, she told me, she learned to see herself and her experiences in a different light. She quit feeling ashamed, because she realized there was nothing for her to be ashamed of. She began to feel strong and resourceful, as she found ways to heal the scars that had been left, and to shape her life as she wished for it to be.

"By the time I knew her, she was a brave, strong, self-confident person. She had taken charge of her life and made it what she chose. She always seemed to me the very picture of success. I admired her a great deal. Admired and loved her. She really made her life her own. The sort of art Dr. Kumar wrote about—well, she really made an art of her life."

Both Paul and Farsan were silent for a few moments before Farsan spoke again.

"So," Farsan said finally, "that's why it's important to notice the models you make—the 'stories' you tell yourself—and to make revisions in those stories, when necessary, to help you create the sort of experiences you want to have in your life." Farsan looked over at Paul, his eyes steady and patient.

"That's why stage one is so important," he added, "because it helps people open windows into themselves, and learn how to see what's there, and—when they wish—to adjust what they find there. When people do that successfully, they're much more able to create the sort of lives they want to live.

"And, of course, as Dr. Kumar pointed out," he continued, "the more people learn to create, in their own lives, the sort of experiences they would like to have, the more the world becomes, collectively, the sort of a world we would all like to live in."

Paul looked over at Farsan and, as he did, it dawned on him that here was a piece of the puzzle of how this world had changed so quickly—of how the people of this world had consciously summoned the New Change, turning it from a distant possibility, to a present actuality.

"So, that's my introduction to stage one—the deluxe version, you might say, because this is your first time here," Farsan said.

He smiled, and Paul smiled back. Perhaps, Paul thought, the three steps practiced at the Retreat might be of more interest to him than he had thought.

"So, the first thing for you to do," Farsan continued, "is to choose how you want to go about delving into your personal experience. I usually invite people to pick something about themselves they would like to better understand, something they're curious about—a reaction, or a feeling, perhaps, that somehow seems out of place, or makes them curious for some other reason.

"It could be something you would like to see changed," he added, "or some experience you might hope you could produce again—something you did, perhaps, or something you felt. But ultimately, it has to be something about yourself that you would like to understand better." Farsan waited for Paul's response.

Paul thought about it. He was a little uncomfortable being asked to come up with something so quickly—but he also had a feeling that there *was* something he had already been wondering about.

It only took a moment for Paul to realize what it was.

"Could it be a dream?" he asked.

As Paul said it, he was surprised at how much he wanted Farsan to say "yes." How many months had it been since he had started having these dreams? he wondered. And how often had he awakened, distressed by one? Even today, his mood had been subtly colored all day by the dream he had had the night before.

"A dream? Do you have a specific one in mind?" Farsan asked.

"Yeah," Paul said, nodding.

"Ideally, it should be something that has some sort of feeling of importance to you."

Paul nodded. "Yes, it does," he said. "I'd like to understand it. I've had some similar dreams, but this one—I had it just last night—and, well, I'd like to understand it."

Farsan nodded his agreement. "Okay, then," he said, a note of seriousness in his voice. "Would you like to tell me what the dream was about?"

"Well, ah—I've been having these dreams. They're mostly about my mother, I guess," Paul said, then added, "She died when I was young."

Farsan listened thoughtfully. "How old were you?" he asked.

"Eleven." Paul frowned. "I've been dreaming about her, and each time, I'm trying to find her. Or I find her, and she won't look at me, even. Last night I found her, and she looked at me. And I could see her face. I could remember her face, and it had been a long time—a really long time—since I could do that." Paul glanced down at his hands. It was hard to say these things to this man, a stranger—and yet it felt good, somehow, to say them aloud.

"Anyway," Paul added, "it didn't stay her face. It turned into, um, well— somebody else's face, before the dream was over."

Paul was silent for a moment.

"Her face turned into someone else's face?" Farsan asked gently.

"Yes," Paul said.

"Whose face did it turn into?" Farsan's tone was very even—calming, somehow. Comforting and steady.

Paul hesitated before he spoke, and for a moment wished he had never brought the subject up. "My girlfriend's," he said finally. "Sheila's."

Farsan nodded, but there was none of the disapproval Paul half expected to see in his expression.

"It sounds like an interesting dream, Paul—an interesting series of dreams," he said. "I can see why you'd want to explore it. Was there anything else you wanted to add about it?"

Paul thought for a moment, then shook his head. "No."

"Okay," Farsan said. "Well, I'll give you some time to reflect on what the dream means to you. Just try to quiet yourself and listen to what's inside. If you have trouble with it, you can come see me again. Feel free to look me up at any time. That's what I'm here for."

Farsan paused, then added, "You know how to find people through the portal?"

"No," Paul said.

"Well, if you need to find somebody while you're here, just open any portal and ask where that person is. The portal will show you where they are on the display. Well, it will actually show you where their room pass is—but most people keep theirs with them. It's a good way to locate anybody who's checked in at the Retreat. My last name is 'Saqqa,' but I think I'm the only 'Farsan' here, so that makes it easy.

"So, look me up if you need to." Farsan stood up. "In any case, we should meet again tomorrow. Will the same time work for you?"

"Two o'clock? Sure," Paul said.

"Okay. Then I guess we're about set."

Paul stood and thanked Farsan for the session before leaving. As he stepped outside, he told himself he should give careful thought to the meaning of the dream, but before he had even arrived back at his room, his attention had returned entirely to his transport project and what needed to be done for it.

18

Paul continued with his project, carefully arranging the parts of his planned transport, checking relative energy requirements, and searching for appropriate adapters to connect one part to another. It was engrossing work, but still, in the back of his mind, he knew there was more to accomplish than this. He was still somewhat worried about how effectively he could aim this, or any other, transport—and he still had no idea how he would provide the huge burst of energy required to run it.

Beyond that—and even more deeply buried in the background of Paul's thoughts—was another worry. As pleased as Paul was at the idea of providing his world with a solution to the endless chain of problems resulting from its excessive population, he was troubled by the thought of what that solution would mean for the world he was now on, as hordes of strangers flooded in from another world, rapidly doubling the population and overstraining the infrastructure. Paul was aware, too, that those countless invaders would carry with them the views and values of the world they had departed from.

As disturbing as he found these thoughts when they hummed and rattled in the background of his mind, he found himself quite capable of pushing them aside—which made the bitter taste they carried with them much more palatable. After all, he had work to do and a duty to perform, even if there were those who might object to what he was trying to accomplish. There were others (a whole world of them) for whom this project would be their salvation—and he would be their hero.

More and more, Paul was coming to believe that he would, in truth, be able to deliver that salvation. The transport, developing beautifully in three-dimensional holographic detail before him, was coming to seem more like reality, more like fact, all the time. Interdimensional-Linking Theory was *probably* correct—and as for the energy, Paul thought—surely, in all this world, some solution could be found.

Paul continued on with his work until the portal flashed its announcement for dinner, then stood back and admired his creation, shining in the air before him. He smiled, walked around it once to better take in what he had accomplished, then asked the portal to save his work and washed up quickly before going to join the rest of the Retreat's participants for dinner in the dining hall.

◻   ◻   ◻

Paul had not forgotten that he had agreed to wash the dinner dishes on Monday, Wednesday, and Friday nights while he was at the Retreat. He stopped by the kitchen on the way to dinner and assured Spence Halwerd that he was remembering and would be there after the meal. Halwerd (as he said he preferred to be called) told Paul that he should come back about eight, when meal time officially ended. Nerida, he said, had rinse duty and would have all the dishes pre-rinsed and stacked for him then.

Halwerd took a minute to show Paul around the kitchen area, where he pointed out the large sinks Paul would use for washing, and the ample racks for drying, beyond them. The kitchen itself was large and bright, with people hurrying about, finishing with food preparation or moving the food for the evening meal to the large dishes used for serving it.

When he was done with the tour, Paul thanked Halwerd, then stepped back into the dining area. Even in the few minutes he'd been gone, the room had filled considerably. With a short, two-hour window for eating dinner, it seemed likely to Paul that most of the residents tried to arrive early, when the food was hot, abundant, and fresh.

Paul got into line for the buffet and looked around. The room was warm and well lit and full of the cheerful din of conversation. It struck him again how many people in the line he was in were holding hands, and how the diners seemed to lean together with an air of convivial warmth. He thought again of the night of the party at Anna and Marco's house, when they had gathered with their friends, and so many in the group held hands or put their arms around one another.

Paul got to the front of the line and filed his plate with an assortment of colorful and tasty-looking foods, then looked for a place to sit near the massive fireplace at the far end of the room. There, a small seating area with overstuffed chairs spread in a semi-circle in front of the fire. Beyond it, tables were arranged behind the backs of the chairs, so they also formed an arc around the fire.

Paul took a seat at one of the tables opposite the fire so he could watch it burning while he ate. He was aware, as he sat down, that the table to his left, the one most directly in front of the fire, had a particularly large number of people at it who were wearing purple vests.

"Yeah, that's basic Kumaric thought," the man seated immediately to Paul's right was saying, as Paul sat down. He looked to be about Paul's age. Neither he, nor the people sitting nearest him, wore vests. "The Divergence made some kinds of situations more painful than they had been before," he commented, then took a bite of food.

"Right, you might say it *deepened* some sorts of pain—like the pain of loss, for example, because they remembered it more—but it wasn't a new *kind* of pain," the woman across from him said.

"Right, right, right—I just said it wrong," a younger man, sitting just beyond the woman, chimed in. "The more people remembered the past and thought about the future, the more, uh," the younger man gestured with his hand at his chest, "the more intensely they felt like those things mattered to them. You know, it was like, *protolife*, and then protolife that got squashed, when things they'd thought about couldn't be."

"Ye-s," the first man said, drawing the word out, hesitantly. "The Divergence made them more focused on the past and the future—right?—and sometimes that increased the depth of the pain they felt, made them more aware of loss. Like, say, when they remembered somebody they'd known in the past who had died, and they knew they would never see them again in the future."

The woman nodded. She was looking at the younger man, also. "Right. It made those sorts of things more painful," she said, "than when they were just living in the present moment, without thinking much about the future or the p..."

"*That's* my point," the younger man cut in. "After the Original Change—I mean the Divergence—*pain was worse*, and not just because of the three impediments. Pain was just, um," he made the gesture by his chest again, "more intense."

"It *could* be more intense," the woman said. "If they built up protolife around those things, and it got blocked..."

"I think we're all in agreement here," the first man said.

"...then it *could* be painful for them in a way it hadn't been before the Divergence, when they were just living in the present moment," the woman finished.

"Yeah, but protolife got fulfilled by the Divergence, too, so there was new joy as well as new pain," the first man commented.

The younger man nodded. "Yeah. Yeah," he said. "It's like this friend of mine. A couple of months ago, his girlfriend left him, and he really felt..." He shook his head, unable to find the words. "It was harsh. You know, it was really painful, because he remembered her and thought they would be together a long time. He had thought about his *future* with her, you know?" He shook his head.

The woman looked at him with sympathy.

The young man took a sip of his water. "But then, he met someone new." He shrugged a little. "I think he's better with her. Seems happier."

"Well, I'm glad it worked out for him," the first man said.

The younger man nodded and took a bite of his food as Paul turned his attention away from their conversation and toward the fireplace at the front of the room. Within its arched chamber, the fire, large and brilliant, flickered and danced. It seemed, in its movements, to be almost alive. But not alive, Paul thought—just releasing the energy that the wood had stored up when it was part of a living tree.

For a moment, Paul thought about how that energy had originally been gathered by the tree from the sun. Ultimately, the wood was just an energy-storage devise—just one more example of solar power being used on this world, he thought, and smiled.

Though the fire offered him no solution to his energy problem, it still attracted and soothed him. He thought perhaps he would go sit in one of the chairs nearer to it, when his meal was done.

Paul took a bite of his dinner and paused to relish its fine flavor, before allowing his thoughts to drift back to the problem of finding an energy supply for the transport. From there they slid on, and soon he was imagining his return to his own earth and the welcome he would receive. How quickly would news of his return spread? he wondered. First thing, upon his return, he would have to get word to the right people in Corprogov. Speaking to Dr. Nakagawa would be a good place to start. He would know who to talk to. Soon, the news would be posted on the Stream—and sent around the world in a flash. Before long, all minds would be filled with the news of what Paul had accomplished and what it would mean for their world.

Paul pictured the people of his world pouring out into the streets to celebrate. He imagined himself wading through their open arms on his way to find Sheila—Sheila who would see him as he longed to be seen—a returning hero, approved of by all...

For a moment, Paul savored the fantasy, then stopped to consider whether it would really go like that, once he returned.

Would people really stream into the streets? Maybe, but more likely they wouldn't grasp the real significance of his discovery until it was their own turn to be sent off world. Few would stop to consider the overall impact on their world.

And what of Sheila? Would she really come to him like that, full of praise and warmth?

She would certainly be pleased, Paul thought—but not especially for the world she lived in. And not really for what it would mean to him, either, after he had strived for this for most of his life. But she would be pleased. She would be pleased at his increased status and at his improved standing with Corprogov, he was sure of that. And she would love receiving all the perks awarded to the most successful Corprogov scientists.

Maybe he would be able to get that large apartment she wanted, then, Paul thought. Maybe when he did, she would finally agree to marry him.

Paul sat staring into the fire, thinking about Sheila, then remembered the dream he had had the night before, when his mother's face had appeared and then become Sheila's.

What a strange dream! he thought.

Paul shifted uncomfortably in his chair as impressions of the dream came back over him. It was distressing to remember the expression on his mother's face, as he had remembered it in the dream—that cold, rejecting look—and equally disturbing to recall the way he had felt when he had seen it: a wretched, brooding heartache, which had permeated the dream and colored his mood long after waking.

Why had she looked at him like that? Paul wondered. Why had he remembered her at all, after so many years, only to see her transform into someone else? And, then—why Sheila?

Paul felt himself tense as he thought about it, then remembered the assignment Farsan had given him, to answer just these sorts of questions.

He knew he should try—but how would he do it?

Farsan had suggested he try to "quiet" himself, hadn't he? But what did that mean, exactly?

Paul took another bite of his dinner, then looked back at the fire. He liked the way the flames leapt and swayed. He liked the calm that he felt, watching them.

Was this what Farsan meant—this "calm," this "quiet?"

Paul wasn't sure. He took several more bites of food, as he sat, watching the flames—but soothing as the fire was, no sudden insight about the dream occurred to him.

After several minutes, Paul tried, instead, to focus his mind on the dream directly. He tried to coax it open like a stubborn lock—but it was like trying to take hold of something slippery. No matter which way he approached it, his thoughts soon slipped off toward something else.

Paul looked down at his plate and realized he had been staring at the fire for some time. He took another bite of his dinner, which was now cold, then glanced around at the area where he was sitting.

The people sitting next to Paul had left, so that now he was alone at his end of his table. It was quiet right around him now, which made the voices from the table to his left seem that much louder. Paul tried to block them out and focus on the flames and on his thoughts about the dream, but after a few minutes one of the voices seemed to separate itself from the drone of background sounds. It got his attention.

It was a familiar voice, Paul realized. He looked around and tried to place it.

Then the speaker caught his eye. It was the woman whose class he'd sat in on earlier that day. She was seated at the next table over, to his left. Jessica—wasn't that what the rugged-looking man had called her? Paul was pretty sure he was right.

"...the three impediments," Jessica was saying to a young man in a yellow and brown shirt, "grew out of the Divergence. The Emergence naturally reverses them. Also, reversing the three impediments helps bring about the Emergence. They're tied together, so it works both ways."

"Right," another familiar voice responded. Paul looked around. It was Farsan. He was also addressing the man in the yellow and brown shirt, one of a handful of people at the table to Paul's left who was not wearing a purple vest. "You could say that Kumaric work is about freeing people from that isolated pinnacle of the self," Farsan said, "or you could say that Kumaric work is about reversing the three impediments—because both roads arrive at essentially the same place."

"As Dr. Kumar wrote," Jessica said, and then recited from memory:

> An expanded perspective has no room for the three impediments in it. It's not insular. It sees deeply enough to find the goodness underlying our motives. It is without the barriers that impede communication.

She finished the quote, then added, "So, if you have an expanded sense of self, if you've really arrived there, then you've left the three impediments behind. Likewise, if you leave the three impediments behind, the place that will carry you to will have an expanded sense of self as one of its features."

The young man in the yellow and brown shirt looked thoughtful. "Yeah, I guess you're right. I mean, I'm sure you're right. I just really hadn't thought of it that way," he said.

"It's helpful to me, when I'm working with people, to keep that in mind," Farsan said, nodding at Jessica. "Often, when people are trying to develop a more expanded sense of self, trying to move from one stage to the next in the process here, I find it's helpful for them to start out by looking for ways to consciously go about reversing the three impediments in whatever context..."

Laughter broke out at the table behind Paul. The conversation there had been growing increasingly boisterous, which was making it harder for Paul to hear what was being said at the table to his left. Paul looked over at Jessica. How thoughtful and patient her expression was, Paul thought, as she listened to the young man in the yellow and brown shirt respond to what Farsan had just finished saying.

For a moment, Paul wondered what it would be like to be involved with a woman like that, so knowledgeable, and so—what was it?—attuned, somehow, or aware. Gentle. Caring.

Paul was intrigued with the thought, but he shoved it aside. Regardless of everything else—his plans, the transport, his relationship with Sheila—he felt certain he was not her type.

Paul looked down at his plate. He was almost done. Again he paused to appreciate how really good the food was here—tasty, satisfying, and plentiful. As he finished the last couple of bites (which were almost as good cold as they had been warm) he wished he could stay at the Retreat longer than the two weeks allowed—perhaps long enough, even, to finish the transport here, where he had a private room to work in and good food prepared for him three times a day.

Paul finished his dinner, then stood up and set his plate in a nearby tray where others had put theirs, then sat back down in one of the armchairs surrounding the fire.

Now the table where Farsan and Jessica sat was behind him and a little to his right, while the fire was ahead and to his left. From where he sat, he could look across the room and see the door to the kitchen.

Paul sat staring into the flames. The chair was comfortable, and he settled down into it. He reminded himself that he would see Farsan the next day and would be expected to have discovered something about the meaning of his dream. It was important that he at least appear to be participating in the program at the Retreat, he told himself, and thought again about Farsan's instruction to "quiet" himself.

As the flames jumped before him, Paul tried again to delve into the dream he'd had the night before. This time, as he stared into the fire, the lock that held the dream closed to him fell open—not fully open, not a clear sight through to the meaning of it all, but enough for the dream itself to return to him, flooding out around him as he sat in the pool of light from the fire—and as it did, the mood he had felt while dreaming it welled up within him.

As Paul sat there, he felt himself again running up the stairs as he had in the dream, with the endless steps rising above him, his legs aching and tired with the long climb. Then, just as suddenly, he felt himself passing through the light and shadows of the apartment, amid the flutter of curtains. The place seemed hollow, empty.

Replaying the dream in his mind, Paul reentered the bedroom, with package in hand. The air was hot and still. The window and curtains closed, the room silent. On the bed, his mother rolled toward him and into the band of light from the open door.

His mother—her face, her eyes, turned toward him. Her eyes.

Paul tensed as he recalled the dream and as the feeling that had come with the dream swept over him again: a feeling of excitement and discovery, of dread and sadness—and of something more, something buried in the complex well of emotion within him, something like...remorse.

He had turned from her, then, he remembered, dreading what he saw in her eyes, hating himself for what he saw there. Then he had turned back, and it was not his mother any longer, but Sheila lying there, and the look on her face was warm and open. It was everything he wanted in that moment—a salve, an escape, a source of solace. She had looked as she had when they had first met, but there was something more in her look, a deeper familiarity...

Now, remembering all this, Paul drew back from the dream, all at once repulsed by the impression of his mother's accusing gaze and drawn to Sheila's alluring warmth—but more than that, confused and disoriented by the emotions that rose with the scenes playing out before his mind's eye.

"It's like that example of Dr. Kumar's," a soft, female voice was saying behind him. Paul looked over at the table where Farsan and Jessica sat, relieved to find some distraction from the dream. A small woman with a green shirt and a purple vest was speaking. She had short dark hair and was maybe five or ten years older than Paul. She sat a few seats from Jessica, who, Paul noticed, was smiling and chatting quietly with a young man who had squatted down to speak to her.

"She wrote about a particularly pessimistic friend of hers, who was...," the woman with the short dark hair was saying. As she spoke, the impression of Paul's mother's face, and Sheila's, fell away—as did the mood that had enveloped Paul while he was remembering them—and he found himself delivered back to the dining hall and its friendly chatter. He glanced around, and noticed that people were drifting by on their way outside, and that the dining hall had begun to clear out.

"...and who believed that most problems were unsolvable," the ES with the green shirt was saying. "So he kept ignoring every problem that came along until they couldn't be ignored any longer—by which point his problems had gotten so bad that they were, truly, unusually hard to solve. He made around him the very circumstances he had modeled within him."

As Paul looked over, he noticed that the scene at the table with all the experienced sojourners had changed. The man with the yellow and brown shirt had gone, and it seemed to Paul that perhaps a couple more had left, as well. Now, at the center of the table, a group of about half a dozen ESs, all with their purple vests, remained. In a jumble of chairs surrounding them were other people without the vests, who sat listening in on the ESs's conversation.

"Right—the whole self-fulfilling prophecy thing," a man with short blond hair and a purple vest responded. "It can be really hard for people to understand that the thing they *know* is true—and which they can *prove* to be true because they've experienced it in the world around them—is only in the world around them because they've modeled it to be there. They've created it around them because they've modeled it inside them—but even so, they think the fact that it exists around them proves that their models were right all along. They don't understand that the cause and effect may flow the other way."

The woman with the green shirt smiled. "Yeah. It exists because they've modeled it. And, of course, that kind of thing can really work *for* you, too. For people who believe problems can be easily solved, for example—well, they just go ahead and take care of their problems. They won't give up easily, because they *know* the problem can be fixed and that things will be better once it is."

"So they nip things in the bud," the blond ES responded, nodding.

"Right, which seems to prove to them that *their* models were right, in just the same way. It's a matter of perspective," the woman in the green shirt answered, then turned as the man next to her began to speak.

"I worked with someone with a problem like the one Dr. Kumar's pessimistic friend had," he said. Paul noticed that he also wore a purple vest, and that he had a dark, neatly trimmed beard. "This fellow was a nice guy, but whenever he began to feel close to someone, it made him feel so vulnerable that soon after connecting with whomever it was, he would react by completely shutting that person out.

"The way he modeled it, he 'knew' that closeness meant trouble, you see. But he was also a really isolated and lonely person, so he'd start to get close to someone because he was lonely, then he'd get scared and suddenly turn and run—shut them out."

Paul told himself he should go back to thinking about the dream—but the truth was that remembering the dream was troubling, and he was curious about what the experienced sojourners were saying.

"He shut people out so completely," the ES with the neatly trimmed beard went on, "that often they would feel hurt and frustrated and wind up getting mad at him and telling him how really badly he was treating them—all before finally giving up and walking away from the relationship. He'd just end up feeling hurt and rejected, and feeling all the more sure that he was right that it was dangerous to get close to people.

"Each time he would begin a relationship, he would end up withdrawing even sooner, and further, and more abruptly—which would make people more and more upset. The breakups kept getting uglier, and he kept feeling more and more convinced that closeness was a bad idea. He couldn't see that he was creating the whole thing by so intensely believing in the problem in the first place—by modeling it that way.

"Eventually, he stopped letting anybody get close to him at all. That's how things were when he came here. Of course, if he hadn't anticipated getting hurt and hadn't started withdrawing from people in the first place, in all likelihood his relationships would have gone along fine. Any problems that came up in those relationships would probably have been resolved, or have blown over, without the rejection and hurt he anticipated—and ultimately created, because he anticipated it."

The man with the beard paused and shrugged, then went on, "But he kept replicating in the world around him the things he had modeled in his mind—and with each cycle, that was just convincing him more and more that his model was true. And the more he believed in it, the more actively he reproduced that very pattern in the world around him. For the longest time, he couldn't see what was going on, because he was right in the middle of it. He couldn't see the forest for the trees."

"So what happened?" Jessica asked. The young man she had been chatting with had stood and left the table a few minutes before.

Paul glanced around and realized that now, with him seated closer to the ESs's table, and with the room having emptied even more, he was having no trouble hearing what any of the experienced sojourners were saying.

"When we met, I asked him about his life. When I saw how isolated he was, I figured there had to be some funny modeling going on there, so I got him talking about his beliefs about relationships. I even asked him to keep a log of whatever beliefs occurred to him on the subject, for a few days—even the stuff he thought seemed too obvious to him to be worth writing down. I also asked him to write down examples from his experience about why he believed each of these things were true.

"Luckily, he was a bright guy. He got the concept quickly, and when he stood back and looked at all he was telling me, it became clear even to him, then, how much his beliefs were generating his experience." The man with the beard looked over at some of the novices listening in. "It was like Dr. Kumar wrote about, from when she was exploring free movement in college," he said to them. "What was inside him, took form outside."

"And it worked out for him? He was able to change those models and have better relationships?" the blond man asked.

"Oh yeah. I ran into him here, again, a year or two later. Lots of things had changed. He told me he was in love. He was here with his sweetheart. They seemed great together. He was so much happier," the man with the beard answered. "Of course, it's not always that easy. Some people really hold onto models that just don't work for them."

"I have to admit, I was doing something like that when I first came here," Paul heard another voice say. He shifted his position in the chair and saw that the speaker was a woman, with medium-length gray and brown hair, and a red shirt beneath her purple vest.

"When I was young, I had a job where one of my duties was to oversee the work of about ten other people," the woman went on. "Each of them was assigned the job of creating a component in a larger piece of technology we were developing. Part of my job was to make sure everything fit together. People were messaging me day and night for some trivial piece of information they needed in order to complete their work. It was making me crazy. I got so that I would just refused to answer the messages for a few days at a time, thinking they could work it out on their own, or find me in person—but by the time I would get to my messages, each person would have messaged me five or ten times with the same question, insistently, like, 'where are you,

I need this answer!' I had a huge backlog of messages to respond to. It really was overwhelming.

"Finally, I got some vacation time, and believe me, I really needed it. I came to the Retreat. It was my first visit. That's when I woke up to what I was doing. I'd modeled the messages as being overwhelming, as being too much to deal with, and so I'd stopped dealing with them—and then they really did become overwhelming. I told people when I got back to only message me *once* per day, no matter how many questions they had in that one message, and that I *would* answer within twenty-four hours. The volume of messages dropped way down after that, and the questions were much more thought out. The very thing that had made my life seem so out of control was actually something I had been controlling—I had been making the workers feel frantic to get in contact with me by making myself so hard to reach, and so they had pushed harder, and I had felt more overwhelmed, so I had resisted more, and so on. I just hadn't seen what was happening while I was in the midst of it. It was important to take a little time and reflect on what was happening."

"'If you answer the call, the phone will quit ringing,'" Jessica commented, "as Dr. Kumar wrote. 'Deal with the problem to remove it, ignore it to preserve it.'"

The woman with the red shirt nodded. "That's what I had to learn."

"The self-fulfilling prophecy thing, again," the blond man commented. "But even when you get the principle, it can be tough for people to catch on, sometimes—to sort out which parts of their experiences are self-generated, and which parts are just the world as it is. I mean, no matter how much you model winter as warm and sunny, you won't stop the snow from falling. But if you model it that way enough, you might travel to someplace that's like that. Part of life is self-fulfilling prophecy, and part grows out of something more basic, that is just the way it is. It can be hard, sometimes, to know which parts are which."

"Um, excuse me, but what is a 'self-fulfilling prophecy,' exactly?" a young woman, whom Paul took to be a novice, asked. "I've heard that term before, but..."

"It means just what it sounds like it would mean," the woman in the green shirt answered. "It's a prophecy—a prediction—that comes true because you believe it will come true. The act of believing shapes the outcome."

The young woman nodded. She seemed to be thinking about it.

"Like the guy Rhett was just talking about," the blond man said, indicating the bearded ES with a tilt of his head. "He predicted (or prophesied, you could say) that he would be hurt—and because he believed it, because he modeled it that way, he behaved in a way that made it happen."

"It can work the other way around, too," the blond man went on. "Like if you think people will like you, then you'll be friendly with them. Because you're friendly with them, then they like you."

The young woman who had asked the question again nodded thoughtfully.

"I'll give you another example," the woman in the green shirt said. "There was a man I worked with once, who was a very angry person," she raised her eyebrows a little, as she remembered. "He was a big guy, and he could be pretty intimidating when he got mad. When I worked with him, I would encourage him to look more closely at the things that troubled him, and he would just throw up this wall of anger—especially if we got close to anything that was painful for him. I wondered why he had even come to the Retreat, he was so," she frowned a little, "so resistant to doing the work here.

"I had no idea how to help him, at first, really," she said, looking now from the young woman to the other ESs, "but finally, I asked him to keep a journal each day. Every time his mood shifted—whenever he suddenly found himself feeling depressed or irritated, for example—I told him he should write down how his mood changed and what he was thinking when it shifted.

"I guess he listened, because he did it. I don't know why, when he fought me about everything else, but he agreed, and he did it. The mental models about himself and his world that were so affecting his state of mind were there, recorded for him to see, in the thoughts he wrote down. It was all laid out right there, a map of what was happening with him. It was hard, at first, for him to see it—because it seemed to him that he had just been writing down *facts*, you know, like Keefe was saying." She nodded toward the man with the blond hair. "He thought they were facts, not models that he had been projecting out onto the world. But he knew enough about Kumaric thought to get the concept, and that helped him make the breakthrough."

"So why was he so angry?" Keefe asked.

"Well, I guess you'd say there was a mistake he'd made, early in his life, and things had gone wrong because of it—things that were important to him," the woman with the green shirt responded. "He'd seen himself as a failure, then, and assumed that others saw him that way. Once that became his model, what I understood was that he just kept perpetuating it—replicating that model out in the world around him. So he was mad at himself for being a 'failure'—and mad at others because he presumed that they looked down on him as one. He expected disapproval, so that's what he perceived. He'd get mad at even the vaguest sign of criticism. He was touchy and hard to deal with, and I'm sure he got real disapproval because of that and lost chances at advancement in his work. He expected disapproval and failure, and because he expected that, that's what he got. It was a self-fulfilling prophecy."

The woman with the green shirt looked over at the young woman who'd asked about self-fulfilling prophecies, as though checking to make sure she'd understood this example. The young woman nodded, and the woman with the green shirt continued, glancing around the group as she spoke.

"Anyway, he'd been telling himself for years how useless and unworthy he was, what a failure he was, and how everybody saw him as one—how other people wouldn't even give him a chance, and that was why he was a failure. He had a real chip on his shoulder, and I'm sure a lot of people steered clear of him because of it. And like I said, I have no doubt that he lost a lot of opportunities that way—so it made it harder for him to succeed."

"Was he able to change those models?" Keefe asked.

"We worked on it. I told him to look back over his journal and create arguments going the other way—against the negative things he'd been telling himself—and to tie those arguments to the foundations of his model of reality so he could deeply invest in believing in them. I told him, whenever one of those mood shifts happened, to notice what he had told himself and to argue back against it. I encouraged him to learn to be a friend to himself."

"It really makes a big difference when you stop driving with your eyes closed and learn to work with your own inner machinery," Paul heard Farsan say. Farsan was sitting with his back to where Paul was now sitting, and Paul had almost forgotten he was there.

Several of the ESs around the table murmured their agreement.

"What do you mean?" a novice seated near Farsan asked.

"Well," Farsan said, turning toward the novice, "it's an analogy Dr. Kumar used in one of her later journals. It's like people start out 'driving through their lives,' so to speak. In a sense, we're all 'driving through our lives,' as we move from one situation to the next.

"Imagine someone who starts out in life," Farsan went on, "not really noticing what they're telling themselves—not noticing what models they're forming about themselves and the world around them, not noticing what their beliefs are. Maybe they don't realize how much difference those things make, how important they are. It's like they're in the driver's seat, but they don't really realize that all these things that their vehicle is doing are results of what *they're* doing, as they sit there in that seat. They move the levers, the pedals, the wheel—but without realizing that it's *them* that's steering, accelerating, and so on.

"Then they crash into something, and they want to close their eyes, after that, wherever they go—because it's scary out there, and they don't want to see the next crash coming. And when I say 'crash,' I mean maybe an important relationship goes to pieces, or they lose an important job. Maybe they say something cruel to someone they love, or have trouble with an addiction—crashes, things that go wrong in people's lives. Sometimes these things will get people to open up their eyes, but sometimes when things go wrong, people want to close their eyes even tighter," Farsan concluded.

"Right, and of course, they still go on driving," Keefe told the novice, "because we're *all* driving through our lives. It doesn't end until your life ends. But when people close their eyes to what's happening in and around them, what they end up avoiding isn't just seeing the oncoming wrecks. They end up avoiding an awareness of the very machinery that could help them to steer without getting into such wrecks in the first place."

"What they really need to do is open their eyes," Farsan added, "and learn how to better use the machinery that carries them through life—that inner machinery that directs how we move protolife to life—to learn to steer it and to 'drive through life' with their eyes open." Farsan paused, then added, "Like I said, it makes such a big difference when they do."

The novice who had asked the question nodded like he understood. "So it's like that stuff about self-fulfilling prophecies," he said. "You create the thing you expect to have happen—the thing you have modeled. So, when you expect a wreck to happen, you close your eyes—and that makes you get into one."

The woman with the green shirt smiled. "Right, and so long as you think that way—so long as you let your inner machinery run like that—you just create one wreck after another, so long as you keep your eyes closed."

There was a momentary lull in the conversation, then Paul heard Jessica's voice ask, "So what became of the angry man?"

"Well, like Farsan was saying—he opened his eyes and took a look at the machinery," the woman in the green shirt replied. "He realized that he was giving himself destructive messages, day after day. He could see, finally, what they were and what impact they were having on his life. 'Like land mines' he said—they exploded his mood every time he stumbled on one—whenever he thought one of those negative beliefs, that is, one of the negative models he had of himself and his life."

She looked thoughtful, then added, "It became plain to him, looking over the record I'd asked him to keep, that this had been happening. He decided he had to change those negative messages—and to change them, he had to change his basic opinion of himself.

"That got him ready to do the real work—to re-evaluate himself, including recognizing the positive motives that had led to the mistakes he had made earlier in his life and trying to see what he might have done, then, differently, to have gotten a better result.

"It was true that he *had* made mistakes—even serious ones—but that didn't mean he had a bad nature. We all make mistakes, I told him. We're born not knowing things, and we have to learn. Mistakes are part of the process."

"Yeah," Rhett said. He wiped his mouth and mustache with his napkin, then pushed the plate away in front of him. "I like to tell people that screwing up is just the stage between acquiring challenges and finding successful ways of meeting them. It's impossible to go through life without passing through that stage—and not just once, but over and over again, as new challenges come up. The test isn't whether you make mistakes, but whether you learn from them."

"That's just what I told him," the woman in the green shirt continued. "I said, if he wanted to feel good about himself, he should learn from his mistakes—and stop being the person who made them."

"And that got him where he needed to go?" Keefe asked.

"Yeah." She raised her eyebrows as she remembered. "It took time, but once he saw the course he had to set, he got to work. He left here a changed man. He still had work to do, but by the time he left, he knew that he could succeed. He had turned that corner," the woman in the green shirt concluded.

She looked thoughtful for a second, then added, "I liked that analogy he used—talking about it as being like clearing land mines—clearing all these buried beliefs which could just explode his mood, these beliefs that were disfiguring him, in a certain sense, and his life. He told me I had given him the tools to detect where they were buried, to dig them up, and to clear them away.

"I felt great," she added, looking around. "It was one of the most satisfying experiences I've had working with people here, because, well, because it helped him so much. But of course it wasn't me. He had to do the work."

"That's great. It really worked out well for both of you, it sounds like," Jessica said.

"Yeah, it did," the woman in the green shirt said, looking pleased.

Jessica nodded. "It's great when people get to a point where they realize that there's a direct connection between what they feel and the messages they give themselves." She glanced around at the novices who were gathered to listen. "It's like our models about what's real—our beliefs—are recordings. They stay in our minds whether we're thinking about them actively, or not. When we tell ourselves bits and pieces of what we believe to be true, it's like we're playing back parts of those recordings, as messages we give to ourselves. When you get it that there's a direct connection between what those messages say and the experience you build for yourself in the world—well, when you get that, you get a lot. It affects so many things—whether you see yourself as a success or a failure; whether you solve your problems, or let them pile up; whether you prepare yourself to be hurt or loved. An event may be factual—like the snow falling—but it will still take on the meaning that you give it. One person's catastrophe is another person's challenging adventure, you might say, depending on what you tell yourself about it."

Farsan smiled and looked around at the people listening in. "That's a big part of how we steer our vehicles—by noticing what those messages are and what effect they have," he said.

"You could say it's how we 'steer our vehicles,' or how we 'program the machinery of self,'" Rhett said. He glanced at the novices, too, then turned his gaze to the other ESs in the group. "I like that analogy. I used it once with a software programmer I worked with," he went on. "It was a perfect fit. She was involved in virtual holography for the Intralink. I said to her, so long as you like the experience your programming creates, then great. But if you don't like what you're experiencing in the virtual hologram around you, then you go in and work on the code—right? It's the same with us, I said. What's in the 'code' or 'programming' we carry inside us gives shape to what we experience around us. If we don't like that experience, we need to rewrite the code of our own programming. That is, we need to rewrite the mental models we hold. I told her, 'We're self-programming machines, and we're all responsible for our own programming.'"

"And that worked for her?" Farsan asked.

"Oh yeah, sure." Rhett smiled. "She said she liked the idea of one of her creations coming to life and being able to shape its own destiny! She said it gave her a wonderful sense of freedom to think of her own life like that—with so much generated on the inside, then taking form around her. After that, it helped her 'keep her eyes open,' you might say—because why crash if you don't have to? She wasn't bad, she wasn't failing—she just needed to tune up the machine. And that was something she knew that she could do."

Paul turned back toward the fire. It had died down some, but was still burning strongly. Something about Farsan talking about learning to steer the vehicle of the self had nudged Paul back to feeling that he should be preparing for his meeting with Farsan the next day.

Paul repositioned himself in his chair so his back would be toward the ES table. As he sat, staring into the fire, he let his thoughts drift. They skipped like a stone from one place to another in his mind. Impressions rose and fell within him: the night on the ledge during his hike, when he had seen the lights of Santa Maria—and the sense of closeness and vast distances he had felt in knowing that this Santa Maria, so close that he could see the glow of its lights, was not his Santa Maria at all, but rather was of a world entirely separate from his own.

He thought about his last night with Sheila and them making love in the darkness of her tiny apartment, touching each other in the most intimate ways while the input from her implant hummed through her mind, holding her attention, a buffer between them.

He remembered how the Retreat had looked the day before, with its rooftops dark and shiny, like pools of water in the sun, when it had first come into sight—and how odd it had felt to see an emblem from the book he'd been listening to in solitude carved so prominently on a door there.

Paul thought about the years of labor he had devoted to building his transport, and the excitement and terror, the joy and horror, he had felt when he had awoken in this world for the first time. What a long, hard trip it had been so far—and how alone he had felt during it!

And now he had a dream to focus on, to reflect on and discover about, he told himself. It seemed trivial and irrelevant, and yet here it was the job before him.

Paul tried to turn his mind toward it, but each time he tried, he felt his thoughts slipping from the topic like water over a smooth stone in one of the creeks he had followed for so many days.

Instead of thinking about the dream of his mother, Paul found himself adrift in a memory in which he was helping his mother unload groceries in the kitchen of the apartment in which he had lived as a child. He was handing things to her from a bag, and she was putting them on a shelf high above him.

"I depend on you a lot when your father is away," she said. She put her hand on his shoulder and smiled down at him. "It means a lot to me, Paul, that you're so helpful when I ask you to be."

Paul smiled back at her.

How old was he? he wondered, remembering it. Eight or nine? Maybe ten? It had made him feel good to think of himself this way, filling in when his father was gone, grown-up like. He remembered how his chest had swelled with pride when she had said that to him.

"It worries me, sometimes, that I ask too much of you," his mother went on, "but I want you to know, Paul, how much it means to me that I can depend on you, when I need to."

Paul picked up one of the bags that had been set on the floor and put it up on the counter. He didn't say anything, but he was smiling.

Paul sat, thinking about this and staring into the fire. At first the memory was pleasant, pleasing, but as he thought about it more, he began to get a terrible feeling in the pit of his stomach, and his eyes welled with tears. The thought was like a purring cat that had suddenly turned on him with flailing claws. Discomforted, Paul pushed it away.

Maybe it wasn't so good an idea to delve into this dream, or to stir up old memories at all, he told himself.

From the table behind him, Paul could hear Jessica's voice saying something about modeling. He turned his head so he could again see what was happening at her table.

"When you get it right, it really makes a big difference," Jessica said, her expression warm and open. Looking at Jessica, now, Paul was again struck with the same impression he'd had before: that there was something distinctive about her—something attentive, gentle, intelligent, yes—but more than that. There was something tender, even loving, in the way she looked at the people around her. And yet, he saw a certain strength in her, as well.

Listening to whatever Jessica had to say was certainly more appealing than trying to reach into the impressions and memories surrounding a disquieting dream. Paul turned now, in his chair, entirely toward her, with his back to the fire. He'd had enough of the dream for one night. He flung one leg over the arm of the chair and leaned against the other arm, with the side of his head resting against the chair's back.

"I worked with a woman a few years ago," Jessica was saying. "She was young—about twenty, twenty-one years old, I think, but she really knew herself and had set her own course in life." A couple of the novices surrounding the ES table had disappeared, but the half dozen or so ESs who had been there from the start remained.

"I guess one way to describe her would be to say she was clear. You know? If she ever had any land mines, they were cleared away," Jessica said. "Really bright, clear energy. She told me how she had always dreamed of having a chance to roam the world. That was her dream—that was the model she had of how she wanted her life to go. She knew she would have to have work she could take with her, that she could do along the way when she needed more funds. She got the idea of designing beautiful gardens for people around their homes. She thought she would do this and then program ecobots to maintain them. She could take this work and move from place to place with it, she thought—going anyplace in the world. But the thing was, where she lived, where she'd grown up, people believed in a strict naturalism—just nature as it was, no human-designed gardens—so at first, there was just no market for her there.

"But she loved the idea so much and saw it so much as a kind of blossoming of natural systems—not taking away from them, but enhancing them. You know—the enhanced-nature philosophy. So she believed in it, and she worked at it. In time, she was able to inspire all sorts of other people in the area she was from to share in her vision—and to hire her to do that sort of work. There's a kind of charisma that comes when you really believe in something, I think, and she definitely had it.

"Anyway, I met her when she stopped here as part of her journey. She was a really interesting woman, and things were working out great for her. I was impressed. She was young, but she really had gotten her purpose and her models lined up so she was creating just the sort of life she wanted. She was definitely bringing her protolife to life and taking a great deal of joy in living."

"That's a great story," Rhett said.

"Yeah," Jessica answered, nodding. "It's so important for people to notice what models they make—and to consciously choose ones that will help them fulfill their promise. Because that's really what it's about, in the end—each of us bringing our own unique gift, our own unique bit of protolife into the world."

Paul watched Jessica as she turned her head and noticed the way her hair fell about her shoulders. He thought again about how she had described the young woman she'd worked with. "Really bright, clear energy," she had said. It seemed to him that was how he would describe Jessica, as well.

Looking beyond the ES table, Paul noticed Halwerd walking out of the kitchen area. Halwerd caught Paul's eye and gestured to him to come over.

They must be ready, Paul thought, as he got up and crossed the room—which was now empty, except for the little group around the ES table.

When he reached Halwerd, Halwerd told him that Nerida would gather up the last few dishes, while Paul got started. She had finished most of the rinsing and had drained the sink—so they wouldn't be in each other's way now. Halwerd told Paul that when he was done washing, he should leave the water in the rinse sink so it could used for the pre-rinse by the morning crew.

Paul agreed, then glanced back toward the table where the experienced sojourners still sat talking, and for a moment reflected on the conversation he'd listened in on that night. Nowhere on his world could he imagine a group of people discussing some sort of "inner mechanics" and their effects on the world around them, while a group of curious onlookers listened in. Nowhere could he imagine them talking about how to use such "mechanics" to bring more fulfillment—more protolife—to life in the world. This was such a different world from his own, Paul thought. In so many ways, this world was so different.

Then he turned and entered the kitchen, where he was greeted by a friendly crew and a tower of freshly rinsed and stacked dishes, pots, and pans.

◘   ◘   ◘

When Paul was done with his kitchen duties, he returned, tired, to his room. As he undressed for bed, he was aware of how weary those few hours of dishwashing had made him, and hoped very much that he would be able to find less physically taxing work to do to earn the money he would need to buy the parts for his new transport unit and the space in which to build it, as well as the food to sustain himself with while he completed his project. His stay at the Retreat, he knew, would pass quickly, and then some sort of job would be needed.

As Paul climbed into bed, he thought again about how difficult it might be for him to get work as a physicist in this world—with no credentials valid in this world and perhaps not even the kind of knowledge expected of physicists here. But he would have to try, he told himself. He dreaded the idea that he might have to earn the large quantities of money that he would need as a laborer, but he knew it might come to that, since his training as a physicist was the only professional training he'd ever had.

Paul set aside those worries for another day, and instead lay thinking about the meeting he would have with Farsan the next day and the sort of insights he would be expected to present then. How could he decode this dream, he wondered, and decipher its underlying meaning?

Could it be that it simply had no meaning? Paul wondered, in the quiet darkness of his room. Might that be so? But as soon as the question was asked, Paul could sense the answer. It meant something to *him*, he knew, just from the way he felt about it—just from the discomfort, the curiosity, and the heartache he felt whenever he thought of his mother, lying there, as she had in the dream, her face turned up toward him—her face, which had, so strangely, become Sheila's.

Why had that happened? Paul wondered, again. And why had his mother looked at him as she had in the dream—with that piercing, cold expression? He remembered her well enough to know that she was nothing like that in real life.

Earlier that evening, while Paul had been washing dishes, he had had time to think while his hands stayed busy with the work. He had passed part of that time wondering if he really wanted to pursue this assignment and if there might be some way around it—a simple lie, perhaps, that he might tell Farsan, to make Farsan think he had completed the assignment.

For a time, as Paul had scrubbed and rinsed the dishes, pots, and pans, he felt regretful that he had ever picked a subject that really meant something to him. Wouldn't it have been easier and more efficient, Paul had told himself then, to have made up some sort of story to tell Farsan from the start and to have never been drawn into the tangle of memories and meanings that underlay the dream he'd promised to unravel?

But now, lying in bed with impressions of the dream drifting past him again, Paul faced the fact that he did, truly, want to know—that he did, truly, want to understand—just what this dream meant to him, and why it had come to him as it had—yet sleep crept up on him before the arrival of any such insight at all.

19

When Paul woke that morning, it seemed like an ordinary enough day. He had no idea how, by the end of it, the whole framework of his life would seem changed, like someone living on the set of an old-fashioned movie, when the backdrop is pulled away, revealing a larger landscape beyond.

Instead, he woke as he had woken often enough since his arrival in this world, thinking about the transport and what he would need to do to find his way home. On this particular morning, he woke thinking about Interdimensional-Linking Theory and how it—or something very similar to it—may have been developed on this world, too. If that was the case, he thought he might be able to locate it through the portal and gain some insight from it. Certainly, he had done the best he could to recall the theory from his world and its supporting mathematics, his first night on the Sojourner's Path—but the fragile nature of memory, and the fact that ILT was, after all, still considered theoretical, had left him with an uncomfortable level of doubt. Yes, it seemed likely that he would be carried home, once he activated his new transport—but the universe was full of inhospitable, deadly environments, and he wanted to do everything he possibly could to be sure he would not end up in one of them.

Glad to have a plan to assuage his worries, Paul sat up, rubbed his eyes, then looked across the room. The text on the wall had changed again, overnight. Now it read:

> *Anyone pulled from a source*
> *longs to go back.*
>
> —RUMI

Paul rubbed his eyes. "Portal," he said from the bed, then proceeded to ask questions of it as he dressed for the day. Once dressed, he sat down in front of the screen and continued searching, until the portal interrupted to announce that breakfast was ready.

Paul hurried through breakfast, then returned to his room and continued to scour the Intralink for the sort of information he needed—all the while worrying about what he would have to do to understand the meaning of the dreams he had been having—and the most recent one, especially.

Paul told himself that as soon as he figured out *how* to go about deciphering his dream, he would stop working on finding an equivalent to ILT, and instead turn his attention to dream interpretation.

Paul asked the portal another question, and a new page appeared, full of mathematical notations, some of which looked like it might be relevant. Even if he didn't find what he was looking for here, he thought, perhaps something on the page would refer him to another piece of research that might be more suitable.

As Paul looked over the mathematics on the screen, his mind drifted. Soon, he found himself thinking about the stories he had heard the day before—the one Farsan had told him about his grandmother, as well as the various stories the ESs had told around the table the night before. In each of these stories someone had taken charge of their own life mostly by observing the "mechanics" of how their mental models helped shape the lives they actually lived.

Paul tried to recall the phrase the young Indira Kumar had written in her journal, when she was a student in Oxford.

What's inside takes form outside—wasn't that it?

Paul turned and looked out his window. Some sojourners were sitting under a tree not far away, talking and relaxing in the sun.

How much had this sort of thing—this becoming aware of interior mechanics—helped to reshape this world? Paul wondered. He imagined people learning to steer their lives in this way. He imagined the practice spreading from person to person—from one sojourner to the next, perhaps—like a wave moving forward, rolling across the land.

Paul looked beyond the meadow outside his window, toward the peaks rising from the next ridge, as the image of that wave played out slowly in his mind.

Wouldn't that practice, spread from person to person, not only have improved the lives of the individuals who engaged in it, he thought, but changed the tone and nature of the society, as well?

Paul looked back at the people gathered under the tree outside. Some of them held hands while they spoke. One, a young woman, lay with her head in another woman's lap and her legs propped up on a young man's knees. As with others Paul had observed, the gestures seemed friendly, comfortable, and relaxed.

Was this the sort of society that would result from those sorts of changes? Paul wondered. Was that part of the secret for how this world had become so different from his own?

Paul sat for a moment longer, contemplating this, then caught himself and directed his attention, once again, back to the mathematics on the screen. All the way down the page were scattered fragments that seemed related to the mathematical proof he was familiar with from his own world, but as was the case on the page before, none seemed really relevant.

Still, Paul thought, the answer could be on the next page—or come up in response to his next query. He might be that close to having the confirmation he wanted that Interdimensional-Linking Theory was true and correct. Then he could count that off his list of the problems he would have to solve before he could find his way home.

◻ ◻ ◻

When the portal announced lunch, Paul was astonished at the amount of time that had passed. He had intended to spend the morning preparing for his meeting with Farsan, and now that meeting was only a couple of hours away.

Paul promised himself that he would work on the dream after lunch, then hurried through his meal.

When he returned, he felt satisfied that he had left enough time to accomplish something adequate. After all, how hard could this be, if something of the sort was expected of all first-time sojourners in the first stage of their work at the Retreat?

Paul decided to try to "quiet" himself, as Farsan had directed. He lay down on the bed and stared up at the ceiling.

He waited like that, then waited some more, but nothing happened.

Paul remembered how quickly time had seemed to pass that morning and looked over at the clock—but only a few minutes had passed.

"Portal," Paul said, "notify me when it's almost two o'clock—at 1:50, this afternoon."

"A notice will be given today, at 1:50 PM," the Portal answered.

Paul closed his eyes. Any thought that came to him, he carefully let drift past. He could feel his thoughts spinning down. Quieter. Good.

Paul hadn't realized how tired he was. Not surprising, though, he thought. It had been a stressful couple of weeks, some of the most difficult of his life.

Now that feeling of quiet was really coming to him, rolling over him like a soft breeze.

Good, Paul thought. It felt nice.

It felt nice.

And that was the last thing Paul remembered thinking.

◻ ◻ ◻

"The time is 1:50," the portal announced.

"The time is 1:50," it repeated, a moment later.

"The time..."

"Yeah, yeah. I hear you. Shut up," Paul said, as he swung his feet over the side of the bed, cursing himself.

Damn, his meeting was only a few minutes away. How could he have let himself fall asleep?

Paul quickly got himself together and left to go see Farsan.

Was this how it was? he asked himself as he walked over to the meeting room—was he going to fail "Sojourning, Stage I"?

Paul knocked on the door. Farsan answered and let him in.

Paul sat down on the sofa. On the wall across from him, it said:

> *You who want*
> *knowledge,*
> *seek the Oneness*
> *within*
>
> —HADEWIJCH II

Paul glanced over at Farsan, as Farsan sat down in the cushioned chair, facing the sofa. Farsan held a ceramic mug in his hand. It looked hand-made.

"So, how have things been going?" Farsan asked, his tone friendly and relaxed. "Have you made progress on that dream?"

"Well," Paul said, hesitating, "um, actually—I don't think I know any more about it than I did yesterday."

Farsan listened, nodding.

Paul felt ashamed. It wasn't like that much had been asked of him. "I mean, I tried, but—well, I fell asleep just now, and, well—I'm not even sure I know what you meant when you said 'quiet yourself.' I'm really not sure how to do this, actually."

"Threw you in the deep end, did I? Sorry, I shouldn't have assumed. That's good for me to know." Farsan smiled, and Paul felt suddenly at ease.

Paul remembered the impression he had had of Farsan when they'd first met. Something about him—his gentleness, perhaps, or his calm demeanor—had reminded Paul of his grandfather, though Farsan was younger than Paul's grandfather had been at any time Paul had known him.

"Well, don't worry, we'll get you up to speed," Farsan said, then added, "Oh, by the way, would you like some tea?"

"Um, yeah. Thanks," Paul answered.

Farsan got up and took a mug from a shelf under the window, then poured some tea from a tea pot he had left on the narrow counter above the shelf.

"Basically, what I was talking about was removing distractions," Farsan went on, as he handed Paul the mug and sat back down, "both external and internal distractions. What I had in mind was, you find a quiet place where you won't be disturbed and set aside any concerns or worries you may be occupied with. That's what I meant—you create a kind of stillness in which you can listen to what's happening on the inside." Farsan tapped his fingers against the center of his chest.

"Then what?" Paul said. He took a sip of his tea. It was good.

"You try to remember the dream. Pull it back into your mind in every detail. When you have it there—its sights and sounds, its emotions and sensations—then you let your attention turn to its individual elements and see what associations you make around them.

"Remember, we begin with certain themes within us: models and patterns that we believe in. Our experience grows out from there. It's a kind of 'seed material' that we make associations around. Those associated elements are given form in our dreams. That form, that expression, can include anything from a book on a coffee table in your dream," Farsan said, gesturing toward the table in front of him, "to a mood that pervades the dream."

"The mood, too?" Paul said, thinking about what a strong feeling had been woven into his dream.

Farsan took a sip of his tea. "Sure," he said, nodding. "Whatever models we hold give rise to emotions." He rested his mug against the arm of his chair with his fingers still through its handle.

"Think about it this way," Farsan went on. "You're driving a vehicle, going down a steep hill in winter, and you hit an icy patch. You begin to lose control of that vehicle. Imagine that in that moment, you are *sure* you are about to slide off the road—to slide right over the cliff at its edge. How do you feel in that moment?"

"Terrified," Paul answered, taking another sip of tea.

"Right. How could you not? Your model of reality says you're about to plunge to your death."

Paul considered this as Farsan went on. "Now, let's say you're a passenger in the back seat of the same vehicle. Your full attention is on your videopod, and you're completely ignoring what's happening on the road. You modeled the trip as a safe one before you started, and the movement of the vehicle on the icy road has *not* gotten your attention. How are you feeling?"

"Well, I don't know specifically, but not terrified," Paul answered.

"Right," Farsan said. "That's true, even though the risk is the same for both the driver and the passenger. *The emotion that you feel is a result of how you model the situation.*"

"Like a kid who thinks there are monsters under his bed—he'll be afraid, even though the monsters aren't real," Paul said.

"Yes, exactly. And someone who thinks they've won the lottery will be excited—even if they read the numbers wrong. Whether our models of reality reflect reality, or not, they are the arbiters of our emotions.

"*So,*" Farsan went on, "our models of reality give rise to our emotions. They do that in our waking lives—and also in our dreams."

Paul sipped his tea and considered Farsan's point. "Okay," Paul said, "so we have models in us, which act as a kind of seed material around which we make associations. And so," he frowned a little and stared at the coffee table in front of him, "if I associate a book with, say, learning—then a book might appear in a dream I might have, a dream that develops around the theme of learning. Or maybe I should say, 'the model of learning?'"

"Right," Farsan said, with enthusiasm, smiling a little. "You catch on fast. So, that dream might have developed around that model of learning—or more likely, though, it would represent a number of models, each being expressed in different facets of the dream—in the same way that multiple models are expressed in our lives."

Paul frowned a little.

"I don't want to make this sound more complicated that it is," Farsan said. He set his mug of tea down on the little table beside his chair. "The idea is basically this: dreams spiral out from their central seed material through a process of association." Farsan held up one hand and gestured around it with the other.

"What you're trying to do," he went on, "is find a quiet place where you can return your attention to the dream and work that process of association in reverse." He moved his hand in the other direction. "You want to follow those same threads that grew out from the seed material, but in reverse, following that same trail of associations backwards—and so, essentially, 'unwind' the dream."

Paul nodded and took another sip from his mug. It was pleasant to have the tea to drink while listening to Farsan talk.

"So, say you remember seeing a book in a dream," Farsan went on. "You focus on the book, just as you remember it from the dream, and notice the associations that come to mind in connection with it. Maybe what comes up are impressions of thoughts or experiences you've had related to learning. So then you decide that the book represented 'learning' in the dream. Like that. It's not complicated."

"And does it work like that with emotion, too? Like, the mood of the dream?" Paul asked.

"Yeah, sure. Emotions are linked to the models that inspired them—same as with the vehicle and the hill. You aren't likely to remember being terrified when you hit that icy patch of road without also remembering the model—that is, the mental image of yourself plummeting to your death—that gave rise to that feeling. If you remember the feeling, then you'll remember the model.

"It's the same with a dream," Farsan continued. "If someone has a dream with a strong emotion in it, trying to return to the emotion in the dream—to relive the emotion from the dream—may be very effective in bringing up the models that inspired it."

Paul nodded while Farsan looked at him thoughtfully. "Was there a lot of emotion in the dream you told me about, Paul?"

Paul continued to nod. "Yeah," he said.

Farsan frowned. "Would you say it was a good feeling?"

"No," Paul said, turning his head a little and drawing the word out.

"A bad one?" Farsan asked.

"Yeah, I would say it was pretty bad," Paul said, and his tone suggested that this was an understatement.

"It wasn't good to see your mother's face after all of that time?"

"No," Paul said, shaking his head.

"Why not?" Farsan asked gently.

"Well, it didn't look like her. Well, I mean, it did. It looked exactly like her, I'm sure—but her expression was all wrong. She never looked at me like that, I think. I don't think she ever looked so cold, so rejecting."

Farsan looked thoughtful. "But you still want to probe into it?" he asked.

"Yeah, I think so," Paul said, and was surprised to hear himself commit to this all over again.

"Okay. Good," Farsan said. He took another sip of his tea, then added, "Sometimes, when someone is having trouble probing into something that carries a strong negative emotion with it, it's not just a problem of technique, as we've been talking about. It can be a little more complicated."

"How?" Paul asked. He drank from his mug, too. He was aware that, somehow, sharing the tea with Farsan made the situation seem less formal and more like talking to a friend. He wondered if that was why Farsan had brought it.

"Well," Farsan said thoughtfully, "sometimes people are just afraid of feeling that emotion—of feeling what they'd have to feel to discover what's behind it. Some emotions are unpleasant to feel, and people veer away from that."

Farsan looked at Paul carefully, then added, "If you think maybe that could be going on here, we could talk about it."

Paul shrugged. "I don't know."

"Well, we could talk about it a little anyway." Farsan ran a hand over his short-cropped hair and looked down at the floor.

"I guess there are a couple of things that are worth saying," he went on. "One is, even if someone's motivated to explore an unpleasant feeling and has decided to do so, the unpleasantness of it can get in the way, like I was saying. The impulse to explore it and the impulse to avoid it can sort of cancel each other out, and so the person just gets stuck."

Paul nodded as Farsan looked over at him.

"If that's going on, you'll want to remind yourself that there's a real value in doing this sort of work," Farsan went on. "The benefits are lasting, while the discomfort is temporary. Whatever the specific cause of an unpleasant emotion, it is a by-product of the models you're building and carrying inside.

"Like I said—our models are the arbiters of our emotions. When we change our models, we change our emotions. When we feel something unpleasant, it's wise to get in there and try to understand what's happening in that 'inner machinery.' Usually some adjustment needs to be made in how you're looking at things—which would allow you to resolve the unpleasant feeling.

"If you don't, you'll just end up saving it for another day—like money in the bank. If someone makes a habit of pushing aside such feelings, they can end up with a really sizable 'bank account'—full of feelings of fear, hurt, shame, and so on. It's not a good idea. In most cases, the wise thing is to go ahead and probe into those feelings, learn from them, and resolve them—and then move past them for good."

Farsan paused, as Paul considered this.

"After all," Farsan added, "pain has a natural value. It's supposed to get our attention and tell us not to do the thing that causes it. If you hit your thumb with a hammer, you don't ignore it and go on hitting your thumb."

Paul chuckled, and Farsan smiled a little. Paul noticed his patient look. Or was it somehow a mixture of patience and warmth?

"The smart thing to do is to try to figure out how not to hit your thumb again, then keep on hammering," Farsan finished.

Paul leaned forward a little. "You said, 'in most cases.' In most cases, it's wise to probe into unpleasant feelings. When isn't it?" he asked.

"Oh." Farsan rubbed his jaw with one hand. "Well, like when you're too close to a situation and can't think it through until you take a break from it. Maybe the emotions are so intense that you just get lost in them; then it can be helpful to back off enough to let the most intense feelings fade—get some distance from them—before coming back at it.

"Or maybe you need to give yourself time to get used to something," Farsan went on. "Like grief, for example. Some things just take time—though there can still be more or less comforting ways to look at them, even then. But, in this case, what I'm basically thinking about is situations where there's some loss of possibility—where you have to give up hope about something you've felt as protolife. It can help to give it time, then, and to focus on new possibilities."

Paul thought about this as he sipped his tea.

"Isn't that all just a different way of working with the machinery, then?" he asked, after a moment. "I mean, like—well, I heard you use that 'driving' analogy last night, at dinner. It's like, sometimes it's good to speed up, and sometimes it's good to slow down—isn't that what you are saying? But you're still driving, right?—even if you're slowing down?"

"Yeah, that's a good point," Farsan said. He smiled at Paul. "Backing off *can* be a way of working with the machinery inside yourself, you're right. But the idea is to try to be conscious about it—to probe when it's useful to probe and to back off if that's really what's best—but not just to run away blindly because it's unpleasant."

Paul nodded. "Got it," he said.

"Anyway," Farsan went on, "I wanted to make a couple of points." He rubbed the back of his neck and glanced down at the floor. "One had to do with people avoiding unpleasant emotions." He stared blankly for another moment.

"Oh, yeah," he said, leaning back in his chair.

"The second thing was, there's another thing that can happen—that can get in the way of probing—when people are dealing with a feeling that's unpleasant for them," Farsan went on. "People sometimes get the idea that if they're feeling something 'bad' (or if they're getting what they think of as 'bad' results from the things they do) they get the idea that there must be something 'bad' about them—something 'bad' inside them—as well. In which case, they don't so much avoid probing into a 'bad' emotion because they don't want to feel it. What they're really avoiding, is discovering what they fear they will find if they look inside themselves."

"Fear? Like what?" Paul asked. He drank some more of his tea and realized it was almost gone.

"Well, like something bad," Farsan said, shrugging. "I supposed it could be anything—but mainly, I think they fear they will find something that they would not be able to accept about themselves."

Paul thought about this.

"Basically," Farsan went on, "they come to suspect, or to believe outright, that they have a 'bad nature'—and they don't want to see that. They don't want to see that because then they would have to dislike or devalue themselves—and that's an awful way to feel.

"So, in case that's any part of the problem here," he concluded, "I'd like to encourage you to work the three impediments in reverse, as you probe into this dream.

"Remind yourself that, one..." Farsan held out his right hand and pushed its index finger down with his left, "...all of life is built upon the foundations of a good nature—and that includes *your* nature, as well. *You* have a good nature.

What people do, we do because it seems desirable to us in the moment we make our decisions. The three impediments may get in the way—they may impede the expression of what's truest in yourself—but when that happens, it's still a *good nature* they impede the expression of.

"Two," he went on, pressing down a second finger, "remember to see from the perspective of others—including prior perspectives of your own, which you may have lost touch with."

"And three," he said, pressing down a third finger, "listen to, and communicate with, yourself—even if what you have to tell yourself, initially, is about an emotion that's unpleasant to feel."

Farsan leaned forward a little. When he spoke again, his voice was slightly softer. "So, that's pretty much what I can tell you about how to go about this—quiet yourself; probe into the dream, along with its emotions; and do not be deterred.

"And one other thing," he said, looking at Paul. "If you need anything else from me, find me. If you have any difficulty, don't hesitate to come knock on my door. That's what I'm here for. Will you do that?"

"Yeah, sure," Paul said.

"Do you have any questions?"

Paul shook his head slowly. "No, I guess not."

"Okay, then," Farsan said, shifting forward in his seat, like he was about to stand. "I guess that will do for today."

Paul drank the rest of his tea, then set the mug on the table in front of the sofa. They both stood, then, and stepped over to the door.

"Meet again tomorrow, same time?" Farsan asked.

"Yeah, that's good," Paul said, and in that moment felt real warmth and respect for Farsan and appreciation for the effort he had put out to help Paul accomplish what was expected of him. He, and the other experienced sojourners, Paul knew, volunteered their time here, and at many other such retreats in this world.

All to help others, Paul thought. But to help them do what, exactly? Expand their sense of self? Put the three impediments behind them? Whatever the details of their practice, it seemed to Paul that repeated small efforts, like the one Farsan was making for him, had, over time, helped to create really impressive changes in this world.

Paul reached over to shake Farsan's hand and was surprised at how Farsan responded—not with a handshake so much as a friendly squeeze. It struck Paul that there was something warm and personable in the gesture—but with no sexual overtone. It was like so many of the physical gestures Paul had seen pass between friends on this earth. He was beginning to think it was nice that there was a context in which such gestures could exist.

Paul said goodbye to Farsan, then stepped out into the late afternoon sun. A small wind had begun to blow. It stirred the needles of the pine trees so that they shimmered in the sun.

How strangely different this world was from his own, Paul thought, as he walked away. The more he explored it, the more he found himself appreciative of it in new ways. However uncomfortable it might be, he *would* push forward into the dream, he told himself, and discover whatever lay within it.

As Paul walked along the path back to his room, he felt the wind tugging at his clothes. In the back of his mind, he felt as though it was trying to pull him away from his course and toward someplace new and uncertain.

◻ ◻ ◻

As Paul let himself into his room, he knew exactly what he needed to do but was feeling restless and, for some reason, not quite ready to begin. Also, he had had some new thoughts about how to search for whatever theories may have been developed on this world that might help him better evaluate the relevance and accuracy of Interdimensional-Linking Theory—so now, instead of lying on the bed and turning his attention toward the feelings he'd had during the dream, Paul sat down in front of the portal and began to search—all the while telling himself that it was the dream he should be pursuing.

Some part of Paul understood that his pursuit of these ideas at this time wasn't so much about his interest in uncovering the validity or shortcomings of ILT (though that was important enough), but was more a reflection of his desire to avoid—if only for a little while longer—the feelings that had haunted his dream and that he had carried with him ever since.

Whatever his motives for following his new search design, the search itself was fruitful. A concept similar to Interdimensional-Linking Theory *had* been developed on this world—only here it was called "Interdimension Relational Dynamics." The math was a little different, but the results were much the same. Both predicted that a bond would be found to exist between certain probable worlds that would create a kind of interdimensional gravity, "linking" or "relating" those worlds to one another.

Though IRD was viewed as an unproven theory on this world—just as ILT was viewed on Paul's—Paul found the arguments for IRD rational and solid. He didn't think he could do much better than that: two worlds and two theories, both arriving at the same basic conclusion. All it took was a little conjecture on Paul's part to conclude that his world and this were linked in just this fashion.

Perhaps, Paul concluded, it would be possible to design a transport unit that could have the capacity to counterbalance this effect, to cut through those bonds, and so succeed in sending someone from earth to a distant world, as he had originally planned to do—but Paul no longer had a desire to accomplish this, even if he could see exactly how to do it. The truth was, he was pleased to find that IRD suggested the same thing he had been thinking—that the bonds between his world and this were strong, and that when he transported again he would naturally return to the world from which he had come—to his home, the world he knew.

The more he thought about it, the more confident he felt that both ILT and IRD were substantially correct. And so, by the time the screen flashed its invitation to dinner, Paul had left this worry behind and had begun to think again about his new transport.

Paul cancelled the portal's alert, then looked up and around. Outside his window, he could see a portion of the wind-swept retreat. The sun had dropped behind the mountains, while the western sky was filled with its fading glow.

Paul had spent more time on his search than he had intended. He got up from his chair and put on his jacket, then stepped out into the gusty evening. He would eat quickly, he promised himself, and get to work on the dream when he returned.

◻ ◻ ◻

By the time Paul got back, it was night, and the wind had picked up even more.

Paul knew that if he let himself turn on the portal, he could easily become immersed, again, in some question or another pertaining to his transport project. But wasn't that just the sort of thing Farsan had warned against?—avoiding the feeling, and so avoiding the process of finding out what was behind it?

Or did his impulse to turn on the portal possibly represent something more? Paul wondered, as he took off his shoes and jacket. Was there maybe some truth he didn't want to discover?

Paul sat on the edge of the bed, trying to feel motivated. *"And do not be deterred,"* he remembered Farsan saying.

Yeah, Paul told himself. He had to at least try. How bad could it be?

He lay down on the bed and got comfortable. From outside, he could hear the sound of the wind buffeting the buildings and the music it made in the pine trees—like the sound of a stream: the wind surging through pine needles.

Paul closed his eyes and tried to remember the details of the dream—tried to remember, especially, how he had felt as each event in the dream played out.

He was running up the stairs, again—the long, unending stairs, with a package in his hand. He had to get it to her. He had to bring her the package.

The stairs seemed endless. Why couldn't he arrive?

Paul remembered the feelings he'd had at that point in the dream: *Anxiety. Frustration.*

Yes, and something more. His feet had been sticking to the steps, his legs heavy. He could remember how it had felt—like he was *being held back from something important. Impeded.*

And then he was in the apartment, going from room to room, looking for her. He should have felt relieved, he had arrived, Paul thought—but he hadn't. Something was wrong. He felt *empty, hollow, anxious.*

He kept looking. Where is she?

Then he was in her room, and she rolled toward him, looking at him with that cold, icy stare.

Yes—and he had wanted to turn away, to leave—to wake again from this dream.

As Paul lay there remembering it, her face started to turn into Sheila's, but he held the image steady in his mind, not letting it turn—looking into his mother's face, staring into it bravely.

He knew that look.

He knew that look.

A shiver ran through him. And then it all came bursting back on him.

He had found her looking just like that: her face drawn, her skin blue with the telltale cast of the *Muerte Azul*, her eyes wide open, turned toward the door, toward him with that unflinching, icy stare—that accusatory look.

He had found her just like that: her eyes cold, unmoving, unforgiving. Her skin pale. Her breath gone.

He had stood there by her bed, the package still in his hand, unopened. His mother was on her side, turned toward the open doorway of her bedroom, as though waiting for him to come—to come and bring her this, the package. But he hadn't come. He was too late, and now she was gone.

It all flooded back over Paul now, and the pain of it was immense.

He remembered sitting on the floor with his head on the side of her bed, holding his mother's hand and crying. Casey was there, lying near her, and he was crying, too. He was so small then! Paul could see him, dressed in his pajamas, his skin strangely pale. Somewhere, Paul knew, their father was away, working for Corprogov outside the quarantine zone.

Paul's head had hurt. His eyes burned. He coughed, and his brother coughed, too—deep, rasping coughs. Paul didn't feel right—and for a moment, remembering it, he thought it was from getting overheated as he'd run up the stairs on his return—but that was in the dream, all that running was in the dream. He hadn't run. He hadn't run *at all*.

Paul remembered that he and his brother had been sick, too. Yes, Paul had been in the first stages—still well enough to go to the store. His brother was worse off than that—but neither had been as sick as their mother.

Paul remembered opening the package and the bottle inside the package, then, and making his brother swallow one of the large red pills inside. Paul had taken one, also, then lay down on the floor beside his mother's bed and looked up at her hollow gaze, as she stared across the room toward the door. She had been waiting for him—waiting for him, and for the medicine.

Paul couldn't stand to see her staring and had reached up, then, and closed her eyes—then lay there on the floor beside her, crying and dozing, dozing and crying, until he had finally fallen into a deep sleep.

Sometime later that night, Paul's father had made it through the quarantine lines and come home to them. Paul remembered being lifted from the floor, his face hot with fever, and put back down in his own bed. He had opened his eyes, then, long enough to see his father's face, which was streaked with tears, and to swallow another of the red pills, which his father handed to him with a glass of water and told him he must take. And he took it, Paul remembered, certain that his father was right. His father knew many things Paul did not. He did important work for Corprogov. He would know what to do now.

Paul sat up in bed, then, in his small room at the Kumaric Retreat, his own face streaked with tears. He burrowed his face in his hands and sobbed hard.

Mama, he thought. *Mom!* and again those feelings of regret, of remorse, rose in him—piercing and deep. *How could I? How could I?* He pushed his face into his hands so hard it hurt. The wind outside battered against the window of his room.

Paul couldn't stand it. How could he stand it? It was this dark, quiet room! It was this space that was sucking this out of him, pulling the poison from the closed cyst within him and spreading it throughout his system.

He needed to get out. He would feel better if he could just get outside.

Paul swung his feet over the edge of his bed and strapped on his shoes, then grabbed up his jacket.

In a moment, he was gone, leaving the dark, empty room behind him.

◘   ◘   ◘

For a time, Paul wandered aimlessly as the wind whipped around him. The Retreat seemed almost deserted, and Paul avoided the few people he did see.

Though he had no intention to go anywhere, Paul soon found himself standing outside the room he had met with Farsan in. He stood quite still, with the wind gusting and grabbing at his clothes.

It was dark inside the room. Clearly, no one was there. Paul pounded on the door, not expecting an answer, then leaned against the door jam, his face pressed into his shirt sleeve, taking in deep gulps of breath. How had he ever gotten suckered into this? He'd been fine before he'd come to this retreat— fine before he'd come to this world!

The door to the next room opened, and light came flooding out.

"Paul?" a voice said in the darkness.

Paul turned toward it. A male figure stood just outside the doorway: Farsan.

"Why don't you come on in, Paul?" he said. He pushed the door back with one arm, then waited for Paul to enter.

Without thinking about it, Paul stepped inside. He heard the door fall shut behind him, blocking out the wild wind.

"How are you doing, Paul?" Farsan asked.

Paul just stood there, unsure how to answer.

"Figured out something about the dream?"

Paul nodded. "Yeah." He wasn't sure he wanted to talk about it, or how he had wound up here, in Farsan's room.

For a moment, Farsan was silent, then Paul's shoulders began to shake.

"Why don't you come sit down and tell me about it?" Farsan put one hand on Paul's shoulder and gestured toward the sofa. Paul sat down, not on the sofa, but on the floor in front of it. He pulled his knees up to his chest.

Farsan sat on the floor near him.

They were both silent as Paul wiped tears away.

"What did you learn?" Farsan asked gently.

"It's my mother," Paul said, staring at his hands. He didn't want to talk about it, but he did want to, too. His thoughts raced frantically around inside his skull, like a cornered animal. Why should he tell this man—why trust him? But maybe it would help. Paul would never see him again, once he left the Retreat. Why say anything? He didn't want to talk about it. He didn't even want to *know* it.

Paul stared at the floor. He could hear Farsan breathing beside him.

Say something! Paul shouted in his head.

What did you learn? The question echoed.

"I killed her," Paul said aloud. He looked over at Farsan, expecting a look of shocked horror. Instead, Farsan looked calm, patient, as though he was trying to appreciate the situation.

"How did you kill her, Paul?"

Paul caught his breath and started to sob again.

"I didn't..."

He tried again, "I didn't...bring her her medicine."

And then it was like a dam bursting, "I didn't bring it to her in time. I could have. I could have saved her. She needed me. She counted on me, and I didn't bring it to her. I walked when I should have run.

"I walked. I walked—damn it. Damn it. I walked and I should have run."

Paul grabbed at his head, making fists as though to pull at the short hair. He sobbed. He cradled his head in his arms and sobbed.

"I killed her. I killed her. She wouldn't have died if I had done what she needed me..." His voice trailed off.

Farsan slid closer to Paul, then gathered him up in his arms and held him as he cried away the bitterest tears of his childhood, now still held within him as a man.

"What did she need you to do, Paul?" Farsan said softly, after a while.

Paul leaned back against the front of the sofa and looked over at Farsan. His breathing was still heavy.

"She needed me to bring her the medicine."

"And you didn't?"

"I got it there late," Paul said. His voice caught in his throat.

"Tell me what happened."

"When I was a kid. It was the *Muerte Azul.* She was sick. My brother and I got sick, too—but nothing like Mom. She had it bad. I went to get her medicine. She asked me to go for her, because she couldn't go herself. My father was away, and so I went. She could count on me. She should have been able to count on me. I wasn't that sick. I walked the whole way. I should have run. I should have run. I sat down for a while, on the curb, I think. It was hot out, and my head was hurting. I got home..."

Paul stopped speaking and stared past Farsan, breathing hard.

"Go on, Paul. It'll help," Farsan said. "Get it out."

Paul caught a deep breath and started crying again. "When I got home, she was dead. She just stared at me, like she was waiting—counting on me—but I never came. I had her medicine. I had *her medicine.* She just stared at me, with this cold, cold stare—like she blamed me!"

"Like you blamed yourself."

Paul nodded, wiping the tears from his face. "Yes. I let her down. And she died," he said. He could feel his throat tighten. It began to hurt.

"She needed the medicine, and you didn't bring it in time."

"Yes," Paul said. "Why didn't she ask me to go sooner? I'd have gone. I could have been back in time. When I was a kid, after she died, every time I thought of her, I remembered her like that—her face blue, her eyes cold, accusing. I couldn't bear it. I didn't remember for years. I didn't want to remember, but now I do. Why didn't she ask me to go sooner? I would have gone. She would have lived." Paul buried his face in his arms.

"Okay, Paul, okay. You've opened it up. That's good. But don't drown in it. I want you to think, too. Keep enough of your head outside of this to use it."

"What do you mean?" Paul asked.

"What sort of medicine was it?"

"I don't know. It was good, though—my brother and I took it, and we got well. But I didn't get it to her in time..."

"And so she died?"

"*Yes.*"

"Are you sure that the medicine was the important thing?" Farsan asked.

"What do you mean?"

"What kind of medicine was it? Would it have made a difference that far into her illness?"

Paul looked up, and his face cleared a little.

"What kind was it?" Farsan asked.

"I don't know."

"What did it look like?"

"They were red. I thought they were big, then. They were kind of ordinary. Oblong."

"Have you seen them anywhere else? What did you ask for at the drug store?"

Paul leaned his head back and looked up at the ceiling. Perhaps a whole minute passed while he sat there, staring upward.

"It was Cycloxip," he said finally, his voice steady and certain. "That's what I was sent to get."

"What does it do, Paul? What's it for? How long does it take to act?"

"I didn't know what it was for, then, but I do now. It's an analgesic. It drops fevers, stops aches and pains. It's just for *symptoms.*"

"And if you had run the whole way? If you'd run really hard?"

Paul looked at Farsan, his eyes growing wide. "If I'd have *flown*, I wouldn't have saved her," Paul said, a look of realization spreading on his face. "People died of congestion. Their lungs filled with fluids. You're right, it wouldn't have saved her." Tears began to fall down Paul's face again.

Paul took a deep breath, then added, "She might have died a little more comfortably, that's all."

"Did it save you and your brother?" Farsan asked.

Paul's look of astonishment spread, as the thought came to him, "No. No, it didn't save anybody. I couldn't have saved anybody. We just got well. Some people just got well."

Paul stared blankly at the wall ahead of him, remembering his father coming back into the quarantine area—his father carrying him to bed, and Paul looking up to see his father's face covered in tears. When had that been? A day later? Two or three? His father must have felt responsible, too, Paul thought, for not having been there for his wife when she needed him, when she lay dying—when his children were left alone in the dark eddies of the *Muerte Azul*. His father had been allowed the inoculation due to the importance of his work—Paul had learned, years later—but he had been unable to arrange it for his own family.

Farsan put his hand on Paul's knee. "Now, I need to ask you this, Paul. You said you killed her. Did you kill your mother?"

Paul turned toward Farsan as the tears ran down his cheeks. "No. No, I didn't kill her. She would have died no matter what I did."

"Did you let her down?"

"Not much," he said slowly. "Just a little bit." He took a deep breath, and a single sob broke from his chest.

"And I was just a kid. I was sick, too," he added.

"Do you think she would have forgiven you for that?"

Paul felt as though he were floating. "Yes. Yes."

"Would she have been right to forgive you?"

"Yes," Paul whispered.

"Good," Farsan said, "then perhaps, now, you can forgive yourself."

Farsan put his hand on Paul's shoulder and leaned a little toward Paul. Paul leaned toward Farsan and let Farsan hug him. As he did, Paul let loose another shower of tears, which swept through him like a mighty river, sweeping away all the guilt he had so long kept locked away inside.

All these years, Paul thought, *I've been running away from that. All these years. All these years, I thought I was responsible. I thought it was my failing.*

◻   ◻   ◻

After Paul left Farsan's room that night, he spent a long time wandering around the Retreat. Everyone had gone to bed, it seemed, and the place was deserted. That was just how Paul wanted it to be—a great expanse he could rattle around in, just as so many thoughts and feelings were rattling around inside of him, just as the wind seemed to make the whole world around him rattle, too.

Paul walked under the swaying branches of the pine trees, in and out of the domes of light that spread beneath the lamps that lit the walkways around the Retreat. Thoughts and feelings rose in him and then drifted away, as though carried on the wind.

Paul thought again about the dream he'd had in which his mother's face had turned into Sheila's.

Why Sheila's?

For a moment, Paul's thoughts turned to Sheila and an evening they'd spent together when she had truly been present with him—the last such time he could remember, though it had been a couple of months since. They had talked about Corprogov, and the Depopulation Project, and how many perks would be granted to Paul if he could really be a success. Sheila had liked that thought, Paul remembered—the vacations, a large apartment.

Paul let the thought drift away. The wind seemed to sweep through his thoughts, loosening one from another, with each new one rolling over the one that came before—impressions of his mother, of his conversation with Farsan, of the quote he had noticed on the wall before he'd left Farsan's room that night, which had read:

Do not be afraid to peer into the darkness,
for there you will also find light.

—THE LITTLE BOOK

Those words seemed at once eerie and beautiful to Paul, as he proceeded through the blustery night.

His thoughts turned again, this time to his time on the trail and all the different forms his dreams had taken along the way. He had been searching for his mother, in one way or another, in almost all of them.

His mother.

His mother, Paul thought. Just to think of her radiated feelings through him that he could barely start to name.

It seemed to Paul almost as though there had been a globe inside of him, tucked away someplace invisible for years—a globe filled with some sort of liquid. Inside this globe, he had held his memories of his mother, all locked away somewhere impenetrable and safe. Now that globe had been smashed, and the liquid held within it had spread everywhere.

Everywhere Paul looked, there were new memories and impressions of his mother, rising like a flood from deep within him. He recalled, in fragments flickering through his mind, the bedtime stories she used to tell, the quality of her laughter, the tenderness of her hugs, the light in her eyes whenever she looked pleased with him. All of these came back to Paul now, *and were his again.*

She *had* loved him. She had loved him, he knew now, without any doubt.

Paul wiped away tears and kept on walking, as the thoughts gathered, and formed, and re-formed in his head.

Paul remembered his grandfather and the comfort Paul had found in his company after his mother's death. He remembered the stories his grandfather had told him about the way the world had been and how it had come to be so changed, with so much less life in it.

It was from his grandfather, Paul remembered, that he had learned about how *Muerte Azul* had been spread gradually up the spine of the continent by bats. He had learned about how the bats had been pushed further and further from their homeland, as the climate changed around them—pushed and pushed by nature gone awry—pushed until they had arrived right at Paul's very doorstep. There they had delivered the disease they carried to Paul's city, to his community, to his family—and to his mother.

Paul stopped beneath a towering pine, as its branches rocked and moaned above him.

Yes, Paul realized, that had been the thing he had learned from his grandfather, as his grandfather had struggled to make sense of his own loss; Paul's mother, his grandfather's daughter, had died because people had carelessly, selfishly, ruined the delicate balance that held the natural world together— that had once kept it brimming with life.

Because people had sickened the natural world (changed the climate so nothing could live as it should, where it should), the natural world, so sickened, had passed its sickness on to humans—had passed its sickness to their bodies and to their lungs, where it has suffocated the life from them—just as people were suffocating the life from the natural world, itself.

Paul steadied himself against the massive tree's trunk as a new realization gathered within him.

And so it had been that Paul was no longer alone in his failing. It was no longer his failing *alone* that had led to the death of his mother.

No, not alone, because, listening to his grandfather talk about lost species—about animals that had once filled the sky, or the oceans, or had covered the land—listening to his grandfather tell about bats, and disease, and climate change, listening to him tell of all the vast and careless damage that people had done as they went about the business of their countless human lives—it had seemed, in Paul's young mind, that human beings formed a kind of swarm. Just as locusts were powerless alone but en masse could clear a field of every living fragment of green in a matter of minutes, human beings threatened to clear the world of every fragment of life but their own. In Paul's young mind, he and his grandfather had stood together in their loss, had stood together against the swarm of humanity, the swarm that had destroyed the right and natural order of the world.

If that right and natural order had been preserved, Paul had understood, his mother would have survived, because the sickness that took her life would never have found her.

If that right and natural order had been preserved, *she would even have survived Paul's failing*, because there would have been no *Muerte Azul* to take away her breath, and her life.

Paul leaned against the tree and began to cry again. He had wanted to right nature, to right the basic wrongness that had taken her from him, to redeem himself by righting what was wrong in the world outside him—though he could never, ever, right the most basic wrong that lay within him.

Paul looked up at the tree limbs swaying above him, buffeted by wind. He felt a thin tremor run through his limbs, as he remembered how he had felt then: it wasn't his fault *alone*—not *alone*—all of humanity was to blame, along with him. And though he could never, ever, undo *his* error, his basic *failing*, he could, perhaps, fight back against the swarm that had so poisoned his world, and poisoned his mother along with it. He wanted to make right what swarming billions of people had made wrong. He wanted to make the world so right, so well, that people like his mother would be protected from clumsy, failed humans like him. If he couldn't resurrect the animals, or block the blinding sun, or re-seed the oceans with life (or any of the other wild schemes he had come up with in those days) then perhaps he could, at least, remove the deadly swarm, or some of it, and so remove at least a piece of the terrible wrongness that underlay his mother's death.

And so he had dreamed of transporting at least some of those swarming billions of humans elsewhere—far away from the earth they had so ravaged, the earth on which his mother had died her unnecessary death, struck down by the clumsiness of people—by the clumsiness of failed people, just like him.

Paul stumbled back toward his room through the windy darkness, his mind still agitated with these disorienting thoughts. He felt like a man standing before a mirror, who found that he was not only wearing new clothes, but new skin, and bones, and sinew. Everything he was seemed new to him.

He had never been culpable—he told himself, now—never for her death, nor for the destruction of his world.

It wasn't his doing, he told himself. It was never his doing.

It wasn't his fault. It had never been his fault.

He had blamed it first on himself, alone, and then on himself, along with all of humanity—but it had never been his failing, at all. He had been a child. *A child.*

Had all his life, his work, been built on this, really?—the desire to make right the wrongness that had torn his mother from him? The desire to make his own wrongness right, to redeem himself for a crime he had never, actually, committed?

Paul entered his room and fell onto his bed, his head swimming in confusion.

If this was his life, then who was he within it?

Who was he, if his whole life was built on something so mistaken?

Paul rolled over and buried his face in the pillow, stricken—and as he did, an answer slowly rose upward from somewhere deep in his mind.

He was his mother's son.

His mother's son—who was never rejected.

Who was always loved.

Who was always loved.

And who deserved to be loved.

20

Paul sat up and rubbed his eyes, then looked across the room at the wall opposite his bed. Once again, the quote on the wall had changed over night. Now it read:

> *Watching the moon*
> *at midnight,*
> *solitary, mid-sky,*
> *I knew myself completely,*
> *no part left out.*
>
> —Izumi Shikibu

Paul sat in bed for a few minutes, thinking about what had happened in the last day. While he did, he ran his hand absentmindedly over his head. His hair was now long enough to feel soft and not so bristly anymore.

Paul got up, then, and showered, before dressing in some of the clothes he had washed out in the sink a couple of days before. Though feeling hurried, he took a few minutes more to wash out his other set of clothes and hang them to dry in the bathroom. Before leaving Farsan's room the night before, Paul had agreed to meet with Farsan at nine o'clock that morning. Farsan had said he wanted a chance to see Paul early and make sure he was doing all right. Now, if he was quick, Paul would have just enough time for breakfast before the meeting.

When Paul arrived for his meeting with Farsan, Farsan told him he had something to share with him. Farsan stepped over to the wall, where he waved his hand in front of the panel.

"It's a quote of Dr. Kumar's. I was trying to remember it before you left last night, but I couldn't remember the exact words. I don't have the advantages of those who use Synaplast. So, I looked it up this morning. It's from one of her journals.

"Here it is," he said, then read to Paul aloud:

> We all deserve love because it is essential to our wellbeing. We all need and deserve love in the same way that all creatures need and deserve air and sunshine.

"I thought you might like hearing that about now. It makes a good foundational belief," Farsan said, as he turned toward Paul.

Paul nodded. "Yeah. I like that," he said. He turned the thought over in his mind, as he sat down on the sofa in the same spot where he had sat on the previous afternoon.

"How are you doing, Paul?" Farsan asked, as he took his familiar place in the armchair.

To an outside observer, it might have seemed that very little had changed since the day before—and yet, they both knew, so very much was different.

"I'm doing much better," Paul said.

"I'm glad to hear it, and to see you looking so well. That was a rough night you had last night."

"Yeah, it was," Paul said.

Farsan nodded. "Well, I guess we should get started—but, well—you've moved forward very quickly, Paul, and I could understand if you felt like that was enough, and you wanted to stop here for a while. But if you *are* ready to go on, I have a question or two I'd like to ask you. Would that be okay?"

Paul thought for a moment. "What are your questions?"

"If I remember right, you started out wondering why you were dreaming about your mother, but also why your girlfriend had appeared in place of your mother in one of these dreams. Do you have any idea now about why that was?"

"No," Paul said.

Farsan looked thoughtful. "What happened, exactly, at that point in the dream, when they switched?"

Paul took a deep breath. "Well, I was inside, looking for my mother. I found her in her bedroom, lying in bed. Her back was to me. Then she rolled over, and her face—for a moment, it was hers. But then I glanced away, and when I looked back, it wasn't hers, anymore. It was Sheila's," Paul said. Even now, something about the dream made him uncomfortable, like he might feel if he had let his hand get too close to a flame. He wanted to pull back from it.

Paul shifted in his seat and looked out the window.

"Can you go a little deeper, like we talked about before?" Farsan said gently.

"I don't know." Paul was silent for minute, as he tried to turn his attention back to the flame. Again, he remembered the way it had felt in the dream, when his mother had looked at him with that cold, hard look. Then Paul watched, as her face changed and became Sheila's. It changed—but not so very much.

Paul looked over at Farsan.

"She looks like her," he said.

"Who does?" Farsan asked.

"Sheila, my girlfriend. She looks like my mother." Paul shook his head. "It never occurred to me before. She looks like her!"

"That's interesting, Paul. What do you think it means?" Farsan asked.

"I don't know." Paul thought for a moment. "I don't know." He rubbed his face with his hands. "I don't think I want to think about it."

"I know," Farsan said. "It's uncomfortable. But if you can look into it, you might learn something of value."

Paul looked at Farsan. He wanted to argue back against this—but he was beginning to understand the power of insight. He was beginning to believe that it was true: we were all self-programming machines—and he, Paul, had gone too long without paying attention to his own programming.

Paul leaned his head back against the back of the sofa and sighed. "You're right," he said. "And I really don't know."

"Okay," Farsan said. "You might spend some time picturing them both in your mind and comparing how you feel about them. Let the associations gather and see what insights come to you. There's some link, or they wouldn't have appeared as they did in the dream."

"Okay," Paul said. "I'll try."

Farsan started to get up, then paused and looked back over at Paul.

"This girlfriend of yours—Sheila?"

"Yeah."

"Would you say that she accepts you?" Farsan asked.

"Oh, yeah, sure," Paul answered, without ever stopping to think about it.

Farsan looked at Paul thoughtfully. "All right, then. Give it some thought and come back—tomorrow? Same time?"

"Okay," Paul said, "9 AM."

◘   ◘   ◘

After leaving his meeting with Farsan, Paul spent time in his room, refining his list of potential parts for his transport and identifying additional bits and pieces that would be needed to connect them. The work was tedious, and in truth, Paul's heart wasn't really in it.

Nothing in Paul's life now seemed to make sense. But still, he wasn't quite ready to turn his full attention to the question Farsan had asked, and the process of refining his list of parts offered him a refuge of sorts while he felt around inside himself for how he would approach the question Farsan had asked him to answer.

Regardless of that, though, after a while, the work began to irritate Paul. He saved his work and turned off the portal, then went and sat on the edge of his bed, where he occupied himself by flipping coins into his hat, which he had put on the floor, and trying to make the coins land heads-side up. As he did, he let his thoughts drift, like a boat floating on a river, carried by unseen currents. Impressions of his fantasy of returning to his world as a hero played through his mind—how the crowds would gather around him, adoring him;

how Sheila would greet him and embrace him with a tenderness she had, in truth, never shown to him before.

Yes, that was how he had always pictured Sheila being, once he returned. She would come to him, proud and radiant, and put her arms around him, holding him close, as though, finally, once and for all, he would have proved himself to her.

Paul replayed the images in his mind, letting them turn here and there—but this time, in Paul's imagination, as Sheila wrapped her arms around him, she became his mother: full of pride and radiance, holding him so close to her. So close.

Paul lay back onto the bed and let the fantasy play out.

"Oh, Mom, I'm sorry," he said to her. "I know, I know it wasn't my fault—but still, I'm so sorry. I wish I could have gotten there in time."

His mother leaned back enough to look Paul in the eye—and Paul was small, there, next to her.

"I know, my darling boy," she said, pushing the hair from his forehead. "My poor, darling boy. You did all I asked. You were sick, too. I didn't want you to run. If I had known I wouldn't last till you got back, I would never have sent you. I'm sorry I put such a burden on you, my darling boy."

Paul lay, then, for a long time, staring up at the ceiling, as tears flowed from his eyes, remembering his mother, and his boyhood, and how hard it had been when she was gone.

Paul spent the rest of the day alone in his room. He didn't even bother to go to lunch. He didn't feel like being around other people, nor did he feel like eating. Instead, he spent the day remembering, and probing, and reflecting on all that had happened. Where before there had been set paths that wound their way through him, paths that he had walked and re-walked countless times—now everything seemed opened up within him, a vast meadow that he now set out to explore every inch of. Everything in his life seemed different. Everything that he touched seemed different, now. It all held a hint of sorrow, and joy, and discovery—but at least now he was free to wander where he wanted, to touch what he wanted, and to see what things really were, and what they really meant for him in his life.

Paul traced back his feelings about his mother and about Sheila, much as Farsan had instructed him to do, following his feelings and his associations and so "unwinding" his dream. Now it seemed to Paul that everything in his life had been wound tightly around the same point, growing out like a filament from his mother's death. He unwound it now—a long, slender thread that he could see clearly, that he could touch, and trace, and follow through himself. It was as though a new line connected up the pieces of his life—and with that new line he found a new story revealed about himself.

It was only for dinner that Paul finally emerged from his room—and only then, really, because he had promised to wash the dishes afterward. (He did, after all, have a travel meal or two still left over from his hike, and so could easily have eaten in his room.)

After Paul finished his dinner, he told Halwerd where he could find him when it was time to start washing up, then went and sat outside the dining hall—where he waited on the grassy meadow, looking up as the sun went down and the sky began to fill with stars.

That was where Farsan found him, after Farsan finished his meal.

They greeted one another, then Farsan sat down next to Paul.

"Good dinner," Farsan said.

"Yeah, it was," Paul said, nodding.

"I didn't see you at lunch."

"Didn't go."

"You doing okay?"

"Yeah. Been thinking," Paul said.

Farsan nodded.

"I think I have an answer for your question," Paul said.

Farsan nodded again. "That's good," he said.

"Sheila accepts me fine—on the surface—but she doesn't love me down deep, like I always wanted her to."

Paul pulled up a stalk of grass that had seeds dangling at one end of it. "I've shown her every devotion," he went on. "I've tried never to let her down—but the relationship is something different for her. She accepts me for what I am *to her*—but what I am to her isn't much. Of the things she wants in life, well, I can give her many of those things. So I'm useful to her, and she accepts me in that way. She even loves me in a way, in her own way—but mostly just for what I give her. She gives me approval when I give her things. She approves of what I give her."

"What do you give her, Paul?"

"I'm useful to her," Paul said, looking over at Farsan. "I give her things she wants. That's why she chooses me." Paul looked down at his feet. "I give her various sorts of things. Vacations. Clothes. Status." Paul hesitated for a moment. "Sex," he added.

Paul wiped a tear from his eye, while continuing to stare down at his feet. "It's a shame, really," he said, with a solemn tone. "I thought I was winning her—that, in time, I would win her heart, truly, really. She does approve of me, I guess—or at least, she approves of me succeeding in the things she benefits from."

Paul glanced over at Farsan. "So that's how it is," he concluded.

"Are you sure?" Farsan asked. "Sometimes, when people are in pain, things can seem worse than they are."

"No, this is true. I've never seen things more clearly in my life. I don't know why I didn't see it before—except that I didn't want to see it. Maybe I needed what I wanted from her too much. But it's not me she loves," Paul said, shaking his head slowly. "She hardly pays attention to me, really. It's what I give her that makes her choose me."

Paul paused, then added, "We were never really close. I thought we would be, could be, if I did things right. But we never really were. She kept it that way. It was how she wanted it, I guess. To have her needs met—but not have too much closeness."

Paul thought about Sheila making love with her implant on, and sighed.

"That's hard, then, Paul," Farsan said. "I'm sorry to hear it. But it's brave of you to recognize it now." He put a hand on Paul's shoulder—a gesture that Paul found surprisingly consoling.

"Thanks," Paul said. "She wasn't like any of the other women I've known. I always had a feeling that she was special, that she could give me something I needed, something that no one else had to give."

Farsan nodded, then said softly, "Like a mother's love?"

Paul looked over at him. "That's it," Paul said.

"She looked like your mother—so if she would accept you, deeply—would love you deeply—it would almost be like your mother doing it?" Farsan offered.

"It's even better than that," Paul said. "You see—*she never would.* She never would have. It's just not who she is. Even if I had given her the world, the *world*—she would never have loved me like that."

For a moment, Paul remembered how he had dreamed of Sheila holding him, when he returned triumphant—holding him like she had never done, like she never would have done—like his mother had held him, when she was alive, before he had lost her and (it seemed) had lost her love, as well.

"It fit, you see," Paul continued explaining to Farsan, "because, deep down, truly, I'd been telling myself I didn't deserve that sort of love. So it made sense to choose Sheila, to seek that from her, and then never get it. It fit the model I had—of wanting and not deserving. So I just had to keep on trying—to keep trying, as though, one day, I might really make myself worthy of it."

Paul sniffed a little. He looked down at his hands, then added, "We could have just kept going on like that for years. We could have spent our lives together, doing just exactly that. I would have tried to please her, to be there for her, to meet her needs—hoping all the while that she would redeem me with her love—and she would have valued all those gifts, all those *things*, but never really me. She could never have loved me like I wanted."

"And so you chose her because with her you could aspire, and maybe even get some of the approval you craved?—but then never really receive the deep love you believed you didn't deserve?" Farsan asked.

"That's it," Paul said.

"That's important to know," Farsan said.

"Yeah, I guess so."

Paul took a deep breath and looked up at the sky, as though searching for something he might find there. Above him was a great blue-black dome, in which the most prominent stars had all emerged. His stars. His sky. The sky he had always known—but somehow fresher or newer, here, as he viewed it now.

Farsan still had his hand on Paul's shoulder. "You know, I've worked with a lot of people here at the Retreat, through the years," he said. "Some people make a lot of headway very quickly, some don't—but I've seen very few accomplish as much, as quickly, as you've done," he said. "You've done very well, Paul. You should feel proud." Farsan squeezed Paul's shoulder, then withdrew his hand.

"Thanks," Paul said, glancing over at Farsan. For a moment, Farsan's warm and thoughtful expression reminded Paul of his grandfather. "I appreciate your help."

They sat together in silence, then, for a few minutes, as more stars gradually appeared above them, brightening the sky.

"You'll come see me in the morning?" Farsan asked finally.

"Sure," Paul said.

"Good. We'll talk about what you can do for stage three, then."

"Stage three?" Paul said. "I thought we were only on stage one."

"Stage one—private self," Farsan listed off. "Stage two—interpersonal relationships. Stage three—the transpersonal self."

"Oh," Paul said, "I see." He nodded a little and smiled, as he realized what Farsan meant—he had passed through stage two by delving into his relationship with Sheila.

"Okay," Paul said to Farsan. "I'll come see you in the morning—9 AM, like we planned."

"Okay. I'll see you then," Farsan said, as he stood up. "Good night, Paul. Rest well."

"Good night," Paul answered, then looked back up at the stars. From inside the dining hall, he could hear the clatter of dishes as the tables were being cleared.

With one hand behind his head, Paul lay back against the wild grasses of the meadow, staring upward. In a few minutes, he knew, Halwerd would come for him—but for now, Paul would just quietly wait here.

◦ 21 ◦

"Hello, Paul," Farsan said, as he opened the door to the meeting room. He again had a mug of tea in his hand and offered to pour Paul some, but this time Paul declined. As they both took their usual seats again, Paul looked up at the wall, which now read:

> *When troubled by your actions, rewrite the code,*
> *and so become someone new.*
>
> *Once that code is revised, you must not blame yourself*
> *for the unfortunate results you got before,*
> *for you are no longer the person who created them.*
>
> *Now you may go forward creating better results.*

———————

> *Be thankful for the problems*
> *that taught you how to be who you are now.*
>
> —THE LITTLE BOOK

"Before we get started talking about what you'll do for stage three, I wanted to ask you a question that I think might be useful for you to consider," Farsan said. He took a sip of his tea.

"Sure, go ahead," Paul said.

"Well, remember I suggested to you the other day that you try to work the three impediments in reverse, as you explored your dream? I was just wondering—have you thought about what you've discovered in terms of the three impediments?"

"No, I haven't," Paul answered.

"Well, I think it can be useful, when trying to understand any sort of problem, to see what role the three impediments may have played in creating it. So, I'd like to suggest that you do that now," Farsan said.

Paul considered this for a minute, before answering.

"Well," he said finally, "first, I guess, I wasn't communicating with myself. I wouldn't even let myself remember what had happened when my mother died, and what it had meant to me."

Farsan nodded. "Okay."

Paul thought for a moment longer. "Second, well, I thought there was something bad in me." Paul frowned a little. "And, third, my perspective was insular—I didn't even begin to see how my mother would really have seen things. She—I'm sure—she wouldn't ever have blamed me the way I imagined her doing, the way I blamed myself. I think she would have felt bad, actually, that I felt bad."

"Okay," Farsan said. "Good. I think you're right about all three. It's amazing how much those three little things can get in the way, sometimes, and muck up the works."

"So," Farsan said, setting down his mug and leaning toward Paul, "like I told you last night, I think we're done with the first two stages. As you probably know, there's a policy here at the Retreat; novices are encouraged to work with at least a couple different experienced sojourners as they progress through the three stages. It's thought that people benefit from being exposed to a variety of approaches."

"So what you're saying is, I need to find somebody else?" Paul said.

"I'm afraid so. I've liked working with you, Paul. I'd be glad to keep going—but at the same time, I think the policy makes sense."

Paul frowned. "Okay, Farsan. I'm kind of disappointed—I thought we made a good team—but that's okay." Paul seemed a little at a loss for what else to say.

"Do you need help finding somebody? I could recommend someone if you like—or maybe you know of someone else you'd like to work with?"

Paul thought for a moment, shaking his head. Then he stopped shaking it. "Could it be anyone?" he asked.

"If they're available."

Paul smiled a little. "There's a woman. I sat in on her class. Her name's 'Jessica,' I think. I think you know her. You were talking to her at dinner the other night."

"Jessica Darrow," Farsan said. "Yes, she's good. Would you like to work with her?"

"Yeah, I think."

"She would be a good choice for you, Paul. She really knows her stuff. She does this work professionally, you know—but still comes to the Retreat each summer and donates her time. You couldn't do better," Farsan said.

Paul nodded.

"Do you need to know how to reach her?"

Paul thought about it. "No—I'll go to her class. I'll ask her there."

"Okay," Farsan said, and for a moment, both he and Paul were silent. Then the two men stood and shook hands. It wasn't the sort of handshake Paul knew from his world, but more a moment of affectionate hand-holding. Then Farsan wished Paul luck, and with a flurry of "thank yous" and "farewells," Paul was on his way.

◙   ◙   ◙

Paul spent the rest of his day refining his plans for the transport and compiling a list of all the parts (from the largest and most important, to the finest bolts and screws) that he would need to piece it together and get it up and running. As he added each item to the list, he asked the portal to give him some idea of the cost, and then added that information to the list, as well. But even as the list took shape on the screen in front of him, Paul found himself wondering what use he would make of all this information. After all, his sense of drive—that feeling that beckoned him back to help rescue his sick and half-starved world—had weakened. He no longer dreamed of some perfect reunion with Sheila, nor did he crave the adulation of crowds, valuing in him what he would not value in himself. He had expunged from himself the poison that had stayed with him since his mother's death, so that now he no longer craved (from Sheila, or an adoring crowd) the antidote.

Beyond the fact that Paul's need was less, he was now convinced that the response he had imagined to his return was pure fantasy. Sheila, he had realized, would never, could never, love him like that—just as Paul now understood that she had never really needed him (though he had wanted to be needed by her, and then to redeem himself by unfailingly meeting that need).

As for the crowds, well, most people probably wouldn't comprehend the importance of his work, Paul now admitted, no matter what message Corprogov sent out over the Stream—and few would have the vision and courage to voluntarily travel to another world. No, for the most part, the people who participated in the depopulation process would probably be chosen by lottery, or sent in clusters of families, or communities, never knowing how lucky they were until they arrived.

So why *should* he complete the transport? Paul asked himself, and the answer that came to him was strong enough—though not as inspiring as his fantasy had been. Because it was needed. Because, for whatever reason, the people of his world, lonely and desperate as they were, had painted themselves into a corner—and he was the only one who had the ability to help them get out. He had a responsibility to complete his project. The truth was no more and no less than that.

It was funny, Paul thought, that he would reach this point in his relationship with the project after finding solutions to so many of what had seemed the most daunting challenges. He was confident now that he could aim the transport to return him to his world. He had figured out how to construct a new transport from specific parts available on this world, almost down to the tiniest screw, and was well on his way to tallying up what the total cost would be, as well. He had yet to figure out how to arrange funding, or to provide an adequate surge of power—but those things, he felt, ought to be doable, one way or another. And yet having come this far, the project seemed to him, now, not so much inspired, as obligatory.

Paul looked over at the wall and read the quote that had appeared that day:

> Create what you love.
> Do not fight what you hate.
>
> Fight creates only more fight.

> —THE LITTLE BOOK

Create what you love, Paul repeated to himself. It sounded so simple, but it seemed to him, in that instant, that nothing could be more complex.

◻   ◻   ◻

Though Paul had spent most of that day in a bit of a slump, the next day he woke in good spirits. At least today, he knew, he would not spend the whole day in his room, nor did he expect to be asked to probe into painful corners of himself. Instead, today, he would visit another of Jessica Darrow's classes and ask her if she would work with him.

After breakfast, Paul showered then dressed in the clothes he had washed and hung up to dry in his bathroom a couple of days before, then took a few minutes to wash out, and hang to dry, the clothes he had been wearing.

Before leaving the bathroom, Paul paused to examine himself in the mirror and was pleased to find nothing particularly odd about his appearance. The bruise on his temple had disappeared entirely, his eyebrows and eyelashes had grown back in enough to appear entirely normal, and the hair on his head was now a carpet of solid brown, with no scalp showing. Yes, his hair was still unusually short, but not, he thought, outside the range of what someone might voluntarily choose for it to be. Finally, Paul felt he could be out among people without being at all self-conscious about his appearance.

Paul looked at the clock. Though he saw no reason to sit through an entire class just because he wished to speak to the teacher afterward, he also didn't want to be late and miss the opportunity, so he planned to arrive about three quarters of the way through the class, as he had done a few days before. Now he had a little time to pass before going.

He sat on the bed, with his back against the wall, and with his legs stretched out on the bedspread in front of him, crossed at the ankle. He thought about all that had changed for him in the last few days. The sort of life he had lived had varied greatly from one time period to the next, but never had he seen a change take place in his own thoughts and feelings—in the basic way things were laid out within himself—so quickly as things had happened within him since coming to the Retreat.

Paul recalled the question he had brought with him to the Retreat, about how it was that the New Change had swept through this earth so quickly, when no particular progress had been made toward it on his own world. It seemed to him, now, that perhaps the two things were related. Perhaps the same sort of practice that had helped him see more clearly and deeply into himself had helped one person after another awaken to new aspects of themselves here. Perhaps this work really could help speed up the development of the sort of "expanded sense of self" Dr. Kumar had talked about as the natural next step in the progress of humanity—the next level that lay before us.

Perhaps, Paul thought, the same sort of practice he had begun, here, had helped billions of people achieve that new level, that "expanded sense of self"—while on his own world, nothing had been done to accelerate that change and so, there, it had proceeded forward on the same timescale as the Original Change had taken place on: a process requiring thousands of years to unfold.

For a moment, Paul wondered how it would feel to really get to that state of expanded consciousness. He could hardly guess—though he did know how he felt so far. He felt lightened and lifted, freed and renewed by this new knowledge of himself.

Paul thought again about his plans to return to his earth and what he would do after his arrival there. First, he would report to Corprogov and let them know his project had been a success. Then he would have to find Sheila and let her know he was okay.

He thought about how it would be to see her then. What *would* it be like? What if she did, really, put her arms around him and held him as he had dreamed of her doing?

But no, Paul thought, shaking his head, she *wouldn't* do that—and not just because it wasn't her way to express her feelings like that, but because, in truth, she had no such deep feelings about him to express.

So what would he tell her? Paul thought. That he was whole and well—and that he had thought a great deal about their relationship while he was gone? That he had come to understand that what he was seeking from her was something she would never give, and that what she was seeking from him had little to do with him, personally?

Would he call it off? Paul wondered.

Probably so, he told himself—and Sheila would be mad, but only for a while, only until she found someone else who would agree to the same terms Paul had agreed to—vacations, status, jewelry—all given in exchange for flashes of approval and the misleading allure that more approval, more love, more acceptance would sometime, somehow, well up from someplace beneath.

Perhaps the next guy would see that there was no next stage waiting to ripen—but that this was the relationship at its full measure, its full depth.

Paul sat for a moment, sadly remembering the many times he had made love to Sheila while she left her implant running—while somewhere, behind her eyes, images of other men mechanically flickered—and all the while Paul had been feeling that if he was just good enough, right enough, true enough, she would turn her full love to him, and the thing that ached within him would be mended.

Paul looked over at the clock. If he wanted to get to Jessica Darrow's class in time, he should be leaving. Paul sat up and put on his shoes, glad to have a reason to stop thinking about Sheila. It was funny, how quickly things could change. Just a few days ago, he had thought of her for comfort—and now, in truth, he didn't really want to think of her at all.

☐ ☐ ☐

As Paul approached the classroom, he slowed to read the words holographically "engraved" on the wall next to the door. The first "engraving"—about four or five lines in length—faded before he got close enough to read it. It was replaced with the words:

MODELING-REALITY CLASS

printed in big, classic letters. In a moment, those words shimmered and rearranged themselves into another phrase:

HOW MENTAL MODELS INFLUENCE EVENTS

Once more, the words cycled and re-formed, so that a quotation was displayed:

What you say will be said back to you.

—BUDDHA

After that, the first "engraving"—the one Paul had missed—cycled back, again. It read:

All the world's a stage,
And all the men and women merely players:
They have their exits and their entrances;
And one man in his time plays many parts.

—WILLIAM SHAKESPEARE

Paul paused for a moment to ponder what he had just read, then took a step to his left and peered into the classroom.

Inside, the lights were dim. A holographic projection of Dr. Kumar filled the front of the room. In the projection, Dr. Kumar was strolling through an open meadow. Behind her, a mountain range with three prominent rock formations rose skyward. Her voice filled the air, though Paul was too busy taking in the scene before him to notice what was being said.

Paul slipped through the door and took a seat near the back of the class, just as the hologram of Dr. Kumar faded and disappeared. As the lights came up, Paul saw Jessica at one side of the classroom, leaning against a table. She had apparently left the front of the class to make space for the holographic projection. Now she stayed where she was and surveyed the class.

"All right," she said, as the last shimmer of the hologram faded from the air, "let's do a little review. Who can name three ways that our mental models influence the events in our lives?" She looked around the class and called on one of the students who had a hand up.

"Well, first of all," a woman with a crisp voice and short graying hair answered, "when we follow our impulses and impressions, we give expression to whatever models we have in our minds—whether we're conscious of what those models are, or not. This happens whether people are making art, or simply living their lives—just as Dr. Kumar described, when she wrote about her college days in Oxford."

"Okay, very good," Jessica responded.

"And that means," a man in a purple vest, who sat to Paul's left, added, "that it's important to notice what you tell yourself—what models you make—because that's the lens through which you'll see the world. Whatever models you have about what's true and real, you'll see the patterns that match those models when you look around you at the world. And you'll be blind to the patterns that don't match your models."

"*Right,*" said a young man in a red and green shirt, "and it's like, you have your mental model—and then you have all these impulses and impressions that grow out of it—and then you have all the actions that those impulses lead to. And those actions make like an echo, like a replica of the mental model. It's like it takes it out of your head and puts it out into the world. It's like when people do art—there's a model on the inside and then they create that same thing on the outside."

"'*In life as in art,*' as they say," the man in the purple vest added.

The woman with the graying hair smiled at the young man, then spoke to Jessica. "And if you have great models, then you'll '*perceive great opportunities from within the vast, scattered star field of life*'—and that's what you'll give form to around you. But if you let yourself hold cynical or unhappy models, then it's their reflection that you'll perceive around you and it's them that you'll give form to through your actions."

"All right, I clearly have a great class here. Those were all excellent answers," Jessica said, smiling at the class. "That makes two of the three types of situations I was looking for—one: we give form around us to what we've modeled inside us; and, two: we perceive around us what we've modeled inside us. That's great. Now, I'd like one more example of how our mental models influence events."

"Casting," the rugged-looking man, whom Paul remembered from the last class, answered from the front row.

"Good," Jessica said. "Would you like to summarize how that works?"

"Sure," he said. "Basically, we draw from people the side of them that matches what we expect. It's like, well, if your mental model of the world is that it's a lousy world full of cranky, unfriendly people and you go out there expecting to have cranky and unfriendly interactions with everybody you meet, then your behavior is going to be calibrated to fit those circumstances, and so the people you meet are going to show you the cranky, unfriendly side of their personalities—however cranky or unfriendly that might be. Through your actions, large and small, you'll instinctively be setting the stage for that.

"Likewise," he added, "if your mental model of the world is that it's full of friendly, nice people and so you go around beginning every interaction as though it is, of course, going to be a friendly, nice one, you're going to draw from other people their friendliest, nicest side."

"And so, whatever you start out believing," a woman sitting behind Paul chimed in, "it's just going to seem proved to you by your experience—even if you're forming that experience. You're going to think it's just *truth*, it's just the way the world truly is, and not a particular pattern of experience that results from a mental model you're carrying."

"Right. Very good," Jessica said. "And why's it called 'casting?'"

"Because," the rugged-looking man said, "it's like we've written these plays in our minds—these scenarios, these stories we've modeled about how the world works, about who we are and why things happen the way they do. It's like we write these plays in our minds and then cast other people in them. It's like we're the directors of our own plays, drawing from other people the performances we have in mind."

"And they're doing the same with us," a young woman just ahead of Paul and to his right said. "They're casting us in *their* plays, also, drawing from us performances fitted to the scenarios in *their* stories."

"I remember seeing a holofilm once," a young man with long brown hair said, "where there were these two friends, both guys. They didn't look that different—I mean, they were about the same amount good looking—but one of them thought of himself as attractive to women, and he would go up to the women he liked and talk to them in this, well, self-confident way, like he had something good to offer, and he was sure they would like him—and they would respond, you know? They'd be friendly. But the other guy had a really negative self image. He wouldn't even go up to anybody, unless his friend pushed him to do it, and when he did, he was really awkward and gave up really fast. It was funny, I guess, but I thought it was sad. Nothing worked out for him."

"That's pungent!" the young man in the red and green shirt exclaimed and shook his head.

"Yeah?" Jessica said.

"Well, it's such a self-fulfilling prophecy, isn't it? That gizmo should open his eyes."

Jessica smiled. "That would help," she said, then turned to the young man with the long brown hair. "That's a great example of casting—each of them got what they expected. Each of them drew from other people performances that matched their models.

"I want to add, too," she said, "that what we're talking about is not just a matter of people eliciting from one another certain behaviors that fit their mental models of reality. We also put out social signals that, in effect, broadcast to others which roles we are prepared to be cast in and which we aren't. Other people pick up those signals and respond accordingly. Those who want something other than what we're offering will move on and look for someone who will interact with them in the ways they want—or at least the ways they expect.

"So, for example, if someone is looking for someone to fall in love with—or if somebody, say, is looking for someone to pick a fight with, whichever it may be—and you're not willing to play either the lover or the fighter in someone else's play, then most likely they'll sense that and move on to someone else who *is* willing to be cast in the appropriate part. On the other hand, if you're ready and willing, most likely they'll pick up those signals too and so the play will begin.

"Okay," Jessica said, as she stepped back toward the front of the class, "I'd like to finish things up with a quote from one of Dr. Kumar's journals. It's from the entry at 2.18.04, I believe. It goes like this," she said and then recited the quote from heart:

> If you see yourself as a victim, others who want to victimize someone will choose you to prey upon. If you see yourself as a leader, those who wish to follow will sense this in you and choose you to follow. We are all like playwrights, casting actors in the stories we write for ourselves. If you want to understand your own story, look around you at the cast you have assembled.

"All right, that's it for today," Jessica said. "Come back next Monday, same time, same place, if you want to join in on another modeling-reality class."

"Great class, Jessica," the rugged-looking man said, as the people in the class got up and began to move toward the door.

"Thanks, Sam," Jessica said.

"What's the next class about?" the woman with the graying hair asked.

"I think we'll focus on rewriting models," Jessica answered.

"Remodeling models," the young man with the red and green shirt chimed in.

Jessica flashed a smile. "Nice, Vic," she said, and again Paul thought how open her face was and how beautiful her smile.

Paul watched her interact with the students on their way out of the room. She looked at each person with such warmth, and each responded by offering such warmth to her.

When all the other students were gone, Jessica Darrow turned that same warm and open face toward Paul.

Paul told himself to speak, but found himself hesitating for a moment.

"Is there something I can help you with?" Jessica asked.

"Well, yeah," Paul said. "My name's Paul Rockwell. I've been working with Farsan Saqqa and have completed the first two stages. Now I'm looking for someone to work with on stage three, and I wonder if you might be willing to work with me."

Paul paused for a moment, then added, "It's my first stay at the Retreat."

Jessica looked at him thoughtfully.

"Well," she said, "I've got three sojourners I'm working with already." She frowned a little, then looked Paul in the eye. Paul could tell that she thought three was enough—but she was still thinking about it.

As Jessica considered, Paul met her gaze and was dazzled all over again by the depth and the gentleness he saw there.

"But that's okay," Jessica said, nodding slowly. "I'll work with you, if you'd like."

· 22 ·

Paul sat down beneath the large white fir and looked back across the meadow that lay between him and the Retreat. He hoped he had found the right tree. All Jessica had said was to meet her "at the tall white fir on the eastern edge of the Retreat" at two thirty that afternoon, and now here he was, ten minutes early, sitting beneath a tall tree with a pale blue cast to its needle-shaped leaves. Though not the tallest tree on the eastern edge of the Retreat, it was the tallest of its kind, with a massive trunk and thick limbs.

Paul looked out across the meadow, which was filled with native grasses, wildflowers, and a variety of other plants (some of which, Paul knew, helped supply the food eaten at the Retreat). After a few minutes, he saw a lone figure start across the meadow, walking in his direction. It was a young woman who moved with a casual grace, strolling in long, even strides with her face turned slightly downward, as though lost in thought. Something in her manner reminded Paul of the way a child might walk happily along with her head full of daydreams.

It wasn't that she seemed to be wandering, Paul told himself, as he watched Jessica coming closer (for now he was certain it was she). On the contrary, she cut across the field in an unerring line, heading directly for the tree under which he sat, walking at a steady pace. Nonetheless, her movements seemed relaxed and idyllic to Paul—the natural stride of someone at peace with herself.

Paul looked around at the meadow speckled with wildflowers; the wide blue sky spotted with clouds; and the clear, sunny day; and took a deep breath of the fresh mountain air. If someone was to feel at peace with themself, he thought, leaning back against the trunk of the old white fir, it would be more possible here than almost anywhere.

When Jessica was nearly to the tree, she looked up and waved at Paul, then glanced around at the scenery, her face bright and cheerful. A moment later, she looked up into the tree and smiled broadly.

"Do you see that?" she asked, as she came to a stop and glanced back down at Paul, who was now only a few meters away. Then she turned her gaze back up into the branches of the tree. Paul followed the line of her sight.

"Do you see it? It's yellow," she said, pointing.

Paul looked harder, then saw what she was looking at, perched on one of the low branches of the tree under which he sat—a bright-yellow bird with a red head and black wings.

"It's a western tanager," Jessica said softly. "A male. Isn't it beautiful?"

Paul smiled. "Yes, it is," he said.

"It's amazing what you can see here," she said, still watching the bird. "What a wonderful place they chose for this Retreat."

The bird hopped, then lifted into the breeze. They both watched as it fluttered through the brilliant air and disappeared into the trees beyond the meadow.

"Western tanager?" Paul said.

"Yes," Jessica said, turning back toward him. "I took a walk two days ago, out along the ridge east of here," she said, gesturing in that direction. "I saw a cooper's hawk and a golden eagle, just on that one trip! Any number of mountain quail. Hummingbirds." She looked thoughtful, remembering. "You can hear coyote at night, sometimes, calling to one another. Owls, too. I saw a mountain lion in the canyon north of here, last summer. They're mostly out at night. Hard to spot. There are bear in the area, too," she finished, still smiling and looking, Paul thought, delighted to remember all these creatures.

"I saw large herds of tule elk and antelope on the way up," Paul said.

"Oh, yeah," Jessica replied, with enthusiasm. "Isn't that wonderful? They're all through the valleys."

Paul smiled at her, and she at him. It was the same smile he had seen her turn toward the students in her class.

Jessica glanced around, took a deep, happy breath, then sat down at the base of the tree, not far from Paul.

"It's a beautiful place, isn't it?" she said. "I love coming here. This is one of my favorite spots at the Retreat. I always feel so, well, connected when I'm here." She glanced around, then smiled at Paul again—a friendly, relaxed smile.

"Well," she added, after a moment, leaning back with her palms against the ground behind her, "we should get to work."

"Okay," Paul said, delighted with her mood and presence.

"You said you covered stages one and two with Farsan?" she asked.

"Yes," Paul said.

"How did that go?"

Paul thought for a moment. "Well," he said, "I learned a lot."

"What did you learn?"

Paul thought again. In the silence, he became aware of the sound of the breeze through the trees above and around him—like a stream flowing—and of the way the light, dappled by the shade of tall trees, splashed down around them.

"Well," Paul said, after a moment or two, "I guess the most important things would be that I'd created some important models—about myself and my life—based on events around the time of my mother's death. Or based on the way I saw those events at the time. I thought I had failed her—my mother—but really, I didn't," Paul said.

He then went on to explain to Jessica about how the work he had done with Farsan in stage one had focused on a series of dreams he'd had—and though it felt personal to talk about them, he decided to go ahead and confide in her openly. He told her about how, in the dreams, his mother had turned away from him, rejecting him—and how, in the last of those dreams, when he had finally seen his mother's face, it had become, not her, but his "old girlfriend," Sheila—from whom, he added, he was now "separated." He told Jessica, too, about the medicine he had been asked to bring to his mother, and about how he had felt, for so long, that if he had just gotten it to her faster, she would have lived.

Retelling it, even then, was hard, and Paul got choked up as he said the words. For a moment his eyes welled with tears—but Jessica looked at him with such consoling empathy that her gaze felt like cool water, carrying the sting away.

He wiped his eyes with the back of a hand, then went on, telling her the rest of the story, about his realization that it was never within his reach to save his mother, and about how he knew now that she had always loved and accepted him and would never have blamed him for getting back when he did.

He had realized, too, he told her, that his father's substance abuse—and the fact that he stayed away so much after his wife's death—were probably his father's way of coping with his own feelings of guilt and loss.

"It wasn't the best way things could have gone—not by far—but I resent him less, now, seeing that he had his own troubles he was dealing with," Paul said.

"So, you've come to see that he didn't have a bad nature?" Jessica asked.

"Yeah." Paul was thoughtful for a minute. "He didn't know how to make his machinery work, I guess—his own inner machinery, I mean," Paul said, trying to use the same terms he'd heard others use at the Retreat. "I guess he just did what he knew how to do, as he tried to escape the pain he was feeling."

"So he was trying to do good, in that small way, at least?"

Paul thought about this. "From his point of view, I guess. I guess escaping the pain was good. Yeah. I just wish he had thought more about what was good for Casey and me. We needed him, too," he said, then added, "Casey's my brother."

Jessica nodded. "So your dad had good intentions, from his point of view, but an insular perspective—and so he didn't see your point of view," she said.

"Yeah," Paul said. He saw what Jessica was trying to do—tie these events to the three impediments. He nodded a little, then added, "And nobody communicated much about anything, either."

"It sounds like it was a hard time for all of you."

"Yeah, it was," Paul said. He looked at Jessica, and she at him, and a certain sense of understanding was shared between them. Then he held Jessica's look for a moment longer, soaking up some sort of solace he found there.

After a moment, Paul felt awkward and glanced down at his hands.

"I think you've done a good job, Paul, learning to see things from his point of view, while retaining your own."

"Thanks," Paul said, looking up again.

Jessica smiled softly. A moment passed before she went on. "You said something before, about your mother turning into your girlfriend in the dream, didn't you? Did you look into that, when you were working with Farsan?"

"Yes," Paul said, then went on to tell her about how he had realized that he had chosen Sheila not so much for what she gave him, but for what she held back—how he had, with her, been trying to earn the love, the connection, the affection he had for so long believed he was undeserving of.

It was hard to retell these things so soon after he had come to see and understand them. It was like pushing on the spot from which a long and brittle splinter had just been removed. The area, cleared of the source of pain, was still tender. If Jessica had been harsh or judgmental at all, it would have been hard for Paul to guard himself against her views—but she was neither of these things. Her eyes were as gentle as those of a doe—deep and comforting—with a spark of lively intelligence in every glance. When she looked at Paul, he sensed something he could not yet name—a feeling running just beneath the surface—a feeling that she was warming to him, to his openness, to his frank discussion of his old burden and pain, and that she appreciated the honesty and bravery required for him to probe into it and to speak of it so plainly to her now, when the old wound, newly laid bare, was still so fresh.

Paul told her how important Sheila had been to him, and how he had imagined himself important to her, too, but that he was coming to understand that they had been like two strangers living parallel lives together.

"It's like what you were saying in class yesterday," Paul said. "I cast her in my play as the one from whom I might earn redemption, acceptance, and love—and she cast me," Paul could feel his eyes welling up again, "as someone who could give her the things she wanted, make her comfortable. I don't think she had any great hopes for life, really." He thought about it a moment more. "And maybe because she had no real hope for the future, she wanted to be sure the present pleased her, if only in a superficial way. She wanted to ignore real life and find something better—better than real life. She wanted to focus on that and ignore all the rest."

"Better than real life," Jessica repeated.

"Better than real life looked to her," Paul said, then thought to himself: better than real life looked to almost everybody on his world.

Paul wiped his eyes with the back of one hand. "What a pair we were." He shook his head. "In a way, I guess we needed each other. And for a while, that was enough." He looked at Jessica.

"And you've just realized this?" Jessica asked.

"In the last few days." Paul frowned, thinking about it.

Jessica looked very thoughtful for a minute. "Well, I'm glad you came to the Retreat, then, Paul," she said.

"Why is that?" Paul asked.

"Because it's helped you and because, well, it sounds like you would be happier in a closer relationship. The self-knowledge Kumaric practice leads to is important in forming close relationships."

Paul looked thoughtful. "I kind of see that, I guess."

"It's like Dr. Kumar wrote," Jessica responded, then added, "If you don't mind being quoted to, I have a quote of her talking about that. It's from *The Little Book.*"

"No, I don't mind," Paul said.

Jessica nodded, then launched into a long quote, recited entirely from memory:

> We cannot, with clarity, reveal how we think and feel to another person until we have first come to know our own thoughts and feelings—for we cannot say what we do not know. Successful intimacy depends on self knowledge.
>
> Each discovery of self involves building new models to define the meaning and significance of what we observe. These models tell us who we are and how we may value ourselves.
>
> When we reveal ourselves to another person before we have a chance to reflect on our own experiences (and in so reflecting, build definitive models for ourselves) we offer that other person tremendous influence, for we are giving them an opportunity (through their comments and reactions) to create for us the lens through which we view and understand our own experiences, and our own selves.

Paul leaned forward as Jessica spoke, his face full of curious interest.

"As we explore ourselves," Jessica continued,

> and reflect on our explorations, we create our own models and definitions of who we are. By knowing ourselves and forming our own models of the nature, purpose, and value of our experiences, we claim the power of self-definition for ourselves. This, in turn, makes intimacy with others both feel and be safer, for though we may then see ourselves through their eyes, our own vision is already present, well formed, and well established.
>
> Intimacy with oneself, therefore, helps build successful intimacy with others for two important reasons: we can only consciously share what we consciously know; and through self knowledge, we gain control over how we interpret and define ourselves, which in turn makes the intimacy we share with others both feel and be safer.

Though Paul had appeared to be listening closely, he had hardly taken in the meaning of the words. "It's amazing that you could remember all of that," he said, when Jessica was done.

"Not so much. I used Synaplast," she said.

"Okay. Well—Synaplast," Paul repeated. The term seemed vaguely familiar, and he wondered if perhaps he had heard Farsan mention it. Paul shook his head. "I don't know what that is."

Jessica frowned a little. "Really?" she said.

Paul could see that she thought it genuinely peculiar that he wouldn't know. He shrugged a little and shook his head.

"Synaplast is a chemical—a protein, actually, I think," Jessica began slowly, looking at Paul with her head tilted a little to one side, her eyes narrowed slightly, as though pondering something confusing. She paused for a moment, then went on. "It's a memory enhancer. For a few hours after you take it, anything you experience will get stuck in your memory. I used it to memorize *The Little Book* and a few bits and pieces of other works in the Kumaric tradition. I've known people to memorize all of *Memories and Reflections* that way, but I wouldn't want to commit quite so much mental space to that." She shook her head. "After all, it's so permanent."

Paul nodded. He understood that he had said something odd in revealing that he didn't know what Synaplast was and so wanted to steer the conversation to another topic as quickly as possible. "Okay," he said, "and you said that passage was from *The Little Book?*"

"Yeah," Jessica replied.

"I saw a quote or two from that book on the wall of my room. It seemed an odd citation. I mean, just, '*The Little Book,*'" he said.

"Yes?" Jessica replied, again frowning slightly.

"Well, I was just wondering, maybe you could tell me more about *The Little Book?*"

"Such as?"

"I don't know. What is it?"

Jessica raised her eyebrows as her mouth fell slightly open. For a moment, neither of them spoke, and Paul realized that he had again stumbled into the wrong terrain.

"You don't know what *The Little Book* is?" Jessica said, as though trying to absorb the idea.

Paul shook his head slowly, unsure of how to escape from the hole he had dug for himself. It seemed to him that her tone would have been no different if he had told her that he had never heard of the *Bible* or of the *Constitution of the United States.*

Paul shifted how he was sitting. What a terrible impression he was making—first the Synaplast gaff and now this! he thought. He tried to assure himself that it didn't matter. He would only be at the Retreat for another week, after all—and his plans for building a new transport were now nearly complete. With any luck, he would be leaving not only the Retreat, but the whole world, soon, anyway. What did it matter what the people here thought of him? But Paul had to admit to himself that he found himself liking this particular person and wanting to make a good impression on her.

"Okay—well," Jessica began. Something in her face, or her manner, reminded Paul of how adults answer the questions of small children: not condescending, but as though she was searching for the most basic terms she could with which to explain something to someone who lacked even the most elemental knowledge.

"After writing *Memories and Reflections,*" she went on, with the look of surprise still discernable on her face, "Dr. Kumar decided she would like to gather up all the insights spread throughout her memoirs and put them together in one place. She wrote that she wanted to put them more succinctly, more precisely—'as one might wish to polish a stone or cut a gem.' The result was a series of journal entries where she reflected on her life and attempted to summarize what she had learned along the way. Some of those passages are very plainly put, others quite poetic, but they all speak to basic truths in some way. That's what she was aiming at.

"After Dr. Kumar's death, when her journals were published, those passages drew special attention. Eventually they—and some other entries from earlier journals, along with pieces of her memoirs—were collected together in a much shorter work, but one with a very long title. '*Notable Reflections: Passages of Special Interest from the Journals and Memoirs of Indira Kumar,*' it was called. It was probably because this title was so cumbersome that people began to refer to it simply as '*Indira Kumar's Little Book*' or '*Dr. Kumar's Little Book*'—and, eventually, simply as '*The Little Book.*'

"Some people don't like it, by the way—it's too dry for them—but I like it, because it gathers so much together in so small a space."

As Jessica finished, she looked at Paul for a long moment, then asked, "How is it that you don't know that? I mean, it's so surprising..." Her voice trailed off.

For a moment, Paul wanted to invent some elaborate lie, to misdirect her, but there was something about this woman—she seemed so genuine, so good hearted. He didn't *want* to lie to her.

"Well," he said, trying to think fast. He knew he couldn't simply tell her the truth—after all, how could she possibly believe him? If she thought him odd now, she would likely think him insane if he told her the truth. Still, he wanted to somehow satisfy her curiosity.

"I was raised differently than most of the people you would know," he ventured, his head spinning with his effort to find the words he needed.

"And I've been very focused on my work," he went on. "It can be a problem, when people get too specialized. We miss out on certain things other people consider an obvious part of life."

The breeze felt suddenly cool against Paul's damp skin, as he watched for Jessica's response. He was relieved, at least, that his reply had been a truthful one. He *had* buried himself in his work for years—leading Sheila to complain, often enough, about how oblivious he was to the things she thought mattered most (such as fashion, popular events, and the availability of goods).

Jessica looked thoughtful. "Yes, I suppose so. It could be like that," she answered. "What sort of work do you do?"

"I'm a physicist," Paul told her, still keeping a careful eye on her response.

Jessica nodded. "Are you associated with one of the universities?"

"No. An independent lab in Strandford."

"What sort of work do you do there?"

Again, Paul was uncertain how to answer. Mentioning the depopulation project was clearly out of the question.

"We do research on the possibility of moving matter in and out of space-time," he said, and again felt relieved that he could provide her with an honest reply, while still not revealing the whole truth.

For a moment, Jessica gave him the same look others had given him since he had arrived on this world—not so much looking *at* him as *into* him. Then she smiled a little and said simply, "That sounds like interesting work"—and Paul saw an opening to steer the conversation away from himself.

"You know more of these passages, then, I take it?" he said.

"Yes, many."

"Could I hear another one?" he asked.

"Certainly," she said.

She seemed a little distracted, but refocused on his question. She thought for moment, then added, "I like this one especially," and recited another passage for him:

> Holding one's heart open is key.
>
> Whenever we hold our hearts open, we help bring about a reversal of the three impediments:
>
> - When we hold our hearts open, we dissolve the insularity of our perspectives—for being open hearted, itself, implies a receptive viewpoint.
> - When we hold our hearts open, we are better able to see the true motives behind our own actions, and behind the actions of others—and so we are better able to see the essential goodness within all of us.
> - When we hold our hearts open, we also hold open the pathways of communication, both by opening awareness within ourselves, and by enhancing empathy and identification with others.
>
> We start life with our hearts open. It is important not to let pain and injury teach us to seal off our hearts.

"That's what I like so much about *The Little Book*," Jessica said, as she finished. "It so clearly names the basic truths Dr. Kumar discovered in her life. So much is said in so few words."

"I like that," Paul said. "Thanks for reciting it."

"You're welcome," Jessica answered, then smiled at Paul so sweetly that he suddenly felt at ease again, as though nothing odd had ever been said.

It occurred to him, then, as he spoke with this woman, that no matter what he said, she was accepting him. Looking at her then, he saw in her eyes something he didn't think he could have recognized before the last few days and all the changes they had brought. She wasn't ignoring him while he struggled to get her to accept him, as he was accustomed to doing with Sheila. She was accepting him, simply and openly.

As Paul sat there talking with Jessica, it gradually dawned on him that he could see this in her, this acceptance—this rare and much-wanted thing, which had for so long been so absent from his life—because, finally, for the first time since he was a boy, he believed he was deserving of it.

How long had this possibility been before him, Paul wondered—in the form of one person or another—while he had only to open his eyes and perceive it?

"It sounds like you and Farsan did a good job covering the basic elements of stage one and stage two," Jessica said, "but you haven't said anything about anchoring or awareness of personal essence. Did you deal at all with those?"

Paul thought about it a moment, then shook his head slowly. "No," he said.

"Well, let's at least touch on them before we move on to stage three, then. Are you familiar with the concept of anchoring?"

Paul hesitated. He didn't want to risk sounding ignorant again, but he really had no choice but to answer truthfully.

"No, I'm not."

"That's okay," Jessica said, as though aware of his hesitation. "Basically, the idea is that the more you become conscious of your models and of the reasons you believe them to be true, the more you become securely anchored to them.

"This kind of awareness can be developed through the sort of work you did in stage one, Paul—or simply through a process of consciously and deliberately exploring and mapping out the models you presume to be true—that is, your beliefs.

"Once you know exactly what you believe and why you believe it, no matter how your beliefs are challenged or brought into question, you can always defend and maintain them, and so remain secure within them. That's anchoring.

"Dr. Kumar compared anchoring," Jessica went on, "with the way a spelunker uses a rope when they explore a cave. They tie one end of the rope to a rock or tree outside the cave and the other end to their own waist. Then, no matter where they go as they explore the cave—no matter how many twists or turns take place in their path—they're always able to find their way back to their starting point. And of course, with anchoring, that starting point is your own perspective—and the set of models that creates that perspective.

"The point is: the more securely you're anchored to your own perspective, the freer you'll feel to explore beyond it—to explore the perspectives of others. And then, like any explorer, you can choose what you want to bring home and make a part of your own life and what you prefer to leave behind.

"I'll give you an example of anchoring at work and of why it can be so important. This was written by Yao Chuan Jianyu, a Kumaric scholar from the middle of the last century. He wrote about the role anchoring played in Dr. Kumar's life. It's another quote—kind of a long one. Are you sure you don't mind being quoted to?"

"No, I don't mind. They've been very interesting so far," Paul said.

"Okay. Here it is," Jessica said. She cast her gaze off to one side and began:

Some have commented on the unusual path Indira Kumar cut through her life. Growing up in rural India at a time when girls received very little education, she nonetheless managed to get one. Some of this can be attributed to the presence of her Aunt Mary, but also to a rare determination in the young Indira herself.

Raised at a time, and in a culture, in which arranged marriages were the norm, she showed remarkable determination in avoiding one. Later, in Oxford, living at a time and in a place where a relationship between two women was seen as an unacceptable aberration, she found her true love in the form of Laura Atherton and again showed remarkable self-determination in embarking on that relationship and embracing the discovery, fulfillment, and joy that relationship would bring them both.

What gave the young Indira Kumar such fortitude? Perhaps to some degree this was a matter of her character, something inborn in her—but another explanation offers itself.

After encountering the Americans who found and returned her family's water buffalo, the young Indira developed a belief in something she called "protolife." That is, she came to believe that it was important for all of us to give life to the promise within us—and that this process of giving fulfillment to protolife underlay the true meaning and purpose of life.

By establishing this model of the world at a foundational level of her belief structure—by integrating it with her concepts of what was good, what was worthwhile, what was right—she anchored herself to it, much as a house is anchored to its foundations. Therefore, no matter how other people's perspectives pushed against hers, she could not be shaken from her own perspective. No matter what others said she *should* do, or *must* do, she had anchored her views to fundamental, foundational belief structures within herself and could not be moved from them. Because of this, she had the strength and determination to continue in school, to refuse an unwanted marriage and, later, to become devoted to the woman she loved. She had anchored herself to a powerful model that lit her path and guided her on it—and that, in turn, formed a guide for others.

"It's really remarkable, if you think about it," Jessica said, as she finished with the quotation. "Modeling has such an important influence on our lives. We shape our lives around the models we choose, and yet, for so long, people paid hardly any attention to which models they formed and to which they held onto—and even less attention to how they could anchor themselves to the most important ones.

"Anyway," she went on, "you can see how important anchoring can be, how it can deepen a person's sense of being rooted to their own perspective and to their own sense of self.

"Anchoring can be important in other contexts, as well. People who are not anchored securely to their own personal models and beliefs may worry that, if they allow themselves to see the world from another person's point of view, they'll lose track of their own perspective—and so, in effect, become separated from the self they know and not be able to find their way back to it. In such cases, those people may resist identifying with others and so develop a particularly narrow and insular perspective. And of course, that impediment can lead to all sorts of problems."

As Paul listened, he had the feeling Jessica was explaining this to him with special care, perhaps since he had shown himself to be unaware of things that were common knowledge. He didn't mind, though. In truth, it was helpful, and though her explanation was careful, there was nothing in the least bit belittling in her manner.

"Is all of this clear so far?" Jessica asked.

"Yes. I'm right there with you," Paul said.

"Good." Jessica smiled a little, then continued. "Anchoring is also important when dealing with someone whose perspective is critical of you or of your behavior," she said, as she bent one leg and wrapped her arms around it. Paul was aware of the way the light fell on her hair and of the patient look in her dark eyes.

"Say you've done something that had some unexpected consequence," she went on, "—a consequence that caused difficulty for someone else—and imagine that that person now resents you for what you did. It's important to be able to understand and learn from that other person's perspective (so in the future you can avoid causing those sorts of problems again) but if you just migrate from your point of view to theirs, you may simply wind up in a place where you dislike and resent yourself for the error you made. Anchoring helps you to remember why your perspective makes sense to you, even when you're receptive to seeing why someone else's perspective makes sense to them—that is, it helps you to be able to see, at the same time, the good intent behind both viewpoints. When you can see both perspectives at the same time, then you can integrate both and come up with a solution that meets both your needs and theirs.

"This is an important step in resolving conflict of any sort and no less so in resolving long-entrenched conflict," she said. "For example, as I'm sure you know, this sort of process was essential in resolving the problems between the Israelis and the Palestinians—finding that balance where each chose to see through the other's eyes, while at the same time remembering their own views and motives. When both sides can do that, then there's no longer a need for conflict. That's when a joint, mutual cooperation can really begin."

Paul was tempted to ask exactly how that conflict had been resolved on this earth, since it still raged on his—a fire that had been burning unquenched for almost two hundred years, with still many bloody deaths occurring—but he dared not ask, since his questions about Synaplast and *The Little Book* had put him in such an awkward spot already.

Paul did know, though, that on his earth both sides were fighting in order to attain something that could, in truth, only be achieved through cooperation: to have a homeland that was both peaceful and secure. He imagined how it might be if both sides could learn what Dr. Kumar had taught—if both sides could expand their perspectives to see through one another's eyes; if communication could be opened up in all directions; and if all involved could understand that the underpinnings of human nature were elementally good, no matter how dangerously misguided or mistaken some actions might be.

"Anyway, that's anchoring, in a nutshell," Jessica concluded. "It has application in quite a wide range of situations, from anchoring new models into place, to feeling secure enough in oneself to allow deep intimacy to take place in a relationship—but for today, that's enough on the topic. Like I said, I just wanted to be sure we at least touched on these things."

"That's fine," Paul said, and thought for a moment. He was wondering something and realized it was something he could freely ask about. "What you said, just now—about feeling secure enough in oneself to allow deep intimacy. Does that really work?"

"Work?" Jessica asked.

"Yeah—knowing yourself deeply and then being able to make relationships come out right—to really be deep, successful?" He was thinking about Sheila and what he had once hoped that could be. "Does it really make relationships deeper? Does it make them work better?"

"Yes, I would say it does. I mean, it definitely does, but that doesn't mean that everything will always work out perfectly." Jessica glanced down at her hands, then up and past Paul, into the forest beyond. Her look seemed far away and tinged with sadness.

"Has it worked well for you?" Paul asked.

"Yes, generally it has," Jessica answered, then turned her gaze back toward Paul. "But I just said goodbye to a man I really love, just a few months ago. It was a wonderful relationship, it really was, but that didn't stop there from being a goodbye at the end of it."

"Where is he now?" Paul asked.

"He's a genetic engineer. He got a grant to work on reversing Batten disease in children—it's a genetic disorder—using a kind of redesigned stem cell, but he had to go to where they had the equipment he needed. He's in Massachusetts now. We thought it would be for a year, maybe two, and we agreed to see other people." Jessica stopped. She seemed sad. "I'm sorry. This isn't supposed to be about me. I'm supposed to be helping you."

"No, I'm interested," Paul said. "Isn't he coming back?"

"He met somebody who's doing the same sort of work he does. He said she shares his passion for it."

"That must be really hard for you," Paul said.

"Yeah, it is. But I'm glad for him, really. Knowing him—it was like watching a flower blossom. So beautiful. He was growing so fast, discovering himself. And part of that discovery was realizing how important that work really was to him."

Jessica frowned just a little, then shrugged and smiled a small smile. "But I think it's really right for him, and I'm glad he's doing it. And I'm glad he's found somebody who will share that path with him."

Paul nodded slowly, not sure what to say. "Why didn't you go with him?" he asked.

"My life is here. I have my work, my clients, my home—family in the area. I didn't want to move to Massachusetts. I didn't want to follow him into *his* life. So I didn't go. And he didn't want to stay." She shrugged again. "I don't regret it. It's just still a little soon, that's all."

"I feel for you," Paul said. "It's not easy, I know."

Jessica smiled at Paul, very sweetly—and for the first time Paul had the impression that the smile was really especially for him and wasn't just the warmth she shared so freely with everyone.

They sat like that for several moments, then Jessica asked, "Are you ready for more?"

"Yeah, I guess so," Paul said.

"Don't worry, we won't go on a lot longer, today. We'll finish this up then work on stage three tomorrow."

"Okay," Paul said.

Jessica smiled her usual warm and unworried smile. "Okay," she said, with a spark of enthusiasm in her voice, "then let's talk some about *sger ngo bo*—personal essence."

Jessica took a moment to collect her thoughts, then continued. "I like the analogy used when Dr. Kumar wrote about this. I'm sorry—if we were in one of the classrooms, I could play this for you as a holoprojection, but not outside here. Do you mind if I recite another passage?"

"No, I don't mind at all. I think it's impressive, actually," Paul said. "I like being impressed."

Jessica looked at Paul with an expression that was, at once, gentle and penetrating, and smiled again.

"This was originally written in Dr. Kumar's journal," Jessica continued, after a moment, "though a very similar passage appeared in *Memories and Reflections*. It's also in *The Little Book*.

"Dr. Kumar wrote this in the spring of 2009. As you'll remember, it was at the end of the previous semester that she had hurt her back in a skiing accident in the mountains outside of Boulder..."

Paul shook his head, almost unconsciously.

Jessica stopped. "No?" she said.

"I didn't get that far," Paul said. "I listened to *Memories and Reflections* on my way here, but I didn't have time to finish it. They were in Zaire, in the Ituri Forest, when I stopped."

Jessica cocked her head slightly. "Okay," she said. "Well, that was quite a bit earlier—1990, wasn't it?"

Paul shrugged and nodded.

"So, well, let me see if I can fill you in some, at least enough so the quote will make sense to you." She thought for a moment. "They'd have been back in Boulder a long time, close to twenty years, by then. Well, more like nineteen. They'd had a couple of sabbatical leaves—one in New Guinea and the other they'd spent in Boulder—and then, late in 2008, Indira and Laura took a trip. They went away for a couple of days just after Thanksgiving, so they could go cross-country skiing.

"They'd been very busy that semester," Jessica continued, glancing off to one side for a moment, then back over at Paul, "—with school and research—and Dr. Kumar had also been wishing she could find the time to start writing her memoirs. But with so much going on, life had begun to seem a bit too hectic for them. And so, when Thanksgiving came, they decided to give themselves a break and take a couple days off to go skiing.

"Unfortunately," Jessica went on, "the conditions were icier than they had expected, and (I think this was on the second day of their trip) Dr. Kumar had problems coming down a hill. She took a spill and had trouble with her back afterward. As I remember, she didn't think much of it at the time—just a pulled muscle, that was all. But later, after she went back to work, she began to have intense back spasms. They were very painful, and finishing up the fall semester was really pretty grueling for her.

"Anyway, she continued to have trouble with her back during the winter break between terms. It continued to be very painful for her, and it didn't seem to be improving. In fact, it was so bad that she felt she had no choice but to take sick leave for the spring semester."

Jessica looked over at the trees past Paul's shoulder for a moment, seemingly gathering her thoughts, then back over at Paul. "Dr. Kumar intended to continue doing research during that time, to try to get done whatever she could even with her back the way it was, but Laura convinced her that she should really take that time off and take care of herself.

"So, that spring, Dr. Kumar spent a little time each morning carefully stretching and going for walks. She also spent some time, in the late mornings and early afternoons, writing up research she'd already done—but most of that semester she spent resting in bed, working on her memoirs using a lap desk that Laura had bought for her.

"She described Laura as being 'like an angel' during that time: always being there with a helping hand, doing all the cooking and cleaning, and insisting that Indira—that is, Dr. Kumar—give her back a break. At that time, Dr. Kumar wrote the following passage in her journal," Jessica said, and then began to recite the passage about 'personal essence' that she'd wanted to share with Paul:

That night, I again lay on the bed, as I had every night since the semester began, feeling like overindulged royalty, while Laura lay hot cloths on my ailing back and then gave me a back rub.

"I hardly know how you can tolerate me," I said, "with me ghosting around the house all day without lifting a finger. I worry that I'm such a drain on you. I get mad at my back for hurting, because I feel like it's hurting you, too."

Laura laughed. "Indira, you must stop worrying. I feel like most of the year we're rushing around and hardly get to see one another. It's nice to be able to spend time with you like this."

"But I can't do anything for you," I said, aware, even as I spoke, of the tight muscles in my back unwinding beneath the soothing pressure of Laura's hands.

"Oh, Indira, don't you know you do something for me every day you're in my life?"

She rested her hand on my shoulder. "Without you, my love, every day would be winter, with the sun a distant spot behind gray clouds. Every day with you in it is like summer breaking through."

I rolled over and looked up at her. Her eyes shone at me brightly.

"It's not just what you *do*, Indira—it's *you*. It's like a kind of warmth you give off, a kind of light. I was thinking about this last night, while I did the dishes, because you seemed so worried about being laid up and what it meant to me. You know how it feels different to be around different people?—and not because of their mood, or something of that sort, but just because of something essential in them? It's like..." She paused, as though searching for the words. "You know how it feels to be out on the first sunny day in spring—like there's something in the air, in that light, and it makes you want to soak it up, to be out in it? I don't know why it feels that way, but it does. Well, you're like that for me, Indira. Just to have you in my life is like having the sun of springtime living here with me, shining on me every day of the year."

I reached up and guided her face towards mine and kissed her. "How could I be so lucky as to have you in my life?" I said. "And you are the sun for me, too, Laura. Whatever would I do without you?"

Laura smiled at me and stroked my face.

"Come, roll back over," she said to me softly. "I'll finish your back."

When Jessica was done, Paul spoke. "That's beautiful," he said.

"Yes," Jessica said, "I suppose that's partially why I chose it to memorize. There are other passages I could have chosen to describe personal essence—but none were so nice as that one."

"So what happened with her back?" Paul asked. "Did it get well?"

"Yes, but gradually. It was much better by summer, and rarely bothered her after that. She credited Laura with her recovery—because she didn't think she would have given herself the rest she needed, otherwise, and also because of the care Laura gave her."

"It was good she had Laura there," Paul said.

"She certainly thought so," Jessica said.

"Anyway," Jessica went on, "Dr. Kumar was interested in this sort of aware-ness, this feeling people have of another person's presence. She wrote that she wondered if this kind of feeling—this feeling that you have around a par-ticular person—was the result of some sort of subtle electromagnetic energy that each person gives off, and which we can all tune into—'like a radio tunes into a station,' she said. She imagined that each person has a unique 'signature'—a kind of 'energy signature' that was unlike anybody else's, that communicates something of our basic selfhoods, our spirits. She believed that if we can become attuned to 'listening' to others in this way, we can become more aware of their feelings, their perspectives, their experiences. She wrote that listening in this way 'helps turn back the impediment of insularity and moves us toward a more expanded sense of self.'

"She used various names for that feeling—for that sense of another person's presence, that feeling that's distinctive to them. Sometimes she referred to it as 'the unique light,' or 'the energy signature' of another per-son. I usually just call it 'the quality of someone's presence'—but you'll see it referred to in different ways in the literature of the Kumaric tradition. I've seen it referred to as 'the quality of light' someone gives off, for example. Also, 'the tone' of someone's personality—or their 'emotional tone,' or 'tonal signature.' Some use the term 'sger ngo bo,' which is a Tibetan term. I use that sometimes, too. It means 'personal essence,' which is another term that's fairly common."

"Kerno-bo?" Paul said.

"Not quite—but that's about the way most English speakers pronounce it. It's three words: 'sger ngo bo,'" Jessica explained.

"Ker no bo," Paul said.

"Closer," Jessica said. "That's all right."

Paul laughed, then looked off toward the Retreat, though his eyes seemed to be looking farther away than that.

"You know," he said, after a moment, "I was just thinking about my brother, Casey. I don't see him very much. Sometimes years have gone by, actually, without us seeing each other. It's just, well, life gets in the way, and we live far apart. But each time I see him and give him a big hug hello, I feel like, 'Yeah, there's Casey. I know this guy.' And I swear, it's just the feeling of him, somehow—like there's a way it always feels to be around him—and I know it; I remember that feeling from childhood. And then I don't see him for a while, and I forget it. But then I see him again, and instantly I recognize that feeling."

"That's exactly what I'm talking about," Jessica said.

"There's an exercise for practicing this," she went on, after a moment, "which we could try, if you'd like. You sit with somebody and hold hands—usually people keep their eyes closed—and you just try to become conscious of the other person's presence and tune into that. Do you want to try it?"

Paul agreed, so Jessica got up and stepped over to where he sat next to the tree and sat down right in front of him. For a moment, Paul wondered if he should read something into the fact that she was suggesting they do this exercise. Was it possible that she was suggesting this as an excuse to hold hands with him? he wondered. But then Paul thought of Farsan and his fatherly warmth and all the many people Paul had seen holding hands since coming to this world, as though it were considered a natural part of friendship here, on this earth, even though it was not on Paul's.

As Jessica reached for Paul's hands, their eyes met and for a moment, again, Paul remembered what he had thought when he had first seen her in the classroom nearly a week before—how there was something in her presence, then, that had seemed to him like a beautiful lake, as clear as the sky above. Now he felt that again, saw it in her eyes, like two liquid pools into which he might dive.

"Now close your eyes," Jessica said.

Paul closed them, and as he did he became aware of the soft air and of the sounds of birds nearby. He could feel the sun on his skin and his heart beating in his chest. He could feel something else, too, something of her, the woman who sat before him, with her hands in his—her tone, her presence—like a song playing sweetly around him, like a melody that called forth the melody of himself, harmonizing with it and unjangling the chords.

Several moments passed, as Paul soaked up Jessica's presence. He felt as though he had been lifted on a current and carried gently away by it.

"Thank you," Jessica said, after a time.

"You can open your eyes now, Paul," she added.

He did, and she was there before him, smiling warmly. In her eyes, Paul saw the same penetrating look that he had seen so often since arriving on this earth; that he had seen in Anna's face before she had invited him—a bald and bruised and barefoot stranger—into her home; that he had seen in the face of the Retreat director, in Farsan's face, and in Jessica's, as well.

It seemed to Paul that Jessica was looking past all the external stuff of who he was and seeing him directly—and he wondered if perhaps his own face appeared like that to her, now—probing, seeking, in that same warm and caring way. Had each of those people seen into him, he wondered, as he now felt himself looking into Jessica?

"It's nice, isn't it?" Jessica said, her hands still holding his.

"Yes, it is," Paul answered.

"You can connect with anything like that," she told him. "I like to do that when I wander through the woods here." She squeezed Paul's hands, then held them for a moment before letting go.

"That's enough for today," she said. "We'll meet again tomorrow—at the same time and place as today?"

"Sure," Paul said, "that would be nice."

Jessica stood and stretched. Paul got up, too. Then they started back toward the Retreat together, talking of small things.

It was late afternoon, with the sun low in the sky before them. As Paul walked along, he kept thinking how beautiful Jessica looked in that light, and how much he would like to hold her hand once more.

◘   ◘   ◘

It was nearly five o'clock when Paul got back to his room. He sat in the chair by the window, staring out at the landscape as the sun drifted down behind the trees to the west, and the clouds above it took on an amber glow. He told himself repeatedly that he had work to do on the transport, but instead of beginning his work, he sat thinking of Jessica and what it had been like to spend the afternoon in her company.

He shouldn't allow himself to take an interest in her, he told himself. He had a hundred reasons not to—another world to return to, a transport to build. And then there was Sheila, whatever that added up to, now, in his life. In any case, this was not his world. His responsibilities lay elsewhere.

Wearily, Paul got up and closed the blinds, then called up the holoprojection of the transport. Following the holographic image as a guide, he used the portal to begin searching for the few small parts he had yet to find. It was tedious work, and though he tried to focus on it, each time he gave his thoughts a chance to drift, he found them returning to Jessica.

Who was this woman? he wondered, as he remembered the sense he had had of her earlier that day: sweet and tenacious, clever and tender, self possessed—and so much more that was ineffable, impossible to name.

Her *sger ngo bo*, perhaps? All he felt certain of was that in his world he had never known anybody like her.

No, there was one other thing he was certain of, Paul told himself. No matter what else, his world still needed him. A whole world still needed him—a world with nearly thirteen billion lonely, desperate people—and he had to remain single-minded and return to it, to that wasted landscape, and offer them the only solution that lay anywhere in sight.

"Portal," he said, "find an adapter that will allow me to connect the parts I have highlighted in red." Then he added, to himself, "I only have a little over a week left at this place. I need to be as ready as I can be before I leave here."

23

When Paul woke in the morning and pulled back the curtains to let in the sun, he saw how much the scene had changed overnight. Where before there'd been open sky with just a few clouds in it, now the sky was filled with tall, knotted clouds. The scene outside Paul's window appeared cooler and darker than the day before, and fewer people were out in it.

Wearily, Paul put on the same clothes he'd worn the day before, then sat down on the edge of the bed to put on his shoes. He was still feeling tired after a late night washing dishes for the whole Retreat. As he bent over to pick up his second shoe, the wall opposite the bed caught his attention. A new quote had appeared overnight:

> *As we allow our sense of self to widen and deepen,*
> *we open doorways to subtle knowledge within ourselves.*
>
> —WASEME YABANN

Paul recognized the name of the Retreat's director and momentarily paused to contemplate her words, then wearily put on his shoe. Maybe breakfast would pick him up some, he told himself, then grabbed his jacket and set off for the dining hall minutes before the portal flashed its announcement that breakfast was served.

The meal was quick and uneventful. When Paul finished, he headed back to his room, where he showered and shaved and put on the clothes he'd washed the day before—and then took a few minutes to wash out the ones he'd been wearing.

The transport plans were nearing completion, and Paul felt eager to get on with them. Now, fed and clean and ready, he drew the curtains on the cloudy day outside, called up the holoprojection he had told the portal to save the day before, and got to work.

◻   ◻   ◻

A couple of hours later, Paul was smiling and walking in circles around the holoprojection. While in truth not especially aesthetically pleasing, it seemed so to Paul—like the beauty of a fine idea made real (or at least made semi-real, in the form of a holoprojection).

It's complete! Paul told himself, hardly able to believe it. He had come to another world with nothing, naked as the day he was born, and, using just what he could find available in this strange new land, he had designed this—a machine that could transport him from one world to another!

Still circling, Paul looked over the design again. It seemed to him remarkably sleek for something built entirely of parts constructed, originally, for other purposes, other technologies. But even though its components came from so many sources, with all of its parts and connectors lined up, it seemed very much one item, one machine. Looking at it now, hanging, fully formed, in 3D in the air before him, it seemed to Paul that he should be able to simply reach out, set the controls, and turn it on.

The current design had much to be said for it, Paul told himself, as he continued to stand and admire his creation. For something pieced together from odd parts, it was surprisingly compact and streamline, and with its straightforward design, it would be simple enough to build. Paul thought he could have one up and running in just a matter of weeks, once he could afford the parts.

Looking over the holoprojection, now, he felt like patting himself on the back. In some ways, he actually preferred this transport design to the original one. In choosing from the parts and subparts available on this world, he'd had to rely on local technology, which, as it turned out, meant that many of the parts were smaller than the equivalent components available on his world. Most of this, Paul had learned, had to do with advances in the field of nanotechnology on this world—which was decidedly ahead of where things stood on Paul's. The effect of this on the transport design was that the main unit was much smaller than the one Paul had designed and built in his lab. That first unit might have fit in a good-sized closet; this one, Paul observed, could fit neatly into his backpack. The transport pad had been pared down, as well. It lacked the hand railing and surrounding chamber Paul had built into his first design—which he now felt to be unnecessary for the one-time use he intended. (Omitting them also helped reduce the complexity of the design, and would therefore help bring down the total cost of construction.) With the further assistance of the smaller parts made possible through advances in nanotechnology, the newly designed transport pad would be only a little larger than a bathroom scale, though a bit more elegant in appearance: a smooth, shiny disk, about ten centimeters thick and roughly two-thirds of a meter in diameter. It would be possible to carry it under one arm, Paul noted, with a smile.

He stepped back from the holoprojection for one final appraisal of his design, then asked the portal to display his list of parts and costs, and to tally it up for him. He then asked to be shown a list of physics-related jobs, along with the average salaries of people working in those fields. Comparing the projected total costs for parts for the transport to the figures on the salary list, it appeared to Paul that he should be able to afford the parts he needed in as few as six months, if he could arrange upper-level work, though it might take as long as two years if he had to accept one of the lower-paying positions.

Paul shook his head and reminded himself that even with a source for funds, success would ultimately depended on finding a power source that could provide the giant burst of energy needed to propel himself from one world to the next. For all his success in designing a new transport, he hadn't made any progress at all in finding a power supply. On a world on which so much seemed dependent on the slow but steady trickle of energy from solar, wave, and geothermal sources, it could well be the case that none of the available technologies could deliver as big a burst of power as he would need.

Paul shut off the holoprojection and felt at once dismayed and quietly relieved, as he thought about this problem. He had done so much work in coming this far, and being held back by a single, possibly insurmountable, detail was frustrating. And yet, the truth was, a part of him had fallen in love with this world, with its broad and vibrant landscapes; its herds of tule elk; its open, friendly people. Paul knew he had a responsibility to the people of his own world to do what he could for them—that he was obligated by this, and that he had to try, and try hard—but the truth was, it was that sense of obligation, and that sense alone, that now beckoned him back to his decimated planet.

Paul closed the portal and pushed open the blinds. He stood very quietly for a minute, looking out onto the gray day. If it weren't for the responsibility he felt, he admitted to himself, he would prefer to remain on this world and never return to his own world at all.

Though Paul joined his fellow sojourners in the dining hall for lunch, his thoughts were far away, recalling what he could remember about the energy production and delivery process on his world. It struck him as ironic that the technology for producing and delivering a large burst of energy might turn out to be harder to replicate on this world than the technology for interplanetary transport.

Paul shook his head. How odd that was, he was thinking. And how strange this world was!

Paul finished his lunch, then went back to his room, where he ignored all the information the portal offered him about energy derived from wind or weather or gravitational fluctuations, and instead searched for evidence of any fossil-fuel-burning power plants still in use. On Paul's world there were few remaining, since nearly all the climate-changing fossil fuels they burned had long since been pulled from the earth and used for energy production. Paul hoped some would still be in use on this world, too—after all, he knew that plants of that sort had once been plentiful on both his world and this, before the branching point that had separated them. But search as he could, he could not find even one fossil-fuel-burning plant in use on this world now.

Paul sighed and looked at the clock. He had to get going. It was almost time to meet with Jessica again.

The thought made him smile. Well, he told himself, her sunny disposition would be a good antidote to the frustration he was feeling.

◙   ◙   ◙

Once again, Paul arrived at the tree before Jessica and sat watching her approach. She crossed the meadow with that same steady, easy gait she had used when walking across it the day before. Just to see her cheered Paul, somehow, in a way he could not name. When she reached him, he was smiling, and she stood for a moment before him, smiling down at him, too. Her dark eyes seemed framed by the tall, gray clouds behind her, as though she, and the world around her, were all lit and charged the same way.

"Well, are you ready for another session?" Jessica asked, as she sat down near Paul.

"Ready," he answered.

"Good. I was thinking about what would be good to do, in working on stage three with you, Paul. As I'm sure you're aware from what you've done in stages one and two, every step in this process is a very individual matter. No two people follow the same path through, here at the Retreat—and it's no different for stage three. Everybody arrives by their own route."

Paul nodded, as he listened. He liked listening to Jessica. Even when she was talking, as she was now, in what Paul thought of as her "teacher mode," there was something so personal, so congenial and welcoming in her manner that it seemed to him as though the words themselves were personal, as well.

"Let me give you a couple of examples," she went on. "I have a friend who was at a concert once, and the audience began to sing along. At first, they were just singing along with the band, and then the musicians on stage stopped singing, and it was just the audience, then, singing together—singing to the band and to one another—ten thousand voices filling the hall, singing as one. She said it was wonderful—this sense of belonging she had with all those people, who had sort of joined together in that moment, shared in it together. But what was really remarkable, she told me, was the way that feeling stayed with her after she left. Everywhere she went, she felt this wonderful connection with every person, every creature she came across—everything that was alive around her. She told me that that was when she realized she had achieved stage three.

"For other people, the turning point may be something much more private. For example, I worked with someone, once, who was very critical of himself. In working through that deep-seated self-criticism—and coming to accept himself, really accept himself, deeply and truly—well, for him, after that, it became easy for him to accept everyone else, as well. For him, that was what brought him to stage three.

"So it's a different route for everyone. Some come to it quickly, some come to it late, but for everybody it's a personal matter, the thing that just happens to work for them."

"How did it happen for you?" Paul asked.

"I was lucky. My parents are both Kumarists, and I grew up in a household where Kumaric thought was just a normal part of life. There was no particular turning point for me—it was more a matter of just growing up into it, as you grow up in other ways."

Paul nodded, and Jessica went on. "When you approached me after class yesterday morning, you asked me to help you work on stage three, and I've been thinking about what might be most helpful for *you*, in particular, Paul—and I remembered the look on your face when you told me about the animals you'd seen on your way here—the tule elk and antelope."

Paul smiled a little as he thought about it. He had noticed the pleasure she took in the animals she'd seen, as well.

"I could see it was something you care about—that you have a feeling for other living things," Jessica went on, her tone bright and cheerful, "so I would encourage you to wander in the forest here, following free movement, and trying to sense the *sger ngo bo* of the life around you. What you're aiming at is trying to feel yourself to be a part of the life around you, the life in this forest—to feel connected to it and to all the creatures in it. When you can expand your sense of connection and belonging that way, it's good practice for reaching stage three.

"I don't want to get your expectations up," she added. "Most people don't come to it overnight, but this is a good place to begin."

Paul smiled at her and she at him. "Okay," he said.

"Good," she said. "You remember the *sger ngo bo* practice we did yesterday?"

"Yes."

"And you recall the concept of 'free movement' from Dr. Kumar's memoirs?"

"Yes, I do."

"Then, just remember—you'll want to pay attention to whatever impulses and impressions come to mind. Let them choose your path for you. Follow them as you walk. The idea is to try to expand your awareness—to do so by feeling a connection to the life around you, while also opening yourself to the deeper, more intuitive layers of yourself."

Jessica was thoughtful for a moment, before adding, "I have a quote I like to share with people who are about to engage in an activity that involves free movement. I find, when I'm suggesting that someone listen to and follow their intuition, it's useful to talk a little about what role intuition might play in our lives."

Jessica looked down at the ground and frowned a little, thoughtfully, before looking up and going on. "As Dr. Kumar pointed out, sometimes an intuitive insight arises out of information we've gathered by quite ordinary means, but have processed in an internal or subconscious way—without, in effect, 'watching' our own thought process. In those cases, the conclusion we've arrived at (through that internal or subconscious process) may drift to the surface and arrive in our conscious awareness without us being aware of where it came from, at all.

"At other times, the source of such a strong feeling or sudden insight might reflect information we pick up, not from a conscious process—nor from a merely subconscious process—but from the greater whole of which we are a part. At such times someone might, say, have a sudden insight that a friend is in need, or perhaps just a strong impulse to wander in a particular direction—and then, afterward, realize that they seemed to have been aware of information that they had no way of knowing by ordinary, physical means.

"Whatever the source of an intuitive feeling, it's important for each person to form their own approach to how they relate to the impulses and impressions that rise up within them—to have some way of distinguishing between the impulses they wish to follow, and those they wish to set aside. In any case, I think this quote does a nice job of addressing that question. If you don't mind, I'd like to recite it for you," Jessica said.

"No, not at all. Go right ahead," Paul told her.

"This is from *Dr. Kumar's Little Book*," Jessica said, then she leaned forward a little, and, staring past Paul, began to speak:

> I stopped by Laura's office after work the other day, since we intended to ride home together. While I was waiting for Laura, I got in a conversation with Ben, a graduate student of hers who has been assisting her with some of her research.
>
> We visited for a while, and in that conversation Ben told me that he battles with himself about whether he should trust his reason most, or whether he should put more trust in his intuition.
>
> "Sometimes I'll just have a feeling about something," he said, "and so I go with it, and it turns out to be right—and not just right, but something I would have never gotten to logically. So then, at those times, I think, 'Wow, this is great. I should really listen to this sort of thing.' But then, at other times, I'll follow some hunch, and it just doesn't pay off, and I tell myself, why did I trust that feeling at all? So I never know where to put the emphasis, especially when my impulse and my logic say different things."
>
> I thought about this a moment, then asked him, "Well, would you say you should trust your reason most, or should you trust your hearing more?"
>
> Ben gave me a funny look, then said, "Well, what I hear gives me information to reason with. So it *helps* me reason. There's no conflict."
>
> "What," I asked him, "if the thing you're listening to isn't very loud—like a conversation people are having in the next room, or a radio station you're listening to that you can't quite tune into right, so there's a lot of static? What if you're listening, but you can't be certain, exactly, about what you're hearing?"
>
> "Well, maybe I'd still listen, but I wouldn't trust it entirely. If what I'd heard seemed important, I'd try to get information in other ways, too," he said.
>
> "And so you'd put all that information together and reason with it?" I asked.
>
> "Yeah."
>
> "Like if you just had this feeling that a friend was in trouble, you probably wouldn't fly across the country to see them based just on that impression—because, after all, maybe you weren't 'tuned into that station' quite right. But then, it'd probably be a good idea to at least give them a call and see how they were doing?" I asked.
>
> "Yeah," Ben said, then rubbed his chin. I gave him a moment to think.

"Does that help with your battle, Ben?" I asked.

"I think so," he said.

I waited again for him to say something, then went on. "If you want some input from me, Ben, I'd recommend you pay attention to your intuition like you would your eyesight when the light is low, or your hearing when the sound is quiet, or your sense of smell when you catch just a whiff of something. Try to get a sense of how reliable that information is, then give it an appropriate weight when you reason with it."

Ben looked at me and smiled his shy, boyish smile. "Yeah, that's it," he said. "There's no conflict—they work together." He paused for a moment, then added, with just a note of hesitation, "Now I know why Dr. Atherton calls you her compass."

Jessica finished the quote, then looked at Paul and said, "So, what I'm suggesting is that, as you follow free movement on this exercise, you keep in mind that the signals rising up within you may be subtle—they may be faint and staticky—but still, try to listen to them and discover what's there and what value it may have for you. Remember, for all of us, it's like a language we've been listening to at the back of our minds for our whole lives. It's there; we can listen in. The more we pay attention to it, the better we learn it." Jessica finished and smiled at Paul. He liked the look in her eye, like a light shining there.

"So, we might as well get started," she said. "There's nothing too ceremonial about it. I'll do the practice along with you. We should both wander off and pick different directions to start with, so we don't interfere with one another. The only instruction is to walk—following your impulses and impressions, going where your whims guide you—and while you wander, try to sense the life around you."

She paused, then added, "Oh, and think about the people you feel connected to, too—think about them, and try to remember their *sger ngo bo*. Okay?"

"Sure," Paul said.

"Okay, then," Jessica said. "We're all set. I'll meet you back here in about an hour. Is that all okay with you?"

"Sure," Paul said again.

"Good. Then you pick a direction, and after you've started, I'll go off in another direction. We'll meet back here when the time feels right."

Paul stood up. "Now?" he said.

Jessica smiled broadly. "Yes, now," she said, then gestured sweetly, as though to wave him away.

Paul smiled back, caught for a moment by the bright look in her dark eyes and by the way her hair moved in the breeze, then he turned and set off into the forest to the east of the Retreat.

◘　◘　◘

Paul walked along the ridge, with the Retreat to his back. Though he was uncertain as to the worth of this activity, he had to admit it felt good to get out of his room, in which he had spent altogether too much time recently, and walk in the woods around the Retreat. He thought a little about trying to feel connected with the trees and birds and with the lizards and squirrels around him in the same way he had felt connected with Jessica the day before—but the idea seemed peculiar to Paul, perhaps silly, and for a time, as he wandered, he found himself thinking about other things, instead: about the work he had remaining, about how much he might be able to accomplish before leaving the Retreat, and about where he would go from there.

After a while, these thoughts circled back to Jessica, and to how much he would like to spend more time with her before the week was up, and he would be required to leave the Retreat.

Thinking of Jessica, Paul noticed that he was hardly following the instructions she had given him. He paused, then, to consider where he felt like walking, and found that he really felt like continuing on along the ridge in the same direction he was going, heading east from the Retreat.

As Paul set out again, he tried to think of who he felt connected to in the way Jessica had described, but he had to admit to himself that there was really nobody in his current life that he felt that sort of connection with. Well, Casey, yes, though it had been a very long time since they had seen one another. Until recently he would have said Sheila, too, but the way he felt now, he didn't really feel like thinking about her much at all.

Paul stopped and, turning to his left, looked off toward the mountains and valleys to the north. This was the terrain he had passed through on the way to the Retreat. Nowhere in it was there a peak as high as the one he now stood on. What rugged and beautiful land, Paul told himself, looking out at the terrain dropping off before him. He thought about his grandfather, then, and what he might think and feel if he could be there with Paul, taking in this sight.

Yes, he had felt that sort of connection with his grandfather, Paul told himself. And with his mother, too.

Impulsively, Paul turned back in the direction in which he'd been headed and continued on along the ridge, away from the Retreat. If he could just remember what they felt like—what he had felt when he was with them, Paul told himself, then he could at least begin to follow the directions Jessica had given him.

Paul pushed himself to begin remembering—but in truth, he didn't want to. They were both long gone, and that was sad enough without him having to remember what it had been like when they were really with him.

That's the problem with this exercise, Paul thought. He was being asked to do whatever he felt like doing, while at the same time being asked to do things he really didn't want to do at all.

Why was he really trying to do this, anyway? he asked himself. Because it was assigned? He didn't come here to study Kumaric practice. He came so he would have a place to stay while he worked on designing and building his new transport. Sure, he'd had to do some of the things assigned to him—but not this. Nobody was checking. Nobody would know what he actually did, or what he thought about, while he was wandering.

Paul stopped again. He stood in a sort of clearing—narrow, sure, but a clearing, nonetheless—at the top of the ridge. From where he stood, he had a particularly clear view of the land to the south, with few trees in the way.

Below him were lower peaks and foothills, a rugged land rolling out for countless kilometers—beyond which, somewhere, he knew, lay the Pacific Ocean.

It was quite a sight. Where Paul stood, he was in the shade of the clouds above, but in the foothills below, the sun had escaped the clouds. It splashed across the lowlands like a sea of light.

Paul looked at the bands of light streaking between earth and sky, and with his eyes followed them up to the clouds above. Just then, he caught a glimpse of lightning flashing deep inside one of the clouds above the ridge. It was followed immediately by the low rumble of thunder.

For a moment, hearing it, Paul was carried back to the last time he had heard that sound—during the storm that had, mistakenly, transported him here. A small shiver ran through him. That one small moment had changed his life so drastically!

Paul looked down from the clouds and at the little clearing around him. Wildflowers bloomed everywhere. Each blossom was rocking gently in the breeze.

Paul turned and looked off to the north, again, back along the route he had hiked on his way to the Retreat. He had come quite far, he told himself. It had been a long hike in—a long hike following the vastly longer, though instantaneous, journey that had brought him to this world. So much had passed, yet so much still lay before him. But he was close to being ready—just the energy supply and the funds to build the transport, and he would be set.

For a moment Paul took in the vision before him: that great open land, through which he had passed—that earth, this earth, so teeming with life. How could he be planning to leave it? Paul asked himself.

And yet he knew that he should—that he must. So much, so many lives, depended on it.

He felt burdened by this thought, and pleased, at the same time: burdened, because so much rested on his shoulders; pleased because, well, because it was satisfying to feel that who he was and what he did mattered so much, to so many.

He looked around. Further up, along the ridge, behind a low-growing live oak, was a fallen pine. Paul had a desire to go sit on the pine log and think a little bit. The spot looked sheltered, and for some reason Paul found the sense of seclusion it offered appealing. He had an impulse to give up the wandering and to go and sit quietly in that sheltered spot. It didn't seem quite fair or right, though—he had agreed to wander, hadn't he? And yet, he had also agreed to follow his impulses.

Paul smiled a little, then stepped out of the narrow clearing and walked beneath the pines for ten meters or so, until he arrived at the private spot. He sat down on the fallen pine trunk there, as he felt like doing, and sat staring out between the gaps in the trees at the uneven hills and spacious valleys that spread out beyond. Sitting there, he thought some more about the transport unit he had designed and what it would take to get it up and running, even as he looked out at the land around him, and took it in. He was glad Jessica had suggested the walk. She was right about one thing—he did like being outside in a place like this.

Thinking this, Paul wondered where Jessica was just then, and where she was going on her walk. He hoped she wouldn't wander to where he was and find him just sitting there. After all, he could hardly tell her that he hadn't really come to the Retreat to study the three stages.

As he thought this, Paul heard a sound on the ridge near him and turned to look back toward the little clearing from which he had just come.

The lowest branches of the live oak next to Paul partially obscured his view. He could see enough to know that there was someone there—but who?

Paul leaned first one way and then the other, trying to see through the oak's branches. He could just make out a figure standing in the little clearing, holding a box of some kind. He looked more closely, trying to get a clear line of view. After a moment, he recognized her. It was the Retreat's director, Waseme Yabann. She was standing at the center of the clearing, with a black box under one arm, looking skyward.

She stood for perhaps a minute, appraising the sky, then took the box (which was no more than a third of a meter in any one dimension), carefully set it down on the ground, then opened the top of it. She bent over the box and put her hand just a little inside the opening, then moved her hand sharply. Whatever she did, the motion was accompanied by an audible click, as though she had just pushed a button or turned a knob of some sort.

Hurriedly, she stepped back from the box and looked up toward the sky. A moment passed, then a narrow beam of white light shot up from the box toward the clouds above.

Some sort of laser? Paul thought. He stared at it, wondering what it could be for. Could it be a signal of some sort? But if so, to whom?

The laser seemed to pulse, almost imperceptibly. It continued to streak skyward for ten seconds, twenty—perhaps thirty or forty seconds, in all—then a bolt of intensely brilliant light spread between the box and sky, as straight in its return as the laser had been when it stretched upward. This was followed almost instantly by a very loud clap of thunder, which dropped from the clouds above and spread across the land.

In an instant, it was over. As Paul sat staring in astonishment at what he had just witnessed, the director stepped forward and closed the box carefully. Then she lifted it under her arm and set off along the ridge, heading back in the direction of the Retreat.

Paul made himself sit still for perhaps a whole minute as he waited for the director to disappear. Then, with Director Yabann gone, he hurried to the center of the clearing and looked around him. There was no mark on the ground where the box had been set, yet Paul was sure the bolt of lightning had made contact there. He looked to the west, where he could just barely discern the motions of Director Yabann disappearing amid the trees, and again Paul pictured the box she had been carrying under one arm.

What was in it? he thought. What was it—a box full of lightning, summoned from the sky above?

Paul's head spun as he looked again in the direction of the Retreat. Had he seen what he thought he had just seen? Was the director of the Retreat really carrying a fully functioning lightning-capture device?

$_{\square}$ 24 $_{\square}$

When Paul woke early the next morning, he opened his eyes and saw the words written on the far wall:

Seek that which gives you joy.

—THE LITTLE BOOK

Paul smiled a little, then rolled over onto his back. So much had happened in the last day! he thought. He had finished his design for the transport and discovered the box that captured lightning, all in one day!

Paul thought back over how the day had progressed. After seeing the box in action, he had finished his session with Jessica, then returned to his room, where he had used the portal to find out whatever he could about the box he'd seen the Retreat director use.

As it turned out, it hadn't taken him long to find what he needed. The information had been there all along, as near at hand, and as easily accessed, as the description the portal gave of the Kumaric Retreat where Paul was staying. It said:

Energy is provided at our Kumaric Retreat through the use of solar-sensitive materials (both photo and thermal) and by harvesting lightning, which we collect via a PLCU (Portable Lightning Capture Unit). Water is carefully recycled, so as not to put excessive demands on the surrounding environment, and then...

Paul stopped the readout then, and asked the portal for more information about PLCUs. Within minutes, he learned that they were constructed around an "ultrananocapacitor," which made them capable of harvesting energy at an incredibly rapid rate. PLCUs were efficient, as well, Paul discovered, at storing energy with minimal loss of charge over time.

All that was good to know, but what really pleased Paul was the fact that such devices could hold up to ten gigajoules of power (far more than enough to run his transport) and were capable of releasing any portion of that energy, at any rate—from a slow trickle, to a single super-powered burst.

What fine luck! Paul told himself, as he looked over the information. He could hardly have hoped for a superior solution to his energy-supply problem.

Paul leaned back in his chair in front of the portal in his room and laughed, as he reflected on having found so easy a solution to a problem over which he had worried so much, and that had vexed him endlessly, even on his own world. This solution was beautifully simple. Portable Lightning Capture Units were sleek, extremely powerful, and easily moved.

Paul asked the portal a few more questions then, and discovered that, although PLCUs were fairly expensive, they were easily acquired, and purchasing one would increase the cost of his project by only about ten percent.

Paul smiled and set aside his recollections of the day before, then swung his feet over the edge of the bed. Now all he needed to do was find some sort of fitting employment, and it would all be easy going after that.

Paul got up and turned on the shower. He knew exactly how he would spend his day. After breakfast he would get to work finding a line of work he would be suited for on this world, and figuring out what he would have to do to prove his credentials, so he could gain employment.

As Paul stepped into the shower, he was smiling and humming to himself. If things went smoothly, he could get all of that accomplished before his next meeting with Jessica, late that afternoon.

◙   ◙   ◙

Paul spent most of the day looking into how he might earn the money necessary for building his transport, breaking only briefly for lunch. Getting hired for one of the lower-paying physics jobs he had learned about through the portal, he concluded, should not be too difficult, as his skills far surpassed what would be required of him. This was assuming, of course, that they accepted his résumé without asking too many questions. After all, he would have nobody to vouch for him on this world, and no school records, even, to back up his claim that he had a PhD.

One of the higher-paying jobs available to physicists on this world also looked like a possibility, though Paul noted that he would have to spend six months or more studying up on developments that had taken place in the field of physics on this world and not on his. Still, Paul thought, if he could make ends meet somehow while he studied, it might be worth it to try for one of these jobs because of the improved earning power he would have with it. Paul felt some excitement about this prospect, not just for the income it would provide, but because he thought it would be fascinating to learn what physicists had discovered on this world that had been overlooked on his.

Paul leaned back in his chair and considered how much had happened since he'd first arrived on this world, and how much he had still to accomplish. As he considered this, the portal flashed an announcement. Paul had asked it to alert him when it was almost 4:30. It was almost time for his next meeting with Jessica.

As Paul walked toward the white fir tree where his meeting would take place, he took in the scene around him. The day was bright, the sky nearly cloudless. The air seemed particularly clear and fresh after the rain that had fallen the night before. Such a different day than the cloud-filled day in which he had wandered for his stage-three exercise the day before!

The sky had been beautiful then, and especially so when Paul was walking back to meet Jessica after having seen Director Yabann collect the lightning. He remembered how the sun had hung in the west, and how it had broken through the clouds in broad bands, washing the land beneath with its amber glow.

Paul had known, then, as he walked toward that golden light, that Jessica would ask him about what he had experienced during his walk, and he had worried about what he would tell her. Certainly, he could not tell her about the lightning-capture box, and what it meant to him to discover it.

It seemed the trip back from his wandering exercise took less time than the trip out, and soon Paul found himself sitting beneath the white fir and the cloudy sky, waiting for Jessica to return from her own wanderings. He didn't have to wait long, for she appeared only minutes later, as though, somehow, she had sensed him there, and so had come when the moment was right.

As Jessica joined Paul under the tree, she asked him how things had gone, and Paul told her simply that he had enjoyed the walk, but didn't think he had reached any new depth in his awareness.

"That's okay," Jessica responded. "It's a lot to expect that a novice sojourner, on their first stay, will achieve stage three the first time out. Stay with it. It will come to you. You have to give it time. It takes practice. Even for people who've reached that level of awareness, it can take practice to maintain it."

"Thanks for the encouragement," Paul said, and to his surprise, he meant it, even thought he had not put any effort into trying to reach stage three. Something in her attitude was so supportive, so warm, that he could hardly help but feel appreciative.

"How did it go for you?" Paul asked.

"Oh, I had a wonderful time. I love to wander here. I think, even if there were no Retreat, I would want to come here. The place—the land—it seems so vital, so alive. I love to feel a part of that. And today, with these clouds—it's so beautiful. The light is fantastic," she said gesturing toward the west, "and there were all sorts of animals out, today, too."

"Yeah? What did you see?" Paul asked, genuinely interested.

"Oh—mule deer and jack rabbits in the canyon," she said, pointing back in the direction from which she'd come, "and I heard a mountain chickadee singing on the way back. It took me a few minutes to spot it in the trees, or I would have been back a few minutes sooner. I hope you weren't waiting long."

"No, not long," Paul said.

Now, walking along on this sunny day, Paul remembered how it had pleased him to see Jessica excited and all lit up the way she had been the day before.

He had wondered exactly what people meant when they talked about reaching stage three, but now he associated it with the way Jessica had seemed in that moment, with the warm light she radiated, much like the sky when it was spreading its bands of gold.

As Paul strolled along now, he thought about this, and about the walk he had taken the day before, and realized he might have been wrong in telling Jessica that he had achieved no progress toward stage three during his wandering exercise. After all, hadn't he been thinking about the sort of energy supply he would need to have to power his transport, and then stumbled on just the sort of energy he needed?

Paul mulled this over. Yes, he had been walking along, following his impulses and impressions, as he'd been asked to do, and had wound up discovering something that replicated just what he'd been modeling in his mind. If Dr. Kumar was right in her assumptions about how free movement worked, this would suggest he had tapped into some deeper awareness in himself.

Was this what he had done—wandered in just the right way to find the sort of power supply he had modeled? Paul wondered. Had some part of him, deep within himself, sensed that possibility, and helped to lead him to it?

Paul hesitated to draw any conclusion at all about how, exactly, he had come to discover the Retreat director with her PLCU, but he quietly felt a certain satisfaction in not only having found a power supply, but in having found it the way he did.

Paul looked up and spotted the white fir, where Jessica had asked him to meet her again—and there she sat, beneath it, waiting for him.

Paul raised an arm to wave at her, and Jessica waved back at him, as Paul hurried forward to meet her.

◻   ◻   ◻

They sat under the fir tree with a soft breeze blowing around them. The location seemed much as it had when they had first met there, two days before, but now there was something different in the atmosphere between them. They were talking about Paul's work on stage three, but something else seemed to be happening beneath the surface of their dialogue. Paul could see it in the soft look in Jessica's eyes and, somehow, too, in her relaxed manner—the way she leaned back against the tree trunk as she spoke to him, the way she picked up bits of leaves or grass and moved them slowly in her hands.

"I wouldn't worry that you didn't make more progress the first time out, Paul," she was saying, echoing the same sentiments she had expressed the day before. "You'll get there. It might take some time, but the door is open for all of us to pass through it. Just keep practicing."

She looked down at the twig she was twirling between her fingers, and Paul had the feeling that she was trying to think of how to help him along.

"The process is really, basically, very simple," she said. "You just keep doing what you've been doing since you came here."

She looked up at Paul. "At the personal level, stay aware of yourself, and of the models you form and carry, and of why you choose them.

"At the interpersonal level," she went on, "practice sensing other people's *sger ngo bos.* Try to see through their eyes. Try to understand why they do what they do—why their actions seem desirable to them, from their own points of view.

"And at a transpersonal level, remind yourself that all people, everywhere—that all life—is seeking for fulfillment of its protolife, and that all of us are trying to do what seems to us to be 'desirable,' or 'good,' as we understand it from our own perspectives."

She leaned forward a little, with her legs crossed and her forearms resting on her knees, and thought about it for a moment longer. "And beyond that, just keep practicing your exercise from yesterday. Try to sense and be aware of the *sger ngo bo* in whatever life is around you. Remember that every living thing has its own experience, and try to be aware of that, of what that experience is—even as you try to stay aware of what you're experiencing within yourself."

She looked over at Paul as Paul nodded.

"In other words," Jessica told him, "choose consciously to expand the range of your awareness, and the range of your identification. Try consciously to expand your sense of self."

She glanced down at the twirling twig again, then added, "And whenever you come across a problem of some sort, remember to work the three impediments in reverse." She looked over at Paul.

Paul smiled a little. Even though Jessica was summarizing ideas he was already familiar with, it was nice to have them gathered together so clearly. What she was describing was, he knew, the most essential elements of the work that people did at Kumaric Retreats. It was, he had to presume, just the sort of practice that, when spread around the globe, had made this world advance so much more quickly than his own.

Jessica smiled back, just briefly, then concluded, "Just keep practicing those things and you'll move forward. It takes time—but if you stay with it, one day you'll wake up and realize you've arrived someplace special. Stay with it, Paul. It will come to you—perhaps at the moment you least expect it, but it will come."

As Jessica finished, she looked over at Paul and, for a moment, held his gaze—and again he saw that deep empathy in her look, that kind of light he saw in her.

"So, that's all our work on stage three, Paul. That's all we do together. The rest is in your hands." She leaned back against the tree again, and smiled at Paul in a way that made Paul feel curious. She had said they were done, but she was clearly not done. He had the feeling she had something else in mind.

"Okay," Paul said.

Jessica looked at him, and took a deep breath. "I would like to suggest something else to you, Paul, now that I'm no longer your ES."

"Yeah?" Paul said. He turned his head a little to one side, listening.

"I see something in you, Paul. I'd like to spend more time with you. I was wondering if you, ah, well—how would you feel about having a madu friendship with me?"

Paul wasn't sure how to respond. He had no idea what "madu" meant, and didn't want to let her see that. What would happen if he pretended he did know and just said "yes?" he wondered. He started to open his mouth to answer, then hesitated.

Jessica looked at him in that same probing way she had done so many times before. "You do know what that is, don't you?"

Paul slowly shook his head. "No," he said softly.

Jessica's eyes widened. "How can that be, Paul? You're smart, you're clearly educated—and yet there are all these things you don't know. Where are you from, Paul, that you don't know what a madu friendship is?"

"Santa Maria, originally," he told her.

Jessica laughed and shook her head. "Maybe so, but I swear, Paul, I sometimes think you're from another planet—no offense intended."

"None taken," Paul said. He had a desire to tell her the truth, to tell her the whole truth.

Jessica smiled at him playfully. "Sometime you're going to have to tell me about this mysterious upbringing you had. Your family weren't Abstanites, were they?" she said, only half joking.

Paul didn't know what to say.

"You don't know what that is, either, do you?"

"No," Paul admitted.

"See? You're not like anybody else I've known, Paul." The way she said it, though, it sounded like a compliment.

"Why don't you tell me about madu friendships," Paul said.

"Okay." Jessica looked at Paul as she paused to gather her thoughts. "The word 'madu' was originally from one of the languages of India—from Kannada. It means 'to join deeply' or 'deep water.' Dr. Kumar introduced the term in her journal to mean a relationship—a friendship—where people connect particularly deeply, but which is still just a friendship. Typically, madu friendships are more physically affectionate than other friendships—but they are friendships. They're not about sex or romance. Typically, madu friends may relate affectionately—they may hold hands, or cuddle, or they may hold one another—but it's not a passionate sort of relationship. It's a friendship, that's all—but a special sort of friendship that's closer and more openly affectionate than usual."

Jessica looked thoughtful. "Dr. Kumar wrote about this sort of relationship in her journal, in October of 1998. The same passage also appears in *The Little Book*. I think it would help make things clearer if I share it with you, even though it's kind of a long quote," she said.

"That's okay," Paul replied.

"All right, then," Jessica said, then recited for him:

I ran into Amica on Pearl Street the other day. She's one of the graduate students helping me sort through the data I collected in New Guinea. She was walking with, and holding hands with, a young man whom I didn't recognize.

Later, at my office, I asked her if she and her boyfriend Dillon had broken up. She said "no," so I explained why I had thought perhaps they had.

Amica laughed and said that that was Rinji she was walking with, and that Rinji and she were just friends—that they hold hands, and sometimes cuddle, but that they really were just friends.

I've always thought Amica particularly open minded, so I guess I shouldn't have been surprised when she said that she and Dillon had agreed to both have close and even physically affectionate friendships with others. She said Dillon was her only lover, and she his, but that they both thought everyone was a lot healthier, both mentally and emotionally, when they had a lot of close and affectionate relationships in their lives.

"You have to be careful when you start that sort of friendship with someone, though," she said. "You have to spell out your intent very clearly, so people won't mistake what's going on and think you mean something else. If you aren't clear, most people will think you're just being really indirect about sex, so you have to be very clear about your intentions."

She thought for a moment, then added, "I had someone tell me once that they thought this was a crazy way to come at things—I mean, why leave sex out? Sex is nice, right?—but if you want to be close to a lot of people and you let sex be part of a lot of relationships, it can get complicated really fast, and usually people end up getting hurt. So, it just seems to me that this works better. Love and closeness without jealousy or broken hearts."

"Hm," I said, "so it works out pretty well for all of you?"

"Yeah—if you're clear about what you're doing, and people don't get other ideas. Of course, people have to stick by the agreement," she added. "You can't tell someone they can let their guard down with you as a friend and then take advantage of that to make a pass at them. That's really uncool. You just have to be very direct about what the relationship is or isn't, or people get confused. But if everyone's definite about what's going on, it can be really nice to have all that extra closeness and affection in your life. I think my relationship with Dillon is better for it, because we don't require one another to meet all of our emotional needs, since we both have such close relationships with other people. It's just better all around, this way, I think—but you definitely have to be very clear with everybody about what's going on."

"What about Dillon, doesn't he get jealous of you and Rinji?" I asked.

"Well, you know," she answered, "I had quite a number of friends like this when we first met, both men and women friends—Dillon did, too—but neither of us were involved with anyone. So, when we got involved, we both knew that of all the people in our lives, we chose one another. I think if it were to hurt Dillon, I would feel very differently about it. I really would. I love him a lot, and everybody I'm close to knows how I feel about him. There's no question about where we stand with one another. I don't think it would be possible for us to do this if that weren't the case."

When I saw Laura that evening, I told her about the conversation I'd had with Amica. I told her that I've often thought it sad how people look and look for one special person to be close to, then find that one person—only to discard so many other relationships with people they've felt some special bond with along the way. Wouldn't life be better, I asked, if we could gather all the people we felt closest to around us, and keep them all throughout our lives?

So many people are starving for connection, for affection, I said, and yet most people hesitate to offer a warm smile or a squeeze of the hand, for fear others will take it as a sign of romantic or sexual intent. It's like we're all hesitating to offer crumbs to the starving for fear they will grab for more—and so people starve more and more in their own personal isolation, while we each offer one another less and less. If only we could set those hesitations aside and shine the warmest light we have on one another.

Perhaps, I told Laura, Amica and Dillon have the right idea about how to go about things. After all, the intimacy we share with others brings so much to life within us. It gives us so much joy. If only we could spread more of that in the world.

"So," Jessica said, as she finished reciting, "a madu friendship is for times when two people feel that a closer relationship would allow them to share something meaningful between them, but where, for whatever reason, a romantic or sexual relationship doesn't fit. Madu friendships can be very close, very affectionate, very intimate relationships. They're just not of a sexual or romantic nature."

Jessica finished speaking and looked at Paul. For a moment, Paul wanted to ask her why she wanted it to be only that, and not something more—but he hesitated, perhaps because he was afraid to hear what she would say. Perhaps, too, he hesitated because he felt he could offer her too little, anyway, since he planned to leave her world as soon as it was possible for him to go. And then there was Sheila, with whom he had felt so involved, even a week before—and toward whom he now felt such detachment.

"I like you, Paul," Jessica was saying, "I like the way it feels to be around you. I see something so good, so kind and true in you. I have this feeling like there are worlds inside you I hardly know, and I want to know you better. I keep having the feeling I'd like to put my arms around you, to curl up beside you, and talk softly with you. So I'm asking..."

"I feel like that about you, too, Jessica," Paul cut in, not really meaning to interrupt. "I'd like it to be like that, too."

"So it's okay? We could be madu friends?"

"Yes," Paul said. It felt good to think of Jessica with her arms around him, and of her in his arms, but part of Paul felt disappointed as soon as he heard himself answer. Had he missed his chance? he wondered. Should he have suggested that something more than this odd "madu friendship" be allowed to happen between them? What a strange world this was—and how strangely people related on it!

Jessica reached over and took Paul's hand. Her face was full of the same light he had seen in her all along. Paul felt a rush, then, of her presence, her warmth—and in that moment, he felt the happiest he had felt in a very long time.

◘   ◘   ◘

Paul and Jessica sat visiting as the sun dropped lower in the sky. Jessica made a point of telling Paul that she would have to be back to her work in the Cuyama Valley in just over a week. Paul asked her then if she enjoyed doing Kumaric work full-time and listened closely as she answered, expressing to him the satisfaction that it gave her to watch people growing and becoming, somehow, truer to themselves.

She and Paul held hands as they talked, with Paul asking Jessica questions, and steering the conversation away from himself.

After a while, Jessica pointed out that it would be time for dinner soon, and asked Paul if he would join her for it.

Paul agreed, and soon they were strolling back toward the Retreat together, hand in hand in the soft evening light.

The dining hall seemed especially crowded to Paul when they arrived, perhaps because he would have preferred for it to be the opposite—a quiet and secluded place, where they could share a private dinner, just the two of them. Perhaps Jessica would have preferred this, too, but nothing of the sort was possible.

As they stood in line for their meal, it seemed to Paul as though everyone knew Jessica, as though she had worked, at one time or another, with practically everyone there, as one person after another stopped to say hello. Jessica beamed at each of them, as warm and friendly as ever. Even when she and Paul took a seat in what Paul hoped would be a quiet corner of the dining hall, others sought her out. Paul's head was awhirl with all that had happened—this strange, new relationship with someone who seemed so ready to accept him, someone who attracted one person after another to approach her, to squeeze her hand, to say a few friendly words.

It made Paul feel special and insignificant, all at once. But finally, he just relaxed and watched Jessica interacting with those who stopped to say hello and with others seated nearby who turned to speak to her. It seemed to him as though they had all drunk of the same elixir, which made them more open and affectionate than he was accustomed to anyone being on his world.

Every once in a while, Jessica would turn back to Paul, and say, "So what were you saying?" or "What was I telling you?" and they would return to their conversation and travel a little further along its branching path, until the next person stopped by their table for a short chat. Interwoven with these bits and pieces of conversation, they talked some about Paul's work and where he had first gotten the idea that extra-space-time travel might be possible.

Paul said it had started with him wishing he could turn back the clock, as it seemed to him that various things had been better in the past. Inspired by this wish, Paul told her, he had begun probing into the mathematics of space-time. He gave up his quest for time travel when he stumbled, quite by accident, on mathematics that suggested that instantaneous travel from one place to another might be quite possible, simply by stepping out of space-time, then back into it.

Jessica found this quite interesting and followed up with more questions for Paul about himself. The two of them talked some about Paul's childhood in Santa Maria and how close he had become to his grandfather after his mother passed away. They talked about Paul's father, and how much his work had taken him away from his family.

Paul worried some that the conversation might slide from his childhood, in general, to what Jessica had called his "mysterious upbringing," but each time Paul grew tense, the conversation seemed to shift naturally from the topic that made him uneasy, either because someone new would stop by the table to say hello, or because Jessica would, in that moment, turn from plying Paul with questions to offering some detail or another about her own life.

Jessica's personal world fascinated Paul. Where he, as an adult, had plenty of coworkers, but almost no family or friends he would really count as close to him—Jessica's life, from what she told him, was much the opposite: she had no coworkers, yet her life was filled with close relationships of all other sorts. While she had no siblings, her parents, aunts and uncles, and many cousins lived in the same small town Jessica lived in. She had there, as well, many friends, both old and new, and many clients she had worked with through the years. She could hardly walk down the street in the main part of town, she told Paul, without running into half a dozen people she knew, and knew quite well.

Jessica was quite happy with her life, it seemed to Paul, though perhaps some little thing was missing—perhaps a sense of excitement, or newness, or scale, as though she longed for some grand adventure within the larger design of her life.

And so the conversation went. Paul would tell a little, then Jessica would tell a little, then they would be interrupted again. During these brief intermissions, Paul had time to worry some about what they would talk about after dinner, when the throngs of people had disappeared, and it was just the two of them together. What would Jessica want to talk about? What would she ask him? Would she want to know why he knew so little about things other people considered commonplace?

Paul thought about this as they left the dining hall and began to walk in the direction of the residences, holding hands as they went.

After a minute or two, Jessica turned to Paul and asked him if he would like to join her in her room for a while.

Paul turned toward her in the faint light, hesitating, then looked her in the eye, and all his hesitation fell away.

"That would be nice," Paul said. Then he walked with her, as she led him home.

As concerned as Paul had been, the problem disappeared as smoothly as his hesitation. When they arrived in Jessica's room, they lay down on the bed together, and Jessica did as she had said she wanted to. She lay beside him and gathered him in her arms, and they stayed like that, then, for a long time, with only a few words spoken, enjoying one another's company quietly—feeling one another's presence.

As Paul lay there, he was aware of the strangeness of it: he had gone from a sexual relationship with someone from whom he often felt estranged, to this affectionate closeness with someone with whom nothing sexual could be expressed.

He had thought this would be difficult, Paul admitted to himself—to be near Jessica and not make love to her—but somehow, knowing for certain that they would not have sex made the atmosphere much less charged than he had expected.

Paul rolled over and looked at Jessica.

"How are you doing?" she asked.

"Good," Paul said, as he felt a smile spread on his face. With one hand, he brushed the hair back from Jessica's eyes. "I think I like maydu friendships," he said.

Jessica smiled, too, and Paul could see she was amused. "It's 'madu,' Paul," she said gently. "'Ma' like in 'mama,' 'du' like in dew on the grass." She rested one hand on the side of his face. Her eyes warmed him.

"Madu," Paul said.

"That's it," Jessica said, then lifted her head a little and looked at the clock.

"Wow, time's going fast," she said. "It's getting late and I've got a class in the morning."

"Oh." Paul lifted his head and glanced around for his shoes.

"Look, I don't know how you'll feel about this, but if you like, you could just sleep here," Jessica said.

Paul smiled at her. It was true, he was liking this madu friendship very much. He nestled his head beside hers.

"I think that would be very nice," he told her.

◙   ◙   ◙

When Paul woke the next morning, Jessica's arms were still around him. He looked at her sleeping beside him, then looked around the room. Light leaked in around the curtains, filling the room with a soft glow. On one wall Paul saw written:

Prosperity is relating, not acquiring.

—Tom Brown, Jr.

Paul smiled, then looked at Jessica, still dreaming beside him. She looked almost like a child, Paul told himself—so sweet, so peaceful. How could he be more prosperous than this, to wake with her sleeping beside him?

He watched her breathing slowly. Even with her sleeping, he could sense her *sger ngo bo*—her presence. The more he was with her, the more beautiful she seemed to him—not just physically, but *her*, who she was. She was like everything he had dreamed of, all rolled into one—intelligent and kind, independent and insightful, lighthearted and serious. And she seemed to care about him and to accept him. How was it that she could see him this way, and not just as some odd sojourner, with peculiar ideas and strange gaps in his knowledge?

How could he be so lucky? he wondered—and yet, for the first time in many years, he had no doubt that he deserved just the sort of warmth she was giving him, and that he, as well, was giving her. What would happen if he were to tell her, truly, who he was? He longed to do it—but only if it could be done right, and she would believe him—and wouldn't conclude, instead, that he was crazy, or lying.

Paul rested his head back against the pillow and thought about his project. Would he really leave her to return to his own world? he asked himself. He hated even to consider it—but at the same time he felt strongly that he had a responsibility to do exactly that. He was so close to being ready to leave this world. He had everything he needed now—the new transport design, the parts and price lists, a more comprehensive theoretical foundation on which to base the aiming—even an energy supply. Once he had the money with which to buy the needed parts, he could quite easily return to his own world.

Paul stared up at the ceiling, and for a moment turned his thoughts to Sheila. If he went back, he would see her, he told himself, but now the thought held no luster. There was nothing there for him anymore—nothing to attach to, to attract him to her anymore. It was done, even if he couldn't tell her now, he would when he saw her next.

He lay staring at the ceiling for some time, then, thinking about his world and the people in it. He had spent time the day before studying the design of the Portable Lightning Capture Units, with the intention of learning what would be required to mass-produce them—so that he could do just that when he returned to his world. It would complete the plans he had been working on for so many years. He could build enough transports to send large numbers of people through to another world, and he could power them, too. Yes, PLCUs would be difficult to construct, as the ultrananocapacitor would have to be produced under exacting conditions, but with sufficient Corprogov funding and enough scientists and technicians on the project, Paul thought it wouldn't take long to accomplish all that was required to put the Depopulation Project into action.

Paul knew that with the PLCU technology successfully transplanted to his world, it would become quite practical to send an endless stream of people through to this world. How many would Corprogov want to send? Paul wondered. One billion or two would hardly alter the pattern of unanswered wants and needs on his world—but if they sent five billion through, Paul calculated, the populations would then be about the same on the two worlds.

Would Corprogov choose to send as many as that? Paul wondered. Probably, he told himself. There would be no reason for them to hesitate. It would be in their best interest to relieve the pressure on their own world, to free up resources and reduce demand.

Imagine how the Upper Crust would live then! Paul told himself. They would have much more than, much better than, true-meat salami and the like. They could live in the sort of endless splendor they had in decades past, before severe shortages had caused even them to curtail their lifestyles.

Surely they must ache to return to those days, Paul thought. There would be nothing to stop them from sending through a full five billion lonely, hungry, unenlightened people to this world.

Lying there, then, Paul let himself imagine it as he had never done before. For the first time, he didn't swerve from the thought of what he would be doing to this world. He no longer needed the project for the hope it could provide him. He no longer needed it to be true, or right. All he wanted now was to see it for what it really was.

The project had been almost like a religion for him, for a long time—a kind of guiding light, a star, a hope he could set his course by—the only possible hope against a backdrop of ruin and despair. In a world moving forward mechanically, resolutely, toward its own destruction, Paul had wanted, needed, for there to be some way to turn the course—to move toward repair, resolution, revival. The Depopulation Project had been that for him—it was the fragment of light, the shred of hope, the one possible solution to all that was wrong. It had been his single prayer.

Now, lying next to Jessica, he wanted something more from it, something different than he had ever wanted, ever asked of it before—he wanted, simply, the truth. How would it be? What would really happen if he returned to his world and opened a passageway from there to here?

It was true, wasn't it? Paul challenged himself. They *would* send through those five billion people—probably chosen because they were, in the view of Corprogov, the least desirable and most expendable: the derelicts, the drug users, the criminals, and dissidents. They would all be rounded up and sent away by Corprogov as they "cleaned up" the earth, their earth, once and for all. One billion, two billion, three, four, and five—and what would cause them to stop there? What would they consider the optimal population of *their* earth to be?

Might it be similar to the population of the world Paul was now in? Why wouldn't Corprogov continue to ship people off world until they got the population low, like that?—a mere three billion? Imagine the sort of selfish splendor they would revel in, then, with all the world's resources for themselves, and ten billion of their world's poorest, saddest, and most bedraggled inhabitants forced into exile on a new world!

What would stop them, if he gave them the key?

Paul looked toward Jessica, then, as she lay sleeping beside him, looked to her as though, somehow, with her native warmth and acceptance, he might find in that some comfort. He sensed her, then, lying next to him—her body next to his, her presence—and imagined for a moment how the world would look through her eyes: her world, full of western tanagers and golden eagles, mule deer and jack rabbits and mountain chickadees, a world of tall skies and clear air, a world full of sane and friendly people, who treated one another (as they treated all other creatures) with care and respect.

Such a world! Such a world was her world—the only world she had ever known—and she was like the blossom of that world, made from it, and made, in Paul's eyes, so nearly perfect.

How would it be for her—for *her*—to have the ravaged people of his world swarming in around her, swelling the ranks of this world until it was as overloaded as his own?

Oh, at first she would welcome them—sad, and lost, and in need of care. She would help to clothe them and to guide them, Paul was sure.

But they would keep on coming then, coming and flooding, flooding and coming, until they would cover the land and blight it, as they had blighted their own world. There would be so many of them then, so many—and instead of giving hope to the newcomers, people like Jessica would have the hope stripped from them, as they saw the world around them stripped of everything that made it lovely, and vibrant, and rich.

This would be his gift to her, Paul told himself—to take away from her everything that she loved, everything she and the others of her world had earned and deserved.

Paul looked back toward the ceiling and pulled the blanket tight around him, as he imagined how it would be when word got around *this* world about what he had done—his "accomplishment," his "gift" to them.

Oh, how they would despise him! he told himself. They would revile him. They would remember him. Yes—they would remember him, always, as the person who had destroyed their world.

◘   ◘   ◘

Paul felt Jessica move beside him and looked over at her. She moved her legs and turned a little, then opened her eyes.

"Good morning," Paul said.

"Oh—hey you. Good morning," she said. She closed her eyes again, and rested her cheek against his shoulder.

For a moment, she lay there like that, then lifted her head suddenly and looked at Paul. "I had the strangest dream," she told him. "You were in it." She frowned a little. "I was so sad."

"Why? What happened?" Paul asked.

"We were someplace—I don't know where. It was dark—the kind of dark where even what's lit looks like shadows. I don't know where we were. It was just the two of us. And then—it was the strangest thing—there was this flash of light. Brilliant light—very intense—and then, suddenly, you were gone."

Jessica looked at Paul. "Such a strange dream," she said. "I wonder why I dreamed it."

"What happened, then?" Paul asked.

"What happened?"

"You said that I disappeared. Did anything happen after that?"

"No. You were just gone, that was all. I dreamed I was with you—and I was happy, in that part of the dream. Then there was this blinding light, and when the light was gone, so were you. It was all darkness around me, then—but I knew you weren't there with me, anymore. You were gone—and I was so terribly sad."

Paul put his hand over hers. "I'm here now," he said.

Jessica looked over at him. "Isn't it a funny dream? I mean, why would I dream that?"

Yes, indeed, why would you? Paul thought. He looked Jessica in the eye. Oh, how he wished he could tell her all that he was thinking, all that he was feeling in that moment—all that he'd been thinking since he woke. Everything in his life was inside out. Everything that had ever meant anything to him, now seemed different.

"Say, what are you doing this morning?" Jessica asked.

"No plans, really," Paul said.

"Well, I've got another modeling-reality class this morning, if you'd like to come. We'll be talking about how to go about changing mental models."

"Changing mental models," Paul repeated, then cocked his head to one side, "and exactly why does this matter?" he said, teasing playfully.

Jessica smiled a little when she saw Paul's smile, but answered seriously, "Because the Emergence depends on people being able to encounter and work with their own interior experience. Choosing what we model—and therefore what we create—is a part of that," she answered.

"The Emergence," Paul repeated.

"Yes," Jessica said.

Paul didn't say anything. Jessica looked at him.

"You don't know what the Emergence is—?" she said, with her tone flat, almost like it was fact.

Paul looked back at her, then nodded, "Yeah," he said, then took a deep breath. He'd done it again.

"But you have read *Memories and Reflections*, haven't you?" she said, then quickly added, "No, I remember—you said you hadn't finished it."

"That's right."

"Well, that would explain it, partly—but it's still hard to understand..." Her voice trailed off. She looked perplexed for a moment, then added. "You really are quite a mystery to me, Paul."

Paul shrugged. He didn't know what to say to that. He could certainly see why she would feel that way.

"So you do know what the New Change is?" Jessica asked.

"Yeah, sure," Paul answered.

"Good," Jessica said, looking at Paul with her head tilted a little. "Okay," she added, then looked thoughtful. "Well, Dr. Kumar started out using the terms 'Original Change' and 'New Change,' but after she and Laura returned to Boulder from Zaire—and she began to talk to other people about these things—she wished she had more descriptive and specific terms to use. After that, she began to speak of 'the Divergence' and 'the Emergence.' 'Divergence' for the time when we all set off on paths of our own, seeking to explore our individuality; 'Emergence' for the New Change, when the real promise and potential of that individuality would emerge."

Jessica cocked her head a little, as though to say, again, "It's funny you didn't know that,"—but instead, she said, "'Divergence' and 'Emergence' are the terms in common use, Paul. People will sometimes refer to the 'Original Change' and the 'New Change,' but you don't hear it that often. 'Divergence' and 'Emergence' are much more common."

"Okay," Paul said. "Thanks." He tried not to feel too embarrassed.

"You're welcome," Jessica said, then smiled at him again, but this time with a look of curiosity in her eyes. "So, you know," she said, "sometime I'm going to have to get you to tell me more about your mysterious upbringing, and the work you've been so buried in."

Paul opened his mouth, then closed it. He felt himself tense a little. He wasn't ready. How could he tell her? Even if she did believe him—which was doubtful—what would she think of him if she knew what he'd really been thinking about and working toward, what he'd really been planning to do, since coming to her world?

"But not this morning," Jessica added. "I've got a class to teach." She got up out of bed. "So, are you going to come along?"

"What—to class? Sure," Paul said.

"Good. I'm going to grab a shower—then breakfast and class?"

"That'd be fine," Paul said, then sat up and swung his legs over the side of the bed. He'd slept with all his clothes on and now noticed how very wrinkled they were.

He looked over at Jessica, who had pulled open a drawer from under the counter that ran along one wall. She took out some clothes, then started for the shower.

"You know what?" Paul said, "I think I'll stop by my room and get a shower and change of clothes, too—then meet you at the dining hall?"

"Sounds good," Jessica said and, as she did, turned and smiled at Paul so sweetly that it made him long for her, suddenly, with a sweeping passion he had not felt, even when she was in his arms.

"Just don't be late, please," she added. "I've got to be at class by nine."

◘   ◘   ◘

Paul hurried back to his room and showered quickly, using the routine he had practiced since boyhood on his water-starved world, and as he did, he thought about Jessica, and about whether it was possible that she felt for him anything as fine as the way he felt about her. She seemed to him like a perfect gem—radiant and flawless.

Surely she had flaws, too, Paul told himself, as he quickly soaped up and rinsed, but that was okay—he just wanted to spend time in the glow that filled the space around her.

Paul finished the shower and stepped out. Still hurrying, he dried himself as he walked out into his bedroom, where the words written on the far wall caught his eye:

> *As we deepen towards union, we pass along our own root.*
> *We have to meet ourselves deeply to meet another deeply.*
>
> —THE LITTLE BOOK

As he read it, Paul thought about Jessica and Sheila in the same moment. It was like thinking, all at once, about a fully unfolded blossom and a knotted bud. For a fleeting moment, Paul felt a surprising affection for Sheila—surprising because it was so unlike the needful longing he had once felt. She seemed to him in that moment not like a lover, but like a friend with whom he had been through hard times. He wished her well. Yes, he wished her well—but that was all.

Paul threw on his clothes, then left to meet Jessica.

◘ 25 ◘

Paul waited outside the dining hall until Jessica arrived, then they ate together and set off for class. When they got to the classroom, Jessica used a feature on her personal player to set new text for the wall outside the door. Once she had it set, Paul watched as she let it play through:

MODELING-REALITY CLASS

it read, then the image shimmered, and new words appeared:

CHANGING MODELS

Paul watched as the words on the wall faded and then took shape again:

> *The only real voyage of discovery...*
> *consists not in seeking new landscapes*
> *but in having new eyes.*
>
> —MARCEL PROUST

Satisfied that she had things set as she wished, Jessica entered the classroom and began checking to make sure the holoprojector was set properly. Paul followed her in and took a seat about three rows back. Soon, other students began to trickle in. Within a few minutes, most of the chairs were taken, and class began.

"Before we start," Jessica told the class, "let's review a little from the last couple of classes. Well, actually, I think it's mostly material from last Wednesday's class I'd like to review before we get started. I think it will help to have that material freshly in mind. If you'll remember, we talked about how, when two or more models pull you in two or more directions, they may act like a tug-of-war, which may leave you stalled in the middle, or otherwise muck up the works.

"Remember, when we talk about mental models and the way they take form in our lives, think of it as being like programming a machine. We're all, in effect, self-programming machines. The mental models we form are like programming. They tell us how to interpret the world around us. They define our perceptions, and the meanings we apply to them. They tell us what actions to take, and why. Without our mental models, we would take in sensory information, but we would see in it no patterns or meanings. We would see the star-filled sky above us, but we would find no constellations there.

"In short, it matters a great deal what models we form and carry, since so much of what we experience is based on them.

"So, can anybody give me an example of how mixed models generate mixed results in our practical experience in the world?" she asked. Paul was impressed, as he had been when watching her teach before, at how quickly and clearly she could make her point.

"Well," a young man in the second row said. He had long brown hair, and Paul remembered seeing him in the other classes. "For example," the man continued, "imagine someone who's a really good singer, who believes in his own talent and that he can make it as a professional singer—but who also for some reason pictures (that is, models) professional singers as all being really full of themselves, like divas, or something. So he tells himself that if he succeeds, he'll become someone he doesn't want to become."

"Right, or maybe," a young man in a striped shirt said, "he thinks that everybody will hate him if he's successful, because then other people will see him as being like a diva, even if he's not."

"Yeah," the man with the long brown hair continued, "either way, he'd be giving himself opposite messages—saying all at once, 'I can succeed—I should do it!' and 'I better not try for it—if I do, things will be bad.' And so he just gets stuck right in the middle. He might go through life finding himself over and over again on the doorstep of success, and then almost without noticing that he was doing it, he'd sabotage it, or come up with some excuse to reject his best opportunities."

"'Cause he'd set his programming to do both—so the two programming instructions sort of cancel each other out," the man with the striped shirt added.

Jessica smiled at them both. "Those are great answers from both of you," she said, then turned toward the rest of the class.

"We also talked some about the cyclical nature of modeling and perception," she went on. "So—let's say someone experiences something new, and in response to that new experience, they create a mental model to represent it. So then they have this new model, and because they have this new model, they generate experiences that give expression to it—that is, that somehow represent or replicate it in the world around them. Each of these replicating experiences, in turn, tends to reinforce and strengthen the new model. That is, each replicating experience makes the new model seem more relevant, true, and real. The more relevant, true, and real the model appears to be, the more it gets replicated in that person's experience—and so on, cycling round and round.

"Ultimately, that model about reality—that is, that belief—may come to be very strongly held. And of course, the more strongly someone believes in a model, the more vividly they replicate it their experience. It just keeps cycling, until finally, in such situations, the thing they have modeled will come to seem to them to be an obvious fact about reality—and not something that they've largely generated for themself," Jessica concluded.

"So, can anybody remember enough about what we talked about last week to give examples for this?" she asked the class.

"Yes," said a young woman with short dark hair. "I was thinking about this after class last week. It's like my friend, Calla. I've known her since we were kids. She won a contest for a science project when we were in, I think it was third grade. It was close, but she came out on top. I think winning it really affected how she saw herself. She saw herself as being successful—a successful person. I've watched her go through life, and she takes that attitude into everything she does. And because she believes she *can* succeed, she thinks it's worth trying, because she believes if she does try, she'll come out on top. She's always been successful at whatever she tries her hand at. She has to work hard for it, but she succeeds. It's just how she sees herself. And I think it gets reinforced with every new success. To her, it's just a fact—she's a success. That's how she is—that's *who* she is—as she sees it."

"It's a self-fulfilling prophecy," a middle-aged man to Paul's right said.

"Exactly," Jessica said. "Any more examples?" She looked around the class. Paul was interested in the discussion, but he nonetheless found himself being distracted by watching Jessica. Her eyes were lit, and she seemed entirely engaged in what she was doing. Her long dark hair seemed to flow around her shoulders as she turned her head to look around the classroom. Watching her now, Paul recalled the feeling of her next to him when he had first waked that morning, the feeling of her presence. What was it that made that feeling be so beautiful? he wondered. Like sunshine on a mountain lake—he just wanted to dive into it.

"It can work in the opposite direction, too," a rugged-looking man said. Paul looked over at him and recognized him from previous modeling-reality classes. A number of the other students looked familiar to Paul, as well.

"Some early failures," the man said, "and the person models themself as a failure. Then they don't put out effort when challenged, because, hey, they're going to fail anyway, right? So the model strengthens, and more and more it just seems like an obvious fact to them, that they were always bound to be a failure, as their life piles up with the 'proof' of one failure after another."

"Right—good example, Sam—and one I would like to emphasize, because it's such a great example of a situation where someone would want to make a conscious effort to change their model—which is the topic for today: how do we identify models we want to change, and how do we go about changing them?"

Paul smiled to himself as he thought about how Jessica was interacting with her students. A "good example," a "great example," she'd said. She was so encouraging toward anybody who made a contribution in class. And everyone responded to her with the same warmth and approval she showed to them.

"Clearly," Jessica continued, "there are good reasons to want to be conscious of and to deliberately choose the models you shape your life around. Most of you were here for earlier classes, so I don't want to spend too much time on review—but I do want to touch on a couple more points. We've already been over some of the basics of how to become conscious of the models we hold. Who can name two primary approaches?"

A young woman in the front put her hand up.

"Yes, Yaima," Jessica said.

"Consciously held beliefs are pretty easy to uncover," Yaima said. "You can make a list—kind of like a beliefs tree. You name one belief, and then you ask yourself why you believe it. Your answer will name other beliefs—other models of reality. You keep asking yourself questions about each one, and they'll branch out like a tree. For each question, whatever your answer is, that's another branch. By listing them all out, you get an overview and become more conscious of what they are."

"That's right," said a woman with graying hair, who was seated behind Paul at the back of the class, "and some of them are going to just seem like statements of fact when you tell yourself about them. But factual or not, they are your models. They tell you, you could say, which constellations you're prepared to see in the night's sky. It may be that to you they're fact, but to someone else—well, they might not see that constellation at all. They might connect those dots differently, make a different picture of them."

"Very good," Jessica said. "Which is much of the reason why people disagree about what is and isn't fact. We can all see the same stars, but we make different constellations of them.

"Okay, and the second approach that we discussed before, about how to become conscious of the models you hold?" Jessica said. "I think you were about to answer, Yaima."

"Yes, some models we aren't so conscious of. One of the main ways of uncovering them is to be very watchful about what you tell yourself—like if, for example, you don't show up for work and so you get fired from your job, and you hear yourself say to yourself, 'Well, they were going to fire me sooner or later anyway,' well, there's a key belief—a model of what you thought was going to happen."

"And so maybe that's why that person didn't show up for work in the first place," Sam said.

"Right," Yaima replied, looking over at Sam, "because if they were going to fire you anyway, why bother to show up?" She shrugged. "Right? But then you create it for yourself. It seems like it's a fact, because it's what you experienced—but it wasn't a fact until you made it one. It happened because you modeled it that way. The model came first. The model made the 'fact' happen. In that context, the model is the more powerful thing."

"Good, good," Jessica said. "So in that approach to becoming conscious of your models, someone models getting fired, and so behaves in a way that actually gets them fired—but is observant enough about what they're telling themself to catch on to what's happening.

"So the point is that you can observe some models—models, for example, that you just take to be fact—first by simply listening to what you tell yourself, and second by noticing patterns in your own experience that you might be curious about, and then asking yourself what your beliefs are about them. So if you keep getting fired from one job after another, for example, it would be wise to ask yourself how you have modeled those events."

Jessica paused for just a moment, then went on. "Paying attention to your dreams can also be useful in uncovering less consciously held models," she said. "If you probe into what your dreams mean or represent, you'll often uncover the models that define those meanings and symbols."

As Jessica spoke, Paul was aware of how conversational her tone was. It was clear that she genuinely wanted to communicate with the people in the class.

"Also, it's helpful to pay attention to shifts in your moods," she said. "If you notice a sudden shift, ask yourself what you were thinking just before your mood shifted. Usually, there will be a belief there—a model about reality, that is—to which you are responding emotionally. And remember, any emotion you feel will be linked to the mental model or models that frame the situation you are responding to emotionally. So if you look behind any emotion, you will find the model that gives rise to it."

She glanced around the class. Most of the people looked thoughtful or were nodding their heads slightly.

"So—wait," the young man in the striped shirt said, "if you're in a house that's on fire, and you feel scared—where's the mental model there? I mean, isn't that just a direct link—there's fire, and so you're scared, with no model? I mean, it's just a fact."

Jessica thought for a moment. "In that case, Vic, I'd say there are at least two mental models at work. One is the perception of the fire itself. The other is that the fire is dangerous."

"The *perception of the fire* is a mental model?" Vic said.

"Yes," Jessica said, nodding, "our mental models allow us to comprehend what our senses tell us. They give cohesion and meaning to what would otherwise be merely a scattered assortment of physical sensations. 'Fire,' as a concept, is a mental model. Fire without the mental model is nothing more than assorted sensations of heat and light. To be scared, you need first to have a conception of 'fire,' as such—and second, to conceive of it as dangerous. Both conceptions require modeling."

"Remember, everybody, modeling is involved at the most basic levels of our perceptions," Jessica said, looking around the class, "Our perceptions of the world depend on our models. As we discussed last week, the stars are in the sky, but the constellations are in our minds. The models we form shape our experience. They motivate our actions and define for us the world we understand ourselves to live in. They interpret, define, and shape the events that we experience."

"Okay, that's enough review. Just remember that the mental models we form about reality have significant influence on the lives we actually live. It matters, therefore, just what our mental models are. If we want to change our experience, the best place to start is with the models we hold."

Jessica smiled as she looked around the class. "So, here's the main question for today," she said. "What if someone discovers that they hold a model that is generating some result they don't like? What steps can that person take to change that model?

"Let's use the person Yaima just described as an example—someone who believes they're going to get fired no matter what they do, so they don't bother to do the things necessary to keep from getting fired. For whatever reason, that's the constellation that that person sees when they look at the star field of their life, and it's entirely real to them—a fact. How would they go about changing their vision of what they can expect from life? How do we rewrite such perceptions, when those perceptions seem to us to simply be factual?"

Jessica tilted her head and spoke into her personal player. The classroom lights dimmed slightly as a holoprojection appeared at the front of the room.

"The answer to this question involves three basic steps," she said, then turned and read the words that were floating in midair at the front of the classroom:

IMAGINATIVELY CREATE A NEW MODEL

ESTABLISH AND BELIEVE IN PRACTICAL BASIS FOR THE NEW MODEL

· THROUGH AN ACT OF FAITH

· THROUGH ANALYSIS AND ANCHORING

· THROUGH EXPERIENCE

DISMANTLE THE OLD MODEL YOU WANT TO REPLACE

As Jessica finished, she turned back toward the class. "Okay, like I was saying, let's imagine that I was working with, for example, a young man who kept getting fired, like Yaima described. What steps could he take to change that model, that expectation that he would just get fired, anyway?

"The first step," Jessica said, answering her own question, "would be for him to create a contrasting model—a model of how he would like things to be. When you do this, you don't, at first, have to believe that the new model is real. Just start off playfully imagining it.

"Start with the ideal. Imagine what you long for, what inspires you. Follow your protolife. If something is truly impractical, you may have to look for a different route or a different way or a different form of what you dream of—but be careful, when forming a new model, not to assume that good things are impossible, because this can then become a self-fulfilling prophecy.

"As you imagine your new model, try to fill in what practical steps would be necessary to make it a reality. This is similar to an artist envisioning a painting they'd like to do, and then going on to consider what sort of canvas and paints would be needed to create it. We're talking about taking practical steps to get the results you want in your life. The more realistic and practical those steps, the more entirely you will be able to give expression to the model you've formed.

"Which brings us to the next step. If you're going to act on your new model, you're going to have to feel confident that it's realistic and practical. You have to be able to imagine it taking form in your life, just as an artist must be able to imagine their vision taking form on the canvas before them. Until that vision, that model, solidifies into a belief, and no longer seems a mere fantasy, you will not take action based on it. Until the artist *believes* their vision will take form on the canvas, they will not act. To bring what you have modeled into your life, you must believe in it, not merely wish for it.

"So, there are three basic steps you can take to accomplish that," Jessica continued. "I'll call them: faith, analysis, and experience.

"Faith is a very basic approach for bridging that gap between fantasy and belief," she said. "It's simply a matter of imagining the new model and telling yourself that it represents how things are or will be. It's handy if it works—often it's not enough to do just this.

"Analysis," Jessica continued, "can be a bit more complicated, but may be more effective at establishing a new model as a belief. Explain to yourself how the old model was generating its old results, and how you will get new results from the new model. Create logical arguments about how the new model makes sense. I'm not, by the way, suggesting you disregard reality. Don't, for example, tell yourself that you can fly just by jumping off a cliff and flapping your arms, and then try to get yourself to believe it."

A few people chuckled.

"But of course, you'd have trouble coming up with a logical argument for believing in that, wouldn't you? However, if you do long for flight," Jessica went on, "don't hesitate to tell yourself that there may be some practical and safe way to simulate that experience.

"What I'm saying is, don't disregard factual reality—but also don't allow yourself to get into the habit of assuming that the particular constellations you've been living with all your life are the only reasonable patterns possible. Sometimes it can be a challenge to decide whether something actually, practically, can be made real—but that challenge is part of the adventure of living. So strive for what you choose to strive for, and if you think it can be made practical and real, then reinforce the model you choose by telling yourself exactly *why* it can be practical and real. Believe in it precisely because you do see *how* it can be made real, or see *why* you know it already is real. Prepare yourself with your paints and easels, so to speak. Take practical steps, think practical thoughts. And do your best to give life to the possibilities brimming within you."

As Paul listened to all of this, he thought about how really remarkable it was that people on this world thought so deliberately about their own "self-programming," and about what they needed to do to get desirable results in their lives and in the world around them. In contrast, on his world, it seemed to Paul, people were mostly trying to run away from themselves, and the harsh world they had collectively created.

Paul remembered what it was like to be out on the street on his earth, and how people would flow past him, their minds filled with the pacifying pabulum broadcast on the Stream. It was so different from this world, where people thought about their "inner machinery" and ways of bringing their own native potential to life.

It seemed to Paul that the publication of Indira Kumar's memoirs had been like a stone sent rolling down a hill, gathering momentum as it went. She deserved a great deal of credit for all that had changed on this world, Paul thought—but so did all the other people of this earth, who had turned that one stone into an avalanche of stones, large and small, all rolling together, all contributing to the transformation of this world.

Paul turned his attention back to the class.

"Which brings us to anchoring," Jessica was saying. She glanced again at the holoprojection behind her. "To really shore up those practical, logical arguments and help them become securely set within the framework of your thinking, anchor them to your most fundamental and basic models of reality—to your foundational beliefs—just as you would anchor a house to its foundations."

A man seated to Paul's right raised his hand. "But, well," the man said, "how do you know which of your beliefs are really foundational?"

"That's a good question," Jessica said, then looked thoughtful for a moment. "We all have a set of fundamental beliefs—fundamental models of reality— that we accept wholeheartedly. These fundamental beliefs act as the foundations upon which we each build a larger network or structure of beliefs.

"So, if you have a model or belief," Jessica went on, "that you feel very strongly about and that is very basic to your viewpoint—that seems, somehow, elemental to your way of seeing things—then that belief is probably foundational for you. You could say that foundational beliefs form the bedrock of your perspective. It's not that foundational beliefs can't be changed, only that—because they are so essential to our way of thinking, and seeing, and interpreting the world— they tend to be especially stable and enduring parts of our perspectives.

"Everybody has their own set of foundational beliefs, though some are quite common," Jessica went on, looking around the class. "Common foundational beliefs might be, for example, that it's good for parents to love their kids, and that indiscriminate violence is bad. Some of mine," she thought for a moment, "are that kindness and affection should be encouraged, and that people should be careful not to cause pain or harm to others.

"Because foundational beliefs are such solid, consistent aspects of our perspectives, we can build on them, just as a house can be built on its foundation. With my foundational beliefs, for example, I might reason out from there that helping a stranger who has—oh, say—been injured and is in need of help, would be a good thing to do. Why? Because it's kind, and it works against pain and harm.

"Because that conclusion is so consistent with my foundational beliefs," Jessica went on, "and because I can see that it's consistent, that conclusion— that it's good to help a stranger under those circumstances—is anchored to those foundations within myself. That conclusion is, therefore, very securely and strongly set in place within myself. It could be buffeted by waves, so to speak, or assaulted by gale-force winds—but it will not be moved. It is anchored to the foundations of my viewpoint, and for this reason it will stay with me as long as those foundations stay in place.

"So, the point here is, if you want to really securely establish a new model, show yourself how that model is a natural outgrowth of your foundational beliefs. Doing this will anchor the new model in place."

Jessica turned again and glanced over the words floating in the air, while Paul watched. He had been taking in every detail of what she said to the class and of her interactions with the students—and had been feeling delighted, all the while, that this warm and beautiful and clever woman had chosen him as someone to form an especially close relationship with.

"So," Jessica said, as she turned back toward the class. For a moment, she caught Paul's eye and smiled a brief, warm smile at him. "If you want to create a new model and make it a stable part of your viewpoint," she told the class, "first imagine that model; then show yourself the reasonable, practical basis for believing in that model; then anchor those reasons, those arguments, to your foundational beliefs.

"Okay, that brings us to reinforcing through experience," she said. "Imagining a new model is an abstract process. When you actually experience a new model, it seems concrete, actual—it seems, therefore, more real.

"So, to really set a new model in place," she went on, "look for some way of experiencing it, as a practical matter, in the real world. If you're trying to see yourself as a success, for example, doing even small things that you know you will succeed at will help set that model in place. If you have a dream that you want to make come true, try to think of other things you have wished for that have actually come to pass. Imagine that your new wish will, then, also come true.

"These sort of tangible confirming experiences can be large or small, literal or symbolic. They may take place in the present, or you may draw on memories of your past. Imagining how future events may give form and action to your new model is helpful, also.

"It can be useful, as well, to surround yourself with other people who already hold the model you're trying to establish in yourself—people's whose viewpoints and beliefs agree with the viewpoints and beliefs you're trying to establish. This will help to reinforce those views.

"In short, in whatever ways you can, create an experiential backdrop for the new model. Put it in context in the practical world."

Jessica glanced back toward the holoprojection. "Removing unwanted models," she read aloud, then faced the class. "Sometimes the first three steps are not enough. Sometimes we go to all this trouble, and then find ourselves backsliding into old perspectives. In those cases, those old mental models need to be identified and deliberately removed.

"If you ever need to remove—instead of simply replace—an old model, you can set about it by doing just the opposite of what you would do to establish a new model."

Jessica held up one hand, then counted off with her fingers.

"First, you have to identify the problem model of reality that you want to change.

"Second, build an argument to prove to yourself that the problem model is not reasonable or realistic. Show yourself how the experiences that had reinforced it were merely the result of a self-fulfilling prophecy.

"Third, remember old experiences that run contrary to it and create new experiences that contradict it.

"If you're still having problems with it, look for ways the unwanted model may have become anchored to one or more of your foundational beliefs. Do the foundational beliefs need adjusting or changing? If so, it is possible to change foundational beliefs—though it may take more work than with other models.

"Let's say, well, that Sam, here, was trying to establish a new model that would allow him to be more forgiving toward people who had treated him poorly.

"I hope you don't mind me picking you for an example, Sam," she said, looking over at the rugged-looking man.

"Not a bit, Jessica," Sam said.

Jessica smiled at him, then went on. "So, let's say Sam was trying to create a new model for his behavior in which he pictured himself being more forgiving, but that when problems came up, he found himself feeling just as bitter as before. He deals with this by asking himself a lot of questions about how he sees these situations, and realizes he is still in possession of a rather antiquated foundational belief, given to him in early childhood—that is, deep down, he believes that some people are just plain bad."

From around the room, Paul heard several people chuckle. He noticed that Jessica also seemed amused.

"Well, you know, I'm just an old-fashioned guy," Sam said dryly.

"Well," Jessica went on, smiling, "he can hardly forgive people who are, at the most essential level, just plain bad, can he? In other words, he has the sort of problem we talked about earlier, where two models get in the way of one another. But now Sam has figured out what the problems is, and he's determined to make progress..."

Sam glanced around the room, nodding and smiling playfully.

"...so he sets about trying to remove this outdated foundational belief from his thinking. He consciously creates arguments to help him dismantle that foundational belief and replace it with another. He works on it for a while, carefully excavating it and setting it aside.

"Of course, when you remove a foundational belief, a lot of other models that rest on it are likely to shift, too—so a lot of things change for Sam, very quickly, then—and, since Sam rid himself of a particularly negative foundational belief, they change for the better.

"My point is, our beliefs—our models of reality—don't exist alone. They're tied together in networks, and may form interesting interrelationships.

"You may all remember, for example, the story Dr. Kumar wrote about late in her memoirs, about her student who was a white supremacist? She refused to take his bigotry seriously, even though she herself was dark skinned—that is, even though his bigotry was directed toward her. Does anybody remember what happened?"

"They became friends—or at least quite friendly with one another," the older woman who sat behind Paul said.

"Could you say exactly why that was possible?" Jessica asked.

"Yes," the woman said, looking thoughtful, "Dr. Kumar was always friendly to him and helped him with his school work whenever he had trouble with it. The way she saw it, he was insecure and that was why he had to keep telling himself that the group he identified with was better than any other group of people. She kept pointing out to him the things he did well, and he got so he really liked her, came back and took another class with her the next semester, and at the end of the year he came to her office and told her how much she had influenced him—that he'd realized that the group he identified with (that is, people of European descent) weren't all better than everybody else, because everybody else included people like her."

"Yeah, and that was okay, he said, because he'd figured out that he was pretty good on his own, anyhow," Vic said. "I liked that story."

"Yes, I liked it, too, Vic," Jessica said. "And as I remember it, Dr. Kumar wrote that if she had simply tried to tell him, from the start, that he was wrong about his white-supremacist beliefs, that it would have seemed to him that she was attacking him—which would only have made him feel more insecure and so caused him to cling all the more intensely to the defense he had erected around his insecurity. That is, he would have clung even more to the deluded belief that he was superior because of his heritage.

"The point I'm trying to make is that sometimes our models of reality are linked together, so that to change one model, you have to also change another that it rests upon. Sometimes one model creates, in effect, a need for another, just as that young man's low self-esteem created in him a need for a kind of antidote. In his case, that antidote took the form of a belief that the group he identified with was a superior group.

"So, if you want to change a model, and you find yourself hesitating to let it go, try to see if it's useful to you in some way, and if it is, perhaps you can find a way to address that need in some other, more constructive, way.

"Okay," Jessica said, looking around the room, "are there any questions before we end the class?"

She waited for a minute, but no one spoke, and no hands went up.

"Well, either that all went especially well, or I have all of you completely befuddled," she said, smiling.

"It all went well, Jessica," Sam said.

"Good job," Paul heard someone behind him say.

"Yes," someone else echoed, as the class in general nodded and murmured "yes."

Jessica smiled and looked all around the room. "Well, I hope so," she said, then added, "We have just a couple of minutes left, and I have a quote I'd like to share with you." She turned her head a little and spoke to her personal player once more. As she did, the holoprojection of the list of ways to establish a new model faded. In its place, a holoprojection of a wall engraving appeared. Jessica read aloud what was written there:

> *Whatsoever . . . you find to be conducive to the good,*
> *the benefit, the welfare of all beings—that doctrine*
> *believe and cling to, and take it as your guide.*
>
> —BUDDHA

When she was done reading, she turned to the class and said, "Dr. Kumar copied that text over into her journal on September 14th, 2016, then wrote next to it, 'Good guide—and a good basis for a foundational model.' I would have to agree. I'll just leave you with that as a little food for thought.

"Well, that's all for today!" she said. "Come next Wednesday, same time, for those who are interested in hearing more on the subject of 'modeling reality.'"

Jessica gave another command to her personal player. As she did, the holo-projection faded and the lights came up in the classroom. The students rose, then, and began to filter out of the classroom, with some stopping to thank Jessica on their way out.

As they left, Paul sat in his chair, watching. He smiled to himself as he recalled having woken, just hours before, in the arms of the lively, beautiful, and intelligent woman he saw before him now. Only a few days before he would have thought such a thing impossible. Now, with the constellation of his life rewritten and his confidence increased, it seemed not so much unbelievable, as simply a very wonderful thing.

As the last students drifted out of the classroom, Paul rose and stepped toward Jessica, even as she turned toward him, her face lit radiantly with an affectionate smile.

▫ 26 ▫

When class was over, Paul and Jessica talked a little. Jessica had a novice sojourner she'd promised to meet with after class, and suggested that Paul join her a little while later, for lunch in the dining hall.

Paul agreed, then returned to his room, where he sat down on the edge of his bed and tried to take in all that had happened in the last few days. It seemed to him as though he had spent his life climbing up a very tall and steep mountain and had, just in the past few days, reached a peak from which he could look back over the land through which he had been traveling and understand the path he had taken through life, and the meaning it had had for him.

Why was it, then, Paul wondered, that he felt so confused while taking in his life from this high vantage point? As rocky and difficult as the path up to this point had been, the way down on the other side seemed, now, to Paul, just as uncertain. If he went forward as he had planned, he would hand Corprogov the keys to this world, and they would destroy it. And if he chose not to return to his own world, and so keep the keys from their grasp, he would extinguish any hope he had ever dreamed of for his earth and the people of it—and they would be lost forever in a mire of their own making.

But Paul's confusion went deeper, even, than that. If he stayed on this world and left his Depopulation Project behind, unfinished, then every ounce of effort he had put into his dream of saving his world would come to nothing. This passion, this purpose, this life's work would, in the archives of his world, amount to no more than a footnote marking a failed experiment—a hapless effort that was never even worth the energy credits spent on it.

Paul put his head in his hands. Maybe there could be some third way, he told himself. If he could not bear to pass through either of these two doors, perhaps some third doorway could be found. Paul thought about the class he had attended that morning. It was clear to him that however he envisioned his future—however he modeled it and whichever model he chose—would have far-reaching implications for the peoples of both his world and this. Whatever he chose, he must choose carefully.

Paul looked up and around the room. A quote on the wall opposite his bed caught his eye. It read:

Face everything with love.

— LAL DED

Yes, Paul thought, these simple aphorisms posted around the Retreat were appealing—but what *practical* path should he pursue now?

Paul stood and looked out the window at the Retreat outside. It was, truly, a beautiful world. He mustn't act recklessly. He would wait until later to decide just what he would do. For now, he had his energy supply, his transport plans, and his price sheet. If he chose to return to his world, all that was left for him to do to accomplish this goal would be to earn sufficient money with which to buy parts, and to actually build the transport itself. And *that*, Paul told himself, would be very simple to do, now that he had done it in virtual form, using the portal's 3D holographic display.

And of course, he told himself, as he considered this further, if he did choose to stay and not return to his own world, he would need money then, too, to live on. It was all the same. In either case, the next thing he needed was to earn money—and to earn it working at the job he preferred, he would need to study physics, as it was known and understood on this world. He would need to become well versed in all that had been learned on this world in the field of physics since the branching point that had set these two worlds on their separate courses.

Yes, this was clearly the right plan, Paul told himself. Whether he chose to stay or to go, that was what he had to do next.

◙   ◙   ◙

Paul met Jessica a little while later for lunch. They took their plates out into the meadow beyond the dining hall and visited in the sunshine. That night, he joined her again for dinner—which they shared in her room, where the crowds wouldn't bother them.

During the days that followed, Jessica taught her classes or worked with other sojourners, while Paul began his study of physics, using the portal in his room to access the information he needed. Having completed his stage-three exercises, he found nobody seemed to expect him to do much more, so he was left on his own to study as he wished.

Day after day, it was like this—Jessica would spend the days teaching, or working with novice sojourners, or engaging in quiet meditation for Kumaric work of her own, while Paul studied in his room, steadily probing the discoveries that more than a century of physics research had brought about on this world.

The evenings were theirs, though—except on those nights when Paul had to wash dishes. He and Jessica would come together, visiting over dinner in Jessica's room, then spend each night tenderly asleep in one another's arms. As this was Paul's only experience with madu friendships, what he shared with Jessica defined for him what a madu friendship was—but for those who knew Jessica and how such friendships normally developed, it was clear to them that something special was going on.

Each morning Paul woke happier than he had the day before. Soon, he found himself wondering how he had lived for twenty-nine years of his life without ever realizing that he could feel such happiness. Sometimes he would think about this odd friendship he and Jessica had created and wonder if it would be more or better if they could physically make love, as well—but he knew it wasn't what she had invited, and so wasn't her choice; and he knew, too, that as long as he might leave her world and leave her behind with it, he had no right to ask her to feel more deeply for him than this. And that's just what he would be asking, he knew, if the relationship went any further.

Often, Paul wondered what Jessica would say if he told her the truth about his world and what sort of life he had come from—but each time the conversation edged in that direction, Paul grew tense, and either he himself turned the conversation away from the topic, or Jessica opened up a new channel through which the conversation could flow.

Once Jessica asked Paul about his "mysterious upbringing," and Paul deflected the question with a joke. She looked at him carefully, then—as she had on other occasions before—then she left the subject behind, as though she understood that, for whatever reason, he wasn't ready to tell her about it. It seemed to Paul that she was waiting, giving him time to come to it on his own.

When Paul wasn't with Jessica or busy studying, he often worried about what he would do when he left the Retreat. He had only a few days left in his stay there and just a little money set aside—not enough to last him long at all. He wondered if he could earn more money mapping fields, like he had done for Anna when he first came to this world, or perhaps find other odd jobs. He would have to live frugally, he told himself, until his studies were done, and he could get a job with an adequate income. Perhaps he could find a small room to rent, someplace, and keep his costs low. He wouldn't need much room in which to live and construct his transport—and certainly he was accustomed to small spaces on his world.

But as carefully as Paul planned out how he would make this all work, he was aware that there was much about this earth he still did not know. He understood that whatever he planned might have little to do with what would actually happen when his stay at the Retreat was up.

And so the week went on, with both Paul and Jessica involved in their own pursuits by day, then coming together after their daytime activities and other obligations had passed.

The week went by quickly—far faster for Paul than the week before—and soon it was Friday. That evening, he and Jessica shared a hurried meal in her room before he left to wash dishes, promising to return as soon as he could—but the mound of dishes, pots, and pans he found in the Retreat's kitchen took him longer to wash then he had hoped or expected.

When Paul finally arrived at Jessica's room that night, he found her already asleep in her bed. He slipped off his shoes, then lay down beside her. Groggily, Jessica rolled over toward him and pulled herself closer to him.

"I'm glad you came," she whispered softly.

"Me, too," Paul said.

They lay in silence for a minute, with her face near his and her arm around his waist. Paul placed his hand over hers, then turned and kissed her lightly on the forehead. Though they were silent, he could feel that she was still awake next to him.

After a minute or two, her voice drifted softly into the darkness, "I have this feeling whenever I'm with you, Paul," she whispered. "It's like there are whole worlds in you I know nothing about. I want to know about those worlds, Paul—the worlds that are inside you. I know you're not ready, yet—but when you are..." Her voice trailed off. Then she added, "I want to discover you, Paul."

Jessica nestled her head against Paul's shoulder, then, as though settling in for sleep—as though, Paul realized, she expected no response.

Paul lifted Jessica's hand to his lips and kissed the back of it.

"Thanks, Jessica," he said, so quietly that he wondered if she even heard him say it.

Paul lay there for several minutes, then, wondering if he should say something more, and listening to Jessica's breathing, until he heard her breaths slow, and realized she had fallen back to sleep.

◧   ◧   ◧

The first light of day crept in around the curtains and lifted Paul from his slumber. He opened his eyes and rolled onto his side. As he looked at Jessica sleeping, he felt happy all over again just to wake beside her.

How was it that she could lift his mood just by being near him? he wondered, not minding at all that he had been pulled up from a deep sleep for this. It wasn't at all like it had been with Sheila, Paul told himself. For one thing, it wasn't Jessica's appearance that inspired him—though in truth, she was quite beautiful. It was the feeling he had whenever he was with her, as though something of who she was washed over him, clearing away doubts and worries, and so brightening each day. With Sheila, he had always felt unsure, swept up in a longing that was never really met. With Jessica, it seemed, what he was feeling was the answer to that longing.

How could he continue to deceive her? Paul wondered. Well, not deceive her, exactly, but leave her out of the truth about himself, and what his life had been. If he did tell her, was there any chance she would believe him? he wondered.

Paul tried to imagine how he would do it, if he did tell her. Would he start by explaining to her the many-worlds interpretation of quantum mechanics, and how it suggested that there are, in fact, many different versions of the universe, and within it, many different versions of earth, all existing like branches growing off the same stalk?

Perhaps. That part, at least, would be safe enough. He could tell her, then, perhaps, more about his research, and his desire to travel to another world, and how this might be made possible by first stepping out of space-time, and then back into it at the appropriate spot.

Yes, he could tell her that much, at least. And if she accepted it, he could tell her that he had tried it, once—by accident—and that he had wound up here, on another earth, on her earth—which was like another branch, different from the world that was his own.

Paul rolled onto his back and stared up at the ceiling. Was it possible that she would believe him? Paul dreaded the possibility that she would think he was lying—or possibly insane.

He looked over at Jessica, again. And even if she believed that, he told himself, that was only half of it, wasn't it? Because she would ask him about the project, and what he had wanted it to accomplish—and that would bring them to what he was doing here, on her world, and what he still thought he might do to it.

No, Paul told himself, shaking his head. He couldn't tell her that, even if she might believe him about the other. He pictured her face as he described to her his plans—and the look of horror as the full realization, as the full import, of what he was telling her settled like a sickening dust around her.

No, he couldn't tell her that. He wasn't ready—and perhaps he never would be ready to tell *that* to her.

Paul raised himself up on one elbow and looked again at Jessica's sleeping face. She seemed so perfect, so precious. Could he really do that to her world? How could he be worthy of this warm and beautiful woman if he would even consider it?

But what if he didn't do it? What if he never returned to his world—never returned at all, and just stayed here?

Paul knew too well what that would mean. That same sickening dust would gather like a cloak around his world, and choke his entire earth to death.

When Paul woke again, Jessica was awake and already dressed. Paul glanced over at the brilliant glow around the curtains and realized he must have slept again for another couple of hours.

Jessica sat down on the side of the bed. "I'm glad you're awake," she said. "I was afraid you'd sleep through breakfast."

"How soon is it?" Paul asked.

"They start serving in, well," Jessica glanced at the clock, "about fifteen minutes."

Paul looked at her.

"Good morning," she said, smiling.

"Good morning," Paul answered.

Jessica sat quietly for a moment, while Paul stretched and sat up.

"Paul," she said, "there's something I was going to talk to you about last night, after you got done—but it got late, so I went on to bed." She paused.

"What is it?" Paul asked.

"Well, you may remember I told you I'd have to be back at work on Monday?"

Paul nodded. He hadn't forgotten. She had told him, on the day she had invited him to be her madu friend, that she would have to be back at work in just over a week. Paul just hadn't wanted to think about how quickly the week was coming to an end.

"This past week has gone by so fast," Jessica said, then frowned a little, while looking down at her hands. Paul reached over and held her hand.

"And what about you, Paul?" Jessica asked. "Your time must be nearly up, too. Will you be going back to your job in Strandford?"

"No," Paul said. "I, ah, I don't need to be back right away."

"How soon, then?" Jessica asked.

"Well, actually, it's, ah, it's sort of open ended," Paul said.

Jessica looked at Paul. A slow, curious smile gathered around the corners of her mouth.

"A job you don't have to go to," she said, smiling fully now. "Interesting. You are such a man of mystery, Paul." She looked at him for a moment, then added, "Okay—well, I was thinking about this last night, before you came over." Paul didn't miss the fact that she had, again, easily let the subject pass.

"I've been liking having you around, Paul," Jessica said, looking Paul in the eye, her eyes deep and dark. "I wish I could see more of you. I've been sad that I would have to leave and that you would go back to Strandford. But if you really do have some free time," Jessica raised her eyebrows as she looked at Paul, "then I was thinking it would be nice if you would come to my house with me. I'll have work to do, but I'll have time in the evenings and on weekends. We could still spend time together."

Paul smiled. If he had been given a choice of any place in the world to go—on this world or his own—there was no place he would rather be than with Jessica.

Paul's smile widened. "How long did you have in mind?" he asked.

"A while. I don't know," Jessica said. "How long do you have in mind?"

"I don't know. A while." Paul squeezed her hand. "I'll come with you, Jessica. I'd love to come with you," he said.

◘   ◘   ◘

The next morning, they both gathered their few possessions together—and just after lunch, they carried them out to Jessica's SPV, which was parked in the long, narrow parking lot at the base of the rise leading up to the south side of the Retreat.

As Jessica set her bag in the trunk, she said to Paul, "I've been thinking about that dream I had the first night you stayed over."

"Yeah—what dream?" Paul asked, pushing his pack in next to Jessica's bag.

"You know—I told you about it. You disappeared in a flash of light." She shook her head a little, as though to say, "how odd!"

"Oh, yeah," Paul said, suddenly remembering the dream. Why had she dreamed *that*?

"I've been reflecting on it, trying to understand what it meant."

"Yeah? And?"

"I think it's about Kade, really—you remember, the man I told you about, who went to Massachusetts?"

"Oh, yeah," Paul said.

"I think it's because I was getting close to someone so soon after he left— you know, like he disappeared, and maybe you would, too? I really hadn't thought it affected me that way—to make me worry like that—but maybe it did." Jessica closed the trunk, then went around to the driver's door of the narrow, low-slung SPV. "Anyway, I think that makes some sense—about why I dreamed it."

"Huh," Paul said. "A flash of light?"

"Yes. It was brilliant. Funny dream, huh?"

"Funny," Paul said.

Jessica climbed into the front seat of the SPV, as Paul took the seat behind hers—then they set off on their drive, winding north through the highlands of the San Rafael Range, down through its chaparral-covered foothills, and on toward the Cuyama Valley, which Jessica called home.

PART V

◧

EMERGENCE

◌ 27 ◌

By mid-afternoon, Paul and Jessica had arrived at Jessica's house, which was outside of the town of New Cuyama, in the Cuyama Valley. Jessica showed Paul around, then they took a little time to get settled in.

They spent that evening dining and visiting with some of Jessica's friends and family, who were all eager to see her upon her return—and who, to Paul's surprise and pleasure, seemed to accept him right away. It was an enjoyable evening, which seemed to pass as quickly as pleasurable activities often seem to do.

That night, Paul and Jessica slept for the first time in Jessica's bed, where they cuddled for a while before falling asleep. Paul woke the next morning, wishing all over again that he and Jessica could be more than madu friends. It seemed to Paul that every hour he spent with her awakened something new in him, something he then wanted to share with her, to give to her. He wished he could be with her passionately, to stroke, and touch, and love her in ways that only a lover could do.

Paul opened his eyes and looked around the room. Light filtered in around the curtains covering the large sliding glass door, which—Paul knew from exploring the house the day before—opened onto the back deck. The room was lit with a soft glow.

As Paul expected, Jessica wasn't there. She had told him the night before that she would have to leave first thing the next morning for an early appointment at her office in New Cuyama, and that she wouldn't be home until late afternoon.

The room seemed somehow empty without her there, Paul thought, then wished again that his relationship with her could deepen. She was so intelligent and gentle, so beautiful and receptive. He longed to be with her in every way possible, to pour himself into her, to let the fire smoldering within him surface and burn through them both.

Paul's thoughts swirled around these ideas, gathering details about how it might be for the two of them to be together. He lay there for several minutes, imagining. And then, abruptly, he pushed these thoughts away. There was no point in thinking about her like that, he told himself. She didn't invite it, and it just wasn't the way things were between them.

And yet, as much as Paul felt sure that that was so, he couldn't help wondering if there was any chance at all that Jessica might feel this way about him, too. He knew, from what Jessica had told him about madu friendships, that he mustn't try to coax her with his body, for in going against their agreement he would damage her trust. He thought about talking to her about it, but that thought didn't seem right, either. In truth, the sweetness Paul had discovered in their simple madu relationship so far surpassed anything he had ever found with a lover that it seemed to him, almost, as though it would be ruined if they ever did, actually, make love.

Paul rose and stretched. Besides, he reminded himself, if he still might transport himself back to his own world, that would mean leaving Jessica behind, here. It was one thing to snuggle with someone and then disappear out of their life forever, Paul told himself; it would be another thing, entirely, to become that person's lover and then disappear like that.

Whatever Paul's actions might potentially mean to Jessica's world, he felt it would be too cruel to treat Jessica, herself, as callously as that. Unless he could commit to staying, Paul told himself, he should accept the relationship as it was. He cared too much for Jessica to do otherwise.

Paul went into the kitchen and fixed his breakfast, then carried it outside to eat on the back deck. The morning was warm compared to the mornings in the mountains, and Paul felt eager to soak up the warmth and sunshine.

As he sat down, he looked around, taking in the view. The land was flat here, stretching out for many kilometers between the Sierra Madre Mountains to the southwest (from which Paul and Jessica had just come), and the Caliente Range to the east and north. Through the long valley between them ran the Cuyama River. Paul had walked down to its bank the evening before (where it lay, not more than a stone's throw from the house) and seen the broad, deep trench it had cut through the land—as though a powerful river flowed there, though at this time, in the summer, it was no more than a stream.

Along the Cuyama's banks grew cattails and reeds, as well as cottonwood trees and willows. Beyond the river, the land was dotted with blue oaks, chamise, and saltbrush—and above all that was the sky, an endless blue, arching from horizon to horizon.

From where Paul now sat, looking out from the deck through the spreading branches of the old cottonwood tree that grew between Jessica's house and the river, he could see the wide expanse of the Caliente Range rising along the eastern horizon and wrapping around to the north. His eye was drawn, especially, to a cliff face to the northeast of where he sat. He had noticed it the day before, gleaming as white as chalk in the afternoon sun. Even now, shaded in the morning light, it still seemed brilliant to Paul, like a jewel set prominently in this rugged and beautiful land.

Paul took it all in as he ate—the spaciousness and vitality of the scene around him—and felt amazed all over again that such a world might exist, and that he would find himself on it.

Sitting there, then, Paul began to think back over the day before. The drive down from the Retreat had been spectacular, with one breathtaking vista after another, as they swooped and curved their way out of the mountains, descending in a little over an hour from a height that it had taken Paul almost a week to attain on his hike. The most remarkable part of all, for Paul, had come when they reached the lowlands and encountered a vast herd of pronghorn antelope crossing the road. They had eased the SPV through the herd, while the antelope leapt and sprinted to get out of their way. Even so, with individual antelope clearing the road so quickly, the herd was so immense that it took Jessica and Paul nearly five minutes to make their way through it.

Paul enjoyed the trip down like nothing else in his life, for it was this land, the same sort of broad and vital land that he had hiked through, that they drove through on their way to Jessica's home—and yet, from the SPV, Paul could take it all in so much more quickly, like a sightseer viewing one vista after another, with his breath stolen by each.

The fact that the trip was so pleasurable made Paul no less pleased to arrive at Jessica's house—a flat-roofed, cottage-size building nearly the same color as the land around it. Paul recalled climbing the steps to the narrow front deck and entering through her front door—and how Jessica had paused, then, to show him the copy of *Memories and Reflections* she kept open on a bookstand in the little entry area just inside the door.

"I was so delighted when I found that," she told Paul, "—a first edition of the actual *physical* book. It's in good shape, too. That's hard to find—they were all passed around so much. I paid a month's income for it—it means that much to me. To think of all that book changed, and all the difference it made in the world, and how this *very* copy was there at the beginning of it all!"

Jessica paused, then added, "I have a copy—a physical copy—of *The Little Book*, too. But it's not so nice. Seventeenth edition, I think that one is, and paperback, not hardback. It's only in so-so condition."

Jessica glanced over at Paul. "If you'll put your pack down, I'll show you around some," she said.

Paul left his pack by the door and followed Jessica. She pointed out a doorway a short way up a hall leading away from the entry area.

"Home office," she said.

Paul stepped over and glanced inside. The room was small and neat, with an Intralink portal at the far side.

"Come on," Jessica said, extending her hand to him.

Paul took her hand and Jessica led him back down the hall and into a large room at the front of the house.

"Living room," she said.

The room was open and well lit. Through broad windows Paul could see the Sierra Madre Mountains in the distance. Facing the windows was a sofa, with a small table in front of it and easy chairs on either side. Behind the sofa was a dining table, and then the kitchen after that. Though the house was actually quite compact, it amazed Paul that one person could have so much space to herself. The whole house was perhaps forty or fifty square meters.

Jessica pulled on Paul's hand and led him through a sliding glass door on the south side of the living room and into a long, narrow room full of green plants. All the outside walls and the ceiling were made of some transparent material—perhaps glass.

"Living machine," Jessica said. She waited a moment, as Paul glanced around.

It was like a rainforest, Paul thought—green, and moist, and full of the soft chirps of crickets—and, yes, frogs, too!

Jessica turned back toward the living room, as though this remarkable room needed no further remark than the brief description she had given.

"Wait," Paul said. He looked at Jessica and frowned a little. "'Living machine?'"

Jessica raised an eyebrow and cocked her head. "Don't tell me," she said, smiling playfully, "you don't know what that is."

Paul shrugged, then shook his head "no." He didn't like getting in these situations. They made him feel tense, uncomfortable.

"Okay," Jessica said, then gave Paul a look that was at once curious and somehow patient. "It's a water-treatment system made of plants and microbes," she said. "It cleans water the same way nature does. It *is* nature, in fact."

Jessica paused, then added, "You'll find living machines like this in most homes, Paul." She said this with a matter-of-fact tone. For a moment she looked at Paul, clearly baffled.

"They're nice because they let you recycle and reuse water," she added. "What I can't reuse, I can return safely to the river."

Jessica looked at Paul a moment longer, still curious, but instead of saying anything, she pushed open the door to the living room and gestured for Paul to follow. They went back through the living room, then Jessica showed Paul the kitchen, which looked out onto the living machine through one of its two windows and the back deck through the other.

From there they went into Jessica's bedroom, which was across from the kitchen. After that, Jessica led Paul outside through a sliding door and onto the deck behind her room, then on up the stairs on the north side of the house, to her rooftop garden.

The roof reminded Paul of the meadows around the Retreat. Its dark, rich soil supported a wide variety of plants. Jessica told Paul that the soil was deep on the rooftop—almost half a meter—and that the plants included some for her to eat and some for wildlife to use.

"'Always give more than you take, from the point of view of whatever you take it from,'" Jessica commented, and Paul had the impression she was quoting, again. "When I built this house, I took some of this land away from the creatures that live here. I like it that this garden helps me give some of that space back."

"That's a nice thought," Paul said. "It's probably a pretty good insulator, too," he added, looking around.

"Yeah," Jessica said, then pointed out an ecobot that was busy tending the garden a few meters away from them and a solar water heater along one edge of the roof.

Paul asked her what the energy source was for the rest of the house. Jessica pointed out the windmill in the southeast corner of the roof. Paul turned around to look at it, while Jessica explained that most of the house was covered with solar-electric paint, and that the roll-out sun screens above the decks made solar-electric power, too.

"All in all, the house is mostly self-sufficient," she said, "and it's pretty easy on the environment, too. And believe me, this land deserves some TLC. A lot of this valley was used for farming and watered with groundwater for perhaps a hundred years, until the water level dropped too low. Then, almost a century ago, it came under the management of the Environmental Reclamation Projects. Since then, the underground aquifers have gradually been restored. That's why the land can be as it is now."

Jessica looked around, then went on. "The river this time of year is fed by springs, which had all dried up before the Projects began. A hundred years ago, the river was dry for most of the year. Now it runs year round. Not so much grew here, then, either. A lot of these trees," she gestured, "have deep roots, and depend on groundwater, too. This whole environment was devastated when the water level fell."

"It looks good now," Paul said.

"Yes, it does," Jessica said. "I like to stand up here, sometimes, when the tule elk come through, and watch them eat the tule reeds by the river. This was their home long before it was ours. I'm glad we've learned to leave space for them, again."

In the days that followed, Jessica fell into the patterns of normal life. On weekdays, she was busy with her clients, while in the evenings and on weekends people were always dropping by. Paul was getting to know Jessica's mother and father, as well as cousins from both sides of her family (many of whom had no siblings, and none of whom had more than one—and yet, they all seemed to feel like they were siblings to one another). Old friends came by, including many whom Jessica had known since childhood. Paul had never known anyone to have so many genuinely close and loving relationships in their life. What an abundance of riches, Paul thought—beautiful land, meaningful work, and such a rich and loving social life.

On Paul's world, people dreamed of attaining the sort of wealth had by Corprogov's Upper Crust—to be able to have what you want, to live where you want, and to do what you want—but no amount of riches on Paul's physically and emotionally ravaged world could begin to buy what the poorest of the people Paul was now surrounded by had in their everyday lives: love and closeness, meaning and beauty. Compared to them, Paul thought, the people of Corprogov's UC seemed the poorest of the poor.

Paul himself was happy most of the time. He enjoyed the time he spent alone, studying advancements in the physics of this world while Jessica was away at work. He enjoyed the evenings and weekends, when the two of them could be together—as he enjoyed each morning and evening, as he woke or went to sleep in Jessica's arms.

Paul took pleasure, as well, in the frequent gatherings with friends and family—but as much as he enjoyed these get-togethers, they took a little getting used to, for Paul was not accustomed to being surrounded by so many warm and welcoming people. He felt, in some ways, like a stray animal taken in by a family accustomed to friendly pets—and yet he warmed to them, too, and soon became the one welcoming them when they came to visit.

It was a different world than his own, Paul knew, and there were many things for him to become accustomed to. Paul found it strange that Jessica never locked her house, since in her world there was no need to do so. He was surprised, too, by the casual way people responded to the sight of a herd drifting by or a flock of birds in the trees around the house. These things, which others seemed to accept as a normal part of life, still filled Paul with a childlike delight each time he saw them.

Nonetheless, as odd as Paul often found the details of his new life with Jessica to be, he had to admit that these were, in truth, the happiest days of his life.

And so one day followed another, and soon weeks had passed. The time slipped by quickly and easily, as though Paul and Jessica had known one another their whole lives, and knew each other's cadences, and how to get along with one another without friction. Each day felt like a gift to Paul, something better than what he had ever dreamed might happen, for here he was, as it seemed to him, living in a perfect world, with a perfect woman, day after day. The only thing missing was that they were not lovers, and yet that was something he felt he had to accept, unless he was willing to decide to stay here forever and give up hope that his own world might still be saved.

As for Jessica, she never asked Paul about his plans or when he would return to his job in Strandford, and Paul never brought it up, either. Perhaps, for Jessica, this was part of her decision not to ask too many questions, or perhaps it was simply the case that neither of them wanted to think about this wonderful time coming to an end.

During the hours when Jessica was at work, Paul stayed busy preparing himself for one of the jobs available to physicists on this world. Sometimes he would stop to think about just which path he would take when he got such a job. Should he stay on this world, or use the money he earned to build his transport? He found himself torn each time, for going, he feared, meant destroying this world, while staying, he felt, meant giving up on his world and sacrificing it to its own self-destructive momentum. What if it was true that he was its only hope? No, he couldn't decide yet, he told himself on these occasions—not until he had to, and that time wasn't here yet.

And so, Paul spent each day preparing himself to have steady, paying work as a physicist on this world, without deciding what would come after—and toward that end, he spent each weekday in front of the portal in Jessica's home, pouring over unfamiliar theories, and diagrams, and mathematical equations.

This process included many fascinating discoveries for Paul, including the fact that on this earth the idea that there existed countless branching points that each resulted in the creation of an infinite number of alternate earths (with each of those, then, placed within an entire alternate universe) was considered more factual, and less theoretical, than on Paul's world, ever since the development of a particularly strong mathematical proof demonstrating this principle. But for Paul, this was only one of any number of remarkable discoveries. Startling advances had also been made in other areas of physics on this world—including quantum gravity, cosmology, and high-energy dynamics.

In the early days of Paul's stay with Jessica, she would come home and find him still at work at the portal in her home office. Quite often she would look, then, at the text and equations on the screen and shake her head at their complexity. It was impossible for her to tell the difference between what she supposed he was working on "for his job in Strandford," and the physics he was actually studying.

Paul would turn the portal off after Jessica arrived, then get up and join her in the kitchen, where they would prepare dinner together. There, in her kitchen, with Jessica as his guide, Paul learned the basics of cooking and found that he enjoyed preparing food with her. In these dishes, they used freshly picked vegetables from the rooftop garden, whole grains and colorful legumes, and also fruits and other foods that Jessica would buy at the market on her way home from work.

Cooking had never really been possible for Paul on his world, as so much of the food available there was one form or another of processed, genetically altered yeast. (As Paul yearned to tell Jessica, "You just warm them up, and then try not to think too much about what it is you're eating.") But here, on Jessica's world, the food was attractive and interesting—fresh and aromatic, vibrant in both taste and color. These foods were remarkable to Paul—parts of the living earth that, in being turned to food, moved some of the earth's vitality into him. Whether legumes or grains, vegetables or fruits, they were all living things with so much flavor that Paul delighted in them every time he sat down for a meal.

As Paul became more adept in the kitchen, he began to spend time trying his hand at recipes Jessica had saved. He would start cooking dinner in the late afternoon and have it ready, and the table set, each evening when Jessica returned home. He enjoyed the process itself, and doing it made him feel better about receiving the gift of Jessica's hospitality, for this way he had a gift to give to her, as well. But it was more than that, even, Paul knew—for it gave him another way to share with her the love that was, day by day, gathering ever stronger within him.

As much pleasure as Paul took in these things, not everything was right with him. No matter how much he and Jessica shared, and no matter how close they got, Paul was always aware of the fact that he was deceiving her. Without ever telling her a lie, without ever saying that he was from her world, of her world, she of course assumed it. So much of who he was and what his life had been, therefore, he was, on every day and in every interaction, concealing from her.

He worried, too, about how she would react if he ever did reveal to her what he had contemplated doing to her world. The fact that he could very easily imagine her thinking him a monster for what he had planned to do was made worse by the fact that he had never really stopped planning to do it. Every day he studied the physics of this world, preparing himself to earn money for—for what, exactly? To support himself while he continued to live on this world? Or to purchase the parts that would allow him to build a new transport, and thus to send himself back to the world he was from—to the world where, upon his arrival, he would open a floodgate through which hungry hordes would pour into Jessica's world, like locusts in full swarm?

Paul thought about this one afternoon, while sitting in Jessica's home office, staring blankly at the portal's screen. That evening, Paul was troubled and quiet during dinner. It felt strange to him to sit with Jessica, then—with her being as she always was, so bright and happy and full of stories of the world around them—while Paul's mind was full of the possibility that he would turn out to be no better than a traitor in her view.

That night, Paul dreamed that he was the commander of an army sent to invade Jessica's world. He watched, somehow powerless to intercede, as his army swarmed across her world and across the valley in which she lived; powerless, even, to act as they forced their way into Jessica's never-locked home on the bank of the gentle Cuyama River; powerless, while they went through her house, touching everything and destroying everything that they touched.

Paul woke, troubled, and spent the day wrestling with impressions of the dream as they lifted into his thoughts over and over again, like an unpleasant aftertaste he could never quite be done with.

That afternoon, Paul decided to set aside his studies and spend some time making up his mind about whether he really should plan to stay or plan to go. He had, he told himself, set the question aside for long enough.

Paul walked down to the river's bank and sat down under the tall cottonwood tree that grew there, as it somehow didn't feel right to think these thoughts while inside of Jessica's home.

As Paul sat there, thinking, a soft breeze rustled the leaves above him, making them flash bright and dark in the sunlight.

Paul thought again about whether there was any way he could help his world without bringing about the destruction of this world, which he had come to know and love. He wondered, for a while, if he might return to his own world and withhold from Corprogov what he had learned about Portable Lightning Capture Units and how to provide enough energy to transport great numbers of people across the gap between worlds.

Yes, Paul told himself, it should be possible to keep that from them, at least until he had Corprogov's agreement to use that technology responsibly and not to send too many people to Jessica's world.

Could he do that, and then return here, to Jessica? Paul wondered. No, no, that would never work. Corprogov would never allow him to return. He would be too useful to them, with his knowledge of transport and lightning-capture technologies, for them to ever permit him to leave.

Paul looked out at the water and sighed. And even if Corprogov somehow didn't view what he had to offer as being so valuable as to detain him in order to keep possession of it, they would, no doubt, take him into custody once he had handed over the plans for building PLCUs—just for having challenged their authority by trying to bargain with them.

In any case, Paul thought sadly, whatever agreement he might coerce from them, they would disregard it as soon as he had handed over the design plans for PLCUs. Paul knew enough about how Corprogov worked to know that they would claim whatever power they had access to and use that power however they saw fit—which, if the past was any evidence, would be to further enhance their own power and wealth, while showing only limited concern for the people, and the creatures, of their world. Paul was certain they would treat Jessica's world even less well than that.

Paul wondered how it was that he had ever believed that Corprogov would use the power of the transport technology responsibly. Blind hope, perhaps— that was all it was. When he had had nothing else to hope for or believe in, he had hoped for and believed in that.

Now, Paul thought, looking around him, there was so much more for him to hope for and care about—and so he could admit the truth to himself now. Corprogov would abuse any power Paul might give it—shipping all the "undesirables" to Jessica's world, without concern for what effect they might have there.

Yes, all the "undesirables," Paul thought—including reformers who might threaten the status of Corprogov's Upper Crust, and who otherwise might offer the best hope to his beleaguered world.

Paul ran his fingers through his hair, then leaned his head back against the tree. Even if his Depopulation Project could lower the population of his world and so reduce environmental and economic pressures, Paul had to admit that his world would still be troubled—burdened not only by an oppressive and irresponsible government, but also shaped and driven by the selfish goals and self-centered views shared by the public in general.

The problem wasn't just that the population of Paul's world was too large— as surely and clearly it was—but that his world was carrying forward the views and values of the Divergence. Its pollution was far more than physical. It was polluted by ideas that gave rise to conflict and bigotry; that gave rise to the destruction of lands and the isolation of individuals; that gave rise to oppressive societies and brutal conflicts; and that gave rise, as well, to loneliness and despair.

It was true—he could not touch what was really wrong there, for the thing that really troubled his world ran far deeper than his project or his technologies could reach. His plans to help depopulate his world would not heal it, Paul admitted to himself, finally—but if given the power to do so, Corprogov would, surely, eventually, bring ruin to this one.

Paul sat beneath the cottonwood tree by the river, choking back his tears. All of his life, all of his work, had been building to this moment. The truth was—the simple and now obvious truth was—that no matter what Paul did, regardless of all his scientific knowledge, regardless, in fact, of the technology that he had developed and discovered, and of all of the power that it gave him, he was powerless to save his world—the world he was born into, the world he had, even with bitterness, loved. The world of his mother and grandfather was lost to him, now. The world on which his brother still resided; the world on which he had worked, and lived, and tried to love—Paul was giving that world up for lost. It had become a patient on which he was prepared to pull the plug—a patient he would no longer try to save. His world was lost to him, now, and Paul knew that he would never, ever, again, return to it.

◘   ◘   ◘

As Paul sat there, trying to come to terms with the fact that he was, really and truly, giving up on his own world, he began to feel other emotions creeping in around the edges of his sadness, like light seeping into a dark room with the rising of the sun.

If he was not going to go back to his own world—if he was going to stay here—then there was no reason why he should ever have to leave Jessica.

The thought spread in Paul's mind, lifting his mood. Jessica, who brightened every moment he spent with her—there was nothing to draw him away from her now! Not Sheila, nor cheering crowds, for he craved neither of them now; not even a responsibility to be of service to his world, for truthfully, there was nothing he could do to save them; not even his brother, Casey (whom he hardly ever saw, anyway), could draw him back there.

No, there was nothing to call him away from Jessica, now.

Paul leaned back his head and laughed—a brief, celebratory outburst, as though with that short exhalation he could release the demons of worry and doubt that had possessed him. Suddenly, everything seemed better: he could stay with Jessica—and he would never have to transport from her world again!

Paul thought for a moment about the dream he had had nearly two months before, when he had been sent, by accident, to an acid planet with an atmosphere that seared his lungs and burned his flesh.

Try as he had, since then, to assure himself that he understood the aiming process, there had always been a residue of doubt. After all, the only thing that had changed, really, was that he thought he understood the principles behind the aiming process better now—but he had made no improvements in the aiming mechanism itself.

What would actually have happened if he *had* tried to transport again? Paul wondered. Where might he have ended up this time? He felt relieved that he would never again have to take that risk—not for any reason, not to go anywhere.

Paul stood up and started to walk the short distance back to Jessica's house. The day was bright—sunny and summery, with a soft breeze singing through the reeds along the river and birds all around joining in that song.

What a world! Paul thought—and now he had no reason to leave it! He could stay here; he could stay here forever. This world was his world now. His world to love and protect. He was freed of any obligation to ever go anyplace else, or to do anything to put at risk what he had found here.

Home, Paul thought. Home. That was how he had felt ever since meeting Jessica—that somehow, in her company, in her presence, he had found the home he had always wished for.

As Paul climbed the steps to the back deck, he thought about what all of this meant. If he had no reason ever to leave Jessica, then he could be with her now, as deeply as she would permit.

From up on the deck, Paul turned and looked back toward the river, taking in the broad scene before him. To the southeast was the cottonwood tree he had been sitting under. Its broad arms reached wide—almost to the spot where Paul now stood. To the northeast was the brilliant white cliff face of the Caliente Range, gleaming in the afternoon sun—while between them, the land rolled out to the east, vital and welcoming.

Home. This place felt like home. This place would feel like home forever—so long as Jessica was here with him. He hoped that they would always be together, and that their relationship would continue to grow and deepen.

Yes, Paul thought, that was what he hoped for—and now, there was no longer a reason for him to hold back from it.

Paul stood there for a minute, thinking. Tonight, he told himself, he would fix Jessica her favorite dinner. Yes, tonight—it was perfect, a Friday, when she would want to relax, and one on which they had not already made other plans. And afterward, while they sat and visited, he would tell her how he felt about her—how special she was to him, and that he hoped their relationship could become something more.

What would her answer be? he wondered. It wasn't what she had asked for, what she had said she wanted—but even so, some part of Paul told him that she, too, wished for something more to happen between them.

And yet, Paul worried briefly, if that was true, then why hadn't she suggested it to him to begin with?

Paul consciously pushed this concern aside and started up the steps to the rooftop garden to pick vegetables for their dinner. As he climbed the stairs, he thought about the path he had taken through life, from all the years he had spent building the transport, to him accidentally being sent to this world. And then, since leaving his world, the long journey he had taken, which had, eventually, led him here, to this place, and even to this dinner he had planned for tonight. It felt to Paul, now, as though his path had always been leading him toward Jessica.

Paul reached the rooftop and looked around. How lucky he was, he told himself, that Jessica was willing to take him as he was and didn't expect him to explain too much about where he had come from, or why he seemed so different from all the other people she had known. It seemed just one more way in which he was lucky to have her in his life.

All around Paul, in the garden, the fruits of vegetable plants were ripening—cucumbers and tomatoes, bell peppers and squash. Paul wanted to pick the best he could find, for tonight would be a very special night.

◌ 28 ◌

The food Paul cooked for their dinner turned out well and both he and Jessica enjoyed the meal. Afterward, they went out on the back deck to sit and visit for a while.

The sun was low in the sky, but the air still bore a portion of the day's heat, as they sat together on the bench seat looking up at the warm glow of the setting sun. Above them, the first stars of evening had begun to shine—bright spots against the still-blue sky.

Jessica was in a particularly good mood that evening. The man she'd been working with that afternoon had had some unusually meaningful insights, and Jessica had been reminded of how helpful and valuable the work she did could be to others.

"It feels so good to know I've helped someone I've worked with—to know that I've helped them to grow and discover new possibilities within themself. I don't think there's anything else in the world I'd rather do than this work, Paul. Well, anything else, except if it could be like this, but on the sort of scale Dr. Kumar worked on. Just imagine all the lives she influenced and all the good she did! Can you imagine how that would have been?—to know that your work had brought such important changes?"

"But it was only possible because there were people like you around to carry it forward," Paul told her.

Jessica smiled that sweet, gentle smile she had. "Yes—everybody participated. The Emergence could never have happened without all the small steps taken in the lives of ordinary people. I know—it's just, I can't think of a more meaningful life than the one she lived, that's all. It seems to me like the ideal life—full of love and adventure and discovery—and a gift beyond value, given to the whole world! What sort of life could be better than that?"

"It seems like you live a pretty wonderful life, to me," Paul said. "Farsan told me you're particularly good at Kumaric work, and I believe him. I'll bet you've made a real difference in a lot of people's lives."

Jessica squeezed Paul's hand. "I love my work. I love helping people emerge. It's just, what Dr. Kumar did..."

"I know, it's the scale," Paul said.

"That's right. So much good done, in just one lifetime. Yes, it's the scale."

"It's also the times in which she lived," Paul added. "The need was there, which meant there was the opportunity." He looked around. "But you're lucky to live in the world you live in."

"The world I live in?" Jessica smiled. "The world we live in."

"Yes," Paul said. "The world we live in."

For a moment, they held one another's gaze, and Paul thought about Jessica, and how much a product of her world she was—a world in which everything had grown right, so true to itself, and how she seemed that way, too.

"I've been wanting to talk to you about something," Paul said. He could feel his heart beating faster as he heard his voice say it.

"Yes. What is it?"

Paul took a moment to gather his thoughts. "I think you're somebody special. You're special to me. I've never known anybody else like you, Jessica." He paused, and Jessica looked at him, listening. She was good at listening. That was one of the things he liked about her.

"I like you, too, Paul," she said, but Paul couldn't tell how she meant it—casually, or in a special way, like the way he felt?

"Do you remember, at the Retreat, when you told me about *sger ngo bo* and about sensing that in another person?"

"Yes."

"I love the way it feels to be around you, Jessica. I keep wishing," Paul paused, and Jessica waited, still listening.

Paul gathered up his nerve to finish. He could feel himself sweating and his heart beating hard.

"I keep wishing there could be something more between us. I know you said you wanted us to be madu friends, but I wish we could be more—that we could be lovers," he said.

"Oh," Jessica said. She nodded and frowned a little, then looked down at her hands. "I've thought about it, too," she said, "but, well—I have reasons to hesitate."

"You have? You do?" Paul said.

"Yes," Jessica said, then looked at her hands a little longer, before looking up at Paul.

"It's not just one thing," she said.

"What is it?" Paul asked.

"Well, you have a girlfriend, you said—you're separated from?"

"Oh—Sheila. Yes," he said.

"I want to know you and be close to you, Paul. I want you to know that, but I also want to do the right thing—and what happens in that relationship, well, that's between you and her, between you and—Sheila?"

"Yeah."

"Well, I want to leave you enough room that if the two of you want to work things out..."

"Oh," Paul said. "Well—I, ah—I don't think that's going anywhere."

Jessica looked at him, and Paul understood that he needed to say more.

"I've been thinking when I see her next, if I see her next, that I, ah—I'll tell her it's all over."

"You have?"

"Yes," Paul said.

"Well, maybe you should do that first," Jessica answered.

"Oh, no, it's ah..."

"What, Paul?"

Paul looked at her. How could he tell her? He hadn't lied to her yet, and he didn't want to start now.

Paul sighed.

"You see, and that's the other thing. You're so sweet, Paul. I see this openness in you. It's like you've been waiting so long to be loved, and to give love, and now you're ready to open yourself up to it like—well, like a flower opens up to the sunshine. It's enchanting, for me, really. You're open—in that way, you're *so* open—but you hold so much back from me, too, Paul. I try to talk to you, and I feel like I'm creeping around the edges of topics you're not ready to talk about. I feel you grow tense, or I hear you sigh, and I leave you alone. But how could we be lovers like that? I want all of you, Paul—your whole heart—and not just little pieces."

"Then you feel...?" Paul started, but wasn't sure how to finish.

"Something special for you? Yes, I do, Paul. Do you think it's every day I invite a man I've only known for a week to come to my home, and then have him stay with me for weeks after—especially a man as mysterious as you are?"

Paul smiled a little. Mysterious! No one in his world would have counted him as such. "Jessica...," he said, but then didn't know how to finish.

"Paul," Jessica said, "I know I told you I would give you space, I wouldn't push you to share things you weren't ready to share. Some people want to be coaxed, want to be pried open—but I've felt you really wanted that space, so I've given it to you. I thought—I hoped—you would learn you could trust me, or you would come to it, somehow, in your own way. I thought you would *want* to share things with me more. But you don't—it's not happening."

"But I *do*," Paul insisted.

"But you don't *say* these things—you hold them back, Paul."

Paul could hardly look at her. "I'm sorry, Jessica. I feel like I've been letting you down."

"Can't you trust me? Don't you trust me?"

"I trust you, Jessica."

"But not enough to tell me whatever it is?"

"No—it's not like that."

"Then how is it?" Jessica asked.

Paul swallowed. "I don't think you'll believe me," he said finally.

Jessica starred at him for a moment, then took his hand. "How do you know until you try me, Paul?"

Paul looked at her.

"Believe you about what?" she asked.

Paul leaned his head back and took a deep breath. It was true—if he told her, she might not believe him—and if he didn't tell her, Paul feared, he might ruin everything that had developed between them.

For a long moment, neither of them spoke, as Paul tried to gather his thoughts.

Finally, Paul lifted his head and spoke. "I'll try, Jessica—but I would like you to agree, before I start, that you'll hear me out, listen to everything I say, before you draw any conclusions."

Jessica gave Paul a long, thoughtful look, and Paul felt again that she wasn't so much looking at him, as into him.

"Okay," Jessica said, very seriously.

"Okay," Paul said, then again took a minute to collect his thoughts.

"Do you remember," he said finally, "the day you first told me what madu friendships were?"

Jessica nodded briefly. "Yes," she said.

"You said something, then. You said, 'Paul, I swear, sometimes I think you're from another planet.' Do you remember saying that?"

"Yes. Paul—you're not going to tell me you're from another planet?"

"No, not another planet, *exactly*—but an earth so different from your earth that you would never recognize it."

Again, Paul struggled to gather his thoughts, then waded forward, unsure of how this would go.

"The earth you know is a beautiful place, Jessica. The land is well. Everybody is kind. Your cities aren't choked with pollution. Your world isn't overcrowded. Your air is good—it feels good to take it into your lungs. Wildlife is everywhere. The countries in your world don't go to war. Your ice hasn't melted. Your oceans haven't risen."

Jessica was frowning slightly. She looked confused. "Paul, I don't understand," she said softly.

"Just listen. You said you would hear me out."

She nodded and looked at him with her full attention.

"I told you about when my mother died. I was living in Santa Maria, then. I didn't tell you that when I was a boy, I used to go swimming with my brother in the ocean there. We would climb up on the roofs of submerged buildings and dive off them. People said it wasn't safe, that the currents were dangerous where the city was submerged, but on a hot day, you'd find all the kids there. There were a lot of kids. The population was always growing. Even with the droughts and floods and famines—even with the *Muerte Azul* and other illnesses spread by the changing climate—the population numbers were always growing."

Paul's eyes were tearing up. He didn't know if she would believe him. She *had* to believe him.

"People ruined everything. We just kept pumping more carbon into the atmosphere, and everything changed. The climate went haywire. Land that was forest became desert. Good cropland turned to dust. The oceans rose— and the cities near the coasts, well, much of them became rooftops for the kids to dive off of. A lot of animals went extinct—a *lot* of animals. Plants, too."

"Paul—" Jessica began.

Paul shook his head slowly and kept on going.

"People were changed by it, too. They sought escape from everything they saw around them. They hid within themselves. It's not like your world, Jessica," he said, his eyes welling up again. He looked at her with a deep, long look, as though to say, *please believe me.*

Jessica's look was stricken, too—as though she was not just listening to what he said, but feeling it along with him. It was a tender, deep look she showed him, full of ache and longing, confusion, and a desire to understand.

"I told you about my work," Paul said, "my research into the possibility of transporting between places by stepping out of and then back into space-time at the appropriate points." Paul frowned, hesitant to say more—but he knew he had to. "My team used a massive, orbiting telescope to look for a world like earth—a habitable world. We hoped—I hoped—to be able to transport people there, to reduce the population, and with it, some of the environmental and economic pressures on the world I knew. We hoped to find a world that could absorb a lot of the population of earth—of my earth—to find a place where we could send billions of people."

He could see Jessica had questions, but he plowed forward. "We had a world picked out. The transport unit was completed. Then one night I was doing some routine maintenance on the transport unit, and there was a storm. Lightning struck. I was on the transport pad when it hit, and I was accidentally transported."

Paul looked at Jessica and she at him. He could see her struggling to make sense of what he said.

"And you were transported?" she echoed.

"To another world than the one I knew—but not to the one we had picked out. I came here, Jessica. I found myself here, on your world—on the world you know—the earth you know. We're both from earth, Jessica, just not the same one."

Jessica shook her head. "You mean this literally, or figuratively?"

"Literally," Paul said, sighing. He wouldn't believe it, either. How could anybody believe this?

Jessica looked very thoughtful.

Paul gave her a moment to think, then thought of something he wanted to add. "Do you remember, in one of your classes at the Retreat, you said something like, 'If you wish you could fly, don't hesitate to tell yourself that there may be some practical way of achieving it. Don't let yourself be held back by believing that the constellations you're accustomed to are the only ones out there.' Well, I believed in this possibility, Jessica. I believed in it since I was in my teens—and I saw the way to make it real. Well, almost—I was aiming at a different world, an unpopulated one. But I'm telling you the truth, Jessica. It's all absolutely true."

Jessica poured herself into his eyes. "I can see that, Paul. You were holding back, and now you're not. You're all right here."

"But it's still hard to believe?" Paul said.

"I've heard that somebody proved that there were other worlds, other universes—like alternate worlds or universes—branching off from ours. It was in the news when I was growing up; they'd proved it. They made all kinds of holofilms about it." Jessica cocked her head a little. "So, if this *is* all true..." Her voice trailed off.

"Is it all true?" she said.

"Yes," Paul said.

"...if it's all true, then you'll be bringing people from your world here?"

Paul took a deep breath. This was the part he had dreaded most. "I was thinking about it," Paul said, determined not to hold anything back from her now. "I was planning on it, in fact. You may think I'm some sort of a monster, to think of dumping half—well, really, more like a third—of the population of my world on yours—but I'm not going to. It wouldn't work anyway. It wouldn't work out well for either of our worlds." Paul shook his head. "But I thought of it. I was going to do it," he confessed. "But I'm not going to, now."

Paul hung his head, and his eyes welled up again. This was harder, even, than he had thought it would be. He braced himself for what she would say next.

Paul felt Jessica's hand as it wrapped around his.

"No shame," she said. Paul looked up and took in her eyes, and he saw that strength he had seen in her from the start.

"You were hoping to do good for your world, Paul—right? Your motives were good," she said and looked at him with that steady, patient strength—and as she did, it became clear to Paul: she wasn't going to reject him.

Tears started to stream down Paul's face. He wiped them away. "I'm sorry. This is so embarrassing," he said.

"No, it shouldn't be," Jessica said, then added in the tone she'd used when quoting from *Dr. Kumar's Little Book*:

> Some may appear tough by suppressing their feelings—but it's tough like ice: it seems hard, but it shatters easily. When we let ourselves feel our emotions, we become like water. We seem soft, but nothing can break us.

It was probably true, Paul thought—but now his tears had stopped, anyway. All over again, he felt dazzled by Jessica. If his transporting to her world was remarkable and amazing, the very fact that someone like her could exist at all seemed more so to Paul—and the fact that she could feel something special for him seemed to Paul phenomenal beyond belief. And yet, here he was, believing in her just as she was believing in him.

Paul sat looking at Jessica's warm and lovely face, then glanced down at their hands, still locked together.

"I want to tell you more about Sheila," Paul said. "As far as she knows, I'm probably dead. I don't plan to go back to my world. I want to stay here." Paul looked up at Jessica, as though to add, *with you*—but he didn't say the words. "I won't be seeing her again. She thinks I'm gone for good—lost on an uninhabited world. Like I said: given up for dead—and that's just how we'll leave it. I'll never see her again.

"I want to be with you, Jessica," Paul added. "It's over with Sheila."

"And your job—will you be going back to Strandford?" Jessica asked, and Paul realized that she had been expecting this all along—for him to leave her just like Kade did.

"No," Paul said. "That job's in the Strandford of my world. I'll never go back to it. The physics I've been studying—it's so I can get work as a physicist in this world. I'm not leaving, Jessica. I want to stay. I want to be with you," Paul concluded, laying everything bare.

"You do?" Jessica said.

"I do," Paul told her.

Jessica gave Paul another long, deep look, then nodded slowly, as though trying to absorb everything he had said. Paul imagined she was sifting through it all, trying to make sense of it, trying to resolve her doubts about the story he had told her.

For several long moments, Jessica was silent, then she told him, "I believe you, Paul. At least, I mean to believe you. It will take a little while for me to get used to the idea. My model of reality doesn't include people traveling between worlds—so I can hardly imagine it, really—but as Dr. Kumar pointed out, reality is bigger than our perceptions of it, so I'm going to try to let my perceptions grow.

"What I'm trying to say, Paul, is that I feel that you're telling me the truth, about it all—and that's enough. Thank you for not holding back any longer. That's what I wanted from you, Paul. That's what I've been wanting."

She took a deep breath, then added, "I would like it if we could be lovers, Paul. I've been wishing it could go that way since we first met. And I think, well, if you can tell me what you've been holding back, then I can be brave enough to do the same with you—and that is: I see something in you, Paul. I've seen it from the start. I've had this feeling all along—and I don't know what you'll think about this, but—I've had this feeling like, somehow, our paths lie together. I've felt this way since you first came up to me after class that first day. I've had this feeling of you and of, well, something I saw in you. I'm not playing around with you, Paul. I want you to know, I'm not just playing around.

"I hope you don't feel like, well, like that's too much, or something—but it's how I feel," she added, a little nervously.

Paul leaned toward her and wrapped his arms around her. "It's not too much, Jessica," he whispered. "I've been feeling, lately, as though every step of my life was just leading me to you. I know that's crazy—but that's how I've been feeling."

Jessica leaned back just a little and explored his eyes with hers. "That's not crazy," she said, then took a slow breath, and added, "I so want us to be lovers, Paul."

She leaned toward him, then, and kissed him, and Paul kissed her back, with a fire rising inside him unlike any he had ever felt before.

After a few minutes, Jessica leaned back and said softly, "Come with me, Paul."

She stood and extended her hand to him.

Paul looked up at her as she stood there, looking down at him, her face radiant with affection.

"Come with me," she said, again, asking. "We'll be more comfortable in my bedroom."

Paul stood and took her hand. They kissed again, and for another minute or two stood there by the bench, their bodies pressed together, immersed in the intimacy of their kiss.

When they paused again to smile and look into one another's eyes, Jessica took Paul by the hand and led him back inside, then down the short hall to her bedroom—where they spent, together, a feverish and nearly sleepless night.

29

Paul woke about dawn to the sounds of Jessica in the throes of a nightmare. Jessica clung to Paul in her sleep. "No. Oh, no," she mumbled loudly. Paul could feel her head turning against his shoulder.

"No," she said.

"Jessica, it's okay. Wake up. It's a dream," Paul said. He put his hand on her shoulder and rocked her gently back and forth. "Jessica, wake up."

Jessica opened her eyes. "Paul?"

"It's okay. It was a dream. You were having a bad dream."

Jessica took a deep breath. "Oh, good."

"Good?"

"It was a dream."

"What happened? What were you dreaming?" Paul asked.

"It was the same dream again. Or almost the same."

"What dream?"

"You disappeared again, Paul. There was a bright light—a brilliant, blinding light—and then you were gone. It was just darkness after that."

Jessica pulled Paul close. "I'm glad you're here."

Paul pressed his lips against her forehead, kissing her. "I'm glad I'm here, too."

"I don't see how I could have been so affected by Kade leaving..." Jessica's voice trailed off.

"Jessica, where were we in the dream?"

"Where? I don't know. We were together, but I'm not sure what was around us. We were outside, somewhere, I think. It was kind of cold out. There was this flash of light, and then you were gone. I was so sad after that. Everything around me was in darkness."

Paul hesitated to say what he was thinking, but after having been so open with Jessica the night before, he didn't want to hold back anymore.

"When I transported here, Jessica, there was a flash of light. That's how the transport works. There's always a flash of light whenever it's set off."

Paul looked at her and could just make out Jessica's face in the soft light leaking in around the curtains.

"Oh. That's so weird," Jessica said.

"Do you think you could have—I don't know, sensed that somehow?"

"Like, from when you came here?"

"Yeah."

Jessica shook her head. "It didn't feel like the past, Paul." She looked at him.

"I'm not going anywhere, Jessica. What I want is to be right here with you."

Jessica rested her head on Paul's shoulder and held him close to her. "I'm glad, Paul. I want you to stay," she told him.

"It's all right," he said. "Just sleep now, and I'll be right here with you when you wake up."

Paul put his hand on Jessica's head. He stroked her gently and thought about her dream. What an odd dream to have! What she had described sounded so much like him transporting—but that was something he would never do again.

After a time, Paul could tell from Jessica's breathing that she had drifted back to sleep. He turned his head and kissed her on her forehead again, then snuggled up to her, still with the same fire for her burning within him, and told himself he should sleep, as well.

◘   ◘   ◘

When Paul woke again, a couple of hours later, Jessica lay still sleeping beside him, her arms wrapped around his chest. Paul lay there for a long time, with his arms around her, as well, amazed at his good fortune. As delighted as Paul had been to discover the natural world so alive and intact on this world, he was far more pleased to discover and to be with Jessica in all the ways he could now be with her. It wasn't just the physical love-making for him, but the fact that he could share with her his most closely held secrets and find that she accepted him still.

Paul knew that after this he would never again hold anything back from her.

After a little while, Paul felt Jessica stir in his arms.

"Good morning, beautiful," he said.

"Good morning," Jessica answered. She lifted her head and smiled at Paul, then leaned forward and kissed him.

"How are you this morning?" she asked, as she rested her head back down on the pillow next to him.

"Glad," he said.

"Glad?" she said.

"Yes—glad we're no longer just madu friends."

"Oh." Jessica looked at Paul carefully for a moment. "Well, we never really were, you know. At least, I never felt about you the way a madu friend feels."

"Oh? How's that?"

"Well, madu friends are just friends, Paul. That's how they feel. I never felt just that way about you. I was always wishing it could be more like this." She pulled him a little closer.

"Me, too," Paul said, and they kissed again, slowly and tenderly.

For a moment, they were lost in one another, then Paul pulled back just enough to whisper, "Thanks."

"Thanks?" Jessica whispered back.

"Yeah. Just thanks—and, well, thanks for believing me, Jessica. I was so afraid you wouldn't."

Jessica looked at Paul with a soft smile. She put her hand on his cheek.

"Well, you don't make sense any other way, do you? And after all," she added, then said with the tone of voice she used when quoting, "'Truth may seem strange to the uninitiated, but that makes it no less true.'"

"Oh," Paul said, thinking about the quote, then added, "What do you mean, that I don't make sense any other way?"

"Well, you are kind of an odd guy," Jessica said. "I don't mean any offense by that—it's just, you're different. I kept trying to figure out how you could be who you were—just what sort of unusual upbringing you might have had, for example. It was hard to make the pieces fit. The explanation you gave me last night was very strange—that's true—but I think all the pieces fit. At least, I—I *think* they do."

"Like what?" Paul asked.

"Well, your accent, for one," Jessica said. "It's subtle, but you have this unusual pattern in your speech—almost like a mild regional difference. Like I said, it's slight, but I've never heard anybody who sounds like you. I'm usually pretty good with accents, but yours I could never place—and you said you were from Santa Maria, so that just didn't make sense. Not the Santa Maria I know. And of course, there's all this stuff you don't know that *everybody* knows—but, still, you're smart, and you know so much about other things."

"Oh, yeah. Anything else?" Paul asked, frowning just a little. It made him a little uneasy, even now, to think of how strange he must have seemed to her.

"Yeah, your hair, for one. Not a normal hair style—not now, anyway. Maybe a few decades ago. And then there's your clothes. I understand why you only have two pair of everything—a lot of sojourners come to the Retreat with very little, because they don't want to carry it—but why don't any of your clothes fit you, Paul? You see, you've been quite a mystery to me."

"My clothes don't fit?"

"They're close, but no." Jessica shook her head.

Paul thought about it a moment, remembering that one set had been given to him by Marco, and the other, well, he'd been tipsy that night and had pulled them off the rack without trying them on at the camp-gear shop in Strandford.

Paul shook his head, too. "No, I guess you're right," he said, and laughed.

"Why don't your clothes fit, Paul? That part I can't quite fit into your story," Jessica asked, and Paul thought a moment about where he would need to start explaining to fill Jessica in on that.

"Also, how did you happen to end up here, if this wasn't the planet you'd been planning on? And why did your earth end up like it did? It sounds so different from here. How did it become that way? Actually, I have a hundred questions for you—I would love it if you would tell me more. I want to hear every detail about you, and your life, and how you came to be here with me. I want to know everything about you, Paul—if you'll tell me. If you'll share that with me."

"I'll share it all, Jessica," Paul said, smiling—glad he could finally tell her everything. "I'd love to," he added, "but could we please get breakfast first?"

◌   ◌   ◌

Paul and Jessica fixed themselves a large breakfast, then carried it out to the table on the back deck to eat it.

Once they were settled and had begun their meal, Paul described for Jessica how he had been working late one night, doing maintenance on the transport pad (which had been left set so that it was aimed at a distant planet), and how a bolt of lightning had traveled down the cabling outside the building, and how it had set the machine off and transported him here, to her world.

Paul told her about how he had awakened, naked and hairless after his transport, and realized that he had been transported. He told her about how confused he had been when he had discovered that the land was the same as on his world, but without all the people and buildings. Then he described Interdimensional-Linking Theory, and how he thought it explained why he had come here.

Paul told her about going first to Anna and Marco's house, and then to The Wayfarer's Inn in Strandford. Then he went on to describe how overpopulated his world was, and how little open space there was in it—and how Strandford was a big city on his world, not the small town it was here.

Paul told Jessica that he had asked himself what she had asked him—about why their worlds had become so different—and that it was his search for an answer to that question that had led him to Dr. Kumar's memoirs, and then on to the Retreat, where he had met her.

Jessica listened with rapt attention to everything he told her. If she had any qualms about believing him, he couldn't see it in her words or manner. Instead, she listened like a child being told an adventure tale, interrupting now and then with more questions for him.

Having already confessed to Jessica that he had thought about invading her world with the excess population of his, it was important to Paul that she not get the impression that he had contemplated doing such a thing without good reason. So Paul tried to make clear to Jessica just how dire the circumstances were on his world.

"Here, you have managed to keep your population numbers low, and to keep climate change from developing," he told her, "but on my world the human population is four times what it is here. Our government is oppressive and motivated by profit, and climate change has run rampant. All over the world, people despair. Everything is so different on my world, Jessica. The difference between here and there is like the difference between day and night.

"You asked me why my world became the way it is," Paul said, then sighed a little. "I know the story, but it's not an easy one to learn about. Corprogov—that is, the government of my world—it likes to keep difficult truths from the public. They want people pacified. They want them quiet and docile. The truth is upsetting. It might rile them up."

Paul shook his head, then went on, and as he did, Jessica listened with serious interest. "I learned some of this from my grandfather when I was growing up. He tried to pass on what he knew—what he remembered from his own life, and what he had read about from long before that. He told me about how the world once was, and about how it had changed."

Paul looked at Jessica. "I remember walking with him when I was a kid," Paul said. "He used to point things out to me that he thought were worth noticing. Like the Santa Barbara Islands—he pointed them out, and told me how they had been cut off from the mainland by rising sea levels and, finally, erosion. He told me about all sorts of things—about how the land had been, and the animals. He taught me a lot.

"When I got older, I wanted to know more. That's when I learned how to access the blacklands of the Stream."

"The Stream?" Jessica asked.

"Yeah," Paul said. "The Stream is kind of like your Intralink, but we don't have portals. We see it though implants." He touched his temple. "The images, the sensations, they light up in people's minds."

Jessica nodded, and seemed to be trying to imagine that. Paul continued, and as he did, impressions of his own world began to flood over him. He was surprised at how strongly he felt, talking about it, and at how much he wanted to tell her—now that he could—every detail about the world he had left behind—and why, as Jessica had asked, it was so different from her own.

"The blacklands is a specially encrypted branch of the Stream," Paul went on, "which Corprogov is always trying to shut down. It's 'blacked out,' you could say, from general public view. It contains a black market, but it's more than that. It also preserves all sorts of information that Corprogov doesn't want people to know about.

"I found out how to access it, like I said. All sorts of stuff is stored there, including the real history of my world—the history that's never taught in school—including the story of how climate change came to be, and how it changed the world.

"It happened mostly because people kept burning things," Paul told Jessica, "because they kept burning coal or oil or gasoline; or using electricity made from burning them; or buying products that required energy from one of those sources, or from some other fossil fuel, for the product to be made and delivered. The whole economy was tied up in it. The whole world."

Paul looked at Jessica, whose eyes were steady, listening. "So, ah—well, the pollutants—all that pollution from all that burning—it went into the air, and it changed the earth's atmosphere. It changed it in such a way that more of the heat from the sun was trapped there—trapped there, inside the earth's atmosphere, as though a blanket had been put over everything.

"The scientists had predicted it," Paul went on, glancing down at his hands. "They had tried to warn everybody—but even they had no idea how quickly it would happen, or how profoundly it would change the world's climate. Over and over again their predictions were too mild, too cautious. Over and over again, when the facts came out, they painted a much more dire picture than scientific predictions had foretold."

Paul shook his head, then looked over at Jessica. He could see, not the childlike enthusiasm he had seen there to begin with, but in its place a look of steady interest and thoughtful concern.

Something about her attentive look resonated with Paul. It felt good to tell this—to tell it to somebody, like this, all at once. It wasn't something people talked about on his world.

"So many animals," Paul continued, as the sadness of it welled up in him, "so many plants that had once fit so naturally in their ecosystems—when the climate changed, ecosystems changed, and a lot of those plants and animals started to die. There were huge die-offs in long chains, where the disappearance of one species would cause the disappearance of another, and another after that."

Paul frowned. "You could think of it as starting low on the food chain, with plants that were dying off as the climate changed. Some weren't getting the amount of rain they needed. For others, higher temperatures meant that pests that fed on them could breed year round. When plants started to die off, then the animals that fed on those plants would die off, too—and then the animals that fed on those animals. Whole ecosystems began to collapse. Many creatures—both plants and animals—began to go extinct, just because of changes in the climate."

Paul shook his head. He felt surrounded by the sadness of it all, as he remembered these things.

"In the past, it used to stay cold in the mountains year round," he continued, looking over at Jessica. "Many of the mountains had glaciers that would melt a little each summer, and grow a little each winter, and so the glaciers were always there, balancing their growing and shrinking each year. Their summer melt fed rivers—sometimes grand and important rivers, like the Ganges that Dr. Kumar wrote about. The warming melted the glaciers in the Himalayas that fed the Ganges, like it melted glaciers everywhere, and once those glaciers were gone, the great Ganges River no longer flowed year round. It went dry in the summertime, and millions of people starved because they couldn't water their crops.

"The same sort of thing happened all over the world, when other glaciers melted. But the problems with crops didn't stop there."

Paul picked up his fork and tapped it against his plate, staring blankly. Then he set the fork back down and continued with what he was telling Jessica.

"Rainfall patterns changed as temperatures around the world grew higher," he said. "In some areas, the heat had a drying effect, and rains that had hardly ever failed, failed to come. Good croplands went barren and turned to dust. In other areas, warmer air passed over water, and because it was warmer, it absorbed much more moisture, like a sponge soaking it up. When that moisture was released, it fell—sometimes as unusually heavy snowfall, slowing commerce and downing trees and sometimes roofs. Other times it came as torrential rains, drowning the land, drowning the crops, flooding people's homes, and carrying away the topsoil. Sometimes the floods came with heavy rains in the summer, and sometimes when the heavy snows that had fallen the winter before melted in the spring."

Paul looked over at Jessica, who held his gaze, her face serious and full of concern. This was what she had asked—how had his world become so different from her own?—and yet, somehow, Paul thought, his answer was more solemn than she might have imagined.

"In many places," Paul went on, "it would be dry one year and then they would have flooding the next, as winds shifted and traveled different routes. Stable climates were replaced by cycles of floods and droughts and droughts and floods. Crops failed year after year, and more people starved."

Paul rubbed his face and leaned back in his chair. "Some areas that had once been moist dried to a tinder," he told Jessica. "The Amazon rainforest was like that—it dried and burned to the ground."

Paul looked at Jessica again, and she held his look, her eyes, now, as sad as his.

"More creatures went extinct," Paul told her. "So many that people entirely lost count. And the water levels rose. Ice was melting everywhere—in the mountains, in the Arctic, in the Antarctic. Like it happens in springtime, they said, when the ice that has lasted all winter suddenly is gone. And all that water drained into the oceans. Coastal cities were destroyed, inundated by the rising water. Their populations fled inland, where there wasn't enough infrastructure—where there wasn't enough food."

Jessica reached over and held Paul's hand, and kept holding it as he went on.

"And all that water had other effects, too," Paul said. "When the ice melted and flowed into the oceans, it shifted the pressure on the world's tectonic plates. The energy built up in that system over thousands of years began to be released in powerful earthquakes and tsunamis, and in violent volcanic eruptions." Paul shook his head, remembering images of devastation he'd found in the blacklands of the Stream.

He seemed lost in thought for a moment, then returned his attention to the conversation. "So, as the climate changed," he went on, "some areas ended up with more water, and some less than they had previously had. Wars broke out over shifting resources, like fresh water and arable land. And those wars created more victims and more refugees."

Paul sighed and took in Jessica's gaze. He had long known the story of his world and how sad it was, but it seemed all the more so telling it to someone whose world had never suffered in these ways. It made it seem, somehow, not inevitable—and therefore, for that reason, more tragic. As hard as it was to talk about it, it seemed easier if he just plowed on through.

"As people moved, they carried disease," Paul went on. "And in the places where people gathered, in those stressed, overcrowded cities or camps, the diseases festered. And in the meanwhile, new diseases appeared. Tropical diseases moved toward the poles, to places where the climate had become warm enough for them to flourish.

"All those problems were made worse by the fact that the population numbers had gotten so high. Even with the famines and the epidemics, the population continued to climb. Families often grew larger than the two children per couple that would have kept the population numbers steady. Even with as few as three children per family, the population was set for exponential growth."

Paul shook his head and sighed. "And amid all this, storms were growing worse—more severe," he continued. "Hurricanes, typhoons, and tornadoes are all fed by the energy rising off of warm water. Just as the polluting gasses had warmed the air, they'd also caused warming in the world's oceans—and so storms grew worse and worse, powered by that heat energy. Monster storms battered the coasts—which were already traumatized by the rising sea water—while tornados, spawned inland, pummeled the land.

"And the sea water itself was changing," Paul added. "The gasses people had released into the air from burning fossil fuels—from burning coal and oil and gasoline, and so forth—well, those gasses got absorbed into the world's oceans. Once absorbed, the gasses turned the water acidic. Creatures with shells could no longer form their shells, because the acid ocean water eroded their shells away faster than they could grow them. This affected all shelled creatures, from the tiniest plankton on up. The shelled creatures died off—and so the creatures that ate them could no longer feed on them. And so those creatures died, too. On and on, it went like that, so that the same sorts of mass die-offs were happening in the oceans as were happening on the land.

"So much of what once made my world vital, and alive, and beautiful has disappeared from it," Paul concluded. "My world is so deeply wounded—and in truth, Jessica, there's nothing I can do to help it."

Paul looked at Jessica, and could see her eyes well with tears.

"That's the saddest story...," she began.

"Yeah," Paul nodded, surprised at how deeply it made him feel to remember it all at once.

"Can't your government do something—couldn't it have done something?" Jessica asked.

"Huh," Paul said. It was almost a laugh. "They did something all right. They saw their opportunity for profits."

Paul paused and thought for a moment, then went on, "My government isn't like your government, Jessica. Your government expresses the will of the people and values an informed population. At least, that's how it seems, from what I've seen through Intralink portals. My government," Paul thought carefully about how to say this, "its goal is to *shape* the will of the people, and to keep them uninformed, or misinformed, so they'll be compliant and be good consumers of its products."

Paul took a deep breath, then went on to explain how Corprogov had come to power. "It started out, in the early days, with corporations trying to protect profits," he told her. "When the scientists warned of climate change and said that certain practices the corporations were involved in, and were profiting from, would have to be changed, the corporations fought back. They used advertising and the control they had over the news media (which they owned large portions of) to mislead the public—to tell them that the scientists were wrong and to ridicule those who believed what the scientists said."

Paul looked at Jessica, who continued to listen closely, a look of intense concern on her face.

"At first they claimed the climate wasn't changing at all," Paul continued. "They would ignore the larger data and do things like—well, like picking out areas where the changing climate had brought about some limited and localized cooling—through increased cloud cover or changed circulation patterns—and then make a big deal out of those completely atypical examples.

"At first, they would use tricks like that, deliberately manipulating and misleading the public—but then, later, when the climate had changed so much that the truth of it could no longer be denied, they admitted that the climate was, in fact, changing, but claimed that the changes weren't caused by human activities—and so, of course, they claimed, no adjustment in human activities—or in *corporate* activities—was needed."

Paul shook his head as he continued. "When politicians spoke out and said something had to be done to stop climate change, the corporations spent heavily on getting them defeated the next time an election came around. Meanwhile, the politicians whom the corporate leaders liked, they advertised in favor of. More and more, politicians depended on corporate approval, as the money and news coverage the corporations could offer could easily decide an election. More and more, governments were made up of people chosen by the corporations, and more and more the governments did the corporation's bidding.

Paul looked at Jessica and found himself feeling sad for her, as he saw in her eyes the sadness she felt for him. He squeezed her hand and went on.

"Even when catastrophes caused by the changing climate began to pile up," he told her, "the corporations stuck to the same strategy. Catastrophes meant profit to them. Storms that wiped out whole areas meant they could move in and buy land cheaply—or sell products or services to a population that was in desperate need, and so would pay any price, after having been stripped of everything they had. Epidemics of disease were the same way; to a corporate mindset, they meant an opportunity to sell vaccines or medicines to a desperate public, who, because of their desperation, would be more willing to part with their cash. They had no desire to fix the underlying problems, as those problems only added to their profit opportunities.

"Oh, sure, the policies, the mindsets, of some corporations were more reasonable, more ethical," Paul said, with a mixture of sadness and cynicism. "Some were even genuinely trying to do good. But even as those corporations resisted, others joined together, growing in power. Hostile takeovers of smaller, less-aggressive corporations became more common. Corporate power became aggregated in the hands of the most ruthless.

"As the largest corporations grew in power, they used their influence over politicians to remove antitrust laws from the books and to dismantle laws preventing monopolies of the news media. And in one country after another, laws that restricted corporate involvement in political campaigns were removed or dismantled, either by legislative action or by court decree.

"And so the corporations grew more powerful, and as they did, they had more power over politicians and governments. Soon, they were not just having laws changed, but were using their influence to change constitutions, as well—and each of these changes added to their power. Gradually, they were gaining control over first a few, and then many, functions of government. In time, whole governments came under their control.

"You might think that democracies would have been slowest to hand over power," Paul added, "but once the Stream was established, and the first free implants distributed, the corporations began sending their ads deep into people's minds. The ads were soothing, reassuring. Though utterly misleading, they gave people hope. In democracies, they were able to sway votes this way, and this also helped them get laws rewritten in their favor. In autocratically run countries, they simply bought their way into power by other means, or stepped in when catastrophes created a vacuum in the power structure."

Paul could see by the look on Jessica's face that she found this all astonishing and distressing.

"Gradually," Paul went on, "corporate structures supplanted government structures around the world. Eventually, one giant conglomerate corporation was ruling the world. Sure, a few small, isolated areas were left out—but they were in poor and remote regions, and nobody listened to or cared about them, anyway.

"And so Corprogov came to power in my world, and has remained the world's governing power in the sixty—ah, sixty-seven years since they were formally established. And of course, they were meddling heavily in government for many decades before that—sowing the seeds of their ascent, you could say."

Paul paused and looked over at Jessica, before adding, "In the blacklands of the Stream, I read about a politician who lived centuries ago—long before Corprogov's existence. He talked about a government of the people, by the people, and for the people. Well, I guess you could say Corprogov isn't about people, at all. Or any of the other creatures on earth, what's left of them. Corprogov is all about profit. That's its driving force. People are valuable in that they help provide profit."

Paul stopped for a moment, then said, "I told you about finding Dr. Kumar's memoirs and how I came to the Retreat. Well, that was the turning point, I think. That was why my world became different from your world, Jessica. For some reason, on my world, Dr. Kumar's memoirs were never published. I never heard of them until I came here. Her gift to your world was never given to mine."

"You never emerged," Jessica said, with shock and sadness in her voice.

"No, we never did." Paul looked at Jessica and held her gaze for a long moment.

"I wanted so to save my world," he told her. Then he leaned toward her as she pulled him into her arms. She held him, then, with all the tenderness and comfort she could give.

◻   ◻   ◻

After a minute, Paul sat up straight, and Jessica looked into his eyes. "You know, Paul, when you first told me, last night, about being from another earth—well, it was like, I believed *you*, but I could hardly believe *it*, if you know what I mean. It was so hard to imagine, to conceive of. But listening to you now, it all seems so vividly real to me—and so sad. It's so sad, Paul."

"I know it is, Jessica. It's true. But can you imagine how it felt to me, coming to your world and discovering all of this?" Paul gestured broadly at the landscape around them. "Clear air. Good water. Extinct animals miraculously alive again. And the people—so kind, so attuned, so present with you when you talk to them. It's a beautiful world, your world, Jessica."

"I know—and hearing what you described just makes me value it all the more. I feel like what you've described to me, Paul, is like a whole world sliding into darkness, while what my world experienced was like a whole world gliding into the light," Jessica told him.

"I know," Paul said. "It felt like that to me coming here. Here was this whole world, so much better than anything I had known. I tried to understand it, to see how it could have happened—and like I told you, I think that the branching point between our worlds was the publication of Dr. Kumar's memoirs—but it's still hard for me to conceive of how so much good grew out from a single point like that. It's like discovering that a whole forest grew from one seed—a lush, vibrant, diverse forest. I've wondered what it would have been like in the years after Dr. Kumar's book was released—in the decades since then. How did things progress that they turned out so much better on this earth than on mine? Can you describe it? Do you know?"

Jessica looked thoughtful. "Basically, I do," she said. "What Dr. Kumar gave us was an understanding of the potential shared by humanity, and an understanding of how we could attain it—and of how each person could reach their own potential, and bring their protolife to life.

"From the text I've heard," she went on, "it was like people who had been in kind of a holding pattern for years, or decades—or even for their whole lives—decided to get up and move toward the promise waiting within them.

"It was a heady era," she told Paul, "after *Memories and Reflections* was released. People read it and were so excited by what they'd read that they would pass their copy on to friends, or family, to other people who would then read it and pass it on again. People said that everywhere they went, people were reading it, and that tattered, beat-up copies continued to circulate, even after having been read dozens of times."

Paul nodded as Jessica continued. "As the book spread, so did the ideas. People were learning that by looking inward they could create more joy in their lives, more meaning—and could help make around them the sort of world they hoped to live in. For a lot of them, it was the first time they had ever imagined that something of that sort was possible."

"And did things change, then, the way Dr. Kumar said they would?" Paul asked, "—the way she said they would when she told Laura about the New Change? I mean the Emergence? You know, when they were driving to, ah—to that place in the Ituri Forest?"

"To Epulu?" Jessica asked.

"Yes."

"Yes, pretty much," Jessica said, nodding. "She did a good job predicting how the Emergence would unfold. As people began to follow Kumaric teachings, they saw more deeply into themselves, and that changed a lot—about how they related to themselves, and how they related to everything else, too."

Jessica paused and thought about it for a moment. "Yes, it was a lot the way she described it. As people looked inward, they began to leave the three impediments behind. It worked then just like it still works now," Jessica said, then started counting off on her fingers.

"As they went deeper into themselves, they became better at communicating with themselves and with others."

She moved on to the next finger. "They saw their own and other people's motives more clearly, and no longer assumed that anyone had a bad or worthless nature."

She pushed down on her third finger. "And in deepening their sense of self, they broadened their perspectives, and so left the insularity of their old viewpoints behind."

"So that really worked?" Paul said.

"Oh, yes. That's what Kumaric practice does," Jessica said, smiling. It occurred to Paul that in her line of work, she had seen this many times.

"Anyway," she went on, "it was like I said, like a kind of dawn coming over the world—with so many people reaching their own enlightenment, emerging, all at once. The ideas Dr. Kumar shared with the world made such a difference in people's lives. They began to feel better about themselves, because they could more easily see their own motives, and therefore the goodness within themselves—and also because they could more easily, consciously, change the things they didn't like.

"People found they could improve their lives and their relationships with others," Jessica told Paul, who sat quietly, listening to every word. "They became more conscious of the mental models they held, and of how those models influenced their lives—and they began to deliberately replace the models that didn't work for them, so that they were consciously choosing the sorts of experiences they had, and the sort of world they made around them.

"These realizations were especially powerful for people during that time, I've heard," Jessica continued, "because, for many of them, it was the first time it had ever occurred to them that they could actually *steer* their course through their own lives."

Paul looked at Jessica as she spoke. She was excited by the subject, he could see—but that didn't surprise him. After all, she had chosen to devote her life to helping people develop just the sort of insight she was talking about now.

"As people came to understand these things," she told Paul, meeting his gaze, "communication improved—like I said—and it became easier for people to see from one another's perspectives.

"And that changed so many things," she told him. "Old prejudices were replaced with clearer understanding. Punitive justice was replaced with restorative justice. Conflicts that had dragged on a long time began to be resolved.

"So, for example," Jessica continued, "family members who had become estranged began to talk, and often found themselves on good terms again. Old friends who had had falling outs finally realized how the other person had seen things. Often they were able to put those conflicts behind them, then, and become friends again. Long-standing conflicts between nations began to be resolved, too, because for the first time those involved really saw from the other's point of view, and really cared that things went well for them.

"People communicated better with themselves, too, and so took notice when they knew, deep down, that what they were contemplating doing was really right or really wrong. And so people learned to listen to their own inner wisdom and to follow it, regardless of what others around them were doing.

"The world changed with a speed that historians say was remarkable. It really was like dawn, with people waking up all over the world. It wasn't that problems no longer existed—new problems will always arise," Jessica said, "—but that the problems that arose were engaged, and addressed, and dealt with effectively. Gradually, the really ancient, intractable problems of humanity began to dissolve away."

"I guess you could say," she added, "that as people's sense of self expanded, they became more likely to answer the question, "What's good for me?" the same way they would answer the question, "What's for the greater good?" because they saw everything and everyone as somehow part of that larger sense of self. They tried to consider the larger effects of their actions, and that made them kinder and more considerate in everything they did. And that helped to make the world more the sort of place it could be."

Paul smiled. It was wonderful to think of a world transforming like that— and not just any world, but *his* world: the world he lived in now. And more than that, he liked listening to Jessica, and especially so when she was interested in and enthused about something, like the way she was now.

For a moment, Paul reflected on what Jessica had been saying. He pictured the changes she had described spreading around the world, as more and more people emerged—and as they learned, more and more, how to leave the three impediments behind.

"So—was there really an archetypal shift, then, when the Emergence began to unfold?" he asked, looking over at Jessica. "I mean, like Dr. Kumar thought might have happened when art and agriculture were first developing, at the time of the Original Change—or, I mean, at the time of the Divergence?"

Jessica smiled and shrugged a little. "Who knows?" she said. "I love the idea, myself. I mean, just imagine it: each person, as they deepen their own personal understanding, contributing something to the collective unconscious— and that contribution helping to establish a whole new way of being that others can then access, and learn from, and use as a kind of template in their own growth, if they wish.

"What an appealing idea!" she said. "Who wouldn't like that idea? I love to imagine that it's true, and that things have really worked that way—that they still work that way—that as each of us travels deeper into ourselves, along what people sometimes call 'the root' of our own selfhoods, that what we find at the deepest point is a kind of collective creation, the treasures left by other people before us—and that we leave our own treasures there, too—that we're all constantly involved in a kind of greater evolution of consciousness."

Jessica smiled. "Anyway, like I said, I love the idea," she went on, "but who knows? The Emergence progressed quickly, relatively speaking, and some people say that's evidence of it—but I say, how could anybody know for sure? Like Dr. Kumar suggested in her preface to *Memories and Reflections*, so much of what's real is beyond our ability to know about for sure. So much of what we wonder about can never really be proven or disproven. I love the idea that that's how it happened, how it's still happening—but what I do know for sure is that, at the very least, each person paved the way for the next person through the normal routes of, well, I guess you'd say 'social discourse.'"

Paul sat up straighter and nodded, thinking about what Jessica was saying.

Jessica looked thoughtful for a moment, then went on. "For example, some people made a point," she told Paul, "of developing mental models of how the world could be, of how it *should* be, in the hope of helping to seed new archetypes—but whether they succeeded in that or not, the models they made helped shape their own actions, and those actions brought practical, tangible results in the world. Also, because they spoke to other people about what they were thinking, their ideas were passed on in that way, too. So, there was a new zeitgeist—a new spirit of the age—but where it came from, exactly, I don't know."

Paul listened with real interest to everything Jessica was saying. After all, her explanation of just how this world had come to be as it was helped answer the central question he'd been asking ever since coming to this world, about how it was that this world had developed so differently than his.

"But the ideas did spread, one way or another," Jessica continued, looking at Paul. "People who had begun their own Kumaric practice, who had taken the time and effort to look into themselves, and so come to know themselves more deeply—who had expanded their sense of self that way—well, they began to help others who wanted to expand *their* sense of self, and who were actively seeking assistance. So each person's discoveries were often passed on in that way, too.

"That's also, by the way, how the Kumaric Retreats came to be," Jessica added. "First friends came together to share and discuss what they'd been learning. And sometimes, when help was wanted, they'd try to help one another along. Gradually, those groups grew larger and took in other people. Eventually, people came together in that way to form Kumaric Centers and, later, Kumaric Retreats."

"What about the sorts of things I told you about on my world," Paul asked, after a moment, "like climate change and mass extinctions? Why didn't those things happen here?"

"It's been a while since I studied that era," Jessica said, "but as I remember, in the early days, before Dr. Kumar's book came out, there were still some of the sort of disinformation campaigns you talked about, that you said happened on your world. They were going on on this world, too, back then. I guess it must have been close to the—what did you call it? the 'branching point?'—between our worlds, when our worlds were still more similar."

Paul nodded. "That makes sense," he said. "So what happened here? What affect did these campaigns have here?"

"Well, as I remember it," Jessica said, "there were these people who were claiming that climate change wasn't real, or that it wasn't human caused—but it worked out like Dr. Kumar predicted. As people began to know themselves more deeply and to expand their sense of self, they began to identify more deeply with others, too—and so they cared more about what others experienced, and that included not just other people, but other kinds of life, as well.

"Once people cared more, they chose to act more caringly," Jessica continued. "And as people began to care more about whether harm was really being done, those disinformation campaigns became less effective—because truthful, factual information was available from other sources. Once people cared, they wanted to know what was really going on, and so they actively sought the truth."

Jessica looked thoughtful for a moment, as though trying to remember more details. "I guess the main thing that happened next," she said, "was that because more people started going to the trouble of getting informed, more people also voted in an informed way. And because of that, more political leaders were elected who shared those concerns, and pretty soon new laws and regulations started going into effect that helped bring climate change to a stop (and that helped, in other ways, as well, to protect the environment). And all of that happened very quickly, once enough people cared to form a majority of the vote. And, of course, the more they cared the more likely they were to actually get out to vote."

"And what about nations that weren't democracies—what happed there?" Paul asked.

"Well, the ideas spread there, too," Jessica said, frowning a little. "They affected individual lives, and those individual lives then affected the world around them. That could happened even with leaders of nations—even non-democratic ones—though how quickly it happened in those places varied greatly. I don't remember a lot of details about that—mostly that in some of those places, things changed surprisingly quickly, while in others it took a long time to change. But still, overall, the pattern was clear—all around the world, people were becoming more conscientious about the impact they were having on other people and other life."

Jessica nodded thoughtfully for a moment. "I've kind of compressed all that, but I think that's about how things went," she said. "Whatever their walk of life, more and more people cared enough to learn what they needed to do—both personally and politically—to help make the world a better place. Even when those actions were small, collectively they made a big difference."

Jessica considered this a moment longer. "Sorry if this is all a little sketchy. Like I said, I've heard text about that era. I even studied it in school—but it's been quite a while since then."

"No, you're doing a great job," Paul said. "But what about the corporations? What became of them here?"

Jessica shrugged. "They just remained corporations—although, if I remember right, the law expanded to allow them to focus on benefiting not just their shareholders, but the whole society, the whole environment. Those were the ones people wanted to invest their money in, to be a part of—the so-called 'benefit corporations.'"

Jessica shook her head, then went on. "There's no remarkable history about the corporations here, really, except that the successful ones were the ones that sought to do some sort of real good, the ones that retooled to make more helpful technology, for example: SPVs, ecobots, carbalizers—that sort of thing. They never gained the kind of power they did on your world, Paul. It just didn't happen here. Maybe that was because people were paying too much attention for them to have the opportunity—or maybe it was because the people running them, and their stockholders, were influenced by Kumaric ideas, too. I just don't know."

Jessica looked thoughtful, as Paul tried to imagine what that time period must have been like on her world.

"But I can tell you," Jessica went on, "that for people, just in general, a lot of what was going on then, a lot of the reason things improved, was just so basically Kumaric. After all, it was this wonderful new era. People were finding fulfillment in their lives and in their relationships. That terrible hollow that Dr. Kumar wrote about—it was getting filled in better ways: in their social relationships, and in other sorts of fulfilling activities. People were just plain happier, and so they didn't mind so much making adjustments in the way they lived in order to help keep the world well.

"After all," Jessica added, "for the most part, they no longer craved having more than what they needed. They understood that filling up their lives and their homes with unneeded things would only distract them—that is, distract them from interactions and experiences that held more meaning, and because of that, brought more joy."

Jessica looked off toward the old cottonwood tree, and it seemed to Paul that she was gathering her thoughts. He didn't mind if she took a little while. He was interested in all she was saying, but he also just liked sitting there with her.

"I remember hearing some text," Jessica went on, "that said the whole economy shifted then. Economists stopped thinking constant growth was a good thing. In fact, if I remember right, they started saying it was like a kind of cancer, constantly growing and consuming. Instead, they said we should seek what they called," she paused and thought for a moment longer, "um, I think it was, 'healthy equilibrium,' where essential needs would be met, and met in a stable way—and that meant not just the essential needs of people, but of all the plants and animals, too."

Jessica looked over at Paul. "And people changed their attitudes about their own spending, too," she said. "They stopped trying to acquire more than what they needed. They tried to have enough, but not too much—to have what they needed, but not more. They tried to think not just about the financial cost, but the environmental cost of each purchase.

"There was a lot of excitement during that time, I've heard. People had a sense that they were participating in something new and wonderful—but there was also some frustration, because the old infrastructure was still in place, and so it was sometimes hard for people to accomplish what they wanted.

"There's a story in my family," Jessica told Paul, meeting his gaze, "about how my—I think it's two 'greats'—how my great, great grandparents wanted to switch to solar energy in their home, but couldn't afford enough solar panels. So each year they bought what they could afford—which was just, like, a sixth of the total number they needed—and they installed them on their roof.

It took them, I think, six years before they could switch over entirely to solar energy in their home, but those small steps got them there.

"The way my family tells it, because people like them bought solar panels when they were expensive and hard to afford, the solar-energy industry had the funds to develop better, cheaper panels later on, and there was enough demand to help bring the prices down. So my great great grandparents were kind of blazing a trail. And of course, eventually, government involvement brought down the prices of solar and other safe sources of energy even further, and that's when sales really took off worldwide.

"But still," Jessica said, "it was small steps like that that really changed the world, as people tried to align their actions with their ideals. Yao Chuan Jianyu talked about small steps like that when he described that era, looking back from the mid-twenty-first century. You remember—I think I mentioned him to you before—at the Retreat? He's a famous Kumaric scholar."

"Yeah, I kind of do—something about anchoring?"

"Yes, that's one of the quotes I have memorized. That was his. I don't have this one memorized, though, but I can paraphrase it. He said the way the world changed was like the way people leave a crowded amphitheater after a concert. Each person takes small steps, little by little, into the space that opens up in front of them. Even though everyone is jammed together, if each person takes what small steps they can, when they can, then the whole crowd moves forward. If everyone just gives up and sits back down in their seat, nobody will go anywhere—but if everybody moves when they can, in whatever ways they can, toward their goal, then pretty soon the whole group will be striding forward. Everybody blazes a trail for everyone who follows."

"Sort of like the way water flows," Paul said.

"How's that?"

"Well, wherever water flows, it cuts a wider channel. It makes more room for more water to flow there later," Paul said.

"Right, it opens up a path. It widens it. That's like what Yao said. 'Small acts change facts,' was a saying back then. And like Yao said, everybody was taking their little steps, going deeper into themselves, and going forward, externally, too, into the sort of world they hoped for—and because of all those small acts, the whole world moved steadily forward."

"It's kind of amazing to think of so many small steps amounting to such immense change," Paul said. He looked off into the distance, trying to imagine it.

"Yes." Jessica nodded. "But that's how it worked. People say that Dr. Kumar's book was like a flame that she set burning—but that it was really all the other people who lit their torches from it that carried that light around the world.

"I guess the point is that her book made a huge difference because it *started* something that other people carried forward," Jessica told Paul. "I only wish it could have started things earlier. Climate change had already begun by the time *Memories and Reflections* was published. I've seen the stage we were at then described as being like toppling a heavy statue—something massive that's been there, unchanging, for a very long time. Once it starts to fall, it's very hard to stop it—but the really dramatic damage isn't done until it hits the ground. That's how things were when *Memories and Reflections* was first published—the statue had been toppled, but it hadn't hit yet. The atmosphere was already greatly changed and the momentum was carrying us in a dangerous direction. We had, somehow, to stop the crash from happening. Reversing that momentum took a great deal of effort and resources. Carbalizers of every shape and form had to be constructed and were erected all over the world. Their job was to scrub the atmosphere of the polluting gasses released by burning fossil fuels. Other devices that reduced the effects of other greenhouse gasses had to be mass produced as well. It was all extremely expensive, but absolutely essential if the climate was to continue to function.

"Other things were tried, too," she added, "ways of shielding the earth from the sun, for example—and some of them helped—but at least by then we had a population that was listening, a population that cared, and was therefore willing to use its actions, its votes, and its voices, to do whatever was necessary. But even those great efforts would have been useless, if the burning of fossil fuels, and the release of other forms of polluting gasses, hadn't been rapidly phased out and eliminated, as well."

"But your world did it," Paul said. "Somehow, it pulled together and did what was necessary. For me, hearing about this—well, it's like if someone you love had died, and then you find out that their identical twin was saved. For me, it's so bittersweet to hear all this."

Jessica reached over to Paul and put her hand on his shoulder. The look in her eyes reminded him all over again of why he wanted to be with her.

"I'm so glad I'm here, with you, on this world, Jessica."

Jessica leaned forward and kissed him, a long, lingering kiss. Then she leaned back in her chair, and they sat together, holding hands and looking off toward the Caliente Range and its brilliant white cliff face, which shone vividly in the light of day.

Paul thought about Jessica's world and the book that had allowed it to become so different from his own.

How remarkable it was that one woman—that Indira Kumar—could make such a difference! Paul thought, then remembered what Jessica had said about her the night before. "I can't think of a more meaningful life...full of love, and adventure, and discovery," she had said.

"I do have one other question for you," Paul told Jessica.

Jessica looked over at him.

"Dr. Kumar—I never finished her memoirs. I'd like to know what became of her and Laura."

◘   ◘   ◘

"Well, I've listened to her memoirs enough times," Jessica told Paul. "I ought to be able to fill you in on that. Let's see—how far did you get?"

"They'd just gotten to the Ituri Forest," Paul said. "All this talk about going there, and I stopped just after they arrived. What was it like for them there?"

"Well," Jessica said, then thought for a moment, "for the most part, they liked being there—and they enjoyed working with the Mbuti. The Mbuti were friendly, and remarkably cheerful. They were always singing. The forest seemed almost enchanted to, ah, to Indira and Laura—as it did to the Mbuti, also. Indira wrote about how much delight the Mbuti took in their experiences and in the world around them.

"Dr. Kumar—Indira—wrote a long passage," Jessica went on, "describing the Mbuti finding a bee hive high up in a tall tree." Jessica gestured with one hand high up in the air. "She wrote about all the singing and anticipation as they worked all day to retrieve the honey—which required real courage and some impressive climbing skills, especially because it was in such a tall tree! Not to mention all the bee stings the climber got!

"So there were some standout events, like that, for them," Jessica said, "but also just the routines of daily life—such as being part of the communal hunting and gathering, or preparing food over an open fire, or the conversations they had with the people they lived with (including interviews they did for their work—conversations about the Mbuti's religion, for example, and their beliefs about the spirit of the forest).

"Neither Indira nor Laura had done much camping out, and in the Ituri they did that for six months. It was an interesting time for them. They both slept in huts made of saplings and giant leaves. They saw okapi and forest elephants. It rained a lot.

"It was quite an adventure for them," Jessica went on, "but they also missed things about home. Oddly, one of the things they found themselves missing most was the sky."

"The sky?" Paul asked.

"Yes, they could only see pieces of it, looking up through the trees. Indira—or Dr. Kumar—no, I'll stick with 'Indira.' She wrote again about feeling like she was underwater. It was a beautiful environment—with everything so green and the huge trees and vines everywhere—but she sometimes felt like she wanted to float up above it all, like floating up to the surface when you're in water. She wanted to at least see something at a distance, every once in a while, and not always feel so enclosed by the trees that were around her all the time. So after a couple of months, she started to feel a little drowned in it—a little drowned in that beautiful green forest.

"But, overall," Jessica went on, "they both did enjoy their stay, and they were both pleased with the experiences they had there." Jessica thought for a moment. "For Laura, it gave her the adventure she had always wanted— and it was also productive for both of them, professionally. If I remember right, Laura published two papers based on her research there, and Indira three."

Jessica put her hand to her mouth, then took it away. "I'm trying to remember whatever else is worth telling you. Sometimes, Indira wished that Laura would be a little less adventuresome. Like the time that Laura picked up a case of ringworm—which she got, Indira thought, because she insisted on wading barefoot in the forest streams. Indira wished Laura would be a little more careful."

"Indira?" Paul said, smiling. "You know, I'm so used to you calling her 'Dr. Kumar.'"

"Usually, yes, I do," Jessica answered, "but sometimes when I talk about her memoirs, it just doesn't sound right to call her that. I mean, she is 'Indira' in the memoirs. But you're right—most of the time people say 'Dr. Kumar,' out of respect."

"So was that a problem, the ringworm?" Paul asked.

"No, it's just a skin infection, really. The Mbuti treated it for her using one of the plants that grew in the forest—which, for Laura, was just more of the adventure. Anyway, they both came back in one piece and felt good about the time they'd spent there. Indira wrote that it was nice to return to the comforts of home when they got back, but that they also both missed the rainforest—mostly the friends they'd made there and that sort of 'cathedral' feeling Indira had written about earlier: that feeling of being someplace where everything around them was alive. But Indira liked returning to the sun and the open sky, too.

"Let me see," Jessica went on, "—oh yeah, and since they had stopped to see Laura's family in London on the way out, they agreed to stop off in India on the way back, so Indira could see her family. It had been years since she'd seen them, and Indira found being there wonderful, and sad, at the same time. Everyone had grown and changed. And yet, there they all were, even if they all were older, or different in other ways. She was glad to be able to see them again and be reunited."

"So what else? I want to hear more," Paul said.

Jessica looked thoughtful. "Well, when they got home, they found their cat, Bubbles, had been well cared for by the family who'd been leasing their home. He seemed content and well fed, and every bit as independent as he'd always been. He seemed happy to see them.

"Uhm, I don't know. She kind of jumps ahead then, if I remember right. She just touches on a lot of small things, briefly," Jessica said. "Years go past, and then, when Indira and Laura have their next sabbatical leaves, it's Indira who first has the idea of doing research abroad—this time in New Guinea."

"Oh, yeah, I remember you mentioned New Guinea before," Paul said.

"Yeah, they went there together, too. Indira was still interested in how the beliefs people hold shape the sort of world they make around them, and her field work in New Guinea related to that. Specifically, she was looking into how changes in beliefs were changing the experiences of people within a particular tribal culture.

"If you remember the sort of things I was talking about in my modeling-reality classes," Jessica told Paul, "they come mostly out of the part of her memoirs that begins there and then continues on over the next dozen years or so. It was during that trip to New Guinea that Indira began to really grasp how truly comprehensive the influence of mental models is. So it was an important time for her."

Paul thought about that briefly, then asked, "And Laura? You said they both went to New Guinea?"

"That's right. They both went. They stayed with a group of people who built their huts way up high in the trees. Indira wrote that she felt like she was in a boat at sea sometimes, when the wind blew.

"So, yes, they both went together, and Laura did research there, too. In fact, as it worked out, their research overlapped. The group they stayed with was

trying to cope with the effects the outside world was having on the environment they had always lived in. They had begun to mix their traditional religious beliefs concerning the natural world around them with beliefs which
came from environmental activists who were not from their culture. That
interested Laura, who'd been researching the ways in which religions all over
the world were evolving in response to external changes, and particularly in
response to changing environmental pressures.

"Indira was interested in those changes, as well—but specifically, in her
case, in how those new beliefs, those new mental models, were creating new
experiences for the people who embraced them," Jessica said, as Paul listened
closely, pleased that she was filling him in on what he had missed.

"So, anyway," Jessica went on, "Indira and Laura spent most of that year in
New Guinea doing research, and the rest of it back in Boulder, writing up
the results."

"And after that?" Paul asked. "What happened then?"

"Well, basically, they went back to the patterns of their regular life in Boulder,
pursuing their research and teaching classes at the University of Colorado.
They saw friends on the weekends. It was a pleasant life for them, but for the
next few years they basically fell into familiar routines."

"But as routine as that time was in most ways," Jessica said, "Indira did
continue to think about the ideas she'd been considering in New Guinea.
She'd thought a lot, ever since her trip to Zaire, about the idea that a 'New
Change'—or an 'Emergence,' as she'd begun to think of it by then—might
be possible for humanity, and how it might be encouraged to take place more
quickly. In New Guinea, she'd thought a lot about how mental modeling
shapes both individual lives and whole cultures. But it wasn't until after that,
in Boulder, that she really began to see how those two sets of ideas might
be combined."

For a moment, Jessica pursed her lips thoughtfully, with one hand to her
mouth. Paul smiled affectionately, watching her.

"It was then," Jessica continued, "that she began to entertain ideas about
the possibly transformative effects of coupling conscious and deliberate self-
exploration with conscious and deliberate mental-modeling. She considered
these ideas to be very theoretical at that time—but she had the feeling that they
might add up to something important. So she kept thinking about them—or
she did, at least, when she could find the time between other obligations.

"As I remember," Jessica said, looking over at Paul, who was still listening
closely, "it was during that time that Indira began to have a desire to write
about the ideas she'd been thinking about—to write about them, and about
the events in her life that had helped her arrive at such insights in the first
place. But she was busy with work and with friends, and she wondered when
she would ever have the time available to write such a book.

"And it really wasn't just her academic responsibilities that kept her busy,"
Jessica added, glancing thoughtfully off to one side, then back over at Paul.
"She and Laura had a lot of close friends there in Boulder. They both valued
those friendships, but those interactions also took time. With so many close
friends in the area, she and Laura both felt like they had one big extended
family there. Not only were they close to their friends, but also to their friends'

families. In many ways, both Indira and Laura were like aunts to the children of their closest friends—which made up a little for them having so little chance to spend time with their own nieces and nephews."

"So they were happy during that time?" Paul asked.

"Oh, yes, sure—their lives were very full and very happy," Jessica answered, "but like I said, Indira had begun to get this itch to write a book about her ideas and her life, but didn't know where she would find the time.

"Let's see, so what else can I tell you?" Jessica said. Paul smiled at the look on her face—so thoughtful and serious. He'd been enjoying watching her; it seemed that he took pleasure in every expression she made.

"Oh, yes," Jessica went on. "She and Laura had another sabbatical leave after that. Both of them were involved in studies of, I guess you'd say, 'a comparative nature,' at that point, studies that required them to have access to a university library and to other people's research. Neither of them had colleagues they were collaborating with then, so they both decided to just stay in Boulder for that leave. It was sort of a disappointment for Laura, though. She complained some about her 'field work' taking her only as far as the library on campus.

"So, anyway, life went on for them," Jessica said, "and it was a couple of years after that—just after Thanksgiving, in 2008—that Indira had her skiing accident, when she hurt her back. The injury was bad enough that she took the following semester off from her job at the University of Colorado. That was when she started working on the book she had hoped to write—that is, on *Memories and Reflections*."

Paul nodded. He remembered Jessica mentioning this before. It seemed different now, though, as Paul imagined all that had led up to it.

"The writing moved quickly during that spring semester and the summer after," she told Paul, "but Indira had to go back to work before she was done writing her memoirs. With the demands of her job and everything else, it took another, if I remember right, another four years for her to finish it—and then a year and a half more, after that, before it was actually in print."

"What was it like for her after it came out?" Paul asked. "I'd think it would have felt kind of strange, to suddenly have a lot of attention directed at her that way—and especially with the book being about herself and her life."

"Well, of course, her memoirs were completed, then, so I can't tell you from that source, but she wrote in her journal that it was sort of a shock to her system, because suddenly so much attention was focused on her and on the book she had written, when she was so accustomed to spending time with Laura, or her students, or friends—but never really being in the public eye."

"So what happened? Did that change the way they lived?"

"Not really. She did say that it was harder for her to do her research, or even just keep up with grading papers and that sort of thing, because people were always streaming into her office—but I think she kind of enjoyed it, too. She liked people, and she enjoyed interacting with them."

"What else about her and Laura? Did they always stay together? They seemed very much in love in the part of the book I heard," Paul asked.

Jessica nodded. "Oh, yes. They continued to be in love for the rest of their lives. In fact, they got married—they married as soon as it was legal for them to do so where they were—but they were both pretty old by then. Can you imagine, it was actually illegal for them to marry before that, just because they were the same sex?! It's hard for me to imagine there ever having been such laws." Jessica shook her head. "They got married right away when the law changed, as soon as it was possible for them to do so. They'd had to wait for decades, though, by then. Indira said sometime in an interview that she and Laura had always thought of themselves as being married, since long before they left Oxford together—and that she had always believed they deserved the same legal rights and social standing as anybody else."

Jessica shook her head again. "It seems strange that she, of all people, was treated like such a second-class citizen in that way, for so much of her life. She and Laura, both."

Paul thought about that, remembering that this world and his both shared a common history of inequity. "And what else?" he asked. "Can you tell me more about what happened in their lives after the memoirs came out? I want to know the rest of the story."

Jessica shrugged. "Well, her journals (which she continued to write) mostly describe a quiet life. In time, she and Laura both retired. They went on living in Boulder after that, with close friends nearby. Occasionally, a reporter would contact Indira for an interview—that sort of thing—but otherwise, in their later years, life slowed down for them and became pretty routine.

"During those years, Indira took time to look back over her life. She thought about the people she'd known and the things that had happened along the way. A lot of her journal entries, in the last decade or two of her life, are about her reflections on earlier times, rather than things going on then.

"She and Laura both lived to be quite old. Indira outlived Laura, but only by a couple of years. Indira had close friends around her, even then, after Laura was gone—and it seemed like, in truth, the whole world wanted to know her. She died in her sleep one night in April of 2043. She just went to sleep and didn't wake up.

"The whole world mourned her passing. There were all sorts of speeches and memorial events. She has always been remembered. And it's funny, because she always seemed surprised by it—by all the attention."

"Your world was lucky to have her," Paul said.

"Our world, Paul. You're part of this world, now," Jessica said, then leaned over the table and kissed him.

After a moment, she settled back into her seat and added, "And I'm lucky to have you, too."

"No, Jessica, that's me. I'm the lucky one," Paul said, and it seemed to him that if Jessica was lucky, that he was a thousand times more so. He was glad he had chosen to share with her all he had told her since their dinner the night before. He was beginning to understand the idea that you have to be willing to share yourself, to be *able* to share yourself, in order to be close to another person—and to understand, too, how wonderful it was when the person you share that with responds as Jessica had.

Paul felt so close to her now, closer than he would have imagined he could ever have felt to anybody—as though there were nothing in the world he wouldn't share with her, nothing in his life, in all the years ahead, that he wouldn't wish to share with her.

Jessica squeezed his hand, and Paul looked at her, smiling—then looked on past her to the brilliant light of the white cliff face, shining in the midday sun.

Whatever the future held, Paul told himself, he wanted to share it all with her.

. 30 .

If things had seemed good between them before, now that Paul had opened up and shared his secrets with Jessica, everything seemed so much better. Not only did he no longer have to worry about what he could and could not say or about deceiving her concerning what he left out, but the sense of closeness between them had expanded greatly. It seemed to Paul now that the closeness he had felt in other relationships amounted to no more than wisps or fragments as compared to what he now felt with Jessica. Each day he shared with her whatever he was feeling, whatever was on his mind, without hesitation, and could see that she loved him all the more for the deep trust and openness he showed her—just as she was trusting and open with him.

But for all that Paul was willing to tell about himself, there was so much more that Jessica seemed so readily to intuit, as though his moods and wishes were as apparent to her as the clouds in the sky or a breeze playing along her skin. It seemed to Paul that she was always having flashes of insight—and could see him with a clarity, quite often, even beyond how he could see himself.

For Paul's part, he saw in Jessica what he had seen from the start—something open and fresh, like a beautiful, clear lake—but he no longer had to dream of diving into it. Instead, each day, he felt himself afloat in her waters and in the closeness they shared between them, while each night they met in a tender and passionate embrace, sharing with and discovering one another, body and soul.

As the days rolled forward, Paul was happier than he could recall ever having been. Not only was he pleased that he had decided to trust Jessica with the whole truth about himself, but he felt increasingly glad about his decision to stay on her world and not return to his. After having shared with her the history of his world, and having learned more about the history of hers, Paul had begun to see his world in sharper contrast to Jessica's. His world seemed the loser in every comparison—the failed twin, with the same starting point as its sibling, but an inability to achieve a fraction as much. Paul was glad to be done with it, to have left it behind, forgotten, and to have moved on. Paul told himself it was right to see himself as successful in his own work and life, and so it was right and natural that he should be here, now—a success-ful person on a planet of successful people—while the rest of his world was simply left behind.

So for Paul, these were happy times, with sunny summer days and evenings spent with Jessica—alone, or with her amid happy gatherings of friends and family. It seemed to Paul as though life could never get better than this—as though his life was like a grand puzzle in which, somehow, wonderfully, all the pieces had fallen, all at once, into their proper positions.

Even Paul's study of the physics of this world was going smoothly. Each day he studied, and each day he made steady progress toward his goal of catching up, in his knowledge and understanding, with the physicists of this earth.

He had previously worried some about how he would be able to prove him-self, once he was done with his studies, as a candidate worthy of being hired to one of the jobs he hoped he might find on this world (since all the references and credentials he could give traced back to his own world, alone), but as Paul continued to learn about the discoveries made by the physicists of this earth over the past one and a quarter centuries, he came to realize that for all that was new to him here, there was also much that was missing—including a variety of things that had been discovered and proven on Paul's world during that time, but not on this one. It would be easy, Paul could see, for him to make a name for himself here, should he wish to do so, simply by introducing this world to some of the physics knowledge from his.

So for Paul, life seemed set. He lived in a world better than any he might have dreamed of, with a woman with whom he shared something deeper and truer than anything he might ever even have thought possible—and now he could see, too, that he would have a successful career as a physicist here, as well. If he had dreamed up the perfect life to live, it could have been no better than this.

Paul turned himself to all of these things, now, so fully that his own forgot-ten world seemed little more than a dream he had left behind. If there was any flaw in the near perfection of his life now, it was that he was not entirely sure he was worthy of all this good fortune, all this happiness. It wasn't that he doubted any longer that he deserved to be loved. As he saw it now, all crea-tures deserve that (just as they deserved light and water and air to breath), and he deserved it no less than they. It was only that he had done nothing to help build this world, nothing to help heal it, or to keep it healed. He was relieved at least that he had not ruined it by letting in a flood of countless strangers. Still, he knew, he was like those strangers in many ways—especially in that he still lacked much of the knowledge and wisdom that had helped shape this world into what it had become.

Paul was all too aware that he hadn't even genuinely tried to achieve a full understanding of those teachings while he was at the Kumaric Retreat. Sure, he had worked hard enough on stages one and two, when he knew others were paying attention, but as soon as all eyes were diverted, he had slid through stage three without effort—and with very little success, as well.

Paul wanted to be worthy of this world, which he had come to love, and to feel more a part of it—to have the same knowledge and understanding that others had. He wished, too, to be more worthy of Jessica, who seemed to him so patient, so wise, so genuinely caring. He wished he could think himself a fraction as wonderful as she seemed, to him, to be.

Paul understood that part of what made Jessica shine with such brilliance and beauty as he saw in her, was the sort of understanding she carried within her, and this made Paul want to expand his understanding, as well. He began to think that perhaps he could improve himself—become more patient, more kind, come to shine more brightly like Jessica did—and that perhaps, in time, he could offer those improvements in himself to Jessica, as a kind of gift to her.

For this reason, Paul began, on an afternoon late in July, to study Kumaric teachings again, quietly, patiently, for a little while each day, while Jessica was still at work. He would leave his physics studies an hour or two early each afternoon and go down by the river, where he would sit by its bank and try to feel himself to be a part of all the life around him.

Paul didn't know if he had expected some sort of sudden breakthrough, but he had, at least, hoped for some more satisfying sense of progress than he had in the first days after he began these studies. But instead of any sudden revelations, mostly what he had felt, at first, was bored. On the third day he had even fallen asleep for a while, as he sat comfortably beneath the cotton-wood tree by the river.

Paul had considered, then, talking to Jessica and asking her advice. This was, after all, just the sort of thing she did professionally—to help people advance in the way he hoped to advance—but Paul liked the idea of this being a sort of surprise for her, a kind of gift he could give to her. Whether it would be given slowly, or all at once, it would be for her, as he thought of it, and not something he would ask her to work on along with him.

So Paul decided to proceed on his own. Instead of speaking to Jessica, he found her copy of *The Little Book* and carried it with him on his next trip to the river. He chose *The Little Book*, and not *Memories and Reflections*, because Jessica had valued it enough to commit it all to memory, which made it special to Paul—made it something he wanted to know, and touch, and understand, as though, perhaps, in understanding it, he would understand something more of Jessica, herself.

Even the physicalness of the paperback copy pleased Paul—a tangible thing he could hold and touch—so different from the sort of text he had (through so much of his life) read on the Stream, or even the audio version of *Memories and Reflections* he had listened to on his hike to the Retreat. This worn old copy of *The Little Book* reminded Paul of the books his grandfather had owned—dusty copies lining the shelves of his room, holding the secrets of bygone days.

Now, sitting beneath the spreading branches of the old cottonwood tree, Paul opened *The Little Book* and glanced through its pages. It was a slender volume, light in his hands. A number of the pages were marked, and Paul recognized the words on several of these as passages Jessica had quoted to him when he was working with her at the Retreat.

Now, Paul turned to one of the marked passages that he didn't recognize and read it slowly to himself:

An expanded sense of self implies that we hold within our awareness not just our own perspective, but a sense and understanding of the perspectives of others.

When we can imagine how life might be through the eyes of another and feel along with what they are feeling, then it may be said that our sense of self has expanded to encompass more.

The broader and deeper that field of understanding—the more widely and fully we allow ourselves to identify and empathize with others—the more truly expansive our sense of self has become.

Paul looked up from the page and took in the scene around him. Nearby a horned lizard was sunning itself on a rock. Paul looked at it and tried to imagine how it might feel. He thought about the roughness of the rock beneath it and the way the sun warmed its body. He wondered if it was aware of him, sitting there, and felt that if he moved suddenly he might scare it. But it wasn't scared now, Paul felt. In fact, he had the feeling it was in a very dreamy, relaxed state.

Was he really sensing it, Paul wondered, or just making up impressions about it? He did have a feeling about it, though, wherever that feeling came from.

Was he sensing the lizard's *sger ngo bo*? he wondered. Was it even possible to sense that in a lizard?

Still, Paul felt that something of that sort was happening.

Paul looked back down at the book. He flipped through a few pages, then read another passage that had been left marked by Jessica:

The first step in the path to wellness is to believe in healing.

If, when we suffer, we believe in healing, then we understand that it is worthwhile to turn our attention to the dark tunnel of our pain, for we perceive the light at the other end of it. It is this expectation that it is possible to resolve the pain buried within us that gives us the courage to probe into it, to find its sources, and to have the diligence to make repairs there. It is, therefore, through this expectation of wellness that we become well again.

When we are confident of our ability to heal, we stride forward in our lives adventuresomely, knowing that if we get burned or bruised along the way, we will heal from those injuries. With this confidence to guide us, when we do encounter pain, we work quickly to resolve it, sure of our success—and so soon move forward again into the bright light of day, still hopeful and ready to engage whatever may come....

Paul skipped a couple of unmarked paragraphs, then continued again in the marked text:

The danger comes when we believe healing is impossible. Then we refuse to probe into our pain to find its source, for such exploration seems, then, not only painful, but purposeless. We shrink back, thinking it pointless to put out the effort necessary to make repairs, and so those repairs go unmade.

When we do not believe that healing is possible, we do not greet life with an adventuresome spirit, but rather shrink back from experience, fearful of the next injury and the presumed impossibility of healing from it. Each injury accrued, then, seems permanent to us—and we insure its relative permanence by our belief that it cannot be healed, and our unwillingness, therefore, to engage in healing it.

Like collectors, we gather up our injuries and keep them boxed and guarded, packed away where nothing may touch them—and, therefore, where nothing may change them. Our inner lives become a museum of unhealed hurts—which seem only to prove to us that injuries go unhealed.

Healing begins when we believe in healing and choose, once again, to hold our hearts open.

Paul looked up from the page. A bird had lit on the branch above him. He tried the *sger ngo bo* exercise with it. It hopped along the branch a couple of steps, then stopped and cocked its head a little to one side before pecking at the bark beneath it.

Insects? Paul thought, then smiled. The bird was enjoying a meal.

Paul knew he couldn't be sure of this, but it seemed to him the bird was in good spirits. He enjoyed watching it as it hopped along the branch, then took wing again and flew off into the willows on the far side of the river.

Paul turned his attention back to the book. He flipped through several more pages, then stopped again at another passage Jessica had left marked:

It is impossible for anyone to do anything that is all good or all bad in its effects.

This is not because of some inherent flaw in human nature, but because the nature of existence is so complex. Every action we take creates an endless cascade of results, some foreseeable, some not, some controllable, some not. Each of these results will be seen from the points of view of all of those who experience them. Within the vast array of effects and side effects of any action, some results will be perceived as desirable and some as undesirable, from some viewpoint, somewhere down the line.

It is good, for example, to provide food for your family—but not from the perspective of the plants and animals that become that food. Likewise, mass murder is a terrible thing—but not from the point of view of the microorganisms that feast on the remains. Each action has such multiple effects, moving out like waves from the original act.

Though perfection may thus be out of our reach, what we *can* achieve is to attempt, in each moment, to act for the greater good—to do our best to take into account the needs and perspectives of all who will be affected by our actions (no matter their station, or their species), for all living things have an experience of their own, worthy of our consideration.

For all living things have an experience of their own, Paul echoed to himself. That was really what he was trying to learn, Paul told himself—to teach himself how to perceive the perspectives, and understand the experiences, of other living things.

In the days and weeks that followed, Paul returned to his Kumaric studies each weekday afternoon, sitting or walking by the river, watching and trying to empathize with the creatures around him, and stopping now and then to read from *The Little Book*.

In the evenings and on weekends, when he was in the company of other people, Paul would try to imagine how things seemed from their perspectives and how they felt about whatever was going on. He found that often people were happy to talk about themselves, and that listening to what they told him helped him deepen his understanding.

Paul enjoyed all of these activities—by the river, and with the people he and Jessica socialized with. He liked being in nature, and he liked hearing what others would share about themselves. And through it all, he felt that his perspective was gradually broadening and deepening, building on the understanding of himself he'd brought from the Retreat—and carrying him, slowly but surely, toward someplace new.

◩   ◩   ◩

And so life went on for Paul and Jessica, moving like this in an easy rhythm from day to day. Paul had explained to Jessica, already, that he was busy each day studying the physics of her world and not on work for his job in Strandford—which was, after all, a whole world away—and how he hoped that, by learning how physics had developed on the world they now shared, he could prepare himself to be hired for the sort of professional work he'd most like to do. Jessica had listened to him as he'd explained, then she'd smiled and told him to take all the time he needed.

And so, as the weeks went by, Paul continued with his physics studies in the mornings and early afternoons, and with his Kumaric studies for an hour or so after that. Each morning, Jessica left for her job in Cuyama, and each evening she returned to her home and a meal already prepared for her.

Though others might have thought their lives routine, both Paul and Jessica were happy and—it was clear to both of them—truly in love. All of Jessica's friends and family, who had always thought of her as somewhat serious, now marveled at how constantly cheerful she had become.

One day, early in October, Paul was down by the river when he heard an SPV pull up in front of Jessica's house. He walked the short distance back to the house and saw that it was Jessica arriving home.

When Paul reached the SPV, Jessica had already climbed out of it and was standing behind it, taking something from the trunk.

"Why are you back so early?" Paul asked.

"Do you know what day this is?" Jessica answered, smiling.

Paul shook his head.

"It's our three-month anniversary!" she said. "It's been three months since we became a couple—three months since the first night we made love."

"How could it be three months already?" Paul asked. "It seems like no time at all."

"I know—time seems to fly by for me, too, since you came here, Paul. But I have to pay attention to the calendar at work, you know. And it has been three months." She kissed him. "So I arranged to leave work a little early today. I wanted to spend a special evening with you."

"I don't even have dinner ready," Paul said, his tone apologetic.

"It's too early for dinner. Have you started it?" Jessica replied.

"No."

"Good," she said. "Because tonight I'm cooking for you. You always cook for me, Paul. It's my turn." She lifted a bag of groceries from the back of the SPV and handed it to Paul, then took out another for her to carry.

Paul followed her inside, thinking about the gift he was preparing for her, and how nice it would have been if somehow it could have been ready for tonight, as well. Still, who knew how long it would take, he told himself. He had to be patient.

Paul closed the door to the house behind him, and as he turned, Jessica's copy of *Memories and Reflections* caught his eye. On impulse, Paul set the bag of groceries down on the little table across from the door and flipped through the pages of the book until he had reached the portion he had yet to read. He kept meaning to go back and finish it, he told himself—he just hadn't gotten to it yet.

Paul glanced down at the page he had turned to. It was the first page of chapter XVIII, and the epigraph written there caught Paul's eye:

> *As ice surrenders*
> *to a brilliant flame*
> *so opens*
> *my heart.*
>
> —G. L. DeWitt

Paul flipped through a few more pages, then stopped again at the beginning of the next chapter:

> *Only the open blossom*
> *feels the sun's*
> *full warmth.*
>
> —Mizuki Inoue

Paul smiled. Yes, he told himself, he would have to get back to this book before too long.

"Hey, where are you?" Jessica called from the kitchen.

"Almost there," Paul called back. He picked up the bag of groceries and carried it in to Jessica.

"You should at least let me give you a hand," Paul said. "We're best when we cook together."

○　○　○

It was a delicious meal that Paul and Jessica shared that night, full of all the foods that Paul had come to love most since his arrival in that world. As had become their habit, they sat out on the deck to eat it, looking out at the warm glow in the western sky, as the sun sank gradually below the distant mountains.

For the two of them, conversation had grown as easy as if they had known each other all their lives—only with the added bonus that there was still so much that they could discover about one another. On that particular evening, they spoke about their childhoods and the dreams they had had for their lives when they were growing up. Paul told Jessica that when he was little he had thought he would like to be a deep-sea diver, because he liked the idea of walking on the ocean's bottom. Jessica told Paul that her earliest aspiration was to make friends with an antelope and then learn to ride it.

Paul smiled.

"I was very serious about it," Jessica said, "when I was, oh, I'd say about seven years old. I would sit outside, very quietly, and wait for one to approach me. I thought if I could pet it, then, well, it would be tame, and we could be friends." She shook her head, smiling and laughing a little to herself. "But none of them ever got close enough for any of that to happen."

"And when you rode it, where did you think you would go?" Paul asked.

"Oh, anywhere. That was half the idea. I could have gone anywhere, you see, after that."

"And instead you became a Kumaric instructor," Paul said.

"They're not so different," Jessica told him. "I'm friendly with people, and then they let me travel inside with them."

"Yeah, I guess maybe it's not so different," Paul said, smiling.

"Why did you want to walk on the ocean's bottom?" Jessica asked.

"I don't know." Paul shrugged. "The bottom of the ocean—what would that be like? And they had equipment for it, for the really deep places. It was kind of new, so the kids talked about it. It was designed for mining, I think, to find there what they'd run out of everywhere else. The pollution from it really spoiled things, I guess, but I just wanted to walk there."

The two of them talked like that, about small things, for a couple of hours, out on the deck, as the evening deepened into night. Finally, with the night sounds rising all around them, they rose and cleared the table. Together, Jessica and Paul did the dishes, then they retired early for the night.

That night, as Paul and Jessica made love together, Paul felt as though he truly were a deep-sea diver, diving into the deepest waters shared between them and walking there with Jessica.

On this night, in particular, their love making seemed especially piercing and sweet, as though the passageways between them had been made completely clear and open by the torrent of love they both were feeling. As that deep passion and tenderness flooded through Paul, it seemed to open, within his very self, corridors that he had never before realized could be opened—and which allowed him to dive, now, even more deeply and encompassingly, into the vast tenderness and love he felt for Jessica.

For all the closeness that had developed between them in recent months, Paul now felt even closer to her, still, so that everything she was, he cherished and gathered to the heart of him—and found, now, within him, in the deepest part of himself.

When they were done with their love making, and those flooding waters that had washed through Paul receded, he found himself changed, somehow—yet still open, as he had never before felt himself to be. He and Jessica lay, then, holding one another, as the moonlight streamed in through the window behind the bed, flooding their bed in its light, and drenching them in it.

As Jessica nestled into Paul's embrace and slowly drifted off to sleep, Paul lay awake, feeling the change that had taken place within him. It was as though something had moved through him and opened up everything in its path—had opened up all his veins and arteries, even, and allowed his blood to flow further than he had ever felt it flow before.

Paul got up and pulled on his pants. Jessica was sound asleep now, and as Paul moved around the room, he tried not to wake her.

Quietly, he pulled open the sliding door and slipped out past the curtain and onto the back deck. The moonlight flowed in around him. He could hear the crickets and frogs singing from down by the river.

Paul slipped on the sandals he kept on the deck and crept silently down the steps and on toward the river. It was as though there were something calling to him, calling him to move outside and into the open spaces—and on beyond them, still opening.

The moonlight, all shiny and cool, seemed to slip over Paul's bare skin, but the air itself was warm, still carrying some of the heat of a summer day.

Paul reached the cottonwood tree where he often sat in the afternoons. He looked up as the moonlight poured itself through the tree's leaves and slid down its branches like rain. From the river's bank he heard a splash, as a pond turtle slipped into the water. The moonlight shone on the water, too—flowing down from the sky and into the river. The voices of the frogs along the river's bank seemed full of that water, too—full of water and moonlight.

What was this new feeling within him? Paul wondered. Everything around him seemed so vibrant and alive—so enriched, somehow. He had this odd sensation that when he inhaled, he inhaled a bit of this vibrant landscape, of this living world, into his lungs, into his body. And when he released his breath, he released it back out into the land, and a little bit of himself went with it—some of his warmth, some of the moisture he had given it, but also something of him: his mood, his essence.

He was taking in, and sharing with, what was around him, just as he had shared himself with Jessica only a little while before.

What a beautiful sensation, Paul thought. It was all so beautiful—everything around him.

Paul noticed the stars shining in the river, then looked up at the stars above. They also shone beautifully—beautiful like everything else in this landscape, but also beautiful in their own way, too.

Paul looked at them and remembered them, then, not just from his months on Jessica's world, but from all his years on his own world, too.

Yes, those are my stars, Paul thought—and as he thought it, he could feel them reaching into him, too—their light beamed from many thousands of light years away, traveling all that distance to find him here, now, in this instant—pouring over him, like the moonlight through the leaves.

His stars, the stars of his world, Paul told himself—and what he had been trying to push away and disown, for months, came flooding back over him. *His world*—and all that he had hoped for, for it. All that he had dreamed of for it. All the people he had known. All the suffering he had seen there. It was all still in him, remembered within him—and he felt for his world, still.

Paul let his eyes fall from the sky and found the stars still there in the river before him. All those people, he thought—all of their sadness, all of their isolation, all of their suffering!

His heart broke, thinking of it.

All their sorrows and pain, their heartaches and loneliness, their destitution and despair—it was all so needless! He could see that now, having lived on this world. Life need not be such a well of sorrow.

It was so unnecessary—and so terribly sad.

Paul stood, staring into the river, with all the stars afloat on it—seemingly millions, no billions of points of light, and each one like the light of an individual human life.

If only they could understand what he had come to understand, Paul told himself. But they don't understand. They don't nearly.

What was it Jessica had said, three months ago? Paul asked himself. What had she said when he had told her about all that had gone wrong on his world?

Paul took a deep breath and tried to recall, letting the memory drift back to him.

Yes, he thought—she said then that his world had never emerged.

That was it, exactly.

It wasn't their fault, Paul told himself. It was never their fault. It was not that they were the failed ones, while this world had succeeded.

No, in truth, they had never really been given a chance.

Paul shook his head.

Dr. Kumar's memoirs were never published there, he told himself. He caught his breath, as the thought seemed to travel on, carried on its own current within him.

They never had a chance to read her book. They never had a chance to learn how to change—how to heal what was in their hearts, how to heal their relationships, how to heal the world around them.

Paul wiped tears away. So sad. All that suffering, all those lost, lonely people—and they'd never really had a chance. The knowledge was never offered to them.

If they had been given the same chance, they would have succeeded, too, Paul told himself. And in a flash, he realized how true it really was—that his world would have been *exactly* like this one, if only it had been given the same opportunity.

The fact was, if that opportunity had been given, his world *would have been this world*—exactly, truly, and entirely—because no branching event would ever have occurred to separate them.

In that moment, Paul felt such love for everything—everything. For all the people of his world, even the most horribly lost and wicked among them. For all the other creatures of his world, destroyed and lost forever because of those very same people. For everything and everyone—for the turtle that had slipped into the water just minutes before; for the tree above him; for the land rolling out from this valley, rolling out across this world; for all of the people of this world with their healed hearts; and for Jessica, especially—who was, now, sleeping alone, only meters from where Paul now stood.

All of these deserved love—all of them. And the lost, lonely people of his world not least of all, but perhaps most—because there was where that love was most sorely needed.

Paul had a feeling in his chest, full and aching, as though his heart were now too large for the space there. He stood, silent, dumbfounded by all that was sweeping through him.

The light played on the water. A breeze rustled through the reeds and through the leaves of the other plants along the river, singing through them. Then, gradually, words returned to Paul. As he stood there, feeling connected to all the life around him, sharing with it a certain intimacy, just as he had been intimate with Jessica only a short time before, Paul felt such love for his surroundings—and felt also, now, a deep love for his own world, piercing and beautiful, lovely and painful all at once.

All they needed was a chance to emerge, he told himself.

That was all they needed.

As he thought about it, a trembling started deep within him and seemed to flow out through him, taking hold at his center and then moving out through his limbs, until he found himself shaking all over.

Paul wrapped his arms around his shoulders, then dropped to his knees in the tall grass.

All they needed was a chance to emerge.

It was so obvious. It was so sweetly, beautifully, dreadfully, painfully obvious.

Another wave of trembling swept over Paul, starting in his heart, and bursting his heart as it moved outward. It carried him along, even as he struggled against it, like a swimmer against a torrent.

But struggle as he did, he could not resist it.

It was so obvious. It was so plainly, truly, brutally obvious.

And so Paul—kneeling there beneath the stars—dropped his face into his hands, and sobbed.

He knew then what he must do, what he had to do, and even just the thought of it tore his heart to shreds.

◻   ◻   ◻

Paul stepped back into the bedroom and slowly slid the door closed behind him. He wanted to be as quiet as possible for Jessica, so as not to wake her, but as he turned away from the door, he stumbled over a pair of shoes that had been left there.

He could hear Jessica roll over in bed.

"Paul?" she said.

He could see her shape where she lay in the bed, turned toward him.

"Paul—why are you up?" she asked.

"It's okay," he whispered. "Go back to sleep." He could hear the sadness in his own voice.

"What is it, Paul? Is something wrong?"

"It's all right," he said, his voice rugged. "Just go back to sleep."

Jessica sat up. "What is it, Paul?" Her tone, though groggy, was gentle and consoling.

Paul turned fully toward her. "Not now, Jessica. In the morning."

"Come here," she said, her voice soft, sleepy.

Paul walked around the end of the bed and sat down beside her. She lay back down. He stroked her face with one hand.

"I'm awake now, Paul. Won't you talk to me?"

Paul swallowed hard. If only he could make his voice sound normal.

"You're sad, Paul," she said.

"Yes," he said.

"Why?"

"My world."

"Your world?"

Paul nodded.

"What about your world?" Jessica asked.

"I, ah, I was restless and went for a little walk. You know, ah—well, you know the only thing that's different between our worlds is that you had *Memories and Reflections* published here. That led to all that followed—and now you have this." Paul gestured toward the sliding door and the world outside it.

"We weren't so lucky," he said.

"We? I thought you felt like you belonged here, now, Paul."

"I do. But not *just* here. You see," Paul said, and his voice grew rough again, "it's like you said, a few months ago, when we were talking, you said my world—my earth—had never emerged. Well, that's why. That's it. That's the only difference between our worlds."

Paul looked at Jessica, tracing her outline with his eyes in the semi-darkness.

"That's what they need, Jessica. They need *Memories and Reflections*—or at least what it holds within it. Maybe that knowledge can do there what it did here." Paul shook his head. "I thought they needed fewer people. But even that would be, at best, a temporary fix. No, you named it. You named what they needed. They need the emergence. They need to emerge."

Paul hung his head. He didn't know how to say the rest to her. Tears began to run down his face. He sniffed. Jessica reached up her hand to stroke his cheek. She could feel the tears there.

"Why? Why so sad, Paul?" she asked.

"If they could only be told. If somebody could only tell them what's possible— what they aren't seeing, yet. They could see it, too—just like what happened here. They could see it—and then..." Paul looked down at Jessica, "What if my world could be well, too? I had thought all was lost. But it doesn't have to be. There's so much suffering there—so much—but it doesn't have to be."

Paul took Jessica's hand and kissed it.

"Oh, Paul. Are you thinking...," Jessica began, and now, for the first time, her voice began to take on some of the ache audible in Paul's.

"I have to try to tell them," he said.

"You're thinking of going. Is that why you're crying, Paul?"

Paul nodded.

"Couldn't you go and just come back?" Jessica asked.

A sob broke loose from Paul's chest.

"Couldn't you?" she asked.

"I would try," Paul answered, after a minute.

"Try? But you came here. Couldn't you just come back the same way again?" Jessica asked, imploring him.

"Maybe," Paul answered, then he looked at Jessica, holding her eyes in his gaze in the dim light. He hardly knew where to begin, but he knew he had to explain to her.

"The aiming," he said. "There's a problem with the aiming."

He took a deep breath, then went on, explaining that he thought he knew how it worked, but in truth, he couldn't be sure it would take him where he intended to go.

"And then there's Corprogov and the original transport unit," he went on. "That unit has probably been dismantled, used for scrap—but even if it hasn't been, even if it's still intact, I mustn't let Corprogov find out that I've returned. If they did, then they would also know that the first transport was a success— and they would continue to pursue the Depopulation Project. They would try to see it through—even if I refused to cooperate, they would still pursue it. And if they succeeded, on their own, like that, they'd invade this world, Jessica. They would ruin it all—and that is something I must never allow to happen," Paul concluded, a deep sadness in his voice.

He shook his head, then went on explaining, emphasizing that he would have to keep his return a secret, and never let Corprogov know he was there. Because of that, he would only be able to take work outside of Corprogov, and outside of everything they regulated and observed.

None of that work would pay much, Paul told Jessica—and so he would never be able to afford all the parts and all the energy credits he would need in order to build and operate a new transport. Even with what he had learned about lightning capture and energy storage in her world—well, that informa- tion would be useless without massive funding—funding sufficient not just to build the parts, but to build the machines that could produce the ultranano components. Even if he could afford, somehow, to buy what he needed to build his own transport there, he would never be able to afford the energy to run it.

Paul tried to explain, to make it all clear to her: the aiming might not work, and so he might not even get there—and once there, it was unlikely that he would ever be able to return.

While he spoke, Jessica listened. She sat up in bed and turned on the small light on the bedside table and gave Paul her complete attention—listening closely, asking questions wherever she needed to in order to entirely understand what he was saying.

"So you would still go, then," Jessica said, wiping away her own tears, "even though you know you'd probably never come back?"

Paul held both her hands in his and looked into her eyes. "I want you to understand. I love you, Jessica. I can't imagine loving anybody more. But what I realized outside, a little while ago, is that it's us—our happiness—against the potential happiness of a whole world. They're suffering, Jessica. They're suffering now and every day—and may suffer for centuries or millennia to come. And I could stop that. Quite possibly I could—just by going back there and telling what I've learned. I could post it to the Stream. It could be anonymous—and it would still get out there. It could spread quickly through the Stream, Jessica. It could really spread fast."

Paul took a deep breath, then added, "If it were just for me, for us, I would stay here, Jessica. I don't just wish I could spend my life with you. I feel, somehow, like if I had more lives to live, I would want to spend not just this one, but all of them with you. But if I go, I could help so many others. It could make such a difference—for now, and for all the years to come. For a whole world, Jessica. For thirteen billion people."

Jessica was smiling when Paul finished, though her eyes still welled with tears. She freed one hand from his, then put it behind his head and pulled him close enough to kiss him—a deep, heartfelt kiss, which, though brief, was full of passion.

"I love you, and I'm so proud of you," Jessica said.

"Proud?" Paul said.

"Paul, don't you see? You've emerged. This is stage three. You're thinking of everyone, feeling for everyone. Oh, Paul, I'm so proud of you." She smiled some more, then her voice caught in her throat, like a laugh, almost, as her tears began to fall again.

"So you'll really go, then," she said.

"I'm sorry, Jessica. I'm so sorry," Paul said. He gathered her in his arms and held her while she cried. Now it was her turn to sob out her sorrow.

Paul held her and rocked her, for as long as it took, crying along with her.

◻︎   ◻︎   ◻︎

After a little while, Jessica sat up straight again and dried her face with her hands. Then she looked at Paul, her eyes full of seriousness. A look both of shock and courage, somehow, was on her face—but something more, too, something steady and solid.

"Paul," she said, "I want to go with you."

"Come with me?" Paul said, surprised. "You would do that? You would give up everything you have here and come with me?"

"I would come with you, Paul."

"You would come with me—when you wouldn't go with Kade?" Paul asked.

"This is different, Paul," Jessica told him.

"How is it different?" he asked.

"When Kade went to Massachusetts—it was different. I loved him. I did. When we were together, he was going through a change—a transformation, really. It was like watching a butterfly emerge from its chrysalis. But the man he became, as beautiful and perfect in his own way as he was—his path wasn't my path, Paul. He belonged in a different life, then."

Jessica thought for a moment, then went on. "I feel aligned with you Paul. I told you this the night you first told me where you were from. Deep, deep within me I feel that we fit, that we're right for one another. The very fact that you've chosen this, to go away from me, only proves to me further that you belong with me and me with you."

Paul smiled. "You're not making sense," he said.

"Yes, I am. Don't you see it? I've built my life around finding ways to help people emerge. That's what happened with Kade—he emerged, and he flew away from me, this beautiful butterfly. And now you, Paul—you've emerged, too—but where you're flying to, that's just where I wish I could go: where the work I do is needed most. You've emerged to become someone who wants to help others along on this path. That's the sort of work I do, Paul— the sort of work I dream of doing: to help not just individuals, but a whole world. We're alike in that way now, Paul, you and I—we share a common goal—and I love you. I want to be with you. In every way, it makes sense for me to go."

Paul's heart soared at the thought. Then he sighed. "Oh, Jessica—but you *can't*."

"Why can't I?" she said. In her voice was a note of defiance.

"No, it's not like you think," Paul said. "I want you to go. But it's just not *possible*."

"It's possible for you," she said.

"No—it's possible for *one* person—not *two*. You don't understand, Jessica. I want you with me, but it just won't work. We wouldn't *survive*—neither of us would."

Paul struggled to find the right words.

"It's the machine," he continued, "the transport. People can't go through in groups. We tried it with mice. What tortured creatures they became, for the few minutes they survived after the transport! The transport thinks in units— in electromagnetically unified sets. That's how it works. That's how it has to work. There's no getting around it. And when you send through a group—a group of mice, a group of people—then the transport will try to relocate them as one unit: as one electromagnetically unified set. The system recognizes bone as bone, brain as brain. It tries to put everything back together as one creature. But it can't—there's no way to make sense of it. All the parts will come through combined, and misaligned, and jutting out everywhere. It's horrible. When we tried it with mice, they never lived long." Paul shuddered. "That's what would happen to us, Jessica—we would be combined, the total sum of two human beings, all mixed together."

"Then couldn't we transport one right after the other?" Jessica asked.

"No—maybe, but maybe not. I'm just not sure about the aiming, Jessica, like I said. I *think* there's a link between our worlds, that wherever we aim the transport, we'd just arrive at the starting point, but on the other one's world—*but I just don't know for sure.* There could be some wild card I haven't guessed at, that I don't understand. I only have *one* transport event to calibrate by. Just *one*, Jessica—that's not enough. We could both go, then end up on entirely different worlds, for all I know."

For a moment, Paul recalled the feeling he'd had when he'd first arrived on this world, and he thought he'd never see another human being again. And then there was the dream he'd had of the acid world. They could both end up someplace like that—or one in one place, and the other in another.

Paul shook his head. "Really, Jessica, it really is too risky. I *have* to go. It's my world. I know how to get around there, how to communicate with them. But there's no reason for both of us to take that sort of risk."

"So you would still go—though you're not even sure if you'd end up where you meant to?" Jessica asked.

Paul thought carefully. "Yes," he said, his voice dry and suddenly quiet. A shiver ran through him at the thought of all that could go wrong. He had been so pleased when he had thought he would never have to risk transporting again.

Paul shook his head. "I have to go, Jessica. I have to try." He steadied his eyes on her. "I'd never be able to live with myself, if I didn't—not now—not now that I know, now that I understand what it could mean to them. It's not just for the present. It'd be for all time going forward. It would change things for them, from that point forward—just like it did when Dr. Kumar introduced her ideas here. If I can do it right, if I can communicate what needs to be said, it would be the same thing, as important as that, for my world, too. I hope you can see that, Jessica. I hope you can understand."

Even as Paul said this, he wished he could take it all back, could take it all back and forget all about it—could fold himself into her arms, and never have to leave them.

Jessica nodded solemnly. "Oh, Paul—how I wish I could argue with you, try to talk you out of this—but I *do* understand. I really, really do. So many lives! So many lives you could help. You could make such a difference." She looked stunned for several moments, then looked up at Paul, bravely.

"Will it be like when you arrived here?" she asked. "You'll be all naked and bald again?"

"Yes," Paul said, nodding.

"It'll be a shame for you to lose all that beautiful hair," she said, reaching up and stroking his head. "You've only just gotten it back." She leaned her head onto Paul's shoulder, then, and pulled him close.

Paul could feel a light trembling moving through her and into him. He held her then—as she held him, each seeking comfort, each giving comfort to the other.

After a minute or two, Jessica lifted her head. "So you can't bring *anything* with you—not even a copy of a book?" she asked. She leaned back and looked at Paul.

"No, it'll just be me, and what I can tell," he told her.

"Then I guess you'll want to use Synaplast, Paul," she said.

"What?" Paul said, though the word sounded familiar.

"Synaplast. It will let you memorize all of *Memories and Reflections*, if you want to," she told him. "It's a lot, but you could do it."

"Oh—yeah," Paul said. He nodded a little as he took the thought in. "That's a good idea. That could help a lot."

He looked at Jessica and could see how hard this all was for her. She wanted to do the right thing. She wanted to try to help, he knew—but he also could see how torn she was, even just to say those few words. It was hard for her to do anything to help him go.

Paul stroked her hair, his hand moving from the top of her head and down over her shoulders.

He looked her in the eye. "We don't have to talk about this now," he told her. "It's late. I woke you. We should go back to sleep. It's best if we both rest, now, I think."

Jessica nodded, and Paul suddenly realized how very tired she looked, much more so than she had when he'd first waked her, just a little while before.

"Come on to bed, then, Paul," she said softly. "I want you here with me."

Paul got undressed and crawled into bed beside Jessica. He knew there was still a lot for them to discuss, but that could wait till morning. For now, he just wanted to pull her close—to pull her close and to hold onto her, still, for as long as he might.

Full of heartache and fatigue, they soon drifted off to sleep together, each still damp with the other one's tears.

◻ 31 ◻

It was hard to face the bright, sunny day with the sadness they both felt, but at least there was comfort in the fact that they both felt it, and both agreed that there was no other choice about what had to be done.

Paul felt, now, that each day he spent on Jessica's world was another day in which the suffering of his own world might have been abated. He felt—and Jessica agreed with him about this, too—that he had a responsibility not to linger longer than necessary with her there, before executing his plan. All that was left was for him to take the practical steps required for his departure.

Paul and Jessica sat at the small table next to the kitchen and discussed all this over breakfast that weekend morning. She told him again how pleased she was, and how proud, that he had reached stage three. It was, in fact, the sort of gift to her that Paul had meant it to be.

They talked, too, about Jessica's suggestion that Paul use Synaplast, and the sort of commitment that was involved in choosing to hold such a large text in one's memory forever. Paul was conscious of the gravity of that decision, but he could also see that it would be the only way to bring the book back with him. He told Jessica that he would do it, but would wait until it was closer to the time when he would leave.

After that, their conversation turned to the question of how Paul could afford the parts he would need to build a new transport unit. He told Jessica what he thought it would cost, then began to discuss what would be required for him to get employment so that he could pay for it.

"No, Paul," Jessica told him. "You needn't do that." She looked down at her empty plate and turned it a little on the table. "I have savings. It's enough to cover the costs you're talking about."

"You have that much?"

"Uh-hm." Jessica nodded.

"How do you happen to have that much saved?" Paul asked.

Jessica shrugged. "I guess you could say I take a Kumaric view of money."

Paul shook his head. "That—I have no idea what that means."

"Well, it means I believe that every creature has a right to what it needs, but not to more than what it needs. Having money doesn't give people a right to take more than their share of the earth's resources. Everything we use means life to something else. I'd rather live in a world where there's more life, than one where I have more things."

Paul had the feeling he'd heard someone say something like that before. Oh yes—it was Zaid, the boy Paul had met on his way to the Retreat.

"Anyway," Jessica went on, "I sort of figured I was saving for the future. Now, I guess maybe it's better if it goes to help the future of your world, Paul."

Jessica looked aside and frowned a little, then looked back at Paul. "I have to admit, I don't like the idea of helping you leave—but at the same time, I think you're right about all this. It's really for the best. You can have that money to build the transport."

"You don't have to do that, Jessica," Paul said.

"No, I don't—but I want to, really. Who ever has a chance to do something this important—to make so big a difference? It's as important as what Dr. Kumar did, really—but this time it's for your world, not mine. I'd really like to help, Paul.

"Besides," she added, "it's like you said—the time we waste now only means more suffering for your world. It will take you too long to earn the money. I can give it to you now." She glanced down at the plate again, then up at Paul.

"Okay, Jessica," Paul said. "If you're sure."

"I'm sure I wish you could go and save your world. I only wish you could stay here, too. But it's decided. You should have the money."

"Thanks," Paul said, and for a moment they both looked at one another solemnly, with shared affection.

"So then what's next?" Jessica said, after a moment.

Paul thought about it. Everything was happening so fast now—he felt as though he were trailing behind each moment, trying to keep up with it. All the plans he had put in place when he had been preparing to go—they were all lined up so neatly now. He felt like everything was in place, and he was sliding toward an inevitable outcome. He must go. He must not stay. And yet, he still wanted so very much to stay with Jessica.

Paul turned his attention back to Jessica's question. "I have a list," he said. "It has all the parts needed to build a transport. I've already put it together in a holographic 3D projection, at the Retreat. It shouldn't be hard to construct.

"I have a price list in the same file," Paul added. "It's on a crystal—a data sphere. It's still in my pack, I think. I'll get it in a little while."

"What else? Is there anything else?" Jessica asked. Paul looked at her. Though she'd slept nearly long enough, she still looked as tired as she had the night before.

It's the sadness, Paul thought. He was sure that was it.

"An energy supply," Paul answered. "We'll need a Portable Lightning Capture Unit. If we can get the parts for it already made, I can build that, too. I've studied the plans."

Jessica laughed.

"What?" Paul said. Jessica was smiling. It was good to see her smile.

"Or maybe just rent one, already charged? PLCUs are easy to get, Paul. You don't have to make one."

Paul smiled back. "Right," he said. "That makes sense. I guess I'm just a little disoriented. I'm getting ready to go. I can't believe it—I'm really preparing to go."

He looked at Jessica. "I wasn't ever going to go. I wasn't ever..."

"I know, Paul," she said. "Me, too."

They both tightened their hold on one another's hands.

"I should get the crystal," Paul said, after a moment.

Jessica looked at him deeply, and he could see the same sadness welling up in her that he felt within himself. At least we feel it to together, Paul thought. There was, at least, some comfort in that.

"It's in your pack?" Jessica said, standing up.

"Yeah," Paul said, as he stood, too. They embraced and kissed. Then Jessica took Paul's hand and together they went to the closet in her room to find the information that would help them send Paul back to the world from which he had come.

After Paul had taken time to review his selections, together, they ordered the needed parts through the portal.

That they were doing these things together felt odd to Paul, as though some special closeness, some special intimacy lay in this careful process of preparing for his departure. Like the closeness of a family preparing for a funeral, he thought—or like falling a long distance. You know you're going to hit, and that it's going to be so painful—but for right now, you're just floating through the air, and everything is lovely.

And everything was lovely, with the two of them together, on a beautiful summer day, working toward a shared goal.

After Paul and Jessica were done with the ordering, they went for a walk by the river, then had a nice lunch out on the deck. It was Jessica's day off, and she had, even before, planned to spend it alone with Paul. Now they were especially glad for that solitude.

For long stretches, then, it seemed as though nothing had changed. It was just as it had been for months before, with the two of them there, together. By the evening, they had set their worries about what was to come aside, and were just enjoying being together, again.

That night, they promised one another their eternal love, even if a whole world kept them apart. Even if both went on to love others, they promised, that love, their love, would still be in them, too.

◫　◫　◫

When the weekend was over, Jessica returned to her job, and Paul had plenty of time to contemplate various ways he might try to return to Jessica's earth, once he had gone back to his. Each scenario he thought of seemed far fetched to him: If only he could suddenly get rich... If only he could find the place the scrapped parts of the original transport had been sold to... Or if it hadn't been sold for scrap, if only he could break into his old lab, without the automated security protocols recognizing him... And if he could get into his old lab, and the transport was still there, if only they had sufficient energy credits available to use...

But then Paul would remind himself that there was still the whole question of aiming, and he would sigh and let his thoughts drift someplace else.

During those days, while Jessica was working and before the transport parts had arrived, Paul would think, sometimes, about how his world would change as it began to emerge. Socially, it would become more like Jessica's, he told himself—but he knew, too, that there were scars it would always bear. The oceans would still have risen, the climate still have changed. And so many animals that had once existed would still be extinct.

Unless. Unless, Paul thought—perhaps one day, when his world had really emerged, he might be able to move freely between his world and this. That time would likely be decades away, he told himself. It might not arrive even in his lifetime, but if it did, Paul imagined himself returning to Jessica, and then traveling back and forth, an old man sending animals from one world to repopulate extinct species on another.

That would be grand, Paul thought—if only they could find a niche for them, still, on his climate-changed world.

Paul found the fantasy satisfying, but he knew that if that day ever did come, it would take time to arrive. And he didn't like the idea of waiting until he was old before he could see Jessica again.

So it was that Paul and Jessica passed the few days it took for the parts for the transport to begin to arrive. Then, together, they began the process of constructing and testing it. It took them a little over a week to put it together, with Paul working alone during the day on weekdays, and the two of them working together on weekday evenings and weekends.

The parts went together smoothly, as Paul had predicted they would, and soon the machine was able to perform the small transport tasks that were possible using just household power. It wasn't long before they had their new transport tuned up and performing as well as the one in Paul's lab had been on the day he had been accidentally transported by it.

For several more days after that, Paul spent his time going over the aiming theory he had developed. Though there was simply not enough data for him to feel that his conclusions were certain, he could, nonetheless, not punch any holes in them. He was as certain as he could be that his theory was correct—but even so, he very much wished he could be more certain than that.

At the very least, Paul concluded, he should be as careful as possible. If his world and Jessica's really were connected as Interdimensional-Linking Theory suggested, then he would arrive back on his world in the same spot from which he had departed from Jessica's, no matter where he aimed the transport. There was, therefore, Paul reasoned, no need to risk sending himself to a distant planet such as G3-97. It was far more sensible to aim the transport more cautiously, and so, to some degree, at least, reduce his risk.

◫ ◫ ◫

One day, during this time, Jessica came home with a bluish powder in a small vial.

"It's Synaplast," she told Paul. "I'm not sure when you'll want to use it, but it will keep for quite a while."

Together, then, they made careful plans about how many hours it would take to memorize all of *Memories and Reflections*, and what size dose of Synaplast Paul would have to take in order to commit it all to memory.

Jessica explained to Paul that for various reasons it was best to do all the memorizing in one session, but that, since *Memories and Reflections* ran for nearly twenty-seven hours, it would have to be speeded up if it was to be memorized in one session of a reasonable length.

"Your personal player will let you speed it up without changing the pitch, I'm sure. Don't worry—it won't sound strange to you. When you're on the Synaplast, your mind will be recording information so readily, so quickly, that everything else in the world around you will seem slowed down in comparison. So it really won't seem as though your personal player is talking too fast. Still, once you start, you'll want to adjust the speed setting until it seems right for you. You'll want to be sure it's set to at least one and a half times normal, though. That should let you finish within about an eighteen-hour window. That's sort of on the outside of how long you would want a session to run, but it should be all right."

Paul and Jessica agreed that since Paul's purpose in memorizing *Memories and Reflections* was so important, that he take enough Synaplast to be sure he was still fully under its influence when he got to the end of that eighteen hours—since that was when he would be memorizing the detailed material in the appendixes at the end of Dr. Kumar's memoirs.

Based on that, Jessica calculated the dose he would have to take. He would start with a partial dose at the beginning, then take a second "booster" dose midway through.

"It may seem," Jessica told Paul, "like it will be hard to stay awake and concentrate for that long, but the Synaplast will make your mind unusually alert. It would be impossible to fall asleep while using it.

"The really important thing is just to be sure you're comfortable before you start," she went on. "Whatever you experience while you're on it will stay with you forever. I knew someone who was bitten by a mosquito when he was memorizing text. It was a problem for him, because the memory of the itching stayed with him and came to his mind whenever he recalled the text, just as vividly as if it were happening all over again. So you'll want to be sure you're comfortable, Paul, and in a good state of mind. We'll find a way to make you as comfortable as possible. You can use the bedroom, if you like—and I'll make sure it's very quiet here that day. Most people recommend doing it in bed, undressed. You don't want lasting memorizes of binding clothing, or anything like that. The weather's still warm. That'll help."

Paul listened carefully. He understood that the drug he would be taking would alter his brain for hours afterward—and in some ways, permanently—and so he wanted to do this right.

"It's a lot to memorize, Paul," Jessica added. "It's a lot to hold within you. Once you do it, you know, it will always be with you."

"I understand," Paul said, looking Jessica in the eye. "What I really wish is that I could memorize you." He smiled. "Then, in a sense, you would always be with me."

For the next few days, Paul rested, and relaxed, and ate good meals, trying to prepare himself for his memorization task. When the weekend came again, Jessica helped prepare the bedroom for him. She tidied up the room, then put the softest sheets on the bed and drew the curtains shut. She also had borrowed from a friend a special sort of headset, which was soft and comfortable, and would block out outside noise.

That Sunday morning, both Paul and Jessica rose before dawn and ate a good breakfast. Jessica placed water and tasty foods by the bed, so Paul could drink and eat when he liked, then she mixed the Synaplast with a little juice and offered it to Paul.

Paul took it from her hand and swallowed down half of it.

"It's almost 5 AM now," Jessica said. "You'll want to remember to take the rest of that at about two this afternoon."

"I know," Paul said.

"And remember to wait until the first dose has fully taken effect before you start the recitation. When you start having the feeling that everything is happening very slowly around you, almost like time has slowed down, and you begin to feel like everything that's happening is very, very familiar, like a sense of déjà vu, then you'll know the Synaplast is really working. That's when you should start the recitation. That's when you'll be able to memorize the way you need to."

"Okay. I've got it," Paul said. "And don't worry—I'll be fine."

Jessica smiled up at him. "I know you will be," she said. "But if there's anything you need me for, I'll be right out here—actually, in the office at first, napping." She yawned. "See?" she smiled at Paul. "But you should wake me if you need me—for *anything*."

Paul smiled back at her. "Thanks," he said. It was touching, all the care Jessica had taken to make sure things went right.

"The next time I see you, you'll have all of *Memories and Reflections* within you," she said, then leaned forward and kissed Paul on the cheek, avoiding getting any residue of the Synaplast on her lips.

"Yeah," Paul said, taking a deep breath. He looked at Jessica with deep affection, then pulled her close and held her tenderly for a moment, before turning and disappearing, alone, into their bedroom.

◘   ◘   ◘

"Memories & Reflections: The Memoirs of Indira Kumar," Kiki recited in the darkened room. "Preface to the Second Edition..."

Kiki's familiar voice drifted over Paul as he lay comfortably in bed. As the words washed over him, Paul turned his entire attention to them. He felt, with the Synaplast in his blood, as though each word hung in the air before him, moving through his awareness with a lazy clarity.

Paul checked his personal player, then turned up the speed. He passed the one and a half speed setting, and had it up to just past one point seven, before the words sounded really right to him.

As the words slipped smoothly into and out of his awareness, Paul's attention bore into every word, and every word bore into him, anchoring itself within him. The sense of déjà vu that Jessica had told him to expect was now in full swing, so that Paul felt not just that he had heard these words before—which he had—but that he had already been in this place, hearing these words, in just this way, before. It was as though every thought that entered his mind, every awareness, stayed there, rebounding around inside him—making every association, every connection, and so locking itself there, imbedding itself in his mind with permanent certainty.

Every word of Indira Kumar's text filled Paul with a sense of vivid perception, as he listened to the preface, then traveled with her through her childhood, then her years in college, her experiences in America, and then, later, Zaire.

Somehow, with his mind so full of such vivid impressions, and with each word latching itself to him with such easy precision, Paul was still able to remember to drink the rest of the Synaplast solution by just after two that afternoon.

Then Paul continued on through the journey that was *Memories and Reflections*, as Indira explored the rainforest of Zaire, returned to Boulder, traveled to New Guinea—and on and on, through the story of the rest of her life.

When that story was finally done, and all the appendixes read and memorized, Paul lay in the room's absolute stillness and quiet, thinking about his plans to go, and how very sad he was to leave Jessica.

Paul was aware that the same feeling of slowed-down time and déjà vu was still fully in effect, and so he knew the drug was still active. He knew that he was memorizing every thought, every feeling that passed through his awareness—and he knew, too that the last thing he wanted was to memorize the sadness he felt at parting from Jessica.

"Kiki, what other sorts of files to do you have stored?" Paul asked.

"A comprehensive collection of articles, reviews, and analyses," Kiki said.

"What sort of articles?" Paul asked.

"They discuss historical context, provide biographical data, evaluate social..."

"Okay," Paul interrupted. "The biographical data—what's that like?"

"I have supplemental biographies for all people mentioned in *Memories and Reflections*," Kiki said.

"Okay—recite the supplemental biography for Indira Kumar." Paul didn't want to use this ability to memorize wastefully, but he thought this, at least, might have some value. After all, people might have questions about the author of the memoirs, once he'd returned to his world.

Kiki's voice poured from the headphones into Paul's ears, filling his mind not just with words, but with the pictures those words painted—images and impressions of Indira Kumar's life. Paul found the details interesting enough, but the recitation—which was done, again, at an accelerated speed—seemed to pass very quickly.

When Kiki was finished, Paul sat up and turned on the light on the bedside table. He looked at the clock there. It was almost half-past 9 PM. By pushing the speed setting up a little more than they had planned, Paul had finished close to two hours early, and even with the biography having taken some time, he still had a good hour and a half during which the Synaplast would be fully active. That would be followed, as Jessica had told him, by another hour or two during which most of what he experienced would still be committed to memory, while the Synaplast gradually left his system.

Clearly, Paul had some time to kill. He sighed and looked around the room, and as he did, he had the feeling he'd been there before, dealing with exactly the same dilemma.

Paul smiled, amused at the illusion. Then, naked, he slipped out from beneath the covers and stepped over to the shelf on the far side of the room. Squatting down, he pulled out Jessica's copy of *The Little Book*. He knew it was generally considered ill advised to try to fit more than one book into one person's head, but Paul reasoned that if he was bound to memorize something over the next couple of hours, it might as well be this.

Paul climbed back into bed between the soft sheets Jessica had put there for him, and began reading, picking out his favorite passages first. Some were his favorites because of what they said. Others had been recited to him by Jessica, and so they reminded him of her.

It took Paul more than an hour to read through these passages. He had just finished them and turned back to the beginning of the book when he heard the door to the bedroom swing open, and saw Jessica standing in the doorway, looking to Paul as beautiful as he had ever seen her.

As Jessica stepped into the room and closed the door quietly behind her, Paul set the book on the bedside table. Then Jessica crossed the room and stood, wrapped in her robe, looking down at Paul from beside the bed.

"I figured you would be done by now," she said. "It's been nearly eighteen hours."

Paul nodded.

"Is the Synaplast still active?" she asked.

"Yes," Paul told her.

"I didn't want you to be alone. I didn't want you to be lonely after you'd finished," she said.

"I'm glad you're here." Paul slid over in bed to make room for her, pulling the covers back.

Jessica loosened the belt around her robe, then let the robe fall from her shoulders. She laid the empty robe at the foot of the bed, then slipped between the sheets beside Paul, naked.

"I'm so glad you're here," Paul repeated.

Jessica lay facing him, and he facing her. He stroked her arm with one hand.

"I didn't want you to have loneliness to remember," she told him.

"Good idea," Paul said. "Now I'll have you to remember."

Jessica snuggled up next to Paul as he put his arms around her. Her skin felt so soft and smooth next to his.

"I thought I'd offer you something else to memorize, until the Synaplast wears off," Jessica said, then looked at Paul, and he could see in her eyes all the love and tenderness he'd ever found there—only, because of the drug, he felt that that loving expression went on and on, pulling him in, then holding him gently afloat within it.

"I'm so glad you're here," Paul said, once more, then Jessica pulled him close and kissed him, and he kissed her back. All the love he felt for her, he felt more deeply, in that extended moment. In that rich now, it seemed to Paul that that love, shared between them, was of all time, and for all time—and that if he could not actually be with Jessica always, he would, at least, remember her, and this, for as long as he would live.

◻   ◻   ◻

One evening, a few days later, Jessica came home to find Paul in the small home office, looking at a map on the portal.

"Dinner's just about ready," Paul said, as he looked up and saw her there.

"What's that you're looking at?" Jessica asked.

"A map of Strandford," Paul told her. "I've been trying to decide what the best place would be for me to arrive when I get back. You can't show up just anyplace without your clothes—and especially if I might pass out from the transport, again." Paul thought about how he had put this, as though he were certain he would arrive back on his world, and not wind up someplace else entirely. He had grown quite uneasy about this in recent days, though he did his best to keep his uncertainty from causing Jessica undue concern. If he had to go, then he could, at least, try not to leave her with the worry that he had arrived at some terrible fate.

"That's not Strandford you have up now," Jessica said, peering over Paul's shoulder at the oval portal screen.

"No—I just zoomed out. We're here, right?" Paul said, pointing as he zoomed in on a spot in the Cuyama Valley.

"That's right."

Paul nodded and zoomed back out again. The map showed the Sierra Madre Mountains—with the Cuyama Valley above them, to the northeast, and Strandford, in the Santa Ynez Valley, below them, to the southwest.

"I'll want to arrive in Strandford on my world," Paul said, gesturing toward the screen, "so that's where I'll need to depart from. It'll take a couple of hours to get there in your SPV?" His voice made it a question.

"Yeah, that sounds about right," Jessica told him.

"Okay," Paul said. He zoomed in on the area around Strandford. "This canal, you see here? It exists on my world, too," Paul said. "I think it's been there a long time. It was probably there before our two worlds branched off from one another."

"And that's why it exists on both?" Jessica said.

"That's what I'm thinking. If I can transport from there, I should arrive in the same spot on my world. Along this canal, here, on my world," he pointed, "are some shops that sell clothes, shoes, that sort of thing. If I transport at night, even if I pass out again, hopefully I'll be able to wake before dawn. I should be able to break into one of those shops, then, and get what I need—clothes, shoes, a hat, maybe even. The store will have an alarm, but if I'm careful I should be able to disable it."

Paul thought about it for a moment. "I'll send them some cash later on, when I have it."

"You should take some System Boost and some Stay Awake before you go. Then maybe you won't pass out—or at least not for as long," Jessica said.

Paul nodded. "That's a good idea."

"When are you thinking of going?" Jessica asked. It was a question they had both put off asking. Neither of them wanted the actual day to arrive.

"I'll want to pick a day when the moon is fairly bright—at least half full, so I can see by it. The soonest that would be would be the beginning of November."

Paul looked up at Jessica and sighed. "It will only get colder after that. I don't want to have to wait until spring. It's already pretty chilly at night."

Jessica put her hand on the back of Paul's neck, then leaned over and kissed him.

"Then it's the beginning of November, my love," she said, as she pulled away, then added, "Oh, Paul—that's not even a week away."

"I know," Paul said. He squeezed her hand. "The moon will be half full on the first."

"The first. That's it, then." Jessica straightened up, then said, "I admire you for this."

Paul looked up at her. "We're both making the same sacrifice."

Jessica nodded solemnly, and it seemed to Paul that she was pushing away tears.

"I don't want to think about it," she said. "This is one pain there's no point in probing into."

Paul stood up and took her hand. "Let's get dinner. Everything's ready," he said.

Together, they went into the kitchen, where the air was scented by the lasagna—full of colorful vegetables and freshly picked herbs—that Paul had prepared for them. For a change, he had set the table in the small dining area by the kitchen. A bottle of red wine stood open on it.

"You know, Paul," Jessica said, as she rested her fork on the edge of her plate, about midway through their dinner. "I've been thinking. If you got sent here by a lightning strike, how do you know how much power will be necessary to send you back?"

Paul took a sip of wine before answering. "As long as we have enough energy to power the transport, it shouldn't matter. I have a pretty good idea how much power is required, from calculations and from tests I've run. So long as it's enough energy to allow the transport unit to break the bonds of space-time, I'll be sent. If I use too much energy, it will just be wasted—I'll have disappeared before it finishes passing through the system. If it's not enough energy, I just won't go anywhere at all."

Jessica nodded. "I've looked into it. A fully charged PLCU can hold around ten gigajoules of power—however much that is," she said. "You can release whatever amount of it you want."

"I know," Paul said. "Believe me, I've looked into it, too. That's way more than enough." He reached over and held Jessica's hand. "It's okay, really. I've thought this all through."

"All right," Jessica said.

Paul took another bite of food, then leaned back in his chair. "It's funny, you know—ever since memorizing *Memories and Reflections*, I keep thinking of quotes from it that seem relevant, somehow, in different situations."

"That's how it is," Jessica said. "Now you have another one?"

"Yeah, this particular one has been going through my head a lot lately. Should I recite it to you?"

"Ah-huh," Jessica said, sipping a little wine. "Please do."

"Okay," Paul said. "It's from when Indira and Laura first came to live with the Mbuti:

I felt as though I had stepped into a world which had developed along different lines than the one I had been living in, one with fewer grandiose schemes, but more of the simple joys that life can offer.

"It's like that living here with you, Jessica," Paul said. "Our worlds developed along different lines—and here, with you, there are so many joys for me."

Jessica looked at him, smiling warmly. "It's like that for me, too, Paul, with you here," she said. Then, after a moment, she added, "What's the rest of the passage?"

"Oh, she goes on with the description," Paul said, then continued with the quotation:

. . . a world where people still slept on bare earth floors and built walls of leaves and sticks; a world enveloped in a single endless moment, which wove in and out of days, and always left room for play and laughter. It seemed plain to me that the people here knew themselves as individuals, as much as we did in the industrialized world, but had never lost touch with the present, in which life is, perpetually, taking place."

Jessica smiled as Paul finished. "I like hearing you quote like that," she said.

"I'm glad you do, because my head's all full of that stuff."

"How is that for you? Is it comfortable?" Jessica asked.

"It's fine. Kind of interesting, that's all," Paul told her. "You know, it's funny—I skipped some of the text, when I read it originally, and didn't finish it until I went to memorize it, but I actually think the way I came at it was better than if I had just read it straight through—like learning about those ideas at the Retreat, and all that."

"Better, huh? How so?" Jessica asked.

"I don't know," Paul shrugged. "Those parts of the book are interesting, but I just think the way I experienced it brought it home even better."

Jessica smiled at him, her eyes bright and warm, and while it was clear to Paul that she was listening to him, he could also see that she was thinking about him, too.

"I wish we could preserve this moment," she said to him. "I wish we could preserve all the moments we've had together."

Paul reached over and took her hand. "Me, too, Jessica. If only we could."

◙   ◙   ◙

On the afternoon of November 1, Jessica picked up a rental PLCU on her way home from her job in New Cuyama. She and Paul shared dinner, as they had so many times before—sitting out on the back deck as the setting sun lit the cliffs to the northeast: first brilliant white, then amber, before the sun disappeared below the horizon.

Paul took the System Boost and Stay Awake, which Jessica had bought for him a few days before. Then they left their dishes in the sink (at Jessica's insistence) and loaded the transport and transport pad into Jessica's SPV, where the PLCU was already waiting. Paul left at her house everything he owned, except the clothes he wore—and even they would wind up in Jessica's possession, for they would be left behind once the transport was activated, and Paul was sent away.

Both of them felt sad as they drove away toward Strandford that night, under the half-full moon. As they rolled along, holding hands when the road would allow Jessica to leave one hand free, they spoke little, and then only of trivial things. Both worked hard not to show their sadness too much, for fear of deepening the other one's sorrow.

The drive seemed to take a surprisingly long time, as they wound through the curving hills to the north, and then to the west, of the Sierra Madres. Paul had the feeling he was turning back the clock, somehow, in returning to the place from which he'd come. So much had changed around him and in him, in the time since he'd first arrived on Jessica's world—and yet, he expected to find his own world essentially unchanged.

When the road turned to the southeast, and they began to near Strandford, Paul stared out at the dark landscape, barely lit by the half light of the moon, and tried to imagine what he would be seeing in the same hills and valley on his world.

He would be there soon, he knew—and unless he was very lucky, he would remain there forever after.

When Paul and Jessica finally arrived at the site by the canal that Paul had picked out on the map, he found trees lining the water's edge, and then nothing but fields beyond that on either side. Jessica parked the SPV as close as she could get it to the canal's bank. Then, in silence, they unloaded the equipment and set it up near the water.

When they were done, they turned to one another and embraced, and the tenderness they each felt seemed to tear through them from the inside.

Paul wiped away Jessica's tears, and she his.

"You're so brave," he said to her.

"No, you are. You're the one who's going," she told him.

They kissed, then, and all that their hearts knew and felt was shared between them.

Like the clearest lake, Paul told himself, as they drew apart again. How he wished he could stay forever!

"I love you, Paul," Jessica said.

"I love you. I always will."

Paul stepped back a little.

"Well," he said.

"Yes," she answered. "There's no use in drawing this out. It will only make it harder."

Paul looked at her for a long moment, then knelt down and rechecked the settings on the transport unit.

"It's all ready," he said, then turned and looked up at her.

"You know, I always wanted to feel worthy of you."

"You always were worthy of me, Paul. And more. I admire you so."

They looked at each other, holding one another's gaze in the fragile light.

"I'm going to start the timer now," Paul said.

"Yes. Okay," Jessica said.

Paul pressed a button—and then, standing, gave Jessica the briefest kiss, before stepping quickly onto the transport pad: a silver disk, shining in the grass.

He turned toward her. "If there's any way I can come back to you, Jessica, I swear that I will."

"Yes—I know," she answered.

Then there was a brilliant flash of light—and after that, only darkness.

EPILOGUE

PAUL ROCKWELL
979 Calle de los Jardines
Santa Barbara, California 93103

Jomei Chandler, Editor
Nueva Alba Press
1154 W. Vista del Pacifico
Santa Barbara, California 93101

Dear Jomei,

I received the email you sent a few days ago, and will try here to respond to each of the points within it.

First, let me say that I am glad you were pleased with the presentation of the story. As you could see in the manuscript I sent you, I decided to try the approach you suggested, including my story along with Dr. Kumar's. I am still a bit uncomfortable with following your suggestion that some of her memoirs be left out in favor of descriptions of my experiences (that is, experiences that introduced me to the same concepts she dealt with in the omitted parts of her memoirs). I am, however, reassured by my own strong sense that the way I experienced these ideas was clearer and more potent for me than what I would have experienced had I simply received those same ideas by listening to Dr. Kumar's book straight through. I hope readers of this book will find this approach superior, as well.

It felt awkward for me, at first, to describe my own experiences as though I were simply a character in the story, as you suggested that I do—but I became accustomed to referring to myself as "Paul" or "he" after the first chapter or two. I believe you are right that this approach will be less confusing to readers than it would have been had some sections of the text been authored by me and others by Dr. Kumar, with both of us referring to ourselves as "I." In any case, I hope I have done an acceptable job in telling my story. (As I said before, I am glad that you seem to be satisfied with what I have produced.)

You asked, as well, that I choose a title for the book. I would like to borrow the title from the quotation I placed at the beginning of the manuscript I sent you (that is, the quotation from Lao Tsu) and so call my book *The Root of Heaven and Earth*. I first saw those lines—which I believe were translated by the Kumaric scholar, Yao Chuan Jianyu—quoted on a wall at the Retreat. They made me think then, as they do now, of Dr. Kumar, and what she offered to her world—how she passed through her own interior "passageway," you might say, and so brought her world an understanding of how, by consciously traveling to the very "root" of ourselves, we may discover, and give expression to, the very best of the possibilities that exist for us. (I feel as though that reference to a "passageway" relates to my own experiences with extra-space-time travel, as well.)

I want to point out that I have made two changes to the appendixes that appeared at the end of *Memories and Reflections*, and which have been included at the end of *The Root of Heaven and Earth*, as well. Specifically, I have added some citations of my own to Dr. Kumar's final appendix (#7) and have added an appendix of my own (#8) after that, in which I have gathered quotations that describe the natural world as it once was. Some of these passages are from books I recall seeing on my grandfather's shelves—books from which he gained some of his knowledge of earth's natural history, and especially of the natural history of North America. I am pleased to have the opportunity to share this material here, as I believe the first step to protecting and restoring the natural vitality of this world is for people to remember how truly vital it is capable of being.

You asked me, in your email, to supply an epilogue to go at the end of the manuscript I sent you, describing what happened after I left Jessica's world and how the book you have agreed to publish came into being. I have given it some thought and have concluded that you are right (as you have been in other matters) in thinking that an epilogue is worth including. So, without further discussion, I will try here to provide the rest of my story, as you have requested:

As hard as I tried to prepare the way for a smooth return to my world, something went wrong with the transport process. I was lucky, at least, that the System Boost and Stay Awake that Jessica gave me seemed to have done their job, because this time I remained conscious while I was being transported. It was extremely fortunate that I did, as it's unlikely that I would have survived otherwise.

As the transport unit was set off, I was aware of a brilliant flash of light. This was followed immediately by an almost entire loss of sensation—no touch, no light, no sound—only an awareness of my own consciousness and of an odd sense of timelessness in which each moment seemed to stretch for an eternity, while also passing with sudden brevity.

The next thing I remember, I was being plunged into cold water. At first, I was aware only of the cold water and of darkness around me—but as I surfaced and caught a breath of air, I became aware of stars and a slender crescent moon overhead, of the salty taste of the water, and of being lifted and gently dropped as swells moved past me.

I looked around, trying to get my bearings straight. Everywhere around me, it seemed, there was only more water (as well as the moon and the stars above) with the exception that in one direction I could see a small, yellowish light burning near the horizon.

I had begun to shiver in the cold water. Seeing nothing better to do, I set off for that one light in the hope that it might mean land.

I have no idea for how long I swam, only that the warmth I generated by swimming was not enough to make up for the creeping chill from the water. In time, I came ashore and found that the yellow light was in fact a campfire. Two men sat by it, dressed in long pants and hooded sweatshirts. Their surfboards lay in the sand only a couple of meters away. A duffle bag (which I later found out held their wet suits) was also nearby.

I covered myself as well as I could with my hands (self conscious not only about my nakedness, but about the fact that I had no hair anywhere on my body) and approached them, trembling violently. They rushed to provide me with a towel, in which I wrapped myself, and some hot chocolate from a pan that sat, already warmed, by their fire.

I was glad that they accepted the explanation I offered for my sudden and surprising appearance on their nearly empty stretch of beach. I had gone for a swim, I told them, and left my clothes on a beach further up the coast. I had then been carried by the current to the spot where I had found them.

After I had warmed up a bit, they offered to give me a ride to where my clothes were. I told them that I had no idea how to find my way back there and that I had left no valuables with them, anyway.

They offered, then, to at least take me to my car. When I told them that I had no car but had been dropped off at the place I had come from, they seemed to assume that I was "hitching" and told me they would be driving south along the coast the next day, heading for a surfing competition in Huntington Beach, and could drop me off someplace along the way, if I would like.

I asked them if they could possibly get me near to the Santa Barbara Islands—as, I reasoned, that would at least bring me into an area I was familiar with.

The smaller one of the two shrugged, then said, "I guess there are islands sort of near Santa Barbara. We could take you to Santa Barbara, if you'd like."

As the warmth had gradually returned to my body, I had begun to worry about why the transport had sent me so far off course. All sorts of things seemed misaligned, out of place—so much so, that I had begun to wonder if, having stepped out of space-time, I had stepped back into it not only at the wrong place in space, but at the wrong place in time, as well. That is, I had begun to worry not just about *where* I was, but *when* I was.

Whatever, exactly, the situation, the men I met on the beach were kind enough to let me camp with them that night. They shared their food with me, and between the two of them managed to give me a pair of swimming trunks, a T-shirt, and a pair of plastic sandals to wear.

I lay awake a long time that night, after the two of them went to sleep. I'm sure it was partly the Stay Awake I'd taken earlier, and partly because I had chosen to try to sleep sitting up in one of the front seats of their van (where I could at least be out of the wind), rather than trying to crowd into the back with the two of them. But I'm sure my sleeplessness was also caused, in part, by the fact that I was deeply worried.

By this point it was clear to me in so many ways (from the unpopulated coastline, to the vehicle my hosts drove, to their response to my mentioning the Santa Barbara Islands—even to the clothes they both wore and had shared with me) that I was somewhere in the past. But just how far into the past I had traveled, and why, I had no idea. I couldn't even know, yet, whether I was in the past of my world, or of Jessica's.

The possibility that I had left Jessica only to be transported, needlessly, pointlessly, into the past of her world—a place from which I could do no particular good—troubled me deeply. And if that did turn out to be the case, I lay awake thinking, what chance would there be of my ever returning to her?

⬚   ⬚   ⬚

The next day my companions dropped me off on a sidewalk in Santa Barbara. Whatever time period I was in, it was clear to me then that the waters had not yet risen on this world, as they had in my time. Standing there on that sidewalk, it felt vastly strange for me to be in the lowlands between the hills of Santa Barbara—between the very islands I had looked down upon with my grandfather, when I was a boy.

My companions had been kind enough not only to allow me to keep the clothes they had offered me the night before, but to hand me five dollars as they dropped me off, just so I would not be completely without money.

I stood for a few minutes, then, staring around me at the streets of Santa Barbara—filled with their strangely dressed people and "automobiles" (which looked much like old pictures I'd seen on the Stream)—then I took charge of myself and set off, looking for a place where I could buy a hat to keep the hot sun off my bald head.

As I went, I wondered if I should really save the money for food, but soon convinced myself that whether I would manage to find a way to stave off starvation or not, the five dollars would probably not make that big a difference—judging from the prices in the small shops I stopped into—and in the meanwhile, I would do well to prevent a serious sunburn.

While searching for a hat, I came across some stands on a street corner. They were made of metal and clear plastic. Inside, they held the first actual newspapers I'd seen in my life. Near the top of the one in front, it said the date was July 17, 2009.

As I stood, bent over, looking at the newspaper, I felt the first wave of nausea I had felt since transporting—though I felt it had more to do with the newspaper than with the transport event itself.

I straightened slowly, then set off down a side street—then turned down an alley, looking for privacy.

There, in the alley, I sat down behind a restaurant and leaned my head back against the wall. I took a deep breath as tears began to slide down my face.

Could it really be true that I had left Jessica *for this?*

Had I really left her, only to find myself pointlessly thrown into the past, nearly *five years* before the branching point?

At this point in time, I couldn't even know which way this earth would branch! Would this earth become my world, or Jessica's—or, conceivably, some other earth entirely? I would have to wait all those years even to find out!

I had known all along that I would miss Jessica, but the very real possibility that I had transported away from her in vain shook me to the core. I rested my forehead on my bent knees and wrapped my arms around my bald head. How could I have ended up here and now? I had planned so carefully! I had tried so hard to do everything right. How could everything have gone so wrong?

I sat there for a long time, caught up in my misery, then gathered myself up enough to deal with the situation at hand. Perhaps I would not know until March of 2014 (when *Memories and Reflections* would first be published in Jessica's world) whether I had arrived in the past of Jessica's earth or mine, but I was alive now, and I had to deal with the present situation.

After giving it some thought, I decided that whatever else I did in this world, I must transcribe the text I had memorized and have it ready to publish when that date rolled around, should it turn out that Dr. Kumar's book would not appear in the world I was in.

As much faith as I had in the lasting effects of Synaplast, I was unwilling to trust my own memory to preserve *Memories and Reflections* exactly as it had been written for as long at it might take for me to know whether or not it would be needed here. Therefore, I wanted to get it down as quickly as possible, while I was still confident that I would remember it precisely.

To do this, I would need a place to stay, and some sort of equipment to do the transcribing. I would need food and some way of paying for rent, as well. In other words, I would need to get myself established in this time and place, no matter what the future might hold—and to do that, I would need income of some sort.

I sat there behind the restaurant, thinking about what sort of work I might get. Not only did I have no credentials at all that would be recognized in this world and in this time period (including no references and no useable résumé), but the only clothes I owned were a blue T-shirt, a pair of bright orange and green swimming trunks, and a pair of brown plastic sandals. My baldness was perhaps not so much of a problem, but my lack of eyebrows and eyelashes, I knew, gave me an odd appearance.

While I was thinking about this, someone carrying a bowl of soup and wearing a white apron came out of the back of the restaurant, then sat down on an upside-down plastic crate that had been left there, and began to eat.

I looked over at him and on impulse asked him if the restaurant had any sort of work available.

He shrugged. "What sort of work do you do?" he asked.

"Well, my last job, I washed dishes," I told him.

He shrugged again. "I'll ask my boss."

He stepped into the restaurant, then reappeared. "No, not now. But check back, if you want."

◻   ◻   ◻

I did stop back there, and at any number of other restaurants during the days that followed. I had spent the five dollars the surfers had given me on a baseball cap (blue, to match my shirt, with "Santa Barbara" written across the front), and had taken to sleeping on the beach, in the dry part above the high-tide mark, covered in sand to help me stay warm.

In the mornings I would rinse off in the ocean, then let my clothes dry on my skin as I made my rounds to the grocery stores, looking for food that had been thrown out behind them. Often I found there food that was only a day too old to be left on the shelves, still in its packaging, set out in a box on top of other boxes in a dumpster behind the store. Often, too, I would find fruits and vegetables that still seemed quite fresh, which apparently had been discarded to make room for a new shipment. Though this food was not quite as nice as what I had enjoyed on Jessica's world, on most days I ate better than I ever had on my own world.

I spent my afternoons going door to door to the restaurants and a few of the shops, asking if they had any work I could do—often returning again to places I had last sought work at only a couple of days before.

After about a week and a half of this, I was told at one of the restaurants that the dishwasher hadn't shown up for work that afternoon, and that if I could start right then I could have a shift dishwashing.

The restaurant was a beachside establishment, which was formal enough for those in fancy clothes to feel comfortable there, but which also welcomed people who had just wandered in off the beach. It had broad windows looking out over the water—and quite a warm, cozy feeling (I found out later) when the fog rolled in at night.

I doubt that that one dishwashing shift would have led to any further work, if it weren't for the fact that the manager was having family trouble at the time, and that I stayed late at the end of my shift and listened while he talked.

It's funny, with all my years of professional training, the one thing that really helped me find work, then, without credentials or even a presentable appearance, was the skills I'd learned while visiting with Jessica's friends and family, and with Jessica herself, when I was trying to learn how to see from others' perspectives and to understand what they were experiencing.

So starting then, because the manager liked me, I was worked into the schedule as a regular dishwasher at what was, in fact, a fairly upscale restaurant—and soon after that, one of my coworkers (who was a particularly agreeable and easygoing guy) invited me to sleep on his couch in exchange for a small contribution to the rent—an invitation that I gladly accepted.

After a few weeks, when I had bought some better clothes and my hair and eyebrows had grown back in enough, I was given a chance to try my hand as a waiter, which then became my regular duty.

Soon after that, I was in a position to sign a lease on a studio apartment in what had once been the stand-alone garage next to a house not far from my job.

After another couple of months, I was able to buy a used laptop computer and some speech-recognition software, and began the work of transcribing *Memories and Reflections*.

I'd had some time to think, by then, about what should be done with the manuscript I would produce, once it was completed. I knew it would be a mistake to publish it so long as there was any possibility that Dr. Kumar might, in a few years, publish it herself. But at the same time, I didn't think I would necessarily have to wait until early March of 2014 to find out whether that was going to happen. The fact was, I had been telling myself, that the difference between whether Dr. Kumar wrote and published her memoirs might be as small as whether she did or did not injure herself on the skiing trip she took with Laura.

I hypothesized that, perhaps, in the past of Jessica's world, Dr. Kumar had zigged when she should have zagged while skiing, and so injured her back—and as a result of that took time off from her work at the University of Colorado and began writing her memoirs—while perhaps, in the past of my world, Dr. Kumar had skied flawlessly that day, had come home feeling fine, and so never got around to starting to write her memoirs.

If it was as simple as that, I thought, then the true branching point might already have been passed. I glanced over at my calendar. It was, by then, late October of 2009—while the skiing trip had taken place just after Thanksgiving in November of 2008.

I was still spending most of my time, when away from my job, transcribing *Memories and Reflections*, and I expected to have it completed within a few months. When it was done, I told myself, I would put it in a safety-deposit box in a bank for safe keeping, then begin my search for Dr. Kumar.

◘　　◘　　◘

I had all sorts of ideas about what I might do if I found her. I imagined her still at work at her job in Boulder. I had been saving all the money I could, and thought perhaps I would move to Boulder and sign up for one of her classes. I could go to her office after class sometime, then, and mention how much I liked reading memoirs, or perhaps make some other comment that might get her to reveal whether she was working on memoirs of her own. Perhaps she would tell me, then, that she had been wanting to write her own memoirs, but hadn't quite found the time—in which case, I would do all I could to coax and encourage her, perhaps even offering to donate my time to free up hers for the project.

I liked these fantasies. I liked imagining meeting her and discovering what she was like. I liked the idea of finding out that I was, in fact, in the past of my world—the world in which she never published her memoirs—and then convincing her to make the necessary change of course. I liked imagining that this was all it might take to keep my world from branching down the wrong path.

And after all, I reminded myself, it would be much better to have her memoirs come from her, actually and literally, than to be published by me.

Having given all this such careful thought, I was, then, not at all prepared for what I would actually discover once the manuscript was done and safely stored away, and I began to search for Dr. Kumar.

I started out by taking some of my hard-earned savings to pay for an adequately fast connection to the Internet, and then, using that, I searched the list of faculty members at the University of Colorado—but she was not listed there.

I followed up with a search for her, as an author, at the sites of the scholarly publications at which, I knew, she had published her research—but could find no mention of her that way, either.

I searched, then, for Laura Atherton on the faculty list at the University of Colorado—and found that she, also, was not listed there.

I expanded my search to other colleges and universities in the United States and Great Britain, searching for both Indira Kumar and Laura Atherton at those, as well—but could still find no mention of either of them.

I moved on, then, to searching the phone listings in all the cities in which they had lived. All I could turn up this way was a phone number for a Laura Atherton in London.

After some nervous pacing around my apartment, I convinced myself to call. I reached her on the third try. As it turned out, she was about the right age and had attended Oxford as an undergraduate—but that was where the similarities ended. This Laura Atherton had never attended graduate school, nor, she told me, had she ever met anybody named Indira Kumar.

I tried, then, to focus my search on finding an Indira Kumar in or around the area of Varanasi in India, but couldn't find the sort of information I needed. From what I could tell, most local records of the sort I needed had not yet made their way onto the Internet.

By this point, it seemed pretty clear to me that wherever Indira Kumar was, she was not on the verge of publishing her memoirs—or at least not memoirs that were anything like the ones I had memorized and transcribed. I was not in the past of Jessica's world, or any world reasonably similar to hers. In this world, like mine, Dr. Kumar's memoirs would not be published, or at least not in any form I would recognize.

As badly aimed as my last transport experience had been, it seemed that one thing had gone right—I had apparently, as planned, been sent across the boundary that separated Jessica's world from mine. It seemed that the linkage had held (as it should have, and would have, if Interdimensional-Linking Theory was correct) and that I had been returned to my own world—to the past of the world from which I had originally come.

I felt certain, now, that there was no reason to hold off from publishing the memoirs I had memorized and transcribed, but I was, nonetheless, still quite curious about what had actually happened in Indira Kumar's life—in the life of the Indira Kumar of my world.

I took the rather extraordinary step, then, of calling India and hiring a private detective there to see if he could locate Indira Kumar, or at the very least tell me what had become of her. I was able to give him quite a few details about her, including the name of the village she'd been born in and the year of her birth, as well as the names of all of her family members. (Much of this information had been in the biography I had had Kiki recite for me before the Synaplast wore off—and which I was, by this point, quite glad to have memorized.)

After waiting a couple of weeks, I heard back from the detective, who told me that while he had not been able to locate anyone named "Indira Kumar" who had been born on that date, he had managed to locate one of her sisters. He then arranged to fax me a letter that that sister had written to him in response to his inquiry about Indira on my behalf—as well as a list of his expenses, including the total fee for his services. He made it quite clear that he considered the case closed.

As you might imagine, I was eager to read the letter, which I picked up from a local coffee shop that offered a faxing service. I took it back to my apartment, where I read it while seated at one of the chairs at my small kitchen table, with light coming in through the kitchen window. I had gotten up early to pick up the fax, as I knew the detective would send it to me overnight, and the light that splashed across the page had the soft glow of morning. The letter read:

> I do not know how it is that the American man who hired you knew my sister, or why he would be asking about her now. Perhaps he knew her through my Aunt Mary, when Indira was living with her and Uncle Anbu in Varanasi. If so, he may remember that she was engaged to be married. After her marriage in 1968, she became pregnant with a child—a son.
>
> I am sorry to tell the American man that my sister Indira died in the late autumn of 1969, when her son was born. There was a great deal of blood, and her midwife could do nothing to stop it. The boy was born healthy, though. He is grown now, and lives in New Delhi, where he works at a branch of the family Import/Export business.
>
> I don't know what else to tell the man who hired you. Tell him I am sorry I have to give this sad news—but Indira has been gone, now, for almost forty years.
>
> Sincerely,
>
> Ananda Sarma
> (formerly, Ananda Kumar)

I sat there, then, in that delicate light, trying to take this all in. I remembered the turning point in Dr. Kumar's young life, when her parents had arranged a marriage for her, and she had struggled with the idea of it—struggled with it under the chinar tree, and as the rain poured down around her, as she walked toward home.

In this world, I surmised, that struggle had ended differently. In this world, it seemed, the letter that the young Indira had written to her parents, telling them that she would not accept the marriage they had arranged for her (that she would, instead, follow her own true calling, her own true protolife)—that letter, apparently, had never actually been written, here, in this world—and so everything that followed after that had been changed, as well.

In this world, in the way things actually happened here, Indira never finished high school. She never went to college. She never left India at all.

In this world, Indira never met Laura, and so she and Laura never fell in love. They never went to the United States together, nor to Africa, nor to New Guinea.

None of those things ever happened in this world—and so this world never received the gift of the insights she gained through those experiences. This world—my world, I thought—never received the book she wrote about her life and about the discoveries and insights she gathered during it.

I rubbed my hands through my hair. Apparently, I was realizing, I had been wrong to conclude that the branching point between Jessica's world and my own turned on whether Dr. Kumar's memoirs had been published.

No, the fact was that the branching point between our two worlds came much earlier than that. The fate of our two worlds turned on whether a young woman—while still in her teens—decided to do what was expected of her, even though she could feel that it was not the right choice for her; or whether she chose, instead, to follow the sweet promise she felt within herself, which beat there as strongly as her own heart.

I sat very still for several minutes, with the light flooding in around me. Yes, I told myself, taking a deep breath—that was it. When she chose to follow her own truth, she opened for the world a window on that truth. When she chose not to open that window for herself, then that window remained closed, as well, for all of us.

⬚   ⬚   ⬚

After several minutes, I set the fax down on the kitchen table, then stood and looked out the window—and as I did, I felt a renewed sense of my own purpose. If I could publish *Memories and Reflections* here, now, in this time period, in this world that had all too soon lost its one and only Indira Kumar, I could do more good than Jessica and I had ever hoped might be achieved by my returning to my world. Now was the time to propagate the seeds of these ideas—now, before all the suffering that might otherwise follow; now, before the waters rose; now, while so many different kinds of plants and animals still existed here; now, when so much was still possible.

I could see that this was, in fact, the time period I should have arrived in—the best time for me to have arrived—the time that I would have aimed at had I only known how to use the transport unit to bring me to this place, to this time, exactly. This was when I had the greatest chance of doing the most good.

Things had gone very right, when I had mistakenly believed that they had gone very wrong. I felt this, and knew it, in a way I had not before. Returning here was the right thing to do—I only wished that I could somehow tell Jessica how really right it had turned out to be. What we had sacrificed for turned out to be of far more worth than either of us had ever expected.

It was, then, in August of 2010, that I began to contact publishers and to show them the manuscript for *Memories and Reflections*—a process that eventually led me to you, Jomei, and to the arrangements I have made with Nueva Alba Press. Thanks to the generous advance you agreed to, I was able to quit my job at the restaurant in March of 2011 and work full time on preparing a manuscript that would include—as you suggested—not just Dr. Kumar's story, but my own story, as well.

Since completing that manuscript, I have had a lot of free time in which to think about the transport event that brought me here, and to give careful thought to the question of why it was that I arrived so far off course—both in the physical location of my arrival, and in the timing of it. I've spent countless hours working and reworking the mathematics underlying my theory of extra-space-time travel, and of the aiming-formula aspect of it, in particular.

As you already know, the sort of travel that I've personally experienced using a transport unit has required a huge burst of energy to set it off. I can now demonstrate mathematically that a burst of energy on that scale, when directed through the transport mechanism, has a kind of "explosive" effect, creating a highly local disturbance just outside of the normal dimensions of space-time. (It is perhaps helpful to imagine this "explosive" disturbance as taking place in the "thin skin" on the "far side" of space-time, at the site of the "rift" generated by the transport event.)

When I first transported from my world to Jessica's, the arc of my trajectory circumvented this turbulence because the transport was aimed, then, at G3-97. I was, therefore, initially propelled away from the transport site, then boomeranged back to it—tied by what I'll call "the elastic threads of linkage" to my starting coordinates, and thus returned to those coordinates by them, much as if a rubber band had snapped me back to my original position—only in this case, because of linkage, that "original position" was transposed to the equivalent coordinates on an alternate earth.

This propelling away and ricocheting back would have taken much less than a nanosecond from the point of view of someone watching from within space-time. As brief as this margin was, it provided a buffer large enough for me to miss the disturbance that was taking place at the outer boundary of space-time—that is, the disturbance that "vibrated" along the "rift" at the site of my departure.

When I transported from Jessica's world to here, I cautiously set the transport to aim at my starting location, hoping to insure that I would not actually end up on G3-97 or some other off-world location. There was, therefore, no way for me to avoid that "explosive" disturbance (which I can see, now, clearly etched in the more subtle mathematics of the aiming formula).

Because I had aimed the transport at my site of departure, I never went far enough from those coordinates (on either earth) to avoid the "explosive" disturbance. It was as though I was, all at once, trying to take off from and land at the site of an explosion, just as a bomb went off. As clearly as I can put it, because of that "explosion," I was thrown off at an "angle" from my intended trajectory—and was sent here, instead, to the correct alternate world, but to the wrong location in both space and time within it. Remarkably, according to my calculations, all of this could have been avoided entirely if I had aimed even a fraction of a meter away from my point of departure.

While certainly there is something somewhat comforting in knowing exactly why I ended up somewhere—and somewhen—so far from what I had aimed at, I had so hoped that the answer to the question of how I came to be here would tell me, also, how to return home to Jessica. Unfortunately, this has not turned out to be the case.

While I had felt sure there must be some useful and identifiable pattern in the "explosive" effect of transporting, the mathematics of the aiming formula, as it turns out, demonstrates that the patterns in the turbulence erupting from a transport event are so complex and variable as to be, essentially, random in their nature. Because of this, I can see no way of harnessing this "explosive" turbulence to send me back to Jessica's time—and worse than that, I see no way of learning how to see a way.

It's still hard for me to accept that the one place where I had some real hope that an answer might be found has turned out to offer me nothing.

I still dream of Jessica most nights. I still wake each morning wishing she were by my side. I still feel her presence in my heart and mind, almost as though she were somehow still near me.

As much as I want to return to her, it's clear to me that I must not try again, unless I can be certain that I will succeed. Here, in this time period, I have the means of building another transport unit—but if I were to try to return to Jessica and randomly, accidentally, make another lengthy jump into the past, there would be no chance of ever getting the raw material together— the essential parts, the basic bits of technology—necessary to build such a device again. I would be stuck in that past location forever, with absolutely zero chance of making it home.

I cannot, therefore, count on more than one chance to return to her. I will keep trying to find a way. I will do all I can. But I will not attempt to transport again unless I can be certain of where and when I will arrive.

I'd like to close with the pair of quotations Dr. Kumar used at the beginning of the last chapter of her book, *Memories and Reflections: The Memoirs of Indira Kumar*. They seem, somehow, to fit here, as well:

A human being is a part of the whole, called by us "Universe," a part limited in time and space. He experiences himself, his thoughts and feelings as something separated from the rest—a kind of optical delusion of his consciousness. This delusion is a kind of prison for us, restricting us to our personal desires and to affection for a few persons nearest to us. Our task must be to free ourselves from this prison by widening our circle of compassion to embrace all living creatures and the whole of nature in its beauty.

—ALBERT EINSTEIN

I want to realize brotherhood or identity not merely with the beings called human, but I want to realize identity with all life.... All life in whatever form it appears must be essentially one.

—MOHANDAS K. GANDHI

Thank you again, Jomei, for your assistance in getting this book into print. Let's hope that the interest it will generate will be enough not only to repay the generous advance you have allowed me, but enough, especially, to spread these ideas as widely here as Dr. Kumar's book succeeded in spreading them in her world. The time is right. May these ideas be like seeds that spread in the wind, taking hold and growing everywhere.

With appreciation for all you have done to help make this a reality—

Paul Rockwell

Paul Rockwell, PhD
Santa Barbara, California, USA
November 18, 2012

PS Jomei—if you would like, please feel free to use this entire letter as the epilogue for the book.

EDITOR'S NOTE

At the beginning of February of 2013, I received a surprising package in the mail. It was the galley proofs I had mailed to Paul only two or three weeks before, still packaged up just as I had mailed them, with my name—"Jomei Chandler"—and address in the upper left, and Paul's address in Santa Barbara in the center, below that. But now stamped in big, red letters next to Paul's address, were the words: "Return to Sender."

Near that stamp, stuck on the front of the package, was one of the yellow forwarding labels the post office uses. It was made out to Paul Rockwell, but the address wasn't in Santa Barbara. It was in New Cuyama.

Apparently, the package I had sent to Paul in Santa Barbara had been forwarded to an address for him in New Cuyama, before being returned to the post office and, a couple of weeks later, to my office here at Nueva Alba Press.

My first thought was to call Paul and find out what was going on, but my call went immediately to his voice-mail service. I left him a message asking him to call me, then went back to the work I'd been doing when the package had first arrived.

I'm not sure for how long I might otherwise have forgotten about it, then— but the package, with its red stamp and yellow label, sat there next to my desk, where it repeatedly caught my attention.

After a couple of days, I tried to call Paul again, but again couldn't get past his voice mail. I tried emailing him and calling him two or three times after that. I even tried to find another phone number listed for him, but apparently the number he'd given me (his cell) was the only one he had.

After that, I just gave up and decided to wait. I was a little annoyed, though. It seemed to me a particularly unprofessional approach for him to take, especially since he had cajoled me into allowing him to take so much of his earnings as an advance, and so little as royalties to come later. Did this give him the idea that he had no further obligation after having been paid? And yet, I knew, this was an unfair assessment. Paul had completed his obligation in almost every way—except, perhaps, for the epilogue, which I still had some hope of him polishing into a nicer form.

Paul had suggested in the letter he'd sent in mid-November that the letter itself be used as the epilogue to his book, but I had some qualms about this. I'd thought he'd done a good job in the letter describing his experiences since arriving here, but it bothered me some that he had, in writing it, switched from referring to himself as "Paul," to referring to himself as "I." Though I could see that perhaps there was some argument to be made in favor of the way he had done things, I was uncomfortable, nonetheless, with him switching from a third-person perspective to a first-person perspective before his story was done.

I had the idea that perhaps Paul had, since finishing the main body of his manuscript, gotten so caught up in reworking the mathematics behind his aiming formula that he really wasn't paying enough attention to refining what I thought was a much-needed epilogue. I thought if I could just talk to him, I could get him to return his full attention to the book for just a little while longer—long enough to provide an epilogue that seemed to be made of the same fabric as the rest of the book. I hoped he would be able to complete this within a few weeks, as everything else was essentially done, and we were nearly set to run the galleys.

The days ticked by, still with no response from Paul. Each day I sat at my desk, and each day the package sitting on the floor beside me caught my attention.

One day in mid-February, nearly two weeks after the package had been returned to me, I looked down at the package for Paul and wondered again what had become of him.

I remembered receiving his letter in mid-November, and then giving him a call in the first days of December. We had made plans, then, to meet a week later at a little café in Santa Barbara, not far from the beach.

It had been a bright day, that day at the café. It was, I remembered, a little less cold than most in that season. I had been in a good mood when I sat down across from Paul—ready to make quick work of the matters we needed to discuss, then make a fast dash across town to another meeting I had scheduled. But as much as my mind was set on work that day, I found Paul focused somewhere else entirely.

While we talked, Paul occasionally interrupted the flow of the conversation to comment on the nature of space-time or to describe (in terms I could not comprehend) some detail about the mathematics he'd been reworking.

At the time, I thought it all unrelated to what we'd met to discuss, and also too hard to follow, and I'm afraid I didn't pay much attention to what he was telling me then. I do recall him saying something about, "it's not just worlds that are linked, but whole universes," and also some comment about "space-time forms a single fabric. Nothing—no two things, no two worlds, no two times—are truly separate within it."

I have the idea that he was also trying to tell me something about constants that weren't constants—or constants that were variables—and something else about how very hard it was "to determine the settings."

It was as though we were having two separate conversations: the one I was having with him, which was about the epilogue, and our publication schedule, and my hope that he would get his revision done quickly; and the conversation he was having with me, which was about physics, and mathematics, and the characteristics of extra-space-time travel.

The only other thing I seemed to recall from his part of the conversation was him saying something like, "The range of possibilities is infinite. *It always was infinite.* If I could only figure out how to *steer* it." I remembered this, in particular, because of the way he said it, with his face turned down toward the table and his fingers pushed into his hair.

I kept trying to redirect the conversation to what I saw as the principle topic. I kept thinking that we had, after all, agreed to meet to discuss his book, which would be in print and ready for distribution in just a matter of months. I hardly saw all this talk about physics and extra-space-time travel as relevant. It wasn't that I was utterly unsympathetic. I understood that what he was telling me was related to his efforts to return to Jessica and that that was important to him—but I also understood, from what he had written in his recent letter, that this effort was sure to prove futile. It just seemed plain to me that he and I would both be better off if he would just leave the subject alone and focus on the matter at hand: which was, of course, the rather pressing question of improvements to be made in the epilogue.

As I sat in my office in mid-February, recalling that day at the café and trying to decide what to do with the returned galley proofs, I tried hard to remember anything else I could about that last conversation I'd had with Paul. He had seemed tired, yes—depressed, even—and he had said something odd just before we had parted. I remembered standing with him outside the door of the café after our meeting. He was unshaven, his hair disheveled. The shadows around his eyes, for a moment, disturbed me. (Had I even really looked at him before that?)

"If I'd only taken the time to work it out," Paul had said to me then. His eyes seemed to look through me, as though I wasn't even there. "Even if it had taken a lifetime, I could have spent that lifetime with her, then traveled anywhere in space-time I chose. There was no hurry, no rush. I could have gone to anywhere, or to any time—and spent all the years beforehand with her."

He took a deep breath, then added, "She was like the clearest lake. I wanted to dive in, and stay with her always."

I patted him on the back, unsure of what to say to him. I really wasn't sure what he was trying to tell me, only that it had to do with Jessica, how he had come to be here, and his desire to go back.

"You'll feel better. Give it time," I told him.

"Time," Paul said.

"I'll send you the galleys next month," I said. "You'll feel better when you see it all in print. Authors always do."

I rushed through the rest of our parting, after that. As I said, I had another meeting on the other side of town and didn't want to be late. I had no idea, then, that this would be the last time I would see Paul.

I picked up the package that had been returned to me from where it sat beside my desk and looked again at all that had been written or stamped or stuck on its front. The fact that I'd had it for nearly two weeks at this point, and that I had yet to hear back from Paul, had begun to trouble me. I was beginning, as well, to feel a little bit guilty about not having listened to him more carefully when we'd met the last time, more than two months before.

Maybe I should really go looking for him, I told myself. I should at least try, it seemed to me—even if it was just to find out what was happening with the book. We'd gone ahead and run the galley proofs without any further input from Paul on the epilogue. (It was good enough, I'd told myself then, even if I did believe it could have been better.) Now I needed to know how soon we could expect to receive his response to the galleys, as integrating any changes he might want to make in the text was the only task remaining before going to print.

We could, I knew, if necessary, move on without his input, but I hoped it wouldn't come to that. I wanted him to at least have that chance to respond. And in truth, I had to admit, I was curious about what had become of him—and a little bit concerned, as well.

I set the package down on my desk, then looked at my watch. It was almost time for lunch. I had a light schedule for the rest of the afternoon, and even that was work I could do from home if I had to. At the very least, I could afford to drop by Paul's address in Santa Barbara, after grabbing a quick lunch.

I told my secretary I would be taking a longer than usual break for lunch. Then I copied over the addresses from the front of the package, before leaving the building.

◘   ◘   ◘

After lunching downtown, I drove over to Paul's studio apartment—which was, as Paul had described it in his letter, converted from a garage that was separate from the main house. I parked a couple of doors up on the residential street, then knocked on his front door. I was not surprised when I got no answer.

Next, I knocked on the door of the main house, then stood for a moment listening to the birds singing in the trees nearby, before the door was opened by a tired and harried-looking woman with a toddler in one arm. When I told her I'd come looking for Paul, she set off on a five-minute rant about how much she'd like to find him, too—as he was late on his rent, and she had no idea where he was, or if he was even coming back. She finished up by saying that she would really like to know if she should re-rent his apartment.

"He's left a mess, too—papers everywhere. I'll show you, maybe you can figure out where he is. At least all that strange machinery is gone. He's been building something here for months. An odd looking thing, but I didn't care—so long as he didn't scratch the wood floors or wake the baby."

She disappeared into the house for a moment, then returned with a set of keys and led me to the small free-standing garage.

She let me in, then stepped in after me. What she had said was true. Though there was hardly any furniture and only a few books or pieces of clothing left lying here or there, the place seemed cluttered—mostly because of all the papers spread about. Each of the papers was covered with diagrams and mathematical equations I could not begin to understand.

On only two of these pieces of paper did I see written something that made some sort of sense to me in normal English—and still these brief notes were cryptic and hard to understand. On one was written:

Clearly, I misnamed Constant-θ.
Constant-θ marks the relationship between her world and here.

A change in Constant-θ in the aiming formula = <u>a change in functional linkage</u>.

No linkage is absolute.
ILT and IRD only mapped small corner…

Is Constant-Q in aiming formula, then, also wrongly named?
Could Constant-Q represent <u>a time-placement variable?</u>

Below that were several lines of mathematical notation—from which I could glean nothing at all. Then a little bit further down on that same sheet of paper, Paul had added:

If true, then theoretically the door is open to any time, any place, in any alternate universe.

The only other piece of paper on which was written something I could make some sort of sense out of, was a scrap I picked up from the chair next to Paul's bed. It said simply:

Can one machine = one electromagnetically unified set?
Transport a transport?

I sat on the edge of Paul's bed (a mattress set directly on the floor) staring at these cryptic notes, while the landlady rattled on about Paul and his unpaid rent. Then I looked up and around the small room at all the other pieces and scraps of paper scattered about, covered in numbers and Greek and Cyrillic letters and other indecipherable notations.

I sighed and stood up, and pushed the two pieces of paper I was holding into my pocket. Then, with the landlady's encouragement, I looked around Paul's tiny apartment a little more.

Most of Paul's clothes, what few there were, still hung in his closet—though a small number of such items were scattered about. In the kitchen, several dishes had been left, unwashed, by the side of the sink—while in the cabinets there were only a few more. The entire space gave the impression of a place not really lived in, but from which someone had not really moved out.

"He got sort of strange toward the end," the landlady was saying, shaking her head. "Ever since he moved in, I always thought he was a nice man—quiet, kept to himself, no trouble to anybody. The last few months, he began staying up most of the night. I know, because I'm often up with the baby, and I'd see his light burning, and sometimes him pacing back and forth, right here across the floor," she gestured, "when the curtain was open.

"He didn't seem so friendly after that. Oh, sure, he'd speak if he was spoken to, but he seemed, well, you know, distracted. All the time. I was sort of worried about him, but, well, what was it to me? He paid the rent regularly—at least he *did*—hasn't paid it in two months now. He was overdue even before he disappeared. I was going to talk to him about it, but he went right by me, muttering something about, 'It's so obvious. How could it have been so obvious, all along?' Like I wasn't even there. Strange man. I mean, I didn't think he was at first, but I do now. If you see him, tell him he owes me two-months rent—and to come get his stuff if he's not going to live here anymore."

By the time I left Paul's apartment, it was just after 2 PM. I stood by my car, thinking for a minute, then decided to make the nearly three-hour drive to New Cuyama. I called my office and told my secretary not to expect me back that day, then programmed Paul's New Cuyama address into my GPS system, and drove away.

The sun had drifted low in the sky by the time I arrived at his address in the open spaces of the Cuyama Valley, nearly ten miles beyond the edge of the town of New Cuyama itself.

I got out of my car and felt the dry breeze blowing past me. There was hardly anything there, just an old pick-up truck and a small trailer home, surrounded by open space. The trailer wasn't large, but it seemed smaller, still, with all that big, empty land stretching out around it. A short, rough grass covered the plains nearby.

I stood by my car, taking in the scene. I had the odd feeling that both the truck and the trailer had been picked up and set there, almost at random, as nobody else lived anywhere near by. All the land around me was flat and open, undistinguished, except for the dry riverbed just a dozen yards to the east—and a bare, chalky-white cliff face, which rose abruptly to the northeast, where it stood gleaming brilliantly in the late-afternoon sun.

As I took in the sights around me, I recalled the descriptions Paul had included in his manuscript, and I realized that this was where Jessica's house was located—or where it would be, in the right world, at the right time, in the distant future.

I walked over to the trailer, listening to the scrunching sound of my shoes against the gravelly soil beneath them. That, and the soft hush of the breeze against my ears, were all that I heard—no birds, no frogs. This was where

Jessica would live—yes, perhaps—but not yet. The water was missing from this valley, and with it much of the life that Paul had described as existing in this place in Jessica's world and time.

I knocked on the trailer's door—but, again, I wasn't surprised when I got no answer. I stood there for a minute or two, looking the place over, then tried the door (which was locked), before wandering around to the far side of the trailer, hoping to find some clue as to what had become of Paul.

Alongside of the trailer there, I found a ladder lying flat against the earth and, looking around, saw that a lightning rod had been mounted to the trailer's roof. A massive piece of cabling had been mounted there, too. It ran down along the side of the trailer and then inside through a half-open window.

On the ground, near where the cable was attached to the outside of the trailer, I found the singed and melted remains of a metal box. I picked it up and examined it in the late-afternoon light. On the side of it was some lettering, which including the word "laser" in small red letters.

I picked up the ladder and leaned it against the side of the trailer where the cabling ran through the partially open window, then climbed up on it. A towel had been used to block the rest of the opening where the cable ran through the window. I pulled it out of the gap and pushed the window open the rest of the way. Inside, I could see where the cable ran down from the window, then over to a large assemblage of odd bits and pieces of machinery that stretched out along one end of the room. From there, another piece of cable stretched to a circular platform in the middle of the room.

I had a good view of the room from where I stood, and could look down at the circular platform easily from there. On it, I could see, quite plainly, were a pile of clothes, some hair, and a quite ordinary-looking paperback book. Next to the book, I could just make out what appeared to me to be the clippings from fingernails. Set around the edge of the platform were snack foods of various sorts, a mug, and what I took to be a half-empty pot of coffee.

I climbed down off the ladder, then surveyed the scene outside again—noting the burnt box marked "laser" lying on the ground, and the heavy cable climbing out the open window and up the side of the trailer, terminating in the lightning rod on the roof. My eye continued on from there, upward, to the clear, blue sky, above.

As I stood there, taking in the scene, it seemed to me that I understood what had happened. I imagined Paul in his small apartment in Santa Barbara, months before, constructing some "strange machinery" and pouring over papers and notations of various sorts, reworking his aiming formula, struggling to acquire an understanding of what had gone wrong—of why, exactly, he had transported to the wrong locations in both space and time.

It would have been after he had answered that question that he had written his letter to me, in which he had described the "'explosive' disturbance" in space-time that had caused him to arrive where and when he had.

Then, clearly, after he had written that letter, he had continued to struggle, trying to find some way around the obstacles that so obviously lay in his path—trying to find a way around or through the sort of "'explosive' disturbance" he had written to me about—still hoping, still striving, to find some way of returning to Jessica.

Yes, I thought, this is what he'd planned all along—to try and keep trying until he found a way back to her. That was why he had wanted so much of his payment for the book as an advance—so that he could afford the time and the materials to build a new transport, so that he would be prepared to return to her, if he ever found answers to all of his questions.

It all made sense; he must have been at work on this project ever since finishing the main body of the manuscript—ever since I had given him his advance. He must have been at work on it long before he had written the letter he wanted me to use for an epilogue, and longer still before he and I had met at the café.

And what had he said to me at the café, that day? I tried to recall.

"If I'd only taken the time to work it out." Wasn't that it?

Yes, he'd said that, and he'd said, "I could have gone to *anywhere*, or to *any time*."

Yes, it all seemed to add up now. I thought it did—I hoped it did, for what I was thinking, I hoped could be true. As I imagined it, he had thought, then, at the time of our last meeting, that it might take a lifetime to refine the aiming aspect of his extra-space-time travel theory—to make it send him to exactly the place and time he chose. But he had glimpsed, by then, the likelihood that it *could* be done. And knowing that, seeing that, he had begun to pour over his work intensely—pounding against the limitations of his own understanding, staying up nights, pacing across the room where his landlady—looking out her window and into his—had seen him.

That's why he had seemed as he had at our last meeting: driven, tired, and determined. He had been pushing—and he had kept pushing, until, in the weeks after that last meeting, he had made a sudden breakthrough.

It hadn't taken a lifetime—just a few more weeks.

What was it his landlady had told me he had said to her as he'd swept past her? "It's so obvious. How could it have been so obvious, all along?"

Yes, perhaps all I was thinking was true. Surely, it was true, I told myself—or he wouldn't have come here and done this.

I looked skyward, again, imagining a much different scene around me. In place of the clear, blue sky above me, I saw in my mind's eye a sky dark and thick with clouds. In that imagined scene, rain looked immanent. Lightning might strike at any time.

Paul climbed the ladder to the roof of his trailer and turned on the laser he had, much earlier, set up for just such an occasion. He turned it on to summon lightning from the sky—not to be captured in some sort of futuristic lightning-capture box, but to come directly down to his lightning rod, where it would be guided along the lightning rod's spine to the massive cable Paul had placed there.

Yes, I told myself—the lightning had exploded the laser's box and sent it tumbling to the ground, but not before it had been channeled by the lightning rod toward its ultimate destination—the cabling, and the transport unit inside.

Yes, the transport unit, which Paul had built with the advance money he'd coaxed me into releasing. He'd built it, and he'd moved it here in the old truck I'd seen parked beside the trailer—and then he had sat there, inside his trailer, waiting on the transport's circular pad—waiting, on a rainy day, or on a rainy night, in January, when the seasonal rains had arrived. He had sat there with all his supplies around him—food, coffee, a good book—everything he would need as he waited for the storm to gather its charge and carry it close enough to his trailer for the laser to guide it home to him—and him home to Jessica.

I climbed up on the ladder, again, and closed the window as far as the massive cable would allow, then put the towel back in the opening to keep the weather out. Then I climbed back down and returned the ladder to the ground beside the trailer. I would leave Paul's place just as I had found it. What else was I to do? Tell the authorities that Paul had transported to another earth, in the future? No, I would leave things for others to sort out, as best they could. I was sure Paul's landlady in Santa Barbara would re-rent his place there, soon enough—and something would eventually be done with this property, as well, I presumed.

I stood and looked again at the cliffs gleaming brightly in the early evening light. While it was true that I would never know for certain what had become of Paul, I really hoped that he had made it. He had, after all, said plainly in his letter to me that he would not try to transport back to Jessica unless he was sure he would arrive where and when he intended. It sounded to me, from the notes I had discovered in his apartment in Santa Barbara, and from what his landlady had told me, as though he'd had some sort of breakthrough, as though he had learned something important by probing the mathematics behind his aiming formula.

Was it really possible that the power to "steer" a transport unit so precisely had been there all along—the ability to control not just the place and time of his arrival, but which alternate universe he traveled to? It did seem to me that that was what his notes suggested. What he had thought was constant, or set, was actually variable, aimable, it seemed. The "steering wheel," so to speak, was not locked, but turnable in any number of directions—he had just had to learn that it could be turned and how to turn it.

If what I was thinking was correct, then he hadn't had to deal at all with the sort of "'explosive' disturbance" he had described to me in his letter. He could have avoided it entirely, simply by aiming the transport (as I recalled him having written in his letter) "even a fraction of a meter" away.

As I walked the short distance back to my car, I imagined Paul appearing late one night in Jessica's yard—at the very spot at which his trailer now stood.

I imagined him quietly letting himself into her never-locked house, then slipping silently into bed beside her—so that when she woke in the morning she would find him there with her, as though, perhaps, he had never really been gone at all.

If, as he had said to his landlady, it was "so obvious;" if it had seemed to him, when he spoke to her then, that it had been "so obvious all along"—if it was as plain as that to him, and as sure as that—then perhaps he was able to get the aiming exactly right this time. Perhaps, where three and a half years had passed for Paul—here in my world and my time—he had, in Jessica's world and her time, managed to reappear only hours after she had parted from him.

Perhaps, I liked imagining, she had gone to bed only once without him after his departure, then woken with him by her side the very next morning—or perhaps even found him, waiting for her, on the front steps of her house, when she returned home after telling him farewell.

I imagined her joy, and his, as they gathered one another in their arms—knowing that never again would any cause be so dire as to force them to part from one another. I pictured them standing there in Jessica's yard, then, holding one another for the longest time, before turning and disappearing together into the soft light of Jessica's home. Their home.

As I got into my car to drive away, I thought about how it might be for them to be reunited—the happiness they would feel as the days opened before them, sunny and countless, their whole lifetimes waiting to be shared—and how it would be for them, as well, to have available a technology that would permit them, quite possibly, to travel to any place, in any time.

I thought about Paul's manuscript and how he had described Jessica in it.

"Can you imagine how that would have been," she had once said to him, "to know that your work had brought such important changes?"

Yes, she had said that—and she had also said, "That's the sort of work I dream of doing."

I smiled as I started my car and drove the short distance out to the main road. I wondered what the future would hold for them and what they would do in it. I imagined the two of them living together and traveling together, going from one earth to the next, with Paul carrying *Memories and Reflections* within him, and Jessica carrying *The Little Book* within her—and the two of them transporting a transport along with them—planting both books like seeds across the vast expanse of probabilities that one world might encompass.

For a moment, I thought about Dr. Kumar, herself, and how thrilled she would have been at so much coming from her work. She had believed that so much was possible, if we could just imagine it—and it seemed that it was true.

Yes, I told myself—possibilities abound, once you believe in them.

Arise and remember...and follow your root.

—THE GNOSTIC *APOCRYPHON OF JOHN*

APPENDIXES

CONTENTS OF APPENDIXES

APPENDIX 1

CITATIONS FOR THE PREFACE
TO THE SECOND EDITION

The following citations refer to the "Preface to the Second Edition" of Dr. Kumar's book, *Memories and Reflections: The Memoirs of Indira Kumar.*

1. Lindberg, David C. "Medieval science and religion," in *The history of science and religion in the Western tradition: An encyclopedia.* ed. Gary B. Ferngren et al. 2000, New York: Garland Publishing; 261.

2. Lindberg, David C. *The beginnings of Western science: The European scientific tradition in philosophical, religious, and institutional context, 600 B.C. to A.D. 1450.* 1992, Chicago: University of Chicago Press; 150–151.

3. Ibid.; 198.

4. Lindberg. "Medieval science and religion;" 259–267.

5. Brooke, John Hedley. *Science and religion: Some historical perspectives.* 1991, Cambridge: Cambridge University Press; 52–81.

6. Gingerich, Owen. "The Copernican revolution," in *The history of science and religion in the Western tradition: An encyclopedia.* ed. Gary B. Ferngren et al. 2000, New York: Garland Publishing; 334–339.

7. Brooke. *Science and religion;* 29–31.

8. Oldroyd, David R. "Theories of the earth and its age before Darwin," in *The history of science and religion in the Western tradition: An*

encyclopedia. ed. Gary B. Ferngren et al. 2000, New York: Garland Publishing; 391–396.

9. Moore, James R. "Charles Darwin," in *The history of science and religion in the Western tradition: An encyclopedia.* ed. Gary B. Ferngren et al. 2000, New York: Garland Publishing; 100–105.

10. Begley, Sharon. "Thinking will make it so: With 'cortical control,' brain waves can move matter." *Newsweek.* April 5, 1999; 64.

11. Lommel, Pim van et al. "Near-death experience in survivors of cardiac arrest: A prospective study in the Netherlands," *The Lancet.* December 15, 2001, vol. 358; 2039–2045.

12. Sabom, Michael. *Light and death: One doctor's fascinating account of near-death experiences.* 1998, Grand Rapids, MI: Zondervan Publishing House; 37–51 and 184–189.

13. Morse, Melvin L. "Near death experiences and death-related visions in children: Implications for the clinician," *Current Problems in Pediatrics.* February, 1994, vol. 24, no. 2; 55–83 (especially 56–58).
    Also discussed in: Schmicker, Michael. *Best evidence: An investigative reporter's three-year quest to uncover the best scientific evidence for ESP, psychokinesis, mental healing, ghosts and poltergeists, dowsing, mediums, near death experiences, reincarnation, and other impossible phenomena that refuse to disappear.* 2d ed. 2002, San Jose, CA: Writers Club Press; 186–210 (especially 187).

14. Stevenson, Ian. *Children who remember previous lives: A question of reincarnation.* rev. ed. 2001, Jefferson, NC: McFarland & Company; 56–93 and 105–120.

15. Stevenson, Ian. "Birthmarks and birth defects corresponding to wounds on deceased persons," *Journal of Scientific Exploration.* 1993, vol. 7, no. 4; 403–410.
    See also: Stevenson, Ian. *Children who remember previous lives;* 101–105.
    The same topic is more broadly discussed in: Stevenson, Ian. *Where reincarnation and biology intersect.* 1997, Westport, CT: Praeger, and most thoroughly explored in: Stevenson, Ian. *Reincarnation and biology: A contribution to the etiology of birthmarks and birth defects.* 2 vols. 1997, Westport, CT: Praeger.

16. Walker, Evan H. "The nature of consciousness," *Mathematical Biosciences.* 1970, vol. 7; 175–176. Quoted in Gary Zukav. *The dancing Wu Li masters: An overview of the new physics.* 1986, Toronto: Bantum Books; 63.

17. Witmer, E. E. "Interpretation of quantum mechanics and the future of physics," *American Journal of Physics.* 1966, vol. 35; 40–52. Quoted in Danah Zohar and Ian Marshall. *The quantum society: Mind, physics, and a new social vision.* 1994, New York: Quill/William Morrow; 75.

18. Haisch, Bernhard, Alfonso Rueda, and H. E. Puthoff. "Beyond e=mc2: A first glimpse of a postmodern physics, in which mass, inertia and gravity arise from underlying electromagnetic processes," *The Sciences.* November/December, 1994, vol. 34, no. 6; 26–31.

19. Stapp, Henry. "Mind, matter, and quantum mechanics," unpublished paper. Quoted in Gary Zukav. *The dancing Wu Li masters: An overview of the new physics.* 1986, Toranto: Bantum Books; 82.

APPENDIX 2

NOTE ON THE ARTICLE ON ANIMAL INTUITION

I'm sorry to say that I have long since misplaced the original magazine article that I began reading in London and finished reading on the plane to Zaire, and that various periodical searches have failed to turn it up. I have, however, found some reference to a few of the stories that were contained therein. The story about wolves keeping track of pack members can be found in *How animals talk and other pleasant studies of birds and beasts*, by William J. Long (1919, New York: Harper & Brothers Publishers; 95–99). The story about the boy and the racing pigeon can be found in an article titled, "The study of cases of 'psi-trailing' in animals," which was published in *The Journal of Parapsychology* (J. B. Rhine and Sara R. Feather. 1962, vol. 26, no. 1; 16–17).

These same references are also cited and summarized in a book titled: *Dogs that know when their owners are coming home and other unexplained powers of animals* by the biochemist Rupert Sheldrake, as is the story of the cow and her calf. (1999, New York: Three Rivers Press; 221–226). It is my impression that the author of the magazine article was aware of Dr. Sheldrake's research, and that it was Sheldrake's data and references which provided the principle fodder for the article I read.

Not only are the references that I've already mentioned to be found in Dr. Sheldrake's book, but his is the only collection of stories of animals warning of impending air raids that I have been able to locate (256–261). He also has a good deal of material on animals who seem to be aware of their owner's state of welfare, even at a considerable distance (105–116), and quite a number of stories of animals who have demonstrated apparent foreknowledge of an event (231–265). Stories of these last two types can also be found in *Psychic animals: An investigation of their secret powers* by Dennis Bardens (1987, London: Robert Hale; 46 and 38–46, respectively). Nonetheless, I have nowhere been able to locate the specific story about the bicyclist and her dog, which I remember reading in the original article I took with me to Zaire, but there are sufficiently similar stories told in both of these two books that I am comfortable retelling the one I remember without further reference. Likewise, I have not been able to place the story about the dog who anticipated her owner's arrival, but stories much like this may be found in Dr. Sheldrake's book (27–90).

All in all, for the discerning reader interested in a more in-depth exploration of this subject, I would recommend the Sheldrake book. He makes a close analysis of the available information and is quite deliberative in the conclusions he draws. And in any case, it makes quite a fine read, front to back.

APPENDIX 3

ARCHAEOLOGICAL NOTES

I. CITATIONS FOR DR. INDIRA KUMAR'S ARTICLE:
"SELF-EXPRESSION AND DISCOVERY IN PREHISTORY"

When Laura and I returned from Zaire, I was preoccupied with compiling and writing up the research I had done with the Mbuti. One thing led to another, and I somehow didn't get back to working on the article I'd planned for the *Huginn/Muninn Newsletter* for over a decade. At that time, I refined the text I'd written on the barge and updated my references. Here are the citations that appeared, finally, in conjunction with my article ("Self-expression and discovery in prehistory") in the *Huginn/Muninn Newsletter* in the fall of 2002, adapted slightly here to fit the earlier version of my article as written on the barge:

1. Feder, Kenneth L. *The past in perspective: An introduction to human prehistory.* 1996, Mountain View, CA: Mayfield Publishing Company; 85, 87, 98, 135–137 and 140.

2. Ibid.; 160–162.

3. Troeng, John. *Worldwide chronology of fifty-three prehistoric innovations.* 1993, Stockholm: Almqvist & Wiksell International; 184–187.

4. Feder. *The past in perspective;* 204.

5. Troeng. *Worldwide chronology;* 188–189, 191–195.

6. Bednarik, Robert G. "Art origins," *Anthropos.* 1994, vol. 89; 175–176.

7. Troeng. *Worldwide Chronology*; 184–187.

8. Brown, Kathryn. "New trips through the back alleys of agriculture," *Science.* April 27, 2001, vol. 292, no. 5517; 631.

9. Feder. *The past in perspective*; 345.

10. Ibid.; 190–191.

11. Harth, Erich. *Dawn of a millennium: Beyond evolution and culture.* 1990, Boston: Little, Brown & Company; 35–42.

12. Bird-David, Nurit. "Beyond 'the original affluent society': A cultural reformulation," in *Limited wants, unlimited means: A reader on hunter-gatherer economics and the environment.* ed. John M. Gowdy. 1998, Washington, DC: Island Press; 119 and 125–126.

13. Smith, Bruce D. *The emergence of agriculture.* 1998, New York: Scientific American Library; 207–214.

14. Feder. *The past in perspective*; 350–351.

15. Gebauer, Anne Birgitte and T. Douglas Price. "Foragers to farmers: An introduction," *Transitions to agriculture in prehistory.* Monographs in world archaeology no. 4. ed. Anne Birgitte Gebauer and T. Douglas Price. 1992, Madison, WI: Prehistory Press; 9–10.

16. Richerson, Peter J., Robert Boyd, and Robert L. Bettinger. "Was agriculture impossible during the Pleistocene but mandatory during the Holocene? A climate change hypothesis," *American Antiquity.* July, 2001, vol. 66, no. 3; 390.

17. Troeng. *Worldwide chronology*; 188–189, 191–192, 214.

18. Ouzman, Sven. "Towards a mindscape of landscape: Rock-art as expression of world-understanding," *The archaeology of rock-art.* ed. Christopher Chippindale and Paul S. C. Taçon. 1998, Cambridge: Cambridge University Press; 33.

19. Rodman, Selden. *Conversations with artists.* 1957, New York: Devin-Adair; 112 and 82.

20. Troeng. *Worldwide chronology*; 184–187.

21a. Europe:

> In "A stylistic categorization of human faces in Paleolithic art" (*Human Mosaic.* spring 1974, vol. 7, no. 2), Amy Gardner explores the apparent lack of involvement the earliest European artists had with the self:

>> The most salient feature of their human representations is a marked lack of individuality.... Any features that did happen to be depicted on the face or head—most commonly the eyes, nose, and hairline—rarely constituted the distinguishing human traits of the figure. Today this might be regarded as...an extreme lack of preoccupation with the self. (30)

> The one striking exception to this pattern is to be found at *La Grotte de La Marche*, which "is full of sketchy, yet amazingly realistic human figurations. Individuals are readily distinguished by their facial features, even by their clothing." (33) In fact, these engravings are so consistent in technique and distributed over so small an area that Gardner suggests they might even be the work of a single artist.

>> The existence of this particular art during the Magdalenian demonstrates that Paleolithic man, was, after all, capable of depicting himself as an individual in twentieth century terms, but that, by and large, throughout the Paleolithic he directed his vision towards the perception of other traits. (33)

b. Asia:

> Though information about the prehistoric art of Asia has been only sparsely available in the West, the figurines selected by Robert G. Bednarik for his article, "The Pleistocene art of Asia" (*Journal of World Prehistory.* December, 1994, vol. 8, no. 4), clearly display the same range of facial features typical of European art of that era. That is, faces are described by a few simple marks, or no facial markings are made at all. (364–367)

c. Australia:

> It is thought that the Dynamic Figures style of Australian rock art dates back about 10,000 years—and perhaps is considerably older than that—and that the Large Naturalistic style predates it. In neither style are facial features included in the human images. (Flood, Josephine. *Rock art of the dreamtime: Images of ancient Australia.* 1997, Sydney: Angus & Robertson; 263, 267–270, and 275–277.) The rich texture and detail present in both these styles reveals the skillfulness of the artists, who, one would imagine, could surely have depicted human faces if they had wished to do so.

d. Africa:

As a general rule, it is difficult to attach specific dates to specific images in rock art, and much of the rock art in Africa has never been dated. Nonetheless, general patterns can be discerned. As David Coulson and Alec Campbell (*African rock art: Paintings and engravings on stone.* 2001, New York: Harry N. Abrams) have written, while "rock art varies enormously from one end of Africa to the other," the images of humans in African rock art can be generally described as "characterless" and "caricatured," and can be said to "rarely... depict actual individuals." (57)

e. The Americas:

The Americas were first populated much more recently than Africa, Asia, Europe, and Australia. While establishing a date for the earliest human habitation of the Americas is problematical, it is clear that human populations did not become both well established and well distributed in the Americas until between 12,000 and 10,000 years ago (Feder. *The past in perspective*; 255–264). It is therefore not surprising that very little art dating back more than 10,000 years has been identified. The next two sections deal with what little information is available concerning representations of humans in the art of the Americas prior to, or even close to, 10,000 years ago.

South America:

The oldest human image of known antiquity from South America was found at *Boqueirão da Pedra Furada* in Brazil. It's on a fallen slab of stone associated with an occupation layer dated to approximately 10,000 BP, and so is at least that old itself. It is a "stick-figure" and has a round, solid head with no facial details. (Pessis, Anne-Marie. "The chronology and evolution of the prehistoric rock paintings in the Serra da Capivara National Park, Piauí, Brazil," in *Dating and the earliest known rock art: Papers presented in symposia 1–3 of the SIARB Congress, Cochabamba, Bolivia, April 1997.* ed. Matthias Strecker and Paul Bahn. 1999, Oxford: Oxbow Books; 41–47.) Through both the artistic style and location of this image, one may infer that it is part of the Northeast Tradition.

While most of the images from the Northeast Tradition cannot be so clearly dated, it is of interest that, within this tradition, human heads are most typically shown as solid areas with no facial features, or as semi-rectangular areas within which abstract designs have been drawn. (Guidon, Niède. "Traditions rupestres de l'aire archeologique de São Raimundo Nonato, Piauí, Bresil," in *Rock art studies in the Americas: Papers presented to Symposium B of the AURA Congress,*

Darwin 1988. ed. Jack Steinbring. 1995, Oxford: Oxbow Monograph 45/Oxbow Books; 121–128.)

I have found no evidence that human faces are ever portrayed within this, possibly oldest, South American artistic tradition.

North America:

What is possibly the oldest art in North America is to be found in the Mojave Desert of California. There, nine petroglyphs have been dated to more than 10,000 BP. These nine petroglyphs include animals images and geometric forms, but no human images. However, these renderings are part of a continuous and little-changing artistic tradition, called the "Great Basin Tradition," in which humans are depicted.

While none of the human images in this tradition have been dated to prior to 10,000 BP, it is nonetheless of interest to note how humans are portrayed within the Great Basin Tradition in general. In it, human heads are usually "either reduced to a small solid circle or shown as a spiral or concentric circle." In other words, no facial details are included. (Whitley, David S. *The art of the shaman: Rock art of California.* 2000, Salt Lake City: University of Utah Press; 44–45, 59, 62, and 65.)

22. Smith. *The emergence of agriculture;* 207–214.

23. Kelly, Robert L. *The foraging spectrum: Diversity in hunter-gatherer lifeways.* 1995, Washington, DC: Smithsonian Institution Press; 19–22.

24. The degree to which modern hunter-gatherers are focused in the moment varies widely and is dependent largely on the climactic conditions within which they live. Some have what James Woodburn describes as "immediate-return" organization, while others have "delayed-return" organization. According to Woodburn, an *"immediate-return system* is one in which activities oriented to the present (rather than to the past or future) are stressed," while a *"delayed-return system* is one in which, in contrast, activities are oriented to the past and the future as well as to the present."

The delayed-return system, as defined by Woodburn, is distinguished by other features, as well, including the application of more complex or labor-intensive technologies for the production of materials used in hunting, the processing or preservation of food, and/or the partial domestications of plants or animals. (Woodburn, James. "African hunter-gatherer social organization: Is it best understood as a product of encapsulation?" in *Hunters and gatherers 1: History, evolution and social change*, ed. Tim Ingold, David Riches, and James Woodburn. 1988, Oxford: Berg; 32.) That such labor is performed at all implies a concern in the present with results that will be garnered in the future.

It's interesting to note that all of the seven immediate-return hunting and gathering societies Woodburn discusses are located in or near the tropics, whereas virtually all of the delayed-return hunter-gatherer societies he makes reference to are located in exclusively non-tropical areas. (35)*

Living in areas where food is scarce for at least one season of the year—which is generally the case outside the tropics—creates pressures in which one must plan for the future in order to insure survival. It's not surprising, therefore, that societies whose members live in such environments are more likely to subscribe to the delayed-return system. (In addition, we might imagine that a move to non-tropical environments inspired, to at least some degree, and for at least some of our ancestors, some of the same sorts of changes in our relationship to time that the advent of agriculture brought forth for others.)

Throughout most of prehistory, the ancestors of modern humans lived in tropical or near-tropical environments, and used only the most basic technologies. It was not until perhaps 40,000 years ago that some of our direct ancestors first migrated to latitudes associated with wide seasonal variations. (Feder, 191) We might therefore assume that at least up until that time, the direct ancestors of modern humans lived largely within immediate-return systems and were focused mostly in the present moment.

Since most of the hunter-gatherers who preceded the first farmers lived in climates with limited seasonal variability and could, throughout each year, find ample food near-at-hand, I presume that on the whole they, also, would have felt little pressure to plan ahead and would most likely have lived lives largely focused in the present.

In relationship to this, it is of some interest to note how the Mbuti, as modern hunter-gatherers who live in the tropics, relate to time. As Colin M. Turnbull has written: "both the future and the past are

---

* The one clear exception, with regard to delayed-return systems, is the Australian Aborigines, whose traditional territory covers both tropical and non-tropical regions—and includes the Australian Outback, with its uncompromising climate. (35)

Another possible exception mentioned by Woodburn is the Okiek of Kenya. However, the Okiek actively engage in bee husbandry, (53) and therefore do not strictly qualify as hunter-gatherers, in the conventional sense.

considered by them as relatively insignificant extensions of the ever-changing present." (*The Mbuti Pygmies: Change and adaptation*. 1983, New York: Holt, Rinehart and Winston; 7.)

Additional Notes—Not Referred To In Main Text:

25. While working on the final version of my article, years after I had returned from Zaire, it occurred to me that some of my colleagues would consider hunting magic to be a better explanation for the general rarity of human faces in art prior to 10,000 BP than the one I had proposed, so I added a brief discussion of that topic at the end of my article before it appeared in the *Huginn/Muninn Newsletter*. I am including that passage below, along with the citations I used for it:

> For a long time it was presumed that the primary motivation for the production of prehistoric art was to improve the odds of a successful hunt. This theory, known as "hunting magic," held that much of prehistoric art was created because the artists believed that, in "capturing" an image of an animal in the form of a figurine or a painting on a cave wall, they had at the same time captured that animal's spirit, and would therefore be able to capture that animal in physical form during the hunt. It was assumed, too, that the general lack of human faces in the art of this period reflected a taboo against depicting the image of a specific human being—for to do so would presumably capture that person's spirit, as well.

> While such ideas predominated for many years, the general theory of hunting magic has since come under greater scrutiny. It has been shown, for example, that while the most common subject matter of prehistoric art is animals, there's no special correlation between the kind of animals represented in the art of a given time and place and the kind of animals actually hunted and eaten by the people of that location. In addition, actual scenes of hunting, which one would expect to be common if the artists were indeed so preoccupied with influencing the outcome of the hunt, are actually quite rare.

> In other words, while the concept of hunting magic may seem attractive as a theory, there's little evidence that it actually played a very large part in the motivations of these early artists. (Bahn, Paul G. "Where's the beef? The myth of hunting magic in Paleolithic art," in *Rock art and prehistory: Papers presented to symposium G of the AURA Congress, Darwin 1988*. ed. Paul Bahn and Andrée Rosenfeld. 1991, Oxford, Oxbow Monograph 10/Oxbow Books; 1–13.)

26. In the final version of my article, "Self-expression and discovery in prehistory," I included a few lines concerning research on self-awareness in animals, and what that research might suggest about the development of self-awareness in human ancestors. I found little to add to what Raymond had told me on the barge, so I see no point in reprinting that material here. I will, however, include the citations I used as my references for that topic:

a. Original research on self-awareness in chimpanzees. (Gallup, Gordon G., Jr. "Self-awareness and the emergence of mind in primates," *American Journal of Primatology.* 1982, vol. 2, no. 3; 237–248.)

b. General overview of self-awareness in a variety of species. (Parker, Sue Taylor, Robert W. Mitchell, and Maria L. Boccia, ed., *Self-awareness in animals and humans: Developmental perspectives.* 1994, Cambridge: Cambridge University Press.)

c. Graphics on shared ancestry between humans and apes. (Ibid.; 423.)

II. STRAY ARCHAEOLOGICAL NOTES

1. These figurines have been found at sites scattered throughout Europe, from southern France to Siberia. Interpretations of the significance of the figurines, and of what portion of them represent pregnant women, vary.

a. Nelson, Sarah M. "Diversity of the Upper Paleolithic 'Venus' figurines and archeological mythology," *Archeological Papers of the American Anthropological Association.* January, 1990, vol. 2, no. 1; 11–22.)

b. Duhard, Jean-Pierre. "Upper Palaeolithic figures as a reflection of human morphology and social organization," *Antiquity.* March, 1993, vol. 67, no. 254; 83–91.)

2. This continues to be the earliest evidence of warfare, as noted in Ferguson, R. Brian, "Archaeology, cultural anthropology, and the origins and intensification of war," in *The archaeology of warfare: Prehistories of raiding and conquest,* ed. Elizabeth N. Arkush and Mark W. Allen. 2006, Gainesville: University Press of Florida; 482.

APPENDIX 4

NOTES ON SEXUALITY

I. SAME-SEX RELATIONSHIPS AND THE BIBLE

When I told Laura I was writing about what she'd said about the Bible at the fire that night at Raymond's bonobo research site, she offered to look over what I had written to make sure I'd put the facts down right, and also to gather together some references to go with what she'd said. What follows is the reference information she provided me with:

Indira,

Your facts all look fine. Here are some sources for the information I gave you and Raymond that night. The first book listed below is one that I was familiar with at that time, while the two that follow came out later, but provide useful summaries of earlier research. I'm also including a list of specific citations for the passages from the Bible that I mentioned then.

Hope this is all you needed, love. Let me know if you want something more.

Laura

John Boswell. *Christianity, Social Tolerance, and Homosexuality: Gay People in Western Europe from the Beginning of the Christian Era to the Fourteenth Century* (Chicago: University of Chicago Press, 1980).

- Details about Sodom and Gomorrah; 92–99.
- On sleeping "the sleep of a woman with a man" and on the meaning of "*toevah*;" 100–101 (including note 34 on 101).

Daniel A. Helminiak. *What the Bible* Really *Says About Homosexuality* (San Francisco: Alamo Square Press, 1994).
- A thoughtful discussion of what the Bible does and does not say about same-sex relationships.

Jeff Miner & John Tyler Connoley. *The Children are Free: Reexamining the Biblical Evidence on Same-Sex Relationships* (Indianapolis, IN: Jesus Metropolitan Community Church, 2002).
- Positive references to same-sex relationships in the Bible; 27–55.

Biblical passages mentioned: Sodom and Gomorrah: Genesis 19; Jesus on Sodom and Gomorrah: Matthew 10:14–15; Sleeping "the sleep of a woman with a man:" Leviticus 18:22; Eating shellfish: Leviticus 11:10; Beating slaves: Exodus 21:20–21; Condoning slavery: Exodus 21:1–11, Leviticus 25:44–46, Titus 2:9, Ephesians 6:5, Colossians 3:22, 1 Timothy 6:1–2; Sex during menstruation: Leviticus 20:18; Children cursing their parents: Leviticus 20:9; Turning the other cheek: Matthew 5:39; The Beatitudes: Matthew 5:2–11

II. ANIMAL SEXUALITY

In the summer of 2001, I began again to work on the article for the *Huginn/Muninn Newsletter* that I had started many years earlier on the barge, and then set aside once Laura and I reached the Ituri Forest. While working on it again, I found myself thinking back to the time Laura and I had spent in Zaire. I remembered the conversations we'd had with Raymond about how commonplace same-sex coupling is in animals and decided I'd like to get more information on the subject.

What I found was a book by Bruce Bagemihl called *Biological exuberance: Animal homosexuality and natural diversity* (1999, New York: St. Martin's Press). It catalogues what is known about the sorts of sexual unions that are formed within a wide variety of animal species, and discusses the influence of social attitudes on both the research performed and the conclusions drawn from it. All in all, it is a valuable compilation of fascinating and little-recognized information about the diversity of sexual expression in animals.

Appendix 5

Citations for Dr. Laura Atherton's Article:

"From Belonging to Isolation: A Multi-Cultural Analysis"

I asked Laura if she would adapt her citations from her paper, "From belonging to isolation: A multi-cultural analysis" (*The International Journal of Religions.* 1990, vol. 37, no. 2) to use as an appendix to my memoirs. She kindly agreed to do so. Her adapted citations follow:

Having read through the chapter in Indira's memoirs that draws on material from my paper, and being unable to use note numbers to match my citation to what she wrote, as I did in my original journal article, I've chosen to present these notes here organized according to which part of the world each traditional story is from.

In addition, each citation is identified by the specific cultural group and location it pertains to (underlined), and is accompanied by a brief description of the story that is being cited. In cases where Indira remembered passages I had quoted in my article, the first few words of each such passage are repeated here to help readers relate each quotation to its source. I believe this approach will be a sufficiently clear means of reference for the reader who wishes to match quoted passages to the sources from which they were drawn or to otherwise explore these matters in fuller detail.

AFRICA:

Barbara C. Sproul. *Primal Myths: Creating the World* (San Francisco: Harper & Row, Publishers, 1979).
- Barotse: Zambia: After making all things, God stayed and lived on the earth, but retreated to the sky to avoid the bad behavior of human beings; 35–36.
- Yao: Mozambique: God retreated to the sky to escape human cruelty; 36–37.
- Ngombe: Zaire: God was driven away by people quarreling; 47.
- Krachi: Togo: God went to the sky to get away from people, who were bothering him; 75.

Andrew Wilson, ed. *World Scripture: A Comparative Anthology of Sacred Texts* (New York: Paragon House, advance copy—later released in 1991).
- Dinka: Sudan: God and the sky were very near to the people, who lived without death, sorrow, sickness, or hunger. Someone who was greedy for extra food made God angry, so he and the sky withdrew to their present location, far above the earth; 307.

ASIA:

Chuang Tzu. *Chuang Tzu: Mystic, Moralist, and Social Reformer*, trans. Herbert A. Giles. 2d ed. rev. (Shanghi: Kelly & Walsh, 1926; reprint, New York: AMS Press, 1974).
- Taoism: China: Describes an early time when people were guided by their instincts, lived with the animals, and when all creation was one; 107–108 (107; quoted passage beginning, "when natural instincts prevailed...").

Wendy Doniger O'Flaherty et al., ed. and trans. *Textual Sources for the Study of Hinduism* (Manchester: Manchester University Press, 1988).
- Hinduism: India: Describes a golden age of harmony, happiness, and goodness when people were focused on the pleasures around them and did not live in houses, but wandered where they wished; 68–69.

EUROPE:

Hesiod. "Works and Days." *Theogony; Works and Days*. trans. M. L. West. World's Classics ed. (Oxford: Oxford University Press, 1988).
- Greece: The first people lived happily and without toil in a plentiful world; 40.

MIDDLE EAST (the Garden of Eden story in three traditions):

The original man and woman live in paradise but are cast out after eating the forbidden fruit.
- The Judaic Tradition: *The Torah: The Five Books of Moses.* 2nd ed. (Philadelphia: Jewish Publication Society of America, 1977); Genesis 2–3.
- The Islamic Tradition: *The Holy Qur'an: Text, Translation and Commentary,* trans. Abdullah Yusuf Ali. U.S. ed. (Elmhurst, NY: Tahrike Tarsile Qur'an, 1987); 2.035–2.036, 7.019–7.025, and 20.117–20.121.
- The Christian Tradition: *New American Standard Bible.* Cambridge study ed. (Cambridge: Cambridge University Press, 1977); Genesis 2–3.

One early Gnostic Christian interpretation of the Garden of Eden story is of special interest in the light of Indira's theory concerning a time when people left behind a sense of holistic belonging to become focused on their own individuation. According to this Gnostic interpretation, the story of the fall described a transition from a state of consciousness in which people where aware of their "divine origin," into a condition of "ordinary consciousness." See: Elaine Pagels. *Adam, Eve, and the Serpent* (New York: Random House, 1988); 65.

NORTH AMERICA:

Richard Erdoes and Alfonso Ortiz, eds. *American Indian Myths and Legends* (New York: Pantheon Books, 1984).
- Cheyenne: American Great Plains: All of the people and all of the animals could communicate with one another. Together, they all lived in friendship; 111–112 (quoted passage beginning, "In the beginning, the Great Medicine created the earth...").
- White River Sioux: American Great Plains: Long ago, many people could understand animal languages, 5 (quoted passage beginning, "Many people...could talk to a bird...").

Knud Rasmussen. *The Netsilik Eskimos: Social Life and Spiritual Culture,* Report of the Fifth Thule Expedition 1921–24; the Danish Expedition to Arctic North America in Charge of Knud Rasmussen, Ph.D., vol. 8, no. 1–2 (Copenhagen: Gyldendalske Boghandel, Nordisk Forlag, 1931).
- Netsilik Inuit: Canadian Arctic: People and animals all spoke the same language; 208 (quoted passage beginning, "Both people and animals.... spoke the same tongue...").

Frank Waters and Oswald White Bear Fredericks. *The Book of the Hopi* (New York: Ballantine Books, 1963).

- <u>Hopi: American Southwest</u>: The first people were happy and pure. In that early time, all creatures could understand one another without speaking, and they all felt as one—but eventually people became convinced of their separateness, and so their sense of happy communion and belonging was lost. Then they became warlike and began to fight with one another; 14–16 (15; quoted passages beginning, "the First People...were happy" and "So the First People kept multiplying...").

SOUTH & CENTRAL AMERICA:

John Bierhorst. *The Mythology of South America* (New York: William Morrow and Company, 1988).
- Story of a tree of life that offers abundant foods ready for the picking and that people eventually chop down. Thus people lose access to this unified source of life-giving nourishment and, in some versions, must thereafter labor to meet their needs. Variations on this story are widely told in the northern-most and central regions of South America, as well as through most of Central America; 12, 15, 18–20, and 79–81.

APPENDIX 6

NOTES ON THE SAND CREEK MASSACRE
& RELATED MATTERS

After seeing that I was, in one way or another, including reference material for most of the sources referred to in my memoirs, I decided to try to contact Joseph Young Bear and see if he might be able to give me some idea what his sources had been for the things he'd talked about on our journey to Sand Creek all those years ago. I found him still living in Lame Deer and wrote, asking for his help. He sent the following letter in reply:

Dear Indira,

It's good to hear from you. It's been a lot of years, hasn't it? I'm not surprised you were able to track me down, though, as I'm living not more than a mile from where I was when Laura was living here. I suppose I should try to get you caught up some, as you were good enough to fill me in with news of you and Laura in your letter. I spent most of the years since you were here doing work similar to what I was doing when we met. I'm expecting to retire next year and am looking forward to slowing down a little, though people tell me I'll wish I had more to do once it happens. I married—got married in 1983. Her name is Cara. We have three kids, all boys, and all grown now.

I'd like to give you more details, but I guess it's more important to be sure this information reaches you before the deadline you mentioned in your letter, so here's the reference information you asked for.

First, let me tell you that you shouldn't worry about asking for my help—I don't mind at all. I'm glad you are writing about Sand Creek. I read through the passage of your book you sent me, and it was something to read about our trip—it really took me back! And yes, I can reassure you that you have got the facts right. (I guess it really does help, as you said, to have kept a journal at the time.)

I'm not really sure where I got most of the information I told you about then, but I've kept most of the books I've read on the subject through the years, so I've been able to find sources for most everything you wrote about, even if I'm not really sure if they are the sources I drew on at that time. (In fact, I'm sure some of them are not, as they were printed after that trip took place.)

Anyhow, here's what I managed to pull together for you:

For information about what happened at Sand Creek, and events leading up to that day, see:
- Grinnell, George Bird (1955) The fighting Cheyennes, The civilization of the American Indian series, vol. 44. Norman, OK: University of Oklahoma Press, chapters 9–14.
- Hoig, Stan (1961) The Sand Creek Massacre. Norman, OK: University of Oklahoma Press.
- Schultz, Duane (1990) Month of the freezing moon: the Sand Creek Massacre November 1864. New York: St. Martin's Press.

For more on what attitudes fueled these events:
- Svaldi, David (1989) Sand Creek and the rhetoric of extermination: a case study in Indian-White relations. Lanham, MD: University Press of America.

For a general history of Indian-White relations:
- Brown, Dee (1973) Bury my heart at Wounded Knee: an Indian history of the American West. New York: Bantam Books.
- Stannard, David E. (1992) American holocaust: the conquest of the New World. New York: Oxford University Press.

For information on the devastation of Indian populations:
- Thornton, Russell (1987) American Indian holocaust and survival: a population history since 1492, The civilization of the American Indian series, vol. 186. Norman, OK: University of Oklahoma Press, most specifically page 43.
- Stannard's American Holocaust (already cited above) also discusses this.

If I remember right, I worked out the figure I gave about how little of our original lands Indians still hold by comparing, I think, Bureau of Indian Affairs land area figures to information I got from an almanac (?) about the land area of the lower 48 states, but that's about all I recall, so I don't have a specific source to give you for that information.

For information on the devastation of wolf populations:

- Lopez, Barry Holstun (1978) Of wolves and men. New York: Charles Scribner's Sons, chapter 9. Really excellent chapter on the slaughter of wolves in America and why it happened.
- Busch, Robert H. (1995) The wolf almanac. New York: Lyons & Burford, Publishers. Has good maps of where wolves used to be and where they are now (pages 4–7, 16–17 and 158). Also talks about the slaughter (pages 99–103 and 109–110).

For information on the devastation of the buffalo population:

- Lott, Dale F. (2002) American bison: a natural history. Berkeley: University of California Press. A map on page 71 shows their former range. Chapter 22 describes their decimation.

I don't remember much about the conversation we had at Deborah's house, but apparently I tried to quote Major Wynkoop for you. A more accurate quote can be found in the Hoig book (page 99), though it's not really so far off from what you have written.

As for other quotes or statements I referred to, Chivington's public statement about killing all Indians can be found in Svaldi's book (page 291), and Downing's statement to the same effect can be found in the Schultz book (page 74). Information about editorials in the *Rocky Mountain News* calling for our extermination can be found in Svaldi (pages 149–150). The passage about the crowd chanting "exterminate them" is also in Svaldi's book (page 188). The quote of the Congressional Record I mentioned appears in Grinnell (pages 150–151).

I hope that gives you all you need, Indira. Like I said, it's good to get word of both you and Laura after all these years. I'm glad things have gone so well for you both. Thanks for including so much news with your note. Well, I guess this is enough, as I want to get this off to you now, before your deadline.

Good luck with your book. Please let me know when it's out in print— I'd like to buy a copy.

All my best to you and Laura.

Joseph

APPENDIX 7

SOURCES OF QUOTATIONS
NOT ALREADY CITED ELSEWHERE

Blake, William. "Proverbs of hell," in *The marriage of heaven and hell: In full color.* 1994, New York: Dover Publications; 8 ("What is now proved...").

Bohm, David J. "A new theory of the relationship of mind and matter," *The Journal of the American Society for Psychical Research.* 1986, vol. 80, no. 2; 129 ("The mental and the material...").

Brown, Jr., Tom with William Owen. *The search.* (1980, Englewood Cliffs, NJ: Prentice-Hall; reprint, 1986, New York: Berkley Books); 146 ("Prosperity is relating...").

(Buddha) Fronsdal, Gil, trans. *The Dhammapada: A new translation of the Buddhist classic with annotations.* 2005, Boston: Shambhala Publications; 36 (10.133) ("What you say...").

(Buddha) Goleman, Daniel. "A conversation between Tibetan lama Tulku Thondup and psychologist Daniel Goleman," *New Age Journal.* September/October, 1996; 76 ("Mind is the main thing...").

(Buddha) as quoted in: "The world's great religions, part II: The path of Buddhism," *Life.* March 7, 1955; 102 ("Whatsoever...you find to be...").

Chuang Tzu. *Chuang Tzu: Mystic, moralist, and social reformer.* trans. Herbert A. Giles. 2nd ed. rev. (1926, Shanghi: Kelly & Walsh; reprint, 1974, New York: AMS Press); 107 ("In the days when natural instincts...").

(Einstein, Albert) as quoted in: Paul Davies. *About time: Einstein's unfinished revolution*. A Touchstone Book. 1996, New York: Simon & Schuster; 70 ("The distinction between past, present and future...").

(Einstein, Albert) Eves, Howard W. *Mathematical circles adieu: A fourth collection of mathematical stories and anecdotes*. 1977, Boston: Prindle, Weber & Schmidt; 60 ("A human being is a part of the whole...").

Emerson, Ralph Waldo. "Nature," in *Essays by Ralph Waldo Emerson: First series and second series; two volumes in one*. n.d., New York: Thomas Nelson and Sons; 141 in second series ("Nature is the incarnation...").

Emerson, Ralph Waldo. *Journals of Ralph Waldo Emerson: With annotations*, vol. 9. ed. Edward Waldo Emerson and Waldo Emerson Forbes. 1913, Boston: Houghton Mifflin; 549 ("People only see...").

Gandhi, Mohandas K. *All men are brothers: Life and thoughts of Mahatma Gandhi as told in his own words*. ed. Krishna Kripalani. 1968, Ahmedabad: Navajivan Publishing House; 153 ("I want to realize brotherhood...").

(Gnostic Apocryphon of John) *The Nag Hammadi library in English*. trans. Coptic Gnostic Library Project. ed. James M. Robinson and Richard Smith. 3rd completely rev. ed. 1990, San Francisco: HarperSanFrancisco; 122 ("Arise and remember...").

(Hadewijch II) Hirshfield, Jane, ed. *Women in praise of the sacred: 43 centuries of spiritual poetry by women*. poem trans. Jane Hirshfield. 1994, New York: HarperCollins Publishers; 109 ("You who want/ knowledge...").

Hesiod. "Works and days," in *Theogony; works and days*. trans. M. L. West. World's Classics ed. 1988, Oxford: Oxford University Press; 39 ("For formerly the tribes of men...").

(Hua Hu Chiang) Walker, Brian, trans. *Hua hu ching: The unknown teachings of Lao Tzu*. 1995, San Francisco: HarperSanFrancisco; 7 ("The superior person...").

Jeans, James. *The mysterious universe*. new rev. ed. 1932, New York: Macmillan Company; 186 ("To-day there is a wide measure...").

Jung, C. G. *The basic writings of C. G. Jung*. ed. Violet Staub De Laszlo. 1959, New York: Modern Library; 287 ("This deeper layer I call...").

(Kant, Immanuel) as quoted in: Henrik Scharling. *Nicolai's marriage: A picture of Danish family life*, vol. 2. trans. "The Guardian," "John Falk," etc. 1876, London: Richard Bentley and Son; 211 ("We see things not as *they* are...").

(Lal Ded) Hirshfield, Jane, ed. *Women in praise of the sacred: 43 centuries of spiritual poetry by women*. poem trans. Coleman Barks. 1994, New York: HarperCollins Publishers; 126 ("Face everything...").

Proust, Marcel, ed. and trans. Justin O'Brien. *The maxims of Marcel Proust.* 1948, New York: Columbia University Press; 181 (no. 349); trans. from: Marcel Proust, *La prisonnière*, vol. 2. Editions de la nouvelle revue Française. 1923–1927, Paris: Gallimard; 75–76 ("The only real voyage...").

Rich, Adrienne. Line from "Ghazal [7/23/68]." Copyright © 1993 by Adrienne Rich. Copyright © 1969 by W. W. Norton & Company, Inc., from *Collected early poems: 1950–1970* by Adrienne Rich. 1993, New York: W. W. Norton & Company; 346 ("When my thought absorbs yours...").

Rilke, Rainer Maria. *Briefe an einen jungen Dichter.* 2009, Cologne: Anaconda; 62; Unpublished translation by William T. Doyle ("Perhaps all who are terrible...").

Roosevelt, Eleanor. *Tomorrow is now.* 1963, New York: Harper & Row, Publishers; xv ("It is today that we...").

Rumi, Jalal al-Din. *Open secret: Versions of Rumi.* trans. John Moyne and Coleman Barks. 1984, Putney, VT: Threshold Books; 59 ("Open every living particle"), 68 ("Rise up nimbly...").

Rumi, Jalal al-Din. *The essential Rumi.* trans. Coleman Barks with John Moyne, A. J. Arberry, and Reynold Nicholson. 1995, San Francisco: HarperSanFrancisco; 3 ("Flow down and down..."), 18 ("Anyone pulled from a source..."), 275–276 ("I am dust particles...").

Shakespeare, William. *As you like it.* ed. Jack R. Crawford. Yale Shakespeare Series. 1919, New Haven, CT: Yale University Press; 42 (2.7.139–142) ("All the world's a stage...).

(Shikibu, Izumi) Hirshfield, Jane, ed. *Women in praise of the sacred: 43 centuries of spiritual poetry by women.* poem trans. Jane Hirshfield and Mariko Aratani. 1994, New York: HarperCollins Publishers; 59 ("Watching the moon...").

Wolff, Robert. *Original wisdom: Stories of an ancient way of knowing.* 2001, Rochester, VT: Inner Traditions; 197 ("All who are in touch...").

Zohar, Danah, and Ian Marshall. *The quantum society: Mind, physics, and a new social vision.* 1994, New York: Quill/William Morrow; 294 ("Each of us, as Jung realized...").

Appendix 8

◉

On How the World Was

,

North America

These quotations collectively paint a picture of the natural world as it once was, in its full and unfettered vitality.

◙   ◙   ◙

Most of the trees in these virgin forests were much larger than any ordinarily seen today. They had grown for centuries, undisturbed.

.   .   .

Until about 1790 trees two to five feet in diameter were common [in the eastern forests] and only as trees passed six feet or reached eight [feet in diameter] did they attract attention.

.   .   .

Large sycamores invariably had hollow trunks.... A very big sycamore could shelter a fairly large number of men—one traveler says twenty or thirty. (Bakeless, 310–311)

◙

[John Muir wrote:] It was a great memorable day when the first flock of passenger pigeons came to our farm.... I have seen flocks streaming south in the fall so large that they were flowing over from horizon to horizon in an almost continuous stream all day long, at the rate of forty or fifty miles an hour, like a mighty river in the sky, widening, contracting, descending like falls and cataracts, and rising suddenly here and there in huge ragged masses like high-splashing spray. (Matthiessen, 182)

◙

But Anza did not loiter to enjoy the pleasing sight. He would drink it in as he traveled. Down the Rio de San Joseph he proceeded past Lake San Antonio de Bucareli, "several leagues in circumference and as full of white geese as of water." (Bolton, 101)

◙

A friend of ours engaged in the cattle trade, informs us, that in going from the Mission of Santa Clara towards San Francisco, in 1850, he accidentally dropped a quarter of fat beef from his cart, while a number of the Condor were in sight. On discovering his loss, after a few minutes, he turned back and observed the Condor in numbers which he estimated at over three hundred, hovering over and near his lost beef.

. . .

In January, 1858, a large Condor was killed.... The bird measured fourteen feet from tip to tip of wings. (Taylor, 19–20)

◙

The grasslands and marshlands of California were home to abundant tule elk when the first Europeans arrived.... Richard Henry Dana in his *Two Years Before the Mast* described "hundreds and hundreds" of these animals on the Marin headlands, which he watched when his sailing ship anchored in San Francisco Bay in 1835.[10]... Early American settler William Heath Davis reported seeing as many as three thousand elk "that swam from Mare Island to Vallejo and back," and John Bidwell wrote of elk "by the thousand" in the Napa and Santa Clara valleys in 1841.[12] (Dasmann 1999, 111)

◙

Though found in nearly all parts of the territory of the United States west of the Mississippi, [the pronghorn antelope] is probably most numerous in the valley of the San Joaquin, California. There [in 1855] it is found in herds literally of thousands. (Newberry, 13)

◙

[The buffalo's] dark forms may often be seen extending over the prairie as far as the eye can reach, a mighty moving mass of life. Onward they rush, moved by some sudden impulse, making the ground tremble under their feet, while their course may be traced by the vast cloud of dust which floats over them as they sweep across the plain. (Kingston, 109)

◙

General Hugh L. Scott, as a young lieutenant, once sat with Benteen...on a high mountain peak giving a view of twenty miles in all directions. The experienced Benteen assured him that there were three hundred thousand buffalo to be seen below them "in one view." (Bakeless, 368)

◙

Once, at dusk an incredible number of bears passed the camp—"a very remarquable thing. There comes out of a vast forest a multitude of bears, 300 att least together, making a horrid noise, breaking small trees, throwing the rocks downe by the watter side."

.   .   .

In New England, at about the same time, John Josselyn remarked that when in rut, the black bears would "walk the Country twenty, thirty, forty in a company." (Bakeless, 145–146)

☐

In the journals of…early explorers there are frequent references to the wild animal life. "In this canyon were seen whole troops of bears."

.   .   .

"Calvin Kinman states that one morning his father counted 40 bears in sight at once from a high point in the Mattole country, where he could overlook a great extent of open land." (Dasmann 1965, 40–41)

☐

In 1497, John Cabot set the tone by describing the Grand Banks as so "swarming with fish [that they] could be taken not only with a net but in baskets let down [and weighted] with a stone." (Mowat, 166)

☐

As John Mason, an English fishing skipper working out of a Newfoundland shore station, noted, "Cods are so thick by the shore that we hardly have been able to row a boat through them." (Mowat, 168)

☐

A record penned by an anonymous mariner of the mid-1500s complains that the worst risk to navigation in the *New Founde Land* was not fog, ice, or uncharted rocks—it was whales of such size and in such numbers that collision with them was an ever-present danger. In the early 1600s one French missionary reported testily that whales were still so numerous in the Gulf of St. Lawrence that "they became very tiresome to us and hindered our rest by their continuous movement and the noise of their spoutings."

.   .   .

Richard Mather, newly arrived in Massachusetts Bay in 1635, reported seeing "multitudes of great whales…spewing up water in the air like the smoke of chimneys and making the sea about them white and hoary…which [sight] now was grown ordinary and usual to behold." (Mowat, 211)

☐

These [tributaries of the Santa Ynez River] were filled conspicuously with Steelhead Trout some two or three feet in length.… Because it not only was unlawful but also because it was very poor sportsmanship, we did not attempt to kill these running Steelhead with stones or with sticks, as we easily could have done. (We were told that some of the local ranchers took them in numbers with pitchforks.)... How many of them there were we made no attempt to estimate. (Spaulding, 113)

◙

During the spring and summer of 1940...more than 525,000 young Steelhead Trout [were rescued] from the drying Santa Ynez River. (Shapovalov, 8)

◙

So singularly clear was the water [of Lake Tahoe], that where it was only twenty or thirty feet deep the bottom was so perfectly distinct that the boat seemed floating in the air! Yes, where it was even *eighty* feet deep. Every little pebble was distinct, every speckled trout, every hand's-breadth of sand.... Down through the transparency of these great depths, the water was not *merely* transparent, but dazzlingly, brilliantly so.... So empty and airy did all spaces seem below us, and so strong was the sense of floating high aloft in mid-nothingness, that we called these boat-excursions "balloon-voyages."

...We could see trout by the thousand winging about in the emptiness under us. (Twain, 162–163)

◙

The lake was full of fish, "seene in the water so cleare as [crystal]."... This was pure rain water, fallen through dustless woodland air upon bare, clean rock or upon a forest floor, where every bit of soil was firmly held by roots, so that the falling rain, as it ran off, took scarcely a particle of earth with it.... Through twenty feet of such water in sunlight, you can see pebbles on the bottom or moving fishes, as if they swam in liquid nothing, the pure, clear water being all but invisible. When the wind is still and these lakes are smooth, they take on the color of the sky, so that the canoes seem to be moving through the air itself. (Bakeless, 151)

◙   ◙   ◙

Bakeless, John. *America as seen by its first explorers: The eyes of discovery.* 1989, Mineola, NY: Dover Publications.

Bolton, Herbert Eugene. *Outpost of empire: The story of the founding of San Francisco.* 1931, New York: Alfred A. Knopf.

Dasmann, Raymond F. "Environmental changes before and after the gold rush," in *A golden state: Mining and economic development in gold rush California,* ed. James J. Rawls, Richard J. Orsi and Marlene Smith-Baranzini. 1999, Berkeley, CA: University of California Press.

---

10. Richard H. Dana, Jr., *Two years before the mast* (New York: Harper and Bros., 1840; New York: Doubleday, 1949), 76.
12. Rockwell D. Hunt, *John Bidwell, prince of California pioneers* (Caldwell, Idaho: Caxton Printers, 1942), 76.

Dasmann, Raymond F. *The destruction of California.* 1965, New York: Macmillan Company.

Kingston, William H. G. *The western world: Picturesque sketches of nature and natural history in Northern and Central America.* 1884, London: T. Nelson and Sons.

Matthiessen, Peter. *Wildlife in America.* 1967, New York: Viking Press.

Mowat, Farley. *Sea of slaughter.* 1985, Toronto: Seal Books/McClelland and Stewart-Bantam Limited.

Newberry, J. S. as quoted in: David E. Brown et al. "An annotated bibliography of references to historical distributions of pronghorn in Southern and Baja California." *Bulletin of the Southern California Academy of Sciences.* 2006, vol. 105, no. 1. Quoted from "Report upon the zoology of the route." no. 2, chap. 1, pp. 70–71, in H. L. Abbot. *Reports of explorations and surveys to ascertain...etc.* 1857, U.S. Senate ex. doc. no 78, vol. 7, Washington, DC; p. 71.

Shapovalov, Leo. "Report on planting of marked steelhead trout in the lagoon of Santa Ynez River, Santa Barbara County, California, 1940." *California Department of Fish and Game, Inland Fisheries Administrative Report.* 1940, no. 40–15.

Spaulding, Edward Selden. *Camping in our mountains: Reminiscences.* [1960?], Santa Barbara, CA: Published for Santa Barbara Historical Society by the Schauer Printing Studio.

Taylor, Alexander S. "The great condor of California." *Hutchings' California Magazine.* July, 1859, no. 37.

Twain, Mark. *Roughing it,* vol. 1. 1913, New York: Harper & Brothers Publishers.

PLEASE JOIN THE CONVERSATION AT:

TheRootOfHeavenAndEarth.com

or come get your copy of the

READING-GROUP GUIDE

CPSIA information can be obtained at www.ICGtesting.com
Printed in the USA
BVOW042006280113

311802BV00002B/16/P

9 781938 960680